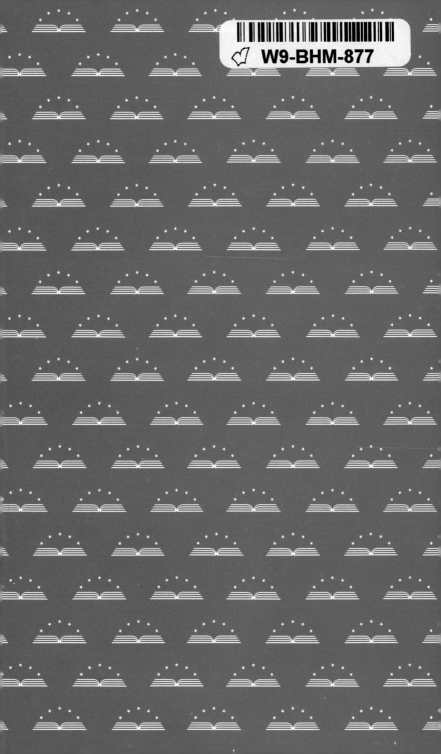

DAWN POWELL

Dawn Powell

NOVELS 1944–1962

My Home Is Far Away
The Locusts Have No King
The Wicked Pavilion
The Golden Spur

THE LIBRARY OF AMERICA

Library of Congress Catalog Number: 00–054596
For cataloging information, see end of Notes.
ISBN 1–931082–02–2

First Printing
The Library of America—127

TIM PAGE

WROTE THE NOTES FOR THIS VOLUME

Contents

MY HOME IS FAR AWAY

For my cousin,
SERGEANT JACK F. SHERMAN

The Man in the Balloon

I

THIS WAS the month of cherries and peaches, of green apples beyond the grape arbor, of little dandelion ghosts in the grass, of sour grass and four-leaf clovers, of still dry heat holding the smell of nasturtiums and dying lilacs. This was the best month of all and the best day. It was not birthday, Easter, Christmas, or picnic, but all these things and something else, something wonderful, something utterly unknown. The two little girls in embroidered white Sunday dresses knew no way to express their secret joy but by whirling each other dizzily over the lawn crying, "We're moving, we're moving! We're moving to London Junction!"

Down the cinder driveway between the Willard house and Dr. Bird's box hedge rumbled the hay wagon, laden with the Willard furniture. The sudden picture of their home, everything that was theirs, yanked out of its familiar roots like baby teeth and stacked up on wheels, made the children stand still, staring, uncertain. There was their little pine bed standing on end, the baby's high-chair hanging by a rope from the corner pole, the big walnut dresser with its front bulging out like a funny-paper policeman's; there were the two big parlor chairs, wide rockers curved in perpetual grins, wonderful for scooting games; there was the couch bought with coupons—bright yellow fuzzy stuff with red and green caterpillars wiggling circles over it so that it always seemed alive and dangerous; there was the pine kitchen cupboard tied on its back to the dining-table as if it had left its little corner only when overpowered by force. Yes, there went their little yellow house itself, for without these things warming its insides, the little yellow house was nothing but empty doors and windows. They watched the wagon wheels roll relentlessly over the pansy-border and leave deep ruts in the soft new grass, but it didn't matter because they didn't live here any more. Like their furniture, now being brushed by the overhanging branches of

Peach Street, they were suspended in space between the little yellow cottage, Number Twenty-Three, and the unknown towers of London Junction. This must be the reason that time, too, was suspended, for no matter how often they ran to ask their mother the time, it was always nine o'clock, a little before, a little after, but not quite starting time. So round and round they swung each other over the grass, as if this example of speed would whip up the minutes.

"We're moving, we're moving, we're moving to London Junction!" they chanted shrilly. This time they whirled through the gap in the hedge into Dr. Bird's front yard. This was a hushed space, shaded with sleek-leafed bushes, wide-spreading locust trees that dripped feathery green over fern beds below. The sun never came here or into the shuttered, vine-covered house; it was an old people's yard with a cool cemetery smell, suitable for an old man and old lady who never came out further than the plaster old man and lady in the tiny weather-house. Old Dr. Bird sat behind the porch vines, shelling peas into a tin saucepan.

"Hold on there! What's all this?" he called out in a high trembling voice.

"We're moving!" Lena answered. "We're moving to London Junction."

"Here," said the old man. "Here you are, girls. Here's a penny apiece."

They flew to his side.

"Dr. Bird," asked Marcia earnestly, "who will hold the string for you to tie up bundles when I go to London Junction?"

"Nobody," said Dr. Bird. "I'll have to do it myself."

"I'm sorry," said Marcia. "I liked putting a finger on the string. I don't see how you'll get along."

"Never mind, here's your penny," said the old man. "Run along or your folks'll drive off without you."

"Say goodbye to Dr. Bird," their mother called from the surrey now pausing in the driveway. "Well, here we go, Dr. Bird."

"Glad, eh?"

"Indeed I am," their mother answered happily. "You see, I'll be there with Ma and Lois, and besides it's a better place for Harry."

"London Junction, London Junction, London Junction!" sang the two girls and whirled each other round and round across the lawn, down the dusty path till they fell in the geranium bed laughing. Their father, a slight, jaunty figure with a little sandy moustache, in a neat brown-checked suit, came out of the little yellow house carrying the baby in one arm and the red telescope in the other. The red telescope was the very thing in which Dr. Bird had first brought the baby. The two girls had looked in it carefully every morning for over a year to see if any other babies had arrived, but so far none had followed Florrie.

"Get in, get in!" shouted their father. "Do you want to go to London Junction or do you want to stay here?"

They scrambled over the wheels into the back seat of the surrey. The horse and surrey were borrowed from the Busby Hotel where their father had clerked until today. It was a handsome outfit, the shining black surrey with tan fringe twinkling along its top, and the gleaming black horse that Papa himself had "broke" in the field behind the hotel. There were leather storm curtains rolled up to be let down in case of rain, and a silver-trimmed whip in a silver-trimmed socket. This elegance so impressed Marcia and Lena that they sat still, proudly stretching their feet in the new Mary Jane black patent-leather slippers. Dr. Bird limped along the box hedge to the gate and watched them.

"Say hello to Lois for me," he called out. "Bring her over if you come down to Reunion."

"Of course we'll come to Reunion," their mother called back. "Ma never misses it, you know that."

She gathered her skirts carefully about her away from the wheel, and leaned over to take the baby from their father's arms.

"Let *us* hold her!" begged Lena.

Their mother stood up and lifted the baby over the back seat to them. They sat her up between them on the tufted tan cushion. In their excitement they clutched her arms so tightly that her big blue eyes welled with indignant tears.

"Don't pinch," admonished their mother, then called out, "Hurry, Harry, or we'll never get there before dark."

Their father went back to the house and to the barn again, then to the tool-shed for no reason at all, except perhaps to say goodbye, just as the sunflowers beside the old playhouse seemed to be nodding goodbye. In this moment before leaving, the clouds stood still and seemed very low, as if they might even be stroked if one stood on the treetop and reached high. Above the clouds somewhere was London Junction, beyond the far-off pine fringe that rimmed this world was London Junction, on the other side of the West Woods, sunset boundary of the world, lay London Junction. The children's eyes widened as the whip cracked and the voyage began.

"Goodbye, Dr. Bird. Goodbye, Mrs. Busby," called their mother, waving her handkerchief. A skinny brown hand waved from the lace curtains of the big gray Busby house. Their mother kept waving her handkerchief all the way down Peach Street, as certain as were the children that the whole world was watching their departure. Sure enough hands waved to them from windows, and passing the marketplace Mr. Charles, the butcher, waved his white apron, and Mr. Finney, the druggist, lifted his straw hat, and the delivery boy from the grocery-store put down his basket to salute them like a soldier.

"Where are the kittens?" Lena suddenly asked.

"In the barn, all right," said their father. "In the barn" sounded ominous to the two little girls who exchanged suspicious glances.

"Where's Towser?" demanded Marcia. "Isn't Towser going to London Junction? We've got to go back and get Towser."

"Poor Towser!" sighed their mother. "OH, Harry!"

"What's happened to Towser?" wailed the girls, and then Florrie began to roar in the alarmingly efficient way she had, at two years old, perfected, so that the horse pricked up its ears and started to gallop, their mother reached back hastily to steady the baby, and Papa swore, pulling on the reins.

"Forget about Towser, damn it!" he shouted above the clatter of hoofs and wheels on the brick pavement. "We'll get another dog in London Junction."

"CITY LIMITS" their mother read out to them from a sign.

"Thirty miles now to London Junction," said their father.

Now they really were past the sunset woods on the edge of the world, and their mother began to sing. They all sang with her. They sang, "There was an old sailor and he had a wooden leg," and "Hark, hark the dogs do bark, the beggars are coming to town," and "A frog he would a woo-ing go." The baby stopped crying. Papa kept the whip out and the horse trotted along at a fine clip. They waved to farmhouses and shouted merry greetings to loads of hay; they waved to children perched on ladders picking cherries and to women at barnyard pumps rounding up geese, for they knew everyone. Mother had been brought up on a farm along here, her brothers' families were strewn all around, and Papa, though he came from another county, knew everyone through managing the hotel and meeting the farmers who hitched every Saturday in the hotel square. But after awhile they did not know the farms; people in fields stared back at them instead of waving. Papa and their mother fell silent.

"I wonder if we'll like London Junction," she said and her voice sounded small. "We don't know anyone but Ma and Lois and the family."

"We'll know plenty," boasted their father. "More people to know, have a better time and have more to do with. They've got asphalt streets in London Junction, and an opera house, and a baseball park."

"But it's so much bigger than Elmville," said their mother. The children, ever watchful, saw that she had taken out her handkerchief. "Of course, I want to be with my own folks, but think of all the people we're leaving. We've known them all our lives. Dr. Bird——"

"Dr. Bird won't have anybody to hold string when he wraps bundles," said Marcia. "Nobody."

Lena was holding Florrie on her lap, squeezing her so tight that now she roared again. The mighty roar that came from this Humpty-Dumpty baby made their father laugh, so they all laughed. Papa leaned over and kissed their mother and for some reason this made the girls laugh all the louder.

"Here," said their father, and handed their mother the reins. "By George, you handle a horse better than any man. Better than me, even."

"Oh no, Harry, not better than you!" their mother protested, quite shocked. "Nobody is as good with a horse as you, Harry—nobody."

Nobody could do anything as well as Harry and that was the truth. The children knew it, their mother knew it, and naturally Harry knew it.

"Well, I like horses," admitted Harry. "And they like me. That's all."

The next village was Oakville, the county seat, and here they stopped to say hello to papa's father, Grandpa Willard, at the Soldiers' Home. The old soldiers sat on benches around the grounds in wheel chairs, either talking to each other or reading, just waiting for gongs to summon them to meals, chapel, or bed. Grandpa Willard was all dressed up in his uniform with the new cork leg his children had given him, and was sitting on a bench busily whittling a whistle out of a stick.

"I been expecting you folks to stop in the last couple weeks," he said. "I made a whistle for each of the kids."

"Getting lonesome for us?" asked Mama.

Grandpa thoughtfully shifted his tobacco to the other cheek, where it made a fascinating egg-like protuberance.

"No time to get lonesome here," he said. "Up early and reading a book or sitting out here figuring, or walking around spotting birds. Seen a couple of partridge back by the creek yesterday. Had a pest of starlings till they let us shoot some. No sirree, they's always plenty to take up your mind without getting lonesome for your folks."

Papa gave him some tobacco, and then mother gave him a new white handkerchief with his initials, R.J.W., which pleased him so much he folded it up carefully in its tissue paper, declaring that it was too fine to use and would have to be put away with his "personal belongings." He called to one of the attendants passing by, to introduce them all proudly, and asked that the event of his son's family calling be written up in an item in the *Home Weekly*.

"By cracky, other folks' families get written up when they visit. I don't see why mine can't," he said with a firm nod of the head.

Papa asked him if there was anything he'd like to have before they drove on, and Grandpa looked rather wistfully at the horse and carriage.

"I sure would like to handle them reins for about ten minutes," he said. "I haven't laid hands on the reins since I been here. Good trotter?"

Papa boasted of the horse's speed, mouth, coat, and general virtues, but then everything that was in any way connected with Papa automatically became superior to all other things of the kind. This horse, he said, was the finest horse in the county, possibly the state. He declared if he had this horse under his care for, say, four weeks he could make her the finest racing nag in the country and Grandpa gravely agreed that this was possible. They examined the points of the animal together and Papa was a little annoyed when Grandpa found a mark on the left hind leg, so Grandpa hastily said the flaw would very likely pass away in a day or two.

"Tell you what, Harry," he said. "You might send me a picture postcard from London Junction. Some of the fellows have quite a collection."

This promise having been given, the old gentleman looked meditatively down at the children and stroked his white moustache. The children beamed back, pleased with his having only one eye and only one leg from the Civil War.

"Harry, maybe you could spare me a little change so as to give the kids something. I don't get my pension till next week."

Their father reached in his pocket and gave him some pennies and a nickel. The old man promptly presented a penny apiece to the two older girls and a nickel to the baby. Marcia and Lena watched their mother pocket the latter.

"Florrie always gets the most," said Marcia.

They regarded their baby sister speculatively.

"Babies got to have money for chewing tobacco," their grandfather said, winking his one eye.

"Thank you so much, father," said their mother earnestly. "I've started a bank account for the baby, and would you believe it, she already has nearly fourteen dollars in it?"

They climbed back in the surrey, while Grandpa made a hurried survey of the grounds to find Captain Somebody who was in charge and a very fine man it would be a pleasure for them to meet. Disappointed in this, he followed them a few yards, calling out last messages.

"Don't bother about the picture postcards if it's going to be too much trouble, Harry," he said. "It ain't a matter of life and death. And say—if they print a piece about you visiting me in the *Home Weekly* next week, I'll send it to you. There's a lot of reading matter in it, so it's worth having anyway. I always save it in my personal belongings."

They thanked him and drove away, leaving him cutting off a chew of tobacco with his penknife.

"I'd like a bank account," said Lena firmly, but her parents paid no heed.

Marcia, too, had been doing some reflecting.

"When I was the baby, I never got any nickels," she stated accusingly. "I would have remembered it if I had."

Marcia's odd and quite useless talent for remembering was a source of astonishment and amusement to her parents. Sometimes in the night her father would pick her out of bed and take her downstairs to entertain the company with her recollections. The company laughed and gasped, but the uncanniness of her memory was not an endearing trait; invariably the guests drew away respectfully from the little freak and warmed all the more to the pretty, unaffected normalcy of little Lena.

"When I was a baby," reflected Marcia gloomily in a louder voice, "Lena got all the nickels because she was the oldest. I only got the pennies."

Lena giggled. Their parents, if they heard, paid no heed but were silent till after they had left Oakville. Then their mother said hesitatingly, "Harry, I felt sorry for Father. None of his own people around. All of you boys, and yet none of you will let him make a home with you. I really think we ought to let him live with us in London Junction when we get settled."

"That's it—when," retorted their father irritably. "No, sir, he's too big a care. He'd drink up his pension and sit around the room all day chewing tobacco. That's all he'd do."

"I get along all right with Father," said their mother. "Don't be hard on him, Harry. Half-blind and only one leg, poor old soul."

The tone of their mother's voice made Marcia and Lena sorry for their grandfather. The things that made him seem wonderful before—the one eye, the cork leg, the charming companions with equally curious characteristics—all these were changed from wonders to sad misfortunes merely by the pity in their mother's voice. Poor, poor Grandpa! And they had forgotten to sing a song for him, and to thank him for the pennies!

"Whoa, Bess!" their father called out abruptly.

They had come to a crossroads, where a grimy two-story house flaunted a sign, "Four Corners House." The sign was nailed to a dead maple tree, with a rusty pail and tin sap tube still attached to the trunk. A stone watering trough and pump were by the hitching post, and a watchdog was tied outside his kennel, growling fearfully at them. The drab exterior of the house was brightened by gay advertisements pinned to the screen door, and by a clothesline hung with red table-cloths. Their father twisted the reins around the post ring and helped their mother to the ground. Perhaps this was to be a visit, too, with even more pennies in the offing. Their father blighted these hopes by motioning them to sit still.

"You kids stay here. We'll take the baby inside with us."

Their mother jumped into their father's arms, laughing secretly. Her new brown sailor hat fell off and the curly brown bangs blew merrily over her white forehead until she had pinned on her hat once more. From the way Papa picked up Florrie and then hurried their mother into the side door of the building, the children guessed some fun was in the air that was only for grown-ups.

"I know what they're having," said Lena calmly. "They're having beer."

Marcia looked at her six-year-old sister, envious of this superior sophistication.

"Whenever they go in the side door instead of the front door of any place, it means they're having beer to drink," Lena enlarged obligingly. "Like in papa's hotel."

The little treat was plainly not a success, for Florrie's indignant bellow was heard from the moment the screen door closed on them. A few moments later she emerged triumphantly in her mother's arms, round face red with rage, fists in mouth. She was only moderately soothed by being jiggled up and down.

"Spoiled," said their father.

"No, dear, it's just that she wants to keep on riding," explained their mother. True enough, as soon as the carriage started again, Florrie fell blissfully asleep in their mother's arms. They did not stop again till they had come to Venice Corners, half-way to London Junction. Venice Corners was a pretty little village with a white frame church on one side of the main street and a fine brick church on the other. In these towns the brick churches were always the Methodist and the smaller wooden ones were Episcopal or Baptist. When they got to London Junction the children had been promised a brick Sunday school, even though they had been baptized in one of the wooden faiths.

Venice Corners had no purring flour mill like Elmville, and no little lake with rowboats like Oakville, but it countered these charms by being placed on top of a hill so that on either side the little houses marched down step by step, each with its hedge moustache, and a red chimney for a hat. It was after the noon hour now and they were all hungry.

"If we're going to see Chris and Isobel we'd better eat first," said their mother. "We mustn't be any bother to Isobel."

Chris was their mother's cousin.

They drew up under a shade tree on the Methodist Church lawn. Their mother took out the lunch basket and passed out hardboiled eggs, chicken drumsticks, and bread and jam. She wiped off their faces with paper napkins. She fed Florrie from her own lunch, and their father petted the horse, making jokes about keeping horse and carriage instead of returning them to the Busbys. Their mother put the baby in the clothes basket to nap, and began to tidy herself for the visit to Chris and Isobel. She fussed with her jabot, a ripple of white lace fastened with her garnet crescent pin over her brown-and-white checked taffeta waist. Papa tweaked her bangs as fast as she pinned them in place, until she begged, "Oh, darling, please!" She straightened the girls' hair-ribbons and smoothed out their mussed sashes of blue silk. Lena had a new blue bonnet with baby-blue forget-me-nots and velvet streamers. This was because she was the oldest and the prettiest and their father liked to have her look like the little girl on the Singer Sewing Machine Calendar, the one where the rosy little girl is bending over a baby's cradle. Marcia wore Lena's outgrown embroidered dress with her last year's faded straw hat, but she was not disturbed because at least she was permitted to wear her birthday locket and besides her feet were the biggest. Florrie, except for a brand-new blue bonnet with lace ruffled edge, wore the freshly starched but faded dregs of her sisters' outgrown wardrobes, and presently justified this economy by throwing up over her embroidered white bib.

"The raspberry jam," said her mother, fixing the damage.

"She always does," said Marcia critically, "even without jam."

Papa watched their mother fussing over all of them, and he frowned.

"You all look all right; what's all this fuss about?" he snapped. "Godamighty, you don't think Isobel has any more than you do, do you? Where's your watch? Why don't you pin it up a little higher? Nothing to be ashamed of. Thirty dollar watch, by God. Pin her up higher where somebody can see it."

Papa was always reminding their mother of her watch, which he and Aunt Lois and their grandmother had bought last Christmas, though in showing it off to strangers he never mentioned his co-sponsors. He had indeed forgotten about them so completely that on Aunt Lois' last visit he had boasted right to her face about the fine present he had given Daisy. Aunt Lois, pink and blond, and wonderfully perfumed, had smiled.

"Yes, it is a lovely watch, Harry," she softly agreed. "But mother and I are still waiting for your share of it to be paid."

For some reason this made their mother cry and their father swear, and the watch was seldom worn after that except when father insisted. Mother obediently pinned it up higher on her waist now, and the girls studied it with earnest admiration again, knowing that to grow up meant this dainty prize, a blue enamelled fleur-de-lys pin holding a blue enamelled locket of a watch to beat right over your own heart.

"I guess you look a damn sight better than Isobel ever did in her life," said father proudly, patting their mother.

"Well, my stars alive!" was what Isobel said when the party walked in the front gate of this relation's home. "If it isn't Harry and Daisy and the girls! Chris! Come on out and see who's here!"

Isobel was just going to pay a call on the minister's wife. She looked so pretty that Marcia secretly wished she was their mother. For instance, Isobel's skin and eyes and hair seemed all of one dusty gold color like a toasted angel's. Then she had pale tan shoes with pretty curved Cuban heels, and she had a rolled-up brown umbrella with a wolf's head handle made of ivory with little emerald eyes; her small feather toque dropped a beautiful veil over her face, so that forever after Marcia thought beauty consisted of long pale lashes on a creamy oval face delicately marked into tiny octagonal shadows by a brown veil. Even more marvellous was the fact that Isobel could talk—very fast, too—through this veil and kiss through it, too. While the parents talked with Isobel and Chris, Marcia invented a game, much to Lena's delight and admiration, called "Isobel." This was merely kissing each other through their handkerchiefs and then, on a better inspiration, through the screen door.

The Wallises lived in a house almost as small as a playhouse at the very bottom of the hill. You stepped down two stone steps from the sidewalk into the tiny yard bordered with conch-shells and red geraniums. The cottage had forgotten what color it had ever been painted and was rain-gray, with a narrow porch decorated with green Chinese shades and a green swing. Unluckily, the grown-ups at once appropriated this swing, so the girls went inside to look around. They saw at once that if Isobel were their mother and this their home there would be very little room for play, since a big brass bed took up most of the space in the parlor. It bore a snow-white spread and pillow-shams embroidered in red; on one sham was worked "I slept and dreamed that Life was Beauty" with a lady embroidered by way of illustration watering a rosebush, and on the other "I woke and found that Life was Duty" with the same lady holding a broom. This was exactly the same as in Dr. Bird's spare bedroom and you did not need to know how to read to recognize the thought even if you did not understand it. The bay window was filled with ferns in mottled green jardinieres, two rubber plants as tall as Lena, and a tiny table of china knick-knacks: a milk-glass setting hen, a little fisher-boy in colored china holding two brown warty fish, a go-way-back-and-sit-down rug, and other souvenirs of Cedar Point, Put-in Bay, and Puritan Springs, so that nobody could possibly play train here in rocking-chairs without knocking things over. The kitchen was twice the size of the parlor-bedroom. It had measle wallpaper—or at least the colored specks looked like measles, Marcia remarked to Lena—and red-checked curtains and a red-checked tablecloth over the big dining table, and a big stove with a dishpan on it of what appeared to be salt-rising dough, from a finger's taste. One good thing about this kitchen was a large headless wire woman in the corner, with some red plaid gingham pinned around her and a tape measure hanging from her neck. Lena and Marcia were admiringly silent before this fine thing, but Lena finally claimed it by saying, "When I grow up I'm going to be a dressmaker and have a Form in my kitchen, too."

"I'm going to be a fireman like Chris," Marcia retorted coldly. "I'll be riding on a train mostly."

This crushed Lena, for Marcia always knew better things to want than she did. They found a stack of Butterick Pattern Books and sat on the floor to examine them, wishing ardently that they could cut out the figures for paper-dolls. Presently Chris came back to make some lemonade for everybody. He was a lean, tall, dark, squint-eyed young man with thick tousled black hair and white teeth. He made you laugh when he winked at you.

"Chris is my favorite relation," Lena said frankly.

"I'm going to marry him when I grow up," Marcia said, and Lena pouted again. But it was really Lena he held on his lap and when he gave them candy he gave Lena the biggest piece. Lena shot a triumphant glance from violet eyes at Marcia, but Marcia again foiled her by turning her head away proudly.

"Keep the candy, Chris," she said tensely, wanting it terribly. "I guess other people like it better than I do."

She marched out on the porch, and without her jealousy Lena found it no fun sitting on Chris' lap so she came out, too. Mama and Isobel were talking in whispers and giggles in the swing, and their father was telling them jokes while he passed the lemonade glasses.

"Come and see us when we get settled in London Junction," said their mother. "I only hope we can get as nice a place as you have. Ma says everything's awfully dear there, so we're staying with her at Lois' till we find the right place."

"We'll probably take the old Furness home on the hill," said their father. "Plenty of room for company there."

"Oh, Harry! We could never afford it!"

"Look here, now, Daisy, we couldn't make do with a little house like this here! What's the sense in moving if we don't improve ourselves. Isn't that right, Chris?"

"The Furness place is pretty big," Chris said slowly. "Biggest house in the Junction."

"We could never afford that much rent," said their mother. "Harry is fooling."

"The hell I am!" shouted their father. "You always seem to think we're not as good as anybody else in London Junction! I'll get the biggest goddam place in town before I'm through. Bigger'n Lois' place, you can take it from me!"

"Costs money, Harry," Chris said.

"I'll get money, don't you worry about me!" their father said, getting madder. "I can go on the road and make plenty any time I say the word."

"Oh, Harry, you won't go on the road!" breathed their mother, wide-eyed with fear. "You promised!"

"I'll do whatever pays me the most, by cracky!" said their father, not looking at her. "Maybe in the factory, and maybe on the road. I'm not going to sit on my patootie, though, and let the other fellas make all the money. I ain't built that way."

There was a quiet, while their mother stared at him, lips trembling, but he would not look back at her. Chris and Isobel swung back and forth in the swing, pretending not to notice how mad their guests were getting. Suddenly the children saw their father jump up from the porch-railing and point upward.

"Look at the sky!" he exclaimed. "It's coming up rain and we've got to get going. Come on, kids."

Their mother and Isobel hung behind whispering, while the girls ran ahead and Chris followed along with their father.

"Did you hear about the man in the balloon?" Chris asked. "He took off from the County Fair grounds this morning in a balloon and they tell me he claimed he'd land in London Junction this afternoon."

A man in a balloon! Lena and Marcia stared from one face to another eagerly.

"Can't tell, we may have to pick up the pieces on our way," said their father. "We had a fellow in a balloon at Elmville last summer. Went up two hundred feet from the courthouse, then came down in Morton's cow-pasture."

"I do hope we see him this time!" said Marcia. "Maybe he'll fall."

"This one never wants to miss anything," laughed their mother, tweaking Marcia's ear.

As soon as they were back in the surrey, Florrie still sleeping, Papa picked up the whip and they started off very fast. No one said anything, for their father's anger had spread around them like a frost. Something had happened that they did not understand and it was somehow Mama's fault. Presently they were in the country again, with the sweet, dull smell of hay, then the damp mossy breeze from the deep woods and hidden frog ponds. Their father put his arm around their mother. She began to laugh, rubbing her head against his cheek.

"Oh, Harry, you kill me!" she chuckled. "The Furness house! Why not Buckingham Palace?"

"All right, Buckingham Palace," agreed their father, laughing reluctantly. "You don't think I mean what I say, Daisy. It makes me mad when you won't believe me. You never think I can do the things I say, but you wait."

"But you won't go on the road, darling," pleaded their mother. "You said you'd take any other job rather than leave me."

"I said I wouldn't go on the road," their father shouted. "All right, if I said I wouldn't, then I won't. That's all there is to that."

Above, the skies darkened suddenly as if a lantern had blown out. A wind blew up, rattling the storm curtains warningly. Clouds as black as midnight rode over the horizon and the baby began to cry loudly. They stopped to put up the storm curtains, but the wind whipped them into their father's face as fast as he buttoned them. Lightning flashed and the horse whinnied in terror. Both the girls were scared but their mother told them to hush. She held the baby tight but it still wept lustily; the horse threw up its head and galloped wildly down the road into the gathering storm. It was barely three o'clock but the earth was drenched in darkness. As they dashed by the farms, horses whinnied, dogs barked, cocks crowed, bells rang in the wind, voices cried out in the fields.

"We can make the edge of town, I think," shouted their father.

"Look!" cried their mother.

When they looked they saw a dark object drifting across the sky like a bat across the ceiling.

"The balloon! The man in the balloon!" exclaimed their mother.

Marcia and Lena, arms tight around each other, looked upward, frightened and fascinated while the balloon drifted slowly downward, barely missing a barn cupola. They could see a dark figure outlined in the ship, a fairy-tale monster, omen of thunder and darkness and nightmares to come. The lightning sprang behind it like hell-fire from the Bible pictures, and the horse reared. It was like that picture in their old dining-room of three horses and night lightning. The children stared helplessly, filled with sick loneliness and fear, as if the creature flying up there had brought the clouds and lightning and the blight to their perfect day, and no one, not even a father and mother, could stop his wicked vengeance.

"I wouldn't want to be up there in his shoes, by God!" yelled their father. Fearfully, they twisted their necks to look back at the balloon which was being driven back by the wind in a circle, though when the lightning flashed again they could see the balloon-man's upraised arms as if he were calling on dark spirits for more terror. Looking back as the galloping horse bore them to the city pavements, they saw the man in the balloon lost in black clouds, sailing higher and higher, roaring prophecies in thunder until he was lost in black sky.

"We'll make it!" their mother called out, for the London Junction signs could be seen as the first big drops began to fall. A railroad ran down the middle of the main street like a street-car track, and they had to pass a switching yard filled with snorting engines and freight-cars which frightened their horse even more. They drove down a wide pavement and dashed in a driveway just as the torrent came. They drove straight into the barn and their father lifted them out on the straw-covered floor.

"Run right in the back door—quick!"

They had no time to look at Aunt Lois' house beyond their fleeting pride in its bigness, but scurried under the grape arbor, through the woodshed and in the kitchen door, which welcomed them with the smell of frying chicken and cake-baking and lights as bright as a church. Aunt Lois came running from the front of the house in a white muslin dress, looking so much like a good angel that they ran to her desperately. She hugged them and they began to cry simultaneously into her lap.

"Why, you poor babies! The storm scared you, didn't it?" Aunt Lois soothed them, drying their tears with her apron.

"No, it wasn't the storm, it was the man in the balloon," whimpered Marcia, still shivering. She buried her moist face in her aunt's soft neck. "Don't let the man in the balloon get us! Please! Please!"

2

Every night in London Junction Lena cried and sometimes their mother rocked her in her arms, big girl that she was, and sang to her. Sometimes she cried, too, leaning over to hide her tears on Lena's yellow curls, and sometimes this sniffling woke up the sensitive Florrie who would set up a great sympathetic bellow and have to be taken up, too. Marcia stood in front of this emotional spectacle, puzzled and unmoved.

"What's Lena bawling about?" she asked repeatedly, and her mother always answered, "She's homesick for the old house on Peach Street."

Marcia tried in vain to understand. Lena had been as excited as she herself had been to come to London Junction. All right, now they were here. They had their wish, didn't they?

Just as they'd made it so often on loads of hay and falling stars. But instead of being happy Lena had to bawl. It didn't make sense. Mama cried, too. Florrie always cried, so that didn't count.

"Well, I do miss Towser," Marcia thoughtfully acknowledged, but she could go no further in comprehending her sister's delicate and doubtless more mature emotions. In less triste moments, Marcia studied her for other signs of the strange difference between them, a difference she longed to rectify, if she could only understand it. Sometimes she begged for a demonstration for the benefit of her playmates.

"Show Georgie how you cry when you're homesick," Marcia would urge, but Lena would only be snappish and run away, blushing.

Marcia was five years old now, fifteen months younger than Lena, but she was half an inch taller because she took after the Willards instead of the Reeds. It was an understood thing that Lena was the pretty one, with her yellow curls and rosy cheeks, but Marcia was proud of having bigger feet so she got new shoes first, and the fact that she could hold her breath longer. She did admire Lena's social poise, her not being afraid of boys but stalking past them, nose calmly in air, and she desperately envied Lena's birthmark, a strawberry basket on her neck, caused, it was said, by her mother's passion for strawberries. Lena, for her part, was envious of grown-up solicitude over Marcia's health, remarks that she looked "peaked" and sickly. Marcia had a memory, too, though this was a matter of wonder and pride to Lena more than envy. Marcia could remember everything that ever happened, almost from her first tooth. She could remember knowing what people were saying before she could talk and she could remember bitterly the humiliation of being helpless. She remembered being carried in her mother's arms to a family reunion and given ice cream for the first time. She had cried over its being too cold and her mother said, "Here, Baby, I'll put it on a stove to warm it." Any fool of even less than two could see it was a table and not a stove, but for some philosophic reason Baby Marcia decided to let the thing pass without protest. If her mother wanted to think a table was a stove, she would just have to wait for a bigger vocabulary to argue the matter. This was the beginning of a series of disillusioning experiences with adult intelligence, and the recurrent question of whether adults were playing a constant game of insulting trickery, or whether they just didn't know much. Lena was gravely shocked by Marcia's spoken doubts, so Marcia kept her thoughts to herself.

Lena went to Primary School in London Junction now and no longer considered Marcia a fit companion in public, but walked home with a girl-friend her own age named Mary Evelyn Stewart. The double name was very fascinating so Marcia changed her own name to Marcia Lily and Lena took the name of Lena Gladys. They tried to make Florrie use her full elegant name of Florence Adeline, but with her customary obstinacy she yelled defiantly, "Me Florrie! Me Florrie!"

"All right, then, be Florrie," Lena Gladys said contemptuously. "But Mary Evelyn and I won't ride you around any more in your go-cart after school."

Lena and Mary Evelyn had a glamorous life in Primary that set them far above Marcia. They had to learn pieces to speak on Exercise Day once a month. Since Mary Evelyn's mother worked in the Fair Store, both children learned in the Willard sitting room, while Marcia, burning with jealousy, played by herself in a corner, cutting out lady paper-dolls all with two names. Marcia couldn't go to school till next term, although she had read and written almost as soon as she walked and talked. This, like her memory, was a dubious talent, for it was not healthy to be different from other children. It wasn't healthy to learn Lena's and Mary Evelyn's pieces the second time she heard them laboriously spelled out, and it was certainly not tactful. Her mother, with a little schoolgirl on each knee, looked down at Marcia helplessly.

"Marcia, you're supposed to be playing paper-dolls!" she protested. "If the girls haven't begun to know their pieces by this time, there's no reason why *you* should."

"She isn't even six," Lena Gladys said coldly to her personal friend, Mary Evelyn. "Now, I'll begin mine again. 'The gingerbread dog and the calico cat——' "

" 'Side by side on the table sat,' " Marcia shrieked, and ran out into the yard yelling the rest of the piece until her mother caught her and boxed her ears.

This correction, not being understood, was forgotten on Exercise Day the next month, when Lena (and of course Marcia) had learned "Little Orphan Annie" with gestures. Mama left Florrie at Grandma's and took Marcia to visit the First Grade. It was an exciting day with the rustle of mothers' best silks, the smell of chalk-dust and newly scrubbed halls, and the squirming of the children sitting two at a desk to make room for the Second Graders. Marcia and her mother sat with the visiting mothers and smaller children in folding chairs on one side of the room. The teacher had drawn a flag in colors on the blackboard, and there were pussy-willows and autumn leaves on her desk. She tapped a little silver gong on her desk when everyone was seated, and she said, "Before we begin the Exercises, perhaps some of our little visitors have a piece they would like to recite for us." Without further urging, Marcia slid off her mother's lap and marched over to the platform, where she recited at terrific speed with glib gestures "Little Orphan Annie." The performance was marked by her mother's horrified face and the sound of Lena sobbing softly into her Reader, "That's my piece! Now I haven't got any piece!"

Even after a punishment for this breach of etiquette and her stout defense, "But Lena didn't know it anyway!" Marcia continued to steal Lena's arithmetic or reader and run easily through the home-work while Lena was patiently working over one word in her Speller. Marcia could not understand why it took her sister or Mary Evelyn so long to learn things when they were like candy—you saw them, ate them, and that was the end. Nor could she understand why it was bad for her to find the books so simple, just because she wasn't in school yet. It was confusing to be scolded for doing Lena's lessons, and then overhear her father chuckling about it to Mr. Friend. These were all matters that would clear up certainly when she started going to school so there was no use puzzling about them.

They lived in one side of a two-family house next to Friend's Grocery Store, after the summer at Grandma's and Aunt Lois' house. Often the children walked past the Furness mansion on Main Boulevard and pretended they lived there just as their father had promised. The big house was empty and they could stroll around the orchard, and even peek through windows of the buildings, unless the old caretaker happened to be around. Through the bars of the cellar windows they could see the basement bowling alley, and back of that the greenhouse with broken panes and cracked flowerpots with dead ferns, for no one had lived in the place since old Mrs. Furness had died. They took their shoes off and went wading on the porch, for the rain leaked through the roof to make delicious puddles and a wading-pool of the garden fountain. The great overgrown lawn was a treasure of four-leaf clovers, mole cellars, garter snakes and hoary dandelions to be blown away in a wish. This was their real home, because their father had said so, and any other place was only marking time.

"It's a good thing I decided not to take the Furness place," their father said to their mother. "I understand the heater used to eat up ten tons of coals a season, and with the laundry in the basement you'd be running up and down those stairs every minute. I'm mighty glad I thought it over again."

"Oh, darling, you know we couldn't—*ever!*" their mother gently protested. "I can't understand your even thinking about it."

But this lack of faith always made their father mad. He was often cross nowadays, and always tired out. Their mother was always shushing them with, "Papa has a lot on his mind at his new job, so do be quiet." There were many nights when Aunt Lois and Grandma came in for what seemed to be a very grave family conference. The children were sent to bed early, but they could hear their father's voice get higher and higher, shouting down Aunt Lois' tense quick words. The nursery was over the living room and by peeking down the open register the girls could see the grown-ups and hear them without actually understanding what these meetings were all about, except that Papa seemed to be the center of them, both leader and victim. Mama sometimes cried, and Grandma's only contribution seemed as moderator, clucking out a "Now, now, there's more to it than that!" Papa usually shouted out the same answers every time. If a fellow had brains there was no sense in his working in a furniture factory for a foreman that didn't even speak English, he said. "I got brains. I got a personality. Carson's a mighty smart man. He's the boss and he knows what's what. If the boss thinks I got the personality for the road, I don't see what you women have to kick about, trying to hold me back." The arguments often had their start before Papa's arrival, with Mama complaining to her mother and sister about something Papa was threatening to do. But as soon as they offered advice and sympathy, Mama went over to Papa's side. By the end of the evening Grandma and Aunt Lois went home annoyed and baffled, and through the register the children could see Mama tenderly embracing Papa, saying, "I know they're my folks, Harry, and they mean a lot to me, but they've no right to criticize you."

"That's all right," Papa growled. "Only thing is, they get you all upset and that's what makes me sore. Carson's been mighty nice to me and you don't seem to appreciate that. He says I'd be worth a fortune to him on the road. You said you didn't want me to work nights at the factory so I told him so. He knows I'm too smart for that. Besides if I go on the road, maybe I can pick up a chance at a big job—maybe in Cleveland, Chicago, Pittsburgh. London Junction isn't the only place in the world."

"Oh, Harry! A real city?" then their mother's voice dropped. "But we've hardly lived in London Junction yet. I'm not sure I'd like Cleveland."

Scraps from these scenes were excitedly pieced together in the dark into whispered clues by Lena and Marcia; they were repeated to Mary Evelyn at recess next day, eventually resulting in Mary Evelyn's mother saying to Lena's mother at the Fair Store one day, "Well, I hear you folks are moving to Cleveland any day now. Your little girl told my little girl." Mama was surprised, then burst out laughing, though later she scolded Lena for telling lies. Lena cried, but Marcia boldly spoke up, "If Papa tells lies, then *we* can tell lies, too!" This brought Mama's wrath on Marcia, while Lena complacently ran out to play with Mary Evelyn.

The mature new life of her older sister was desperately fascinating to Marcia, now constantly left out. On Sundays she hoped to have Lena to herself for Sunday school, but even there Mary Evelyn came first. One Sunday they were dressed up in their green nun's veiling jumper dresses with polka dot blouses and felt tricorn hats, ready to march off to the First Christian Church, a penny in each little crocheted purse. But at the corner of Maple and Fourth they met Mary Evelyn.

"Hello, Mary Evelyn," said Lena.

"Hello, Lena Gladys," said Mary Evelyn.

"Hello," Marcia said breathlessly, but Mary Evelyn paid no attention, just staring at Lena as if they had a secret together.

"You go on to the Christian Church," Lena directed Marcia, firmly. "I'm going to Mary Evelyn's Sunday School."

"But you can't!" gasped Marcia. "Mary Evelyn is a Presbyterian, and they sing different songs."

"Is she a tattle-tale?" Mary Evelyn asked Lena, as if Marcia was a doll and couldn't talk for herself. Mary Evelyn was tall for her age. She had a velvet dress and a locket with an opal and asafetida in it, a prayer book with a lock, and a nickel for collection. She had very red cheeks just as Lena had, and a fat black braid down her back with the ends tightly curled. She had a pink velvet hat with a big bow under her chin, for her mother bought all her clothes from a catalogue. She did not care to walk in public with anybody younger than she was, so Marcia was obliged to keep several steps behind the two older girls. As she kept shouting remarks to them, the conspicuity was almost worse than letting her come along with them. Lena threatened to tell Mama and this stopped Marcia for a minute or two. Still, she would rather be lectured for walking behind them than go all by herself to the First Christian Sunday School. Presently, crushed by criticism and threats, she stood on the corner watching unhappily while Lena Gladys and Mary Evelyn stalked proudly down the street toward the Presbyterian Church. She wanted to get even by going home and tattling, but she didn't quite dare risk their scorn. Her pride was shattered by being treated like a baby, but more than that she was mystified by the difference between herself and Lena. What made Lena have the courage to step into a strange church, knowing she might get spanked for doing this without permission? What made it more fun for Lena to do things without permission, anyway? Marcia hopscotched by herself on the corner, pretending to have a good time in case they turned around and looked, but they did not seem to care what she did, providing she didn't bother them. Desolately she saw that they were actually turning in the Presbyterian Churchyard and leaving her. She had only to turn up East Maple and go to the Christian Church, but she couldn't bear to go all alone. Suddenly, with a little gasp at her own daring, she began running in the direction of the other girls, and as the last bell chimed, she fell over the brownstone steps of the Presbyterian Church, tearing a big hole in the knee of her stocking. A strange big man with whiskers lifted her up and carried her into the assembly door just as they began singing, "I washed my hands this morning, so very clean and white—." The big man put Marcia down on a chair where she sat rigidly, her heart pounding almost visibly under her jumper. If it had not been for the encouraging sight of Lena standing smugly in the front row with Mary Evelyn, and the fact that the great door was closed, she would have rushed wildly out again, back to her proper church. She saw that she was in a row with boys, too, some of them giants of eight or nine years old, and this threw her into fresh panic. She kept her eyes fixed on Lena, standing so calmly, her yellow curls prettily ruffling out from under her felt hat; she ached with envy of this marvellous poise. Then she thought of what Lena and Mary Evelyn would do to her when they found she had tagged, and this prospect was worse than fear of her mother's scolding. She thought, too, of what the stained glass God of the First Christian Church would do, if he found her in a Presbyterian Church, and it was no comfort thinking he might do the same thing to Lena because clearly Lena did not fear Him. She saw Georgie Hollis from across the street making faces at her and even read his lips, "What are you doing in my Sunday School?"

Then everybody sat down and a very big, very old woman rustled up to the platform. She had mixed yellow and gray hair that looked like old corn silk piled in ropes on her head and loose downy cheeks that wobbled as she walked. Moreover, she flashed a sparkling lot of gold teeth, a black-ribboned pince-nez and a ruffled blouse covered with brooches, and chains that clinked with authority. There was a silence as she looked over the audience. Marcia hoped her heart did not thunder out her guilty presence.

"I am going to tell you little folks about Sin," said the lady in a sweet, whining Sunday-school voice. "Look what I have here. A glass of pure water, a white rabbit's foot and a bottle of black ink. The rabbit's foot represents the purity of your souls when you are little children. The ink is black like sin and the pure water is the Spirit of Goodness. Does everyone see?"

Marcia craned her neck and saw the rabbit's foot held up.

"Now, the rabbit's foot I dip in the pure water of goodness and see? It stays as white as snow. But then I dip it into the ink of Sin and look! Sin makes the soul black."

This turned out to be absolutely true and there was a murmur as the lady dangled the black rabbit's foot before the astonished audience. Marcia gripped her seat, feeling faintly sick with the knowledge of her own rabbit's foot soul turning black with sin inside her. She heard the slow sugary voice drone on, "Now, children, what do we mean by Sin?"

No one answered. The lady looked around, frowning impatiently.

"Come, come, children, I'm sure we know what Sin is. Come, Mary Evelyn, you've been coming to Sunday School regularly, what is Sin?"

"Ice cream," said Mary Evelyn hopefully.

Someone tittered.

"No, no, ice cream isn't a sin, except when it is forbidden," said the lady sharply. Mary Evelyn pouted. Marcia felt her own hand going up almost of its own accord.

"There's a little hand. What is Sin, dear?"

"Going to the wrong Sunday School," Marcia said clearly.

This was even worse than ice cream for an answer. The lady was scowling as if she wished she had never dirtied her nice rabbit's foot for the benefit of these young stupids. Furthermore, it made Lena and Mary Evelyn turn around and look at the offender. Marcia felt her face burning hot, and her stomach felt as if she'd been riding on a streetcar. She wished urgently that she might drop dead, but then someone opened the door and called out, "Are you through, Miss Marshall? The children may go to their classes now, and we can resume the discussion at Collection time."

With a burst of desperation Marcia ran for the open door and hurtled herself into the great outdoors, falling down on the same step as before and bruising her other knee. She ran down the street toward home, certain of being chased by a pack of Presbyterians and was only reassured at the corner of Maple by the Kandy Kitchen sign. This cheery sight reminded her that she still had her penny so she went inside. At the candy counter she hesitated between a licorice shoestring and a chocolate peppermint that might have a penny prize in it. She chose the peppermint and was rewarded by biting on a coin at once, which allowed her to have a second candy. She loitered over this one, making it last till she had finished a wonderful funny paper the Kandy Kitchen man had opened up over the ice cream table. Instead of being about Buster Brown and Mary Jane, this had a magical story about some one named Little Nemo. Marcia pored over this, happily sucking on her peppermint. She felt mature and independent now, ashamed that she had ever been so childish as to tag after Lena and Mary Evelyn. Suddenly she realized that she was biting on a second penny, unheard-of good fortune, and this reward gave her an inspiration.

"Mr. Kitchen," she said to the bald top of a head on the other side of the counter, "do you sell rabbit's foots?"

Mr. Kitchen's hand scratched the bald top and he said no, but if he ever caught a jackrabbit he'd give her a foot for luck.

"I don't want it for luck," Marcia explained. "I want it to play Sin with like the Presbyterians do. I guess maybe I can make one."

She could hardly wait to run home and make herself a rabbit's foot out of cotton and string. She decided she would have to get the ink out of Papa's desk while he was mowing the back lawn. Planning this treat, she saw Lena and Mary Evelyn marching primly around the corner, so she ran out, following them at a few paces, forgetting her vow.

"Tagtail," said Mary Evelyn loudly without turning around.

"Pooh on you," answered Marcia.

"Don't pay any attention to her," said Lena.

"She'll never go to heaven and be an angel like us," said Mary Evelyn, primly.

"I don't care, then I'll go to hell and play with all the little devils," said Marcia fiercely. "I'd rather."

This awed her elders into silence, though she could see them exchanging a look of shocked horror. Her own words had even frightened herself and she had a panicky feeling that the man in the balloon might have overheard.

"Let's not let her play house with us," said Mary Evelyn.

"I don't care, I don't care!" shrilly answered Marcia. "I don't play baby games like house. I'm going to get me a rabbit's foot and play Sin. Right now, too."

The two other girls whispered together over this, clearly intrigued. Finally Lena stopped.

"All right, you can walk with us," she said graciously. "We'll play Sin, too. How do we do it?"

"Come on and I'll show you!" Marcia jubilantly cried. If it had not been Sunday they would have run all the way home to start the game. It was too bad Mary Evelyn spilled ink on her dress, but if everybody was going to get spanked, Mary Evelyn might as well, too.

3

In the double-house on Fourth Street next to Friend's Grocery Store, there was a dark hallway between the two apartments and a common staircase to the second floor. The Friends' rooms were on the right side and the Willards' on the left. The Friends' baby had died but they still kept its bedroom upstairs with the Madonnas and infant Jesus pictures all over, and Mrs. Friend allowed the Willard children to look at them once in a while. But she got angry when Marcia asked if Jesus was real why the various pictures of him looked like different people. She asked, too, if they could play with the little Madonnas. After that, their mother told them to stay on their side of the hall. Sometimes Charlie Friend, a nephew who delivered groceries for Mr. Friend after high school, came over and walked down the banister in his stocking feet, waving his arms to balance himself, but when Marcia and Lena tried it, they fell downstairs. Mrs. Friend blamed Charlie for this. She said he was too big a boy to play with little girls because he always made them cry. Charlie got mad and Lena and Marcia were even madder, because Charlie swiped candy for them and penny sodas in six different flavors to dissolve in water.

The Friends gave Florrie a big white cradle, and every night Marcia and Lena took opposite sides of the cradle, rocking it and singing at the top of their voices until Florrie, for some reason, would fall asleep. Sometimes their father got out his shining yellow guitar and sang with them, teaching them to take different parts. When Mama had finished the supper dishes they had quartettes. Their father's songs had many verses and were usually sad, with old men grieving for their childhood homes across the sea, mothers lamenting their dead children, little girls lost in the snowstorm, beautiful ladies dying because they had gone to the ball with a hectic flush, poor little Joe in the cold, cold night, and above all the honest Irish lad unable to get work in the city. The last was the favorite of all and they knew all the words. It went—

> Our little farm was small
> It would not support us all,
> And one of us was forced away from home.
> So I bid them all goodbye
> With a teardrop in my eye,
> And sailed for Castle Garden all alone.
>
> When I landed in New York,
> It was hard to get work;
> I roamed about the streets from day to day.
> I went from place to place
> With starvation in my face—
> Nobody had any work, they'd say,
>
> Now I'm an honest Irish lad
> And my home is far away;
> If pleasing you I'll either sing or dance.
> I'll do anything you say
> If you'll only name the day
> You'll give an honest Irish lad a chance.

It was all Marcia could do to keep from howling in sympathy, as they sang, although Lena did not seem at all affected by these melodious tragedies. After Florrie had fallen asleep, the girls were allowed to go downstairs another hour to look at their picture books, Puss in Boots and Cinderella. But the most fun was when their mother told stories. On such evenings their father made a party of it. He would rap on the Friends' door for them to come over and listen, and he would arrange the chairs as if for a show, all of them facing Mama's chair. There was always an excitement about their father; his laughter, his rages, all of his movements were sudden; anger and pleasure exploded without warning or clear reason. When he invited the Friends, it always meant he was in a fine humor, proud of his family, tickled with everything Mama said or did.

"Come on in," he'd say, "Daisy's going to tell the kids stories."

But the stories were really for him. He would put the children into their nightgowns and red Christmas robes with rabbit slippers, then plant them in their small rockers before the big stove. Mr. and Mrs. Friend settled themselves in their appointed chairs, waiting for their host to finish his preparations for the supper to come later—sardines and cheese and beer, or maybe an oyster stew.

"Harry's a better cook than I am," their mother always said. "Harry can do anything he puts his mind to."

"By Jove, I can't tell a story the way she does and that's a a fact," their father chuckled. "She can raise the hair on your head—even yours—Friend, ha ha! Go ahead, honey, begin."

Mama took the big chair and crossed her legs under her, tailor-fashion. She looked like a little girl this way, blowing her curly bangs out of her eyes, which were shining wide. The stories she told in a hushed voice were all about ghosts in churchyards, the wind going woo-oo—ooo, the dogs howling in cemeteries, the dead dancing over their graves to violins played by skeleton figures. Papa would wink at Mr. Friend, fat little Mrs. Friend would clutch her husband and gasp, "Oh, my God!" Mr. Friend smoked a pipe and whenever Mama's voice sank to a whisper as it did when the story approached its climax, he would take the pipe out of his mouth and hold it motionless, shaking his bald head in amazement. Then, as Mama sat back triumphantly, Mr. Friend would chuckle and nudge his wife, "Who believes such things? Amy, you're crazy! Nobody ever saw such things, don't be foolish."

Lena always sat rocking back and forth happily, her blue eyes fixed on her mother's flushed excited face, pleased that it was a party and that she was the oldest child. For Marcia, however, each word was agony, sowing seed for terror in darkness. She would not be surpassed by Lena, though, so she clenched the arms of her rocker and tried to shut her ears to her mother's voice. One time, unable to bear the part where the Feet dance by themselves on the treetop, she ran out of the room with her fingers in her ears. Everyone laughed at her, the way they did at Mrs. Friend, so after that she steeled herself to laugh whenever she was frightened. This fooled and pleased her father, who picked her up and held her on his knee.

"Can you beat that?" he exclaimed proudly. "She knows it's funny, already."

So Lena laughed, too, but Mrs. Friend continued to be scared, no matter how often she heard the stories, and she always cried, "Oh, my God!" with a frantic clutch at her husband's arm.

"Do you wonder why I married Daisy?" their father said, arm around his wife. "Why, I'd rather listen to Daisy than go to a show."

This Lena repeated proudly to Mary Evelyn Stewart who told it to her mother, who said there were no shows in London Junction anyway, which Mary Evelyn then told Lena who told her father, who said angrily that he did not like the idea of his daughter playing with the daughter of a woman who worked in a store. This, in reverse order, went back the same route and so for two or three weeks Mary Evelyn and Lena did not speak to each other, and Lena took "Gladys" off her name because she said two names looked silly, and she went back to her own Sunday School.

Their father was a Travelling Man, now, for the London Furniture Company. He came home Thursday nights and stayed till Sunday night. On Thursday the children would stay awake, waiting for him. They could peek down through the register and see their mother sitting at the window, waiting. Then there would be the step on the porch, the exclamations and laughter. Their father and mother would embrace joyously and, still holding each other, start waltzing around and round the room faster and faster, their father not even stopping to take off his hat and coat. When they could stand it no longer, the children tore downstairs, barefooted, and took turns climbing up their father, ending up one on each shoulder. It was fun having your father a Travelling Man because he brought home presents. He brought hats for Mama from Cleveland, funny fans and joke books, miniature decks of cards, perfume, hair-ribbons, boxes of candy, soap rabbits, pencils, calendars, and once he brought Mama a fur capelet. Another travelling man was going to sell it to him cheap if Mama liked it. Mama showed it to Aunt Lois and Grandma and Mrs. Friend, but made him take it back the next trip.

"We can't spend that much money, dear," she protested, fondly. "The kids all need winter coats and we need a new carpet."

"Better keep it, Daisy," advised Mrs. Friend. "If you don't take it, Number Two will."

This got to be a family joke. Their father would pass the meat platter to her and say, "If you don't take it Number Two will." But when he went on his long trip—the Southern territory, and was gone three weeks—Mrs. Friend said, "You should have taken the fur cape because you see you didn't get the carpet or the new coats anyway. You've got to take what your man has a mind to give you of his own accord, because he's never going to give you anything you ask for, and that's the man of it."

"The trouble with Harry being on the road," Mama said to Aunt Lois, "is that he makes more money than he would here in the shop, but he hardly ever sends me any."

"Write and ask him," urged Aunt Lois.

Mama shook her head.

"I don't want to hurt his feelings. Harry's feelings get so hurt when I have to tell him about money."

"All men's feelings are hurt there," Aunt Lois said, laughing.

Aunt Lois' visits, frequent though they were, were always exciting. She wore pretty clothes, furs, and kid gloves, beads, handsome combs in her fair hair, and her skin was soft and pink like the big dolls' in the toy store. Lena was supposed to be the spit and image of her. She had beautiful teeth and was always laughing, perhaps for that very reason. One grudge she still bore against her absent husband was that he had exploited her beautiful crinkly gold hair to advertise his own manufactured hair tonic "Blair's *Blondina*"; and since word came that he made quite a sum out of his formula Aunt Lois was all the madder. She always entered in a state of excitement about something, so it made her calls very thrilling. She brought presents, a bag of peanuts, a cake, some chewing-gum, every time she came, but usually Mama or one of the children was in tears by the time she left, just out of excess excitement. There was nothing half-way about Aunt Lois. She was ecstatically approving or violently disapproving, never merely tolerant. She thought Mrs. Friend was an idiot, and she thought all the members of Papa's family, particularly his sister Kit, were big-heads. She said once, and she'd say it again, that Mr. Putney was the man Mama should have married. Mr. Thorburne Putney, the distinguished lecturer. Outside of his personal and financial qualifications, it was always a good thing to have a prominent man in the family, a man who'd been all over the world. Mama only laughed at mention of this past suitor, and reminded her sister of so many ridiculous stories of him that Aunt Lois ended up weeping from laughter.

If Aunt Lois seemed in a tolerant mood, Mama would confide her worries. Aunt Lois would start criticizing Harry, saying it was always a bad thing for a man to go on the road—it always meant trouble. Then Mama would be hurt and stay away from her for two or three days, making Mrs. Friend her confidante, until Mrs. Friend would say it was just exactly the way she had prophesied, as soon as a man got to travelling he forgot his responsibilities, so this criticism sent Mama back to Aunt Lois. There was a great deal of talk about money, and usually Aunt Lois or Mrs. Friend would insist on leaving some with Mama. After these visits Mama would be depressed but the moment their father's step was on the porch, everything was all right again.

"God damn it, I'm too busy to think of every little thing," the children could hear their father say after the first joyous waltz and the gossip had begun, "I wish you wouldn't talk to Lois or Mrs. Friend. They just upset you, honey."

"I don't know why I do, Harry," their mother guiltily confessed. "Maybe I'm just lonesome for you."

"Lonesome!" shouted their father. "I'm the one that's lonesome. Come home every night to a cold hotel room. No wonder, I feel half sick all the time. I'm a home man, damn it, but I got to take this job to *make* a home! I wish folks would get that in their heads!"

The next time he went away on one of his longer trips, their mother sent Marcia and Lena to Kraus' Store to see if they could use corn muffins and biscuits once a week. The Krauses said yes, so three times a week their mother baked and they took the baskets after school to Kraus'. Mr. Friend ordered some for his store and other families in the neighborhood ordered regular supplies, too.

"Only don't tell my husband," their mother would beg. "Harry is so proud, he'd kill me."

She couldn't keep the secret herself, and finally told Aunt Lois.

"I won't have to ask him for any money," she said gleefully. "That will make him wonder, I'll bet."

It was fun having a secret from their father, but they waited for him to ask questions in vain. Instead, the girls heard their mother ask him playfully after a while, "Don't you think it's funny I don't need any money?"

Their father patted her tenderly and said, "Honey, you're finally learning how to manage, that's all. That's my girl!"

There was the time he brought home the high Spanish comb and the candied ginger and the talking machine with records. They played it nights for Aunt Lois and Grandma, but Aunt Lois was bad-tempered, spoiling it all. In the middle of "Oh the moon shines tonight on pretty Red Wing as sung by Edison Records," Aunt Lois said, "Harry, how much did that thing cost you? Don't you think your family might like a few comforts before you spend your money on trash like this?"

Papa looked so bewildered and abused that Marcia felt a hot surge of anger, and she cried out in a choking voice, "We don't want any comforts, Aunt Lois! We like the talking machine best!"

"Hush, dear," said Mama, her face red.

"I'd send it back a-flying, if I was in your place, Daisy, and take the money instead," said Aunt Lois firmly.

"You're just jealous, Lois," their mother cried out hotly. "Harry loves me and brings me presents and your husband hasn't written you in ten years. I *love* the talking machine! I'd rather have it than anything in the world and Harry knows it!"

She threw her arms around his neck, sobbing, and he patted her, but his face was still dark and aggrieved.

"That's what a fellow gets when he tries to do something nice for somebody," he grumbled. "Always plenty of people to criticize."

After Aunt Lois went, Mama comforted him, and even sent him out to the saloon for a pint of beer. That night the children heard him playing the guitar long after they were asleep. He sang, "Oh, Bedelia, oh, Bedelia, I've a longing for to steal you, oh, Bedelia." When they heard the gramophone playing again, "Oh the moon shines tonight on pretty Red Wing," they rolled into each other's arms to sleep, happy because he was happy again.

4

Wherever Grandma stayed was "Grandma's house," though the London Junction place was really Aunt Lois', left her by her absent husband's father, and a great burden to her in size and taxes. But while Aunt Lois whisked briskly up and down stairs with mop and broom and a towel around her head, eternally busy at keeping the big house in order, Grandma rocked on the side porch with her darning bag, visiting with her friends and keeping up an air of gracious leisure. Ever since she had given up the Elmville farm she talked of having a place of her own, "being independent" as she said. But her children balked her in this by making her stay for a while first with one and then the other. She managed to sustain a feeling of independence at Aunt Lois' by making plans for a millinery store, a tea-room, or a dress-making shop. Aunt Lois was always catching her with the grass blinds of the porch drawn, in low-voiced conferences with furtive little people who had a store to let or a business to sell. Aunt Lois recently had taken in schoolteachers as roomers, but one time she found that in her absence Grandma had admitted two night workers from the Foundry.

"They can use the teachers' rooms while the teachers are away," Grandma explained. "Don't you see, Lois, they can sleep daytimes while the teachers are at school?"

When Aunt Lois expostulated that the teachers wouldn't like it, Grandma explained, "They needn't know. My goodness, Lois, I could nip upstairs and wake them before the teachers got home, couldn't I? My glory, Lois, don't you want to make a little extra money? I don't want to just work for nothing all my life. Never mind! Let it go! I'll have a place of my own one of these days."

A fine thing about Grandma was that she never seemed to admit any difference between children and grown-ups, so she was as apt to confide her career plans to Marcia and Lena as to anyone else, or if she stayed with them to let them stay up till it was her own bedtime. Marcia played here while Lena was at school, and Grandma let her stir cake batter or peel potatoes or help make beds while she talked about her plans.

"Lois has had a lot of trouble in her life, what with losing her baby and having Charlie run off on her like he did," she said. "But on the other hand there's plenty Lois don't understand. A person can work their fingers to the bone on a farm, doing chores and raising ten children, all for nothing, and that's all right. But a body with a little more ambition is supposed to take a back seat. It's not fair."

"No," Marcia gravely agreed. "It's not fair. If I was you, Grandma, I'd run away."

"I will," her grandmother said resolutely. "I'm not going to take a back seat all my life. No matter what my own flesh and blood think. Why, I got more get-up-and-git in my little finger than the lot of them. I'll show them."

She had a friend, just as Lena had, a lady named Mrs. Carmel who used to run a millinery store in town but now lived in Cleveland. Mrs. Carmel had written her to come to Cleveland and start a rooming house, as there was a perfect fortune in it. It would be a real treat, Mrs. Carmel's letter said, to have an old friend there, and she needn't mind missing her lodge work as there were plenty Lady Maccabees and D.A.R.'s and Eastern Stars in Cleveland as well as a Women's Relief Corps. Every time Aunt Lois made objection to something Grandma did, Grandma would go up to her big front room and read over Mrs. Carmel's letter sometimes aloud to Marcia.

Grandma confided a great deal in Marcia and sometimes in her daughter Daisy, whenever Daisy was mad at Aunt Lois. But when her two daughters made up, Grandma knew it was no use talking to either of them for they sided against her. Either Lois scolded or Daisy slyly teased her. Strangers and Marcia were, however, constantly sympathetic. It was mean, they felt, for Aunt Lois to lose her temper whenever Grandma stopped Mr. Sweeney going by. Grandma's voice talking to Mr. Sweeney was very different than when she talked to anybody else, and Marcia finally discovered that all grown-ups used different voices for different classes of society. The voice Grandma used for Mr. Sweeney was a very elegant one, and furthermore with him she never used the words "me" or "her" in a sentence. "I and my daughter Lois get very lonely here, Mr. Sweeney, especially at nights. It is very hard for she, especially being a widow you might say, and a lovely looking girl as anybody can tell you. It's hard for a woman, Mr. Sweeney, when her man is a sick man. Yes sir, my daughter's husband was taken with an old disease they call walking fever ten years ago and we haven't seen him since. Very hard for both I and she. You know how a mother feels, Mr. Sweeney. It would be a privilege to me to see some lovely widower like yourself pay her a call now and then." Mr. Sweeney had a reddish face and was always dressed up with a big black-brimmed hat over his bald head, a cane, and a large thick gold watch fob resting on his tight tan vest. He even carried thick kid gloves sometimes, for his affairs took him into fine places in distant cities. He lived in the London Junction Hotel and rented his former home on Willow Avenue to which he and Grandma referred in sacred tones as "the property." He had property in Cleveland, too, and in Lesterville where his wife's parents had been very well fixed.

"A real gentleman," Grandma told Marcia, "and your Aunt Lois don't even appreciate what I'm trying to do for her. It's enough to break a body's heart."

"My daughter Lois wondered what your opinion was of the present situation," Grandma would say, just to keep Mr. Sweeney another few minutes. "She was saying to a party the other day that Mr. Sweeney is about the only person you can talk to in this place, I mean the only person who gets around and knows."

Mr. Sweeney would stand a little closer to the porch, careful not to disturb the spot where grass was planted but never grew, raise his big hat and mop his head thoughtfully, replace handkerchief in back pocket and cough. "It's likely we're in for some more hard times, Mrs. Reed—*but*, we got some good men in the country, J. P. Morgan, John D. Rockefeller, Andrew Carnegie—I guess we can trust them to look out for the common people in a pinch."

What made Grandma mad was that Aunt Lois would peek out and see who was there and go right back in the house, which hurt Mr. Sweeney's feelings so that he would lift his hat and go on his way with dignity. It made Grandma mad to be teased by her daughter Daisy as if Mr. Sweeney was *her* beau, when she was only trying to interest him in Lois. Even Marcia disapproved of her mother's ridicule of Mr. Sweeney, her defense being a matter of bribery largely, since Mr. Sweeney had given her a half dollar one day for bringing him a glass of water. Grandma discussed business in a low secret voice with Mr. Sweeney, and her plans to run a rooming house in Cleveland as her very clever friend, Mrs. Carmel, had advised. "It will leave my daughter very lonesome, Mr. Sweeney," Grandma confessed. "I trust you as the person she admires more than anyone else to sort of look after her. She's young and inexperienced, you know." But in spite of Aunt Lois' supposed reverence for Mr. Sweeney, she always ran away when he was there and scolded Grandma afterward, until Grandma would get red-faced and go upstairs to write other relations or—better still—Mrs. Carmel.

One day the children's mother got sick and all of them, even Florrie, were brought to Grandma's to stay, while Aunt Lois went to the Fourth Street House to nurse her sister. It was a wonderful vacation. Lena played hookey from school and Grandma let them eat cookies and milk every meal with bananas and oranges in between. They could play "Run,

Sheepie, Run," in the streets after dark with the neighbor children, and Florrie stayed up till she fell asleep of her own accord and threw up unheeded after every cookie. The teachers had fun, too, for Grandma let them have beaux all over the house at all hours and cook fudge late at night.

"My daughter Daisy is a very sick girl," she said, shaking her head. "I'll have to ask you ladies to help me with the house while Lois is nursing her."

The children could empty all the drawers and trunks they liked, dress up, play opera house—anything. They got out the family album bound in green plush with an inset diamond-shaped mirror and a tasselled gold lock, and one day Grandma patiently went over the whole family gallery for them. For instance, this pretty, full-cheeked, curly-haired brunette with the lace bertha and fan was Grandma's first-born who died at the Chicago World's Fair. This plump little girl, eager, laughing, with a ball held up in her hand, was not a playmate for you at all but your own great-grandmother who was to grow up to have four babies, one of them stolen by Indians, the others dead. This smiling handsome young man in the high collar, checked vest and thick curly black hair was the great-uncle who ended up insane, tied to a post and chain in an asylum; he was Great-Uncle Samuel and he had been a postman leaving one family in Rhode Island to start another in Massachusetts. "Amnesia, they call it now," said Grandma. "He left your Great-Aunt Nell and all the children and was gone thirteen years, forgetting his name and home. When he remembered he came back and took a razor to his wife and children, so they locked him away."

This story hung over Marcia's mind—that laughing youth should grow up into misery and horror, that to grow up did not mean rewards but anguish; even she might go crazy, with a post and chain and a razor. It was terrifying to look at the picture of her great-great-grandmother, the little girl with the ball, and think of her running through dark Indian forests crying, "Baby! Baby!" and the woods crying back, "Baby! Baby!" and far off the sound of a baby crying, lost forever. She thought of her great-grandmother always as a little girl with the ball, not as the later picture, the bent old lady in cap and shawl with the tired sad face. "Did she have nice things happen to her finally?" begged Marcia. "Please, Grandma, didn't nice things happen?"

"Died in the Elm County Poorhouse," said Grandma. "People didn't have the money then they have today." It was like Papa's songs and Marcia felt that there was not enough room in her chest to bear such woe.

"Who's this one?" Lena asked, pointing to the next page, a strange foreign gentleman who seemed to have a head coming out of his stomach.

"That is an Oriental prince," Grandma's voice now swelled with pride. "He was a Siamese twin and his sister grew out of his stomach. My sister Sarah Rebecca met him on a boat trip to Italy and he very kindly gave her his picture."

"No, no!" Marcia choked. "Don't tell me any more, Grandma. No more!"

She ran out the door into the back yard, into the woodshed where they wouldn't find her slapping her own eyes to keep back tears. But tears were inside her, crying Baby! Baby! oh, Indians, give back the little girl's baby!

5

During their father's longer absences, the children and their mother spent more and more time at Grandma's. Aunt Lois turned out one of the teachers and let her sister use the room for her family on the many nights they spent there, for Daisy was not so much afraid as lonesome at night. When some tiff with Aunt Lois—always about Papa—made her stay home in the house on Fourth Street for a few nights, she moved a cot into the children's room. She pushed the dresser against the door, and put Papa's revolver under her pillow. Then she wrapped her red Chinese kimono around herself and sat square-legged on the bed—her curly brown hair over her shoulders, telling stories long after bedtime. When a lightning storm came she was really happy and not at all frightened. She said burglars wouldn't be out on a night like this. In the middle of the night the thunder would begin and the rain pour. Lena and Marcia would cry out with fear and hold tight to each other. But their mother would jump out of bed and pull a chair up to the window. "Come, kids, watch the lightning!" she would cry and sometimes picked them out of bed, snuggled in blankets to sit in the chair by the window with her. It was something special to be gotten up in the night so the girls tried to be worthy of the honor but they could hardly keep back their cries of terror at each new thunderbolt or rip of lightning. They put their fingers in their ears and shut their eyes, peeking once in a while at their mother, whose eyes were shining in her rapt face, as if the storm was a story or a song to her.

"But lightning kills people," Marcia quavered.

"They would die anyway," said their mother. "If lightning didn't kill them they'd drop dead of something else. Green apples maybe."

It was fun having Papa away, a Santa Claus about to pop in with surprises any day. Besides, their mother let them do almost anything they liked. She showed them tricks she'd never showed them before: card tricks, how to twist your legs behind your neck, how to play the mouth-organ, and how to dance while she played the talking machine. She let them taste coffee and tea and told them jokes about two Irishmen, and two Dutchmen. She didn't even scold them when a lady down the street reported that the children played train with her bread loaves when they delivered them. They tied a string around the loaf and dragged it very conveniently to the store or home that had ordered it from their mother. She made them a little wagon with a board and thread-spools for wheels so the lady no longer complained.

One disadvantage in Papa's longer trips was that they missed the Saturday night celebration of paying the grocery bill. Papa had made a custom of taking all three children over to Friend's Store right after Saturday night supper (always tea and toast and applesauce). The store was crowded with farmers in hip boots, leather jackets and stocking caps, buying their week's supplies. Marcia and Lena, with Florrie grasped between them, stood close to Papa so as not to get lost in this great crowd, and also to indicate their preferences in the "treat." The bill paid, Mr. Friend then took a brown paper bag and tin scoop over to wooden buckets on the floor filled with different candies, hard candy in one, rather grayish chocolates in another, horehound drops in a third. Mr. Friend made a show of letting them choose, but no matter what they said there was always a preponderance of hard candy and never enough chocolates. Marcia saved her chocolates till bedtime, but Lena ate hers at once, shrewdly enough, since later on Marcia would have to divide hers with her or be reproached as selfish by Mama. Now three Saturdays sometimes passed with no treat, and Mr. Friend's informal generosity at other times did not make up for the loss of this ceremony.

Mama was restless and moody during Papa's absences. Once Aunt Lois promised to cheer her up by taking her to Lesterville to see a show with a friend of hers. London Junction had an opera house, but it had been condemned by the Fire Department ever since the last stock company's visit. The fire hazard had been recognized only after the leading man had run off with the mayor's niece after the last act of *Dr. Jekyll and Mr. Hyde*, but after that London Junction drama lovers must travel to Lesterville for their fun. Aunt Lois' friend was an insurance man named Wilson, a business acquaintance she said, who occasionally took her to supper when she had shopping to do in Lesterville. It would be a pleasure to meet her sister. Mama was excited, and decided to take one of the children.

"I know it won't be me," Marcia said stoically. "The middle one never gets took anywhere. It's always the baby, or Lena because she's the oldest. The middle one never gets took anywhere."

Mama weighed the matter gravely, but made up her mind when Aunt Lois reminded her that Florrie would cry all the time and that Lena had just shaved off her eyebrows at Mary Evelyn's suggestion and looked peculiar. It was luck at last for the middle one. Lena was left to sulkily look after Florrie, and Marcia was fixed up in a new plaid hair-ribbon, Lena's coat since it had no patches, with white mittens strung through the sleeves for safety. Aunt Lois and Mama did each other's hair in new ways before the mirror and borrowed each other's gloves, neck-ribbons, belts and furbelows, convinced that a good time as well as *chic* depended on the wearing of borrowed trifles. Mama wore her best brown broadcloth with black velvet buttons and a short cape, and Aunt Lois wore a handsome black velveteen with narrow fur edgings at the hem and bodice. They had sachets of flower petals pinned to their underthings and Marcia was allowed a drop of perfume on her handkerchief.

Lena looked after them with a long face, pressing it against the window as they left.

"I'll probably have a bad earache when you get home," she predicted. "It hurts bad already."

They took the five o'clock streetcar to Lesterville, ten miles away. For a long time before they got there, Marcia saw the dark sky illumined with flames; like a Fourth of July celebration. These were the steel mills, Mama explained. The car stopped at every other corner to pick up the workers with their dinner pails on their way to or from the mills. Riding past the gates you saw men bare to the waist outlined darkly against brilliant fire of blue or red or white, looking like the saints in stained-glass windows. The men crowded on the car smelled of dirt and sweat and pipe smoke, but more than anything else of power. Marcia withdrew into her mother's arms, afraid of these silent men, puzzled that her mother and Aunt Lois seemed unaffected by them.

"Mr. Wilson spoke of getting tickets for 'Colonial Dames' at the Lyceum," said Aunt Lois. "We can take turns holding Marcia on our lap."

They got off at the White Hotel on the Square. It was Marcia's first trip to Lesterville and the biggest town she'd ever seen, but she did not want people to suspect this, so she took care not to show interest in her surroundings. They went into a palm-decorated corridor, with a marble floor and large leather chairs lining the walls with cuspidors beside them. As they entered two gentlemen got up and removed their hats with the most gratifying reverence. One was dapper and swarthy with curling black moustaches and luxuriant black curly hair brushed back in a pompadour. He carried a rich brown topcoat over his arm, neatly folded, and wore a flower in his lapel. Marcia was so overcome with the stylishness of this Mr. Wilson that she had only a mild surprise to see that his companion was Mr. Sweeney. Mr. Sweeney bent low over Aunt Lois' hand, with the solemn dignity of one about to lead in prayer.

"I had business in Lesterville with Wilson," he said, "and when I heard you and your sister were coming over, I seized the opportunity to make it a party—my party, if you please."

Aunt Lois was very redfaced and gave Mama a deep look that was evidently meant to say volumes.

"Sweeney took charge of everything when he found you were coming," Mr. Wilson laughingly told Aunt Lois. "He says supper at the Chinatown, then out to Luna Park to see the Gaiety Revue."

Mama looked helplessly at her sister, and then at Marcia who was unable to conceal her rapture at Mr. Wilson's words and elegant manners.

"Isn't the Chinatown a little—I mean—" stammered Mama.

"I have been looking forward to such an opportunity as this for a long time," Mr. Sweeney said, fixing a look of worshipful admiration on Aunt Lois. "It is most opportune, most opportune, indeed."

It was clear that Aunt Lois' silence and rising blushes were not due to coquetry but to mounting indignation. Would the gentlemen excuse them for a moment, she asked ominously? Marcia found herself hustled out to the Ladies' Parlor where a serious conference was held.

"You stay, Lois," Mama said earnestly. "I had no idea it would be like this. Marcia and I will take the car back. If I'd realized it was to be a party of four—oh, Harry wouldn't like it at all! No, I can't stay, I just can't."

Aunt Lois said testily that she had no intention of staying either. She did not think it was any of Harry's business if his wife wanted to have a bit of innocent pleasure, but what made her so mad she could spit was that old goat Mr. Sweeney butting in.

"Ma told him I'd be here, I just know it," she declared angrily. "I'll bet a million dollars she planned the whole thing, she's so set on him. I can't stand him. He'd spoil any party. I wouldn't go with him if he was the last man on earth. I could kill him right now. It's not Walter's fault, of course, but wouldn't you think he could have done something to keep Mr. Sweeney off?"

Mama said she thought Walter Wilson looked awfully fast, and that for her part she'd trust Mr. Sweeney a great deal more than she would Mr. Wilson, but she simply couldn't stay another minute on account of Harry. Going with her sister and a friend to a show was one thing, but a foursome! Lois tartly replied, running a chamois over her crimson face, that Mama was acting like a fool, and that Walter Wilson was a perfect gentleman which was more than Harry Willard would ever be. Mama said haughtily that would be quite enough, thank you, and she would take Marcia away at once, if Lois would calm down enough to explain that Marcia had been taken sick. Aunt Lois put on her plumed black hat at a more dashing angle over her curly blond hair, but this was not for purposes of allure but a gesture of warfare. They stalked back to the gentlemen who appeared to sense some cloud on the horizon for they looked apprehensive. Mama explained that her little girl had suffered a bad stomach spell, and she'd have to take her home at once. Mr. Wilson hoped Aunt Lois could stay, but Aunt Lois said stiffly that she must help her sister. In this awkward conversation, Marcia felt the need for a tactful word from her, and as she was being pulled away she managed to smile reassuringly at Mr. Wilson and say, "Of course I'm not *really* sick."

They got on the seven o'clock streetcar going back past the steel mills. Marcia kept her face pressed against the window, blinking hard at the red glaring sky to hide her tears. Aunt Lois and Mama wrangled for a while as to whose fault it was the evening had been spoiled, Harry's, or Mr. Sweeney's, or Grandma's. Then both ladies stared into space with tight lips, and did not speak to each other the rest of the trip. Marcia's heart was heavy with disappointment. This would never have happened to the oldest or youngest, she bitterly reflected, just to the middle one.

6

In the spring London Junction turned into a real city, with crowds on the street and the trains bringing in strangers every day. This was due to visits from the carnival, Sells' Circus, a medicine show, and later on a tabernacle with revival meetings. There wasn't room in the London Junction Hotel for all the visitors, so the townspeople let out their spare rooms for fifty cents a night. Aunt Lois rejected Grandma's urgent advice to make room for Rosetta, the Rose Dancer from the carnival, but the children's mother was finally persuaded to give up her own bedroom to her. This was not so much Grandma's persuasive powers as the fact that Mrs. Willard was snatching at every penny she could earn and was lonely without her husband now that his trips lasted so much longer.

For once Lena was jealous of Marcia who didn't have to go to school, and could be petted by the glamorous roomer, could even spend an afternoon in the tent dressing room, peeking at the Rose Dance performance through a hole in the canvas. Rosetta's Rose Dance was the high-class act of the carnival, but there were many other wonders hidden in tents along the street and in the railroad lot, all pointed out by her mother on an exploring expedition the very first day. There was the white horse that could count and spell, the fortune-teller in the gypsy clothes, the snake-charmer with the boa constrictor pet, the sword-swallower, and the midgets. There were two midgets dressed like a king and queen who rode in a tiny royal coach drawn by midget ponies with midget footmen and coachmen in white wigs and knee-breeches. They drove through town every day at noon so that the school children might see them. Marcia was so excited over the midgets she ran away to follow them through the streets back to their tent. But she got into the wrong tent in her confusion and found herself before a long glass case wherein lay a huge snake. The snakes' eyes were on a level with her own, and she stood hypnotized with terror, unable to look away. She was saved by the arrival of Charlie Friend. "I'm lost," she babbled.

"You ran away, you mean," Charlie said. "Come on home and get your whipping."

The presence in the house of Rosetta saved her from punishment, although the snake itself had punished her enough already. Rosetta gave her a popcorn ball and called her "darlin" so that Marcia at once became her slave.

Rosetta was a sharp-faced tall thin woman but she turned into a fairy princess in a golden wig, long curls falling over her shoulders, her skin coated with white powder, and dressed in the pink changeable silk skirt which she lifted up and down to simulate rose petals while a violin played "Hearts and Flowers." Mama came to see her once and sat in the front row of the tent with Marcia. They were very proud to be friends with the artist. Mama said she certainly wished Harry could be home to see this beautiful performance.

Every night at midnight Rosetta's step was heard on the porch. Their mother sat up waiting for this, reading the *Yellow Book* or sewing. The children could hear her calling up Aunt Lois earlier in the evening, begging her to come down to go with her to the carnival, but Aunt Lois wouldn't come and Mama was too shy to go alone at night. She sat on the front porch stoop with Mrs. Friend on the other side of the dividing railing, and watched the carnival lights far down the street. When the merry-go-round in the B.&O. depot lot played something familiar she and Mrs. Friend would softly sing the words to this distant accompaniment. "Just because you made those goo-goo eyes," and "Won't you come home, Bill Bailey," and "Two Little Girls in Blue." As soon as Rosetta came in, often with a man, there was excitement downstairs, enough to waken the two older girls who immediately peeked down the floor register. There was a smell of fresh coffee, the subdued rattle of dishes as if it was daylight, and sometimes the voices went on and on far into the night. They could hear their mother laughing sometimes or talking excitedly—always about Harry, Harry, Harry and then Rosetta's twanging voice with its "darlings," "honeys" and other pretty pet names she used for everybody. Rosetta was a secret, and nobody was ever to breathe to Papa that there had been a stranger in the house, that shameful thing, "a *boarder!*"

"I'll tell him myself sometime when he's in a good humor," their mother assured Aunt Lois and Grandma, "but if he hears it from anyone else he'll just kill me. You know how Harry thinks of his home."

"You'll tell him the first thing," said Aunt Lois. "You tell him everything the minute he sets foot in the house."

Their mother laughed guiltily.

"I know. I just can't keep a thing from Harry. And anyhow he sees so many things all over the country, I want him to realize that we've got things happening right here at home, too. He'll be mighty surprised when he finds I know an actress, and I didn't have to travel on the road to meet her, either."

The carnival ended Saturday night but Rosetta stayed all day Sunday, too, on Mama's invitation. Mama mended her rose-petal costume, and Rosetta showed Mama and Mrs. Friend how to shampoo their hair with the white of an egg. The three ladies in their kimonos took pails of water and basins out in the back yard Sunday afternoon and washed each other's hair, and compared lengths. Rosetta told them stories in a low voice that made Mama laugh and made Mrs. Friend exclaim admiringly, "I don't see where in the world you pick up such things." Mrs. Friend, being fair, was given a lemon rinse with the white of egg, and Mama, being brunette, was recommended vinegar. Rosetta herself put peroxide in the water and wrapped her short hair in a towel.

"I wish Harry could walk in right now," Mama kept saying. "I'll bet Harry's never met anybody like Rosetta, don't you, Mrs. Friend?"

While the ladies were drying their hair in the back yard among the elderberry bushes and sunflowers, Lena and Marcia took turns trying on the performer's rose costume and flapping their arms about to make a rose, until Marcia put her stout boot through the silk where mama had mended it, so they hastily put the whole thing back in the trunk. Florrie had whizzed around in her walker and gouged out the chocolate frosting on a newly baked cake that Mama had set on the window sill to cool, so the children, chastened by their misdemeanors and aware of imminent correction, tried to entertain themselves in more pious ways, such as washing dishes. On Marcia's inspiration they tried shampooing Florrie's scanty blond curls to shrieks of rage. When the three ladies came in, still giggling from mysterious secrets, Mama was so excited she did not notice the mischief they had created. The women sat before the dresser mirror in the downstairs bedroom trying their hair in new ways Rosetta recommended from pictures in the Sunday *Cincinnati Enquirer*. Mama read aloud *Durandel's Gossip* and *Clarabelle's Chatter of Women and Their Ways* from the paper. Rosetta ordered some soap from Mama's Larkin Soap Catalogue and enough geranium toilet water to win Mama the special premium of a hand-painted jardiniere. She would send the money from Mansfield where the troupe was performing next week.

"Don't forget to look up Harry," Mama said. "He'll be at the Parker House till Wednesday. Harry Willard, care of London Furniture Company."

"It'll be a real pleasure, dear," Rosetta assured her warmly. "I'll have George give him free passes to all the tents. I'll tell him you suggested it, dear."

Mama was beaming at thought of the pleasure Harry was soon to have all due to her, and perhaps at the thought of this indirect way of being in touch with him. She and Mrs. Friend sat in the bedroom talking excitedly in their kimonos long after the carnival man had come to take Rosetta and her trunk away. They cut up the cake Florrie had ruined and Mama only laughed about it because she was so excited at what a thrill Rosetta was going to have meeting Harry and how astonished Harry would be at meeting such an unusual friend of his wife. Before dark they washed their hair again to get the white of egg out of it because, as Mrs. Friend ruefully put it, the egg dried like glue in the hair, no fault of Rosetta's of course, their own for not doing it right.

That night Mama moved back in her own bedroom and she let Lena sleep with her because she had an earache. Marcia stayed upstairs alone for a little while and then came down purposefully.

"I have an earache, too," she stated firmly.

Her mother laughed.

"All right, climb in, rascal," she said.

But Mama didn't stay in bed. Instead she put on her kimono and went out on the front porch where Mrs. Friend was sitting rocking in the dark.

"I kinda miss the merry-go-round music," she said to Mrs. Friend. "It makes everything more lonesome now, doesn't it?"

Papa came home three days later in a new blue suit with a checkered tie and a cane and his moustache shaved off so that Florrie didn't know him and wouldn't go to him. This time he had brought a necklace of shells from Atlantic City for Mama and salt water taffy and a little box with two white mice in it and a big bath towel named Gilsey. The children played with the mice while Mama sat on his lap in the big chair. They forgot about their secret until suddenly Papa said, "A funny thing happened to me in Mansfield. An old trollop from some street show there came up to me in the Parker House and claimed she knew me. Said she was a friend of my wife's. I knew it was some kinda funny business so I walked off and next thing I see her working the same thing on Hartwell of the Eugenia Candy Company. You meet a lot of queer ones, travelling around."

"Oh, Harry!" Mama said in a low voice. Then she said, "There's something I want to tell you. You children had better go to bed now."

Marcia and Lena hung around, wanting to hear and help tell all about Rosetta's visit, but their father hoisted one of them to each shoulder and marched upstairs, whistling "Marching Through Georgia," leaving Florrie in the crib downstairs as usual.

"But we wanted to tell the secret!" Lena protested as he tumbled them on their bed.

"I can spell shampoo," Marcia said. "I can read it, too."

"You help your mother, that's all I ask," said Papa.

Later they heard their father's voice getting louder and louder downstairs, their mother's more pleading.

"But I had to get the money, somewhere, Harry," their mother was saying. "That's all I took her in for."

"So you don't trust me!" their father shouted. "If I've told you once I've told you a dozen times that I'm going to send you some money, but oh, no, you believe your mother and Lois and neighbors, take their word against mine every time! Take in a carnival trollop in my home to make some cash as if your own husband didn't look after you! Daisy, I don't understand you! Don't you love me any more, Daisy; is that it?"

"Oh, Harry, you *know*—" their mother's voice was muffled now, very likely on Papa's forgiving shoulder. "I wouldn't hurt you for anything in the world. It's all my fault, darling. But look—here's the three dollars!"

"Keep it," Papa said gruffly. "Buy yourself a porterhouse steak with it tomorrow."

7

One of the curious things about everybody else, to Marcia, was their need for a Friend. Lena had to have a Friend, Mary Evelyn; Grandma had to have a Friend, Mrs. Carmel; and even Papa had a Friend. A friend was someone who did everything differently from you and was a source of unending fascination. It was an honor to have a Friend call on you, or praise you, and you talked about your Friend proudly because a Friend was always richer, handsomer and wiser than you— at least at first. A Friend gave you advice, sometimes presents, and his lack in any respect was well-advised, in fact a virtue.

Papa's Friend was a very important person named Hartwell of the Eugenia Candy Company and they met frequently on the road as they both had the "Eastern territory" and stayed often in the same hotels. Mr. Hartwell lived in a club in Lesterville. He was not married but went steady with the company's cashier there, a very lovely woman who had expressed the wish to meet Mrs. Willard and get acquainted.

"Why don't they get married?" Mama asked one day when Papa was speaking of his Friend.

"They've gone together so long, there wouldn't be any point in getting married," Papa explained in some exasperation.

Mr. Hartwell, who after a suitable period, was called just Hartwell and presently Ed, persuaded Papa to join the Elks, and also the Masons, as he himself was a 33rd degree Mason. It was a wonderful thing in business, Papa said, to flash your lodge pins on a customer and find that they were brothers. It paid back the dues it cost you. He'd gotten many a new customer since he'd joined these organizations, just for that very reason. Besides, there were the social advantages—smokes, stag parties, picnics, fishing trips. As these social advantages usually delayed Papa's homecomings, Mama was a little troubled about them. She was not even sure she would like Hartwell, in spite of the complimentary messages he sent through her husband to "the little woman." Hartwell bought his suits from a Pittsburgh catalogue which sent samples in return for his measurements, so Papa bought his suits there, too. People in London Junction said that Mr. Willard was a very snappy dresser. Mama and the children were very proud. When Papa came home with his new pepper-and-salt outfit and a stiff katy like Hartwell's, he was so tickled with himself that he said Mama should take herself and the children down to the Fair Dry Goods Store for new outfits.

"I guess we don't look good enough to go around with you," Mama teased him, a little ruefully, but Papa kissed her and said he had the prettiest wife and the finest family in the world. He said they would always look good to him even in rags. He said he'd seen plenty society beauties in Cleveland and Philadelphia and Buffalo that couldn't hold a candle to his Daisy in spite of their fine jewels and satins.

Mama took Lena and Marcia down to the Fair Dry Goods Store with the five-dollar bill Papa gave her. This was the store where Mary Evelyn's mother clerked and where Mary Evelyn was now proudly sorting ribbons in a box for the Saturday sale. Marcia and Lena stood on the other side of the counter watching this delicate operation in silent envy while their mother looked around. Mary Evelyn had her hair in rag curlers, and wore a ruffled black sateen pinafore over her pink checked gingham dress. She wore curlers, as many other children did, every day except for Sunday schools, parties, and Exercise Day when they were released into half-braids with reluctantly curling ends. Marcia and Lena had real curls but regretted not being allowed to wear rag curlers like Mary Evelyn.

The Fair Store was a long narrow store with only one window and a curious smell of shoe leather and wool in it, somehow identified pleasurably with new clothes. Mr. Brady owned it. He was a bald, polite fat man who always dressed in black as his wife had been dead many years. His manner was grave and dignified, for he always kept in mind his duties as president of the Chamber of Commerce, head of the School Board, and superintendent of the Methodist Sunday School. He talked to Mama for a while and then with a bow turned her over to Mrs. Stewart.

"I declare, Mrs. Willard, you're the only person in London Junction that can make Mr. Brady laugh out loud," Mrs. Stewart whispered to Mrs. Willard, unfolding a bolt of goods on the counter. "Now here is percale, eight cents a yard, but I have some lovely bengaline for dress at forty-five a yard. I made one myself for Mary Evelyn, though I usually get her the store clothes."

"What color percale would you like?" Mama asked Lena. Lena and Marcia exchanged a look of mutual understanding.

"We'd like store dresses like Mary Evelyn," Lena said.

Their mother pretended not to hear them but went on comparing materials.

"Four pairs of Black Cat stockings for them," said Mama. "I'd better get that and their underwear first. Two panty-waists—gauze."

"Mary Evelyn doesn't wear Black Cat stockings," said Lena clearly. "She wears socks. That's what we want."

"I don't wear panty-waists either," stated Mary Evelyn. "I wear suspenders."

Mrs. Stewart laughed indulgently, but Mama firmly stuck to her order. She ordered ten yards of percale.

"My cousin Lydia from Venice Corners is a seamstress," she said. "She made a trousseau for Mr. Brady's niece last year. She'll come over with her pattern books to help me make these up, because she keeps up with all the latest styles."

"I'd rather have a store dress," said Lena. "I'd rather have a store dress and a black sateen pinafore."

"I've got in some darling little dresses from Chicago," said Mrs. Stewart helpfully. "Lena Gladys would look sweet in a blue one just the color of her eyes."

"I'd rather have a pink store dress," said Marcia, feeling left out. "A pink 'cordion-pleated one so I could do a rose dance."

"I want that, too," Lena exclaimed jealously.

Mama bit her lip.

"Then I'll take twelve yards of the Val lace for trimming," she said, "and six yards of rickrack for the baby's dress."

"Anything for yourself, Mrs. Willard?" asked Mrs. Stewart, taking scissors out of her black apron pocket and snipping busily. "A pretty shirtwaist, maybe—peekaboo style?"

Mama shook her head. She said her husband had brought her some special material from the city which her cousin Isobel was going to help her with as she had a sewing-machine and a form. She thought the girls should have Sunday slippers and this surprise almost made up to them for not getting the store dresses. She looked a long time at the shirtwaists and said she might be back for the blue French tucked one with net inserts and velvet bows, but four dollars was a lot of money. When she paid for the shoes and other purchases it took all the money from her purse, her five dollars and even her bread-money except a quarter with which she bought Papa a fine handkerchief. They had to hurry home to get Papa's lunch, as he was to be home for two weeks now, "taking inventory." Lena and Marcia wanted to stay and help Mary Evelyn sort ribbons, but Mary Evelyn refused their offer.

"I'm the only one that knows how to do it," she said, airily. "Mr. Brady won't let anybody but me handle these ribbons."

"My, everything is dear now at Mr. Brady's," Mama murmured, hurrying them down Fourth Street. "You need a fortune in that store."

This remark Lena told Mary Evelyn at recess the following school day, who told her mother who said that people without money shouldn't go shopping in a high-class store, which was then repeated via Lena to Papa and Mama. This resulted in Papa flying into a rage and going down to Mr. Brady's store all by himself. Mr. Brady was a brother Mason and that afternoon Papa, beaming with triumph, flung a paper package at his wife. When she opened it there was a shirtwaist, not the one she had wanted, but a black satin one with a high neck and lace bertha, besides a pair of white kid gloves and a cut-steel belt-buckle with slipper buckles to match.

"I want you to wear them to the Elks Banquet next week," Papa said, when Mama had embraced him in gratitude mixed with consternation. "By God, I'm not going to have this damn town saying anything is too dear for my wife."

"But how did you do it, Harry?" Mama cried.

"Listen, Brady gives any lodge brother all the credit he wants," boasted Papa. "I could have had the store if I asked for it. As I say to Hartwell, nothing's too good for my Daisy."

It took Mama four months of extra baking to pay the Fair

Store bill, but anyhow Papa had her picture taken in the new finery just to show people. It was almost the only time she ever wore it.

8

In the summer, Papa and Mama went on a trip up the Great Lakes with Hartwell and his lady-friend. They left Florrie with Aunt Lois and Grandma, although Grandma complained she had no time for them since she was packing up any minute to move to Cleveland. Lena and Marcia were to stay on the farm near Elmville with Aunt Betts and Uncle Louie. Uncle Louie was Grandma's step-son and almost as old as she was. His wife was Grandma's first cousin, brought up with her like a sister on the old Medrow County home near Bethel.

Uncle Louie drove up to London Junction in a fine new rubber-tired buggy prepared to collect the children. He invited Grandma to come back with him, but she said indeed not, that she was branching out soon as an independent woman in Cleveland. She said her good friend Mrs. Carmel and her astute business adviser, Mr. Sweeney, were behind her in her new venture, and she did not give a snap of her finger for what Louie or Lois or Daisy or anybody else had to say. She also didn't give a snap whether she ever set foot on a farm again, because she was a body that liked to be where something was going on, where you could hear some good talk, learn something, and make a little spare cash. Uncle Louie brought in head cheese for her and a fried oyster sandwich from the London Junction Hotel and said he didn't blame her for kicking about the farm and fire away all she liked.

Uncle Louie was a thin wiry man with sandy hair, more of this in his great moustache, eyebrows and sprouting from his nose and ears than actually on his head. He was so tall that the effort of talking to a much shorter wife and other people had made him humped so that his sharp chin seemed to rest far down on his flat chest and the back of his neck bent over almost horizontally. His face was weather-beaten and red, with his eyes as round and blue as the sky, only red-rimmed and edged with fair downy lashes that looked like chicken feathers. There was a good deal of the rooster in Uncle Louie

which was only natural in a farmer and very fascinating to observe. When anybody talked he cocked his head gravely and
kept his eyes fixed on them with a rooster's suspicious curiosity. Then he winked solemnly, and scratched his stomach as if
he was scratching for corn. He talked little but listened to
everybody intently, suddenly bursting into a rafter-shaking
laugh that was half-cackle and half-whinny, and made everybody else laugh, too. He carried money in the sole of his boot
and took it off to pay Papa for a brass bed he ordered from
the London Furniture Store. As they rolled down the road
toward Elmville he took off his thick boot again to pay for a
corn-shucker in the New Amsterdam Hardware Store. When
he wanted small change for drinks of "Moxie" or hard candy
at corner stores, he had to unbutton his shirt where a cotton
tobacco pouch was pinned containing his small change or
"chicken feed." From the beginning Marcia was his favorite
because she spoke up to him.

"You're my girl, Old Socks," he said, with a wink. "Pussy
here can be Betts' girl."

"Will we have anybody to play with?" Lena asked. "I don't
want to have to play just with Marcia all the time."

Uncle Louie cackled again, and tweaked her curls.

"Why, Pussy, you got more to play with than there is in
Buckingham Palace. There's Billy, he's a goat, and Old Tom,
he's a bull, and one hundred sheep and six cows and Tiddley-
Winks, the biggest Eskimo dog you ever saw, and a few hundred chicks, not counting the ducks and turkeys and geese
and the rabbits and woodchucks and chipmunks and Almedy
and the twelve Chapman kids two miles down the pike."

Lena frowned, for she hated being teased.

"How old's Almedy?" asked Lena.

Uncle Louie considered this.

"Almedy's pushing sixteen," he decided finally. "When you
get them from the orphanage you can't tell, so we just let
Almedy pick her own birthday."

"I'd like to pick my birthday," Lena sighed. "What did
Almedy pick?"

"Almedy picked Fourth of July last year but this year she
picked Decoration Day." Uncle Louie said, "Being an orphan
she can pick a different birthday every year."

"Are you sure you haven't any children of your own for us to play with, Uncle Louie?" Lena persisted, still frowning, for Almedy sounded far too grown up.

"Why, Godamighty, Puss, our boys ain't been home in ten years—Carl's ten thousand miles away in Mexico and Phil's somewhere in China in the Marines, married to a Chinee, for all we know. We never hear except on Christmas. The girls both are raising families in Ioway."

Marcia's and Lena's eyes glowed with the pleasant but improbable prospect of little Chinese cousins to play with.

"Anyway, we've brought our Flinch deck if we don't have anybody to play with," said Marcia with a sigh of resignation. "We can play Muggins."

"Sure you can play Muggins, and Pit and Old Maid and croquignole," agreed Uncle Louie. "Your Aunt Betts'll teach you how to churn, too, and there's berrying and horse-riding. You won't be homesick."

"Lena will," said Marcia, a little jealously. "Lena's always homesick."

Reminded of this talent, Lena screwed up her face to cry but was as yet too interested in the ride to manage any tears. They would come later.

Uncle Louie took a different route going down to Elmville than they had coming up because he had to stop on farm business in both New Amsterdam and Willardville. New Amsterdam had windmills and a Dutch Reformed Church and when they stopped in the Ice Cream Kitchen, the waitress talked Dutch. "What nationality are we?" asked Marcia. "Dutch and Welsh and English," Papa said. "A good mixture."

The town blacksmith was a relation, so they went to the forge down a cobblestone alley between two stores. Uncle Louie let them come inside the charred, dark stable to watch the sparks fly while the smith, Uncle John, hammered out a shoe. This was a wonderful and terrifying spot, like a cave in a goblin woods with the floor half earth, half boards, black with pitch and covered with sawdust. The big furnace in the middle seemed like hell-fire, spitting out brimstone, growling and roaring so that the smith was like Satan himself, dealing in fire and darkness. There was a half-loft over the back end of the place with a cot on it, a washstand and a pine corner cupboard. Little crescent windows high under the eaves let in light and permitted barn swifts to flutter in and out.

"Step up to my parlor, Louie, and have some schnapps," Uncle John roared above the din of his hammering, so Uncle Louie helped the girls up the home-made pine ladder to the loft. Uncle John, it seems, was a bachelor and though he had a room at some niece's house, he preferred to stay mostly in his own shop. The children sat on the cot, speechless with pleasure. They looked down in the pit below at Uncle John, wondering whether he was really black or whether it washed off. Certainly the black mop of oily curls and the vast black moustache would not come off. A half-grown boy ran around barefoot, fetching water and doing errands, and he too was either black or wonderfully dirty. Lena decided after scientific observation that this was dirt since he kept gaping up at her and then wiping his sleeve across his cheek leaving small areas of almost white. Uncle John talked to him in Dutch, and called him Hans, so the girls decided that this must be Hans Brinker himself or the little boy who saved the dyke. They smiled at him but this seemed to scare him, for he ran down the alley and didn't come back. They saw him peeking at them from behind the hitching-tree when they left and this time he grinned and thumbed his nose at them. Uncle John heaved himself up the loft. He took out a jug from his corner cupboard and before he said a word to them he threw back his head and drank with gurgling noises and an active play of Adam's apple. Then he passed the jug to Uncle Louie who drank a little, made a face and spat it out.

"You don't need to tell me how you make your schnapps, John," gasped Uncle Louie, and both men cackled loudly. Uncle John opened the cupboard again. He took out a stone jar of oatmeal cookies which he passed to the children. Then he lifted them up to see other treasures inside the magic cupboard, little wooden windmills, boats with little sailors in them, little wooden dwarfs with nails made into anvils, all manner of toys he had carved or forged himself. Marcia hoped he would give them some but he dusted them off with a red handkerchief and tenderly put them back. Before they left he hammered crossed nails to make scissors for each of

them, so it was a profitable visit after all. Lena and her friend
Mary Evelyn Stewart often put crossed pins on the street-car
tracks behind the London Junction school for the car wheels
to crush into scissors, but the big nails in the forge made
them much better. They were so pleased that they tried not to
hurt Uncle John's feelings by screaming when he swung
them, first one and then the other, high in the air. They
carried the bruises of his iron fingers on their ribs for days
afterward.

Back in the buggy they rolled swiftly down the cobblestone
street on to the dusty road. Uncle Louie gave his attention to
the horse which was almost running away in his eagerness to
get home. Once in a while Uncle Louie would burst into a
loud yodel of joy, a few bars of some song that had no words
but "Hi dee hi dee hi oh de hi de hi do ho oh." Then he
would wink at them and say, "How about a song, Old Socks,
hey, Pussy?"

So they would sing all the songs they had learned from
Papa and from Sunday school and from Lena's school. They
sang, "Can you bake a cherry pie, charming Billy?" and "A
frog he would a-wooing go," and "Three blind mice," while
Uncle Louie chorused with a "hi dee hi dee hi dee ho" and
the horse whinnied. Approaching Willardville, where Grandpa
Willard's folks all settled, they began smelling something
queer, which Uncle Louie explained was the Rubber Works.
There was a big factory here with one big store and a row of
little yellow frame houses all alike, two saloons and a public
square with a bandstand pavilion in it. There was a new brick
hotel by the depot with a stuffed bear in the yard, standing on
its hind legs. A red automobile at the curb was a rare sight,
indeed, but as all the other sights were rare to the girls they
accepted it as no stranger than the stuffed bear or the smell of
rubber. In spite of these wonders, the town seemed to begin
and end all in one spot, huddling all its pretensions to importance in the square, the streets branching off from it being no
more than country lanes.

Uncle Louie left them in the buggy while he went into the
Big Store to get them each a pair of boys' overalls to play in,
a pickle crock, a sack of meal and a big tin of tobacco, all of
which he put in the back of the buggy where his corn shucker

was tied. He had a bag of licorice jelly beans for Almedy, too, he said. Almedy, being an orphan and helping with the chores, liked a treat now and then. Maybe she was too big to play with them, he said, but she'd help them keep their bibs and tuckers clean.

They were nearing East Elmville Township where Uncle Louie lived and coming to Uncle Louie's neighbors. As they approached each farm, no matter how far back the house and farm buildings were from the road, Uncle Louie slowed the horse, leaned far out and yodelled "Hy-yi, Dolphie!" or "Hy-yi—Charlie!" From the distant cornfields or from the barn an echo would come back, "Hy-yi, Louie!" These echoes rode miles on the wind and were mocked by the horse's whinnying to the neighbor horses who whinnied back from fields, galloping along pasture fences beside them to the next dividing rails. On the wind, too, was the sad sweet fragrance of clover, the dusty smell of wheat, of new-cut wood lying in the green woods, of unseen fish ponds and fresh-ploughed earth. They passed the Chapmans' farm, ramshackle unpainted house and sheds all leaning against each other as if one big grunt from the sows running around in the mud would blow them all down. Uncle Louie waved the whip and yelled in greeting. Innumerable heads popped up from a row of currant bushes.

"Company!" yelled Uncle Louie, "You kids come over!"

The answering yell from a dozen throats sounded savage and derisive to the children but was probably friendly.

"Fine kids," said Uncle Louie. "Pack of hellions."

Now they came to the lane and there was no holding the horse. Lena and Marcia, gasping, hung on to their hats. Uncle Louie stood up shouting, "Hi, yi Betts, hi yi!" A woman's voice halloed back. The horse galloped through the gates, which Aunt Betts had barely lowered in time, and ran straight into the barn. Hearts pounding, the children were lifted out; the panting horse whinnied triumph to her sisters and brothers and they whinnied welcome. Roosters crowed, hens set up an excited din. Aunt Betts—small, black-eyed, rosy, and roly-poly—came running up with her checkered apron over her head, calling greetings. The cows, now ambling up from the valley for milking, mooed, dogs leaped about them and barked, the turkey cock ran up gobbling, the whole country-side brayed and sang a welcome to the two girls.

Aunt Betts hurried them up to the big jolly house, shooed the flies off the kitchen screen with her apron, and whisked them into the big kitchen. Marcia sniffed cherry pie baking and there was a fine chocolate cake smell, too, coming from the stove. She began to jump up and down in ecstasy, but suddenly there was a bleating noise from Lena. She had her face screwed up, her underlip thrust out, and her fists in her eyes. Aunt Betts picked her up on her lap and started rocking her just as if she was Florrie.

"What's the matter, honey girl?" Aunt Betts cried out, worried. "Where does it hurt? Let me get you some peppermint."

Marcia looked on this tender scene with a cold scowl.

"She's homesick," she said flatly. "I knew she would be."

Anything to get the biggest piece of pie! Anything to get rocked and petted and called honey girl! I wish I was an only child, thought Marcia bitterly; I wish I was an orphan with a different birthday every year and no home.

9

"What does the downstairs smell like?" Lena asked, as if it was a riddle.

"Like chicken and pie in the kitchen," Marcia answered after a moment's intense pondering. "Like a churn in the parlor, and upstairs like a trunk."

"Aunt Betts smells like a churn, too," said Lena. "Uncle Louie smells like a barn, and Almedy smells like cows and strawberry patch."

They sat at the edge of the cornfield in their blue overalls and straw hats, barefooted, contemplating the universe. Marcia was very happy because Lena had no one else to play with and was forced to make a chum of her sister. They made up secrets, and played school with the cornstalks as pupils. Marcia was allowed to play principal sometimes instead of always being just a teacher. They had boys' rows and girls' rows and named as many as they could manage. They had teachers' pets, usually the smallest cornstalk in the first row, and then there were the big boys in the back who had to be scolded. They took turns being Miss Browne, the first-grade teacher, and Miss Sutton, the principal. Each stood at the head of the field four rows apart and conducted the corn in singing, numbers, spelling, and recess. The boy pet in Miss Browne's class was called Maurice and the girl pet Violet. In Miss Sutton's class there were other pets. Pets were always addressed in honeyed tones and permitted to run errands, and were lavishly praised.

"Violet, you may take this note to the principal in Room 42," the teacher would say sweetly, and then, changing to a stern voice, add, "We will have a test in numbers while Violet is absent."

Teaching also involved tiptoeing up and down the aisles and "catching" the pupils. Except for the pets, they were a cheating, whispering, disobedient lot, inclined to throw paperwads, chew gum, pass notes, and copy answers. Then the stern disciplinarian would come out. Whoever was Miss Browne would say in terrifying accents, "George Barnes, report at once to the principal's office!" Miss Sutton would be prepared for this with a fierce lecture and a switch. Miss Browne would simulate a snivelling, abject George Barnes, and then a recess would be declared with the two teachers eating green apples, ostensibly brought to them by their devoted "pets." This education in school technique as outlined by Lena made Marcia wild for September to come and real school to begin. On the other hand, the fun was all in being the teacher, and in the vast expanse of cornfield. Sometimes they would open up new schools in the rows further off—a third grade and a fifth, even, though the courses were necessarily the same as the first grade, mixed with Sunday school. The corn stretched for miles, and it seemed a pity that only the section nearest the house could be educated. Uncle Louie said they could play in the corn but not to touch it, so when Almedy found Marcia whipping an unruly stalk for being truant, they almost had to give up the school, except Almedy finally promised not to tell if they wouldn't tell about her fellow.

Almedy's romance was almost as much fun as the corn school. Every day they walked with her down the lane to the mailbox to wait for the mailman. He came in a little white wagon and rang a dinner bell at every gate. The head of the Chapman lane was opposite the gate to Uncle Louie's lane, and Almedy's fellow was the second Chapman boy, named Elbert. He was almost a head shorter than Almedy, but he was her fellow anyway, she said. He rode on a plough-horse barefooted to wait for the mail. Almedy tried to get to her gate first, then she'd wait for Elbert, even when the mail had already been left. She would always speak first.

"Hello, Elbert," she'd say.

"Hiya, Almedy," he'd say, and that was the only thing he said to her.

He pretended not to notice them at all but he stood up on the horse like a bareback circus rider and jumped up and down. The white horse stood still as if nothing was going on at all, though it switched the flies with its long tail and sometimes this whipped Elbert's bare legs, so he said bad words. He sometimes hoisted himself off the horse to the branches of the great maple trees on either side of the gate and he swung from them by his knees, yelling, "Whoa, there, Moll! Plague on you, don't you run away or I'll whip the Jesus out of you." Moll, far from being the wild, uncontrollable colt Elbert fancied her, was so fat and old she needed no bridle, and tranquilly grazed the weeds or gnawed the leaves of the bushes. During Elbert's argument with his horse, Almedy and the two children stood attentively on the other side of the road. Marcia and Lena looked from Elbert to Almedy with grave absorption as a model for conduct in future courtships of their own. Almedy giggled every minute as if Elbert was a clown but evidently Elbert did not know anyone was watching, for he never looked at her, just yelled at the horse and did acrobatics. Finally, he would settle down on the horse, usually after a far-off admonitory shout from a distant field, reach down in the mailbox for the batch of farm papers, catalogues, samples or what not. The clank of the tin mailbox shutting again was the signal for the horse to wheel around and thump back down the Chapman lane. Almedy would stop giggling at once, and keep her thin scarred brown hand over her eyes, watching him till he was lost in the trees. She would stand for two or three minutes just looking down the

Chapman lane, her sharp, plain brown face suddenly desolate and drawn up as if she too was going to be homesick. Marcia and Lena watched her, puzzled that this everyday routine should mean so much to Almedy when nothing seemed to happen at all.

"How do you know when a boy is your fellow?" Lena inquired.

"Oh, you know all right," said Almedy.

"But how?" persisted Lena.

"Oh, he walks home behind you from church or picnics," Almedy finally answered. "Elbert walks home behind me."

"What do you say to your fellow?" Lena anxiously asked, running a little to keep up with Almedy's long strides.

"Nothing," said Almedy.

"Doesn't anybody ever talk to their fellow?" asked Lena.

"No," said Almedy. "What's there to talk about?"

Almedy was so busy milking or washing or working in the fields that she was a disappointment to the children as a companion. She spoiled their games, too, just like a boy would.

"I saw a fairy in the churn today and it was turning the butter into vanilla ice cream," said Marcia.

"That's a lie," argued Lena. "*I* saw that fairy and it said it was churning chocolate fudge."

"Did your fairy have on a purple hat with a silver bell?" Marcia asked. "Mine did, and a plume too. I saw it."

"You saw your father's shirt-tail flying around the corner!" snapped Almedy, so the game was spoiled.

Almedy was thin and hunched like Uncle Louie, with a sharp nose and chin, and sharp, sly, brown eyes. When they went swimming in the brook she looked like a boy because her hair was short from the typhoid epidemic at the orphanage the year before. Dressed up on Sundays when the neighbors stopped to take her to church, since Uncle Louie and Aunt Betts wouldn't go, she looked more like a boy than ever, for the light blue straw hat sat up high on top of her shorn head and the made-over faded blue poplin dress hung limp on her thin scarecrow figure. The neighbors didn't bring her all the way home but let her out a mile down the road, so Almedy always took off her shoes and carried them this distance to save them. Marcia and Lena would run down the lane to meet her, but Almedy never seemed glad. She showed them her colored Sunday school cards which she saved up, but she kept gloomy silence the rest of the way.

"What happened at church?" the girls would cry.

"Nothing," said Almedy.

"Who was at church, Almedy?" Aunt Betts would ask later.

"Nobody," Almedy said.

Some people had luck with their orphans, Aunt Betts said again and again to Uncle Louie, but Almedy was no comfort at all. You could get no more out of her than you could out of Tiddley Winks, and never a word of gratitude for their giving her a home. She was as good as gold in her way, but no company. Never mind, Uncle Louie said, she was a good worker, as good as a hired man in the fields and she was about the fastest milker he'd ever seen. He'd say that much for Almedy, and that was more than he could say for other folks' orphans.

An orphan was different from people. It looked like people, ate like people, and could talk a little, but it was more like a horse or dog. Orphans were nearly always ungrateful and after you gave them a home and raised them they usually got into trouble or ran off with some fellow and you never saw them again. Marcia and Lena wondered how soon Almedy would run off with Elbert. When they saw her sitting out on the orchard fence every night after the supper dishes were done, her thin arms folded over her chest, skinny bare legs hooked through the rails for security, they wondered if she was planning to run away tonight. She kept her back to the farmhouse and faced the lane, though even in bright daylight she could never have seen beyond the thick trees to the Chapmans' gate. She just sat there till bedtime.

"Whatcha looking at, Almedy?" Marcia came up and asked.

"Turtles," said Almedy.

Marcia shrank back a little, for it was true. Two mottled turtles could be seen crawling around a mossy log under the acorn tree.

"Don't you want to come play drop-the-handkerchief?" urged Marcia.

"Naw, I like turtles," said Almedy, stonily. "I like turtles better'n anything."

IO

The finest feature of life on the farm was the vacation from manners. Voices were never lowered; indeed, a normal tone was regarded as city affectation, and a suspicious attempt at secrecy. You could hear Uncle Louie talking far off in the barn to visitors, and even in the very same room he and Aunt Betts shouted at each other as if they were acres apart. It may have been that this constant noise kept them from being lonesome. At any rate, the shrill nasal pitch maintained indoors and out by the couple and all their neighbors managed to convey hearty good humor, open hearts and solid virtue. Marcia and Lena tried to achieve the same effect in their speech but it evidently took years of training to get your voice to come twanging through your nose that way, and when you tried it your very palate seemed to whirr like a banjo string. A good heart and honesty seemed to be so completely a matter of noise that whenever any deals with the butcher or milk company were under way you could hear the honest fellows half a mile away doing their best to out-shout each other and show how aboveboard the transactions were. Fancy table manners were also suspect, indicating a desire to seem better than ordinary folks. Such airs as "Please pass the butter" were almost insults, and likely to be reprimanded by Uncle Louie saying "What are your arms for?"

Meals were served in the big sunny kitchen on a table spread with green oilcloth, with a flypaper as a centerpiece. Jars of conserve, catsup, piccalilli, cole slaw, pickled beets and sugar were left on the table all the time, covered between meals by a red-checkered tablecloth. A person could pick up her plate and carry it outdoors to eat on the kitchen stoop if she liked. Almedy never did sit down at table, but took her plate and a chunk of bread out to the springhouse where it was always cool. Like Tiddley Winks, the dog, she did not like to have anyone watch her eat. It was Lena who discovered after judicious investigation that Almedy ate everything, even mashed potatoes, with her fingers.

Food was different here than any place the children had ever been. For breakfast there was oatmeal, mashed potatoes covered with mixed corn and tomatoes, fried ham or sausage and gravy, soda biscuits, and sometimes corn-meal pancakes and apple pie. Aunt Betts worried because the young visitors could not put away all that was placed before them. She said they both looked peaked and needed fattening up, but when they obediently tried to stuff down more they ended up with stomach aches.

Aunt Betts and Uncle Louie had such a good time eating that they kept Lena and Marcia in giggles all the time. Aunt Betts liked to sit by the stove, eating out of the pots with a big pewter spoon. Uncle Louie used a knife exclusively with fascinating dexterity. Each time he finished a plateful he'd shout, "Betts, by God! More, by God!" Often for supper, which was around five o'clock, they had mugs of hard cider or homemade wine brewed from elderberries or dandelions. They would talk about things they remembered and roar with laughter till tears would stream down Aunt Betts' rosy round face. They told the same things over and over with never-failing enjoyment. There was the time the English Quaker family came all the way from England to the Quaker settlement down by the covered bridge. They had slept on the bare parlor floor on hay, with the old grandfather waking them up all hours of the night shouting, "Liverpool! Don't miss the boat!"

"Liverpool! Don't miss the boat!" gasped Aunt Betts, holding her sides, her plump bosom quivering with mirth. "Liverpool—oh, my! Oh, my sakes, Louie, stop it or I'll die laughing!"

Uncle Louie would throw back his head and cackle till the dog would run up from the barn to peer in the kitchen door, panting with sympathetic delight. The children would stand gaping, uncertain of the joke but highly pleased.

The pie races were the most fun. Aunt Betts would cut great wedges of pie for Almedy and the children. Then she would set three pies in hot pie tins down on the table, their berry juice still bubbling up through the flaky white crusts. Aunt Betts and Uncle Louie, each with a knife in hand and shaking with suppressed glee, would eye each other steadily for a moment, then cry out together, "Go!" Then their knives laid into the nearest pie, scooping it into their mouths, seeing who would get to the middle pie first. Uncle Louie always won because Aunt Betts got out of breath from laughing and had to unloose her belt, even her collar. One night they finished the cider barrel between them, drinking from the bung, and they must have had a race on the pantry too, for the fried squirrels and corn pudding were all gone by morning.

Almedy went up to her room at dark when the children did, but Uncle Louie and Aunt Betts could often be heard shouting with laughter in the kitchen till late at night.

The children's bedroom had sloping ceilings so that a grown person could stand erect only in the middle of the room. The window was very small, covered with mosquito netting which glistened like a spider web when the moonlight came through it. In the enormous black walnut bed the two girls lay awake listening to the country night noises that seemed to have smells as well somehow woven into them, a hot melting honeysuckle fragrance or the smell of rain on cedars, of wet maple leaves and dew on lilacs all mingled with the musty mothball aroma of their featherbed. A million crickets ticked out the darkness, a barn owl hooted, a loon laughed, frogs croaked down by the spring, sleeping birds gave tiny clucks, sometimes a horse let out a lonesome whinny.

It was too bad Almedy would not play with them. She would never sing with them or tell stories.

"They're all lies," Almedy stated briefly. "Songs and stories is all the same—lies."

"We could play a game," Lena would plead. "We don't have to go to sleep yet."

"Games is sinning," Almedy said, and marched up to her attic bedroom. She never read books. The only time she ever joined them was when they played ghosts once with sheets as shrouds. She entered into this game so zestfully that the children went to bed shivering with terror. After that Almedy would say grimly, "Want to play ghost?" so that they would hastily retreat, leaving her to her favorite relaxation of looking over her colored Sunday school cards.

Papa came down to take them back home in August. Marcia and Lena were so gloomy at leaving that their father was irritated. They wanted Almedy to come home with them as a souvenir of these happy days. Papa grumbled that he guessed it would be all right for Almedy to visit them, but Uncle Louie said the farm couldn't get along without Almedy.

"Don't you want to come home with us, Almedy? We've got white mice and a gramophone." They tried to coax her.

Almedy smiled, crookedly.

"When I leave this here place it won't be for no visit," she said.

Papa took them home on the train. They chattered all the way about Uncle Louie and Aunt Betts until their father sharply ordered them to hush. Aunt Lois, Grandma, Mama and Florrie were waiting in the sitting room when they got home. For some reason, after the first rejoicing their mother acted worried.

"They've lost all their nice manners," she said ruefully. "They've turned into regular little Indians."

"Betts is nobody to handle youngsters," their father agreed. "Wait till you see how they eat."

"I can eat with a knife," boasted Marcia.

"See what I mean?" said their father. "I guess next time we take a trip we'll have to leave them some place else."

Everything that had seemed so magical about their summer was now tarnished by their parents' disapproval. After they were sent to bed, Marcia and Lena gloomily listened to the family council downstairs.

"Never mind, Betts and Louie are all right," Grandma was saying, consolingly. "They never hurt a fly."

"You said once they used to drive around together before they were married, drinking in every saloon in the country," Aunt Lois reminded her. "Everybody knows Betts used to lay around with every travelling man that came to town."

"They tell me half the kids at the Chapman farm, next to Louie's, are Louie's," said Papa, chuckling. "Look like him, too, the old devil."

"Remember when Betts was carrying on with that old bachelor at Four Corners?" said Aunt Lois. "Then when he got to wanting younger women she sent her own daughter up to him, just to keep him in the family. That was Ede, the one that went to Iowa."

"Louie still runs after a pretty girl," said Grandma. "He still sneaks off to town to see that little milliner, but then Louie's got a heart as big as all outdoors. I think he just wants to help her."

"That Almedy is going to be a handful from what the neighbors say," said Aunt Lois.

"What's Almedy got to do with this conversation?" indignantly inquired their father. "She's not even in the family."

Marcia and Lena lay in bed, puzzling over these remarks, torn between loyalty to their parents and love for Aunt Betts and Uncle Louie.

"It spoils everything," Marcia complained resentfully.

People didn't like to see other people happy, that was all. If children were happy, especially away from home, their parents insisted it was bad for them. Fathers wanted you to be disobedient so they could correct you. Mothers wanted you to be sick or sad so they could console or protect you. Marcia longed to grow up fast so she could defy them all. She would have a dress with a train, a watch with a fleur-de-lys pin, unlimited licorice beans, and she would eat with her knife faster than anybody.

II

The first thing Marcia got from school was measles, which she passed on to Florrie. In return for this Lena acquired chickenpox and got the whole family quarantined, a condition that lasted a long time, as one would get it just as another was getting well. Mr. Friend put their groceries outside the kitchen door every day with pots of soup and stew made by his wife. Mama had not caught the germ and was determined to keep up with her baking, in spite of the doctor's orders. She baked a dozen loaves of bread in the middle of the night to escape his attention, then left them in the hallway for Mrs. Friend to deliver to her customers. When Mrs. Friend, speaking through the closed door, cautiously suggested that the bread might spread chickenpox Mama indignantly replied that good fresh bread never hurt anybody. If the doctor heard about it and objected, she would simply tell him she had to keep her bread customers in order to pay his bill, and that ought to settle his hash. Mrs. Friend reluctantly took on the secret duty of delivering what she insisted was tainted goods. She was not amused by Mama teasing her later about her qualms.

"Any spots on old Mr. Krug today?" Mama giggled through the door. "I'll bet that bald head of his looks funny with chickenpox."

It was Mrs. Friend's turn to triumph when their father was forced by the Health Officer to stay at the London Junction Hotel when he came home from a trip. He visited the house every morning and evening, talking to them through the kitchen window, making fun of their spots and assuring them that feathers would sprout out next. This separation made their mother almost sicker than chickenpox itself could have done. Papa's hearty efforts to cheer her up did no good. In his new winter coat with the velvet collar, his red silk muffler, derby hat and kid gloves, his nose red with cold, he sat on the overturned washboiler outside the kitchen window, while Mama sat in the little sewing-chair inside, wrapped in a blue wool robe. The children had been moved, beds and all, to the dining room to make the work easier for their mother, and to keep them warmer.

"Don't worry about me, Daisy," Papa urged, his face pressed to the window pane. "The Junction Hotel serves a damn nice steak dinner for fifty-five cents. I could have the stew for thirty-five, but, hell, the difference is worth it. I got running water in my room and I sleep like a top. Last night a couple of B.&O. train dispatchers and some drummers from an eastern concern dropped in the room and we played poker till midnight. Went out afterward and had as good a Welsh rarebit at the Greek's as you could get at the Hotel Statler."

"Didn't it upset your stomach?" Mama asked, jealously.

Papa reassured her happily on this point. As further cheer he told her that the boss, Mr. Carson, had hinted in so many words that he was the best man he'd ever had on the road, and not to feel that his superior talents went unobserved. This must mean a raise, Papa deduced, for Mr. Carson was far too shrewd a businessman to risk losing him to some bigger firm in a larger city. Say what you would, a man with the brains to build up a business like the London Furniture Company, known all over the world including Canada and California, as makers of the finest merchandise, not excepting Grand Rapids even, was not one to let a man like Harry Willard slip through his fingers. The fact of the matter was that a certain burled walnut dining room set, red tapestry upholstery, eight pieces, was almost certain to be awarded to Papa at Easter time as a reward for salesmanship.

"I don't know where we'd put it," Mama said wearily. "There's no room."

"We'll throw out everything else then and make room," expostulated Papa. "Don't stand there and tell me you'd turn down a beautiful burled walnut, Empire style, eight-piece dining set—our Number 842A, the finest number in the catalogue—just to keep a lot of junk we bought once in Elmville at an auction! How do you think Carson's wife is going to feel when Carson tells her Harry Willard's wife doesn't appreciate Harry getting the salesman's grand prize for the year? Daisy, I'm surprised at you."

Either the reproach or the increasing strain of her nursing duties brought tears to Mama's eyes and this was too much.

"I come here to cheer you up. I stand outside my own home, freezing to death with a cold coming on, just to cheer you up, and you have to cry!" Papa angrily exclaimed. "That's all the thanks a man gets."

For some reason Mama did not react to his fit of temper in her usual contrite way, but permitted him to dash around the house to the street without calling him back. She quietly gave the children their supper in bed on a bread-board, rocked Florrie to sleep without singing. When they were almost asleep the doctor called, and later there was a loud banging on the door. It was Papa. He came inside and hugged Mama, in spite of her protests.

"The doctor says you might catch it," she protested.

"He don't need to know I'm here," Papa said. "What kind of a doctor is he, anyway, trying to separate married people? I've got to look after things here; you can't manage all alone. Here, I brought you something. Just won it at the Kandy Kitchen raffle."

It was a five-pound box of candy, and what the children minded most about having chickenpox was that even the thought of candy made them really sick. Marcia was even too sick to get up and peek through the portieres when Lena

reported that Papa was wrapping Mama up in blankets in a
chair by the stove, and was treating her as if she too was sick,
and that in spite of the quarantine Mrs. Friend was there
too, putting a hotwater bottle on Mama's stomach. Papa and
Mrs. Friend tiptoed back and forth through the dining
room, now the sickroom, from living room to kitchen all
night, carrying things to Mama. It was not these odd activities that frightened the children into the conviction that their
mother was sick; it was the fact that for the first time their
father's voice was lowered to a whisper.

After a while they got used to Mama's sick spells, and there
were compensations. Isobel would come over to look after
them for a few weeks. Grandma, with wistful protests about
her Cleveland plans being delayed, stayed with them for a
while, and when Papa was home he did the cooking and nursing because he was the best cook and nurse Mama ever heard
of. She said she was well just hearing his voice downstairs, and
sure enough she stayed well quite a few months.

12

"Sing it again," their mother begged.

So Lena and Marcia sat on the edge of her bed and sang it.

> "I'm an honest Irish lad, and my home is far away,
> If pleasing you I'll either sing or dance——"

Every afternoon after school they came to visit their
mother, but the rest of the time they stayed with Aunt Lois
during Mama's sickness. They enjoyed a gloomy prestige at
school by their mother having consumption, but Mary Evelyn
tried to spoil it all by boasting of her father dying of double
pneumonia. She pointed out that it ought to be double consumption then to equal her claim to distinction.

Grandma took care of her sick daughter most of the time,
but presently the doctor said a trained nurse must be called
in. Mr. Carson had permitted Papa to exchange routes with
another salesman, which enabled him to get home every
night to relieve Grandma. Each night he brought home new
medicine that some of the fellows had recommended, and he

tried them all out on Mama from the onion plaster on the chest to the mustard pack on her back. He was exasperated with everybody for the failure of these remedies, and annoyed that the doctor ordered a trained nurse, annoyed, too, that Mrs. Friend seemed to regard this as ominous.

"It just means that she's getting better," he said. "The doctor doesn't want to trust her any more to the old lady and Lois. They make Daisy nervous. I told the doctor so myself. I came in yesterday after her mother had been looking after her and Daisy was so upset she was out of her head for a while. Didn't even know me."

"Daisy's a mighty sick girl," Mrs. Friend said, solemnly. "I only hope she pulls through."

These awesome words made Lena and Marcia look anxiously at their mother, who lay on her side with her eyes fixed on the window, paying no attention to the conversation passing over her. Her small hands looked bluish white against the covers, and the nails seemed almost gray. It was queer to see them lying so lifelessly beside her, fluttering slightly like lame birds when a sudden noise reached her.

"Maybe when she gets well she'll have a dimple like Florrie," Lena observed. "Or a scar like Marcia's got from chickenpox."

"Poor kids," said Mrs. Friend, patting their heads. "Well, I'll pray twice as hard to the Blessed Virgin and maybe the trained nurse can pull her through."

"We're not Catholics," said Lena coldly. "It wouldn't do any good for you to pray to the Virgin on our account."

When their mother roused herself again she had them sing some more, and even tried to sing herself. Their father was so exuberant over her good spirits that he dashed out to get her a present and came back with several parcels which he dumped proudly on the bed.

"Open 'em up," he commanded, rubbing his hands. "I bought out the whole damn Fair Store, honey. Wait till you see."

Mama shook her head, smiling, so Mrs. Friend had to open up the packages.

"Why, Harry Willard! Silk stockings!" she gasped. "And a real silk nightgown and a pink chemise with hand embroidery.

And a gold mesh pocketbook. Why, it must have cost a million dollars!"

"Brady's a brother Mason, that's all," Papa explained, proudly beaming. "Try 'em on, Daisy. It'll make you feel better."

The children jumped up and down on the bed, pleased with the celebration, but their mother, in spite of Mrs. Friend's assistance, could not seem to keep her head above the pillow. She did put one leg out from the covers and they got one silk stocking on, but then she turned her face listlessly to the wall, whimpering, "Where's Harry? Tell Harry I want to go back to Peach Street."

"The children had better go back to their aunt's now," said Mrs. Friend. "She's sinking."

"She'll feel better when she gets a good look at that gold mesh bag," their father declared positively. "I may be no doctor but I do know my Daisy. You're coming around all right, aren't you, honey? Daisy, listen to me. Hartwell's lady friend was asking about you. Isn't that nice of her? She says her brother had the same thing and now he weighs two hundred pounds. Are you listening, Daisy?"

"I want to go home," repeated their mother, staring dully out the window. "I want to go back to Peach Street. I want Harry."

"Here I am, honey," their father said, leaning over her, but she looked past him as if the Harry she wanted was nowhere near. The children were half-persuaded that this was a new kind of game their mother had invented, but this time it was a game their father did not like at all, for he scowled, then picked up the presents from the bed and dumped them into a dresser drawer.

"She's too sick to appreciate things," Mrs. Friend consoled him. "She'll enjoy them when she gets well."

"I'll bet if I could get her downstairs, sitting up, she'd be all right in a jiffy," Papa said. "I could pull her out of this if I was in charge, doctor or no doctor, but every time I do anything Lois comes in and starts raising Cain with me. Says the doctor knows best."

"You'd better let the doctor handle it," Mrs. Friend said. "You keep on cheering her up, that's the main thing."

Papa nodded a thoughtful agreement to this.

"I guess she'd snap out of it if I got that dining room set I promised her," he said. "She'd be so tickled to see that eight-piece set moving in here she'd like as not jump right out of bed."

Mrs. Friend said not to worry about new furniture. The thing now was to get the new trained nurse.

Papa met the Columbus train the next day that brought the trained nurse, and since the depot was near Aunt Lois' house he escorted her there at once to meet the family. The nurse was a small, thin woman in her late twenties, with a thin pointed dead-white face, colorless lashes and brows that made her eyes gleam like dark grey marbles. She had a trim figure in her white uniform when her blue cape was thrown aside, with a tiny waist accented by a tightly drawn belt. In spite of her small stature, her hands were large, knobby and red. Conscious of this, evidently, she kept putting them under her apron, or twisting them nervously around the long chain on which she carried her pince-nez. Her hair was faded blond and obviously prized, for she had gone to great pains with an elaborate frizzed coiffeur of pompadour, nests of curls, and many combs. Papa was very proud of her and appeared to be working hard to impress the city person favorably. His efforts won him the only smiles she was willing to spare.

"Meet the second Mrs. Willard," was the way he had jovially introduced her, much to Aunt Lois' glowering disapproval.

Her name was really Hawkins, first name Idah, spelled with an h, if you please. She had a low, cautious voice, and she murmured that she hoped to be of service, although the Lord gave and the Lord took away. In any case she would not tarry over supper but would hasten at once to her case and do what was in her power, though she admitted she was merely human and could do no more than she could.

"I feel better just having her around," Papa confided in a surge of new spirits, but Grandma and Aunt Lois looked with hostile eyes at the intruder who knew more than they did about Daisy.

That very night Florrie, who had been weeping steadily and with almost mature understanding for her mother, was allowed to go see her, in the care of Mrs. Friend. Marcia and Lena had gone to bed, when the telephone ringing awoke them. Presently their aunt came upstairs and instructed them to get dressed. Their mother had had a spell of loneliness and wanted to see them at once. This rare suggestion, coming after ten o'clock, was most exciting and seemed proof that their mother, as always, was arranging a special treat for them. They struggled into their clothes, with leather leggings and rubbers, for a heavy snow was falling. They wanted to take along their Christmas skates, even though they hadn't learned to skate, but Aunt Lois brusquely refused this. She would take them on the sled, she said, unless the snow was already too deep.

Outside was a magic night of crisp twinkly stars, snow-muffled cottages and white trees. Aunt Lois drew the sled down the middle of the icy pavement, for the sidewalks were filled with drifts. This was indeed growing up, Marcia felt, to be out after bedtime in the dead of night and in the middle of the street. She sat in front on the sled with Lena's legs around her and a blanket tucked around them both, their breath curling out in the frosty air like smoke. Sounds were grown-up sounds, too, at this hour; the constant jangle of engine bells, a warm jolly sound that cut through blizzards and darkness like a dog's welcome bark. Aunt Lois' arctics crunched swiftly over the snow, and the snowflakes whirled like tiny stars around the street lamps. Down the street they could see their house with all the lights on, downstairs and up, as if it was Christmas Eve. Night was the best time of all to be outdoors, they thought, especially in winter and in London Junction where the smell of train smoke mingled with the tangy snowflecked air and tickled the nose. Darkness, snow, smoke and stars made a special London Junction smell, just as mittens and their wool mufflers drawn tightly up to their noses and moist from chewing had a fuzzy snowball taste.

At the door of the house they were met and shushed into silence by Mrs. Friend. Miss Hawkins stood primly by their mother's bed, and Doctor Andrews was gravely holding their mother's wrist. Grandma sat in the sewing-chair in the corner, tears sliding down her cheeks, silently rocking Florrie.

"Mama doesn't like Florrie rocked any more," Lena stated. "Florrie's too big now to be rocked to sleep every night, Mama says. It will spoil her, won't it, Papa?"

No one paid any attention to this. Papa sat on the other side of Mama, staring at her with an expression of bewilderment and pain. It was clear that something dreadful was happening but it seemed to be happening to Papa instead of to their mother.

"Do you want us to sing, Mama?" Lena asked. Marcia was proud of Lena's efficiency. She knew what to do more than the grown-ups did. When their mother did not hear, Lena repeated the question louder, and this time the sick woman turned her haggard face toward them.

"Little pickaninnies," she murmured. "Come on, hop on the wagon, pickaninnies, we're going back to Peach Street."

Delighted with the game, they climbed on the bed beside her.

"Give her the whip, Harry, we've got to get there before dark," urged their mother. "Hang on, pickaninnies, here we go. Hurry, hurry, hurry."

They could almost feel the bed rising in the air like a fairy-tale carpet, and they hung on to it tightly, their nervous giggles dying in their throats into whimpers at the sudden strangeness in their father's face. He knelt by the bed and put his head in his hands.

"Don't do it, Daisy, don't do it," he whispered. "I'll give up the road. I'll get you the Furness place—I swear I will. I'll have the dining room set put in there right away. I'll do anything you say, Daisy."

"Don't fall off," cried their mother harshly. "Harry, where are you? Look!" She raised herself up on her elbows, her eyes staring fixedly ahead. "Look, it's the man in the balloon! Look out!"

Their father caught her in his arms and laid her back on the pillow. Miss Hawkins pulled the children abruptly off the bed and pushed them into the hall, closing the door on them. They could hear Florrie burst into a panic of sobs.

"This is it," they heard the doctor say, but they could tell no more, for Mr. Friend took them back to Aunt Lois' at once. They did not know what "it" was until late the next day.

13

The funeral people suddenly filled the Fourth Street house, their dim unknown faces haunted the dark hallways upstairs and down, the murmur of their funeral voices rose and fell like the sighing of the wind, their catfeet slipped back and forth on whispering errands. The minute a heart stopped beating, these shapes assembled as if this was the cue that brought them to life, and the final clang of the iron cemetery gates would shoo them back into designs in the wallpaper and shadows behind doors. The first of the funeral people to materialize was a large shapeless whispering woman in black serge, with woolly black hair and eyebrows and fat moist hands, scaly red cheeks, swollen legs (she wore rubber stockings under her black cotton hose), and a mighty black cotton umbrella which might well have been her means of transportation from funeral to funeral. She was wonderful with funerals, everybody said, and she didn't need to be told to come, but had a sense that informed her of death and even of its direction. Like a hawk circling over the dying sheep, Aunt Lizzie circled over sick relatives, ready to pounce at the right moment. She said she had been packed for a week for Daisy's funeral and Something told her, the way Something always did, that this was the day. She went to the deathbed at once, and after a sibilant conference with Mr. Fanzer, the undertaker, she took charge of Daisy, bathing her, combing her, permitting no one else in the room, not even Papa or Grandma. Marcia heard her talking, and peeked in, wide-eyed, to see if Mama had come to life.

"I always talk to 'em," Aunt Lizzie said comfortably. "They's always a chance they can hear."

The children were ordered to stay at Aunt Lois', but Marcia hung back and hid under the living room couch to watch the funeral catfeet shuffle to and fro. She could tell Aunt Lizzie by the soft, heelless kid shoes with holes cut out for bunions, but even without opening her eyes she could recognize Aunt Lizzie by the mouldy smell scattering from her black skirts.

"Like cellar rats," Marcia thought, sniffing again to make sure there wasn't a faint whiff of sheep barn in it, too. She could hear the insistent questions, "What's to become of the children? Who's to take the children?"

Isobel and Chris came, Grandpa Willard came, Aunt Betts and Uncle Louie came, and all of them changed into funeral faces, so it was as if you had never known these favorites any more than you'd known the other innumerable aunts and uncles.

"We wanted to be with you in your sorrow," they all chanted to Papa, Grandma and Aunt Lois.

So this was Sorrow. Sorrow smelt of carnations and cellar-rats and potato salad. People sat in the kitchen eating potato salad at all hours of day and night, as fast as Aunt Lizzie made it in the washboiler. Sorrow separated you from everyone else and Sorrow was a puzzle with no answer. Sorrow wasn't bad or good; it was just there making each person strange and lonely. Sorrow made Lena keep her face screwed up, sniffling, as if something hurt her.

"Where does it hurt?" Marcia asked, mystified. "Is it like being spanked?"

"It doesn't hurt exactly," Lena replied. "It's more like being homesick. You ought to cry, too. I heard people say it was funny you didn't cry."

"I didn't cry because I was glad to see Aunt Betts and Uncle Louie," said Marcia. "A person can't cry when they just can't."

Florrie was noisier than ever in her grief. She cried steadily until Mrs. Friend was afraid she'd have a convulsion. Her little body stiffened, a look of wild terror was on her face, and she refused to be fed or let anyone touch her without screaming. This manifestation was looked upon by all the funeral people as highly satisfactory, and Marcia heard many say, "The baby is the only one who realizes. The middle one hasn't any feelings at all."

It was a commendable thing to have feelings, for feelings were to feel bad with, and feeling bad was what everybody liked to see. Marcia watched Florrie and then Lena to find the secret of feelings, but her only sensation was one of limitless wonder at why people were different from herself. She thought maybe she was bewitched, for she was sure her secret self, the one with no feelings but intense sensations, was utterly separate from a little girl in a blue hair-ribbon named Marcia Willard. The little girl named Marcia could be pinched or bruised without feeling pain, because she was filled with the numbing fragrance of death, an immense thing by itself, like a train whistle blowing far off, or an echo in the woods. There were no people in it, not even Mama, here or gone. But nobody knew this. Nobody knew it but Marcia's secret self, and it filled her to the brim with such a tangle of desperate wonder there was room for nothing else.

Miss Hawkins stayed on for the funeral "at no extra charge," Papa told everyone with deep appreciation. She even wore a black dress like a member of the family, having brought the garment along with this occasion in mind. What moved Papa the most was that Mr. Carson, the president of the London Furniture Company, sent a pillow of pink carnations, a token of the esteem in which he held Papa even more than a tribute to the dead. Papa showed the pillow to the girls with tears in his eyes.

"I want you girls to realize the kind of man your Papa works for. I want you to remember this when you grow up, and if Mr. Carson ever needs a friend and I'm not here I want you to take my place."

The worst thing for Marcia about the funeral was having to sit on Aunt Lizzie's slippery lap (it had no shelf at all) and seeing grown-up people cry. Now she had feelings, Marcia thought, when the quartette of Papa's brother Masons sang "Rocked in the Cradle of the Deep," but it made her angry to have feelings and lose the strange sense of sorrow. She didn't like to see her father crying on Aunt Lois' shoulder, either, because feelings seemed to have made him forget that he didn't like Aunt Lois one bit.

Their father held them up, one at a time, to look at their mother, lying on the pillow of carnations in the clothes Papa had gotten for her at the Fair Store that time.

"Doesn't your Mama look beautiful?" Aunt Lizzie crooned, standing behind them.

"I don't like her looking that way," said Marcia stiffly. "I don't like her hair fixed that way."

They weren't allowed to ride to the cemetery because Florrie was still screaming, and the two others had to wheel her around the house in her gocart. The undertaker's men came then to take away the rented chairs. Aunt Lizzie made a final boilerful of potato salad and then vanished with her massive umbrella, never to be seen again in London Junction. Florrie was whisked back to Aunt Lois', and the two girls were put to bed in Mama's own bed. It smelled of disinfectant and carnations, and Marcia couldn't sleep. In the night she suddenly knew what she wished. She wished Mama had taken her with her and let her lie on the carnation pillow, but of course it would never have happened that way. It would have been Florrie or Lena, because the middle one never got taken any place.

PART TWO

The Shepherdess in the Snowstorm Ball

14

HODGE STREET was the greatest adventure since the day they moved to London Junction. Hodge Street was in Cleveland and was the particular location that Mrs. Carmel, in her infinite wisdom, had chosen as the ideal spot for Grandma to "branch out." The old lady was a little chagrined to find her young kin moving in on her new-won independence, but Harry, as she confided with a sigh to Mrs. Carmel, could always get around her. Somebody had to look after the poor kids. After their mother's funeral the children grew accustomed to being addressed as "you poor kids" with sad head-shakings. They grew accustomed to hearing their problems discussed candidly wherever they went, and were surprised to discover their future was not a matter of their own choosing but dependent on who was "willing" to look after them.

It was embarrassing to find that their favorite relatives were not responsive to suggestions of living with them. There were arguments as to whether it wouldn't be wiser to separate them instead of trying to farm them out in a lump. Lena favored this, because there was a chance she might be allowed to live with their darling Isobel and Chris, but thoughts of separation left Marcia stricken. Papa said no, their mama would never want them separated. During these conferences, they huddled together, even Florrie numbed into silence by their new importance, the sense of which overwhelmed them to the exclusion of grief.

Aunt Lois finally volunteered to keep them, reluctant as she was to make things any easier for Harry, until Harry made permanent plans. She said poor Daisy would turn over in her grave if they had to go to an orphange, which was where they would end up if it was left to Harry, because he was certain to neglect them just as he had neglected Daisy.

Lena, with her new authority as female head of her family, suggested Uncle Louie's. Uncle Louie himself said regretfully that he thought he and Betts were getting too old to manage a new family. Aunt Lois said that nothing would upset their mama up in heaven more than the thought of them turning into heathens at Uncle Louie's. Busy as she was with her School Board work and her two teacher boarders, she would look after Daisy's family, providing Harry could be made to "do the right thing." If Harry had "done the right thing" in the past, poor Daisy would be alive at this minute. This phrase nettled their father mightily. He said nothing would upset poor Daisy up in heaven more than the idea of her children being bossed by Lois. If Lois had looked after her sister better when Papa, through force of circumstance, had left her in her own kin's care, poor Daisy would be alive now. He haughtily announced he would leave his brood in the care of Mrs. Friend until he found a suitable housekeeper. He had arranged for Isobel to make them each a purple dress and coat from a bolt of serge he had thoughtfully purchased on the Big Four out of Columbus, from another commercial traveller. He mentioned that he proposed to give Lena music lessons, a wish of poor Daisy's. He sternly advised Mrs. Friend to try and break Florrie of nail-biting, and to teach Marcia to answer when she was called, instead of acting deaf and dumb.

Mrs. Friend, much moved by this trust, took over her duties with tears in her eyes. They stayed in their old rooms with the two apartments thrown into one. She petted Florrie, deferred to Lena's authority as the Oldest, and taught them all to be good Catholics. Papa came home only once a month, usually bringing Mr. Hartwell to cheer him up. After a few months Papa got righteously indignant at Mrs. Friend's suggestion that he buy shoes for the children and contribute a little to their board. Papa's feelings were so deeply hurt by this lack of confidence that he ordered the children packed up at once.

"Blood is thicker than water, Mrs. Friend," he declared sternly, and forthwith carted Florrie to Isobel's in Venice Corners, and escorted the older two up to Cleveland as a surprise to their grandmother.

He did not fully explain his reasons for breaking with the Friends, but hinted that it was a religious matter.

"She was bringing them up Catholics," he said, and Mrs. Carmel, present at the time, was even more horrified than Grandma, and promised a safe refuge here from popery, every opportunity on the other hand to attend the beautiful new churches for Christian Science and Spiritualism. Harry, with grave injunctions for them to go to whatever Sunday school Grandma suggested—but, please, no rosaries for Mama's sake—then departed on a business engagement with his friend Hartwell, whose main factory was fortunately right on Hodge Street.

Hodge Street was barely half a dozen blocks from the Public Square and not far from the lake docks. While some carping souls would not have regarded Hodge (including Hodge Lane, Hodge Court, and Hodge Alley) as a proper location for the rearing of children, Marcia and Lena found it ideal, with the constant noise of trains reminiscent of London Junction, the froggy boat whistles, and the fragrant presence of the Eugenia Candy Factory, which perfumed the very air they breathed with fumes of sweet chocolate. Up and down side streets off Hodge were rooming houses whose tenants varied from genteel widows with pensions to shrill females who sat on the narrow porches in Japanese kimonos and kid curlers till dusk. "Light housekeepers," Grandma called them. These females kept the porch blinds discreetly low, and were prone to hastily pull their kimonos together at a man's approach, but this pious symptom of modesty never carried itself to the point of going indoors and dressing. Such a step would have meant losing a few neighbors' remarks, missing a street accident, or being the butt of gossip oneself. These ladies preserved their social standing by referring to each other as Mrs. M., Mrs. B., Mrs. R., and so on, as if the full use of the last name was too great a liberty. They were mostly of middle age, and although they maintained a well-bred reserve about their earlier life and never "gave away" anything, there must have been a basic similarity in all their experiences to have brought them to the same tastes and same habits. Whenever anyone passed, these females hushed up, but barely had the somewhat self-conscious passerby got out of hearing before every detail of costume and bearing was laid open to discussion. The high standards of fashion and figure verbally expressed by these ladies was particularly surprising, since they themselves so rarely put on a corset or dress, though to hear their morning critical consideration of the May Company advertisements you would have imagined they were about to make some impressive purchases that very day.

It was Grandma's habit to go down one of these side streets and back the other on her marketing in order to exchange a little gossip with as many of these ladies as possible. She was sorry that the purifying presence of her grandchildren limited the scope of her own roomers' conversation. Mrs. Myers and Mrs. Benton (better known as Mrs. M. and Mrs. B.) lapsed into morose silence when Marcia and Lena took over the porch as playground. With their bare feet usually adorned with Blue Jay corn-plasters, thrust in lopsided worn mules, they clattered in to Grandma often to complain that the doll clothes, banana peels and orange rinds scattered over the porch made the place "not look nice," particularly since this was Hodge Street proper and not one of its cheaper tributaries.

Aunt Lois visited the children to make sure "Harry was doing something about them." She demanded of her mother what these women did for a living, a query much resented by Grandma who coldly explained that they were women bereaved by law or death of their husbands, too high class to take employment or to let themselves go to seed in some hick town like London Junction. Aunt Lois wanted to know if and how Mrs. B. or Mrs. M. paid their board, to which Grandma indignantly replied that both ladies received registered letters every few weeks, indicating to any idiot that they had property somewhere, or an income coming in somehow.

"Do they pay you?" Aunt Lois relentlessly insisted. "Do you see any of this big income?"

Grandma said that in Cleveland you did not do business that way. In Cleveland you didn't ding and ding at high class people (like Mrs. M. and Mrs. B.) whose status was established; you gave credit. Otherwise, as Mrs. Carmel herself would tell you, you lost your customers. Grandma suggested that her daughter go to Mr. Sweeney for corroboration of this

statement, since Mr. Sweeney was the only man in London
Junction with a grain of sense. Growing heated, Grandma
added that she was on her own now, an independent woman
at last, thank God, and she wouldn't take any criticism from
any child of hers, because if such a child was so darned smart,
why hadn't she known how to hang on to a husband? Aunt
Lois flushed and changed the subject to her late sister's husband. Did Harry tell her what he planned for the children and
did he send her any money for their keep? Did he get them
the shoes they needed? Did he stay with them when he was in
Cleveland or did he hang around the Eugenia Candy Company as usual all day with Ed Hartwell? Grandma said that
Harry was more like a son to her than any of her own blood.
It was a pleasure to have him in the house and Mr. Hartwell,
too, a true gentleman who did her the honor of taking a
room when Harry was in town, as they were devoted friends,
and a finer man never breathed, except possibly Mr. Sweeney.

"Mrs. Reed," Mr. Hartwell had said, gravely shaking her
hands only a few evenings ago on coming in rather late, "I
apologize from the bottom of my heart for my condition. I
can promise you as a gentleman to a lady and a mother, God
bless her, that you will never see me in this shape again."

"So he was drunk," said Aunt Lois, with satisfaction.
"Harry too, of course. No respect for poor Daisy, not dead a
year. I wish they'd both walk in right now. I'd give them a
piece of my mind."

Not ten minutes later her brother-in-law actually did walk
in, bearing white silk scarfs for his daughters, and accompanied by his friend Hartwell, both in a praiseworthy state of
grave sobriety. This put Aunt Lois out of countenance.
Grandma went on knitting a green hug-me-tight for Mrs. M.,
hiding a demure smile as Mr. Hartwell turned his masculine
charm on Aunt Lois. There was no use denying that Papa's
friend made a good appearance, with his broad shoulders,
square jaw and big white teeth, carefully oiled brown wavy
hair and large Masonic diamond ring. He wore his red pin-
dot tie knotted in the latest style, bulging the exact degree
out above his vest and secured with a conservative onyx pin
rimmed with chip diamonds. His collar and cuffs were stiff
and snowy, though no whiter than Papa's, Marcia jealously

noted, and from the way his watch chain, hung with an elk's tooth, lay across his vest, Mr. Hartwell was on his way to acquiring a bread-basket as distinguished as Mr. Sweeney's. Papa was proud of his friend's elegant appearance but particularly proud of his rich fruity baritone. He watched admiringly the effect of this magic sound on Aunt Lois, for she could not disguise her pleasure in its resonant flattery.

"Willard, you never told me your wife's sister was the spit and image of Lillian Russell," exclaimed Hartwell in a reverent tone. "The very same complexion, the flaxen hair, the same figure! I'll bet you have a lot of strangers staring at you in the street, Mrs. Blair, taking you for Lillian Russell. A younger Lillian, of course!"

Aunt Lois blushed, giggled, and tossed her head. Grandma winked slyly at her son-in-law, who was luckily escaping a "good talking to."

"That reminds me. Eddie Foy is playing here at the Hippodrome," said Hartwell. "Willard, I'm going to ask a favor of you. Will you give me permission to escort your sister-in-law there tonight? We might have a little supper afterward at the Hofbrau."

Under the spell of Mr. Hartwell, Aunt Lois forgot her plan to give Papa a "piece of her mind." In her effort to do her hair more like Lillian Russell's, she forgot even to continue her probe into Grandma's business.

Lena and Marcia were relieved that Aunt Lois was not going to take them away this time or to scold Papa. They were unhappy and bewildered that anyone should accuse him of being an indifferent parent, for he brought them, in addition to the scarfs, a bag of oranges and a box of Eugenia Chocolates, discarded from Hartwell's sample case as being a little stale.

Papa took them in the kitchen, leaving Hartwell to Aunt Lois and Grandma. As soon as he was away from the radiance of his friend, he grew silent and moody. Marcia and Lena tried to cheer him up. They liked Cleveland, they said. They would like Florrie to come up there and all of them live there together. They didn't need anything, in spite of what Aunt Lois might tell him. To further reassure him of their loyalty Marcia put out her scuffed shoe.

"These shoes are still good, Papa," she said earnestly. "So are Lena's. We put paper over the holes. We don't need new shoes anyway because we don't go to Sunday school here."

"I like your brown suit," Lena said, trying to add to his pleasure. "Now you've got a blue suit and a gray suit and a brown suit just like Mr. Hartwell."

Papa gloomily patted her on the head.

"You'll both have new outfits, from head to foot, next time I come in," he declared. "I told your grandmother last time I was here to take you down to May Company and get you outfitted right, regardless of expense. I'm too busy to do it. She could have done it, and charged it."

"Maybe they don't charge in Cleveland," Lena suggested.

Papa noticed Lena's hair now and said disapprovingly that it looked dirty and had lost its curl.

"Nobody brushes it," Lena explained readily. "It got into such a big tangle that Marcia had to cut it out in two places. Marcia got fleas in hers."

Marcia beamed.

"Not fleas, nits," she corrected. "We got nits in our mattress. It was from the Hunkies that stayed here."

"The Hunkies wouldn't pay their bill because they said they was bedbugs," Lena amplified. "Grandma got the policemen after them but they got away. Then we found the nits, so we have to shake the sheets hard when we make the bed."

"Grandma and Mrs. M. put gasoline on the mattress," Marcia added happily. "Now it smells like gasoline all night."

This brought a look of deep annoyance to their father's face. He got up and paced up and down the kitchen, stroking his chin.

"How long are we going to stay here? Are we going to go back to London Junction? When are we going back to school? Are you going to live with us?"

Their father threw his hands up impatiently at this flood of questions.

"Never mind, I'll get a housekeeper myself, if your own flesh and blood can't look after you any better," he vowed. "You kids need looking after. I'm surprised at your grandmother. You ought to be in school. By George, it's a goddam shame you can't trust anybody to do the right thing! Mind you, keep on saying your prayers every night, even if you don't go to Sunday school, and don't forget God bless Mama."

They asked him where his guitar was and if he wouldn't sing something. The guitar was at the Friends', he said, and he didn't have time to sing right now, for he was up to his ears in work. He had to do the work of ten, he said, because Mr. Carson depended utterly on him to keep the business going. They were cudgelling their brains to think of other intimate details of life at Grandma's, when he patted their heads abruptly and sauntered out to the porch. They heard him out there in a quick change of mood joshing Mrs. M. and Mrs. B. He wanted to know what a couple of good-looking women like them were doing without half a dozen fellows hanging around, and had they heard the new one about the drummer and the chorus girl? Mrs. M. and Mrs. B. could be heard chuckling with the special secret kind of laughter that follows a special kind of joke, until Mrs. M. cried out coyly for him to stop before they died laughing.

"Did you hear what Mrs. M. just said to Papa?" Lena whispered later to Marcia in amazement. "She said he had two of the darlingest little girls she'd ever seen and anybody'd be mighty proud to be a second mother to them!"

"Maybe she won't chase us off the porch after this," Marcia said hopefully. "Maybe she'll stop picking on us."

Listening at every keyhole during their father's brief talks with Aunt Lois and Grandma, they could not gather what the plans for their future were to be. They did deduce that their grandmother had no intention of keeping them there for good, and that Aunt Lois would let them live with her only on condition that "Harry straightened out and did the right thing." It seemed they were a big responsibility—not a desirable one, either. They sat on the back-stair steps meditating glumly till bed time, Marcia getting her cue for gloom from Lena, who scowled and wouldn't talk.

"I'm good and mad," Lena finally said mysteriously.

"So am I," said Marcia, not knowing what there was to be mad about but anxious to share her sister's mood, and not to betray such ignorance as to suggest a game of jacks when this was the moment for gloom.

"They all pick on Papa," said Lena. "What do they mean, he don't treat us right? He brought us oranges, didn't he, and candy?"

"My piece had a worm in it," said Marcia.

"That's what you get for taking the biggest," said Lena. "Let's go to bed without being told, just to spite them."

They rather hoped their father would come in to their room to see them before they really got to bed. Their dark mood did not prevent their jumping up and down on the bed for the customary interval, followed by the conventional pillow fight. Later they were wakened by thunder and with one accord they rushed to the window to watch the lightning, hugging each other fearfully at each roll of thunder. It was thus their father found them when he came up to say good-night to them.

"Your mother used always to love lightning and thunder," he said.

"That's why we always do, too," said Lena. "We always watch it ever since."

He took them on his lap and they sat in the dark, quietly watching the storm the way Mama used to do.

15

The children didn't have to go to school while they stayed with Grandma. Marcia was worried that this meant she wouldn't "pass" and moreover they had to hide when the school inspector came around. When he saw them, Grandma explained that "my daughter's children are visiting me for a few days before they go back to their school in London Junction. The poor kids have lost their mother." Other inspectors called regularly, too. When the gas inspector came the children had to rush through the house warning tenants to detach the rubber hose connecting the pipe with a one-burner gas plate, since this was against fire laws. The police inspector called, too, after a Mr. Barmby had skipped his bill one dark daybreak, leaving a suitcase containing a revolver and several bolts of brocade stolen from a nearby merchant. The police called again to confer with Grandma on the two young ladies with red cheeks in the light housekeeping front bedroom, who were not young matrons as they claimed but fourteen-year-old runaways from Chicago. Things were always happening at Grandma's, and the old lady was happy as a lark, whispering in the halls with Mrs. B. and Mrs. M., listening at doorways to strange sounds, pattering and puttering about, visiting with her friend, Mrs. Carmel. She lived in fear that Aunt Lois would pop in some day when she was having trouble with a roomer, or explaining some little difficulty to a policeman, or taking off Mr. Hartwell's or Papa's shoes when they came in late so exhausted that they fell asleep on the floor or bed with all their clothes on. Aunt Lois might call all the family together to get Grandma back to the propriety of private life in London Junction, a flavorless prospect for a woman now hell-bent on an independent career. If Daisy had only lived, she sometimes sighed, Daisy would have approved of her new life. Daisy never would have nagged her mother; Daisy would have pitched right in and helped out; Daisy would have sung and told stories such as Mrs. B. and Mrs. M. had never heard. Go ahead and tell them, Marcia; tell one of your mother's ghost stories now to Mrs. B.!

The children were permitted real grown-up duties such as making beds, except for changing sheets which wasn't necessary often anyway, for a little wrinkle or bits of grime in bedclothing never killed anybody. An Irish girl named Mary did the hard work, to a constant flow of instructions from Grandma.

A fascinating feature of Grandma's residence was that it was one of fourteen three-story frame houses, all exactly alike, and joined together at their foundations. The cellars had connecting doors, allowing the exploratory young visitors to wander almost a full block in an underground labyrinth of coal bins, jam closets, gray furnaces with swarming pipes, wood piles, broken furniture, trunks and rat traps.

The back yards of these houses were separated by high weatherbeaten picket fences. Here were garbage pails, ash heaps, clothesline props, the lines sagging constantly with grayish washings. Lean tomcats scurried about, city cats with business on their minds, so they tolerated no petting. A tramp from the Union Station train yards would rest occasionally on a sloping cellar door, eating his handout. Grandma declared that Cleveland tramps were not as high class or as educated as the London Junction tramps, who usually paid their way either in wood chopping or instructive conversation about the government.

In the basement of Grandma's house lived Uncle Wally, Grandma's oldest brother, who had suddenly come home from several years' wandering in the Far West. His daughters and sons in Elmville refused to take him in because, they claimed, he had turned Unitarian in his travels, so he took up quarters at Grandma's. He indicated his intention of staying, by thoughtfully taking charge of the furnace the very hour he arrived, then mending the washing machine, almost the last lick of work he did, once he was established on a cot in the furnace room. He was sixty-five years old now, and didn't care much about anything but a warm bed and plenty of coffee. He kept his own coffee pot piping hot always on the furnace. He had a big arm-chair beside the cot and kept his treasures on the broad sill of the barred cellar window. These treasures consisted of a deck of soiled cards for solitaire, a Holy Bible rusty with age, and a stiff collar which he was saving for his funeral. Under the cot was a slop jar with a pink crocheted lid, a cuspidor, and a tobacco box. When the children prowled through the basement, they found him usually sitting on the bed, hands on his knees, staring at nothing. If they made too much noise he snarled at them, but otherwise paid little attention to the busy life going on around him. Papa's visits cheered him up, and he usually would say something that would keep Papa chuckling for a long time.

"Martha used to say a man was too dirty for a house. Keep him in the barn or the cellar, she said, and by golly maybe she was right," he once volunteered philosophically. "Course every man's bound to have some woman at him, wife or daughter; he might as well get used to it or clear out like I did. The thing is to hold on to your temper, keep out of the way, and keep your hat on."

Next to Uncle Wally's furnace room was the laundry with the washtubs, an ironing board and a mangle in it. It was always filled with the smell of steaming Fels Naphtha soap and of wet woolens. The children were frightened of being caught in the mangle, as Mrs. Myers was always warning them, but could not be kept out when the tubs were emptied to drain off the cement floor and the opportunity for wading barefoot was at hand. Grandma padded in and out in the bedroom slippers her aching feet demanded, telling Mary to hurry, hurry, there was plenty work upstairs waiting. Roomers sometimes came down with a shirt or nightdress, calling out, "Put this in, Mary, will you? It won't cost any extra, now that you've got the suds there." The children had learned that in any spot where women were at work they were bound to scold about everything. Another point was that any time women were at work meant a clear field for mischief or adventure in other quarters. It was the time to idle away with ball and jacks on the front stoop until the ice cream sandwich man could be seen wheeling his cart far down the street. Then Lena delegated Marcia to creep into Grandma's room and get two pennies from the saucer of change on the walnut highboy. Lena wouldn't get it herself, because she said it was stealing. Money secured, they raced down the street with a pack of other screaming children who burst out of alleys, gutter drains and thin air, holding high their pennies in tight fists. The fresh smell of the lake was in the wind, and steamer smoke, train smoke, a smell of wheat dust and coffee warehouses, threaded with the dim far-off clamor of the docks.

"I wish we could stay here for good," Marcia said sincerely. "It's fun doing as we please."

"I don't like Mrs. M. and Mrs. B. always bossing us," objected Lena. "Besides I want to stay with Papa and Florrie. I want to live in London Junction again and see Mary Evelyn."

Whenever they asked Papa if he had found the housekeeper he told them to hush up and stop bothering a busy man, all tired out from trying to make a living for them. On his rare visits he sat on the porch with Mrs. M. and Mrs. B., chuckling and teasing them. When a new roomer brought out a guitar they heard Papa singing to them, "Our little farm was small; it would not support us all." Mrs. M. and Mrs. B. both commented many times on what a card Mr. Willard was, and he certainly would have no trouble getting a mother for his little ones. Mrs. M. said three was, to her mind, the ideal number of children, as they sort of looked after themselves, leaving the parents, who might be still full of life, to go on good times together. Or for that matter the children could be left a good deal with their relations. Mrs. B. said that from Mr. Willard's dressiness she judged he made a nice little salary and could afford help to look after the children, leaving the new mother free to shop or go to her card clubs and keep up appearances. Both agreed that those little girls certainly needed a mother's care. But when Ed Hartwell was with Papa the two men made a bee-line for downtown and spent very little time with the roomers.

Mr. Hartwell made some side remarks to Papa about Mrs. B. and Mrs. M. being Battle-Axes. Soon afterward Marcia asked Mrs. M. what a battle-ax was, and received a sound box on the ears. The girls tried to keep awake till their father got in, but sleep usually overtook them. In the morning he was cross if they waked him, and often he left without a goodbye. "He's just like a chicken with his head cut off without Daisy," said Grandma to Mrs. Carmel. "He don't know what to do with the kids because he's just a kid himself."

16

Grandma's first year on Hodge Street was a great success, she often stated, and she could never thank her friend Mrs. Carmel enough for her excellent advice. No one who applied for lodging was ever turned away, though this resulted sometimes in older tenants being forced out of their beds or else to sharing them. Living room and dining room were divided by screens or calico curtains strung across into dormitories for three or four people, and in especially busy times Grandma slept in the dining room in the folding bed with the children, since a private room for them was now out of the question. In spite of the number of lodgers and light housekeepers, there seemed a lot of financial difficulties. Grandma had mixed fears, one that Aunt Lois would come up and see her serious difficulties, and the other that she would *not* come up and help her out. Aunt Lois came up scolding once a month, forcing Grandma to admit that very few people found it convenient to pay their bills. Aunt Lois said it was an outrage that

Harry never paid any board either for himself or the girls, and she would give him a good talking to. Lena and Marcia heard these accusations with gloomy forebodings, not lessened by Aunt Lois buying them underwear and shoes with the remark, "Your father will have to pay me back for these." Sensing trouble ahead for their father, Marcia insisted they needed nothing; if they did, then Papa would get it at the right time. When their father was told of Aunt Lois' action, he was angry at the implied criticism.

"Besides, the shoes hurt us," Marcia willingly declared. "Anyway the underwear isn't the kind Mama used to get us at the Fair Store."

Papa at once took them out and bought them new hats and hair-ribbons, the kind their mother would have liked, he said. They overheard him having a long talk with Grandma about what was to be done with them, but while the plans seemed exciting they also seemed confused. He was going to take a house in London Junction with a housekeeper, he was going to board them at the London Junction Hotel, he was going to send them to boarding school, he was going to move to California and take them there, also he was going to take an apartment with Ed Hartwell in Lesterville and have Ed's girl look out for them. These contradictory plans satisfied Grandma, and the five dollars he gave her as token of good will completely won her.

"Harry and I could always get on," she told Mrs. Carmel. "Harry and I never had a word."

She was gratified to hear that Mrs. Carmel respected Harry, and that she agreed with Grandma that Lois was too hard on everybody. Mrs. Carmel reminded Grandma that Lois had always tried to stand in her way, and hoped Grandma kept in mind that the Cleveland venture was all Mrs. Carmel's idea.

"I'm a business woman myself," said Mrs. Carmel. "I recognize a talent for business and you've got it. Your daughter doesn't see it."

Grandma was so flattered that she saw no need to mention Lois' required contribution to her business success.

Mrs. Carmel ran a millinery store in East Cleveland. She was a gaunt, dark woman always draped in innumerable black shawls, capes, veils, rustling skirts all blowing out like bat

wings when she scuttled down the streets. She held her elbows stiffly out as if tacking to the wind for speed, but actually this posture was to secure many bags, large black ones,
crocheted or velvet, all stuffed to capacity with old letters, ancient cancelled bankbooks, receipts and recipes, gumdrops,
sewing kit, samples of brocade, bone hairpins, tangerines,
Butterick patterns, keys to long-forgotten rooms in long-lost
houses, photographs of owlish children naked on bear rugs or
heavily muffled up on bamboo chairs, but in either case long
since grown up, addresses, stamps, obsolete coins, streetcar
tickets, ribbon remnants, pincushions, and many other useful
objects which could not be left in bureau drawers for thievish
servants. Mrs. Carmel veered and zoomed around street corners as if wound up by the toymaker and liable to be stopped
only by direct collision with an immovable object, and the curious motor noise she made as she zoomed was her mutter-
ings to herself with parched lips smacking and false teeth
clacking. These mutters were as documentary as the contents
of her bag, "May Company, Baileys, Taylor Arcade, Wood-
land car, half a cup of sugar, picture postcard," passersby
would catch as she poised on a curb before flight to another
corner, and often they took a second look at the eagle's beak
under the black veiled bonnet, the sturdy wart with curling
tendrils on her chin, the beetling black brows and restless
beady eyes. Some superstitious strangers even crossed themselves or made a wish as she brushed by, but for all this
strange appearance and behavior Grandma stated that Mrs.
Carmel was as bright as a dollar, with a heart as big as all outdoors. Her girls worked their fingers to the bone for her and
were rewarded in their "bad times" by a nice nip of gin which
Mrs. Carmel herself was obliged to take medicinally to keep
up her strength. It was amazing that Mrs. Carmel made a living, amazing that any customer could be found in any walk of
life for the bonnets which she gorged as generously with odds
and ends as she did her pockets.

The shop was so tiny, it was squeezed out of existence by
two larger stores. Inside there was only one counter, and that
as well as the shelves was stacked with hats of all ages for all
seasons. A large bin in the corner held untrimmed felts, and
in spite of the overpowering smell of camphor fat dingy

moths waddled comfortably in and out of this perpetual banquet. The darkness of the showroom and the smallness and
dullness of the mirror aided sales undoubtedly, and since Mrs.
Carmel never bought new stock but churned her old frames
and ribbons about seasonally, the overhead could not have
been great. Some people, including Grandma, were certain
there was a secret treasure hidden in one of the black bags, indeed were so convinced of this hidden security that they
gladly handed over the fifty cents or so Mrs. Carmel requested, usually after a busy clawing through her purse and
the preface, "I seem to be a little short of cash."

Mrs. Carmel, called Em by Grandma, seldom talked above
a coarse, rasping whisper or at best a croak, because all of her
conversation was strictly confidential. She did not like large
groups and even in a small company she would wring her
hands restlessly, protruding upper teeth gnawing at under lip
till chance permitted her the exclusive attention of one person, usually Grandma. These teeth were incidentally purchased for the long-deceased Mr. Carmel the very day of his
death, and as an economical measure his widow instantly had
her own fangs removed and wore these new teeth which
might not fit perfectly but stayed in fairly well and worked a
little better than her bare gums. They provided, too, an interesting sibilance to her speech, and heightened the air of secrecy to her remarks. She usually looked around the room in
the middle of a sentence, to whisper, "*She* wouldn't be at the
door, would she?" After the first greeting the secrets began,
with some such opener as, "Well, I saw the Party finally and I
passed on that remark I heard about our Friend. Well, I wish
you could have seen his face!" This was a game dear to
Grandma's heart and part of Mrs. Carmel's fascination for
her. "No!" Grandma would cry, edging up her chair. "I wish
I could have been there! How did the Party take it?" Mrs.
Carmel would click her teeth and permit herself a windy
chuckle. "They gave me a kinda funny look and then this
other Party spoke up and mentioned such and such a price for
the property—wait till She hears that!" Grandma was as delighted with this mystery as a child and all but clapped her
hands at each fresh clue from her guest.

"You mean She didn't know the Property was for sale?"

Mrs. Carmel nodded twice very slowly. "She still goes to that Place I told you about."

"No!" cried Grandma, flushing with excitement. "How in the world did you know?"

"I saw the letter," whispered Mrs. Carmel, with a cautious glance at the door. "I ran into the other party's lawyer at the Lecture, and he showed it to me."

It was Grandma's turn to throw a bombshell and she drew back in her chair as if to give it more power.

"Well, don't repeat this for the world, but this Party I told you about from Akron told me yesterday she knows for a fact the will's been changed in *his* favor."

"That's a lie," Mrs. Carmel said stoutly. "I can't tell you who told me but I can assure you the will is not changed one iota in any way, shape or form."

"You don't mean—!" gasped Grandma, eyes sparkling, and now beginning to rock her chair happily to and fro. Such code information was exchanged between Mrs. Carmel and her friend at every visit, leaving both participants glowing with secrets only half revealed. The children, sometimes discovered too late in the closets or under a sofa, could make neither head nor tail of what they heard, nor for that matter could any adult intruder, so that Mrs. Carmel's intense fear of eavesdroppers was quite unnecessary.

Mrs. Carmel carried grudges among her other impedimenta. She was in a constant state of war with the landlord of her tiny place, and he was forever doing something that "made her hot French blood boil," for she was French by marriage and proud of it. When the children came to live with Grandma they stood in a row, jaws agape, staring at Mrs. Carmel, watching her chin waggling in perpetual croaks and sibilants, half anesthetized by the camphorous lavender sachet exuding from her drapes; finally Mrs. Carmel would tweak their cheeks with bony claws and cluck, "I always get on with little folks. No, sir, I never have any trouble with children, never, not an iota."

A gumdrop apiece, flavored faintly with mothballs, and then off she zoomed into the night. They would press noses to the front window, watching her nebulous black wings fluttering under the street lamp, then plunging suddenly homeward into darkness. No one else was ever able to bring such glamour to Grandma's busy life or to leave such a gratifying afterglow of intrigue, subrosa, entre-nous-innuendo.

It was a pity Mrs. Carmel finally sided with Aunt Lois in saying the children were too big a handful for Grandma. There was a noisy conference one week-end with everybody crying about poor Daisy, Aunt Lois sternly accusing, Grandma vacillating, Mrs. Carmel stating that Grandma could put a little shop in the space occupied by the children and make a mint of money. The word "imposition" occurred several times.

That very night Papa, red-eyed and desperate, packed them up and took them to the station. It was a shock to find nobody at Grandma's was desolate at their sudden departure.

"Run along with your dad," said Uncle Wally. "Maybe there'll be some peace around the place now. Keep your noses clean."

Mrs. M. and Mrs. B. were equally stoical about their loss.

"I hope somebody teaches them some manners," said Mrs. M. "The younger one is as impudent as they come. Battle-Ax!"

"Will we see Florrie?" Marcia begged to know as their father hurried them through the Union Depot. "Are we going to London Junction?"

Papa didn't get their tickets at once but stood chewing a cigar thoughtfully for several minutes. They didn't know where they were going till they got on the train, but they were glad to be with Papa again.

17

"When I set out to do a thing, I do it," stated Papa several times and with increasing complacency. No one, least of all his three doting daughters, could deny this. There they were, almost by magic, so swiftly had Papa acted, back in the London Junction Hotel for the season, under the eye of the manager's wife, Mrs. Purdy. They had been escorted by Papa to the school superintendent's office and examined for their proper places in school, Florrie admitted to the kindergarten. They had been regally outfitted on credit at the Fair Store;

they had been assigned a small, unpainted table in the hotel
kitchen for their private use; and Papa and Mr. Purdy had sat
up late, vowing friendship over a bottle of whiskey. Friendship
was what men had as protection from the cruelties of women
and fate. Mr. Purdy declared that in all his twenty years of
hotel business he had never come across as decent a fellow as
Harry Willard, and he didn't care who heard him say it. He
said it was a rotten shame that life had treated him so badly,
leaving him helpless with his family, but then life was, as that
piece said, like a game of cards. The figure was so apt that he
and Papa soon vanished into a distant chamber with a pair of
Chicago shoe salesmen to check on the simile. The girls, still
dazzled by their swift re-establishment, didn't see Papa again
for a week; but the Purdys, in fact the whole hotel, took good
care of them.

The hotel was in the middle of town, with the train tracks
running directly in front of it and the ticket office opening off
the hotel lobby. The freight office and yards were further
down, connecting with the ticket office by a long covered
shed. An all-night cafeteria was on the other side of the ticket
office, and here those railroad men who were not dressed for
the privileges of the regular hotel dining room might feel at
ease. Train talk was the thing in both places, however, with
the daily schedules of Number Nine, Number Forty-six,
Number Six, etc., all discussed as if they were race horses instead of engines. Indeed, these engines panted and snorted as
joyfully into the very doors of the London Junction Hotel as
if they were pet stallions showing off for their proud masters,
anxious for a pat of approval. Their records hung conspicu-
ously in both cafeteria and hotel lobby, and were studied intently by everyone, regardless of any plans for travel. "Did
you hear about Twenty-six? Broke down twenty-two minutes
out of Columbus, had to back up for repairs, got in an hour
and forty minutes late. Shorty was firing. Old Hank in the
cab." The commercial travellers liked to know all these
things—something to season their conversation while they
were selling.

The hotel was four stories high, of red brick, with glass-
walled lobby, behind which the residents lolled in Morris
chairs and viewed the passing trains, or, as they shifted from

view, the marketplace on the other side of the tracks. Mr. Purdy, owner and manager, was a man of forty, thin, beak-nosed, bald, with a nasal eastern voice and general air of cosmopolitan distinction, due to a neatly cropped brown moustache, rimless glasses on a black ribbon, and a fur-collared greatcoat. He kept his wife and other family details tucked away somewhere in the back of the house, and was known to freeze Mrs. Purdy with a look when she ventured into the doorway of the lobby. The rule was that she was to use the back entrance, and though Mr. Purdy dined with his guests in the dining room, and so did Mrs. Hazy, his house-keeper, Mrs. Purdy was protected from this commercial scene by being screened off with her offspring into a corner of the kitchen. Far from being displeased, Mrs. Purdy basked in the special protection provided for her, not at all resentful that it was her money which had bought the hotel so that she might have deserved some say in its management. The isolation had further point in that the Purdy offspring, at two years old, showed signs to all but his mother of being imbecilic, though in a silent, unobtrusive way.

Papa had engaged a large corner bedroom for his family, with two big brass beds in it so that when he was at home he could sleep there too. In the mornings the chambermaid helped them get ready for school. The older girls brought Florrie home from kindergarten at noon and she was permit-ted to tag at the chambermaid's skirts the rest of the day. Mrs. Purdy's niece, Bonnie, the cashier, also took a personal inter-est in Florrie, and allowed her to play in the lobby under her fond but casual eye. Florrie took turns sitting on the laps of the various residents, ate limitless bonbons and cookies, and showed off.

"Where is your Mama, Baby?" the gentlemen would ask, and Florrie would point heavenward. This always resulted in someone pressing a coin upon her, and a display of handker-chiefs with several sentimental bachelors blowing their noses ostentatiously. As Mr. Sweeney, who was frequently present, said, "There are times when a man isn't ashamed to shed an honest tear."

Bonnie Purdy was a trim, complacent little figure, very styl-ish, since she had a pass on all the railroads and could make trips all over the country on the spur of the moment to see shows, buy hats, or go to parties. She was considered full of life, admired for her jauntily swaying hips and high-stepping when she was fixed up, and the intimations of plumply curved legs revealed by her skirts. She was no chippy, the men respectfully declared, but a fine little girl, high school and business college graduate, a little lady even if she did work around men. She was up on all the latest songs and taught them to Marcia and Lena, accompanying them on the dining room piano. She even took them with her to Eastern Star entertainments, where she had them sing. She was an earnest performer herself, specializing in musical recitations. For these she looked particularly fine, wearing a white Greek-style wool dress with a red collar that set off her smooth black hair, parted in the middle and drawn smoothly back like pictures of the Madonna. Her cheeks were full, her eyes large and expressive, her mouth childishly pretty but solemn. She sat on the platform in a large arm-chair, and recited "Sandolphin, the Angel of Mercy, Sandophin, the Angel of Prayer," while a lodge sister played the Flower Song on the piano. It was considered a very refined performance. She always came up to say good night to the children, bringing them glasses of milk, and anxiously assuring them there was nothing to be afraid of. But no one could be afraid with the genial trains romping in and out of the room all night—or so it seemed—and the friendly male voices in the halls or outside on the train platform.

Florrie still sobbed in the night for her mother. Marcia, too, had one recurrent dream of her mother. She saw her crossing a street, in her dream, bent over with a bushel bag of potatoes on her back, and her face so tired it did not even smile. Another time she saw her mother carrying her bed on her back, again all bent over like an old woman. In her dreams her mother never smiled, but was always bent with a heavy burden, so Marcia dreaded these dreams and was glad if Florrie woke her up with her crying. Then she would manage to keep her quiet by telling her stories, never-ending stories, in the course of which they both fell asleep. The stories were about a boy named Niky who was a million years old and lived in a tree, with a Whistle Fairy who could transform him anywhere in any shape when Niky whistled. If Florrie was fretful, Marcia made extravagant promises of producing Niky in person, though at the crucial moment she announced he had been disguised as the tangerine Florrie had just eaten. As Lena considered this sort of thing childish, Marcia tried to save it for the nights Lena spent at her friend, Mary Evelyn's.

It was to be expected that Aunt Lois was perturbed over Harry's solution to his domestic problem but, as the other relatives felt too, she realized that interference meant taking on the responsibility oneself, and she had worry enough with Grandma. She insisted that they spend Saturdays and Sundays with her, scrubbing them from top to toe, mending and darning them, and looking over their report cards. She wanted to keep Florrie, indeed everyone wanted to keep Florrie, even Isobel and Chris, poor as they were, for Florrie was a "little doll," they all said. But Papa vowed poor Daisy would never want the girls separated. Besides, it was Florrie who looked after him, trying to do all the things she had seen her mother do, bringing him his matches and ash tray, admiring his neckties, worrying over his frowns, lisping consolation.

"She's a second Daisy," declared Papa fondly. "I wouldn't take a million for her."

The kitchen help at the hotel provided spontaneous entertainment and occasional discipline for the children. Their love affairs, the town and hotel scandals were freely aired, and later conducted to school by Marcia and Lena for the recess secrets with their classmates. Mrs. McGuire, the cook; Pete, the pastry cook; Kitty and Fanny, the two helpers, knew everything that was going on in town, and were not afraid to make suitable comments. Sometimes on the Friday night Knights of Columbus dances in Eagle Hall, they took Lena to sit by the orchestra and watch the dancing. In good-humored idle hours they taught the children to waltz and two-step and schottische, and twice they took all three girls to the dances to show off Marcia and Lena dancing together and all three singing "Absence Makes the Heart Grow Fonder." After school they rode in the engines in the switch yard with the engineers, and played in the telegraph tower with Oley, the Swedish operator. He let them hang on to wires and get electric shocks unless the inspector or dispatcher was around to chase them.

"I hear you're going to get a new mama," the trainmen and the kitchen girls were always saying. "Is it that chippy in Newark your dad's running with?"

"Your papa's sweet on Bonnie, isn't he?" the kitchen girls demanded, curiously, and receiving an astonished negative from Marcia they pursued the point with, "What was he doing with her at the Luna Park picnic last Sunday, then? What does she look after you kids for then? Believe me, it ain't for money."

It was true that every few weeks their father drew them on his knee for a grave conference.

"How do you like keeping house for your papa?" he would ask earnestly.

They would chorus their pleasure. Then he would whip out a cabinet photograph of a lady from his pocket and ask, "How would you like this lady for your new mama?" Ever pleased at any dramatic change they always expressed approval, though the ladies varied from the one in a long white robe with her hair down, seated at a harp, to a pop-eyed plump brunette in a black picture hat, leaning on a parasol. Whenever they confided excitedly in Bonnie about these ladies, Bonnie got cross and, one time, burst into tears. They couldn't imagine what was the matter.

"It just goes to show," Bonnie, weeping, explained. "A person does the best she knows how but all the good it does! A person could eat her heart out for a kind word for all some people care!"

"My papa likes you, Bonnie," Florrie volunteered one day.

"Your papa hates the ground I walk on," she stated darkly. "You can tell him I said so."

Mr. Hartwell came over often, sometimes with his lady-friend Mabel. On these occasions Papa borrowed a screen from Mr. Purdy to place around the children's bed, while he acted host to his two guests and Bonnie when she got off duty. Mabel was definitely stout, "a fine figure," as Papa declared, with tightly curled bangs and yellow hair, a pink and white face, and two gold teeth. She had been Mr. Hartwell's lady-friend for ten years, and was still half dazzled and half resentful of his hold on her, so that she divided her time between rumpling his glossy hair in her two plump little fists and cooing, "Whose honey sugar are you?" and next minute snapping, "Oh, shut your big mouth, you big fourflusher. I said Shut Up." Mr. Hartwell usually remained polite toward her during both these treatments, since, as he often said, he had too big a respect for a real lady like Miss Purdy and his friend Willard to kick her rump right through her shoulder blades as many less cultivated men might do on similar provocation.

A card table was set up during these gay evenings and Five Hundred enjoyed with a pitcher of beer, pretzels and cheese. Papa kidded Bonnie about all her beaux and treated Mabel with the cagey respect due a pal's lady-friend. Sometimes he played the guitar for Bonnie to recite or sing, but often in the very middle he would stop abruptly and put the guitar away. "I guess it reminds him of Mama," deduced Marcia and Lena, in bed listening but pretending for their own purposes to be asleep.

Mabel slept in Bonnie's room on these occasions, and Mr. Hartwell tucked in the other brass bed with Papa. They snored and filled the room with fumes of cigar smoke and beer. In the night Florrie always stumbled into her father's bed. Mr. Hartwell and Papa were usually waked up by Florrie putting her feet in their faces or butting them in the stomachs in her restless tossing. These were good times, the children thought, being part of Papa's life, but after his parties he was silent and moody. Bonnie was always finding some reason to call when he was home, but he never seemed glad to see her when no one else was around.

"How's Mr. Willard today?" Bonnie asked gayly. "I don't suppose any power on earth would make him take a poor girl to the Elks' dance in Lesterville tonight."

"An old family man like me's got no business at a dance," Papa answered. "All I can do to get around on crutches as it is."

"You wouldn't have to dance," Bonnie said. "I don't give a snap about dancing, myself, but I enjoy good music. Maybe you'd like to walk down to the Band Concert later, when I get off. It always cheers me up."

"I don't want to cheer up," Papa said. "I got a lot on my mind. You get one of those young fellows from the Yard. You don't want an old boy like me to tag along."

"Mr. Willard, you're not much past thirty," Bonnie tremulously protested. "I suppose you think I'm too old, too, being twenty! You don't need to always act as if you were my father."

"You're a nice girl, Bonnie," Papa said. "You go have a good time."

"I pressed your suit, Mr. Willard," Bonnie said, standing in the door, unwilling to leave without a friendlier contact. "No, don't bother to pay me. I was pressing my own things anyway, so it was no trouble. Well, so long."

Still she didn't go. Papa started dealing himself a round of Solitaire on the bed, pretending not to notice Bonnie's uncertainty. The children, laboring over their school books, glanced up curiously at this scene, not understanding Papa's gayety in crowds and his moodiness when alone with their gay, beloved Bonnie.

"I suppose you'll be gone three weeks this trip," pursued Bonnie, swinging her keys nervously. "Maybe I might be running down to Columbus next Saturday, myself."

"That so?" Papa listlessly said.

"Oh, something else," Bonnie pursued, watching his face anxiously. "The lodge is putting on a show next Thursday night in the hall, and I thought the girls could sing 'Go to Sleep, My Little Pickaninny,' then 'Hello, Central,' for an encore. They'll get paid fifty cents."

Papa beamed now, and looked over with pride at his offspring.

"Their mama would be tickled to hear that," he exclaimed. "By George, they're getting to be real professionals."

"I taught them," Bonnie reminded him. "I thought it would be cute if they had Florrie in a cradle, rocking her for the first song."

"Blacked up like a pickaninny?" Marcia asked, excitedly.

"She's too big for a cradle," said Lena.

"I am not," wailed Florrie, clinging to Bonnie's skirts. "I want to do what Bonnie says."

Bonnie consoled her, finding a solution to her own vague embarrassment by picking her up to take downstairs with her.

"No objection to my sitting at your table for lunch, Mr. Willard, I hope?" she asked jauntily, and when Papa only shook his head she went away humming, with Florrie on her shoulder.

"Bonnie's awful good to us, Papa," said Lena. "Sometimes she reminds me of Mama."

"Hush! Nobody's like your Mama," Papa said harshly. He got up and put on his hat. "Get to work on your lessons now, no more fooling!"

No matter how gloomy he was, alone in the room with them, he changed as soon as he entered a group. They tiptoed down the back stairs to listen outside the lobby or dining room door while he told stories and joked with the other men and the waitresses. No matter how quiet the place would be, Papa's entrance made it immediately merry. His daughters huddled in the back hall, listening to the roars of laughter and their father's contagious chuckle, not knowing what was so funny but proud as Punch when somebody cried out, "By George, you can't beat Harry Willard! No, sir, he can't be topped!"

The hotel and the intimacy with Papa was exciting for a while, but then it grew lonely, for the longer his absences were the more brusquely people treated the children. Mrs. McGuire and the kitchen help found them underfoot too much, and scolded, till their only refuge was in swiping cookies and oranges from the icebox and having some really good reason for a scolding. Lena stood up haughtily to the constant, though not really bad-tempered, nagging and regarded herself as an adult, not to be confused with her two younger sisters. She had a dignified private life with her friend Mary Evelyn, and made personal visits to the Friends', and to her Aunt Lois to discuss family affairs and receive rewards due her advanced years in trinkets, small change, new bonnets and ribbons. When Mrs. Purdy commissioned her to look after the idiot baby, Lena proudly announced that she was no nursemaid and stayed at Mary Evelyn's for two days. The job therefore fell to Marcia. Even though Mrs. Purdy gave her twenty-five cents a week, it was humiliating to be caught by her classmates, wheeling the Purdy baby up and down back alleys. Florrie was a comfort, in that she liked to wheel anything, and ran along beside, begging to push the gocart. Eventually Marcia perfected a scheme whereby she let Florrie wheel the empty gocart around and as soon as Mrs. Purdy got out of her apartment for her missionary committee work, Marcia plumped the baby on the living room floor, barricaded it with chairs, and then sat on a stool outside the pen, reading all of Mrs. Purdy's books. School work was easy to the point of boredom, but here in Mrs. Purdy's overfurnished parlor was the culture of the ages. "Last Days of Pompeii," the works of Mrs. E. D. E. N. Southworth, "Lucille," Miss Mulock's works, "The Old Mamzelle's Secret," "Three Musketeers," "If I Were King," "Wormwood," Henty stories, Horatio Alger books—all these Marcia devoured in a state of ecstasy unmarred by her inadequacy to digest many hard lumps of language or meaning, for the thrill was in the reading. Florrie loyally warned her of Mrs. Purdy's approach, so the books and chairs could be replaced and the ever-ready explanation given that the baby cried so she brought it inside. When they weren't counting the days till Papa returned, Florrie and Marcia were wandering up and down past Mary Evelyn's house, hoping for Lena to come out.

But whenever they were fortunate enough to catch her, Lena was quite likely to strut past them with Mary Evelyn (dressed as nearly alike as their totally dissimilar charms would allow), and if she did speak, it was in no friendly spirit. "Go home and wash your face," she was likely to admonish Marcia curtly. "You ought to be ashamed going around with your petticoat showing. For heaven's sake, take Florrie home and blow her nose, and don't you two come tagging around Mary Evelyn and me, or I'll tell Papa."

Dashed but not discouraged, Marcia and Florrie swiped sleeves across their faces, jerked at their offending skirts, yanked their garters and, after gawking at their fashionable sister's progress down the street with her proud friend, they followed doggedly, utterly fascinated by the busy life Lena was able to make for herself. Lena and Mary Evelyn took walks to gather violets or mushrooms, they went to Epworth League meetings, they joined the Loyal Temperance Legion, a mysterious secret society that met after dark and sang songs and took pledges never to touch rum. Lena and Mary Evelyn did their studies together and made fudge, and they sewed things, on the sewing machine. Marcia and Florrie were a little unhappy at Lena's individuality, but proud and astonished too at her initiative. They tried to think of games to rival Mary Evelyn's inducements, but the only thing that would hold Lena was Marcia's final desperate offer to spend her quarter on ice cream, instead of saving it for the *St. Nicholas Magazine.* During Papa's visits Lena gave up her friend, in case Papa would offer some treat which she might miss. She felt her responsibility, too, and usually devoted the first evening with Papa to a grave report on the bad behavior of her two sisters. Marcia was kept after school twice for not answering when spoken to, she was sent home by the teacher to wash her hands, she was slapped for impudence when she called the teacher a chippy. Florrie had bawled all during Sunday school, so they said she couldn't come again, and she had jumped on the bed till it broke the slats. Lena then produced her report card with an A in deportment, which she felt offset the C's in her studies, and partially convinced Papa, so that he saw only the D in Marcia's deportment and not the A's and B's in studies.

"I don't like deportment, that's why," Marcia belligerently explained. For her part she was able to tell Papa that Lena visited Aunt Lois all the time and told her everything that Papa was doing, so that Aunt Lois was madder than ever at him. She added that Lena now swore, and said "Lord" and "For heaven's sake," just like Mary Evelyn. This retaliation impressed Lena with her sister's strategic abilities, so she treated her like an equal for fully three days.

Papa didn't go on a trip for over a month. When Mr. Hartwell came over they didn't celebrate, but talked in low voices far into the night. Bonnie Purdy came in at midnight, bringing coffee and sandwiches which she declared were just going to waste in the icebox. The children sensed something queer was going on from Papa's silent spells and letter writing. One morning Bonnie came in at daybreak in her dressing gown to wake Papa for the Chicago train. He was gone two days. When he came back he had his hat once again cocked on the side of his head and chuckled at everything. Bonnie ran in the room after him, and they saw her reach up and kiss him warmly.

"I knew you'd get it," she cried. "You can get anything you ever go for, Harry Willard, if you'd just listen to me!"

Since there was no other audience available, Papa was obliged to do his talking to his small family. He paced up and down the room, with his thumbs in his vest, and said, thank God, he didn't have to slave for a flathead like Carson any more, a man who wouldn't trust an old employe, criticizing expense accounts, pinching pennies like no first-class company ever did. He was glad he could lift his head up again on his trips, hold his own with other men representing high-class firms such as the London Furniture Company could never be with a dumbbell like Bert Carson at the head, a spying, suspicious old cheapskate who didn't appreciate what a hell of a lot of guts it took to build up a business on the road. He should have listened to Hartwell two years ago and quit then instead of waiting for this kick in the pants. But you couldn't keep Harry Willard down, no, sir! He was signed up now with the Emperor Mausoleum Company, travelling out of Chicago, working for one of the biggest men in the business, Colgate Custer.

"You can tell that to your Aunt Lois next time she tries to pump you," Papa instructed Lena. "Just say your father's making twice the money and working for Colgate Custer. I'll drop in on your grandma next week and tell her. She's the only friend I've got in the whole damn family."

He went off next day in high spirits, without saying when he would be back. Mr. Purdy came in to see him and was surprised to find him gone.

"Did he leave anything with you?" he asked Lena.

Lena said no, and Mr. Purdy, after a thoughtful look around the room, went out, stroking his chin.

"I suppose Papa never paid this bill, either," said Lena, scowling. "I get sick and tired of it!"

Florrie and Marcia stared in horror at this evidence of rising disloyalty to Papa.

"Aunt Lois says we owe everybody in town," Lena stated. "Mary Evelyn's mother said Papa never's paid a bill in his life, and the only reason the Purdys let us stay here, never paying, is that Bonnie Purdy is stuck on Papa. Aunt Lois said Papa borrowed fifty dollars from Mr. Sweeney for the first month we were here and never paid anything since."

Florrie began to cry. Every word Lena said hurt Marcia. Even if it was true, you couldn't come right out and say such things, not, oh never, about Papa. Lena's pretty, rosy face was drawn into an angry frown, her lips pulled tightly together. She looked almost grown-up and very much like Aunt Lois, with her hair frizzed and pulled back into a bun.

"I don't believe what Mary Evelyn's mother says," Marcia said. "She's just a store clerk."

This high-handed attack again impressed and surprised Lena so that she looked at Marcia with grudging respect. Carried away with her success Marcia made so bold as to ask Bonnie outright, before Lena, if Papa owed a lot of money.

"He'll pay it back, don't you worry about that," Bonnie said firmly. "You children ought to be ashamed criticizing your father. Why, your father is one of the finest, loveliest men that ever breathed."

"What will Mr. Purdy do with us if Papa doesn't pay the bill?" Marcia asked.

Bonnie merely tousled both girls' heads, and looked fondly down at them.

"You poor kids worrying that way!" she exclaimed. "But don't you go worrying your papa about things! He's got enough on his mind, three motherless children, nobody but strangers willing to look after them, poor man!"

As usual Lena's pride was roused.

"We have plenty of relations, we don't have to have strangers," she said with a toss of her head. "We've got Chris and Isobel and Uncle Louie and Grandpa Willard, and plenty other relations."

"They never come to see us," said Marcia candidly. "When Papa wrote we were coming to visit them they never answered."

"They were just afraid they'd have you on their hands for good," Bonnie suggested. "It costs money to bring up three children, and they maybe weren't sure they could afford you."

"But we only wanted to visit them," Marcia said. "Papa told them."

"I guess they didn't believe him," Lena said.

Bonnie shook her finger at them.

"Not another word about your father, now! Lena, don't you listen to that bad Mary Evelyn. Your father's doing the best he can; he's a wonderful man and don't you forget it."

Lena was as pleased as the others to have this reassurance. She punished Mary Evelyn by staying home and allowing Marcia to spend her ten cents on nougats which they ate playing Casino on the floor.

18

It astonished Marcia to discover that other children lived in an almost incomprehensibly different way than they did. It took a long time for this fact to penetrate, since she spent very little time with her schoolmates. They played silly games at recess, like Water, Water Wildflower, and Crack the Whip, all involving a lot of running and whooping around, when the time could be spent in the school library, reading books not recommended, or studying words in the big dictionary. Lena always walked home with Mary Evelyn and an older new friend, Myrtle Chase, who had just moved to town from Detroit and was an object of worship to Lena and Mary Evelyn. Marcia walked home alone, carrying on imaginary conversations with characters in the books she was reading. The other children had birthday parties, which filled Marcia with vague dread, for everybody else knew what to do and, besides, she never had any presents to give. They had peanut races, and the mothers told them what games to play, and to save their favors for "memory books," whatever they might be. These children had pretty little bedrooms, doll houses, little pianos, all kinds of story books, and sometimes they had bicycles or ponies or rabbits in the back yard. They lived on Park Square, far from the railroad center of town, or on Main Boulevard; they took dancing lessons every Saturday from a Miss Brumby, and music lessons, violin or piano, from a Miss Cory from Oberlin. Their fathers were at home all the time and owned a grocery store, a real estate business, a hardware store, or were executives in the furniture factory, the banks, or the telephone company. At the parties something awful usually happened. The mother would ask Marcia where was her "hankie," and, finding she had none, would take her upstairs to lend her one. Or she would exclaim, gently, "Little girl, is that a nice way to eat? Just look at your frock—or was that stain on it before?" Dishes broke as soon as they reached Marcia's hands. Some adult would usually draw her out of the group to say, "That's not nice language for a little girl," with Marcia sulkily uncertain of what word had been wrong, only knowing that the kitchen help and the lobby gentlemen at the hotel always chuckled when she said it.

In school she was looked upon with suspicion, and her quick answers usually brought out whispers of "Cheat! Cheat!" until she learned not to answer. Lena was frankly ashamed of her, though she rose valiantly to her defense when the teacher punished her for copying in a test, unable to believe Marcia remembered whole pages word for word almost in one glance. Lena assumed her authority as Oldest, and called on Marcia's teacher for redress, saying with dignity that her young sister was the smartest girl in class and the teacher ought to know better, and if she didn't stop picking on Marcia she, Lena, would take it up with the principal. On this happy occasion Lena elected to march home holding on to Marcia's arm protectively, and she showed her how to crochet as a special favor.

Papa, at their urgent request, packed up all three of them to go to Uncle Louie's that summer, and he said maybe he'd have a house when they came back. This time everything was different. Uncle Louie had had bad luck with his crops, Aunt Betts' rose cold turned into a siege of asthma, and Almedy worked so hard she had no time for company. The girls missed the careless freedom of the hotel, and country games seemed silly after the grown-up pleasures of London Junction. Florrie got a rash from sliding down the haystack on her bottom and all three got poison ivy. Uncle Louie and Aunt Betts weren't as jolly this time, and didn't seem to want them.

"How long did your father say you were going to stay here?" asked Uncle Louie, at the end of a week.

"As long as we like, he said," Lena reassured him.

"I guess that's the size of it," said Uncle Louie moodily. "By George, he sent along all your winter clothes, too, mittens and skates even. Does he think we have to be responsible now for you?"

"Now, Lou," Aunt Betts wheezed, "it isn't the children's fault. Like as not they didn't know a thing about it. Don't make Florrie cry." For Florrie always wept at criticisms of Papa.

"That's so," granted Uncle Louie. "Harry's got a hell of a nerve, though, not even asking by your leave. If he can't raise his own family, why don't he put 'em in a home? I like the kids all right, but I'm not going to let Harry impose on me on that account."

As usual, Lena's pride rose up again, though Marcia was only mildly uncomfortable at these discussions. Lena laboriously wrote a letter to Papa and another to Aunt Lois, stating "we don't want to stay anywheres we're not wanted so pleas send us tickets." Aunt Lois was frantically adjusting Grandma's affairs in Cleveland, and Papa was in the West, so after waiting impatiently two or three days Lena announced they were leaving that very day for London Junction. Uncle Louie was abashed, and tried to coax them to wait till Papa wrote, but Lena was firm. She packed up the trunk again, herself, and saw that Marcia and Florrie got into their train clothes. "You'll have to buy our tickets, Uncle Louie," she said stiffly, as he drove them to the train. "Papa will send you the money later."

Uncle Louie was disturbed by their sudden departure, but afraid to tempt Fate by forbidding it. They didn't need tickets after all, for a freight train ambled along with an engineer and brakeman from the London Junction yards, so they rode free in the caboose, singing all the way for the edification of the other occupants, the county sheriff and a swarthy gentleman handcuffed to him, en route to the state penitentiary. The swarthy gentleman was stimulated to sing "Santa Lucia" and "Funicula," in Italian, and readily taught them to the girls, so they felt the trip was highly worth while.

"What'll we do when we get there?" Marcia asked as the train came into the switch yards. "Mr. Purdy said he had to have our room for the stock company this month."

"You wait and see," Lena said mysteriously.

Florrie and Marcia watched their competent leader with satisfaction. At London Junction she held up a hand for the cab.

"Drive us to Mrs. Lois Blair's," she commanded, and after they got in she said, "You're to charge this to Mr. Harry Willard, please."

"Oughtn't we to run in and see Bonnie?" Marcia asked.

Lena shook her head.

"No, sir, we're not going any place we're not wanted," she declared. "I'm sick and tired of it. Aunt Lois will have to keep us because she's our aunt, isn't she?"

They were all excited at the idea of moving into Aunt Lois' big house, and all pleased with Lena's masterly management. Aunt Lois, just back from Cleveland, was caught in the right mood, much impressed with their Italian songs. She laughed appreciatively over Lena's account of their difficulties. They did exactly the right thing, she said. Whenever they were in trouble they must come straight to her. She'd manage somehow.

19

At this time Aunt Lois was thirty-four years old, buxom and handsome and, according to Papa's grumbling admission, worth nearly ten thousand dollars! Apart from her house, she had done well with her stock in the Lesterville Steel Mills, even though she was always being tapped by all of her relations for loans (never to be repaid). She enjoyed her position as leader of the family, feeling that her generosity entitled her to dictate the lives of all her dependents. She kept in touch with all the northern Ohio relations, passing on their marriages, schools, diets, jobs, pleasures, and clothes. Each year she had one hobby which she obliged the rest of the family to share. One year she insisted that the cure for all diseases was to wear Ground Gripper shoes, the next year it was a front-lace corset which she would have gladly foisted on the men, too. Then came the fireless cooker year, the cooking-in-paper-bags year, the linoleum-over-the-whole-house year, the cement porch year, the shower bath year, and each one of these obsessions received the passionate devotion of a new religion, working its way into her conversation on any subject, and invested with powers little less than magical of renewing health, wealth and happiness. The relations, bound by debt to Aunt Lois, had to admit the common sense of her advice, and permitted themselves to be badgered into following her commands, particularly since her zeal led her to advance further loans for carrying out her wishes.

The only rebellious members of her family were her mother and her brother-in-law. "Mother is slippery as an eel," she said. "She won't argue, always seems to agree, then she goes right ahead doing what she pleases." She itched to regulate her brother-in-law's life, and was irked that the children's hotel life carried them out of her control. But now they were under her roof, and their dependence on her gave her a gratifying hold on their father. She wrote him immediately that she was taking the children, "straightening out the absolutely shocking effect on their manners and language of their life at the hotel," and she would expect regular sums for their support. For answer Papa sent them a large box of salt water taffy from Atlantic City and a series of pictures of himself and Mr. Hartwell wearing false noses and opera hats on the sides of their heads. Aunt Lois did not share the children's delight over the communication.

They missed their old liberty, but their new life seemed to be a step upward in respectability, besides being luxurious beyond their wildest imaginations. They were convinced that nowhere in the world existed advantages superior to Aunt Lois' home. There were no teachers rooming there now, though Aunt Lois did make extra money by selling insurance policies in her spare time. One of her recent whims had been to sell all of her old furniture and do the entire downstairs over in stylish Fumed Oak. The big parlor had gas coals in the fireplace, a Story and Clark player-piano, an elegant rainbow-tinted glass chandelier with a red bead fringe, a bust of somebody (possibly Ulysses S. Grant), a bowl of goldfish with a wondrous castle inside, leather cushions with pictures of Indian maids burnt on them, a rack containing the piano rolls, sheet music out of the Sunday supplements, *Etudes*, and magazines old and new—*Burr MacIntosh's, Ainslee's, Munsey's, Delineator, Young's, Smart Set* and the *Blue Book*. Most of these had been marked by Aunt Lois, and the favored poems or epigrams were carefully memorized by Marcia and pondered upon in the night. "Love is a flower, passion's a weed"; "Men love women, women love love"; "Gods weep, the half-gods can only laugh." These fruity thoughts gave a pleasingly theatrical background to Marcia's impression of Aunt Lois' house. Lena and Florrie were more impressed with the fireless cooker and the piano, where Lena, with Aunt Lois' help, learned "Shepherd Dance," the "Weasel Waltz," and "Dorothy, A Country Dance."

Much to their surprise, the children discovered that not only did Aunt Lois find Mr. Sweeney tolerable now, she even welcomed him as a regular caller. She instructed them not to mention this to their father, who would be sure to put an evil meaning to it, and as further safeguard she sent them upstairs during his calls. If they escaped banishment by reading quietly in the corner, they found the conversation fully as baffling as Mrs. Carmel's. Mr. Sweeney always stood for a moment in the doorway, head bared and bowed as if scarcely daring to enter the sacred presence of Pure Womanhood. Receiving Aunt Lois' hand, he bowed low over it and entered with grave dignity. He placed his hat, cane, and gloves on the hall table; then, with another bow, presented Aunt Lois with a large, beribboned box of De Klyn's Bon Bons, or for variety Chandler and Rudd Salted Almonds. These rites observed and properly applauded by Aunt Lois, he then drew up a straight chair to Aunt Lois, who implored him to take the big chair. Her entreaties, based as much on the demands of his bulk as on politeness, finally prevailed over his humble wishes, and with a "May I smoke?" he relaxed comfortably. Aunt Lois, who could never be idle, crocheted or mended, and in low tones vibrant with conspiracy the two murmured such phrases as "six per cent," "common," "two hundred shares preferred," "stockholders' meeting," "dividends." The quality of their voices was so charged with excitement and secret pleasure that it was hard to believe money, and not romance, was its cause. Aunt Lois' fair head bent breathlessly toward Mr. Sweeney's flushed heavy-jowled face, and when he left she sat smiling abstractedly at her work as if words of love instead of mere financial profit still lingered on the air. Whenever Marcia reminded her of the old jokes between Mama and her about Mr. Sweeney's pompous airs, Aunt Lois reddened and said sharply, it took a long time to appreciate some people.

"Don't you tell your father I said so," she added.

Every Saturday Aunt Lois went to Lesterville on business, and these were the days Papa elected to call on his children if he was in town. He stayed at the Elks' instead of the hotel because, he said, things were getting too thick at the hotel.

One time Lena boldly asked him if he was intending to pay board at Aunt Lois' as she had insisted. A look of hurt surprise came over his face as he regarded his daughter reproachfully. Then he took out his checkbook and wrote out a check for twenty dollars. Later, Aunt Lois said the check was no good, which wounded Papa even more.

"Looks like a man can never suit some parties no matter how hard he tries," he said, wistfully, so that even Lena felt ashamed for her forwardness. He brought them red tamo'-shanters, and fur-topped boots for Florrie, and a sample picture book of famous mausoleums erected by his company in all parts of the earth. He talked of buying a mausoleum for Daisy, too, when Lena said Aunt Lois thought Mama should have a gravestone. He brought them a song book from Bonnie, advising them not to tell their aunt from where it came, and taught them "Take Me Out to the Ball Game." They were confused and sorry when he left, for he criticized Aunt Lois, and they were already mixed up in their feelings by Aunt Lois' steady attacks on him. Florrie remained steadfast, vowing complete adoration of Papa, unmarred by her devotion to Aunt Lois, but Lena swayed from one to the other.

There were more secrets to be kept, later on, when who should be found lolling on the parlor sofa one day but Mr. Hartwell, Papa's friend. Mr. Hartwell gave them each a quarter and told them that under no circumstances were they to tell Papa of this visit, while Aunt Lois sternly admonished them never to speak of it to Mr. Sweeney. Mr. Hartwell's visits, which became regular, and took place usually while they were at school, were quite different from Mr. Sweeney's. Aunt Lois laughed a lot at everything Mr. Hartwell said, and he followed her around when she cooked, patting her shoulder and tweaking her curly yellow hair. He, too, brought candy. He saved pictures of Lillian Russell to show how much she looked like her, and made her blush by calling her his "Evening Star." He was very much at home around the place, taking naps in the downstairs bedroom when he came in from the train, and helping himself in the icebox. Aunt Lois was always cross after his visits, scolding the children for eating the cake she was saving for him, and complaining of how tied down she was, just at the age when she could have a good time. There was something very secret about Mr. Hartwell's visits, and he frequently used the back door because it was handier, he said. Once some woman telephoned there for him, and Aunt Lois answered that she knew no such person as Hartwell. None of the children liked Aunt Lois' change of manner under Mr. Hartwell's influence. Usually arrogant and dignified, she giggled and flirted and blushed in a silly way, not becoming an elderly woman. Lena said she had a good notion to tell Papa on her, but when she did she was taken aback by Papa's roar of delight.

"The old son-of-a-gun!" he kept chuckling. "Wait till I get hold of him! By George, I'll tell him I heard it from Mabel. That'll serve him right for being so foxy!"

His opportunity did not take this form, but gave him even more satisfaction. Aunt Lois was home when he called one day, "full as a tick," as she described him later to Mr. Sweeney. She promptly attacked him for his snappy new topcoat when the girls needed clothes; she wanted to know if he seriously intended to pay for Lena's piano lessons as Daisy had always wished; she also wanted to know what about all this talk about Bonnie Purdy chasing all over the country to meet him, making herself the talk of the town, staying in the same hotels in Cleveland and Toledo with him; what kind of father was he, after a wonderful wife like Daisy, chasing a chippy like Bonnie Purdy, so that his little girls would grow up with a bad name?

Papa got white at this, unable to speak for a moment. When he did his voice trembled.

"I can't help where Bonnie Purdy goes," he said. "At least I'm not taking her away from somebody. You can't talk, Lois, while you're fooling around with Ed Hartwell. You know he's got Mabel. You mind your own reputation. I'll look after mine. People are talking about you more than they are about me."

Aunt Lois must have been stunned into silence by this; certainly she acted strangely and secretively after that, and was snappish at the children. Mr. Hartwell did not come any more, but on her weekly trips to Cleveland she always brought back a box of Eugenia Candies, and a *Cosmopolitan*, his favorite magazine. Though she said these trips were to visit her mother, she was vague in her news of Hodge Street, and was preoccupied a great deal of the time. She did not like Lena bringing Mary Evelyn home after school, finally forbidding it outright because Mary Evelyn's mother was a gossip and troublemaker, she said. Lena was not to be denied her social life, and visited Mary Evelyn's home instead, because her papa said she could. When Papa said she was not to wear her Sunday shoes to school, Lena answered that Aunt Lois said she could, so she was able to manage an agreeable state of independence.

It was Lena's fault that Mary Evelyn was present and able to inform the town, the day Mr. Hartwell's Mabel called on Aunt Lois. Lena had defied Aunt Lois by bringing Mary Evelyn in for cookies, inasmuch as Aunt Lois wasn't expected home from Lesterville till six. Marcia and Florrie were playing jacks on the front stoop when a large blond woman, dressed elaborately in velvet and feather trimmings, came up the walk. Marcia was pleased to see this was Mabel, part of the old hotel parties. But Mabel was in no state for friendliness.

"Where's your aunt?" she asked.

Marcia and Florrie reported in unison that she was away. Mabel set her jaw and said she could wait. And wait she did, sitting upright in the parlor without taking off her kid gloves or hat for nearly an hour. Lena and Mary Evelyn peeked at her from time to time, curiously. A few minutes after six o'clock a cab drew up and out stepped Aunt Lois, laden with bundles, accompanied by Mr. Sweeney. As soon as they entered the house the lady visitor began to shout. There was a scream from Aunt Lois, a sound of bundles dropping and panting voices, with Mr. Sweeney softly exclaiming, "Ladies! Ladies!" Presently Mabel came running out, red-faced and dishevelled, many tears streaming down her cheeks, muttering, "Oh, oh, oh, oh my God!"

Mr. Sweeney consoled Aunt Lois, who lay back on the sofa white as a sheet, trembling.

"I really believe she had a gun," said Mr. Sweeney. "What on earth was she after you for? What was she shouting about her man and who is she? I'd better call the police."

"No," said Aunt Lois briefly. She drew her hand restlessly away from Mr. Sweeney's soothing touch. "She's some crazy woman that mixed me up with somebody."

"I'd better stay here to see she doesn't come back," said Mr. Sweeney gravely, patting her hand again.

"Oh, for God's sake, leave me be!" cried Aunt Lois desperately, pushing him aside. "Can't you see I'm upset?"

Mr. Sweeney was so offended at this ungrateful suggestion that he got up, buttoning his coat with great dignity across his broad vest and walking majestically out of the house.

"It's not my business, of course," he stated at the door. "But I must say I do not understand this incident, not in the least, Mrs. Blair."

Other people in London Junction were more astute, easily making interesting deductions from Mary Evelyn's fortunately detailed report. At school the new girl, Myrtle Chase, told Lena she was not allowed to play with her any more, and the mother of Marcia's seat-mate requested that her daughter's seat be changed. Papa unexpectedly took Aunt Lois' part in public discussions and went so far as to tell Ed Hartwell that Mabel was not a lady in any sense of the word. Ed replied sorrowfully that sometimes a fellow found that out too late. He said that when a woman like Mabel came right out and refused to be a lady, she ought to have her bucket kicked right up between her shoulder blades. He said if she ever laid a finger on Lois again he'd do that very thing, in spite of being the best-natured fellow in the world.

20

Mrs. Jane's rooming house in Lesterville was on West Park Street, convenient to the markets and to the steel mills, which was perhaps the best that could be said for it. On one side were warehouses, old houses made into bake-shops, and stores with rooms to let upstairs, and on the other side the offices and outlying buildings of the steel works began, ending far off in the glaring sky above the mills themselves. Mrs. Jane's had been mentioned to Papa by a stranger in the station, so it was here the Willard family found itself, bag and baggage, as suddenly as it had found itself once before, on Hodge Street. The reasons for this move were similar too—vague reprisals on Aunt Lois, Fate, and all the other elements that forever challenged Papa. The children were puffed up with pride at being claimed by Papa and almost keeping house for him, you might say. Papa was working now for the High Class Novelty Company of Lesterville and was to be home nights—at least, he wasn't to travel on this job for a time.

"I want a rest from the road, get my health back," he said confidentially to Mrs. Jane when they moved in to the parlor floor. "The fact is, those cold hotel rooms and drafty trains can get a man's constitution down in time. Many's the night I've sat in some damn hotel room, shaking from head to foot with a chill, first hot, then cold, hands shaking so I could hardly hold a glass. Only thing for it is to carry a little brandy on you, take a swallow every five minutes or so till the spell is over."

Mrs. Jane said she had spells of terrible dizziness, much the same, and found brandy the only cure. As Papa appeared on the verge of a chill and Mrs. Jane seemed to sense a dizzy spell coming on, they had a glass of brandy then and there, as they settled the fees and privileges of the new living quarters. The chief advantage of the new arrangement was that Mrs. Jane had lost three children herself—stillborn, accidents, and "cholery morbus," so she was particularly well equipped to keep an eye on three motherless little girls. (Both Papa and Mrs. Jane wiped their eyes here and looked mournfully at the three girls who were comfortably playing Robber Casino on the bed.) Mrs. Jane had plenty to do, with her millhand roomers, night and day workers, but she would make these three little dolls her special care, provide from her own table for them, at least once a day, see that they washed their ears and didn't run the streets like hoodlums. So the deal was set and Papa said with satisfaction that he could stand just so much criticism from certain people, then he liked to step in and show them up.

"You write your grandma and your Aunt Lois to keep their hands off; your father is looking after you now," he instructed the children, and with a promise to install them in the proper school the next day he put his hat on the side of his head and was off to the Lesterville Hotel, where Mr. Hartwell was stopping, because he didn't have much chance to see his old friend any more.

The children examined the rooms curiously, wanting to be pleased but a little bewildered. The room which was to be their bedroom, living room and kitchen still bore traces of its original purpose, which was an old-fashioned family kitchen, but parlor and bedroom perquisites had been added for lodgers' needs. There was a bird's-eye maple folding bed with a bulging front for the children, a worn Morris chair, a richly carved, black walnut arm-chair (some of this carving proved later to be examples of petrified Spearmint), a clothes rack in a niche formerly used for the stove. The floor was camou-flaged with a mottled, scuffed, brownish linoleum, which stopped at the middle door to join a scuffed, greenish linoleum. A card table with dangerously inclined legs was disguised by a tasselled plum velvet drape, the stain in the middle almost hidden by the pewter dish of colored clay fruit from Mexico. This room opened by lofty arched sliding doors into the dark alcove, formerly dining room, in which Papa's brass bed and an enormous black walnut wardrobe were wedged. Another sliding door leading to Mrs. Jane's own rooms was boarded up with odd pieces of water-soaked beaverboard. In here a small, high window was hung with ruffled dimity curtains, dusty and fly-blown, but as coy as if they gave on some sunny daisy field instead of an airshaft. A black stovepipe came mysteriously in one aperture near the ceiling, crooked an elbow and went out another for no pur-pose but decoration, since whatever stove was ever connected with it had long since been junked, but Mrs. Jane said the pipes looked better than holes in the plaster.

Mrs. Jane was a thin, flabby woman of forty-five, with a putty-colored face, liverish lips permanently curled up in what was meant to be a heartening smile, ready to widen into a merry cackle the more honest because it revealed palate, bridgework and tonsils without affectation. A tendency to jaundice gave a yellow cast to her eyeballs and patches of brown spots on her lean neck. She had a high, little girl voice and a way of fondly cocking her head to one side, but this coquettish effect was only to reassure the suspicious, and not to lure the opposite sex, because, goodness knows, as she made haste to explain to Papa, none of her men lodgers needed to worry about her setting after them. She'd had her chances, still had; but just because she felt sorry for a nice looking young man with three motherless children didn't mean she was looking for a man. Papa said a woman with her figure didn't need to look far and she agreed that he had certainly said it. Mrs. Jane spoke often with pleasure of her figure, though it was seldom revealed to proper advantage. She wore a bungalow apron and lace boudoir cap for marketing, since her head was always armored in steel curlers. For household chores she wrapped her head in whatever dustcap, towel or napkin was handy, and shuffled around in bedroom slippers, bare legs and a ragged crepe kimono, flowery sleeves pinned back on her shoulder. This working costume gave an impression of slavish domesticity, but like many a dustcloth around the head often indicated merely that there was a lot of work to be done but not right now. A scrubbing pail of suds was usually abandoned on the hall steps; a mop, broom, or carpet sweeper leaned against a door to clout the unsuspecting as they entered; a dustpan of debris sometimes sat all day on a stair step; a washing half done in the back yard, a stew burning dry on her stove—these were ambitious projects started at breakfast by Mrs. Jane and deserted for others that occurred to her: an attic cleaning, a bargaining tour of the markets. Lodgers commented on Mrs. Jane's industry when they saw her implements about, and Mrs. Jane, possibly abandoning all for the daily paper in the porch rocker, would reply in a cheery whine, "Woman's work is never done." This uproarious *mot* sent her into peals of laughter.

A great deal of Mrs. Jane's time was spent in locating her pet, a large tiger cat appropriately named Tommy. Her voice could be heard wailing, "Tommy! Tommy! Where are you, Tommy dear? Come, Tommy!" from morning to midnight, and scarcely a day passed that she did not have a few hours' anguished conviction that Tommy had been stolen or run over. The cat's chief pleasure seemed to be in providing this daily drama for his fond mistress. During her distracted calls and search for him, often accompanied by sobs, Tommy lay blinking under the porch or on the roof, observing her frenzy with what might be a sardonic masculine smile, and after pleasuring himself with the sight of his dear madam making a fool of herself over him he stretched himself and ambled leisurely to his cushion on the back stairs where, in due time, she would find him manicuring his nails and tidying his whiskers as if nothing had happened.

"They know!" Mrs. Jane declared proudly, indicating the intelligent animal. "You'd be surprised how they know!"

Mrs. Jane felt that the Willard children were almost like her own, she said, which meant they had to run errands and help her with the chores. "Get your beds done now, girls! Have you done your baseboards, Marcia? Have you dusted your dressers?"

Marcia hated this use of "your," not wanting any connection with household unpleasantness. "They're not *my* baseboards," she would mutter. "They're *hers!*"

After the first genial conference, Papa and Mrs. Jane did not further the intimacy, though Mrs. Jane did her best. She asked questions of the girls. "I guess your father's got a sweetheart some place," she said. "Some young girl, I suppose, young enough to be his daughter. Your father's got a lot of snap to him, the way he steps, the way he wears that hat of his. I guess he shows the girls a good time all right. One of these days I'm going to fix myself up, branch out in a new navy blue suit. I'll bet he takes notice then, by golly! I still got my figure and I got all my teeth, that's the mainest thing."

Mrs. Jane talked of a day to come when she would retire to sunny California and lie around one of those bungalows in a bungalow apron, in a hammock all day. If she found the right man, maybe some widower with a little snap to him, she would hand over her savings and off they'd go. If the widower had any children she'd be a second mother to them. These implications depressed the children and made Papa wary, even though deceptively genial. When Mrs. Jane suggested opening the sliding doors between their suites, he generously declared he wouldn't permit it because lots of people would get something in their heads. Some people had that kind of mind. Mrs. Jane said she was old enough not to care what people said, especially if she liked a person, but Papa told her she wasn't fair to herself. He said a person in her position in the community couldn't be too careful and he intended to help her keep up this respected position.

After that he spent some time pushing the wardrobe against the sliding door to Mrs. Jane's room, in case the beaverboard strips might not hold against the hurricanes of circumstance.

21

Papa sat in the carved chair, knees crossed, eyes gazing dreamily upward, and plucked at his guitar.

"Picture tonight, the fields are-a snowy-a-white," he sang tenderly. "Come on, Florrie, sing it after me. The other kids know it."

Florrie sat on the foot stool directly in front of her father, her small hands clasped, and her large earnest blue eyes fixed worshipfully on him.

"Pitcha taneye, a feelsa sowee why," she dutifully sang.

"After this let's sing 'Honest Irish Lad,' " urged Marcia, and Lena said, "Then 'Poor Little Joe.' "

"How the old folks would enjoy it," went on Papa, ignoring them.

He scarcely ever would sing the old favorites. When the girls sang them he would interrupt with a command to go on an errand, or he would himself go out, frowning. It was as if these songs were buried in the Mapleview Cemetery with Mama, all covered with myrtle and graveyard flowers. Marcia shut her eyes sometimes and saw Mama behind those final iron gates, wandering forlorn, eyes blind with death, the heavy pack on her back, the homeless Irish lad beside her, and poor little Joe shivering in rags. About these three the snow danced and swirled as it did in the glass Snowstorm Ball on Mrs. Jane's mantelpiece, the storm finally engulfing them just as it did the little shepherdess in the glass ball. Maybe, thought Marcia, this was the way Papa, too, thought of the old songs, and wanted to forget.

"How about a new song?" asked Mr. Taylor, Papa's new friend.

"That's the trouble with giving up the road," Papa complained. "You get behind the times. By the time a song hits this town, it's a hundred years old."

"I heard a pip in Columbus last week," boasted Mr. Taylor. "Name of it was 'If I Had a Thousand Lives.' Fellow came out and sang it in a full dress suit, then in a kinda frame-like behind him some girl would light up like a picture. Made you all choked up. End up with her coming out of the frame and walking over to him, so they walked up and down together, her in front of him, ahanging on to his arm. They musta sung it five, six times."

"How'd it go?" Papa asked, interested.

Mr. Taylor scratched his nose.

"If I—no, it was lower than that. If I—dum de dum. Well, hell, a song's just a song. Those fellas are always singing something or other. I pay no attention."

"I'll take Detroit any day in preference to Columbus," stated Papa, resuming his guitar. "I've seen some of the finest shows in the world in Detroit, Michigan. I'll say that much."

"I guess you've never been to Detroit, have you, Mr. Taylor?" asked Marcia brightly.

Mr. Taylor looked moodily at her.

"How about the kids going out to play?" he suggested, whereupon all three girls favored him with a reproachful frown.

Mr. Taylor was Papa's new friend for Lesterville. He was a dried, sandy little man with a long, pointed nose like a rat's, a feature that seemed to fascinate him as much as it did other people, for he was always tugging at it, then squinting down to see if any change had come over it. Between these diversions he wrinkled it into a perpetual sniff, accompanied by rapid blinking of his small, raisin eyes. He sniffed at words and people as if his nostrils did the work of all other senses, and he could sniff out a thought or even a person's financial status quicker than a beagle could smell a fox. He lived in a men's hotel down the street, and was proud of it because it was called The Hermits' Club, just like the one in Cleveland, though the Lesterville Hermits were bound by no convivial ties, only by their common need for a hall bedroom cheap. Mr. Taylor had several calling cards printed up with his name and club on it, which he passed around to strangers unfamiliar with the "club." Its privileges, apart from a bed and the use of the elevator, were so limited that he came over to the Willards' rooms frequently, especially on Sunday, where he could have room to spread out the funnies. His favorite was "Hee Haw! And Her Name was Maud," and he often used that expression to clinch an argument.

He never took off his cap, a baggish, greenish plaid number with a big visor sliding down over his nose, and he kept a match behind his ear as a precaution against any delay in getting a smoke the instant the desire struck him. He wore a bow tie and a brick colored Norfolk suit. He had one silk shirt which Papa said he never took off, but his vanity entitled him to snap his fingers at Papa's other friend, Ed Hartwell, the finest dresser Papa ever saw.

When Papa first brought Mr. Taylor to the Lesterville rooms the children burst out laughing, for he was small and droll like a monkey. But like many a droll, twinkling-eyed little man with a funny, nasal, cracked voice and clownish ways, he was not funny at all. He had a way of eating the best candies Mr. Hartwell brought to them, of pinching their cheeks, pulling their curls, and ordering them about as if he was a teacher or a relation instead of just a fellow worker at the High Class Novelty Company.

"Mark my words, the novelty business is here to stay," he said, nodding wisely. "You wouldn't catch Charlie Taylor traipsing around the country selling tombs like you did, Willard. Stay in an up-and-coming boom town like Lesterville and get in the novelty business; that's my advice to anybody."

Papa agreed heartily, in fact too heartily, that there was a lot in this clever statement. He didn't intend to stay in Lesterville all his life, but it was a relief not to be kicked around by a cheap outfit like the Mausoleum Company, run by a big crook like Colgate Custer who, it was said, had Negro blood the way all the Southerners did; you could tell by the fingernails. Naturally, a high-spirited fellow who'd been all over, as Papa had, knew what it was all about, missed the cosmopolitan advantages of the road. The latest songs, for instance, oyster cocktails—try and get one in Lesterville!—lobster New-burgh, peach melba. Still, they weren't everything. At the High Class Novelty Company a man was treated like a gen-tleman, even though he didn't get the jack you got on the road. But you got a chance to know everyday folks and there wasn't a finer man in the business than Troyan, a foreigner, yes, a Bohemian, but the Bohemians were the finest class of people when you got to know them. They didn't try to catch you up on expense accounts; they knew how to appreciate a first-class salesman. Mr. Taylor silently twigged his nose dur-ing Papa's praise of the boss, venturing no answer but, "A fel-low's got to work for somebody, what the hell? It's either that or starve, what the hell?"

Marcia and Lena resented Mr. Taylor, for either he inter-fered with their games by his presence or made their evenings lonely by keeping Papa out, usually, it would appear, at Stein's Saloon over by the Steel Mills.

Papa defended his new friend by saying he was a man who had a lot of trouble—wife ran away with another man, leav-ing him with a little boy, of whom Mr. Taylor didn't see much. He had efficiently deposited him on his erring wife's mother who had been made to feel it her duty to do penance for the scandal in the family. Now he sat on the arm of the battered Morris chair, whirling his watch chain around, whistling out of tune, spoiling Papa's song. Marcia sat on the floor, legs crossed, writing in her composition book, and Lena played Solitaire, waiting for their turn to sing with Papa.

The remains of Sunday dinner, canned beans, buns and weenies, were in the sink in the corner, and steaming on the gas plate was a teakettle for dish water. The kettle was a rusty, misshapen affair, wearing another larger kettle's lid which slid down over the snout, giving a startling resemblance to Mr. Taylor.

"What the hell, Willard, you going to hang around here all day?" Mr. Taylor restlessly demanded.

Florrie's lip began to tremble.

"I want to learn the song!" she began to sob, so Papa hastily resumed the lesson, for Florrie was his pet.

Mr. Taylor picked up his coffee cup with the spoon in it and rattled the spoon around, scraping the last bit of sugar from the cracks, and watching the children meditatively as if, Marcia bitterly whispered to Lena, he was planning to eat them if no other plan for their disposition presented itself.

"Make yourself at home for a spell, Charlie," urged Papa. "I got to quiet the kids for a while."

Mr. Taylor put down his coffee cup on the floor and rattled his keys. If he couldn't rattle or scrape something he tapped on whatever was handy, or snorted, coughed, whistled, anything to cheer himself up and make his presence felt. Now he got up and helped himself to the one piece of candied fruit Lena and Marcia had been quarreling over. He glanced down at Marcia's composition book.

"Copying something?" he asked.

Marcia gave him an icy look.

"I don't copy," she said. "I make up."

Whistling jauntily at the rebuff, Mr. Taylor made a leisurely tour of the rooms now, peering in the wardrobe, tapping the pipe, and looking through the kitchen curtains at the high black wood fence barely two feet away. A trickle of noonday sun lit up this pleasant prospect, accenting tenderly a tin ash pail now being investigated by Mrs. Jane's cat, Tommy.

"What do you pay for this hole?" Mr. Taylor inquired, wrinkling his nose.

Papa put the guitar back in its case and the girls cast reproachful eyes at the intruder.

"Seven-fifty a week," said Papa. "It's an outrage, but then the old lady keeps an eye on the kids. Why, we had one of the prettiest little homes in London Junction for only ten dollars a month, when my wife was alive. The best furnishings. Fact was I had a brand new dining room set ordered the very day Daisy died. She always wanted the best. Wait a minute. I got a picture of an actress here, looks just like her. Found it in last week's *Leader*."

He produced from his vest pocket a newspaper clipping and the children ran to look over Mr. Taylor's arms. It did look a little like Mama. The name here was Mabel Taliaferro, but Papa had clippings of other actresses who reminded him of Mama, either in the bangs or the tilt of the head, or a little expression around the eyes. The children fell in with this habit, saving pictures of every beauty in the news, disappointed if Papa silently shook his head after a study of them, justifying their mistake by pointing out that the watch or the ribbon or the earring was like Mama's. Mr. Taylor scrutinized or rather sniffed the clipping indifferently, then handed it back to Papa.

"Don't look like nobody to me but this Mabel Whatsername here, what the hell," was his comment, but Papa looked again at the picture, holding it up to the light with a stern, searching expression as if he was commanding it to be Daisy herself. Then he put it carefully back in his pocket.

"Why didn't you leave the kids with their aunt back in London Junction?" asked Mr. Taylor. "None of my business, but this is no place to raise kids, what the hell."

"Their grandmother got in some trouble in Cleveland and Lois had to stay up there for a while," said Papa, but the children knew there had been another quarrel between Aunt Lois and Papa, mutual accusations resulting in Papa's hotly packing them off to Lesterville.

"Roomer at their grandmother's left a cigar burning and burned down half the street—fourteen houses," said Papa, referring to the catastrophe which had ended Grandma's Hodge Street adventure. "Law got after the old lady, besides her losing all of her furniture, and most of the roomers beat their bill in the middle of the excitement. I guess Lois has her hands full, but the old lady's bound to start in again. Going in the millinery business now with a friend of hers."

"We'll get free hats," prophesied Lena.

Mr. Taylor shrugged impatiently at these family details.

"Let's go over to the hotel and get Hartwell," said Mr. Taylor. "Cook up a game there. Let the kids go play, what the hell, no good their sticking in here all the time. They're big enough to amuse themselves, ain't they?"

Marcia and Lena again looked resentfully at him and Marcia made bold to pull her nose in angry mockery, so Florrie had a fit of giggles, very irritating to Mr. Taylor, suspicious of its cause.

The truth was that they didn't know how to go about playing in Lesterville. In Cleveland the Hodge Street district had been a little village in itself, but Lesterville, in bursting from village into busy, industrial town, was too big for one center and too small for several centers. At the big West Park Street School everybody belonged to "the bunch" except the foreigners, who kept to themselves. There was no welcome in either group for strangers. Lena and Marcia dreaded recess, when their isolation was most conspicuous. Fifth graders didn't mix with fourth graders, so Lena would not dream of easing her own misery by sharing Marcia's. In Marcia's class a big, athletic girl named Burnadetta dictated the games, the fashions, the catchwords ("Oh, that'll be peachy!" "Oh, you kiddo!" "If you don't like it, lump it!"). The stone-paved schoolyard rang with the cries of her devoted followers: "Come here, Burnadetta! Look at me, Burnadetta! Where's Burnadetta? Oh, Burnadetta, Burnadetta, Burnadetta!" A name like Burnadetta is as good as a pony or a big play yard for prestige, or even a roguish nickname like Jerry, that of the tomboy leader of Lena's class. Whatever qualities besides appealing names these girls had for leadership the outsiders could not guess; they could only be fascinated audience to the inner circle's fun, tagging behind while the eager slaves jostled each other for the privilege of walking next to the idol. "I'll carry your books, Burnadetta! . . . I'll draw your map for you, Jerry! . . . You can copy my composition, Burnadetta! . . . Oh, you kiddo! Oh, oh, what'll we play next, Burnadetta, Jerry!"

Lena and Marcia dreamed of strange, incredible adventures in which Burnadetta or Jerry said, "Hello," and even walked through the school gates with them, to the envy of all. This, they felt, could be accomplished if Aunt Lois in all her beauty and efficiency would suddenly come to school for them, showing these children of plain mothers that a beautiful aunt was much more desirable. But these were dreams and not to be counted upon.

School clothes were different here, too, being Peter Thompsons or middy suits, purchased in the Juvenile Department, and not at all like the grown-up hand-me-downs made over by Isobel and sent over twice a year. Lesterville school children had allowances, ate lunch in the school cafeteria, and travelled back and forth to school in "bunches" on the streetcar, or went to The Sugar Bowl for banana splits at recess. Uninvited to do this, even if they had the money, Lena and

Marcia hid in the basement toilet at recess or pretended to have nosebleed, and at noon walked all the way home for bread and milk and ginger snaps. Florrie, being in the first grade, and completely trusting, was fortunate enough to be Teacher's pet, so she was launched in games by her patron and often invited to share Teacher's lunch. Saturdays and Sundays were days when other children had mysterious club meetings, picnics, picture shows, visits to the park or menagerie; Papa had to work Saturdays, so there was nothing to do but skip the rope in front of Mrs. Jane's house or just sit on the stoop in silence. They were afraid of the busy street clanging with streetcars, factory bells and ear-splitting whistles, and crowded with the steel workers jostling each other along with grim, intent faces, sometimes shouting bad words that made the very air shiver.

So they sat on the narrow front porch which jutted past Mrs. Jane's fern-filled bay window, two steps above street level. They made up guessing games and thought of what they wanted most in the world, like high heels, a croquignole board, a lavalliere like Burnadetta's, a visit from a relation or Bonnie Purdy. On Sundays they had Papa for a little while unless he'd been out all night with Mr. Taylor, after which he lay in bed all day, shouting to them for God's sake to shut up. They were afraid to go to the big stone churches because here you had to wear gloves and carry a Bible or prayerbook and have patent leather slippers. Lena noticed these religious rules and decreed that they must not try to break them, even though there was a Membership Campaign on at the East Park Presbyterian Church, and Burnadetta herself had asked them to sign up on her team ("the Blues") so that she could win a star.

"You have to give a dime there," Lena disclosed gloomily to Marcia. "Even the juveniles can't give pennies."

At least Papa was home on Sundays, so they could sing; that was a comfort. But here was Mr. Taylor ruining their one day by suggesting that Papa leave, and that they "go play."

"Why don't they go down to that new Athletic Club just opened on the Square?" persisted Mr. Taylor. "Swimming pool, sand piles, games. I seen kids running in and out. Free, too."

Papa hadn't heard of this and listened with interest. To the girls, the idea sounded so entrancing that they looked at Mr. Taylor more favorably, and were glad when Papa urged them to get into street clothes. In Papa's impressive company, they were positive no snubs could occur. Papa led them straight to the big new building with the football field beyond it and tennis courts in front. At the "Children's Entrance" he bade them have a good time and he'd come after them at five to take them home on the streetcar. Lena, with a great show of assurance, led them to some stairs marked "Swimming Pool" but a buxom young woman in a bathing suit said they must bring bathing suits for the Pool. Having none to command, Lena then led them to the Gymnasium, where children were riding stationary bicycles, tumbling on mattresses, climbing monkey cages, chinning themselves, and playing ball. They did not need to be told that here also a costume was necessary, since all the girls wore bloomers and middies, absent from the Willards' wardrobe. Florrie, unconscious of this, flung herself joyously into a double somersault, exposing her underpants to the jeers of some small boys until Lena hastily dragged her away. Another room yielded a group listening to a Story Teller, but a glance indicated that these drab, bespectacled, morose little folks were the doomed ones, left out of everything else and unpopular, so to join them would certainly be admission of defeat.

"That old story!" Marcia scornfully exclaimed as they withdrew. "Everybody knows 'Peter Pan'!"

"I don't," said Florrie, hanging back.

"Come on, then, I'll tell you," Marcia said, and inasmuch as she had heard of Peter Pan only dimly she made up a hasty story about a magic boy who lived in a skillet and granted wishes to a kitchen slavey when anything beginning with a "b" was cooked in the pan, but caused an earthquake if by some horrible chance cornmeal mush was ever cooked in it.

Wandering through the bare whitewashed corridors, they peeked in several rooms where gym classes were in progress, but there seemed no possible way of joining any group. These other boys and girls seemed to have been born in bunches, happily complete, looking with indifferent, even hostile, gaze at the three strangers. In one room an empty ping-pong table inspired them to experiment with the game, but two young ladies appeared and calmly announced they had "signed" for that hour. They finally found a Reading Room with a checkerboard in it but no checkers or any reading matter as yet, equipped merely with empty shelves and a long table and a *Silence, Please*, sign.

"I'll bet Mr. Taylor knew all the time it would be this way," said Marcia, as they sat down on the chairs. They played "I Love My Love With an A" for a while, then strolled out to the hall where a lady sat at a desk, with a green reading shade over her eyes.

"Did you sign up for what hours you want to use the pool?" she asked in a brisk, metallic voice. "Tuesday afternoons and Sundays for children."

Lena, with an important cough, immediately took the pencil and put down, "Sundays, 2–4," to the immense admiration of her sisters; then wrote all their names in the proper column in the new backward-slanting handwriting the girls in her class used.

"Willard," repeated the lady, running her finger down a big list. "Is your father George Willard?"

"No, Harry Willard," said Lena. The lady frowned.

"We have only one Willard here. How long has your father been a member?"

Lena looked blank, so Marcia stepped up.

"About six months," she said.

The lady then shuffled some index cards, shaking her head.

"Perhaps he's been dropped for non-payment of dues," she said. "I don't see you children down as Junior Members, either. Have you paid your fee?"

"I don't remember," stammered Lena, getting very red. "How much was it?"

"The regular membership fee is ten dollars, and two dollars a month dues," said the lady. "If your father had paid that up, your Junior fee would only be five dollars a year. Otherwise——"

"Does everybody have to be a member?" asked Lena.

The lady now removed the reading shade and passed a hand over her harassed brow, regarding them with some thought.

"Monday is Free Day," she said. "Get your schoolteachers to write a statement that your parents cannot afford regular membership. That entitles you to all the Privileges on Free Day."

"We'll come Sundays, if we come, because our father is a member," said Lena loudly. "Somebody here made a mistake, I guess, and he'll have to see about it. We don't want to come on any Free Day."

She pushed Marcia and Florrie ahead of her out the front door, her lips drawn tight to keep from screaming her fury. They stood outside the front door, waiting for five o'clock to come, but Papa didn't come back, and finally at half-past they straggled home, asking the way from a dozen people. It was Mr. Taylor's fault. They restored a little of their spirits by imitating him with such success that when their father came home in an extraordinarily hilarious mood himself he found them in shrieks of laughter, pulling their noses and blinking their eyes and shouting "what-the-hell" in unison.

"I guess you kids had a good time," he said, and they laughed some more.

22

"I hate Lesterville! I hate Lesterville!" Lena was the first to come out and say it, though it was in a low mutter that only her sisters could hear. If only they could have stayed in dear London Junction, they mourned, and Lena went as far as to write firm letters to Aunt Lois and Mrs. Friend, suggesting that a long visit to the Junction would be appreciated.

"There is no use our going to school any more because the bunch just talks about the new Athletic Club and we can't go there because we're not members. Marcia's teacher won't pay attention when she holds up her hand to answer, then she gives her *F* on her grade card. Florrie hasn't any party dress, so she can't go to parties when she's asked. Nobody asks Marcia and me, ha ha. There is a rat in the kitchen. I wish Mama was alive. Mrs. Jane is mean to us. If somebody doesn't take us away from here we will run away, anyhow me."

Marcia was disturbed over this candid letter, since she had

just sent a long letter of her own of a far more romantic nature, describing her beautiful new wardrobe (seen in the Smith Store catalogue), and telling of gay parties in the fashionable homes of Jerry (Lena's chum) and Burnadetta (my chum), Papa's eminence at the Athletic Club ("he is president of it") and her own and her sisters' triumphs in the Epworth League, Dancing School and Gym Club. She dared not admit her guilt to Lena, and trusted to the usual delay in Lena's acquiring a stamp.

It was true that life in Lesterville seemed a series of misfortunes. Marcia's teacher suggested calling at her home to talk over grades, and inquired who looked after their homework. Marcia said, "Our housekeeper." When the teacher did call she reported to the Community Charity Service that the children were neglected and, to their mortification, a box of groceries was delivered in the Charity Service truck.

At sight of this, Mrs. Jane assumed that Papa had lost his job and harried him every night for back rent and advance as well. The cashier of the Bakery Lunch, who roomed on the third floor, lost a cameo ring and said one of those fresh little girls had stolen it. Lena talked back to her and was slapped in the face. Later Florrie found the ring in the hall, but Lena wouldn't let her give it back because the woman would be all the more certain of theft. At school Marcia got first prize in Composition but was ignominiously retired to third prize because the principal, who was judge, said the theme showed she had had outside help. And Florrie had broken Mrs. Jane's glass Snowstorm Ball because the shepherdess looked like Mama and she wanted to save her.

It was no good telling Papa these woes, because they made him so mad he banged out of the house and stayed out all night playing poker with Mr. Taylor. He was gloomy whenever he was home, and always gloomier after a visit from his old friend Hartwell, now back on probation with Mabel. Mr. Hartwell said Papa was too big a man to be stuck in a cheap outfit like the High Class Novelty Company. A first-class salesman was going to waste, he declared, and it was a damn shame. He brought messages from the waitress at the Toledo lunch room, from Kitty over in Detroit, from the Clark crowd in Akron, and he described gay parties in fashionable roof gardens ("don't mention this to Mabel") where Papa's fund of anecdotes would have been highly prized.

"No, sir, I'm through with that," Papa declared a little more emphatically than was necessary. "I've got a good thing here, a raise promised. Had a hint from Troyan the other day I might be asked into the firm. I've had plenty of offers to go back on the road but not me. Got a letter just today from my old firm wanting me back. No siree."

Later on Lena found the letter and showed it to Marcia in alarm. The Mausoleum Company wanted to know when Mr. Willard was going to make good the funds he had collected and been unable to account for at his dismissal. The sum was one hundred and four dollars, and they were wasting no more time on letters, but would bring action at once. Meantime they would refuse references in the event he sought work elsewhere.

"I wish we'd stayed in London Junction!" Lena said, as if that was the only thing to be said in this fresh catastrophe. They worried about the hour when police would close in and cart them all off to prison. Papa's worry took the form of scolding them, until Lena talked back again and Florrie cried. The night steelworkers sleeping in the room upstairs banged on the floor. "Shut that brat up!"

How wonderful in the middle of these adversities to see Bonnie Purdy suddenly appear one Saturday afternoon at their door, a little plumper but as jaunty as ever. They rushed to her as if here was salvation, and Bonnie did not hesitate to promise anything they asked. Would she stay with them, would she take them to the picture show, would she ask Mrs. Jane to let them have the cellar for their playroom, would she take them back to the London Junction Hotel? Poor Papa's face lit up when he came in from work and saw Bonnie. "I happened to be passing," said Bonnie, "and just happened to see the number and I thought I'd drop in. Now that I'm here I might as well fix the place up a little."

"We don't need anybody to fix us up," Papa said. "If you just dropped in to criticize you might as well leave."

Bonnie reddened.

"I wasn't criticizing, Mr. Willard, only the children—the place—well, those stories going around in the Junction made me so cross. I thought I'd come over and help."

"So you happened to pass by," said Papa disagreeably. "You can tell anybody in London Junction to mind their own goddam business, and I'll do the same."

Bonnie bit her lip and then decided to ignore Papa's mood. She gave a gay laugh.

"I'd be sore if I didn't know you were always kidding, Harry Willard!" she said. "You wouldn't be cross to an old friend like me. I know you like me too much for that. Just for spite, I'm going to give you a big kiss."

This was done, with some embarrassed remonstrances from Papa, and then suddenly capitulating he waltzed Bonnie around the room in a tight embrace, to the delight of the girls.

"Just like when Mama was alive!" they exclaimed in chorus.

Papa stopped abruptly, leaving Bonnie dizzily hanging on to a chair, laughing breathlessly.

"Bonnie looks like Mama, doesn't she, Papa?" said Marcia.

"Not a bit," Papa said. "Your Mama never painted her face."

Bonnie rubbed her cheeks.

"I guess the first Mrs. Willard was a mighty pretty woman," she said.

"First and *only* Mrs. Willard," Papa corrected. Having succeeded in making Bonnie dab at her eyes with a handkerchief, he seemed cheered.

"I hear you're going steady with every fellow on the Big Four," he said, smiling. "Got to have your good time, I guess, haven't you, Bonnie?"

"I don't like to sit around being lonesome for anybody," Bonnie said, chin now going in air. "Speaking of paint, I don't lay it on the way certain Lesterville women do, folks you seem to think are all right or you wouldn't be chasing them, from stories I hear."

Papa laughed amiably.

"I'm not chasing anybody," Papa said. "If I was chasing anybody it wouldn't be somebody that got herself talked about in every saloon from here to Cincinnati."

"I don't know who you have reference to, Mr. Willard," Bonnie said, voice trembling.

"Getting engaged to three fellows at once, dating up a dozen others on the side," Papa said. "Not that it's anything to me. I just hate to see a nice girl make herself look cheap."

"I can't help who says they're engaged to who," Bonnie said. "Personally, I don't intend to get married, ever. Not on a bet."

"That's fine," Papa said. "Anybody that gets herself talked about can't expect a decent man to marry them."

"A decent man doesn't hang around those girls in Stein's Cafe," Bonnie said. She was trying not to cry. "A decent man doesn't get a girl started caring for him, then act huffy when she shows a little affection. If he acted a little nicer, maybe she wouldn't go round trying to have what little pleasure she can."

"Staying all night at Cedar Point," Papa said, musingly. "A fine thing."

Bonnie burst into tears.

"If you knew so much you could have stopped me, Harry Willard," she sobbed. "What have you got against me, anyway? What have I done except be a friend?"

Papa was at a loss over this, and looked scowlingly at the floor.

"It's your coming over here to criticize," he said. "All I get everywhere I go since Daisy died is criticism. By God, it's more than a man can stand, working night and day, doing his best, taking care of his family all alone, friendless——"

"Ed Hartwell is over at Mabel's," Bonnie said. "They're your friends, aren't they? To tell the truth, I was on my way there this minute."

She began pinning on her hat, her lips still quivering.

Papa said nothing and at the door she turned.

"Any message for Ed?" Bonnie asked. "Maybe you might drop around. Far be it from me to suggest."

"Couldn't do it," Papa said.

The girls watched Bonnie leave, resignedly. No picture show, no streetcar ride, nobody ever kept promises, not even Bonnie. And Papa had been cross with her, so perhaps she'd never come again. He didn't even say goodbye to Bonnie when she went, but after a little while he picked up his hat and left. He didn't come back that night, nor was he back the next morning when Aunt Lois marvellously appeared, just as Lena had begged.

"You mean your father hasn't been home since yesterday afternoon?" she exclaimed, after the first joys of reunion. "What did you have for lunch this noon?"

"We made hot water soup," said Lena. "You boil the water and put in salt and pepper and buttered crackers for oysters, so it tastes like oyster soup."

Aunt Lois looked thoughtfully around the rooms, made no comment while they admiringly described the details of Bonnie Purdy's costume, and the news that she was visiting Mabel and Mr. Hartwell. Presently she accosted Mrs. Jane in the hallway and there was a low-voiced conference, clicking of tongues, shaking of heads on both sides, sighs, shrugs, sorrowful glances at the girls, all ending up in Mrs. Jane helping Aunt Lois find a suitcase into which to put their clothes. Lena nudged Marcia. "We're going back to London Junction," her lips formed the words.

"But we can't," Marcia lamented in a whisper. "The truant officer will come after us tomorrow if we don't go to school."

"We'll be in school there," said Lena rapturously. "With Mary Evelyn."

"Put on your coats, you're coming home with me," said Aunt Lois, buckling the straps of the wicker suitcase. She shook her head significantly at Mrs. Jane. "It's beyond me. I honestly wouldn't have believed it, well as I know Harry Willard. I advise you to get your money from him, Mrs. Jane, before he skips. That's the way Harry is. Oh, you poor kids!"

There was delay in leaving, eager as the older two were to go anywhere and have something happen, anything at all. Florrie sat on the floor and sobbed that she would not leave Papa, that she wouldn't leave Mrs. Jane's tomcat, Tommy, and that she had to look after her dear Papa because he had said so. Marcia suddenly remembered she had two library books out, *The Green Fairy Book* and *The Blue Fairy Book*, and unless she took them back tomorrow she would have to pay four cents or else the police would come to London Junction and get her. Mrs. Jane promised not only to deliver the books but not to give her address to the police in case of delay. Florrie stuck to her guns till the threat of leaving without her brought her, weeping, after them. The faint twinges about Papa's reaction were lost completely in the unexpected treat of being driven all the way back to London Junction in Mr. Sweeney's new Winton car. The three sat in the back and sang the songs they knew, very loud when they passed Burnadetta's house on East Park. Aunt Lois sat in front with Mr. Sweeney, talking earnestly in the low emphatic tone which always meant "something was going to be done about the girls."

PART THREE

Home Is Far Away

23

THERE WERE different kinds of happiness, Marcia decided. What most people wanted was the happiness of having what other people wanted. Then they had brief moments of an inferior happiness when they only got what they themselves but nobody else wanted. This rather spoiled things. Some people made mistakes in their opinion of what other people wanted, but if they didn't find out they managed to be happy, maybe wondering a little once in a while what everybody wanted this for. Others wasted so much time trying to have what other people wanted that sometimes they never knew they were perfectly happy without it. The biggest jolt in growing up was to discover that you didn't like what others liked and they thought you were crazy to like what you liked.

Marcia thought the greatest happiness was to be left alone. If anybody was around they kept you from thinking or reading or else made fun of your diary or whipped you or scolded you about something. Lena wanted everything other girls wanted, whether she really liked it or not, and since these were all tangible objects costing money, Lena was unhappy a good deal of the time. Florrie's happiness consisted in having people love her and fondle her and refrain from unkind words about anybody. There were definite barometers for people's happiness, too. You could tell Aunt Lois' by the sudden richness of her laugh, and the way her blond curls kinked up of their own accord. You could tell Grandma's by the way she smiled secretly to herself over her mending, moving her lips and nodding complacently as if at her age she knew better than to have her pleasure spoiled by telling it to some jealous confidante. You could tell Papa's by the cocky set of his hat and by his walk.

It was evident that Papa was pretty happy about something that summer of 1911 because his stiff straw hat sat snappily on the side of his wavy brown hair or else tilted itself merrily over one eyebrow. His hat was as sensitive to the master's temper as Aunt Lois' hair was to hers; it seemed to rejoice all of itself in a happy secret, rearing itself up at the slightest touch of the hand, never sedately straight as in his somber moods. Papa's shoes, too, seemed to dance along by themselves, and in these happy moments his footsteps coming down the sidewalk sounded like a tap dance. He had a travelling job again for the Cleveland Excelsior Cement Company, working for a Mr. Balzer who, he declared, was just about the biggest man in the cement business, as well as a hell of a fine man. Give him a German any day, he said, in preference to these Bohemian novelty men; he'd said it before, and he'd say it again: the cement business, when managed by a superior fellow like Oscar Balzer, was about the most exclusive and up-and-coming business a man could get into. He visited his daughters every three or four weeks on his London Junction trip, and usually brought them a box of Chandler & Rudd salted almonds, or peppermint candy hearts, or joke books. He almost pacified Aunt Lois' prejudices by presenting her with a box of Mama's jewelry, including the fleur-de-lys watch and pin, and the garnet pin and her garnet earrings. They both cried over this, and said how pleased Daisy would be at his disposal of her jewels. Aunt Lois said it was about the sweetest thing Harry had ever done.

"You'll find out the kind of man I am one of these days, Lois," Papa said, wiping his eyes. "I'll betcha anything Daisy knows how I try just as well as if she was alive. You've always criticized but you'll find out I'm always looking for some way to do what Daisy would want of me, and that's all I ask. Well, by George, I think I've got a chance right now to please Daisy, and when I do it you can bet your sweet life Daisy up there is going to be tickled to death."

Aunt Lois said cautiously that she didn't know what he was up to but she sincerely hoped it would be for the best. She said so far as she was concerned she'd never had anything against him, except the way he ran up bills and neglected his children, but she'd always said he'd come through in the long run. At least she hoped so. She said Daisy had always thought the sun rose and set on him, and that was why it seemed a shame, seeing him run around with girls like Bonnie Purdy, who couldn't be mentioned in the same breath with dear Daisy.

"You're absolutely right and I'll shake on it," Papa agreed solemnly. "You know what's what, Lois, in spite of being so bull-headed about everything. Yes, sir, I may have had too good a time now and then, but something always held me back from getting in too deep. It was like Daisy was whispering to me, 'Now, wait a minute, Harry. Think of the kids. Is this the right thing for them?' And I'd back right down. That's the way it's been from the day she died and that's a fact."

Aunt Lois pinned the fleur-de-lys pin on her fresh pink poplin dress, and Papa looked at it with moist, sentimental eyes. Suddenly he said, "Tell you what, Lois, I'd better get that watch cleaned and repaired before I give it to you."

"I can have it done right here, Harry," Aunt Lois said.

"No, I know a fellow in Cleveland who'll do it for nothing as a favor to me," Papa said. "I happen to have done a few favors for him and he'll be glad to fix it up good as new. The clasp is a little loose, and I wouldn't want you to lose it."

"We—ell——"

Aunt Lois reluctantly handed over the watch, which Papa quickly wrapped in the chamois bag and pocketed with a suspicious air of finality. This put a little dampener on the reconciliation, especially since Papa immediately left the house, whistling "The Whistler and His Dog" as he jauntily stepped down the walk. Aunt Lois looked moodily after him.

"I don't know what's got into him to be so darn tickled with himself," she observed, and repeated the incident to Mr. Sweeney, later on, over a plate of oysters he had brought from Lesterville.

"Some woman, take my word for it," said Mr. Sweeney.

This turned out to be the truth. Papa was about to get married. As he frequently boasted later on, the news of the wedding was written up all over the country, in three newspapers to be exact. He had the clippings to prove it. Aunt Lois thought the children should have been invited to the wedding, especially since the bride's own child by a former marriage would be present; however, it meant railroad tickets and new dresses, so Papa vetoed the suggestion. Besides, the bride said that one child underfoot at a wedding was enough; time enough to take the others on after they were settled. Aunt Lois held out that Florrie at least should go, being Papa's favorite and a decoration to any gathering, but Papa was too impressed with his new wife's family to agree. In his preliminary discussions of the marriage he had proudly boasted not of his fiancée's beauty or virtues but of her folks.

"Finest people in Daleport," he stated. "Genuine old Western Reserve stock, not like London Junction folks at all. Originally from Vermont, fine old New England folks."

Aunt Lois, ruffled by the turn affairs had taken, retorted that most everybody came from New England at one time or another, because there was no place else to come from unless they were immigrants, and the reason they came was they were such mean skinflints they wanted to get whatever property they could for nothing, and if they were so fine they wouldn't have needed to leave Vermont in the first place. Papa was dashed by this for a moment, but he would not have his triumph spoiled. He reminded Aunt Lois that the new Mrs. Willard was second cousin to J. B. Hawkins of Ashtabula, one-time Congressman. Aunt Lois replied that this didn't make Mrs. Willard a Congressman, and she didn't see what was so wonderful about being cousins, especially *second* cousins of anybody, because second cousins never left you anything, and besides she'd read in the *Literary Digest* that the entire white race was thirty-second cousins of each other. The onion being the cousin of the lily didn't make it any posy, she said, or smell any the better.

Papa had brought his news to her in a genial, all-forgiving mood, certain that at last he was doing the right thing, so that Aunt Lois' testy reaction gave him more sorrow than anger. His proud, beaming smile changed to an expression of grieved bewilderment.

"I don't understand you, Lois," he said, shaking his head. "You've been raising Cain for years about my running with the wrong women, so I go out of my way to get a real lady, someone Daisy would be sure to say would make a good, refined mother for the girls. And already you're giving me hell for it. If they aren't too tough for you, they're too refined; that's about the size of it. God damn, what's a man to do, trying to do the right thing and always getting kicked in the pants for it?"

He stalked out of the house, glowering, leaving Aunt Lois to pursue her unfavorable reflections aloud to the children. They were puzzled as much as their father had been by her indignation, since she had often darkly hinted at the day he would some day disgrace them all by marrying Bonnie Purdy. Marcia and Florrie had hoped this disgrace would happen, but Lena, who was more socially advanced now, had primly informed Papa one day that she would run away if he married Bonnie, because Mary Evelyn's mother said Bonnie wasn't nice. Papa was a little afraid of his oldest daughter, but he said he guessed Bonnie Purdy was about as nice as Mary Evelyn's mother, but he had no intention of marrying either one. When news came of the new marriage, Lena gravely thanked her father for following her advice. Marcia was glad of any change, but Florrie wept that she did not want any new mama; she had only one mama, and nobody could make her have another one. Eventually they received souvenir postcards of Niagara Falls and the three clippings of the wedding.

"Friends of Harry Willard in London Junction," said the *London Junction Register*, "will be interested to learn of his recent marriage to Mrs. Idah Hawkins Turner of Daleport. Mr. Willard has recently taken a position as manager of the London Junction Furniture Company's Retail Store and Funeral Parlor on Main Street. He is the brother-in-law of Mrs. Lois Blair, long a resident here, with whom his three children have made their home."

The *Daleport Sentinel* said, "Mrs. Idah Hawkins Turner, age 36, became the bride yesterday of Mr. Harry Willard, 37, of London Junction, in a small but tasteful ceremony at the home of Mrs. Turner's mother, Mrs. Minnie Hawkins. The bride was formerly a trained nurse in Columbus, but retired three years ago to marry the well-known Daleport dentist, Dr. Ephraim Turner, who died last year at the age of 61, leaving one infant, little Minelda May. The couple was attended by Mr. Ed Hartwell of Lesterville, as best man, and the bride's sister, Mrs. Burns, as matron of honor. Reverend Timothy Thompson was the officiating clergyman, and delicious refreshments were enjoyed by all."

The *Elmville Republican* said, "News has reached friends here of the second marriage of Henry Willard, formerly of Peach Street, and the Busby Hotel. The first Mrs. Willard, affectionately remembered here as Daisy Reed, passed away six years ago leaving three little daughters. Mr. Willard's new bride attended his first wife's last illness in the capacity of nurse, and after her first marriage resided in Daleport, where the present wedding took place. She is the second cousin of former Congressman J. B. Hawkins."

The big news, such as to stun Aunt Lois into silence, appeared in the London Junction paper two weeks later. "The Main Street Realty Company announces the sale of the Furness house, long vacant, to Mrs. Idah Hawkins Willard, recently married to Harry Willard. Mrs. Willard has been negotiating for the property for some time, and on a recent flying trip to the Junction arranged for its repair. It is expected the property will be in readiness for the couple on their return next month from a month's honeymoon."

"The Furness house!" gasped all who heard. "So Harry married money! Well, what do you know!"

Aunt Lois eventually found the right answer to this.

"Money, of course she has money. Why else do you think she put her hooks into that dentist, an old man twice her age? Everybody in that part of the state says he was dying when she nailed him and had him sign over everything to her on the wedding day. Left her close to fifteen thousand dollars! At that, she got a bargain on the Furness house. Trust Harry Willard to land on his feet!"

This made Aunt Lois madder than anything else. Now Papa was reaping rewards for extravagance and mismanagement, while she, who had made up to his family for his delinquencies, could barely keep her head above water. As she said to Mr. Sweeney, Daisy would turn over in her grave if she but knew.

24

Everybody in London Junction talked about the second Mrs. Willard's trousseau, and several ladies had even paid formal calls for the express purpose of examining it. There was her off-white satin wedding dress with the short, pearl-sequined veil, her fawn-colored broadcloth travelling suit trimmed in brown soutache, with a peg top skirt, brown horsehair toque and gloves to match, her purple taffeta petticoat and umbrella, her peach-colored *crepe de chine* party dress with beaded panel down the front and baby blue velvet forget-me-nots appliqued around the flounce, and her big horsehair picture hat weighted with huge roses. For every day she had the clothes left over from her mourning period for the late Dr. Turner. Her early weeks in London Junction were marked by magic transformations from mousy little grub by morning into radiant butterfly by dusk, radiance graded to suit whatever occasion was on hand. Papa strutted when he escorted this fashionable figure down Main Street on Saturday nights to the picture show or on Sundays to the First Methodist Church, wheeling little Minelda May in the very latest gocart from the Store. Marcia, Lena and Florrie followed at an admiring distance, proud of the stares at their new mother's city dresses, and shocked to hear later that their own shabbiness was as much a subject of comment as their stepmother's elegance.

It was like a dream to walk home from school straight up the Furness front walk. After a while Mrs. Willard ruled that they were to use the back alley and back door, because they tracked up the new broadloom carpet. Their first rapture over the change in their fortunes was not easily quenched. It was true that the Furness place, after years of neglect, was no longer the show place of London Junction, but it was still to them the fairytale castle it had been when Papa first promised it to Mama, and they had played there, pretending to own it. It was far too big to refurnish, so several rooms were shut up. The three girls used one big bedroom, with a cot in the alcove for Florrie. Their new mother said that girls' rooms shouldn't be cluttered up with a lot of junk, so, to tell the truth, it looked more bleak than the house's exterior grandeur would indicate. Downstairs, the big parlor was decorated with the very latest in furniture, rugs and drapes from the Store (payment deducted from Papa's salary for the next thirty months), with a grand piano in the middle of the room. A purple plush scarf, with gold roses painted upon it, added a royal richness to the piano, crowned in addition by a funereal-looking amphora of gilded wheat. The piano was queen of the parlor, with two bright blue plush chairs, overstuffed and tasselled, as its duchesses. These were placed before the fireplace (made up-to-date with artificial gas logs) and their dignity enhanced by a stiff hand-embroidered sofa cushion laid against each right foreleg. A vast blue davenport between the chairs was so rigidly overstuffed that its cushions popped up waist high. The parlor seemed made not for living inhabitants but for these regal pieces of furniture which frowned at any violation of their lofty privacy and brooked no touch but the reverent dusting ministrations of their priestess, Mrs. Willard.

Behind the davenport was a mahogany refectory table bearing a top-heavy gold pagoda of a lamp. On one side was placed a limp leather volume of Whittier's *Snowbound*, and on the other a silver framed photograph of the wedding party, with Minelda's diaper showing. The "changeable" wallpaper of purple into rose permitted but two works of art to "mark up" its distinction, one of these a small violently colored view of a rose-covered cottage doorway, the other a large gold-framed copy of a shallow brown brook with a deer peeping through brown willow branches beside it. Culture was modestly represented by an old golden oak bookcase reclaimed from the Friends' attic and properly hidden behind two potted palms. The old books were there as they had been in Mama's day, but to save wear and tear they were locked up. Florrie's big doll was locked in here so she wouldn't break it, and also her sisters' gilt-edged diaries, because Mrs. Willard was a careful woman and felt that all possessions were better locked up, since it was regrettably impossible to lock up their owners.

"I want to teach the girls to take care of things," she told Papa. "They've lived such a helter-skelter life, they've got to learn how nice people act. Supposing some of my relations, like Cousin Jay from Ashtabula, would come to visit us. Why, he'd think they were little hoodlums."

"That's the ticket," Papa agreed, with satisfaction. "I want you to make ladies of 'em. God knows, I can't do it, because it takes a lady to make 'em act right. That's what their own mother would want."

The girls were in a daze over their sudden ascent in the world. Imagine living in the big Furness house, with a piano and pictures and balconies and thick rugs. Every day there was some new luxury added to the household. Mrs. Willard considered it stylish to subscribe to a magazine of some sort, and, after discussing the matter for several evenings with her husband and callers, settled on *The Delineator*. A magazine rack was immediately purchased for this, and to keep it company the *Lesterville Weekly Courier* and the London Junction Furniture Company catalogue. The girls were not allowed to touch this collection, however, because they would muss up everything. At first they were too awed by their new splendor to resent the rules for its protection. At school they boasted of their new mother and their new house, the dumbwaiter, the big empty stables, the fountain that didn't work, the iron dog. Lena, always more courageous than her sisters, even planned and issued invitations to her classmates and teachers to a big party (with favors and games and prizes like Myrtle Chase's parties), date to be determined later. It was just as well that she had a fight with Mary Evelyn over the invitation list, because it gave an excuse for calling the whole thing off with no loss of dignity. Their new mother, they announced, was richer than anybody in London Junction; she had a whole cedar chest full of Philippine embroidered underwear; she owned a cottage at Silver Lake where undoubtedly they would henceforth spend their summers lolling in rowboats and collecting shells; she had a fabulous brother Vance who spent a year or two in military school, and had been to New York City, and she had relatives of great consequence in the East, in addition to her cousin, the Ashtabula Congressman. Papa overheard these vulgar boasts and reprimanded the girls severely, though he himself was making important references to these advantages at his lodge and around the Store.

Papa was actually walking on air, between his residence in the Furness house and his magnificent new title as manager of the Store. He had cards printed with his name and a new middle initial he had added for style—"Mr. Harry J. Willard, General Manager, LONDON FURNITURE STORE, LONDON JUNCTION. YOUR HOME IS YOUR CASTLE, LET US FURNISH

IT. *Undertaking Parlors.*" The Store was the newest business building in the Junction, with plateglass windows on one entire side, and the wholesale offices and catalogue department located on the two floors above. A great billboard advertising the Store rose above the roof, giving a respectable impression of a five-story building to fascinated passengers whizzing by on trains. Papa took his daughters down to look over his new headquarters very soon after he settled there, but on the advice of his wife finally forbade them to come in the Store except on the most vital errand. It was too bad, for all three had spotted wonderful corners for play in the great showroom. There was a smell of varnish and new wood as soon as you stepped inside, and an impressive vista of glossy dining tables, buffets, Windsor chairs, settees, crowds of fat overstuffed chairs adorned with tassels, fringes, tapestry insets, and so pompous in their newness and overstuffedness that it must have taken great courage to invite one to take its place in a simple parlor with lesser pieces. Floor lamps and table lamps of all shapes and sizes were lit all day to demonstrate their charms; some were ingeniously attached to the arm of a chair, a smoking stand, or built into a center table. A mezzanine floor with elegant gold-trimmed balustrade held the many styles of beds from veneered bronze maple to burled walnut. The place really got its elegant tone, aside from its artistic furniture, from a Chinese incense burner hanging in the living-room suite department, blending its Sen-Sen and strawberry shrub fragrance with that of furniture polish and glue, also from the huge Victor Talking Machine with megaphone which boomed out richly over the Store and on to the street a perpetual chorus of "Come, Come, I Want You Only." It was worth the price of admission just working in a place like that, Papa said happily, and with a treat like that on the premises he didn't see how he could keep the customers out. His old Lesterville friend from the High Class Novelty Works dropped in one day (Mr. Taylor), and after a tour of the place shook his head and said it was too rich for his blood. He was so awed by the sight of Papa in white collar, black suit and shiny black shoes, moving gracefully among all this luxury, changing the Victrola needle, relighting the incense burner, conferring with the mortician glibly on choice of coffin linings, that he skulked out of the place while Papa was still showing off, and was never seen in the Store again.

All in all the Willard girls felt that they had come into a fairytale world, and the town itself was impressed. Papa adopted a brisk but somber manner suited to his new position, kept away from the Elks' Club and the London Junction Hotel, spoke to his former cronies from his travelling salesman and railroad life with the proper mingling of friendliness and aloofness. It seemed to him that every person he met in his day's work was looking at him with awe and inwardly exclaiming, "Harry Willard, of all people! A self-made man, by George, a living success story. Said he'd make good and darned if he hasn't. Leading citizen, topnotch businessman, well, well, well!" His daughters looked at him with reverence for this magic he had wrought. They bragged about it to their schoolmates and by night they gloated over it to each other.

But the adjustment to good fortune is sometimes as hard to make as the adjustment to bad fortune. Anxious as they were to live up to the new standard, there seemed to be not one single thing they could do to suit their new mother. They didn't even know why it was wrong, because she just stood shaking her head in despair and sometimes throwing up her hands as if there was no coping with such stupidity. They didn't open or shut doors right, they walked on their heels instead of their toes, they wiped their hands on their napkins or else they didn't, they sat on the bed, they sat on the chairs, they sang till the place sounded like bedlam, they went around in old clothes, looking like perfect little tramps and shaming their elders, or else they wanted to wear their best clothes and ruin them. Efforts to do right in the face of these confused complaints seemed hopeless, and even Papa was unsympathetic. Coming home at night beaming with his new triumphs, he was righteously annoyed to be brought down to earth by his wife's complaints about his children.

"I'm surprised at you girls," he scolded. "I got a fine new home for you, just like your own mother always wanted for you, and you don't know how to act right. You don't say 'thank you' and you don't mind. If you don't try to behave yourselves, I'll send you off some place, I swear. You got to learn to appreciate what people are trying to do for you. Lena, you're the oldest.

I'm going to count on you to keep the others toeing the mark. You're growing up and it's time you learned how to be ladies."

But it was Lena who made the first big mistake. She was anxious to be the new mama's pet, so she earnestly tried to ingratiate herself by relating the defects of her younger sisters with gloomy prophecies of what would become of them if they didn't follow her own example. She said that Marcia did not wear her galoshes or mittens and hid them in a tree trunk on her way to school, and that in the school cloakroom she rouged her face with red crepe paper. She said that Florrie was always dragging around a dirty kitten named Snowball and hiding it in the bedroom until she, Lena, was afraid they'd all catch the mange from it. She was afraid they'd catch roup from the sick chicken Florrie had carried around for a day or two, too. The new Mrs. Willard approved of Lena's helpful information and instructed her to punish these misdemeanors if they came up again. Heady with power, Lena brought Mary Evelyn home one day to show off the house, taking care to do so when she thought no one was around, so she could take her in the front door.

"This is the parlor," she said with a wave of her hand. "Twenty-two by thirty."

Mary Evelyn could not disguise her admiration and envy for a moment, then inquired with a mean smirk why the piano was locked, and was it because nobody was allowed to play it. Taunted by this, Lena was driven to look for the key in the kitchen cabinet, where unfortunately she did find it in the broken sugar bowl. She haughtily invited Mary Evelyn to join her in a duet and they were seated playing "Chopsticks" when suddenly a figure loomed in the doorway. It was the new Mrs. Willard in her fawn-colored suit. Her face was white and stony, her marble eyes sparked with fury. Not quite sure what was wrong, both girls froze at this image of wrath. The lady stalked over to the piano and shut down the keyboard almost on their very fingers.

"Give me that key," she commanded in a low hoarse voice, and as Lena weakly obeyed she said through her teeth, "You are not to touch this piano, never, do you hear?"

"I was only——"

"None of your impudence!" Mrs. Willard snarled. "Who

told you you could come in this room? I won't have you little demons trooping in and out, pawing my good furniture with your filthy hands. Your father will hear of this."

Mary Evelyn was out of the door and half-way down the block in a flash. But Lena, after her first shock, stubbornly stood her ground.

"I guess I'm supposed to have my music lessons, like my father promised," she said haughtily. "Where am I supposed to practice?"

"I don't know and I don't care," muttered Mrs. Willard. "Just stay out of this room with your dirty boots."

On the front porch Minelda, still in her carriage, wailed loudly to be brought inside.

"Let her yell," Lena said in a loud voice, and ran to join Mary Evelyn.

The former Miss Hawkins stood for a moment darting her eyes about the room, studying what must be done to repair the desolate ruin that twenty minutes of invasion had wrought. Without taking off her hat—it was the big one with the flowers—she ran for a dust cloth and began frantically to polish away imaginary stains from the piano. She tested a few notes to see how much out of key the abuse had left the sensitive instrument, then for a final test sat down to play her one and only selection, "Work for the Night is Coming," with one hand. The notes seemed unimpaired, but she shook her head, convinced that some interior damage had been done, then she locked the keyboard lovingly. She got down on her knees to wipe from a very red rose in the carpet the mud tracks she fancied must be there. It took her several minutes to arrange *Snowbound* at its proper angle on the refectory table, and even then her earnest inspection could not inform her whether its contents had been violated by the intruder's eyes. In the midst of these repairs she suddenly realized that Lena had actually drawn up one of the white shades, and this atrocity brought from her a moan of genuine anguish. Her eyes were red rimmed when Papa came home, and when he asked what was wrong, she put her head on his shoulder and sobbed, "Oh Harry, Harry, what am I going to do? I can't stand seeing our home wrecked by these children. You've got to speak to them, dear, before they pull the whole place down around our ears!"

25

After her first difficulty with her stepmother, Lena refused to take any orders except from Papa. She said she was too big to be looking after other people's babies, and if anyone had to wheel Minelda after school it would have to be Marcia. Marcia did not mind this chore very much, since it let her out of playing games with the school children, and besides she felt there was no use arguing about it. She got a book out of the library every day and read as she wheeled. If Minelda yelled too loudly, she was sometimes exasperated to the point of giving her a good pinch. Minelda was two and a half, sickly and inclined to whimpering, brought on by the thorough manner she was bundled up by her devoted mother, even in summer. Minelda tossed and squirmed under her usually wet woolens, suffering from prickly heat, and her pinched little face was white to the point of blueness. Her steady squirming and tugging at her little harness did not penetrate Marcia's consciousness, absorbed as she was in her book. Even when Minelda managed to wriggle half out of her gocart, her little caretaker paid no attention, since the sobs presently subsided into chokes and gurgles as she hung herself by her strap. Sometimes a book would be so entrancing that Marcia, resting the open book on the buggy's handle bar, would be wheeling for several minutes peacefully before noticing that the gocart was empty. Emerging from her daydream, Marcia would presently recognize distant shrieks and there would be Minelda, far back in the ditch where an unexpected jolt had thrown her. As soon as they were near home Minelda set up a defiant howl proclaiming all these indignities until her mother rushed out of the kitchen to snatch her up into protective arms.

"You poor, poor baby, what has that bad girl done to you?" she cried out, which set Minelda off into new sobs and indignant glares at Marcia. "Where did this bruise come from? And just look at the way she's dirtied up your nice clean pillow! Get a rag and wipe off these wheels this very minute, Marcia Willard! I never saw such a disgraceful sight. No wonder the poor child cries!"

Attention being directed to the damage done the gocart and Minelda, Marcia registered mild astonishment on seeing that there were dents in the carriage where she had absent-mindedly banged it into a tree or wall. Remnants of twigs and gravel on Minelda's bib indicated a misguided feast on definitely inedible items.

"She'll be sick!" moaned her mother. "Why did you let her?"

"I can't help it if a person wants to eat caterpillars," Marcia argued in self-defense. "If that's what she likes, I can't stop her."

"Wheel her down the paved streets after this," Minelda's mother commanded. "Why must you always take these back alleys?"

"Because my dress is torn, that's why," Marcia said.

"I'd be ashamed to be so vain," said her stepmother. "Nobody is looking at an ugly little girl like you, anyway. Wait a minute, now, what are you hiding under your jacket? Is that a book?"

The crime was out, try as Marcia did to conceal her book. Mrs. Willard snatched at it.

"That's why you're so careless. Head so full of nonsense and silly stories you don't even know you're alive. No wonder! Well, I'll see to it you get your library card stopped."

The glamor of their new life slowly sifted down to its disagreeable reality. Here they were in a fine big house with a new mother who had pretty clothes and a piano, and with their father a dignified public figure "out of the woods" at last, as he himself proudly put it. Mr. and Mrs. Harry Willard were mentioned at least once a week in the *Register* as being present at the Masonic Banquet, guests at Mr. Carson's Memorial Dinner, patrons of the London Junction Boosters Annual Minstrel Show, with invitations to be members of the Bridge Club, and Mrs. Willard elected second vice-president of the Women's Century Reading Club. Such social prominence was more than the family had ever dreamed of, and was commented upon enviously by all the relations. But try as they would, there seemed no place in this charmed life for anybody but Papa, Idah Hawkins Willard, and possibly Minelda. The night the Willards took their turn at entertaining the Bridge Club (refreshments of beer, pretzels, ice cream and cake; prizes, a hand-embroidered muffin towel and a burnt leather wallet) the children were instructed not to show themselves downstairs under any circumstances. Marcia and Lena exchanged a look of consternation, having boasted for several days to their schoolmates of this great event.

"When it meets at Mrs. Carson's, Barbara passes things," Lena said.

"Maybe they could come down and sing something," Papa suggested.

"What would they wear?" his bride inquired. "They'd look like little tramps and nobody wants children running around at a nice party."

The Bridge Club was a really devastating blow. Lena and Florrie had invited their intimate friends to come play with them during the party and they were desperately wondering how to ward them off. Lena sneaked down the back stairs during the party and brought back cruel reports of the party's progress. Two of Florrie's classmates had been brought by their parents to play with Florrie, and were seen enjoying ice cream and cake. Furthermore, Lena had heard her stepmother explaining that the reason Florrie couldn't come down was that she was sick. Worse yet, one child was permitted—even urged—to render her piece, "Angel's Serenade," on the piano, when Lena could play it much faster if anybody would ever give her the chance. This shocking event brought gloom to the bedroom when Lena reported it.

"Didn't Papa do anything about it?" Marcia asked.

"Papa clapped," Lena said. "Then he and Mr. Chase said they would go downtown and get some more beer, and they haven't come back yet and She is mad as hops. She keeps getting up from the card table and emptying the ash trays even when there's nothing in them."

"I'm not a bit sick," Florrie brooded, sitting up in bed. "She oughtn't to tell lies about me. I won't even try to call her 'mama' like she said we should."

It was the beginning of calling the new mother "She."

26

The bridal chamber was on the second floor, and was so beautiful that the door was kept locked. No matter how often the bride went in and out She carefully took her keys from her pocket and shut off this paradise from prying little eyes. As the bookcase, parlor, piano, icebox, clothes chests and closets were also kept locked, the girls were resigned to the bedroom's beauties being denied them. They had viewed it once on a tour of the house with Aunt Lois, and once Florrie had taken a little colored girl of her acquaintance up over the porch roof to peer in the window, for the secrecy had persuaded her there must be fairy queens and magic carpets there. But there was only the canopy bed left from the Furness estate, draped in pink silkalene, and the new bride's gold dresser set and knicknacks. At night they could hear the door being locked and what seemed sounds of quarrelling—"Now, Harry! Harry, now stop! Harry, if you don't stop, now, I'll never forgive you. Now, now, now, Harry, stop!"

The second Mrs. Willard had changed very little since her first appearance in London Junction as Idah Hawkins, nurse to the first Mrs. Willard's last illness. Motherhood had added no curves to her slight figure, so She resorted to modest padding here and there for style, and Lena on a snooping trip reported that the lady's suit with weights and paddings actually weighed more than She did. For dressy purposes there was a jar of Hygienic Vegetable Rouge, which She rubbed carefully into a small circle in each cheek. Her faded scanty hair was decorated with switch, curls, and other devices of a richer golden hue, and when other ladies admired the coiffure She modestly boasted that it took three-quarters of an hour to get it that way. She said most women didn't have the patience, but She had always taken pains with her appearance and saw no reason for a real lady to let herself slide. She liked her little girl to look nice, too, and it was funny to hear the poor child cry just because the other girls had dirtied her up. When someone referred to her first encounter with Harry Willard, a twinkle came into her pale marble eyes and She tittered, "I had my eye on him right off, even then." It seems that when her first husband, Dr. Turner, passed on, the very first thing She had done was to buy some stock in the London Furniture Company. Then She asked Mr. Carson, the company president, what had happened to Harry Willard and Mr. Carson said, by George, he needed a man like Willard again, so he sent for him. That was how it started, what with her business trips to the Junction, and Mr. Carson trying to locate Harry again, old differences forgotten.

"Well, it takes a lot of courage to marry a widower with three little girls," Mary Evelyn's mother said, the day of her call, for which she had had fifty new calling cards specially engraved, in addition to purchasing a new Alice blue suit with red buttons and trimming to show that other ladies in London Junction besides the new Mrs. Willard knew the styles. The new bride gravely acknowledged her guest's compliment.

"The thing is not to let them take advantage," She explained. "They've been spoiled so, it's going to take a lot of managing, but it's just like I told Dr. Turner when I found out how spoiled *he* was. 'Your mother may have let you spill your ashes all over the floor, but she's dead now, and if you are set on smoking you take it right out to the garage where it belongs.' You have to let 'em know where you stand right at the start."

In spite of this statement, Mrs. Idah Willard's "stand" was so elaborate, and involved so many contingencies, that her new family despaired of ever getting it straight. First, they were to stay out of the house except for sleeping and eating. Second, they were not to sit out on the lawn mooning where everybody could see them, nor were they to go visiting relatives or school friends or have them call. They were not to use their school paper for games, because it cost money, nor were they to keep reading in their school readers for fun after their lesson was learned. They were to make themselves useful, instead of ornamental, but on the other hand She'd rather do all the housework herself than have them singing songs while they made beds or washed dishes. Their duties were to pick up scraps on the front lawn, tend to Minelda, and run errands. They were not to go places where townspeople would talk about their ragged clothes, but they were not allowed to use their sewing boxes either, because needles and thread cost money. They might sit in the old carriage barn, but they were to just sit there, not pretend they were riding or indeed pretend any other kind of nonsense, and if they tracked in mud when they came in to supper She would straighten them out. The "straightening out" was unpleasant, since She was so small She had to resort to tricks for her force, such as pinching them or cracking their heads with her diamond ring. Marcia found a handsome silver-tasselled little whip in the street after the circus parade, and this She at once appropriated, saying grimly as She locked it in the closet, "You'll get your whip when you ask for it." When Marcia stiffly refused to react to her whippings, She complained to Papa that he would have to punish the girls, since they were so wayward they wouldn't even cry. Florrie had croup and She tied a coal-oil bandage around her neck which burned her fearfully all night. Marcia and Lena sat up all night thinking maybe Florrie would die of pain but they were afraid to call out or tell Papa because they were sure this was part of Her plan. In the morning, She took off the bandage and when the skin came off with it She tittered, "My goodness, I forgot to put vaseline on first." There was no use telling these things to Papa, because She always told him something else first, and as he often said, it looked like his sister-in-law, Lois, was putting the kids up to mischief just to spoil the first break he'd ever had. She was afraid to whip Lena, however, since Lena threatened to tell Mr. Carson's daughter, Barbara. Lena was pretty independent, and all She could do was grind her teeth when Lena did as she pleased. Lena wouldn't come straight home from school, because she was organizing an exclusive after-school group of three into the "Buckeye Girls Sewing and Secret Society." The organization didn't have anything to sew so they changed the name to "B.L.G." (Buckeye Lark Girls), a purely pleasure club. Some boys found out the secret meaning of B.L.G., so the club met again to change its name to U.K.U.K. (U-Know-Us-Kids).

After this last monumental step forward, the club sagged into inactivity, till Myrtle Chase's mother took a kindly interest. She suggested they make it a nice little reading club like her own Century Club. To make it more fun and grown-up they should observe "parliamentary rule," which they could learn out of her own *Roberts' Rules of Order*. After a gloomy session with Mr. Roberts and Mrs. Chase's copy of *Tales of a Wayside Inn*, Lena said that if people's mothers were going to butt in they'd give up the whole project. Just then She got wind of Lena's secret society and told Papa Lena belonged to a club whose purpose was to read dirty books. Papa's nerves were ragged from the friction in his family, so he lost his temper and ordered Lena to come right home after school instead of getting herself talked about with her dirty books. Lena indignantly confided this to Mary Evelyn, who eagerly asked where you got those "dirty books" and that was a fine idea for a club, much better than Mrs. Chase's. They decided, after pondering the matter, that if Lena's stepmother knew so much about them she must have some. This incited Lena to further daring. She stole the house keys again and after earnest prowling discovered a book in her stepmother's bureau drawer called *Sex Talks*. She sneaked this out with palpitating heart, and soon had a much larger reading club than Mrs. Chase had anticipated. Since any type of reading was a chore for Lena's group, and this book was full of big words, they were only kept going by the conviction that anything hidden must be worth while. Besides, at last they had a secret. Finally, She discovered the secret, and this time Lena was whipped reluctantly by Papa at Her insistence. He was mad at Her, though, afterwards, and went out alone that night, slamming the door. When he came home, the girls heard him coming upstairs on his hands and knees, and they heard her crying out, "Oh, Harry, you've been drinking! You can't even walk upstairs."

"I can walk upstairs if I want to, God damn it," shouted Papa. "Anybody can walk upstairs, but *this* is the way I like to go upstairs, and this is the way I'm *going* to do it."

All of these domestic upsets grieved Papa.

"No matter how hard you try, something's always going wrong," he said, but he couldn't be down long. He was too dazzled by his new importance as a solid citizen, actually on the Chamber of Commerce, on the Church Entertainment Committee, and manager of the remodelled Retail Furniture Store and Undertaking Parlor. Whoever managed the furniture salesmen automatically became assistant undertaker, since the duties had always gone together like those of jeweller and optician. The simple facts of embalming, selecting a coffin, and directing the funeral procedure were passed on by his predecessor, and Papa was ecstatically pleased over his emergence as a professional man, respected by all, particularly on those sorrowful occasions when he tiptoed about in his new funeral black, wearing white gloves and whispering consolation to the bereaved. "A more cheerful personality than Fanzer has," Mr. Carson himself said, referring to the undertaker in charge. These personal advantages in his career so intoxicated Papa that he was enraged to hear doubts expressed on the wisdom of his marriage. Mrs. Friend told him old friends of Daisy thought his new wife favored her own child at the expense of her acquired three. Papa vowed he would never forgive such an impudent comment. He swore that Lois had put the children up to mischief because she was jealous he had the Furness place. He forbade the girls to visit their aunt. But there seemed no way of keeping his children up to his own social level. On Sundays, when he and his stylish bride wheeled Minelda in her Sunday best down Main Boulevard, he was sure to meet his three daughters wandering glumly and shabbily down the street. Could they have money to go to the picture show or to the Kandy Kitchen? By George, he indignantly replied, he was not made of money. Let them go home and catch up on their homework, instead of running the streets.

"Can we have the key?" Lena impertinently asked. "How can we go home if we're locked out?"

Mrs. Willard murmured to Papa that they wanted the key just to scratch up the piano and muss up the Sunday paper. She said they took such poor care of their clothes She personally was ashamed to have passersby see them on the front porch, so they had better keep in the back of the house. Papa almost hated them for their silent, gloomy faces, for their interfering with his just rewards, and for their unconscious reminder that his new affluence was not sound. There wasn't any more money than there ever was, for the upkeep of his wife's house took three times more than he had ever dreamed. And, as She herself said, you couldn't expect her to spend the late Dr. Turner's bequest and her own little savings on those three spoiled kids. There was an end to even her patience, She declared.

27

Grandma was back in London Junction "on her own, too," as she jubilantly boasted, definitely not living with kin. After her Cleveland disasters which she blamed mysteriously on politics, she had been obliged to make a visiting tour of her children, a very disagreeable experience for a lady who had once branched out into a career.

"Not one of my children ever minded me," she complained. "I don't see why they think I should mind them now."

They expected her to live with them and look after their children.

"A grandmother doesn't like children any more than a mother does," she declared. "Sometimes she's just too old to get out of tending them, that's all, but I'm not. Never felt better in my life."

It was that fine man, Mr. Sweeney, who came to her rescue with a loan, just as before. Since Aunt Lois had paid him back the last time he had come to the rescue she was mad enough at this new negotiation to take a train for California, where Aunt Betts had gone for her asthma. She said if Grandma wanted to get in hot water again she would have to get herself out this time. She said she would not forgive Mr. Sweeney for aiding Grandma's wildcat scheme.

The present wildcat scheme was a collaboration of Mrs. Carmel and Grandma. Rheumatism had hampered Mrs. Carmel's gift for hat trimming and idleness made her restless. They would go in partnership in a notion shop in London Junction. With Mrs. Carmel's savings and Grandma's loan from Mr. Sweeney, they would make a fortune. They took an apartment over the Fair Store, with the living room as their shop. The notions consisted of knicknacks from Mrs. Carmel's bags, ancient handkerchiefs slightly yellowed, silk remnants also somewhat sun-faded, postcards, dusty marchpane fruit with a pungent flavor of mothballs, patterns, mag-

azine subscriptions, hairpins, fans, souvenir spoons shined up
to look like new except for a dent or two where some baby
had teethed on them, bibs, and sheet music. The sheet music
was far from being the latest thing, and had been sampled by
mice and moths so that a page crumpled away at a touch.
However, for a genuine musician there were many treats here,
vocally and instrumentally, "The Little Romp Quick-step,"
"Father is Dead, and Mother's So Poor," "Velocipede Gallop," "Stay Home With Me Tonight, Tom," and "Mama,
Why Don't Baby Cry?" As Grandma said, at least it made a
nice showing. By way of a specialty, they sold home-made
candy, butterscotch, peanut brittle, and sea-foam. The candy
was inspired by finding among Mrs. Carmel's treasures an old
paper-backed volume called *Young Folk's Candy and Good
Times Book.* Recipes were adapted to the unscientific cook,
reading "add some water, a little more sugar if it seems too
thin, stir only if necessary but not too much, dash of flavor-
ing to taste, set aside to cool and cut up into squares." If the
results were good, Grandma dipped into them until there was
scarcely enough for three customers at twenty-five cents a box
but a careful packing job could spread it out to five, what
with each piece wrapped in waxed paper and an extra cardboard at the bottom.

The Fair Store was right in the busiest section of town,
around the corner from the railroad and directly opposite the
bandstand. From their front bay window they could watch
the crowd at the band concerts, and from their side windows
they could watch the passing trains. With proper lighting conditions they could even see some life going on in the back of
the London Junction Hotel. Across the corridor from them
was the Odd Fellows Hall, the scene of dances and banquets.
Sometimes a dance orchestra competed with the band concerts, so that Grandma, relaxing happily under the spell of all
this music, could produce a humming arrangement of the
"William Tell Overture" all mixed up with "Give My Regards
to Broadway." She liked a good tune to hum and felt aggrieved that she could never get beyond the first bar of "Oh,
You Beautiful Doll," because the 8:41 Cincinnati Express always roared through the rest of it.

The apartment had a big square front room with pine

woodwork and a light wallpaper mottled with an intricate design of bilious morning glories. Shelves had been built along one side for their wares, and a counter placed beneath them. A wax head decorated the counter, wearing a blond transformation made apparently of rope rather than hair. A Perfecto Cigar Box served as cash register. A dark closet opening from the front room turned out to be the kitchen, from which issued the smell of escaping gas and burnt sugar. Another door led to two small cubicles which were called bedrooms, and were also used for fitting of corsets. Mr. Brady, owner of the Fair Store, allowed the ladies his Irregulars. Grandma felt that most women's figures were irregular anyway, so they might as well save money by buying irregular corsets. It only took a jiffy to cut off the garters from the bust section and sew them on the right end.

The arrival of Grandma in London Junction had a devastating effect on the Willard girls. A person goes through life accepting his lot with equanimity, till a moment of complete happiness reveals to him that he has up to now had a perfectly wretched existence. Marcia and Lena and Florrie had reluctantly adjusted themselves to their stepmother's rule, working out their own routine for dodging her displeasure. Suddenly Grandma was in town, and the flash of hope this brought made them see their life in the Furness home as unendurable torture. The possibility of escape to Grandma's and a revival of the easygoing days on Hodge Street made them look with mutinous indignation on their lot. Why must they be made to feel guilty of some crime? Why must they wake each morning with leaden hearts, tiptoe glumly downstairs to breakfast, waiting for the almost certain morning greeting from Her, "Don't dig your heels into my new waxed floors! Don't put your filthy hands on my clean tablecloth! Stop coughing; your cold's all gone!" If Minelda had a rash or stomach ache or sore throat, it was ascribed to Marcia who had in her wickedness let Minelda eat a banana, walk on the grass, or throw her bonnet on the sidewalk.

"I'll tell Grandma," Lena and Marcia whispered to each other in the dark. But how could they when She wouldn't let them visit her? And how could they when it might bring criticism on Papa? They sat upstairs in the dark, forbidden to read because lights cost money, forbidden to sing, forbidden to play games because it might shake the floor, forbidden to go out because they'd track mud back indoors. If Lena boldly ventured downstairs to ask Papa's permission to sit in the kitchen or to unlock Florrie's big doll from the closet, Papa flew into a temper.

"What's the matter bothering me with fool questions like that?" So She always won out, smiling crookedly down at her mending as Lena had to retreat back upstairs.

"Our own Grandma in town and She won't let us see her," Marcia and Lena muttered angrily. Grandma in town gave Marcia confidence to creep downstairs and sneak *Parlor Recitations for Young People* out of the bookcase without asking permission. Caught red-handed just as she was learning "My Mother Calls Me William," she was jerked by her arm into the kitchen, and her own silver-tasselled whip was administered smartly. Stonily impassive during this punishment, Marcia looked contemptuously at the former Miss Hawkins, who sank back flushed and trembling into a chair.

"Next time you'll cry," she gasped. "I'll get a bigger whip."

"I don't care how big a whip you get," Marcia said coldly. "Just don't touch me with your hands, if you please."

She stalked upstairs triumphantly in spite of the red whip marks across her cheek and arms. This she did mind, for now everyone at school would know that she, a big girl of nearly twelve, was still getting whippings. Everyone would make fun of her.

When could they visit Grandma, they begged their father, trying not to seem too eager or She would find a way to stop them completely. Papa gruffly told them whenever their mother gave permission.

His wife tightened her lips and cast her pale cold eyes around the three with a look of satisfaction.

"No sense in their picking up bad manners again," She said. "I've had a time breaking them of all the bad habits their grandmother taught them, and their Aunt Lois and, goodness knows, who all. They only want to carry tales. If their grandma wanted them around she'd have sent for them before. Nobody wants three young ones around; oh, no, they leave that kind of dirty work to me."

Papa was fidgety between his wife's complaint and the steadfast accusing gaze of his daughters.

"It's her place to call on me first," She went on in a thin fretful tone. "Harry, I'm surprised you aren't offended by her not calling."

"That's right," acknowledged Papa, glad of a reasonable stand. "She ought to call on us first."

"Why?" asked Marcia.

Her stepmother threw up her hands.

"There! That's the back talk I get all day from these girls!"

Papa was glad to get out of the house on pretext of mowing the lawn. But Grandma's presence in town had its effect on him, too. Every night he told trivial anecdotes about things that happened long ago on Hodge Street, cautiously sifted recollections of episodes in Grandma's life, expressions she used, samples of her generosity and good nature, with head-shakings over her business innocence and how often his advice had saved her. His wife listened silently and clamped her jaw grimly when finally, to no one's surprise but his own, Papa announced that, disagreeable as the task was, he supposed he owed it to the old lady to give her the benefit of his advice in her present undertaking.

"I might as well go down after supper and get it over with," he said, lowering his eyes to hide the sparkle of eagerness. "The old lady will think it funny if I don't drop in for a talk, and nobody else can handle her the way I can. Besides," he was inspired to add, "when she goes I'll probably come into quite a lot of property because she always claimed she'd leave it to me."

"How much has she got?" his wife asked with interest. "We could get a machine, maybe. We could go on a tour. Why don't you find out?"

"I'll feel around," promised Papa, glad to have the matter closed amiably. "I'll take the girls over right after supper if they can behave themselves!"

It turned out there was another reason for Papa's eagerness to leave the house that night. He grasped Florrie by one hand and sped down the street, beaming, Marcia and Lena breathlessly skipping along behind. At Jake's Saloon near the hotel he stopped and peered in the door.

"By George, there's Ed Hartwell in there!" he exclaimed in profound surprise. "You kids wait while I go and say hello. He must be making the Junction on his new route. Well, well."

He hastily ducked inside and the immediate burst of laughter from inside was like old times. Marcia and Lena exchanged a comprehending look.

"He knew Ed was here," stated Lena. "He knew he didn't dare ask him to the house so he made up this excuse."

Hello took some time so the three girls walked back and forth impatiently in front of the saloon.

A fog of stale beer fumes surrounded the place, and from inside they heard "Too Much Mustard" jangling on the mechanical piano. Some boys from Lena's class came along and yelled "Hello, sweetheart," at Lena, who tossed her head indignantly. Marcia wished they would yell at her, too, but boys never looked at anyone but Lena. If they had a home like other girls they could have parties at night and make fudge and play Post Office. Marcia mentioned this to Lena as a prospect for their possible future at Grandma's, but Lena suddenly drew away and said with a far-away look, "Maybe only one of us can stay at Grandma's, and I'm the one because I'm the oldest."

It was half an hour before Papa emerged from Jake's, arm in arm with Ed Hartwell, and chuckling away in the highest spirits. Mr. Hartwell was even more elegant looking than before, for his sideburns and moustache were now lightly tinged with gray, and his figure had increased impressively. It seemed that Mr. Hartwell felt that he, too, should call on Grandma.

"Harry, your mother-in-law is one of the finest," he declared warmly. He shook hands with the girls, picked up Florrie to carry but found his wind not up to it, so put her down. He gave each of them a quarter on the spot, and pinched Lena's rosy cheek with an exclamation that, by George, she was getting to be a little beauty. He patted Marcia's head and observed that she looked bright as a little button.

Both men repeated complimentary remarks about the old lady, and what guts she had, and how anxious they were to see her. However, they delayed the visit a little longer by recollecting some private matter that needed attending in the

Elks Club. In spite of their impatience at the second delay, the girls were cheered to hear Papa laugh again all the louder, and to hear him saying things that made Mr. Hartwell roar with deepest appreciation.

"By George, there's nobody like you, Willard!" Mr. Hartwell declared, slapping him on the back. "I don't know whether your wife realizes how lucky she is, and you can tell her I said so."

"How's Mabel, Mr. Hartwell?" Marcia asked, politely. "Are you married yet?"

This set Mr. Hartwell and Papa into another fit of laughter right in the middle of the street. Mr. Hartwell shook his head admiringly.

"That one always hits the nail on the head, don't she, Harry?"

Marcia was pleased but mystified at the merry reaction to her question, and seeing her puzzled frown Mr. Hartwell hastened to say that Mabel was in the best of health and gaining steadily, at last report weighing two hundred pounds and fit as a fiddle.

"A bull fiddle," said Papa, which convulsed his friend.

It was nearly eight o'clock when they reached the Fair Store building. A dark doorway led to the upstairs apartments and ballroom. A small blue light at the landing gave a grisly glow to the hall, dimly indicating a rotten board in the floor and a broken banister. Bad plumbing and the circumstance of street cats using the vestibule for a comfort station lent an intimate aroma to the place, not particularly mellowed by the Corylopsis incense burning in the ballroom's Ladies' Parlor. On the first door of the second floor was a placard bearing the news, "Odd Fellows Dance. Admission Fifty Cents, Ladies Free," and issuing from this spot could be heard sounds of an orchestra tuning up. Other doors led to the Fair Store stockrooms, a Christian Science Reading Room, a dentist's office, and at the end of the hall the Novelty Shop. This was Grandma's new headquarters. Marcia clutched Lena's arm as they heard the well-remembered slippered footsteps coming to answer their knock. Lena jerked her arm free.

"Remember what I told you," Lena whispered sharply. "I'm the one that's going to stay here."

It was always discouraging to have others calm in moments your own heart was thundering with wild rapture, and Grandma was as calm as ever at sight of her callers.

"Grandma. Oh, Grandma," cried Marcia, flinging herself at the old lady the instant the door opened and trembling with delight. But Grandma's pleasure in seeing her family was in no way proportionate to the visitors' estimation of the joy they were bestowing. She accepted their embraces with moderate warmth and welcomed them into her parlor with more pride in a parlor of her own than in the callers.

"They can't take away my independence," she said, patting Mr. Hartwell fondly on the arm. "So long as I've got friends like Mr. Sweeney and Mrs. Carmel here I don't need to take anything from my family."

Mrs. Carmel, it seemed, was busy in the kitchen over a large iron pot of fondant, muttering like a witch as she stirred it. She hoped they would excuse her for continuing this chore, because the truth was their chocolate fondant had caught on like a house afire, and they had to be on their toes every minute, meeting the demand. London Junction might be behind the times in some ways but not in its candy tastes.

"You folks have a good talk," she benignly advised, and then with a wheezy chuckle, "you gentlemen take a good look at my partner there and see if you notice anything."

At this Grandma blushingly stroked her hair, and all exclaimed at once on this startling change. Yes, she said, it was true she was wearing a transformation. For years it had been recommended to her by friends who found it astonishing for a woman of her youthful appearance to have gray hair. A purchase of a box of oddments from a fire sale had yielded this wig, and since no one wanted to buy it Grandma had appropriated it for her own use. Moreover, in this business, closely connected with fashions as it was, a woman had to look her best. The wig was nut brown and reared up in luxuriant tiers to a crown of tight curls falling neatly over a high amber comb.

"By Jove, you don't look a day over thirty-five!" exclaimed Papa.

Grandma explained that she dared not wear the device all the time, for fear her daughter Lois would see her in it and go

into a jealous rage. She might be obliged to give it up altogether if a customer should take a fancy to it. She said she had
happened to learn from a high-priced authority in Cleveland
that this very transformation represented the finest workman-
ship of its kind outside New York City. Little experiences
while wearing it had borne out this theory. For instance, on
streetcars in Cleveland perfect strangers would stare and then
accost her.

"Excuse me, madam," they had said more than once, "that
is one of the most beautiful wigs I ever saw." Parties would
cross the street, staring, and say, "You don't know me from
Adam but I just have to ask you where you got that wonderful transformation. I've never seen anything like it and I've
travelled all over the country."

"I feel younger in it, too," confessed Grandma. "Mrs.
Carmel's been after me to get my teeth pulled out too and
get a set but that means money."

"I tell her if she wants to beautify herself, might as well go
the whole hog," whistled Mrs. Carmel, chuckling so that the
velvet bow she wore in her own hair fell in the pot of boiling
candy and had to be fished out with a dipper.

The strains of the orchestra came through the walls and a
drum roll shook the floor.

"Dance," Grandma explained complacently. "There's
something going on here every minute. Sometimes two
things."

She produced a bakery cake and a pot of coffee from the
stove, and passed these around.

"You can't beat bakery cake," she said. "Nothing tastes
better than good bakery bread, too. I like being up to the
minute. I don't listen to all that talk about old-fashioned
home baking. I've tasted plenty of soggy home baking, I can
tell you."

Mr. Hartwell and Papa examined the wares with professional interest, recommending a touch here and there. Mr.
Hartwell recalled that by chance he had a bottle of whiskey
on his hip he had happened absentmindedly to pick up in his
room and begged permission to serve himself and friend
Willard. Permission was granted at once.

"A drinking man don't feel right when he's not drinking," Grandma stated. "That's why Wally never felt good."

"Where is Uncle Wally?" asked Marcia.

"Went back to his daughter in Elmville after the fire," Grandma said. "Slept in the barn there, and when he didn't show up for meals for a couple of days they went out and found him lying there in the hay, dead as you please. Martha said the horses wouldn't touch the hay for days."

Marcia thought of poor old Uncle Wally all still and cold in the haymow, nobody missing him for days. That was what people did to old men, maybe old ladies too, only women were stronger.

"Well, we all got to go some time," Grandma added comfortably.

Lena was singing "Wrap Me in a Bundle, Dear, and Take Me Home with You," with the orchestra next door. She and Marcia danced to it, counting carefully. Florrie sat on a stool in the kitchen, greasing pans for Mrs. Carmel. Florrie loved helping, but her stepmother wouldn't let her. She wanted to pick up some hairpins scattered over the floor, but Grandma said no, that if she needed a hairpin she knew right where they were, one under the counter, one under the big rocker, and one under the sink. Once you started putting things where they belonged you never knew where anything was.

Mr. Hartwell said Grandma had more common sense in her little finger than most women had in their whole body. He applauded the two girls' dancing and nudged Papa.

"I'll take your daughter in for this dance," he said. "How about it, Lena?"

"But it's not free," Lena protested.

"Nothing's free," Mr. Hartwell merrily answered. Marcia watched, in an anguish of jealousy while Mr. Hartwell took Lena across the hall to the Odd Fellows' Dance. It was some consolation to think of how mad it would make Her when She found it out. Marcia went out to stand in the hall, watching. She saw Bonnie Purdy dancing with a tall man from out of town. You could always tell people from out of town because they looked better and had a mysterious swagger. Maybe everybody looked better out of town. Mr. Hartwell was holding Lena off proudly as if she was a little doll, and Lena was tossing her head and pointing her toes carefully, pretending not to notice Marcia watching.

When the dance was over Mr. Hartwell didn't bring Lena back but stood in the middle of the floor tapping his foot and clapping his hands for an encore. Marcia went back to Grandma's. Papa was sitting on a stool by Grandma, holding her hand. They both looked very weepy.

"No, sir, Harry, there'll never be anybody like Daisy," Grandma said. "I remember when I sat up with her over the third baby. When she came to I said, 'Well, Daisy, that makes three.' And she said—she was always teasing me—'All right, mom, isn't it about time you told me the facts of life?' "

"We were always laughing, having a good time over something," Papa said, wiping his eyes. "Sometimes I think we shouldn't ever have left Peach Street."

"No, sir, I don't think you should have," Grandma said, solemnly shaking her monument of curls. "Things wouldn't have turned out this way if you'd stayed there. Well, you've got a new wife now. I hear she's got a nice appearance."

"And we've got the Furness house," Papa said. "I always told Daisy we would but she wouldn't believe me. Maybe I tried to do too much for Daisy."

"Maybe you did, Harry," Grandma admitted. "All Daisy ever wanted was you. I guess you wanted to spoil her."

"I did," Papa said, wiping his nose. "I wanted Daisy to have everything, but Daisy didn't need fine clothes to look good. She looked good in any old rag."

Mr. Hartwell brought Lena back, with a deep bow of thanks. She looked, he said, more and more like her Aunt Lois. It was time to go, and Mrs. Carmel gave the girls each a bag of candy mixed with salted peanuts. Mr. Hartwell and Papa had a final drink out of the bottle before leaving, and they both informed Grandma that she was just about the finest woman they'd ever had the pleasure of knowing. Mr. Hartwell said he would give a thousand dollars if his own mother, also a wonderful woman, could meet her. He hadn't seen his mother for five years, he said, and a man felt pretty bad when he hadn't seen his mother for five years. Grandma said it was too bad his mother didn't live nearer to him, but he said it wasn't that, but every time he was in his home town, Chicago, he was so head over heels in work he didn't have a chance to run out to see her.

Marcia and Lena waited with falling spirits for a chance to tell Grandma their own problem but there wasn't any way of getting her attention without Papa hearing. Glumly, Marcia wondered if Grandma would save them anyway. Nobody was interested in anybody much but themselves. Maybe Grandma would take sides with their stepmother.

"I'll call on your wife one of these days," Grandma said to Papa. "Soon as business lets up I'll drop in. I've never been through the Furness house."

They left Mr. Hartwell at the Elks House, and almost at once their gaiety vanished. Marcia walked behind, thinking her heart would break. Mr. Hartwell had danced only with Lena, and if anybody was to stay with Grandma it would be Lena. There was never any hope, anywhere. Even Papa's steps lagged as they approached their house, their good time forgotten in the apprehension of what was awaiting them. It was after ten and the house was dark. The girls started for the back door but Papa harshly ordered them to follow him up the front walk to the front door. He took out a key and unlocked it as his wife, in a night hair net and blue flannel kimono, turned on the stair lights. "You're not bringing them all in the front way, Harry!" She cried out. "Wait, I'll open the back door."

"I'll come in any damn door I please," shouted Papa. "I'll come down the chimney if I damn well like."

He tramped upstairs, roughly brushing her aside. The girls tiptoed up behind him, careful not to scar up the stairs or the banister, but their stepmother followed them on her knees, wiping each step. Papa went in the bedroom and banged the door.

"Did your father stop anywhere on the way to your grandmother's?" She asked Lena sharply.

"No," said Lena.

"No," said Marcia.

"No, Ma'am," said Florrie, lips trembling. "Oh, don't whip Papa, please!"

28

"I feel sorry for Her," Florrie said one day, in troubled tones.

Her older sisters regarded her with a baleful look. They had been forbidden to leave the house or to play cards, because it was Sunday, and they could not go to Epworth League meeting because word had gotten round that these services ended up in kissing games in the choir loft. (Lena had taken a prominent part in these activities, though Marcia had unfortunately not been invited.) They could sit on the porch if they liked, but they didn't like because they had been forced to change from their Sunday dresses to patched blue calico, and someone might see them, especially since it was their gloomy conviction that She made the patches big on purpose. So they sat in their room, sulking in the twilight.

"What are you sorry for Her about?" demanded Marcia. "She slapped your hands for crocheting, didn't she?"

Florrie acknowledged this.

"She cries all the time, though," she said.

"Let Her cry," said Lena, scowling at the tenderhearted little sister. Then curiosity overcame her and she added, "What does She cry about?"

"It's about money, and Papa cries too, I think," Florrie said. "Her eyes are red all the time, and She never puts her rats in her hair any more. She even scolded Minelda, too."

"She's getting meaner every minute, ever since Grandma's been in town," Marcia said. "She shook you for coughing tonight, and said you just did it to make Papa worry. I don't see why you feel sorry for Her."

"I feel sorry for Her because She can't help being mean," Florrie said guiltily, knowing this confession of weakness would not please her sisters. "Marcia can't help spilling things and breaking things, and Papa can't help his temper, and She can't help being mean. I guess that's why Papa doesn't get mad at Her; it's because he knows She can't help it."

Lena and Marcia frowned into space, speculating on what mighty catastrophe could cause tears in Her eyes. The muffled voices of their father and Her in their own room down the hall encouraged Lena to creep down the hall to listen. She came back, nodding with satisfaction.

"It's about money, all right," she said. "She keeps saying, 'Oh, Harry, why didn't you tell me before? You know I trusted you.' Papa's getting sort of mad. He keeps saying, 'Can't I get it through your head that I wouldn't have touched a penny of your damned money if I hadn't thought I could put it back? How many times have I got to explain it to you?' She says She can't get over his lying about his salary, and now that She's used up all her money She can't run the house on what little he makes, and pay taxes and pay his old bills. He says nobody would be after him about the old bills if he didn't live in this big house, and that's Her fault."

"Maybe we'll get sent to an orphanage," Marcia said hopefully.

"Florrie, maybe, but we're too old, I think," Lena said.

Marcia took a turn at eavesdropping next and was able to report that there was mention of Grandpa Willard coming, and something about his pension coming in handy. This was cheerful news, because there was the fond belief that a visitor in the house would keep Her from nagging at them. The third floor rooms might be unlocked then, too, and She wouldn't dare refuse them books or magazines if some relative was around. Things would certainly be different.

The next day Papa dragged out one of the attic mattresses to be aired, indicating that a visitor was expected. Marcia disobeyed the order not to go to Grandma's except with special permission, and played hookey after morning recess in order to inform her grandma of the happy prospect. It was disconcerting to have Grandma shrug off the news with a patronizing comment that the old man was better off in the Soldiers' Home. Later, when Grandpa Willard appeared in brand new civilian clothes Marcia heard him inquire benignly of Papa after the "old lady."

"Is she still alive? Well, well!" he exclaimed, shaking his head in amazement. "Got all her faculties still? Well, I'll be doggoned. When I saw the old lady ten, twenty years ago, it seemed to me her memory was beginning to fail a little. Well, well, thank goodness I got my memory."

Old men didn't like old ladies any more than old ladies liked old men; far from common experiences making them sympathetic, it made them even gleeful over a contemporary's infirmities, as if life was a see-saw, the other going down made you automatically go up. Marcia resented this contempt her grandparents had for each other's antiquity, and caught her grandfather in a memory lapse, after his slighting reference to Grandma Reed's failing. Grandpa gravely considered her accusation.

"No, my memory ain't going one bit," he declared. "It's just that there's a lot of things I never knew right in the first place, that's all."

Grandpa and Papa had a talk on the back steps after supper. Papa said the way he figured was that it was lonesome spending your last days in a Home when you had children ready and willing to board you. Daisy had always wanted him to live with them, but it never worked out that way. But now that they had this big house Papa figured it would tickle Daisy to know Pa was at last staying with them. He could mow the lawn and help around the garden, and take it easy the little time remaining to him. Staying with his folks he got his full pension instead of the Home taking most of it, and he could pay board. Grandpa said money never meant anything to him and he'd just as soon turn the whole pension over to Harry and just keep out enough for tobacco and reading matter, maybe a beer now and then. He didn't want to be any trouble to anybody, and She might as well know that right away. He'd make his own bed and keep his own room tidy, and get his own meals. Papa said he'd send word to the rest of the family around the state to come see him there, but Grandpa said that would make trouble for Her and not to bother.

It took Grandpa very little time to gather the situation, especially after his new daughter-in-law had hidden his pipe tobacco, thrown out his pile of the *Home Weekly*, and put newspapers over the floor of his room so he wouldn't step on the parquet. Without saying a word to anyone he took his cot down to the cellar and fixed up a corner by the bowling alley for his room. Papa didn't say a word when he came home at night and found this change made, but he rummaged around the attic for a washstand and couple of chairs to add to the cellar room. Neither did his wife mention the move, but silently set to work scrubbing and fumigating the little bedroom which Grandpa had just vacated. She did think of little things each day to remind Grandpa that a room in the cellar was no excuse for slovenliness. He must keep the windows locked so that burglars wouldn't get in that way, and he must not go prowling in the potato bins or the preserve closet, for sometimes things would turn, just having sick old folks breathing on them. He wasn't to smoke in there either, because what with his pipe chugging away and his pile of old dirty papers, like as not he'd set the house on fire and they'd all be burned in their sleep. Grandpa promised to step outside when he wanted to smoke, and keep his part of the cellar clean as a whistle. He got up early in the morning and went out, nobody knew where, and came home at supper time to smoke out in the yard. Marcia and Lena sat beside him, Florrie on his lap, asking for stories about when he was a drummer boy. If the occasion was opportune, they told their own stories about Her. Grandpa listened discreetly to these confidences, offering neither advice nor consolation. He wasn't any help at all, the girls decided, any more than Grandma Reed was. Old folks were just as afraid as children were; you couldn't count on them for anything. Marcia, reflecting on this, felt a sudden wave of fear. Supposing when she grew old—that is, providing there would ever be an end to this awful eternity of childhood—she would have a daughter just like her stepmother, and the daughter would make her sleep in the cellar like Uncle Wally and Grandpa had had to do.

"I won't have any daughters then," she decided. "No family at all; that's the only safe thing."

She spoke of this to Lena and Grandpa when they were raking the grass. It was fun raking, but they had to pretend it wasn't or She wouldn't ask them to do it. She already suspected that this chore was not sufficiently in the nature of punishment, for She peered out the kitchen window and called out, "For goodness sake, don't ruin that rake, and there's no need chopping into the turf that way! Looks like a herd of buffalo had been let loose on it."

"We've got to walk *some place*. We can't fly over it," Marcia said in a loud enough tone to be considered audacious by Lena, but not loud enough to reach the kitchen.

Grandpa had a crick in his back and took time out for a chew of tobacco.

"If you don't have any family you'll just be an old maid," Lena said crushingly. "How do you think you'll like that, smarty?"

"I'd like it fine," Marcia boldly replied, hoping God wouldn't hear this and take her seriously. "I don't see any sense in getting married and having a lot of family to be mean to me."

"You get used to it," Grandpa said comfortably. "If it ain't your own family it's other people's. Might as well be picked on by your own flesh and blood."

"Marcia's going to be an old maid whether she wants to or not," Lena said complacently. "The boys don't like her because she's so crazy."

This had such a ring of authority that Marcia kept a moody silence. It was a fact that boys sent Lena notes all the time and followed her home from school as far as they dared. The only boy who sent Marcia notes was little David Gross, who was only eleven, small for his age, and called sissy by the class. Even the high-school boys and railroad men in the Elks Pool Room whistled at Lena as she passed, but Marcia walked past much slower and oftener with never a whistle. If she had heard one she would have shrieked out her delight, "Oh, thank you, thank you, thank you!" It was Lena's yellow curls that did the trick, and then her rosy cheeks. Nobody ever liked hair-colored hair, straight at that, like Marcia's. The future looked very gloomy so far as romance was concerned. Probably there'd be nothing left for her but to be rich and famous. But even famous people, married or no, often ended up with cruel landlords and mean uncles throwing them into institutions, locking them in attics, or putting them on the street. Marcia thought very likely Lena would be the one to turn on her in her hour of need and order her off to a cot in the cellar. Lena was sometimes almost as bad as her stepmother. Lena walked on the other side of the street rather than walk to school with Marcia, and whenever Marcia told her anything Lena exclaimed coldly, "Oh, you're crazy." If it was something Marcia had read in a book, Lena said it was just poppycock, because the only persons Lena trusted were Mary Evelyn and Myrtle Chase.

Grandpa was a great reader and discussed books with Marcia. His son's wife was fit to be tied when She found out he had brought a box of paper-backed novels from the Soldiers' Home. There was no way She could forbid his lending them to Marcia, however, because She did not dare say all the things she'd like to Grandpa—not yet, anyway. Marcia read countless novels by E. P. Roe, Charlotte Braeme, Bulwer Lytton, Mary J. Holmes, and others, but they left her baffled and angry.

"The lord always marries the governess," she complained earnestly to Grandpa, "but it turns out in the end she is really a princess anyway, so it doesn't prove anything. I'll bet he wouldn't have married her if he didn't know she was going to turn out to be rich and noble. No, sir, there isn't one story where the governess stays just a governess, because if she did nobody would ever marry her."

"Now, don't be so critical," rebuked Grandpa. "Read all the books you like but don't go round criticizing."

"Well, I just don't see any sense in the way these people in these books act," grumbled Marcia. "I should think if anybody could marry whoever he pleased it would be a lord, so what do they make so much fuss about it for?"

"You don't know what you're talking about," Grandpa stated flatly. "The party that writes up all these stories ought to know whereof he speaks. If that's the way he likes to have people act, he's got a right to make them act that way."

"Marcia's always crazy," said Lena.

There was no use talking to anybody because nobody understood anything, except maybe Florrie, who was so anxious to be obliging that she agreed with everybody. Whenever you said outright what you were thinking people stared at you curiously, as if thoughts were something you should keep to yourself.

Still, there was David Gross, even if he was a sissy. Marcia hoped her stepmother wouldn't find out about her secret intimacy with the Gross family. Lena might tell. Florrie knew about it because she went there with Marcia often. The

Grosses lived in the brick house behind the schoolhouse, so that Marcia and Florrie could run in and out (the front door, too, and without knocking, at Mrs. Gross' own insistence) during recess or any time they had a chance. David and Marcia acted out stories they had read or made up together. David's mother taught Florrie to crochet and to play the piano, but Florrie had to keep her new accomplishment secret from her stepmother for fear She would scold, fearing some future violation of Her own piano which was for looks. David's mother read out loud to them and let them sit in the living room or play games anywhere in the house, make fudge in the kitchen, race up and down stairs or take any books they liked out of the bookcase. Nothing was locked in the Gross home. They had a gramophone and Mrs. Gross explained the stories of operas to them when she played the records. She was a soft-voiced, plain, gentle woman with curly gray hair and ruffled dresses. Florrie worshipped her because she let her hug and kiss her, a privilege Florrie was denied by her self-conscious sisters and even by Papa, since it irritated Her so much to see. She did not look like other mothers in London Junction, but seemed more like somebody's sister, or like their Cousin Isobel. It was certain that Mrs. Gross was not beautiful the way Aunt Lois was, or like Isobel, but her way of talking and smiling with her eyes, which had unusually heavy lashes, presented a new definition of beauty. It must be Eastern graces, Marcia decided, and determined that she too would go to Philadelphia or Washington when she grew up and learn little ways like Mrs. Gross.

The Grosses had moved to London Junction from Washington, but after the first excitement over a new family in town, with the local ladies leaving cards, the different ministers' wives calling, and invitations to town functions issued, they were left to themselves. Mrs. Gross had not responded to the welcome and, without being rude, had quietly established her family as being self-sufficient. David did not join in the school games, and was too clever in his studies to be regarded with anything but contempt and suspicion. Moreover, he was almost two years younger than the others in his class and a head shorter than Marcia. He wore thick glasses, braces on his teeth, in addition to pronouncing grass "grahs" and

water "wottah" instead of "worter." His doom so far as popularity was concerned was sealed the day he came running
into class late, apologizing to the teacher, "Pardon my dishevelled appearance, but I've been in the woods collecting
some botanical specimens." A low hiss went around the
room, in which Marcia joined, though she was secretly impressed with this bold speech. A few days later she settled her
own hash by using "feminine prerogative" in a composition
and was met with the same hiss when the work was read
aloud. Compositions were exchanged for students to grade
each other and David wrote on Marcia's, "100% plus." So
they were obliged to be friends, quietly, and helped each
other with their compositions. David explained to Marcia that
"*Helas*" was not a girl's name, and Marcia explained to David
that the seven sisters in his story could not be just three or
four months apart in their ages. It was a stimulating and helpful friendship, even though Lena jeered at it.

There was in the Gross family an older sister named Fannie
who was hump-backed and painted copies of famous masters
in a room she called her "studio." (She gave Marcia her copy
of the Rosa Bonheur picture that used to hang in the Elmville
house.) Then there was a little old lady in a wheelchair, called
Aunt Rachel, who muttered in a foreign language and had a
mat of fuzzy white curls. Hump-back, foreign language
speaker, and sissy in the family were social hurdles that even a
fictional noblewoman could not take without some embarrassment, so Marcia and Florrie endeavored to disguise their
intimacy with the new family. Mr. Gross never appeared because, David explained, his family, with the exception of Aunt
Rachel, who was a little crazy, had never forgiven him for
marrying a Gentile. So, to conciliate his aging parents, he had
gone back to stay with them in the East.

"But Fannie and I aren't Gentiles," David proudly explained. "Mother has Aunt Rachel teach us our Bible and
once a month she takes us to Cleveland to the synagogue, because she knows it pleases Father. When he comes back he'll
be proud of us."

Florrie wanted to know what a Gentile was, and Marcia impatiently explained it was some kind of people in the Bible.
Mrs. Gross, in spite of being a Gentile, seemed like anybody

else, so that except for the soft speech, different from the nasal shrill voices of other London Junction women, she had no strange Biblical characteristics. Marcia was puzzled when David declared she too was Gentile, and hastily assured him that she was no such thing, being First Church of Christ and part Welsh and English and Dutch. Later she asked Grandpa about this, and after some reflection he said they might be Gentiles when you got right down to it. He gave her a little dictionary for her birthday so she could look up things. She kept this in the carriage seat in the barn so nobody could take it away, and also her composition books where she wrote down things that nobody, not even Grandpa, would discuss. Mrs. Gross loaned her new novels to let Grandpa read, such as *The Calling of Dan Matthews*, *The Beloved Vagabond*, and *The Girl from the Limberlost*. Sometimes she was so deep in these worlds that she hardly noticed she was still being whipped for not answering when spoken to. Florrie did her crying for her. They didn't tell the Grosses about their stepmother, because they were ashamed. It would be terrible if people got to feeling sorry for them the way they were for the barefoot poor children who lived in shacks along the railroad. It would be terrible, too, if people wondered why Papa didn't notice what was going on, but Lena's theory was that he did but he didn't know what to do about it, especially since She was good to him at least. After they went to bed, She tiptoed in their room, and while they pretended to be asleep She noiselessly went through all their dresser drawers and took away anything she thought was nonsense, such as Lena's La Blanche Face Powder and the samples she was always sending away for. She finally found Florrie's crocheting and took that away, and even after Marcia hid her novels under the mattress she reached under and took them out, so the only way she could get them back was to say they belonged to the Church Library.

"As if I would still be reading the church library books," Marcia later exclaimed to her grandfather. "In those books the moral is always that the poor boy can go to heaven quicker than the rich boy, but then the story has the poor boy get a lot richer than the rich boy, so finally there isn't any moral, except you'd better get rich to be on the safe side."

"Well, that's the way books are and you gotta take 'em that

way," Grandpa advised her. "If books was anything like real life nobody'd want to waste time reading 'em."

Florrie had nightmares from being waked up by creeping hands under her pillow, so she was punished for this. She sometimes walked in her sleep and it made it all the worse for her when she yelled, "Don't let the witch get me, don't let her." She didn't dare tell Mrs. Gross the crocheting had been taken away, so she said she got tired of it. But secretly she got a piece of twine and a bent hairpin and hid it with Marcia's notebooks in the carriage seat. She couldn't resist bringing it in the house one night and hiding it under her pillow. It was going to be a penwiper for Marcia, she promised, when she finished crocheting it. But in the morning it was gone. The next night Florrie cried herself to sleep and then walked, in her sleep, straight into Papa's bedroom and shouted in an awful voice, "Give me my string and hairpin; I want to crochet. You give it to me or I'll tell the devil on you."

Papa woke up, frightened out of his wits, and picked up Florrie. Minelda in the crib started to bawl, too. Florrie woke up at Papa's voice and burst into hysterics, telling the whole story about her crochet hook and the string. Papa was very quiet and asked his wife what this was all about.

"Of course, I put it away," She said stoutly. "Florrie's fidgety enough as it is without giving her more things to fidget with. Next she'll have St. Vitus' dance."

Papa carried Florrie back to her bed, where she sobbed, trembling for hours. Lena and Marcia were afraid they would catch it on Florrie's account but they heard Papa arguing in the next room for a long time, and in the morning their stepmother's eyes were as red-rimmed as Florrie's, and she was more subdued than they had ever seen her. The next day, however, Marcia could not find her notebooks or dictionary and her stepmother found her looking for them all over the barn.

"If you're looking for that trash of yours, I just burned it," She said shrilly. "I'm not going to look after a loony child in this family."

Marcia's chest filled with murderous fury. She felt faint with the desire to kill Her. She looked around to see if Grandpa and Lena had heard her precious things called "trash" and burned, but they pretended not to hear. That was the trouble with everybody in the same boat; they wouldn't lift a finger to help you because they were afraid of catching it themselves.

"That was a twenty-five-cent notebook," Marcia said icily. "My father gave it to me."

"It'll be a long time before your father gives you another twenty-five cents to waste on such junk, when you're needing schoolbooks," She said, her eyes glittering. She started to go indoors, but decided to round off the discipline.

"Mr. Willard, you don't need to sit out front gabbing with those girls so everybody can hear you a block away. Anybody eating us out of house and home ought to make themselves useful."

"You can't talk that way to Grandpa," Marcia shouted, shaking her fist.

"Hush," said Grandpa quietly. He didn't look at Her as She locked the screen door to prevent them coming indoors without permission, but scratched his head thoughtfully. Then he stumped down the front walk, holding himself very straight, the way a drummer-boy should. Marcia and Lena did not look at each other. Marcia shut her lips tightly together. Make yourself numb, she said to herself, draw deep breaths. Pretend you're dead. If you're dead it doesn't matter about notebooks or dictionaries or crochet hooks or Grandpa. Nobody can hurt a dead person.

It was some satisfaction to have Papa worried about Grandpa not showing up for supper, and Her sullen uneasiness. She chewed her fingernails every time Papa went down the cellar to look for Grandpa, and gave a gasp of relief when the familiar step was heard on the front walk, finally.

"Your father's been drinking, that's what," She said loudly. "Listen to the way he's walking. Well! Just one thing more on my shoulders!"

29

The miracle that had failed to take place with Grandma in town and with the arrival of Grandpa Willard actually occurred when Vance Hawkins moved in with them. Next to Minelda, She prized her younger brother Vance, and talked about him so much that Papa often got jealous. Vance had been everywhere. ("A lot of other folks have travelled around, too," Papa said to this.) He had spent a year in military school, so that he had many rich friends contacted there. ("Why doesn't he go stay with them then, if those rich people are so crazy about him?" Papa inquired.) Brother Vance was an expert telegrapher and was going to work in the London Junction Western Union office for sixty-five dollars a month, temporarily, of course, since his opportunities with his rich friends were unlimited. He had dropped telegraphy to work for the National Cash Register people in Dayton, but some girl named Mildred started chasing him and blaming things on him that were none of his doing, so he had to clear out. In Detroit he had worked for Ford Motors at thirty-five dollars a week, if you please, but had been lucky enough to catch his toe in some machine and received $3,000 damages. "It's not a fortune," he had modestly written concerning this triumph, "but it's a start. You don't need a big toe to walk with anyway." The reason he said he was taking the London Junction job was that he had invested his little sum so shrewdly and in such a tight way that he could not get at it somehow. He wrote quite frankly that he wanted to make sort of a visit with his favorite sister instead of boarding at some stranger's, because he wanted to save his salary with the purpose of settling in California.

Papa said the family was big enough as it was.

"It's all YOUR family," his wife plaintively answered. "It's not mine. If you see fit to have your father live with us in the house my money paid for, I certainly have a right to ask my only brother. Goodness knows, it's time I had some of my own kin around for protection. As near as I can make out, Harry, you want not only all your own family but your first wife's family living off of us. If I didn't put my foot down I'll bet you'd have old lady Reed move in on us."

She liked to talk that way about Grandma because it annoyed Papa as much as it pained the children.

"Will Vance stay in the cellar with Grandpa?" Florrie innocently asked.

"There's an old mattress in the potato bin. He could fix himself up pretty comfortable there," Grandpa chuckled, fondly patting Florrie's head.

But Vance was to have not only the biggest bedroom on the third floor but the freedom of the house as well. The girls first recognized the miracle when they came home from school one day and found a young man reclining easily on the parlor davenport, with his feet thrown over the arm. They peeked in, mindful of their place, and were shocked when he genially urged them to come on in and get acquainted. Their stepmother impatiently nodded permission. She was flushed and smiling with pride in her visitor, so excited she forgot to scowl warningly at the girls as they walked gingerly over the broadloom carpet. Even the piano was unlocked and had three pieces of sheet music arranged on it as if anybody that wanted could sit down and run through these gems, "Till the Sands of the Desert Grow Cold," "Put On Your Old Gray Bonnet," and "Come, Josephine, in My Flying Machine."

One good thing was that Vance did not look like his sister Idah. That was something. He was long and lean, with a way of leaping around as if he was made of rubber. He had a hook nose and fishy gray eyes set astonishingly close together for the simple reason that his narrow face left no room for them to spread out. His long head, in fact, seemed to have a dimension missing, being all profile, rising from lively Adam's apple over the nasal hump and up to the peak of his scalp, from which a fountain of greasy yellow hair sprawled in all directions. It was a pity he did not have his sister's cosmetic privileges, for his skin was decorated with a pink rash which, She explained to Papa, had been faithfully his since infancy.

"His blood is too rich," She explained proudly. "All the Hawkins have rich blood."

As if these charms were not enough, he had a habit of holding his mouth agape in a half smile, revealing an extraordinary set of pale salmon gums studded with cigarette-stained stumps of teeth. The reason for keeping his mouth open appeared to be no vanity over his remarkable expanse of gums, but a convenience for jumping into the conversation with no loss of time. It was plain that listening to anybody was a hardship; he could scarcely wait for his chance to hop in, usually with an anecdote prefaced by the phrase, "like the fellow in the show." His words were lost in uncontrollable chortles in which Papa, coming home early to welcome his in-law, only feebly joined. Vance had a baffling way of darting his eyes around and behind you, so that you found yourself following his gaze uneasily, half expecting some strange tropical bird to be wafting about your head, or possibly some psychic phenomena to be manifesting itself. His sister could not restrain her pride in him, and nodded triumphantly around the room at every remark he made. There, that's the way to talk, she seemed to say; here's a party that knows what it's all about.

Papa made a polite effort to be amused by the newcomer, but it had never been his nature to be impressed by anybody but himself, so in due course his basic irritation betrayed itself.

"I guess there's not many towns of any size in this country that Vance hasn't seen," his sister declared. "It's an education just listening to him tell it."

"I covered a good deal of territory myself," Papa reminded her. "I guess I've been around as much as Vance here."

Vance said, all joking aside, his mind was pretty set on making California his permanent home. With his damages he could live pretty well, working when he felt like it, laying off when he pleased. There was a chance of getting more damages too, he said, if anything should complicate the condition of his foot. He'd seen to that, all right, and didn't need a lawyer to tell him. Papa said personally he didn't give a snap of his little finger about California, or Dayton, or Detroit either for that matter. Give him a real town like Cleveland or, say, Atlantic City, or Buffalo. Or if you wanted good climate and plenty of sun take a little place like Elmville, where the sun shone all the time and a man could raise a family on the fat of the land for fifteen dollars a week, eggs twelve cents a dozen, all the berries you could put up free.

During the evening Grandpa listened for a while silently, then disappeared. The girls were pleased with this new life in the house and the change in their stepmother. Vance was taken with Lena, ogling her with open admiration. He called her "Blondie" and pinched her cheeks. He held Minelda on his lap until she dampened it, a crisis that brought an angry oath to his lips and resulted in Minelda being dumped wailing on the floor.

"My best gray suit," he said reproachfully, shaking his head. "I got two others but this is my best. Always wear gray 'cause it don't show the dander like blue."

The episode brought an end to the gala evening and reminded Her that the girls had been neglected in discipline, so they were sent off to bed with instructions not to horse around up there and bring the house down.

"How about me and Lena taking a little walk first?" Vance asked, but his sister said, a little sharply, that Lena was no age to be going walking with boys, especially a grown man of twenty-six.

After the first excitement of the new arrival, the family settled down to normal; that is, She made it clear that Vance's freedom with the house was no reason for the others to follow suit. He had a front door key and sometimes when he came in late at night he even brought company with him. They could be heard rattling around the kitchen, eating snacks. When Papa heard this he would go to the head of the stairs in his nightshirt and roar down, "What's going on down there? That you, Vance? Can't you let people sleep, damn it?" This would wake up the rest of the house. Minelda would start bawling and asking for a drink of water, or her teddy bear, or the washcloth she chewed herself to sleep on. Her mother would protest that Harry mustn't be too hard on Vance; he was just a kid. Papa would say kid, nothing; at twenty-six he himself was raising a family. The girls would sit up in bed, whispering conjectures about what Vance was up to, and morning would find everybody sullen or irascible.

Vance brought presents to Lena, and could not, as he himself cheerfully confessed, keep his hands off her. He went to dances in Lesterville and brought her souvenirs from there, and heart-shaped candy boxes tied with big blue satin bows. He even asked her to go with him to dances, but Papa wouldn't allow it, much as Lena wanted to go. But he got them in trouble by inviting them to come in the parlor. His sister came in one day and found Florrie playing "Glow Worm," taught her by Mrs. Gross, while Vance taught Lena the schottische, with the carpet rolled up. As might have been expected, Vance did not take any blame for this outrage, but watched with a shrug while his sister hustled the girls out of the room, Florrie by the ear.

"You take things too serious, Idah," he said, dropping on to the sofa again with his copy of *Argosy.* "You're way behind the times."

Papa did not talk much when Vance was at supper, because Vance did all the talking, with his sister's approving interpolations. Grandpa did not even come to meals. Papa said he thought he was living on the free lunch at Jake's Saloon, and bags of gumdrops he kept in his dresser drawer. It was just as well he didn't come, because meals were skimpier and skimpier. Suppers were half-cooked potatoes fried in lard, a few gray little sausages, some stringbeans or peas, also mysteriously gray and greasy, and burnt cookies or maple syrup and soda biscuits, so consistently overdosed with cream of tartar that the girls thought it was deliberate. Papa did not eat much, and his daughters found out that it was because he dropped off at Grandma Reed's before coming home every day, and had a bite. They knew he did not like Vance being the kingpin in the house, but he did not quarrel with him. Having Papa gloomy made him seem closer to them now, and his irritation at Minelda's whining seemed something in their favor.

Marcia stopped in the Western Union office whenever Vance was on duty, and he let her read all the telegrams, and showed her how to type on the Oliver Invisible Typewriter. Next door to the telegraph office was Chase's Music Store, and in no time at all Vance had made an intimate friend of Gertrude Chase, the young lady who demonstrated sheet music. He let Marcia run the telegraph office while he went next door and sang, "Give Me Once More the Sunshine of Your Smile," through his nose, with Gertrude earnestly banging out the accompaniment. Marcia was to tell any impatient customers that the operator was checking on some mix-up at the tower, the railroad telegraph office, but anybody could tell this was a lie, hearing Vance's adenoidal warble echoing through the piano showroom next door. Nobody else in London Junction had time to hang around a music store singing the new songs. As many of the telegrams were concerned with Papa's business, saying "Aunt Sade low, come at once," or "Funeral Tuesday at four," or "Order coffin for Father at Carson's," Papa had even further reason for annoyance at his house guest.

"He's costing me a fortune," Papa declared, "just by never being on the job. Why, God Almighty, he spends hours at a time in the music store. You can even see him leaning over the piano there any time of day, through the plate glass window."

"I guess if any harm was done the inspector would let him know," said Mrs. Willard. "He's quicker than most boys, so he can do his job a lot quicker."

But She confessed frankly that she was worried about all the town girls chasing after Vance. They just wouldn't let him be and one of these days he might give in to one of them, he was so good-natured. Papa said he guessed Vance could take care of himself if they started taking his clothes off. Vance himself declared the London Junction girls were pretty slow. The girls in Toledo knew how to show a fellow a good time, and when you got in the right crowd in Erie, Pennsylvania, you could have the time of your life. As a matter of fact, Vance said wherever he went he tried to get in with the right crowd right away, because it made all the difference in the world. The trouble with London Junction was that there wasn't any right crowd. You met the same bunch at the Odd Fellows' dances that you met at Sunday school picnics or Cosmopolitan Club balls. It made it hard for a fellow just come to town to pick out his bunch. Papa sarcastically replied that he guessed Vance had picked his bunch all right when he took Sadie Murphy behind the freight house and paid her off with two poker chips, so Sadie had indignantly told the town.

The more Vance burgeoned out as the town beau, the more depressed Papa became. Grandma Reed told the girls she hadn't heard Harry laugh since the night he and Ed Hartwell came to see her. Papa said it wasn't up to the manager of a furniture and funeral parlor to go round laughing at every little thing. The fact was that laughing took your mind off business and a fellow pushing forty didn't feel much like laughing anyway. At his age a man with Papa's responsible position had to watch his step. He got disgusted with these flybrains that ran around town with out-of-town girls, or

went on excursions to Cedar Point with ladies who were far
from wives. It was a shame, honest to God, to see some of
these men his own age get into a room at the London Junction Hotel and drink and play poker all night. You could tell
they didn't have the right kind of wife and home. Papa said
the young women were getting worse all the time, too. He
could see them passing the Store on Saturday nights, letting
some fellow hold on to their round, bare arm, knowing damn
well what he'd be after next, but these modern girls didn't
seem to care. He said when he walked home late Saturday
nights from the Store he could hear the couples spooning and
giggling on the dark porches, sometimes lying down together
in the hammocks. No yelling of "Now, now, stop! Now, I
warn you. Stop, I say!" with which any decent woman repelled a man's vulgar approaches. It made Papa shocked to
find that there were so many girls in town who let these
young fellows get away with murder. Take the family that
lived in the double house on Fourth where he and Daisy used
to live. The daughter there wasn't much older than Lena, but
she had some fellow kissing her on the porch and playing the
banjo every night. If Papa had been the girl's father he'd kick
the chap out before he got her in trouble.

This was Papa's new moral attitude brought about by
Vance's presence in the house, and Vance's doing all the
things Papa used to like to do. But the really staggering blow
came when Papa and wife and four daughters came home
from Minelda's baptism at church one evening and found
Vance sitting on the front porch with Bonnie Purdy and another couple. Papa turned pale and could not even speak for
a minute in answer to Bonnie's teasing "Hello, stranger." The
girls flung themselves on Bonnie rapturously till Papa harshly
ordered them to go indoors.

"Can we sit in the parlor while Bonnie is here?" Florrie
asked eagerly. This innocent betrayal of her stepmother's rules
annoyed both Her and Papa, especially since Bonnie laughingly said, "Isn't she darling? As if it wasn't her own home!"

After this remark there was nothing to be done but invite
the whole group into the parlor, where Bonnie gayly played
the piano for Vance to sing, and the girls sat, carefully motionless so as not to spoil anything, on the sofa. Papa wouldn't

look at Bonnie, because Vance sat on the piano bench with his arm around her.

"Come on, Harry, get out your guitar," Bonnie urged. "Girls, do make your father play like old times. I don't get to London Junction much any more, and I'd like to hear him for old time's sake."

Papa said brusquely that he had no time to tinker around like that any more. His wife sat stiffly on a straight chair, biting her fingernails and glaring at Bonnie's taking liberties with the piano. She could not resist getting a cloth finally and wiping off the keys the minute Bonnie took her hands off of them. The other girl who had come with Bonnie sat on the lap of her escort quite as if it was a matter of form rather than pleasure. She and Bonnie had come over from Lesterville, where Bonnie now worked, in the young man's automobile and they were driving back late that night. Bonnie was still pretty, but had new city ways such as crossing her plump legs rather high, showing her clocked black silk stockings and a pleated ruffle of purple taffeta petticoat. She had a purple silk scarf wound round her head for motoring, with strands of black hair looped out over her pink cheeks, and she had a rose silk jersey suit.

"Going with the boys yet, Lena?" she asked, which caused Lena to look in hasty apprehension at her stepmother.

"Yes, she does," Marcia jealously answered for her.

"I do not!" Lena flared up, glancing from her father to stepmother.

"Lena's my girl," Vance said. "Prettiest girl in the Junction, if you ask me."

"Florrie's my favorite," Bonnie said, picking up Florrie affectionately. "Remember when I used to look after you, Florrie? Remember what fun we used to have at the hotel—you girls and your father and——"

"Florrie was too little to remember," Papa said in a harsh voice.

"No, no, I do so remember," Florrie cried out. "I remember Bonnie because she was always good to us, always, always."

"I'm glad somebody remembers me," Bonnie said. Vance pinched her cheek and Papa abruptly got up and left the room.

"Hey, Harry, how about fixing us a little treat?" Vance called out. "I bring in some company; you might treat 'em right."

Minelda, who had enjoyed being the center of attention at her baptism, began to whimper at Florrie being petted, so her mother took her off to bed. At the door She paused, trying to catch Marcia's or Lena's eyes and thus convey a disciplinary silent warning, but both girls carefully avoided this opportunity, because they wanted to stay up with Bonnie.

"I don't think we're very welcome here," said Bonnie's girl friend. "Your sister glared at me as if she could eat me alive, Vance."

"She does that to everybody," Marcia reassured her.

"Oh, she does?" Bonnie asked, with lifted eyebrows.

"Come on now, let's have 'On Mobile Bay,'" Vance said, pulling Bonnie down to the piano bench again, this time on his lap.

Papa came back in the room with a plate of gingersnaps, and stopped dead in front of the piano just as Vance was nuzzling Bonnie's neck.

"God damn you, don't you know how to treat a lady?" he said in a trembling voice.

Bonnie giggled.

"Don't worry about Bonnie; she's been kissed before, plenty," Vance said easily, and this time turned Bonnie's face around for a real kiss. The next minute Papa had yanked him off the piano bench by the coat collar and knocked him down. The children screamed, Bonnie and her girl friend clapped their hands in terror, and She came running downstairs into the room to find her pet brother sitting on the floor holding on to his jaw, with a foolish look of utter amazement. Papa stood panting beside him.

"Not in my house you can't do that sort of thing," he choked. "Not by a damn sight!"

"Your house?" his wife shrilly cried. "Your house? You ought to be ashamed of yourself, Harry Willard. Oh, poor Vancie, did he hurt you?"

"He couldn't hurt me, not him," Vance said sullenly, getting to his feet and stroking down his hair. "He's just going crazy, that's all. I won't stand for it either."

"Then get out. Get out and stay out!" shouted Papa, eyes blazing.

"Oh, Harry, please!" Bonnie murmured, pulling at his arm. "He didn't mean any harm. You know it didn't mean anything."

"I'd be a fool if I thought that," Papa said.

"What business is it of yours if Vance wants to make love to his girl?" demanded Vance's sister.

"That's what I'd like to know," Vance added.

"I just don't like it, that's all, and that's enough," Papa shouted. "Now get out before I throw you out."

"I don't need to be told that more than once," Vance said. "Come on, folks, I'm getting out right now."

He pulled Bonnie and her friend toward the door, Bonnie with averted face and the other girl pop-eyed. Florrie began to cry, but Lena and Marcia were highly pleased at the privilege of being present at this show, even if they were frightened at seeing their father in such a fit of temper. He stood there shaking visibly while Vance and his friends left, and did not move when his wife came back in.

"All right, throw my little brother out. Two can play at that game," She said in a cold fury. "I told your father next time he came in late I'd lock him out and this is the time I'm going to do it. You'll be sorry for what you did to Vance, Harry Willard!"

She ran out and they heard her feet clattering down the cellar steps. Papa did not pay any attention, but wiped his forehead finally and muttered, "Get to bed, all of you."

This was the night, then, that Grandpa came home in the pouring rain and found the doors locked. He must have been drinking, it was said later, or he wouldn't have wandered all over the Junction switch yards the way he had. Mr. Purdy called them up before breakfast the next morning and told them the old man had been killed by a third rail.

"She killed him," Lena and Marcia whispered to each other. "She'd like to kill all of us."

Vance's moving to the hotel was lost in the shock of Grandpa's death. It served a purpose, in a way, for She dared not nag Papa for putting out Vance, since she had admitted in front of everybody that she was going to lock out Grandpa.

She didn't dare talk as much as she wanted about the four hundred and sixteen dollars Grandpa had left to his children, though she made it clear the money would repair the roof and get a new furnace and washing machine. Papa merely said that he had written to the rest of the brothers and sisters scattered around the state, and said he was using Grandpa's fortune to get him the best goddam coffin the Carson Furniture and Funeral Parlor could supply. It was the least they could do for the old man, he told them, and though there were some whimpers from some of the relations it was too late. Papa himself got a new suit for the funeral and made a down payment on a Ford. He urged them not to deliver the car yet, as it wouldn't look right for him to go riding around so soon after his old man died. Even so, his brothers and sister continued to write him nasty letters for years.

"There's no pleasing your own relations," Papa said, shaking his head. "You can do and do for them but still it ain't enough."

30

Marcia was planning to run away. Florrie knew about it, but they didn't tell Lena because she was sure to tattle to Mary Evelyn and it would get back to Papa. Marcia had made this decision after the Speaking Prize trouble. Every year at commencement time, a prize consisting of a brass medal on a red satin ribbon was awarded to the best recitation at the Grammar School Holiday Exercises. This had been awarded to Marcia for "The Raven" (expression and gestures coached by Fanny Gross). The winner of this medal was then invited to represent her town in the Mid-Summer Educational Conference in Lesterville, where the county winner would win an even larger medal and ten dollars. The participants would receive a handsome certificate merely for competing. They were to be judged by the *Courier* editor, the Methodist minister, and the high-school principal. The requirement that loomed most important to Marcia was that the girls were to wear white dresses and white shoes and stockings.

Since she had no white dress or white shoes, Marcia asked

Papa to buy them, a request that enraged him. He had just paid his taxes, he said, and if he bought for one he would have to buy for all three. Business was poor, now that these young men left town as soon as they got a girl in trouble instead of marrying her and buying furniture. As for the undertaking end, folks were all going to some new quack doctor in town and getting cured, instead of patronizing old Doc Franks, who knew his business. Besides, it would take two or three dollars for carfare and to spend the day in Lesterville, so he didn't see that ten dollars would be any profit supposing she did get it, which wasn't likely. It was a terrible blow to Marcia. Even Lena was generously indignant, but in making her complaint to Papa she did not improve matters by stating that they all needed white shoes and stockings anyway, and she thought she'd better accompany Marcia on this important mission. She explained that she would be in the contest herself, since she spoke every bit as well as Marcia, but for the fact that her teacher was so dumb she couldn't make the students remember anything, so that Lena had broken down in the middle of her piece. Papa scowled over these supplications, and was definitely set against it when his wife called out that if he was going to buy white things for the girls he would have to pay the laundry bill, and the laundryman had just been around for his last bill. So here was her great opportunity nipped in the bud by Papa himself, and Marcia made up her mind to run away. She would somehow find a way to enter the competition and get the cash prize, so that she could live comfortably in some distant city until she got work. Other girls her age worked, and it must be a fine thing to have dollar bills in your pocket and no one to tell you how to spend them. It seemed to her, on a judicious study of herself in the mirror, that she would look about sixteen with her braids wound around her head and high heels; wearing glasses might help too. She was certain she knew enough to teach school, knowing more than any grown person she had ever met so far, if people would only give her a chance to tell it. David Gross recommended that she go straight to his father in Washington, who would employ her at once, but Marcia said she didn't want to go to anybody's parents, as parents were bound to cause trouble, no matter what you did. She could address envelopes anyway, the way they advertised in the papers, or she could sell magazine subscriptions and make all kinds of money. She hinted to Mrs. Friend that she was contemplating taking a position. Mrs. Friend wanted to know what sort of position. Marcia said she had thought of being an amanuensis to a famous author or else a companion to a wealthy old lady, travelling abroad and bringing her wraps on deck when the evenings were too cool. Mrs. Friend gave her a quarter to copy some letters, and Marcia put this in a special sachet bag toward her carfare to Lesterville. To leave no stone unturned in the way of future career in case she didn't get the ten dollars, Marcia also copied drawings in magazines which said, "Copy this cartoon and win a free scholarship to the International Cartoonists' Institute in St. Louis, jobs to graduates guaranteed." This took a lot of paper, in fact almost the whole quarter's worth, since so much erasing wore holes in the drawing, and Florrie, usually slavishly optimistic about Marcia's genius, thought so many smudges might count against her.

"Will you come back to London Junction ever?" Florrie asked tremulously.

Marcia shook her head firmly in the negative, and Florrie sobbed over this imminent parting until Marcia promised to come and get her some day. If she won the Lesterville County Elocution Prize, she would take up acting instead of art, and she promised that Florrie could see all her shows free.

While Marcia was desperately plotting ways to run away, and an immediate means of getting to Lesterville for the big day that would open all the gates, the Chautauqua came to town. Mrs. Gross took David and Marcia to a Dramatic Reading. One lady took all the parts in "The Lion and the Mouse," changing her voice, jumping up and sitting down all over the stage, conjuring up invisible scenery, until Marcia was in an excited daze, resolved that this would be her chosen work. She managed to find a copy of the play at the library and read it softly in the toilet (changing her voice marvellously and stopping dead when anyone came in), and she hoped to hear more of the lady's talents, but the next performance was on the "Poetry of Rabindranath Tagore," and Marcia decided it couldn't be much or the Woman's Century

Reading Club wouldn't be going in a body. The high-school boys did odd jobs around the Chautauqua tent, and there were college boys who travelled with the management. This was all that interested Lena and Mary Evelyn, who managed to hang around the grounds making acquaintance of many strange boys by the simple process of cutting across the road to walk in front of them in dignified conversation, sometimes pausing to frown at the boys "following" them, until a sparkling interchange of repartee ensued. Lena walked with one boy and Mary Evelyn with the other. Lena stayed all night with Mary Evelyn on these occasions, and Papa did not dare forbid this for some reason, in spite of his wife's protests that Lena was having dates. She reported that her brother Vance, now staying at the hotel, said he and a tony friend from Lesterville had dated up Lena and Myrtle Chase one night and gone riding all over the country. Papa said he didn't believe a word Vance Hawkins ever said, so no action came of this. To make up for this leniency he forbade Marcia and Florrie to go out nights to watch people coming and going from the Chautauqua.

Marcia eagerly followed the billboards announcing the daily offerings of cosmopolitan entertainment: The Trouville Opera Company, in scenes from "Cavalleria Rusticana"; Mr. Abner Snively, World-Renowned Humorist, in Monologues, Assisted by Consuela Chapman, Concert Violinist; The Occult Sciences and Philosophy of the Orient, by Dr. Cass Bittner of the University of Virginia; Italy and the Dalmatian Coast, with Slides, by Sir Wade Frisbee, Explorer, Naturalist, and World-Traveller. Mrs. Gross took David and Fanny every night, and Marcia listened enviously to their accounts. Lena said the whole thing was too much like church, and she wouldn't be caught dead inside the tent. Papa said it wouldn't look right if he, as a leading citizen, stayed away from this community treat, so he selected Abner Snively, the World-Renowned Humorist, and the next day Mary Evelyn's mother told Lena she never heard anybody laugh so much in her life as Papa did. Papa told the jokes over and over again at supper, tears rolling down his cheek as he told about Pat and Mike, Rastus and the Colonel, Hans and Fritz, the Native and the Missionary Lady. He declared that in all of his experience he had frankly never heard such a genius as Snively, and he guessed he had heard the best of them, of course before he settled down. His wife said she thought, if you were to ask her opinion, that Mr. Snively got pretty close to being off-color sometimes, but maybe that was the type of thing Harry liked. Marcia said that if she were to take the County Elocution Prize she would very likely go around the country with a Chautauqua, telling jokes and giving dramatic readings. This made Papa sober up, and he said he wouldn't have any daughter of his charging around the country performing like some actress, and so far as the County Prize was concerned she might as well get it out of her head because he had talked the thing over with Idah and there was no point getting any white clothes for Marcia anyway, because she'd have them dirty and torn before she got there.

Marcia wanted to write Aunt Lois out in California for the white dress, without which no talent could be heard, but it would take too long. Mrs. Gross finally heard of the trouble and said she could fix over a dress of Fanny's for her, though she wasn't much good at fixing, and Marcia could stuff some cotton in her own white shoes. She stole a visit to Grandma and explained the situation. Grandma said if she had the money for the fare she'd give it to her in a minute, but the fact was it took every penny she and Mrs. Carmel had to get their business on its feet. They were doing fine, understand, and stood in the way of making hundreds, maybe thousands, but it just took a little time, and until then she couldn't do what she'd like for her grandchildren. She couldn't even spare the change for a Chautauqua ticket, since she'd had to borrow from Mr. Sweeney again for the Women's Relief Corps picnic last week, a pretty dressy affair held in conjunction with the G.A.R. Reunion in Elmville. (A pity Grandpa Willard wasn't alive for it, Grandma said, since the other old gentlemen, many of them over seventy, seemed to enjoy it so much.) After this unsuccessful interview Marcia wandered wistfully over to the Chautauqua tent and studied the program for the afternoon. Through a flap in the tent she saw that half the seats were empty and there was no reason why a person couldn't just go in and sit down, but she didn't have the courage. The picture of the afternoon's speaker was of a blandly beaming middle-aged man, long thin hair parted in the middle, pince-nez dropping a black ribbon elegantly down his face, Chester-field overcoat buttoned up to his wing collar, and stylish top-hat in white-gloved hand over his heart. The name of this personage was Thorburne Putney, F.R.G.S., B.A., International Authority on The Art of Living.

"Thorburne Putney," Marcia repeated, pleased with the euphonious syllables. Suddenly she remembered the house on Fourth Street, and Aunt Lois telling Mama she should have married Thorburne Putney. "Thorburne Putney," she repeated with immense satisfaction in the coincidence, and an immediate impulse to make good use of it. She would wait at the gate of the grounds until he came out, and he would suddenly look at her and exclaim, "Good heavens, who are you? You are the spit and image of my long lost and only love, Daisy Reed. Can it be possible?" Then, skipping all details, Marcia saw herself immediately adopted by the great man and whisked off in a huge automobile, going from town to town on the Chautauqua circuit as his pampered daughter, and sometimes assisting him on the platform with a special recitation of "The Raven." Visions of a glamorous future occupied her agreeably as she sauntered back and forth before the gate, and she was so deep in them that Mr. Putney and a red-haired massive woman were almost upon her before she recognized them. Recalling herself rudely from a grand ball in the White House where she was presiding at tea as the adored daughter of President Putney, Marcia looked up suddenly and let out a scream. The great man stopped and bent over her in alarm.

"Are you hurt? What happened?"

"I—I twisted my ankle," Marcia gasped, forgetting her carefully planned approach. "I do it all the time. My mother used to know you."

Mr. Putney and his companion stared at each other blankly.

"My mother's name was Daisy Reed and I look like her," Marcia babbled on. "Papa got married again and we live in the biggest house in town and I'm going to go on Chautauqua tours just like you after I get the County Elocution prize."

The great Thorburne Putney shook his head in amazement, and began to laugh. It was not a jolly laugh, for he bared his teeth and shook the laugh out raspingly; it was like a rusty bucket on a rusty chain being fetched up from a dry well. Still, it was a laugh in its own way, and Marcia took it as great encouragement. She was disappointed that he gave no start of astonishment at hearing the romantic name of Daisy Reed once more, but passed a hand across his brow thoughtfully. The lady, who had the reddest hair that was ever seen on land or sea and a bosom on which she laid a variety of trinkets without even needing to fasten them, was much more friendly.

"So you get elocution prizes. Isn't that nice?" she said. "That's just how you got started, isn't it, Thorburne?"

"Maybe the way I'll end up, too," Mr. Putney said sourly. "Twelve people in the tent this afternoon. All looked like idiots. What did you say your mother's name was?"

"Daisy Reed," said Marcia. "She's dead."

She felt tears coming to her eyes and thought with surprise that she did so have feelings, no matter what Lena said.

"Poor kiddie," said the lady.

"Maybe she wouldn't have died if she'd married you," Marcia said solemnly to Mr. Putney, who stared at her.

"Daisy Reed, of course," he said. "Daisy was a dear. I took sick in a little town here once some fifteen years ago or so, and Daisy's family harbored me. Poor Daisy. Dead, you say."

"You're a nice child," the lady said, patting Marcia on the head as if she was Florrie instead of practically grown-up. "You know what you want to do with your life and that's a lot. If my little girl had lived she'd be just about your age and your coloring. How old are you?"

"Thirteen," said Marcia. "Tomorrow's my birthday but I never get any presents except underwear and shoes and stuff like that."

Mr. Putney was oiling up his laugh with pleasanter results now, and the lady's laugh shook all of her trinkets.

"That's too good to pass up, Burnie," she said, and with a giddy sensation that she feared might be fatal Marcia saw her reach in her chain handbag and extend a tiny coin, too little even for a dime.

"Here's a birthday present," she said.

Marcia looked at the coin with a sinking feeling. It was just a medal or something.

"What is it?" she asked, trying not to show her disappointment.

"A five-dollar goldpiece," said Mr. Putney. "Haven't you ever seen any before?"

"Oh, sure, but I get them mixed up with ten-dollar goldpieces," Marcia stammered, joy leaping once more through her body. "Oh, thank you, thank you."

"Write to me what you do with it," the lady said, and handed her a card. "Here's our regular address."

They walked with Marcia to the railroad tracks before the hotel, Mr. Putney half-amused, half-sarcastic at the lady's sentimental insistence that her own Dorothea would have been exactly like Marcia had she lived.

"I never expected Dorothea to turn out a beauty," she said seriously. "She was too much like her father for that. But she was bright as a button from the time she could talk, just like this one."

Marcia was getting good and tired of being bright as a button, to tell the truth, but if that was the only compliment she was ever going to get from people she might as well resign herself to it.

"There are buttons and buttons," Mr. Putney said, pronouncing his words in a carefully clipped way, like an actor would. You could tell when he was meaning to be funny, because he put his finger to the side of his nose. "For instance, there is the wool-covered button. Not that Daisy's daughter is that type of button; I merely suggest that you watch your figures of speech. Watch them like a hawk, my dear Beverly."

"There are hawks and hawks too, Burnie," the lady said, a little roguishly. Marcia decided they must be married. She was so dizzy from this marvellous adventure that she did not know what she was telling them, and afterward she thought it was certainly not the sort of cosmopolitan talk of which she fancied herself capable, because Beverly laughed too much. Beverly talked too, and afterwards fragments floated back to Marcia's mind, but at the time one phrase boomed away in her head, drowning out every other impression—Five-dollar goldpiece, five-dollar goldpiece, five-dollar goldpiece. She wanted to bolt down the middle of the street shouting this miracle to the whole town, though she could not very well

break away from the flattering attention of Mr. and Mrs. Putney. She was glad Lena was not around, for if they ever saw
how much prettier Lena was than she they would probably
take back the five-dollar goldpiece and give it to her. No one
had ever made so much fuss over her, and these were great
and famous personages too. They had a home in Cleveland
and almost in a dream Marcia heard herself being invited to
visit them, because they were very lonely when they weren't
on the road. Mr. Putney inquired after Grandma Reed and
declared he would like to call on her if he had the time, but
they were leaving the next day. He presented Marcia with his
pamphlet, *The Art of Living Richly*, with his autograph, "To a
very bright little button," which rather spoiled it for Marcia.

She ran all the way home and seeing Lena and Mary Evelyn across the street shouted her news at them.

"You'd better not tell Her you have the money or She'll
take it away from you," Lena cautioned, and added thoughtfully, "Maybe you'd better let me keep it for you."

"Why don't you go visit the people and get one yourself?"
suggested Mary Evelyn, and this seemed such a practical idea
that Lena at once accepted it. Marcia watched them go off in
the direction of the hotel with some uneasiness. Lena was always spoiling everything. She would probably tell Mrs. Putney that Marcia's birthday wasn't tomorrow at all, but six
months off. Lena was tricky that way, always telling on everybody. It turned out that on the steps of the hotel Lena and
Myrtle ran into Vance Hawkins, who took them to an ice-
cream parlor, so they didn't have a chance at the Putneys.

It was Florrie who really made trouble. She had been
whimpering every night at the idea of Marcia running away
forever, and when she heard about the five dollars she was
certain that this would speed up the parting. She went to
Papa and begged him to let Marcia go to the Lesterville Prize
Contest, because Marcia was sure to win, and maybe if she
wasn't allowed to go she might run away and get killed like
Grandpa Willard. Papa flew off the handle at once, and said
he wasn't going to take any criticism on the way he was raising his family, no, sir, not even from the family itself. He said
he and the children's mother had gotten along without traipsing around the country speaking pieces, spending a fortune

on white dresses, and so on, and carfare, and he guessed his children could do the same. He said that if he caught Marcia out of the house on the afternoon of the exercises he would give her the hiding of her life. Marcia went upstairs and sulked over this, but Florrie tried to appease her by saying Papa wasn't really mean, he was just mad that he didn't have money for the white outfits and carfare, and it made him madder that he didn't dare ask his wife to buy them, so he had to take it out on somebody. Marcia told this to David Gross, who said if she wanted to run away right away he would help her. He said Destiny had sent Thorburne Putney to London Junction at this crucial moment in Marcia's career, almost as if her dead mother had willed this to happen, and to allow anything to stand in her way was sacrilege. Marcia scarcely slept that night, planning and planning ways of escape, and when she did doze off she dreamed of Mama crossing the road with the burden tied to her back, and no matter how hard Marcia willed her to turn around and smile she could not make it happen until the last instant. Then her mother's face blended into Bonnie Purdy's face and Cousin Isobel's and Mrs. Gross', until Marcia thought with consternation she had forgotten her mother's face, and now it would never come back to her.

The day before the Lesterville Exercises, Marcia's great inspiration came, approved by David Gross and Florrie, but a deadly secret from everyone else. The most important thing in the competition was, after all, reciting the piece and wearing the white dress before the three judges. There was no use hoping to get to the exercises after her father's warning, but she would take the car to Lesterville early in the morning while Papa and his wife were at the Carsons' making preparations for Mr. Carson's mother's funeral. She was supposed to be in charge of Minelda during their absence, but Florrie thought she could manage her. Once in Lesterville she would make straight for one of the three judges' addresses, wearing her white dress which was now hanging in Mrs. Gross' bedroom; she would recite her piece, get the prize, and take the next car home before her absence would be noticed. Then with her prize money she would run away. Florrie's awed doubt that she would ever dare do this strengthened Marcia's courage. Next morning she wanted to confide in Lena, but fortunately they had a fight over a box of cactus candy Aunt Lois had sent from California, so they stopped speaking to each other. Marcia got into Fanny Gross' made-over white dress, which still dipped quite a lot on one side in spite of all Mrs. Gross could do; the shoes stuffed with cotton didn't wobble too much, and anyway they were white, which was the main thing. David kept a lookout for anyone who might tell on her until Marcia had gotten aboard the eight o'clock streetcar, five-dollar goldpiece in her hand.

The conductor could not change the five-dollar goldpiece and said she didn't need to pay. It was a wonderful thing having money and going into the world by yourself. Everybody smiled at her; a man gave her a chocolate bar, another man told her where the *Courier* office could be found; in fact, the world was filled with marvellous strangers all devoted to you, who would take your part against your relations on any occasion. Marcia looked out the window, passing the steel mills and Mrs. Jane's house, and fancied she saw Mrs. Jane herself sweeping off the front stoop, with a handkerchief tied around her curlers. She waved her hand and it really was Mrs. Jane but she looked up blankly at the streetcar, not recognizing Marcia in the white dress. Marcia got off at the Square, as the man had directed, and there was the little *Courier* office. It was not open yet, and Mr. Andrews was not likely to be in for some time, the janitor said, because the paper came out the day before and the rest of the week Mr. Andrews took it easy. Marcia stood in the hallway waiting, however, and murmuring "The Raven" to herself over and over, to insure herself against stage fright. It was nearly ten o'clock when a Ford drew up and Mr. Andrews arrived. He was a gloomy-looking, gray-complexioned little man with an unexpected little potbelly which he patted constantly as if he feared it might slip away. His suit seemed wrinkled and a size too large, wrinkling around his ankles till he hitched up his belt. He seemed uneasily conscious of his appearance, for he looked around pugnaciously the minute he got out of the car, ready to face down any criticism. Seeing only Marcia, he got out his keys and swung them around uncertainly.

"I can't come to the exercises, but I've got my piece and I

came to speak it for the judges before the exercises," Marcia said. "It says you get a certificate and the prizewinner gets ten dollars. Here's my Lesterville medal."

Mr. Andrews was baffled by this, to the extent of taking off his shapeless gray hat and running his hand over his bald head. He took his swivel chair at his desk and frowned at Marcia.

"I guess since you made the trip specially I could give you a certificate," he said. "No need to speak the piece though. Not for me."

"Oh, yes, I have to," Marcia hastened to correct him. "It says here in the rules that you have to be heard by the judges and wear a white dress and white shoes before you can get the certificate. I'll begin."

Mr. Andrews shook his head uneasily and opened his mouth about to protest once more, but Marcia had firmly planted herself before him. The janitor came in and began sweeping around the musty shadows behind the file-case, and Mr. Andrews looked hopefully at Marcia to see if this interruption would distract her, but she was sailing into "The Raven" in her best platform manner, waving her right hand over this word, pointing upward at that, and lowering her voice to a croak on the "Quoth the raven, nevermore." Mr. Andrews fixed his eyes steadily on the back of his hand, which he had placed over his knee so that he missed the best part of the expressions and gestures. At the end of every stanza he made a motion to get up, then relaxed despondently as Marcia sailed briskly on. She didn't forget a word or a gesture, humping her shoulders and ducking her head like a raven on the last phrase. The janitor stopped sweeping and applauded briefly at the end of the piece, while Marcia stood before Mr. Andrews with her hand outstretched for the certificate.

"I suppose I have to go to the principal's office now and recite it before I can get the certificate," she said after a pause, during which Mr. Andrews drummed moodily on the table without looking at her.

"No, no, you can't do that," he hastened to say, reaching out to hold her back in case she tore out the door on this ambitious errand. "This isn't regular at all, and I don't know who gave you the idea that it was. But you speak real well, and you went to the trouble of this trip, so maybe I can get the principal and Dr. Bosley on the phone about it. If they say it's okay I'll give you your certificate right now."

Marcia wanted to ask what about the ten dollars, but she didn't dare. She listened with pounding heart while Mr. Andrews made his phone calls, explaining that there was a kid in the office reciting pieces like a house afire, because her folks wouldn't let her come to the regular exercises, and was it all right to give her the certificate. Apparently this was all right, for he started shaking his fountain pen over an impressive document.

"What put it in your head to want this certificate anyway?" he asked, stealing a curious look at her.

"Because I want to get a job, and it shows what I can do," Marcia explained, "especially if you aren't in high school yet."

Mr. Andrews allowed that that was right, and after thoughtfully drumming on the table some more said there wasn't anything he could do about the prize without his two fellow-judges, but he was pretty sure they'd be glad to chip in with him on a private award for ambition, and here was five dollars. He advised her to put it aside in a savings bank as a start towards college, maybe a great career—look at Edison who came from a little town not a hundred miles off. Mr. Andrews began warming to his subject, which was evidently a familiar one, possibly the very speech he had delivered at the public school commencement exercises. It was Marcia's turn to look embarrassed as the sole recipient of this inspirational talk. In the middle Mr. Andrews even got up and pounded his desk when he mentioned the government, which he said would never be the same until we got Teddy Roosevelt back in office. Marcia wiggled from one foot to the other, wondering how much more she would have to listen before she got the five dollars. Mr. Andrews stopped abruptly in the middle of a sentence and sat down, mopping his forehead. Not knowing exactly what to do Marcia clapped her hands, which embarrassed the editor to the point of hastily handing her the five dollars and muttering something about work to be done.

On the streetcar going back to London Junction, Marcia thought she might have won even more money by going to the other two judges, but it was too late, and besides she would be getting home before noon. It was a great day. It was too bad she couldn't show off her white dress to Lena, but the best thing was to leave the outfit at Mrs. Gross' and go home in her checked gingham in case She was home. She was so full of excitement that it was a blow to come into the kitchen and find that Minelda and Florrie had not only tipped over a pan of biscuit dough on the kitchen floor, but had tracked it into the forbidden rooms. Marcia angrily set to cleaning up the mess, knowing she would get scolded for letting it happen, then for not cleaning it up right. It was awful the way your home and your family could take all the joy out of life.

31

How old must you be before you learn to hide yourself completely and thus protect yourself? When Mrs. Gross stated that she was going to ask Mr. Willard personally if Marcia couldn't share David's French lessons next fall, Marcia was bursting to say, "But I won't be here this fall. I'll be working some place far off, because the first chance I get I'm going to run away." But she dared not even trust Mrs. Gross. Mrs. Gross might say that nice children didn't run away, and think how it would hurt her parents' feelings; then Marcia might blurt out something about Her and being whipped and all the things that no one should know or they would feel sorry for her, and the worst thing that could happen to anybody was public pity. Mrs. Gross was likely to report her plan to Papa "for the best," and Grandma might tell "for the best," too. Either people spoiled your plans because they were downright mean or because they meant it "for the best." When Marcia felt her secret unbearably near her lips, she started talking giddily about a riddle, a book she had read, or something that happened a long time ago. Her stepmother declared she never heard so much nonsense in all her life, and there wasn't a truthful bone in Marcia's whole body. Marcia did not shake inside with rage at this the way she used to do, because she had ten dollars pinned in a sachet bag to her undershirt, and ten dollars was better than the Holy Bible to make you feel calm and safe from wounds. She woke up often in the night with a shock of fear, remembering that she was going to do something tremendous, something was going to happen to her, to her alone, not to Florrie and Lena. This wasn't pretend either. It was as if she was bewitched by that other person inside her making her do something instead of pretending. She didn't know how or when she was going to do this, but every day seemed the last. Every moment sharpened her sensations. This is the last time I will pass the burned Holy Roller Church, she would think every day; this is the last time I'll wait by the Gross barn for the wind to shake down crab apples; this is the last time I'll start numbing myself coming in the back door in case She's laying for me with a switch or scolding; this is the last time I'll walk past Mary Evelyn's front porch hoping she and Lena will wave and ask me to come and play with them. It was funny knowing you were gone, but not knowing where, and having other people treat you as if you were still present. It was funny having that other person inside you, strong and invincible like Lena, when outside you were resigned to whatever came up. The very wind, heady with dying lilacs and the constant smell of train smoke, apples rotting in roadside ditches, the heavy sweetness of preserve kettles boiling over in hot kitchens bore a solemn warning to Marcia that this is the last summer, this is the last time, the very last. She saw each familiar face and spot with the desperate clarity of farewell and this time she knew it was not pretending. She tried to remember when she found out pretending was no good. Was it when she gave up waiting for Aunt Lois or Grandma or Cousin Isobel to come rescue them, or was it the day she met the Putneys and discovered that reality could be as good or better than pretending?

She knew the day had almost come when the newspaper told the details of the new school and set Papa to raging. It seemed that the town fathers had decided to charge tuition in the new high school. Papa stormed about this at supper time, declaring that between Lena's and Marcia's fees he'd go bankrupt. He said the best people in the Junction had gotten along without any new expensive schools (gymnasiums, domestic science and manual training departments, business courses, and all those newfangled ideas), and he guessed his daughters could do the same.

"You mean we have to quit school?" Lena asked, eyes wide. Bad girls and poor children who had to work in the mills quit school. "If we don't go everybody will think it's because we're too poor to pay the tuition. All the other girls are ordering gym suits and domestic science aprons from the Fair Store already. Oh, Papa, we just *have* to go."

"Aprons! Gym suits! I never heard the like," gasped Mrs. Willard, eyes darting from one to the other and resting sympathetically on Papa. "Harry, I do think you ought to get up at the Chamber of Commerce meeting and give them a piece of your mind! The way youngsters now are pampered; why, I never in all my life! And what good are they at the end? A lot of good-for-nothings that expect you to do and do for them the rest of their life! The house needs painting, we have to make a payment on the car before they'll deliver it, there's our lodge dues, and our vacation expenses next month at Silver Lake, and the new washer; but, oh, no, we have to take our last penny to buy school trash for the girls!"

"But everybody in town is doing it," wailed Lena.

Marcia looked stonily into space.

"Lena's so full of boys and dates behind the schoolhouse— oh, yes, don't think I don't hear all about it!—and Marcia's so full of crazy ideas she moons around like a lunatic, don't know anybody's talking to her half the time. No siree, Harry Willard, you don't need to ask me for my money, and I won't have you taking the household money either. No siree. They're not my flesh and blood. Let them go to their Aunt Lois or their grandmother or some of those relations they're always telling about. When it comes to laying out any more money I wash my hands."

As this outburst said all and more than Papa had in his mind, there was nothing left for him but to glower at his plate.

"What's the good of us getting high honors if we can't go to the new high school?" Lena inquired. "Our own mother wouldn't want us to quit school. I'll bet we don't get allowed to ride in the automobile when we do get one. I'll bet only Minelda gets allowed in it."

Minelda's mother's bony hand flashed across Lena's cheek in a smart slap which brought Lena to her feet, scarlet with indignation.

"I won't stand it! I'll go away and never come back, never! I'll tell Aunt Lois, I'll tell everybody!" She ran out of the kitchen door, giving it a good bang. Papa got up and walked slowly toward the door, not looking at his wife. She sat gnawing her fingernails nervously. Florrie got up and went over to Papa, slipping her hand in his. Minelda screwed up her little white face into crying position and made whimpering demands to go bye-bye. Marcia could see Lena running down the street toward Mary Evelyn's or maybe Grandma's. Now Lena would be the one to run away, and that meant she'd have to stay, at least for a while. Lena always got first chance at everything.

"Goodness only knows what stories she's started telling this very minute," muttered Mrs. Willard. "I won't dare lift my head by the time she's started her lies."

Marcia thought Lena wouldn't tell though, because Lena didn't want the town feeling sorry for them any more than Marcia did. With a sudden sinking feeling she remembered that Lena had borrowed her five-dollar goldpiece that afternoon to show Myrtle Chase. Now Lena would keep it. She'd run away with it, and it was just like her, Marcia thought with rising wrath. She had even guessed that Marcia was planning to run away with it, but Marcia wouldn't confess it when she challenged her. So now Lena would run away with it. You couldn't trust anybody. Well, she would show her soon enough that two could run away as well as one.

"Never fear, she'll be back, Harry," said Mrs. Willard. "Come and finish your supper."

Papa sat down and nobody said anything. Marcia hoped he would mention the rice being burned and the bread being mildewed, but he didn't seem to notice, or if he did his wife's bad cooking was by this time no cause for comment. Suddenly Florrie began to sob softly.

"I hope Lena won't get killed like Grandpa Willard," she moaned. "Can't you do something, Papa?"

But Papa only took out a cigar and smoked morosely, never looking up to meet his wife's watchful eyes. At dark he went out. Marcia and Florrie went upstairs whispering, and watched the front window for his return.

"Maybe she ran away to California to Aunt Lois," said

Florrie. "Do you think maybe she's gone to live with Mary Evelyn? Maybe Grandma will let her stay with her."

When Papa came home they heard him haranguing his wife in the bedroom, and in the midst of this they thought they heard something about Mary Evelyn's mother saying Lena was spending the night there. Mary Evelyn's mother had had the nerve to tell Papa he would have to do something about the way his children were neglected, especially Lena, before she, Mrs. Stewart, would even advise the child to go home. Papa was pretty mad at Mrs. Stewart, who he said had always had her nose in everybody's business from way back, but he was mad at his wife too. The girls could hear her protesting, "But, Harry—" and finally Papa shouted, "God damn it, why can't you cook rice without burning it? I don't ask for any Hotel Astor cooking; all I ask is a little rice that's not burned once in a while."

Florrie was desperately worried about Lena, but Marcia's concern was for her five-dollar goldpiece and the way Lena always got there first, and the way Lena never got reality and pretending mixed up, but went straight out and did things. She and Florrie could hardly sleep for the fear that Lena would never come back and they would never see her again. Now she was out in the world maybe, like the honest Irish lad or poor little Joe. Marcia thought of the time their hearts had been wrung with woe over these sad songs; maybe it wasn't the songs but the dim knowledge that the same fate was waiting in the future for themselves.

The next day Lena did not come back and Papa said he was not going to give Mrs. Stewart the satisfaction of asking her where his daughter had gone. At noon he came home early to see if there was any word from Lena, but there wasn't. Mrs. Willard buzzed around him uneasily, telling him that Lena had been getting out of hand lately anyway, and was up to plenty of mischief that Papa didn't know about. She said many was the time she had spotted Lena and a girl friend walking down dark streets with boys on evenings Lena was supposed to be at Epworth League meetings or doing her homework with Mary Evelyn. She said that her brother Vance had told her that everybody in town knew Lena left her home looking one way, the way a girl should, but as soon as she got

to Mary Evelyn's she put paint on her face and did her hair
up and put on high-heeled slippers. She never intended to
mention this to him, since he wouldn't ever listen to any criticism of his children, but did Papa know that Lena had been
buying clothes and charging them to him at the Fair Store?
Just ask Mrs. Stewart that, if you please, and see what she had
to say. Maybe it was just as well the young lady had cleared
out when she did. Maybe she had reasons of her own, but had
aggravated people on purpose so as to put the blame on
them. If Papa wanted to find out the sort of goings-on Lena
had been up to this last year, just take a look at her diary, the
one she had stolen out of the parlor bookcase and kept hidden—or rather thought she kept hidden—in the pocket of her
winter coat. Papa listened to this without comment, scowling
into space. Marcia and Florrie were surprised at the cleverness
of their older sister as they heard this report; Marcia felt hurt
that she hadn't been allowed to share all this intrigue and that
Lena had shut her off utterly again. She hastily went upstairs
to get Lena's diary, but Papa came up for it before she was
through.

The entries in Lena's diary, written in purple ink, were not
too revealing of her criminal tendencies. They went along
pretty much in a monotone: "May 9—From this date on I am
going to keep a record of everything that happens to me. May
10—Nothing doing. May 11—Ditto. May 12—Nothing doing.
May 13—Ditto. May 14—Cora Bird's party. Not invited. May
15—Nothing doing. May 16—Circus. Not allowed to go. May
17—Nothing doing. May 18—B. G. walked home from meeting with me. May 19—B. G. and L. F. came to Myrtle's
house. May 20—Had fight with B. G. May 21—Nothing
doing. May 22—Ditto. May 23—Made fudge at Mary Evelyn's.
We raised Cain. May 24—N. D. May 25—Ditto. May 26—
Made up with B. G. May 27—Meeting of U-No-Us-Kids at
Myrtle C's. We raised Cain. Pinocchio. We made a rule to
keep diaries all our life, so we can show our children. May
28—Nothing doing." There was never any mention of anyone
in the family, Lena's private life deliberately excluding these
necessary evils. Papa stood in the bedroom doorway frowning
over the little book, then tossing it on the dresser.

"Where'd she get this book?" he asked.

"We both got them from Cousin Isobel for Christmas but She—I mean Mother—locked them up and wouldn't let us write in them," Marcia said. "I guess Lena took hers out anyway."

"Where's your Aunt Lois now?" Papa asked.

"She's coming home pretty soon, I guess," Marcia said.

When night came there was still no word of Lena. Papa didn't come home for supper, but went to Grandma's and called at the Fair Store, where Mrs. Stewart gave him a suit box.

"You can give these old rags to Mrs. Willard," she said. "They're the clothes she had Lena wearing while she herself went around in all her finery. I fixed up Lena to look decent just like I would my own Mary Evelyn, and you can tell your wife I said so. You'll get the bill, never mind."

Papa was in such a rage that he vowed if Lena came home he wouldn't let her in the door, making him the laughing stock of the town. This scandal was as much as his job was worth, he said. His wife was openly pleased to find him in this frame of mind, and told Florrie that her cot was going up in the attic because from now on she would sleep with Marcia. It was as if Lena was gone forever.

32

The London Junction newspaper gave the news away and everybody in town, especially Grandma Reed and Mrs. Carmel, said it was just about the most romantic thing they'd ever heard of. "A little bird has just told us," said the newspaper, "that Mrs. Lois Blair's long sojourn in the West has not been entirely for the purpose of installing herself in the real estate business out there. On the contrary, Cupid has had a hand in delaying her homecoming. A few months ago Mr. R. L. Sweeney, noted realtor of London Junction and Lesterville, decided he too needed a western climate, and the gist of the matter is that he settled in Pasadena where Mrs. Blair was located, and the two were secretly wed over four months ago. Friends and relatives of the pair were only today notified of the union, inasmuch as the Sweeneys are expected back immediately to take up residence in Mrs. Blair's home here. The couple were met in Cleveland by Mrs. Sweeney's niece, Miss Lena Willard, who will make her home with them, according to rumors around town. Congratulations, Mr. and Mrs. Sweeney, and may you not regret your choice of London Junction as your future home in preference to the Golden State."

"I'd like to see Ed Hartwell's face when he finds that out," Papa chuckled to Grandma Reed. He had beckoned Marcia and Florrie to come with him the minute supper was over. He told his wife this was a family matter and before he went to Lois' to bring Lena home he wanted to have a talk with Grandma, and the girls might as well come along. As usual, as soon as they got off the Furness property, he began to whistle and step quickly, almost as if a chill strong wind issued from his home, blowing him away without any effort on his part. He was plainly delighted that Lena had not taken refuge with Mary Evelyn's mother and for a moment hesitated at the corner, muttering something about dropping in to tell off Mrs. Stewart.

"At least it's all in the family," he repeated several times, after they got to Grandma's.

Grandma was sitting in her bay window in a house dress, fanning herself with a large souvenir palm leaf fan decorated with a lively picture of Teddy Roosevelt leading the Rough Riders. She was not wearing her transformation, but had her gray hair done in curl papers, with a black velvet bow thrust in the midst to brighten it up. She had the newspaper in her lap, and kept looking at it and shaking her head.

"Lena must have gone straight to Cleveland and met their train," Papa said. "Now how do you suppose that little devil knew when they were coming when nobody else did?"

"Maybe she stopped in the telegraph office and Vance Hawkins showed her the telegrams," Grandma suggested. "I can't get over their getting married without telling me. Goodness knows, I've been trying to bring them together for years, then I just gave up. Mr. Sweeney has always been mighty lovely to me though, mighty lovely indeed. I don't know where I'd be without him."

Mrs. Carmel's head popped out of the bedroom door. She

was taking a "bird bath," as she expressed it, and continued to push a washcloth over her sharp old face as she talked.

"I tell Mrs. Reed she could have got Mr. Sweeney any day she held out her little finger," she declared. "What that man didn't do for her!"

"Now, now," Grandma said, blushing. "I don't say Mr. Sweeney didn't say a great many things to me that sometimes made me think. But Lois is more up and coming, and when she sets out to get somebody, anybody else has got to take a back seat."

"It takes a load off my mind about Lena, I can tell you," Papa confessed. "That kid is just as pig-headed as her Aunt Lois, and hell knows what she would do when she set her mind to it. I haven't slept a wink till I read this."

"Children always turn up," Grandma said comfortably. "Mine were always running away, and for that matter some of them stayed away, but there was always plenty more running around asking for cookies."

"It ain't the ones that run away you worry about," Mrs. Carmel interpolated, popping her head in again. "It's the ones that stay home. They're the ones, all right. Never get married if they're girls, never keep a job if they're boys. No, sir, the ones that run away do all right."

Papa asked Grandma if Ed Hartwell had been in to see her lately, and if he ever did show up to be sure and tell him about Lois marrying Sweeney. He said it was one on Ed, all right.

"Ed was pretty stuck on Lois," Papa said. "Lois was pretty soft on him too, but they couldn't stand up to Mabel. She'd have filled them both full of buckshot. A fella ought to think about the future when he takes up with a girl like Mabel. They ain't so bad when you marry them—I mean, take a girl like Mabel—but when you don't you're in for it. I don't think Lois ever cared for Sweeney the way she did for Ed. I guess she just gave up, being on toward thirty-six, seven, and figuring that Sweeney has plenty of dough."

"Lena'll have a good time living with Aunt Lois," Florrie said thoughtfully.

"Who said I'd let her stay there?" Papa cried wrathfully.

"Aunt Lois will let her go to high school," Marcia said.

"I'd let her stay there, Harry," Grandma advised. "The minute you start fighting over children, you lose out. If you start a rumpus and make her come back, then something'll happen to make everybody sorry."

"Folks'll talk, now that it's already printed in the papers that she's staying there," Mrs. Carmel obligingly put in. "You don't want to set folks talking."

"Maybe Aunt Lois will let us all stay there again," Florrie said hopefully.

Papa looked sorrowfully at his youngest and shook his head.

"That's the way your children turn against you," he observed, but he was too relieved about Lena's return to get really angry. "Florrie is the one I thought I could always count on too. She's the most like Daisy. So you like your Aunt Lois better than you do Papa, eh, Florrie? Didn't we always have good times together, Florrie?"

Florrie's brows met in an anguish of decision.

"We used to," she answered truthfully. "Only you don't play the guitar and sing any more."

Papa laughed. He shook the ashes from the cigar on the floor and leaned back in his chair. Marcia thought it was funny about places and people; the way certain places and certain people preserved a person at his happiest and best, and other places and people distorted him into a grim stranger. With Grandma Reed, Papa was young and gay again, kidding about his troubles, relaxing in Grandma's easygoing sympathy. But with his wife he had to be on guard all the time, reminding himself that this was the right life, nice people didn't joke and whistle, nice people worried about money, appearances, tidiness, possessions, and naturally you wanted to be considered nice people. It was too bad it was impossible to be nice people and enjoy life at the same time. It was too bad, too, that if you wanted to be nice people you couldn't like the companions you naturally might prefer. So Papa felt guilty enjoying himself at Grandma's, but at the moment the guilt sensation intensified his pleasure. It would worry him later when he had time for it.

Mrs. Carmel, refreshed by her toilet, and anxious not to miss any tidbit, emerged complete from the bedroom now, wearing a rusty black poplin high-necked dress which wafted a musty, attic breeze about the room, aided by Grandma's fan. Over her finely tucked bosom she wore a variety of brooches and dangling knicknacks, explaining to Papa that if London Junction folks didn't know enough to buy genuine up-to-date jewelry when they saw it, she herself had the good taste and common sense not to let it go to waste. If Papa saw anything on her chest that he fancied as an adornment to his wife, however, Mrs. Carmel would be glad to surrender it at the lowest possible price, since he was like a real son to her partner. She was in the middle of saying that she was sure her partner thought more of him than she did even of her new son-in-law, Mr. Sweeney, when she was taken with a sneezing attack, quelled only after some magic operations with a large blue bandana handkerchief somehow whipped out of her blouse and a bottle of lavender smelling salts which she inhaled with shut eyes and a prayerful expression.

"This climate don't agree with her like Hodge Street," Grandma explained. "I tell her any day she says the word we'll pack up and go back there. I'd just as soon now anyway if Lois is coming back. It'll be criticism from morning till night, every little thing I do, when she gets here. I wouldn't be a bit surprised if she'd put it up to Mr. Sweeney not to help me any more."

"I told you you should have nabbed him yourself," Mrs. Carmel gasped, with a flourish of her bandana before replacing it in her blouse. "Why, Mr. Willard, when this woman here was wearing that transformation she could have got any man in town. Why didn't you wear it tonight?"

"I'm not going to wear it any more," Grandma said sorrowfully, and picked up the newspaper again with the picture of Mr. Sweeney.

Papa took out his watch and said he had a good notion to meet the seven-thirty Express in case the bride and groom came in on it. He thought he'd leave the girls for a little visit and stop back for them. Maybe he'd bring back Lena, he said. Mrs. Carmel, who had dressed up especially for her friend's son-in-law, urged him to stay and talk over the business and goings-on around town. She said she and Grandma were kind of disappointed in the Junction, things being so slow. Of course, that business about Bonnie Purdy had stirred things up a little, but being cooped up in the shop all day they didn't get a chance to hear news that a person like Papa, in an undertaking parlor, would hear. Papa had his hat on the side of his head and a hand on the doorknob, but he paused to look questioningly from Grandma to Mrs. Carmel.

"What about Bonnie Purdy? Isn't she still at the Gas Company in Lesterville?" he wanted to know.

"Not now. The party she used to run with, not to mention any names, went to her boss and got her fired after this other party stepped in. Told the whole story, so Bonnie got the sack." Mrs. Carmel happily wheezed out her information, interrupted herself to take a tremendous snort of her smelling salts, thrusting it dangerously up a nostril and placing a bony finger on the other one for maximum effect. "Don't say I said so, but Mrs. Stewart down in the Fair Store says there's other parties mixed up in it. My, what won't these girls do next! As I say to my partner here, I'm not sorry my own daughters are under the sod when I hear these stories. Why don't you ask your company to stay and have a dish of pickled pigsfeet, Mrs. Reed?"

Papa said they had just eaten supper but he might have a snack when he came back in, a suggestion which pleased both old ladies. Grandma talked a good deal about how much she hated her early farm life, but she carried its routine in a small measure into whatever quarters she found herself. The apartment always smelled of cooking, a quart of berries being preserved, a few beets being pickled, a cheesecloth bag of sour cream dripping into a pan under the sink, later to emerge as a cupful of cottage cheese, and stone crocks of various leftovers of meats being pickled, jellied or ground into sandwich paste. The room was so overwhelmed with these housekeeping demonstrations that its original commercial intent was quite obscured. The same lady in the rope wig guarded the cigar-box cash register, and the same pile of ancient sheet music was piled beside her, but Mrs. Carmel's large sewing basket sat on top, filled with patterns and half-finished garments from many years back. She selected her latest effort from the basket for her evening's work, a child's coat of a singularly unwieldy carpet-like material. It was just a remnant, she said, from a sale in a big store in Paris, France, and though she had no particular child in mind, one would turn up come cold weather.

Papa stood in the doorway, quietly brushing his coat sleeve.

"I didn't hear anything," he finally said. "What happened to Bonnie? Is she back in town?"

"The only folks she could go to were her relations at the hotel. I guess they don't know about it yet. Well, live and learn, I always say."

Grandma was rocking back and forth, fanning herself and looking moodily out the window. Florrie and Marcia were playing double solitaire on the floor but enormously interested in Mrs. Carmel's cagey conversation. Papa evidently decided not to give her the pleasure of more questions, for he abruptly bolted out the door.

"There's a mighty fine man," stated Mrs. Carmel, nodding her head rapidly at the large needle she held in her hand to be threaded. "He puts me in mind of Mr. Carmel, just as full of ginger as they come, right up to the age of fifty. I'm glad he's got a nice little wife now; she's a trim little party judging from her looks, seeing her across the street."

"I don't like a woman with little feet," Grandma said, the Rough Riders dreamily waving back and forth before her face. "I've never known it to fail, there's something mean about a woman with little feet. Not that some with big feet aren't mean too, but just the same a little-foot woman is likely to be nasty in little ways."

Florrie and Marcia kept watch out the window to see if they could catch sight of Lena and Aunt Lois when the seven-thirty came through. Florrie swore she could see Papa—she could tell him by his hat, she said—in the back room of the hotel, but Marcia didn't think he'd be there on account of the money he still owed Mr. Purdy. They wondered if Lena could be made to come home again, and if Papa and Aunt Lois might not have a fight right there at the station. Aunt Lois might want to fight, they decided, but Papa cared too much about appearances. He'd pretend it was all his idea, Lena staying with Aunt Lois, and he'd tell everybody around town that it was something he'd talked Sweeney and Aunt Lois into doing, since they weren't likely to have any children of their own, and Lena was a favorite with them. When they heard the train coming in, they begged Grandma to let them run over to the station and see.

"Go ahead," she said. "But you don't catch me going. I'm a little cross with Lois for putting this over on me. Lois has hurt my feelings just once too often."

Sure enough, there was Mr. Sweeney, resplendent in an all-white suit and a Panama hat, holding open the door of the taxicab. Aunt Lois was pointing out her bags to the baggage-man, and she too was all in white linen, with a big Panama hat and white oxfords. Lena was standing demurely by Mr. Sweeney, and it was a blow to see that she too was in brand new clothes, pink linen and pink hat to match, with a little pink crocheted handbag. Florrie ran over to her and clutched her frantically, but Lena disengaged herself.

"Don't get me all dirty, Florrie," she said.

"Hello, Lena," said Marcia jealously.

"Hello," Lena said, and looked away frowning as if here was horrid reminder of a sordid past.

"Where's my five-dollar goldpiece?" Marcia said in a louder voice.

"My goodness, are you going to harp on that all my life?" exclaimed Lena petulantly. "Can't you see Aunt Lois and Mr. Sweeney want to get home?"

There was no sign of Papa. Aunt Lois hugged them and told them she would come and bring them presents from California as soon as they got unpacked, and tell Grandma she was coming down there and straighten her out first thing in the morning. Florrie and Marcia hung back while the distinguished little party drove off, Aunt Lois blowing kisses to them, Mr. Sweeney trying not to look too swollen up with pride, and Lena pursing up her lips and folding her hands demurely in her lap.

"When I run away, I'll take you with me," Marcia said after a long silence. "How would you like that?"

"I wouldn't want to leave Papa," Florrie said doubtfully. "But if you want me to go, Marcia, I will. Can I come back when we get there?"

Marcia looked at Florrie critically for the first time and saw that as usual Lena had grounds for her snubbing. Florrie's fair silky hair was all tousled over one eye and her jumper had a portion of raspberry jam embroidered over it. In the station window she saw that her own petticoat was showing a good three inches on one side, and two buttons were off her blouse.

"Well, I don't see how a person can be expected to think of every little thing," she muttered aloud.

They started back toward Grandma's, cutting across the back way to come up the back steps. This was an error in taste, for Papa and Bonnie Purdy were engaged in deep low-voiced conversation in the shadow of the back stairs. Bonnie was doing all the talking and Papa was listening, earnestly nodding his head. The girls crept around the front way un-observed and waited a long time at Grandma's till Papa came to get them. They spent the time describing Aunt Lois' cos-tume over and over again for the old ladies' amazement.

"Travelling in white—well, I never!" ejaculated Mrs. Carmel several times. "You wouldn't see me doing it, even in my prime."

33

Marcia and Florrie were forbidden to visit Lena at Aunt Lois'. Their stepmother said if Lena wanted to see them she could come and call on them, and, for that matter, just let that young lady show her face in the door. Setting the whole town against her own folks, causing talk, and even ruining people's confidence in her own father, so that only this very day Mr. Friend had called in an undertaker from Lesterville to attend his sister's passing. That was the sort of thing your indepen-dent young ladies could do to their own fathers. She was not saying anything, Mrs. Willard added, about the damage done to her good name by the situation; she was used to it. Stories got back to her, and she knew exactly whom to blame for not being invited to join the new Social Club. Her brother Vance had obligingly told her that the town gossip was that the Willards expected to be invited places but never returned hos-pitality, they were so afraid of someone dirtying up their dishes and upholstery. Well, anyone with half an eye knew who started that talk, and the somebody was right in the family, or was till she saw fit to run away to an aunt who had as good as said she was through looking after other people's children. No, declared Mrs. Willard, she would not lift a finger to bring Lena back to her proper home, and if her father tried to do so, she, Idah Hawkins Willard, would pack up and go straight back to Daleport, taking Minelda with her and the household linen which was all her personal property, proved by her initials. Lena's adventure and triumphal return under the enemy's flag seemed to have unleashed a whole horde of venomous thoughts in her stepmother, for she ranted at the table, fixing a glassy oyster-colored eye on first Florrie, then Marcia, and muttering angry monologues around her work, relieving herself of a perfect mint of bitterness, scathing memories of all the family traits—Marcia's sarcastic silences, Florrie's pouting face, and Lena's brazenness.

"I shouldn't be a bit surprised," she said, shaking a knobby red forefinger at Marcia, "if somebody right in this family didn't tell the whole town that I'm not a good housekeeper. Yes, sir, I'll bet neighbors down the street whisper behind my back, 'There goes a woman that sweeps the dirt into closets.' I'd like them to step in here and I'd show 'em every inch of the house, clean as a whistle, except when you children are around."

She took care to say nothing about Papa, for she was respectful of his temper and not a little afraid he might bolt out of her life forever. When her patience was too tried with him, she shut her jaw tightly, lips white under compression, and she was deeply hurt that this visible effort at self-control irritated rather than pleased Papa. She talked so much about Lena insulting her own father by not even coming to see him that Papa was reluctantly obliged to confess that Aunt Lois and Lena had come in the store, and they had talked over the whole matter. As might have been expected, he took the position of the whole arrangement being his idea.

"I told Lois right to her face that there was no reason she shouldn't take a little responsibility, now that she's settled down with Sweeney," Papa said. "Naturally, I wouldn't let my daughter live with strangers, and I wouldn't let her live with people that couldn't give her advantages that I couldn't give her. But, by George, Sweeney is worth plenty of money and he might as well spend it on my daughter as on some orphan from an asylum, some kid with bad blood maybe that'd turn on 'em in the end. I've got a hell of a lot of expense right now. I told Lois for the time being I don't mind somebody else in the family taking over part of the burden if it's all right with Lena. It won't be like her own home here, but it'll be a good experience for her. My dad sent me to live with my Uncle Bill when I was about Lena's age. Best thing that ever happened to me."

"She'll lose whatever manners I've drummed into her," his wife moodily said. "I can just hear them talking about me, telling lies and putting people against me. I noticed Mrs. Chase had a tea yesterday and not a word to me. Every time I go to market somebody makes some remark that shows stories are going around. I'm almost afraid to go downtown."

So their sister was gone forever, Marcia and Florrie thought with a sense of terror. They met her at Grandma's after Sunday school. Grandma was having a celebration dinner for the bridal couple, and the girls sneaked in on their way home. This time Lena was very gracious and let Marcia wear her new coral beads all the time she was there, and gave Florrie a red handkerchief with the words, "Twenty-Three Skidoo," printed on it in yellow. She confided that she had heard about Aunt Lois' train through telegrams Vance Hawkins had transmitted, and she generously suggested that both sisters run away as soon as possible—"not to Aunt Lois' though," she interpolated. She said she wouldn't stand being bossed by That Woman a second, and they were dummies to take it, and so was Papa. She said so far as she was concerned she was absolutely through with Papa, and it was just like Aunt Lois said, he was a big windbag, always blowing off about something and never really doing anything. Marcia and Florrie exchanged a stricken look over this shocking irreverence.

"Don't, Lena," Florrie begged tearfully. "Please don't talk about Papa that way. Mama wouldn't like it."

Marcia longed to confide in Lena that she too was going to run away, but she could not be sure whether Lena would be sympathetic or suddenly go to the grown-ups' side, blabbing everything so that Aunt Lois would taunt Papa with it and then she'd be locked up. It was a pity you could never trust anybody.

Mr. Sweeney, now kingpin in the Willard and Reed family, bore himself with the dignity of a man elected to a public office far above his dreams but one for which he knew himself, in all humility, to be perfectly equipped. He nodded thoughtfully over Grandma's and Aunt Lois' exchange on family matters, voiced his judgments with an impressive hemming and hawing, and all in all accepted his promotion from family adviser to head of family with suitable gravity. It was a shame that a man of such majestic manner should have to perspire like any ordinary fellow, until Aunt Lois implored him to take off his coat even if he did wear old-fashioned suspenders. The ladies asked his opinion on the seasoning of the succotash, the state of the nation, the band concert programs, and all private problems, with flattering deference to his resonant decisions. There was none of the laughter such as was occasioned by Papa's presence at a family party, though Mr. Sweeney was not without proper appreciation, observing "Very humorous, yes," to many things that were said. He addressed Aunt Lois deferentially as "Mrs. Sweeney" or "my dear," referred to the first Mrs. Sweeney as "poor Ivy," and rather annoyed Grandma by occasionally testing out the word "Mother" on her, until Grandma observed that the small difference in their ages made this form of address a little ridiculous. At sixty, she said, she could hardly have had a son of fifty-three even if she'd wanted one.

Marriage had completely altered Aunt Lois' queenly attitude toward Mr. Sweeney. She fluttered anxiously about him, patting his big red hand as it lay on the table, lighting his cigar, bringing him a glass of lemonade when he mopped his broad red forehead, filling his plate before Grandma could ask if he wanted more, putting all the white meat from her own dish onto his, and looking at the other plates with a frown as if she would like to give them all necks and gizzards just so that her master might have the daintiest bits. She buttered his buns, and slid her own coffee to him when Grandma said the second pot would take another minute. In short, she behaved as a wife should, who recognizes the authority of her master and his superior requirements. All domineering traits seemed to have been melted by marriage, and Aunt Lois deferred completely to her husband now, explaining that wherever they went in the West there was always someone who mistook him for a senator or colonel or bigwig of sorts, and treated them both accordingly. It made travelling a pleasure. Both bride and groom had expanded in waistline and referred affectionately to many good dishes they had found in the West. Californians were fine people, they said, not at all stuck up like you'd think. True, they ate their lettuce first, that is before soup, and with mayonnaise instead of sugar and vinegar, but then every state had its own customs that looked funny to other states. The Sweeneys expected to take a two months' vacation in the West every year, and might even put Lena in a boarding school out there.

"I might visit you myself," Grandma said, "I've always had a hankering for California."

"I understand the climate cures arthritis," Mrs. Carmel said.

Aunt Lois brushed aside these suggestions.

"Ma, now you know you'd never leave Ohio," she said. "Why, every time she's ever been in Indiana or Kentucky, Mr. Sweeney, she is miserable. She can tell the minute we're on the Ohio state border, and then she perks up. Besides, that kind of a trip takes money, Ma, and this shop doesn't look to me as if there was that much profit in it."

Grandma was about to say in some irritation that she could always put her fingers on cash when she needed it, but bethought herself of her daughter's probable policing of Mr. Sweeney's checkbook and was silent.

There was a great deal of talk about Papa, Aunt Lois declaring that if he tried to make Lena come back home she would have the law on him for neglect. Grandma said Harry wasn't to blame, he'd always had hard luck, and whatever had gone wrong was the fault of his wife. Aunt Lois said he had picked his wife with his eyes open, and she could well remember the day poor Daisy died and Harry brought this nurse in saying, "Meet the second Mrs. Willard." That was the sort of thing you couldn't forget, with your sister lying on her deathbed and the three children scared out of their wits. She wouldn't be at all surprised but what the second Mrs. Willard had fixed up the medicine for Daisy just so she could get Harry.

"You mean this party poisoned her?" Mrs. Carmel exclaimed, beady eyes glowing with pleasure.

"Now, now, Mrs. Sweeney," Mr. Sweeney remonstrated, shaking a finger fondly at his wife. "Don't exaggerate."

Aunt Lois tossed her head sulkily, and compromised by saying Harry could have married lots of girls who would have made lovely mothers, good-hearted, hard-working girls, say, like Bonnie Purdy. Aunt Lois said, much to her nieces' astonishment, that she never could understand why Papa hadn't married Bonnie anyway, because Bonnie was fond of the children and was by no means stupid.

"But you always told him not to, Aunt Lois," Florrie said wide-eyed.

"I may have said something once in a while, but, my goodness, I never tried to run his life one way or another," Aunt Lois replied. "A real man never takes anybody's advice anyway, if he has any gumption. No, sir, Harry should have married Bonnie. If he had, the whole family would be better off and Bonnie wouldn't be in the fix she's in right now."

Marcia asked if it was true Lena would go to the new high school, and Mr. Sweeney said naturally, that was the plan. Brooding over this for a few moments, Marcia stated that she personally was going to get a job and make a lot of money maybe, she hinted, not in London Junction either. When Mr. Sweeney benignly asked her what she could do, she said she had learned the touch system at the telegraph office when Vance Hawkins let her use the typewriter. Aunt Lois wanted to know what the touch system was, and Marcia explained it was "not looking at what you're doing."

"I should think you'd make a lot of mistakes that way," Aunt Lois said.

Marcia admitted that the type did sort of jumble up, but that's the way you had to do it; you looked up at the ceiling and banged away, and that was the touch system, the first thing required of an office worker. She didn't see how anyone could be expected to have the finished product perfect when they wouldn't let you look at the keys. She also didn't see how she could be expected to be an expert when her stepmother had forbidden her to hang around the telegraph office any more, because she made trouble for Vance, telling customers that he was practicing in the music store or had stepped out to take a walk with Bonnie Purdy, until a warning came that he might be fired, all due to Miss Know-it-all.

Marcia was settling into a cozy chat when the clanging of the twelve-fifty Cincinnati Express brought her to the realization that they were already late for dinner and would have to make up some excuse for being late. She snatched Florrie's Sunday school hat and jammed it on the tousled head, yanked her out the door and flew down the street. Lena left the table to stand in the bay window and watch them as far as the turn in the street. When Aunt Lois reminded her that Marcia had forgotten to give back the coral beads, Lena said she guessed she'd let her keep them, because she liked her blue beads the best anyway. She resumed her place at the table in a rather gloomy mood, which she maintained the rest of the day. Aunt Lois did not like Mary Evelyn and disapproved of Lena going around with her. She said Mary Evelyn painted her cheeks and chased after boys, both of these occupations appealing enormously to Lena too. But if you couldn't play around with your bosom friend, you might as well play with your sisters. Only now she was an only child, Lena thought, something she had always longed to be, but it wasn't much fun really, except for the clothes and the presents, and half the fun of even these rewards was in showing them off to your sisters. Nothing ever turned out perfect.

34

In another week school would open. David Gross told Marcia of the new courses there would be in high school, the new things he was going to learn.

"General history," he said, dreamily staring into space through his thick glasses. "That's about Nebuchadnezzar and his hanging gardens. I'll take that, and so would you, Marcia. You and I would probably be the only ones that would like it."

"I know," said Marcia gloomily.

"English literature," pursued David. He got out a pencil and began writing it all down on the back of the parcel he was about to mail to his father (some fudge his sister Fanny had just made).

"I've read it all," Marcia said. "I've read more than Miss Burlington has anyway."

"Yes, but there's a new teacher taking her place, somebody from Ohio State," David said. "Everything is improved, they told Mother at the school meeting. It won't be any fun learning new things without you. And there'll be prizes and scholarships."

"Maybe Lena will get some," Marcia said.

David shook his head.

"No, she won't, because all she cares about is boys. She isn't like you."

Marcia said nothing, half glad that her own passionate interest in the boys was not obvious, since it was not a reciprocal matter, and half disgusted with David for being so dumb as not to see this. David was like Lena said he was, a little old man. He might be very bright and all that, but Marcia felt there must be something the matter with a boy that thought she was the most beautiful girl in town. She hoped nobody ever heard him saying this or they'd make fun of both of them. It was too bad he was half a head shorter than she was, and what with always talking like a book and wearing knickerbockers when the other boys wore long pants, David was worse than no boy friend at all, even if they did make up exciting stories together. Now that was over, and the fact that David felt so forlorn about it made Marcia more philosophical. Maybe going to the new high school would just have meant that she would have to be mean to David, because she would want to go to the dances and parties and David would never fit in there; if you felt a misfit yourself you just wouldn't dare go around with another misfit. She wouldn't be allowed to go to any of the high-school parties anyway, what was she thinking of? She reminded herself. She wouldn't have the class dues: or the right dress or permission to go with a boy. Even meeting David accidentally in the postoffice, on an errand for her stepmother, they had to talk at the writing desk, pretending to be waiting for stamps, for fear word would get back to her home. It was lucky she was there this day, for the postal clerk stuck his head out the window after a while and called to her.

"Here's a card for one of you Willard girls," he said. It was for her, and was a picture of Edgewater Park, Cleveland, with a few lines on the back from Mrs. Putney, "We'll have a pic-nic supper in this park if you have a chance to visit us this summer. Bring your bathing suit."

This exciting message was shared with David and all its pos-sibilities gone over breathlessly. She would go to Cleveland when she ran away, and it would have to be soon now, before school began. She would go to Mrs. Putney's and get a job from there. How wonderful that the postcard hadn't gone home where perhaps she would never have received it or, even worse, her stepmother would have had to find out all about the Putneys. Marcia was so excited she wanted to tell Papa, Grandma, everybody, but David reminded her that this would spoil all her plans.

In front of the London Junction Hotel bar she caught a glimpse of Papa laughing with a big man who must be Mr. Hartwell. This was the Papa they never saw any more, the gay laughing Papa with hat on the side of his head and the half-smoked cigar in his hand. Marcia looked at him a long time, feeling lonesome for him, as if he'd been away a long time. But even as she watched, the two men separated; Papa looked at his watch, straightened his hat, waved his hand, and as Mr. Hartwell took his sample case inside the hotel Papa seemed to change. His shoulders slumped, his footsteps dragged slowly and he walked with his eyes bent on the ground.

When she got home Marcia knocked on the back screen door, was let in silently by her stepmother, gave her the stamped envelopes She had requested, and tiptoed carefully up the steps, being careful not to touch the railing or put her heels on the stairs. She was supposed to wash her hands and clean up Minelda before lunch, a touchy chore, since Minelda screamed whenever anyone washed her, and her mother kept calling up frantically to stop torturing the child, sometimes dashing up to cuff Marcia and finish the job herself, unconvinced even when Minelda yelled all the louder at the change in hands. Marcia thought of the hanging gardens of Nebuchadnezzar as she combed Minelda's skimpy locks; they were all mixed up with the new high-school playground with the fountain playing in the center. In one of Grandpa's books, now locked in the parlor bookcase, there were pictures of ancient Babylon and all the places described in general history. Grandpa had given the book to her, but She had taken it away at his death and locked it up even though he'd written "Marcia's book" on the flyleaf. Marcia felt an overwhelming urge to have this book, to hide it and take it with her wherever she went, so that some day if she should meet David Gross she could say, "I know about those things too." Minelda was calm today and Marcia left her without any tumult, creeping down the front stairs into the dark parlor, reaching with trembling fingers into the vase where Florrie said the keys were now kept. She found it and with pounding heart was about to unlock the bookcase when she heard the voice of Vance in the back hallway. Marcia frantically slid behind the huge arm-chair, fortunately placed in the corner, and with an awful sinking sensation heard Vance and her stepmother come into the room.

"I don't want Harry to find you here, Vance; you know how he is," Mrs. Willard murmured fretfully. "Goodness knows, I've got my hands full without bringing on another fight. Now what is it? Hurry, before he gets here."

"Keep your shirt on," Vance replied in an aggrieved tone. He lit a cigarette and threw the match at the fireplace without a word of reproach from his sister. Marcia was relieved that they were sitting down with their backs to her, at least, but she was afraid she might cough and nothing short of death would be the penalty for being discovered here.

"Oh, Vancie, I can't stand it if you're in trouble again," Marcia heard her stepmother moan.

"It isn't my fault, damn it," Vance muttered.

His sister hastened to reassure him.

"I know it isn't, Vancie, but you do have the worst luck. Some woman again, I'll bet. I'd just like to lay my hands on her."

There was a moment's silence and then Vance began talking quickly and quietly, interrupted only by smothered exclamations from his sister.

"I've got to skip town and I've got to have money. A girl I've been running around with got herself in trouble and the wire just came through the office to her relations that she died in the doctor's office this morning in Lesterville. It'll be all over town by tomorrow. I've got a guy's Ford down by the office and I'm going East, only I've got to have some dough. How much you got here?"

There was another moaning sigh from his sister, and then, "You might as well tell me the rest, Vancie. Who's the girl?"

"Bonnie Purdy," Vance said, "your husband's old girl friend. If you want to know so much he gave her the dough for the operation too. I wasn't going to get hooked when she came to me, by George."

"Harry gave her money? Harry Willard?" her voice was incredulous. "It must have been the money for the car. That's why they haven't delivered it. Of all the dirty tricks!"

"I told her to go ahead and go to him when she came after me about it," Vance went on angrily. "He was so damned careful of her he didn't want anybody else kissing her. I guess he could be careful enough of her to pay for her doctor. No girl is going to trap me that way, believe me. Only now she's conked out, everybody knew I was going with her, she told people about it, so that lets me in on a fine mess. Girls always got to blab and get a fellow in a jam just when he's getting his feet on the ground."

"But Harry— I can't get over Harry giving it to her."

"Yes, and he can pay for her funeral expenses too, he's such a gentleman," Vance snorted. "He can lay her out, if that's any satisfaction to him, and pay for the pleasure. Only that isn't going to get me out of town."

"If Harry has the money unbeknownst to me to pay for Bonnie Purdy," said Mrs. Willard tensely, "then I guess I can find some to get my brother out of trouble."

"That's the old girl," Vance exclaimed, much relieved.

There was a rustling of paper. She must keep her money in her blouse, Marcia decided, not daring to peek, and praying that they would both get out before her breathing could be heard.

"Go on, now, quick, out the front door," Mrs. Willard urged.

"I knew I could count on you," Vance's voice came back jubilantly. "I'll write Mom and she'll tell you where I land. Bye, old girl. Don't let on. You think I'm killed or something, that's the ticket."

The door closed softly, and Marcia pressed both hands over her heart to keep it from thundering too loud. She shut her eyes, waiting for the high-heeled footsteps to cross to the back hall, but after a full moment in sudden silence she opened them. For a moment she did not realize what was wrong. Then she knew eyes were upon her. Before she met them, she knew what it would be. The two marble eyes fixed on her were filled with implacable hatred. Her stepmother was bending over the chair looking down at her.

"I wasn't doing anything," Marcia choked.

"Spying. Sneaking." The voice was deadly calm, and Marcia thought this then would be the end of her, death from fright. "Trying to find out things that are none of your business so you can tell everybody lies. Well, this is one time you won't. Come out of there, and go in the kitchen."

Unable to speak and unable to move, the grim fingers gripped her wrist and yanked her briskly into the kitchen, opened the screen door and pushed her outside, locking it again.

"Wait," said her stepmother, and her steps could be heard flying upstairs. Marcia had to wait, for she did not know what to do or how she could get her legs to moving anyway. If Papa had come up the path then, she would not have dared tell him what was happening, any more than she'd dare tell anyone. In almost no time, the high-heeled slippers flew down the back stairs, and this time there was a crooked smile on her stepmother's face. She handed out the door, a big square bag, indeed the very telescope, now mouse-chewed and shabby, that the Willards had moved with to London Junction, the "telescope" in which Dr. Byrd had brought Florrie ten years ago.

"There's your things," She said. "Never come back here again. I'll tell my story of what happened, and it's not going to be the same as yours, so the best thing for you to do is clear out. Don't you dare open your mouth about anything you heard and don't you dare go to your father with any tales. You'll pay for it if you do. Get out!"

Marcia stood stupidly for a while, even after the door clicked. She didn't know what to do, because Myrtle Chase was walking past and would see her being put out of the house. When Myrtle turned the corner, Marcia picked up the telescope and ran as fast as she could across the vacant lots between home and the railroad tracks. She took the freight tracks because they didn't run through the center street but switched off a side alley till they came to the depot. She ran so fast that she fell down in the cinders once and bruised her hand. She could see the end of the street where Aunt Lois lived, and she desperately wished she dared stop to see Lena, but she might tell and then she'd be killed or might be taken back home. Coming to the station, there was a passenger train coming in and Marcia knew she would have to take it no matter which way it was going. If it was going toward Elmville she would go to Aunt Betts', though she knew their house was full of half a dozen grandchildren now and Aunt Betts was sick. If it was going toward Cleveland—! She asked the conductor and he said it was Cleveland, and Marcia stumbled onto the coach. She dragged her bag into the women's room, so that anyone getting on from the Junction wouldn't see her and try to stop her. She stood in there trying to fix herself up and wiping away tears of fright.

Pretty soon she came out and took a seat. She felt in her waist to see that her five dollars was still pinned to her underslip, with Mrs. Putney's postcard picture of Edgewater Park. The card and Lena's coral beads were lucky, she thought, breathing a little easier as the train rolled along. She was still scared, but she felt light-headed and gay, the way Papa did when he was going away from home. She thought she must be like Papa, the kind of person who was always glad going away instead of coming home. She looked out the window, feeling the other self inside her, the self that had no feelings and could never be hurt, coming out stronger and stronger, looking at the fringe of London Junction and the beginnings of Milltown with calm, almost without remembrance. In a back yard past Milltown Village, a woman was chopping off the head of a chicken, and Marcia thought if Florrie was along this would make her cry. She thought she ought to cry just a little, out of loyalty to Florrie. She'd come back and get Florrie some day, just like she promised. But maybe Florrie would never leave Papa. It was as if Florrie would always have to protect Papa instead of the other way round.

The porter came in with the last call for lunch, and passengers began moving forward. Marcia remembered she had no lunch, but she didn't know how you acted in a diner. When a boy came through with fruit and candy she asked him how much each of his wares was. Nothing was under ten cents. As he was about Marcia's age, she did not want him to think she couldn't afford this, so she asked him how much lunch in the diner would be.

"You don't want to spend all that money," said the boy, a thin freckled boy with several teeth missing. "Look. Take this, and don't say anything."

He handed her a pear and an apple, and dodged hastily down the aisle before the conductor could catch him at this unprofessional conduct. A young lady came in looking, Marcia saw at once, as a young lady on her own should look. She was not pretty like Lena but she looked like pictures in magazines. She had black hair parted in the middle and drawn sleekly back to fine little snail-like coils on the back of her neck, from ear to ear. Marcia studied this coiffure intently, pretending to read the Want Ads in the *Leader* at the same time. "Mother's Helper—oh, no! Secretary—maybe, why not? Telephone Operator—that ought to be easy. Be a Trained Nurse—maybe. Cash Girl in Large Department Store—maybe . . ." Presently Marcia went back to the women's room and undid her long braids. In the face of some urgent pounding on the door, she finally got her hair twisted up into what seemed a similar set of coils. She looked at least sixteen, she thought with pleasure. She rubbed some red paper on her cheeks the way Lena and Mary Evelyn did, but an old lady stared at her so sternly she hastily wiped it off the minute she got back to her seat.

It was not long after noon but it was dark and raining outside, so there was not much to see. Marcia thought about what she would do when she got into Union Station. She would take a streetcar to the Putneys, and she would say she was looking for a room. She was sure they would be good to her, because strangers were always good to you. The light rattle of the rain on the coach roof made her drowsy, and she thought about telephone operating, being a salesgirl in May's, being a secretary with the touch system, and presently she was in a half dream reciting with Mr. Putney, only he changed into a very old man, so she had the platform all to herself and was taking all the parts in a play called "The Lion and the Mouse." Lena and Florrie and Papa and Aunt Lois were all there in the front row gazing worshipfully at her.

The rain came louder, beating across the window. Marcia rubbed a spot on the pane and saw they were already at Union Falls, miles and miles from London Junction. The rain covered the spot, and Marcia took her forefinger and wrote "MARCIA WILLARD" across the foggy pane.

THE LOCUSTS HAVE NO KING

*The locusts have no king, yet go
they forth all of them by bands.*
PROVERBS

CONTENTS

I

. . . journey into the juke-box . . .

WHEREVER he went that night people insisted on confiding in him. Perhaps some fear of his fellow-men gleamed in the young man's intense blue eyes that made them want to reassure him that they, too, were unarmed. Perhaps his eager haste suggested a mission of love, so circumstance must conspire mischievously with people to delay him.

It began when he stepped confidently into a taxi at Fourth and Bank, gave the address on East End Avenue, suddenly felt in his change pocket, then in his wallet with an expression of acute chagrin, impatiently crumpled his hat under his arm and stepped out on the street again. Frowning he considered Umberto's Grotto lettered in white on a blue canopy tilted up to street level like a tea-pot snout. He dashed down the stairs but the man he sought had just left. While he hesitated in the doorway his taxi escaped and pudgy Umberto clutched his lapel to lament how grievous had been the mistake of listening to relatives, adding a garden and Muzak, and how much happier he, being a simple man of simple tastes, would be if only his worthless wife and children could have fallen in the East River. A man should never marry, said Umberto, and would gladly have revealed more, generously offering a glass of chianti and a toast *"Salut e figli masci!"* but Frederick pleaded that his emergency would permit him to waste no time. Perhaps he could find Murray in those spots further east, suggested Umberto following him up the steps and making a wide gesture toward the lights beyond Sheridan Square. Pulling his topcoat around his neck, Frederick hurried out into the chilly March rain. He had lived long in the neighborhood but everything looked strange and new tonight, a little terrifying to a man just emerged from seven years' burial in the dead ages. Tonight the work was completed and it was as if he had just returned from a long voyage and must grope eagerly but a little uncertainly for the old familiar landmarks. Each block toward the bright lights seemed a century's step through a tunnel of darkness toward Lyle—and life. Names of bars mentioned by Murray flickered vaguely through his memory, and he stepped tentatively into one called the Florida.

It surprised him that everyone knew Murray. Everyone knew Murray Cahill and his nocturnal habits far better than did the man who had shared his apartment for years. This was Murray's world. In the Florida Tavern a long-nosed girl with sleek head, chin sliding into a gaunt length of black sweater and slacks, looked up at mention of the name. Her long feet in ballet slippers hooked over the rungs of the bar stool.

"Try the America's bar two blocks over and up," she suggested. "He goes there first. How about sticking around here for a while? Have a drink. I gotta talk to somebody. No? Okay, okay."

Hurrying across the street the misty golden lights made faces blur as in a dream, shine brightly for a second, then fade into a half-smile, a moustache, harlequin spectacles, wide red lips. Little dark streets waited for footsteps, invited shadows to creep back to forgotten ages; cats' eyes peered up from cellar windows, watched from sloping roofs for some signal from the hidden moon. Frederick felt like the banquet guest in the fairy-tale who took the wrong overshoes and stepped out into another age. He wondered if his disguise was adequate, if his toga showed. He wondered if the day would ever come when he would cease being the stranger, the solitary wanderer, the observer without passport or knowledge of the language. Like a shy but curious nursery child in adult wonderland, he peered into the Americas whose blue neon sign cast a warning green shadow on each new arrival. The bar was long and narrow with a juke-box glowing like hell-fire in the back, bellowing demon songs to the damned. No Murray in sight.

"Murray ought to be in the Barrel about now," said the waiter. "He doesn't get in here till around two as a rule."

"Have a drink," said a man at the bar, a bald fat man in a plaid shirt. "I think I'm being stood up but I'm waiting to make sure. She said she'd be here, but that's the way she is. This isn't the first time. You look like an intelligent guy, I'd like to ask you a question. Now I'm a married man. My wife—here, take a seat."

"I'm sorry, I'm late," Frederick apologized and hastened into the street again, darting in and out of the cafés of Rubberleg Square, so-called for the high percentage of weak-kneed pedestrians. Rough bar, fancy bar, bars with doormen, bars with sawdust floors—Murray was bound to be in one of them, but which? Frederick was astonished at the variety at first, and then at their inevitable sameness.

Wherever he went he found advertising men all weeping into their Bourbon of happy days when they were star reporters on the Providence *Journal*. They yearned to tell him their dreams and disappointments. Sometimes they were with petulant wives, who, if from the South, had been the prettiest girls in Tallahassee; if from the Middle West their folks had the biggest house in Evansville. Sometimes these men, happier by far when cub reporters than now with their twenty thousand a year, were not with wives but with stylists, camera ladies, women's-angle-women from their offices, all emotionally fulfilled by making fat salaries, wearing Delman shoes and Daché hats, and above all being out with The Office and talking shop. These were the women who had won the war, the spoils were theirs; these were the women who had found a swansdown paycheck warmer in bed than naked Cupid. Wherever he went Frederick found the new race of men and women, the victors who had won by default, who had sold a pint of Type O for the merest gold-mine. Wherever he went his sobriety induced warm overtures from total strangers unable to make friends by day.

Hopefully looking around the bar of the Barrel, most regal of the neighborhood bistros, he was pounced upon by a man from the K.G.R. Advertising Agency whose tears over good old newspaper days were mingled with belligerent pride in cigarette campaigns.

"Just wait till you see what I've done with Hazelnut," the K.G.R. man boasted, detaining Frederick by the lapel. "Just a woman's hand holding a flaming match and the line 'Let Me Give You a Light.' Just that one line, mind you, but it sings. Hazelnut knows it. K.G.R. knows it. They've got to admit it. 'Let Me Give You a Light.' And the match playing like a searchlight over a pack of Hazelnut Cigarettes up in the sky. It's good, damn it, if I do say so myself."

"Excellent," Frederick said, wary as he always was with genial men, not wishing to rebuff them but dreading their intrusion.

The K.G.R. man removed his right hand from the lapel, loosened his hold on the highball glass, readjusted his foot on the rail, and swaying briefly at the loss of support transferred his grip to Frederick's reluctant hand. He smiled engagingly.

"Hi, fella. I like you. You're all right. You know what it's all about. Got a poker face but I can tell you catch. Jack, give this guy a drink. Here, fella, sit down here. I had a girl but she blew. Where'd Dodo go, Jack?"

"Thanks, I won't have any more," Frederick said, and in an effort to discourage further intimacy turned to the bartender with a stern, almost accusing voice. "Where's Murray?"

Suddenly he felt foolish. It seemed to him that customers and bartender looked up suspiciously at his haughty tone. It seemed to him they must guess at once that he was a stranger to these places, queasily dismayed by the revellers clustering around the little red piano lustily singing old songs and spilling their drinks on the colored pianist; the smell of ancient tombs and crumbling ruins must be about him; Latin footnotes and ravellings of doctors' theses must be swarming in pursuit of him like hungry moths. Prudently he said no more when the bartender, ignoring his previous protest, placed a drink before him.

"Murray's hat's still checked," said the bartender coldly. "He'll be back."

He knows, thought Frederick, that Murray's roommate doesn't belong, plays no part in the neighborhood's midnight antics; he recognizes a discreet, sober man certain never to drink except within his means, to resent amiable offers of treats and therefore not to reciprocate; here is a man unlikely to create the mirage of gaiety that impels customers to magnificent gestures; here is a man who would remember that tomorrow was Rent Day when it was his turn to buy a drink, a man who would not admit the compulsions of bar room etiquette. Here is a man who ought to get out and make room for the genuine members; maybe he speaks a dozen languages but he doesn't speak ours. "Nor understand," Frederick admitted, listening to the strange phrases fly back and forth around him.

"*The Detroit Free Press? . . . Good God, old man, then you knew Jack Huberman? . . . You did? . . . Well, I was on the Post-Dispatch by that time, then I went to Ivy Lee . . .*"
"*What—you were with Ivy Lee? . . . I left there for J. Walter Thompson . . . what? . . . no! no! . . . Have a drink! . . . You were? . . . No! No! . . . You were? . . . Have a drink . . .*"

He turned to thank the K.G.R. man but the latter had found a more congenial attachment at the other end of the bar, another old newspaper man now in public relations. Hazelnut campaign was forgotten in the joyful exchange of old encounters with Huey Long, Ford; intimate anecdotes of front-page names; fond reminiscences of the great hearts of Hearst, Howard, Munsey, Patterson, McCormick. Frederick listened, meditating on the curious way newspaper men, despite their apprenticeship in realities, end up convinced by their own romantic inventions, respectful of the celebrities their own lies created, teary over sob-stories they had made up themselves, doffing their plumes reverently to whatever powers had kept them down. The public relations man, a stout little chap named Mooney with a trim moustache, spoke sardonically of the prostitution of his journalistic genius, but as he heard himself sneer at the first-water phonies whose reputations he preserved, stuffed, and mounted, he was moved to awe at his own power and its fabulous possibilities. He might be engaged in the world's most degrading occupation but at least he was better at it than anyone else. He called to two ladies in a booth to affirm this, both of them high in the business world—one in Gimbel's or Altman's department store, the other in real estate. The ladies paused in the midst of their comparison of income-tax to declare that Mooney was certainly the best there was, and they only wished they had his accounts.

Mooney gratefully shook their hands and even went to the trouble to explain that he was the soul of honesty, refusing to touch certain large sums that clients had placed at his disposal into which he could have dipped without the big saps knowing the difference, but which, in his ridiculous honesty, he never even considered touching, unless, of course, it was absolutely necessary, and in view of how much money the particular clients had a person need really feel no compunction about rewarding his honesty with a little extra dividend, what the hell, we're all in business, we know what time it is. The K.G.R. man lurched up to receive equal attention, jostled Public Relations aside to lean across the table and recount his Hazelnut inspiration, was so overwhelmed by their polite attention that he ordered more drinks to add to the regiment of glasses before them, drinks consumed, drinks started, and the drinks Public Relations had ordered; he invited them to dance, to sit at the bar, to go up to the Blue Angel where Arturo knew he was a person of consequence, to visit his home in Greenwich any time, any hour of day or night. The two men hovered over the table, vying with each other for the approval of these splendid influential women who were not flibbertigibbets but real guys, pals, people. They patted the pals on the back, dropped cigarette ashes and an occasional cinder down their bosoms, waved their drinks at perilous angles over their heads, shouted with resounding laughter over every word even before it had been said, were generously happy in the pleasure their company was surely giving. Frederick watched the innocent scene in the bar mirror, and speculated on how long this fine new friendship would last, and what would happen if the ladies really should appear sometime in the dead of night in Greenwich. One of the ladies waved to him, and he bowed gratefully, since he knew few people. Probably one of his students at the League.

He thought of Lyle waiting for him, reproached himself for not starting out sooner. Each morning his waking thought was "How soon will I see Lyle today?" but he was always late; wanting wings to fly to her he must always punish his desires with barriers of his own creation. He had promised to meet her at the Beckleys' at ten but at ten he had been putting the last fond period to his manuscript. Then he had been obliged to think about clothes, an outrageous tax on the brain, to rummage for dress shirt and silk socks. Moths had embroidered their initials on the trousers of his dinner clothes, dress hose were in threads, so he had to switch back to tweeds. He found he had enough cash for his own carfare but not enough to be an evening's guest at a millionaire's house; that meant he had to find Murray. A burst of anger swept over him at the sheer inconvenience of being in love with Lyle, and at the demands her group made on him. Be on time. Dress. Be discreet for these are friends of my husband. Please take home all unescorted ladies, pay for the night-cap in the fine café they select, use your breakfast money on a check-room tip, walk home when your small funds give out. All for love. All for the incurable need of seeing Lyle whenever and wherever he could. How often he had rebelled at the bond-age of his love, said goodbye forever, then rushed back to her sweet forgiving arms, begging for his chains. He had refused the easy teaching job in a Southern college, all for Lyle; and now the only way he could celebrate the comple-tion of his work was to follow her to her own world and hope for a word with her. He would know no one there and be in-tensely uncomfortable, all for Lyle.

"But you ought to know Ephraim Beckley better, darling," she had said. "I don't expect you to like him, because nobody does, but after all he is a power, grandson of one of the great publishers. You ought to have a little scientific curiosity. You can't stay in another century every minute. It will do you good, darling. Ephraim spoke of you particularly!"

Frederick professed immense gratification at the compli-ment, adding that, for his part he always enjoyed being in-troduced to Ephraim Beckley and considered the Beckley amnesia in the presence of unknowns nothing short of genius.

"But he didn't realize you had written the *Swan* essays," Lyle said. "He probably thought it was only *Swann's Way*. He meets so many Prousts. Do come. Even if it's horrible it's something you ought to know. You do have to know the world, dear!"

So he must promise to meet her there, half annoyed and half touched by Lyle's transparent efforts to bring him out of his shell. She was always mistaking his retreat from life as loneli-ness that must be assuaged, or else she was chiding him for not liking people. She was wrong, he felt. People amused him, and safe in her arms he did not fear them. He wanted to be specta-tor, that was all, not actor; if possible he wanted a glass wall be-tween him and other human beings and he was happy when Lyle joined him in the observation post, unhappy when she was on the other side of the glass. It made him uncomfortable when the actors addressed him, as if Myrna Loy should sud-

denly reach out of a moving picture to shake his hand. Still he
would go where Lyle bade him, knowing he would hate it,
knowing he would be unable to curb his misery at seeing her
surrounded by admirers and belongers. Above all, he would be
obliged to think about money. That was the thing that was always coming between himself and Lyle, the expense of being
good to the rich. His own poverty never inconvenienced him;
his ascetic tastes required little more than enough for dinner at
Umberto's or the Chinaman's, coffee and a sandwich in
Whelan's, a beer or two, a concert, a book. But no, for Lyle's
sake, he must forage around trying to borrow money enough
to visit or sup at some rich man's home, be prepared for the
little accepted duties of Extra Man. "Be good to the rich." Why
couldn't the rich mind their own business, divide expenses
with each other, invite each other to dinner and feast on each
other's fruity conversation? The truth was that they feared
other rich might be richer than they were, a horrid thought,
for if they are not the richest, what are they? So they must have
artists, scientists, economists around them to feed their bleak
minds and to verify their superiority; yes, yes, they are the
richest, sing hosanna, and so far as they know are leading a
cultural life as well, since the finest minds have been bemused
by their cellar.

He brightened at the thought of a decent supper, but suspected that the Beckleys ate well only when they were alone,
so as to save the feelings of guests less fortunate. Some lonely
artist might have a tantrum at sight of a whole beef from their
deep freeze, and the injustice of a first-rate label on a bottle
might send him sobbing to the cloak-room. One mustn't tantalize the poor. How much gayer the old Ward McAllister
days must have been, when the rich really clinked, had silver
sleigh bells on their streams of consciousness, and ermine diapers on their young! But today, each Mrs. Beckley had One
Good Black Dress like any stenographer, and only when a
dangerous law suit shook the coffers did she feel poor enough
to wear all of her diamonds.

Frederick toyed for a moment with the idea of staying away
from the Beckleys'. He would only document his prejudices
and hurt Lyle's feelings. He would not be good to Beckley,
probably would not even speak to him, curious as he was

about the monster, but would lurk in some corner, contemptuously bored, impatient with Lyle for enjoying such people.
He wondered if his slumbering bitterness could be merely
jealousy of her professional success, since the rewards of his
own work were so limited. But hers was not the kind of success he wanted, if he did want success. No, he thought, his
resentment came from the way she unconsciously made his
otherwise good life seem a pitiable failure. After all, he wrote
what he chose in the manner he chose for a limited and highly
respectful audience; he lived an independent scholar's life
which was a boon in itself, and he had his love. He was far
too sensible to ask that she divorce Allan and marry him. He
loved solitude and Lyle next; she loved the world and him
next. They told this to each other. They never mentioned
Allan's invalidism or his dependence on Lyle. No, they declared their reason for not marrying (at anyone's cost) was
their sensible awareness of the basic difference in their tastes.
But being too reasonable to wish for complete fulfilment did
not keep the denial from corroding inside you, until the constant analysis bared a torturing sense of injustice. Even in this
resentful mood he could not stay away from her, must follow
her to any party, be introduced again and again to people interested only in flamboyant success, be conscious of his inadequate tailoring, lack of small talk, and find himself shamed by
a fretful desire for millions merely to avoid adolescent humiliation. It was as if all these people mocked him with "Thirty-
six years old and no more money in his pocket than when he
was twelve!"

He was considering what he would do if he didn't find
Murray, when Murray came in the door. Whenever he caught
sight of Murray in public he was reminded of how little they
knew of each other in spite of sharing an apartment these last
few years. How odd to believe the careful protection of each
other's privacy complete proof of deep spiritual sympathy!
Murray's tempestuous marriage had left him grayer and more
stooped than his forty years warranted, but there was something boyish and sweet in his square ruddy face with its snub
nose and wide, wry mouth. Frederick wondered if it was the
defiant swagger and independent air that challenged women
to clutter up his life. Certainly basic kindliness would not be

a bait. More likely it was his passion for bars, poker, and a womanless world that drew them; perhaps he was irresistibly cruel and double-crossing in his dealings with them; borrowed their money, betrayed them marvellously with their best friends, left them crying their eyes out. The girl who came in with Murray was unknown to Frederick, but then he had met only Judy, his regular girl, and Gerda, the ex-wife.

Murray lifted eyebrows in surprise at sight of Frederick drinking and came over to inquire into the cause of such deviltry. His girl stood by an empty booth, smiling at them both with her head cocked in a determined roguishness that made Frederick nervous. He had a feeling that one kind look would have her leaping at them like a too exuberant puppy.

Murray did have cash and if that wasn't enough he would be glad to okay any checks Frederick might sign, having the sound prestige of owing a considerable sum to The Barrel. Frederick confessed to a prejudice against using credit in cafés, on his small salary; a few small bills in his wallet was all he asked.

"Mur-ray!" a voice called. "Remember me?"

"What's the idea of stealing my girl?" The K.G.R. man was slapping Murray on the back. "Where'd you two disappear?"

"The new place down the street," Murray confided. "They got a juke-box and drinks only forty cents. I was just saving money, Larry."

"Okay, but you were stealing my girl," said the K.G.R. man. "I don't mind your stealing her but why do you bring her back just when I'm having a good time? Hey, honey, come on over here."

"I don't want to sit at the bar," pouted his honey. "I want to talk to Murray. Mur-ray!"

"Ought to be a law keeping women on a leash in bars," Murray muttered to Frederick. "I swear these guys bring them in just to get rid of them. Don't get me wrong. Dodo's a nice kid, known her for years, but hell, I got other things on my mind. Tell you in a minute."

Dodo came over, finger in mouth in an attempt at little girl sulks. She was evidently proud of her extreme slenderness for her gray-striped green wool dress followed every bone and sinew snugly, and from the demure way she thrust out her high-pointed breasts you would have thought they were her own invention, exclusive with her. Even on close view her face had no distinction to warrant her obvious satisfaction with it, but then Frederick granted that he had never been a judge of beauty. That she had no misgivings as to her value was clear for she wriggled between the two friends with a spoiled, little-girl giggle.

"Why can't I meet this good-looking man, Mur-ray?" she demanded, cocking her head up invitingly. "It can't be that terrible man you live with, Mur-ray. You said he never went out."

Murray nudged Frederick.

"This is the lad, himself, Dodo. Frederick Olliver. Dodo Brennan. Larry down there brought her to dinner with me. I knew her in Baltimore. Lay off this man, Dodo, he's off to a party with big folks."

Miss Brennan put her head back, half-closing her eyes in a knowing, teasing smile that Frederick recognized as the "I - know - all - about - you - naughty - man - and - your - secrets - and - I'm - every - bit - as - smart - as - you - are - I - can - see - right - through - you - this - very - minute" look. She put out a small, elaborately manicured soft hand and laid it in his as if it were a dear little dove. Frederick was startled to find that the skin actually did have a silken feathery texture that affected him not disagreeably. She had a small, neat-featured face with tidily-pencilled green eyes, smoothly pancaked skin, low forehead, daintily chiselled nose with that half-moon flare of the nostrils that meant something or other. Her hair was black and drawn tightly back into a thick gleaming roll at the nape, a green-spangled snood with a jewelled spider comb doing hat-duty. Her complacency and the way she waved one fancy, long green glove indicated a proud conviction of being the ten best-dressed women in New York.

"You're visiting here?" Frederick asked.

"Pooh on you," she tinkled in pretended indignation. "If you mean I look like an out-of-towner, I'm living here, if you please. At the Barbizon till I find an apartment. Murray's go-ing to find me a husband, too, aren't you Murray?"

The dear little dove stayed in his hand trustingly until Frederick placed it around the daiquiri before her. He

noticed, or her careful maneuvering brought it to his attention, that her legs were gracefully slender, another matter for
her private satisfaction. It struck him that he had never seen a
woman so pleased with herself; this satisfaction was so
tremendously out of proportion to its cause that you were attracted by it and not by the appearance itself. Conscious of his
monastic tastes, his long bondage to Lyle to the exclusion of
other loves, Frederick admitted that he would probably never
know what the heartier males really stalked. This girl must
have gotten her assurance from superior connoisseurs; she
couldn't have cooked it up out of her own vanity. Instead of
being just a neatly groomed, undistinguished woman as he, in
his worldly inexperience thought, she must be a beauty in the
eyes of most men or she would not have this manner. There
was the way she stroked her slim hips and tenderly powdered
her face as if they were treasures on loan to her from the royal
collection; the way she smiled lovingly into her compact
mirror and then back at her image full-length in the booth
mirror as if "Oh you darling, you, you perfectly adorable
creature, you!" Frederick felt an odd mixture of scorn and respect for this self-satisfaction. He bowed to what must be a
majority taste, a little pleased at himself for actually studying
any other woman but Lyle. It might be due to his curiosity
about Murray's private tastes or there might be a hint that his
terrible, lovely enslavement to Lyle might have an end, someday. (But how could he bear it?)

"Murray showed me things you wrote," Dodo said, both
little doves encircling the daiquiri as if it was a baby's mug of
milk. She grimaced. "Oh, but how dull! Really, honestly,
truly, Mr. Olliver! Deadly! You're not really that serious—
you're too handsome—you just can't be that awful!"

"Why not?" Murray asked. "Look here, Dodo. You could
be just as awful if you put your mind to it. You only half try,
that's the trouble."

Dodo thrust her chin in the air.

"I could do better than that without trying a bit," she said
playfully. "Nobody wants to read all that tiresome blah about
old dead people nobody ever heard of. Please, Mr. Olliver,
don't do it any more, or we just can't be friends. And you do
look so *darling*, doesn't he Murray?"

Frederick looked at his watch embarrassed.

"You're going to a party, you lucky you," Dodo sighed, and now the little dove hands were outrageously tweaking at his tie. "I don't see why you don't take me. You know perfectly well I'm nicer than anyone you'll see there. Come on, do take me. Look at that horrible Larry down there; he'll talk about his old Hazelnut all night, and Murray says he has to go someplace. I'll be all alone! Please! Where is the party?"

"Biggest house you ever saw, honey," Murray said. "Take your skates along. You've heard of Ephraim Beckley, haven't you?"

Well, for goodness' sake, she hoped Murray didn't think she was a complete dunce! She may have been in New York only a month but she could read the papers, thank you, and what with Beckley libraries, Beckley Foundations, and Beckley stables, she guessed almost anyone would know who Beckleys were. What was more, another girl from her home town had met all sorts of people at a Beckley party. By this time Dodo had both little doves tugging at Frederick's sleeves, and as usual he had no idea how to extricate himself. But if Lyle hadn't insisted he come up there he would not have had to hunt for Murray, and none of this would have happened. He looked around for escape as Murray's little friend began jumping up and down in a delicate, kittenish way, moaning, "Oh Frederick, if you don't take me, I'll call you Mr. Olliver! I will so! I'm in a party mood and I don't know any parties. The Beckleys are the dream of my life! Please."

Frederick had a fleeting picture of himself entering the Beckley drawing-room with the bold little stranger. He could see Lyle's astonished face knowing well his panic before importunate ladies. He could picture Dodo running wild in the august gathering, squealing banalities, buttonholing, flinging legs and bosom in all directions tossed from man to man like an animated beanbag. With a shudder, he took advantage of her momentary switch to Murray and started for the door, as hastily as he dared. A cab had drawn up at the curb to deliver a pair of very young sailors and Frederick got in as they paid their fare.

"Any girls in there, champ?" one asked him with a nod toward The Barrel entrance.

"Only one—" Frederick started to warn them, since The Barrel could scarcely boast of any female customers of suitable age for these hopeful youngsters, but even as he spoke a girl ran out and pushed past them into the cab. It was Dodo, merry and triumphant, giggling archly at him as she settled herself in the cab. There was nothing he could do in the face of the watching sailors but to handle the situation as Murray might have done.

"You know perfectly well you wanted me to come along," Dodo pouted at him. "You've got to take me, now don't you look so cross! That party is the dream of my life!"

"I would not want it said I deprived anyone of the dream of her life," Frederick said. He gave the address to the driver.

"I never saw anyone so mad!" Dodo cried delightedly.

"Mad with joy," Frederick corrected her, managing a gallant smile. "This seems to be my lucky night."

2

. . . the human dynamos . . .

It was Ephraim Beckley's father who had had the real editorial genius to amass a fortune, but the heirs had been shrewd investors and knew a few tricks themselves. Now that the old gentleman was gone, biographers engaged every decade to rewrite his life (since it could not be re-lived) had difficulty spotting any sensitivity to literature in the records, his immortality as a great editor resting, as one embittered Jewish chronicler wrote, in "Yankee-ing" down his competitors and in making a good thing of his associations with great authors. His collection of intimate letters from Poe, Whitman, Clyde Fitch, Jack London, Ambrose Bierce, Frank Norris, O. Henry, and lesser lights, had sold for a fortune. None of the letters was witty or in the writer's best vein, running largely—*"I must apologize for coming to your house last week in such a deplorable state of shabbiness that your butler was asked to dismiss me, but the truth is I must ask again for a small sum to buy food for myself and family. I realize you have principles about loaning money to private individuals and cannot blame you for your attitude on drink. I hope, however, that you will not ignore this request as you have the others, since I am in desperate need . . ."* etcetera.

The Poe letters, largely in this vein, sold separately for thousands being in excellent condition and exquisite handwriting. The Beckley offspring, with this impeccable literary tradition, had no difficulty in placing themselves in important civic and publishing positions. Soon they had their own collections of autographs—from international figures, minor and major poets, inventors, painters, all asking for loans. Having learned from Papa that a courteous reply curtailed the collection they never answered, thus sucking out four or five letters per poet and providing future profits for their own heirs. Papa had a nice sense of humor and his favorite family joke was, "If I'd given every author five dollars the first time he asked for it you children would be in the poorhouse." It was as good a slogan for success as any, and the children did not quarrel with it.

Frederick Olliver had brought his resolute companion into the Beckley house with an assumption of poise he was far from feeling. The guest of a guest had no right to bring a guest even if he had the desire. But when he caught sight of Lyle, in the midst of her admirers, and as soon as he had received his host's clammy handshake and heard him mispronounce his name he took mischievous satisfaction in unleashing a Dodo. He had a flare of annoyance at Lyle for having said "Beckley's dying to see you" when obviously Beckley had no idea who he was unless he was Olivier, the actor. Lyle had wanted him to be there to see herself in her element; she wanted him to appreciate her sacrifices in preferring him, no matter how embarrassing his own position there might be. (He was being unfair but he wanted to be.) He saw her eyebrows raise a question about Dodo but he ignored it. Let her think the incident was of his own choice. He was considering taking Dodo over to introduce her but was relieved to find the young lady had darted after a famous name in a corner and he escaped to the third floor, following the invitation of his publisher, Benedict Strafford, the only person he recognized there. Presently he was peacefully wandering around the Beckley library in the upper reaches of the house, looking at the glass cabinets of rare manuscripts, viewing the sumptuous canyons of books, the portraits of beagle-nosed Beckleys each firmly clasping an exquisitely bound book as if to keep the artist from stealing it. Here he could forget Lyle, Dodo, and the disagreeable flavor of the entire evening for no one in this literary household had thought of the library but Strafford and himself.

Mr. Strafford, bald and bullish, sprawled in a vast white leather chair smacking his lips over a drink of his own mixing. His imperious voice and decisive manner suggested big business far more than did the pallid, whining host, although Strafford's struggles to keep in publishing savored of a reckless loyalty to Art. Strafford himself was constantly torn between respect for the praise of Frederick's work by foreign readers with convenient large estates for him to visit, and the incontrovertible fact that his sales were never over twelve hundred copies. At least, it was a relief to know that an Olliver book usually took years to perfect, and even more pleasant that the author's wants were met by weekly lectures at the League for Cultural Foundations and his essays in the *Swan Quarterly* and similar magazines. Feeling somewhat guilty every time he thought about Frederick, Mr. Strafford soothed his conscience as a fatherly publisher by offering him a room in his offices where he could write. This suited Frederick admirably, providing stenographic assistance and convenient access to a research library. He worked slowly and was glad Strafford never rushed him or made dutiful attempts at friendlier relations. They kept out of each other's way except for necessary encounters, and tonight at the Beckleys' was the first time they had met outside their business requirements. Both were astonished to discover themselves linked in the warmest friendship by mutual dislike of their host. To Strafford, his first visit to the Beckley home was a needling reminder of his own inadequacies in business. This was the way a publisher should live—country home right in New York, innumerable servants, trained nurses for distinguished diseases, buttons everywhere to turn off the radio, drawing-rooms stuffed with celebrated guests all deliciously bored, opera boxes to leave empty, the finest brandy hidden away. The pretty panorama stirred Strafford to a sense of injustice; it pointed out that here was the only decent way to live. The thought that at the age of sixty it might be too late to achieve it made him withdraw from the company to brood. The sight of Frederick gave him the first pleasure of the evening; here was his author, by George, here was someone who could testify to his power, such as it was. Frederick's feelings were similar; in Strafford he saw the only person here besides Lyle who remembered his name and respected (without quite understanding) his talents. Furthermore, say what you would about the man, he had the good taste to be a bad business man and the innocence to be civil to authors if not utterly baffled by them. The two gentlemen strolled amiably arm-in-arm away from the center of chatter, pausing to consider a huge Zorach marble mother-and-child on the landing flanked by massive urns of chrysanthemums. They examined in silence a special corridor lined with Beckley best sellers, each shelf equipped with a special light for close study of these nine-day wonders. Determined to discover the secret of success Mr. Strafford spent several minutes searching for and adjusting his reading glasses and one minute in a swift glance up and down the collection, observing tersely that every fifth one was an historical novel. Something could be learned from that, surely. A statue in evening dress turned out to be no work of art but a watchful servant who advised them they would find themselves comfortable and alone in the adjoining library, a room to be bequeathed, panelling, chandeliers, portraits, and all to a western university already negotiating to sell it. After blinking incredulously at the grandeur of the room and noting an adorable decanter of brandy on a coffee table, Mr. Strafford remarked that it was certainly a well-chosen library. Frederick replied that a "well-chosen" library usually indicated that someone, not the owner, had selected it. In the case of Beckley, he stated that the shelves would reveal his real literary attachments by being lined with United States bills. Mr. Strafford pointed to an open volume of Juvenal on the desk. Frederick replied with a shrug that the maid must have been reading it; he disagreed that any clairvoyant insight into any human being may be gained by a masterly glance at the books they leave around. Might as well judge an actor by the wigs and costumes hung in his dressing-room. Of course, as in tea-leaf reading, the truth was sometimes struck by accident. Mr. Strafford weighed this dissertation and began to fidget.

"I was just thinking of the idea anyone would get of me by a peek at my desk," he said uneasily. "Good heavens!"

"You mean you left out that little court memoir you're publishing," Frederick guessed.

Mr. Strafford shook his head. Evidently suppressing a confidence with great effort he picked up a pocket magazine that lay on the table, a silk bookmark calling attention to an article called "Ephraim Beckley, The Human Dynamo."

This served to release pent-up indignation and break down his discretion in one instant, for he pounded his fist on the quaking coffee table.

"*The* human dynamo, my eye!" he muttered hoarsely. "What about there being *two* human dynamos? Beckley isn't the only man with ideas, granted he ever had any of his own. He has the capital to get other people's brains and other people's ideas. I don't. But let me tell you I've got an idea as good as any Beckley ever had and if I had the right man for this project— Say!"

Something about the glint in Strafford's eye as he regarded him made Frederick distinctly uneasy, and the word of a new "project" as Strafford called the fancy sideline ventures into which he sometimes entered, filled him with foreboding. He was further dismayed by the sound of a reflective whistle emanating from Strafford's lips, a cheery sign that ideas of an ominous nature were bubbling within.

"What do you know about a magazine named *Haw?*" asked Strafford mysteriously.

Frederick recalled that the words "*Haw*, Periodical" were on the door of the office below Strafford's.

"That's what's on my desk this minute," Strafford burst forth. "Last twelve issues frozen. You see I own it."

"But what on earth can you do with it?" asked Frederick, astonished.

"I just decided," Strafford whispered. "Run it, begad. On the q.t. maybe. Probably bad if it got around the Strafford name was tied up in it. But, by George, that's where the money is these days. I didn't know why I bought it but sometimes I have a hunch. And just this minute it all clears up for me. I'm going to run it and you're the man that's going to help me with it."

"Me?"

"Why not? We understand each other. I don't want the average sort of fellow around for the job, you know, I wouldn't want the *Haw* sort. Why, this can make our fortune. You're the man, Olliver! I got a hunch."

Frederick looked at Strafford incredulously. The gentleman sat biting the end of a Beckley cigar with as much gusto as if it had been Beckley's ear, bald head thrown back, face beaming triumphantly at him.

"I mean it," said Mr. Strafford benignly. "Don't try to talk, boy, I know you're surprised. But you're it. Why, the thing'll be a sensation. On the quiet, of course."

Frederick, quite speechless, pondered the peculiar logic that had inspired his chief to consider an obscure scholar with a passionate indifference to what the public ate as the ideal assistant in this rowdy venture. Mr. Strafford's innocent idea that the undertaking might be a sensation but at the same time a dark secret further nonplussed him until he identified it as the same logic the gentleman was rumored to use in his cautious flings at sex. While Mr. Strafford blew smoke rings dreamily at the panelled ceiling Frederick recalled the Strafford legends, of how he always took his ladies to dine on the mezzanine of the Vanderbilt where he considered himself invisible instead of to the lower dining-room where he conducted his more respectable guests. His manner on these occasions had often been remarked by acquaintances he did not see; it was so charged with sinister implications that the wonder was he was not arrested on sight. He kept his jaunty felt hat pulled down well over his eyes, coat-collar up around his ears, and he pushed the lady through the revolving doors with the veiled eagerness of a wolf about to fling her onto a perfumed bed instead of into a *petite marmite*. Clutching her arm doggedly, he hustled her to a table, pushed her into a chair in a dark corner as if he was locking her in a private bedroom. He ordered a cocktail, whispering the order to the waiter as if mixed drinking was as scandalous as mixed bathing; and after the dinner he hurried the lady out, hovering about her protectively, as if to hide her nudity from the leering crowd. His splendid air of guilt was retained all the next day at the office, and came from nothing more than the naughty fact that she was a woman and he was a man, that they were out together like other men and women, and that other men and women were probably doing mischievous things that he and she were not doing but very likely could do.

"Well?" prodded Strafford, and as Frederick was still speechless, he went on plaintively, "By George, Olliver, I'm tired of men like Beckley hooking all the plums. This is just the sort of thing he'd snap up if he knew about it. There's a mint in it."

"How did the owners happen to sell?" Frederick asked.

"Bankrupt. I got it just for taking over their debts," Mr. Strafford said with an extremely foxy leer. "Didn't have to give out a penny."

There was no use in commenting on this typically Strafford coup. When Strafford continued that he had been hung by his regard for prestige all his life and was going in from now on for Sure Things, Frederick demurred that no prestige plus a proven financial flop might not be classified as Sure Thing, Strafford brushed the objection aside as sheer modesty. Frederick didn't realize how much confidence Strafford had in him. All you needed to put the thing over was brains, and surely Frederick would admit his and Strafford's brains were superior to Beckley's.

"It's the sort of thing he's always done to pick up a quick dollar," Strafford assured him.

"I don't think it would help the firm's prestige," Frederick murmured weakly, causing Strafford to give an impetuous snort. "Isn't it just cartoon strips?"

"Of course it is! But how would Beckley have prestige except by making money? Look at your own situation. If your own books had sold half a million copies you'd have all the prestige of a Santayana. We can both make something out of this, Olliver—you'll get your prestige, alright, don't you worry about that. But I can tell you that you don't get prestige in this country with a frayed shirt-cuff. Excuse me, old man."

Very red and abashed by the slip that happened to be a true observation Mr. Strafford hastily gulped a brandy, and Frederick pulled down his coat sleeve with a wry smile.

"I know, I know," Strafford pursued, appeasingly. "You don't care about anything but getting your own book out. But the public doesn't want highbrow books now. I'm thinking of your own good, old man, in putting off publication for a while. What the public wants now is *Haw* and that book of ours, *I Was a Court Lady*. You've got to wait till the time is right. Meantime you can be polishing up the rough spots, say, but making a little money on the side. Let's say we let Miss Jones do the routine chores on *Haw*—clip stuff, paste-up, stick in a murder between jokes. All you have to do is drop down there once in a while to shape up things, look after my interests. Suppose I put you on the pay-roll at seventy-five a week. It's a snap for you and a favor to me. It means I've got somebody in there I can trust and I can keep clear of it, personally."

"I appreciate your faith in my business ability," Frederick managed to reply with due gravity, preposterous as the suggestion was, "but——"

The doors opened and Strafford held up a warning finger.

"Mum's the word on this," he whispered. "Mustn't let it out that the firm has anything to do with it. But, by George, I'll show Beckley yet. Try to see it my way, old man."

Lyle came in the door.

3

. . . the invulnerables . . .

As soon as Lyle sat down beside him Frederick's smouldering resentment vanished. He was ready to confess that bringing a strange girl to her friends' party had been punishment, not pleasure. No amount of cold analysis could dispel his sense of utter completeness when he was with Lyle. The corrosive thoughts which sheathed and armored him against the world melted; disarmed, he was content. Here was Lyle, and nothing else mattered. Without looking at each other, without touching, their love flowed between them and around them. Incredible that they could ever quarrel, incredible that a little while before he had felt stonily hostile towards her for no better reason than that her friends and her pleasures were not his, incredible that he should ever question this peace. Here was the rock on which all his life was built, here was love invincible, indestructible. Strafford and the whole room faded when their eyes finally met.

"We'll have a chat later, perhaps," Mr. Strafford said, vaguely aware of this, and with a courtly bow to Lyle, he strolled toward the hall. At the door he turned to give Frederick a meaning nod, finger to his lips.

"He does look like a bleached bull," Lyle murmured. "What's he like, out of the arena?"

Frederick looked away from her, longing to take her in his arms. These public encounters were torture.

"This party has brought out the tycoon in him," he tried to answer calmly. "I don't know what he's like any more. Tonight he has me baffled."

His head began to swim with the necessity for control, familiar as the demand was. Now for the clenched heart and the small talk, the interminable words that must veil their love. One of these days he would kick the screen of words aside and let the lightning strike, even, he thought desperately, at risk of it striking their love itself. He felt a blaze of anger at Lyle for demanding this endurance of him.

"It's you who baffle me tonight, dear," Lyle said. "Who is this girl you brought?"

He had forgotten Dodo completely in his anxiety to tell about his book being done. He had expected Lyle to ask the question of course, and he had intended to tell her the whole story. But now he hedged. After all, was there any reason he should not bring along insurance against being a wall-flower? Hadn't Lyle noticed that he usually stood around on one foot at her friends' parties, waiting for a word with her? Why shouldn't he show a little independence by bringing along someone to talk to him? The fact was, however, that he had left Dodo Brennan almost as soon as they arrived. At first he had been amused by her wide-eyed queries—"Not really Harry Kooney, the arranger? And my, so many countesses and every-one talking French or German! Poor little me!" Then he was mightily relieved when she forgot him in her quest for bigger game. He hoped she would forget him the rest of the evening, too, but he did not want Lyle to guess this. His terror of young women always secretly amused her. Before he could frame an answer Dodo came in, pointing a playfully accusing finger at him. He was sure Lyle guessed his discomfort; she must know he was comparing the younger woman's brassy smartness with her own soft, casual grace. He could never say whether the impression of beauty Lyle gave to him was valid or whether he was only admiring in her the memory of his own love. The pile of pale red hair reminded him of its silky softness against his own cheek; the slender white arms had been cool around his neck, the wide blond-lashed dark eyes spelled unquestioning love for him, the sulky crooked mouth remembered his. He was, he admitted, an Ephraim Beckley in his own way, gloating over his possessions because they were his, reasoning that if this object had been desired and won by such a fastidious collector as himself, then it was axiomatically priceless.

"There you are, you awful man!" Dodo cried, tweaking his ear impudently. She made a wry face at Lyle. "He brought me here and then he ran away before he even told me who people were. Is it true that somebody here wrote that play *Summer Day*?"

"Mrs. Gaynor and her husband wrote *Summer Day*," Frederick said, and motioned to Lyle. "Mrs. Gaynor. Miss Brennan."

Dodo clapped her hand over her mouth and made wide eyes. She used her face as she did her voice and the rest of her body as if this was her favorite doll and she could make it do all sorts of things. Then she put out her hand to Lyle in the sweetly respectful way a good little girl says goodnight to Mummy's friends.

"I'm so sorry I didn't know. Of course I've heard of the Gaynors but I got mixed up hearing everyone talk. I just loved *Summer Day*. I saw it twice when it opened in Baltimore."

Lyle murmured something and gave Frederick a glance he knew well enough meant a plea for escape. The next minute Dodo had drawn up a stool to Lyle and was saying, "Oh, Mrs. Gaynor, I don't see how you do it! She must be a perfect whiz, mustn't she, Frederick? All those plays! I've simply got to sit at your feet! Frederick, you tell her I really mean it. Seriously."

"She means it seriously," Frederick said, unwilling to catch Lyle's eye.

"You mustn't spoil me," Lyle said, wanting to punish him.

"But you should be spoiled! Even if you do only half the work, you deserve loads of credit."

Suddenly Dodo leaped up and impetuously straightened Frederick's tie and flicked his sleeve with a possessive assurance. She looked over her shoulder at Lyle.

"He could be really handsome if he had the right tailor and would smile sometimes," she said archly. "Did you ever see such blue eyes? But, please, don't you ever smile, Freddy?"

"Freddy," Lyle repeated under her breath.

"I have my elfin side," Frederick answered.

Dodo looked at him suspiciously.

"Pooh on you if you're trying to be clever!"

She turned her attention to the room, her eyes roving the balcony and lofty windows, frowning at some object that should have given a cue to its value by a price mark, blinking hard as if to make the secret pop out.

"A man said the library alone cost a fortune," she murmured. "I don't get it."

Strafford came back in, looking devilishly complacent with two actresses from the Gaynor play. He began to lecture loudly on the incunabula in one cabinet, tossing in an aside or two that hinted of easily detected forgeries and the charming gullibility of the owner. As the ladies moved past them, jewelled, fragrant and beautiful, tinted porcelain faces and lacquered golden hair suggesting residence on some angel planet, they waved lightly to Lyle. Dodo stared at them as if Fate had sent these superior beings to tantalize her personally. Confidence in her own charm vanished at the comparison; her little artifices dropped from her like a shabby cloak and left her standing forlorn, a plain fretful little woman childishly in doubt for the first time. Frederick observing this had a rush of pity for her bewilderment. The fleeting glimpse of something genuine in her roused his curiosity. He watched her eyes travel jealousy over the women, pause at each jewel. He saw her glance back to Lyle, and at the tiny chinchilla cape behind her on the sofa, at the jewelled vanity in her lap. Anger blazed in the girl's face. Her hands clenched.

"I wish I had a million dollars!" she exclaimed passionately. "I wish I had ten million dollars! I—" She recovered herself quickly and finished with an apologetic murmur, "I mean so I could buy a lot of books and things."

Frederick heard Lyle smother a soft laugh but he would not share it. Lyle was invulnerable, but the stranger, like himself, was not, no matter how desperately she pretended. All these guests were Lyle's people, a success clique; there was nothing about them he liked, understood or even cared to understand. The half-a-minute revelation of the young outsider showed that she belonged with him, never with them. She was on the outside and always would be. He was sorry for her, for wanting something she could never name, and for that painful moment of doubt in her own beauty. He watched her trying to recover her saucy confidence, lighting a cigarette with lips curved in mocking, jaunty smile, eyelids lowered to hide the torment of envy they might betray.

Lyle, too, was watching Dodo curiously. She had been struck by the eyes before, thinking of the many times she had seen that expression. It was in the jealous eyes of old Southern women as they watched young debutantes dance as if here were their thieving rivals not their successors. It was in the cold, measuring eyes of a woman who makes a business of being a woman. Skeptical, hard, relentless eyes, they divide all visible assets in the rival by a thousand. If another woman is beautiful these eyes grudgingly admit that she is not ugly, no more than that; if she displays wit the eyes significantly find a wine-stain on her dress. But when the other's toilette reveals free access to a fat purse, then the eyes are unmasked and flash with righteous indignation; this is the end for which a woman is a woman. Beauty, brains, position are enviable, not in themselves, but for their purchasing power; if crutches won masculine rewards these women would break their own legs. Flaunting of luxuries was testimony to superior power over men, medals of practical victories. So Dodo's eyes flashed with bitterness as they priced the other women's trophies. When Benedict Strafford came back to the group she winked at him merrily to show the others she had valuable connections of her own there. Strafford was taken aback by the wink and looked from Dodo to the others to see if he had missed something.

"Excuse me, Olliver," he said. "I just saw Tyson Bricker in the music room."

He paused to stroke his jaw, pushing his face to left and right as if it was a rubber mask that needed adjusting. Frederick, fearing some new inspiration, waited in silence.

"Bricker was mentioning how much he liked your work in the *Swan*. Said you had classes at his League. It struck me that he might listen to you if you asked for a little boost on that Court Lady novel of ours."

"I'd love to meet Tyson Bricker." Dodo was all of asparkle once more. "He lectured at my mother's club in Baltimore once. He was marvellous! Better than Sinatra. Where is he?"

"I doubt if he'd trust my word on anything like that," Frederick said, "especially since I can't lie very well. I've barely met Bricker, and I didn't read the book."

"You could thank him for what he said about your own work," Mr. Strafford said wistfully. "Just say you're doing work for the firm now and happened to notice he had been neglecting our books. Well—never mind. It just seemed a good chance to take advantage of his interest in you. I don't quite dare approach him myself."

"I'll go along with you," Dodo offered eagerly.

Mr. Strafford looked alarmed.

"I'm sure Mr. Bricker would like that better," Lyle said.

"Dear me, no. Olliver is the only person who could carry any weight with Bricker," Mr. Strafford protested. "I don't mean to go after him in a pushing way, of course. Maybe, if you just strolled up and said 'Thanks for your good words, old fellow. Why not get together sometime for a little chat?' All the Beckley authors are at him now, no reason one of my authors shouldn't edge in."

Frederick's manifest horror evidently discouraged him for the publisher hastily changed the subject.

"Funny how you can always tell a Beckley author," he turned to Lyle. "The men always look like solid country squires—dogs, trout, good roast beef, that sort of thing; wives always pregnant in dirndls, pardon me. The women all three-name writers always crazy to wear low necks then get a bunch of tulle to cover up, saying interesting things so fast you can't hear yourself think. I'm not against them, mind, I just think it's funny how you can always spot 'em."

"Dennis Orphen looked different," Lyle said.

"That's right, he looks more like a soda jerker," Strafford granted. "The way a writer ought to look, eh, Olliver?"

Dodo was tugging at his sleeve roguishly, being very much the little-dirl-wiz-big-mans.

"Come on, let's you and I go talk to Tyson Bricker," she coaxed, pulling the publisher toward the door where he turned and waved goodbye with a helpless shrug of his shoulders.

"He was really serious about your sucking up to Tyson, wasn't he? Does he think you're the go-getter type?" Lyle asked as they left. "Or does he think that's the proper social approach?"

"This house has a strange effect on its guests," Frederick explained. "It's put Strafford into a frightful state of ambition. It's made the young lady lust for millions, and it's made me want to go home."

Why had he come, anyway? he wondered angrily? There was almost no chance of persuading her to come home with him for she was always cautious around Allan's friends.

Lyle put her hand over his, smiling ruefully. No, there was no chance.

"Is it that bad, darling? I thought you'd be amused."

"The things that amuse you usually infuriate me," Frederick said. "I can't be amused at the spectacle of an idiot like Beckley in control of so many first-rate brains. Is that so funny to you?"

Rebuffed, Lyle withdrew her hand and lifted her head stubbornly.

"Yes," she said. "I find it hilarious. And he's not an idiot, he only looks that way. It's his Uncle Hector who's the idiot. Old Hector Beckley. He's the dean of all idiots."

"He sounds like an old dear," Frederick said, eyes flashing his hurt at her silent refusal.

"He presided at the annual Beckley dinner last week," Lyle chattered, pretending not to see. "All the sons and sons' wives and grandsons. Uncle Lex, he's the bad boy, Ephraim's brother, was stinking, of course. Ephraim made everybody all get back into their uniforms, World War I and World War II, and old Hector sat at the head of the table under flags of all nations and one big Beckley flag with dates of all our wars on it. It was to show that Beckleys were only in business to help their country instead of to get rich. Hector is senile, of course, and sat playing with some chessmen and gurgling while every one read speeches to his business genius and leadership. Then he cried because he dropped his cake on the floor and they wouldn't let him pick it up. Uncle Lex tried to make everybody sing *Dearie* and *Everybody's Doing It.* Cordelay, the youngest son, refused to say a word during the whole evening. He was mad because he was too fat for his uniform but he had to wear it anyway."

"Fascinating," Frederick said. "I don't see how you lived through it."

They would quarrel, as always, not over the real thing but something, anything else.

"I'm trying to show you how really amusing they are," Lyle defended herself, flushed, rising to the bait. "Must people be in print? Does the whole living world have to be translated into book form before you will look at it? I wonder if I will ever understand you—or if I should."

"Perhaps we should be content to baffle each other," Frederick said distantly. "No use my trying to understand the

Beckleys or why you always want me to meet them. I find them criminally ignorant and dangerously unfunny."

"You are so determined to have a difficult life, aren't you?" Lyle said quietly, but her cheeks flushed, as if by a slap, and betrayed her feelings. "A little courtesy, a little interest in human beings, would make everything easier for you. But you would rather have your difficulties so that you can stay bitter and oh, so misunderstood and I can stay worried about you. Does your artistic integrity require you to be rude to Tyson Bricker and Beckley, anyone who could be valuable to you? Is it a crime for me to want to help you? And how can you understand another century if you refuse to even look at your own?"

Frederick stiffened. It angered him that she should think his career was, like hers, something to be coddled by social contacts, little flattering gestures, an eager nod in the right direction. She had not even asked if he had finished his book, so he would not tell her. He was piqued, too, that she had betrayed no flicker of jealousy over his bringing another girl to the party. She accepted his love and his career as matters for her to take up when she liked, mould as she liked, dictate what terms she liked. Having coaxed him to meet her here to test again how much he desired her, she would not reward him by going home with him. She had wanted him to come in order to "contact" Bricker or Beckley—she was almost as bad as Strafford! Lyle saw his face harden and put her hand over his, pleadingly.

"You're so much better than any of them, darling, that's why," she whispered. "And you won't do anything right, that's why I love you. But it could be so easy . . ."

"I think we'd better stay in our separate corners and not try to understand each other's business," Frederick said coldly. He was ashamed but stubbornly silent when her hand dropped from his and she drew back like a beaten child fearing another blow. She tried to smile.

"Let's go," Lyle proposed, fastening the little cape over her shoulders. "Perhaps this house does have a bad effect on all of us. I'm acting like some agent arranging a little deal. Come on."

"My place?" Frederick said, challenging her.

Lyle would not meet his eyes.

"I'm supposed to stop off at our leading lady's apartment down the block to console her. Allan asked me to. She's not 'happy in her part' after the notices, now they're on the road, are all going to Louise. After all she was the New York hit. Can you wait—or shall I telephone her instead?"

"You mustn't forget your professional interests even if I do forget mine," Frederick said, blazing as he always did at the primary importance of her work, work that bound her to her husband even more than did duty or pity. "In any case, I shall have to look after the lady I brought here."

This, he saw with mingled satisfaction and horror at his own words, had its effect. Lyle looked at him, unbelievingly.

"That Dodo girl? That Pooh-on-you girl? But she wants to stay and meet all the wonderfuls. I heard her say so. We can ask Ephraim to see that she gets home safely or dangerously, whichever she likes. No reason you should have that bother."

"It's no bother to look after an attractive twenty-year-old girl, my dear," Frederick said perversely.

Lyle's color rose.

"Imagine her being only twenty!" she said. "It usually takes a woman years to acquire that polish. Goodnight, then."

It was a triumph to disturb Lyle's poise, but he hadn't intended to carry it this far. She had walked out of the room, head high in the air, before he could bring himself to call her. His chest ached with love for her and his smouldering hurt that she should always assume he was the failure that needed her help. He had been unfair, but she had hurt him, too. He picked up the brandy she had left on the table and drank it. Through the open door he heard dance music and the sound of farewells from the hall below. He could hear a high, artificial baby-laugh above other noise. Dodo, of course. A man came in and started removing ash-trays and glasses, and Frederick, feeling ashamed and defiant over his childish scene with Lyle, followed the noise downstairs to the music-room in the back of the house. Lyle and the actress, Vera Cawley, had left, as had most of the Beckley regular crowd. Only the guests other guests had brought were staying, making the most of their first and last visit. The mulatto pianist was holding forth on the virtues of the Schillinger method in

composition, idly improvising a combination of the *Second
Tchaikovsky Concerto* and *Two Little Girls in Blue*, stopping to
jot down notes. In the glass alcove where gleaming green
plants under blue lights made evil jungle shadows on the
black glass he saw Dodo with Tyson Bricker, laughing shrilly
at Ephraim Beckley. Ephraim's hands were flapping together
behind his back like fish fins, and his wide fish mouth was
making futile efforts to join in the laughter, though his bulging
oyster-colored eyes betrayed private fury. Dodo was poking
him with her little fist and backing him into the plants.

"Come on, Mr. Beckley, what makes you such an old
stuffy?" Dodo was gaily teasing. "My daddy's just as good as
you are but he knows how to have fun and you don't. Why,
we have bigger parties than this in Baltimore every day, and
bigger houses, too. Come on, now, let me teach you the
rhumba!"

Frederick hesitated but it was too late to retreat. Dodo
caught sight of him and shook her finger at him.

"There's that terrible Olliver man! You won't look after me
but Tyson will, won't you, Tyson?"

Mr. Beckley's eyes directed a rocket of hatred around the
group that landed with regrettably negative results on Dodo.
He slid out of the room, locking his smile back up in the
deep-freeze as he did so.

"I'll gladly look after the young lady, but I shouldn't want
to scrap with Olliver," Tyson Bricker said with his gusty
laugh. "How are you, old chap? Not leaving?"

"If the young lady is ready," Frederick said. "I gather that
our host won't protest too much if we all leave."

The young lady, offended by Ephraim's exit, decided that
she would leave if she could be taken back to the Barrel. It
was only half-past one and the Barrel was wonderful then.
Absolute bedlam. She insisted on the company of the
arranger and the two plastic men (they were the best plastic
men in the trade—Hollywood was raving over what they did
with The Last Supper). As Tyson Bricker lived in Gramercy
Park and as Dodo kept a firm hand on his arm they all went
down to the Barrel together. Frederick was deeply thankful
that Lyle could not witness his undignified finish as one of
five escorts, the least important one at that.

The K.G.R. man had left for the new bar when they arrived at the Barrel, and Murray had started on his usual rounds with midnight cronies. Dodo made the arranger play a duet with the colored pianist and ordered double Scotches for everybody. The bill was handed to Frederick and the three dollars left from Murray's loan paid the tip.

"Murray will okay this," he said to the waiter as he signed for the twenty-six dollars. He had a dizzy feeling of doom, for he was desperately afraid of debt and its testimony to his practical incompetence. But after all there was that salary Strafford offered for that idiotic *Haw* job. Perhaps his incompetence was not so obvious, after all. He must be a little tight, but his head felt quite clear—strange but clear. He was glad when Dodo insisted on going to hear Roger Stearns up at the One Two Three with the Plastic Men and the arranger. She wanted Tyson to come, too, but Tyson looked doubtfully at Frederick.

"What about you, Olliver? Shall we go?"

Frederick saw that Dodo was already at the door, standing with her head on the arranger's shoulder, and her hand cuddling one Plastic Man's chin.

"Why not let them go along, and you and I have a nightcap here?" he said to Tyson, and heard himself adding genially "There are some things I'd like to talk over with you, old man."

4

. . . a dozen white shirts . . .

NEW YORK was a city named Frederick, Lyle thought. Walking down through the Park from the Metropolitan Museum she reflected that her pleasure in the Chinese show had been based on *his* pleasure in it; the Boat-house down yonder was nothing in itself but a spot that had amused Frederick with its fantastic night-life of shy sailors and terrifying bobby-soxers. Coming out on Fifth Avenue at Fifty-ninth she read his name into whatever she saw; down that street was the restaurant where they must go for the curried dishes he loved; further along was the motion picture house with the Italian movie he wanted to see; here was the gallery with the Marsh show he would like; here was a shop to order slipcovers for his furniture; here was the refugee shirt-maker she had recommended to him. She remembered hearing that the man had just received fresh supplies, and that he had Frederick's measurements. The excuse for making him an intimate present pleased her, and she hastened into the building and up to the little shop. It was possible to get white material soon, she was told, and she might even order a dozen. But as soon as she had made out the check, she had the familiar sinking feeling of having made a mistake. She walked down the three flights to the book-store on the first floor and wandered through it, unseeingly.

Frederick would not wear the shirts, of course. After a few weeks, noticing the same frayed collar and cuffs, she would try to ask tactfully if he had received them and he would say, "Oh, those? Oh yes, but of course I don't need them. Much too good for my purposes. I never need anything that luxurious."

And she would have to pretend her feelings were not hurt and try to be reasonable. First, he would consider the gift a criticism of his poverty as well as of his appearance, and he was satisfied with both. He was a meticulous man, but he believed that an austere shabbiness within one's means was proper for a gentleman. Second, he would suspect that the present had been suggested by one of her friends, say a Beckley, and that would start the old bitterness—you-and-your-fine-friends and me-and-my-simple-tastes. Third, she was opening herself to the wound of his chronic ingratitude. She would stay awake for nights wondering if he really loved her or anyone, if he had any capacity for feeling whatever, and why he should wish to deny her the simple joy of giving a present. She would torture herself with analysis of him, taking each virtue apart and finding its cruel base, then in the deep necessity for preserving a love without which she could not live, taking the cruelties apart and finding the noble base. Hers was the real crime—for having a flair for happiness, for being spoiled by luxury and friends, for taking good fortune as her due, surprised that anyone else should expect the same.

Supposing he did sneer at her gift. Ingratitude was not a vice. You were not compelled to give and you were not compelled to be grateful for another's pleasure in being generous. Frederick had always made it clear that he disliked being beneficiary as much as he disliked being benefactor. He had often declared his admiration for honest ruthlessness; it meant that the person knew what he wanted and went after it openly. Unselfishness, he had said, was a form of confusion. The person gave away what he was not sure of needing for himself. Later when he found he did need it, he demanded gratitude. In summer he threw away his overcoat and in winter sought gratitude. Instead of accusing himself of lack of foresight he pinned the fault on the innocent victim of his own folly.

This was the cold logical reasoning that always hurt her in her lover; his indifferent dismissal of her impulsive warm gestures, his fear of losing himself, his caution, his painful reticence. Was it reticence, or was this all there was? Granted that taciturn people through no fault of their own are always credited with deep reserves of emotion; then, as the guards hold so relentlessly for so long, the suspicion dawns that there is no feeling there at all; and they are berated for monstrous insensitivity in their later years, as if it was their crime that natural coldness was construed as controlled passion. He was sexually passionate but emotionally afraid perhaps. She must forgive that. After all, what would she do if he were reckless enough to demand she leave Allan? Yes, she was to blame there, for

her bondage to Allan was not so much love or pity as work—
Allan represented her work and this was her love and her
necessity, which Frederick only dimly understood. He understood and disliked her discretion, but it was for the sake of
their love as well as for her own self-preservation. Would she
love him if his demands prevented her from writing, if his dislike for the stage obliged her to give up its gay tissue-paper
people, its fantastic but dear extortions? Then there was his
contempt for all her friends, begrudging her the pleasure in
small things, as if it was unworthy of her to enjoy anything
but his love. Yes, he was arrogant, but wait! Wasn't his arrogance a phase of the mental and personal integrity she loved?
Wasn't his caution a scorn of throwing waste to the mob? As
for her own "generosity," she had always had more of everything than most people. Did she ever deprive herself? No.
Candidly, she believed she was capable of doing so, but sacrifice had never been required. Except the sacrifice of being unable to divorce Allan and marry Frederick. What she was sure
she could never bear was what Frederick endured with such
dignity—professional obscurity. She knew of no one else who
accepted this fate without shrill breast-beatings, bitter envy
and cries of "Unfair!" Strafford had treated him shabbily,
postponing his book, doling out consolations, denying him
the simple reward of critical recognition. Her heart ached for
him, but whatever he suffered he would not tell or let her
help. He withdrew almost slyly from her sympathy; he would
not be her hurt little boy. For that matter, he would not be
her true friend, either; he was lover only, an emotional gourmet selecting from her heart whatever dainty morsel that he
needed, then withdrawing to his private world. But supposing
he submitted to her completely, bared his wounds, begged for
pity, wouldn't she despise him? Wasn't his elusiveness the secret of her gnawing disease for him? Wasn't it a challenge in
its way equivalent to her own iron-barred marriage?

There were excuses for his eccentricity. There had been his
mother who had squandered her own and her sons' money
on gay companions, there were the gambling debts left by his
older brother. Fortunately his scorn for the hollow laws of
sportsmanship saved him from the silly martyrdom of making
good these debts. There was his precocious childhood, one

school after another, never a real home, that kept him always lonely and shy until his pride furnished armor; there was his detached curiosity about all human beings as if they were books to be studied, answers to be found by mathematical formulae. Tragic, since he had no ability to communicate with ordinary people. A farm boy on a country road nodding a greeting would freeze his tongue. As a little boy he had the feeling, he had told her once, of being under ice unable to push through or make the world hear his cry. Thinking of all of this, Lyle felt an overwhelming surge of love for him. Love was not for the virtues or vices of the beloved, but for his dear childhood, his lost desires, his memories; it was a never-slaked curiosity about that lost world, the mystery forever unsolved. Loving was partly the quest (how much of the unsolvable lost boy can I recover) and part acquisitiveness (the greed for another life to live besides my own).

Suppose she did love too much. Suppose she was the one who gave, who pursued, who made the overtures after every quarrel. There was nothing either wonderful or tragic about loving too much, any more than there was in eating too much; no need to take a Byronic bow on pure greed. This was the kind of reasoning Frederick would use, Lyle thought, and she felt happy again. It was the way she changed her thinking around with each new character in a play, trying to think like a thief, a tart, a general, an empress. It was a gift valuable in collaboration with Allan but it was actually more of a child's game than talent. Here was a toy playhouse of dolls to which she could retreat when her heart might break. Allan, constructionist, built the toy house, and she made the dolls—that was the part of her marriage she could not give up even for Frederick. Allan needed her dolls and she needed Allan's doll-house. And now she had made Frederick into one of her dolls, a doll with a dozen custom-made shirts. She set him, mentally, in several dramatic situations; she saw him as inventor too proud to sell to Industry, as monk obliged to enter worldly life to rescue fallen brother; amused with her game she tried him as high-minded reformer posing as king of the underworld, as disappointed poet turned successful thief, as aristocratic scientist turned jitterbug by empty-headed bobby-soxer. Here Lyle stopped herself with a shock

of acute pain. The girl Frederick had brought to the Beckleys'!
The girl he said he had to see home! His curtness had
wounded her feelings and they had parted angrily, but she
had had no doubts of his fidelity. She had never had a doubt
of his love. He might have been piqued into hurting her feelings, but he never, never— —But then she would have said it
was impossible for him to have tolerated such a silly girl; as a
doll in her play she could not deny that such a character
might welcome the oddest temptations. Lyle felt weak at the
doubts crowding to her brain. She walked to the curb, raising
her hand for a taxi, trying futilely to keep the play from unfolding in her facile imagination. The shock of surprise last
night when she had caught sight of Frederick entering the
Beckley hall with a strange girl, a girl who clung to his arm
with a coy burlesque of stage-fright while Mrs. Beckley made
the introductions. A girl named Dodo! A girl aglitter with artificial postures, mincing mannerisms, lisps, pouts, goo - goo -
eyes, shy smirks of oh - I'm - just - a - little - nobody - and -
you're - all - so - big - and - wonderful - I'm - scared - weally -
twuly, then burgeoning under liquor into brash insolence.
She had wondered why Frederick, who tolerated few people,
had never mentioned knowing the girl, then she had smiled,
understanding that this was one of Frederick's sardonic
jokes, producing for their mutual edification a fly in the
Beckley ointment. She had blamed herself for the final quarrel. Her possessive attitude that he could not be interested in
anyone else (newer and younger, at that!) was not flattering
to a male ego. After all, the darling was attractive, definitely
male, not so eccentric that he did not have the usual man's
aversion to being considered an open book. She should have
been clever enough to hide the fact that she knew him by
heart. Oh she did, did she? Why, she didn't even know her invented characters by heart! They were always doing something unexpected. What stupid complacency was this, anyway?
Her daily routine was complicated and unpredictable, but his
was unchangeable, she had always thought. At this very
minute he was having lunch with Edwin Stalk down at the
Swan Café. Just as this crossed her mind Lyle heard her name
called and saw Edwin Stalk getting out of a taxi before her.
Stalk, editor of the *Swan*, was part of the Olliver life she never

penetrated. He couldn't be more than twenty-eight she thought, a dark, strikingly handsome lad.

"Do you want my cab, Mrs. Gaynor?"

"Thanks, yes," she said and could not resist adding, "Do you know if Mr. Olliver went back to his office? I understood him to say he was lunching with you."

"He telephoned to cancel the appointment," Stalk said, his always mournful dark eyes registering the minor social blow as if it was a death in the family. "He never breaks appointments, either, you know."

"I know," said Lyle, smiling. "But he's not too old to learn."

"I'm glad to see you," Stalk said simply, holding open the door of the cab for her and looking at her with childish admiration. "I am always glad to see you, I think."

Lyle murmured the address to the driver, so preoccupied with her thoughts she paid no heed to Stalk standing on the curb, hat in hand, watching her drive off. She did not know her lover by heart, after all, was in her mind. For all she knew he had broken the date with the *Swan* editor to lunch with Dodo. Dodo! Plot Number 486—Bobby-soxer changes stately scientist into jitter-bug! Very well, it served her right, Lyle told herself, for cutting up friends and lovers into stage dolls and walking them through her pasteboard plots. Maybe they wanted to make their own plots. Maybe she had always been so blindly sure that she had lost the capacity to observe. She huddled in the corner of the seat, drawing her furs around her, cold with strange new fears. There would surely be a message from him when she got home, but when she rushed in the hallway there was Pedro saying Mr. Gaynor wanted to go over some notes and was waiting in his bedroom. She must call Mr. Sawyer at once as to whether she could put up the visiting English star and her husband, Mr. Gaynor's masseur wanted to speak to her about a new specialist at Medical Center doing wonders with bone diseases. The *Post* wanted her to do Allan's theatrical memoirs and awaited her call. Mr. Beckley wanted her to reconsider the invitation to go South. Had Mr. Olliver telephoned? No. Lyle wanted to telephone him at once but Pedro said Mr. Gaynor was very nervous. He had waited so long for her today. If she would hurry right in to him, please . . .

"Of course," Lyle replied mechanically. She was not to be allowed one moment hunting for the vanished lover—not even if he were dead, floating face-upward down the Hudson, unclaimed in the Morgue or Bellevue, she thought with a fierce upsurge of rebellion, walking toward Allan's door. For the first time it seemed to her that she was a prisoner.

5

. . . the prisoners in great form . . .

ALLAN was sitting up in his specially designed writing chair, which indicated he had had one of his bad days. He always felt personally affronted by these attacks and deliberately forced himself to sit up, work, entertain, do everything to show he was undefeated. Visitors who did not understand this were prone to exclaim, "Why, Allan, you're your old self again," and Allan would smile proudly as if Pain, overhearing, would withdraw, properly chagrined at having met its match. Deprived these many years of the theatre, he revelled in his own theatricalities, affecting a bottle-green velvet house-jacket, white scarf under his ruddy jowls giving him the appearance of a Dickensian country squire. He was a big-shouldered, florid man, moustache still black though his thinning hair was iron-gray shading to wings of white above the ears, contrasting effectively with the crooked black eyebrows above the black, unrevealing eyes, shades, rather than windows to the soul. It amused him, further, to have his room with its dark oak chairs, panelled walls, and high frost-paned windows, seem more of the taproom than bed-chamber. "I like the idea of playing Elizabeth Barrett in a *Student Prince* set," was his explanation. It was a matter of pride with him to have none of the invalid look or trappings about him, just as it had pleased him in his younger days to be taken for a stock-broker or full-back instead of an actor. In his presence Lyle felt herself and often saw others wilt, as if his greed for life left no oxygen for anyone else.

Sam Flannery, for twenty years Allan's business manager, press-agent, slave and whipping boy, was sitting on the oak settle by the fireplace. He was a tidy, little man with a rosy choir-boy face, pretty blue eyes anxiously searching for rebuffs that the eager perpetual smile sought to deflect. Lyle had come to accept Flannery as one of Allan's necessities though he represented a truth she hated, that Allan would accept any-one who would toady, ridicule them though he did. Curled up gracefully on a cushion at Allan's feet was a frail wisp of a blonde whose thick, black-rimmed spectacles must have been all that kept her from blowing out the window when the door opened. A small audience, thought Lyle, resigned, but still an audience. She was sure from the set of Allan's jaw, high color and glittering eye, that he had been having one of his annual Master-Mind days, when he suddenly revolutionized their affairs, changed butchers, demanded linen inventories, planned musical revivals, insisted on financial reports, and switched the leading character in whatever they were working on from man to woman. Flannery always supported him in these brainstorms.

"Don't tell me you've decided to come home, my dear!" Allan exclaimed. "It's barely four o'clock. I'm afraid you've cut short your luncheon with the other debutantes, dear, dear! Surely not on our account, my love?"

"Not at all," Lyle answered. "I simply ran out of reefers."

"You poor child! And the other girls were mean and teased you, I suppose. But how was the meringue glacé?"

"Yummy," said Lyle. "Buffy and Booboo and Bunny and I all had four helpings with our Southern Comfort. Oh—lush!"

"Nothing like old school friendships, Flannery," Allan said, shaking his head wisely. "Same class, came out same year, engaged same week, all married in pink—bridesmaids in black, of course, very chic—same wedding-day."

"Same man," Lyle said.

It was their standard manner of masking mutual irritation and Lyle saw from the exchange of smiles between Flannery and the girl that as usual the audience thought it indicated a merry rapport between them.

"Sawyer says your first act hasn't any heart and isn't funny," said Allan.

"I say the same of Sawyer," she said. It was *her* first act when anything was wrong. She didn't care today what was the matter with the new play. All she cared about was finding out where Frederick was and if he had really taken the pooh girl to lunch.

"Oh, I forgot. This young lady is stage-struck. Marianna, is that right, my dear?" Allan waved to the girl at his feet. "Says she's planning to study ballet, voice, percussion and How to

Read Fast at the League for Cultural Foundations. I've just recommended her to drop all that and give her secretarial services and her body to a playwright as the best way to get ahead. Don't you agree?"

"I've always found it worked," Lyle said.

"I knew she'd bear me out," Allan said. "Back to your notes, now, Marianna."

The girl flashed Lyle a smile of intense sweetness, and when she spoke her voice showed such cautiously refined diction as to hint of some fatal native coarseness.

"I can't type, you know. Not yet. I'm just writing in pencil what he says."

"The real trouble is her thin legs," Allan said. "Eyes too far apart, too, shoulders humped. Have to dress her in wings to hide that hump."

Lyle saw that the girl regarded this as good-natured chaffing and was blushing with pleasure. They never knew, she thought, any more than she had known when she was a stage-struck girl delighted to be object or victim of the great man's attention. Poor Marianna. Poor Allan, with his savage efforts to balance his frustrations by frustrating others.

"I've got a wonderful idea, Lyle. What about making Martin a woman?" Allan asked, and indicated the notes on Marianna's lap with his pipe. Lyle smothered a sigh of dismay. Allan's master-mind always messed up everything. "He might like the change—eh, Flannery?"

Lyle hated the days when he chose to be funny about Flannery's homosexual leanings; they were times when his own physical difficulties galled him into taunting everyone else with their undesirableness, impotence or unnatural tastes. She knew he was suffering but today she was tired of pitying; she did not care to be even polite about his inspiration.

"Too trite. There've been hundreds of dowagers saying damn and cracking their canes around the props," she said. "I like a good mean old man."

Allan frowned thoughtfully, then changed the subject.

"Flannery says you can get white shirts now. He said he gave you the address of a man."

Lyle looked at him blankly and then the familiar feeling of guilt came over her—not for having a lover but for always thinking of Frederick first in the matters that meant most to Allan and least to Frederick. She wondered if the tailor would even let her have more white shirts.

"Maybe Martin could be a woman, after all—someone like —well, say a female Roland Young or maybe a female Ernest Truex," she conceded, guiltily. "Yes, I see it."

"Stick to your side. I like him better an old man, now that I think of it," Allan said reflectively. "Eh, Flannery? I saw something in the paper about a birthday party at an old man's home. Some old boy's hundredth birthday. Had outlived six wives and forgot their names. Reporter asked him as an expert what he thought of a wife two-timing him and the old boy said it was a fine thing once in a while. 'Makes her more chipper round the house,' the old boy said."

Marianna and Flannery screamed inordinately at this. "True, too," Allan added. "All faithful wives are nags. Nag because they haven't had a chance to be unfaithful, or else passed it up."

"Put that in," Flannery urged. "It makes sense, doesn't it, Lyle?"

Lyle felt her face flushing.

"If it's funny and shows heart," she said.

"Flannery says we can get Schafer dough for this if we play our cards right," Allan said. "Mrs. Schafer is crazy about interesting people. They also like sailing and the Museum of Non-objective Art and lobster at Billy the Oysterman's."

"He's an awful man," Lyle said. "He has a notebook full of risqué stories and he can remember the story of his life besides. Anyway, he tells everybody 'the Gaynors are terribly overrated.' He told Sawyer so."

"We'll just have to agree with him," Allan said. "Remember what it says in *The Knights*. 'To steal, perjure yourself, and make a receiver of your rump are three essentials for climbing high.' Flannery knows that."

She could not stand his badgering Flannery any more, but Flannery's vague smile masked any resentment he might feel. He said that he was sure Lyle was mistaken about Schafer's prejudice because he was a shrewd man and therefore certainly must know that the Gaynors were the hottest bet in town, the greatest team since—since—"Beaumont and Fletcher," assisted Allan. Flannery nodded admiringly.

"Marianna, this guy knows everything in the book," he said beaming. "There isn't a reference he doesn't get. I've said it before and I'll say it again,—the Gaynors are the biggest stuff in the American theatre and they've only just got going."

Lyle hoped this flattery would stop Allan, but on the other hand she supposed Flannery was well-enough protected, having the complacent ego of the ignorant. He might be obsequious to his clients but on the outside later he would be bragging of how he had just told off the Gaynors and how he not only kept them from bollexing up their business but practically wrote their plays himself. He handled a musical star and a concert-violinist and his reports on what he did for them indicated what he must claim for the Gaynor success. Celebrities were kind to him because he seemed honestly to like and deeply appreciate their qualities, but this was not devotion but an insatiable curiosity about their luck. He saw no superior talent in them, merely a mysterious magnetism for luck. His violinist client scoring a fabulous hit in Carnegie Hall made him puzzle anew over the fellow's fool luck. He himself could have done it better, if he had ever learned to play the violin, but the thing was—how did they manage to attract luck? That was the admirable thing. He made a good living out of these lucky folk but he should have been an artist. "The reason I never went in for painting is that I'd want to do it so much better than anyone else," he stated once. "My great ambition has always prevented me from doing anything." Frustrated by his perfectionism he consoled himself by circulating around favored ones unfettered by high ideals. He had a strong faith that luck might be contagious and that someday he would catch it and astound everyone by blossoming forth artist, musician, poet laureate and movie-tycoon all in one. Until that day he was their abject slave with a valuable knack at figures and a soothing imperviousness to insults which made him ideal for Allan. Lyle did not know how she could have managed without Flannery as buffer. She needed him but there were times when she thought it was Flannery, not Allan's helplessness, that kept her bound to

Allan. Flannery, constant reminder of the dozen different bars to her escape.

"Can I change my clothes?" she asked. She would telephone Frederick's apartment, she thought, then Strafford's. He'd have to be at one place or the other—he always was on Thursdays. If he wasn't it would mean . . .

"Good God, we've been waiting for you hours while you were probably furbishing up your rhumba at Arthur Murrays!" Allan exclaimed impatiently. "Listen, my beauty, we happen to have struck gold and we've got to ride our luck while we've got it. Don't forget I was in this business when you were in that pretty silver cradle of yours, and I know we can't let the grass grow. You can't just run around celebrating and re-arranging your laurels, you sweet child."

"Right," said Flannery. "As I was just telling that dumb soprano of mine . . ."

"Or was just wishing you could tell her," Allan laughed genially. "Never mind, Flannery, old boy, someday you can kick out your soprano and have a whole stable of tenors. Like my naïve little wife, here, with her stable of intellectuals —good God, not one of them could put her to bed. Intellectuals, but so dumb they don't know what she really wants."

"What I really want is coffee," Lyle said and went to the halldoor to call Pedro.

"Oh she doesn't know she wants it, I grant you," Allan pursued, suddenly wincing as the pain whipped his thighs, and his voice went on in a shrill gasp. "Why would a little spoiled darling from a second-string finishing school know what she wanted anyway, outside of her name in the columns and a foot on the stage? I'll tell you one thing, Flannery, any woman of my own generation would have had enough red blood in her to have given me a hundred horns by this time, and by George I'd respect them for it, I respect decent lust in a woman, yes, even in a pansy . . ."

"Personally I lust for respect," Lyle said calmly, "and coffee. Do you remember a book about a woman in love with an orchid? She used to creep out in the greenhouse at night for a rendezvous with it. Would you really like horns from an orchid—especially a green orchid so that you wouldn't know how the child would turn out? So unfair, too, when he'd start going to school and be called orchid by the other children."

Allan was distracted only for a moment. Lyle went to his bed-table and brought him the bottle of capsules, but he shook his head impatiently, angry at the assumption his sarcasm was only a pitiful defense against pain. She left it at his side, nevertheless, knowing he would take it when she pretended to look at his page of notes. His voice was calm again next time he spoke.

"I console myself in my affliction, Flannery," he said mockingly, "by the knowledge that it was my reputation and not my sexual ability that won the lady. Her martyrdom is not so amazing since the reputation at least is bigger and better than ever and fortunately she is herself in the best of health and can distribute autographs all over the town without a twinge. Isn't that fine, Flannery? Isn't that ducky, Marianna?"

"I'm getting lazy, though, Marianna," Lyle said, smiling. Poor Allan, poor Allan, oh poor Allan, she thought, her pity clutching her heart or was it her heart clutching for pity? "I want to sleep late and let somebody else run around delivering autographs. Maybe in a little closed carriage like *Rosemarie-Confiseur*, with a coachman—a green orchid in livery maybe."

"Oh Lyle, you're wonderful!" Flannery burst out in his high giggle of exaggerated appreciation. "Oh you two are in great form, today, you really ought not to waste it on Marianna and me."

"Do you hear, Allan? Flannery thinks we ought to write a play. Next he'll be suggesting we move to New York City— Greenwich Village, maybe, where all the angels live."

"Oh Lyle!" shrieked Flannery, laughter dying uncertainly as he saw Allan suddenly lie back in his chair, arm thrown wearily over his eyes. "Well, I guess I'll leave you fellows to your conference. Bye now. I'll take you down street for a sandwich, Marianna, if you're through. Maybe a drink."

"Sure. Take her. Put a little nourishment on her bones," Allan said without moving. "Wore out my energy waiting around here for Lyle, I guess."

"I'm sorry," Lyle said. "I was held up at the Museum looking up those costumes."

A lie. She was held up ordering shirts for her lover who had been having lunch with somebody else, somebody new, somebody who was not bound to a cruel duty. Somebody who could call him up whenever she chose, who wasn't afraid of her husband's reputation. Or where was he? She had to find out. She could tiptoe out now and telephone all the places he might be, just to hear his voice, just to know she was wrong. If Allan would only fall asleep—or die? . . . Die? She'd never thought such a wish, never before. . . .

Marianna was hesitating beside Allan's chair, being very much the shy child, a little frightened of the king. They always pretended to be shy, once they'd battered their way in; one needn't bother to reassure them. Without the mighty black spectacles for restraint her fair hair fell over her eyes in careful disarray, and she was standing in a manner to exaggerate her humped shoulders, now that they had been noticed.

"Here are my notes, Mr. Gaynor," she said timidly. "If you want me to come and work for you again I'll be awfully happy. Flannery knows where to find me."

The notes, Lyle observed, consisted of half a dozen words to a page written in the carefully standardized boarding-school script considered suitable to recommend Marlboro Cigarettes. Her lip curled but then she remembered the dreadful requirements of the stage, the need to act every moment, to conceal every genuine ache under a mock one. If the girl wanted a job, it was certainly wiser for her to appear artless, timid, and fey than to cry out her hunger and deep necessity.

"Marianna's alright, isn't she, Allan?" Flannery wanted to know.

"She has enough intelligence not to try to show any," Allan granted wearily, the two guests chuckling happily. "Something my dear wife has yet to learn."

After they left, Lyle poured herself coffee from the tray Pedro put on the table, and Allan sat up slowly and painfully.

"Let's go away from New York," he said abruptly. "Let's go to Mexico. I've always wanted to live in Mexico."

"I know," Lyle said, her heart dropping at the mere suggestion of being separated from Frederick. "But it might be bad for you. Oh no, we mustn't."

"The doctor says the Southwest would be fine. I might even be able to ride. I could ride through the mountains, join up with the Penitentes, maybe, offer myself for crucifixion, really enjoy myself, for once."

"You wouldn't enjoy yourself away from New York, you know that," Lyle murmured, already suffering the anguish of farewell forever to Frederick. No matter what one sacrificed there was always one more great renunciation that was demanded, the one wish that could not be granted.

"Never mind. I'll get there," Allan said. Her silence suggested to him that he may have carried his needling too far today in the glow of his appreciative audience. He seldom nagged when they were alone.

"That bastard Flannery got on my nerves today, you know," he said. "Imagine a little punk like that making a fortune out of our brains—yours more than mine, dear, I freely admit. The old bean's getting rustier and rustier. And then the little punk has to hang around boring the pants off me till you come."

"I know," she said.

Allan looked at her furtively.

"You look tired," he said solicitously. "Maybe the best thing is for you to take a little rest now so you'll be fresh. Yes, that's the idea. You run along and take a nap. We can put off this talk till later."

"Thanks, I will do that," she said.

Allan never wanted to work except before an audience, too. But she could thank him for making her fatigue his excuse. She went upstairs to her own room and dialed Frederick's apartment again. There was no answer and she was afraid to call the League or Strafford's to ask for him. Allan might someday take it into his head to listen on the extension.

6

. . . moonlight on Rubberleg Square . . .

THE real night does not begin on Rubberleg Square till stroke of twelve, the moment after all decisions have been made and abandoned. The reformed citizens who have cautiously stayed home reading four-dollar books that instruct as well as entertain, and have even gone to bed because tomorrow is a big day at the office, suddenly rear up in their sheets, throw on their clothes once more, and dash out for one night-cap to ward off wagon-pride. Couples who have braved Broadway to attend a solemn play concerning injustice out of town are smitten with an irresistible craving for the proximity of barflies, wastrels, crooks. The artist's model who has been doing uptown nightclubs in her room-mate's mink has had as much splendour as her Irish blood and whiskey content can endure and has escaped in a taxicab to the Florida bar downtown where her amazing hair-do and evening clothes make a gratifying glow in the dingy room and her amorous whim is satisfied by a genial merchant mariner more than it would have been by the elderly broker who was her dinner host. Here, on Rubberleg Square, the four dark streets suddenly come to life with running feet. "BAR," in red or blue neon lights, glows in any direction as if it was all one will-o'-the-wisp, same bar, same Bill, Hank, Jim, Al pushing Same-agains across the same counter. The whisper of light love is in the air; plain women brushing past are beautiful in veils of heavy bedroom perfume; men's eyes darting through the mist are ruthless hunters; hands touch accidentally, shoulders brush, smiles are smuggled in the dark to shadowy strangers. On Eighth Street the Russian shops, Chinese shops, Mexican Craft shops, Antique Jewelry, Basketweave, Chess, Rare Print and Rare Book Shops all darken simultaneously and life begins.

Rushing from Blue Bar to Red Bar to Blue Bar two sailors support an inanimate companion, his feet dragging as their grip on each arm loosens. A gentleman in somebody else's hat balances himself carefully down the middle of the Avenue of the Americas, as if it was a slack wire; his head thrust forward like a hen's, his arms flapping, his knees buckling, he tacks from curb to curb and finally flutters into the safe cove of "BAR" like a clumsy pigeon. Another gentleman with a frozen, waxy face drags an enfeebled lady behind him by her arm; her pocketbook swings from a long strap in a wide vigorous circle and slaps passers-by with a rhythmic thud. Cats lope purposefully along the gutter, alleycat and runaway pet hunt together, shying away from doting ladies with growls of jungle hatred. Taxis slide noiselessly through the damp streets, their doors swing open; a man and woman catapult from a restaurant canopy into one of these roving love-nests, are locked in an intense embrace before the door bangs shut; the taxi speeds into midnight. From unseen cellar nightclubs comes the sound of tom-toms and hidden revelry, though if you were to penetrate one of these caves you would look in vain for gaiety; you would find a bare half-dozen unsmiling guests, a dozen frowning waiters, an unhappy orchestra. The unseen mirth must be piped in from absent proprietors, or perhaps the walls are laughter-conditioned.

This is the hour when the four Pillars of Rubberleg Square collide, astonished to see each other at the usual places. Why, hello Caraway, hello Marquette, hello Doctor, hello Rover! The idea of something for the road occurs, is pounced upon as a brilliant epigram that must be celebrated. From now till closing time the Four are inseparable, examining other bars, retracing the steps each has taken singly before. The four Pillars know everybody, everyplace, and everything. The four Pillars are Mr. Marquette, trim, gay, plump, an ex-postal clerk who drinks because his wife is a lady; ("A fine thing. Look at you, a respectable man with a bank-vice-president in the family, staying up all night, keeping the neighbors awake with your groans and carrying on. What would my people say out in St. Louis? For shame!"); Dr. Zieman, lean, hawk-faced, Van-Dyked, who gave up teaching English literature for rum when his wife's juvenile *Wootsy, the Bad Cricket* was compared to something or other with the success that invariably follows any comparison; Mr. Caraway, an old New Yorker who has been sipping away for years at a small trust fund that permits him neither to go very far or stay very long anywhere. Lastly there is Rover, spit and image of the younger John Drew, up on all stage, radio and film small talk, has influential friends named Herman, Brock, Terry, Bogey, Jasper, and Norman through his wife, a prominent off-stage noise named Clarice. The lives of these gentlemen seldom cross by day but by night they unite in the business of inspecting and reporting on selected bars in the neighborhood. Earlier in the evening they have found plausible errands for themselves in different blocks, and at the final round-up they are able to piece together the activities of almost anyone you can mention.

At the Florida bar they begin comparing notes. Someone inquires whether anyone has seen Murray Cahill tonight. Why, yes, Marquette happened to be dashing past Barney's at six-fifteen and caught a glimpse of him in the bar having a double whiskey sour (no cherry) with a tall legal-looking chap in a London gray snap brim, bow-tie, ruptured duck on lapel. Being in a hurry Marquette could not tell whether it was a friend from his O.W.I. days or a bar stranger. Caraway saw him around eight at the Lafayette having onion soup and a ham sandwich reading the sport page of the *Telegram* all alone. He said hello, that was all, then paid his check ($3.40, so he must have had a couple of drinks too), made a local call in the phone booth on the way out, probably what he came in for, because he was never a Lafayette man. Last Caraway saw of him was standing on the corner just as that K.G.R. advertising man who always buys drinks all around came along with some cutie and the three went up the street together.

Is that a fact! Dr. Zieman, for his part, on his way to the lending library for a reserved copy of *I Was a Court Lady* as an antidote for *Wootsy* had seen the advertising men and the girl draped around the pianist in the Barrel all singing *Chickery Chick*. No sign of Murray, but he might have been in the boys' room or out with that Polish girl of his only he never took her out. At this point, a square-set lady in a good Brooks Brothers tweed suit comes into the Florida with the harassed air of someone called in at the last moment for an emergency Caesarian; she settles herself on a bar-stool, burying herself intensely in the *Swan* magazine and an old-fashioned. The Four Pillars lift their hats to her, respecting as they do the

dignity of the magazine she carries. Caraway recalls that he has seen her some weeks before whacking a well-known abstractionist with an umbrella in the benign shadow of the Jefferson Market jail shouting "Stalinist!" at the top of her lungs. Rover says she is a Character on the Cape, but rich. They are willing to accept comradely overtures from her (name of Hammerley, Rover recalls) but the lady is absorbed, in fact, blind. Things are dull at the Florida tonight, and it seems advisable to penetrate further into the interior of the Square. With a grave nod to Hank, the four pull hats firmly down over their ears against the light rain and file out like decent pall-bearers, heading with one accord for the America's Bar where they order four rye and waters (five cents cheaper than with fizz) just as the bartender, in one of those inexplicable spasms of bartender morality, is throwing a customer out of the place for drinking and using a profane word in his temple.

The Four Pillars digest the new scene with quiet pleasure, have a word with the manager at the back, a drink on the house, a wink at the manager's wife who patiently sits over the cash register as if she expected to hatch a brood of gold eagles. They exchange further queries and answers as to events of the evening previous, and what happened to each after they separated. Sometimes it is necessary to consult the bartender for accurate data on Last Night. The Florida bartender, Hank, is a gloomy man for six hours but curiously vivacious from then on to closing time, describing customers and situations that he, with his almost psychic powers, has "sized up." He can size up at a glance, it seems, particularly if he mops up the counter steadily in front of the customer listening to what is being said. He freely gives the Pillars the fruits of his uncanny research. On the other hand, the bartender at the New Place, where they next pause, is something of a snob in his way, enjoying the spectacle of Names making fools of themselves in his place; and he shares with the Pillars his satisfaction over having "told off" a certain big shot last night, of having refused to serve you-know-who, saying "I don't care who you are, I'm trying to run a decent place here."

It is here that the leading man from that play *Summer Day*

came in stinko last night, drinking rye Presbyterians, waving hundred dollar bills till he passed out and that good-looking girl from A.A. stepped up and took him home, either for sex or reform or both. This elicits from Marquette the news that he saw Allan Gaynor, *Summer Day* author, twenty years ago in his own stock company, a good actor but a chaser. Got mixed up with a banker's wife in St. Louis—Marquette's home town, hushed up, of course. Caraway used to see Gaynor's wife, Lyle, when she went to Stokely, the girls' school in the Connecticut village where he spent summers. Talented kid, quite a beauty, her family and the Beckleys ran the Beach Club. Naturally, with that background, the school had to give her all the prizes, especially in their dramatic affairs. Seems Gaynor's company stayed at the Beckleys' where Gaynor met her and first thing they were married, she being stage-struck and he being society-struck. Not much dough on her side but solid. The collaboration started with her writing a play, Allan doctoring it, then along comes his accident and he has to give up acting. She's smart and gets him to concentrate on writing. And now look at them—half a dozen hits, well not big hits but carriage trade, prestige. Rover complains that his wife had auditioned unsuccessfully for *Summer Day* but it was her dog who got a job at thirty-five bucks a week to sleep on the sofa during the second act. It burned up Clarice to have her theatrical career end as stage mother for a dog, and she blamed the Gaynors. Marquette wonders humorously how Gaynor casts his ingénues, now that he's crippled up, and the Doctor chuckles that maybe Mrs. Gaynor has to do double-duty in casting, now. Caraway remembers having idly observed the lady ordering a lot of plants, philodendron, he thought, at George the Florist's sent to a Bank Street address. It was nothing to him, heaven knows, but he could not help remembering that he'd seen her going in Murray Cahill's apartment over there once, and since Murray was out—"Must be that professor that Murray lives with," agreed Marquette. The bartender of the New Place is as indifferent to the Gaynors' private affairs as are the Pillars, and the subject yielding no more fruit in spite of intensive concentration on their individual wishing wells, he finally observes, "Everybody's got to come from someplace, I don't care how big they are. They can't always have been up there in those top brackets. It ain't the way of the world. And in the long run you'll find everybody's only human."

At each bar the Four Pillars act as quasi-owners, frowning on newcomers who do not behave, who complain of portions or ask for extra olives; they stare fixedly at bounders who try to engage lone ladies in conversation, they report dubious activities to the manager in a low voice, demonstrating that they might by chance drop in a bar for a refresher once in a while but they are by no means habitual drunkards, they are gentlemen, by George, and accustomed to behaving like gentlemen in all circumstances.

It is a pity that tonight Dr. Zieman succumbs to his tendency to fall asleep in unexpected places, obliging his friends Marquette and Caraway to give up further work and drag him across the Square long before closing-time, their six rubberlegs so desperately involved that the friendly policeman could not tell who is taking whom home. Rover stays on at the bar. The incident is not anything to be ashamed of, he explains to no one in particular. Dr. Zieman happens to be troubled with insomnia, that is all, and has to take his naps whenever they come. On this particular evening he had fallen smack off his stool dragging down a lady writer who had been pinning on material so long that she fell into a grateful doze herself as soon as she hit the floor and had to be removed before the Doctor, snoring peacefully, could be extricated.

"Boy, he sure had insomnia bad tonight!" the bartender exclaimed.

Someone had laughed, but Rover restored the group dignity by stating in a clear Barrymore voice that rebuked the entire bar, "Insomnia is a terrible thing, let me tell you, especially for a professional man like the doctor. You never know when it's going to hit you."

"The bald-headed old boy is a worse lush than the doc," the bartender said. "He fell down himself going out."

Rover was roused to further defense of the dignity of his friends. "The bald-headed gentleman happens to be a very close lifelong friend of the Allan Gaynors," he said haughtily.

"It wouldn't be a very good thing for this bar to have it get back to the Gaynors that their friend was called a lush. They certainly would never let him come here again or at least *they* wouldn't come."

"Oh, forget it," said the bartender. "How about the match game? And this time let's play it right! No funny-business."

7

. . . the hide-out . . .

WOMEN were always infuriated at the Murray-Frederick establishment for it hinted of a permanent stronghold against marriage. "You lucky bastards!" married men friends always cried enviously. "What a hide-out!" The apartment on Bank Street was ideally arranged for keeping out of each other's way, yet each could use the other as protection against encroachments of ladies. They had separate entrances on the first floor of an old house; bath and kitchenette were off a connecting hall between the two large rooms so that days could pass without sight or sound of each other. Frederick kept his outer and inner doors locked except in summer when his access to the garden was used by Murray. Murray's doors were usually open to any number of friends and chance acquaintances, whether he was in or not. The two men had no friends in common, no joint social engagements, and only the most meagre idea of each other's private life. This did not prevent Murray's ladies from wondering how much Frederick Olliver knew of their secrets. His ex-wife, Gerda, was so sure Murray had told Frederick all about their troubles, that she made elaborate confidences to Frederick when she met him, asked intimate questions, and took umbrage at his silence, thinking he was being cagey and hostile instead of embarrassed. Murray's regular girl, Judy Dahl, had more complicated reactions to Frederick, certain that he was responsible for Murray's elusiveness, though she managed to maintain a superficially friendly attitude. She had a habit of wandering around the place naked in summer, and Frederick was often disconcerted to find her in the raw casually frying her lunch in the kitchenette or painting at her easel when he came out from a shower. Murray allowed her to use his big room for work since she had only a tiny hall bedroom at a girls' club on Abingdon Square. Frederick wished Murray would ask her to dress when he wasn't around, but the encounters were seldom and he finally perfected a technique for ignoring her.

The presence of the telephone in the middle hall and the fact that Judy always answered it, when possible, gave her a few clues to Frederick's habits. Mr. Stalk had called and would be at the *Swan* office at three to discuss the new article; Mrs. Gaynor had called and would be free at six; the League office had called and was transferring his class from Room 20 to 28 this week.

The night after the Beckley party Frederick was working in his room, trying to concentrate in spite of recurrent stabs of guilt at his foolish quarrel with Lyle. He wrote a note to her. "Darling, it must embarrass you as much as it does me that I have never been unfaithful to you and never will be. Do forgive this blind spot." He thrust it in his pocket, decided to telephone instead, then frowned on hearing Judy moving around next door, which prevented him from going in to telephone in privacy. Usually Judy went home at night if Murray failed to return, but this night he heard her answer the phone when it rang, and then she knocked on his door. She was clothed, fortunately, and busy building up the fire by the time he came out in his dressing gown to answer. He hoped it would be Lyle but instead an operator asked for him and then he heard Murray's voice, low and guarded.

"Don't say it's me if Judy's still there. Look, Gerda is back in town. She told somebody she was on her way down to my place, but if Judy's still there, there's bound to be fireworks so I'm keeping out. See if there's anything you can do to get Judy out before things happen. Tell her you want my room for a friend. I'll call later to see. Right now I'm by way of getting plastered."

"I'll do what I can," Frederick said, and hung up. He knew quite well this was no situation he could handle and Murray must know it too, but he hesitated a moment. He saw that two women were sitting on the day-bed in Murray's room, with highballs and he heard one of them whisper, "Judy, ask him if he wants a drink." When Judy paid no attention to this suggestion, he realized he must have established himself long ago as a hopeless snob or boor to her, someone she had finally given up inviting, certain of his customary refusal. If she made no move to speak to him he did not see how he could find any deft way of asking her to go home, no matter what

excuse he could invent. He assured himself that Murray was merely nervous and the chances were that Gerda would not appear at all. The sight of Judy's square, uncompromising back made him sorry for her and he wished he had made her believe in his friendliness. He did not know why he wanted Judy to understand him, and he knew she would be astonished to discover he had ever given her more than a passing thought. Even a slight knowledge of Murray indicated that the ex-wife, Gerda, was still top woman and that Judy meant probably no more to him than a boiled dinner. Patient, stolid, and devoted, Judy at twenty-four seemed older than either of the men, more like a mother in her pride in Murray's waywardness and success with women. Frederick saw a mirror of his own withdrawn proud misery in her, and seeing the mistake of it he wanted to show her how to be otherwise. He wanted to say something that would show he was friendly no matter what might happen but as soon as he heard the other woman's voice murmur, "Judy, make him stay. If you don't I will." He gave up and hastily went in his room and locked the door. Let Murray figure it out himself. He had his own rift with Lyle to worry about.

"For heaven's sake let him alone!" he overheard Judy say to the others, and that settled it. "Murray won't stand for anybody disturbing his highness."

While Frederick tried to retrieve his ideas at his desk, the two ladies who had called to see Murray became intrigued, as was always the case, by the idea of an Extra Man wasting away on the other side of the hall. They were confident that here was a lonely male Cinderella wistfully hoping the beautiful ladies would invite him to join them. Judy curtly dismissed this idea with the authority of five years' experience during which dozens of Murray's guests had been rebuffed by this Cinderella. Murray had defended his partner with the statement that if Frederick was decent enough to ignore their noise, they should be decent enough to respect his privacy. Judy now took grim pleasure in protecting the laws of the house. After all, the ladies were Murray's friends, not hers.

"You can't tell me he's a stuffed shirt when he's lived with an old rounder like Murray Cahill all these years," said Miss Drake. Caroline Drake had come in at seven, swearing that

Murray had invited her to dinner at the Barrel and had never showed up. She was a silverware stylist and had met Murray when she was organizing a fashion show at Marshall Field's and he had been running a trade magazine. She had known his ex-wife, too, and gloomily decided that maybe Gerda had been right to leave him if he broke dates this way. Judy provided Caroline with high-balls while she waited and meantime Lorna Leahy, who lived next door, walked in to ask why Murray had not called for her as he had promised. Both ladies, being old friends, after the initial awkwardness of running into each other in these circumstances, settled down for a good time cutting up Murray. Caroline was a hearty, big boned woman, groomed to the last follicle, and not at all flattering in her assumption that Judy's position in Murray's life could have nothing to do with sex. Judy was used to this and bore no grudges. She was secretly pleased by the arrival of Lorna Leahy, commercial artist, who declared loudly that she, too, had a date with Murray, and Judy listened to the two ladies out-do each other in possessive anecdotes about Murray, who, when all was said and done, had stood up both of them. For this small favor Judy thanked her absent idol. Nevertheless, she was offended that they were more than ready to pounce on Frederick as a substitute.

"He's so distinguished looking!" Lorna Leahy exclaimed.

"I could go for that proud-faced hard-to-get kind," Miss Drake stated, stretching out her large, beautifully manicured hands as if one wrench from them would finish the hapless prey. "There was a fellow in Santa Fé like that on my Western trip. A cowboy. Same blue eyes that look right through you. Never said anything but one look and you turn straight to water. He joined the rodeo and once in New York I ran into him at the Ringside, drunk as a coot. A wild horse had thrown him and he was punch-drunk but he still had those sad eyes. He sure looked pretty in those tight pants and that fifty-dollar satin shirt."

Lorna Leahy, ruffled that Murray should have made a date with her best friend and not appeased by the joint stand-up, said that of all people in the world to compare with a cowboy Mr. Olliver was the last. She considered him aristocratic looking rather than handsome, with that faint fleck of grey at the temples, sensitive face and those blue eyes. She said it made her laugh to think of Caroline's cowboy, when Frederick Olliver was such a—well—such a highbrow. His essays were published abroad and in the *Swan* and the last book of his was out of this world. As for asking him to join them she wouldn't dream of it; that click of the key was enough for her. She'd learned something about men from her marriage, mistake though it had been. Caroline, quite humbled by this rebuke, asked eagerly for more information on Frederick's work, admitting generously that travelling around the country so much made a person a terrible dope.

While they discussed this subject Judy reflected bitterly that Murray kept Frederick as a protection against herself more than anything else. The only comfort was that it protected him against other women, as well. She silently went on darning Murray's socks, resolved not to leave these callers to wait for Murray. She could outstay anybody. She was a self-contained, honorable young woman, who had no hesitancy in admitting she had been the pursuer, dogging Murray's footsteps, earnestly trying to prove her usefulness until he allowed her his bed and the privilege of forgiving his other affairs, looking after his clothes and room and hangovers, cooking for his friends when he permitted, and waiting for his anecdotes about parties with other women. She was sure Murray needed her and she thought he loved her in a way without knowing it. She might have a baby for him someday and then he would give in to her completely. Or maybe not. He had not liked her painting any better for her winning a prize last year; he hadn't liked it any better than he had when he met her sketching on a Maine shore and stopped to kid her about her color. He thought she was foolish, spending her salary from clerking nights at the stationery store on lessons and art supplies, and he said she ought to marry some farmer and have a dozen kids. But he was kind to her and let her use his room. She thought that if Frederick Olliver did not have the back room it would be easier for her. She could live there and look after him. The way it was now Judy blamed Frederick for Murray's trouble with his ex-wife; if she had the back room she could throw out Gerda. She knew she was unfair to Frederick. She was not even sorry for him, as

Murray was, that he was tangled up with a rich married woman, and with all his brains could barely make enough to eat. He was the one obstacle in her stolid pursuit that patience and perseverance could not conquer. She thought about him as much as she did about the women in Murray's life, for it was his presence there that gave them full sway. She thought he must be comparing her to the others whenever he looked at her. She was a country girl and didn't care who knew it. She had a round, scrubbed blonde face and white pigtails hanging or else wound round her head, a square peasant body and a deep agreeable voice. Everybody liked and trusted her; push-cart merchants and shop-keepers gave her the best at smallest prices; dogs and babies leaped to her lap; women were never jealous of her; and fellow-painters liked her to pose for them even though they could not praise her painting. Judy did not mind their silence since she had never heard painters praise each other, anyway; moreover she knew she was slow. It would take years for her to do what others did quickly. She was content with small consolations along the way. Murray's open pleasure in a well-dressed woman did not incite her to any effort to compete. She never went anywhere fancy, so why should she? She wore her brown slacks, ski shoes and sheepskin-lined jacket in the city as she did in the country, a blue butcher's apron over her sweater to paint or cook. Murray used to laugh at her, suggesting an occasional change to more frivolous dress, then he got so he never mentioned it. Once, when Frederick came into Ticino's with Mrs. Gaynor, Judy had suggested that they might share a table with them but Murray had looked pointedly from Mrs. Gaynor to Judy's dirty fingernails and shook his head, laughing. Judy blamed Frederick for that, too. Mrs. Gaynor's life was complete without Frederick just as Murray's life was complete without hers. Frederick, too, was a silent lonely person waiting for crumbs, but it was no bond between them. She scorned him for the patience and silent acceptance of little that was like her own. When the telephone rang once again for him she recognized Mrs. Gaynor's voice and despised him for being in to receive it. Why wasn't he out in bars with mysterious other women the way Murray was, instead of always waiting for this dry crust? How much better to be like Murray, having the other person always worried while he laughed in bars with his private friends, unless he was being shoved into some scented boudoir by one of his stylish ladies! Judy was so disgusted with Frederick that she asked Lorna to rap on his door, fearing her scorn would show in her face.

Frederick came out to the telephone, stalling for time by lighting a cigarette, guessing that Murray was checking up on what he had accomplished. From the silence in the living-room he knew that the three ladies were waiting eagerly to hear whatever he had to say, and he knew he was helpless. But this time it was Lyle and before he could make a discreet suggestion to meet her somewhere she startled him by demanding, "Frederick, where were you lunching today that you had to break your date with Stalk?" The tone, accusing and peremptory, was not at all like Lyle and for a minute he could not answer for sheer bewilderment.

"I didn't have time for lunch today," he began, and was about to say he had taken a part-time job but stopped, feeling three pairs of interested female eyes boring through the walls at him. Lyle knew where the telephone was; she knew a personal conversation was impossible when Murray's room was full of people. The pangs of guilt over his silly behavior last night vanished in his exasperation.

"Darling, I can't get it out of my head you were seeing that Dodo girl again," now Lyle's voice sounded high and strained, and pleading. "I simply had to know if it was true."

"I said I was too busy to go out for lunch," he kept his voice low and casual because of the listening women, but he was really angry. He had sometimes been piqued that Lyle was never jealous of him in the fierce exhausting way he was jealous of her—of her marriage, of her all-absorbing work, of her suitors, of her simple joy in living. But now that she was acting like any ordinary woman, accusing him of secret meetings with a stupid girl he never expected to see again, and all in the presence of three curious friends of Murray, Frederick was genuinely outraged. Wild horses would not make him admit now that the girl was an unavoidable accident, someone whose very name, crazy as it was, he had forgotten until she brought it up.

"Supposing I telephone you around noon tomorrow?" he suggested.

"Do forgive me for being a fool," Lyle gave a breathless little laugh. "I just turned silly, that's all. I only needed your voice. Pretend I never said a word, darling, will you?"

"Of course," Frederick said.

When he hung up the receiver his cheeks felt hot and burning, either at the inferior object of Lyle's suspicion, or at her apology for having suspected at all; he was not sure which. In either case he felt too embarrassed to face the three ladies who must have gathered, judging from their smug smiles, that some misunderstanding had been going on and withdrew again to his room, too disturbed to work or to remember the little diplomatic task Murray had asked of him. He fumbled in his pocket for the note to Lyle and crumpled it up.

Caroline Drake and Lorna Leahy seized the telephone as soon as Frederick left and made telephone calls to several bars, local and distant to locate Murray, not guessing that Murray's motto, known to all bartenders and likely to be engraved on his tombstone was: "If a lady calls, I'm out." To disturb a man in his bar was as bad as to walk in on his bath. Women ought to be gentlemen, he had often complained. Judy knew this and did not enlighten her companions. She could not forgive their disloyalty in switching from Murray to gushing praise of Frederick. She thought all women ought to be true to Murray. She was too grateful for Murray's irregular favors to risk being jealous, though she knew he liked Lorna Leahy. He often mentioned his admiration for Lorna's magazine covers and illustrations, saying rather cruelly that at least Lorna knew how to make the most of a clever commercial gift without kidding herself into being a bad Cézanne. Judy was not at all offended, admitting that she did not know enough about commercial art to appreciate Lorna's work. Moreover she did not think Murray, her wayward darling, knew enough about art to know whether she herself was bad, but she did not say this. It might hurt his feelings.

"Let's get Frederick to go over to The Barrel with us," proposed Caroline.

"You all go and I'll wait here," Lorna Leahy said.

Judy gave her a measured look but said nothing. She had no intention of leaving the place, regardless of appearances. Subtlety had never gotten her anywhere and certainly would not with these purposeful women.

"Let's have another gag first," said Miss Drake, pouring herself a generous slug. "Here I am, stood up by a dear old friend I just located after years. Of course I felt a little guilty dating up Murray, having been such a close friend of Gerda's. But you always stick up for the man in separations. I do. I always adored Murray anyway. I did, anyway, till he stood me up. Have a gag, ladies. Cheer ourselves up."

"What was Gerda like? I'm always curious about ex-wives?" asked Lorna.

"Gerda," said Caroline, weighing her words judiciously, "was an absolute fool. She looked clever and talked a lot of intellectual, arty claptrap but she had a kewpie brain."

"What made her so mean to Murray?" Judy could not help asking.

"Gerda wasn't mean. She wasn't smart enough to be mean," Caroline answered. "Intellectually and morally she was a mess, but you couldn't say she was mean. Just a fool. Good God, I should know. She was my best friend, wasn't she?"

When the doorbell suddenly rang Judy was against answering it, but Miss Drake had high hopes of the unexpected and leaped to the door. Judy and Lorna heard her astonished exclamation in the hallway.

"Gerda!"

"Why, Caroline Drake, what in the world are you doing here?" cried a fluty voice.

This was the moment Judy was always dreading, the return of the ex-wife with baggage. It was the only thing that could shake her stolid calm, and all she could do was to stare stupidly at the door, paying no attention to Caroline Drake's shrill squeals of introduction.

The latest caller was a tall, thin, olive-skinned woman with radiant, heavily mascaraed eyes, a spangled green scarf wound round her head, massive white mouton coat flung over

paisley blouse and green slacks, gold-painted toe-nails protruding from metal-trimmed sandals, and as vibrantly intense
in her movements as if she had been sprung from a bow into
the room. Her heavy make-up, bracelets, huge rings, and glittering appurtenances securely camouflaged whatever reality
might lie beneath and made even Caroline Drake, in spite of
her meticulous grooming, seem a blowsy milkmaid. Judy
looked at her with deep distrust and a sick sense of defeat,
noting the small red leather bag that was ominously larger
than a mere jewel-case.

"A party! How marvellous!" cried Gerda, in a throaty theatrical voice that trailed final syllables and last words like veils
in the wind. "I'd adore a spot of sherry. But where's the
host?"

"There isn't any sherry," Judy said.

"The host's gone to bed," Lorna said with a brilliant inspiration, pointing toward Frederick's door. "We couldn't keep
him awake."

"Murray's out, of course. Not that we care. Come on,
Gerda, have a gag."

Caroline's voice was crassly Middlewestern compared to
Gerda's, and it was elaborately folksy now. Lorna tried to exchange a sly look with Judy but Judy remained coldly un-
responsive.

Gerda directed her bright eager eyes toward each of the
ladies; her near-sighted concentration gave an impression of
ingenuous curiosity.

"All I really care about is that extra bed there," she sighed.
"I'm dead. Plane, train, bus—and then I can't get into my
apartment till goodness knows when. My sub-tenants. I was
so clever to think of Murray, wasn't I?"

"Yes," Judy said as she tied her jeepshawl under her chin.

"And how lucky to find my old chum here, all in one
stroke!" Gerda said, dropping the coat on the couch, then
turning to Caroline she said in a tone of mild inquiry, "I had
no idea you were in New York, Caroline. But of course it's
been years. Five years, yes."

"Gerda, do you know how long it's been? Five years and six
months!" Caroline exclaimed, pouncing on any detour
around her hot embarrassment.

"Five years and six months!" marvelled Gerda. "I can't believe it, Caroline, it can't be! I must have had my mink then."

"You did!" enthusiastically agreed Caroline. "You had the mink—and of course Murray."

"Of course. But five years and six months without so much as a word between us!" Gerda turned to the others with a helpless shrug. "I simply can't believe it. Caroline and I were best friends, you see."

"We were!" Caroline affirmed. "It was a honey-colored mink."

"You must have lots to talk over," Lorna said politely, and received a suspicious glance from Caroline.

"Caroline testified for me in my divorce," Gerda laughed reminiscently. "She said Murray was a confirmed alcoholic and was mentally cruel. She said he was always asking where things were when they were right under his nose, until my sanity was jeopardized."

"She did?" Lorna asked, again seeking and receiving no sympathetic support from Judy.

"She simply couldn't endure poor Murray!" Gerda pursued. "He wasn't that bad, Caroline, even if he *was* my husband. Does he know you're in New York?"

"I'm having a night-cap if nobody else is," was Caroline's answer to this, pretending not to notice Lorna's slight attack of coughing.

"I think it's about time," Lorna said, holding out her own glass.

Judy tucked her sketchbooks under her arm and marched to the door.

"So long, everybody," she said, and walked out, not really minding that none of them suspected or would even believe she was Murray's girl, the only one of them with a right to the room, and the right to wait for him. She did not care that they were chattering at such a pace they did not bother to call her back, but she did mind the thought that Murray would be glad to find Gerda there, trouble and all, and she did mind the prospect of his sarcastic irritability when Gerda would leave, as she always did. He would be upset all over again at having lost her and angry at Judy for just being herself. He would get over it as he had the other times but it would be bad for a while. That was the only thing that hurt Judy and made her clench her fists turning the corner of Greenwich, longing to kill Gerda. There was not even a mischievous consolation in the thought that Murray, blithe as he might be in some tavern at this moment, was sooner or later coming home to a hornet's nest.

8

. . . the banquet-beagles . . .

FREDERICK may have learned a technique for ignoring Judy in the apartment, but there was no possibility of ignoring Gerda. She assumed the role of charming hostess who must urge the shy houseguest to join them on all occasions. She insisted on bringing a tray of rather bad coffee and a brioche in to him in the morning. She borrowed his victrola to play her new Mexican dance records. When Murray went to his office she chose to sit in Frederick's room, sitting cross-legged on the floor sewing up her costumes for dance recitals never to be given. "You look so lonely," she explained. He did not dare invite Lyle to visit him because Gerda knew too many of the Gaynor friends. He was increasingly anxious to clear up the misunderstanding with Lyle for she represented his whole outside life, apart from his work. He knew she was still hurt and knew also that they needed only a quiet evening in each other's arms to banish their wounds. He began to hate Gerda as the obstacle to this peace of mind, just as Judy hated him for the same reason, and when Gerda finally did depart for her own place he could barely bring himself to say goodbye. The minute the door closed on her—gayly ordering a subdued, unhappy Murray to carry down her Mexican drums—he telephoned Lyle to come over. They rushed into each other's arms as if their separation had been six years instead of six days, and in a little while both were laughing helplessly over the Dodo incident. How naïve Lyle had been, for all her worldly wisdom, not to have known his horror of the type!

"A pooh-on-you girl!" he reproached her. "You might have known how scared I was of her. Good God, darling, give me credit for choosing a more worthy rival for you than that."

"I was an idiot," Lyle freely admitted. "It's what always happens when I try *not* to be an idiot. Forgive me, darling."

It was a pity their reconciliation had to be cut short by Frederick's classes at the League for this was the night when he taught from 7 to 11. He would have to come to her apartment off Washington Square around midnight if he was to see her again before tomorrow, and this would be unsatisfactory because the Beckleys would be there. Allan Gaynor, being an invalid, had company around constantly even if Lyle herself was not entertaining. Lyle's home was never anything to Frederick but a reminder of all the barriers between them, and particularly when filled with the Gaynors' joint friends, emphasizing the indestructibility of marriage and the hopelessness of love.

Shying away from this basic problem as he always did, Frederick chose to direct his irritation at the League which had prevented him from enjoying at least an hour more of Lyle's company. It had depressed him almost from the very start but there had been nothing else for him to do. Now, on his way there, it occurred to him that he no longer needed that money. He pondered over the possibility of getting out of his contract and the nearer he got to the building the more odious everything it represented seemed to him, and the more imperative it was for him to leave it. "League for Cultural Foundations," he found himself muttering aloud savagely. "That's America for you. Words. Meaningless words!" The League seemed suddenly the whole basis for his quarrel with Lyle. It was the barrier between them. It was a dragon to be destroyed, though he was obliged to admit that leaving Lyle out of the question, it was a mighty monster in its own right.

It was as lecturer in the English Department that Frederick Olliver was connected with the League, receiving his rent-money in exchange for classes four hours a week in Contemporary Novel, International Literary Progress, Classic Reading, and Poetry. Four hours had seemed a small price to pay for a roof over his head with the rest of the week free for his own work, but after a while he had a desperate feeling that he was being bribed to distribute cancer. The only assuaging thought was that no one in his classes would have known the difference between cancer and culture anyway, and if they had had the hazards of achieving the latter explained to them would gladly have chosen the former.

The League for Cultural Foundation occupied a brownstone house in the West Twenties, specifically to the west of the feather belt, an area where the Hudson Dusters had appropriately enough once dominated. If the neighborhood's Polish bars rang out with slivovitch cheer far into the dawn, there was the cultural balance of Lillie Langtry's historic residence and of a great poem ("Twas the Night Before Christmas") having been penned almost within blotting distance of the school. Distinguished members of the faculty might have to wade through truck-loads of aigrettes, plumes, coq feathers and peacock tails to get to their missionary tasks, but at least they were within walking distance of a Cavanagh steak and could pay calls after class on pleasant little couples in London Terrace or on eccentric celebrities flapping their bat wings through the monastic stained glass corridors of the Hotel Chelsea. If visiting savants occasionally paused to wonder exactly what they were accomplishing by the exhibition rather than the sharing of their intellectual wealth they were reassured by the knowledge that New York's most publicized cultural leader, Tyson Bricker, was the nominal head, the thing that made the League tick.

And tick is what the League did. It had begun ticking long before the war backed by an anonymous millionaire, with small classes of ambitious under-educated young office-workers who craved a conversational mask for their deficiencies without the labor of basic correction. During the war the classes bulged with middle-aged students anxious to get an idea of what it would be like to have an idea; servicemen's wives resolved to be prepared in case their warrior husbands had learned something suddenly; out-of-town teachers on brief cosmopolitan vacations anxious to thrust one toe in the ocean of fine arts. There were courses in Radio Appreciation, Radio Gag Writing, Radio Advertising; Contemporary Art Appreciation (involving the memorizing of names and addresses of art galleries, art critics, current exhibitions, and review quotes). In the Music Department business men, who had found tone deafness and absence of musical sense a handicap in salesmanship, were taught self-control during concerts and the names of composers. Students who could read music took courses in arranging, learning to disguise familiar songs by contrapuntal twists, since it was typical of the age that actual creative composition was impossible and therefore undesirable. In the field of literature were short courses in ghost-writing, short short writing, serial suspense, and contemporary novel-writing. The last-named involved a careful survey of the Sunday book review magazines and keeping up with guest authors on radio programs for inside information.

It was during his ten o'clock Novel class that Frederick made up his mind to see Tyson Bricker that very night and ask for release from his contract. His new duties at Strafford's took up his time, he intended to say, and between the League and *Haw* he foresaw himself being driven to either mass murder or suicide. He looked around the classroom objectively, feeling better now that he proposed to leave it, but marvelling afresh that so many grown-up, self-supporting people should be eager to spend time and money studying not a subject in itself but methods to conceal their ignorance of it. Some of them travelled hours on the subways from far-ends of boroughs for this evening of Books, but so far as he knew not a one of them read anything but *Lil Abner* and *Bruce Gentry*. To open a book with intent to read was as preposterous as to actually go into the Metropolitan Opera House instead of happily standing outside watching the suckers go in. Frederick had soon given up any effort to change this state, merely giving assignments and conducting symposiums. Listening now to the discussion which he had cleverly put in the hands of an ambitious young salesman, he discovered that one man did read at least enough to interfere with the others' pleasure in learning.

"Now what did you think of that new book *The West Waits* by that fellow Nackley, Miss Corey?" Frederick heard the chairman ask.

"It was long-winded and not what the public expected of Nackley," Miss Corey stated. "It didn't live up to the promise of his other book, *The Nevada Moon*, at least not to me. That's what the New York *Times* said."

"I agree!" declared a solemn young man in dark glasses. "I read the *Eagle*."

"I liked it," said the fat overgrown ex-sailor from Sunnyside. "I liked it fine. I read the book."

Chairman and class glared at the interruption.

"It was pretentious, too, the style," said the chairman severely. "The New York *Tribune* said Nackley evidently was not aware what has been going on in the West today. Nackley's no Kenneth Roberts, either. The *Tribune* and *Times* both said that."

"I liked it," said the fat boy placidly. "I read the book. I read Kenneth Roberts, too. I liked him fine."

"I suppose you'd set up your opinion against the nation's leading critics," the chairman said sarcastically. "I don't need to read the book to know it isn't up to standard, at least not to us studying here at the League."

It was clear that the book-reader was throwing a monkey wrench into the literary discussion of review-readers, and it was equally clear to Frederick, if it had not been ere this, that there was nothing he had to offer these earnest seekers. If the bluebird of happiness were offered to them they would still be searching for its prefabricated duplicate, forever prizing the mechanical simulation to the unpriced, unmotored, therefore cheap reality. Unable to endure more, Frederick stole out into the hall and lit a cigarette. On the stair-landing a door had been cut from the League's house into the adjoining loft-building where larger classes were held, and he saw on the door a placard announcing that Tyson Bricker's class, "Motion Picture Criticism," was in progress. He might catch him at the close of this class. He wondered how Bricker "packaged" his motion picture culture, decided to listen in on him, and stepped inside the class-room. This course being Bricker's only class, was such a favorite that the room was packed with standees—some using their neighbors' backs as desks for note-taking. Tyson, trim, gray-haired, well-dressed, gray pin-striped suit, black tie, black cigarette holder, was giving his class an example of critical ease by lounging in a large red leather easy-chair, coffee-table with silver pot and cup beside him and a disarming absence of textbooks or notes. A young lady in a stupendous pompadour, was summarizing a current picture.

"So she thinks if that's the way he feels about it she'll just drop out of his life, so she takes a job in the department store to support herself and the child. All the time he doesn't know the child is his, he doesn't even know where she is and he's through with her anyway because he thinks she's bad after he saw her in the nightclub with Ricky Moller, the gangster;

so he throws himself into his work and never will have anything to do with any women because the way he feels is that they're all no-good. Finally, the head of the department store falls in love with her but she won't have anything to do with him because she still loves the father of her child, but he doesn't know he is. Finally at the airport a call comes to rush some serum to a sick child, a dying child, and he is supposed to fly the governor personally to some big affair but instead he gives up the honor to another pilot and he jumps into the only plane left and the fellows all say, 'You can't fly that old crate,' but he says, 'A child's life is worth taking a chance,' and he flies the old crate with the serum and all the time it's his own child and she forgives him and quits work in the store."

"Your summary has occupied just twelve minutes longer than the picture itself," Tyson said in his pleasant Hoosier voice. "And you offer no criticism."

"I didn't read any," explained the student. "You didn't tell us to read any this week."

"You can take mine down and then read it," Tyson said, smiling. "Write down 'A touching story of a mother's sacrifice and of a man who found himself. An old story, but perennially true, perennially moving.' "

Frederick wondered whether Tyson was only kidding his class or whether an occupational disease derived from dusty clichés had affected his brain. A bell rang dismissing the class, and Frederick backed into a corner to allow the earnest pack to follow the scent through the halls to other troughs of wisdom. Just then he felt a hand tugging at his sleeve.

"Hello, there, you," said a girl.

He did not recognize the child in orange sweater, brown corduroy slacks, beaver jacket carelessly hanging over one shoulder, tight pigtails swinging. But the tilt of her head and the mocking half-smile and twinkle were familiar. Dodo, of course. He was surprised to find himself almost relieved to see her, perhaps because she seemed a normal note in a phoney world. She smiled up at him impishly.

"You're mad at me because I went off with those other men that night," she accused him. "I think you're mean. I've got to have a *little* fun, haven't I, when I may have to go back to Baltimore any minute?"

To assure her that her departure that evening had been a pleasure would have served no good purpose, so Frederick countered by asking how she happened to be at the League.

"I'm trying to get a job in a broadcasting studio and Tyson thought this would be good for me," she said. "But I haven't met a soul so far who could do me any good. The students are all *terrible*. So tacky, honestly. Tell you what. You can take me to the Barrel for one teentsy night-cap but no more, not unless you'll be fun."

Frederick politely explained that he was to discuss a business matter with Tyson Bricker and would have to forego the privilege she suggested. At that moment Tyson saw him and came over.

"How do you like our little school-girl, Olliver?" Tyson asked, lightly spanking Dodo. "Pretty sharp-looking, I think. One of these days I'm going to keep her after school. How about a minute's chat, Olliver? Let's just step in my office a sec and then we'll go."

"I did want to see you," Frederick said.

Frederick had been wondering how Dodo could be disposed of, fearing her ability to attach herself, but it was evident that Tyson knew how to handle these problems. Tyson must have to brush off eager students every day.

"Darn business!" he exclaimed ruefully. "Why do we have to work, Olliver, when we ought to be taking this sweet kid out for a good time?"

"Can't I talk business, too?" Dodo asked plaintively.

"With that pretty little puss?" Tyson chucked her under the chin. "We'd bore you to death, sweetie."

"Pooh on you," said Dodo merrily, and wagged a finger at Frederick. "You too, Mr. Stuffy. Be seeing you."

She scampered down the hall, blowing impudent kisses at them. Tyson handled that neatly, Frederick thought enviously; Tyson could handle anything. Everybody could handle simple problems better than Frederick Olliver.

The two men came to the general offices behind the lecture room to the door on which was the name "*TYSON BRICKER*," as it was on the door of at least a dozen other offices in the city, for he was publishers' consultant, broadcasting adviser, promotion director of universities, newspapers, magazines and liberal organizations. On banquet menus the name TYSON BRICKER was as familiar as fruit-cup. Colleagues, without his gift for "mixing," declared that Tyson could smell a business dinner with its opportunity for a speech and publicity a thousand miles away. He was, they claimed, what Ben Jonson called a banquet-beagle. Since the ambition of the League's students was to become small-time banquet-beagles he served a special purpose as model. Uncertain as to what was his prime qualification for this career but having sublime faith that it was all exterior, some students copied his vocal inflections, some followed his example of black or orange ties with gray suits, and some gave up the natural lethargic shuffle of youth for his jaunty middle-aged swagger.

Frederick had noticed a dozen Bricker imitators in the halls as they went into his office. Although it was after ten a desperate looking elderly secretary was frantically typing in the outer office, and handed Bricker a sheaf of messages as he came in.

"That's a nice kid, that Dodo," Tyson observed, glancing carelessly at the notes as if they were the usual fan mail. "Money running out, so she's trying to get some kind of foothold here so she won't have to go back to her folks in Baltimore. Lives in dinky hotel room, drugstore lunches, beaux buy dinner, you know the struggle. Must be from pretty good people or she wouldn't have been invited to the Beckleys'—that's where I met her. I've tried to be nice to her on that account. Like to know Beckley better myself. That's right, I met you there, too."

"I think I remember the evening," Frederick said. Obviously, Lyle had been right insisting that he come to the Beckleys'. It must have been the reason for Bricker's sudden interest in him.

One memo roused Tyson's interest, and he begged Frederick to have a seat while he made a call. Nice kid waiting for him to telephone, didn't want to disappoint her. He slicked back his gray hair, adjusted tie and quizzical smile as he picked up the telephone.

"Hello, sweet thing," he said into the transmitter. "About time you called me, young lady! Now let's see when I can

take you out to dinner—wait a minute, Miss Wells is right
here. What about Wednesday—no, I'm talking at the News
Editors Banquet at the Waldorf that night." (Miss Wells
handed him a notebook which he leafed through rapidly,
stopping abruptly at something the sweet kid was saying.)
"What's that? You can't go out to dinner anyway? You're
married now? Oh, you mean that nice kid in the Marines is
back? Well, hooray for you. . . . Why, honey, I don't know
of anything at CBS that he could do right now. Let me think
it over. Nice of you to think of me, Gertrude. So long."

Tyson was fifty-two and had been spoiled by the war into
believing that young girls really adored him. It still baffled
him that the sweet kids who used to rhumba and jump for
balloons with him at the Stork Club now called him up only
to get jobs for their returned soldiers. It made him throw his
weight very vigorously on the side of bigger armies and more
wars. He had been such an industrious fellow all his life that
he had only begun having fun in his forties, and the best part
of it was taking sweet kids out dancing or sipping champagne,
laughing at old codgers on the dance floor being made fools
of by young girls. He disliked heavy drinking but did not
mind getting a little tiddly over champagne, providing it was
in gay, youthful company, and he found naughty stories, if
broad enough, utterly irresistible. His essays into domesticity
had not been successful. He usually had one wife packed up
ready to go and one ready to step in. Since his official ménage
was an estate far up the Hudson he saw it only seldom so that
his marriages never interfered with the gay bachelor life he led
in New York.

The little telephone interchange brought a little wrinkle of
annoyance to Tyson's brow and he pored busily over papers
on his desk to cover his momentary deflation. Frederick
thought he detected a slight venomous smile on the thin lips
of the elderly secretary, a smile that vanished the minute
Tyson recovered his poise.

"Those darn kids!" he laughed, looking up at Frederick
with a rueful shake of the head. "I love 'em, I do, I love 'em,
but what a lot of trouble they can be! Ah me! Just another sec
here, Olliver, and I'll be with you. Get out that Olliver manuscript, will you, Miss Wells?"

With considerable surprise Frederick saw Miss Wells place on the desk the red-bound manuscript of his own book. He knew that Strafford had spoken of having outside readings of it by learned authorities but he had not thought that even Strafford would deem Tyson Bricker a competent medievalist. Evidently Bricker was all things to all learning. Scornful though he was of the man's opportunism Frederick did believe in his beagling ability, and his being able to nose out quarry in any terrain no matter how unfamiliar. He accepted and lit the cigarette Tyson handed him.

"A fine job you've done here, Olliver," Tyson now stated gravely. "Strafford called me in for a consultation on his spring list, you see. I doubt if anyone with the possible exception of Helen Waddell could have handled your subject more sensitively. It's an outrage that you're not more appreciated. The years you've put into this sort of research, but who knows it? I was telling Strafford what a crying shame it is that a man of your caliber can do fine work all through life and never be recognized, while any little flash-in-the-pan with only one-hundredth your ability but with the human touch, let's say, is all over the place."

Nothing is more nettling than to be told you are unappreciated, and likely to be so all your life, so Frederick made no response to what his colleague seemed to feel was a pretty compliment. He restrained an impulse to retort that it was only Mr. Bricker's own lack of appreciation that made him think it universal, and that there were thousands far better equipped than he to appreciate Olliver. So far as that was concerned Olliver had admirers in far places where Mr. Bricker's own glossy name could never penetrate. But Tyson had meant well, as his warm friendly smile indicated. He beamed at Frederick with the honest affection one could feel toward a man who will never be a rival, a man one is sure will never be anything but a distinguished failure, a man one can praise freely and honestly without danger of sending him zooming up the ladder ahead of oneself. Frederick read all this in the fond smile and thought he would be able to feel encouraged about his future only when such people as Bricker snarled at him. He had misgivings already concerning the publication of his book, picturing the grave conferences between Strafford and Bricker, the repeated protestations of reverence for such scholarship, such fine prose; the lamentations over the vulgarity of the reading public, the noble statements that the dissemination of such work would constitute their life work had they only their own tastes to think of; then the solemn reminder of their practical duties as publisher and as teacher-critic to the underprivileged public (which had a right to "escape reading" regardless of literary standards), and to the masses whose tastes must be fed; finally, the mournful decision that the luxury of pandering to their fine personal predilections must be denied them; the Olliver book must be put aside if not abandoned altogether to some more selfish and fortunate firm.

"It struck me that a foreword in a popular vein might help a little to put it over," Tyson went on. "I'd be glad to do what I could in view of our association together here at the League. We can come to some arrangement if you like the idea."

Frederick was mystified by this offer, as well as embarrassed. He needed no foreword but would have felt bound to have one, if any, by Edward Stalk in whose magazine some of the material had been printed. As Stalk and Bricker were firm enemies he did not mention this but murmured his thanks evasively.

"I only wish I could take time off and do my own book, my Jane Austen," Tyson sighed, picking up his hat and giving a final wave which combined Miss Wells and his cluttered desk as if the two would merge magically into order. Tyson was famous for his passion for Jane Austen whom he quoted in every possible connection, though he had not read her for twenty years and if he ever should do so again would be astonished at what he did not know about her, and at the number of sagacious things she had never said. However, it was a dignified harmless passion and entitled the distinguished fan to write introductory paragraphs to many works on the lady. These volumes were all listed as "Bricker's Austen," and the card catalogue in the Forty-second Street Public Library had a dozen Austen and Bricker cards cross-filed quite as if he had already made his definitive study.

"What I was about to suggest, Olliver," Tyson said as they came out on Eighth Avenue, "was that you take on a few more classes at the League, to tide you over. That sort of book won't ever sell, as you know. Mrs. Gaynor was saying to me the other day . . ."

"I couldn't possibly," Frederick answered. Had Lyle been trying to help the poor failure again? He had not told her yet about his job on Strafford's magazine because he was half-ashamed, but now he told Bricker about it defiantly, suddenly proud that he could be considered as cleverly corruptible as the next one and not too unworldly to do some purveying to the masses on his own hook. A little wildly he informed Tyson that *Haw* was a certain success judging by the first issue he had gotten out, that he expected to make a great deal of money out of it inasmuch as Strafford was giving him an interest in it, and that he had no need of being "tided over" in spite of Mrs. Gaynor's thoughtful suggestion. To Tyson's exclamation of astonishment that he could do such work, Frederick replied that he enjoyed it very much indeed, that it was a satisfaction to be giving the reading population the sort of thing it craved, and that with due deference to Tyson's idol, he doubted if even Jane Austen could give the joy that *Haw*, with its murder stories, raffish jokes and raucous cartoons, was giving. He expected Tyson to resent the veiled sarcasm, but instead saw a look of awe in the other's eyes.

"That's the stuff! You've got your feet on the ground, old boy!" Tyson said approvingly. "I had no idea you had that much common sense. By cracky, Olliver, I knew we would get on if we got to know each other. Why, I feel as if I knew you better in these last five minutes than in all the time you've been at the League! Look here, I have to pick up a dame at the Plaza at one-thirty, but I've got an hour or so to kill before then. What say we chop over to the Barrel for a highball first? I'd like to hear you talk more, Olliver, by George, I would."

That was how well he managed things, Frederick thought hopelessly. He wanted to insult someone and the fellow was entranced; he wanted to resign and was offered more work; he wanted peace and quiet with Lyle and was on his way to uproar at the Barrel. In a last spurt of protest he told Tyson he had to check on an engagement first. There was a bare chance that Lyle might now be alone. But when he stopped in the corner cigar store to telephone he was told by Pedro that Mrs. Gaynor had gone out. In a state of numb resignation he accompanied Tyson to the Barrel and there was Dodo, sitting alone at the bar, sipping a stinger. She was watching the door and waved eagerly as they entered.

"I just knew you two would come here!" she cried, patting the empty bar-stool beside her imperiously. "I told Al here I wasn't alone, didn't I, Al? I said I was waiting for someone. Wasn't I bright?"

Tyson lifted eyebrows toward Frederick in wry amusement.

"You were, indeed, you sweet thing," he said and motioned Frederick to a seat on the other side of Dodo. "Two Scotches and another stinger, Al. Say, it's pretty gay here tonight."

An old gentleman in a checked suit with a bowler hat and spats, handlebar moustache pasted under his nose, was dancing around the piano, wheezily singing *A Bicycle Built for Two*.

"New talent," Tyson said.

The bartender leaned forward confidentially.

"Know who that is? Rich old crackpot. Always comes in with a big party. Likes to rig himself up like that and pays the pianist to let him carry on. Let's see—what's his name, now?"

"I wish he'd stop," complained Dodo. "I want *Day by Day*. Go make him shut up, Freddie. Make him go sit down at his own table."

"Beckley, that's it," the bartender said. "Lexington Beckley. Quite a character around town."

"Beckley?" repeated Frederick with a vague premonition.

"Look, he's with Mrs. Gaynor's party over in the corner," Tyson exclaimed. "I think she sees us, Olliver. Let's go say hello."

In the bar mirror Frederick could see Lyle's eyes fixed on him with an expression of hurt bewilderment. Of course it looked queer for her to find him with the very girl he had explained away a bare four hours before. But she would surely believe it was an accident even if she might not see the humor of it. He followed Tyson over to the corner booth where Lyle sat with half a dozen of the inner Beckley circle. She barely spoke to him and his case was not helped by Tyson.

"Just the person I wanted to see, Mrs. Gaynor," he exclaimed. "Olliver and I have a little pupil from the League with us over there and I'll bet you know how we can get her a film job. Anything at all, just to get a foothold. Maybe a word from you at Paramount. I'm not in good favor there myself now. Dodo Brennan. That's the name."

"I'd be glad to speak to Evan about her," Lyle said sweetly. "I'm sure she'd make a good receptionist."

"Anything," Tyson said. "The poor kid just wants an in, isn't that so, Olliver?"

"I'll mention to Evan that you and Mr. Olliver cannot recommend her too highly for any position whatever," said Lyle.

"Good!" Tyson laughed. "Lucky for all of us we know a big shot or two so we can help out some of these sweet kids."

"Lucky for them, too," said Lyle.

She was flushed with anger and her flashing eyes refused to see Frederick, and as she addressed herself in a low voice to Tyson there was no opportunity to explain that Dodo's presence was not part of a mischievous plan. Dodo was beckoning from the bar and Lyle pointedly called Frederick's attention to this. Desperately he leaned over Cordely Beckley's head and said to her, "Perhaps I can walk home with you when you're ready to leave."

"My goodness, I wouldn't dream of taking you away from your little protégé," Lyle answered brightly. "She'd never forgive you."

"Tomorrow, then," Frederick murmured, growing hot with anger at Lyle's unfair condemnation of him on circumstantial evidence.

"Tomorrow?" Lyle repeated, frowning, and then exclaimed, "Oh no, I'm flying down to the Beckleys' in Carolina with Allan for a couple of weeks. We're considering buying a place down there."

One of the younger Beckleys clapped her hands at this.

"Lyle's changed her mind! She's coming with us!" she cried.

Knowing why she had changed her mind Frederick could not speak for indignation. She was punishing him, in a highhanded, arrogant way that permitted no defense. She was strong in the midst of her special satellites, the people who protected her from him, the people who came first. She was reminding him again that the "we" in her life meant Mr. and

Mrs. Gaynor and that they were about to cement this invincible fort even further by new plans and home-buying that showed the indestructible harmony of their union and the insignificance of any intruder. She was revenging herself for his having, as she thought, deliberately chosen Dodo's company, and so far as that went why shouldn't he? She had her fine separate life with Allan, why shouldn't he have Dodo? Tyson had crowded into the seat beside Lyle but Frederick was still standing. He bowed goodnight stiffly to Lyle and ignored the others just as rudely as they were ignoring him. Lyle looked icily past him without response, and he stalked back to the bar. He made no move when Dodo tugged at his sleeve and squeezed his hand. She hung her head looking up at him sidewise, mockingly, thick black lashes quivering like legs on a green spider.

"You're a bad boy leaving me all alone," she pouted. "Don't you know you can't run away from me like that, you old naughty?"

"I'm afraid that's true," he said.

After Lyle's injustice the little dove hand in his seemed friendly and consoling. It was Lyle who had forced this situation on him, he thought bitterly. Tyson had helped, but it was primarily all Lyle's fault. Not his. Not Dodo's. He and Dodo were the wronged ones.

"Let's get out of here," he said explosively.

"Let's," agreed Dodo, jumping off the stool eagerly.

As they went out the door he felt a rush of mingled elation and fright as if his ship had just lost sight of land.

9

. . . young Olliver . . .

"L<small>ET'S</small> go to someplace like the Stork Club," said Dodo, "Let's celebrate."

She sat on Frederick's day-bed combing her hair as casually as if nothing had happened. With her bare legs thrust in high-heeled black sandals and her tight black satin dress accentuating whatever curves were not exposed she looked like an *Esquire* picture, Frederick thought. What on earth is an *Esquire* picture doing in this somber, book-lined room, he wondered? And very much at home she was, too, full of suggestions as to changes in furniture and curtains. He laughed indulgently over her criticisms of the Bracque drawing over his fireplace, allowed her to boast of a cousin of hers in Salisbury, Maryland, who was the best artist she ever knew and who had had things in the school paper that everybody said were better than anything in New York. Everything she did not understand, such as the Bracque and his article in the *Swan* magazine made her feel personally affronted. But Frederick only chuckled, for she was a mere child, after all. For the same reason he did not refuse sarcastically her desire to celebrate, as he would have, had the suggestion come from Lyle. After all, he had to remember that Dodo was young, and an outsider, with the natural curiosity of both. It occurred to him that an excursion into the night world he loathed might have a certain piquancy if one was in the role of guide to a naïve stranger. He had been forced to accompany Lyle on some occasions and his position as nobody in the wake of a glittering group was no pleasure. The experience had its value, however, for at least he knew his way around, that was something.

"Turn your back while I dress," he commanded Dodo.

"Why should I turn around?" Dodo wanted to know. She twisted her hair over her neck with one hand, and pulled the spangled net over it. "You have a terribly nice body, much better than other men your age."

Never having thought about his body, and never having anticipated compliments on it from a young woman he knew only in bed, Frederick smiled. The implication that Dodo was familiar with many other male bodies, far from disturbing him, made him feel safe and even flattered, for it showed he was not unique in surrendering to this particular temptation.

"I'll have to find a decent shirt," he muttered. Lucky he had his salary in his pocket, shirt or no shirt, for Dodo took for granted that he was a man of means. Oddly enough he liked this, too, for the misconception was more flattering than Lyle's thoughtful consideration for his poverty.

"You're so poky! It's midnight already!" Dodo scolded.

She smoothed out the bed, arranged the red corduroy couch cover. While Frederick was pulling out one drawer after another she impatiently searched through the clothes closet. He could not help an inward amusement at himself for his pleasure over what would normally seem an invasion of his privacy.

"You silly man, here's a whole box of shirts!" she cried out. "All brand new and expensive! I should think that a man who went to all the trouble of buying shirts like these would certainly remember them! Honestly, Freddie! Just look! They must have cost you plenty!"

She had found Lyle's gift and it was no time to explain that he had intended returning them as soon as Lyle got back. But Dodo's awe over his possession of such luxuries changed his mind. It would only have added insult to the injury he was already doing Lyle, he reflected. Rejecting them would be a disagreeable and unnecessary gesture, he thought, the sort he could never control. He was always ashamed of the angry pride that was his curse, that always hurt himself as much as it did Lyle. Now he experienced surprised gratitude to Dodo for saving him from another humiliating expression of his weakness. Of course he would keep the gift.

Dodo had on her coat and had fastened the gardenias he had bought her at dinner in her dark hair. She was all impatience to be off and skipped out to the hall. While he tied his tie—a present from Lyle—Dodo attempted a tap dance before the hall mirror. He knew Murray and whoever else was in the front could hear her and would know it was not Lyle.

This pleased him. He wondered why he had always been so secretive, almost ashamed, of his one great love, and now so proudly exhibitionistic of its betrayal. He wanted everyone to know he was not that vulnerable figure, a faithful lover, but a normal, regular fellow unhampered by any civilized emotions—carefree, uncapturable, faithless. Instead of tiptoeing out discreetly he made no effort to lower his voice. "Haven't you ever been to the Stork Club, Dodo?"

"Oh yes, Larry's taken me everyplace," Dodo answered impatiently. "But he always passes out. Besides I want to go with someone that knows who's who, like you do."

In the vestibule he pulled her to him and kissed her cool cheek.

"Let's go back," he whispered.

"Oh, Freddie, don't be silly!" Dodo expostulated, drawing away. "You promised we could go someplace and have fun!"

"Then come back afterwards and stay for breakfast," he urged.

"Maybe," Dodo shrugged. "Don't crush my gardenias, please!"

It was one of the amazing things about the new self Dodo had awakened in him that he was not at all embarrassed to be caught by Caroline Drake who came out of Murray's door at that moment. He was grateful again to Dodo, for release from his idiotic shyness. Caroline inordinately redolent of Shalimar and fine Bourbon, was so surprised she looked twice.

"Why, Mr. Olliver, for goodness' sake!" she exclaimed in bewilderment. "I didn't recognize you."

Aware of having been clumsy she dashed out to the street in great confusion.

"She heard you ask me to stay for breakfast," Dodo said resentfully. "You shouldn't say things in front of people. They might talk about me."

"Nonsense!" Frederick laughed.

It struck him that he laughed a lot for a man whose great love affair had crashed a bare two weeks ago. He had always felt that if Lyle were ever to forsake him he would die, but instead he felt as if he had just come to life. It was as if he had suddenly been admitted to The Club, and was from now on privy to secrets of which he had never even dreamed, secrets that all other men had always known. The first time Dodo had spent the night with him had revealed a new world and a new self and had shocked him with the awful thought that he might so easily have gone on forever without this simple knowledge. All his years with Lyle had given him not the faintest desire to be unfaithful. The very handicaps to their complete relationship—his all-absorbing work, her untouchable marriage, and her social and professional life, had made him want to keep perfect what half-portions he did have. But now he saw that he had been badly nourished, and it seemed to justify his surprising lack of conscience. Here at last was an affair that need not be hidden—he was a free man; Dodo was a free woman.

It was as if chains, gags, and blinders had been removed. He had no duty here to be respectful of her husband's name or her own public reputation, no need to conceal every natural feeling. He could ask her to take a trip with him, stay to breakfast, have dinner publicly with him every night since she had no husband or superior friends to be constantly appeased. With Dodo it was he who called the tune. He knew well enough that it was her picture of him as a person of importance that had made the easy conquest, but that bolstered his vanity even more. He scarcely thought of Lyle in the wonderful excitement of his new game, and when he did think of her it was to be glad she was away, glad she was angry with him, glad of anything that delayed the necessity of a decision. Above the marvel of discovery there was a wild jubilation of senses in merging with youth, a girl eighteen years his junior. He would have laughed scornfully at such a cliché until it happened to him. Actually the extraordinary delight of their love-making had nothing to do with physical or emotional fulfillment, being more tantalizing than satisfying. For Dodo it was a sexual triumph over Fame, for Frederick it was a triumph over Youth. It left him exhilarated for days afterward, eager to get up in the morning to begin savoring the memory and the anticipation. Everything had new vitality and flavor. The sun shining, the taste of coffee or cigarettes, the sound of a song in the street, the simplest sensations elated him. He had always had a detached literary curiosity about strangers he passed; now he was moved to ecstasies of appreciation of all mankind. The lethargic, gloomy janitor of the block saying, "Looks like the government is having its troubles same as us common folks," made Frederick ponder with delight on the exquisite rightness, the absolute Americanism of the working-man. When he crossed the Square at Eleventh Street, usually a hazardous, infinitely annoying venture, he paused now to contemplate with something approaching glee the stately disorder of the street arrangements, the possible mischief in the minds of the city planners. He saw his own street and his own apartment as if for the first time, with admiring surprise. It was odd that his heady glow had no effect on his original picture of Dodo, as he had seen her that first night with Murray at the Barrel. It was odd that he could be so enchanted by her yet retain his reservations complete in a separate compartment of his consciousness. He found her conversation as commonplace as on first meeting, and speculated (with amusement now instead of with impatient hostility) on how she was able to fancy herself an irresistible wit. It surprised him mildly that the vibrant youthful nervousness of her physical movements should be combined with such a rusty mental machinery. Though any sudden glimpse of her gave him quick delight it did not persuade him of her superior beauty. Her breasts were too sharp and close together, he thought, her hair too coarse and sleek, her trimness a cause for approval without admiration. Whatever effect she had upon him had nothing at all to do with her qualifications. She could have been plainer and far more stupid without lessening her attraction for him. Yes, her very ignorance was flattering to him. It implied that his appeal to her was a basic male superiority which overshadowed the handicap of mere academic virtues. His new injection of youth made him notice girls on the street for the first time, contemplating the possibilities of adding even further to his new knowledge. His blood pounded when he thought of last night; he went through his day's work thinking of making love to her again. How curious, he thought, to have thrown open every door to this stranger when he had kept so much of himself from Lyle! Dodo boldly pranced from Murray's quarters to his, and Frederick sensed that he was going up in Judy's estimation as a result. He was a regular fellow, now, like Murray. The news, relayed to Dodo by Judy, that Frederick had a serious secret affair made him all the more valuable to Dodo. The third time she stayed with him she hinted of marriage, and it pleased Frederick to be laughingly evasive, as other blades were, on this sacred point. From his pleasure at her pouting hints he realized how unhappy he had been at having the mere idea of marriage closed to him for so long; he could not marry Lyle, he could not marry any one else. He wilfully kept Lyle out of his mind quite aware that there would come a day soon enough when decisions must be made. He felt that each minute until then must be devoured greedily and in a vague way hoped and feared that perhaps the delirium would have vanished before the day of reckoning could come. Had the memory of his first meeting with Lyle faded or was it really true he was now happy for the first time? Dodo's dates with Larry, her coy allusions to mysterious other suitors did not stir him at all for he seemed to feel no jealousy, just simple sensual delight in whatever he gained. Her idea of being amusing was to ridicule him in public but this, too, flattered him, as if dignity was a chaperon well lost. She was irritable after their love-making, for his immense delight made her suspect she had given away something worth more than she realized. But Frederick was not hurt by her peevish jibes, his senses still singing of his triumph.

At the Stork Club—he must certainly be bewitched to have consented to such folly—he saw that the producer of Lyle's play was entering behind them. If he had been with Lyle he would have kept haughtily aloof, seething with resentment at having to share her with these professional admirers, contemptuous of the respectful flurry their presence made around other diners. Now, he was relieved to be recognized by the man for he was awarded a good table on the strength of the association.

"Why didn't you introduce me?" Dodo whispered, as they followed their waiter across the floor. "You're so mean, Freddie!"

Everything about the place reeked of the life Lyle led, the people she knew, of the things he had never understood and therefore disliked which meant so much to her. Tonight, however, he was glad to be able to name the figures Dodo pointed out.

"It's just like being at a show—especially when you know who everybody is!" Dodo exclaimed and squeezed his hand gratefully. It suddenly struck him as strange to be sitting on the outside enjoying the show instead of being part of it and bored. For a second he was not sure he liked the new role but Dodo's hand persuaded him.

"Look!" Dodo cried out. "Do make him come over here!"

Frederick saw Tyson Bricker, resplendent in the gayest of evening sportwear with a group nearby. Tyson's reverent manner indicated that he was with very valuable contacts indeed and his smile of recognition was of the vague preoccupied sort usually intended to keep lesser lights at bay.

"Tell him to come over with us," Dodo insisted. "He's an old friend of yours, isn't he? He likes me, too. Waiter, tell the gentleman at that table I want to speak to him."

"No—" Frederick interrupted hastily, then stopped. Why not? Dodo had as much right to express herself as Tyson Bricker did. But Tyson merely smiled evasively at them and appeared absorbed in some compelling discussion. Very different, Frederick thought sardonically, from the times when Tyson spotted Lyle Gaynor. Then he would have attached himself to her table for the evening. In a fit of petulance at the slight Dodo was ready to get up and accept a drunken stranger's invitation to dance, till Frederick remonstrated.

"I don't see why I can't have some fun even if you don't dance," she sulked. She was further aggravated by being absent in the Powder room at the time Tyson chose to come over to their table.

"I'm with Cham Bellaman, you know," he explained. "Just bought the Barton publications. By the way, they say the Gaynors are expected back Saturday. Give them my regards, will you? I see you're taking charge of our little student. Sweet kid."

But he was gone by the time the sweet kid got back, and she was only appeased by being told Cham Bellaman himself had been with Tyson.

"He was all over last week's *Life*," she marvelled. "And I didn't even recognize him!"

The mere mention of fine names had subdued her. When her old friend Larry, from the K.G.R. Agency started toward them Dodo was feeling so superior that she murmured, "Let's not let Larry join us. He gets so noisy he'll spoil everything!"

"Hey, you people!" Larry called out, pushing past tables toward them with a determination that knocked chairs and glasses to the floor. "What are you doing here?"

"I don't have to wait for you to take me places, Larry," Dodo said haughtily. "I know other men, plenty of them."

"So I see," Larry amiably replied. "Where's old Murray? Is he here too? What say we tool down to the Barrel for a night-cap?"

"Too tired, Larry," Dodo said. "Why don't you go on home, yourself? You're really disgusting!"

"So my wife was just saying," Larry agreed and shook Frederick's hand a second time fervently. "Not so disgusting as I'd like, hey, fella? You know, Dodo, I like this guy. He's alright. I like that deadpan of his. Shake, old boy."

Frederick shook.

"So that's your wife," Dodo observed, frowning across the room. "I notice you didn't get as good a table as we did. Freddie knows people, that's why. Come on, Freddie, let's go home. Freddie don't have any wives to keep us here, thank goodness."

"Good deal!" Larry laughed genially. "Well, so long as they keep us, hey, fella?"

"Pooh," said Dodo coldly. "I wouldn't advise you to be humorous, Larry. Goodnight."

When they got into the taxicab Frederick discovered that the outing had made Dodo highly pleased with him. He was glad now, that he had been trained, however reluctantly, by Lyle to know the way around in such places, since it had set him up in Dodo's eyes. She hummed happily for a while, then snuggled into his arms and fell asleep like a kitten, her gardenias drooping over one eye and her arm tight around his neck. Frederick gave the driver his address with an exultant feeling that in his arms was something entirely his own, dominated by him, awed by him. It was a delicious sensation, unmarred even by Tyson's words flickering dimly in the back of his mind, "I hear the Gaynors get back Saturday."

10

. . . lesson in acting . . .

THE joke was always on women, Lyle thought. Their lives
have become too complicated to be managed either by reason
or instinct. Each path blocks every other path and goals are
reached only by blind luck. It seemed to her that all the problems of her own life were rushing together in a wild dance,
riding her like trolls, their clamor drowning any single voice.
Whenever Frederick had hurt her before, she had been glad
of the refuge of hard work and the impersonal frivolity of the
friends he despised. But this time, it was different. It was not
only another woman, but the fact that he had cruelly and deliberately mocked her. He had made a fool of her, made her
laugh over her suspicions as if they constituted a preposterous
joke between them, and this was monstrous. It hinted at deep
wells of sadistic evil in him; it tainted their entire past, made
her doubt that love had ever existed. Bitter as she was towards
her lover the weeks spent away from him at the Beckleys'
Carolina place did nothing to restore her. All her worlds were
shaken at once. Nature itself, turned enemy; the silence of
country nights was sinister, made her fears roar the louder
through her brain, and sleep was won only by nembutal, even
that magic deserting before daybreak. Outside her window
the forests of elms hoary with Spanish moss shuddered with
windy prophesies of lovers betrayed, lovers dead, woe and
desolate age to come. At the hour of dawn there was a terrific
tuning-up of song birds in tree and barn but it was as meaningless as a press-agent's drum-beating for the sun never
really appeared. After the fanfare of color in the sky, the rose
and orange clouds parted for the favorite's entrance, but, like
a spoiled star, one peep told the golden one there were no
photographers on hand, no crowd really, so she retreated
sulkily, drew the bat-gray shades, let it be known she refused
to go out in public, was a recluse really. Gray days and chill
mists drove the Beckley guests to the idle pleasures of the interior, but this was even more unsatisfactory than the out-

doors for at this moment when Lyle was so anxious to find consolation with her own friends she was bewitched into seeing them as Frederick saw them. Ephraim, making ponderous pronouncements on art once outrageously funny to her, now appeared as Frederick saw him—a vain, stupid man presuming that an inherited fortune entitled him to intellectual authority. There was Mrs. Ephraim, so steeped in her Boston antecedents she had needed no further education, coasting on her harmless belief that the earth was pear-shaped, the Beckleys and Boston at the big end, Art at the little stem. How could she have tolerated them! And how right Frederick had been in estimating their hollowness!

Their group of guests—talented folk since Ephraim supported his father's belief that talent around meant free and guaranteed entertainment—seemed only the lucky gamblers Frederick had declared them to be. If Barlow's opera had not had Koussevitsky to make it the season's talk who would have deferred to his banalities on politics? If Everitt's novel had not been a best-seller who would have considered his insults a sign of wit? Her lover had stabbed her, Lyle thought, and had taken away her anodyne besides. He had taken away, worse yet, the sense of guilt which had given her patience with Allan. She was suddenly tired of pretending Allan's perpetual jeers at her conventional upbringing were an amiable family joke. She hated their game of being Happy Couple. Allan seemed now a selfish, egocentric burden, a burden that Frederick, she realized now, had made possible for her to bear. Angry at Frederick, disgusted with her husband and her friends, Lyle stayed in her room pretending to be working over the new play Sawyer was expecting from them, but there was nothing in any corner of her mind but speculations about Frederick. How many weeks, months, maybe years, had he carried on with this girl? And before that how many others were there? Always so smug, she mocked herself, always so certain that it was the same with him as it was with her. How did she know what went on in his apartment when she was not there? Murray, his companion, had dozens of women around. No reason why Frederick might not have shared them. It was true as Frederick had often complained, she recalled remorsefully, that they had had little time together actually. Her fault. Their moments were what was left over from her full life, she forced herself to admit; time she could spare from rehearsals, Allan's requirements, the things she put first, relying on Frederick's taste for solitude since it convenienced her to do so. It was convenient to be blind, convenient to believe their love needed no reassurances, their understanding needed no words.

Thinking of the person Frederick was revealing himself to be, Lyle wondered what else was to be found out, how long had he despised her own talents for instance, as he did those of her friends. He had always admired—or *pretended* to admire—the way she made the puppets in Allan's bare outlines into real people. It delighted him, he had said, the same way improvisations on a musical theme delighted him. He had often urged her to do a play entirely her own, but that would be the supreme disloyalty to Allan. Allan had been her teacher. He had opened every door to her, he had made her discover her own self, he had applauded each step, staged her, plotted her happiness the same way he plotted a play. When he cracked up physically, and then for a frightening interval, mentally, she had been able to repay him, never allowing him to give up, assuring him that his confinement did not lessen his value to their collaboration, though the worry of rehearsals, revisions, try-outs and casting was now entirely on her shoulders. Actually this was the best thing that could have happened, and resulted in their increasing success, for Lyle was thus given opportunity to humanize and twist the rigid conventional framework of Allan's plots. She always insisted on the superior importance of his share, however, and saw now with her newly disillusioned eyes that she had convinced him that almost any amateur could take over her contribution. It was Frederick's fault, she thought, during the cocktail hour with the company grouped around Allan's bed, that she noticed for the first time Allan's constant reference to "*my* last play," the play "*I'm* working on now." Of course he had said this for years, but now it seemed significant, part of the plot against her. Every one knew she did most of the work, of course—or did they?

"I must never take anything for granted again," Lyle thought.

The longer Allan delayed their return on the basis that they were working just the same as if they had been at home, the more her long-buried resentment towards him rose, the more detestable the Beckleys seemed, and the more dim her lover's guilt, until wild jealousy melted into mere sorrow. She could scarcely wait to see Frederick and tell him she forgave him, that she understood at last the loneliness of his position, the position in which her loyalty to Allan had placed him.

She knew these affairs were only trivial, she would say, and he could rely on her understanding because she was the one at fault, the one who had failed him. Then, on the plane coming up it occurred to her that again she was taking too much for granted. Perhaps this Dodo business was serious. Perhaps he would even admit as much. Unable to face such a possibility, Lyle decided to act as if nothing had happened. She would telephone him for lunch and keep up a gay, friendly front, demanding no explanations, leaving their course completely up to him. That is, providing he did not suggest that their paths separate. Facing the chance that he really might want release, Lyle determined to show him that she asked nothing, that everything would be conducted his way. She would be casual, and if his manner revealed the dreaded wish to be free she would plan a next meeting with others present, his own friends, Edwin Stalk, say, to reassure him.

The program was not so easily carried out. She telephoned him the night she arrived, thinking that he might have been as wretched as she and want to see her at once, all things forgotten. But there was an ominously long pause between Murray's answer and Frederick's voice. He sounded cool and enigmatic, as if he had taken time to prepare a defense against her.

"I wanted to catch up on all that's been going on," she plunged. "Did you give up your League job the way you planned?"

No, he had decided to fulfill his contract, Frederick answered, and went into detail as to Bricker's new plans for the League, and the advantage of seeing them through. Lyle made haste to agree completely with the wisdom of his decision, and Bricker's need to back his opportunistic inspirations with other people's brains, as Frederick had often said——

"Oh, Tyson's got brains, alright," said Frederick, all contrariness, and Lyle quickly amended her remark, changing the subject to the boredom of Carolina and her discovery that the Beckley set was fully as dull as he had said. Frederick appeared to relax at this concession, and then struck a blow to her heart by saying, "You must tell me all about it. What about having cocktails tomorrow?"

"Tomorrow?" she echoed stupidly. Tomorrow. Not tonight. Not this minute. But it was even worse as he went on.

"What about meeting me at the Ritz, say, around six. You probably have a dinner somewhere later."

The Ritz. Not at his apartment, but in public so they must be casual. And at six instead of five because she might have a dinner date relieving him from enduring more than an hour or two with her. Very well, then.

"The Ritz is so quiet!" she protested. "If we're going to be so grand let's go to the Savoy Plaza. I've just spent three weeks in the quiet!"

She would out-do him in casualness.

"Very well," he said and was about to ring off but she could not let him go without saying, "I'll have to leave early because I've asked crowds in for dinner."

There! She thought, as flushed and breathless as if she had been boxing. There! She had not begged him to come to her dinner as she always had before, with invariably sarcastic or wry refusals from him. She had not told him who was coming so that he would have the opportunity to ridicule them, either amusingly or jealously. She had shown no surprise at the unprecedented extravagance of his invitation, nor asked what success had come his way to warrant the change of habit.

It was serious, she thought, and her heart seemed to rock in broken glass.

"I'll invite Edwin Stalk and Benedict Strafford to dinner," Lyle thought fiercely. "I'll invite every one he admires so he'll wish he had been here. I won't have any of the people he thinks I'll be having. He'll be surprised."

It was such a silly little consolation that she found herself laughing hysterically.

II

. . . the revenge on love . . .

After living together for seven years and keeping a gentlemanly distance, Murray Cahill and Frederick Olliver were
suddenly intimate friends. The reason for the new relationship
was as justifiable as that for some marriages between antipo-
dal personalities—that is, those involved had one major experience together: they were in the same hurricane, the same
war, or the same spotlight at the same time. Murray was in a
jam with women and conscience; so was Frederick. Murray
was changing his routine; so was Frederick. Murray's difficulties made it necessary for him to avoid his usual midnight
cronies but not his midnight habits. He found new bars, and
sometimes sat around Umberto's or the Jai Alai bar, neither
place being on his usual agenda. Frederick's habit had been to
work in his room nights, but after his rebirth he had an aversion to returning to his cocoon. He looked back on his years
of self-imposed isolation with wonder, and he did not want to
be alone remembering the cause. Sometimes, when Dodo was
punishing him for a few days, he wanted to stay home to
await a possible call from her, but there was the other danger
that Lyle might find him and he was still unwilling to face the
issue. He could not bear to be cruel, he could not say no, he
could not say yes, nor could he bear to promise renouncing
Dodo. He wanted reckless flight, but he wanted no bridges
burned. To postpone definite decision he kept out of his
apartment at the hours Lyle used to call and took to coming
into Umberto's directly from his office, lingering over some
wine and a dinner. In the usual manner of men sensitive to intrusion, he and Murray pretended at first not to see each
other in the little restaurant. After four or five encounters,
during which they warily circled each other like strange dogs,
they found themselves at the same table, speaking of general
matters together, in due course approaching the remotely
personal, and after awhile having night-caps together in their
apartment, tacitly ignoring door-bells or telephone, providing

341

alibis for each other. Men are understood to be absolutely silent with each other on personal matters but this is only when they are asked direct questions. Then they remember that men never talk, men never gossip, men never betray a friend—certainly not for such a small audience. But, unquestioned, they are apt to reveal their own secrets as well as those of their friends, and are goaded on to all sorts of incriminating revelations by a look of indifference in the listener's eye.

Since Frederick showed no interest Murray revealed that he was attempting to relieve himself of Judy's overwhelming devotion, and win back his wife, for no other reason, he confessed, than that Gerda had been on his mind so long he couldn't have any peace until he'd gotten her back.

"I'm not in love with her any more, I don't think," he said as they sat before the fireplace in Frederick's room with a cold winter dawn breaking outside, and hot rum drinks thawing out their secrets. "I know she only wants me around to bolster up her ego, and I've an idea she sleeps with anybody that's around but maybe not. But she got her hooks into me twenty years ago and every time she takes them out it hurts so that I want them back in, that's all. I run around with other women but it never leaves a dent. And Judy's a damned nuisance. Damn it, I want an adult woman. You know when you're a kid and playing around with the other guys, somebody's always got a little sister tagging along that's always losing her didy or having to have her nose wiped or falling out of the tree so nobody can have any fun? Well, that's the way I feel about Judy. A young girl's a hell of a responsibility and when you try to pry 'em loose it's like getting chewing-gum off your shoe."

Frederick did not say that for his part it was more like trying to catch an eel in the open sea without even liking eels. He was the more sympathetic of Murray's predicament since he saw no beauty in either Gerda or Judy. And Murray was the more sympathetic towards Frederick since he regarded Dodo as a little tramp and an affair with a married woman of Lyle's professional preoccupations as very small pickings indeed. Frederick obligingly reassured his friend that he was not treating Judy badly by trying to ease her out. She was young, he said, wrapped up in her ambition, and it was doing her a decent service to make her free for marriage and a family. Murray was glad to hear this angle, which coincided with his own and hoped Judy would some day appreciate what he was doing for her. He made a point of having other people around the place as much as possible, and contrived to have Judy leave with them or faked an errand outside himself, but these tricks couldn't go on forever. As to Frederick's situation Murray persuaded him he need feel no guilt toward Lyle.

"She can't expect you to go through life waiting in a corner drugstore for her to finish her parties or her family duties," he declared. "You say she was shocked to hear you'd taken over that *Haw* magazine job. Hell's bells, she ought to know a man's got to make a living. You can't go on living on a little critical prestige all your life. It shows how little she understands what you're up against. I'll say this for Gerda, she was the first to make me get out of feature writing into something that made dough."

It was a relief to Frederick to think of Lyle as thoughtless and blind to his interests. Indeed her behavior since her return to town bore out the accusation. She did not mention their quarrel when they met. She appeared engrossed wholly in writing her new play, asking about his own new work with perfunctory politeness. After her first outburst about his job on *Haw* she made no comments. After a while her thoughtful questions as to how the magazine was succeeding, and her considerate "How nice to be in work you enjoy" made him angry that she never asked when his book was coming out or how his new series in the *Swan* was being received, or why he avoided seeing her alone. Yes, Murray was right, Lyle had failed to sympathize with his work and he should not feel the dull weight of remorse when he saw her. Curiously enough, he felt most hostile and righteously aggrieved with Lyle at the times Dodo was eluding him. Why shouldn't he have other loves, he argued; Lyle never considered getting a divorce for him! But when he had just spent the night with Dodo he was able to call on Lyle or lunch with her with a detached pitying appreciation of her qualities. He was happy; she, whom he had once loved deeply, was not. He found the new pallor emphasizing the contrast of brown eyes and red-gold hair and the aura of secret sadness made her extraordinarily beautiful. It excited him as something he had caused and it tempted him to comfort her but there was no comfort to give without committing himself again. He confined himself to complimenting her on her appearance, the wisdom of whatever she said, the value of her work and the great future open to her. One day Lyle sat very still as he repeated the favorable remarks being made at the next table about the Gaynor play and the great charm of Mrs. Gaynor, an opinion that was universally held, Frederick assured her, else why would she have so many distinguished friends and satellites? Lyle's rigid silence made him uncomfortably conscious of the strangeness of his attitude. He had never called her friends distinguished nor had he been given to delivering obvious bouquets when he had been in love. He saw Lyle staring at him, clutching her purse as if it was a life preserver. Then she gave a choking gasp that turned into a hard little laugh.

"Your flattery will break my heart," she said. "It's like the compliments exchanged by nations just before the declaration of war."

He pretended not to understand, and retreated into a pose of wounded feelings. He had been puzzled at first by her silent acceptance of their new status but then he thought bitterly that it showed how little his love had meant in her busy life. Finally, a wave of remorse would engulf him that the light by which he had lived for years should have been quenched and replaced by a will-o'-the-wisp.

Frederick and Murray had fortified their stronghold by a program of joint engagements. Murray explained to Judy on these occasions that Frederick was using the entire apartment for a party, and finally said that they were planning a joint housekeeping arrangement which prohibited Judy's free use of the place. She patiently moved her properties back to the little room on Abingdon Square.

"That little moron of his seems to be making Frederick human late in life," she observed, adding hopefully, "it might be a good thing if he married her."

"Good Lord, no!" Murray exclaimed. "It's nothing but an affair."

"Nothing but an affair," Judy echoed mechanically. "Oh."

The "housekeeping arrangement" consisted of occasionally having morning coffee together or uniting in the expense of a casserole of *paella valenciana* from Jai Alai for intimate little home dinners either for Dodo and Gerda or other ladies. After each man had confessed his attachment to one love, and had revealed how cavalierly he was treated by his lady, he felt the contradictory necessity of demonstrating his independence. Certainly, each boasted, nothing would induce him to seek consolation from his older love, when the present one was recalcitrant, but neither was he one to be inconvenienced by such female capriciousness. If Gerda was chilly, as was usually the case, or Dodo mysteriously occupied for days, Murray did not resort to Judy nor did Frederick to Lyle; there was Lorna Leahy next door or Caroline Drake, or personable ladies encountered in Umberto's or elsewhere. Sometimes men are tremendously set up by cementing a new friendship, more than they are by a new mistress, and since Frederick had never had an intimate friend, he found his new life a continuous adventure. This was the way other men were, this was the way they lived. Murray's acceptance of him as a regular fellow, not a highbrow or stuffed shirt, was wonderfully gratifying, and his assumption that Frederick was not allowing his infatuation with Dodo to spoil his pleasures elsewhere was flattering though not quite true. Murray slept with Judy once in a while "to keep from hurting her feelings" and obliged other ladies indiscriminately for the same reason. His fixation on Gerda had very little to do with sex, anyway, he said. For his part, Frederick could barely bring himself to touch Lyle's hand, partly because of the dreadful pang of guilt over a passion gone dead, fear that it hadn't gone dead, and would flare up compelling him to end his adventure. He wanted to go on anticipating or remembering Dodo's electric effect on him as long as he dared. This state of excitement, though it deliberately short-circuited Lyle's appeal for him, made him for the first time find all kinds of women desirable, although his old shyness kept him silent even when they made all the overtures, as he was astonished to find was frequently the case. When he saw Lyle he took satisfaction in mentioning numerous engagements and new interests. She was not the only one whose life was full. He felt almost viciously triumphant as if he had conquered an enemy instead of a love. He was no longer the orphan lover, he wanted her to know, waiting for what crumbs she could spare him, a man whose simple habits she could always count upon, and whose preference for solitude insured her his faithfulness. No, he was a man she had subtly prevented from being himself as he now was. He had been a guest of Bennett Strafford at a broadcast—("I thought you detested radio, Frederick!"); he had been to a gay cocktail party at Tyson Bricker's—("A cocktail party, Frederick?"); he had been to the theatre and enjoyed it—("But you always said you hated the stage, Frederick! You never will go with me.") It gave him a cruel pleasure to report having visited or encountered friends of her circle, implying that he did not require her sponsorship, and exaggerating the degree of intimacy to such an extent that Lyle felt they were no longer her friends but wholly Frederick's. She felt the sly reproach when he said, "I've heard you speak of your friends, the Bellamans, and so I was especially interested in being invited to dinner there last night." She had selfishly refrained from taking him there, his tone hinted, but he was welcomed there on his own merits, nonetheless. He had refused so often to go all the places he now went or to mix with the people he now praised that she had given up asking him, long ago. They were hers and Allan's friends, anyway, and she used to reproach herself for being a little relieved that Frederick's interests seemed elsewhere. One day lunching together (at her suggestion), she seized upon his new taste for the theatre to invite him to join her that night in the Beckleys' box; but he declined. The pleasure, she thought sorrowfully, was in the company not the event, and his quick refusal stung her. Would he like to see *Billion Dollar Baby*, then, tomorrow night? She had just gotten tickets, and before the doubt in his face could crystallize into a negative she deliberately tortured herself by saying, "I can't go, but if you could use the tickets—" His face brightened. Splendid. He thought at once of Dodo's passionate desire to see that show, and her childish delight if he produced tickets.

"I've wanted to see it," he said brusquely, pocketing the tickets Lyle thrust at him.

"Since when?" she inquired, smiling to cover her disappointment. "You said you hated musicals."

"I understand this is different," he said impatiently. He could scarcely wait to call up Dodo and report what seemed a personal achievement on his part and not at all connected with Lyle. Dodo was always boasting of other men taking her to the theatre, and now she would see he was just as obliging.

"I'm beginning to believe you're taking a Dale Carnegie course, Frederick," Lyle said with an effort at lightness. "In another six lessons you'll be such a good mixer, you'll be running for office."

Frederick saw a welcome excuse for a quarrel in the remark and stated that he had been reproached for unsociability by Lyle for years and now that he was profiting by her criticism to come out of his shell he was being unjustly attacked. He had been buried in work for years, as she must have known, and he was surprised she begrudged him the natural reaction from such gruelling concentration.

Placed in the wrong, Lyle nervously tried to placate him. He was surely joking, she said, and perhaps she was tactless from the strain of the new play which was not coming on right at all. Indeed, she secretly hated the theatre now for its stern demands that prevented full attendance on one's love life. Frederick allowed himself to be calmed, and Lyle tried to talk of neutral subjects. She had a misgiving that admission of her work faltering pleased him as if he were a rival playwright. She was aware that he wanted to find her at fault in dozens of minor ways as an excuse for leaving her, and she was angry at herself for accepting the guilt—she was the unfaithful one, the one to ask forgiveness. She knew he was waiting and dreading the underlying questions, "Don't you love me any more? Why won't you see me alone any more except in public places?" But then she suspected from his uneasy glances that he was beginning to wonder why she did not ask. Mystery, then, was the only protection for her pride and she was stubbornly determined to tear her heart out rather than accuse him or try to woo him back, or comment on his new behavior. Each morning she woke with the sinking thought of nothing to live for. Everything else in her life seemed hateful. She could not work. Allan's sarcasm, forgiven before in her guilty love, now made him seem a galling burden that had caused her present plight. She had no heart for the curtain of banter they had maintained to hide the crueller truths of pain and sacrifice. She had once felt that in spite of everything, at least she and Allan had always been able to laugh together. But, she wondered, had they really laughed at the same jokes? After some fleeting hint of an abyss of icy hatred in him she wondered if he had only laughed at the naïve folly of her own laughter; he was enemy laughing at captive. She had other moments, as Frederick did, of considering her lover the real enemy, for whose present triumph she must be revenged. The strength of her pride enabled her to baffle him by an apparent indifference to his coolness. It was her weapon but it could be used against her. Finding no expected reaction to his hints of new friends, Frederick made his allusions more definite, spoke of mysterious private plans, referred to feminine names she did not know, determined to have her wince or explode in anger that would restore his advantage. Lyle submitted to the sharper wounds, managed to agree that Caroline Drake was a most interesting woman without inquiring how Frederick happened to see her, but finally she was goaded to venture on the thin ice between them.

"By the way, Tyson Bricker reminded me to get some kind of a job for that friend of yours, the Baltimore girl, Dodo something or other," she said, looking intently into her coffee cup. "He thought she'd be happy doing anything in any kind of theatrical or film office. I believe Kerry is going to take her on. I must tell Tyson or perhaps you will."

At her first sentence Frederick had stiffened himself for the big scene, but as she finished all he could think was how helpful he was about to prove himself to Dodo. His friendship for Lyle Gaynor was winning Dodo her long-craved job. He was able to do more for Dodo than her advertising big shot from K.G.R. or any of the beaux who merely took her dancing. He couldn't dance but he could get her a job in the very office she most wanted. And he had tickets for the show she most wished to see. Frederick was in such a glow of satisfaction that he forgot Lyle's part in it. He wanted to find Dodo as soon as he dared leave, and savor her delighted gratitude. It was a delicious thing to be able to grant heart's desires to the one you loved. There had been so little he could ever do for Lyle.

"I'll be calling you," he answered Lyle and made an absorbing job of paying the check, refusing to let her pay her share as she used to do. She was going across the street and he got on a bus to go back to his office. He caught a glimpse of her from his window and before he was conscious of it the old aching rush of love for her swept over him. He saw how thin she was, how sad her face, and as he watched she made a troubled gesture toward her eyes. He wanted to cry out to her, to beg her to wait, only wait—but for what? Tears came to his eyes as the bus carried him on.

12

. . . cats out of the bag . . .

THE ménage of Murray and Frederick was a never-failing source of discussion to those two bosom friends, Caroline Drake and Lorna Leahy. They kept a ready file of information on the activities of both gentlemen and used it as a sort of reference book for all masculine behavior, professional or personal. Lorna, living next door to them as she did, could report on encounters with their guests, chats with their mutual janitor, and the conduct of the servant they had just acquired. Caroline, as a figure in the business world and lady about town, heard tidbits here and there about Frederick's connection with Lyle Gaynor. (Like columnists' gossip, the news of the affair broke after it was all over.) Caroline was in Gerda Cahill's misguided confidence, too, so she could describe to Lorna the efforts of Murray to win back his wife, and Gerda's counter efforts to win every other man as a lover.

"She even took on some twenty-year-old poet or other," Caroline declared. "She said to me, 'My dear, you must try him. Marvellous! He stayed with me eighteen hours straight!' I said, 'Goodness, Gerda, how did you do it? You must have had a yo-yo.' "

"You were mean," Lorna beamed.

"She doesn't get it," Caroline said. "Gerda is so nuts about herself it never strikes her that anyone can be mean. I give her a good crack now and then about Murray having affairs of his own, but she just sighs and says, 'Poor darling, he's so unhappy!' "

"Sweet," Lorna said. "Maybe, if you and I had been as dumb as Gerda we'd still have our husbands."

"God forbid!" Caroline exclaimed sincerely. "I'd rather put the money in a business of my own."

Ever since their marriages had exploded Caroline and Lorna had been in each other's confidence, sharing a bottle of an evening in Lorna's studio or Caroline's penthouse. In fact they had been telling each other everything for so many years over their cups that they'd never heard a word each other said. When Caroline's marriage was breaking up—(he was jealous of her superior success in the same store) she was kept going by Lorna's understanding support. Lorna had been in the same spot herself, in a common-law arrangement with another artist, George Leahy, who had no push and was ungrateful to Lorna for turning over her surplus jobs to him. Eventually, Caroline's Arthur left and she happily resumed her maiden name; Lorna, not having enjoyed the legal right to it previously, adopted her mate's name as soon as they parted. In spite of their relief at getting their freedom the two women in their endless confidences were increasingly sentimental over lost love. They told each other of their years of fidelity—(if only they had Gerda's frivolous nature!) and each lamented the curse of being a one-man woman. Men always took advantage of this virtue and Caroline agreed with Lorna that honestly, if it could be done over again, she'd sleep with every man who came along instead of wasting loyalty on one undeserving male. After a few drinks, Caroline finally said she *had* slept with maybe forty or fifty men but only because she was so desperately unhappy. Lorna said she didn't blame anyone in Caroline's domestic situation for doing just that, and many times wished she had not been such a loyal sap about George, but except for a few vacation trips and sometimes being betrayed by alcohol she had really never—well, anyway, she didn't blame any one.

Caroline liked to go straight from work to her modernistic Murray Hill apartment, fling off her smart office clothes, and after a brisk shower settle down in handsome house pajamas for leisurely home drinking. In winter she refreshed herself and callers before her huge living room fire or had friends gather around the great white bed in her bedroom where she lay with a tray, a polar bear rug thrown over her and cannel coal sparkling merrily in the fireplace. In summer the setting sun found her on her terrace—(she raised corn and tomatoes as well as flowers and grain spirits there). She always wanted Lorna to visit her but Lorna was annoyingly reluctant to change her working clothes to come up to Caroline's neighborhood and taxed Caroline's good nature with challenges to give up her comfort and come to Lorna's place for less and worse to drink. Lorna proudly confessed to being unable to afford the best (as Caroline could) and Caroline was obliged to declare heartily that hell, it wasn't the liquor, it was the intelligent companionship she was seeking. Lorna was selfish with her inferior beverages, too, filling her own glass constantly—(it was her whiskey, wasn't it?) with seeming absentmindedness as she talked, then drifting off into a light doze when it was her guest's turn to reveal the mysteries of her secret nature. When she was uprooted and planted in Caroline's garden Lorna's dim resentment of the superior advantages made her keep her eyes fixed on the bottle as she drank, experiencing a sense of great achievement, even revenge, as the contents sank lower and lower, below the Canadian Club letters, below the label, down, down to the last dregs. "Maybe we'd better eat something," one or the other might say, but this seldom came to anything for they were solitary eaters, ice-box snatchers, greedy to have that entire chicken all alone no matter how generous they were with liquids. Frequently they lost interest in dinner once they had descended below the bottle's label and then a remarkable inspiration would come to open a second bottle and repeat the revelations they had been repeating for years to glazed eyes and deaf ears.

"No, you don't mean it! Why have you never told me this before?"

"Didn't I? How strange! I was positive I had told you. In any case, now the cat is out of the bag you might as well know the whole story. Well, this dealer and I took the plane to Mexico City——"

"No! I can't believe it, Lorna! You actually——"

"I swear it, Caroline!"

"No!"

"Yes, yes!"

As the sun set and the stars and moon or for all they knew a typhoon came up the voices grew louder and shriller, neighbors listened by necessity and Caroline's colored maid, Johanna, was known to observe "Everybody listens to them ladies talk except theyselves."

Cats safely out of bags, the friends separated, either for private dinner or a tasty sleeping pill and oblivion till another working day.

As is often the case their indulgences kept them fresher and younger-looking than their hard-working, respectable contemporaries, since they spent so much more time taking care of their faces and figures than did their righteous friends who worked, spurned temptations, and foolishly trusted God instead of Elizabeth Arden to reward them with a complexion. Caroline was hard and fit, a trim size fourteen, with a fine jaw-line, carefully tinted dark-gold hair, and except for too pale near-sighted eyes and a wide mouthful of strong white teeth that seemed capable of crunching the bones of her human obstacles, she could pass as an attractive thirty-five instead of forty-two. Lorna was small, with a brown pixie face and a mop of curls that she ruefully termed "prematurely white." For years she had threatened to dye her hair but always yielded to her friends' obliging plea not to touch it! That white hair is the most striking thing in town! Of course the only person who sincerely liked the white mat was Lorna herself, but she was happy in her conceit and seldom wore a hat, shaking her curls like a restless pony until someone said "Do you mind my saying you have the most individual hair I've ever seen?" In spite of their years of intimacy the two friends belonged to different sets. Lorna, the artist, sometimes went to Caroline's parties and sat aloof with an extremely mean pixie sneer for Caroline's wholesale jobbers, visiting silverware buyers, and department store heads. When Caroline tried to bring good-natured guests over to Lorna's corner Lorna snubbed them curtly. Sometimes when the party was at its gayest with no one noticing her aloofness Lorna would pass out just for spite and whatever gentleman was being the life of the party would be called upon to walk her around the block, take her home, or do something for her that would disrupt the general gaiety. In spite of her own commercial success, Lorna's friends were mostly poor or pretentiously Bohemian, loudly literary or artistic, and at her own rare parties one of them invariably managed to make some crack about Caroline's expensive get-ups which would either send Caroline home in a rage or keep her apologizing to them for hours for her superior earning powers. "Caroline can be such a Babbitt," Lorna told her friends. As for Caroline she had taken to making bets at her own parties on just how soon Lorna would "do her stuff" and just who would be drafted into service. She knew Lorna's moment for vapors was bound to come when some talented guest was about to take the center of the stage by song or dance; she knew, too, that having spoiled the show Lorna would revive suddenly if the wrong man was pressed to take care of her, holding out for the party's key man with extraordinary genius, passing out, reviving, and fading again until she'd gotten the man she (and usually Caroline) wanted.

Both ladies talked in confidence of their frustrations in the quest for love, but the truth was they had gotten all they wanted of the commodity and had no intention of making the least sacrifice of comfort for a few Cupid feathers. The men with whom they occasionally dined had a way of needling them or as Caroline said "getting her ego down" because men were jealous of a woman's financial success. Men forgave genius, or a *succès d'estime* in a woman, but her financial advantage infuriated them. Women forgave success in business but never forgave success with men. One thing Caroline and Lorna had in common was an overpowering reverence for high-brows, no matter how obscure. Each had met friends' friends of great erudition who dazzled them with thoughts and phrases gloriously beyond their own intellectual means, something they could wonder at with neither envy of the possessor nor the desire to buy. Since they were able to afford what material objects they craved, they missed the innocent female joy of window-shopping, admiring something without the disappointment of possession. On their rare opportunities to worship an articulate Brain they listened raptly; the facile conversation on politics, philosophy and particularly scholarly facets of literature they rubbed in their scalps as earnestly as if it was a new tonic and tried the phrases on their mouths like the latest lipstick. They were as proud of their respect for learning as if their awe in itself was a credit to them, an achievement close to magic. They were both gratified to have made the acquaintance of Mr. Frederick Olliver and lived in an enjoyable state of suspense as to whether he would recognize them, snub them deliciously, or have one of his darling moods of Old World charm. Caroline had been so impressed by his arrogant sarcasm whenever she had met him that she bought his last book and read five pages of it every night before sleeping, no matter how tight she was. Cozily embarked on her own fortune hunt she thought it was enormously chic of Frederick Olliver to scorn commercial offers—Murray reported he had been urged to accept large sums in Hollywood as research expert on an historical film. "Privacy is the only luxury essential to me," he had said, "and I see no logic in giving it up in order to make money to buy it back."

In spite of being awed by the unfamiliar elegance of Frederick's mind Caroline's natural aggressiveness usually rose to the fore and she invited him to call many times until he surrendered. At first he consented out of courtesy to a friend of Murray; at that time they were becoming such great chums. Later he found a stubborn satisfaction in a life neither Lyle nor Dodo could enter or could even imagine. He talked of parties at Miss Drake's to Lyle in order to mystify and annoy her; when Dodo eluded or tormented him with talk of marvellous engagements it was consoling to call on Caroline and be welcomed with such obvious pride. Once Caroline frightened him by becoming amorous over old-fashioneds. Her fingers clutched his thigh with the iron determination of a medieval torture device—(he was literally black and blue for days) and she pulled him toward her by the coat-lapel so relentlessly that he was in great fear for his worn suit, and also of being devoured by the competent big white teeth. Just as he was resigned to a mighty kiss fragrantly concocted of *Fabulous* and *Old Granddad* Caroline released him and burst into tears. "Oh what's the matter with everything?" she moaned. "Everything's so horrible. There ought to be something. Something ought to be right. For God's sake, get me a drink, before I go absolutely nuts." In his relief and surprise Frederick was very kind and gentle, and after getting her a drink, a compact and cigarette, he held her hand for a while and kissed her lightly on the forehead, when he said goodnight. Caroline, he was amused to see, was too solidly realistic to be in the least fooled by this demonstration.

"That means a hell of a lot, now, doesn't it?" she said gloomily, lighting a new cigarette on the one he had just lit for her. "You think I'm a lady Babbitt and that's all you do think of me—if you ever did think of me, and the hell with you."

Frederick thought about this episode in the middle of the night and several times next day and each time it made him chuckle. He was so taken with this evidence of Caroline's essential hard shrewdness contrasting with Lyle's subtlety and Dodo's coquetry that he called on her the next day with a small Victorian corsage of violets and sweetheart roses. Caroline was too astonished to be grateful but she told Lorna that he must have meant it as an apology for trying to "make" her.

"But I never thought of Frederick in that way!" Caroline explained dreamily. "So when he started making passes naturally I——"

"Well, how was it?" Lorna rudely inquired but Caroline didn't think that was a bit funny.

13

. . . the octopus named Virgil . . .

FREDERICK'S worst fear was that Lyle would find out somehow the sorry chase that Dodo was giving him. The depths of his humiliating defeats were in proportion to the heights of his raptures. Cautious of money by nature or rather frightened of insolvency he was goaded to extravagant gestures by Dodo's loud complaints of stinginess. As soon as he had agreed to take her to a "gay place," the Barrel or uptown, he offset his first sense of panic by inner arguments making the cause of his folly seem worthy. Then, having surrendered gracefully enough, and anxious to disguise his unbecoming poverty from a young lady who thought all men over thirty-five made twenty-thousand a year, he was given the privilege of sitting alone at a table while Dodo made friends at the bar, or else engaged in merry repartee with occupants of the next table. Sometimes she invited a few strangers, mostly men if possible, to their table where she edified them by stories of men in Baltimore who were crazy about her, silly fellows who never got onto the fact that she would let one take her home and go right out with another one. On rare occasions one of her listeners would have heard of Frederick Olliver and praise some essay. This was the moment for Dodo to interrupt petulantly, "Honestly, I can't understand a word Freddie writes and I don't think he can either. Nobody wants to read that sort of bunk."

Frederick only laughed indulgently.

Now that she had the job in the Paramount office Dodo was constantly thrilled by proximity to wonderful actors, writers, producers, all crazy about her. Frederick's reward for what he considered his service to her was to be denied her favors, because of her superior new opportunities. He was tormented by her callous boasts to him of new conquests, but even more by her elusiveness. He knew his only advantage over his rivals was her conception of him as a social superior, someone mysteriously regarded as distinguished by others. It was therefore up to him to build up this advantage in order to hold her interest. He must never admit that the days he could not find her were hopelessly empty. He accepted invitations from any quarter especially any that might sound desirable to Dodo, aware that Dodo's idea of a successful society man was one whose book was full, no matter with what. It was dimly consoling to discover that his years of comparative isolation made his company prized the more highly. To Lyle he found it diplomatic to give the impression he was discreetly interested in many women instead of in one, and he mentioned every feminine name but Dodo's. Naturally, Lyle must guess there was someone else but he could not bear her to think that all was over between them, nor for her to know who her successor was. On the other hand he freely spoke of the Gaynors to Dodo because she was much impressed by them and tolerated him more because he knew them. Dodo's complacency did not give way to jealousy but rather to envy of his opportunities. If she voiced the familiar suspicion of other women Frederick was ready to reassure her until she would pout, "Well, if you aren't sweet on her why can't I go visit Caroline Drake, too? I like penthouse parties, too."

He saw that she was contemptuous of his bondage to her and he knew that she respected masculine infidelity just as Judy did, but he was congenitally unable to pose as a Casanova. His greatest advantage was his stubborn silence when she spoke of marriage. Other men she'd liked were already married but he had no such excuse. It mystified and piqued her that an old bachelor so excited over her should be so cagey about marriage, and once she made this surprising discovery she nagged about it constantly. She didn't want to marry him but she wanted to be asked. It showed he was not really subjugated and that kept up her curiosity even while she was annoyed. Frederick suffered a shock of horror whenever Dodo hinted at marriage. The only idea of marriage he had ever had was with Lyle and he was astonished that circumstances didn't alter this desperate conviction. Lyle was the only woman he could ever marry, and the feeling persisted in the bottom of his being like an underground river, fathomless, eternal. The mere word on Dodo's lips seemed a violation and he was as puzzled at his reaction as was Dodo. He couldn't make love to Lyle, but he couldn't marry Dodo. He admired Lyle and wanted to hurt her for the unworthiness of her rival; he despised Dodo and wanted to be hurt by her. He knew he must seem a ridiculous figure in groups where Dodo jibed at his age and shouted out the small sum he got for the essays a few admired in the *Swan*. She compensated for this by carrying a copy of *Haw* around to show strangers, explaining that her escort was editor but never got credit for it. She pointed to Frederick's embarrassed face, giggling, "He's ashamed of doing anything that everybody else likes, he's such an old stuffy, but *I* think *Haw* is wonderful. Everybody likes jokes and murder stories and comic strips. Wouldn't you think he'd be glad to give the public what it wants?"

She still enjoyed attending the League class where she could display for other students' envy her familiarity with members of the faculty. She had not gotten over her first impression of a League course as a badge of intellectual distinction, and wanted everyone to know she was not only enrolled there but was on cozy terms with the League heads. Whenever she was impressed she betrayed it by deriding the object of her awe insistently, unable to leave it alone or disguise her awe by simulated indifference. She wanted to bring whatever it was down to her own level so she could dismiss it. Frederick could not reproach her for lack of perception concerning the League since he had himself been taken in by its pretensions at first. Now his distaste for it was numbed by its service to his love-life. Dodo liked it. Dodo liked to exploit her intimacy with him, and walk past the less fortunate students with Dr. Olliver, and if possible Mr. Tyson Bricker. Frederick was glad he had not resigned. He was glad he had the *Haw* job too, not only for the money to oil his new courtship but for the defense it gave him against any accusations of pedantry. Dodo was vaguely irritated by his serious writing and baffled by its effect on other people. She was therefore exhilarated to have him humbled by an ordinary job. She teased him by demanding why on earth he took such a silly job as *Haw* anyway, then switched to the statement that at least it was better than making a fool of himself writing for magazines that never paid anything. There were moments when Frederick was inclined to agree with Dodo, particularly as it became clear that Strafford was postponing publication of his book on the flimsiest pretexts. Other times he found himself longing for Lyle's reassurance after a long spell of Dodo's nagging. He needed consolation after Dodo's strategic attacks of headaches that prevented love-making but were miraculously alleviated by visits to gay spots where other men could be found. Frederick wished there was some way of having Lyle's sympathy for the wounds he received from Dodo but he dared not make an overture, now that their relationship was so conveniently casual. A false move might mean too much and then he would not be free when Dodo was in the mood to be kind. He had been relieved to have Lyle telephone less frequently and he thought it fair not to make any gestures but to leave her to suggest meeting. He had avoided her house and it was some time before it dawned on him that she no longer invited him there. She had spent years pleading with him to join her parties and evidently gave up just at the time he was changing into a social person. It was only logical of course. He tried to justify his twinge of envy whenever he heard Dodo talk of someone who had dined at the Gaynors. It marred his standing with Dodo to be neglected by the Gaynors.

"But I thought you were *in* with the Gaynors," Dodo said many times. "I'd just love to go to their place and meet all those people. I don't see why they don't ask you. They ask Tyson Bricker."

Frederick consoled himself by reflecting that even for Dodo's esteem he could not go through an evening that would re- mind him of the countless unhappy hours of looking across a crowded room filled with the distressingly permanent- seeming belongings of the Gaynors, waiting to meet Lyle's eyes as his only reward. But there should be some other way of regaining at least the benefit of the understanding and deep admiration that had been underneath and seemingly apart from their physical relationship. At the first of his new social life he had braced himself for running into Lyle, but when the situation never occurred he began seeking it delib- erately, and finally wondering, with a sense of panic, if the door was really shut. He pictured chance meetings in crowds which absolved him of intimate words but permitted a continuation of the old sympathy. The door must not be entirely closed. So he went with Benedict Strafford to one of the Beckley Thursdays but Lyle was not there and he heard that she seldom came. "Lyle seems to have buried herself, completely," he heard, and was curious as to whether this meant misery or unknown celebrations. He followed the openings of art shows where the artist was an old friend of hers. Murray mentioned having seen her at Gerda's and he accepted Gerda's invitation to a supper in the secret hope of exchanging a few words with Lyle, pretending to Murray that he dreaded such an encounter. But Lyle was not there and he dared not bring up her name. On two Sundays Dodo's evasiveness drove him to Friends of Music concerts, knowing Lyle had season tickets. But he saw no one he knew except Edwin Stalk, the *Swan* editor. After the second time he walked out with Stalk for dinner at the Blue Ribbon. Frederick was surprised to hear that Mrs. Gaynor had presented Stalk with her own tickets. Lyle knew the Stalks only through him and Stalk had always professed a scorn of the Gaynor theatrical and social set. Frederick felt childishly jealous of Lyle's encroachment on his former private life. After all Stalk was *his* special property, part of the meager private life he used to have to offset Lyle's full one. He expected to discuss the *Swan*, and his own contributions during dinner, for Stalk had always been completely preoccupied with literature. But Stalk was moodily silent, barely answering Frederick's attempts at their usual exchange. He was a thin, dark, tragic-faced young man, brilliantly self-educated, and oblivious to everything in the world that was not printed, so oblivious that women of all ages pursued him, flung fortunes at him for his literary projects, presented him with theatres, houses, honorary degrees and fitted bags. He lived with a White Russian woman, older than himself, who was kept in a constant agony of jealous insecurity never certain when Edwin's professional needs might require the exchange of his body for some financial backing, never certain how long his indifference to worldly pleasures would protect her. Frederick had been so tortured by troubles of the flesh that he was relieved at the idea of an evening with Stalk, discussing abstractions, literature, anything that provided surcease from love. But tonight Stalk stared into space,

crumpled breadcrumbs over the red-checked tablecloth with
delicate long fingers, neglected his sauerbraten and drank
three seidels of Michelob, an unprecedented dissipation for
him.

"People ought to go to concerts in individual sunken
bells," he said fretfully. "They interfere with music. They
want to compete with it. Did you see that woman standing in
the aisle beside me? All during the second movement she was
scratching her bare arm, as if she was tuning up a fifth instrument. I heard nothing else. And the man beside me. Moving
his lips as if Wolfgang Amadeus himself had commissioned
lyrics. I couldn't look away. I wanted to say, 'Louder, please,
if you have a secret libretto to this quartette, in the name of
God, out with it and no mumbling!' "

"The anesthesia wasn't strong enough for you," Frederick
suggested. "You should have had a full orchestra and been
blindfolded."

"Maybe. Maybe. I'm immunized now to chamber music,"
Stalk admitted. "I begin to notice the musicians and pick out
a favorite by his mannerisms. Like an amateur at the races. I
picked the cellist today because he wagged his foot." He
shrugged his shoulders and fixed his eyes with sudden intentness on Frederick.

"You've known the Gaynors a long time, haven't you?"

"Several years," Frederick said, "why?"

"How did you come to know them?" pursued Stalk.

Surprised at any display of interest in personalities from
Stalk, Frederick answered that he had met Lyle when he was
attached to an Eastern university and she had come to the
town to stage a try-out of one of the Gaynor plays. When he
returned to New York he had called at the Gaynor home, the
play having become their first success.

Edwin listened carefully, selected a cigarette from a ruby-
encrusted silver case—(gift of some lover of *belles lettres*)—
and tapped it thoughtfully.

"I remember it was you who brought her to the *Swan* luncheons some time ago. It seemed to me I'd seen you with them,
and I wondered why I never run into you at their house."

"I didn't know you went there," Frederick exclaimed surprised. "Personally I don't care for that circle. Broadway and

Hollywood tangled up with Wall Street and Park Avenue. Not in my line."

Edwin lifted his eyebrows.

"I never see that element there," he said. "Mrs. Gaynor has too much discrimination for that sort of thing. I daresay Gaynor himself would like it. He's a disgusting beast."

Frederick was astonished first at Stalk expressing such interest in any human beings who had nothing to do with either the *Swan* or his own mental processes, and second that any one should refer to Allan Gaynor as a disgusting beast. Allan had the invalid's immunity from criticism, and in all the years he had been the barrier to Frederick's happiness the latter had never judged him as he would have an ordinary rival. Allan was invalid, a middle-aged person whose conduct and tastes were dictated by his misfortune, a person to be pitied and excused if not liked, an unanswerable argument against Lyle getting a divorce. But here was Edwin Stalk of all people violating this unwritten code.

"Beast?" Frederick repeated.

Stalk shrugged thin shoulders and lit a cigarette.

"Why doesn't he bump himself off?" he said coldly. "He's nothing but a burden to her."

"He's a great favorite in their group." Frederick found himself in the extraordinary position of defender. "They tell me he knows more about the theatre than any one except Nathan, and he's still able to write damn good plays."

"She writes them and pretends he helps," Edwin Stalk said, then he asked abruptly, "You're not letting Strafford's have your new book, are you? Haven't they forfeited it by postponing it?"

Frederick did not think so. Besides Strafford's had the best name for his sort of work.

"Not any more," Stalk said. "That *Court Lady* best-seller didn't help them any. I hear they're making pots and pots and are going to specialize in that sort of trash. They're cleaning up on some cheap magazine, too, *Haw*. Won't do you any good to have the Strafford imprint, I would say."

Frederick was glad Stalk did not know his connection with *Haw*, although he doubted if it would affect any opinion of his *Swan* writing.

"How's *Swan* doing?" he countered.

"Ups and downs as usual," Stalk said carelessly. "Attacked for being non-political, political, academic, revolutionary, reactionary, dirty and squeamish. Your piece on Hrosvitha struck some as a recommendation of chastity for women dramatists. I was telling Mrs. Gaynor. As a matter of fact, I find her exceptionally helpful regarding the magazine. I never dreamed she was so brilliant outside her own field. Extraordinary woman."

"Very," Frederick agreed, nonplussed, wondering what had brought about the change in Stalk, shrewdly suspecting that Lyle had put money in the magazine. He was about to suggest a brandy but Stalk had reached for his black Homburg, an affectation, Frederick thought, to make him seem the continental artist. They walked toward Sixth Avenue and Frederick anticipated the usual visit to the Stalks' upper west side apartment and an evening of discussion. Instead Stalk hailed a south bound taxi at the corner and got in.

"You go down, don't you? I'll give you a lift. Or perhaps you're going to the Gaynors too."

"No," said Frederick, getting in the cab beside him. "I'll get off at Eighth Street."

"I've arranged to meet a Mexican poet at the Gaynors'," Stalk said. "I can't talk to any one in my own apartment. Solange always wants everything translated for her so she can argue too. She thinks every person of talent is my enemy and she must defend me, by insulting them. Mrs. Gaynor feels she's helping the magazine by letting us use her apartment from time to time. It's a godsend, of course."

Frederick murmured something. He had always been careful to take no liberties with the Gaynor home and was taken aback by Stalk's words. He was annoyed at the empty evening ahead of him as well and further bewildered when Stalk said meditatively, "Love is curious, isn't it? You could go through life thinking you know all about it but when it really happens you realize you have never really known it."

Frederick was on the verge of laughing at this gem issuing from a young man who had hitherto seemed adult enough to mock at such profundities.

"You won't come on down?" Stalk said when Frederick got

out. "I'm sure it would be alright. After all you've known the Gaynors much longer than I."

Frederick shook his head and waved goodnight. He was conscious of a sense of injury that he was not free to call at the Gaynors'. He decided that Stalk was getting to be a bore and was sure Lyle must find him so, too. He recalled her having remarked about the doleful young man on first meeting him, "But he looks like a ham Byron, a stock company heavy. Is he really just solid brain as you say?"

He would like to have repeated to her Stalk's sententious thought on love but was suddenly struck by the implication that Stalk was in love with Lyle. The idea amused him tremendously and he was sure it would amuse Lyle if she knew. He bought cigarettes in the drug-store, smiling to himself and then amusement gave way to a smouldering indignation. Lyle was deliberately wooing the few old friends that belonged to his private life. She had no interest in them before, now she courted them and shut him out, her little revenge for his change toward her. It was only through him she had met such people as Stalk and the *Swan* intellectuals. Now she took advantage of her charm and professional standing to woo them away from him, to show they were as easily bought as the friends of hers he had ridiculed. He could almost see the *Swan* group lounging comfortably about Lyle's huge living room, Stalk, if you please, lolling back in Lyle's pleasant little study with the one object of his interest (Stalk could talk to only one person at a time); Allan Gaynor somewhere in a corner with his usual special little audience, smiling inscrutably at the somber discussions over the *Swan* problems. Frederick walked along Eighth Street, scowling, glancing in open bars unconsciously to see if Dodo might be there. He could walk over to the Americas and see Murray, perhaps, but he didn't want Murray to suspect the disadvantage of his position. Their masculine solidarity was based on the mutual difficulty of avoiding importunate females, not on sympathy for being abused by them. Frederick felt his bitterness toward Lyle rising; he thought of his wasted years of loving her, and now her undermining of his only intellectual support, making Edwin Stalk fall in love with her so that he preferred an evening with her to an evening with himself. He felt that he hated Lyle, and it soothed his conscience to find new justifications for his unfaithfulness. When he looked through the door of the Barrel and saw Dodo at the bar with Larry he was so filled with bitterness toward Lyle that there was no room for jealousy over Dodo. He felt only relief at finding Dodo again under no matter what circumstances, and had no hesitation in walking in to join them.

"I wasn't lying when I said I was going to Baltimore for the week-end," Dodo said defiantly, then giggled, "I guess I meant I was going to *Barreltomore!*"

"Can you bear this?" Larry asked Frederick, nodding toward Dodo who had buried her face in her hands in a convulsion of merriment. "It must be those double Scotch Mists she's been eating."

"I'll have one myself," Frederick said.

"Tell Freddie about the octopus!" Dodo cried. "Go on, Larry."

"Well, these people found an octopus in their swimming pool and it took such a fancy to them that they made a family pet of it, called it Charlie," Larry obliged. "Listen, this time I'll call it Virgil. Well, Virgil was a great help around the house —squeezed all the oranges, made all the beds at once—hey, you have to have another drink for this. Waiter!"

Frederick woke up the next morning with a frightful headache, fully dressed, but with a vague conviction that he had done something wonderful. He had gotten blind drunk for the first time in his life and now he remembered why. It was to show Dodo he was no more stuffed shirt than Larry. Her shrill giggle still rang in his head and he had a fleeting memory of her cry, "Larry, Freddie's ordered another Scotch Mist! Isn't he terrif? Come on, Freddie, now *you* tell about Harry, the Octopus. Come on! Show how he played the bagpipes again, go on!"

His hand was sore and bleeding and it took a long time for him to remember why. It had happened when he got out of the cab at his place and had tried to pull Dodo out with him. She had bit his hand till he let go and he could still hear her giggling as she drove on with Larry. He had stood dizzily hanging to his gatepost listening to the bagpipes. They were in his ears for days.

14

. . . voyage through the sky . . .

ALTHOUGH he had had a part in only a few hits Allan Gaynor was numbered among the city's leading theatrical figures for he had been a successful actor-manager before his accident had confined him to writing. The fact that he had never done a creditable play by himself was nothing against him since most of his colleagues required at least one collaborator unless they were shrewd enough to merely purchase plots and hire a stable of hacks to do the actual work. Allan knew his theatre, kept up with the new names, knew the traditions and was actor enough to hold that the manner of the great man was more effective than the proof in attracting a following. Lyle had nourished his ego and attended so carefully to his affairs that he had come to regard her contribution as nothing more than an extension of his own brain. He recognized the quality she brought to his collaboration but it never occurred to him that she had the major task of production problems nor that she might have succeeded all alone. He was comfortably unaware of managerial suggestions that she do her own play, or that it saddened more than flattered her to be told that his obdurate technical pattern handicapped her fluid approach to modern problems. He was impatient with her, lately, for the new play seemed to be getting nowhere and he had no intention of facing his own inadequacy when he could conveniently put the blame on someone else. What was the matter with her, he was finally stirred to demand, whenever reviews of a new play reminded him that they had none to offer? Didn't she realize that desirable actors were taking other jobs, theatres were being sewed up, new names were crowding them? Questions on plans from the theatrical columnists irked him with the vague reminder that he could promise nothing without Lyle. Lyle pleaded time to work at a kink and he consented, but he had an apprehension that the trouble might be more than a kink and that there might be serious danger to the arrangement that gave him a luxurious idle life and yet full credit for worthy work. He became more observant of his wife's habits, looked for reasons for her apathy, criticized and accused her of faults he actually did not believe in the least. In his irritability at a possible hitch in his smooth life he often hit the target without knowing it. You would think she was a lady crossed in love, he mocked. She must have had her feminine vanity badly hurt, he said, by having old Olliver no longer mooning around. Maybe it was too much for her, hearing that one of her swains preferred chasing some little cutie from Tyson Bricker's school to her mature charms. Or maybe she couldn't work because she was spending too damn much time with that *Swan* crowd, talking abstract art, existentialism, Marxism, surrealism, instead of theatre. It seemed ridiculous that his play, all ready to be put in rehearsal except for the routine business of writing it, should be held up merely because a pretty woman was finding her court dwindling. Without the armor of guilty love Lyle found herself seething with murderous indignation after such attacks. It was Frederick's fault for making her thus vulnerable but it was her husband she hated. She hated him for being a cripple and binding her to him; she hated him for the revelation of his underlying cruel self-interest. The graceful façade of their life together cracked daily. He was apt to be politely sarcastic to guests whom he felt were flattering her and distracting her from her duties. Lyle, in self-defense, met her friends in bars sufficiently inconspicuous as to run no risk of encountering the Gaynors' joint friends who might tell Allan. What was there to tell except what no one could guess—that she was desperately trying to reconstruct a life that would allow her to forget anguish for perhaps twenty minutes?

Every morning when he woke, Pedro brought Allan his breakfast, dressed and bathed him, wheeled him to the elevator and thence Allan proceeded to his study on the roof, where he remained till two o'clock undisturbed. The study was a small one-room shack originally used by the janitor but the Gaynors had begged for it, pleading Allan's need for sky and fresh air as well as his professional need to "get away." He could sit outdoors and get the grimy city sun and see far over the town, and in these brief hours alone Allan relived his life, rebuilding past triumphs to support him against the active world of downstairs. Some days he sat in the little cozy room where no one else was allowed to enter except the maid, and looked over old photographs, files of old programs with his name scattered all through them, letters from admirers, notes of play ideas, a genealogical chart of the Gaynor family, souvenirs of ladies, histories of the stage. His "concentrated work" here was pure fabrication as Lyle surmised, for all working conferences were held in her own study downstairs. But well men went to offices away from their home and so must Allan, and it was here on the roof that he really lived completely, not in the drawing-room below, as people thought, conducting his famous conversations, graciously accepting cues for his reminiscences, rewarding an epigram with his quick nod, basking discreetly in the respectful admiration of his chosen company. Here was a special world, swung like a great cage over the city, ten stories above the walking, riding world. Here he could lie back in his chair and see smokestacks on the East River, avenues of roof tanks advancing or retreating like giant chessmen far toward the downtown canyon, northward to the Chrysler tower and castle ramparts of mighty skyscrapers brought low by distance. When he wheeled to the east or west walls he could look down on the little streets of tenements and shops, their flat or gabled roofs raised or slanted for skylights protecting the asparagus or art beneath. Across the northern areaway he could see into the window of a loft sweatshop where fluorescent day lights showed girls at looms winding red and blue cord over giant spools. On warm days the girls brought their sandwiches and cokes to the fire escape barely a dozen feet away from him; he loved this proximity to alien life. Sometimes when a girl crawled out of the loft window all by herself he called to her softly or smiled a greeting, but none ever smiled back or did more than stare indifferently. They could not know who he was or that he could not walk; he might be anyone taking a sun-bath for all they cared, a wax dummy. He did not like to think their coolness was due to any other factor but the unfairness of his infirmity; he did not want to think that even if he were strong, he would still be a baldish man in his fifties, with little remnant of the good looks that had won him so many favors years before. Impatient with his failure at mild flirtation he pushed his chair to the opposite wall, watched the wind chase ashes and smoke over other roofs; he followed cloud shapes trailing after passing planes, idly composed melodies on the intricate radio wires that scored the sky. In a high wind, the buildings swayed like ships, the tanks and towers were smokestacks of great liners and Allan carried on imaginary conversations with other passengers, strangers in whom he confided as one only could in strangers. On vivid days, the sun had a way of spotlighting a balcony or distant terrace that brought old associations into sharp focus; long ago events played again, costumed by memory, dialogued and emphasized by reflection. A suddenly illumined dormer window must be where he had once lived; he could almost look in and see himself making love to a girl named Carrie who was always afraid that someone perhaps on this very roof might be watching. He described Carrie to his imaginary shipmate, he described his room as a struggling young actor at Madame Blanchard's (long since torn down) and Carrie's husband whose jealousy was so innocently appeased by being given a bit part in Allan's company. Allan was reminded by the charming imaginary stranger's sympathy of all the places whose chimneys he could almost identify, where he and Lyle had first sought apartments, each trying to suit the other's taste. There was the penthouse hardly a block away (he was sure he recognized the latticed wall and garden) which the woman wanted to sublet because "her husband left her alone so much at nights." Lyle had not liked the place, but that very night Allan had been impelled to go back to see the blonde Polish woman who was too pretty to be left alone. Call it rape, if you like, for she did struggle, but afterwards she was only ominously silent. Baffled by the tacit scorn he had defensively said that she was not a virgin, after all. The woman had frostily replied, "Certainly not, but I like to choose." He had gone back again to erase the unpleasant sense of defeat and fathomless contempt, trying to make it over into a gay sophisticated adventure, but her cold, scornful face reduced him to babbling helpless apologies. He had been strong and good-looking, then, too, but the girl had looked at him with the same cool indifference of the girls from the sweatshop, so that there was no triumph, nothing but angry shame in the victory even now, fourteen years later.

In his life on the roof he seldom thought of his physical handicap or of his life with Lyle but of everything far back, before the year of his affliction.

He sometimes napped, putting himself to sleep counting or trying to count, the women he had slept with and it pleased him to have a forgotten name or incident bob up each time. His taste had been for the bizarre adventure rather than for romance, quantity more than quality, and he regretted that the demands of his fame had forced him to surrender to ladies of social and financial value to him, renouncing the gambling-sport of chase and capture to be had only in servant quarters and territories that might have jeopardized his position. He spoke of this to his invisible shipmate and sighed over the waste of his energies.

"Rape, good God, it's the man who is raped. The actresses, heiresses, hostesses, I've had to make love to in order to save a play. The ugly women, old women, lonely women I've had to sleep with to save their feelings! The women I've hated that I've had to go on with to keep them from breaking up my marriage! A man in public life like myself is always raped or blackmailed into bed. His own lusts are a luxury he can't enjoy without terrible cost. Like refusing an autograph. He's always being backed against a wall and being had. He can't be the hunter—he doesn't have time or energy for the pure sport of normal sex, once he's arrived. He can't go foraging in strange ice-boxes—everything is brought in on a tray, like it or not,—cold when it gets there, never what he wants at that moment."

Allan had grown accustomed to having his end of the roof to himself through all but the summer months. Even the maid who cleaned his room was allowed to do so only at night when he was downstairs. He was startled, therefore, to have one of his intimate discourses with his shipmate ap-plauded by a tinkling laugh.

"Don't mind me, mister. I talk to myself, too," said a woman's voice. "Everybody says it means you're crazy but I say it's just that they're so crazy you can't talk sense to them like you can to yourself."

The woman was shaking one of his rugs over the wall, and the door of the shack was open so Allan concluded she must be a new servant from his own household. She was a buxom little mulatta with a soft moon face, an oddly babyish mouth with baby teeth and a prim baby voice. Servants were hard to get or her indifferent fluttering of the rug would have proved her inadequacy at once. Allan was on the point of scolding her for daring to approach his room during the hours he had expressly forbidden it but she forestalled him.

"Mrs. Gaynor said I was to come up at night to do you but my husband won't let me go out at night. I guess it don't matter if she don't know. She ain't around anyways. I'll just drop in when it's handy. Just so long as it ain't dark because my husband's awful upset if I'm out after dark. Don't tell Mrs. Gaynor on me, please."

Allan hesitated, irritation melting into curiosity at her impudence.

"What's your name?" he asked.

"Mrs. Bender. I don't usually work around but my husband's the furnace man next door and your Pedro asked me just as a favor. Just one room I don't mind. Of course I wouldn't work for Jews or foreigners but I don't mind this. Only I can't come nights . . ."

"Alright," Allan cut in, impatiently. "Come in the afternoons after three, then, when I'm not in."

The girl's futile manipulation of the rug stopped. She appeared to ponder for a moment then she shook her head with a gentle smile.

"I'd be afraid to come to a place all by myself here all alone, mister," she said. "It wouldn't look nice, me being a married woman and then, too, anything missing you'd blame me. And my husband'd get mad. He's from Trinidad. Wouldn't you rather I was around for company? You act kinda lonesome lying up here nobody but yourself to talk to."

She gave him another bland smile and Allan looked at her more carefully, a little puzzled.

She might be thirty or she might be much older, he couldn't tell. She was not pretty and her figure was stolidly matronly though her legs were long and shapely. Allan was mentally reproaching Lyle for permitting this intruder on his privacy but then it struck him that for the first time in years something was happening to him and only to him. For Lyle

and other free people days were filled with dozens of little adventures, little trivial brushes with tragedy or romance, ex-
changes with strangers, fleeting glimpses of unknown worlds.
But his day held no surprises, his hours and even his friends
were arranged carefully beforehand. Nothing as remarkable as
a strange Negress addressing him on the roof had occurred to
him in ages and Allan felt a sudden excitement out of all proportion to the episode.

"It's kinda chilly out here, don't you think, mister? Maybe
now would be a good chance for you to show me just how
you want things done inside. You just explain everything, because not working around I may not do it your way without
your telling me. Don't it get on your nerves anyway those
girls over there in the shop spying on you? People ought to
mind their own business." Before he could answer she was
pushing his chair toward the door of the shack and he was
silent with inner amusement at her boldness. He was almost
invariably annoyed by loquacious servants and certainly this
one had said nothing extraordinary, yet the plaintive cajolery
in her voice gave vague other meanings to her words. She was
certainly a petty thief for she said, pushing his chair through
the door, "If you weren't right here, see, you might think I
took that brandy over there but being as you're right here
you can see the bottle's almost empty anyway. And don't you
worry about leaving your wallet around because I never take
money from anybody. I never take anything that ain't freely
offered, especially from a gentleman, because my husband
wouldn't let me."

There was nothing to explain about tidying the room,
nothing more than the usual admonitions about leaving papers as they were and taking care of breakables. Mrs. Bender,
in fact, did not appear to listen as he began to tell her, but
seated herself on a leather hassock before him, her soft
opaque eyes fixed on him with her vaguely knowing smile. He
could not disguise his surprise when she lit a cigarette, but she
misconstrued the cause and said hastily, "No, I didn't take
yours. I always carry my own cigarettes, no need to worry
about that."

She had finished the room, evidently, but made no move
to go. Allan wondered uncertainly, if she was waiting to be

paid or if she was under the delusion she was to act as a companion.

"I like it up here, you know, off by ourselves this way," she
said, comfortably blowing a ring of smoke. "Living in a basement like I do this is a nice change. Quiet and private. Not
like working in a regular home. I guess you and I can get
along alright. Of course my husband wouldn't let me work
for anybody unless it was a perfect gentleman."

Allan could hear himself imitating the baby lady voice for
the benefit of Lyle and his evening's guests.

"Would your husband allow you to accept the brandy?" he
asked.

Mrs. Bender considered this, he was amused to see, with
great seriousness, blowing several smoke rings into space and
finally studying the bottle as if the answer would come from
some genie within.

"Tell you what," she decided, "he might not like it if I
brought the bottle home, but it would be alright to drink it
here. I guess you'd like some, too, kinda brace you up after
being outdoors in all that wind."

"The glasses are in the little corner cupboard," he said,
smiling openly now. "Very little for me, please."

"Now you're talking," Mrs. Bender said, quickly stamping
out her cigarette in the tray and producing bottle and glasses
with unexpected alacrity. She sat down with her glass, drawing her chair nearer to him, and looking at him with her odd,
watchful smile.

"I'll just kinda relax and take my time if it's all the same to
you," she said. "If I got home too soon my husband would
think I hadn't done my work right and he wouldn't like that.
He wouldn't want anyone going around saying his wife didn't
do her work right."

It was too amazing, and so basically feminine, Allan
thought, in its peculiar way—shuffling chivalric husband and
standards of etiquette for her own curious purposes. He was
exhilarated by something—no matter how trivial—happening
to him now instead of always in the past, or in his reading. He
felt alive again.

"You're too fine-looking a man to be wasting away up here
all alone, mister," she said, sipping her glass.

It would make a funny anecdote at dinner; he was particularly good at imitating odd accents, and it would show he had a life of his own in a way, still open to the unexpected. But for some reason Allan did not mention the episode at dinner that night. When Lyle asked him how he came to spend so long a time on the roof, he answered that he had happened to find himself in particularly good form for working.

15

. . . the trade analysts . . .

WHAT do we mean by the name "Strafford's?" Or rather, what do we think when we use the word "Strafford's?" What flashes across the mind—the very first association, that is—before we have time to think? What does "Strafford's" *stand for*, perhaps I should put it that way? Without stopping to connect it consciously with publishing do we think Permanence, Quality, Usefulness, Luxury, Escape, Jewelry, a style of dress, perhaps . . . ?

These were the solemn questions under discussion in the conference room of Strafford's increasingly affluent company when Frederick, at the urgent behest of Mr. Strafford, reluctantly appeared. He had been aware of the brainstorm that had recently visited Mr. Strafford, resulting in carpenters, painters, new faces and great batches of important inter-office memoranda all over the place. Miss Jones, the wizened young-old firm fixture who handled the routine details of *Haw* with one hand, while brewing a canned stew over a sterno with the other, had informed Frederick some time ago that Strafford's was being "stream-lined."

At first the process revealed itself in the form of millions of memos in triplicate (one for your desk, one for your files, one for checking and returning to the sender) snowing over the employees warning against paper wastage, and appraising all of changes in personnel which they had already noticed. The memos stated that hereafter, as part of the firm's progressive policy, the receptionist was to be called Contact Manager, the switchboard operator was Traffic Co-ordinator, the file chief was Chief Co-ordinator, the salesmen were Traction Engineers, the office boy was Intercommunication Chief, all clerks were Junior Executives, stenographers were Communications Executives, and Mr. Strafford himself was Operations Chief or "O.C." if you wanted to save the company's time and paper and indicate a cozy familiarity between boss and workers. Accustomed to Mr. Strafford's periodic attacks of business genius (coincident usually with a splendid hangover, remorse and resolutions) Frederick paid little attention to these manifestations, expecting them to blow over in due course. The changes did not affect the *Haw* office, since the firm's connection with this seedy sheet was still a secret. But after a few weeks it became apparent that this revolution was something out of the ordinary; heads were rolling, brisk new chiefs and executives replaced what the memos referred to as "deadwood;" desks whizzed through the halls, a loud speaker croaked out messages and calls to conference from the O.C.'s office and the Intercommunication Chief rushed from office to office in this busy bedlam pinning up large placards saying "THINK." Frederick was not to escape participation in this, for after his ignoring dozens of peremptory calls to attend Policy Change Conferences, Miss Jones informed him that his presence was now obligatory, not as *Haw* of course, but as one of the book department's Editorial Advisers.

"Strafford's is being analyzed now," Miss Jones gloomily stated. "That woman who's always flying around here with her hat on and types memos standing up with one glove on is doing it."

"Mrs. Caswell," Frederick remembered. "I thought she was publicity or something."

"She's from Berghart and Caswell, Trade Analysts," corrected Miss Jones. "They analyze institutions and stores. They did Beckley's Jubilee Year and it seems it's the talk of the trade. So of course the boss had to have them, too. Her name's Eva Caswell."

Frederick glanced idly at the latest memo on his desk, ignored up to that point.

"Mr. Olliver, *please!*" read the dashing handwriting in green ink. "What happens to Strafford's concerns you just as much as it does everyone else. In order to get a clear picture of Strafford's as a whole we need your help. *You* as much as anyone else *are* Strafford's. Now that we've cleared out the deadwood and gotten focussed on our objective, do let's work together on the new structure. Four o'clock today in the new conference room, then, for our final week of crystallization. P.S. Dear, dear Mr. Olliver, I know very well you're busy, but this is the big moment in our firm's life, so big we're inviting our most important friends in for today's conference. I know you will come. Yours, Topsy."

"Topsy?" repeated Frederick.

"She signs her personal notes Topsy," Miss Jones explained. "It's just a cute way of saying her name's Eva."

"I see," said Frederick. "Why do I have to go?"

"I guess to make a show for the editorial department," Miss Jones offered. "There is so much sales and promotion and advertising that I guess it doesn't look right to have hardly any editors. Ever since *Court Lady*'s been a best-seller Strafford lets the sales-force pick the books. He always goes a little nuts when he makes money or goes on the wagon. We just humor him."

Frederick was in a dour state of mind since the *Haw* job, which was to be such a casual affair, was requiring more and more of his time due to its outrageous success. It seemed to prove that a magazine with no staff, no taste, no conferences or danger of improving the reader's mind, could run on greased tracks. He spent an hour or two every morning in the office then left the routine with his instructions to Miss Jones and the make-up man. He was free to ascend the stairs to Strafford's proper and devote the rest of his day to his own work, but what use was it? It disgusted him that he could handle *Haw*, which he hated, with belligerent efficiency, but was powerless to promote his own work. He checked and polished his own manuscript, planned his work for *Swan*, commented on works of other authors, but was corroded with the bitter conviction that he was victimized. His worst obstacle was his success with *Haw*. Strafford, he knew, realized that publication of his book with no more than his usual laurels, would ruin the golden goose. Frederick was too proud to push his own cause, relying on his haughty modesty to elicit eventual justice. Moreover, the disturbed condition of his private life made him fear a direct showdown with Strafford. He mocked himself by sudden bursts of studying *Haw*'s success with the seriousness of Larry attacking a cigarette slogan for Hazelnut. That morning he had found sardonic amusement in discussing a new comic strip with an ex-convict's ghostwriter. He described the moral value of a serial about a two-cent crook who was always caught and he spoke of the great artistic merit of such a project. He dictated a note to Miss Jones on obtaining a strip to popularize the adventures of Candide. He added a pompous editorial foreword on the intellectual beauties of the comic strip, the international good-will engendered, the crimes prevented, the seeds of social conscience planted through sheer economy of articulate or literate thoughts. He smiled inwardly when Miss Jones, who had her own opinion of a man whose books contained no conversation suddenly looked at him over her notebook with the dawn of reverence. At last, her expression said, you have seen the great light, you really aren't such a dope after all. You can learn . . . "Mr. Olliver," she breathed, "you're a genius." Art is a cigarette ad, then, Frederick mused, literature is a soap opera, integrity is getting your claptrap done by payday so you can take some trollop to some clip joint where she can double-cross you.

It seemed to him that Dodo's capricious treatment of him was somehow responsible for the dismal confusion of his life. The effort of justifying his infatuation was tainting his whole reasoning processes. He blamed Strafford for taking advantage of his weakest moment; he blamed Lyle for allowing him to fall in love with another woman and again for not consoling his vanity when Dodo injured it; he blamed Dodo for keeping him in such spasms of uncertainty that the affair had no chance to burn itself out. (Where had she been last night and the night before? In what gay place had she been gay with what stupid rival? Had she forgotten it was he who had gotten her that movie job that offered her such splendid pastures? He dialed her office. "Freddie, please don't bother me when I'm at work," she said primly. "I'm terribly busy. One of our West Coast producers just got in and I have to show him around . . . Well, for goodness' sake, you must have heard of Eddie Fargo! . . . No, I can't meet you at the Barrel, I'm going to La Rue with Eddie. It's business and besides I've never been to La Rue . . . Oh Freddie, stop being such a silly goon. We're not engaged!")

And now, smarting under all these wounds he must be further tortured by attending an asinine seance concerning the "stream-lining" of Benedict Strafford's business. Yes, and there was no use blaming anyone else for his fix, disagreeable as this admission was. He was furious with himself for being the gull, for lacking the offensive capacity for personal promotion. He was the nice little fellow who was always the scapegoat in the school prank, the respectable gentleman who always got snow-balled, the good husband who always got the horns. Always the target, never the archer, he berated himself. Frederick tore up the note signed *Topsy* and flung it viciously in the waste-basket. Only six months ago he had been a free man—now look at him!—so tarnished with compromises that he dared not demand his simple rights. He could not free himself from Dodo but at least he could resign from *Haw*. He would, yes he would resign; moreover he would insist that his manuscript be published without further delay. He would have an understanding with Strafford at once, today, and give up once and for all the naïve notion that one gentleman behaving with modesty and forbearance induces another to recognize his undeclared rights.

"Trade analysts," he mocked as he went up to the conference room.

Berghart and Caswell had evidently been at work on every phase of Strafford life, for the once dank, mission-panelled old room was now air-conditioned red-lacquered and glassbricked, artificial daylight oozing from the happy walls illuminating with impartial precision the doodlings on every memorandum pad. In the diffusion of false sunshine Frederick saw a complete wax works conference set around the long center table—the university president, the magazine editor, the venerable explorer, the refugee professor of note, faculty brothers from the League of Cultural Foundations and behind them, a dozen departmental figures and other gloomy countenances of undoubted leaden weight in the world of letters. Mr. Strafford motioned him to a vacant chair with an air of grave responsibility.

"Mr. Olliver, of course you know," he whispered loudly to the gentleman beside him. "A special editorial consultant for us, distinguished writer as well."

"Extinguished, he means," Frederick thought.

He observed with distrust Mrs. Caswell and her assistant at the head of the table. You would know them anywhere, he thought, as the robot engineers of a vast machine, oiling and guiding it to work with the speed and tireless futility of an exercise horse. Mrs. Caswell's bisque face, electrically-controlled twinkles, dimples, smiles, frowns, and laughter were phenomenally and impressively unlife-like—the business mama-doll, call me Topsy for business camaraderie, Eva for formal intimacies. Business mama-doll, Iron Virgin, chromium Lorelei, the camouflaged Vacuum Cleaner ready to clean any vacuum. Her assistant bore similar traces of terrifying robot leadership—a keen-eyed young man in chalk-striped business suit, black-rimmed spectacles, a well-exercised, well-Turkish-bathed, well-groomed, well-disguised steel model for success, who slipped notes under the nose of big chief with mechanical regularity. Mr. Strafford, directly between his two experts, looked winningly apoplectic and human, even juicy, and Frederick speculated on how much juice the two Fruit-masters could really squeeze out of him. He would be popped in the lady robot's jaw of Hollywood-capped teeth and come out the male robot's jaw of powerful porcelain, all canned and labelled for distribution. Mrs. Caswell acknowledged Frederick's arrival with a flashing smile and wagging of a pink-gloved finger.

"Our truant," she said. Faces of salesmen, and other departmental furnishings of Strafford's turned to Frederick with a dull apathy engendered by six weeks of daily pep-talks. Frederick thought he caught a flicker of scorn from the Traction Engineers who must be recalling the difficulty of selling his last book.

"Mrs. Caswell is giving us our final analysis today," Strafford announced in a solemn voice. "We want to restore the firm's name to its original significance. To do so we have had Mrs. Caswell, our expert, analyze our conception of the firm's original status and then compare with its present one. We have slipped, boys and girls, if Mrs. Caswell's report is to be trusted and of course it is or she wouldn't be here—we have gone far off our proper course. All very well to be making more money than ever before but what of our seventy-year-old reputation as intellectual aristocrats?"

Mrs. Caswell graciously allowed the publisher to have his say, then tossed aside the wisps of pink veil over the gay, crazy hat that showed she was woman first, executive second according to the latest robot rules.

"Like any private analyst we make no definite suggestions. We only help you to help yourself. We add up what you yourselves have said and show you the final figure. In this case, after six weeks of study and daily get togethers we submit our findings. Do you know what the name Strafford's now stands for—or is beginning to stand for? Tell them, Vincent."

"Sex," said her assistant and Frederick heard a stunned voice behind him murmur "Good God!"

"Ever since the novel *I Was a Court Lady* has rocked the country and incidentally put our company in the black, we have been attacked from pulpit to lecture room as purveyors of obscene literature," Mrs. Caswell continued. "Mr. Strafford himself actually admits he has been refused membership in a very fine club because of his connection with the book. The quality of manuscripts submitted to us has dropped to the level of pulp fiction. We have censors after every book we put out as if we were in the erotica business. Since this is the first major success in forty years the firm has many enemies to help capitalize on the unpleasant reputation. Mr. Strafford realizes that he owes a great debt to the ancestor who founded the firm, and must repay it by restoring the original prestige at any cost. How? Let's hear from our distinguished visitors."

The university president, well known as a guest on Invitation to Learning pitting his er-er-ers against those of the most erudite, now obliged with the famous clearing of throat that blew the cobwebs from his mental wine-cellar, and declared hoarsely that the answer was obvious. Strafford's must counter their errors by publishing treasuries of profoundest significance and give them promotion equal to the *Court Lady*. Mr. Strafford looked vaguely distressed, thanked the doctor, and said hopefully that he was sure Tyson Bricker, the well-known molder of public opinion might have an even better, more definite solution.

Mr. Bricker, never one to be caught napping, sprang to his feet.

"I would suggest getting hold of something—say like Nietzsche or Shaw—something new and controversial, something with bite, then push it to the skies. I agree with the doctor that now is the time to show you dare be an intellectual. Furthermore . . ."

Jingling his keys with his right hand and stroking the back of his gray hair with his left, gazing dreamily at the ceiling, Mr. Bricker was the picture of a man-thinking-out-loud, a feat for which he was famous.

"The original Strafford dared publish many uncommercial books," he pursued in a gently musing bed-side manner, a manner that allowed him to switch to the opposite view if it seemed more advisable. "Why not recapture that old spirit of daring? Dare to be long-hair, as the saying is." Looking about among the impassive faces for a sympathetic response his eyes lit on Frederick and he went on more urgently, "Olliver, there, ought to have some ideas. I'm sure he'll agree with me that if Sex is dragging you down on the one hand you need Brains to bring up the balance. Start an intellectual revolution, Benedict. Let Strafford's be our leaders, show us the way out of materialism and nationalism, give us a new philosopher or a poet—something to build a new culture upon. Come on, Olliver, a seasoned scholar like you ought to give us a definite lead to work on. What about some hook-up between the Renaissance and today—you know that field better than I do. Who's our man—what's our angle?"

Frederick felt the blood rushing away from his body, veins and arteries being filled with a torrent of tears, hot and searing. This was the time when he should have robot molten steel coursing through him, this was the time he should rise and say, "Gentlemen, this firm has the answer in your safe at this moment, a work by Frederick Olliver on the seeds of thought planted in ancient and medieval monasteries, the roots that grew in the earth when the flowers were scorched by wars and tyranny, the roots that produced tranquillity and beauty after centuries of despair, the tree that never dies that bears peace and salvation forever. The book you want is mine, gentlemen, and the man you want is Olliver."

For a fleeting moment the thought seemed to communicate itself to Tyson on whose face a sudden light dawned. He pointed at Frederick, then snapped his fingers triumphantly, in a gesture of inspiration. It could not be, Frederick warned himself, trying to hold back the wild hope. Was there possibly a chance that his hour had come at last?

"By George, Olliver, you *are* the man," cried Tyson. "That manuscript of yours gives a hundred and one lights on this very problem. I swear, people, that if any one man can give us a definite lead on the kind of book we want it's Frederick Olliver. Obviously, if we've gotten a reputation for vulgarity we regain prestige by throwing our weight behind some classical work of high aspiration. Let's look into Oliver's work for suggestions."

Mr. Strafford, looking increasingly red and uneasy, asked, "Have you anything to suggest, Olliver?"

Frederick rose unsteadily, gathering steel from the bright glitter of the eyes of Mrs. Caswell and her assistant. He was weak with a helpless rage of which he had not dreamed himself capable. The hopes he had buried each year deeper and deeper had risen shamefully to the surface at Tyson's first appeal to him, betraying him again, weakening him to cruel disappointment, making him once more the eternal gull, vulnerable, prey to every false dream.

No, he would not hope, he would not be party to any hope, no one could say he was open again to despair.

There was an exchange of notes between Male and Female robot as he rose to his feet. Before he could speak Mrs. Caswell leaned forward to ask with great intentness, "What about this manuscript of yours, Mr. Olliver? Perhaps that's the very thing we're after."

"Hardly. The money to be offended at failing prestige," Frederick said, smiling coldly, "was obtained by publishing an offensive novel. I suggest that Strafford's publish as many such books as they can find until their integument is gilt-proofed against shame."

There was a ripple of laughter, a reproachful shake of the head from Tyson, and then the Traction Manager got up applauding Frederick's suggestion. Frederick felt as if he was choking to death, as if his familiar enemy, himself, had burnt his throat with the mocking words. The only power over his life that he had, he thought, was the power to ruin whatever meant most to him, to show he had discarded hope before hope had left. It was impossible to stay in the room any longer not knowing what fresh damage he might do himself, either by his mockery or the folly of new hope. He pushed out the door, glad of the voices raised in argument that cloaked his exit. He ran downstairs to the *Haw* office to snatch his coat and hat. On the street he started to hail a cab, but, after all, where was he going? Some place, where he could cry out. *But I didn't believe them, you see, I wasn't fooled this time, I was smart enough to know it was a trap and I didn't fall. But wasn't it a cruel joke?*

I have no one, no one, he thought more with surprise than self-pity, and the fault is in me because I have always hidden myself, because I never learned the secret of communication with human beings, because I have always been afraid and have worn armor and a foil on my rapier, never trusting treaties, my friends, enemies or myself . . .

Lyle was the only person in his whole existence before whom he had laid down arms, whose identity with himself was safe and implicit, but now that was gone . . . You rejected me, she would say, and now you are rejected and you expect me to console you for this justice? There was Murray, at this very minute in all probability standing at the bar in Bleeck's for his first five o'clock exhilarator, but how could he describe to him his fierce self-defeat without first explaining who he was, what the real self beneath his Murray-self was? In a crisis there was no one who even knew you—there was no eye that would not cloud with bewilderment if not contempt that what meant nothing to him should mean everything to you. I have no one, Frederick thought—even if I were sure of seeing Dodo there is no language between us, she would understand only that something had defeated me and she would rejoice as if in some way it exalted her. In a way he felt the elation of complete destruction, himself, just as Dodo would. He was as much his own enemy after all as was Dodo. He was conscious of walking toward Times Square, hurrying, as if he were late to a definite destination and realized he was on the way to Dodo's office in the Paramount Building. He suddenly wondered what bribe he had for her favor, as busy parents wonder, coming home late with no toy for the spoiled child. He was ashamed for himself and for his love that he should immediately think of promising her an introduction to Edwin Stalk of whom she had recently been hearing, or he would take her to the night's opening and point out, even introduce her to important people. He would not talk of his own desperation, but he would have the consolation of making love to her. That much, at least, he thought. Dodo was standing at the reception desk, her hat on, green sport coat jauntily over her shoulders, absorbed in painting her lips when Frederick came in. (She was hoping for someone else, he guessed, but he might do.)

"How'd you know I'd be here this late?" she wanted to know. "I always leave at five but Carter Tenafly, you know, the English writer that wrote the book of the month is in with J.B. so I waited to see if they needed me for anything."

"Come down to my place for tea," Frederick said, trying to sound casual, knowing that a hint of his urgency would put her out of reach at once. "We can celebrate later."

Dodo looked at him curiously.

"You look sort of funny, did something happen?"

"Yes," Frederick said wildly. "I've just come into some money, in fact a small fortune. Of course it's a secret."

Dodo's eyes widened. With a squeal of delight she slipped her hand under his arm.

"Freddie! How wonderful! Oh do let's celebrate! Oh I wish you'd let me go in and tell Mr. Tenafly and J.B. Oh Freddie, do let me tell them . . ."

"No, no, it's a secret!" Frederick said, pulling her toward the elevator, his hands trembling and his whole body shaking with the shame of his lie and the necessity for it. Dodo looked reluctantly back toward the door where the great men were conferring. Frederick knew she had been waiting, as she always did, for the men to come out, find her alone there, and in a burst of after-hours geniality, perhaps invite her to join them, drink with them, sleep with them—whatever would seem the greatest social honor to her. But he didn't care. He didn't care what monstrous lie had won her sudden change of heart, making her snuggle tenderly in his arms in the taxi all the way downtown. Once there, shades drawn and door bolted, nothing mattered, but the marvel of her happy complaisance, her return to her original role of eager seductress, flinging off her flimsy garments, pouting naughtily over a difficult fastening, kicking her slippers across the room to land on his hat. I do have this, this much at least for this minute is

mine, Frederick thought, his head throbbing fiercely. But after a little while he lay with his head in the pillow, aching with
the agony of further defeat, and Dodo swiftly and ominously
dressing herself, face flushed with rage.

"Dodo . . ." he murmured. "Wait . . ."

"For what?" she said harshly, putting on her hat without
even looking in the mirror. "Life is too short to wait for a
miracle. I'm going out with a real man."

He heard the door bang viciously. He had no one, no, no
one and he despised himself fervently.

16

. . . the black magic . . .

GERDA CAHILL had a knack, everyone said and she admitted it herself with perfect candor. She was a born salonnière. She could, she laughingly confessed, turn a seat on a Greyhound bus or a roomette on a train into her own salon at the drop of an olive. She could move into the most barren cellar in the dreariest alley in Europe, any place from Telegraph Hill to Savannah—(you should have seen her place there on Factors Row), toss a scarf over a broken box, simply fill the umbrella jar with fresh green branches or possibly claret cup, cover the rat holes with Aubusson scraps, and in no time everyone who was anyone for miles around would be drawn there magnetically, crying out that there was no one in the world with such a knack as Gerda. It was a knack that had annoyed and fascinated her ex-husband, since he understood neither her motives nor their rewards. For years she had maintained an attic at thirty dollars a month in a condemned building far over by the East River, in the Thirties. Inconvenient of access as it was, the minute she was back in town guests came and went, found the key to the mailbox if no one answered their ring, brought their compositions for her piano, their poems for her desk, their tears for her shoulder, their friends for her supper. Gerda accepted each new talent at its owner's own appraisal with the good-natured tolerance that comes of ignorance and serene indifference to everything outside one's self. Her little geniuses sometimes found that her seeming appreciation was merely a mirror giving back no more than it received. At least she was never disillusioned or angry when they arrived at a position to drop her, and often in more discriminating salons they missed Gerda's amiable unanalytical applause.

She had the easy self-confidence of having renounced high society in her youth, preferring the bohemian life, and she still spent a great deal of time assuring everyone that she would never, never go back or ever regret the place in Tuxedo. As is usually the case with those who throw away titles or position to champion the peasantry she had trouble convincing these chosen friends that she was even an equal; they suspected her of coming up from even lower depths, fruit of the most depraved miscegenation. However, Gerda was blind to this, and would scarcely have understood such skepticism in any case.

Auctions at Flattau and Park Bernet had yielded her a dozen tremendous pieces of formidable furniture, bargains because no respectable home was large enough to house them. A great square piano and a gold-painted sedan chair were lavishly useless but impressive; in the corner tottered a huge rococo wardrobe closet decorated with life-size Cupids chipping off like old love itself, the loose doors popping open at the sound of any bell or automobile horn as if to allow refuge for half a dozen secret lovers instead of for the gaudy costumes packed within. Chairs were never less than thrones and quite as precarious; divans were sumptuously pillowed to atone for dead springs; rugs were deep-piled, ancient, choking up with dust as if with tears, at the least footfall. Caroline Drake thought everything looked frightfully buggy and usually gave herself a thorough brushing the minute she got outside, but then Gerda privately thought Caroline's own glass house was very Gimbelish looking. One good thing was that there were always lots of men, new men, at Gerda's, though Caroline said it was no wonder; any woman who stayed home all day, kept the latch open and always had a pot of soup on the stove and a thimble of liquor could have the place teeming with men. Caroline herself usually managed to bring home from Gerda's parties some young choreographer, poet or percussionist willing to forget his sexual preferences in exchange for her Scotch. There was always the fun of seeing poor Murray trapped there, too, glaring around to see what people liked about this sort of thing, prepared to take a poke at anyone who might be making fun of Gerda when she began speaking foreign languages or discussing world affairs.

"Gerda doesn't want him there and he hates it but he just can't stay away," Caroline said to Lorna Leahy. "I think he comes because he's a frustrated martyr. He wants to be in a bar bellyaching to the fellows about his wife nagging, making him come to her parties and damned if he will. It baffles him

horribly to have her beg him to stay away, so of course he has
to come."

Caroline thought she might inveigle Murray out if the
crowd stayed on, but there was an even better prospect today
for Gerda had sworn to produce Frederick Olliver, always a
prize to be fought over with Lorna. Frederick had started out
by mocking at Gerda's artificial postures but had ended by
discovering an admirable basic sincerity in the tremendous to-
do she made over him. He was almost sure to be there. This
was the reason Caroline waited half an hour in the pouring
rain for a cross-town bus, unable to get a cab, her brand-new
brass-gold curls wilting by the minute. She was sure Lorna
would be there even if she had to swim because she was so
damned afraid Caroline would grab off Frederick. First it had
been Murray Cahill, now it was Frederick. Silly to find yourself practically breaking up an old friendship over a man who
didn't care, really, about either of you and whom, for that
matter, neither of you really wanted. It was all Lorna's fault
for being so underhanded. When Caroline asked Frederick to
dinner she used to ask Lorna too, until she discovered that
whenever Lorna rounded him up she kept him smugly to herself to crow about later. The result was that Caroline was unwilling to pass up a chance to get ahead of Lorna. In addition
to bucking the storm she had to carry two bottles of rye
under her arm (Gerda wouldn't have anything but wine and
everybody had to chip in on anything else), and by the time
she had gotten off into the flooded gutter and her umbrella
had blown inside out, Caroline was in no mood for carnival,
longing to step into a vestibule and swig her bottles all alone.
The rain was coming down in torrents, a garbage can had
overturned and was shipping grapefruit rinds down the
streaming street, people with sense were darting under the El
posts or into shops, newspapers over their heads; no one
would dream of being out on such a night except a woman
looking for a man.

"Even Lorna won't come," Caroline thought. "It would be
too obvious."

She struggled with hat, bottles, and umbrella across the
street, dodged the careening garbage-can lid as it sailed past
her, and blinded by the cutting rain was almost felled by a

taxi-cab skidding to a stop before Gerda's address. Caroline muttered a sincere oath as she reached the door of the battered building and was discomfited to see that the occupant of the taxi-cab was following her and had heard her. Anyway it meant that there was another fool besides herself today—a woman too, of course. To her surprise she recognized Mrs. Gaynor, no one she ever expected to see at Gerda's and who probably wouldn't remember having met her once in a restaurant with Murray Cahill, but this was no day for coy reserve and Caroline reminded her at once of their former encounter. Mrs. Gaynor was openly grateful for a kind word in this unknown world. Almost in the same breath they apologized for having braved the tempest for such a slight occasion, as if their presence was a shocking confession of loneliness and scarcity of opportunities. Caroline suddenly remembered that this was rumored to be the woman in Frederick's life, and thought happily, well if she gets him away today she'll be taking him from Lorna as well as herself. They climbed the four flights of stairs—good heavens, what fools! Tornadoes, four flights of stairs, anything for a man! They passed the show-room for artificial limbs on the first landing, the chemical laboratory with its mysterious smells on the second, the photographer's studio on the third. The contrast of rotting stair-case and feeble light on mottled walls only intensified the seedy grandeur of Gerda's carpeted, incense-filled hall, her door gaily hung with sleighbells.

As they waited Caroline studied her companion furtively, reflecting that she was losing her looks, thank God; that radiant red-haired pearly-skin glow did wear out faster than less sensational types. (Mustn't be too critical, though, the rain had probably washed out her own looks as well.) She still had a figure, *faux-maigre* as the copy called it, feathery light but curved. Having no bones helped, of course, Caroline reflected enviously, wishing some magic would melt down her own rawboned hips. Lyle, for her part thought here was one of the women who now figured in Frederick's life, here was someone who was closer to him than she was and she wanted to cry out "What was it he wanted that I couldn't give him and you others could? Where did I fail? What made him change, or was he always looking for something else and I didn't guess?" She wondered if the reason for her unusual presence at Gerda Cahill's was completely obvious, if the other woman guessed at once that her life, without her lover, was spent in tracking down remnants of him, taking up whatever person was said to be now in his confidence, gathering mournful solace from merely hearing his name spoken, piecing together a Frederick she had never known from scraps of strangers' talk. Analyzing, rehearsing accusations and then apologies, puzzling over the change in him, she thought the truth must be that one never changed, one was merely found out. She had been blind, that was all, cruelly blind. She had reproached him for his resentment of her kind of life and his unwillingness to take part in it or wait on the outskirts for her spare moments; but she herself had never made an effort to enter his life, beyond the confidences he offered, until he was gone. Only then did she comprehend the vast ocean between them, the ocean she always expected him to overcome. At every step of her road backwards to reconstruct a man she had never known she found new cause for penitence. No wonder he disliked her circle! No wonder he hated the Beckleys, the nightclubs, the parties, the first nights. It was easier to admit her own cruelty than to bear the burden of his. Lyle only hoped that her new knowledge of him would not cause her to fling herself at his feet for forgiveness if they should be left alone.

How sweet of them to come on such a day, Gerda cried, spectacular in a sea-green velvet robe, both hands reaching out to them through twin cylinders of tinkling bracelets, while the eyes of both guests leapt past their welcome into the dark corners of the room to see if He was there. Lyle could see the *Swan*'s Mexican poet lying on the floor playing with Iamb, the cat, pulling its claws over his thick black hair, laughingly inviting bites and scratches. Lorna Leahy, in gray slacks and tight purple sweater, emerald bow in white curly mop, was very much at home as hostess-assistant, stirring up the great vase of wine and fruit mixture with a baton.

"I put rum in it this time," she whispered loudly to Caroline. "After all it's a celebration, isn't it?"

Frederick was not here but this was part of the life he liked, Lyle thought, and looked eagerly around. In a corner by the Franklin stove she saw a little pallid blonde with the intent vague expression, coronet of braids, high cheek-bones and firm calves of the dancer, earnestly demonstrating some sort of Oriental contortion to two fragile young men in plaid wool shirts.

"It's the story of Ramajana, the Demon King of Sanka," Gerda explained to Lyle. "Then she's doing something perfectly extraordinary on the Krishna dances during the Monsoon Rains. I want Miranda to show them to Frederick Olliver especially."

"He's coming?" Lyle asked involuntarily. Gerda slipped her bracelets up and down her arms and Lyle was not sure the sound of bells was from them or from the sweet syllables of Frederick's name.

"Of course," Gerda said. "I had to coax him but by this time I know he adores parties; he just wants to be coaxed."

Another thing she had never guessed in her cursed complacency, Lyle reflected.

The windows shook with the lash of rain, fog-horns bellowed from the bowels of the earth, the long narrow room in candle light with the giant furniture and fluttering draperies seemed a vault for musty treasures and guests from beyond. Yet the sleighbells on the door quivered with newcomers, the reality of the tempest was admitted by the growing mound of galoshes, proof that there were dozens of foolish citizens who were glad to give up lonely security in their own rooms for danger in company, the bare chance of finding the lost love or the new. Years of war were sponged off, those who must have been involved avoided its mention as if they were on probation for a crime they hoped would be forgotten. But then these were days when the gift of forgetting was a treasure in itself.

Caroline Drake was obliged to greet Lorna Leahy with exaggerated joy, and Lyle, left alone, saw no one she knew. She was ashamed and frightened that no one, except Padilla, the poet, recognized the name Lyle Gaynor, or if they did there was none of the respectful murmur she had not realized she took for granted as her due. She regretted that she had not taken more pleasure at the time in the critical praise for *Summer Day*, whose advent last year was overshadowed by the success of half a dozen subsequent hits. But she had been too cautiously cynical in her theory that the press had only the power of veto. Drama critics in the city, she often said, were like an old married couple; they had lived together so long they looked and thought alike, they disagreed only on the details of the funeral—burial or cremation? They compared plays with other plays, never with life, for they sent the second-string reviewers to that; a play was true to "life" if it conformed to other plays on the same subject. Life, in fact, was a lady in front asked to remove her hat so they could see the play. Sometimes they took a sabbatical year but only to travel; a theatrical gesture in itself. The Gaynor plays, they chanted, were gay, bitter, revealing studies of sensitive moderns, true pictures of modern society. How would they know, Lyle had queried, except that they recognized the sets from the last play of modern society? But she had profited by their dream world and knew she had received far more applause than she deserved. At least she had *thought* she knew that, even when she was most contemptuously ungrateful in her mind. But now that she seemed in danger of being obscured merely for an hour or two she was dashed, even hurt. If she was to see Frederick again here she must have her usual, undeserved, court. For the first time it came home to her how comfortably she had counted on reputation to make up for minor personal disappointments. A crutch, a cushion, a veil, a safety net for all missteps, that knowledge of work recognized and admired whether she was old or young. Without it she felt vulnerable and exposed, a woman in her thirties whom no one knew, an everyday woman with no protection of love or fame, with no banner to bear but that of pleading mistress begging for a crumb. Left standing unnoticed for a moment it struck Lyle how soft and spoiled she was, never venturing on any path that was not especially paved for her, innocently astonished that the paving could wear out and torches on dark corners would not be lit. And she had been hurt because Frederick was no braver than she!

"I didn't get the name." Someone was repeating Gerda's introduction, but even when it was repeated there was no sign of recognition or interest. How perfectly idiotic to expect any, Lyle thought, but, after all, she had been spoiled and Frederick had been too kind to tell her even when he knew it was a wall between them. It was as silly as an old romance where lovers separate forever because, incredibly enough, she has not explained to him that she is a duchess or pregnant, and he has not explained that he has tuberculosis or a mad wife.

With a wave of relief she saw that Tyson Bricker had arrived and with his usual quick appraisal of the contents of a room had elected her as the one of most importance. Accustomed to being the aggressor, if not the intruder, he must have been surprised at the cordiality of her greeting, not realizing that he was rescuing someone from a desert island of self-analysis.

"Who would dream of finding you here, dear lady?" he exclaimed, drawing her hand under his arm and stroking it fondly. "Gerda's is the place for promising talent, not for the already-arrived."

"Should I be offended or flattered?" Lyle asked, warmed with mere recognition. She had long ago accepted Frederick's disparaging opinion of the man as a relentless, if shrewd, climber, but at least he was familiar.

"Not yet published, exhibited, heard or seen are the entrance requirements for membership here," Tyson murmured in her ear. "We grown-ups are allowed only on sufferance and must expect certain youthful insults. I never find you at home any more, you cruel creature. Everyone says the Gaynors have begun to lock their door to the old friends. Where does one find you these days?"

"Here today," answered Lyle. "How do you happen to be here, yourself?"

Tyson squinted at his wrist watch after another lightning calculation of the room's value in human possibilities.

"I promised to pick up Frederick Olliver here. No taxis and I have the car outside unless it's floated down the river. Interesting chap, Olliver. I remember now you used to try to sell him to me."

"What finally sold you?" Lyle asked.

Tyson produced cigarettes and a lighter with a thoughtful frown.

"I already had him at the League, of course. But it was what he did with that *Haw* magazine that really sold me on the man. Phenomenal. Not many know he's at the bottom of it, of course."

Lyle said nothing. Poor Frederick. She should have understood how the ironic success of *Haw* had only pointed up his other failures and made him dash with almost suicidal frenzy into anything new or different.

"I only know his other work," she finally said. "You must admire that, of course."

"Admire it?" exclaimed Tyson. "My dear lady, I've finally succeeded in putting it over! I must say it's been a tough job, too, when you consider how difficult Olliver himself is. When you hear about it I'll bet you anything you'll have to credit me with one of the sweetest deals in my whole career."

"You've persuaded Strafford to publish his book?" Lyle guessed.

Tyson looked pained.

"Strafford! Oh yes, of course he'll want to take all the credit! But I'm sure Olliver realizes who is responsible. Don't ask me any more questions because it's not to be told yet. But it so happened I was in a position to pick anyone and I put my money on Olliver. I wonder where he is. Coming here was his idea, confound him."

Lyle wondered how it had come about that Frederick should be a frequenter of this environment. His Pooh-girl was no part of it, clearly. She was tantalized by his name leaping out of conversations around her and tried to trace which one had said it and what there was about him or her that fitted into Frederick's present tastes. Which ones had he made love to, what did he talk about when he was alone with Caroline Drake or Gerda or the pixie-faced woman passing out glass cups of whatever it was? Tyson gave her a warning shake of the head as she took the cup, and ever mindful of his expensive stomach he inconspicuously produced a flask for her to share, but Lyle thought this would mark her as an outsider and drank the punch. She saw Murray Cahill in a corner, backed there by Caroline Drake who appeared to be serving her own whiskey to him and other applicants. At least Murray made Frederick seem more imminent, but she was afraid he'd come in and find her standing around like Alice Adams, fixed smile on her face, all too obviously waiting for him. She had two more quick drinks to give her courage to talk to these strangers who ignored her. But one had no right to feel offended at the snubs of the poor or unsuccessful. What?—the hostess failed to introduced you, someone spilled wine on your gown and stepped on your toes? Why not, you are sufficiently famous, as much in public domain as if you were a civic institution. But mind your own manners, let's have no reprisals from you. The Spanish poet, holding the cat around his shoulders like a fur-piece with its bushy Persian tail flicking his cheek rhythmically in delicate protest, came over to kiss her hand and speak to Tyson. He was incredibly handsome as well as gifted, and Edwin Stalk had occasionally brought him to her house. Lyle wished she had dared let him make love to her but the memory of love stood between her and any consoling surrender like the Church itself. She was becoming more and more impatient with her body's stern fidelity that remained like a perfume long after the vial was empty. In her old age, she warned herself, she would look back on this continence with regret. No, she thought again, the nuns had something; there was more voluptuous satisfaction in having been desired and withholding than in indifferent squandering and unhappy quests for something beyond the immediate gestures. The real cause for regret in old age would be that one had met no love great enough to command fidelity.

"Padilla refuses to be translated," Tyson said, amused.

Padilla stroked the cat's mouth. (He would be the kind of lover, Lyle thought, who was happier in the exhibition of his skill than the quality of his conquest.)

"Because everything becomes sinister when translated into English," he complained. "Edwin Stalk tells me he will do it very painlessly but it frightens me and I am not going to consent. The Anglo-Saxon poet is always possessed and I am not ready for the devil. Supposing I am translated into a poet who cannot go three blocks from my own door? In Spanish, I am always safe. Maybe I fear that fourth block beyond my door. Never mind, in Spanish the people of the village would have a sweet pepper here, some wine a mile further, good morning, here's a new baby, good-day professor, advise us on philosophy and the weather. Presently I am miles from home, maybe drunk, but at least not Anglo-Saxon. No, I stay Spanish, I tell Edwin Stalk. I am afraid of translation into English."

"The fear itself is a good Anglo-Saxon neurosis," Tyson Bricker said briskly. "Maybe you're already translated, young man. The worst is over."

Lorna Leahy was beside Lyle with a fresh glass, part of Gerda's knack for hospitality being in letting the guests provide for each other as well as for her.

"He was for Franco, you know," Lorna murmured in Lyle's ear. "Can you imagine Gerda sleeping with him? I think we should shave her head, honestly, but of course no one cares about that sort of thing now the war's over. So long as we don't sleep with the French or English or Russians. Really, Mrs. Gaynor, doesn't it seem absolutely mad? We don't know ourselves or anyone else from one day to the next, things are changing so fast. I'm so glad to have this opportunity of meeting you. Will you have a new play for next year?"

"I'm afraid not," Lyle said eagerly, amazed at her childish pleasure in being noticed, almost as if she was through, an old-timer long forgotten.

Lorna watched Caroline's corner jealously and confided to Lyle that Murray was getting absolutely rigid, thanks to Caroline, and Gerda certainly wouldn't take care of him, throw him right out in the teeth of the hurricane, like as not. As a matter of fact, she, Lorna, thought it would be a good thing to have him take her home where she could look after him before Caroline got him too plastered to move. Not that she expected any thanks, either, for looking after him. The chances were he would probably walk out on her and go see that Judy girl, that little square he always had hanging around. Did Lyle know her? Judy Dahl, new winner of the Hazelnut Cigarette prize, God knows why.

"Obvious," Tyson explained with intent to console. "Like all lady artists she uses her sex to get ahead in her profession, don't you agree, Mrs. Gaynor?"

Lorna was not entirely gratified by this explanation, implying as it did that she herself did not have proper sex appeal to get ahead, and Lyle murmured that women had as much right to use sex to get ahead professionally as men had to use their professional success to get ahead sexually.

"Thinks she's a genuine artist just because she knows the difference between the canvas and the brush," Lorna went on indignantly. "Of course I'm just a hack, you see, that's the idea, because I'm good enough at it to make a living. But she's the real thing, a regular Picasso, because she can't make money! Disgusting! Second prize, mind you! Two conch shells on a table with a doll's head and an alarm clock! Will somebody tell me what that has to do with art or cigarettes? When Hazelnut gives *me* an order I have to make the cigarette look like a cigarette, of course, but little Miss Judy Rembrandt gets a prize and two thousand bucks just to leave out cigarettes. How chic! Yet even Murray himself says she's lousy. Honestly, is it any wonder we drink? Here, let me give you another. God knows it's not champagne but at least it's got rum in it today. I couldn't have stood claret lemonade on a day like this. Excuse me, I have to mix some more."

This was the way Frederick must have felt all these years at her parties, Lyle thought, grateful for an occasional kind word, then left alone thinking, "I'm really an idiot to expose myself to this kind of embarrassment." She tried to detach herself and see everything as Frederick saw it. Obviously he must be the best-known person in a group like this, more than Tyson since his work was elegantly free of mass appeal. They made him feel as young as they were, too, for there was youth in an insecurity with the world ahead; she and Tyson were established and had only the toboggan ahead. That is, if it was for appreciation of his work Frederick came here. She pushed her reservations back in her mind resolutely, attempting very carefully to study every angle of this picture for what it gave him, and she told herself it was unfair to say this was an inexpensive reprint of a Beckley evening, the flaw for him in the latter being that she was central figure and the virtue in the former being that she was not. She saw that Tyson was already bored with the number of guests arriving whom he did not know and who did not know him, or if they did, seemed to regard him as a merely respectable representative of an older, stuffier order. He was not at all pleased when Padilla said to her, "Do you think we could get Edwin Stalk to come to Gerda's sometime? She would be so flattered, but then he doesn't like crowds. If we could get him, it would be amusing."

The punch was making her feel dizzy and a little sick but conscious of Lorna's apology for its not being champagne she felt obliged to drink it whenever it was passed. She must show she could be gracious with Frederick's friends in spite of his making no effort with hers. He had criticized her friends relentlessly and in the end she was seeing them as he saw them —smug, dead, selfish, opportunistic, hollow . . . She tried to see the superiority of these friends of his with his eyes as well, doing her best to keep down the impression that she had seen, heard and discarded all this before in her life-time. In the ballet-lovers group which had grown steadily a lean dark snake-headed girl in a Mexican sweater, velveteen dirndl and thick gaucho boots, leapt to the piano bench every few moments as if to settle some verbal argument by an instrumental rebuttal. "Isn't this the sort of thing you mean, Miranda? Isn't this it?"

Tinkering over the treble chords hopefully, waiting for an invitation to play that never came she presently slipped willy-nilly into a Chopin prelude, head bent submissively over the keyboard, lips moving until she got the right connection when she rolled and gyrated on the piano bench in a pelvic ecstasy, eager to conduct worthy phrases over the doubtful rocks and rills of Gerda's bargain piano. She bent over the tiny runs with a tender smile, letting the smaller Pomeranian chords have the run of their leash, then bending back suddenly as if to keep the big bass hounds from jumping on the grass. Throughout she was the fond, responsible disciplinarian conducting the doggish romp—down Towser, down—come on Peewee, jump, Peewee, down Towser, down, down, down! "It's that mood you want, isn't it, Miranda—" but Miranda wasn't listening.

"Frederick Olliver said Renée—" of course her name was Renée, Lyle thought, overhearing—"made Gerda's old Beckstein sound like a harpsichord."

So there was something else Frederick found amusing, though he had found nothing rewarding in creditable compositions played by experts of renown in her company. Maybe the mere fact that a person or talent was properly appreciated spoiled it for him, reminding him of his own failure; these inferior demonstrations built up his pride of superiority. Poor darling, oh poor darling, she thought, how unhappy he must have been to have been comforted by such modest fires.

Outside, thunder and the rumble of the El rolled like breakers in a stormy ocean over the tinkling music and shrill beat of voices that carried only the skeletons of words, though Lyle could hear someone crying repeatedly for the medieval Breton whaling song—"the one Frederick liked so much." Who said that, she wondered? She went to the window and drew aside the moldy green velvet draperies which Gerda used to shut out the days. Gerda's costume, belted in silver, she realized was contrived from the same fabric, probably once in Isolde's own chamber, along with the baronial furniture and Gerda herself. The rain was coming down in a fine, almost invisible curtain now, veiling the street, throwing up spray from the gutters, giving wavering lights the look of lanterns on ancient fishing boats. A strange glow from somewhere above or below transformed the street outside into the lonely sea itself with a dim moon rising in dim clouds above it, far away, long, long ago. The high choir-boy voice she heard behind her was followed by the twanging of a lyre and she was Isolde herself, waiting for the lover's ship, or was she a maid on the Breton coast peering through the fog for the lost fisherman? She felt a hand on her shoulder.

"Look," she exclaimed. "Do you see it, too? It's like black magic! . . . Now it's gone, of course, the street is back."

"When you say the words, whatever you saw goes away," Tyson informed her, concisely. "You ought to know enough about black magic to know that, dear child. It's probably that black magic punch you're drinking, frankly. At the moment, you look like a slightly drunken angel—adorable, of course."

"Thank you for the 'slightly,' " Lyle said, following him back into the room.

"Come over here by the door," he urged her in an undertone. "I always like to have a foot outside in a party like this. What's keeping Olliver, for pity's sake? By George, I'm going to run him down. I want to leave. I don't know these people, really."

"I heard someone say there's a telephone downstairs," Lyle said. He looked dried, and tidily insignificant, it struck her, as if air and life went out of him in a foreign element where he was not an important personage. (Was she affected this way, too?) He would telephone Strafford's, Tyson said, though it was long after six, and the office was only a few blocks away.

"If you can't get in the booth downstairs there's one in the bar next door," Gerda cried out, and then as he left, "But why is Tyson Bricker so nervous? I want him to hear Victor sing some more."

"He's nervous because he stays up all hours without drinking," Caroline Drake loudly stated. "I know because I tried it once. And last night I saw him—he never sees me, of course—at the Stork Club. It cost him a forty dollar check for the little drip he was with to win a bottle of California sherry out of a balloon. No wonder he's nervous today."

"I prefer the pet shop next door to the Stork Club," Padilla said, thrusting a macaroon at the cat on his shoulder. "It's more exclusive. There is the same rope to keep out the wrong people, and you stand there waiting to be recognized by some celebrated bird or dog in a cage. You wave and sometimes they bark back and you are allowed inside the rope. I am *persona grata* there because my *chihuahua* lives there now. I find no place to live, of course, because I am only a poet. But Manuelo has a whole cage to himself because he's of royal blood."

Lyle stole a look at herself in the fly-blown mirror by the door and was surprised at her flushed, disheveled appearance—red hair kinked up out of its careful coiffeur by the rain, one earring gone, lipstick awry.

"Why, I do look drunk!" she thought in consternation. "Blowsy!" Like Tyson, then, part of her good looks came from the knowledge of belonging. But no sooner had she fumbled for her compact than she saw Frederick entering the door behind her and there was nothing for either of them to do but shake hands politely. He looked remarkably well, of course, even with the rain dripping from his hair and his shabby old raincoat trailing puddles over the floor. Six weeks and five days since they had met, she recalled, in a crowd at the Museum opening of course—six months since they had lunched alone.

"It's been awfully wet," she said tentatively.

"Awfully," he replied, shaking himself.

So long as she could smile when he greeted her. So long as she could keep from crying out, "Oh darling, at last you're here. See how nicely I fit into your new life! See how much your friends like me. See me drinking this stuff and not minding it at all. See how little I miss the things you thought were so important to me!"

How glad she was to have Padilla come back with Gerda at that moment, Padilla bringing a hassock for her so that he might sit at her feet! That, at least, was some indication of her right to be there. But Frederick could not even take off his raincoat, he explained to Gerda; he had only time to pick up Tyson and get on his way. At first he avoided looking directly at her when he spoke, but when the others came up his eyes rushed to Lyle's, unable to look away, and she felt herself drowning, unable to save herself. She knew well enough that he would not have dared sit beside her on the hassock, when she instinctively moved over, if Padilla and Gerda had not been there to make the gesture safe. She knew he would not have pretended to support himself by an arm half around her if he hadn't been certain of immediate departure. But she knew, too, that he must feel the need again to be near her, no matter how he covered it with talking to the others, and she could not speak for joy. She moved slightly so that she felt his heart beating against her back, his very breath on her neck. She was afraid to look at him for fear a conscious contact would frighten him away.

"But everyone has been screaming for you!" Gerda protested. "Murray swore you would come! I'll have to punish Murray for making everyone come out on such a day for nothing. If it's a sweetheart why didn't you bring her here? Never mind, you must stay for one drink. A toast to the book. Besides Tyson may be gone for hours, hunting for a telephone."

"Then the book is coming out?" Lyle murmured over her shoulder. Their hands, unexpectedly touching on the leather seat were held together as if by an electric current.

"I thought Tyson had told you," Frederick said, flushing. He had not been able to find an easy way of telling her, though he knew he should have. "It's the International Award——"

"Frederick!" She glowed with triumphant pride in him and he drank it in thirstily.

"Strafford's are using it to square themselves for that *Court Lady* success," he went on. Telling it to Lyle made the fantastic news seem true to him for the first time. "They've been scouting around for something like it. International usually picks a European or Englishman. It was just luck Strafford's needed my kind of thing and International needed to make up to America."

Their hands tightened silently, each pretending to be unaware. He's happy, now he's won, Lyle thought, and it seemed that his reward was all she had ever wanted for either of them. She reminded herself that he had not sought her out at once to tell her this sudden culmination of all they had dreamed. This was the hour they had dreamed of but the dream was all she was permitted to share. The reality excluded her. She must not let herself think he was hers again. Gerda was clapping her hands, insisting that everyone toast Frederick's success and the ladies all rushed up to embrace him. Everyone knew about the award except herself, Lyle thought. This was really cruel. She thought of the nights they had spent going over each chapter, a part of their love-making. The fact that she shared her own work so completely with her husband and a public made her the more loyally absorbed in Frederick's. Was there no kindness in him at all that he must bar her from even the smallest compensation?

"It's the most important work of our generation, oh by far," Renée shouted and pulled Frederick into the center of the room.

" '*Our* generation'?" Tyson repeated sarcastically in Lyle's ear. "I declare I hadn't expected that. No wonder he wanted to come here."

He folded his arms, scowling at the young ladies fussing merrily over Frederick.

"This amuses me, it really does," he drawled, with an attempt at a smile. "The man hasn't done anything different than before when they paid no attention to him. Then I knock myself out to put him over—I could have picked anybody else, mind you—with absolutely no cooperation from him, as you might expect. And now he gets the credit. I hope he realizes how funny it is."

He must have known it was funny, Lyle suspected, not only the sudden female adoration but Tyson's ruffled envy over the tributes from youth. He flashed her a half-smile, as Miranda and Renée tried to comb his wet hair. This was the last straw for Tyson who called out impatiently, "Come on, Olliver, we'll be late, let's go."

"He doesn't seem to realize what it means to be asked to dine at the Beckleys'." he complained.

Lyle could not believe she had heard aright. It could not be that Frederick was surrendering to the Beckleys of his own accord.

"Beckley is out to get him away from Strafford's eventually, I suppose," Tyson said, with another glance at his watch. "You know how they always like to claim every new fish, after somebody else has proved them. I asked myself along because, by Jove, I deserve some thanks after all the time I've put in building him up. No help from him, either—excuse me, I forgot he used to be a friend of yours."

"Yes, he was," Lyle said. "I think I will have some of your flask now if you don't mind."

Tyson whisked it out of his pocket.

"Here, keep it. I was here once before and knew I'd need it. Look here, you're an old friend of the Beckleys, why not nip along with us and barge in?"

"No, I wouldn't dream of going without being asked," Lyle said, thoughtfully. "I really don't care about their parties any more. I like it better here."

She was pouring Tyson's flask into the punch when Frederick came up to say goodbye to her.

"Please!" Tyson expostulated from the doorway, waving Frederick's raincoat. "Olliver, for Pete's sake, hurry. It isn't everybody who gets asked to the Beckleys' for dinner. A small family dinner, mind you, at that!"

"What luck!" Lyle said smiling at Frederick brightly. "Nobody there but the morons as you used to say."

"Come, come, they're not that bad," he reproached her without thinking. "When you get to know them—alright, Tyson, I'm coming."

Lyle picked up the baton and stirred the punch.

"Now why did that monster make Frederick go to the Beckleys'?" Gerda cried, throwing up her arms in a theatrical gesture as the door closed on the two men. "He hates that sort of thing."

"Does he?" Lyle's lip curled.

"He must hate it to drive up there in this tempest," Padilla called out from the window. "Cats and dogs! Look!"

Lyle walked over and looked out as he held back the curtains. Once more she heard the roar of the surf on the legendary coast and she saw the spume of the stormy sea, black and lonely, with the moon in mourning above. Far out, the lantern on her lover's boat bobbed up and down and was lost.

. . . the foul weather friends in fair weather . . .

"I suppose you'll be pulling out of this joint any day," Murray said, without looking up from the *Tribune* comic section.

"Me?" Frederick asked, startled. "Why?"

Murray rattled the page and raised himself on an elbow to sip at the cup of coffee on the end-table by the sofa. He had not been dressed for days, nor shaved, and now at five o'clock was still in striped purple pajamas, feet slipping out of sandals. The apartment had not been cleaned for some time so that the spring breeze had the opportunity to chase a herd of ghostly floor "pussies" back and forth across the bare floor. The part-time maid had not been in and, Frederick feared, was gone for good, since Murray refused to get up to let her in. The paucity of rugs and furniture in the front room kept it from appearing really dirty, but the sink in the alcove was full of cups and saucepans in which dregs of coffee or canned soup had ossified. Frederick kept his own room tidy but he was afraid to touch the other end of the apartment after overhearing Murray's indignation at Judy's attempted interference. If he and his room-mate needed any goddam housewifely supervision they would ask for it, he had shouted; the reason they didn't was that they hated bang and clatter when they were trying to think. Since then Frederick had been cautiously tiptoeing around his friend's jitters, aware that he was in some way responsible for them.

"I'm surprised Strafford doesn't make you put up at some fancy uptown hotel. He could get you in," Murray went on. "Fellow in your position can't afford to live in a fleabag like this. You gotta give 'em a show for their money. Ought to get some new clothes, too, old boy."

Frederick was in the hall between their rooms, brushing his suit with a whisk-broom. He decided, after a moment's uncertainty, to treat this as a joke.

"Do you mean to insinuate that peg-top pants have gone

out?" he laughed. "No, Murray, I'm no good at 'shows' even if they wanted one. This isn't my show anyway."

"Take all these saps busting in here for interviews," Murray said. "Half the time I have to throw them out. God knows I'm not trained to be a gentleman's gentleman. Wish I was. Telephone ringing every minute. They all figure you can pay for a snappier set-up than this."

"I realize it's a nuisance," Frederick answered awkwardly, not sure what Murray was driving at but the word "saps" and "pay" hinted at adulation dishonestly come by and honest poor folks deprived of a humble abode by a stingy rich man. "I'm waiting for a private phone. Or do you mean you want my room for someone else . . ."

"Who, for instance?" Murray laughed mirthlessly. "No, I'm thinking of the position you're in right now. I'm trying to say you wouldn't be letting me down, so far as your rent is concerned, if you wanted to move. I've got unemployment insurance and plenty of prospects."

This was the kind of tension between them ever since the papers had announced Frederick's good news, and Frederick was at a loss how to handle it. Their loyalty had been cemented by difficulties in common, but now Frederick was removed to unknown heights, an unconscious betrayal of friendship, since Murray was in depths of trouble. Murray could not deny it was his own fault but this did not keep him from blaming others. He had gone on a week's binge as was his annual post-Lenten habit, but this time he had lost his job, a thing that simply never happened and certainly should not happen at a time his creditors were pressing him. It meant he could not go on with the quiet arrangements for the summer cottage at Pomfret Gerda had wistfully admired. He had counted on renting it for her as a quixotic way of compensating her for Judy's prize (a matter about which Gerda neither knew or cared). Judy's silent satisfaction over her Hazelnut Cigarette triumph struck Murray as vaguely unfair to Gerda who had the womanly grace to win nothing but what he gave her; now that he could make no gifts she did not complain, nor, for that matter, had she ever thanked him, being under a hazy delusion that one casually reached into whatever pocket was nearest just as others reached into yours. If he could not be of use to her he had no right to hang around, she felt and he knew. Usually an amiable fellow the recent twists of fate kept Murray with a constant supply of chips for his shoulder and plenty of time to keep them polished. His room-mate's bright prospects made him feel even more wronged.

Frederick was discovering that no matter how generous friends are in your failure, they do not easily forgive your success. He found the only way he could mollify Murray was to feed him delectable tales of hard luck everywhere and he made the most of every possible shadow in his own glaring sunshine. He turned into a veritable papa robin industriously bringing home jucier and uglier worms to cheer the fledgling. Let's see, he would think on the way to the apartment, what lovely bad news had he heard today? Ah yes, Strafford was said to be drinking again and had, in fact, been tapped for A.A. instead of the club he wanted; Umberto was selling his restaurant because the OPA and his family were conniving to ruin him; the *Swan* magazine had a nasty run-in over rights with the English *Horizon*, Lorna Leahy had a calcium deficiency, bones turning to pure water or worse, someone had cancer, someone was fired, sued, dead, arrested, caught frightfully unaware in a hydrangea bush one night at the Botanical Gardens. Eagerly Frederick plied his friend with these choice proofs of human incompetence until Murray relaxed into a state of modest satisfaction, and even looked on Frederick with a return of the old fondness when as a final frosting for his cake Frederick generously confessed that his love life was in a desperately unhappy state.

"Ah, you're lucky, getting out of that Dodo mess, from what I hear," Murray consoled him. "Of course, I don't really believe she's a nympho as they say; she just thinks she's got enough lollypops for everybody. I could have told you at the start all about that baby but you were in too deep."

Frederick debated whether to give his friend further comfort by an all-revealing question as to why women were always being nymphomaniacs for everybody but you: however Murray might be just touchy enough to think he might mean Gerda. No, there was no use trying to regain the old camaraderie after the crime of good luck. Bad weather friends were as undependable as fair weather friends in a crisis, the relationship in both cases being dictated by conditions of fortune instead of mutual tastes. How could he possibly have imagined himself close to a man who followed the funnies, Frederick asked himself with a touch of irritation; a man who used the book section to gather up a broken high-ball glass? There had been a perfectly good reason for their having kept discreet distance all those years; the peacefulness of their relationship had been in acknowledging no common ground. He had always known that Murray shrugged his shoulders over the eccentricity of a man who read or wrote anything but detective stories; therefore his demonstration of practical success in an unpractical field was in itself a kind of insult to a man's common sense. There would have been none of this veiled hostility if they had only stayed in their separate corners. Now the very air was charged with the blackmail of confessions soured, wounds foolishly exposed; each looked vainly for the door marked *private* which they had so blithely unhinged. When Murray dropped and broke his cup he looked reproachfully at Frederick as if even his hangovers were no longer his own secret. I'd better get out, Frederick thought, but where could he find companionship that would permit him to be his old self, without the strain of consideration for rivals, enemies, flatterers? He longed to be able to speak his natural tongue instead of the diplomatic idiom of success, the false humility, the pretense of gratitude for ignorant praise, the tactful turn of the other cheek to unfair attack.

"Have you seen the Hazelnut Exhibition yet?" he asked, seeking to deflect Murray's attention. "How was Judy's picture?"

Murray flung the paper aside with a gloomy sigh.

"I took a look at it a couple of times while she was painting it, but she knows my opinion by this time. The kid's no artist, she's a little farmer—ought to be cooking for some fisherman back there in Maine. I've told her so, but seeing all those phony bohemians vacationing up there in Rockport every summer gave her the art bug. She thinks a couple of prizes means she's good. Hell, there's more sheer art in this *Penny* strip here. Judy hasn't got the temperament. Take Gerda. Gerda's never done anything, but just the way she

fools around with music or dancing shows the real temperament. I'm glad the kid got the prize, of course, since it means
so much to her, but I hate to see her wasting her life on a
pipedream."

The airing of this point of view seemed to relieve Murray
and he sipped his coffee quietly for a minute.

"You feel alright?" he asked suddenly. "Seems to me you've
gotten pretty skinny. Color not so good."

A little surprised at this solicitude Frederick admitted he
did not sleep well.

"Too much celebration, too much running around. People
always did wear me out," he confessed. "Just an hour or so
trying to talk to strangers goes right to my stomach. I drink
more than I ever did and I don't enjoy it particularly."

"Cracking up just like me," Murray said gloomily. "Old
age. I used to think old age was a kind of feather bed you
gradually sank down into, but it's not. It's a goddam stone
wall you butt your head into till it cracks. Ever think about
dying? I mean, who would you want notified in case it happened? Here we are, living together all these years and we
wouldn't have any idea what to do with each other's body."

"Don't go to any trouble with mine. I'll just take pot-
luck," Frederick said but a spasm of childish terror struck
him. What to do in case of death? Who would care? Who
would grieve? Not Dodo, he guessed. What was he heading
for—Murray, too? Two old hermits, perhaps, starving together; loving privacy all their lives they have it for bride in
death.

"I think about it sometimes now with a hangover," Murray
said. "Maybe we ought to exchange cards. I have a brother in
Wheeling. That's the only things relatives are for, isn't it—to
look after remains? I don't think we could trust each other to
handle a demise properly. You're too thin now to lift me and
I have the shakes so I'd probably drop your cadaver in the
gutter. Well, cheerio, there's still Schenley's Black Label. Stick
around."

"I'm late for a date," Frederick answered, knowing he was
offending Murray by rejecting his overture, but he had to see
Dodo if he could possibly find her. He did not want to give
away the uncertainty of his engagement by telephoning her

where Murray could witness a possible rebuff. He would go outside to a booth.

"Give Judy my congratulations," he said.

He left Murray silently pouring himself a slug of rye.

18

. . . the brick in the bouquet . . .

FREDERICK liked to think that no matter how much she
ranted against him Dodo did enjoy sharing the outward aspects of his rise. The headwaiter bringing a pencil with the
check as if his picture that week on a magazine cover had
transformed him at once into royalty too fastidious to have
pockets soiled with vulgar cash. Such touching tribute neces-
sitated his paying for whatever friends Dodo brought with
her, and his shock over a two hundred dollar bill from one
restaurant, was almost compensated by her excited approbation. It was something, he thought. It was something that she
boasted about him, too, and carried newspaper clippings
about him to show to strangers, even if it did make him
blush. The poor child, at least, was being her natural self. It
was something that she called him "Freddie" and teased him
with intimate possessiveness in public, even though, alone
with him, she went into sulks and accusations that left him
hopelessly defeated. He found it faintly ironic that she must
remind him not to be kidded by compliments, it was only because he was in the papers. She could not have understood his
horror at the salaams the city made, not to Mind but to the
negotiable evidence of it. The shameless reverence for noto-
riety of any caliber, criminal or cultural, was frightening, the
more so because he could so easily not have been its object.
It was his luck not his work that was esteemed; his horse had
paid off, the slot machine had showered him with gold, and
such robot honors magically changed the man. It seems he
was a wit, a genius, a beau; though no one knew exactly what
wonder he had performed. The exaggerated sum of money
declared as his mental weight was wonder enough. He could
not imagine how he could maintain a decent ego when it was
his luck not his work that was admired. But it helped justify
him to Dodo. Sometimes he marvelled at himself in public
whenever Dodo spotted a Name and artlessly introduced herself, showing clippings of her escort as a ticket of admission,

explaining the finer points of Mr. Olliver's work, what some-one at Harvard had said about it and what she—(very mer-rily)—privately thought about it. He was pleased to be of such use to her, glad to make up in some way for the emo-tional confusion that affected his whole body, glad even to suffer her sudden reversions to vindictiveness.

"You think you're so smart when you're just dull, dull, dull!" she had cried only the night before in the Barrel, "Larry has more brains in his little finger than you have with all your luck. He knows what people like and that's more than you do. You just get all the luck because you know the right people and he doesn't."

It was as if his good fortune had been at the expense of half a dozen worthier rivals and he must atone for it or be accused of pure arrogance.

The night before his penance had been to listen to Larry's idea for the new Hazelnut campaign and to simulate Dodo's enthusiasm over these remarkable inspirations. He did not disagree with Dodo's assertion that he had all the breaks whereas Larry had to fight the whole K.G.R. Agency and the entire tobacco business before he could come into his own. Hadn't Larry originated the idea of an art show, the Con-temporary Masters series (*"There's art in cigarette-making, too, gentlemen!"*), yet some guy at B.B.D.&O. took all the credit. Lone dreamer that he was, unappreciated by his firm (you couldn't call thirty thousand a year appreciation)—he had to go ahead fighting, bravely solacing his wounds with a friendly bonded Scotch, watching the other fellow always get the gravy. As he was about to go, Dodo, moved to tears over the world's injustice to genius, pointed her finger accusingly at Frederick:

"You see what some people have to go through while someone like you gets away with murder just because you know the right people? You ought to be ashamed of yourself acting so smug and superior when Larry has such a hard time."

"Don't go, old man," Frederick urged in desperation, sens-ing the punishment he would receive if left alone with Dodo. "Stay, have another drink."

Wherever he turned it was the same—the winner must

feign humility, thank fools for praise, maintain a sweet temper in the face of bores and insult, expect the brick in the bouquet as his just desert, struggle to conceal his natural shyness and undemocratic tastes. He was obliged to admit to himself that the only place he could relax was at the Ephraim Beckleys' among wealthy dilettantes amiably eager for any new kind of lion. Tyson Bricker, when they met at the League, was too self-assured to acknowledge jealousy, but took a quizzical, patronizing attitude of you-know-and-I-know-old-man-this-is-just-one-of-those-amusing-flukes-and-we-won't-let-it-turn-our-head. Benedict Strafford looked upon him more as bank collateral than person, a testimony to Strafford publishing shrewdness. ("I had such a fine tribute from Lindsay of Chase National," Benedict boasted to Frederick. "'It's men like you, Strafford,' he said, 'who carry the banner of our American traditions of clean mind, and clean body. Let's have more books like *The Treasure.*' And you should have heard the ovation I got in Hollywood!") He rather wistfully hinted at the possibility of siphoning the censored sex in the *Court Lady* film into the abstractions in Frederick's book and making it more of a "property." *Lady*, as the much discussed chronicle of madcap love and youth was now familiarly called, was being filmed with the youthful lovers played by Hollywood's leading off-screen grand-parents, their heady raptures sternly leashed by the Johnson office and arthritis. He spoke of high praise offered everywhere to the talented publisher of *The Treasure* and congratulated the world for perspicacious bestowing of credit. In his brand new sartorial splendor—(a man carrying the banner of American tradition had certain obligations to fashion)—Mr. Strafford was busy as the White Rabbit, consorting with the press, bankers, brokers, politicians, and Palm Beach widows. Olliver? Frederick Olliver? Oh yes, an excellent property.

No wonder Fortune's favorites took to speaking of themselves in the third person, Frederick reflected, for it was the masquerade costume that won the prize, never the person beneath, nor did one ever dare to remove the mask and breathe again.

After Frederick left Murray pouring himself a shot of rye, he hurried over to the Greenwich Avenue drugstore to tele-

phone Dodo. She had told him she had a breakfast date at the
Plaza with an actor from Hollywood who thought she was
much too smart to be just a receptionist, and she ought to be
in Hollywood where a good head was really appreciated. It
was now five o'clock and Frederick wondered bitterly on what
pillow the good head was resting that she hadn't gotten home
yet? But next minute he was thinking the poor child wasn't
really responsible, she deserved what pleasure she could find.
His nickel brought a response this time and he was relieved
that she was in a gay humor.

"I've had champagne all day, Freddie," she giggled. "Now
Tommy and I are looking for a party. Look, he says a friend
of his is invited to the Gaynors' today and I said you knew
them and you could take us there. Will you, Freddie? I
promised him you would so you've got to."

"I'm not invited myself," Frederick said. "I . . ."

"Now, listen, Freddie, you're such an old friend you could
take us there without asking! Don't be such a stinker!"

He was relieved that rumors of his affair with Lyle had
never reached Dodo's ears, suspecting she would be more apt
to claim social privileges from the facts than revenge.

"I really wouldn't dare presume—you see I . . ."

"Alright, don't!" Dodo was angry again. "You're in a position to do anything you like and you're being mean. Alright,
Tommy and I will go some place else! Pooh on you!"

She hung up and he mopped his forehead, in a relief that
he was saved from being pressed into some horrible situation,
even if rescue had come from her wrath not his own courage.
He walked eastward toward Washington Square, his feeling of
humiliation giving way to an unexpected elation. At least he
would not have to suffer a threesome dinner, acting the part
of hell-of-a-fellow, decent extrovert, always happy to share
friends and mistress with any plaid coat and suede footwear
from the West. Good God, what a desert he'd been in, he
thought, how thirsty he was for merely adult minds, what a
world of perpetual juvenilia he had deliberately elected!

He found himself looking in the direction of the Gaynor
apartment, musing that at last he was in a position to enjoy
the kind of company they kept for he had proved himself one
of them, hadn't he? There would be no need to appease or

make apology for others' frustrations; here would be people seasoned and humorously knowledgeable in the ways of worldly approval, banded together, you might say, against the savage enmity of the hungry mob. He wished there was some plausible way of re-opening that door. He longed to exhibit his innocence to Allan, as well as to the group. "My dear fellow, I no longer resent you; in fact I appreciate you fully for the first time and see why your wife could not leave you for another man. See how splendidly I can look you straight in the eye, more honorable than any man present for I am innocent of intentions toward your wife (all the nobler for having been a sinner once)—and am ready to help protect your home against any lusting stranger." To the friends he could indicate his freedom from all the old jealousy—"of course you love her and no reason she should not enjoy your company for she deserves every happiness." And to Lyle he could pay the compliment of asking only for her sweet friendship, adding himself to her list of devoted, undemanding worshipers. He saw himself already in the big, friendly living-room being at ease at last, but the vision of a Frederick gaily chatting with the Gaynor guests faded quixotically into the new Frederick facing the old unhappy Frederick and growing hysterically genial to offset the chilly scorn in the latter's eye. He almost saw himself whispering to Lyle, "Why do you have that fellow scowling around? He acts as if we were all responsible for the doom of civilization, putting down everything we say in his judgment book, he being self-appointed judge just because he's no good at our games? He seems envious of crowns we haven't even won, discontented over failures he hasn't even had. I've done him no harm and my ruin would do him no service." Frederick tried to hold the vignette, tantalized by the picture of the person he once was, inwardly chagrined that it was so grim, hoping for a stranger's glimpse of some grace he never knew he had. All he got was a nostalgic stabbing sensation in his chest, an echo of the ache of desire for Lyle—or had it been only the desire to prove himself superior to her friends and work? He *had* proved superior, come to think of it, but had he proved it to *her*? For a moment an idea tempted him, then he turned his head in the other direction. The whim to test his strength might lead him into embarrassing pitfalls. He would call on the Stalks, instead, he thought, and a moment later was telephoning and being urged by Solange with unexpected warmth to come up at once.

The Stalks lived west of Central Park not far from the Hotel des Artistes in an apartment of sufficient rococo gloom and space to accommodate relations of Solange as fast as they arrived from various corners of Europe. Bald and frowsy heads of all ages popped out of doors down the long corridor as Solange admitted Frederick. He caught the aroma of many diverse highly spiced dishes being stewed or roasted as if many quarrelling palates must be appeased. If Stalk had been any other kind of man the encroachments of his mistress's relatives would have indicated female domination of the worst sort, but his utter preoccupation with affairs of the mind and treatment of his co-household as if they were subway strangers gave him a pedestal not to be assailed. Guests from Russia, Paris, and Germany had crowded him into the front parlor which he occupied as bedroom, study, and reception room. Here nightly political arguments took place, complaints of betrayal by their leaders, the betrayal consisting in tyrants refusing to confine their oppression to minority groups. If Hitler had only pursued his purge of radicals and the unprotected instead of threatening the great middle-class, taking away *our* property—*our* very ideals as it were—the whole war could have been averted. Here Solange led Frederick, two miniature toy poodles and a huge Siamese cat padding along behind. A refectory table, covered with fine yellowed lace, stood in the bay of the ceiling-high front windows, and on it were samovar, percolator, and chafing dishes quietly bubbling beside platters of smoked salmon, kippers, herring salad, red caviar and pastries. This was what he disliked about Europeans (he meant Solange's Europeans)—the obscene worship of food, the groaning tables of indigestibles at all hours, the conviction that full mouth and stomach make for love, gaiety, peace and mutual understanding. Bars inspired brotherly goodwill because there was the implicit sharing of vice whereas the unctuous assumption of saintly virtue in pandering to the belly and storing up juicy treasures for worms made for individual complacency positively dangerous to fellowship.

Solange enjoyed the role of hostess but could not conceal her jealousy of all Edwin's friends and enthusiasms, feeling perpetually cheated that he (as well as all her family) could not be swallowed whole by her. She encouraged his hypochondria as her ally, and her happiness would have been complete if she could have kept him under sedatives in bed, dependent on her for everything—food, opinions, and carefully rationed friends. She was eighteen years older than Stalk and had managed to capture him simply because he had been unprepared for danger from such a quarter. Aside from her relatives she brought to him a *dot* of intimate literary lore gleaned from famous men she claimed as lovers. She candidly boasted of having stolen the young man's virginity while he was under the spell of an extremely absorbing story about Annamites frolicking in Jean Cocteau's closet. She used her reminiscences as the children's photographer uses the birdie and had unpacked her trunks in his apartment, chattering steadily and hypnotically before he realized what was going on, and then he was too indifferent to struggle. She freely confessed that she talked to keep people from noticing her ugliness, though she made up for this disarming modesty by frequent assertions that she could get any man she ever wanted, competing with Hedy Lamarr or any beauty you could name because as Wells (or was it Bennett or Shaw or Stalin or Heinrich Mann or Picasso or Molnar?) had said, she was not mere woman but absinthe (or was it aphrodisiac, marijuana, ambrosia or Dr. Pepper?). Frederick found her more than a little terrifying and wondered if even death would loosen her passionate clutch on Stalk. She had a thin treacherous clown face, long self-absorbed upper lip, narrow wolfish head, thin nose, suspicious black rat eyes set close together betraying a routine of madness and secret hysteria. Light showed through the crevices in her elaborate hairdo, its red far redder than red hair, perhaps, he thought, because she adored blood, its color, perfume and texture. He thought of her as totally dead, needing a lash to feel a feather, vibrating rustily only to Inquisitional tortures, smelling of graveyard flowers, indeed carrying herself like a newly embalmed corpse wound up to live motion by some secret devilish drug. She had mummified herself with self-worship and was forever infuriated that no one else recognized her god, so her black eyes (doll's eyes that clicked back in her head when she lay down, he thought) bubbled and glowed with hatred. He was repelled, even while admitting to a queer drug-like fascination about her, and the luminous opalescent sheen of her skin did give her a ghoulish beauty. He saw with dismay they were to be alone, that not only was Edwin absent but that she shouted down the hall something in Russian that must have meant "Stay out" for the heads immediately popped inside their cells, doors hastily banged shut. He was not reassured by her long ringed fingers remaining on his arm, guiding him to the Victorian loveseat in the darkest corner, where she bade him sit beside her, motioning her pets to sit quietly at her feet, and insuring their obedience by flourishing a box of dog-biscuit.

"I want to see you alone, Frederick," she stated in her hoarse bronchial voice. "I don't want Edwin to know because it is about him I wish to speak. You think I do not like you, perhaps. It is not true. I like you very much. I *wish* to like you much more if you know what I mean. As a friend. Now! Allow me to tell you in secrecy that Edwin is in great, great danger and you must help me."

Frederick fixed his apprehensive gaze carefully on the opposite wall wishing a door would suddenly open and kind demons snatch him off to some safe hell away from what was certain to be embarrassing confidences. And shouldn't he have said, "I like you too or at least about as much as you like me?"

"You are a man of the world, a man of many love affairs, perhaps, while Edwin is a child," Solange said, forcing his eyes back to her with the ferocity of her will-power. "I know him better than he knows himself. I have made him what he is, whether he says it or not. He is a child and a genius. I make him eat coffee and cake when he doesn't know he is eating. If necessary I open his mouth and feed him with the spoon. I have put the very clothes on him when he might forget he was in pajamas in his concentration. I keep the world from nibbling at him. I am all around him, inside, outside, fighting his enemies—he could not reach out a hand without finding me there to help him. It is a terrible struggle for me,

Frederick, against everyone, even Edwin himself. And now comes this disaster that I have only discovered lately. This is how I first knew. Look."

She produced a small volume and held it open at one page for him.

"The Satirical Epigrams of the Greek Anthology," Frederick said, glad to find any remark that did not commit him.

"Yes. We are both very fond of this particular volume and pick it up often. I was reading it only a month or two ago. Now, let me make one thing clear. Edwin has such regard for books that he never underlines a favorite passage. He has notes, perhaps, clipped to the pages, but never does he pencil a line here and there. Never."

Should he say he was very happy to hear this, Frederick wondered?

"When I picked up the book a fortnight ago I found this," her long forefinger indicated a heavily underscored paragraph. "What would you think if you were a woman almost eighteen years older than your lover, Frederick?"

Frederick read the words of Parmenion: *"It is difficult to choose between famine and an old woman. To hunger is terrible but her bed is still more painful. Phillis when starving prayed to have an elderly wife, but when he slept with her, he prayed for famine. So the inconstancy of a portionless son."*

"Does it mean something?" he asked uneasily.

"Two nights later this too was underlined," Solange went on in a choked voice, leafing to another volume. " 'And what is the evening of women? Old age and countless wrinkles,' Macedonus the Consul. Am I really so wrinkled and in my evening, Frederick? Of course, I knew at once there was someone else younger and made it my business to find out who it was. This time, I tell you, it was dangerous. So I ask your help. You must go and explain to her that Edwin Stalk cannot exist without me. This woman must not ruin his life, all his hopes for his future. I am his future. I am Stalk! Edwin is with her this very moment—perhaps in her arms. He seldom comes home till morning, so I am not at all deluded. You know her. You must beg her to give him up, for without me he will have nothing. Her name is . . ."

Frederick had a desperate last hope that he would be spared definite information but Solange was relentless. ". . . Lyle Gaynor."

He seemed to be falling through space, and surely someone had kicked him hard in the stomach, numbing him momentarily to the knife in his chest. Lyle! What in heaven's name had he expected, after all? Was his male vanity so colossal he had actually fancied a woman would be forever true to him through all his other loves? As if he were examining broken bones after the wreck he tentatively put his hand on his heart, trying to diagnose his sharp pain—was it jealous love, unquenchable, or was it shock, outraged ego, perhaps an unsuspected priggishness offended by word of female promiscuity? Whatever it was Solange's next complaint, accompanied by weeping, came to him from some far distant planet. Death, that was what he was experiencing, he decided; he had been on a voyage but the harbor had always been there. Now harbor itself was gone, and he was no longer voyageur but exile.

"Edwin has never believed in marriage," Solange's voice beat against his unwilling consciousness. "I know, because of course many women have tried to get him and I've not been afraid because his ideas are too fixed. Now I am told she is planning to divorce her husband, and marry Edwin."

If the first news had numbed him the last shocked him back to consciousness, and wild anger. Lyle could do this? What about those years of loneliness he had spent, believing in the impossibility of her divorcing Allan? How miraculously he had escaped a whole life under such a delusion! How lucky to have gotten out before the brutal awakening when she would have found no barriers to marrying someone else! The weight of remorse he once experienced at thought of Lyle was blasted by Solange's words and the harsh laugh that echoed through the room seemed to come from that other Frederick, now mocking him.

"You don't believe she wants to marry Edwin?" Solange asked, startled. "You laugh at the idea?"

"I believe it; that's why I'm laughing," Frederick bitterly replied. A thousand horns from Dodo could not have made him burn with outraged pride as this news had done; he could not recover calm to study its authenticity. He wanted to dash out of the house straight to Lyle and accuse her, not of unfaithfulness, but of thieving from his life, deliberately seducing from him his stout armor of cynicism the better for him to suffer, traducing him into belief in her so that pleasures away from her were poisoned by conscience. His indignation mingled with a savage joy in vindication. See, he wanted to cry out to invisible accusers, this is the very treachery I anticipated unconsciously! Can anyone blame me for fortifying myself against it? Solange's ringed hands clung to his hand like a chained falcon's claw and reminded him that Lyle had wronged this splendid woman, as well as Allan and himself.

"Edwin admires and respects you, Frederick," Solange said, her voice rasping with tears controlled. "I would ask you to speak to him but I think it best you go to her. She is so interested in him and in the *Swan*—tell her the best way to help both is to give up, go away. She is a woman of the world—he's not used to anyone like her. An infatuation, if you know what I mean. She has dozens of other lovers. She can turn to them."

"Of course," Frederick agreed, amazed at the fatuous complacency that had never before permitted a doubt of Lyle's fidelity. Being obliged to admit such peaks of masculine vanity heightened his anger, drove him to the other extreme of suspecting a thousand other deceptions.

"Then you will go see her?" asked Solange eagerly, oblivious to the poodles which had leapt to her lap and were tearing at the box of dog biscuit.

"Yes," Frederick said. What was he promising, he asked himself, his head swimming with rage, confusion and Solange's own mesmeric gaze.

Solange gave an exclamation of delight and rose to her feet, the dogs tumbling to the floor.

"And now we'll have a little supper. Hermann! Katya! Natasha! Frieda! You've met them all." He could hear the cages down the hallway opening with happy cries in many languages and reached hastily for his hat, a little afraid that Solange might move him into one of the rooms, lulled into subjugation as Stalk had been.

"But you must not leave now that we are such friends, for we are, aren't we?" protested Solange, her hand still clutching his wrist and her little eyes searching his face avidly for some clue to his feeling.

"I want to plan how best to help," he explained, lamely. "I agree that Edwin is too valuable to risk his going off the deep end this way. I want to think for a little while."

He ran out of the house as if he were scrambling out of a pit and started walking at a furious pace through the Park. At first he had a burning desire to face Lyle with her crime which grew uglier whichever way he looked at it. He had credited her with loyalty to Allan, a loyalty he had been obliged to bear, too, but the truth was she had only been waiting for the right man. He, Frederick Olliver, had not been considered as worthy as Edwin Stalk, that was all.

"Stalk, good God!" Frederick mocked. "Stealing him from the dead, you might say. What kind of man is he, anyway, to be dominated by that witch for years? So Lyle thinks a zombie is worth getting a divorce for!"

How gullible he had been not to have seen all this as inevitable! Thirty-seven years old and as naïve as a child. He asked himself if there was any hope of his ever learning, if age and experience could ever teach one anything but to pretend they did.

19

. . . Sunday-School for Scandal . . .

THE coolness between those bosom friends Lorna Leahy and
Caroline Drake was a great inconvenience to both of them
and stemmed from nothing more than a fortnight on the
wagon which gave them the opportunity to dispassionately
observe unpleasant traits in each other. Caroline had listened
with seeming sympathy to Lorna's tirade about Judy Dahl's
Hazelnut prize, the injustice of an amateur (call it Fine Arts,
if you liked, it was sheer Communism!)—getting more kudos
than a hard-working professional—the years Lorna had
worked to perfect her technique only to be by-passed by a
clumsy whippersnapper with pull!—(Judy Dahl had slept with
the judges, of course she had!) At the end Caroline had said
with a maddening, dreamy smile, "You know I always liked
that kid!" which sent Lorna off in a dumb rage. Then Caroline
had staged a series of silverware demonstrations at the Waldorf,
hiring actors and stage directors to put on luncheons, cocktail
parties, buffet suppers and so on to demonstrate the proper
use of silver and glassware. She had suggested Lorna sketch
these affairs for the trade, with the horrid result that Lorna
Leahy got all the credit with her picture looking like Freddy
Bartholomew printed in *Home Styles*, and not a word about
Caroline Drake.

"I expected that," Caroline said to Gerda, "but imagine her
never even thanking me for the publicity!"

She gave a large party for the express purpose of leaving
out Lorna, and when Lorna made grieved reproach later she
replied heartily, "Oh, but you hate my friends so much I was
sure you'd be bored silly!" Lorna retaliated by telephoning a
glowing report of her box party at Carnegie and laughing, "I
would have invited you but I know how you *loathe* music!"
They were too civilized, thank goodness, for open quarrels,
contenting themselves with a little friendly candor about
wrong choice of hats, food, doctors, dressmakers, and words,
when they did meet ("It's *regardless*, Caroline, not *irregard-*

less," Lorna said gently. Caroline huffily replied that *regardless* was a footless, weak word and got you nowhere, that on the other hand you threw in the word *irregardless* and won any argument hands down. She added that there were a lot of people going around New York saying *regardless* who couldn't make the living she could with all her ignorance). Tacitly they agreed on the definition of the word "climber," which as they now secretly applied it to each other meant "a person enjoying the company of others besides one's self."

Between unsatisfactory meetings they telephoned each other of small triumphs;—Lorna had lunched at *Le Pavillon*, Caroline had moved up two on her firm's vice-president list, Lorna had four marvelous invitations for this week-end in the country, Caroline was buying a Packard black-market, Lorna had a terrible time with a total stranger telephoning obscene proposals to her (she couldn't imagine where he'd heard about her!)—Caroline had drunk *fundador* all night with that gorgeous Spanish poet and goodness only knows what happened. Naturally nothing was as annoying as the preference each exhibited for insincere flatterers who praised her virtues to an honest friend who could point out her faults. Lorna described the thrill of going to Sammy's in the Bowery, how really sordid she found it personally but "of course *you* would have loved it!" Caroline retired for a few days' rest after this *coup*, explaining when Lorna eventually telephoned that she'd been doing the town with Benedict Strafford, the publisher, having been inspired to tie up his *Court Lady* book—you know the one the censors fussed over—with a *Court Lady* silver design.

"You *would* think of that!" Lorna replied plaintively, adding in a voice close to tears, "I've wanted to meet Benedict Strafford for ages. Honestly, Caroline, I don't see why you don't let *me* meet people like that?"

Caroline was familiar with this reaction, but determined not to be taken in by it this time. "Why don't you let me meet So and So," from Lorna indicated no interest or sympathy but was a sort of animal cry, meaning "Why aren't these people thrown to me for nourishment? I want to see how different they are from your unperceptive description. I want to see what there is about them I wouldn't like. I want to see how wrong you are in believing they like you. I want to sit with my lip curled preparing my future criticism while they do the awful things I was positive they would do. Oh, do let me meet them that I may tear them to pieces!" No, Caroline thought regretfully, she would not be wheedled by her clever friend into giving her such advantage, but on the other hand nothing was much fun without the mulling it over with an old friend later. Supposing it was true that Lorna, regarded soberly and dispassionately, was a vain, hypocritical, super-rayfeened bitch; had these shortcomings prevented them from having twenty years of good times together? Maybe it was the difference in their faults rather than the similarity in their virtues that bound them together. You seldom noticed good qualities in a close friend anyway; you took them for granted and used your eyes to pick out the flaws. Caroline, finding the maintenance of a grudge much against her easy-going nature, and having accumulated a cumbersome stock of secrets, threw caution to the winds and invited Lorna to come over and meet Mr. Strafford for Sunday breakfast. Lorna at once demurred, most aggravatingly, saying she was booked so far ahead and for this Sunday had promised to go driving out in the country with Gerda and a wealthy friend, but—well— she did hate disappointing Gerda's friend but—well—since she had only accepted *tentatively*—yes, she would do her best as a favor to Caroline to come for breakfast. Now, pondered Caroline, how could she produce Mr. Strafford, for their relations were not nearly as cozy as she had led Lorna to believe. Being a sound business woman, however, Caroline set to work on the technique of promotion and contact. She telephoned the business manager of a magazine which was waiting eagerly for her store to enlarge its advertising appropriation and asked ("this is purely social, Tom," she explained) if they would not be interested in a future article on Benedict Strafford, the great publisher. Tom declared nothing gave him more pleasure than to do her this personal favor, showing he liked her as a human being not just as a prospect. He was astonished that the magazine's editorial department had been too dumb to think up the idea, and he would push it right through. Murray Cahill had once done features for them so Caroline suggested the interview be assigned to him. This

also seemed a perfect inspiration. Caroline then contacted
Murray, advised him to contact Tom, then contacted Mr.
Strafford with the flattering news that *People* wanted to feature him as Man of the Week, and wouldn't it be pleasanter if
he met the interviewer at her apartment for a quiet little
Sunday breakfast? Mr. Strafford was enchanted at the fresh
evidence of public appreciation, thanked her profusely, and
Caroline with a sigh of satisfaction laid in enough Bourbon
and sausages to accommodate the greediest Sunday school
class. She had looked forward to propitiating Lorna by providing an intimate little foursome, just the two ladies and the
two beaux but at noon Murray called up and asked if he
might bring Judy Dahl, the reason being that she was coming
down with flu and apparently would be enormously improved
and cheered by passing around the germs.

"That fixes it!" groaned Caroline after polite cries of pleasure. "Lorna will be furious to see Judy and will catch the flu
from her besides!"

She provided herself with an invigorating ounce of medici-
nal spirits before adding a fifth place to her attractive table,
wondered whether she dared telephone Lorna and confess
the dilemma, decided that the best thing was to round up another man as buffer for possible quarrels, telephoned several
Extra Men, extricated herself as deftly as possible on finding
that each Extra Man was inevitably equipped with two or
more Extra Women, all happy to come, decided to let bad
enough alone, and hoped at least that Lorna would descend
from the wagon long enough to be human. The lateness of
her guests gave her time to think about Benedict Strafford,
and she speculated on why he had never married. Either he
had a convenient little nest somewhere in the wilds of Staten
Island (some peasant type unsuitable for marriage), or was a
confirmed sporting-house type (probably sneaked up to
Harlem or Chinatown the way so many of those intellectual
men did, never guessing that any lady of their own class had
a similar apparatus), or he might be as Padilla insisted, a well-
integrated fairy. She could question Frederick Olliver about
this except that she sometimes had similar suspicions about
him. Padilla, of course, suspected everybody, proclaiming that
it was not the fighters but the Four F's who had won the war

with their five years to slip into the absent 1-A boss's shoes. Padilla declared that our boys had returned to find the whole Horatio Alger democratic system of economics shifted;—the bright young man no longer got the job by marrying the boss's daughter but by sleeping with the boss himself. A funny idea, Caroline had to admit, and that led to wondering if Padilla's own excessive lady-killing wasn't a sign of "protesting too much"? A pity amusing men were invariably on the wrong side socially or physically or financially—Padilla being possibly all three. Good heavens, she thought in consternation, what kind of an age is this anyway where a woman suspects a man of disguised homo tendencies just because he wants to sleep with every woman he meets? Those big football-playing he-men must have started that sort of rumor to justify their own disappointing performances. The arrival of Benedict Strafford at half-past one put an end to these maiden reveries and introduced a new problem for he had taken the liberty—he was sure Miss Drake would forgive him—of bringing a lady friend, none other in fact than little Miss Dodo who had heard so much of Miss Drake's wonderful parties he could not refuse her plea to be brought along.

"Of course we have met before but only in crowds," Dodo cried.

Caroline vaguely recalled the new guest as someone who was always being brought places by men who didn't know her last name, and other guests were always stumbling on her hugging their husbands in back hallways, giving her telephone number to gentlemen without pencils, or emerging from dark terraces demurely soignée with bewildered gentlemen all tousled and rouge-smeared. The young lady was darting eagle eyes about Caroline's apartment as if memorizing the terrain for future strategy, and Caroline determined immediately to keep all possible hiding spots locked. There was something ominous, Caroline thought, in the business-like way the girl stripped off her long black gloves in the bedroom, removed her large black crownless hat deftly, tightened the wide fancy belt of her rose-printed black silk, and patted her sleek black hair, as if "*Now!* Get in there and start punching!" Damn these cagey bachelors, Caroline thought, always so scared to go anyplace alone!

"This young lady is a friend of the chap who's coming to interview me," Benedict explained, rubbing his hands happily at sight of the large room with the May sunshine glittering over breakfast table and fine bar. "My, what a beautiful view you have here!"

"I've known Murray Cahill for just ages!" exclaimed Dodo. "He's one of mother's oldest friends in Baltimore! They graduated together."

"How sweet!" Caroline said, wishing with a burst of the old affection that Lorna could have been there to hear about Murray being "one of *mother's* oldest friends," and giving a quick critical survey of Baby's neck and chin with the satisfactory conclusion that Mummy must have graduated at the age of nine to have a daughter this mature. It appeared that Dodo had just accidentally acquired Mr. Strafford an hour previously at a public broadcast sponsored by the League for Cultural Relations, (Mr. Tyson Bricker, presiding) where he had discussed "Can the Post War Generation Be Taught to Read." As publisher of *The Treasure* Mr. Strafford had voiced an enthusiastic affirmative and highest hopes for the young people, only shaken in the Question Period by Dodo's asking what made him so sure any member of the Post War Generation had ever read or purchased *The Treasure*.

"She had me there," Mr. Strafford confessed to Caroline, chuckling ("He would have strangled any female his own age piping up with that" Caroline thought), "so I had to bring her along to think up an answer."

It was refreshing to see that the arrival of Judy Dahl with Murray eclipsed Miss Dodo temporarily. Mr. Strafford had a literary man's curiosity about feminine workers in the graphic arts, and Judy looked her part. The childish lack of make-up, careless blonde hair, stubby nails, scuffed shoes, faded "Levis" and blue sport shirt struck the right tone for Artist-Too-Successful-To-Give-a-Damn, hinted at many summers on fashionable beaches snubbing the Bourgeoisie, and made Dodo and Caroline look like suburban respectability. Naturally, the impression Judy made might have been less interesting if no one had heard of her prize, but this gave her curt manners the charm of a royal snub and her monosyllabic replies the weight of epigrams. Lorna will be positive I invited her just for spite, Caroline thought, and began wishing the phone would ring saying Lorna was on her way to the country after all. Still she did need Lorna to hold her own against these too fortunate younger women. If she was to be forced into the Chaperon's corner it would be less mortifying if Lorna were there alongside her. Since she had been mistakenly inspired to show off her own cooking the maid Johanna was not present and the extra guests obliged Caroline to stay in the kitchen stretching the omelette with more tomatoes, watercress, mushrooms, while Murray acted as bartender. Very happy he was, too, in these duties, for he could drown out with fierce rattlings of the shaker Caroline's tactless shouts about Gerda, and Strafford's pompous compliments to "our charming little artist here." One of the most sordid demonstrations of masculine opportunism, Murray found, was the way men clustered around Judy Dahl now, and he was put to it as an old friend to keep her head from being turned. If he had not reluctantly invited her to come along today a couple of other guys would have asked her out and he couldn't get it into her thick little head that all they wanted when they flattered her about her painting was to get her in bed. Judy did not worry at all over their sincerity; at least it blackmailed Murray into taking her out with him as if they were any married couple. Maybe Caroline Drake was one of his women and probably Dodo at one time or other, but at least she, Judy, was the one he had brought today. Quite content, Judy folded her legs under her on the white leather sofa and applied herself earnestly to a perusal of *Life* magazine, emerging from this trance only when Murray shouted with cold exasperation, "Judy, you're being spoken to!"

"I was merely asking if you saw the Peter Blume exhibition at the Durlacher Galleries," Benedict Strafford was saying, so taken with the charming little artist's no doubt typical artist ways, that Dodo felt aggrieved and flounced over to tinker sulkily with the small ivory piano.

"No," Judy answered, adding loquaciously for Murray's benefit, "I don't go to exhibitions any more."

Mr. Strafford was enchanted.

"You make it sound as if you'd outgrown dolls!" he chortled. "Delightful!"

"Judy only means that now she's a big enough artist to ignore her contemporaries," Murray said, adding morosely as he poured a daiquiri into the publisher's greedy goblet, "They always get that way. It's 'Me and Michelangelo but not Me and my rivals.' "

"A wonderful career for a lady," Mr. Strafford said, beaming paternally at the young lady's healthy bosom as emphasized by her open shirt. "Painting is so much more suitable for them than writing, pardon me for saying so. Women who write all day have a theory they have to talk all night, and of course the training in finishing their sentences absolutely spoils them for any interruption. Oh, I have many brilliant women on my list but I've often thought how much pleasanter for everyone if they'd just gone off in the woods and painted quietly. However did you begin, dear child?"

"Representationalism," Judy answered, biting into an apple from the table's centerpiece since she was very hungry and the sizzling of sausages on the kitchen stove had only just begun. "Like everybody."

"Of course, of course," Benedict nodded sympathetically.

"I'm in my intermediate period right now," Judy amplified not sure whether Murray's frown meant she was talking too much or too little or merely to the wrong person.

Dodo had been revenging herself by poking out *"Cha Ta"* on the keys with one finger as if she was prodding a drowsy trick elephant that might bellow satisfactorily with due stimulation. This display of musicianship failing to attract attention she added vocal power not at all deterred by ignorance of the lyrics.

"She had 'em, she had 'em," she chanted, "Dum dum dum de dum."

"I hate to bring up business before breakfast," Caroline shouted from the kitchen, "but why don't you two boys decide on what angle you want in this article?"

"Any suggestions, Strafford?" Murray inquired in a hostile voice, significantly frowning at the arm the gentleman had casually placed across the back of Judy's seat.

"What—oh—er—" Strafford closed his eyes to down his third daiquiri at a gulp. ("A lush," thought Murray with the stern contempt of one drinker for another.) "I—let me see, now. To be quite frank with you I'm sometimes referred to in the trade as a human dynamo."

"Oh, Murray, that's *cute*!" cried Dodo, quite bowled over by the expression and jumping to her feet. "You *know* it's cute, Murray, it's so absolutely right! Admit it, now!"

"Can't you leave that damned magazine alone?" Murray answered, snatching *Life* and her apple from Judy's hands. At this moment the shock of the door-bell ringing caused a sudden crash in the kitchen, Murray's gesture knocked Judy's drink into the publisher's lap, and with a silvery sweet halloa Lorna thrust her gray curls coquettishly in the door.

"I'm late—I know I'm late," she crooned, allowing Caroline's warm kiss to fall somewhere midair, "but look at the wonderful surprise! Look, Caroline, Lyle Gaynor! She was going to drive Gerda and me out to Cobb's Mill for the day but Gerda's sick so here we are!"

"They'll all have to eat on their laps," decided Caroline with a rueful glance at her beautiful table, and began her introductions. "Lorna, this is Dodo—er—anyway she's one of Murray's mother's oldest friends, and Mrs. Gaynor—that's right, you two must know each other through Frederick Olliver—and this is Judy Hazelnut—oh dear, Mr. Strafford, let me mop you up, did something get upset?"

20

. . . the baby skin . . .

As Caroline told Lorna later she was so rattled by the way her party was going that she didn't know the difference between Lyle Gaynor and Eleanor Roosevelt. All she did know was that the wrong people were being thrown with the wrong people at the wrong time and there was nothing she could do about it, so she simply decided to have a good time and the hell with everybody else. She was grateful for her divine gift of making her mind a complete blank which she did as soon as she grasped the full horror of the Dodo girl (of course, now she recalled she was Frederick Olliver's private cutie)— flinging herself upon Lyle Gaynor (what was that tale about Lyle and Frederick she'd heard?)—and squealing, "Lyle Gaynor, just the person I've wanted to know better! I'll bet you don't remember the time Freddie Olliver introduced us at the Ephraim Beckleys' party. Did Freddie ever tell you how thrilled I was at meeting the author of *Summer's Day*? I've been dying to know you ever since. Do let's sit over here and talk."

Lorna, for her part, later recollected that at this moment her great prize, Mrs. Gaynor, had looked desperately around for help, had backed toward the door and then had given her, Lorna, a look from those lovely hazel eyes of such profound reproach that Lorna couldn't think for the life of her what she had done. Mind you, Lorna had not had to urge her to come along; she had just had a funny hunch there at Gerda's that Mrs. Gaynor was blue. God knows a woman like that wouldn't be leaving her own crowd for Gerda's crazy set-up unless she was in a pretty low state of mind about something. Lorna hadn't known Dodo would be there and all she knew about Lyle and Olliver was that there had been whispers, but no one was sure. So she hadn't noticed what was wrong at first. Anyway she had been too amused at Murray's trying to keep Mr. Strafford away from Judy, at the same time dying to find out who was staying with Gerda and if she was really sick this time. Trust a man to never want anything to fall through his mitts! Of course Lorna had been a little disappointed in Benedict Strafford, she told Caroline, for he was not at *all* what Caroline had described; much older than she had imagined and utterly and completely bald.

"I love him for it!" Caroline had cried. "Men getting bald is the only thing God ever did for women. It evens things a little bit."

Strafford being acquainted with Lyle had saved the situation for a moment and kept Dodo from jumping right on Lyle's lap. Without realizing what was going on, both Lorna and Caroline could see (hours later) that Lyle was in the awful position of fending off that always unwelcome deference to age from tactless youth. You would have thought from Dodo's manner that Lyle was grandma in a lace cap, and no matter how she tried to duck her the kid clung to Lyle like Death itself. It was because there wasn't any man for her to grab. She was going to get something out of this occasion, Dodo was; if it wasn't a new man it would be a new name.

"You should have heard our broadcast this morning, Mrs. Gaynor," babbled Strafford. "Do you know Tyson Bricker told me afterwards I had a first-rate microphone personality? There was some talk of being on a regular weekly program, literary quiz sort of thing. You theatrical people aren't the only ones, ha ha!"

"Tyson said he was much better than Ephraim Beckley," Dodo eagerly contributed. "And Freddie Olliver was simply awful when he was on—he hardly said a word and you couldn't even hear him. I'll bet you get hundreds of fan letters, Mr. Strafford."

Mr. Strafford stroked his left cheek, reflecting on this with judicious modesty.

"I don't know. I confess I had a moment or two of what you call 'mike fright.' I'm afraid I committed the unpardonable sin of ending several declarative sentences with prepositions," he confessed, ruefully. "I may be caught up on that by the radio audience, eh, Mr. Cahill?"

Mr. Cahill sourly assured him that the radio audience did not care whether a sentence ended in a preposition or a rout. He added, shaking up a fresh batch of daiquiris, that the

speech had probably made a pleasant obbligato to all the nation's papas spelling out the Sunday funnies to their howling
young. Mr. Strafford decided to consider this very amusing,
exclaiming to Judy that here was a most delightful chap, certain to be a crackerjack journalist if he took up residence in
New York, and how strange he had not met him before.

"He's lived here with Frederick Olliver for years," Judy
said, reaching for a pear but giving up at Murray's coldly disapproving eye. "Olliver never introduces people to other
people, that's all."

"Will you pipe down?" Murray muttered menacingly.

Mr. Strafford looked again at Murray, this time with less
enthusiasm, concluding with an old New Yorker's cynicism,
that anyone around for years that he hadn't met after a lifetime of circulating was probably not worth meeting anyway.
Murray's pointed statement that Lorna Leahy, too, was an
artist, made Mr. Strafford affirm once more his interest in the
brush. He asked Lorna, poised elfishly on a footstool before
him, if she, as an older professional, was not excited over the
fine new talent turned up by Hazelnut's art show? He gave
Judy's knee a fatherly pat, absently allowing his plump hand
to rest there as he waited for Lorna's considered opinion.

"Don't let's pay any attention to them. They're talking
art," Dodo urged Lyle, conducting her to the piano bench.
"You know that suit is awfully smart, I really mean that. You
know I hear lots about you from people at Paramount, people from Hollywood. Do you know Tommy Ramus? Do you
know Alfred Sutter? Do you know Archie Bleisher? I've heard
about those wonderful parties you have."

"Thank you," Lyle said helplessly, feeling herself reddening
under Dodo's curious inspection, suspecting she must be
looking badly to have Dodo compliment her, for the girl was
no one to make up to a more alluring female. Had Frederick
confessed his former love, Lyle wondered nervously, and was
Dodo trying to be nice to a defeated rival? Or had he never
told and was her pointed attention sheer coincidence? Either
theory hurt.

"You and I are the only ones that don't care about art,"
Dodo whispered, and to demonstrate their solidarity she applied her kerchief to dusting an infinitesimal speck from Lyle's

shoulder. "I'm going to get myself a suit, too. I think nothing looks nicer. Where do you have your hair done? Do you see why they're making such a fuss over that artist girl? If I'd known this was going to be such a dumb party I wouldn't have come at all. I just came to spite a boyfriend of mine. I just want him to find out I don't need to wait for him to introduce me to his friends. Is your apartment modern like this?"

Now that she was caught in this jam Lyle had to face the fact that she had secretly wanted to meet Dodo during the shameless year of pursuing Frederick's new life. Yes, she had to admit that she had prayed for a chance to see the girl away from him so that she might study what magic she herself had lacked. But Dodo's unexpected overtures left her confused and speechless. The girl had no business appealing to her, she thought hotly. If she didn't guard herself she would be advising Frederick's preference in clothes and perfume just because she was a fool in love, ready to accept anyone the lover (even decamping) loved. She stiffened, however, at Dodo's presumptuous hands twitching, tweaking, and clutching her in friendly possessiveness. After all she was not old or plain enough to be liked by a rival! She steeled herself to hate Dodo. Everything about the Pooh-girl was repulsive to her— the pointer's nostrils, the sleek, taut little body squirming proudly in its sheath, the coarse pomaded black hair and tiny ears, the indefinable animal quality, an invisible hairiness about her, the even white squirrelish teeth, the slender, long-nailed hands, forever caressing her hair, hips, waist. The singsong nasal Southern baby voice offended her even if what it said had not done so. These unfavorable observations should have a tonic effect, Lyle told herself, and should help her to forget a lover with so little discrimination.

"I wish my hair was red," Dodo was saying generously, belying the compliment by complacently stroking her own smooth black coiffure. "It wouldn't suit me the way it suits you. I don't see why Murray and Mr. Strafford pay so much attention to that goon when you're a lot better-looking. I really mean that."

Lyle thought this would be cruelty in a clever woman but must be pity in Dodo's case. She gave a start at the unexpected touch of Dodo's little hands at her throat.

"What a marvellous scarf—!" Dodo gushed. "I've been looking for that shade of turquoise; it looks like a spider web."

"Do keep it," Lyle said, loosening the gossamer material, as if it already choked her, "I never liked it."

"Oh, really, now, Mrs. Gaynor! I *love* it. Even if it doesn't go with my dress! What *is* that wonderful perfume?"

"*Je reviens*," said Lyle.

"Murray, why don't you take Benedict into the bedroom for your interview," Caroline shouted, pushing a teawagon of breakfast remains into the kitchen. "If you wait too long you'll both be too high and don't forget, I'm responsible for this piece. It'd better be good so I can get special rates out of *People*."

"So I'm part of a deal, well, well! Glad to be considered so valuable," laughed Benedict.

"With these career-women everybody's part of a deal," Murray growled, unable to keep from snapping at somebody even though Caroline was the only one present who did not annoy him. "God, how I hate them!"

"I beg your pardon, Mr. Cahill?" his hostess remarked frigidly.

As Caroline had loaned him hundreds of dollars over a period of years and had only half an hour before slipped two twenties in Murray's pocket she felt justified in giving him a fruity wedge of her mind. She stated icily that nowadays men wanted a woman to work but not to be too good at her job— just good enough to pay her own way and not bright enough to add up what men owed her, not bright enough to see when she was getting a bum deal; they wanted her clever enough to admit his brains and ability when he shot his trap over world affairs but not bright enough to realize it was the liquor bought by her salary that was loosening his tongue. In fact men used the term "career-woman" to indicate a girl who made more than he did and who was unforgiveably good at her job when he was not able to hold one. Having thus cleared the air Caroline rushed over to Murray contritely and kissed him for she knew he couldn't help being a porcupine when he wasn't working, the old dear!

"Now you two get in there and get to work!" she ordered,

ashamed of her outburst. "That leaves us a hen party but all the better, isn't it, girls?"

The belligerence of her question made Lorna declare that she loved nothing more than a good old hen party, and besides it was the first chance she'd had to talk to Judy since her prize. ("Good Heavens! Now what?" Caroline groaned apprehensively.) There were so many things they had to talk over since they both had studied with Miller and both knew Larry Glay at Hazelnut, a darling as ever was. Lorna said roguishly that she, for one, was not at all surprised when Judy got the prize because she had heard Larry rave about Judy's figure and complexion. Dodo's face had brightened at the first mention of Larry Glay, and she leaned forward ready to shine with inside information if knowing Larry was the key to popularity. But Lorna's "tradelast" for Judy made her sink back with an expression stricken and incredulous. Lyle, observing the change, looked around for the cause. Dodo sat frozen, swallowing the rum collins Caroline now produced as if her throat hurt her. Staring fixedly into space she said presently in a strained voice, "Everytime I go around in any old thing then everybody else is all dressed up so I feel silly. Then when I'm all dressed up nobody else is. New York is so funny that way. Sometimes I wish I'd never come."

"Is that the only thing you have against us?" Lyle asked, thinking how strange that she could not repeat this minor tragedy to Frederick who would have found it amusing, once. The girl's lip was actually quivering.

Dodo stared balefully at Judy who was sitting cross-legged on the sofa, streaked ashen lock falling across her face, stolidly munching an apple as she listened to Lorna. Occasionally she grunted an answer.

"Larry Glay simply raves over your baby skin," Lorna was again declaring.

"You never can tell what men are likely to go for in this town," Dodo burst forth, her brows knitting unhappily. "There just isn't any point. You could read *Harper's Bazaar* and *Vogue* all day long and still you couldn't tell. I just hate men. New York men, I mean. This dress cost eighty dollars but I might as well have come here in shorts. I wish I had."

She whipped out her compact and painted her lips savagely,

pausing and slowly replacing the unnecessary lipstick as if reproached by the sight of Judy's pale mouth. She tied Lyle's scarf carefully in a new bow, and this appeared to restore her confidence. Caroline, having efficiently placed her dishes in the washer with loud protestations of needing no help, came back in the room and seeing that the hen party was pairing off poured herself a drink and nipped slyly into the bedroom to join the men, raising her voice from time to time in such happy howls of glee that the ladies looked up jealously.

"Caroline just loves a hen party," Lorna tinkled, "for other women, that is."

The suspicious quality of the ladies' merriment reaching Caroline squashed her own glee, allowing her a good guess as to who the victim of the unheard joke might be.

"You see what I mean," Dodo went on to Lyle, endeavoring to sound calm. "A man takes you to a party and then starts making passes at somebody else. If you call *that* a baby skin! I just don't get it."

Quite mystified Lyle followed Dodo's jealous eyes again to Judy who had risen and was blowing her nose with artistic fervor. What could Dodo be talking about? Whatever its cause there was no mistaking the sincerity of her emotions for she had difficulty controlling her voice and her twitching lips. Certainly it had nothing to do with Frederick Olliver or even Strafford. It must be, Lyle concluded, that Dodo was pathologically jealous of every other female any man admired. She studied Judy too, wondering why Judy gave no sign of having met her before, then remembered they had never exchanged more than a cool nod, even though they knew all about each other. She watched furtively for some sign of astonishment on Judy's, Lorna's, Caroline's face at seeing her and her successor in a confidential huddle and felt a pang of dismay that they showed no surprise. It was one thing to have conducted an affair with such discretion that no one knew when it was over, and she had been grateful that Frederick had meticulously observed the rules she had laid down. But now she was the only person who could remember that there had been love and for her would always be. She should have mistrusted a love that was not stronger than a gentleman's code; she wished with all her heart that he had shouted her name in all the bars, confessed his love to every passing stranger. It would have made the memory less a dream, and she would not be cursed with the dreadful doubt that she had ever been important to him. Waves of shame for her own stingy caution came over her, for it had been she who dictated the terms, and the day had come when she wanted heavenly forgiveness for cowardice in her sinning more than worldly approval of her virtue. There was a stinging implication, too, in Murray Cahill's casual treatment of her, that he considered her only one of many women in Frederick's life. Ominous above all was Dodo's singling her out for special friendship. A woman in love could always sense a rival, predecessor or possible successor—when it was important. She had not been important, face it, that must be it. Dodo, if she sensed anything, evidently dismissed her. How humiliating to inspire no jealousy in a rival—and how bitterly revealing!

"I have a friend in Baltimore who's a better painter than anybody around here, and everybody who knows anything about art says so," Dodo confided in a low tone. "Of course he's a man so I don't suppose that old lecher in there would like him. That's another reason I hate men. You're the only person here I like. I knew I'd like you but Freddie Olliver would never take me to any of your parties. I came here today just to spite him, he's always going on so about Caroline Drake's apartment but oh no, I can't come here. And oh no, I can't go when he's with his old editors. I can't wait to see his face when I tell him I came to Caroline Drake's with Benedict Strafford and met you here, besides! I think I'll call him up right now. Only then I'd have to have dinner with him and I'd never get rid of him. You know how he is, always wanting you to himself, so you can't have any fun."

"I've always admired his work," Lyle said weakly.

"Oh, *that!* I'll tell him you said so," Dodo said, glumly, and then clapped her hands in inspiration. "I know what. I'll pretend you made me jealous then I can have an excuse for ditching him. I feel too blue to be stuck with him all Sunday evening. If he'd take me to a party, it would be all right, but oh no he thinks he's so interesting I have to have him all alone! Don't you hate men like that?"

For this Frederick had left her, Lyle thought, with mounting fury. No wonder he hid from her, knowing as he surely must, how wasted his new love was. She could not listen longer to the little monster who had elected her ear for confession. She was afraid she might cry out in indignation. ("How dare you not love my lover who loves you more than he does me?") She was saved by Benedict Strafford suddenly springing out of the bedroom door looking on the verge of apoplexy. He had his hat in his hand and made a stiff, unsmiling bow in the doorway, carefully avoiding a direct look at Judy.

"Thank you, thank you very much, Miss Drake," he said formally. "Thank you all and good day!"

"I'll drop you," Lyle said, leaping up.

"But—" began Caroline. He sidled out the door skittishly as if he expected or had just received a sound kick in the seat. Lyle followed him exclaiming, "I'm sorry but I must drive Mr. Strafford home. Do excuse me."

The flight left Caroline's jaw agape. "What'd I do to her, for God's sake," she wailed. "Murray, what happened?"

"I told the old goat off," Murray said, coolly as the outer door banged. "Who does he think he is, anyway? Human Dynamo! Caroline, for God's sake, where do you find people like that? I'm damned if I waste my time building him up, even if I do need the dough. Pawing women!"

"If Judy ever buttoned up her shirt he wouldn't have pawed her," Caroline shouted, exasperated. "Blame her for not wearing a brassière, don't blame me. *I* didn't ask her here to put her dirty little shoes on my white sofa!"

"Come on, you little idiot, don't you know when you've been insulted?" Murray yanked Judy to her feet and toward the door, his round boyish face flushed with indignation. "Let's get out of this."

"Take the service elevator or you'll run into them," Caroline called out, furiously, then turned on Dodo who was looking wide-eyed. "What? Haven't you been insulted yet? Am I losing my grip?"

"What did she say to Mrs. Gaynor?" Lorna wailed. "Caroline, I feel so *responsible!* Did Dodo say something to upset her?"

Dodo rose.

"Listen, Lyle Gaynor is a friend of mine," she said haughtily. "If she goes I go. Besides, I don't want to get mixed up in other people's fights."

"That's just fine! Here's your hat," approved Caroline shrilly and barely two minutes later she was pouring a pair of very stiff ones, indeed, handing one to Lorna. With a huge groan she kicked off her shoes, collapsing on the sofa, hand over eyes. Lorna sprawled cozily in a big chair with an equally weary sigh.

"I don't know why it is men never get insulted till they've finished your dinner or your liquor or your pocketbook," Caroline whimpered, and suddenly tears streamed down her face, making white ruts in her thick tropical make-up. "We're just a pair of soft-headed old career women, Lorna, you and me. Well, here's to us!"

In no time at all they were embarked on four weeks' worth of pent-up confidences. Lorna told Caroline what she liked best about her was her marvellous flair for parties. Alright, supposing guests did quarrel, it was never boring, and she almost died laughing when Caroline came out with that crack about not having invited Judy. Of course the girl was alright, Lorna had nothing against her. Caroline generously replied that she thought Judy was awful and never the artist that Lorna was, but since Lorna liked her she would try not to be too hard on the kid. She added that as far as she was concerned the only nice thing about the party was Lorna being so sweet as to bring Lyle Gaynor. Lorna insisted that she deserved no credit, and furthermore, in her opinion, Lyle Gaynor acted stuck-up. Lorna wished to apologize here and now for not asking Caroline's permission first to bring such a wet-blanket. Caroline would not listen to any denigration of any friend of Lorna's even if Lorna herself did the denigrating. She only wondered if Lorna would ever forgive her for introducing that old bore, Benedict Strafford, into her life. She only hoped he wouldn't start persecuting her. Lorna promised that if he ever presumed on the slight acquaintance she would not hold Caroline in any way to blame.

What a satisfaction to have the place to themselves, letting their hair down like old times, clinking glasses, and passing judgment on the recently departed! There was nothing like old friendship, no matter how tried or trying it often was.

Naturally you couldn't love anybody twenty-four hours a day; in fact it was during the periods of coolness that you appreciated your friend the most, and returned with all the more pleasure. Lorna dashed off some sketches of Mr. Strafford that seemed to Caroline at the moment the most brilliant works of genius she had ever seen, and whether Murray did his piece or not she was certain she could sell these drawings to *People*. Lorna said she valued Caroline's artistic criticism more than anyone's, and she would rather appear in *People* than in the Metropolitan Museum. At seven o'clock that evening they were deep in familiar confidences and Lorna had cured Caroline's hiccups by efficiently fixing up a magic concoction of lemon slices soaked in sugar and Worcestershire sauce.

Caroline's amazement and admiration of her friend's unexpected domestic lore was boundless.

"Lorna, what I like about you is you have so many sides to your character," she said with deep feeling. "Who would guess you could cure hiccups! I never even dreamed you were such a home body!"

21

. . . variations on a juke-box theme . . .

The Four Pillars of Rubberleg Square sat at the bar in the Americas viewing their future in the bar mirror and drinking up their past and present. The juke-box was aglow and bursting with joyous booms of *You Won't Be Satisfied Until You Break My Heart*, and whenever it heaved into silence a fragile girl with a Veronica Lake blonde bang drooping over one eye and a blonde fur coat over her shoulders got off the bar stool with great care to extort more jubilation from the obliging instrument. The nickel always dropped on the floor, the coat slipped down, and the bang had to be thrust back in the ensuing search before the same song boomed out again with the girl replacing herself on the bar stool with suspicious care. The Four Pillars had contemplated this routine with placid enjoyment for some time as nothing else had happened since a Labrador retriever brought his master in for a drink then dragged him out precipitately when challenged by little Queenie, the bar cat.

"Don't let that dame horn in on you, ever," warned Rover addressing his friends in the bar mirror as was their custom since they always sat side by side at bars and probably would not have recognized each other face to face. "She drinks beer when she's on her own but stingers when it's on anyone else. I've seen her around. Came from some whistlestop down East to go on the stage."

"Maybe she thinks this is it," said the doctor.

Instead of their usual custom of keeping separate accounts, tonight Dr. Zieman had insisted on being host to the other three and for persuasion produced a remarkable roll of bills with elaborate casualness. Caraway whispered to Marquette his guess that the doctor's wife must have finally sold *Wootsie the Bad Cricket* to Walt Disney for a fat sum; but Marquette had read somewhere that *Wootsie's* little sister, *Betsy the Good Grasshopper* had just been published and Schwarz's toy shop was bringing out the two lovable little insects as a Twin-Toy

sensation. This reminded Rover that his own wife's talents
produced no profit, her present assignment as walk-on or
dance-on, in the Ballet rewarding her (and him) with only a
free backstage view of three productions weekly. ("What do I
get out of watching her get pushed around by a bunch of
fags?" he often complained.) He spoke wistfully of her artistic
heyday when her cat made thirty-five dollars a week in the
Gaynor play, and inquired of the doctor whether the story of
a stage cat wouldn't make a wow of a juvenile book, if he
could only deflect his wife's energies to such a task. This
made Caraway reflect favorably for the first time on the advantages of having a wife and for a moment all four were
silent, contemplating the pleasant prospect of being kept
drunk for years by the kiddies. Everytime the doctor displayed
his roll, gartered with a wide rubber band, Marquette was impelled to avert his face with the curious feeling that he was
spying on Mrs. Zieman's intimate garments, a fancy that for a
moment gave his rye and water a disagreeably woolly taste. In
a little while, however, all three of the doctor's cronies experienced a pleasurably relaxed sense of riches and personal
achievement and moved their stools closer and closer to the
doctor the better to inhale the heady fragrance of folding
money. They ordered Canadian Club instead of bar rye—only
fifteen cents more, what the hell—and this automatically
raised the level of their conversation; they spoke of art. Dr.
Zieman quoted several lines from Gerard Manley Hopkins,
graciously pointing out the sprung rhythm; Marquette gave
an opinion on world affairs and mentioned India; Rover had
new secrets from Brock, Herman, Miriam, Jasper, and Bogey.
The simple bar was transformed into a most exclusive club,
and in compliment to the occasion Mr. Caraway, first trum-
peting the hint that his own reserve had melted by much
nose-blowing and coughing, revealed certain episodes from
his past life. He mentioned summers in Old Cove, Connecticut, a quiet, healthy resort he could recommend to anyone
needing a change of air; i.e. there was a vast difference in the
air of fishingtown saloons from Greenwich Village saloons.
He spoke of having watched the playwright, Mrs. Lyle
Gaynor as a girl, driving her ponycart down the beach-road
with her pale auburn hair flying and all the boys mooning for

her. Prodded by the Pillars he gave the inside story of her romance with Gaynor. "I never have mentioned this and perhaps I shouldn't—" he began hesitantly. Naturally no one could reply that indeed he had mentioned it dozens of times. Besides the familiar anecdote sounded much finer and more intimate than it usually did under less affluent conditions. Mr. Marquette, as if for the first time, was then moved to divulge details of a scandal in Allan Gaynor's earlier life in St. Louis, while his friends exclaimed, "No, you don't say!" as if they had not been fanning their drinks with these same tales many times over. The repetition did serve, however, to bring the two Gaynors closer and closer to the Pillars' lives, and even Dr. Zieman, the only one who had no fingernail hold on these public figures, now referred to "Lyle" and "Allan" and tonight added to the script his opinion that Allan would probably end up losing his mind. At this point the sensibilities of all four were unpleasantly jolted by a mocking laugh from the jukebox girl.

"That's all you know about it," she said, tossing back the fair locks. "Don't you worry about Allan Gaynor's mind. Allan Gaynor happens to be alright. I happen to know Allan Gaynor personally and I can tell you right here and now that he happens to have more brains than you four creeps put together."

The Pillars could not have been more startled if Gaynor himself had popped up behind them, though the chances were that they would not have recognized him in spite of their boasted acquaintance with him. Rover catching the doctor's eye in the mirror, lifted a wry eyebrow, Mr. Marquette and Mr. Caraway exchanged expressionless glances and drained their glasses.

"Allan Gaynor!" the girl repeated with her musical laugh. "A lot you know about Allan Gaynor. Allan Gaynor's a genius. You wouldn't know that, naturally."

Ladies in their cups or forced by circumstance to do their pubcrawling solo were invariably outraged by the spectacle of four men free to enjoy themselves without visible feminine chains, and the Pillars were usually complacently prepared for illbred insults and reproaches. But this was different. The girl's hint of deeper and more recent connection with the subject of their conversation brought them down with embarrassing suddenness from their lofty reminiscences. They examined their empty glasses which seemed to chorus a suggestion to move on, but at that moment the advertising man named Larry Glay leaped jauntily through the door and the Pillars could not bear to miss whatever fresh drama he might bring. The advertising genius had not been around for a time and looked as if he'd been through the wringer, ears laid back, hair slicked to the bone and the general skinned and plucked appearance of a man who had submitted to purification by shower until all color and juice had been drained from him. He darted a swift look around the booths. "Looking for that Dodo kid," whispered Rover to the doctor.

"What's the matter, Spike, losing all your trade to the Barrel?" Larry asked the bartender genially. "Nobody around tonight."

"Suits me," was the curt answer. "Who you looking for?"

"Me?" Larry repeated evasively with a second glance around. "Well, who you got?"

"Your friend Murray hasn't been around," Spike, the bartender said. "I got a bouncer of his here. If you see him, tell him."

"I'll warn him to keep out," said Larry. "Say, I feel terrible. Can't you cheer me up?"

After a whiskey neat he was sufficiently refreshed to take an interest in the juke-box girl. There was the customary procedure (after another survey of the room to make sure nothing better offered) of merry remarks seemingly addressed to the bartender and accompanied by disproportionate hilarity, and sidelong glances at the girl who responded by smiling sardonically into her beer.

"Where would that little tramp get a fur coat like that?" Rover muttered to the bartender. "Last I heard was she couldn't afford any more diction lessons."

"Some Coast Guard boy friend gave her the dough to get a cure," Spike whispered happily, "but she decided she'd have more fun with a fur coat."

"Well, you can't have everything," Dr. Zieman reflected philosophically, stroking his beard.

His three friends laughed heartily at this, repeating it over and over with such unaffected enjoyment that the doctor felt justified in ordering another round at once. They were not too engrossed in their own fun to ignore the activities of the K.G.R. man and nudged each other as he ordered a stinger sent to the young lady. For her part the tribute to her charm made her increasingly haughty and very much the lady, dallying with her drink indifferently to offset any impression that it was of any consequence to her. Her lips curved in a quizzical dreamy smile suggesting private amusement at the idea of herself, of all people, being in this sordid spot with these sordid people.

"Haven't seen you down here, much, lately, Mr. Glay," the bartender said. "What's the matter, going Park Avenue on us?"

"His wife doesn't like his sweetie, that's all," spoke up the girl, pointing at Larry. "Isn't that so, Jackson?"

"Hey, now, you're talking to an old married man," Larry protested with a wink at the Pillars. "What would I be doing with a sweetie?"

"I bite. What?" said the girl, and after a moment of concentrated thought added that whatever he would be doing with a sweetie somebody else was doing right now and serve him right.

"Serves everybody right," said Larry. "Service, that's what I like. One more for me with two chasers of the same."

"Now watch her get nasty," Rover nudged Caraway. "Get a load of this."

"I suppose you wonder how I happen to know so much," pursued the girl with a faint smile and (as the Pillars noticed) suddenly remembering to get her money's worth out of her diction lessons and becoming very pear-shaped indeed. "Naturally you happen to be the type that doesn't know what's under your own nose."

"Sure I do. It's *Old Granddad*," said Larry happily and downed his three whiskeys with accompanying incantations of "See no evil, hear no evil, do no evil."

"Oh, I could tell you plenty if I cared to, my fine simian friend," the girl continued in her best dowager voice. "I happen to know the world, myself——"

"I'll say she does from what I hear," Rover nudged the doctor.

"—and nothing amuses me so much as you married men thinking nobody else can get away with it. Oh, you're so clever! I could tell you a few things." She leaned her chin on her hands with a look of infinite sorrow for human error.

"What about more of the juke-box and less of the gypsy, honey?" suggested Larry uneasily, fishing for coins in his pocket. He selected an attractive fifty cent program divided fair and square between *You Won't Be Satisfied* and the *Anniversary Waltz*. After a brave attempt at a soft shoe routine, forefinger pointed skyward, while the juke-box burst with rosy apoplectic song, he edged toward the Four Pillars who were sternly minding their own business by staring fixedly in the bar mirror.

"Oh, please don't feel you must sit with me, Mr. Hazelnut," the girl said huffily. "I'm sure your four ancient friends will appreciate your conversation more than I possibly could. After all, I happen to be used to Allan Gaynor's conversations."

"I can see you're a kid that likes her conversation alright and plenty of it," Larry gaily conceded, looking around hopefully for other and friendlier companionship. "Say, this place is dead tonight. What's the matter with old Murray anyway? Any you fellows seen him? What's he up to these days?"

"I haven't the faintest idea, I'm sure," Dr. Zieman said, gesturing to the bartender for another round on the kiddies. "I believe it may have been Murray I saw an hour or so ago with that Pollock girl, your prize artist. Having gin rickeys and a little quarrel in Barney's, as I recall. I just happened to glance in the door."

"The guy he lives with, he was here last night at closing time. Olliver, that's his name," volunteered the bartender. "With that kid, Dodo."

"See what I told you, Jackson?" cried the girl, nodding her head, at Larry. "And you married men are so sure you know everything."

"If I don't, you're insulting my wife!" said Larry. "She should have told me more."

"Frederick Olliver's a big shot now," stated Caraway. "Yes sir, he must be taking in a lot of dough right now. Smart fellow, I like him."

"I figured he must be rich, never buying drinks," meditated the bartender, polishing his nails on his cuff, "except when that Dodo kid runs up the check on him, and, boy, can she do that."

"See?" said the girl, triumphantly. "Sometimes a girl can get away with just as much as you can."

"Now what'd I ever do to this woman?" complained Larry. "Or didn't I?"

He appealed to the Four Pillars but their faces remained impassive. The girl burst into her most musical laugh and pushed her face close to Larry's.

"Snap out of it, silly boy, can't you tell when you're being kidded? I dare you to take me over to the New Place for a nightcap. I dare you."

As a gentleman accustomed to overcoming female reluctance by bold attack Larry Glay was obviously confused by counter-attack. The girl rubbed her cheek affectionately against his shoulder.

"Come on, let's get away from these creeps," she indicated Dr. Zieman and his guests. "Your girl-friend's out with other people, don't you worry about her."

"Honey, you're the only girl I'd ever invite to break up my home. I thought you knew that." The advertising man gallantly surrendered, clapping his hat on his head, and crooking his elbow for the lady. "Excuse us, gentlemen, we're off to a small, middleclass hotel where a lady can lose her good name in comfort. What *is* your good name, anyway?"

"You are clever, you know," the girl said, sweeping her cloak about her frail body. "Marianna Garrett. You remember Marianna."

"Isn't that something?" observed Caraway watching them through the door. "They're crossing the street. I guess she's taking him to the other bar. Funny seeing a wise guy like that get trapped. I wouldn't have missed it."

"What'd she mean she worked for Allan Gaynor? Was that on the level?" inquired the doctor.

"Say, I was just thinking," said Rover. "Maybe she was planning to meet that guy here all along and they just put on that act for our benefit."

"No, he was looking for somebody else," stated Marquette. "He was trapped, that was all. Serves him right. He thought he was doing so well when she let him buy that first drink. So trusting and so proud, it makes me laugh. Like sticking his head in the lion's mouth."

They were going over the incident with increasing pleasure when Frederick Olliver and Dodo came in and stood at the bar. Dodo was gotten up in a tight tweedy coat of purple plaid, a high stovepipe felt hat swathed in veils, magenta gloves, shoes, and enormous shoulderbag, her small neatly chiselled face shining under a smooth layer of gypsy foundation cream, her Fatal Apple lips pouting sulkily. The ensemble gave an impression of garish simplicity and still smelt of the shop in spite of the heavy sprinkling of Tabu. The Pillars sat back, expectantly. She ordered a Bourbon and sipped it in silence. Frederick Olliver looked gloomy staring at Dodo who looked haughtily away from him. Must have been wrangling, deduced the Pillars. You couldn't get a girl like that to keep her trap shut unless you managed to make her mad. She was annoyed, that was clear, and with reason, so Dodo felt. Here was the first chance she had to wear her brand new outfit and she had waited for a really exciting date, refusing Frederick, then no one else had called her and at the end she was obliged to fall back on him, for which naturally she would never forgive him. He had taken her to three or four places of her choice but no sooner were they seated than she was dissatisfied and wanted to leave; this too was unpardonable in him. Finally they came down to Rubberleg Square where surely someone could be found to admire the new clothes.

"What makes everything so dull tonight, anyway?" she demanded peevishly of the bar-tender. "Where is everybody? It's so dead."

"I wouldn't say it was bad as all that," Spike answered. "We been having fun, haven't we, fellas? You shoulda been here when Larry Glay and the blonde were going at each other. First I thought she was going to conk him, next thing she's out to make him. Funny, wasn't it, fellas?"

"Larry?" Dodo said, eyes widening. "How long ago?"

"They just left," the bartender said. "Five minutes."

"I told you we should have come here first!" Dodo whirled on Frederick, petulantly. "Where'd he go?"

"The blonde wanted him to go to the New Place at first," Rover offered. "But I don't know."

"You mean he brought his wife?" Dodo asked sharply, her nostrils quivering, like a mouse's moustache on the scent, Frederick thought with that detached scorn part of him always felt for his love.

"No, this was just a girl around here," the bartender said casually, squinting at the glass he was wiping. "They got to talking. She——"

But Dodo was out of the door in a flash. The Pillars forgot themselves so far as to turn around and gape after her. Frederick stood still, frozen.

"What's with her?" the bartender exclaimed, and scratched his jaw, the friction evidently producing inspiration for he clapped a hand over his mouth.

No one said anything. Frederick reached for his change pocket and laid the money on the bar. He strolled toward the door.

"I wouldn't go over to the New Place if I was you, bud," called the bartender. "Looks to me like you'd be running into bad news."

"Thanks," said Frederick stiffly, and the Four staring through the window, saw him hesitate outside then saunter in the opposite direction.

The Four waited a suitable length of time and then with one accord rose and filed out. Their discretion had betrayed them, though, for when they got to the New Place there was no sign of Dodo, Larry, or the juke-box girl. All that the bartender would tell them was that he was trying to run a decent place and some things he wouldn't tolerate. Give him a Bowery bum, sterno can and all any time, in preference to a drinking lady. The Pillars were grieved to get no more than that for their trouble.

It was days before they found out that Dodo had bolted into the bar and after a seemingly polite encounter with Larry and the blonde had slapped the blonde and thrown a highball in Larry's face. The blonde had run out in great dudgeon, Larry had disappeared out the back entrance, and Dodo after long conferring in the telephone booth, was finally called for by Mr. Olliver in a taxicab. What a pity Dr. Zieman's celebration had cost the Pillars their grand-stand seat at such a juicy show!

22

. . . the blue plate reunion . . .

THE Swan Café had been ruined or made by the eminence of its patrons, your point of view depending on whether you were patron or proprietor. Created in the cellar of a Chelsea delicatessen during the prohibition era by the inevitable ex-Mouquin waiters, one a Swiss cellist, it managed to survive the depression by the unvarying plainness of its fare—lentil soup, sauerbraten, sulze vinaigrette, potato dumplings, apfel strudel and pineapple-cheese pie. New patrons were deeply resented by the old faithful customers. It was these faithfuls, after all, who had kept the place going all during the bleak days of prohibition and depression; here, as precocious undergraduates, they had created their little magazine, graciously permitting the proprietors to invest in it. Here they used tables as editorial desks, booths as conference rooms, the dark hallway and garbage-strewn courtyard as trysting ground. Their battered felt hats moulded in the dark cellar closet, forgotten; their bills, I.O.U.'s, and bouncing checks, yellowed and dignified with age, popped out of the dusty roll-top desk in the kitchen. They had seen Fanny, the kitchen cat, through a dozen litters, adopted her children, glorified her in cartoon and story. During the magazine's periodical slumps they were cheered by drinking coffee in the little cellar room while the chef took out his cello and played for them. When Edwin Stalk miraculously took charge, bringing distinction to their magazine and its restaurant home, they loyally continued their patronage and even paid an old bill occasionally. They felt justified in their indignation, therefore, when the faculty members of the nearby League for Cultural Foundations began crowding the place, ordering lavish meals, demanding "spritzen" instead of beer, demoralizing the waiters with tips, and referring to the seedy Prohibition *decor* as "amusing" or "quaint." The faithfuls had to wait for tables only to find the sauerbraten crossed off the menu, the lentil and sausage soup watered down to thin bean juice. True, their corner table was still reserved but it was no longer dominant. Workers from nearby lofts once entertained and bewildered by loud quarrels approaching fisticuffs over nothing more than a dainty problem in aesthetics, were more interested in watching for radio notables or queer bearded foreigners among the League diners. Talk of the changes over two decades made small impression on Edwin Stalk, the *Swan's* saviour, for he was rarely conscious of surroundings, never certain whether people or places were real or something he had read. Neither active in nor responsible to his own generation, the Swan Café and the Mermaid Tavern merged for him into one picture. His friends, with clothespin heads for all he knew, were pegged in his memory by the particular subjects he liked to discuss with them and he thought of them not by names but as Poetry, Ballet, Minor Prophets, Western culture, Russian Soul, Swedish Architecture and sought out one or the other as he would a special book, according to his mood, closing it at his will, and vitally disturbed if Subject did not stick to Subject. His memory of his own youth was not of foundling home, rich foster-mother, travel, doting women, and many honors but of the time and place he had first read Proust, Joyce, Pushkin, Freud and Spengler. Women had taken possession of him early, fought over him until the day Solange had established her firm clutch, and Stalk accepted the victor with passive indifference and even relief. The *Swan* was the first great reality—it was mother, mistress, child, past and future. He never admitted into his consciousness the fact that the magazine had been struggling into shape for some years under other hands before he had adopted it. Whenever anyone made reference to a poem by T. S. Eliot or an essay on The Word Revolution by Jolas in the old *Swan*, Edwin's handsome brows arched together in a look of pain as if: "You are not speaking of *MY Swan* and therefore I think you are being rude." He had the same grieved expression when someone firmly fixed in his mind as Southern Agrarian escaped his category and spoke of unrelated matters. Whatever appeared in the *Swan* seemed his very own, accidentally put into lucid even jewelled words by his contributors, just as carpenters and masons carry out the architect's dream without making it any the less his. Edwin was not aware of unreasonable egotism; he believed he was giving absolutely selfless devotion to a cause, liking and tolerating human beings in proportion to their belief in the *Swan*, interested in events and talk only where it might feed the *Swan*. Indeed he thought he was unconcerned with his pocket and the needs of his body; you might call him totally unaware, too, of the feminine dither over him except for the fact that he had always taken it for granted and would have come to sharp attention if a sixth sense informed him that women's eyes were not upon him. Already Edwin Stalk was credited with being a Great Editor, and if this réclame implied possession of antennae sensing and pseudopodia enveloping all varieties of spiritual caviar then the reputation was deserved. If it meant his profile and an unerring instinct for sponsor appeal had drawn capital into the wizening coffers, then it was twice deserved; if it indicated a royal faculty for getting other people to attend to the labor and steady grind of producing, then the term was merited even more. He was fortunate in having that convenience, familiar to Great Editors, the Magazine Mama, an enormous girl with a profound and hairy mind, a body so huge and unwieldy for general group arrangements in office, taxicab or theatre, that her steadfast anonymity was astounding. It was Josephine Carey who had been with the *Swan* from its feeble inception, even setting type at one time, paying its bills from her own modest allowance, trudging on messenger duties, keeping books, reading manuscripts, attending to correspondence, meeting lawyers and subpoenae-servers, offering a memory stocked with encyclopedic information, keeping herself wonderfully in the background through all sorts of staff changes. Her services for Edwin Stalk were performed so unobtrusively that he was scarcely conscious of her presence, and often forgot her name, looking up sometimes from his desk with complete bewilderment at the shapeless hulk padding about, her billowing draperies wafting a smell of musty hay and soy sauce. Her garments were always the same—dark greenish black serges or crêpes with flowing bat-wing sleeves, always mussed, always showing a cerise slip below the hem and chewed bits of shoulder-straps at the neck. She lived for each issue and on the occasion of its tenth anniversary number was caught by the printer in the act of pressing a passionate kiss on the gold-lettered cover.

Josephine was as sublimely unconscious of her great size and clumsiness as Stalk was of his beauty. If no one stopped her she was all for tucking herself up on the smallest footstool, attempting to squeeze dangerously into the child's chair or onto the arm of the frailest antique sofa, wedging into the most crowded bus or elevator, unaware that anything beyond her wee whisper required accommodation. Though she spoke little during office hours, it was Josephine who answered all queries at the weekly luncheons, providing statistical ballast for both sides in all arguments, whether they concerned the Bolivian tin dynasty, European literary criticism during the *Sturm and Drang*, or the pet charades of the Goncourt circle. It was her habit to arrive before anyone else at the Café corner table and take her place at the remotest corner to avoid inconveniencing others, but since she drank gallons of coffee she was obliged to excuse herself frequently for the ladies' room, squeezing herself back and forth past the chairs of late arrivals with gasping apologies. The demands of the body embarrassed her dreadfully and she was only consoled by remembering that the great minds she revered suffered from similar interruptions. Her vast fund of general information saved her from trivial interchange and when anyone threatened to become too personal she had been known to deluge them with the figures on some ponderous subject, talking rapidly for what seemed hours, not as an exhibitionist but as a desperate defender of her own privacy. Some spy from the human race might spot her vulnerability, so barriers of statistics must be piled up like sandbags to protect the small shy bird within. It was a good thing that she did not suspect others of any more interest in the physical than she herself had, for it saved her from any inferiority; her evident impression that she went from head straight into winglets like a seraph resulted in astonishing displays of bare porky thigh and generous bosom. The unexpected treat combined with her majestic mind and soft creamy skin sometimes tempted neurotic young men to bury their faces in the cool buttery curve of throat, only to be chilled by the deadly flow of portentous information issuing from the face above.

On the occasion of the special Olliver issue of the *Swan* Josephine, armed with bulging briefcase and wearing a mangled brown moleskin cape of the Valeska Surratt era, padded into the Swan Café before twelve and was surprised to find no one present but Editor Stalk who sat in her own special corner. He was lost in thought and did not even notice Josephine wedging her bulk heroically through improbable apertures. A pale lemon glow filtering through the barred cellar window behind him softened his dark, sharply chiselled face and gave it boyish wistfulness. Josephine was stirred with vague yearnings to cheer him with some rare offering, some little-known anecdote of Tallyrand's life, say, or a well-documented tidbit concerning André Chénier. Nothing of the sort occurring to her she resorted to office news.

"The International Committee is ordering ten thousand copies of this issue for foreign distribution," she said, and repeated it when Stalk looked up at her blankly. "That pays the printer. And the ads we got from South America will carry the Padilla poetry number."

Stalk lifted his shoulders indifferently and Josephine sought for other subjects. "Too bad nobody's here today," she said. "Padilla was coming but I guess everybody else has gone to the country. And Olliver's so puffed up nowadays he's forgotten we gave him his start. He never shows up any more."

"I don't care," Stalk said. "The only person I wanted to see today was Mrs. Gaynor. I hope she got my message."

A cloud passed over Josephine's face. She, too, had been questioned by Solange about Mrs. Gaynor. Josephine had been offended by the intimacy of the question as well as by the danger of Stalk's beautiful mind being defiled by normal masculine preoccupations. And she always shuddered when a wife's grisly shadow crossed the temple stairs.

"Do you think we can get money from her?" she now asked. "I read that her play folded on the road and there was no film tie-up."

Edwin brushed this aside as irrelevant.

"I don't want money from Mrs. Gaynor," he said impatiently. "All I was hoping for was the benefit of her kind of intelligence. We tend to get too academic. To expand we need someone with Mrs. Gaynor's experience with large audiences."

"She hasn't done anything for ages, has she?" Josephine murmured. She unlatched her briefcase and drew out a batch

of notes with a certain setting of her round jaw that would indicate to anyone but Edwin Stalk her dismissal of the lady's
intelligence and a quiet resolution to barricade her intrusion.
An angry button in a strategic frontal position rebelled at the
strain of duty and popped off as she sat down.

"It's our academic following that's built us up so far,"
Josephine contented herself with adding, oblivious to her
calamity. The editor smiled radiantly. Not for her, it seemed,
but at the sight of Mrs. Gaynor pausing uncertainly in the
dining-room door, her marvellous intelligence being marked
with interest by alert gentlemen accustomed to the *Swan's*
drabber feminine trade. Not often had they seen mind so
elegantly packaged in soft sables, rusty-feathered hat blending
charmingly into rusty gold curls. Edwin Stalk, usually languid
in motion, startled Josephine by bounding up like a boy and
running toward the guest. He was pushed into the background by Tyson Bricker suddenly rising from a table and
seizing Lyle's hands.

"What is this charming creature doing in this end of the
world?" Tyson exclaimed, deftly managing to present his exquisitely tailored gray back to Edwin Stalk. "I never see you.
No one sees you. Is this old saloon to be the background of
a new comedy? *Are* you working? What are you and Allan
doing?" His fine eyes assumed the grave accusatory look he was
wont to direct at writers to remind them that he, as critic and
teacher, was still boss, waiting to catch them up on tardiness
and mischief.

"Perhaps I need a course with you at the League, first,"
Lyle countered, flushing at his keen gaze which might see
through her flimsy pretext for being there.

"They have introduced a course in Fast Reading at the
League," Edwin Stalk maliciously interrupted. "Bricker starts
them off by showing them how to keep their minds a blank,
and they can read like the wind, unless, of course, thinking
sets in. How do you cure that, Bricker?"

"Ah, Stalk, how are you? Stalk has never appreciated what
we're trying to do," Tyson acknowledged his enemy's presence with a curt nod, "any more than I appreciate what he's
trying to do. For instance, he believes in keeping a Frederick
Olliver just for his fifty or sixty readers. I believe in giving fifty

or sixty thousand the privilege of reading him. Never mind, old chap, you'll learn just as Olliver has. Saw him only last week out at Oak Ridge, by the way."

"Oak Ridge?" Lyle repeated. "Not Cordelay Beckley's country place?"

"The very same. They turned over a guest cottage to Olliver to work in whenever he likes," Tyson sighed enviously. "Lucky boy! Surely the Beckleys told you."

"I haven't seen them for a long time," Lyle said. She was conscious of Edwin tugging at her arm like a spoiled child and was glad to be excused from more questioning by Tyson. She had come, she pretended to herself, because the editor had urged her. Actually, it was only to hear talk of Frederick even if he was not there. She was getting shameless in her need, she thought, utterly shameless.

In the *Swan* corner the Spanish poet had just arrived and insisted on placing Lyle beside him. He was in a jubilant mood, freshly pomaded, manicured, and gaudily sport-coated. He embarrassed Josephine by kissing her hand passionately. "Thank you for the twenty dollars, I hope," he whispered loudly in her ear.

"You must all be good to me today," he explained, "because I am celebrating my metamorphosis. I am about to become a breakfast food. In six delicious translations. Stalk here brings out a Portable Padilla. At once Tyson Bricker, whom I just saw, promises to bring out a Padilla Omnibus. Stalk hates Bricker so he must come back with a Padilla Treasury. Tyson retaliates with a Pocket Padilla. What about a Pick Pocket Padilla, Edwin? Eh? Next will come the Potable Padilla, the Edible Padilla, the Medicine Chest Padilla. I have not written a line since I found out this secret of success. My fortune is as good as made. I am already famous."

"Are you sure it's your fortune?" Lyle asked. "Tyson's and Edwin's pictures will be on the cover, not yours. And it will be Stalk's Padilla Portable and Bricker's Padilla Omnibus, you know."

It appeared that Padilla had already considered this.

"They are good enough to let me have a small percent," he reassured her. "I have their word on that, bless their hearts."

"Only a verbal agreement?" Lyle teased him.

"Certainly," Padilla answered. "An ironclad contract would be too easy for them to break."

Suddenly Frederick Olliver had come in and slipped into the bench next to Lyle.

"What expert has been giving you such masterly advice?" he asked Padilla.

"A Miss Marianna Garrett," answered Padilla and seeing the blank expression of all he added, "She is writing a play with Allan Gaynor. Doesn't that make her an expert?"

"No. Every female budding playwright in New York thinks marriage to Allan Gaynor would fix up her career," Stalk said, impatient of Padilla's frivolity. "But Lyle's talent is what they need."

Lyle's joy in seeing Frederick and wild flicker of hope when he came straight to her side had vanished abruptly at Padilla's remark. The odd behavior of Allan and his barometer, Flannery, during the last weeks suddenly came to mind. The two men had long ago stopped arguing with her for a Hollywood season ("Everyone else goes there when they can't work and they clean up")—and in her relief at being left alone Lyle had not questioned why. She found it increasingly easy to keep to her own suite and was grateful for Allan's mysterious preoccupations whatever they were. Sometimes she ran into the little thin blonde in the hall looking smug and guilty but she was accustomed to his lady visitors making much of the great man's harmless flattery. That there was a conspiracy against her in the house, however, and a new writing collaboration under way had never occurred to her. Terror made her pale at the hint of secret enemies—Flannery, Pedro, the other servants, Sawyer, too, perhaps—traps being laid for her. ("So you are definitely against going ahead with the Reno comedy? . . . So you think it's better to wait another season to finish the musical version of *Summer Day*? . . . So you think we're both too used up to tackle the new idea before fall?") She had discovered an unconquerable aversion to every contact, even mental, with Allan, and her old career of decorating and concealing his stock company plots with her own lacy twists and feminine wisdom seemed actively nauseating to her. No, she could never endure the double harness again, but the news that it was not even offered, that she was being locked out of prison, disturbed her frightfully. Enemies, enemies every-where, even here, she thought.

"Does that mean you are working alone at last?" asked Frederick in surprise.

"Evidently," Lyle said in a low strained voice that made him sense something was wrong and that it had to do with Padilla's word of Allan's new collaborator. The old habit of consoling her for outbursts of her husband's insensitivity came over him and he struggled against the instinctive im-pulse to take her hand, disarmed by the unexpected glimpse of Lyle at a disadvantage.

"I'm looking forward to Mrs. Gaynor's first solo flight," Edwin Stalk said, gazing yearningly at Lyle. "I think it's the best thing in the world that Gaynor has found someone else for his factory. He'll probably find dozens more in Holly-wood, as Padilla says."

"Did Padilla say—" Lyle exclaimed, almost betraying her incredulity. So there were more and more conspiracies against her. Everyone knew about them. She was angry that Frederick should know, too, and deliberately drew back from the un-derstanding pity in his eyes. She could not bear him to be kind or that she should need kindness.

"We'll do our best out there," she said.

"But Padilla said the other day you weren't going," Edwin said plaintively. "Olliver, we mustn't let her go."

"I doubt if anything could ever persuade Mrs. Gaynor to leave her New York," Frederick said easily, turning to her. "Of course it's not true, you're not leaving?"

Why couldn't she, Lyle thought wildly, her shattered pride flaring up at his calm assumption of knowing all about her. The affection in his tone and manner wounded her, remind-ing her of the months she had longed for it in vain. That it should come because he found her betrayed by others as well as himself made her indignant. Why didn't it occur to him that her love could change as his had? Even if it couldn't, she would not want him to be so sure. She had never wanted to leave New York because of him, and he dared assume this was still true. She thought of how he had turned her against the Beckleys, then blithely accepted them for himself. Betrayal all around her, she thought.

"I think the atmosphere out there will be ideal for work," she said haughtily. "Not so chic as a Beckley guest-house, of course."

"Which Beckley is it that has the seismograph in the cellar that shows where and how the guests have been sleeping?" Padilla asked eagerly. "Have you been warned of that yet, Olliver? Amusing idea."

Frederick's face had crimsoned at Lyle's sarcastic rejection of his overture. He picked up the menu and studied it silently.

"I could publish the magazine in California, couldn't I?" Stalk demanded. "That's exactly what I will do. Wonderful!"

"Ideal," agreed Lyle. She was suddenly crushed against the table as Josephine Carey wriggled out behind her chair with a hiss of "Sorry. So sorry."

"Must telephone," muttered Frederick and sprang to his feet.

23

Dodo hated him, she would never forgive him, she wished he would stop telephoning her, her dearest wish was never to set eyes on him again. This time it was goodbye for good, she was going away, far away, or back home to Baltimore; she might even kill herself but she knew that would please him too much! As these threatening words climaxed a quarrel lasting half the night, through nightclubs, taxis, streets and bed, Frederick was exasperated into retorting, "For God's sake, go then! I can't stand any more!" She did, and an hour later he was trying to find her, telephoning her room and eventually her office, frantic for her voice, despising himself for his weakness, arguing in excuse that the only cure for him was satiety. If he could just see her when and where he chose for just one week, say, then he would be free again, but Dodo must have half-guessed this for she kept him always wondering. He would have given up anything to see her, even if only to quarrel again, but she was nowhere to be found. He remembered telling her that he might go to the *Swan* luncheon, and he went there in the faint hope that she might call him there, or even burst in on it. His nerves were exhausted, he did not feel like *Swan* talk; off-guard, his first instinct on seeing Lyle was the old relief that here was refuge; the hint that she too was in trouble stirred him, but in a few seconds he sensed her coldness. In his disappointment at Lyle's unfriendliness, and then at Dodo's not calling, he concentrated on analyzing his luncheon companions as if they were to blame. Clearly there was something between Stalk and Lyle; Frederick considered Stalk disparagingly, annoyed that he should be ten years his junior. Too young for Lyle. Was he such a remarkable editor, after all? He was definitely reactionary, ridiculously ivory-tower for the times, and childishly befuddled by infatuation, even if all one believed was his doting eyes apart from Solange's warning. The magazine would suffer. In fact its studious aloofness from present-day problems seemed dangerously political, even seditious, to Frederick, reminding him that its editors had almost always been only two or three generations removed from Europe. Yet they had no patience with the "melting pot" idea, snubbing any manuscripts that smacked of steerage, peasantry, or labor, pouncing greedily on Henry James, for instance, as if their approval elevated their own ancestors and granted them hereditary rights to elegant drawing-rooms. Obviously this style of literary social climbing was dated, Frederick mused, glowing with a democratic passion now that his own work was proclaimed to have a message for every class. He no longer needed hot-house protection and forgot he ever had. He disliked the *Swan*, its restaurant, its editors, and was sorry he had come.

He went out to telephone every few minutes all to no avail and Dodo's cruelty made him the more angry at Lyle. Now that he was ready to turn to her for forgiveness and renewal of sympathy she belonged all too clearly to Stalk. She had deliberately snubbed him. If Allan was taking on a new collaborator it must mean Lyle had someone else. Her slur about the Beckleys brought back all too vividly other difficulties only last night on the same score. And how dare she invade his private domain anyway? The *Swan* was *his* field, admitted so by her in the old days where everyplace else was hers. Even in the midst of their affair he would have resented her presence, and how much more so because another lover was responsible for her visit! Padilla's innuendoes proved that Solange was right, she had other suitors. It relieved him to find some cause besides Dodo for his restless misery. Perhaps this was a game Lyle was playing to punish him, quite apart from her interest in Stalk. Of course! Wherever he went nowadays, it dawned on Frederick, he came up against her sabotage, for it must be that. The more he thought about it the more he could see nothing but intent to injure in her adopting his old friends and interests. Why should she have been at Caroline Drake's except to make mysterious trouble in that small corner of his life? Why was she seeing Benedict Strafford and even Gerda Cahill except to harm him in some way? None of these represented her kind of life; they could not amuse her nor could she claim they were Allan's friends. Frederick thought of Allan with pity, a man admitted by Lyle as responsible for her career, yet here she was brazenly flaunting her hold on young Stalk, and flirting with Padilla, dominating the luncheon as if it was her own little tea-party. He thought of poor Solange, too, who had done so much for Stalk, and wished to do more but he would not have her interfere in his work; Lyle alone was allowed to do that. Frederick wished for his old advantage of proud poverty that he might punish her for presuming on her position. He had introduced her to this very table years ago; now she wished to edge him out in the subtle ways known so well to her, show that she could always have an ascendancy over him.

And to what evil end had she dressed herself for a *Colony* luncheon so that Edwin Stalk could not take his admiring eyes away from her? It affronted him for her to glow with that suspicious radiance of a woman in love or beloved. Her nearness to him, obliging frequent contacts, made him remember with bitterness old days of longing for just this proximity, old days when he had foolishly fancied himself her one love. He told himself that no matter how savagely Dodo treated him, at least it was direct, and his present pain was nothing to the long-hidden anguish of his years with Lyle. It was a pleasure to take the role of victim rather than offender. He welcomed the idea that it was actually Lyle who had caused last night's final vicious quarrel with Dodo. Lyle had plotted the whole thing and must be gloating over it. It might even be she who had suggested that Cordelay Beckley offer him the cottage, so beautifully equipped for work, friendly companions whenever or if he chose. Lyle must have foreseen how this would complicate his relations with Dodo! Why couldn't she go out to this wonderful spot, too, Dodo had immediately protested, making such a scene every time he intended going that he had to stay in town, only to have Dodo punish him by stubbornly denying him her company. If she wasn't good enough for his friends she wasn't good enough for him, thank you. He was thinking of her reputation, he lied. Thinking of his own reputation, Dodo had mocked. She chanced on revenge by acquiring her own Beckley, no other than Uncle Lexington, whom she met at the Barrel in an excessively amiable mood. He was old, and maybe he liked to do dumb things but at least he was a Beckley. A Beckley took her to the zoo, she could boast, a Beckley took her bowling, a Beckley gave her jewelry and an oil painting when she pretended it was her birthday. Some men thought she wasn't as smart as they were but now she had a Beckley beau, thank you, and a millionaire knew what was what. He was always borrowing money from her, but alright, a rich man like that had to keep all his money in trust funds and stocks and things like that. A rich man had funny ways, you had to take that into consideration, for instance the way he always carried a little bag with that checkered coat and false moustache and bowler so he could put it on in nightclubs and sing Gay Nineties songs. Sometimes he paid the orchestra leader a hundred dollars to let him do it, so you couldn't say he was stingy. Dodo's triumph ended when her discreet attempt to sell her gifts brought out the fact that bracelet and clips were false, the painting cut out from *Town and Country* and framed personally by Uncle Lex.

"Why did you do this to me?" she tearfully reproached him. "You took advantage of me because I'm poor."

"Just shows you don't need money to be happy, by Joe," Uncle Lex gleefully retorted, "if you don't know the difference in things. I had you fooled for a while, didn't I? You can't beat the Five and Dime. Why, I always give girls presents from the Five and Dime and they never know the difference."

"But coming from you, Mr. Beckley—" Dodo had wailed, and later blaming Frederick for the whole misadventure she complained bitterly, "And he isn't even crazy, that's the worst. Making me meet him at the Plaza just to go stand in the Zoo watching that Barbary sheep jump for nothing!"

Last night she boasted of Caroline's party. ("You weren't invited, I noticed!") He surmised she had crashed it by thrusting herself on Benedict Strafford, and was resigned to the worst. But he was unprepared for her trump card when she crowed that Lyle Gaynor was there, and had been simply darling to her, devoting herself to Dodo alone, in fact she couldn't have been sweeter; no one in the world had ever been as sweet to her; and their talk was so interestingly confidential that Dodo would not give Freddie the least hint of what it was about, no she wouldn't. Didn't he wish he knew, though? Why should he act so jumpy simply because an old friend of his liked her? The implications of Machiavellian strategy on Lyle's part maddened Frederick beyond all discretion.

"She couldn't possibly have liked you," he was stung into shouting. "She was just being bitchy. You should have seen through it."

"And why couldn't she possibly have liked me?" Dodo inquired, pausing ominously in the midst of unzipping her dress for she had finally been cajoled into his room.

Frederick saw defeat ahead already but his nerves were beyond diplomacy.   .

"Because she never likes people like you," he floundered wildly.

"What do you mean—'people like me?' " Dodo leapt at the phrase suspiciously, her slim body in the half-unfastened purple jersey as taut as an arrow about to whizz through him.

"I mean anyone natural and simple, anyone outside her circle—." He saw with despair that she was zipping up her dress with finality.

"So I'm simple! I don't know I'm being snubbed!" Dodo cried. "Nobody could ever possibly like me, they just pretend they do to be bitchy! That shows what you think of me. You're the one that hates me! Well, I hate you, too."

She was pulling on her jacket and he tried to stop her, trying to appease her with kisses but she kept her face averted haughtily, the green eyes glittering and the jaw revealing its unexpected hardness as it did in these encounters. Why couldn't he learn to wait till afterward, Frederick scolded himself, but even while he strove for command Dodo tempted him to fresh folly by tying on the cloudy blue scarf which was so unmistakably, significantly Lyle's.

"Lyle Gaynor gave me this scarf," Dodo said proudly. "She insisted that I take it!"

"It's not becoming to you and she knew it!" he could not keep from retorting, furious at Lyle's revenging herself by such a devilish joke; she must have known in her infinite feminine wisdom that Dodo would always wear it as an excuse for boasting of her new friendship, that the delicacy of its fabric and design and its familiar fragrance would be reminders of another love. Whatever he said to persuade Dodo to discard the scarf made matters worse, seeming proof positive that he wished her to have no friends and no pleasure.

"You think I'm not good enough to marry you!" she sobbed. "Other men better than you want to marry me, if they could get a divorce, but you don't even have to get a divorce. You—you—why you won't even give me a ring yourself yet you won't let anybody else give me a little scarf. Pooh on you, Freddie Olliver, you wait!"

"I didn't know you wanted a ring," he shouted after her, not caring whether Murray heard or not, and hurrying into his clothes. But a taxi speeding away into the dawn was all he saw when he got down to the street . . . Lyle's fault. How diabolical a clever woman could be with a naïve rival, he thought, yet not so clever after all, for Lyle's victory steeled him with a fierce protective desire to avenge Dodo, who could never be a match for a woman like Lyle. He glared at Stalk and Padilla as if they had already made a slighting remark about Dodo, or perhaps were *thinking* one, comparing her unfavorably with Lyle, as of course would be the case. It seemed to him that they were the ones who tried to keep Dodo from her simple good time at Beckleys or even from this very luncheon. What right had they to sit in judgment on a poor child who merely lacked education and sophistication? He forgot that neither Padilla nor Stalk knew Dodo: their attention to Lyle seemed a tacit criticism of his own preference. He would atone for all this to Dodo, he thought, and when he went out to the phone booth he was resolved to beg her to come down there so that he might defend her from others corroborating his own secret opinion of her. He would tell them she was to be his wife, and he would really mean it! That was all she wanted, poor child. The resolution frightened him, revealing how firmly he still resisted the ultimate surrender. But the hour for it had struck and his reasoning process, after the first shock, rushed to perform its duty, contriving an argument that marriage would solve everything. At least it would solve the immediate problem.

She had not reported at her office yet; so he forced himself to telephone "Tommy," "Dick," and the young whippersnappers she always talked of, and he grimly accepted their veiled amusement at his query. No, they had not seen her.

She had no girl friends but eventually a girl answered her room number.

"I've taken Miss Brennan's room," the girl said.

She had really gone?

"When will she be back?" he asked. "Did she leave a forwarding address?"

The girl could tell him nothing. He hung up the receiver, noting absently that his hands were shaking frightfully. He made his way back to the Swan dining-room, not wanting to go back but incapable of any other choice. Tyson Bricker stopped him as he passed his table.

"Have a drink with me," he urged. "You look as if you needed one. Hangover?"

Frederick sat down.

"What do you know about that sweet kid kicking up those pretty little heels all over the tabloids? You can't tell about these children, can you?"

Tyson pushed the newspaper toward Frederick. The photograph of a blonde Mrs. Lawrence Glay of Riverdale meant nothing to Frederick at first nor the news that she was suing for divorce. She was naming as co-respondent one Miss Dorothy Brennan, of Baltimore, identified by reporters as the girl on the plane for Bermuda that very morning. Mr. Glay was staging a Hazelnut style show in Hamilton, it seemed.

"Says it's been going on for five years," Tyson chuckled. "Claims the kid followed her husband up here, from Baltimore and made a hell of a row. I never even heard of the guy. I thought she was just another sweet kid on the make. Glay's his name. Ever know him?"

"Hazelnut Cigarettes," Frederick muttered idiotically. "You know. 'Let me give you a light?' Just the one line."

Tyson looked baffled.

"Just the one line, mind you," Frederick said mechanically, "but it sings."

24

. . . the calendar slogans . . .

LYLE rapped on the door of Allan's room but there was no answer. Either he was asleep or staying up on the roof late. It was too bad for any delay might make her falter in her decision. Or *had* she decided? Nobody ever decided anything. Situations were solved only by other situations. She could take no credit. The sudden light that had made her past mistakes and her future correction so simple might fail any moment and leave her struggling again in her eternal puzzle. She was strong enough right now but there was no guarantee she could hold out. She needed props—love, security, success. She went into her study and stood looking at the work neglected for months on her desk. The notes clipped to some typescript seemed incomprehensible to her, though they were in her own writing. She must get back to work. She glanced at the pages of dialogue and thought how silly they sounded. In the folder were a dozen variations of this same scene; she might better have occupied herself writing some copybook maxim a hundred times. She crumpled up the pages and tossed them in the basket. She would never write that play, or perhaps any other. The thought frightened her. But why should it? Once she had found out the sham of her profession she was no good at it. The Show Must Go On. She laughed scornfully remembering how Frederick had mocked the sentimental phrase. "The Show Must Go On" so the old trouper clowns on till he drops dead. No, it was *not* just for the manager's profit, she had argued, and was angry that she could never articulate her emotional reasons to match Frederick's crisp logic. But if you did not believe the Show Must Go On what did you have left?

The desk calendar was turned to a date weeks ago, evidence of her indifference. As for copybook maxims there was one printed on the calendar, "Thursday the 12th. Darkness Comes Before Daylight." She could not help smiling, leafing through the pad for further philosophic gems, but why smile when the

Platitude was the staff of life, the solace for heartbreak, the answer to "Why" even though the oracle spoke in the priest's own hollow voice. Underneath the woes of the world ran the firm roots of the platitudes, the calendar slogans, the song cues, a safety net to catch the heart after its vain quest for private solutions.

"I must be old at last," Lyle thought, but she had known that before. A woman was old the day her lover left her.

To keep up her courage she decided to telephone a lawyer, but she could only think of those Allan had used. Cordelay Beckley was a lawyer but he was now Frederick Olliver's friend. She didn't want Frederick to know until the divorce was final. He might think she was getting it as a trick to win him back. But it was to prove something to herself, at no matter what cost to her. Before, it had been Frederick who paid. If it had not been for his love she would have left Allan years ago, paradoxical as the reasoning was. The more intense their relationship grew the more bound she had felt to make up to Allan in other ways for never having desired him. All the time it had been Frederick who was being wronged. No sooner had he withdrawn from the triangle than the two remaining figures fell apart, their whole security based on his presence. He had been used, and her blindness to it, and the fact that he had been willing to be used did not condone the crime, Lyle thought. Without him, her sense of obligation to Allan vanished; she felt dislike, even revulsion for him, and days passed when she could not bear to see him because it was he, not Dodo, who had devoured her happiness. Whether she ever wrote again, she knew she could never work with him, and this certainty with what Padilla had told her made divorce more plausible. She would not have dared come to the decision if it had not been for that.

Going through the halls the whole apartment seemed hostile and unfamiliar. Even the maid on her knees scrubbing the kitchen floor was one she had never seen before. The curtains had been drawn for months in the big dining-room, and the long dark room reproached her for neglect. No more gay dinner parties, no casual Sunday night suppers, no after-theatre buffets. One would have thought it was the host who had departed instead of the hostess's lover. Curious that the parties she used to love and defend to Frederick had turned tasteless and as boring as he had said when she no longer needed to defend them. She had enjoyed them, perhaps, knowing that when the last guest left she would find Frederick waiting for her the more eagerly. Curious that her sentimental duty to Allan was so unimportant without the argument over it with Frederick. As soon as she had made up her mind to leave him his independence of her seemed justification enough. He had his own social life, now. Hadn't Padilla indicated he was making plans without her help? She would give up this place, of course, and as soon as she made up her mind it was intolerable to spend even another week there. She would go to Reno or wherever she must and come back to a small studio apartment, like Frederick's, she thought. The thought of working without having to propitiate Allan's fixed notions excited her. But what would she do until she was ready to work? The question frightened her and she wavered. She had never been alone in her life. Everything had always been arranged for her—first there had been her father, then her maiden aunt, then her guardian, Cordelay Beckley, then Allan. Maybe she should wait—but she recognized her old sin of evasion. She must make her own decisions and clear everything with Allan this very day if possible.

The phone was ringing again when she reached her bedroom, and went on ringing, indicating that Pedro was out, and for some reason no other servants were in the house. Even the kitchen maid had vanished, apparently. Lyle let it ring on. She remembered that an actress from *Summer Day* was going to call about the prospects of a new play and there was nothing to tell her. This reminded her that she had helped the girl arrange for her own divorce last year, hiring a man Sawyer knew. The very person, Lyle thought, and rang his office at once. He remembered her, showed no surprise at her request, assured her of immediate action. As it was late in the day he was willing to meet her for tea whenever and wherever she suggested. Lyle named a hotel near his office and hurried out. As she stood before the house waiting for a cab, she saw the colored janitor watching her from the basement entrance.

"He ain't back yet," he said.

He stumbled towards her, and stood watching the doorman put her in the cab.

"He took the car," he said, grinning. "Your man took the car."

She understood then that he was referring to Allan. Allan found all travel so difficult he used the car only under necessity and she wondered why now.

"Be sure there's someone on hand to help him when he comes back," she said to the doorman, but the janitor spoke up with a disagreeable smile.

"That's alright, he's got somebody."

Flannery and perhaps the little Marianna, Lyle guessed. She did not like the way the man was smirking at her, and there was a definite insult in his mocking laugh as the taxi door closed. She would have Allan ask the agent about him, but right now she had more important matters on hand. She did not think about him again until three hours later when she returned, her mind filled with the ominous step she had just taken. The dark man was still standing on the basement steps as if he had been waiting for her.

"He ain't back yet, missy." His voice startled her into turning and seeing his mocking smile. "That's one cripple that ain't coming back, either, if he knows what's good for him."

The man was crazy, Lyle thought. Allan would have to—no, she would have to ask the agent about him herself. She would be alone from now on. She hoped someone would be in the apartment, for the madman might follow her. She was afraid of everything now. No sign of Pedro but the telephone ringing was encouraging. It was Cordelay Beckley. He had been trying to get her all day to tell her about Allan.

"Yes?" she said almost knowing.

"Lyle, you mustn't think I'm on his side in this. There was just nothing else I could do, considering his condition, and considering the jam he was in. Naturally, I couldn't tell you but believe me I didn't think he would walk out—good heavens, Lyle, how could I guess when he's been laid up so long? But then still waters as they say——"

The voice in the transmitter went on though Lyle had dropped it and lay on the bed staring at the ceiling.

25

. . . the buzzard is the best flyer . . .

WHEREVER he went that day and that night he found people
were either strangers or enemies and he had no protection
against them. Eyes everywhere appraised his strength, plotted
against his weakness, waited for his surrender, as if his destruction was their salvation. Round and round about the
streets he walked swiftly and mechanically, heeding no traffic
lights, fancying sounds of smothered laughter and mocking
whispers. Round and round about, the Boyg in *Peer Gynt* had
commanded, go round and round about, young man, round
and round about. The awful loneliness and fear of his fellow-
men that had cursed him up to the day he had first met Lyle
was upon him. He could have wept with longing for all-
forgiving, all-excusing arms, and he muttered aloud alternate
pleas and reproaches to Lyle for having deserted him. It did
not seem unreasonable to expect comfort from her for Dodo
having left him. At every corner cigar-store he paused with
the old habit of trying to find Dodo, and he was overwhelmed with memories to find his pocket filled with nickels,
a cautious habit he had formed of being prepared to telephone her any moment without the delay of making change.
In his notebook he had only yesterday added a new telephone
number where she might be traced, a hair-dresser on Madison
Avenue she had mentioned. It was a strange use for his research training, he reflected, and a damning record of his
insecurity—the pages of names and numbers where she might
be hiding from him. Folded neatly inside the notebook were
news clippings of nightclub openings, musical shows, indoor
polo games, restaurants, every possible inducement for her favor. Carefully concealed in his wallet as safeguard against her
scornful jeers was announcement of an honorary degree to be
conferred upon him by an Eastern university. Frederick stood
still re-reading the note which had arrived that morning and
which he had immediately hidden as if it was evidence of
some crime. His first feeling of satisfaction had been lost in

hasty assembling of defenses against Dodo's jibes. "No, it really means nothing, no of course I shan't go, no, of course I don't care about it, and of course I realize it doesn't signify I'm any better than your uncle who is the best lawyer in Cumberland or your second cousin who is very high up in Washington." Now there would be no one to taunt him and he should feel relieved instead of bewildered and lost. He must keep on going, he told himself, as if he was frozen and only constant action would ward off the end. It fooled the enemies, too, into believing he was still alive. It surprised him to discover himself in the Strafford office at four o'clock, the exact hour of his appointment with the head, though he was not conscious of having remembered it. Benedict Strafford's door was slightly opened and Frederick pushed in. The Human Dynamo was fast asleep in his swivel chair, hands clasped under his cheek like a child, feet on desk. His three telephones were ringing simultaneously but he slept on.

"Oh dear, I'm afraid that's my mistake," a feminine voice cried out contritely beside Frederick.

It was Mrs. Caswell, black eyes gleaming full power through blonde veils, an extraordinary covey of lovebirds atop her menacing topknot of bronze braids. She slipped a beige-gloved hand into Frederick's, flashing him the special hundred percent porcelain smile.

"I thought I'd discovered Benny's D.Q.—" she said, adding archly, "Drinking Quotient. Two brandies at lunch. No martinis. I had it figured out that his brain is at its best around three-thirty if he's had two brandies, no more, no less, and he had such a wonderful inspiration to discuss with you. But perhaps it should have been three o'clock."

"Or three brandies," said Frederick.

The publisher sprang out of his chair belligerently.

"As I was saying to Mrs. Caswell," he boomed, "we haven't been on the best seller list for two weeks and something's got to be done. My idea is this——"

"I was right after all," Mrs. Caswell murmured, seating herself on Benny's desk, and adjusting the small silver-backed pad and pencil that hung from her wrist.

"I've done all I can to put you over, Olliver," said the publisher, earnestly, "and I know you appreciate it. That's why I feel free to ask your help now. I'm sure you'll agree that it's not fair for an author to make more out of a book than the publisher, and what with all these plagiarism suits on *Court Lady* I've been doing a lot of thinking. Our trade analysts here, Mrs. Caswell—Topsy, I mean,—has been analyzing best sellers with me and by George, I've finally got something."

Frederick heard the words but they meant nothing.

"Ever come across an old paper-back periodical called *People's Home Journal?* Or *Family Journal?*" Mr. Strafford lowered his voice craftily. "Used to run novels about lords and ladies and governesses and seduction in the old manorhouse. All unsigned. All like *Court Lady* and every other damned best seller period romance. My idea is to hire a stable of hacks here to bring them up to date with certain movie stars in mind. We create a firm author—say a Hazel Poysonby Dart— Mrs. Caswell's idea—. The stuff's in public domain so all rights are ours. No author trouble, no split profits. What do you say?"

"Isn't it wonderful?" Mrs. Caswell cooed.

Mr. Strafford chuckled and took out a cigar.

"By George, the idea tickles me, I must confess," he said. "I get a hunch now and then, they've got to grant me that, after what I did with *Haw*. This little lady helps, of course."

"Mr. Berghart and I didn't expect to go into the publishing business so intensively when we first took the Strafford account," Mrs. Caswell confessed. "We've made it worth while, though, and I'm sure we'll be able to handle future publishers much better because of our investigations here."

Mr. Strafford patted her vigorously on the back.

"You bet you will. Olliver, not only have they analyzed best sellers for the past five seasons but they've analyzed reviewers, so we put in special features to attract each reviewer. None of them care about fiction, we've discovered, so we put in bits about gardening, cooking, baseball, sailing—whatever hobby they fancy. By George, I do think we've got something."

"It's confidential, of course," Mrs. Caswell warned, squirming out of range of Mr. Strafford's friendly grasp.

"Beckley's agent tried to buy stock in *Haw* and I'll venture they'd want to buy into this if they knew about it," Strafford chuckled, and then pointed his cigar at Frederick. "It's what you did with *Haw* that makes me know you're just the man for this job, too, Olliver."

Frederick's wandering thoughts came alert at the last words.

"Me?"

"I could hire somebody who would do what I told 'em, but no more," said Strafford. "You, on the other hand, can give a plain business idea class. The public is ready for class. You gave 'em Voltaire and Homer in comics and now that you're leaving the job don't be surprised if we feed 'em your own works in funnies, eh, Mrs. Caswell? You could set up the new enterprise in your own way, just the same. Give you a free hand. Show him the rough plan we worked out, Topsy."

"I'm afraid I wouldn't be interested," Frederick said.

Strafford held his cigar at a distance and examined it reproachfully.

"I know you didn't get the money out of *Haw* that you should have. I admit it," he said. "But this time it's different. Big dough. I should say at the outset we could pay——"

"It isn't the money," Frederick interrupted.

"Heavens, Olliver, you can't live forever on what you made out of your book!" Strafford said impatiently. "And if it's the extra work you object to that's where you're foolish. A little extra work never hurt anybody, does a man good. When you get to be my age you'll find work a damn sight easier for you than pleasure. Take the way you've been going in for night life. And the money it costs besides."

"That's over," Frederick said, embarrassed. "I can get along on very little when I choose."

"Shouldn't have to," objected Strafford. "A man ought to want more money."

"He doesn't feel it," Mrs. Caswell shook her head regretfully. "But what shall we do? We can't just have anybody."

"Try Tyson Bricker," Frederick said.

"He'd claim the whole idea was his," Strafford said. "He takes all the credit for *The Treasure* getting the award when everybody knows I'd had Olliver here under contract for years. No I won't cut Tyson in on this, damned if I do."

"Still—" mused Mrs. Caswell. "If Mr. Olliver definitely refuses——"

"Definitely," said Frederick. "I have two or three years of research ahead of me."

"A new *Treasure*, eh? That's splendid," said Strafford, his face lengthening. "Of course we can't expect a great whopping prize on everything you do from now on, you know, old man. Some things happen only once in a lifetime."

"I know," said Frederick. "I think I'm old enough to realize that now."

"Man of integrity, Mrs. Caswell," Strafford nodded toward Frederick with a deep sigh. "That's what I admire,—integrity. But it does make people hard to get along with."

"Think it over," implored Topsy, as Frederick rose to go. "Look how disappointed poor Benny is. Poor Benny."

Benny did look disappointed. Frederick had an uncomfortable impression overhearing a suppressed squeal that the publisher was forcibly pulling the trade analyst onto his lap for consolation as the door closed behind him. He walked down to the *Haw* office and collected his belongings in a brief-case. The numbness of losing Dodo gave way to elation, the false elation experienced sometimes in a bereavement, an uncontrollable animal joy in personal survival with a vulture glee in wolfing the departed's share of air and light and joy. The memos on his desk to call Gerda Cahill, call Caroline Drake, call Lorna Leahy, call Mrs. Beckley, made him think how strange it would be to have no battle with Dodo over each of these invitations, whatever they were. A copy of *Horizon* with an essay on his work reminded him that he would not need to grin indulgently while Dodo jeered at the respectful praise. He was so exhausted that he could not trust his sense of relief. It was the relief of the tired mother when the baby stops crying at last; the realization of its death comes much later. He could not trust his curious indifference to her relationship to Larry Glay. It seemed to him now that he had always known that. He tried to think back when it was he had guessed, and decided it was the very first night at The Barrel. Even when Larry had been at the other end of the bar and she had been between Murray and himself they had each stopped talking to close-harmonize sentimentally when the pianist played *Who*. He had never dared think about it before, but that was the moment. He could never claim to have been deceived. The mere sight of the telephone on his desk reminded him of the hours he had spent trying to find her, plead with her, explain, apologize, implore, bribe. He took out the tabloid from his pocket with Mrs. Glay's picture on page three and Dodo's on page four. Miss Jones, coming up behind him, startled him.

"Funny how often it's the wife who's the good-looking one," she said, critically pointing to Mrs. Glay's picture, and then to Dodo's. "This one looks like a weasel. Maybe she's got money, though. Honestly, *men!*"

It was not even necessary to start disliking Miss Jones for saying Dodo looked like a weasel, he thought. Larry Glay would have the chivalrous duty of defending Dodo from now on.

"Mr. Strafford says you're giving up *Haw*," said Miss Jones. "I suppose I can carry on by myself for awhile but I wish you'd give me some ideas."

"I haven't any," said Frederick sincerely. He could not imagine how he had ever had any ideas. He thought suddenly of an ancient Latin fragment called *The Pumpkinification of Claudius.* He wondered if this was what had happened to him, and if some classical Dodo had caused the process in the eminent Claudius. The idea amused him.

"You might try to get Al Capp or Caniff started on a dumb boy named Claud who has the best of intentions but always takes some wrong step that turns him into a pumpkin," he said, and then noting Miss Jones' blank expression added, "Never mind. Mr. Cahill will have plenty of new angles when he takes over. He knows a great deal more about this business than I do, I assure you."

Strafford had taken his word on Murray's capabilities for the job, agreeing to hire him before he remembered their former unpleasant encounter.

"But you'll come in from time to time, won't you?" she asked.

Indeed he would, Frederick answered, knowing that he would never set foot in the *Haw* office again if he possibly could avoid it. The mere sight of the bound volumes of the year's issues made him acutely sick, and he could scarcely bear to spend a minute more there. He hurried out with the exuberance of someone just rid of a monstrous burden. How had he endured it so long, he marvelled. It was a weight to balance the weight of Dodo, he knew. He could not have borne the one without the other. He was about to take a cab but he felt utterly incapable of any decision, where to go, whom to see, what to do. His chest felt empty, and he found himself touching it experimentally from time to time as if something was lost, though he was conscious of neither pain nor sorrow. His feet carried him along through the streets, in and out of bars, through daylight into night. Dodo and Larry were already in Bermuda, he thought, and saw them wrangling in some magnolia-shaded garden, Dodo with a scarlet poinciana in her black hair; he could hear her berating Larry for the handsomer costumes of the other women, and could see these beauties flirting with Larry while Dodo stormed and sulked, jealous that it was not she who was getting attention. He could see her furiously making up her face, repainting her lips, pitching her giggle higher, patting her nice little body invitingly, making raucous fun of Larry's latest advertising triumphs to rival ad-men at the bar, struggling belligerently to out-glamour the lovely creatures now surrounding Larry. She had her match, Frederick reflected; no pity for her childishness and ignorance would ever weaken Larry; he was as ready to answer any other call to love as she was. Frederick could almost hear strains of orchestras, juke-boxes, street-musicians and the pair of quarrelling voices blend suddenly into close harmony, *The girl that I marry*— He touched his chest again, curious that he still felt no woe, nothing but a detached wonder that he had ever been concerned in such a farce. He thought of Miss Jones' calling Dodo weasel-faced, and it struck him that his past year had been a year of destruction, of rodent gnawing away at everything he valued in himself. He had accomplished nothing on the *Treasure's* sequel, honor and pride forgotten in the delirium of his foolish chase.

It seemed he was in the New Place bar finally with chatter all about him and stately prints of old Knickerbocker days dignifying the flyblown walls. A red-haired girl named Buffy was weeping loudly that she had been double-crossed by Larry Glay, but one thing she would bet her bottom dollar on, was that he would never marry that little tramp who followed him onto the plane, because he had told her personally that was all off. Anyway his wife had gotten divorced from him twice before and they always got married again.

"You'd think they'd get tired of the blood tests," she said.

A stout lady with iron-gray hair under a mannish felt hat adjusted her mighty rear to the frail bar-stool next to Frederick, and ordered a double old-fashioned. She raised a lorgnette to the pictures above the bar, stating to no one in particular that the proprietor was to be congratulated on maintaining the quaint atmosphere of old New York. The old-fashioned itself she pronounced a miracle of delicacy and superior to any mixture she'd sampled at the Florida or other bistros she had just renounced because of the offensive presence of those four old goats you saw everywhere. The bartender acknowledged his lofty standards, priding himself on always washing the glasses, meticulously removing all insects before serving a potion, throwing out any customer who had 'had enough,' and often refusing to serve customers who came in only because they had been tossed out of every place else in the neighborhood. However since few patrons appreciated his stern code, he hovered gratefully before the lady, his eyes searching the room for an opportunity to demonstrate his finicky ideals. A small newsboy entering with a few morning *Mirrors* was all that offered and the honest fellow ordered him out peremptorily, declaring that his customers were not to be annoyed in their pleasures and it was time every little bum was in bed, anyway. He ignored the obscene gestures of reprisal made by the wistful little chap from the street. A burly truckdriver declared that he would back the new place and Jack, the honest bartender, against every bar in town, and the test of a customer's loyalty was whether he came around to you for his belt before breakfast same as for his nightcap, a sentimental routine he hoped Jack appreciated. The stout matron winked at Frederick and produced from her armpit a copy of the *Swan*, which she placed on the bar before her.

"Interesting characters around here," she whispered, and then blinked at her magazine which bore a drawing of Frederick himself on the cover. She looked again at Frederick, then extended a sturdy hand.

"A real privilege," she said and vowed that she had read

every bit of Olliver she could lay her hands on. Frederick gave a quick apprehensive glance around as if Dodo might suddenly materialize with shrill deprecations of the work admired. In his relief he thanked the lady fulsomely, even ordering her a drink. He looked at the red-haired girl, speculating whether Dodo could hold her own against her. The burly fellow construed his look as admiration for he nudged him, muttering, "No dice. I took her out the other night and boy is she dumb." Frederick nodded, pondering the grievous lack of brains in a beauty who refuses, though she becomes axiomatically brilliant if she surrenders. The girl was prettier than Dodo but all Larry cared about was quantity and variety. He wondered how Dodo could get along with a man even more irresponsible and unpredictable than herself.

"The buzzard is the best flyer," he heard the navy pilot at the end of the bar saying, and it seemed an answer to his own query. "You watch the buzzard and see how he picks his air-currents, makes his landings—beautiful sight, really. If a flyer could only learn the buzzard's secret——"

"He's always after something, that's why," ventured the pilot's companion. "Something for himself and nobody else. That steers him. A bird always looking out for himself can fly straight and fast and never gets lost."

Two ladies passing by stopped to peer through the glass and make mysterious gestures, but Frederick was idly listening to an argument on whether the Naval Ordnance manual on ballistics did or did not scan for one whole chapter.

"They're speaking to you," the stout lady said to Frederick.

Caroline Drake and Lorna Leahy gave up their efforts to attract his attention and came inside.

"We couldn't believe it was you," Caroline exclaimed. "I just can't picture you in this dump. We've been taking the new course in Fast Reading with Tyson Bricker over at the League. Marvellous! We decided you must be waiting for Murray too, or you wouldn't be in a place like this. We stopped by your house but beat it when we saw what was going on."

"Judy Dahl was helping unload something in front," Lorna said breathlessly. "Do you think Murray knows?"

"Do you know what she got with her prize money?" Caroline demanded gleefully. "A Bendix! And it was going into Murray's and your apartment, believe it or not. We nearly died."

"We couldn't have been more shocked if it was a baby-carriage," Lorna said. "I went right up to her and said what in the world do those boys want with a Bendix and she said, 'I don't have room for it at the Y.' We simply screamed."

Frederick was glad to see them, glad they clung to him, glad that somebody obviously liked him. He invited them to have a drink. Lorna cast a significant look about the bar.

"I wouldn't want to be seen in here myself," she murmured deprecatingly. "Of course Caroline doesn't mind but——"

"Oh shucks, let's go up to my place and get some good stuff," Caroline interrupted impatiently. "We can telephone around for Murray from there unless he's gone home and got caught in the Bendix already. Say, what do you know about Larry Glay?"

Lorna let out a peal of laughter.

"Go on and tell Frederick what we heard tonight at Nino's. He'll die."

"Somebody said you were engaged to that girl, Dodo Whatsername," Caroline obliged. "We nearly died. Imagine you marrying that!"

Frederick managed a sympathetic laugh that sounded so convincing he kept it up for several minutes, with the ladies joining in.

"Excuse my broken heart," he chuckled, and it really seemed to him that nothing in the world could be so preposterous as the idea of himself and Dodo.

"Larry's a fool if he marries her," Caroline declared. "She'll sleep with all his accounts and the wives will murder her. He might as well kiss his job goodbye, poor guy."

"Poor guy," Frederick said. The fantastic wish that it was he in the poor guy's shoes—if only for twenty-four hours—overwhelmed him. He was afraid to speak for fear the words might pop out so he kept on laughing as they went up the street together.

"That Bendix!" he repeated in the greatest glee.

"The joke is that Gerda's the one that's likely to use it," Caroline chortled. "We just left her and she says——"

"Caroline, that was confidential!" rebuked Lorna. "If you're going to tell about her psychoanalyst——"

"Confidential, hell," Caroline zestfully went on. "It's a riot. Gerda's been occupying her bird-brain with being psychoanalyzed and what does this Groper finally tell her but that she needs her husband."

"The Groper thought she was sex-starved!" giggled Lorna.

"Or else he thought she ought to be," Caroline amended. "Anyway Judy had better take her Bendix out of Murray's room because the Groper's sending Gerda down to take over. Wouldn't that kill you?"

They went into fresh gales of laughter. Frederick swore he'd never laughed so in his life. His heart was broken, Mrs. Glay's heart was broken, Solange's heart was broken, Judy's was probably about to be broken—in fact the world was so full of jokes the three friends were kept laughing far into the night.

26

. . . more like sisters . . .

MURRAY and Frederick were friends again, since Frederick had graciously allowed Fate to reduce him to Murray's own state of cynical resignation. Once again they united in barricading the apartment against rapacious females, but as usual all nature conspired against their safety. Murray had borrowed a thousand dollars from Frederick to pay for Gerda's psychoanalyst, but immediately Judy announced herself pregnant and Murray had to deflect the money for her abortion, not at all sure but that the resolute girl would go ahead and have the baby anyway. The portion saved for Gerda was immediately lavished by that lady on providing a recital for a Voodoo dancer from Haiti who had taken up his quarters with Gerda. "I'm really disgusted with her for the first time," Murray gloomily admitted. "Gerda's always been a *lady* before, but this sort of thing looks so awful. And no one will believe it isn't sex unless they know Gerda as I do."

As the only man who had ever devotedly loved Gerda, Murray was the only one persistently rebuffed, but his delusions of her incredible frigidity were all that saved his pride. The latest episode really hurt, although it coincided fortunately with a counter-dilemma, namely Judy's marriage proposal from none other than Mr. Strafford himself.

"I'm being shoved into the old halter and nobody knows it better than I do," said Murray. "Of course I'm not fool enough to think Gerda and I could have hit it off on a second try even if that dumb doctor did put the idea in her head. Still, I knew what to expect and when a man's getting on in his forties that's something. Then Judy pulls this *or else*. She wants to marry somebody and she's perfectly satisfied to marry old Strafford and palm off my baby on him. Olliver, I swear, there's no limit to what an honest woman won't do to get a man or a baby."

He'd marry Judy, especially since Gerda's hi-jinx with the Voodoo man made the idea less grim. He assured Frederick, however, that it would be merely a gesture to pacify Judy; she was reasonable enough to demand no change in their habits. She'd keep her room and he'd continue with his independent bachelor life. No sense in a man getting in any deeper than necessary. He requested that Frederick keep the wedding news quiet as Gerda would get upset if she heard about it. Frederick did not answer that Caroline and Lorna had already reported Gerda's sublime indifference to the project.

"She's so darned sure he'll always come arunning no matter how many other women he marries," Caroline had said. "It couldn't be a better arrangement since Judy doesn't care where he runs so long as she's got him nailed legally and his twins under her belt. I give him six months after the ceremony to find himself in a Ludwig Baumann bedroom suite out in Queens all lined up with the Parent-Teachers' Association for Friday nights."

"If he makes good at that job maybe it'll be a little house in Rye," chortled Lorna. "I can just see Murray's first night at the Dads' Club."

The ladies guffawed over their prophesies like a pair of jovial witches, giving Frederick an uneasy suspicion of their merriment over his own masculine bungles. Knowing from his personal experience that whatever he might say would be wrong he carefully agreed with Murray as to the common sense of his plans, showed no skepticism when told that no matter what happened there'd be no need to worry about Judy taking over their nice bachelor quarters. He accepted Murray's comments on Dodo without invitation, for he found himself needing co-operation in the little unpleasant dilemmas that followed her flight. Strange male voices on the phone claiming to be Baltimore cousins or family friends wanted to know if Mr. Olliver could give them Miss Brennan's new address. Frederick was not sure whether he was being made mock of by his many unknown younger rivals of whom Dodo was always boasting, or whether their concern was legitimate. He was glad to have Murray relieve him of this embarrassment by brusquely answering that Miss Brennan's activities were no concern of this telephone number; he maliciously suggested inquiring at the K.G.R. Advertising Co., or at the Paramount's Hollywood office. The worst happened when Dodo's mother came to the apartment in person, a calamity so much more painful than any of Murray's that he forgave Frederick for everything, and after vanquishing the intruder the two men repaired to Umberto's below and sat with the proprietor discussing life in the large over a bottle of consoling grappa. Dodo had often referred to Mama, a Southern gentlewoman of such refinement and moral apprehensions that Dodo could scarcely smoke a cigarette or apply a lipstick without sighing, "Mama would *kill* me if she saw me smoking. Of course, she's a terribly good sport about things and is more like a sister than a mother but being always idolized by Papa and brought up in cotton wool, you might say, she does get shocked sometimes." Frederick had no delusions concerning the lady, surmising that if she were any credit her daughter would have allowed her to visit her in New York. Three days after Dodo's exit, Mrs. Brennan appeared at the Bank Street apartment with a small handbag, arriving as Murray was unlocking the door. Daughter had written her about her distinguished gentleman friend, Mr. Olliver, and knowing Murray from Baltimore Mama could not resist the impulse to talk things out, knowing Mr. Olliver must be as upset as she was over a scandal in the family. She was in the living-room, hat, white cotton gloves and silver fox jacket off before the men could collaborate on defense.

Frederick had not been outside the house since his night with Lorna and Caroline. He could scarcely drive himself to get out of bed, exhausted as if by a long fever, oddly relieved of the burden of his infatuation, but ashamed of his defeat even though no one really knew how much he had been involved. It surprised him that he should experience only a wave of tired relief the moment Dodo's step seemed final. At last he need not fear offending the jaunty blades who telephoned for her, the ones who called her "Dee" or "Brenny" from some secret other life she lived, and spoke to Frederick with the careful respectful tones of thieves addressing the warden. Even if any longing for her remained the visit of Mrs. Brennan would have acted as a shock cure. The lady was a plump duplicate of her daughter, a cartoon of her mannerisms and defects. The small tidy features, half-moon nostrils enlarged as if by long practice in sniffing out valuable contacts, green marble eyes with the roach antennae lashes, pencilled brow arches, querulous bee-stung lips were all incongruously centered in a wide, flat face; the black hair was even blacker and coarser than the daughter's and drawn back to a thick knob at the back of the short bullish neck. The hands were soft and tiny and meaningless as Dodo's were, swelling into slender arms that swung curiously from the thick shoulders. She addressed her image in her compact mirror as lovingly as Dodo ever did, and seemed fully as confident of her power over men. She was nearing her fifties, according to Murray, but sighed regretfully over the tragedy of her approaching birthday.

"I can't *believe* I'm thirty-six next Tuesday, I swear, honey, I swear I just can't believe that old writing in the family Bible! Married at fifteen and all—well, I guess Dodo's told all about me. She always says I never grew up, just stayed like the day I was married, and excepting for putting on six pounds—but thank goodness I still wear a size twelve. I guess Dodo told you how we're always swapping dresses when we have dates, not that I go out except when I get blue and Dodo says 'Mama, for goodness sake, get out and enjoy yourself, you can't live on memories, people will think you're stuckup.' So I go to some of the real nice functions, exclusive little parties, or maybe some high-class hotel. Always with somebody like Judge Haggerty, or the Davenanty lawyers, gentlemen everybody looks up to so there's no talk."

Frederick sat helplessly as the lady prattled on, mentioning fine names of friends and forbears, her voice sweetening and diminishing into a terrifying burlesque of Dodo, and he brushed aside hastily the picture of himself legally attached to these two gentlewomen. Murray handled the situation by pouring out several drinks for the lady and thoughtfully telephoning for hotel reservations in a distant part of the city.

"I just had to tell Mr. Olliver not to break down on account of my little girl running off in that naughty way," said Mrs. Brennan, swigging her drink with a little finger daintily crooked. "Us being more the same age we have to understand how hot-headed youth can be, and I know my daughter did admire you because she sent me lots of clippings about you, knowing how crazy I am about writing and books, especially historical, not just trash, if you know what I mean. I don't want to raise any false hopes, but from all I hear it isn't too certain she'll marry Larry after all. Not that I don't think he shouldn't pay through the nose, though, dragging our family name through all this scandal—well, alright, I'll have a tiny drop more, Murray. Murray's just like family to me, Mr. Olliver, and that's why I didn't hesitate to come right down here, because I knew if hotels were full as they said Murray would want me right here."

"We got a room for you, though," Murray reminded her with a look at Frederick. "Mustn't forget to check in before eight."

Mrs. Brennan declared she was having such a good time getting acquainted that she'd just as soon skip the old hotel and make a night of it with the two gentlemen which Dodo would tell them was certainly a compliment as she was almost too fussy about making friends, probably her convent training and widowed so young with so many important men courting her, and for the sake of the little girl she'd had to be so careful. But she could let herself go, seeing that her little girl wasn't there and these were men of her own generation, maybe a little older, but she thought the man ought to be older than the woman, anyway. Sort of protect her like a daddy, and speaking of daddies, no one had a nicer, sweeter daddy than she had had, a cultured millionaire who lost everything to a less cultured partner but—my goodness, Murray needn't be in such a hurry, they had time for a teentsy night-cap, this time a real power-house, please, on the rocks as Daddy used to say.

Murray's patience with the visitor was doubtless due to his appreciation of Frederick's embarrassment, and an undeniable delight in the astonishing similarity of mother and daughter. For Frederick each moment of the familiar baby voice and gestures, genteel boasting to an obligato of lapel twigging, knee-patting and seemingly casual brushes of her body against whichever man was nearest was hideous burlesque of his recent love's tricks. He dared not picture the two women together, nor think of how near he came to a lifetime of defensively enduring the double cross. When Murray peremptorily wrapped the silver fox cape around her reluctant body, softening the blow by a sly pat on her grateful hip, Frederick sank back in his chair with a shudder. He heard the too-familiar voice in the hall gurgling coyly over Murray's simulated flattery. He heard her cry that her daughter would simply kill her if she heard Mama had been in a bachelors' apartment, but she'd simply had to talk things over with Mr. Olliver, his being an older man of her own generation, actually more apt to be a beau of hers than her daughter's but don't let on she said that. And they knew where to find her if they wanted to go to some quiet little place where people with nasty minds wouldn't talk and they could have a few drinks and a few laughs because she loved a good laugh and had a memory for a good limerick—nothing off-color understand, but just a teentsy bit risqué—cute things the Judge had told her and what a story-teller he was to be sure! And sweet! Leave it to an older man to know how to be nice to a woman, that was one thing she'd tried to drum into Dodo's head, and when she first told her mother about Mr. Olliver it looked as if she had learned, but my goodness, now look what happened! If she'd guessed what was going on Mrs. Brennan declared she would have marched right up to New York City months ago, only Dodo had kept putting her off—honest to goodness she shouldn't be saying so but she honestly believed her Mamma would get her beau away from her—her own Mamma, mind you, but more like a sister, of course. Murray briskly reminded her that the hotel must not be kept waiting and Frederick heard the voice cry petulantly "If you're trying to get rid of me, Murray Cahill, pooh on you, I can get my own self a taxi, you just run right along—" then the hall door closed on Murray's soothing words and her coquettish giggle. Incredible, Frederick thought, trying in vain to shake off the nightmare. He went to the bathroom to turn on a tub with a desperate longing to be cleaned of the curdled musky atmosphere of Dodo's Mamma and all she represented. Judy's gray flannel house-robe hung on the bathroom door, two pairs of her white socks were on the towel rack, a can of turpentine with paint brushes in it under the bowl. No, there was to be no change in their bachelor arrangements with Murray's wedding, Frederick reflected sardonically, no change except that the bride was moving in. He pondered over some paint-smeared garment soaking in the tub, then gave up the idea of a bath as he heard Judy herself come in the door. She was laden with brown parcels and was obviously about to engage in some domestic enterprise involving the front half of the apartment. She greeted Frederick with unaccustomed warmth.

"Murray's bringing up some wine from Umberto's in a minute as soon as he gets that woman a cab. Why don't you have some supper with us after a while?"

The invitation made Frederick the more conscious of being an intruder, an outsider even in his own quarters. He saw that Judy was in a mood to talk and deduced that the procuring of the marriage license had evidently produced a simultaneous speech license. He foresaw a switching of roles with Murray the silent partner and Judy released by happiness into perpetual chatter. That she was happy, there could be no doubt, for her round, blonde face glowed with it, and her usually shy, almost sullen eyes were radiantly friendly.

"It was nice of you to turn your job over to Murray, Frederick," she said. "He thinks he'll like it even if he doesn't like Mr. Strafford. Aren't you going to keep any regular job? I heard someone say you resigned teaching at the League, too."

"I have to catch up on a year's research," Frederick answered, though each time anyone questioned him he was filled with fresh doubts of his future without a regular income, solitary, and now insecure even as to his living place. Even if he did have enough money put aside for three or four years of modest living, it had been rash to abandon both League and Strafford's as soon as Dodo left him. They seemed unpleasantly linked with the whole betrayal and since he could not revenge his own folly on anyone else he wanted to punish himself. If he hadn't taken the *Haw* job Dodo would have been out of his reach, and if he had given up the League job as he had first planned she would never have disrupted his life with Lyle.

"I'm doing some work near Boston this summer, where I can read, too," he explained, and reading Judy's eager expression astutely went on, "I may stay on the college staff all winter if I like, which would give Murray my room here, of course."

Unable to disguise her satisfaction at this prospect Judy changed the subject.

"I can't remember who that woman is I just saw outside with Murray. I know I've seen her and I remember her voice but I can't place her. Oh yes, here's a telegram for you I just signed for."

Frederick took the yellow envelope she extended from under a bag of oranges and went into his own room. The visitation of Mrs. Brennan made him feel physically ill and he sat down on the bed, his hands over his forehead. Not only that but the feeling of being gently pushed out of his home made him desperately lonely, his whole being crying out for Lyle at any price—love, understanding, peace—home. Too late, now, to try to patch things up. With all her kindness she would not accept the sorry overtures of a man publicly rejected by her rival. She would be foolish indeed to take him back on those humiliating terms when Stalk offered fresh, untarnished adoration. Frederick felt his head suddenly bursting with jealousy and cold hatred for the young editor. He vowed to himself that no matter what happened he would withdraw from the *Swan*. A new quarterly had appeared in Boston under distinguished international auspices, and there he would publish his new work—when he got down to it—and let the *Swan* go its way with its too-clever Padillas and young Western aesthetes.

The sight of the ruffled purple satin bolster which Dodo had given him distracted him momentarily. He picked it up gingerly between thumb and forefinger without thinking and pitched it out the open French windows into the general region of the garbage pail. It made him feel better and he tore open the telegram, half sensing what it would be. It was a cablegram from Hamilton, Bermuda. *"Freddie darling Please Forgive Horrible Mistake Please Cable Plane Fare Back Will explain love Your Dodo."*

For a split second a wild rush of joy came over him but it was lost in blazing anger. He tossed the crumpled paper into the grate, wishing it were something that could break with a thunderous crash. His temples pounded with rage and he cast his eye around for further outlet. There was her cute little collection of china and glass monkeys to be swept into the empty fireplace, there was the moustache cup marked "Daddy" she had mirthfully gotten for his Valentine, there was the red satin nightie with pink chiffon jacket she liked to hang over his pajamas when she felt magnanimous, and liked even better to pack up to punish him. Frederick flung the mementoes into the grate, tore the nightgown off the hook into rags and tossed a lighted match into the fireplace after it. He could hear himself panting hoarsely as if he were pushing away some giant boulder, and perspiration dripped from his forehead. The flames were slow to start and he used the Cape Cod lighter and bellows on them till the pretty nightgown swelled out first like a Hollywood pin-up model. The smoke curled above it into a vague ghostly face, sharp nostrils, wolfish lips and then the smoke spread into the wide, flat expanse of head, features now a vague, tiny pocket in the middle, then lost as the flames covered them. The heat brought out the perfume and the room filled with the sickening poisonous incense of Dodo—or was it her mother? Frederick threw open the other window and the garden door. He heard Murray's rap and then a conspiratorial chuckle.

"How about a quick snort now the old girl's gone? A toast to Southern womanhood, suh."

"Thanks for handling her," Frederick managed to say. "I'll be right out."

He stood at the open garden door drawing long deep breaths of the June night. He looked up at the soft innocent sky and remembered the first time he and Lyle had stood in that doorway, admiring the surrounding gardens and sun porches, the budding ailanthus and scrubby ivy vines, exclaiming rapturously over the tropical beauties of Manhattan summer even in near-slums; the remarkable magic of the air, the stars, the view, but most of all their love, newly-minted and shining bright forever. He saw himself as he was then, wretchedly solitary, withdrawn, haughty, shy, carrying himself carefully secret as he had from childhood in a routine of polite helplessness, bursting through the prison only in his work. He remembered the joy of finding Lyle and his reluctant doors opening to unbelievable happiness. Lyle. After a little while he lit a cigarette, closed his doors and went in for the quick snort with Murray. Judy was busy defrosting the dinner, her drink beside her in the kitchenette.

"I don't know who keeps the old girl but she still manages to make 'em fork over," chuckled Murray with the usual masculine good nature over a friend's embarrassment. "Funny thing if you shut your eyes—no, by jove, even if you keep 'em open a little bit, you'd think it was Dodo. Dodo in ten years, anyway. You should have heard her when she got taken with family pride, all mixed up with being jealous of Dodo. Jealous of her own daughter for being younger, can you beat that? She said, 'I'm worried about her good name because Dodo's not a young girl any more. She says she's twenty but she's really twenty-five. You see I was only thirteen when I married!' Here's to our Southern belles, Olliver, you can't beat 'em."

"I guess women are the same all over," said Judy laconically, and Murray winked at Frederick with an approving nod. Judy made sense and had a funny, dry humor when you got to know her, he whispered to his friend. There were lots of things about Judy quite aside from her fine talent.

Even if there weren't, Frederick reflected pessimistically, you could always pretend there were if you were bound to marry her anyway. He did not trust himself to accept the dinner invitation but hastened out, wondering as he locked his own door how long before Judy would ask if he minded her keeping the baby in his room—just while he was out of course. He hesitated outside Lorna Leahy's apartment, hearing Caroline's voice inside, knowing they would welcome his call. But lonely as he was he didn't want to see the ladies. He didn't want anything in the world but Lyle.

27

. . . the mosaic . . .

THE round-faced rosy little fellow waiting for a taxicab in front of the Jefferson Market looked familiar but Frederick did not recognize him as Sam Flannery until he eagerly saluted him.

"You've come up in the world since I last saw you, old man," Flannery exclaimed, pumping his hand. "Over my head, of course, that stuff you write, but give me credit for knowing my limitations. I understand you're coming out in a syndicated strip just like Knights of King Arthur. Congratulations!"

"How are the Gaynors?" Frederick asked.

Flannery's cherub face clouded and he drew Frederick aside, waving away a taxi just drawing to the curb.

"You mean you haven't heard?" he asked. "I thought everybody heard and was blaming me, on account of my being the manager and knowing the girl and all. But Allan Gaynor's a deep one, you know, nobody can handle that guy after a certain point. I covered for him, well, you know how a guy has to cover a client especially when the wife's somebody like Lyle—a lady and collaborator too, part of the picture in every way."

"What are you talking about?" Frederick asked. "Do you mind walking?"

Flannery had just been calling on Lyle, it seems, or trying to but she refused to see anyone. It must have been a shock to her. And Pedro had gone with Allan, there was no maid around, so Flannery didn't know really how she was taking it. She was in, alright, the doorman said, but she didn't answer the door. Fortunately she didn't know the whole story and if luck held it wouldn't get out.

"I still say she was a little to blame, letting things get out of hand," Flannery said plaintively. "She just took no interest in anything for months there just when I told them both they were hot and ought to be producing. I told them. I said— well, anyway, he thought he'd train a new collaborator on the side. He'd kinda got the idea he was like that guy in *Pygmalion*. This Garrett kid seemed willing enough, just a little tramp, but ambitious, ready to take anything. When this other jam came up, he lined up a private train, put it up to the Garrett girl, and they beat it to Palm Springs. He always wanted to go West and Lyle never would, and I fixed up a kind of picture deal—mind you, I don't consider I'm to blame. I just saw which way the cards were falling——"

"He was strong enough to do all that when he wanted to, then," said Frederick. "She—none of us needed to have been so sorry for him, evidently."

"It leaves me in a nice fix," Flannery complained bitterly. "After I stood by and sort of helped, then he doesn't even let me in on the other thing. Having that Trinidad woman up on the roof all the time until her husband—the janitor, mind you, came in and stabbed him! A frame-up if you ask me, but no fool like an old one! Mussed him up so he had to clear out, left me to pay off the couple and shut them up. Lyle doesn't know about that. All she knows is his running off with the other girl. I don't know how much she guessed about what a chaser he was when he got a chance. Any skirt, anything at all."

"I didn't know—" Frederick began.

"Nobody thought he could, of course," Flannery said gloomily. "A tart could always guess or someone like this janitor's wife. I'm telling you because you're an old friend and I'd like someone to appreciate what I've done, hushing up a juicy bit like that. I might know he'd try to doublecross me if he could, because he's got his own idea of what's funny. Lyle could tell you that but I guess you know. I'm kind of afraid she doesn't like me any more and I can't very well tell her what I've done for her. You might put in a good word. When all's said and done I'm the guy that put those two on the map. I deserve a break from one or the other and she's the one I could really sell, if I could get her to working again. He's through except for riding on the old name in Hollywood, maybe. He isn't kidding anybody but himself and maybe that dumb cluck."

They were approaching the Square and Frederick was no longer listening. His whole being ached and throbbed with the unaccustomed idea of Lyle in trouble, Lyle betrayed, alone, needing him as he had always needed her, but too proud as always to call for help. He could scarcely bear to listen to the peevish chatter of the rosy young man who had outsmarted himself by working against Lyle.

"Who helped him get away?" Frederick demanded, concealing his dislike as best he could. "A man in his condition must have had pretty powerful co-operation all along the line to be able to run away. Not able to move but able to make a getaway across the country."

"Your friend Cordelay Beckley," Flannery replied. "You were bound to hear it from him anyway, being down at his place as I've heard. I wouldn't have said anything if I hadn't been sure he would have told you, anyway."

Frederick stopped abruptly.

"I go in the other direction," he said. "So long."

He crossed the street, aware that Flannery was standing on the corner gaping at him, chubby choir-boy face dismayed and bewildered.

Poor Lyle, he thought, always protected but now with no one. He hurried down the street, and when he reached the apartment house he stopped and lit a cigarette, trying to think, but in a way it was better not to think. The fat white-haired Irish doorman recognized him and pushed the automatic elevator button for him.

"That's the way they'll do it tomorrow with the atom bomb," he said, beaming. "Just press a button, they say. A wonderful age we're in, Mr. Olliver. Just press a button and blow up a whole country. My wife declares she's afraid to even listen to it on the radio. Says maybe the whole world will blow up, not just Bikini."

Frederick nodded impatiently. The car shot upward and he got off on the third floor in the Gaynor foyer. He rang the bell but there was no answer. After a few more attempts he rapped on it with his knuckles and called her name.

"It's alright, Lyle," he said softly, hearing a faint motion from within, and his heart smote him that he should have contributed to her terror of facing a visitor. I won't hurt you, this time, I will be very careful of the wounds I have already given you, you can count on me for that much kindness. . . .

The door opened and he saw Lyle, pale and defiant in a dark gray trailing negligee, eyes unsmiling, shadowed with purple from headache, weeping, or illness. They stood looking at each other, silently. Frederick tried to speak but only his lips moved and besides there was nothing to say. Slowly she opened the door wider and he took a step inside. She seemed smaller or it might be that he had never seen her helpless and bewildered before. It was like taking a child in his arms.

They had said all these things to each other a thousand times before. They had told each other over and over of the loneliness they had known until they met; they had confided often the half-life inadequacy of all experiences, joys or triumphs away from each other, the way nothing in their days was complete until they had told it to each other; they had marvelled for years that all pain vanished when they were in each other's arms, and they had told each other the little remembered woes of childhood for the other to console. Yet all Sunday morning they said these things again, listening eagerly even with amazement.

"Until I met you," Frederick said, "I thought of myself as a kind of spectator at all human antics, never a participant. You were like the beautiful prima ballerina who stopped in the ballet to pull me into the carnival."

"You taught the ballerina the meaning of her dance, my dear," Lyle said, and did not add that the lesson had gone so deep she could not dance again with the meaning gone. They did not speak of Dodo. Whatever they repeated now, however, was new for they were different people. Before, in the confidence of their love they had scarcely listened to words or meanings, hearing only the beloved's voice and delighting in his presence, certain of knowing and loving each tiniest wish or thought. Then, suddenly, they found they were strangers, each was capable of desires and deeds beyond either of their imaginations. Now they listened and fell in love anew at words they knew by heart. Frederick lay in her bed, and whether it was herself or the image of his lost Dodo to which he had made such violent love Lyle did not ask, knowing only that he was hers again, that it did not matter who found him here or saw their love, now that they needed each other so desperately. It was Sunday and they made their own coffee and talked of Frederick's new plans, of Lyle's first play, of an apartment in Boston for a while, perhaps, and he spoke of wasted sacrifice.

"The same things would have happened even if I'd divorced Allan years ago and we'd married," Lyle said. "I wonder now if I was sacrificing anything but you to Allan. Whatever it was, I don't believe anybody but the sacrificer really gets any value from the sacrifice. He always wanted to go to the Southwest and he's gone. I must have been unsure not to have faced the whole truth before. I must have. The way I never faced the fact that you were a young bachelor, in a woman's world so that any new face——"

"You created the face yourself," Frederick said. "You created your own enemy, not believing, suspecting——"

"Must we remember it?" Lyle begged. "Must we?"

Frederick drew a deep breath.

"Darling, I was unfaithful to you," he murmured, "but it was my own heart I broke. I could never stand it again. No, there are things I couldn't bear."

Lyle, combing her hair at the vanity table, smiled at him in the mirror. She could bear anything, she thought. There was never too much that a person could give or endure in love. Frederick was idly fiddling with the bedside radio and there was a sputtering of words and confused noises.

"It's the Bikini test—the atom bomb the elevator man's wife is afraid of," Frederick said.

"When you hear the words—'What goes here' that will be the signal——" said the faraway voice, and suddenly Frederick was filled with fear, too. He went over to Lyle and held her tightly. In a world of destruction one must hold fast to whatever fragments of love are left, for sometimes a mosaic can be more beautiful than an unbroken pattern.

THE WICKED PAVILION

*". . . oh this wicked Pavilion! We were kept there till
half-past one this morning waiting for the Prince,
and it has kept me in bed with the head-ache till
twelve to-day. . . ."*

Mrs. Creevey to Mr. Creevey
from *The Creevey Papers*

CONTENTS

PART ONE

. . . *entrance* . . .

SHORTLY after two a sandy-haired gentleman in the middle years hurried into the Café Julien, sat down at Alexander's table as he always did, ordered coffee and cognac as he always did, asked for stationery as he always did, shook out a fountain pen and proceeded to write. Considering that this was the very same man who spent each morning staring, motionless, before a typewriter in a midtown hotel, it was surprising how swiftly his pen moved over the pages at the café table. At five, just as the first cocktail customers were arriving, he paid his check, pocketed his papers and went to the desk in the lobby.

"Keep this for me," he said to the clerk, handing over the manuscript.

"Okay, Mr. Orphen," said the clerk, and opened the safe to put it with Mr. Orphen's other papers.

The sandy-haired man went out, buttoning up his overcoat in the flurry of snow over Washington Square, hailed a taxi and drove back to the hotel room where he sat for a while staring at the empty page in the typewriter until he decided it was time to get drunk.

That was the day he had written on the Julien stationery:

There was nothing unusual about that New York winter of 1948 for the unusual was now the usual. Elderly ladies died of starvation in shabby hotels leaving boxes full of rags and hundred-dollar bills; bands of children robbed and raped through the city streets, lovers could find no beds, hamburgers were forty cents at lunch counters, truck drivers demanded double wages to properly educate their young in the starving high-class professions; aged spinsters, brides and mothers were shot by demented youths, frightened girls screamed for help in the night while police, in pairs for safety's sake, pinned tickets on parked automobiles. Citizens harassed by Internal Revenue hounds jumped out of windows for want of forty dollars, families on relief bought bigger television sets to match the new time-bought furniture. The Friendly Loan agent, the Smiling Banker, the Laughing Financial Aid lurked in dark alleys to terrorize the innocent; baby sitters received a dollar an hour with torture concessions; universities dynamited acres of historic mansions and playgrounds to build halls for teaching history and child psychology. Men of education were allowed to make enough at their jobs to defray the cost of going to an office; parents were able, by patriotic investment in the world's largest munitions plant, to send their sons to the fine college next door to it, though time and labor would have been saved by whizzing the sons direct from home to factory to have their heads blown off at once.

It was an old man's decade.

Geriatricians, endowed by the richest octogenarians, experimented on ways of prolonging the reign of the Old and keeping the enemy, Youth, from coming into its own. Pediatricians were subsidized to strengthen, heighten and toughen the young for soldiering; the eighteenth-birthday banquets were already being planned, the festive maypoles of ticker tape set up, the drummers hired, the invitations with government seals sent out, the marching songs rehearsed. The venerable statesmen and bankers were generously taking time off from their golfing, yachting and money-changing for the bang-up affair that would clear the earth once again of these intruders on old-men pleasures and profits. Some who had triumphed too long were deviled by fear of a turn of fortune and besieged their psychoanalysts for the expensive reassurance that they were after all boss-men, superior to their victims and the ordinary rules. When the stifled conscience croaked of justice to come they scuttled feverishly to the Church and clutched their winnings behind the King's X of the sacred robes.

In the great libraries professors studied ways of doing away with books; politicians proclaimed reading and writing unnecessary and therefore illegal, for the action of written words on the human brain might induce thought, a subversive process certain to incite rebellion at robot leadership. All the knowledge required for the soldier generation could be pumped in by loudspeaker; eyes must be saved for target practice, hands preserved for bayonets. Why allow an enemy bomb to blast our accumulated culture when we can do it ourselves by government process?

In the city the elements themselves were money: air was money, fire was money, water was money, the need of, the quest for, the greed for. Love was money. There was money or death.

But there were many who were bewildered by the moral mechanics of the age just as there are those who can never learn a game no matter how long they've been obliged to play it or how many times they've read the rules and paid the forfeits. If this is the way the world is turning around, they say, then by all means let it stop turning, let us get off the cosmic Ferris wheel into space. Allow us the boon of standing still till the vertigo passes, give us a respite to gather together the scraps of what was once *us*—the old longings for what? for whom? that gave us our wings and the chart for our tomorrows.

There must be some place along the route, a halfway house in time where the runners may pause and ask themselves why they run, what is the prize and is it the prize they really want? What became of Beauty, where went Love? There must be havens where they may be at least remembered.

The shadow that lay over the land was growing mightily and no one escaped it. As in countries ruled by the Gestapo or the guillotine one must only whisper truths, bribe or be bribed, ask no questions, give no answers, police or be policed, run in fear and silence ahead of the shadow.

. . . a young man against the city . . .

At half past nine that February evening the Café Julien around the corner from Washington Square was almost deserted. Solitary gentlemen on the prowl strolled in expectantly, ready to crowd into any corner if the place was jammed, but horrified into quick retreat at sight of the empty tables. Three young teachers, briefed by *Cue* Magazine on how to have a typically French evening in New York, had cast a stricken glance into the bleak expanse of marble tables and mirror walls, then backed out.

"This can't be the place," one cried out. "It looks like a mausoleum."

The remark brought complacent smiles to the grim-faced old waiters, guarding their tables with folded arms like shepherds of old. The Julien waiters were forthright self-respecting individuals who felt their first duty was to protect the café from customers, their second to keep customers and employers in their proper places. The fact that only two of the marble-topped tables were occupied was a state of business perversely satisfactory to these waiters, who had the more leisure for meditation and the exchange of private insults. A young Jersey-looking couple peered curiously in the doorway looking for some spectacular rout that would explain the place's cosmopolitan reputation, then drew back puzzled at seeing only two patrons. Karl, the Alsatian with the piratical mustaches, turned down a chair at each of his three empty tables, indicating mythical reservations, folded his arms again and stared contentedly at the chipped cupids on the ceiling. The more excitable Guillaume, given to muttering personal comments behind his patrons' backs, flapped his napkin busily as if shooing out flies, and shouted after the innocent little couple, "Kitchen closed now, nothing to eat, kitchen closed."

The two solitary diners who remained at their tables after the dinner crowd had departed smiled with the smug pleasure of insiders at such a typical demonstration of the café's quixotic hospitality. The plump monkish little waiter, Philippe (said by many old-timers to resemble Dubois, the celebrated waiter of Mouquin's where the artist Pennell, you may recall, hung a plaque in his honor, "*A boire—Dubois*") turned from his peaceful contemplation of the old fencing studio across the way to twinkle merrily down at his favorite patron, Monsieur Prescott. He liked Monsieur Prescott first because he loved youth and beauty, seldom found in this rendezvous dedicated to testy old gourmets, miserly world travelers, battered bon vivants and escapees from behind the frank-and-apple-pie curtain. Philippe liked Monsieur Prescott above all because he had the grace to appear only every two or three years, while other customers were exasperatingly regular. Philippe felt young and refreshed just looking at Ricky Prescott, a young man built for the gridiron, wide of shoulder, strong white teeth flashing above square pugnacious jaw, long legs sprawling under the table, hard black eyes ever looking for and receiving friendship and approbation. Other Julien visitors were always asking Philippe who was this breezy young man, so obviously from the wide-open spaces, and what did he do.

"It is Monsieur Prescott, a very good friend of mine," Philippe always replied with dignity, as if this covered everything. Hundreds of people all over the world would have given the same answer, for Rick had the knack of getting on with all classes and all ages, ruling out all barriers, loving good people wherever he found them. Stray dogs followed him, office boys called him by his first name; cops, taxi drivers, bootblacks never forgot him, nor he them. He had been back in New York for several weeks and had been popping into the Julien almost every day. Tonight he and Philippe had gone through their usual little game of ordering the dinner.

"What do I want tonight, Philippe?" Rick had asked.

"Blue points in *sauce mignonne*, *pommes soufflées*, squab *sous cloche*," Philippe had said, straight-faced.

"Fine, I'll have pork chops and Schaeffer's light," Rick had answered, and as always during this routine Philippe had demanded to know why a strapping fellow with the appetite of a bear and no taste for good food should ever leave those big steak-and-pie places on Broadway. Why did he choose to come to the Julien anyway?

"Why does anybody come here?" countered Ricky.

Philippe gave this question some judicious thought.

"They come because they have always come here," he said.

"Why did they come here the first time, then?"

"Nobody ever comes to the Julien for the first time," Philippe said, and as this was a thought that appealed to him hugely, his plump little body shook with noiseless chuckles. Recovering his gravity he leaned toward Ricky's ear and asked, "You tell me why you come here."

Rick frowned.

"I guess because something happened to me once here and I keep thinking it might happen again, I don't know what, but—well I'm always expecting something I don't expect."

He grinned with a confidential wink that captivated

Philippe, whose inner chuckles began all over, this time ending in a little toy squeak.

"Maybe you expect Miss Cars, hey?" he said slyly.

Miss "Cars" (and Philippe was tickled to see that the young man flushed at the name) was a young lady romantically identified with Monsieur Prescott, indeed the real reason for Prescott's devotion to the Julien as both of them well knew. It was on Prescott's first visit to the café that he had met Miss Cars, it was Miss Cars he sought in the café every time he returned to New York. It was here they quarreled and said good-bye for ever, it was here they made up after long separations, here they misunderstood each other again, and here Prescott once again was seeking the lost love.

"Oh, Miss Carsdale," Ricky said. "How is Miss Carsdale, Philippe?"

"I no see Miss Cars, like I told you," Philippe sighed. His feet were too tired after a lifetime of carrying trays to and from the distant kitchen to tramp out the final syllables of long words. He would have liked to be able to produce Monsieur Prescott's little lady or at least to give him advice on how to find her again. He had a vague recollection of some scene last time the two had been there and of Miss Cars running out of the café alone.

"Maybe Miss Cars think you not nice to her," he ventured vaguely.

The young man was righteously offended.

"Me not nice to her?" he repeated bitterly. "After all she got me into?"

He was about to recite his grievances to Philippe, decided they were too complicated, and allowed Philippe to waddle away for another beer while he sat brooding. It was undeniably Miss Cars who had made him reject the fine job in Calcutta after World War II for the simple reason that he was wild to get back to her. It was Miss Cars's fault he had got tangled up with three other women just because of her maddening virtue. Yes, there was no question but that Miss Cars, fragile and sweet as she was, had precipitated Rick Prescott from one mistake into another. It was her fault entirely, and this was how it had happened.

Seven years ago in the excitement of our-regiment-sails-at-dawn, Monsieur Prescott had made a heavy-handed attack on Miss Carsdale's virtue on the spittle-and-sawdust-strewn staircase of an old loft building on East Eighth Street where she rented a work studio for her photography. Whenever he remembered that night Rick cursed the mischievous jinx that had twisted the most magical day of his life into a sordid memory. It was the first time he'd ever been in New York, the city of his dreams, the first time he'd worn his officer's uniform, the first time he'd been drunk on champagne. New York loved him as it loved no other young man, and he embraced the city, impulsively discarding everything he had hitherto cherished of his Michigan boyhood loyalties. In Radio City Gardens he looked up at the colossal Prometheus commanding the city's very heart and thought, Me! He wandered up and down in a kind of smiling daze, slipped away from the buddies and home-town friends supervising his departure, and strolled happily down Fifth Avenue, finding all faces beautiful and wondrously kind, the lacy fragility of the city trees incomparably superior to his huge native forests. Under the giant diesel hum of street and harbor traffic he caught the sweet music of danger, the voices of deathless love and magic adventure.

My city, he had exulted, mine for these few hours at least, no matter what comes after. He wanted to embrace the Library lions, follow each softly smiling girl to the ends of the earth, bellow his joy from the top of the Empire State building. Wandering on foot or bus in a joyous daze he suddenly came at evening upon the treasure itself, a softly lit quiet park into which the avenue itself disappeared. Bewildered, breathless, as if he had come upon Lhasa, he walked around the little park, seeing couples strolling, arms about each other, windows of vine-covered houses lighting up, hearing church chimes, as if the city outside this was only a dream. The sign on the canopy of a corner mansion, CAFE JULIEN, told him he was in Greenwich Village and this café was the very place he was to meet his friends for dinner. And here they were waiting for him, not believing that he had stumbled there by chance, not even believing his day's adventure had been with a city and not a girl.

He kissed all the girls enthusiastically, regardless of the men in the party who were all spending the war comfortably in

Washington or at 90 Church Street. He was handsomer and younger than they, and grateful for his departure they sang his praises while the girls found patriotic excuse to stroke his black hair or urge soft thighs against his. Rick loved them all, loved the café, loved even war since it had brought him here. With each fresh champagne he looked for the wonderful surprise, the special adventure that the city had surely promised him.

All around the café he could see little groups chattering happily, new arrivals being joyously welcomed, tables joining other tables, and though eyes strayed to the good-looking young soldier, Rick had a pang of knowing they were complete without him, they would be complete long after he had left on his unknown journey. Tomorrow night these very friends of his would celebrate without him; even Maidie Rennels, who felt she had home-town rights to him, was already planning a theatre party with someone else. The city he had fallen in love with would carry no mark from him, this café would not know he was gone. Impatient with these glimpses of future loneliness he suggested going to other spots, gayer and louder, where tomorrows could be drowned out in music.

"But we have to wait for Ellenora," Maidie Rennels kept explaining. "Don't you remember I wrote you all about Ellenora, the girl I met when I was studying at the League? She has a studio around the corner and we told her we'd be here."

"You mean Rick doesn't know Ellenora?" someone else asked, and shook her head pityingly.

You may have observed that whenever you enter a new group there is apt to be constant allusion to some fabulous character who is not present, someone whose opinions are quoted on all subjects, someone so witty or unique that you find yourself apologizing for not having met him or her. You may think you are having a perfectly good time, but how can you when this marvelous creature is not present? The name "Ellenora" was dangled before Rick until he began working up a foggy hostility to the absent one. Ellenora was everyone's darling, all painters wanted to capture her charm on canvas, and she herself, a child of artists, was wonderfully gifted, studying art on money she earned as a photographer. How exciting for her to be engaged to marry Bob Huron who had proper security to give an artist wife, and who adored her as she deserved. What a pity Ricky might never be privileged to meet her! Ricky began to feel that her absence was a subtle snub to him, and her being engaged to another man without even waiting to meet Richard Prescott was an insult. Then the sudden arrival of Ellenora in person changed everything.

"Darling—you did come after all— Look, here's Ellenora. See, Ricky, here's Ellenora, the girl we've been telling you about—"

"Just for a minute," Ellenora had said, as they pulled out a chair for her. "I'm on my way to the studio to pick up some proofs but I had to stop in to say hello."

Ricky's unreasoning prejudice wavered at first sight of her radiant little face. He had braced himself for a blasé beauty from a Hollywood picture of artists' life, a too clever poseur, full of arty talk and sophisticated repartee. This girl was nothing like that nor was she like any girl Rick had ever known. She had a delicate, quaint femininity that belonged to the past and seemed all the more striking in the New York setting. All in a moment the others seemed blowzy, their gaiety heavy-handed, their friendliness aggressive, their flattery obvious. He marveled that he had ever found hearty Maidie Rennels even mildly desirable. Ellenora had the teasing fascination of a light perfume, hovering in a room long after the unknown visitor has vanished.

She disarmed him by being no beauty, yet he couldn't keep his eyes away from the luminous pallor of her face, the delicate, humorously tilted nose, the tender, voluptuous coral mouth, the wide-apart eager hazel eyes with the soft babyish shadows beneath and the fine silky blond hair drawn sleekly up from the pretty ears, from which hung heavy topaz earrings. Whatever it was she wore—the tiny brown chiffon hat with its scarf falling over the shoulder of the cinnamon wool dress, the unexpected glimpses of bright emerald green silk somewhere in the lining of her brown cape—seemed special to Rick and made the other women appear drab. Whatever it was she said made the others seem stupid. They sounded shrill beside her soft breathless voice that seemed to quiver on the verge of either tears or laughter, just as the gentle comments she made seemed halfway dolorous and halfway comical but always miraculously right to him. At that time there was a special vocabulary college girls used as a precaution, it would seem, against communication. But Ellenora talked, as many articulate artists do, in terms of visual imagery and it was new to Rick. Even her long narrow hand fluttering to secure a stray lock of hair or to stamp out a cigarette in the ashtray bewitched him, hinting of the sweet helplessness of long-ago ladies.

He felt himself back again in his schooldays, a halfback when he wanted to be a bookworm, always too big for his age, clumsy and oafish, hands and feet all over the place. It angered him that she should have this effect on him, reducing him to the old boyish sense of inadequacy. He felt rebuffed when she took a seat on the other side of the table, and to show how little her presence affected him he found himself directing idiotic taunts at her, which she received with polite indifference. There was a lacy unreality about her that reminded him of the ailanthus branches or the Chrysler Tower he had admired. He suspected she must be amused by his too obvious subjugation, and he tried to restore his happy self-assurance by challenging every remark she made until the others cried out, "Rick, stop picking on Ellenora, she's such a darling!"

Any person experienced in love recognizes these outwardly hostile first encounters between a man and woman as the storm signal of immediate attraction, but fortunately for the two, the ordinary bystander reads only the exterior antagonism. Ellenora, only recently engaged to her nice young broker, was immediately conscious of the electric bond between her and this soldier and it frightened her that whatever this new feeling was—reckless, dizzy, ecstatic—she had never had it for Bob Huron, the man she was going to marry. Even when each of them spoke to someone else they were saying something wild and dangerous to each other. Ellenora tried to tell herself that it was the young man's situation, not the man himself, which was shaking her emotions as they had never been shaken before. He was going away to war, that was all. She hated the other men, her friends, for their safe jobs. She hated the tenderness with which the gods protect mediocrity while the rare irreplaceable specimens must be tossed into danger. She wished it was Bob Huron who was saying good-bye and as soon as she found herself thinking this she knew she could never marry Bob, never, never, not even if she never saw this soldier again. These strange sensations and thoughts filled her with terror. She did not know what she was saying, when she spoke, except it must be something he willed her to say. She kept her eyes from him lest they fill with frightened, revealing tears, and it relieved her that he construed this as a snub. Let him think she disapproved of him rather than guess that her lips must be guarded to keep the word "Love!" from flying out to him. The more he mocked at her sobriety in contrast to the merry party the more shaken and foolishly bewitched she felt. Nothing like this had ever happened to her in her twenty years and surely this kind of sudden sickness must betray itself to everyone else if not to him. Bob Huron, she thought, appalled, how could I ever have thought of marrying him when I know there is this man somewhere in the world? She would have to leave, before whatever in the air swelled into an explosion.

"I have an early appointment tomorrow and have to leave," she said, rising. "You know I told you I had to pick up some work at my studio and couldn't come along. But I couldn't resist saying hello—"

"See what you've done, Rick," the Barnard girl exclaimed. "You've teased her so much she's going."

"I told you I had to leave early," Ellenora said almost sharply.

Rick's face looked suddenly desolate.

"I won't have it said I drove away a lady," he said and pushed back his own chair. "I'll walk her to her door to make up for it."

Going out the café door they had walked along in a tense silence that was like a fierce embrace. These things did happen, one did meet the one love, knew it at once, fought it, surrendered to it, stayed forever true.

"Where have you been all my life?" he finally asked and the question seemed brilliantly original to the bemused girl.

"Nowhere, I guess," she answered helplessly.

"What will you be doing until I get back?" he asked.

"Nothing," she murmured and they were hushed as if they had just exchanged solemn vows. They walked slowly along Eighth Street, hand in hand, and the silence seemed to fill in everything that Ellenora wanted said. She was beginning to wonder if she dared risk asking him up to the studio, for legally the students and artists were not allowed at night in these condemned old buildings except for emergencies. If they did manage to creep up there, if she could manage to build a fire in the fireplace—for really this was an emergency, once in a lifetime you might say—

"Here we are," she whispered at the entrance to the bleak loft building where she had her studio. At that instant, without warning, Rick made a wild predatory lunge toward her. When she pushed him away he backed into an ashcan that tipped over in the gutter with a tremendous clatter and suddenly the spell was broken and Rick was roaring with laughter.

"Please be quiet, Rick, or I'll lose my studio!" she cried.

The humiliation of his chasing her up the dirty staircase where any passer-by could see the clumsy struggle, her shame at her own sentimental expectations when all of their friends back at the café must have anticipated just such shenanigans made Ellenora give a heartbroken sob and a slap that sent him off balance tumbling down smack into the ashheap. She bolted the door behind her and stood there trembling, afraid to go on upstairs now and afraid to go out and back home to her apartment on Irving Place until he had gone. Everything that had seemed true between them now seemed a romantic schoolgirl distortion. He was just a soldier on leave, nothing more. She should have expected nothing more. He must have thought she was a complete fool. And she was, she was! She would never forgive him, but now she would never marry anyone else, never.

Prescott, for his part, was furiously disgusted with himself. The moment she had said "Here we are" he realized this was the end and he had swooped on her like some cave man, fully as astonished at himself as Ellenora had been. The ashcan episode restored him to his senses but then in his disappointment and embarrassment he had worked up a rage at the girl who had led him on to believe she had the understanding of angels. Didn't she realize that finding the city of his dreams and dream girl to match on the very night he plunged into nowhere was a miracle no man could handle? He was twenty-six, decent, already an officer, and if he was good enough to be killed for his country he deserved some help in his emotional crises even if he had acted like a lumberjack. More unfair still was the fact that he, a prize marksman and athletic champion, should be sent hurtling down ten dirty steps into a garbage pile, forced to spend his precious hours before sailing in a doctor's office having three stitches taken in his head, all caused by a feeble little tap from a small white hand.

So this was Love at First Sight. So this was what happened when you met the dream girl. Brooding over this with mounting indignation on the flight to England, Ricky had celebrated his first night there by gallantly getting engaged to a Liverpool barmaid, also disappointed in love, who had listened sympathetically to him and who did him the inestimable favor of eloping with a corporal before he had his first leave. Three years later the armistice brought him back to New York and since New York was Ellenora he was in a fever to find her again, past error forgotten. He was so sure she had not married, so sure his own mark was on her, that it did not even seem chance to find her in the little art shop near the Julien. Of course he would find her. Of course she had not married. Of course she would meet him whenever he asked. And of course everything would be the same as before.

They met every day at five at Philippe's table in the Café Julien—same place, same waiter, same table as their first meeting, for they must start all over from scratch they tacitly agreed. They laughed a great deal, spoke very warily of personal matters, maintaining the gay exterior intimacy possible only in café relationships, where a man is as rich as his credit and a lady is as glamorous as her hat. Ricky, reduced again to being overgrown boy with tiny dainty woman of the world, knowing too well the sudden wild impulses that carried him away, tried to maintain his masculine poise by cagily indicating that this relationship was only a delightful oasis in his otherwise full life. Ellenora, being all loving and as dangerously bemused by the young man as before, guarded her susceptibilities by behaving archly worldly and mysterious. The very violence of their attraction for each other put them fiercely on guard, as often happens to people who use up their resistance on one great desire and have none left for the mildest of future temptations. They skipped gracefully around the edge of love, retreated when it compelled them to look into its blinding face. Avoiding major issues they found minor ones turned major wherever they turned. How strange that they had both read *The Life of the Bee*, odd that they both knew Cummings' poetry by heart, rather uncanny that they preferred the bare charm of the Café Julien to uptown gayer spots. Prescott had a dim idea that Ellenora had come to New York to study art from somewhere in New England; Ellenora gathered that Prescott stemmed from Michigan, and that he had studied some kind of engineering.

They asked no questions of each other, barely mentioning other names or other places in their lives but finding each other out in a kind of breathless, intoxicating hide-and-seek. And the truth was that everything else faded away in the excitement of each other's presence. They would have forgotten to eat or drink if Philippe's affectionate supervision had not nudged them. Wary of allowing strong drink to betray his emotions as it had at their first meeting, Rick suggested vermouth cassis for the first week of their postwar cocktail meetings, and they parted discreetly at seven with great checking of wrist watches to imply other important claims. The second week, confident of their civilized control, they graduated to the pernod that was just coming back on the market, and though this heightened their pleasure in each other they still pretended that their daily meetings were accidental, a continuous lark maintained as a joke on the friends who thought they hated each other. A little more lax under pernod they did not look at the clock until the tables were filling with diners, tablecloths being whisked over marbletops. Then with little exclamations of alarm each must rush out to the hall to telephone explanations to importunate dinner companions waiting elsewhere. The third week they did not even try to part but stayed until the café closed and then Ellenora allowed him to take her to her door.

Ellenora's feminine pride made her take pains to indicate that though she enjoyed his company, her availability was

purely accidental; she was by no means a girl to be forgotten
for three years (war or no war) and then picked up at a moment's notice. She hoped he would never find out that the
day after he had sailed she had broken her engagement to
Bob Huron. She hoped he would not hear about the young
doctor she had been on the verge of engaging herself to
just at the moment Rick next came into her life, changing
everything. She was afraid to risk seeing him alone in her
studio, not for fear he would take advantage of her, but for
fear this time she would surrender too easily. Rick was smart
enough to make no demand, his own pride (as long as he
could hold on to it) was in demonstrating that he never made
the same mistake twice. The fourth week they discovered
French Seventy-fives, a seasonal favorite concocted of brandy
and champagne which made them laugh long and loud at
their new-found wit, reach across the table for each other's
hands over some delectable comment, find each other's eyes
suddenly and stop laughing for a breathless moment. By this
time Ellenora was recklessly putting all her eggs in one basket,
refusing dates with nice fellows who adored her, and arranging for special permission from the landlord to live in her
work studio since the apartment she shared with two other
girls left no privacy for love. She intended to resist stalwartly
of course, but she was desperately eager for the opportunity
to show her strength.

One night they were in the café dawdling over French
Seventy-fives, putting off the moment of parting, when some
army pals of Rick joined them. Ellenora hoped they would go
for she had decided this was to be the night, but Rick kept
urging them to stay. Their drinks were two dollars apiece and
the check was bound to be big enough to send an ordinary
young couple on a week-end honeymoon (for Ellenora was
ridiculously thinking on those lines), but what really stabbed
her was hearing Rick, who had told her nothing of this, carelessly mention to his friends that he expected to take a job in
Chicago next week. Stunned at the foolish dreams she had
been building on this man for a second heartbreak, mortified
at the thought of how close her surrender had been, Ellenora
sipped her drink, smiling stiffly at the loud jokes about other
girls in other places, Rick's record as a wolf, and how they

might have known he would hide a creature as lovely as Ellenora in some out-of-the-way place like this where no one else could have a chance at her. It was then that Rick, a little disturbed perhaps by his friends' obvious interest in Ellenora, took it into his head to relate the story of their ashcan romance, embellishing it to his advantage, declaring that he had noticed this kid had had One Too Many and had gallantly offered to take her home from the restaurant.

"I was drinking Coca-cola that night," Ellenora had protested, but the men paid no attention and she realized that every one of the warriors would have told the same story in the same way so she couldn't really blame Ricky too much. But when it came to the payoff, the part where one little tap from her sent him sprawling, Ricky's version for the boys was that this poor sweet kid couldn't make it up the stairs and he had tried to carry her upstairs so her folks wouldn't be worried—

"My folks!" Ellenora had interrupted in indignation. "They weren't even living there!"

—then the girl, whose name, mind you, he had not even caught, took her purse trimmed in heavy gold and slugged him with it so he had to have eighteen stitches taken, all because these New York girls insisted on mistaking simple kindness as attacks on their honor. The loud laughter of the men, Rick's humorous admission of getting his only war wounds from a five-foot virgin infuriated Ellenora, fearful as she was that Rick might guess the thought of him was all that had kept her a virgin in his absence.

"At least he came out alive," she said, managing a sweet smile. "What Rick never knew was that I was trying to save him from getting killed by the man waiting for me upstairs."

With these words, which she noted had the effect of turning the laughter on Rick, she picked up her coat and said, "That reminds me, somebody might kill me right now if I don't get home. Good night, everybody. And incidentally, Ricky, I'm five-feet-five."

It was such a mean trick to humiliate him in front of his pals, implying that he wasn't getting anywhere with her and had been so naïve as to think her a virgin, that Rick did not even rise for her departure, merely saluting her with smiling fury.

"A second round for you, my dear," he said. "I assure you there won't be a third."

Having successfully ruined her own good name and future happiness Ellenora marched out victorious, all ready to embark on months of weeping nightmares over her insane act. That was what happened when you held on to your normal impulses so rigidly, your whole being got deranged and trained for every other kind of self-destruction. They had ruined the reality with their foolish little game. Grimly flinging himself into a two-day binge Rick took one buddy's drunken challenge to fly to Texas next day. There he signed up with the fellow's oil company, and generously married his sister, a good-natured big girl who had tearfully confided men didn't like her because she had no mystery and didn't play little games. In another year she was no longer good-natured (having been praised for that alone too often) and he was a free man again, celebrating the annulment in New Orleans during Mardi gras, when the desire came over him for Ellenora. He was in his room at the St. Charles, drinking sloe gin with a lot of fine strangers in masquerade costumes, when his forgotten long-distance call came through, and when Ellenora heard all the babes giggling she hung up, thinking it was one more cruel joke. This time he didn't come to his senses till a month later in St. Croix with a girl he had taken along for a Mardi gras gag (after Ellenora's brush-off), and it took plenty of time and legal business, for this babe was no fool, to get rid of her and then, happily, a transfer to the New York office. He was still with the Glistro Oil Company, doing very well, though he knew and had in fact known for some time that the job bored him, and each unasked for promotion depressed him. His friends and family irritated him by their praise of his success with Glistro Oil as if this was a loftier career than they had ever dreamed of for him. In these moments of unreasonable dissatisfaction he longed for Ellenora, as if Ellenora and New York would resolve his future, Ellenora would somehow illuminate the wonderful road he was destined to follow. Until then he must mark time, venting his unrest in wild ruinous ways, and someday they could not be undone. Ellenora was his future, his dream, his harbor.

He still hated to admit her spell over him, and he put off surrendering to it, certain she would be around and available, and he could save his vanity by letting her make the first steps. Again he would make it a casual reunion, he thought, strolling into the old Julien café and running into her. Only this time it didn't happen.

At first in this 1948 winter he didn't even ask for her, just took to occasionally dropping into the café, then daily as his stubbornness got aroused. Finally he asked a question idly here and there, and at last he made a definite quest. From a walk down Eighth Street he saw that her old studio was torn down, from the janitor of her old apartment house on Irving Place he found that her two roommates had married without leaving their new names, from a telephone call to her old fiancé, Bob Huron, he received the chilly news that neither Mr. Huron nor his new wife had kept in touch with Miss Carsdale. From the corner florist he learned that flowers had been sent to her at some uptown address a year ago but he could not discover by whom. Nor was their mutual friend, Maidie Rennels, to be found at her apartment. By this time Rick was leaving messages, in case anyone met her, to call him at his office or leave word in care of the Café Julien. He moved from his hotel to a furnished apartment near the Julien, not admitting to himself that he proposed to trap her in there before she could get away next time.

"You're sure you haven't heard anything about her?" Rick asked Philippe, the waiter.

Philippe shook his head.

"Maybe she got consump," he ventured politely.

"Funny she should stop coming here," Prescott said.

"I no see Miss Cars for maybe two year," Philippe told him as he had several times before. "Maybe she come on my day off. Maybe she got married. Hah. Monsieur Prescott married, no?"

"No," Prescott said impatiently. "I got enough wives already."

"Maybe Miss Cars got husband and big family, too," Philippe suggested mischievously.

Prescott gave a short laugh. He was not worried about her being either dead or married because he simply would not have it so. He was not unfeeling in his conviction that she was in no trouble, he was merely showing his profound faith in Ellenora's powers over destiny. That little slap that had felled him had left an enduring respect for Ellenora's might. He could tease her with his anecdotes of other women, leave her, but she would always be the winner, and while this angered him it also continued to fascinate him. It bewildered him, too, that he could not settle down to the flirtations and pleasures of his New York life until he had got Ellenora pinned down. A fancier of beauty, wit and flamboyance in women, he could never understand why he had pegged Ellenora as his special property from the minute he laid eyes on her. He never could remember her features and sometimes thought perhaps she hadn't any—just a couple of smoky eyeholes in that sort of luminous Laurencin mask. She was taller than you thought and plumper than you thought; he had reason to know she was stronger than you thought. He had a couple of photographs of her but they didn't look anything like his inner picture of her. He knew he laughed most of the time he was with her but for the life of him he couldn't remember a single funny thing she ever said. He liked a sleek flawlessly tailored woman and it was strange he was so amused and delighted by Ellenora's penchant for feathers, ruffles, tinkling jewelry, softly swishing silks. They were so definitely and ridiculously ladylike in an age of crisp business girl ensembles. Like a peacock, he thought, silly and lovely; she walked like a bird, too, fluttering along the street helplessly and prettily as if her feet were made for perching on high branches and not for walking.

In distant places it disturbed him that he had so little to remember about Ellenora, for after all he knew little about her. She was homesickness, he knew that much, though God knows she represented nothing secure or known. It was New York he loved and he guessed Ellenora represented New York or his idea of New York the way the mind arbitrarily elects some unsuspecting cruise acquaintance to embody the hopes and glamorous expectations of a Caribbean trip. He would be in some deadly dull little southern town or on some desolate ranch and suddenly he would ache for Ellenora—not Ellenora as a body, mind you, but Ellenora complete with name band,

Blue Angel, Eddie Condon's, El Morocco, Chinatown, Park
Avenue cocktail party, hansom ride in the Park, theatrical
lobby chatter between the acts, champagne buckets beside the
table, keep-the-change, taxicab characters, and ha-ha-ha, ho-
ho-ho, kiss-kiss, bang-bang, tomorrow same place. This was
Ellenora, who, as a matter of actual fact, was not tied with any
of these memories. He had never even danced with Ellenora
and if he had been to any nightclub with her would certainly
have been too polite to leave his drink sitting alone at the
table while he whizzed Ellenora around the floor. Very likely
the reason she represented this fictional and legendary Manhattan to him was that they had spent too many hours in one
spot postponing going someplace else until what they had not
seen together was more real than what they had.

The Ellenora who figured in his dreams knew everything
about him, for he had long soul-satisfying conversations with
her, telling her everything and being understood completely.
She knew that he was meant to do something finer than just
bury himself in business. He'd even told her—in these imaginary conferences—the dreadful way his mother had let him
down, doting as she had been, too, on his twelfth birthday
when she asked him what he intended to be when he grew up.

"A foreign correspondent," he had whispered almost
choked up with the awe of putting it into words. It was the
year he was reading Vincent Sheean and Walter Duranty, and
besides he had been made sports editor of the school paper.
His mother had burst into spontaneous, crushing laughter,
and then explained to him fondly. "But Ricky, darling, nobody in our family is ever a journalist. We've never been the
least bit clever that way. We're always lawyers."

"What about Grandpa Weaver?" he had shouted furiously,
angry at her laughter after he had opened his heart so foolishly.

"He wasn't able to finish law so he went into business," his
mother said. "And that's lucky for us, because now he can see
you through law school."

"He doesn't need to," young Ricky had said, obstreper-
ously, "I'll go in business myself since you think I couldn't do
anything else."

But Ellenora knew he could have done anything, this
Ellenora he always carried with him. Later whenever he found

the real one it was a surprise to have her not know, for it was fixed in his mind that his thousand mental confessions had miraculously reached her and most of the time it really seemed as if they had. But what had gone wrong with the connection now? He had to find her. She *must* know that.

On this February eve Prescott had been drifting in and out of the Julien since five, sitting down for a while, then wandering up University Place to the stationer's, glancing over the magazines, exchanging track news with a messenger boy, getting his shoes shined across the street, anything to pass the time till he might enter the café again, all primed to see Ellenora seated at a table. He would act as if he didn't know her at first, he decided, one of the harmless jokes they used to have; pretending the other one had made a mistake, summoning Philippe, always in on the joke, to please remove this presumptuous stranger.

But Ellenora never came, and disturbed by this defection Rick drank fast. A person traveled, knocked around, liked to see new places and make new friends, certain that the harbor was always there safe and sure whenever the mood came to return. It was outrageous to find the shore line changing behind one, no lamps waiting in windows for the returned wayfarer. Let everyplace else in the world change but let Manhattan stay the way it was, his dream city, Rick insisted in his thoughts, the way it had been that first day, the day he met Ellenora, the way he pictured it in far places. He was not a man to admit things could be other than he wished, and now, he thought, let other lovers default as they would, if he sat tight and willed it the world would stop at the spot he insisted—*here*, *now*, with Ellenora smiling across the table.

He would give chance a little more time, he decided, and summoned Philippe.

"Save our—my table," he said. "I'll be back."

Outside once more for the restless stroll down the block, a peep into the Brevoort, a look into the Grosvenor, then back to the Julien stubbornly hopeful. She wasn't there, and he wavered between childish resentment that he couldn't *make* the wish come true (this was Ellenora's fault and if she walked in this minute he would not even look up, just to punish her) and the uneasy suspicion that he was making a fool of himself.

He ought to shrug his shoulders and call up Maidie—there
were dozens of girls, thousands! Still, now he was here, no
reason why he shouldn't stay on and have dinner, and after
that wait just a little longer. He knew this was only an excuse;
he was chagrined to find himself still dawdling there hopefully
at half past ten. For a full hour there had been nothing worth
observing in the place except the patron at the opposite end
of the room whose beard showed above his French newspaper. Earlier in the evening the relief telephone operator, a
majestic blonde, had been emerging from her switchboard
every half hour with the regularity of a cuckoo clock to stand
at the café door and cluck "McGrew? McGrew? A call for Mr.
McGrew." Each time Prescott was hopeful that one of his
messages left in every possible place, from delicatessen shop
to Art Students League, had reached Ellenora. But each time
the lady's eyes rejected him, traveled thoroughly up and
down the room again, not at all convinced by the bareness of
the room. Each time she raised her hand to her eyes and
peered at the red velvet curtains, the cuspidors, the cupid-
strewn ceiling, as if clues were concealed there by mischievous
colleagues. At ten-thirty she appeared again, but this time she
stood in the doorway quietly scratching her blond chignon
with a pencil and staring intently at Rick Prescott. Hopeful
and happy he started to rise.

"A call for Prescott?" he asked.

"No," she said haughtily, "Mr. McGrew."

It was too much. Rick sent her a look of deep reproach followed by a burst of plain fury, as if the poor woman was personally responsible for telephones refusing to ring for him.
Whoever McGrew was he hated him, too, for it seemed to him
they all must have guessed the depth of his infatuation; they
must have sensed that his desire was now so violent he would
have begged Ellenora to marry and stay with him forever if
only she would walk in the café door this instant. They thought
he was making a fool of himself once again, and they all knew
Ellenora was deliberately teasing him, trying to see to what
lengths he would go to catch her again. How they would laugh
when she came into the café with her fine New York boy friend
and there would be the old Middle Western yokel waiting at
the same old table with his silly heart on his sleeve!

All right, let them laugh! He would laugh, too. Fully as outraged as if Ellenora had publicly mocked at his honorable offer of love everlasting, Ricky leaped to his feet and followed the operator back to the switchboard.

"Is the same lady calling McGrew who called before?" he inquired.

The girl nodded, and he said briskly, "I'll take the call and tell her where she can find him."

A lady disappointed in not finding a McGrew might be in the same reckless mood as a man disappointed in an Ellenora. He was in Booth One speaking into the telephone before the operator could make up her mind whether this was permissible.

. . . *the man behind the beard* . . .

It was a matter of supreme indifference to the tall Catalan waiter at the opposite end of the café that his lone customer, Dalzell Sloane, was making the decision of a lifetime. For the Catalan every hour of his life had held a problem of terrific moment, whether to punch a fellow worker, throw a plate at a customer, resign his job, present all of his possessions to a daughter momentarily the favorite, enter a monastery, return to Spain, go west, east, north; all problems ending in the decision to have another cup of coffee in the kitchen.

But Sloane, so it seemed to him now, had never had to make a decision before in his life. There were always two paths, and if you stood long enough at the crossroads, one of them proved impassable. There were always two women, but one of them wouldn't have you or one of them kidnaped you. There were two careers but at the crucial moment one of them dropped out, something happened, somebody made an appointment, and there you were. For Dalzell, destiny had shaped itself only through his hesitation. But though he had hesitated over this one problem, waiting for chance to decide, it would not solve itself. Something must be done, once and for all, and tonight. This necessity had produced in his head nothing more constructive than a kind of perpetual buzz that was like a telephone ringing in some neighbor's apartment.

He tried to draw counsel by detaching himself from his body, watching the bearded stranger in the mirrors across and beyond, assuring himself that such a calm, distinguished-looking citizen could have no real worry. He knew the beard made him look older than his fifty years, but at least it made him look successful, and after half a century one has the right to at least the appearance of success. If someone were to ask, "What have you done with your fifty years, Dalzell Sloane?" he could answer, "I have failed in love and in art, but I have raised a beard." The beard had given him credit and character references, for people assumed in a vague way that a man with a beard had traveled everywhere, knew all about art and science, had influential friends and doting ladies tucked away all over the world, and was securely solvent. Dalzell had only to look at himself in the mirror to be almost convinced this was all true. "Thank you, beard," he saluted it silently, marking that the gray was beginning to dominate the brown as it did in his thick hair, though his brows were still as dark as his eyes.

The beard, like everything else in his life, owed itself to no decision of his, but had grown of its own accord during a long illness, and all that had been demanded of him was to select a cut from the page of style offered by a Parisian barber. Later his fellow painters, Marius and Ben, took turns cutting it during their merry parties, shouting hilariously all the while. Old Marius and Ben, Dalzell thought, the three of them always together then, and now Marius dead, Ben lost for years.

A group of diners emerging from the large dining room beyond the café paused to stare in the door, pleased to discover a bearded bohemian philosophizing over his glass, even though it was not absinthe, and he wore no smock or beret. Dalzell looked steadily into his glass, trained to tourist curiosity. He had noticed them earlier in the evening when they came in, the pouting, red-mouthed, bare-shouldered young girl in blue taffeta with the white camellias in her blue-black hair, the tipsy, pink-faced fiancé, the two busty, gray matrons in their mighty silver fox capes, the large, purple-faced, responsible men of affairs. Thirty years ago he would have noted it as an effective idea for a canvas. Family Outing,

Engagement Dinner. Now he had learned to reject such in-spirations on the spot as he rejected any flare of desire, thus protecting himself against the certain failure. Family parties such as this were familiar to the big dining room, usually cho-sen by the host as a place where the appetite was king, undis-turbed by music, glamour or youthful pleasures. The young were inevitably bewildered and disappointed as they discov-ered that the excited clamor of happy voices did not mean gaiety and dancing but sheer middle-aged joy over bouilla-baisse, venison, or *cassoulet Toulousaine* with its own wedded wine. Dalzell was sympathetically amused at the youthful im-patience with stomachic ecstasy, and it amused him, too, that the naughty word "café" made responsible men herd their families into the respectable safety of the dining room. Where did they get the money to feed Julien dinners so casually to five mouths? Thirty dollars at the least, more than he spent for food in six weeks, Dalzell thought.

There were people, and Dalzell was one of them, who were born café people, claustrophobes unable to endure a definite place or plan. The café was a sort of union station where they might loiter, missing trains and boats as they liked, post-poning the final decision to go anyplace or do anything until there was no longer need for decision. One came here be-cause one couldn't decide where to dine, whom to telephone, what to do. At least one had not yet committed oneself to one parlor or one group for the evening; the door of freedom was still open. One might be lonely, frustrated or heartbro-ken, but at least one wasn't sewed up. Someone barely known might come into the café bringing marvelous strangers from Rome, London, Hollywood, anyplace at all, and one joined forces, went places after the café closed that one had never heard of before and never would again, talked strange talk, perhaps kissed strange lips to be forgotten next day. Here was haven for those who craved privacy in the midst of sociability, for those whose hearts sank with fear as the door of a charm-ing home (their own or anyone's) closed them in with a known intimate little group; here might be the chance com-panion for the lonely one who shuddered at the fixed en-gagement, ever dodging the little red book as a trap for the unwary. Here, in this café, were blessed doors strategically placed so that flight was always possible at first glimpse of an undesired friend or foe's approach. Here was procrastinator's paradise, the spot for homehaters to hang their hats, here was the stationary cruise ship into which the hunted family man might leap without passport or visa. Here in the Julien it was possible to maintain heavenly anonymity if one chose, here was the spot where nothing beyond good behavior was expected of one, here was safety from the final decision, but since the doors closed at midnight sharply, a bare two hours from now, Dalzell began wondering from where his solution would come. At this very moment in the dining room there might be someone he had known and forgotten years ago, now risen to great consequence in the world, and this person would pause at the café entrance to cry out, "Dalzell Sloane, as I live and breathe, the very person I'm looking for!" Or a theatre party, dropping in at the last minute for a nightcap, would carry him off to someone's apartment for midnight music, and one o'clock would pass, two o'clock, three o'clock —he would have missed the train, not the first time his future had been determined by negatives. But then what about tomorow? Ah well, even if nothing else would be accomplished, at least he would have closed a door.

Dalzell had been sipping *mazagran*, for the strong coffee with the twist of lemon served in a goblet for twenty-five cents seemed less odiously economical than the same brew in a cup, but now he remembered that the last time he had been at the Julien with Ben and Marius they had drunk *amer picon citron*, and just as Marius had insisted, it had had a curiously magical effect on him, alcosomatic perhaps. It seemed to seep delicately through his bones, detaching his mind from his body, transforming him into a cool, wise observer of himself. Since he wished to observe instead of to be, he recklessly decided to spend eighty cents on a glass of the magic potion. He would step outside himself, perhaps change into Marius watching from the other world. Almost with the first sip his mood changed into a Marius-like desire for genial companionship. He was lonely. He'd been lonely for months, years. He regretted that he had been systematically avoiding people for so long, afraid they might guess his circumstances, or that he might be foolish enough to confide in someone. He had

taken the back corner in the café to hide from possible discovery, but now that he was changing into the boisterous
Marius he wanted to be found. He didn't want just anybody
—the gray little half-people resigned to failure and poverty
who had been creeping through his life all too long, demanding nothing, giving nothing. He wanted the bright
beautiful wonderful ones, the stars in his dark sky whose fleeting presence raised him to their firmament. He thought of
Andy Callingham, photographed only last week on arriving at
the Ambassador. "Dalzell, you old son-of-a-gun, I'll join you
in fifteen minutes," he pictured Andy as saying over the telephone, but that was nonsense. Andy would never go anyplace
where there were no columnists, no gaping admirers, no publicity for his last novel. He wouldn't even pick up the phone
except for Zanuck or a Rockefeller. Dennis Orphen, then, but
this would be what Dennis called his "drunk time" and he'd
bring all of his convivial cronies. Dalzell began berating himself for his folly in keeping up with his valuable friendships
only when he was in the chips and didn't need such support,
then scuttling down to Skid Row at the first drop in fortune,
cowering under cover guiltily as if bad luck was a crime or
contagion that must isolate one from all humanity. If the bad
luck stayed on, as it usually did with him, you cut off all
bridges back to civilized living and the chance of revival.

How long had it been, Dalzell pondered, was it months or
years, that he had kept his door locked to his old friends as if
Despair was a lady of the streets hiding in his room? A familiar voice on the telephone, a glimpse of an old friend on the
street, was like a dun; the simple words "Let's get together"
filled him with panic, as if "hello" committed him to horrify-
ing expenditures—twenty cents worth of cigarettes, a beer, a
cup of coffee—all these were obligations he could not face.
After his emergence from his underground hiding—and how
could he explain what had brought about his release?—the
habit of friendship was hard to regain. The connection could
not be won back with a simple phone call, the loving path was
now overgrown with thistles and angry brush. Forget the solace of the old, then. Dalzell decided whatever was to save
him must come from the new and unpredictable.

With a vague idea of tempting the unknown, Dalzell rose

and strolled out into the little lobby that was now as deserted as the café. He observed the café's other customer emerging from the first phone booth. The other stood for a moment at the café door hitching his belt around his middle with the nonchalant pride of a big guy who knows how to keep in trim, knows what he wants, goes after it, gets it. There was something familiar-looking about him, and it struck Dalzell that he might be a film actor choosing this spot to get away from fans. Yes, he looked like that star Monty Douglass, and Dalzell was warmed by his grin, envisaging a quick friendship over a nightcap, an impulsive putting of cards on the table, a miraculous solution to everything. Childish dreaming, Dalzell scolded himself, and he went on his way down the stairs to the men's room.

He was slightly bewildered to find there a tall bushy-browed beagle-nosed man, coatless in a fancy mauve shirt and scarlet suspenders, his pinstriped gray jacket dangling from the doorknob, solemnly flexing his right arm with a regular rhythm before the mirror.

"Feel those muscles," commanded this gentleman, without taking his eye from the mirror, apparently not at all perturbed by an audience.

"Like iron," said Dalzell obediently.

"Of course they're like iron, because I keep them that way. Golf. Tennis. Sixty years old. I just put my arm through the door. Take a look at the other side. Right through. Wanted to see if I could still do it."

"You must be a professional athlete," Dalzell said, properly awed by the jagged hole in the door.

"Think so?" beamed the man. "Believe it or not, I'm in the advertising business."

"No!"

"I'm telling you. Here's my card, Hastings Hardy of Hardy, Long, and Love. I just don't let myself get soft, that's all."

It was the name of a leading advertising firm, one that had saved the lives of many a struggling artist by its sweet temptations. Dalzell himself in a low moment had offered to be corrupted there, but with no success. Maybe this was the time and this the opportunity, if only he knew how to make it work.

"Another thing, I eat right," said the tall man, patting his stomach. "The best food and not too much of it, three times a day, or don't you agree?"

"I do, indeed," said Dalzell.

"By best foods I do not mean health foods, understand," said Mr. Hardy, looking at him sternly. "Do you think I could have busted that door with my fist on a diet of health foods? I've always had the best food and liquor, and as a result how old would you say I am, sir?"

"Forty-four," Dalzell said, and was rewarded by a hand-clasp of deepest affection.

"Sixty next month," said Mr. Hardy, pleased to see Dalzell's expression of suitable astonishment. He took his coat from the door knob. With considerable care he managed to get the right arms into the right sleeves. After a complacent glance in the mirror again he looked at Dalzell.

"You look to me like a mighty intelligent fellow," he said. "I like a man who *looks* intelligent. What do you do?"

The beard again, Dalzell thought.

"My name's Dalzell Sloane. I paint."

This seemed to strike Mr. Hardy with tremendous force for he took a step back to stare at Dalzell.

"An artist? What do you know? As a matter of fact I'm talking to somebody right now about having my portrait done."

He seized Dalzell's hands and shook it vigorously, and then Dalzell saw that his eyes were brightly glazed like gray marbles staring straight past him.

"Look here, what do you say to joining my wife and me for a brandy when you come back up? We're with my daughter and her fiancé's family and we're arguing about the portrait right now. I'm going to tell them you're the man to do it. Sloane, eh? Frankly Sloane, I like you. I'd like to regard you as a friend. And what's the use of old friends if you can't do 'em a favor? We'd just about decided on some little chap I forget, oh yes, Whitfield. He did the president of Bailey Stodder, our biggest client. Did vice-president of General Flexmetals, too, hangs right there in the bastard's private office. Whitfield, that's this artist's name. Know him?"

The artists who make the most money from the bourgeoisie are usually never even heard of in the art world, and this name was unknown to Dalzell.

"I suppose he's good on tweed," Dalzell said, tentatively.

"The best in the field," declared Hardy. "On the Bailey Stodder job you can almost spot the tailor's name, it's that good. But why shouldn't I have a man of my own, why should I have to have Stodder's fellow? Come on back and join us and we'll talk it over. By George, I like to make my own decisions."

"That's mighty nice of you," Dalzell said, and again they shook hands. "I'll settle up first in the café and then join you in the dining room."

This was it, then, Dalzell thought with a deep breath, this was the crazy chance that was going to settle everything. After all these years Fate had decided to make him a portrait painter. Okay, Fate, this time he'd take whatever came. He washed his hands, turned back his frayed cuffs, flicked tentatively at his suit and decided he'd look better covered in topcoat, and then he followed his new friend back upstairs. The clerk was back at the desk in the lobby and the telephone girl was at the switchboard. Dalzell looked at the clock. Eleven. He tried not to let his hopes rise too insanely.

In the café he settled his bill, six eighty-five, as much as he had spent all last week. In his wallet there was still the eighty dollars he had reserved for his ticket from his—well, call it stolen profits—and it struck him that under the circumstances Alex deserved a larger tip so he drew out a dollar bill and left it in place of the seventy-five cents, but habit was so strong he could not leave the cigarette pack even if there was only one smoke left in it. Matches, too, went in pocket. He put on his loose brown topcoat, its shabbiness forgiven, he thought, by its English cut and the wide white scarf around his neck. He strolled through the center hall back into the dining room, surprised to find that in spite of all his experience hope was rising once again. The conviction that this-is-it was so strong that already he could visualize the rich portrait of Hastings Hardy, the belligerent marble blue eyes, the grasshopper jaws about to clench the biggest steak *Chateaubriand* or the biggest contract, the three-hundred-dollar suit, the twenty-dollar necktie (flight of ducks, black, *à la* Frank Benson in formation on a blue and white ground), the thirty-dollar fountain pen in hand signing the million-dollar contract nattily unscrolled to look like the Magna Carta— Oh no, not that way, Dalzell caught himself hastily, and altered the picture in an instant to a stern but wise executive, the mandibles parted in a paternal smile, the eyes and forehead Jovelike.

Hastings Hardy Hastings Hardy, he repeated to himself like a charm as he looked over the dining room, searching the small inside banquet room, then with mounting apprehension, the inner alcoves.

Every table was deserted.

He realized how firmly he had fastened on this last fantastic hope, because it took so long for his mind to admit that there were only waiters left in the darkened room.

"Mr. Hardy's party?" he asked incredulously of the waiter who was busily pushing a wagon of dishes toward the kitchen.

"But the dining room has closed," replied the waiter, as the last lights dimmed on the ceiling. "Everyone has left, as you can see."

Dalzell stood for a minute, a kind of panic coming over him. If Fate was sending him perfect strangers to play jokes on him at this late hour, then he would be compelled to make some move for his own preservation. He would go back to the café and summon enough assurance to invite the other lone customer for a final drink. In the café he looked all around but the other table was deserted.

"Has Monty Douglass left?" he asked Philippe who was going through the unmistakable signs of clearing up the table for the next customer.

"My gentleman?" countered Philippe. "That's not Mr. Douglass."

Now there was no one who might rescue him, and his fear returned. It might mean that at twelve o'clock, the very minute the last chair was piled on the last table, Dalzell Sloane must take a train to a lonely far western village perhaps for ever, perhaps to die and drop like a dried apple into the family graveyard, or—and the dread of making a choice brought a dizzy seasickness over him—go back to the lie that would eventually devour him.

Quite pale, Dalzell sat down abruptly at Karl's table by the door. There was something ominous, he thought, in the mockery of last-minute hopes being raised only to be dashed.

The furies indeed must be after him. He raised his hand to signal Karl for another drink but Karl, his arms folded majestically over his little chest, was staring fixedly at a poster advertising the skiing pleasures of the Bavarian Alps which hung above his table, and he made no move to ask the patron's pleasure. He was, in fact, asleep, in the manner he had perfected after forty years of avoiding the customer's eye. He was startled into attention by a sudden shout of laughter and blast of cold air from the outer hall as a clutch of ladies and men in dinner clothes plunged in, the valiant survivors of some party who must make a merry night of it now that they were in Greenwich Village.

"Dalzell Sloane, as I live!" boomed a male voice that could belong, as Dalzell knew, to no one but Okie, the indefatigable, omnipresent, indestructible publisher, refugee from half a dozen bankruptcies, perennial Extra Man at the best dinners, relentless raconteur, and known far and wide as The Bore That Walks Like a Man. "I've been trying to get hold of you for months."

Wonderful Okie, Dalzell thought joyously, dear, deadly, boring Okie, the friend in need! Fantastic that the day should ever have come when the sight of old Okie would make his heart swell with fond affection. And the beaming lady with him was none other than Cynthia Earle, Cynthia with new short ash-blond curls clustering around her narrow once brunette head, which swiveled, snakewise, in a nest of glittering jewelry. As her arms reached out eagerly to embrace him the thought leapt between them that he still owed her six hundred dollars.

"Darling!" she cried, flinging her arms about him. "We've come to this place dozens of times hoping we'd find you. Where on earth have you been all these years?"

"I've telephoned," said Dalzell evasively.

Her friends were busily drawing up chairs, tossing their wraps on neighboring tables, pushing Dalzell back into his seat against the wall until he felt himself plunged straight through the mirror, saved only by Cynthia's purposeful grasp on his arm.

"We've just escaped from a funny little dinner and I brought everybody here for a nightcap, only I haven't any money," Cynthia burbled on. "Do tell the waiter I want to cash a check. Waiter!"

But Karl was rudely obstinate about cashing Cynthia's check. He insisted that the Julien would cash checks only when sponsored by a trustworthy customer such as Monsieur Sloane. Cynthia's face reddened at this insult to her credit, and she looked on incredulously as Dalzell, equally appalled and embarrassed, wrote his utterly worthless name on the back of her check. It was such a typically Julien incident, so endearingly French-foxy, that he would have burst out laughing if he had dared. Cynthia, worth millions, whose mere name gave her credit any other place, must have her check certified by a man who owed not only her but the Julien itself for years past, and who could not even afford a bank account! He saw Cynthia looking at him half mockingly, her lips curled tightly to keep back some taunting query. She must be thinking he had had a great windfall and had been neglecting her, as other favorites had, because of brighter opportunities. He was on the verge of setting her right but if he said he was no better off than ever, then she would be on guard against impositions. People like Cynthia enjoyed observing the ups and downs of artists' lives but they became bored and irritated when it was all *downs*. One could not blame them. Dalzell himself was bored by the monotony and shame of always needing fifty dollars, forever needing fifty dollars, fifty dollars to go, fifty dollars to stay, fifty dollars to pay back some other fifty dollars. Cynthia's eyes were covering him sharply after Karl's rebuff to her and he fancied she recognized the topcoat as the one he'd worn in London fifteen years ago. The sudden withdrawal of her radiant emanations told him—how well he knew the signals!—that she regretted mentioning "checkbook," cautiously anticipated a request from him, and a minimum sum had already lit up in the cash register of her mind. You didn't have to be a mind reader to know the reasoning of the rich.

No, he couldn't endure it, Dalzell thought angrily. Better be considered ungrateful, forgetting true old friends in his heartless climbing, rather than be found beaten, tired and afraid. Let them think he dined regularly on Julien squab and Moselle with only the richest and noblest. To confirm their suspicions he smiled vaguely across the room at new groups of visitors crowding into the café.

"How are things going, old man?" Okie asked, throwing an arm around Cynthia's slim shoulder as if to protect her from contagious poverty.

"Very well indeed, judging by his credit here at Julien's," Cynthia said dryly.

"When you never hear from a fellow, you can figure he's in the chips, ha ha," Okie told her.

"I did have rather a run of luck in Brazil," Dalzell said.

He had always found it saved pride, on emerging from retreat forced by poverty, to claim in London great success in Hollywood, in New York to boast of Continental favor, and in Paris or Rome to ascribe his disappearance to ethnological pioneering in unknown isles. Better to have people jealous and skeptical than pitying or scornful.

"I thought you looked disgustingly cocky," Cynthia answered. "No wonder your real friends never hear from you."

There, he congratulated himself bitterly, he had delivered himself into their hands. They could blame him now for chronic ingratitude but not for chronic poverty.

"Wouldn't you know it?" Cynthia exclaimed petulantly. "I never see them when they're having their success. Okie, you are so right. About them."

Them, of course, meant the artists she had "subsidized" in the past, the subsidy consisting, as Dalzell well knew, of never more than a hundred dollars a month for a year or two, which gave her a fine philanthropic reputation, dictator rights and the privileges of the artist's bed and time. He himself had been a bargain, having been young and naïve enough to think he was really in love with her and that she really admired his talent. Later, of course, he and Ben had laughed over the printed interviews in which Cynthia had modestly excused her largesse to artists: "I don't want to spoil them, really. I just think a little security doesn't hurt real genius."

Security! As if even Cynthia herself had ever had it! She kept her iron fingers on his arm possessively, and he recalled an old trick of hers of fondling one man publicly while planning to sleep with someone else. He wondered which one of

these others was her present lover and was surprised to discover he was still capable of a twinge of jealousy.

"You might at least have answered my letters!" she reproachfully hissed in his ear.

What would he have said in answer to that last letter of hers
six years ago? *I am not pretending that I need the money,
Dalzell, but if you are in the chips now, as someone who saw you
in Paris was telling me, why not return at least part of the loan
so I can pass it on to some young artist who really needs it?*

"Order up, everybody," Okie roared genially. "Cynthia
Earle's money is no good here, but Dalzell Sloane's is, ho ho."

"Allow me," Dalzell said calmly and motioned to the
waiter.

Now he was in for it. He was into his ticket money already
just because he couldn't stand Okie's needling. It was going
to be Okie, then, who decided his future and he resented this
intrusion even though it was all his own fault. He could see
that Okie was showing off his intimacy with Cynthia, reveling
in his new eminence as right-hand man to rich lady, a role
that allowed him to regard the rest of mankind as beggars,
borrowers, swindlers, pennypinchers and imposters.

Okie had become important through the passage of years
merely by never changing, loyally preserving every trait, however disagreeable, of his youth, adjusting them to his spreading figure and whitening hair until he exuded the mellow
dignity of an ivy-covered outhouse. For years he had been a
last minute telephone call, an emergency escort, for Cynthia
in bleak periods between her lovers and marriages, until finally these caesurae in Cynthia's life totted up to more than
the big moments and here was Okie at long last Cynthia's
Man—not lover, scarcely friend, but reliable old Stand-In,
glorified by garlands of snubs from the best people and bearing his scars from Cynthia's whip as saber cuts from royal
duels.

His bulging frog eyes were beamed at Dalzell and then at
Cynthia with the permanent anxiety for her approval. Do we
insult him or is he going to insult me? Do we like this person
or should we put him in his place? Do Cynthia and he gang
up against me? Dare I count on Cynthia to gang up with me
against him or may I have the delicious relief of ganging up

with him just for a moment against dear Cynthia? Who moves first? Do I jump on his lap or at his throat? The throat is always the most fun, but what if the mistress's whim was the opposite?

Dalzell was sensing Okie's problem when Cynthia's lips tickled his ear once more.

"Talk to Severgny," she whispered urgently. "He's been trying to find you for weeks."

A dealer looking for him? Dalzell's heart beat faster.

"We talked about you all evening," Cynthia said mysteriously. "Wait, I'll tell you about him, while they're yakking about the drinks."

The sudden influx of last minute customers created a din outside the din at his own table and Cynthia was obliged to shout introductions. No one heard or paid any heed to the names and all Dalzell could hear was the loud buzz of Cynthia's voice in his ear sometimes punctuated and sometimes obscured by a wild squeal from one of the ladies or a bellow from Okie. It was easier to study them in the looking glass in tableaux whose titles were zealously furnished by Cynthia.

It was the looking-glass world, at that, he thought dazedly, and it must be that he was the rabbit.

"Severgny is the new proprietor of the Menton Studio, getting a terrific reputation in moderns and everyone thinks he's French but of course he's just Swiss," Cynthia buzzed in Dalzell's ear, "and he would never have been anything but an interior decorator except for the war, and he spent that in Hollywood painting monster murals over those monster beds, but it's all paid off as you know. The woman beside him talking about this café's Old World charm—" she nodded toward a gaunt spinster in bony but dauntless décolletage—"is Iona Hollis, steel mills and Picassos, you know, and that egghead is Larry Whitfield, the portrait painter—Laidlaw Whitfield, that is—"

"Indeed," murmured Dalzell. The tweed specialist himself, no less.

"—and the little cotton-haired dried-up doll is Mrs. Whitfield. He had to marry her in order to meet the right people, of course, but the joke was the Social Register dropped her right afterward." A sudden lull in which Mrs. Whitfield bent toward her made Cynthia continue shamelessly, "As I was saying, there we were at this strange little dinner tonight."

"I've barely met Jerry Dulaine and I can't imagine why she asked me to dinner," Iona Hollis' deep voice sounded, "or why I went."

"Come now, we went because we wanted to meet Collier McGrew," Okie said benignly. "It was a damn fine dinner even if he didn't show up, but Elsie Hookley drove us out, that's all."

"I was positive that any party a girl like Jerry Dulaine would give would be really wild, in a chic way of course," Cynthia complained. "But it was as stuffy and correct as one of Mother's own dinners. I wouldn't want her to know I said so but she must be disgustingly respectable at heart."

"Do you suppose she or Elsie had something up their sleeve?" Miss Hollis pondered. "Why should anybody throw a party like that for nothing?"

"I'm sure there was some reason we were asked and some reason McGrew backed out," Cynthia said. "He's no fool. I'm sure we were about to be tapped to back a play or a little magazine or adopt some refugees. I noticed Elsie's brother wasn't there, whatever that meant. Anyway it was worth coming down for just to run into Dalzell here at the old Julien."

"I've been most anxious to see you." Severgny leaned across the table toward Dalzell and Dalzell's heart missed a beat. A Fifth Avenue dealer anxious to meet him? More people arrived with more introductions and Cynthia's documentary going on and on in his ear, but Dalzell was thinking only about Severgny, waiting for the moment to resume conversation with him, wondering if this was the chance he had known was coming to him. Feverishly he tried to think of plausible excuses for being without a dealer at present. He could do himself no good by confessing he'd broken with the Kreuber Gallery because Kreuber insisted on charging him storage rates for holding his canvases, so dim was his faith in them. In his mind he began sorting out pictures suitable for his first one-man show in fifteen years. There would be the terrible cost of framing, at the outset. . . .

Cynthia's elbow dug into his ribs.

"Severgny is asking you a question," she said.

Dalzell made the effort of jumping back through the looking glass and directing himself toward the trim little mustached gentleman leaning across the table towards him.

"Could I count on having some of your time very soon, Mr. Sloane?" Severgny repeated, and before Dalzell could answer he went on, "I understand you and Ben Forrester knew more about Marius than anyone else."

Marius? Dalzell came down to earth.

"Severgny's working on a big memorial show for Marius," Cynthia explained. "It's to be the same month Okie's definitive biography of Marius comes out."

"We need your help in tracking down certain canvases we know existed," Severgny pursued while Dalzell arranged a smile to conceal his stricken hopes. "Did he leave a large body of work in Rome, for instance, or where would you say he left most of his paintings?"

"Ask Household Finance," Dalzell replied grimly. "Ask the Morris Plan. Ask the warehouses and landladies all over the world who sold it as junk to pay storage rent, or else took it along with his furniture and clothes to auction off when he couldn't pay."

"Not literally!" Okie laughed. "He's joking, of course, Severgny. Dalzell, surely you have an idea of where his stuff is. You have some yourself, I know. If Marius had only been like Whitfield here, who keeps a record of every scrap of work he ever did!" Okie exclaimed.

"Can you imagine anybody ever caring?" Cynthia whispered in Dalzell's ear maliciously, though she might have shouted without giving offense, for two new young men were crowding around the table exchanging shrill introductions, more chairs were being drawn up until Dalzell, squeezed against the mirror, was dizzy with claustrophobia. Severgny was trying to tell him something and Okie was obliged to relay the words.

"Severgny got hold of Ben Forrester," Okie said. "He reached him through a San Francisco dealer, and he's promised to help us with the Marius show."

Dalzell's first thought was of the burst of new hopes that

must have flared in Ben's breast at the urgent summons from any dealer, and the double disappointment on finding the call was not for Forrester, the artist, but for Forrester, bosom friend of Marius! How well he knew that hurt flash of jealousy on learning that Marius had been the one to win the Grand Immortal Prize of death which opened the gates closed in life to all of them! Marius is my dear friend, Ben must have said just as Dalzell had, and he is a fine painter, but what has he got that I haven't got except a coffin? The feeling had lasted with Dalzell for days after the first funeral fanfare in the papers, a perfectly ridiculous resentment at Marius for "selling out," quite as if he had started toadying to patrons and critics, dropping his old friends merely for the publicity and success of death. Then reason had set in, and as the definitive articles and kiting of Marius prices grew, the affair became a wonderful joke, something Marius himself would have loved. Ben must have gone through all these stages, too, thought Dalzell, for in the old days Ben had more intermittent bouts with success than any of them. If they could only meet, check the comedy step by step, wipe out all the bitterness with wild laughter! If Ben were really in New York—

"Remember when Marius would have been glad to take a thousand dollars for everything he had in the studio?" Okie was shouting. "Yet that little oil we saw tonight in Miss Dulaine's—just a boy's head looking up at clouds—would bring five thousand. Remember? The brown eyes, torn blue shirt, the clothesline—"

Did he remember? Dalzell gulped down his drink.

"Marius had his different periods, too," Okie was pontificating, waving a cigar at Severgny, "but as I point out in my book, they were not right-about changes, they were logical transitions and all consistent with his marvelous gusto and what I refer to as his greed for beauty, that is to say beauty complete—to be *completely* drunk, *completely* mad, and that reminds me I want you to give me a few of those wonderful anecdotes about him, those bawdy—ha ha ha—Rabelaisian, ha ha, sayings of his we all used to love."

In his ears Dalzell could hear again Marius mockingly mimicking Okie, *My sense of humor is as good as the next one but I find nothing funny in bawdiness for the sake of bawdiness, after all, Marius, one is a gentleman first and a clown last and I must ask you to leave my room if you will not be a gentleman.*

"My theory on Marius' final use of white—" said Okie, and suddenly Dalzell felt that he must get out of here, he must find Ben and laugh before the joke became too ugly for laughter. What did these people know of old Marius? The mere circumstance of Okie knowing a woman rich enough to back a magazine for him made him a mighty critic of all the arts with trespasser rights to all of them. The fact that Severgny knew how to bargain (it might have been real estate or canned beans for all he cared except that he liked the social advantages of more elevated wares) gave him the right to encourage or discourage Titian himself. Cynthia Earle's ability to buy a porkchop for an artist or writer when they were hungry endowed her with the most exquisite perceptivity and the right to judge their work. Marius was dead and these were the people who had killed him, these were the demons who had destroyed him as they were destroying himself, too, Dalzell thought. These were the embalmers, the coffin salesmen, the cemetery landlords who carved up the artist. There was some consolation, though, that had Marius's success come during his lifetime he would have had to play the idiot success game with these buzzards. He would have been obliged to listen to Okie's asinine pronouncements on technique, he would have had to defer to Severgny and to Cynthia; the stench of success would have risen higher than that of his moldering carcass. Still, let's face it, he would have had the satisfaction of knowing he was good, his talent would not have been corroded and crippled with doubt.

Or would success have corroded and crippled, too, as some said it did? It was a risk he himself was willing to take, Dalzell reflected. If his integrity, morals and whole spirit were to be corrupted, why then let it be by Success for a change.

"Think about it and make memoranda of canvases you remember and where he did them," Severgny said. "Ben Forrester is doing the same thing."

"Funny Ben hasn't looked you up yet, now he's here," Okie remarked. "Such old pals." Ben here? A quick apprehension struck Dalzell.

"I'm not surprised he didn't look me up," Cynthia said

plaintively. "I know artists better than you do, Okie, and they never look anybody up unless they need them. And when you need *them* you can never find them, because they're always hiding out someplace from creditors or wives or something. And lies! Once I gave a marvelous party for Dalzell and Marius when they were going to Spain, and then they told me the wrong ship so I couldn't find them to see them off!"

Dalzell suppressed a faint grin, remembering that the name of the ship had been that of a Staten Island ferry and their Pyrenees had been the hills around Tottenville. It was one of their jokes that whenever the going was too tough they could discover havens within subway or ferry fare from Manhattan. Rooming houses in the Bronx, abandoned beach cottages, river barges, the wastelands of Queens—how often they had announced some proud foreign destination and then merely disappeared in a subway kiosk until luck turned!

"Ben didn't give us his address," Okie said. "I sort of gathered there was a lady friend. All I know is he took the Queens subway at Fifty-Ninth."

"I'll bet Dalzell knows perfectly well where Ben is," Cynthia said. "They always covered for each other. You do know, don't you, Dalzell?"

Why then, perhaps I do, Dalzell thought with a sudden glimmer of light. Perhaps . . . Before Cynthia could tease him further a new couple entered the café and there were screams of recognition, more introductions, more chairs pulled up at Cynthia's insistent invitation. Guillaume crossly insisted the place would close in ten minutes, but even with this repeated warning, the same three young teachers were in again, pushing past him purposefully, convinced that the mounting uproar indicated something exciting was surely about to happen.

"We'll all go up to Cynthia's," Okie shouted. "Dalzell, you'll come."

"Later," Dalzell said.

In fifteen minutes his train would leave, but for him it had already left. Through his mind raced a series of pictures, the closing gate to the Sunflower Special in the Station, the certain desolation in his heart as the train sped westward to that old attic bedroom looking out over the peaceful prairie, the burned church with the ruined cemetery (the painting that had won him the prize money to leave home) and his sister's face smiling a tired welcome to the prodigal, home at last in final defeat. Dalzell shivered. In the confusion of last minute noise he rose and slipped out to the hall.

The porter was talking excitedly to the clerk at the desk.

"I tell you, someone has broken the door downstairs! Ah, Monsieur Sloane, you were downstairs, yes, did you see what had happened?"

"No," said Dalzell, and went out the door. He had to move fast before his courage failed him, but whether it was the *amer picons*, the idea of having escaped Cynthia and Okie, the thought that soon the train would be moving westward without him, liberating him, as it were, for whatever might happen, or whether it was the thought of having at last made a decision, feverish elation possessed him. It carried him along East Eighth to the B.M.T. station where he had to compose himself for a moment, trying to bring back that long ago— had it been ten or twenty years?—address. Uptown, under the river in the subway, or over the Queensboro bridge on the bus, the last stop, then the local bus—no by George, he'd take a taxicab to—where? Keane, wasn't it, but what number?

"Something about the Battle of Hastings," he remembered, and then laughed aloud triumphantly. "Ten Sixty-Six Keane Place."

Unexpectedly for this hour and this neighborhood a taxi's lights came toward him from downtown, and taking it as a sign Dalzell hailed it. At least a three-dollar tariff but magic was brewing—that is, if the driver happened to be in the mood to transport anyone to another borough.

He was. He happened to live in Queens and was on his way home.

It was his lucky night, just as Dalzell had known it would be. He would have thought so even if he had known that Mr. Hastings Hardy at that moment was back in the Julien looking for him.

. . . ladies of the town . . .

In the living room of a charming made-over brownstone house four blocks north of the Café Julien and one block west of Fifth Avenue there sat this very evening two ladies in the most festive of evening dresses in the most profound of melancholies. The scattering of half-filled coffee cups and liqueur glasses about the little tables, the atmosphere of mingled perfumes and cigar smoke, the grouping of the chairs hinted of recently departed dinner guests; the gloomy faces of the ladies, the earliness of the hour—it was not yet eleven—and the visible signs of elaborate expectations indicated all too clearly that the party had not "come off." The dresses and even the living room had the look of stage properties about to be packed off to the warehouse now that the play had failed.

Whatever had gone wrong, the fault had certainly not been with the *mise en scène*, though the eyes of the hostess had traveled anxiously over every inch of the room, looking for some guilty flaw. The wallpaper was the correct silvery-patterned green; the crystal-beaded lamps glittered with suitable discretion; the shining striped satin of the sofa and chairs, the unworn blond rugs, the cautious blend of antique and modern furniture all murmured of "taste" or that decorator's strait-jacketing of personal revelations that is accepted as taste. Through an arched door could be seen a dining room, china cabinet, chandeliers and all, a daring gesture toward formal tradition for such a small apartment, and a soft coral light on the opposite side of the entry hall led not to the wings but really and truly to a white and gold little gem of a bedroom.

"When you think of how long it took us to cook up this party," mused Elsie Hookley bitterly, "then to have us right back where we started in just three hours! Look at the place! You wouldn't know anybody'd been here, even!"

"Did you expect them to wreck the place?" inquired the other tartly.

Of the two ladies you might have surmised that the older, ferocious-looking one was chaperon, singing teacher or stage mother for the other, but then Miss Dulaine looked far too glossily self-sufficient to need such protection, and Elsie

Hookley (she had dropped the "Baroness" along with the Baron Humfert himself) was the merest babe in the wood, as she admiringly confessed, before the younger woman's knowledge of the world. Consider them as bosom friends by necessity in spite of the twenty years difference in their ages, bound together by a common foe and at the moment by defeat. They had known each other hardly two years, they had nothing in common but a profound distaste for women friends and a passion for private life, but friendship had spread under them like an invisible net waiting for the certain catch. Both had moved from more fashionable sections of New York into the Washington Square quarter at the same time, with identical motives for marshaling their resources while unobtrusively retrenching. Being the only solitary ladies in the Twelfth Street house they spent months fending off possible neighborly advances from the other. Finding themselves on the same bus they carefully hid behind their newspapers, bumping their carts into each other in the A.&P. Supermarket with identical cocktail crackers, club soda and red caviar, they looked carefully past each other; hands touching at the Sixth Avenue newsstand as they reached for the same columnist's newspaper they did not exchange a single smile.

Months of this wary circling finally persuaded them that they had nothing to fear from each other, and extravagantly relieved, they backed into a minuet of neighborliness, courting the casual encounters and excuses for the very conversational exchange they had formerly spent so much time in avoiding. Elsie looked for her neighbor's name or picture in gossip columns; Jerry was impressed by society page references to Elsie's family. Without being aware of it they fell into a companionship that on the surface made no demands or encroachments but consisted of confidences over nightcaps when they arrived home at the same hour, intimate revelations one makes to someone safely in another world or in another country. They felt completely safe with each other; neither could conceive of the possible intrusion of the other in her own sphere. They could tell about their own sins or those of their dearest friends with all the pleasure of spilling the beans and without the attendant fear of just reprisals. Never going to the same places they exchanged little worlds like party favors whenever they met, cheered and amazed that their offerings were so highly prized, their discarded and discounted currency so valuable. Each was fascinated by the vice the other wished most to hide; in Elsie it was her respectability; in Jerry it was her lawlessness. They had never known anyone like each other, but in their blind progress towards opposite goals they had reached a simultaneous stalemate, and the temporary collision seemed a rare union of minds. Whatever it was they wanted in life, they were confident it was not the same thing; they would never be rivals, but between them they might play a winning hand.

Like shipboard acquaintances they confided freely everything about themselves except what they did last night or were going to do tomorrow. Elsie talked about Boston, to Jerry's great delight, for Elsie was an escaped Bostonian, in perpetual and futile flight from everything that city represented, as obsessed with it as any excommunicated Catholic with the Vatican. She derided her brother Wharton for being a proper Bostonian, horrified by the democratic waywardness of his sister, and she chose to fancy herself voluntary renegade instead of involuntary exile.

"Boston is supposed to be the center of culture, but there's no place on earth where money is so much worshiped. Talk about Chicago or the oil cities! Good God!" Elsie was wont to rant. "In Boston a family is supposed to be distinguished if some scalawag ancestor socked away enough loot to keep the next five generations in feeble-minded homes and keep their lawyers in yachts. Nobody's ever read a book in Boston, they just have libraries. Nobody likes paintings, they just buy them. They go for concerts in a big way because all real Bostonians are deaf as posts so music doesn't give them any pain. I tell you in Boston the word 'ignorance' just means no money in the family. That's the way my brother Wharton thinks. Boston! Ugh! I'm ashamed to admit the twenty-five years I spent there trying to conform. But give me credit for pulling out finally, even if I had to marry a European crook to do it."

Elsie could not understand that the more elegantly eccentric she made her family out to be the more delighted Jerry became. The running stock of tidbits about family quarrels, scandals, lawsuits, feuds and hidden passions opened a curious world to Jerry and she followed it, fitting pieces together as she might have a jigsaw puzzle. It seemed that after Elsie's marital debacle brother Wharton felt it was her duty to stay with Mother in the great house on Marlborough Street, but Elsie absolutely refused, so Wharton and his family had to live there and of course simply ROBBED dotty old Mama. Finally Mama, with her last shred of intelligence, had put the house up for sale and went to live in happy senility at the Hotel Vendome with an ancient dependent. Brother and sister continued to accuse each other of filial neglect but Elsie didn't feel a bit guilty because Mama had never forgiven her for the scandal about the Baron. And Mama and Wharton had been so gaga about him at first, so dumbfounded that it should be Elsie the barbarian who had brought the Almanach de Gotha into the family and vice versa. And even after the Baron von Humfert had gotten into that swindling jam and had to be bought out, brother Wharton still enjoyed baronessing his sister in public until Elsie, just for pure spite, had dropped the title.

"Of course the man was a crook," she quoted Wharton as fuming, "but the title left us a little dignity. But oh no, Elsie won't leave us even that little shred of pride!"

Elsie swore that wild horses would not drag her into her brother's stuffy clutches now that he had taken up residence in New York on Gracie Square. But after a few months when it became apparent that the Wharton Hookleys were in no way importuning her to be one of them, Elsie began to worry. Perhaps she had been too blunt. She heard everywhere of their social activities, so evidently they did not need her introductions. A furtive familiar that she usually took to be her conscience reminded her that blood was thicker than water, a brother was a brother and then there were the children, her nieces. God forbid that she should ever be the snob her brother was, but the fact was those girls soon to enter society needed the experience and guidance of an aunt who was a woman of the world. Nita, their mother, was nothing but a child herself.

So Elsie had nobly decided to make the overtures and sacrifice herself. She called and magnanimously offered herself as chaperon for the older girl who had just come out.

"I would be perfectly willing to take Isabella shopping or driving," she reported to Jerry she had told Wharton. "I have lived in New York for years and therefore know everyone and would see that Isabella got to know them too. I could arrange little parties for her—take her to the right galleries, the right plays, the proper restaurants, in a word prepare her for a successful marriage."

And what do you think Wharton, the stinker, had said?

"My dear Elsie," he had said, and in repeating her brother's incredible words Elsie gave him a quavering sort of village idiot voice just as in quoting herself she used an ineffably dulcet, benevolent whinny, "what in the world would it do to my daughter's future to be seen about with your sort of friends? I'm sure they're the most interesting people in the world to you but what would it do to little Isabella's reputation?"

Those were her brother's very words.

This absolutely killed Jerry, though Elsie thought the story merited indignation rather than laughter. On second thoughts she decided it made her feel better to be amused by Wharton rather than insulted so she joined heartily in the laughter.

"But believe me, my dear," Elsie sighed, "these are the moments I just wish I'd kept the Baron."

She said this as if the Baron was a wool hat she'd given away not knowing a blizzard was coming.

From Elsie Jerry got the general impression that the best Bostonians rattled their family skeletons at each other as proudly as Texans flashed their jumbo diamonds. She concluded that Elsie's whimsicalities were a proof that the Hookleys were gloriously rich.

But if Jerry was spellbound by Elsie's Boston legends, Elsie was even more entranced by her peep into Jerry's world—a world without trust funds, no windfalls from forgotten relatives, no estates to be settled, no wills to fight, no salary, no family, yet a world illuminated with vague opulence. How on earth did a girl without a boat, so to speak, sail triumphantly through life, knowing the best people and the best places? It couldn't be that Jerry was merely a shrewd manager for she was always tipping grocery boys in dollar bills for bringing up a quart of milk, or handing out five dollars to a taxi driver and saying to keep the change. When Elsie rebuked her for this folly Jerry shrugged.

"I just remember what a thrill it was when some uncle gave me a buck when I was a kid," she explained. "And then I figure that anybody in a three-thousand-dollar mink coat hasn't got any right to be waiting around for eighty-five cents change from a cabby."

No, Jerry was certainly not the shrewd type. Of course a good-looking girl with a figure for clothes and a model's opportunities (for that's how Jerry had started) could always assemble a fine wardrobe on credit or gravy, and have unlimited dates, but how had Jerry managed to collect so many important men as close friends? Gossip columnists never seemed able to link her name in shady romances, her escorts varied from Cabinet members to industrialists, bankers, yachtsmen, and for bohemian relief older editors of *Fortune*, *Life* or play angels. How could a girl without family or social sponsors acquire such a circle? Elsie could not rest until Jerry would consent to clear up this mystery. It took Jerry a little time to figure it out herself.

"I guess I learned a lot watching the other girls make mistakes," she finally confessed, rather enjoying the luxury of being candid about herself. "I'd see how some of the girls scared men, big men, I mean. I knew big shots want to have fun the same as anybody but they're awfully skittish. They're afraid of their jobs and publicity and their wives and their children, and of being used. If a new girl flatters a man too much he's afraid she's going to move in. If she finagles a couple of drinks out of him he's scared she's going to stick him for a sable coat. You've got to calm him down right away like you would a nervous virgin. He feels easier if he finds out right away that you know bigger shots than he is and could introduce him to them, or tell him about them. You ask his advice about business. You show him you're not on the make, you're just trying to make friends with him because you admire him. Maybe you surprise him by buying him a tie or a book. Look, he says, here's somebody doing something for me at last, instead of me having to do something for her. After that he relaxes with you—and he can't do that with many people, see."

From a sharp little lawyer Elsie sometimes consulted and whose work gave him the opportunity to observe Jerry Dulaine's rise, Elsie heard another angle.

"Jerry's antecedents and background are so hopelessly low grade she's never had anything to lose," he explained. "Nothing surprises her, nothing awes her, and never having made any particular class in society she's at home in all of them. Like genuine royalty, you might say—or the oldest peasantry."

Elsie congratulated herself on providing herself with such juicy nourishment for she had devoured most of her old friends, her enthusiasms were thinning out, and she had reached a time of life when the zest for adventure properly takes itself out in belaboring a daughter-in-law, ruining a grandchild or defending a worthless son. Having been denied these natural channels for her robust energy she had satisfied herself in years past by feeding on younger people who had talent, or a capacity for unique mischief. She liked to be in the midst of uproar without leaving her rocking chair, and for her chosen ones she was always ready with a shoulder to cry upon even though it was often she who had to make them cry. Certain disappointments in the last few years had made her more cautious but had not lessened her appetite, and after her preliminary reserve she plunged into Jerry's private career with the single-minded gusto of a folio collector. It delighted Elsie that there should be individuals like Jerry, wild cards, you might say, being anything the dealer named, anything that was needed for winning.

It was the first time she had encountered one of these girls so inexplicably in the city spotlight, girls everybody seems to know or ought to know, whose names invariably euphonious or amusing, ring a very faint bell, and rather than admit ignorance the businessman assumes she is a débutante, the débutante guesses she is an actress, the actor deduces she must be rich, all credit her with distinction in some field of which they are ignorant. With no letters of introduction she builds a kind of social security for herself simply on the importance and dignity of her escorts. Here was democracy, Elsie thought, a joke on the bourgeoisie, particularly a joke on her brother, who for all his position and influence, could not know half the great names in Jerry's date book. She chuckled to think of the elaborate hocus-pocus he would have to go through to get suitable matches for his daughters when little Jerry Dulaine, runaway girl from a Kansas small town, could know anyone she wanted. It was a pleasure, at those times when Wharton used the outrageous excuse of having some very important visitor, too important to risk meeting his sister, for Elsie to mention that she had just met that very gentleman on her doorstep escorting her dearest friend home from the races. Wharton could not disguise his helpless irritation that a sister he liked to reproach as surrounding herself with cheap wastrels and Bowery bums should have contacts he himself had made with difficulty.

"He's always knocked his brains out for something you take right in your stride," Elsie chortled privately to Jerry.

It was just as well that Elsie was completely in the dark as to how her young friend had gotten her start "taking everything in her stride," miraculously keeping her name above water at the same time. Jerry herself could not disentangle that first introduction from the chain of subsequent introductions that had been her staircase. The fact was, her success, such as it was, stemmed from an error made fifteen years ago.

This was what had happened, only a few months after Jerry had landed in New York.

A young couple of some social distinction, pondering their financial woes in the bar of a midtown hotel, remembered that an elderly uncle, high in government affairs and rich in oil, usually kept a suite at this hotel. Brave with double Manhattans and last hopes of fortunes, they rushed up to his suite to surprise him, which they did indeed, for they found him entertaining a personable young woman, two gay goblets on the coffee table, a serious-looking bucket of champagne on the floor. In the ensuing embarrassment the young couple hastily stated that their visit was for the purpose of inviting Uncle George to Oyster Bay for the week end with some marvelous people, and of course they would be delighted if Miss Dulaine would come too. Miss Dulaine went, and since her appearance and deportment were perfectly acceptable, the girl wearing the proper clothes, saying the proper things, playing tennis and swimming well, she interested influential men who issued invitations to places where she met higher figures who moved her further along, and no one ever discovered that Uncle had picked her up in the lobby of his hotel a bare thirty minutes before his nephew's call. Even if they had discovered this, it would have been too late to matter, for Jerry was already being mentioned in gossip columns on the fringes of both glamour and fashion.

A likable, good-looking young woman without affectations, on speaking terms with the leading names, can always get along in New York, and Jerry got along. She was blessed with that easy confidence that all men are men and everybody's only human that often induces the world to behave as if this was true. She had quit high school in her Kansas home to come to New York on her father's railroad pass (he was a fireman on the Southern Pacific Railroad), met another girl in the Grand Central Station ladies' room who got her a job in a wholesale garment house where she modeled. Tessie also took her to her rooming house on West Fifty-Fifth, invited her on a couple of double dates with a press agent boy friend and a photographer, and Jerry was started. She made enough money, had a good time, and was happy enough for a few months.

But the social popularity she began enjoying after her successful début in the Biltmore lobby made the demands of her job seem increasingly oppressive. Staying up all night in the best nightclubs with the easiest spenders, who themselves need not get up next day till dark, made Jerry's own alarm clock seem a cruel dictator. She had quickly picked up the standards and patter of the garment trade, could appraise within a dollar every rag on every back, see through fur and leather to the designer's label, nose out makeshifts and imitations until her tastes and needs were elevated hopelessly beyond her ability to satisfy them. Her modeling job, well paid as it first had seemed, became merely a means of meeting spenders, and the truth was that as a model Jerry was not as pretty as others at that time (that radiant sheen of youth came to her much later) and she was much too grateful. Older men liked to take her out, because a more conspicuous beauty would have caused gossip. Jerry looked like just a nice girl. She had the clean healthy look of a Western niece or the

suburban bride of some junior associate. Her friend Tessie
and other play girls in her shop and hotel called on her when
the party required another girl who could be trusted not to
encroach on their special game. Wives did not bristle jealously
at her presence, or if they did they were reassured when some
respectable older citizen spoke to her. Older men were flattered that she seemed to prefer them to younger, hotter
blood, and Jerry really did. Younger men demanded too
much, drank too much, cost too much, and got you nowhere,
as Jerry had seen by watching her friend Tessie's occasional
lapses into love. A floater herself, and from a family of
floaters, Jerry reacted to a man of fifty or more, of established
reputation in business or public life, securely solvent, the way
most women react to a fine masculine physique. She cut out
pictures of such men of affairs from *Time* and *Newsweek*,
pinned them on her mirror, and if opportunity came to acquire a personally autographed photograph she framed it in
silver for her dresser.

But the camera lens was cruel to sleepy eyes and her modeling jobs dwindled as more and more men depended on her
ready assent to last minute calls, "Come on over to the Stork
and help me get rid of a branch manager, Jerry, atta girl."
What had first seemed her chief asset turned out to be her
misfortune: looking like a nice girl who would never accept
diamonds or foreign cars, these were seldom offered. Even
the ordinary negotiable loot of a popular girl got less and less.
Open-handed men of substance, half tempted to settle a good
sum on her, looked into her clear, honest blue eyes and
switched to vague offers of marriage (with a big home and
ready-made family out in Nebraska) or else proposed a regular job with fine opportunities for a girl with personality. Her
girl friend, Tessie, who had launched her so kindly, was no
longer her friend for Tessie had counted on some gratifying
male skepticism at her loyal claims for Jerry's beauty, brains
and wit. It was a betrayal of confidence, Tessie indignantly
felt, that her men friends were taken in by her praise and soon
went so far as to prefer Jerry to her prettier self. Jerry had
naïvely thought her sponsor would be proud to see her accepted, but to her surprise she soon saw Tessie's eyes fixed on
her with unmistakable hostility, lip curled in accusing scorn;

and presently Jerry realized that Tessie's fondness had been based on her unflattering faith that Jerry was merely a good foil, and could never make out without Tessie. There were bitter words. No, Jerry discovered, you could not depend on girl friends in this little world, not after you moved up into their class. Just remember not to grieve over them, but save your tears for that ominous twilight when their flattering jealousy turns to kindness.

The girls separated, Tessie to marry a natty-looking promoter named Walton simply to stop him making passes at Jerry, who honestly detested him and had not wanted to offend Tessie by rebuffing him. They knew too much about each other to dare be enemies outright but each felt, when they divided their joint possessions, that she had been robbed. They spoke to each other only when they chanced to meet head on, once or twice a year. Catching a glimpse of each other in a crowd they made a swift estimate of the other's appearance, saw that muskrat had replaced mink or vice versa, wondered a little, and ducked out of sight.

Jerry who had moved to the Pierre slid back to Lexington Avenue hotels. She took to leaving the receiver off the hook mornings to block early assignments for work. The simple truth was that with her increasingly extravagant tastes she really could not afford to work. A miserable hundred or so a week (taxes and social security deducted), did not pay the upkeep of a job like hers. As for settling for the safety of marriage, that seemed the final defeat, synonymous in Jerry's mind with asking for the last rites. Then suddenly—all in a day, it seemed—men friends were looking at the girl next to her instead of at her, and were saying, "Who was that attractive girl in your party at the Café Julien the other night?" or "What a little beauty over there at the corner table!" Not daring to analyze these warnings signals Jerry was only conscious of a growing desperation, hidden and solitary, a desperation never to be faced openly but nevertheless lurking for her in mirrors and in men's eyes. She found herself hiding iodine and sleeping pills from herself, avoiding edges of penthouse roofs, afraid.

It was Uncle Sam, the one with the red, white and blue pants, who eventually cornered Jerry. One of the pleasanter tasks he had assigned his internal revenue men was a secret investigation of the patrons of expensive restaurants, shops and entertainments. The larger spenders were, of course, able to come to a gentleman's agreement, or else were lavishly protected by distinguished lawyers or politicians, so the industrious officers must make up their records with names of minor lone unfortunates whose clothes, companions, residences and checks were out of all proportion to their avowed incomes. Jerry Dulaine was one of these, and like a sporting fish showed such guilt, terror and impudence as to guarantee her constant persecution with fines, threats, warrants, super-fines for not paying fines. In particular there was a cadaverous Mr. Prince in the Empire State head offices who had made Miss Dulaine's tax deficiencies a gruesome case for the government far more evil than the million-dollar lapses of mighty corporations. Nothing less than a small fortune was needed to appease these bloodhounds, and Jerry had observed that nobody reaps a fortune nowadays from working union hours or even double-paid overtime. As for saving for these quarterly raids, if such a thing were possible any more, the slogan of the new economy was "Save the pennies and the bank will charge you double to take care of them." Luckless citizens with no genius for major crime were obliged to apply themselves to figuring out quick-profit schemes unique and complicated enough to elude tax classification. There must be a Gimmick, they told themselves, and toiled night and day to find how to make the quick dollar without toil. They were constantly goaded onward by news of a lady relaxing in her bubble bath who thought up a perfumed chewing gum and made a fortune; a retired but restless black marketeer bronzing his pot on Miami Beach thought of a dolls' roller derby and was back in big business; a radio bit-player, between shots, thought of a sound-skip device that would eliminate all voices but the one desired; a bartender on Rubberleg Square thought up the idea of a juke-box psychoanalyst, two backward students at Penn State thought of a Baby-Naming Personal Service. All through the night and all through the land the geniuses, the bums, the experts and the birdbrains were pecking away for the golden gimmick that would fell the great enemy, Taxes.

Jerry Dulaine, who knew everyone, learned by listening,

introduced Ideas to Capital, shuffled contacts personal with contacts professional, joined the quest for the Gimmick. She got a bank ten good clearing-house days away from her New York bank, took a $500 option on a $100,000 business block, "sold it," "bought" a suburban movie theatre, borrowed on it, "bought" a textile works, traded it for a piece of a musical show, wangled advances to pay past losses, her distant checks passing her local checks on slow trains, one deal juggling the other, all maneuvered so swiftly that the eyes never quite caught up with the prestidigitator's hands.

For the past five years—Jerry was now thirty-four—she had lived perilously on the brink of disaster, but she had lived well and still clung to the brink. It was still a good show, Elsie Hookley declared, mystified and admiring. But Jerry was beginning to wonder. How much longer could she keep it up and where was it leading? Instead of the game being easier it was getting tougher. She was calling up more men than called her up and, worse yet, some of these gentlemen belonged to the older and lower part of her ladder. And there were the lunches every day with other girls whose luck was running out except for restaurant credit.

Elsie, once Jerry's apprehensions had penetrated her consciousness, was far more disturbed than Jerry. Taxis, instead of private cars, were bringing Jerry home, and earlier besides. Jerry's doings had filled Elsie's life and made her forget her uneasiness about her own. She had countered Wharton's victories with Jerry's and if the show was not to go on forever then she must see that the curtain came down on a triumphant finale that would pay off both star and audience. Elsie made wild plans in her worried sleep to rent a bigger, finer house than her brother's where she would bombard his finest guest list with royal dinners at which Jerry would shine. She would pick up the old exclusive club memberships gaily discarded decades ago and install Jerry in the inner circle. She would rent a palace in Capri or Rome where Jerry would preside over international royalty.

"It wouldn't do," she always had to sigh before resigning herself to sleep. "I'm too old and too tired."

The great inspiration came at last on the morning she had carried Jerry's mail up to her from the hall table and found

the young lady sitting cross-legged in bed absorbed in scis-
soring a photograph out of *City Life*. The sight of the world-
ling's tousled head bent over her paper-doll cuttings,
shining black locks loose, brow knit, pajama coat carelessly
unbuttoned down to the twinkling childish navel, charmed
Elsie. An innocent little devil-child, she thought, her innate
generalissimo instincts deeply touched. Oh yes, she vowed,
she would fight to protect this happy picture. Who would
dream that this dear child, so simple and guileless-looking
without make-up, pretty mouth puckered in concentration,
small pink bare foot peeping out of blankets, had been probably night-clubbing all over town most of the night?

Elsie looked fondly about the room. There always seemed
such order in its disorder, the dresser drawers always half open,
the satin puff always sliding to floor, coffee cup with cigarette
butts always on night table, a book always face-open on the
floor where it had slid, mottoes and cartoons that had appealed
to Jerry pasted on the mirror. ("It's just our club motto," Jerry
explained, seeing Elsie puzzling over one card: The Lady
Flounderers Club. *They said* I *couldn't do it so* I *didn't even try*,
Fishback, Elsie read, and saw pasted below this inspirational
thought, *Better half-done today than not at all tomorrow*.)
These touches, with the jet slippers toppled wearily in a corner
where dance-tired feet had kicked them, gave the place a jolly,
inviting air, as cozy as a kitchen fireplace.

At the moment Jerry was carefully inserting the clipped
photograph into the silver frame that always contained her
Man of the Week. Elsie dropped the letters on the bed, noting from the corner of her eye that the envelopes had ominous cellophane windows, and then looked at the latest idol,
relieved that this one's face didn't look like a trail map
through the Badlands as the *Time* cover men always did.

"Collier McGrew?" she exclaimed and took a second look.

"Isn't he a dream?" Jerry demanded happily. "The most
marvelous man I ever met in my life."

Elsie sat down, shaking her head in speechless amazement.

"I knew you got around," she finally sighed, "but Collier
McGrew! Where on earth did you meet him—the White
House?"

"Why shouldn't I meet him?" Jerry asked, squirming off

the bed and sliding her feet into rabbit-furred mules. "He's in public domain. Let's have some coffee."

"But he doesn't go to nightclubs or any gay spots. How did you meet him?" Elsie eagerly followed Jerry into the kitchen and took two cups out of the cupboard as Jerry adjusted the Chemex.

"I had lunch at the Julien the other day with Judge Brockner and he was there with some Congressman Brockie knew," Jerry explained. "Brockie and the Congressman had to go to some meeting and McGrew and I had a brandy and he walked me home. Then there was that benefit fashion show. I was with the fashion people and he was bored with his benefit people so he took me out for dinner. Just a quiet little steak house. He hates crowds he said. Then last night a drip I knew took me to a newspaper party and there was McGrew with some Washington big-shot and bored stiff. I was the only person there he knew, he said, so he and I slipped out and had a quiet snack, then he drove me home."

"Well!" Elsie exclaimed. "When I think of everybody in the Pentagon and U.N. after him, my brother Wharton quoting him on everything and bragging about how close they are, and then you walk away with him just because everybody else bores him!"

"The most attractive man I ever met," Jerry declared with such an unwonted dewy look that Elsie gave her an approving thump on the back. They carried their cups to the living room and Jerry dropped on the sofa.

"I could marry a man like that," Jerry said, dreamily stirring her coffee. "I swear I could."

Much to her surprise Elsie did not take this as a joke.

"Now this is something I'll buy!" Elsie shouted, and clapped her hands as the idea began burgeoning in her brain. "Don't you see it? You've been wasting your time on small stakes, but this is the time for the big kill. You're thirty-four and still gorgeous. You've got a chance at the biggest man you've ever met and you ought to play it big. How would you like to be an ambassador's wife?"

Jerry's answer was to burst out laughing. How would Elsie herself like to be Pope, she countered. Who wanted to get married, for heaven's sake? All anybody asked was some ready cash and a good time, and besides McGrew wasn't any ambassador.

"Everybody says he will be," Elsie insisted, her eyes beginning to glitter and her nostrils dilate at the whiff of the marvelous mischief she was about to launch. In her excitement she began to stride about the room, holding her cigarette aloft like a torch and waving it about as she swooped back and forth until it seemed to Jerry the room could not possibly contain this mobile statue of Liberty. "And let me tell you something about marriage, my dear girl."

"Now Elsie!" Jerry cried in alarm. "Not the facts of life!"

"You don't realize what a future there is in marriage," Elsie said, ignoring the interruption. "Why, I've seen women without looks and no talent for anything else be perfect geniuses at marriage. They really clean up. You marry your man, pop a baby right off the reel, enter it in Groton or Spence on its christening day, have the father set up a trust fund for it right off with you as guardian, get your divorce, marry the next guy, pop another baby with trust fund, repeat divorce and same deal all over. Finally you're living high on the income from four or five trust funds, without lifting a finger."

"Like a prize stud," Jerry observed. "Frankly I don't see myself as a breeder, old girl."

Elsie was obliged to admit that it might be a little late for Jerry to get into that field, but there were other ways of making a business out of marriage.

"You work it out like a big merger," she said with a large gesture. "After all a girl like you has a lot to offer and you expect top price. A man like McGrew needs a woman like you and you need a man like him."

"He's done all right for himself all these years without a wife," Jerry objected. "Why should he need one now?"

Elsie could answer that one. First, everybody said he should marry and mothers all over the world were throwing their daughters at him. He had been so busy dodging daughters ever since the New Deal had flushed him out of an aristocratic private life into public service that he'd been afraid to marry. But now that he was rising in importance, honored from the Pentagon to United Nations and Wall Street, he needed a hostess to help share his tremendous social obligations.

Brother Wharton said so and Elsie was positive he was grooming his eldest daughter for the job, a little goon like that, mind you! When obviously the one woman in the world equipped to handle such a man of affairs was Jerry. And the great part of it was that evidently McGrew himself had recognized this.

"Tell me again just what he said," she urged.

Jerry looked dreamily at the photograph.

"He said I was the first woman he'd met in years he could talk to without feeling she was either a competitor or a responsibility," she said in a faraway voice, and then remembered something fresh. "He said I was plastic, that's it."

"Plastic?" Elsie queried doubtfully.

"Not like Dupont products, silly," Jerry said, impatiently. "He said he was frightfully tired and bored and I had a plastic charm that gave to any mood. He thanked me for refreshing him, he said."

"That does it!" Elsie cried. "He admits you've got the quality he needs. If we follow this up right you'll be Mrs. McGrew and all your future will be solved."

"What do you want me to do—blackmail him into it?" giggled Jerry. "Elsie, darling, don't be an idiot."

"There you are!" Elsie exclaimed. "You just don't know your own value. Believe me, I've been around enough to know how high you could go if the right person handled you. Why, I could put this across myself if you'd let me handle you and do just as I said."

Jerry's continued amusement made Elsie the more resolute. She swore she was going to study this problem and map out a campaign that Jerry would have to follow. The idea of Elsie as marriage broker and talent manager kept Jerry in hysterics for several days, but she stopped laughing when she had to buy her own dinner two nights in a row and another envelope frank-stamped from the Collector of Internal Revenue arrived. This letter turned out to be a warrant form with penciled-in threats and rebukes by the clerk. Hopelessly Jerry tore up the letter and turned to Elsie. The hour had come for her to put her destiny in someone else's hands.

Elsie, seeing that she had made her impression, set to work. She devoted herself to planning her strategy with the thoroughness of a long pent-up housewife going after a belated college degree. She pried all the information about McGrew she could get out of her brother by the ancient technique of disparaging the man so that Wharton would angrily blurt out everything he knew. By poking around she ascertained that little Isabella was studying cooking at a fashionable cooking school (McGrew was a Chevalier du Tastvins); little Isabella was also boning up furiously with tutors in French, Spanish, and Persian (there was a rumor that McGrew might be sent to Iran on a government mission); little Isabella was having a second début in Washington, D.C., on the excuse that Hookley cousins there demanded it. Obviously Wharton was doing his best to land McGrew and Elsie's nostrils quivered happily at this familiar challenge.

McGrew was to leave that week for Florida, Elsie learned, for conferences with certain politicos there and best of all he was to spend some time, at Wharton's insistence, with some Palm Beach Hookleys. They were her cousins, too, Elsie joyously cried, and they could just as well sponsor *her* friend as they could Wharton's. Jerry would meet McGrew under finer auspices than she ever had in New York and a different background often acted as a forcing spot for romance. A long-distance call arranged for ten days at the cousins' estate and after that Jerry could bide her time at a hotel—McGrew's hotel, if possible.

"My cousin's set is the last word in stuffiness," Elsie said. "I want McGrew to see that you can handle a stuffy set as well as you can a party crowd. A diplomat's wife has to know all kinds. But above everything else she has to know food and wines. I'll teach you."

"Nobody has ever complained that I didn't know how to order a fine dinner," Jerry laughed.

"I mean to serve it in your own home," Elsie said. "Why else do you think Wharton and Nita are forcing their poor daughter to study gourmet cooking when all she knows is chocolate malties? But leave this to me. I'll arrange everything."

While Jerry was away Elsie was to have decorators do over her helter-skelter apartment into a tasteful background for a lady of discrimination. Good books, a fine modern painting or two, and the ultimate in equipment for serving such dinners as would melt away all barriers of class and race in any capital where a diplomat might be sent.

"I'll loan you my Iola to cook for you," Elsie said. "We will stage a marvelous demonstration dinner for McGrew the minute you get back just to sew him up if Florida hasn't already done it."

Jerry was ready to do anything or go anywhere that was financed. Cheered by Elsie's generosity, she set out with a fine southern wardrobe privately sure she could get McGrew one way or another. Hadn't he refrained from making any passes at her? Wasn't that how you knew a man had seriously fallen for you? At her door he had kissed her good night, a sweet, warm, sexless sort of kiss that had left Jerry absolutely dewy-eyed, knocked for a loop as she admitted dizzily to herself afterward. This must be It. No groping, no clutches, just a boy-girl kiss. Jerry was thankful she hadn't been in the least tight or she might have been fool enough to make a pass or two herself. But McGrew or no McGrew she had a few private ideas for making the most of a Florida trip, though Elsie, suspecting that in her present state Jerry might give up the game at the drop of a hat, gave her last minute warnings.

"Don't you dare forget this deal isn't just a flop in the hay," Elsie said severely. "It's a roll in the orange blossoms. So don't get mixed up with any fly-by-nights down there, don't get plastered except with the best people, don't forget you're not there to have yourself a good time but to build a respectable marrying background for yourself. You've still got a good reputation, God knows why. You've had sense enough to know you can have more fun with better people that way, but that Irish in you is beginning to come out more and more so watch out for it. You be working on being top drawer down there while I get the nest all ready. When you get back you're going to start making your name as hostess in your own home instead of party girl."

"But I hate staying home," Jerry complained. "I hate ending up in the same place I started out and with the same people."

"There you are!" Elsie exclaimed, quite shocked. "Don't you know that no matter how many men you get by being seen around all the spots with all the big shots you only get a husband by having him see you in your own home? You've got to give dinners—fine dinners. Once you've got people at your own table you've got the edge on them. They've as good as admitted they're your friends and are committed to stand by you. Wait till you get back and see all the things I've planned for you. It's a new life, my chick."

So off Jerry went, glad to be away from creditors, returning weeks later radiantly bronzed, confessing to many happy hours with McGrew and allowing Elsie to deduce she had practically won her game when the truth was she had, to her own bewilderment, merely been playing McGrew's. He was too experienced a bachelor to permit any pressure, and she sensed soon enough that her appeal for him was in her demanding nothing but being *there* when he chose to see her. No use hoping to rouse his interest by her popularity with other men of his rank, for he would not compete. If he was so delighted to find her alone with no plans, then she would be that, like a back-street mistress, she thought, without the romance. He was a new kind of fish to her, and for the life of her she couldn't understand why she would feel so flattered and elated after a perfectly harmless swim or ride with him. She knew most men would class her as desirable but McGrew gave her the dizzy delusion that she must be intellectual, and that was a new sensation indeed.

Just as she persuaded herself she was getting someplace she found that the gentleman had left for New York without so much as a good-bye. A curious man, she reflected, slightly chilled by his efficient use of her for exactly what and when he liked, with no loose ends or wasted time, just as he dropped being charming to order the dinner, then resumed charm the minute the headwaiter left. She did not betray her doubts to Elsie when Elsie suggested she give a dinner for McGrew as soon as she got back to town. It gave her an excuse to telephone him, and he was in the mood to find it amusing to be invited to "test her new cook." Happily relieved, Jerry made out a guest list but Elsie immediately crossed off all Hollywood or Broadway names and substituted more worthy ones.

"I hardly know these people," Jerry protested at Elsie's list. "Why should they accept any dinner invitation from me?"

"On account of the guest of honor, silly," Elsie said. "You'll see."

Indeed it had been funny, Jerry admitted, the way people hemmed and made excuses till the McGrew name was mentioned and how fast they accepted then. But now the masterly plan had been tested, the dinner was over, and at eleven o'clock the two ladies, deserted, knew they had failed. Jerry had known it was a flop for hours but Elsie refused to admit it till the last guest had fled. Then she decided to be philosophical about it, for she feasted on catastrophe, and there had been so many subtle angles to the evening's failure that she anticipated a whole season of warming over tidbits, souping and hashing. She enjoyed her power as secret entrepreneur of a grand comedy. She was not vain enough to expect gratitude from Jerry or personal applause if the game had succeeded; all she had dreamed was a slow trickle of fury through her brother's future thoughts. She did not think yet about the financial loss to herself, not because she was generous but because she was vague about money, blind in arithmetic and only spasmodically foxy. For her it was chiefly a dazzling, amusing scheme that had missed fire. It had occupied her energies for a while very nicely, and she did not realize how serious it was for Jerry. Her young friend's gloom gave her the opportunity for a few cheerful words on errors in strategy. She felt there might be consolation in analyzing the whole situation, now that the show was over.

Which Elsie proceeded to do.

. . . evening at home . . .

"At least my husband was a gentleman," Elsie Hookley suddenly announced, helping herself from a decanter of Jamieson's Irish which she had drawn within cuddling distance. "What if he did ruin my life, the bastard? He had a great many women, true enough, but he was a gentleman and he treated them like ladies. He paid them and he paid them well. All right, what if it was my money? The way he put it was that a real gentleman expected to pay and a real lady expected to be taken care of. That's your European aristocrat for you."

"So McGrew isn't a European aristocrat," Jerry Dulaine replied crossly. "So I don't get paid. It still doesn't explain why he didn't show up."

"And not one word out of him," Elsie said happily, for she was beginning to enjoy the enormity of the catastrophe. "Not a telegram. You're sure he understood he was to be guest of honor?"

"He's known it for two weeks," Jerry said wearily, for they'd been all over this a dozen times. "You know perfectly well he told me his favorite dishes and you had Iola make them especially for him."

Elsie nodded sadly.

"Guinea hen, broccoli in creamed chestnuts, wild rice—my God, my brother would do murder for a dinner like that! And Iola all gussied up in turquoise corduroy uniform from Clyde's! I had counted on McGrew telling Wharton all about it just so he'd burn up." She thought of something new. "You're sure he never came to your apartment before we fixed it up? He's such a wine and food man he might have been afraid your dinner would be a weenie roast."

"He brought me home but he never came up," Jerry said.

"You're sure you remembered not to sleep with him?" Elsie asked with a meditative glance at her friend.

Jerry had a flash of righteous indignation at this insult.

"I told you this was *serious*, Elsie," she exclaimed. "I told you it was his never making any pass, just saying little things to me—never anything personal, too—that made me know he meant something serious."

"You mean nothing really happened when you were with him so much in Florida?" Elsie asked as reproachfully as any designing mother. "For goodness sake, what did you do when you were alone?"

"Talked, like I told you," Jerry muttered.

"What about, for God's sake?" Elsie demanded.

Jerry shrugged and lit a cigarette.

"Art," she admitted defensively. "He buys paintings, doesn't he? And I asked his advice a lot about investments and—oh, things. He liked my ideas, he said."

She lit a cigarette and looked at herself in the mirrored wall, thinking back ruefully of how important it had seemed to get exactly the right white taffeta to show off her tanned shoulders and enhance her violet eyes. Every square inch of that sleek bronze skin cost a good fifty dollars if you measured it in Florida hotel rates, and when you considered that this gilding encompassed her whole body you realized that here was indeed complete folly. Staying on down there week after week just because McGrew was there, borrowing and charging right and left to anybody she could think of (particularly Elsie), writing post-dated checks on bank accounts she'd long outspent, counting on one big throw of the dice to recoup. Even so, she wouldn't have got in so deep if she hadn't been carried out of her depth by Elsie's enthusiastic urging. Elsie had really shoved her into this mess, and God knows Elsie had certainly made the whole evening a hundred times worse, but you couldn't say that.

"I know you wish I'd go home," Elsie said, kicking off her slippers and stretching out her long bony legs in their stockinged feet to the fender, her skirt pulled up above her knobby knees in the careless sexless way that always obliged people to look studiously away. "You wish I'd gotten out sooner, so you could have gone out with the others. They wouldn't invite me of course, because they couldn't stand me. I don't care. Right now, I feel like a little cozy post-mortem. A party that's a flop is more fun to talk over than a good party. Now get yourself a drink and sit down."

She wants me to drink with her so I'll blubber out more troubles and it'll cheer her up, Jerry thought. She knew Elsie loved her best when she played her cards badly and any other time she would have humored her by reporting a whole book of errors, the way pretty women mollify their enemies by stories of childhood freckles and miseries. But tonight she could not bear consolation or advice. She wanted Elsie to go home, for the sight of the gaunt, brassy-haired confidante of her misadventures, like the half-filled glasses left about, the inordinately festive profusion of fresh flowers (forty dollars' worth) smote her with the grim evidence of the evening's disaster. She didn't even dare put her fears into words; she could say it, but if she ever *heard* it she would surely gobble her bottle of Nembutal on the spot. It wasn't that she had counted too much on this dinner party to which the guest of honor had failed to come. It was the hint that her luck had run out and would never come back, that this was the beginning of worse disasters to come, of situations her blind knack could not manage. Already she could see the sunken black eyes of the dreadful Mr. Prince of Internal Revenue, wagging his bony finger at her and thundering, "If I can't afford to buy my wife or girl friend dresses like yours, then you ought to be in jail!"

In another minute she might burst into tears, Jerry thought with horror, and then where would she be? You didn't start sniveling until you'd given up hope of getting anything out of life but pity. Hastily she poured herself a stiff highball and sat down on the rug, doing her best to suppress her ungrateful exasperation with her friend. It was turning out to be exactly as she had always feared intimacy with a neighbor would turn out—and she should be kicking herself instead of blaming Elsie.

The trouble with accepting Elsie's devotion in an off-guard moment of need was that she moved in on you, so to speak. You should have been prepared for that. It was only reasonable. You thought it was fine that you knew how to spend beautifully without knowing where your money was coming from, but unfortunately Elsie, who had it and was willing to back your imagination, had to have an orchestra seat at the show. Elsie saw no unfair irony in herself wearing a ten ninety-five rayon crepe from Klein's-on-the-Square while Jerry wore a two-hundred-dollar dress she'd charged to her account at Bergdorf's. That was perfectly natural, Elsie thought. Pantry and cellar were her only indulgences, her sole requirement of clothes being that they should either be or at least look like basement bargains, but she placed no limit on what Jerry demanded for her proper setting.

"I should be grateful," Jerry reproached herself.

Of course it had to be a boomerang. Elsie financed you to a party designed to settle your whole future, then she queered everything by attending it. It was the first time they had attempted to fit together the odd sections of their social jigsaw, and in spite of all the knowledge they had of each other through after-hours confidences, they appeared to each other before an audience in a completely new light, like summer lovers suddenly popping up in winter clothes. Elsie, for her part, was more than satisfied with Jerry's easy manner in handling a large dinner party, and her loud compliments with hearty pats on the back made guests and Jerry wonder just what vulgar hi-jinks she had anticipated.

"Would you have dreamed that Jerry Dulaine could have managed a thing like this?" Elsie crowed again and again. "Isn't she marvelous? Just see what Colly McGrew is missing!"

Even if he had come, Elsie would have bollixed everything, Jerry knew. The more Jerry tried to pass off the slight from her missing guest the more Elsie insisted everyone should be mortally insulted. McGrew had decided they were none of them worth his while, Elsie reminded them again and again, and she just wondered what lies her own dear brother Wharton had said about Jerry Dulaine to keep McGrew from coming.

Jerry was accustomed to making a party go under the most trying handicaps, and after the hour's delaying of dinner, beautifully prepared and served by Elsie's precious Iola, she expected to salvage a pleasant enough evening for the others, with no further reference to the truant guest, loss though it was to herself. But she had never bucked against Elsie Hookley, and seeing her on show, so to speak, for the first time, Jerry thanked her stars that Prince Charming had not come, for if he had, Elsie would have driven him off forever. In those friendly hours when they had let down their hair, Jerry had taken for granted that Elsie, like herself, put the locks up in public. The picture Elsie had given of herself was of a worldly-wise gentlewoman, obliged by her station to put up with certain silly conventionalities, carrying on properly with straight face, but all the time saving up her real democratic feelings for the private orgy of honesty. Now Jerry saw that Elsie not only let her hair down in public but pulled out everybody else's hairpins as well. The spectacle of a few people dressed up to go through the motions of a genteel social routine inflamed Elsie, as she saw in it a masquerading dragon sent by her enemy, Boston, which she must attack with fiendish vigor. No simple exchange of amenities could pass without suspicion, the merest mouse of a polite compliment to the hostess must be harpooned and held up as deadly rodent. *Don't believe him when he says this is the finest Montrachet he's ever tasted, Jerry, he's got too good a cellar himself to kid anybody, though fat chance anybody ever gets of sampling it these days.* . . . An escape of talk into general fields while Elsie enjoyed a bite of fowl had her stopped only momentarily and then she was loudly declaring that were she the hostess, God forbid, she would never speak to anybody present for their neglecting to appreciate the marvel of the cooking, the equal of which she defied them to find short of Julien's, the *old* Julien's of course, not the new one her dear, dear brother Wharton continued to be so devoted to.

The fact was that Elsie was being herself, never less than overwhelming. Youthful years of excessive shyness, awkwardness and suppressed desires had fitted her out with a perfect treasure chest of home-truths conceived too late for their original cues but all waiting for some victorious day when they could be uttered. There was something pernicious, she felt, in the efforts of the others to pretend the party was a success; she felt she must prove her contempt for society's emptiness by emptying it before Jerry's very eyes. By the time they had arrived at dessert general conversation had been pretty well blocked, Elsie tackling, single-handed, every sentence that ventured down the field. The withdrawal to the living room for coffee offered a dim hope of loosening Elsie's grip.

"By George, that's an early Marius," Okie, the publisher of *Hemisphere*, had exclaimed, studying the painting above the fireplace. He had been invited as the last of a vanishing race, the Extra Men, and moreover Cynthia Earle, whose family background paralleled McGrew's, was using him these days as escort. Jerry nodded modestly to him, hoping Elsie had not overheard his remark for she would certainly declare that the picture was hers and that she knew more about it than Okie.

"An early Marius, at that," Okie went on. "You are lucky, Miss Dulaine."

"You must come in the gallery sometime and talk to me about it," murmured Severgny, the art dealer who sometimes employed Jerry as decoy to bring into his place certain rich collectors. "I am extremely interested in Marius right now."

"Let me tell you what Marius said the time I bumped into him at the Whitney—" Cynthia Earle began.

"But Marius is dead!" Elsie Hookley had boomed.

"This," Cynthia had patiently conceded, "was *before* he was dead. I mentioned his Paris show and you know how terribly, terribly funny Marius always was—"

"But Marius hasn't had a show in Paris for years!" shouted Elsie.

"This was 1939," Cynthia continued graciously. "The year before I met him at the Whitney as I was saying—"

"I can't understand why the Whitney didn't buy more of Marius," Elsie said. "They overdid on Ben Forrester, if you ask my opinion, and then only one little Dalzell Sloane. And speaking of Dalzell—"

"So you met Marius." Jerry raised her voice pointedly to Cynthia, not only to get the ball away from Elsie but because a certain idea for a profitable deal with Severgny had just occurred to her.

"Oh I wish I could remember the exact words. It was so— so *Marius*." Cynthia's little-girl Tinker Bell laugh at this moment was a tactical error for she had barely got on to her story again before Elsie charged.

"Oh I admit Marius was funny, oh screamingly funny. But Dalzell Sloane was a genius and a gentleman." Elsie placed one hand on the tense knee of Park Avenue's pet portrait painter and fixed the others with a beady blue eye. "I know geniuses aren't supposed to have any decency, they're supposed to be just sexy and funny like Marius, but let me tell you, Dalzell could paint rings around all of them. Just because he was too much of a gentleman to *use* people, the way you have to do, Mr. Whitfield—"

"Cynthia is telling a story about Marius," Jerry chided without conviction, and then since everything was already lost she gave up to a mild speculating on whether Cynthia could ever get the ball any nearer goal against Elsie's overpowering tactics. Cynthia had resolutely started her anecdote all over again when suddenly Elsie snatched the Whitney Museum from her lips and whooped down the field scoring a touchdown with a big inside story about a Hookley ancestral connection with the museum in Boston, a city where Collier McGrew's great-great-grandfather's South Boston wife had been unable to write her own name, and how do you like that, you people who think he's so perfect. Cynthia gave up, as indeed did everyone else, for Elsie was trimmed to take on every verbal offering, shaking an argument out of the merest name, questioning the pronunciation of a word before the speaker had gotten out the last syllable, finding political affronts in the first sentence of some attempted joke, pouncing on some orphan cause barely mentioned as needing noble defense, cutting through whispered asides like a school monitor, finally managing to keep the conversational ball on her big nose and batting it up and down like a trained seal. No use, Jerry thought, almost admiringly. No use, concluded the guests, and surrendered to glazed apathy as Elsie triumphantly regaled them with detailed grudges she had had for years against characters they had never known and never wished to know, delicately prefacing her remarks with a "Jerry's heard me say this before but since I'm on the subject—" convinced she was making the talk general by keeping one hand on Whitfield's knee, the other on Cynthia's back and addressing herself across the room to Jerry as if she was in a distant cornfield.

Yes, Elsie had been in great form and the guests had fled as from a tornado at half past ten, and not one of them had invited Jerry to come along with them for a store nightcap for fear Elsie would come too. Let them go and the hell with everything, Jerry thought, she was a gone goose now, anyway.

Being sorry for herself Jerry spared some morose speculations on poor Elsie, who, it was evident, was a comforting flannel nightgown for lonely winter nights but not to be worn in public. There were people like that whose shoulder-chips, spiritual ulcers or painful vanities were fluoroscoped by a party, though the weaknesses never came out in everyday life. A kind of disease, really, and you simply ought to make allowances. It couldn't be any fun being fifty-four years old with no men left in your life, being sore at the world for the mistakes you had made in it, feuding forever with your an-

cestors while you boasted of them, sitting up there in your
family tree dropping coconuts on yourself.

Poor, angry, honest, openhearted old Elsie, lavishing love
and gifts on chronically unworthy, ungrateful wastrels! ("I'm
as bad as the rest of them," Jerry guiltily admitted, "but how
can I help myself and anyway if it wasn't me it would be
somebody else"), then shrieking for vengeance when they behaved as she had so wonderfully predicted. Poor old Elsie,
Jerry thought, she's so proud of having kicked over that fine
old family and being so democratic, yet every time she meets
a title or a millionaire she wishes she could mow them down
with superior lineage. Instead all she can do is to bellow at
them. And it was funny to see her heckle everybody like an
old eagle, sort of brave, really, poor mad creature. They said
she had once been rather striking, in that old Boston warhorse way, six feet tall with flame-red hair and legs right up to
her shoulder blades as some contemporary had remarked.
Her hair was now on the pink side, frizzed in front and
looped into a limp bun on top. Her eyes were brilliantly blue
and if she would use creams instead of a careless washrag her
skin might have been more human-looking. As it was, her
striding walk, her great height, her icy glare and booming
voice quite terrified people and it was always necessary to reassure those who were backing away—"You know she comes
from a very old family, the Boston Hookleys, you know, her
brother's Wharton Hookley—he got the mother to do poor
Elsie out of her proper place in the old Marlborough Street
home just because Elsie refused to live in Boston—some legal
twist, and of course she could call herself Baroness but she's
so democratic—"

Good old Elsie, indeed, but that didn't give her the right
to ruin everybody's evening and a great deal more than that.
Now that it was all over there was no point in regrets or
reproaches. Besides Elsie seemed blissfully unaware that she
herself was responsible for anything going wrong. She sat
there wiggling her toes before the fireplace and sipping her
drink with the pleased expression of a day's wrecking well
done.

"Did you hear me take down that little museum monster
when he said, 'I had no idea Miss Dulaine did herself so

well!'?" Elsie asked. "I simply looked him in the eye and said, 'Just what kind of an evening *did* you expect from Miss Dulaine, may I inquire?' and of course he was on a spot. And as for Okie—"

"You made him mad, too," Jerry acknowledged. "You told him he knew nothing about art."

Elsie's blue eyes widened in honest astonishment.

"Why should that make him mad? God knows Okie has always been the dumbest man on earth but at least I gave him credit for *knowing* it. Now *really!* Look, do you think I should telephone around some more for McGrew? Just in case—"

"No, no," Jerry hastily protested, for one of Elsie's tricks had been to keep telephoning various clubs and restaurants during the evening to track down the missing guest so that all present should realize all was lost without him. It might be funny someday but right now and tomorrow it was serious, so that Elsie's sudden chuckle as she comfortably poured herself a dividend made Jerry's kindlier thoughts switch to resentment that a girl of her own looks and capacities should have to sit around in a handsome new evening dress with a noisy old girl just because she owed her a fortune. The favors weren't all on Elsie's side. She had been bored and lonely for years until her frustrated appetite for holocausts had been gratified by Jerry's magnanimous sharing of her ups and downs. It was just as she was thinking this that Jerry's downstairs bell rang.

"I knew he'd come!" cried Elsie clapping her hands. "Just let me give him a piece of my mind."

But suddenly Jerry's cheeks flushed and her eyes began to glow.

"Pull your dress down, Elsie," she commanded briskly, giving herself a quick glance in the mirror. "This may be somebody else."

"But who—?" Elsie began, bewildered, and then she stared at her friend with dawning suspicion. "You telephoned somebody a few minutes ago, didn't you?"

"I told you," Jerry said evasively. "I called the Julien Café again just as you suggested and talked to a man who said he was looking for McGrew, too. He asked where I was—"

Elsie threw up her hands.

"And you invited him up," she accused incredulously. "Good Heavens, Jerry, what's the matter with you? He might be a ripper or a lunatic. I can't understand you."

For no matter how thoroughly she approved and felt she understood her young friend there was always more to be found out. It was her turn to look with bewilderment at the change coming over the other, for if an audience brought out Elsie's disease the prospect of a strange man brought out Jerry's.

In any great crisis, financial or emotional, that would send most persons to the bottle or out the window, it had long been Jerry's habit to turn to a new man as restorative, someone unknown, hazardous, unique. She took care to maintain most circumspect relations with any man whose valuable friendship she knew was an important asset, not to be traded for a transient affair with awkward aftermaths. But a moment of pique, a broken date, a lost earring, an unpleasant interview brought out a wild lust for compensating abandon, the more fantastic the better. Elsie had her own outlets which she kept to herself, and she had gathered from cryptic references to "characters" and low barroom types that Jerry, too, favored piquant contrast in her conquests. All very well and a woman's only human, but tonight was more than a mere broken date, it was a whole future, and weren't they in it together? But Jerry seemed slipping from her grasp, needing neither her sympathy nor her company. She tried to make Jerry meet her reproachful eyes but the young lady was busily spraying *L'Amour L'Amour* on her hair and wrists and humming happily.

"I always can tell you're up to something when you start singing 'Where or When,'" Elsie accused her. "I just wish you'd learn the rest of the words."

"There aren't any other words but where or when," Jerry said, and then exclaimed impatiently, "Listen, Elsie, this night has sunk me. But I'm going to have one good time before I give up and maybe this is it."

"With a total stranger!" Elsie gasped. "Don't you know this sort of caper will finish you with McGrew? You can't play high and low."

"That's how I play, old dear," Jerry said.

"I will not be called old dear, not by anybody," Elsie said as she stalked proudly out the door, a little miffed not to be called back.

The hall light was out and it was too bad she could not get a good look at the stranger as she passed him on the stairs. She stood outside her own apartment door listening for a moment as Jerry opened the door to him. Prescott was his name, Elsie overheard him announce.

"At least he sounds human this time," she reflected. "No *deses* and *doses.*"

That the late guest must look as satisfactory as his accent Elsie could deduce from the sudden dovelike flutiness in Jerry's voice, a change she had observed before when her companion would be interrupted mid-sentence by a husky delivery boy or dreamy solicitor. The change in voice was accompanied, in these moments of fleeting lust, by a telltale glitter in the gray-green eyes that made the pupils tiny pinpoints of desire and the color go hard and unrevealing.

"The little devil," Elsie marveled with a chuckle. "I wonder how much longer she can get away with it."

The old great Dane, whose fur had a pinkish tinge similar to his mistress's hair, was waiting inside Elsie's door, and he rose with arthritic chivalry when she entered. Her living room looked small and untidy after Jerry's brand-new grandeur. Still, it was a cozy dump, Elsie thought, with the garden outside and the jolly little dining corner where Iola daily displayed her priceless culinary treasures. Elsie strode into the kitchen, which was larger than the living room, indeed had to be to house the extraordinary collection of copper and clay utensils, graduated pots and weapons and lordly equipment of herbs, groceries and general fodder sufficient to pacify the fussiest chef and feed a tribe of gourmets. Elsie opened the huge icebox with a fond pat on its belly as if it was the favorite stud in a fine stable, and reached in for her inevitable nightcap of beer—this time a good Danish brand—and a prize hoard of chicken livers for Brucie.

"What'll you bet!" Elsie mused aloud with a reflective glance upward, another shake of the head. But it wasn't funny, come to think of it, it was downright asinine for a girl of Jerry's potentialities and opportunities to throw her body and brains around as if there were plenty more where those came from. Elsie had always muffed her own chances and took for granted that she always would, but it angered her now that Jerry was bent on doing the same thing, no matter how a person tried to help her.

Now what satisfaction is that going to be for her to wind up this mess in bed with a strange man? Elsie thought, exasperated. How is that going to fix up everything? If she'd only have let me stay and thrash out things we might have figured out something.

She picked the *Evening Post* out of the wastebasket to read Leonard Lyons' column in bed and her eye caught the pile of unopened bills she had thrown there earlier. It was an outrage to have to think about money. It crossed her mind that her quixotic vanity would ruin her some day, that idiotic pride she took in being regarded as a woman of unlimited means. Whatever they might criticize in her looks or brains she would not have it that anyone dared be superior to her financially. Even with her brother Wharton, who was supposed to be guardian of the family fortunes, Elsie had all sorts of little dodges to make him think she had mysterious other sources of revenue of which he could not guess. She switched off the kitchen lights and carried beer and paper into the bedroom. The fine glow she had experienced in carrying off the evening in such bold style, delivering so many good punches at possible detractors of her protégée, faded and she felt rebuffed for a moment. Brucie followed her to the dresser where he stood beside her like a watchful valet while she skinned off the blue rayon satin dress, the pinned-up magenta slip—imagine anybody paying more than two ninety-eight for a slip, though come to think of it a Hattie Carnegie slip for Jerry had cost thirty-odd dollars—the elastic girdle, the incredibly long nylons. It occurred to Elsie to study her naked length in the dresser mirror thoughtfully as if she was viewing it for the first time. The truth was she thought of herself seldom in physical terms, and even soaping herself absently in the shower she was as likely to wash Brucie's curious snout thrust through the shower curtains as her own bottom. She shook her head now in quizzical dismay over the roll of fat over her stomach and the lack of padding in proper places. No one can remain dissatisfied completely with one's body even if all one can honestly boast is a rare birthmark. So it presently struck Elsie that her upper thighs were evenly matched, her knees if knobby were knobbed in the right direction, and even if dressmakers did complain that her behind seemed to slope down all the way to her knees, still her shoulders were quite remarkable for her age, not too bony and certainly not flabby.

"Not so bad, eh Brucie," she asked her dog complacently.

Maybe she had given up too soon, she reflected. Maybe instead of fixing up Jerry Dulaine's lovelife she should have another go at her own. Maybe she could have hung on to that Portuguese lad on the Cape a little longer, maybe she should have given him the car he kept pestering her for. She'd gotten him away from her mulatto maid by promising him a secondhand motor bike with a fire horn but of course that was when the little bounder was in oilskins and before she'd put him into a Tuxedo and taught him to carry fancy canes. Yes, she could have kept him from that Gloucester widow if she'd given in about the car. Not a Buick, of course, but say a used Chevy.

"I'm just too damned Yankee, that's my trouble," Elsie sighed giving her hair a couple of licks with the brush. "I could have strung along that little monkey another summer or two just buying him a couple of flashy shirts and a Tattersall vest. I always get stingy at the wrong time. Darned if I wouldn't like to have the little rat around right this minute."

Musing on love, Elsie gave another deep sigh and hopped into bed, thrusting her long bony feet over the edge to make room beside her for Brucie.

. . . the telephone date . . .

Rick hurried purposefully up Fifth Avenue, savagely proud of having conquered his weakness for Ellenora. It was no good telling himself that she had no way of knowing he had been waiting for her; he felt as righteously injured as if she had deliberately stood him up to make a fool out of him. At the corner he hesitated just a fraction of a minute, half turned to catch a dim glimpse of some people getting out of a cab in front of Longchamps, firmly dismissed the wild idea that the girl might be Ellenora (which indeed it was) and pushed onward. He knew perfectly well he was about to get into trouble, the way he always did, as if spiting himself would make everybody else sorry. Chasing up some unknown dame from a phone call like a dumb freshman, he mocked himself, but nothing could ever stop him in these stubborn moods. You had to see these blind adventures through to the bitter end, though they were never worth the trouble and could ruin your life. Still anything was better than sitting on in the Julien waiting for someone who would never come.

When he saw the handsome girl who opened the door of her apartment he knew he was having the luck he didn't deserve. Jerry was congratulating herself along the same lines.

"Looks like a party," he said. "How nice."

"How do you do," Jerry said with a shrug. "It's all over and it was not at all nice."

"Then I'm sorry I missed it," Rick said. "I see McGrew isn't here yet. I was expecting him at the Julien, myself. That was why I suggested we might as well wait for him together."

"Of course," Jerry agreed.

Eying her new guest with increasing appreciation she felt cheered and elated. If she could produce a beauty like this out of thin air in her very darkest hour, then she was certainly not done for. The hell with McGrew, she thought.

"I gather you had important business to discuss with him," she said politely. "Will I be in the way?"

Rick hesitated and then grinned at her.

"Not as much as he will be," he said, and then they both laughed shamelessly, understanding each other.

"You never even heard of him," Jerry accused.

"I've heard of nothing but McGrew all evening," Rick defended himself. "Everytime the phone rang at the Julien it wasn't for me, always for McGrew. I answered it to put a stop to it, that's all. A man like that can get dangerous. I only wanted to warn you in case he is really a friend of yours. By the way, is he?"

"Of course he is," Jerry said. "Friend enough to stand me up."

"So that was it," Rick said. "I thought you were making it too easy for me, telling me to come on over. But I was getting tired of being stood up myself."

"Not you too!"

"Every night for two months," Rick said. "I'm damn sick of it."

"I'm sick of everything myself," Jerry said. "I was trying to get rid of the last guest so I could put my head in the oven."

"Could I help?" Rick asked. "Just show me the oven."

"It would have to be the pressure cooker," Jerry said. "Mostly I was considering pills, being a lazy girl. Then I rather hoped you'd turn out to be the killer type and save me the trouble."

"No, I'm just as lazy as you are," Rick confessed. His experienced eyes had taken in the carefully decorated look of the place, the kind of impeccable taste often used to mask the dweller's secret life. Kept, he thought.

"I wouldn't want to mess up such a pretty room," he said.

"Oh it's not paid for," Jerry said, and then to her surprise tears came to her eyes, and suddenly she was gulping and choking away like any Southern belle with the vapors. She snatched at the handkerchief her guest quietly handed her and would have started to bawl in earnest except for the curious fact that the young man showed no disposition to stop her. Indeed he was looking over a book casually as if the lady had asked him to look away while she fixed a garter.

"Thanks for not saying anything," Jerry said, surprised. "How nice of you not to say it will make me feel better to cry because it never does."

"I could have said things can't be as bad as all that," Rick admitted, putting the book aside to look at her. "But probably they're worse. I warn you, though, if you tell me anything I'm likely as not to blab it."

"If I did tell you anything I'd make out I'm just crying over a broken heart," Jerry admitted, "but it's much more important than that. To tell the truth—"

Rick put up a protesting hand.

"Can't we be strangers?" he asked.

"Then let's get out of here," Jerry said.

"Back to the Julien?" Rick asked.

"Too chummy," Jerry said. "I feel like loud company. Dingy bars with fine low types who could never do me any good. I know a few spots."

"I know a few myself," Rick said. "Better change your costume."

Jerry started for the bedroom door but turned to look at him.

"Do you always know the right way to handle people's troubles?" she asked curiously.

"That's what they tell me," he said. "Trouble is just what I'm good at. I have a feeling I see it coming at me right now."

"Let's not look, then," Jerry suggested. "Let's get even with everybody and have one good time before we die."

"Hurry up, then," Rick said. "We've only got all night."

This was the way it always ended up, he thought, resigned. Every time he tried to blot out Ellenora he wound up blotting out himself. He wanted to have a light gay adventure to make up for his romantic wounds but it always bogged down into his feeling sorry for somebody and getting himself in a mess trying to help them out. As if he was God's gamekeeper, his mother used to scold him.

Gourd's grimekipper, Geep's Godkimer, Gam's keep—he was muttering it angrily to himself hours later.

. . . one good time before we die . . .

THE electric light in the middle of the ceiling sent a steady unrelenting warning and it was this, more than the rhythmic moaning sound, that finally opened Jerry's eyes. What she saw was a dream, she knew, and closed her eyes again, reaching out an arm to the light she knew was by her bed but which somehow now was not there so she slowly opened her eyes once more. Her room would be a mess, she knew that from the fierce throbbing in her head which meant that she had drunk too much of something terrible, and of course her clothes would be thrown all over the place and probably the lamp turned over. But this bulb in the ceiling? The pale

woman with long red braids lying in the other bed? The funny-
looking windows with no curtains—dungeonlike windows—
yes, with bars.

Suddenly it struck her that she must have done it—taken
poison or dope pills just as she had been afraid she might.
This was no dream, this was a hospital.

How had it happened, how long ago, and where? Frightened, she sat up in bed abruptly and the sudden motion made
her sick. She leaped up to go to the bathroom but the door
was shut.

"There's not even a doorknob," she gasped, and then saw
the little pane of glass on a level with her own eye in the top of
the door. It was a hospital corridor outside but she saw no one
pass until a young mulatto nurse hurried by, paying no heed to
Jerry's pounding on the door and outcries. Frantically Jerry
looked around for a basin or sink but there was nothing in the
room but the two beds and only one sheet. She was stark
naked and there was no sign of her clothes. Her hands were
bruised and she realized that her rings had been torn off.

"What kind of hospital is this?" she cried out.

The girl in the other bed, with the sheet pulled up to her
chin and her braids lying on it, turned quiet empty eyes on her.

What had happened? Where had it happened and with
whom? Another stab of pain in her head made her snatch the
sheet and vomit into it. She rolled it up and sat on the bed-
ticking, shivering. Think, she commanded herself, think hard.
There had been the dinner party and Elsie's voice booming in
the dining room, Elsie's voice booming in the living room,
people sitting around, but clearer than anything else she remembered the sick desperation in her heart, a feeling that this
was a wake for her because this was the end. She remembered
being alone with Elsie, slipping to her medicine cabinet to
count her sleeping pills, praying that Elsie would get out.
Well, had she gone and was this waking up in hell? No, there
was something else. Then she remembered the doorbell, the
arrival of the angel, it seemed at the time, named Ricky, a
crazy good-looking stranger who made her forget the medicine cabinet. They had compared notes—each was in a mood
to kick over the traces, each was ready to trust the first passing stranger or, if requested, take a rocket to the moon. Oh,

they had met at the precisely right moment for anything to happen. They had decided to go out on the town—not to the uptown places but to all the dives—Monty's on Houston Street, the Grotto down by the bridge, the Sink, the Bowery Lido—

The Bowery Lido. Suddenly Jerry saw it again.

The band was booming out "Rose of Washington Square," the grizzled chorus boys in straw hats were shuffling-off to Buffalo, arms around each other's shoulders, the Lido Ladies, old variety hoofers and stompers and ripe young strippers, were prancing off the stage, the mission derelicts were peering in the windows at the uptown slummers whooping it up inside, the cops were getting their handouts at the bar—this was the real New York, the real people, the good people, the bitter salt of the earth. None of the phoniness of Fifty-Second Street, or the fancy spots. "Isn't it wonderful? Isn't it fun?" That was what she and Rick kept saying to each other and whatever strangers they invited to join them, the Chinaman, the old streetwalker they prevailed upon the waiter not to throw out, the old hunchback. And then she remembered Tessie. That must have been when it started, she thought, pressing her hands to her head. Imagine seeing Tessie in a G-string and transparent fan marching along in the Lido chorus line, Tessie, her old roommate who had married a respectable customer's man and moved to Mount Kisco! Tessie, who had advised her ten years ago to give up the gay life and settle down before it was too late. Tessie, obviously fifteen pounds over model size sixteen and with the silveriest blond dye job on her too long flowing locks, strutting past the customers and so flabbergasted at sight of Jerry she had forgotten their past differences and shouted, "My God, Jerry!"

"Tessie!"

Next Tessie was sitting at their table and they were hugging and kissing each other like long-lost sisters, so Rick could never have dreamed that they hadn't been speaking to each other for a good ten years, and the waiter was bringing round after round of whiskey and fizz with Tessie sending drinks to all her buddies in the floor show and inviting them all to join them. What happened then? Was Tessie here, too? What had become of Ricky?

Jerry ran to the barred window and shouted their names into the stone-gray daybreak. A great animal roar answered her, lunatic laughter and a sustained inhuman moan that seemed to come from the stone walls shuddering into the new day. Jerry ran back to the door and peered out the aperture, pounding on it furiously. This time she saw two eyes in a dark face in the peephole of the door opposite. Whoever it was shook her head as if in warning and then lifted dark wrinkled hands to the peephole, spelling out in sign language "W A I T." The eyes appeared again and the head nodded. At least someone was a friend, Jerry thought. The mulatto nurse hurried down the hall and this time she came in the room.

"Shame on you, dirtying your bed, I'll teach you," she cried out, and smacked Jerry smartly. "Shouting and carrying on, you dirty thing, running around naked, disturbing everybody."

"I want a nightgown, I want to go to the bathroom," Jerry said carefully.

"Oh yes, a private bathroom and a lace nightie, oh sure," the nurse smacked her again. "When it's time to go to the bathroom I'll let you know, you filthy little tramp, you."

This is a dream, Jerry said out loud over and over, this is a dream but why don't I wake up?

"Shut up," said the girl. "If you behaved right you wouldn't be here, you tramp."

"Can't we please have the light out?" Jerry begged.

The girl gave a jeering laugh.

"That light stays on, so if one of you gets killed I can look in and see which one did it."

The door closed behind her.

A dream, a dream, Jerry chanted, pulling a corner of the wet sheet across her nakedness, a dream, only all she could think of now was of how to choke the nurse to death. She went to the peephole again and her friend across the hall winked this time and again spelled out "wait" with her hands.

The stone walls were still moaning; it was a hollow, beyond-pain baying noise like beasts at the water hole, but now the sky was a lighter gray and there was the croaking of river tugs, the clatter of delivery trucks, and garbage cans. Out the window she could see the stone court surrounded by bigger gray stone buildings with barred windows, and there was a smell now of dead river rats, sour coffee grounds, boiling hay or mush, and Jerry vomited again into the sheet. No, this was not a dream, but what was it? She felt a little better now, except for the pain in her head and the sudden piercing desire to kill the nurse.

Back to Tessie and the Bowery Lido she pushed her thoughts. They had talked about what wonderful times they used to have, the limousines sent to take them to house parties in Bucks County, Saratoga, Montauk Point, New Haven —anywhere, private planes toting them to masked balls in Palm Beach, Hollywood, New Orleans, Texas, the big spending gentleman buying a name band to amuse them on his Miami-bound yacht, champagne raining all the time, oh the happy, carefree, days of old, the dear wonderful good good friends whose names were either forgotten or never known, ah those pure, unclouded happy times! And those two loyal, devoted, true-unto-death friends Tessie Baxter and Jerry Dulaine, such friends as neither had ever had before or since, all of which made this chance meeting here in the Bowery an occasion for unlimited celebration and hosannas.

"I'm just working here for laughs," Tessie said. "I wanted to get in off the road, no matter what I had to do. I've got the most marvelous midget, a real clown. You'll die."

Jerry tried to concentrate on what happened after Tessie's midget brought up the two punks who wanted to dance with her. Then Tessie took her backstage and they sat there gabbing, not listening to each other, until she remembered to go back in and look for Rick. But the place was suddenly in an uproar, full of cops and shouting. Someone snatched her arm and somebody else grabbed her when she struggled—that was as far as she could remember.

The door of her room opened and the nurse stood there.

"Well, get out to the washroom and on the double. Throw that sheet over you, you can't be running around here naked, you dirty tramp!"

Jerry's fists clenched but the open door was there and she ran out, the soiled sheet bunched in front of her, joining the sudden horde of half-naked women running down the hall, her red-haired roommate being shoved and yanked by the mulatto nurse. They were nearly all youngish women except for the tiny dark Porto Rican called Maria who Jerry realized must be her friend from across the hall. It was so wonderful to be in the washroom, able to wash and have a turn at the comb with the others that Jerry's murderous rage changed to the humblest gratitude for this privilege.

"That nurse wouldn't give me a sheet or open the door last night," she murmured, waiting behind her friend who was combing her short shaggy gray hair.

The little woman smiled.

"If she open door maybe you try to run out of place naked," she explained. "Maybe you get to next floor then they lock you up for crazy and maybe long time before you get out, like happen to me here once."

Jerry shivered, knowing it would have happened just like that because now she knew anything could happen. Everybody else seemed to be old hands here, calling each other by name—Babe, Chick, Bonny, Bobby, Flossie, Sally—taunting each other with having boasted that last time was to have been the last time and now look. It was amazing how quickly the human mind adjusted, she thought, for she felt more bound to these women than to any other group she'd ever known. When the day attendant, a hard-faced white woman, came in with a clean sheet for her to wear she surprised her with her burst of gratitude. And when the woman put down a cardboard box of used lipsticks, Jerry's joy equaled that of the others.

"Doctor says you tramps can put on lipstick this morning," the nurse shouted out. "But don't forget where you are and start making passes at him or it's the lockup for the lot of you."

"Where are we?" Jerry asked Maria.

"What's the matter, you forget?" said Maria. "City hospital."

"I never was here—" Jerry started to say but from the mocking smiles around her knew no one would believe her. What frightened her most was the curious way she felt in the wrong, as if the mulatto girl's cruelty must not be questioned, nor did she have any right to a gown, or any right to be any-place else but here. She saw that there was a bump on her temple and remembered something.

"The policeman hit me, he hit me with his club," she exclaimed, and there was a titter from the others.

"They always do," said Maria. "The bump will go away before you get out."

"What do you mean?" Jerry asked. "I'm going home as soon as they give me my clothes."

"That'll be when," said the tall sixteen-year-old named Bobby with the translucent white skin. "Where'd they pick you up?"

"The Bowery Lido," Jerry said. "I don't know what happened, if I got sick and doctors brought me here or—"

"What are you talking about? The cops brought you, girl," Bobby laughed scornfully. "Same as they brought all of us. For cripes sake, what made you try anything in the Bowery anyway?"

"I wasn't trying anything."

"Break it up, you tramps, and come and get it!" the nurse yelled through the door, and again they ran down the hall, some in hospital shirts, bare-bottomed and barefooted, some, like Jerry, with sheets held in front of them or dragging behind. They slid onto benches at a bare table at the end of the hall, a bowl of watery farina and a cup of cold tea in front of each. The nurse and a new attendant went from one to the next, popping pills in each mouth. Bobby resisted hers and was slapped. Jerry held hers in her mouth, and slid it out on her cereal spoon.

"They have no right to hit us," she said.

Maria shook her head at her.

"They got all the right they want," she whispered. "There's nothing anybody can do."

"When do the newspapers come?" Jerry asked, thinking that there might be some explanation in the news, but all heads turned to her again with a mocking smile.

"No reading's allowed here," Bobby said. "That's why they take away everybody's glasses. No radio either. They always take away Sally's hearing aid, too, and then when she doesn't hear what they say they let her have a good wallop."

"I like to read," stated the quiet, waxen-faced woman about Jerry's age with the chrysanthemum bob of black hair and the carefully manicured white hands. "I went to school when I was a kid and I was always reading."

"I know the school you went to, Bonny," jeered the nurse.

"Shut up, you creeps," said Bonny quietly, as everyone hooted with laughter.

"Some school," taunted the one named Chick. "Sunday school."

"I taught Sunday school class once, damn you," shouted Bonny, rising.

"Break it up, girls," the day nurse ordered. "The doctor's here. Good heavens, Bobby, this is the third time you've been in since Christmas."

"I had a fit in a subway station," Bobby said.

"She had a fit in the Hotel St. George, don't let her kid you," said Chick, winking at Jerry. "It scared this sailor she was shacking up with and he got the cops."

"Men are all jerks," said Bobby. "A girl has a simple everyday fit and they start screaming for the cops. A fellow I knew had a fit once, we were sitting on a bench in Prospect Park, and I was only a kid fourteen years old and did I call the cops? No, I stuck my handbag in his jaw so he wouldn't bite off his tongue, and the dumb cluck bit through the bag and got pieces of my mirror in his windpipe and darn near killed himself. But it was the right thing to do."

"How do I telephone?" Jerry asked.

"Are you kidding?"

"But people will be looking for me," Jerry said, and then stopped. Who would be looking for her? Creditors, maybe. Rick Prescott must have thought she had skipped out of the Lido when she stayed out so long with Tessie. What had happened to Tessie?

She could tell that some of the guests or patients or prisoners were locked in their rooms for the attendant was carrying trays in and out.

"Can you find out if my friend, Tessie Baxter, came in with me last night?" Jerry asked the nurse. "Is she here now?"

"That's none of your business, miss," said the nurse coolly, and everyone laughed. Obviously this nurse was regarded as a wag. "If your friend is the same kind as you she'll be here sooner or later, I can tell you that much."

"Are we allowed to telephone?" Jerry asked meekly.

"Sure, we all have private wires," said the one called Chick.

She sat on the bench beside Jerry and suddenly patted her on the cheek. "I like you, kid. When we get out let's see what we can do together. Where'd you get your hair done?"

"Elizabeth Arden's," said Jerry and realized it was the wrong thing to say for there was a silence till Bobby said, "She had Elizabeth Arden fix her up so she could go down to the Bowery and get herself a man."

"I was kidding," said Jerry.

"There's a phone booth in the hall but your pocketbook's in the office safe so you won't have a dime to call, anyway," volunteered Maria. "Maybe somebody will call and leave a message for you. Whatever name you told them when you were brought in."

Jerry knew it was no use trying to remember how she had come in or what she had said.

"Anybody want me to do any phoning for them when I leave this morning?" she asked.

"Who told you you were getting out?" asked Chick. "Tell me the truth, where'd you get your hair done like that? I like your fingernails. What shade is that?"

"Opalescent," said Jerry.

"You certainly did a job on yourself just to work the Bowery," said Bobby, admiringly. "Look, girls, the toenails yet!"

"Opalescent," repeated Chick, giggling. "Opalescent toenails!"

"It's nice." Maria nodded to her kindly, and Jerry felt a wave of love for her, as if here was the dearest friend she had ever had, one she would cherish forever.

"Would you like me to tell your family where you are?" Jerry asked her, wanting to do something wonderful for her.

Maria looked alarmed.

"No no, please," she said. "My husband will come wait for me outside and beat me up."

"Maria's old man gets drunk on Porto Rican rum and starts whamming the kids around and Maria clobbers him with everything she can lay her hands on," explained Bobby, while Maria smiled apologetically. "The neighbors call the police and they cart off Maria yelling her head off so they bring her here. Then her old man lays for her to get out so she doesn't care how long she stays here."

"I don't know maybe this time I killed him," Maria said thoughtfully. "Better for me maybe to stay crazy."

The girl with the red braids who had shared Jerry's room was standing in the hall facing the open door of the bathroom. The day nurse had stood her there like a window dummy and she had not moved.

"She's making up her mind to take a bath," explained Bobby. "She'll stand there maybe all day and all night unless somebody lifts her in."

"The doctor's ready, girls," shouted the nurse, and the mere thought of a man around excited everyone to fever pitch. "Come on, you, he wants to see you first, miss."

Jerry got up, trying to cover herself with the sheet, and made for the office. The doctor was a young man, disguising his youth behind a short black Van Dyke. He had a card in front of him and looked at her over this briefly.

"Well?" he asked crisply.

"I want to know how I got here," Jerry asked quietly. It was funny how fast you learned. Any protest of injustice brought on more injustice, so you must be quiet, accept outwardly whatever punishment the powers give, and wait, as Maria had told her, just wait.

"You don't remember?" the doctor said skeptically, then nodded. "That's right, you were in such a state the cops said they had to give you a shot to quiet you. The report says you and some other prostitutes were picked up in a Bowery joint with a hunchback who peddles reefers which you were smoking—"

The blood swam in Jerry's head.

"He passed us cigarettes, I didn't know they were reefers," she said faintly.

"You gave him a five-dollar bill, they said," said the doctor. "You wouldn't give that for a pack of Camels."

"I thought he was poor, that's all," Jerry said.

The doctor looked at her still skeptically.

"Are you so rich? Anyway there was a clean-up all over town last night. Some of the girls went to jail and the ones that were hysterical were taken to alcoholic or psycho wards in the city hospitals."

"What made them think I was a prostitute?" Jerry asked evenly.

The doctor looked at her again and then shrugged.

"The place you were, the people you were with, the reefers," he answered. "The hunchback is a procurer in that section and you gave him money."

"I told you I was sorry for him being a hunchback," Jerry repeated. "Was he arrested?"

The doctor gave a short laugh.

"I doubt it. Those places always pay protection for their regulars. When there's word of a clean-up the cops go after the strangers."

"Is that how those other girls out there were brought here —just to cover for the really guilty ones?" Jerry asked, trying to keep her voice steady, concealing the anger with which she was filled.

"That's not my business," said the doctor. "I'm the doctor, not the law. I can tell you that most of the girls out there today are brought in regularly—usually drunk or hopped up, either a little weak in the head like Bobby, or so long in prostitution that they don't even know it's a bad word and knowing no other life and not learning it's considered a sin they go right back in it."

"Those aren't bad women," Jerry said. "I'll bet you always get the wrong ones and they are too scared to say so."

The doctor was annoyed, and tapped his pencil on the card.

"It's not my business to prove their innocence or guilt," he said.

"Oh we're all guilty, I know that," Jerry said bitterly. "I know now that you become guilty and you feel guilty as soon as someone treats you as guilty. The only innocent ones are the accusers so all of you try to accuse the other person before you're found out yourself. You know it will *make* him guilty."

"I can't give you more time, Miss—" he referred to the card, "Dulaine. I agree with some things you are saying, but I advise you to take care where you say them. You made the office downstairs very angry last night screaming accusations at them and at the police, and threatening to report them all to your fiancé, Collier McGrew, who would order a big investigation. He's on our board, of course."

Jerry drew a long breath.

"I said that?" she murmured. "I can't remember."

"Reefer smokers think it's funny sometimes to pass their cigarettes to greenhorns. They get a kick watching their reactions," the doctor said. "I'm surprised you didn't suspect that. It usually creates delusions of grandeur. Maybe that's what made you boast of all the important people you thought you knew."

"Yes," said Jerry. There were evidently a lot of things she had said and done that it would be better not to know. But bringing in McGrew's name! Her fiancé! She felt weak with shame.

"I'll see if we can get you out of here as soon as possible," said the doctor. "That's all for now."

His phone rang and he picked up the receiver. He motioned Jerry to wait as he answered and when he hung up he smiled at her.

"Well, that's one on me," he said. "It seems you did know Collier McGrew. You insisted on his being notified last night, and he has sent his car for you and arranged for your release. The nurse will bring you your clothes, and your valuables are down in the office. I can only advise you to stay in your own class after this, Miss Dulaine. Stick with the people you know."

"Thank you," gasped Jerry, plunging out the door, tears in her eyes thinking of how good everyone was, how incredibly kind people were. The other women were standing in line outside the door waiting their turn with the doctor and the nurse stood by with her clothes over her arm.

"I'm going, I'm getting out!" Jerry cried out to the others. "Tell me what I can get for you outside, whoever you want me to see. I'll telephone your office and say you're sick or maybe there's somebody you want to come get you."

"Listen, those tramps got no offices," muttered the nurse.

"You're all right, Jerry," Chick called to her.

"Send me a newspaper or something," said the quiet-looking one named Bonny. "I'd like to do a little reading instead of sitting around yakking with these creeps."

The pale girl was still standing looking into the bathing room, her red braids over her shoulder, the slender legs bare from the thigh down posed in an arrested step like the statues of Diana. Jerry hesitated beside her, wanting to do something.

"Your hair is lovely," she said but the blue eyes looked calmly, patiently off as if waiting for a magic word to waken her.

"She's all right, she feels no pain," the nurse said impatiently. "Here's your clothes, now get into them, you're so anxious to get out."

She tossed the clothes on the bed, frowning, not wanting to show her curiosity and respect for someone able to escape so quickly into a world outside her authority. Jerry hurried into her clothes, overwhelmed with the privilege of wearing stockings and shoes, powder, her own comb. It was a dream that she was really getting out—she must make the most of it before she wakened and found herself back in this room with no doorknob on the door. She was glad she had changed from party clothes to street wear before she went out for that good time last night with Rick Prescott.

The girls were lined up outside the doctor's office as she passed and Bobby ran up to her, her sheet dragging behind her thin bare childish body.

"Got any rouge?" she whispered.

Jerry took out her compact and gave it to her, and handed the others her comb, lipstick, perfume vial, handkerchief.

"She'll take them all away tonight but we can hold them till then," said Maria, nodding toward the nurse down the hall.

Jerry followed the attendant down the corridors and out, thinking of the doctor's advice to stick to her own class and with the people she knew, and she thought these were the people she knew, this was her class.

A chauffeur in livery was standing in the office waiting for her.

"Mr. McGrew's car is outside," he said. "I'm to drive you to your home. He asked me to give you this note."

She opened the note, sitting in the back of the car.

I could not reach you last night as my plane from Texas grounded in the desert and the relief didn't get me in till this morning. My secretary took the hospital's message and tried to straighten out what seems to be some fantastic error, or was it a joke? It will be amusing to hear all about it from you. Can I make amends for failing you at dinner last night by having Swanson pick you up at seven tonight?

As ever,
McGREW

Jerry smiled faintly as she crumpled the note. Elsie would certainly get a bang out of that, she thought, though it seemed a long time ago and of no matter to herself. She caught a glimpse of a man standing in front of her apartment. A process server, she thought, and decided to ask McGrew's chauffeur to drive on but it was too late. He had already stopped and opened the car door for her.

"Any message for Mr. McGrew, Miss Dulaine?" he asked, as she got out. "He thought you might want me to call for you later."

Jerry hesitated. It was too late, she thought. Everything happened too late. There wasn't anything she wanted of McGrew now.

"Thank him and tell him I'm not free tonight," she said and walked bravely up the steps. But it wasn't a process server at all, she realized, just her good friend of last night.

"I was just about to dredge the river," Rick said to her, taking her keys from her hand. "I've been chasing all over trying to find out what happened to you. I went backstage hunting for you and Tessie. Then there was that raid on the place and they shooed everybody out of the joint. All of a sudden I sobered up and remembered you said you were going to jump in the river."

"Me?" Jerry asked with a tired grimace. "I thought I said I was too lazy."

"You look pretty rocky," he said, surveying her doubtfully.

"Someday I'll tell you about it," Jerry said.

"Don't," he said. "I could guess when I saw the limousine."

"It wasn't that way at all," Jerry said. "That was just the happy ending that happens a day too late, at least that's the way I always fix it."

"That's the way I fix it, too," Rick said. "Born that way. Has something to do with the middle ear. Can't change it."

"Don't look so scared," Jerry laughed. "I won't faint."

"Sure you're all right?" He hesitated, about to go.

"Now I am," she said. She saw her mail on the hall table, topped by the long envelope from the collector of internal revenue, and sat down on the bottom stair suddenly, her head in her hands.

"Ever play crack the whip?" she asked, quite dizzy. "I feel like the one on the end that gets whirled off the faster they go."

Ricky turned and helped her to her feet.

"We'd better go make some coffee," he suggested. "We need a bracer. Let's face it, we had one hell of a good time even if it kills both of us."

He had intended to go back to his apartment, shower and shave, and get to the office around noon. But she was a nice kid and he couldn't leave her like this, half in a daze. It was just another one of those things he had started and had to see through.

Waking up in Jerry's bed later on, much refreshed, he asked Jerry why she was smiling.

"I can't get over that doctor taking me for a prostitute," she said.

PART TWO

. . . gentleman against women . . .

WHARTON HOOKLEY had the most profound admiration for his sister Elsie's incorruptible character, and he often dreamed of the monuments and even scholarships he would institute in her name when she died, the Elsie Hookley Club for Art Students, the Elsie Hookley Orphanage, the Elsie Hookley Woman Travelers' Aid (all inspired by his sister's latest vagary and worked out in systematic detail by his insomnia), but the trouble was that Elsie never would die. This put her brother into a most exasperating position, for almost every time he saw her or heard about her he got into such a sweat that he was bound to betray the very opposite of those emotions he wished to have. How could he eulogize his sister's classic candor until it was conveniently silenced once and for all? How could he state that no matter how unconventionally Elsie had lived and through whatever gaudy gutters she had trailed the Hookley traditions, she herself was the soul of honor when he was forever hearing that Elsie bore him no ill will for doing her out of her rightful inheritance? "Wharton really *cares* about possessions and I don't," she had generously said—no sense in doubting this report for she often made the same statement in his presence—"Grandmother's diamonds and the Maryland and Boston homesteads really mean something to Wharton, and I don't deserve them since I don't appreciate them, so let him keep my share, I have all I need in my little income."

The fact was that Elsie's outspokenness was Wharton's hair shirt, or rather one of his hair shirts as he had rather a full wardrobe of them, mostly the gifts of women as such unnecessary sartorial luxuries are apt to be. For most of his lifetime he had been able to maintain a Christian forbearance in the face of such vague aspersions from his sister's bohemian adherents, the kind of gentlemanly poise possible when one is sure the world is wise enough to wink at these fabrications. Wharton had been so confident that everyone agreed with his own exaggerated admiration for himself that he felt he could afford to excuse, even publicly defend his sister's eccentric doubts about his honesty. Elsie had never been well as a child, Elsie had been taken in by an early marriage to a titled foreigner, Elsie had been a child beauty and then, at the age of twelve, shot up to a grotesque six feet and been obliged to compensate.

But too late it was borne in on Wharton that the world secretly believed Elsie. Who put on the big social show in Boston and New York, after all, and how was it Wharton, with four expensive daughters, could live and travel in grandeur, fling around pews, stained glass windows and cemetery lots in endless memoriams to related Hookleys, unless he was nibbling away at Elsie's proper funds? Wharton, who had always been fiendishly meticulous and efficient in money matters, rued the day he had inherited the management of the family estate (though he would have cut his throat if anyone else had been given the nerve-racking privilege). Elsie, caring little as she did about diamonds, forgot she had casually changed them into bonds on which she now drew interest, and all that her loyal supporters saw was that Wharton's girls wore the diamonds. So many people felt guilty for finding Elsie Hookley's excessive heartiness and belligerent bohemianism almost intolerable that they pounced gratefully on any chance to prove they were not snobs, and after being chased into the most queasily genteel position by her excessive earthiness they were happy to proclaim their essential democracy by denouncing her brother for lack of it. Often Wharton found himself waking in the middle of the night accusing himself of dishonesty, remembering that he had forgotten to notify Elsie of the sale of five acres of timberland in northern Maine, and he would get up and paddle to his desk in his bare feet to jot it down right then and there at his desk. These careful notes referring to the sum of $304.64 being deposited to her account only made Elsie, who hadn't even known of any timberland, speculate sarcastically on how much Wharton was holding back from her on the deal. The more Wharton heard of Elsie's reflections on him the more slips he made, like a child who's been told it's clumsy, until he sometimes wondered if he was not being slowly tortured into unconscious chicanery, and at these moments he fiercely cursed his sister for puncturing his good conscience. A fine head for figures and careful bookkeeping being his particular vanity, slurs on these were all that worried him; like someone so absorbed in boasting of his abstinence he doesn't know he's sipped away a pint of bourbon, Wharton was so engrossed in his careful bookkeeping accounts and business management that he never seemed to notice that all the family furniture, silver, china and other accouterments of solid living unobtrusively found their way into his possession. In all her life Elsie had never noticed whether she was eating off a gold plate or a picnic pasteboard and besides, with the hit-or-miss life she led, what would she do with things?

That was why her request for the cane was so astounding.

It was one of the days when Wharton Hookley felt he owed it to his peace of mind to sojourn down to the Café Julien to lunch alone in state, for Elsie's note about the cane had been the last straw. The only thing that soothed him in moments of stress was to buy himself and nobody else a lavish lunch in an expensive restaurant, and look about him at all the people buying expensive lunches with money they were obliged to earn themselves, whereas he did not have to work for his lunch money and therefore must represent a superior order of mankind. It always surprised him that acquaintances, seeing him exhibiting his superiority in this fashion, did not envy him but often attempted to join him under the fantastic impression that he was lonesome. He ordered with the loving care he always bestowed on his stomach, starting off with a solitary Gibson, and a green turtle soup with Madeira. Sipping his wine with a complacent survey of an adjoining table where three businessmen were feasting on what must have taken them a good half day's work to earn, he felt sufficiently composed to take out his sister's note.

"I hate to have to keep after you about Uncle Carpenter's ram's-head cane," the large flowing handwriting said—now why must she dot her r's and h's, he wondered pettishly— "but honestly, Wharton, this must be the tenth time I've asked you for it during the last few years, and why on earth you hang on to it when you know what it means to me on account of Uncle Carpenter being my favorite relative—etcetera, etcetera."

The fact was that every time Elsie remembered Uncle Carpenter's ram's-head cane, Wharton knew something nasty was in the wind. He and his older sister were poles apart, had never understood one thing about each other's nature, lived completely different lives that crossed only occasionally, on the surface of things meant nothing to each other, but somehow had never been able to make a single move unless they were convinced it was the exact opposite of what the other would do. Even when they were not in the same country they had some kind of radar that told them what the other was up to, always something extraordinarily wrong and inducive to a countermove carefully planned to cause equal irritation on the other side.

Take the matter of Uncle Carpenter. For several summers, Wharton had sent his younger daughters up to Uncle Carpenter's big place at Narragansett, and once in a while Wharton would have a faint twinge thinking that Uncle Carpenter was half his sister's property, too, but still if she didn't have sense enough to feather her nest he wasn't going to do it for her. On the old man's death the place, technically, was half Elsie's, but since she showed no interest—of course if it was ever sold, Wharton always said, she would get her half—he continued using it for family purposes, carefully deducting repairs and general upkeep from Elsie's as well as his own estates, fifty-fifty fair and square. Then—just as he was vaguely expecting some much more justifiable alarming demand—he received Elsie's request for Uncle Carpenter's cane. In his relief he was about to send it to her post-haste when a shrewd second thought came to him. Just what was there about that cane, one, incidentally, which he had never even remembered? He went through a hundred ancestral canes in the Narragansett attic until he found the one with the little ugly jade ram's-head. The eyes and horns were studded with emerald and diamond chips and it was made of some perhaps remarkable Malaysian wood, the head unscrewed for a dagger, but it was an ugly thing at best and certainly of no great value. Wharton did not remember ever having seen his uncle use it, and at first he just sat there

looking at the damn cane shaking his head and thinking what
a fool Elsie was. Why on earth did Elsie want it? Was it a museum piece, was there something about it that made it worth
a king's ransom, and what mysterious enemies were behind
Elsie in this strange request? Wharton hung on to the cane,
reading up about cane collections, asking questions here and
there, with Elsie making repeated demands. Something more
important always came up and the cane would be forgotten,
but maybe after two years of silence up popped the matter of
the cane again. The worst thing was that he couldn't think
of any reason for not giving it to her so he always promised
to hunt it up. He went to Uncle Sam's Cane Shop on Forty-
Sixth Street with it and they said it might be worth something
as a curio, the ram's horns were remarkably carved and the
end capped with a miniature hoof was a quaint conceit, but
even though it might be worth five hundred dollars to some
collector the cane shop would not offer more than two hundred at most.

"Why should Elsie have Uncle's cane?" fretted Wharton,
and looking around at the bustling lunchers who surely could
not enjoy their armagnac when they knew it was the sweat off
their own brows, it seemed to him they were all his enemies,
all of them knew what there was about the cane that made
Elsie want it and they were all laughing at him. Well, she
wouldn't get it this time, either, he vowed, and see how they
liked *that!* He saw that everyone was laughing today and he
wondered if maybe it wasn't the cane, but something else,
something somebody might have said about him in Boston,
for instance, or something about Nita, his wife—

The thought of Nita popped up like a jack-in-the-box from
the bottom of his conscious mind, the way it had been doing
lately, and it would not go away no matter how he tried to remind himself that it was not Nita but Uncle Carpenter's cane
that was bothering him.

At the age of thirty-five (having lived dutifully with his
mother in the Boston house during all of her strokes, pursuing his private eccentricities with the utmost discretion)
Wharton had found exactly the right bride and had married
her. She was the sixteen-year-old daughter of a Peruvian dig-
nitary, so the step had none of the hazards of a union with

some overeducated, wilful American woman but was like taking on a sweet, dutiful daughter with none of the inconvenience of creating her. Wharton was a frustrated mother, and far from having a mother complex, had only enjoyed his own mother when she was too feeble to resist his maternal care and dictatorship. Mother now retired, Wharton found Nita gloriously childlike, a blank page as so many carefully reared and protected South American young girls are. She had been an obedient daughter and except for occasional wayward weeping fits of nostalgia for tropic skies and convent playmates, tried hard to be an obedient bride. Wharton had never been nor wished to be a ladies' favorite, for the young ones were like his sister, arrogant and superior, and moreover he had constantly before him that particularly terrifying breed of Boston women, unsexed by age and ugliness, hairy with old family fortunes, the spayed witches of subterranean bank vaults, perpetual demonstrations of the Horror of Femaleness.

Wharton himself had been no beauty, licked at the start by a nose that did seem an outrage, a mongrel affair beginning as the Hookley Roman then spreading into Egyptian, and possessing a perverse talent for collecting lumps, iridescent scales, ridges and spots so that it seemed to reflect half a dozen colors simultaneously, ranging through bruise-purple, cabbage green, mulberry red, baby-bottom pink and chalk white. Wharton had such a terrific reputation for efficiency that many friends swore that the reason his nose changed colors before your very eyes was because of an elaborate Rimbaud color code, indicating varied reactions to his surroundings. But middle age had been kind to him, for nose, mottled skin, prim mouth, grim chin and irritable grape-green eyes were blessedly dominated and softened by luxuriant, wavy iron-gray hair and eyebrows. "Distinguished" was the word for Wharton at fifty-five at exactly the time in his life when the overpowering egotism built up by his marriage was being dangerously punctured. Ah, what a stroke of genius it had been for him to have found Nita! How happy he had been on his honeymoon and for years afterward basking in the safety of Nita's childish innocence where his intellectual shortcomings, sexual coldness and caprices—indeed his basic ignorance—would not be discovered. He corrected her language, manners, dress, aired his opinions on all subjects as simple gospel, but particularly he enjoyed her gasps of bewilderment when he lectured her on some new angle of art, literature, psychoanalysis, or perversion that had secretly shocked him. He was well aware that many men of his quixotic moods preferred young boys, but he dreaded to expose his inexperience to one of his own sex, and after certain cautious experiments realized that his anemic lusts were canceled by his overpowering fear of gossip.

Marrying Nita was the perfect answer, just at the moment when Boston had formed its own opinion of him. Against the flattering background of Nita's delectable purity he blossomed forth as the all-round-He-man, the Husband who knows everything, the reformed rake (as Nita's tradition informed her all husbands were) who was generously patient with her backwardness. He soon taught her that snuggling, hand-holding and similar affectionate demonstrations were kittenish and vulgar. He had read somewhere, however, that breathing into a woman's ear or scratching her at the nape of the neck drove her into complete ecstasy, and this was something he did not mind doing, lecturing her at the same time on the purpose of this diablerie so that the dear gullible child did a great deal of dutiful squealing. This success led him into reading many frank handbooks on the subject of sharing one's sex with women, his own instinctive revulsion neutralized by Nita's disapproval. In due course Nita bore him four daughters, a sort of door prize for each time he had attended. This was again fortunate since any male infant would surely have terrified him with the hint of future knowledge surpassing his. Nita allowed him to assume the position of hen mother, clucking and clacking rules for their every moment, herself in the role of conscientious older sister. But when the youngest turned six and Nita herself was thirty-two, looking, to tell the truth, a bare nineteen, she suddenly blossomed out before Wharton's horrified eyes as the complete American girl.

Wharton had grown so complacent in his role of tutor that it never occurred to him that his pupil might graduate. Nor had it ever struck him that the ideas he pronounced purely for dramatic effect would really take root in virgin soil. Suddenly he found his wife utterly changed, as if seduced by his worst enemy. The charming little doll wife was his Frankenstein monster confronting him with all the sawdust with which he himself had stuffed her. He groaned now at the idiotic satisfaction he used to take in nagging her for her convent shyness (he being a very shy man himself), telling her that now she was an American and must learn American confidence. He dared not remind himself of the daring new books, plays, pictures, philosophies which secretly appalled him that he maintained (against her shocked protestations) were necessary for the modern thinker. "You must learn the ways of the world, my dear child," he had patronizingly instructed her, smiling kindly at her naïve outcries, "this is the world, this is life. You're no longer a child and you're no longer in Mother Clarissa's convent in Peru. You're a woman of the world, a wife and mother, and an American!"

The first time Elsie had demanded Uncle Carpenter's ram's-head cane was the very year Nita had burgeoned forth with the bombshell that as an American woman of the world she could naturally waste no more time in the wilderness of Uncle Carpenter's Rhode Island estate or the Hookley morguish manor in Boston. A New York establishment was indicated as the suitable headquarters for the midwinter season of an American matron whose four ugly daughters were safely tucked away in boarding school, and in his consternation Wharton found himself doing exactly as Nita directed him, unable to answer her query as to whether he wasn't pleased with his little pupil, now that she had become the kind of wife he wanted.

Nita had learned more than he intended, and in that maddening way women have, had not been content to leave the knowledge in print the way it was supposed to be but must put it into practical use. She was enthusiastically modern now, frighteningly knowledgeable on all the matters he himself had pretended to be, as worldly and bold in her conversation as any American woman he had ever feared. Wasn't he proud, she demanded, that she was no longer the little provincial prude he had so patiently brought up? Now she could carry on the most fashionably free conversation with any man; wasn't he flattered when he saw how his years of patient criticisms had finally taken effect? It must make him laugh to think of the way she used to embarrass him by slipping her hand in his in public as if he was her papa, as he often said in scolding, and the way she had been afraid to talk to men, turning really pale when the conversation turned openly on sex! How sweet and patient he had been, reading to her, explaining and scolding until she was now—as you see—a genuine woman of the world. She no longer drew back in consternation when some male guest kissed her or casually caressed her, for she knew her husband would mock at her foreign backwardness, and if necessity arose she could breathe in their ears and scratch the napes of their necks like any other proper American woman.

Baffled as he was, Wharton was certain she had not gone to any lengths with any other man because if she had—and it tortured him to face it—he had a terrible conviction that she would never have returned to him. With a herculean effort he adjusted himself superficially to the new order, saw with newly opened eyes that his wife was not regarded as an appropriate detail in Wharton Hookley's properly furnished background, but as a powerful little female in her own right, holding sway over a circle of admirers who listened respectfully to her shrewd worldly conversation. Overhearing her at times Wharton groaned inwardly at the world-weary comments on love and sin with which he had often delighted to shock her now being repeated, contrasting so devastatingly with her charmingly childish figure, bright innocent eyes, Latin lisp. People must surely get the wrong idea from her talk, he thought desperately, but there had been too many years of gentle scolding her for prudery, ignorance, and convent-narrowness to start reproaching her for the exact opposite. He dared not remember the evenings in the country when he had read aloud to his four daughters and Nita, carefully explaining all hidden meanings, scatological or sexual (nothing to be afraid of, let us face these matters openly), insisting on his superior masculinity, furious at himself for blushing or stammering when the five female faces remained dutifully blank and unimpressed. Now he found his wife's vocabulary astonishingly racy, and when some involuntary reproach escaped him she would mildly remind him that these were good old Anglo-Saxon words long in use, and he was perforce silenced by this parroting. Sometimes a glib quotation from some radical nincompoop, some facile praise for an anarchistic artist or philosopher exasperated him to the point of screaming protest, his sensitive nose glittered like a rock in Painted Desert and it seemed incredible for Nita to answer, troubled and wide-eyed, "But, Wharton, have you changed your opinions, then, after you worked so hard to make me see things your way?" Every scarecrow that had ever appalled him from his sister Elsie's mental pastures he had held up for Nita's fright, but it turned out his scarecrows scared nobody but himself; they leered at him on all sides, from sister, wife, and even his four little daughters.

You couldn't trust women, Wharton thought, sipping his brandy, moderately soothed to see fellow diners taking out watches and hastily paying their checks to get back to their wretched desks while he, one of the master men, could dawdle all day if he liked without losing a penny. Still, it was his second brandy, a rare indulgence for midday, and with a sigh he signed his check, placed the exact tip on it and strolled to the checkroom. The checkroom girl was helping a young man into his overcoat, the young man, being a little drunk, waved his arms clumsily and winked at Wharton. Wharton allowed himself a discreet flicker of a smile in response and when the lad gave an impatient oath Wharton inclined his head sympathetically. To tell the truth the young man had a sudden and utterly unreasonable appeal for Wharton, perhaps because his thoughts had been so overrun with women. It seemed to Wharton that there was about this young man, as there had been about himself at that age, absolutely nothing that would capture a woman's fancy. He was a swarthy, undersized, wiry little chap with wide ears, a knobby black-thatched head, close-set beady little eyes, a comedy button nose, crooked mouth, and an outthrust impudent chin—a little monkey you might say, and his arms swung about like monkey arms, too long for his body. Wharton wondered how he happened to be in such a place, for he looked as if he belonged on the other side of an all-night lunch counter, maybe in a turtle-necked black sweater with a dirty apron tied around his waist. Here was a young man who must have been born knowing everything; there was nothing you could tell this one, judging by the knowing mockery of the face. You wouldn't catch this one being harassed by the complexities of femaleness, or cornered by his own weaknesses. Here was the kind of son he should have had, Wharton thought, the ugly essence of masculinity itself, arrogant, fearless, raw. There was something familiar about him, and it was as he was smiling involuntarily at the outlandishly big coat the boy was getting into that Wharton realized the familiarity was in the coat itself.

"Why, that's my coat!" he exclaimed, startled out of his good manners.

The young man laughed, shrugged, the girl hastily pulled off the coat and handed it to Wharton, who found himself apologizing ridiculously for claiming his own property, even though there was his name woven in the lining for all to see.

"But you didn't have a coat when you came in, Mr. Hookley, I'm sure," the girl murmured, confused.

"Perhaps I left it here last week," Wharton graciously allowed. "Usually I wear—"

As a matter of fact usually he wore his new topcoat. It came over him that he hadn't worn the one in his hands for at least a year. In fact he could have sworn he'd left it in the country. Mystified and embarrassed he tipped the girl and followed the young man out the hallway to the street. Not at all perturbed by the episode the young man was swinging jauntily down the street, a derby hat on the side of his head, twirling his cane like some old-time vaudevillian.

Wharton's eyes followed the cane. It was a ram's-headed cane capped by a dainty little goat's hoof.

. . . the animal lovers . . .

THE enormous portrait of the four Hookley girls which hung in Wharton's library was an unfailing comfort to everyone and well worth the ten thousand dollars extorted by the artist, Laidlaw Whitfield, that charming gentleman-painter whose exhibitions were reviewed in the society columns instead of on the art page. Wharton's plan had been to have the four girls, great galumphing grim replicas of himself, curled, and socked, and pearled, grouped around their mother in the Boston garden. This turned out to be such an ungentlemanly enterprise, the lovely little Nita amid the four gargoyle girls forming a satirical fantasy that would have ruined the artist's social success, that the four girls were done alone, long heavy locks and costumes given especial attention to soften the reality. Visitors, unable to compliment the children, could speak effusively of the beautiful painting, the velvet so "touchable," the lace so *real*, the sunlight on the flowers so charmingly done, Bluebell, the great Dane, so true to life. Wharton could look at this soothing idealization and flatter himself on being superior to all women for he had produced four himself, and could honestly boast, conscientious mother that he was, that he had plotted, planned and guarded every thought and move of their lives. It was he, not Nita, who directed their diet, dentistry, reading, recreations, dress, friends, schools, manners, and when they were at home he was at them indefatigably every minute, so that he seldom heard their own voices except the docile, "Yes, Father," "Thank you, Father," and "Good-morning, Father." Their aunt Elsie, who had heard them conversing beyond this point, loved to report elsewhere the delicious news that these exquisitely trained girls spoke a most regrettable, and probably incurable Brooklynese caught from their first nurse (medically irreproachable), and their riding master (a jewel, also, in his own field). Further reports from Elsie were that her brother could not distinguish between his daughters, so similar were they in appearance and so abysmally ignorant was he of any shades of difference in the female character, anyway.

"Just four junior Whartons in different sizes," she jubilated. "I think he had them by parthenogenesis."

Elsie, teeming with a marvelous new idea, had taken it into her head to drop into her brother's duplex on Gracie Square without warning, quite aware that to have pinned him down to a definite appointment would have put him on his guard. Whenever she popped in like this, Wharton was furious with himself for not forestalling this inconvenient visit for it was always inconvenient, as everything about his sister was and always would be. Nita was never any help in these difficulties, and today she herself was put out. She was expecting guests at six and Wharton was already cross because they were part of the new group he did not know. She was sure Elsie would stay and make everything worse by shouting family matters at Wharton. It was long after five and for special reasons she wanted to spend more time arranging her charming little person to perfection. The maid reported that Elsie had brought her great Dane which had started the dachshund yapping, and it so happened that the children had brought in Bluebell herself, Brucie's mother, to see the vet. Out of sheer high spirits Bluebell had immediately disgraced herself at sight of the new Ispahan in the hall and was at the moment confined upstairs to the children's bathroom, refreshing her fagged old gums with some nubbly bath towels and wet nylons.

"Elsie will have to wait till after my bath," Wharton called out testily from his bedroom. "She knows she should have telephoned me first or come to see me at my office."

"It's *your* sister, Wharton, dear," Nita called back from her mirror-walled dressing room. "The sooner you see her the sooner she'll go away."

"Why couldn't Gladys have told her I was out?" Wharton asked peevishly.

"Darling, you know Gladys is absolutely petrified of her," Nita retorted. "You *must* get down there, and do try to keep her from staying."

Elsie was not at all unconscious of the flutter her calls always occasioned. The instant her firm voice sounded at the door, "Tell Mr. Hookley I'm here, Gladys," there were scampers and scurries and whispers and tiptoeings all over the place as if it was a prohibition raid. Then the cautious stillness, indicating that everyone was in their hiding place holding their breath. Elsie knew something special was afoot by the way the Hookleys' ancient retainer Gladys recoiled from the door, palsied hands uplifted as if this was the devil himself.

"And how are you these days, Gladys?" Elsie raised her voice a good octave to the eminence she deemed proper for addressing inferiors. This kind inquiry set Gladys to trembling all over again though she managed a terrified smile even as she backed away, quavering "Q-q-q-q-uite n-n-n-ic-e, madam," her faded blue eyes begging for mercy. Gladys had worked in the Hookley homes for fifty years out of sheer terror. She was afraid of all Hookleys and everything else. She believed the world was a lunatic and she was its trembling nurse. If she only could manage to coax and soothe it it might not leap at her, but on the other hand it might, just as Brucie or Bluebell might. The slightest overture found her backing warily toward any door with a fixed oh-I'm-not-afraid-a-bit smile, wide frightened eyes and little gasps of Yes, please, it is a warm day, oh *please*, yes of course it is, dearie, now, now, of course you know best, and please, oh *please* I'm very well, and there, there, everything's going to be all right, please—oh dear—*Yowie!*

Today's encounter with Elsie and Brucie, coming so soon after the *affaire* Bluebell, left the poor woman shaking like a leaf, knowing she was to blame for everything, even for Brucie's instant recognition of his mother's traces on the rug and dutiful lifting of leg to follow example. Having set the household rocking on its heels Elsie stalked straight into her brother's library, Brucie loping behind with poor Gladys scampering around for mops and Airwick.

Elsie selected a cigarette from Wharton's special hoard and seated herself before the portrait of the Hookley daughters. This never failed to amuse her, and she sat there smiling at it, till it occurred to her to torture Gladys further by shouting for her to bring a bowl of water for Brucie and a double Scotch for herself. Gladys was apparently too spent to accomplish this mission alone and it was Williams, the butler, who bore the tray, obviously resentful of being hurried from his own tea into his party coat.

"Thank you, Williams." Elsie ascended the scale to the master voice again. "Thank you very much. Leave the bottle."

She critically studied the drink Williams had poured and then added a proper amount more and was resuming her artistic pleasure in the Hookley portrait when she realized that she herself was being examined. Eight-year-old Gloria, already five feet tall, Hookley-nosed, baby fangs fearsomely clamped in steel, lanky fair locks dripping about her head like an inadequate fountain, legs bruised, bitten and vaccinated, startlingly bare from ankle socks to bloomered crotch, stood in the doorway.

"Did my mother invite you to her party?" the tot inquired without preamble, her eyes disapproving first of Brucie sitting on the love seat with Aunt Elsie, and then of Aunt Elsie sitting on the love seat with Brucie.

"Not a bit," Elsie answered genially, pulling off her gloves and adjusting her Filene's basement hat with great care at an angle leaving only one eye diabolically visible. "How are you, Gloria?"

"Very well, thank you. Did my father give you that hat?"

"No, dear. Your father did not," Elsie answered, and then, as she was really sorry for her nieces, foreseeing a grim girlhood for them either under her brother's thumb or on their own sparse merits, she said, "You look very nice today, Gloria."

"Thank you very much, Aunt Elsie," said Gloria, graciously seating herself on the ottoman opposite her aunt. "You have very nice new shoes. Did Father give them to you?"

"Indeed he did not, darling," replied Elsie, thinking the girl has no more business wearing bobby-sox than I have.

"Did my mother say you could have that highball?" Gloria went on politely, her attention focused on Brucie's pursuit of fleas. "Would you like me to bring you something to eat?"

The girl is too damn tall, Elsie thought, you feel like snapping at her as if she was a grownup. She always had to remember not to get angry, for the children always asked these same questions of everybody as a kind of courteous repartee. Where did they learn it? No matter what faults Wharton had, or Nita, either, they certainly never credited themselves publicly or privately with grandiose benevolences, and it was strange where the girls got the idea that their visitors were thanes of the family. Cooling her irritation by trying to figure out the source of this childish obsession Elsie concluded that it was born in them, as it was born in all rich people, excepting, of course, in rogue elephants like herself. All friends and relatives of other rich people are supported by them. ("I met a nice little couple at the Lambreths' the other day; they drove me home in their new Cadillac." "What? So the Lambreths are buying Cadillacs for their protégés now!") The Born Rich eye strips every other guest in a friend's house of talent, beauty, personal ability and independence and makes them at once the dependent of the other Rich—else why

should they be there? What other bond is there between human beings? It entertained and soothed Elsie now to reflect
on the industrious instruction Wharton had lavished on his
wife and children, and how Nita had learned something un-
foreseen from it, and the daughters had allowed it to roll off
their knobby little skulls like tropic rain, leaving the basic I.Q.
undisturbed by any philosophy except I-AM-RICH, WE-ARE-
RICH, YOU-ARE-NOT-RICH.

A strange moaning sound echoed suddenly through the
upper hall. Aunt and niece exchanged a nod as Brucie pricked
up his ears.

"Bluebell?" asked Elsie.

Gloria nodded with a beam of anticipation.

"She's locked in my bathroom, but she always smells
Brucie, doesn't she? Will you let Brucie visit her again this
summer, Aunt Elsie?"

"I doubt if your parents will allow it," said Elsie. "You
know what always happens."

Aunt and niece were silent, smiling reminiscently, united
for the moment in pleasant memories of the glorious days
when Brucie visited Bluebell's kennels in the country. The
great dogs had to be locked up separately but there was always the day when one or the other broke loose and freed the
other and they streaked off to town, rejuvenated, like sailors
on leave. They loped joyously down the highway, chasing
anything that moved in the bushes, stripping clotheslines of
the day's wash in back yards, scattering chickens, detouring
traffic, and heading always for Mulligan's Bar at the edge of
town where they had once been taken and been made much
of by a highly temporary former gardener. Police, state troop-
ers, veterinarians and sundry public officials were alerted by
indignant or frightened citizens, the Hookley home was soon
called and in a matter of hours the mother and son, tired but
triumphant, were back in their reinforced kennels while
Wharton furiously wrote checks making amends for lost laundry, broken bottles and glasses in Mulligan's, lost chickens,
rabbits and sundry properties.

"They have fun together, don't they, Aunt Elsie?" Gloria
said dreamily. "Big dogs like to play the same as little ones,
don't they, Aunt Elsie?"

"Of course, my dear," Elsie said, looking at her niece more kindly.

Wharton came into the room, cloaked in the manner he reserved for his sister, that of a preoccupied, harassed, weary man of Christian patience and forgiveness, resigned to any personal slurs or impositions, a man not too well and given to pressing a throbbing temple or overworked heart but never mind, it's really not your fault, it will be quite all right if you will not tax him too much with your idiotic demands. He kissed Elsie tenderly on the brim of her fedora, patted Brucie and Gloria twice each on the head and said solicitously, "I hope nothing's wrong, Elsie, to bring you away from your colorful little cocktail bars." Having established his impression of Elsie's slavish devotion to bars and the fact that her visit would have to be a matter of life and death to excuse it, he remained standing with an arm around Gloria's shoulders, smiling carefully at his sister.

"I came for the cane," Elsie said briskly, with the easy confidence of one who has the power of being a nuisance. "You've been so frightfully busy and couldn't get it to me."

The sound of guests arriving in the outer hall saved Wharton, and the next moment a loud wail from upstairs provided distraction. Brucie threw back his head and yowled back.

"My dear Elsie," Wharton exclaimed sharply, "you know how often I've asked you not to bring Brucie when Bluebell is here! There's always bound to be trouble!"

Elsie put a fond restraining hand on Brucie's collar.

"My dear Wharton," she replied easily. "Bluebell is Brucie's mother after all. Can't you ever forgive or understand animals having family feelings even if human beings don't? Brucie and I will be off in a minute, as soon as you give me Uncle Carpenter's cane, there's a dear boy."

More guests were arriving and at last Nita's voice could be heard greeting them in the living room. Wharton threw out his hands in a gesture of polite exasperation.

"Really, Elsie, for someone who has never taken any proper pride in the family and has done her best—yes, I'm going to say it!—to belittle the name, this sudden sentimentality about Uncle Carpenter is too ridiculous. As I recall only too well you were too busy chasing after that phony Count of yours to even come to Uncle's deathbed and now—"

"Phony, Wharton?" Elsie interrupted ominously. "You refer to the Baron Humfert as *phony* in just what sense, may I inquire? I too can recall all too well the offensive way you used to roll out all the Humfert titles and connections to impress your friends. Surely you're not trying to imply his title is phony just because he's no longer in the Hookley family."

Hypertension, watch out for hypertension, Wharton strove to watch himself.

"You know perfectly well what I mean, Elsie, my dear," he said with a steely smile. "He was phony in the sense that he was not a true royalist at all, insisting on giving up his title and joining the underground like any peasant. We've been over this too many times for you to pretend you didn't know he used the money we settled on him to promote all sorts of uprisings."

"I think it was the finest thing he ever did, Wharton," declared Elsie ringingly, who thought no such thing and had a private conviction that her ex-husband would have joined any church or any cause, even a good one, for a price.

Wharton controlled himself with difficulty, maintaining his patient smile which he directed now significantly at the drink in his sister's hand.

"Is that stout you're drinking, my dear?" he asked. "It's very dark for Scotch, isn't it?"

"I like it dark, old boy," Elsie shouted, "just the way your mother always liked it and all the red-blooded women in the family, right back to the original Hookley barmaid in Lancashire. I hope you've told little Gloria here all about that great-great-grandma."

"No, he didn't, Aunt Elsie," Gloria piped up, her beady little eyes leaping hopefully from father to aunt while she stroked Brucie's hide vigorously.

Wharton's emotions were now discoloring his nose just as she feared, and he raised a hand for truce, even though he would have found great relief in a real out-and-out-no-holds-barred fight with Elsie.

"May I ask you to lower your voice, Elsie?" He was mad enough now to be able to use his most dulcet tone, even though he knew it acted like a red flag to his sister. "We have guests here, nice people if you'll forgive my using such an old-fashioned expression, gentlemen and ladies, if you please, who wouldn't want to be subjected to the inside story of the Hookley barmaid even by her reincarnated descendant. Now, let us get to the point of this visit, Elsie, as quickly and quietly as possible."

Elsie swallowed her drink and put down the glass.

"Gloria, dear, I know you love Brucie but would you mind not pinching him? He still has his teeth, you know." She spoke very kindly and then composed herself in her chair leisurely before answering her brother. Lighting a fresh cigarette provided a further delay. "I have come to the conclusion, Wharton, that you must have lost Uncle Carpenter's cane and that indicates that perhaps a great many more of his treasures, which, as you know, are half mine, may be lost or misplaced. I'm not accusing you or Nita, of course, but you have had sole use of his house for all these years—"

"I grant you that, Elsie. I've always told you I can't understand why you've chosen to live in comparative squalor instead of in any of the family houses at your disposal," Wharton said impatiently. "If you choose to pass up your legal rights—"

"Don't be so sure of that," Elsie interrupted with a pleasant nod at little Gloria. "Your peculiar attitude in refusing to give me poor Uncle's cane, a simple little memento like that, has made me realize it's about time I should protect my other rights."

Wharton stiffened.

"And might one inquire just what it is you are proposing to do?" he asked with a glacial smile.

Elsie pulled her felt brim further over her right eye and then flung her head back sidewise, in a regal gesture revealing half an eye beamed ominously at her brother.

"I propose to look over the Narragansett property myself and select what items I wish in order to realize cash on them," she stated. "Moreover I shall then go to Boston and talk to Mother about reopening the Marlborough Street house. I see no reason why I should not spend a season or two in Boston after all my years in squalor as you call it."

Wharton whipped out his kerchief and pressed it to his lips to stifle a scream of rage.

"Elsie! You know Mother's condition!" he shouted. "You know she has a stroke every time she sees you!"

"Nothing major," corrected Elsie calmly. "May I ask you not to raise your voice unless you wish to excite Brucie? As for an only daughter wishing to visit her ailing mother, only a man without human feelings like yourself could regard it with such astonishment. How do I know if Cousin Beals is doing the right thing for her?"

"Cousin Beals is doing everything that can be done for a senile old lady in her eighties," Wharton said, breathing heavily but getting himself under control. "She won't recognize you, and if you attempt to move her from the Vendome you'll kill her."

"It's a chance you yourself have often taken, Wharton, when it suited your book," Elsie said, lowering her head to give him the benefit of the full crown of her hat.

He was outmaneuvered and he knew it. He had been braced years ago for Elsie's illogical brainstorms but today he was prepared only for the silly cane struggle. He dared make no objection to her demand for the Narragansett property, though after exclusive use of it for so long Nita had come to regard it as completely theirs and he knew she would scold him for surrendering anything in it. He was licked, but at least the battle was over temporarily, he did not have to explain the cane mystery, and perhaps she would change her mind about the monstrous Boston plan. At any rate she would go away.

"Why not call at my office and pick up the Narragansett keys?" he suggested, knowing his calm surrender took away part of her pleasure. "Naturally there is nothing I can do to keep you from upsetting Mother if that is your peculiar desire. And now forgive me if I join Nita's guests. I would ask you to meet them but you know how insupportable you always find our friends, my dear. A pity we will have so little time to see you what with this being Isabella's first season out."

"I'll run up and see Isabella now," said Elsie, but Wharton raised his hand hastily in protest.

"The poor girl has worn herself out already," he said. "She has taken to her bed and doesn't even join in our family meals."

"You drove her too hard," Elsie said firmly. "Absolutely barbaric to hound the poor child to land a husband the first year. The whole town's talking about it."

"I can trust you to keep me informed on the town talk," replied Wharton, smiling brilliantly.

Both rose, feeling a little regretful that they could not extend their always bracing quarrels, and though the room still seemed to reek of gunpowder they looked at each other with a kind of fond admiration. Gloria, who had been enjoying the battle, turned away in disappointment and petulantly gave Brucie a good pinch. With a howl Brucie bolted through the door, an echoing howl resounded from the upper floor, and the next moment Gladys could be heard screaming as she streaked, white-faced, down the stairs. The noise had electrified the quiet little group just assembled in the great living room though Nita had laughingly explained it was only the dogs.

"Bluebell and Brucie always have wild reunions," she was saying in her fetching Spanish lisp. "Sit down, everybody, they won't hurt anybody, they just want to get at each other. It is just a little incest like anybody else. Wharton will quiet them."

Fortunately Bluebell had not succeeded in breaking down the bathroom door because Brucie was trying to break it down from the other side. Elsie, with great presence of mind, took a tray of caviar, whipped sour cream and smoked salmon from Williams as he was bearing it to his mistress and took it upstairs as lure for Brucie. The strategy proved effective and the hors d'oeuvres dulled Brucie's filial passion to the point of allowing Elsie to lead him downstairs again with amiable docility. Wharton, mopping his brow wearily, paused at the door of the living room. His bout with Elsie and Brucie left him with little strength to face Nita's guests, for this was one of the newer cultural groups which always had him at a disadvantage anyway. Nita hurried out into the hall, sparkling and happy seeing that her sister-in-law was about to leave with no further disaster. She was looking even prettier than ever, hibiscus in her black hair and a huge cluster of scarlet taffeta flowers at her tiny waist and trailing down the white skirt to her hem. She embraced Elsie tenderly, reproaching her for not staying with them for dinner when there were such nice people here.

"Now, now, darling," Wharton interpolated with a warning look at his wife, "you know Elsie always finds our friends too respectable for her."

"Oh I don't know. I might have one highball," Elsie said just as he had feared, hooking Brucie's leash on to the newel post with dreadful finality.

As she strode into the living room Wharton transferred his irritation to his wife who should have known this would happen.

"I don't even know some of these people," he muttered crossly.

"Do be nice to Mrs. Grover," Nita whispered to him. "In blue over by the window."

But Wharton had stopped short as Nita went forward with Elsie. A curious puzzled expression came to his face and he did not seem to hear people greeting him, his eyes fixed on a swarthy young man standing by the mantelpiece, thumbs thrust nonchalantly in a fancy waistcoat, short legs spread apart and bowed as if astride a horse, a black lock falling over his low forehead, a crooked smile quivering on his lips.

"This is Elsie, Wharton's sister," Nita was saying, looking very tiny beside Elsie. "Elsie, this is Nigel di Angelo. He was in my art class and we're in the same dianetics group now."

"Pleasure," mumbled the young man.

Elsie blinked. Now really. No, it simply could not be.

"Nigel?" she repeated. "Did you say Nigh-jell?"

The young man returned her stare with a defiant grin.

"Nigel di Angelo," Nita said. "You've no idea how gifted he is."

Elsie nodded with a faint smile.

"I believe I'm familiar with his work," she said musingly. "I think Mrs. Jamieson in Gloucester has his very first oil painting."

The young man tugged at his lock as if it was a bell rope and evidently memory answered the summons.

"That's right," he said. "I remember. Four clams on a green plate. Let's see, this Mrs. Jamieson you mention—"

"Had a Buick," Elsie said, obliging him to meet her significant gaze.

The young man blew a smoke ring at her, unperturbed.

"I picked out an M.G. for her later," he said nonchalantly. "I like English cars."

"Of course," Elsie said. English cars! Nigel! "I wish you'd help me pick one out sometime."

It was fun to see the greedy little black eyes sparkle at that.

"Be glad to," he said. "Let me get in touch with you."

An overwhelming desire to laugh came over Elsie and to Wharton's great relief she snatched the drink he offered her and gulped it down.

"Must get Brucie home," she gasped, making for the door.

"I was sure you'd find it too dull for you," he replied. As she untied Brucie's leash from the newel post he glanced around the hall and coatroom, glad to see no sign of the young man's cane, but wondering why he had not carried it today and what this signified. Nita's new interests were increasingly curious, he thought wearily, and this odd young man's presence here was as baffling as his having the damnable cane and his own topcoat.

Elsie managed to get out on the street with Brucie tugging at his leash before the laughter came.

Niggy of all people! And calling himself Nigel, if you please. Memories of that fantastic summer on the Cape came back to Elsie, and since they were naughty memories a fond smile curled her lips. Niggy had been the Portugee of the year, and the summer ladies, always undermanned, had talked of nothing but Niggy. It was Niggy this and Niggy that. They fought over him in bars, they ruined his fishing by following him in their speedboats; they gave up husbands, jobs, reputations, for the Niggy chase. Elsie recalled her disgust at the hysteria, not having yet seen him, and picturing a slumbrous-eyed Latin of incredible beauty and delicious stupidity.

And then her prim, hymn-singing, Baptist Iola, the best cook on the eastern seaboard, had tried to kill herself for love of this hero. Outraged, as well as mightily inconvenienced, Elsie had taken it upon herself to confront the cad and bring him to account. She was astonished to find the heartbreaker one of the ugliest little monkeys she had ever laid eyes on. How did he get away with it? Evidently good girls are forewarned against wickedly handsome males but their guards are down before such disarming ugliness, so before they knew what was happening he had them all—the maids, the arty spinsters, the bored matrons. Elsie well remembered the stern scolding she had given him to leave poor Iola alone if he did not mean marriage, and to protect and console Iola she had sent her, virtue only slightly nicked, flying back to New York City to recover.

The day after she had straightened out Iola's problem, Elsie had strolled down to the docks to watch the fishing boats come in. Intellectual curiosity was what she termed it, as she stood watching the ugly little monkey scrabbling around his wretched little boat, always grinning, always legs sprawled apart astride an invisible beast—porpoise or billy-goat, perhaps. He looked scared to death when he spotted Elsie standing there, tall and formidable in her oilskins.

"Want a fish?" he asked tentatively.

"Bring it to the house tonight," Elsie had commanded regally.

He was there, grinning, after dark, amused to be at the front door instead of the back, and just as he had impishly guessed, the fish was not mentioned.

He was impressed with the way this tall lady ordered him around, and he was respectfully awed by her superior gift for mischief on a grand scale. She didn't give a good damn, he marveled! He was glad to give up his fishing future to trot at her heels, cruising around at her expense, learning something all the time.

Elsie chuckled as she remembered how she had arrogantly forced the higher circles of the lower Cape to accept Niggy, and his own delight in her instructions. A real monkey he was, learning the art and music chatter as she fed it to him, learning the book talk, the patter about places. You get a higher type of girl that way, she had explained, and was rewarded by his grateful industry in bed.

He learned too much too fast, Elsie reflected. I'll never forget the day I told him he could have that secondhand motor bike for his birthday. "I want a Buick!" he kept yelling at me, absolutely furious. So I lost him and now it's an M.G. To tell the truth I did a lot better with him than I did with Jerry Dulaine. I wonder if I couldn't—

She was so absorbed in her sentimental meditations that Brucie had dragged her half a dozen blocks down the East River Drive before she remembered she hated this part of town and hailed a cruising cab.

PART THREE

. . . journey over the bridge . . .

He should have taken the subway, Dalzell Sloane reflected, watching the taximeter jump with what seemed to him a kind of demoniacal complacency to a new pair of ciphers led by a proud figure three. Still, he might never have found the place at this hour, for once they left the lights of Flushing the road was pitch-dark. It had started to drizzle, too, and the sharp wind coming up from the river reminded Dalzell of the winter he had spent in these very environs with a fearful bronchitis, one that lasted even after he was able to get back to Manhattan, and everyone said, "You have one of those Paris colds, it's those old buildings!" He squinted out the window, rubbed the mist off the glass as they passed a street lamp, and saw the hulk of an old mansion in a tangle of bushes and broken walls, the impressive stone steps and arched entrance still standing proudly, the side walls and chambers scattered about in odd heaps of bricks, tin cans, pipes, rubble. Nothing had been done to it in all these years, indicating a civic reverence for antiquity, Marius used to say, that Europeans don't credit us with having.

"A few yards more," Dalzell instructed the driver, who was twisting his head around to scrutinize his fare suspiciously and who now said, "Say, mister, we're getting into the wilderness here. Have a heart, I gotta get back to the other side of town. I hope you're not counting on my waiting on you if your party ain't here."

"No," said Dalzell, thinking how fantastic of him to count on the party being there. He hadn't been near the place for nearly eight years, and that time it had been Marius who had suddenly walked in the door in the middle of the winter night with a big loaf of Bohemian rye bread, a blackjack of salami and a bottle of genuine rotgut bourbon. It had been his own fourth week of hiding out, Dalzell recalled, and he was down to a very clever schedule of taking his one meal of a can of beans or chile with a solitary glass of hot wine at midnight so that the gnawing in the stomach was lulled to sleep until time for the next day's pot of coffee and carefully doled out pieces of bread. Marius was down and out then, too, but when two of them were in the same condition it seemed almost like success. Together they had the courage to tap Ben for a touch, and on the twenty-five dollars Ben managed to squeeze out of his wife—this one fortunately had a regular salary as a schoolteacher, owning a cottage in Maine to boot where Ben lived cozily, leaving the Queens dump to whatever hobo cared to fix it up—they roared with laughter and drank and worked and bragged and argued for a good two months, when Marius' dealer came through with the money to buy a suit, pair of shoes and a ticket to some midwestern university where he'd been offered a teaching job. Dalzell had gotten some money from Cynthia Earle—or was it from his brother-in-law?—to go to Arizona, and later, when he tried to find Marius, his only answer was a vituperative letter from Marius' mistress—the German one who produced all the children for him—saying that she was not going to have Marius ruined by his parasitical friends when his children needed care and even if she knew where he was she wouldn't tell his evil companions, particularly Dalzell Sloane or Ben Forrester who were notorious for their devilish attempts to force liquor, naked women and godlessness on a decent family man unable to make a living anyway, what with his obstinate devotion to painting.

"Old Trina," Dalzell murmured aloud, and thought she certainly must be dead, too, or she would have been stampeding around the town, unless she was still afraid of his legitimate wives popping up.

Three dollars and ninety cents, the driver said, stopping the car, and from his voice it was clear that nothing less than a dollar tip would avert the ugly business for which the neighborhood was noted. Dalzell got out in the rain, handing the driver the exact sum with the suitable tip, nothing to elicit a thank you but satisfactory enough to draw a "Some neighborhood you got here, brother, some neighborhood," and the headlights of the taxi swept over the can-strewn lot, past the fallen oak and uprooted dead bushes left from old hurricanes, and recognizing these old landmarks Dalzell would not have been surprised to see the same old goat carcass as of long years ago, but rats or buzzards must have disposed of that, certainly the local authorities could not have done so. The lights, as the taxi turned, covered the big house at the top of the slope, showed the broken windows, the chimney bricks tumbled on the porch roof, the drainpipe dangling uselessly from the eaves.

So the place was still there, Dalzell marveled, his heart beating fast as the vanishing tail lights of the taxi bumping down the road reminded him of past encounters in the night with unsavory derelicts. The wind from the water was brisk, the rain cut like hailstones and he pulled his muffler over his ears and chin, standing still for a moment until he could get his bearings, remembering the unexpected ditches and garbage pits underfoot. He sniffed the old smell of burnt or rotting wood with the whiff of river rats and the drowned, the moldy cemeteries of ancient burghers. "Paris!" Marius had cried out—was it in 1928?—like Columbus discovering America, "this is the smell of Paris, and this will be our Paris!"

There were the soft, furtive sounds of footsteps somewhere nearby, the low growl of night-prowling mongrels, whisperings, and a car without lights slithering by, but these were not the things Dalzell feared, these were not oblivion, disgrace, poverty, loneliness, these were the friendly, human sounds of footpads, burglars, gangsters, killers—these were not *Things*. *Things* were what lay in wait in his familiar places, certainly in that cozy room prepared for him in his sister's midwest home. He stumbled up the pathless bank of weeds and his feet found the remnants of the gravel path, they crunched on broken gin bottles, tripped over tangles of barbed wire and dead bushes where tree-toads yipped rhythmically as if it was their industry that produced the rain. He felt movement under his feet, toads, rats, lizards, snakes, perhaps, and they cheered him as if these materializations exorcised the intangibles. The garage doors that had dangled by a thread for years had finally fallen, he noted, and the roof, too, judging by the rain falling through. There used to be a door from the garage into what had once been used as an office, and if this was still open, a closet would lead to the middle portion of the mansion that had remained solid through decades of fires, bankruptcies, storms, lawsuits, and other scavengers. In the eighteen-nineties this had been Ben's grandfather's home and the seat of his small coal business; when the business went the place was left to neglect and quarrels among the heirs all over the country. As a child Ben remembered playing among the ruins, later on camping out for days there with amiable young women. The city had threatened for years to sell it for taxes but until it did this was the last retreat for the three friends. Evidently the city had still forgotten about it.

He groped his way along the muddy wall, found the step to the old office, and even the door, which pushed open. There was the fireplace wall, more broken glass underfoot, then the place for the closet door—yes, it was there, and Dalzell gave a little laugh of triumph! But it did not push open as of old, and he realized something must be shoved against it on the other side. Someone was there, then. Indeed he could smell coffee boiling. He tried to look out through the paneless french windows to see if some ray of light outside might guide him, and he saw a faint glitter as water dripped from the eaves onto some gleaming metal. He lit his cigarette lighter and peered out, saw that the narrow old porch was still there but the railing had fallen off, dragging down the dead ivy vines. This side of the building faced a dumping lot that stretched through swamps and sewers to the old wharf, and now Dalzell could see the lights on the bay winking throughout the mist, and after a full minute of incredulity he saw that the little pinpoints of glittering reflection he had observed were raindrops on the metal of an automobile parked by the porch. In the late twenties such a sight merely indicated bootleggers or highjackers making use of the place as a temporary hideout, and later it had meant some adventure-loving heiress involved in a temporary amour with Marius or Ben. Dalzell had no idea what it meant now, beyond the fact that somebody was obviously making use of the place. He heard sounds of furniture being moved on the other side of the closet, and quickly collecting his thoughts knocked vigorously on the door, rather than be caught as a snooper suddenly when it opened. The bureau or whatever it was on the other side was being pushed aside and the door opened suddenly. A man stood there and Dalzell put up his hand, shading his eyes from the glare of the flashlight on him. Behind the man a ship's lantern on a charred work bench flickered over a mottled plaster wall and the strips of oilcloth blocking the windows. The fumes of a rusty old oil heater blew out from the room and while Dalzell was blinking the other man reached out to seize his hands and pull him into the room.

"Sloane, you old son of a gun, how did you know I was here?"

"I knew in my bones, I swear!"

The next minute they were roaring with delighted laughter, slapping each other's shoulders, trying to look each other over in the dim light. Then for want of sensible words, bursting into laughter again, and shouting that it was just like it had always been, how one would arrive at the Cavendish not knowing anyone else in London and next day the other breezes in from Marseilles; and the time Marius was being thrown out of his studio on the rue Mazarine, the concierge shoving his easel out the door, when up the stairs comes Ben, pocket full of dollars, just arrived from New York, and two hours later in pops Dalzell, just landed from Rome, innocently looking for the vacancy advertised on the front door. Never needed to write each other, those three, let the years pass without a word between them, then they get a hunch and hit the same spot again—sometimes the three of them, sometimes two.

"I'm not surprised to find you here, not one bit," Dalzell said, looking around. "What does surprise me, though, is that the place hasn't fallen apart."

His eye went from the paint bucket sitting in the fireplace to catch the rain dripping down the chimney to the opened door in the corner hinting of snugger quarters further inside. At least they were still able to patch up a couple of rooms for shelter.

"Wait till you see how fine it is," Ben said, pushing the chest of drawers against the outer door once again. "Marius must have been here since I was last. An old ferry captain shacked up here, they tell me, till his wife found him and dragged him back to the village."

Ben had a bad cough and in spite of his boast that the old dump had never been cozier Dalzell noted that he was in several worn sweaters under the patched jaunty sport jacket. His beard was only a gray stubble, now, and he was bald as an owl, great frame shrunken, worn face with sunken eyes hinting at no cushioned past. He must have had it worse than I did after his spurt of luck, Dalzell thought; at least I didn't have wives and mistresses and children dragging at me along with all the other troubles. Ben was pushing him peremptorily through the corner door into a smaller room, fitted out very handsomely indeed, Dalzell saw with appropriate exclamations, for the walls were soundly weatherproofed with panels of old doors, their hinges neatly dovetailing; the floor's deficiencies were covered by layers of carpets and linoleum. A big four-poster bed, wood blocks taking the place of two missing legs, was in an alcove with a motorboat's tarpaulin draped over it, humorously ribboned as if it were the finest lace canopy. Other loose doors were latched together to make a stout screen around an oil cookstove and it was from this makeshift kitchen the smell of boiling coffee came. On a long oilcloth-covered table were two lanterns illuminating a stack of plates, jelly glasses and mugs of all sizes.

"Looks as if Marius himself might be here," Dalzell exclaimed, pulling out a packing box to sit upon.

"I've been sorting out all the junk and cleaning up," Ben said.

"Must have found traces of Marius," Dalzell said. "He was the one last here."

Ben flashed him a sharp questioning glance.

"He left a batch of work here, yes," he answered curtly.

"As soon as I heard they were having trouble locating his canvases I thought they might be here," Dalzell said. "How do they look—mildewed?"

Ben took the coffeepot off the burner and poured it into two cups.

"Most of it snug as a bug under the tarpaulin up in the dry closet," he answered. "Mucked up here and there but easy enough to touch up. When Marius was alive and getting nowhere, being misunderstood, I thought he was a great painter. But do you know, now that he's dead and so damn well understood I don't find this stuff so wonderful. He must not have been satisfied with it himself," he added defensively, seeing Dalzell's reproachful look, "or he wouldn't have dumped it here, most of it half done. Why, remember that sketching trip we made on Staten Island around Richmond and Tottenville? He's got some half starts on those old taverns and street markets that aren't any better than mine—or yours."

"What are you going to do with them?" Dalzell asked, uncomfortable at the disparagement of their old friend.

"The fact is," Ben said deliberately, "I intend to finish them and touch up the others and tell the blasted dealers Marius left them with me in a trade."

He folded his arms and looked defiantly at Dalzell.

"Go ahead," he urged as Dalzell silently puffed a cigarette. "Tell me I'm taking too big a chance and so I'm a crook, go ahead and say it."

"I was only about to tell you I'd like to help out," Dalzell answered. "That's why I took a chance on finding you here. The two of us together could do better."

"Fine," said Ben. "Pardon my overestimating your scruples."

"A dealer who wouldn't give five bucks for my work bought three thinking they were Marius'," Dalzell said dryly. "I could have gone on, but I decided if the only way I could get by was to pretend to be somebody else I'd better go back where I came from. Now that I've seen you I feel differently."

"It looks like this is the only way out for both of us," Ben said. "I've had nothing but bad breaks for the last couple of years and when I got the message from this guy Severgny I snatched at the chance to clear out. Left a note for Martha and one for my girl friend, then hopped in the jalopy and took off."

"I'm as good as gone myself," Dalzell said. "My trunk's in Grand Central Station. I've got about sixty bucks of my ticket money and that's all."

"You're a godsend," Ben said. "I've got about eight. We can hole in here for almost nothing. We'll work over the stuff and let it leak back little by little. I told Severgny I'm rounding up what canvases I know exist. First cash we get we can move back to Manhattan."

"Marius would think it was a big joke," Dalzell said.

"We're doing him a big favor," Ben declared. "He'd be glad artists were making a living off of him instead of dealers. All we want is enough to give ourselves a new start on our own, isn't it?"

"A fresh start, yes," murmured Dalzell.

He looked around him, filled with incredulous joy that he was here instead of on the train bound for surrender and death. His eyes took in the old rope-bound trunk at the foot of the bed with the same old *De Grasse* stickers on it, the black-painted initials M.M.M., the dangling broken lock. He got up and went to the middle partition, pushed the improvised paneling of doors gently till one of them tipped forward and showed the ladder of boards leading upstairs just as it used to be.

"This section upstairs is still fairly solid," Ben said, "if you're wondering how soon the place falls in on us."

They stood for a moment looking each other over, Ben reading the ups and downs of Dalzell's life in the familiar old topcoat, the souvenir of love in the expensive gaudy muffler, the hope and havoc in the still youthful eyes; Dalzell seeing the challenge still burning in Ben's defiant gaze in spite of the stooped shoulders.

"If we're not too old," Ben murmured, half to himself. "Good God, Sloane, we *are* old!"

Dalzell shrugged.

"We were always old part of the time, Ben," he answered. "Not Marius, of course."

"Never Marius," agreed Ben. He studied Dalzell fondly and silently for a moment, then banged on the table suddenly with his fist until the big lanterns shook. "But now we're beginning all over again, Sloane, my boy, we're young again!"

"Thanks to Marius." Dalzell lifted his glass, and then the memory of Okie's pompous words came to him and he began to laugh, sputtering out the story, all about his ticket money, Cynthia's new blond hair, the chase to ride on Marius' chariot, the five thousand dollars Okie would give for the brown-eyed boy looking at the sky—

"No!" gasped Ben. "The best thing you ever did and he thought Marius did it! That shows how easy it's going to be!"

They began to laugh again, tried to talk but couldn't stop laughing. It was wonderful to have fear and loneliness transformed at last into a great joke between friends.

. . . *the waters under the bridge* . . .

How Marius would have loved the joke, Dalzell and Ben kept crying out to each other every day! Here was a merry vengeance for everything the world had made him and his two friends suffer, and they could almost hear his deep laughter in the echoes of their own. Camping out in the old Queens property, not an hour from Times Square, they were as safe from invasion as if they were cruising on some yacht in mid-ocean, while they were being sought all over New York. Someday, Dalzell was sure, when they confessed their secret, it wouldn't be funny. But for the first week of their reunion everything was funny.

"Tell me again how Okie claimed he could tell that boy's head of yours was an early Marius," Ben begged. "I can almost hear him."

"First he knew it was a Marius because Marius always got that sense of starry yearning in his children's eyes," Dalzell tried to imitate Okey's pompous lecture-hall voice, "and then there was the quality of the white paint that Marius was using at one time after he thought his old whites were fringing off yellow."

"Very good," approved Ben.

"It never struck him that we used each other's supplies, of course," Dalzell said, "and since I hadn't finished the picture I hadn't signed it. The museum scout who turned it up in that antique shop swore it was Marius and by the time Okie got through describing the special Marius touches to it I almost believed he *had* done it. I certainly would have gotten nowhere trying to prove it was mine."

"Supposing Trina shows up with whatever he left with her," speculated Ben. "She was the only dame shrewd enough to have saved anything. Remember the Sicilian model who ripped up everything in his studio and then set it on fire when she found him in bed with somebody else?"

"If Trina's anywhere in the world where she could have heard about his new reputation she would have been throwing her weight around long before this," Dalzell said. "And if Trina hadn't shoved Anna out of the picture we might look forward to Anna popping up to claim all rewards—that is if she's still alive."

"His women are all dead or they'd be brawling over his grave," Ben said.

It seemed to Dalzell that it was he and Ben who had died and gone to Heaven and not old Marius at all. That night at the Café Julien he had stepped out of his old life completely, and here in this ghost house he felt as if he was preparing for a new birth. To wake to the sound of birds, river tugs, or flapping of loose boards on the roof instead of to the creditor's knock was a kind of heaven. They had stocked up their shelf with groceries and bare necessities, and for Dalzell it was luxury to begin the day with coffee and bread that did not require his shaking out all his pockets for the pennies to buy it. Each day was opened fresh for painting instead of being snarled and gutted by arguments and futile plottings of the mind as to ways and means of getting through this day and tomorrow. For Dalzell this was a security he had not had in years, and for Ben it was the same at first. They worked over the Marius sketches and canvases diligently, planned how they were to be presented, and made notes for their own work. They took long walks along the water's edge, scarcely believing that across the river from the old abandoned ferry slip was New York itself, the city that had rejected them but would sooner or later receive them. At night they relaxed over Chianti or brandy, remembering the past, filling in the lost years. They wondered that they had done without each other so long, and even if they had only troubles to tell each other how much easier they could have borne them together!

Telling Ben about all the promised fellowships that had fallen through, the planned exhibitions that had dissolved at the last minute, the honors and commissions that had inexplicably melted before his grasp, down to the Hastings Harding misadventure, made the disappointments seem comical pranks of Fate. Dalzell dredged his memory to find more hilarious catastrophes to keep them laughing, and now it seemed to him that they were marvelous clowns who had cleverly planned their pratfalls for the grateful amusement of the world.

"Of course I had better luck than you or Marius at the outset." Ben was so cheered up by Dalzell's chronicles of frustration that he began to swell with the feeling of being a child of Fortune himself, only temporarily sidetracked. "Dough in the family, and I knew the right people. The only trouble was that whenever I was on the upgrade Martha would start being the old helpmate, shoving me down people's throats, till I'd get so embarrassed the deal would fall through."

"No!" Dalzell observed, as if he was not well aware of Martha Forrester's reputation as the aggressive agent-wife.

"Marius was the lucky bastard, though," Ben said. "I know, he had to die to make a living, but the fact was he never even tried to get anywhere. He didn't want to be anybody. All he wanted to do was paint what he liked when he liked, have the dames he liked, get as drunk as he liked. You and I tried to act decent once in a while, at least. But Marius just insulting the best people made them think he was a genuine genius. Remember when he threw Piermont Bradley out of his own house and next day Bradley buys one of his pictures?"

They roared with laughter as if their entire lives had been delightfully spiced with mischief instead of spiked with mistakes. They talked of their women, picturing themselves as pursued and bedeviled by avid females who fended off more desirable creatures. It was true that all three had left a trail of shrews, for they were the genial type that makes shrews of the gentlest women anyway in order to have their peccadillos condoned by society. Even if the ladies had been sweet and unreproachful these gentlemen preferred to sit in taverns boasting of angry viragos waiting for them with frying pans lifted, for it made their dawdling in bars and wenching more brave and manly. Dalzell, whose nature had been far from bold, was aglow with the honor of being classed with Ben and Marius.

"You were always pretty sly about your lovelife," Ben accused him now. "Smart, too, keeping from getting hooked."

"I don't call it smart always falling for somebody out of my reach," Dalzell said.

"Now there's the difference between us!" Ben exclaimed, relaxing in the luxury of candor under alcohol. "You just don't know how to go about it, that's all. I'm a perfectly frank person so let's be honest with each other—"

Dalzell had a momentary impulse to say he'd never seen bold Ben fetch down any birds that weren't already on the ground but he knew that the one thing a perfectly frank person cannot take is frankness, so he allowed Ben to continue unchallenged for a moment.

"You're just too soft, Sloane," said Ben. "When things get tough you just fold up, nary a whimper, as if you had no right to anything better. You're too damn modest, Sloane, and that's no good for an artist."

"Modest!" Dalzell shouted, suddenly outraged. "How can any man who has the gall to put a brush to pure white canvas be called modest?"

Startled by this outburst Ben retracted.

"Anyway you're not egotistical—" he started.

"I am enthusiastically egotistical," Dalzell interrupted hotly, "or else abysmally suicidal. I pride myself most on a kind of oafish stubbornness that gets me from one state to the other."

"All right, you're not modest," Ben conceded. "But you can't say you're a go-getter. Everytime a streak of luck aims at you you have a trick of deflecting it, as if you were some kind of lightning rod, so you end up with nothing but a hole in the ground. Now with me, whenever luck struck I managed to grab it by the horns and ride it till it threw me, at least. With the right breaks I could have been a first-rate businessman."

Dalzell was about to match this but decided it was neither the time nor place to boast to each other of their fine flair for business.

Ben was sick of women, so he claimed, and dismissed his wives and mistresses as such a pack of avaricious, ignorant harridans clamoring for gold, bed and babies that one might marvel how such a strong intelligent man ever fell afoul of them. But after a while a certain wistfulness crept into his voice and Dalzell suspected he was casting about for new chains as soon as he could find some.

"I married Martha because she was educated, a lady, understand, not like the arty bohemian tramps I'd been sleeping around with," Ben explained. "Nice New England family, a little money. How did I know she'd break with them on my account and turn artier than anybody? Finally I had to go on living with her because I was too broke to get away, and she could always get a teaching job. Then, out in Santa Fe, I got this girl Fitzy, a hospital nurse."

A fine, upstanding, simple country girl, Fitzy, Ben said, good drinker, good model—big hips and bosom with tiny waist on the Lachaise style. But the trouble was that after listening to him a few years she started talking art, too, just like your other women, all the stupider for finally knowing the names of all the things to be stupid about. Fitzy and Martha would have a beer and start fighting, not over Ben, but about art.

"All Martha knew about art was what she heard from me when we first married," Ben complained. "All Fitzy knew was what I'd come round to thinking later. I got it on both sides—Martha nagging at me for not being a good enough painter to earn a living, and Fitzy pitying me for being too good to make money. Then that Hoboken scene of mine that I gave Marius on a trade got printed in the papers as his and that did it."

"The girls recognized it as yours?" Dalzell asked.

"Hah!" snorted Ben. "That was the test I gave them. I was sore as the dickens at the mistake and wanted a little loyal sympathy. So, without saying anything, I showed the reproduction to Mart to see if she spotted the mistake. She just bawled me out for not being able to paint a good picture like that and make some money. I didn't say anything, just showed it to Fitzy next day and what does she do but tell me how lousy it is and why should this Marius be so famous when I could do a million times better. That finished me. When Okie started hunting me down I was ready to run out. I had a lot of Marius canvases. I threw them and my own into the old chevvy and started driving East. I'd made up a plan then what I was going to do."

"I didn't plan. It just happened in my case," Dalzell said. "When the demand began after his death I was broke and sold a couple of Marius sketches to a decorator. Then when the guy came in my studio and saw a little water color of mine he said, 'How much for that Marius?' I just swallowed hard, said 'A hundred bucks' and he took it. Next time it happened I got scared. I said to myself if the only way I can get by as an artist is by pretending to be somebody else then I might as well give up and go back where I came from, raise chickens, teach country school, be a grocery clerk. I was scared."

"I'm not a bit scared," Ben answered. "When the idea hit me I thought it came straight from old Marius himself, a kind of bequest. Whatever we get out of it you can be sure the dealers and chiselers will get a hundred times more, but at least it gets us out of the woods and ready for a new start on our own."

"I want to pay back Cynthia Earle, damn it," Dalzell confessed.

"Are you crazy?" Ben asked. "Nobody ever pays back Cynthia. Cynthia's had her money's worth, never fear."

Yes, he would pay back Cynthia, Dalzell thought, every last penny. She had never expected it and would be vexed to have no more excuse to patronize him. Once the debt had been removed between them he might be able to clean her out of his mind. For Cynthia had been his one great love. The flame had stayed alive for years, giving no warmth, merely illuminating the falseness and unworthiness of the beloved, cauterizing him against other surrenders. Knowing all about her, viewing her with cynical detachment as the enemy of everything he believed in, he had still felt slaked in her presence at the Julien the other evening. You lived and learned what a fool you'd been and wise, at last, continued to be a fool.

At twenty-six he had fallen in love at first meeting with Cynthia, braced though he was with warnings and devastating reports of her eccentricities. All the other artists knew her and none spoke well of her, but speak of her they did. She was rich and commanded you to dinner like a princess royal, but expected you to pay. She was a nymphomaniac and could easily have appeased her needs by taking you into her silken sheets, but oh no, her perverse pleasure was in climbing up your dark tenement steps and wallowing in straw ticking and dirty blankets. She could have introduced you into the soft lights of her world but it always ended with her invading yours. She promised fabulous favors but changed her mind at a minute's notice. She inveigled the best pictures out of you as gifts and in return was as likely as not to coyly send you her garter! In spite of all these legends, Dalzell had longed to meet her if only to be in on the joke. It had struck him, too, that her detractors were only too glad to hasten to her parties. Marius knew her, Ben knew her, and it seemed to Dalzell it would be an achievement just to be able to add his own personal criticisms to the common legend.

But he had capitulated at the first meeting. He was prepared for someone thoroughly pretentious, vain, and evil. Her affectations came as no surprise, but what enslaved him were certain mannerisms of which no one had told him and which seemed therefore for him alone. She was not ugly as they said, but handsome in a swarthy, gamy, medieval way. She was overtall but had a coy way of ducking her head to look up at you with a bashful little-girl smile, hands clasped behind her, all but twisting her apron strings, and she spoke in a tiny tinkling Betty Boop voice. To his surprise he found the contrast of her little-girl posturings with her full-bosomed woman's body enticing, and the sophisticated talk in the baby voice curiously piquant. He was convinced she had perfectly good brains but she seemed to make a deliberate effort to keep her conversation on an arch débutante level. Her pet artists, ungrateful by vocation, amused themselves by imitating her gestures and baby-talk. They drew private cartoons of her underlip pulled out in a bad-baby pout, wounded little raisin eyes blinking when someone had crossed her certainly full-grown will. They imitated her arch way of clapping a hand over her mouth after saying a catty or naughty phrase. She was notoriously avid for lovers, aggressive in pursuit of each new flame, primly genteel about other people's morals, but knowing all this, and seeing even more faults than had others, did not save Dalzell. He found her very vanity a virtue, and something magnificent in her never suspecting men's love for her was for anything but her own self. He had the good sense to speak of her half mockingly just as his friends did for he knew to admit anything else would be to expose himself to ridicule. He did not mind what they said about her for he exulted in a secret belief that he alone knew who and what was under this mask.

Perhaps she represented Art itself to him, and her kiss was admission ticket to the world of immortals. She represented

the World, too, for he had never before met any millionaires
with yachts, castles, ranches and noble kin all over the world.
The stories Marius and Ben had told him of her promiscuity
did not lessen his triumph when she leaped into his bed, for
it seemed a proof that he was at last deemed a real artist. He
saw her pretentiousness, her disloyalty and trickery, but when
she finally banished him he was so stricken he could not paint
for a year. Art had dismissed him. For years and years he had
moments of wild thirst for her, and it was no relief to dismiss
it as merely a sex need for she had been singularly unsatisfactory in that respect, eager and indefatigable though she was.

It is curious that some men lust all their lives for a woman
who leaves them unsated. They are challenged by visions of
unexplored delights ahead. Cynthia had obsessed him and always would, but whenever he spoke of her it was with the
cool detachment of her other protégés. He had forgiven her
other lovers but he had furiously resented her husbands. Why,
he often asked himself? Everyone said she only married a man
because she didn't want to sleep with him. There was a kind
of flaunting of her basic snobbery in her marriages, for she
wed only bankers or titles. All very well to amuse oneself with
artists, but good heavens, one didn't marry them any more
than one marries the grocery boy. Every time Cynthia was divorced Dalzell had a perfectly ridiculous feeling of victory, as
if one more banker down the drain was proof of artist superiority. But he had never wished her unhappy, and when other
flames of her past chuckled over her growing defeats in love,
recounting gleefully some futile campaign, Dalzell felt only a
twinge of sadness and reproach for the inconsiderate male
who dared deny her. He couldn't be still in love, ever so
slightly, with her, but it was odd how old jealousy remained
long after the name and face of love have been forgotten. And
here he was, bitterly jealous of dull old Okie who had never
been either lover or husband and therefore had never been
banished! Male vanity at its worst and most unreasonable,
Dalzell told himself sternly: he wanted to be succeeded by superior men to make the object of his love more worthy and
the reason for his years of desire more justifiable. He certainly
didn't want to be in Okie's shoes.

He could still tingle with shame at his obtuseness to what

had been transparent to everybody else at the time. Cynthia couldn't abide love in the abjectly adoring form he offered it. She must chase and snatch reluctant men from their wives or mistresses, flaunt her victories before her less powerful rivals, wear a new artist every day as Marius had once said of her. She must have been through with him, Dalzell forced himself to admit, the instant she found he had willingly given up all others for her. How blind and stupid he had been to her persistent efforts to banish him! He managed to smile a little ruefully when Ben reminded him of that moment of cruel revelation.

"Do you remember the time Cynthia summoned her whole stable to bring her that California painter, What's-his-name?" Ben asked one evening. They were drinking strong coffee laced with bourbon while they put finishing touches on two canvases Ben was going to take in to Severgny the next day.

"The blond beast," Dalzell said, laughing as he had trained himself to do at this bitter recollection. He had had no idea at the time why she had been cross with him, picking quarrels on every occasion, accusing him of infidelities and other defections as an excuse to avoid him. Then came the day she had a pang of remorse and allowed him a quick kiss, saying, "Now stop being silly and run along. Of course I'm not angry any more, silly, I'm in a frightful rush to get out to Mother's and you keep bothering me. Now run back to the studio and stay there in case I phone you to come out to the country tomorrow."

He had stayed in the studio dutifully, happy at the reconciliation, not daring to stir outside for fear of missing the call. The next afternoon Ben and Marius had burst in, shouting with laughter. It was a wonderful joke on Cynthia, they said.

"You know that big Swede she's been chasing, the one that paints bridge builders all looking like himself," Ben said. "You know how she's been pestering all of us to bring him up every time she invites us, because he refused to come by himself. Well, she finally beat him down last fall and set him up in a fine studio in Carnegie Hall with the biggest allowance she ever gave any of us—"

"Five hundred a month he held out for," Marius chuckled.

Dalzell remembered still the sickness in his stomach and the terrible effort to laugh.

"The woman's crazy," Ben had gone on. "She got me in a corner at the Julien the day after she'd managed to make him and you could hear her all over the café bragging about Swedish technique. Her husband, the big stiff, sitting right there all the time, not even knowing what she was talking about."

"All the waiters did," Marius said.

Last fall, Dalzell had thought dumbly, this has been going on for months. So that's the quarrel she has with me.

"She always spent weekends in his studio," Ben went on, and both men shouted again with mirth at what was to come. "Then today they were having breakfast when a big blond girl walked in the room. Asked if Oley had made his proposition yet. Seems she and Oley had gotten married as soon as he started getting the allowance, but it wasn't going to be enough when they had the baby. So Cynthia would have to double it."

"Ha," Dalzell managed to say weakly. "And did she?"

"Cynthia give any money without priority rights?" exclaimed Ben. "Are you kidding? She scrambled out of the place as fast as she could, said she'd have to send the check, and then she marched in on Marius and me at the Julien, mad as hops. Outraged decency. Artist having the gall to marry somebody. Wife having the gall to have baby. Bad manners. Simply frightfully bad manners even for an artist and Swede. Well she blew off steam and we made her all the madder by laughing, then she started bawling and we put her in a cab and sent her home. Marius promised her a new doll, a young Polish sculptor."

"How about you, Dalzell?" Marius had demanded teasingly. "Or have you done your time?"

"I've done my time, thanks," Dalzell had said and he found he could laugh very convincingly. After all these years he could still feel inside his chest how much that laugh had hurt.

"That's right. We used to call him Oley, the blond beast," Ben mused now as they remembered. "He was a pretty fair painter till Cynthia got hold of him. Then he and his bride found out they could get along a lot better just selling his Swedish technique and nobody's ever heard of him since."

"Okie's her consolation prize, now," Dalzell said, casually.

In another week he and Ben were going to take an apartment in town. Gerda Cahill was going to Mexico again and would let them sublet her cold-water flat in the East Thirties. They would have money, this time, they rejoiced. Even so Dalzell dreaded New York and fervently wished he could stay hidden in the safe kindness of the rat-ridden old mansion forever.

. . . the Marius assignment . . .

The greatest favor Marius, the man, had ever done for Marius, the artist, was to die at exactly the right moment. Many men have triumphantly exploited a minuscule talent through life only to ruin themselves by muffing their deaths. Missing their proper exit cues they have hung around like dreary guests at a party, repeating themselves until it is made clear to all how little they ever had to say.

But Marius, bless his heart, had made death his great achievement. He had fumbled gloriously every chance in his lifetime, wantonly antagonized all who could help him, been stubbornly loyal to every outcast or dungheap that enhanced his mischievous nuisance value, stood valiantly in his own light, and then, by wonderfully timing his death, removed the enemy shadow, Marius the man, allowing Marius the artist to step into clear blaze of sun. He had been away from New York so long that journalists and art dealers had stopped smarting from his bawdy insults, husbands had lost the zeal to avenge their honor, harassed old friends once goaded into barricading their doors, beds and cellars when the big man stormed into town with all his bar friends, ladies and lads of the town, with the inevitable disasters ending in hospitals or jails, could breathe easier. Everyone was filled with the Christian pleasure of giving full praise to a man without requiring police protection from him. How considerate of him to die far away in Mexico so no one had to pass the hat for the funeral. How brilliant to choose a month barren of news fit for publication so that editors had to pad their pages with broadsides against the plague of surrealism and existentialism, the sure causes of juvenile delinquency, homosexuality and suicides! The coincidence of a news magazine reprinting Marius' painting of a Hoboken Square the very day Hoboken's oldest building burned down gave feature writers and Sunday critics a nice lead into large thoughts on our American art heritage, the neglect of our native great men, and fulsome appreciation of the true-blue American realism that had been wickedly pushed aside by decadent foreign influences. Checking up on the artist they found that he had just been killed in Mexico. Marius' death was a national catastrophe, they said, and there were suggestions that he be disinterred and given a burial in Arlington. To the very end, they wrote, Marius was an *American* in every sense of the word, regardless of his foreign studies and travels.

It happened that for some reason—perhaps an extraordinarily dry decade creatively—there had sprung up from American university campuses, European pastures for grazing scholars, and other academic preserves a ravening horde of cultural necrophiles. Wars, planetary bombings, invasion by Martians and such fears of premature destruction were driving these opportunists into snatching chargers of long-proven might on which to steal quick rides to glory. Intelligent enough to concede their personal inability to get anywhere without a celebrated mount, and too lazy to take the bellboy's job for which they were fitted, they rushed to stake claims on the great names of the past, boasted with a genuine sense of a deed accomplished that they were about to write a book on Dostoyevsky, Tolstoy, El Greco, or Bach, and dined out with dignity on nifties panned from the richly plummed legends. Some, who had the chance, stalked aging celebrities who might do them the favor of dropping dead and providing juicy material for future memoirs. Sometimes a subject who had been buying Scotch and steaks for a permanent entourage of doting biographers had the bad taste to live on and on, getting politically or socially *de trop* and allowing the biographers' rightful property, you might say, to deliberately deteriorate in value, making the once prized treasury of private journals and personal anecdote plain rubbish. Worse yet, sometimes the subject lived beyond his bad period and betrayed old followers, who had dropped him, by dying in a blaze of new glory, with new riders in at the death.

Marius, at the last, had proved his worthiness and generosity. Anyone who had once hoped to ride on his name and been brutally thrown, or else had given up, could claim whatever valuable connection he chose, for his long absence equalized all their claims. They could vie with each other without loss of face in anecdotes about long ago days when they, and they alone, had stood by the man against his enemies, heard his secrets, indeed provided him with advice and inspiration. "You working on Marius?" they cried in astonishment to each other. "I'm working on Marius, too, but of course you knew him at a different period."

The increasing number of those who claimed to have been the dearest friends of the artist was causing a great deal of bewilderment to an honest young man named Alfred Briggs, who knew nothing of either Marius or art till his discharge from the Navy four months before when the news magazine *City Life* hired him to give a "fresh angle" to the traditional neglected-artist story. Briggs had stayed on in the Navy as a warrant officer after World War I for he was having a good time and was not at all sure of where he would fit into civilian life. The decision to be a writer had come over him while the fleet was cruising in the Caribbean, pausing in St. Thomas, Montego Bay, Port-au-Prince and other playlands where he met fellow Americans and British ladies and gentlemen lounging around swimming pools with tall frosted drinks in their hands, being fanned by tireless natives.

"Who are these people?" Briggs had asked, and on being told that these fortunate folk were all writers—novelists, playwrights, journalists—Briggs cried out, "Then that's the life for me! How do I begin?"

With the flattering letters these genial professionals obligingly wrote for someone they felt could never be a rival, Briggs had no trouble in landing the magazine job when he got out of the service. His honest statement that he had never written anything but clear, straightforward reports for superior officers charmed the *City Life* editor. Briggs had hoped for assignments in the field of sports but the editor felt that literary training and education were required for that, whereas art was a department where inexperience and ignorance would not be noticed.

Pleased as he was to have a regular job which would permit him to return soon to the Islands with some dream girl and live like a lord, and flattered as he was at the outspoken envy of free-lance writers, Briggs found himself utterly bewildered by the first assignment. It had seemed like a breeze, at first. Nothing to do but call up or go see a list the editor gave him of people who would tell him about Marius, and all he needed to do was to write it down like a day's report. But no sooner had one person given him a tasty anecdote about Marius than the next person would deny it.

"I can't imagine where you heard such a ridiculous story," one man said on being asked to verify a legend. "From Dennis Orphen? Why, Marius hardly knew the man. I myself knew Marius for years, here and in Paris, and never even heard him mention Dennis Orphen. He must have gotten it from the Barrows and they weren't even there when it happened."

"Then something *did* happen?" Briggs would press patiently.

"If you mean did Marius take a love seat from a house on Gramercy Park and set it up outside the Park gates for some Bowery pals of his to have a bottle party," said the old friend who was named Ainslie Flagg, "something like that did happen in Prohibition days but it wasn't Gramercy Park, it was Gracie Square and he didn't steal it, he simply took it and why should people spread these nasty stories about him just because he drank too much?"

"This happened when he was drunk?" Briggs asked.

"Now don't go making this a big drunken story about Marius," protested Flagg angrily. "He's dead and no reason to drag his name through the dust. Of course he was drunk. When he wasn't painting he was always drunk. Anyhow the next day after this thing happened he got all dressed up and went back and made a beautiful apology, I give him credit for that."

"Then it did happen or he wouldn't have apologized?" craftily pursued Briggs.

"As I say it was a handsome apology only it seems he picked a different house by mistake this time and they thought he was crazy and had him thrown out so he landed up in jail."

"Jail?" Briggs pricked up his ears. "Marius was in jail once?"

"He was always in jail for something or other, how do you think he got those jail pictures?" the loyal friend shouted. "And let me tell you I'm absolutely disgusted with people pretending to be Marius' friends and then rushing to tell you newspapers every scandal about his private life. I refuse to be part of such a dirty deal, I don't care how big your magazine is."

Baffled, Briggs called on the next friend on his list, explained his purpose, said he had just talked to Ainslie Flagg about Marius.

"Ainslie Flagg?" the latter repeated, knitting his brows. "I don't think he was ever a close friend of Marius. Oh yes, he's the rich old crock who tried to have Marius arrested once. I've forgotten what it was about, something about stealing his sofa or some silly thing. No use trying to get any information about Marius from *him*."

Small wonder that young Briggs was beginning to think those hibiscus-wreathed fortunates lolling around tropic swimming pools had betrayed him into a most maddening profession. Marius was supposed to be worth four installments, yet how could you get anywhere forever crossing out? And what could you do when so many times he had barely mentioned the object of his call before the old friend would brush him off hastily with "Frankly we'd done all we ever could for Marius and if his wife told you to ask us for funeral expenses we'll just have to refuse." This sort of answer stopped after the publicity started really rolling, for after that everyone was eager to talk. Briggs knew nothing of the art world so he had to copy down very carefully every phrase he heard and every explanation of Marius' technique, and when the next person contradicted this he crossed it all out with equal care.

"At this rate," he meditated gloomily, "I'll have crossed out all four installments before I've got even one written."

Then came the lucky day he visited the museum which had managed to flush four large Marius canvases out of its basement and was displaying them with proper pomp in its best room, one on each wall. It was the first time he'd ever been in a museum and he was more concerned with how to behave in a big mausoleum than he was with the pictures themselves.

Huge clumps of marble in the main hall studded with a recognizable human eye or navel made him glad that at least he was not required as yet to have any dealings with this form of art. He marveled that the young visitors trudging through could take so calm a view of these amazing creations, which he feared would bring on a fit if he looked twice at them. He was relieved to reach the Marius room without mishap and to be smoothed by the simple, almost photographic pictures. But again he saw how backward he was in his reactions, for here the jaded young visitors suddenly came to life, gazing in incredulous amazement at the walls, seemingly paralyzed by their emotions. He listened to their excited cries, their bewildered comments.

"Look, it's a real room!" one said. "Out the window you can see the bridge so it must be around Fifty-Ninth Street. Look, there's that corner store where my uncle works. Imagine a fellow painting a real room like that in a real place. What do you know?"

"This one called 'Burlesque,' " another young man said. "A naked girl right there. I read somewhere that they used to have these shows right on the stage with live naked girls."

"It looks real, all right," granted another. "It couldn't have been here though. Must have been Paris or Chicago or someplace like that."

Mr. Briggs got out his notebook and jotted down these comments and then sought out the young lady in charge of public relations. She seemed very cross since it was almost six, closing time, and Mr. Briggs had already asked questions of a sort to indicate he would do the cause of art no good whatever he might report.

"All right, all right," she said irritably. "This new generation was brought up on Picasso and Modigliani and they think women have three heads and two guitars. Naturally when they see Marius' paintings they are all bowled over—like people were when moving pictures started talking out loud."

"But look, Essie, this dining-room table has real spaghetti on it!" someone was exclaiming.

"Next they'll be trying to dig it out," muttered the museum girl to Briggs. "You should have been here when we showed Harnett and some early American primitives. We caught a screwball trying to get a revolver out of one painting to shoot himself right here."

"What imagination to have a real little girl with a real doll in a real rocking chair!" another voice exclaimed in awe. "You can almost see it rocking."

"They always go for that one," said the girl, as she turned to leave. "Real chair, real girl. He called it 'Little Ellenora' first, then changed the title to 'The Live Dolls,' I suppose because the doll looks as if it was being squeezed to death. The way it's pushing its arms out as if it was trying to get away."

Studying this picture Briggs felt an almost irresistible temptation to push the child's pale brown hair out of her eyes. He looked around hastily, hoping no one had guessed his naïve reaction but the visitors had marched on and there was only the girl in blue seated on a marble bench in front of the portrait. He looked at her twice, puzzled, for there was something exceedingly familiar about her. She looked away from him and rather self-consciously lifted her hand to push back a stray bang. A light burst on him.

"Why, you're the Live Doll!" he exclaimed. "I know you are."

He was pointing a forefinger at her as accusingly as if he'd caught her red-handed digging out one of Harnett's convincing props.

"Can't I be allowed to look at myself?" the girl inquired. "How did you guess?"

It must have been the gesture of pushing back the hair, Briggs reflected, then he wasn't sure. The girl was now in her twenties but she had the kind of special little-girl face that some women carry from the childhood to the grave. He realized he had been conscious of her sitting there as motionless as the picture, ever since he had come in the hall, and there was the same waiting expectancy in both. He was pleasurably amazed at his new perception. He had actually recognized someone from a painting by detecting an identical inner quality in picture and model. Briggs was thrilled, prouder of his own newborn perception than of the painter's. His eyes behind the thick, black-rimmed spectacles sparkled.

"I didn't know I was that smart," he exclaimed excitedly to

her. "It's funny what goes on in the back of your head without your knowing it, I saw you sitting here when I came in, then after I look around you're in the same position and—well, all of a sudden it just hit me. Something said, that's the girl. Isn't it uncanny?"

The girl looked at him with amusement.

"It is, except that after you go to galleries a lot you usually can tell that the person sitting very still in front of a portrait is either the artist's wife, the owner, or the original," she said, and hastened to add kindly, "No, really, it was clever of you and I'm sure no one else ever could have guessed."

"Of course you're wearing the same shade of blue as the child," Briggs acknowledged, peering closer at the portrait, "and the nose is the same, a special kind of little tilt to it—well, maybe it wasn't so smart of me. Only you see I'm writing a piece about Marius and this is the first time I've gotten hopped up about him. Look. When he paints a room like that one over there you just know the kind of person who lives there. You almost know who's going to come in the door. It's real, but there's something else he gets—like past and future. A sort of magic key."

The girl smiled a little.

"Maybe that's it," she admitted. "Let's see if you can tell the past and future in my picture here. What's my key?"

Briggs looked from her to the picture and back again.

"Believing, that's what it is," he said, and scratched his head. "I mean like always believing in Santa Claus, always believing everything is on the up and up, just—well, just believing."

He was a little disconcerted at her burst of laughter.

"You're absolutely wonderful," she said. "I really believed he was going to change me into a fairy princess, just as he promised. I went on believing it ever since, without ever seeing him again. But I'm glad I got over that."

"Oh no you didn't," Briggs said positively. "You've still got it."

She looked at him, quite startled and he could see he had impressed her.

"Oh dear, I suppose it's true," she said ruefully. "So that's my jinx."

"Don't lose it," Briggs begged her. "Nobody has that look any more. It's beautiful."

He felt unreasonably pleased with himself and intolerably brilliant. He could see by her face that she thought he was brilliant, too, and he wished he could go on shining for her, but she had risen and was pulling on her gloves.

"Good luck with your piece," she said.

"Oh please!" Briggs cried out impulsively. "I mean I was hoping you wouldn't leave me. I don't know much about Marius or art and you clear things up so wonderfully. Couldn't you give me about half an hour—have a drink with me, say?"

Ellenora hesitated.

"It would help so much," he said. "You really must."

"There's a place next door," Ellenora said. She sighed, thinking that here was another example of how easy it was for anybody to bully her. Once you had your feelings hurt badly you couldn't bear to hurt even a passing stranger.

"Let's go to that place Marius used to like," Briggs urged eagerly, hurrying her through the hall. "That will give me the atmosphere don't you see? What's its name—the Café Julien?"

"The Café Julien," Ellenora murmured uneasily. "It's pretty far downtown and I have to be back uptown."

"So do I. I'll bring you back," Briggs promised. "I have to cover a shindig in honor of Marius that a Mrs. Earle is giving so I won't keep you long."

A taxi slid conveniently to the curb beside them and Briggs had firmly helped her in before she could change her mind. He was so pleased with his conquest that it was several blocks before he remembered he was supposed to pick up Janie at six to take her to the Earle party. He could telephone and explain he was detained by an unexpected assignment but he'd have to think up something good. Janie wasn't the believing type herself.

. . . the portrait found and lost . . .

"MAYBE you have some objections to the Café Julien," said Briggs tentatively. "Maybe you know some other place he hung out."

"Objections to the Julien? Oh no, of course not," Ellenora feebly assured him.

Unless you counted it as an objection that she had tried to avoid the place ever since she had fled from it that last night with Ricky. Unless it was an objection that she looked upon it as an old friend who had betrayed her. Unless you called it an objection that the mere mention of the café reminded her that here she had all but offered herself to a man who was already planning to leave her. Idiotic to go on blaming places and people for your own weaknesses, she scolded herself. Besides she was cured now. At least, almost. No one could ever know, of course, that once or twice a year in the middle of a gay party she gave in to an insane, uncontrollable impulse to telephone the Café Julien and ask for Mr. Prescott. Luckily he was never there.

"Marius always went to the Julien when he was in town," Ellenora informed the young man. "When I was a student we saved our money to go there just to spot the older artists."

"They told me to hang around there for the right Marius atmosphere," Briggs said. "I tried to get something from the waiters about the good old days. I asked them did Lillian Russell eat there? Was it true that Scott Fitzgerald and David Belasco and T. S. Eliot and Wendell Willkie used to go there? This one waiter just looks at the other one and shrugs his shoulders. 'Why not?' he says. 'Everybody's gotta eat somewhere, maybe here, I don't care.' "

"That's the way the Julien is," Ellenora laughed.

Briggs shook his head.

"I give up," he said. "I can't picture Marius there, a guy supposed to be full of life. A bleak old dump like that."

"It's the way it strikes you at first," Ellenora said defensively. "Then you find yourself coming back again and again, not quite knowing why. The tables look bare, the lights cold and bright, so the people and the talk become the only furnishings, and you come back to find just that."

"I guess you love the place," Briggs said.

Ellenora was silent, thinking that everything had begun and ended in the Julien. Each time she had started up with Rick she had entered the café an eager, confident woman, and after each breakup she had left it with her pride and love shattered. It did no good to tell herself she had expected something that had never been promised, for then she felt ashamed for assuming he was as caught as she. After each parting she had deliberately set to work to build up a completely new Ellenora. She changed her work, her friends, her neighborhood, her coiffeur, and above all tried to stamp out the damaging softness—yes, the young man was right—the "believing" in her nature. She taught herself to lunch with Maidie Rennels and not wait for mention of the beloved name, not even to ask, because she was foolishly afraid all of his friends must have guessed her infatuation—perhaps he had boasted of it himself so she must babble of serious beaux for them to report back to Rick. This did not work out with good old Maidie who said one day, "I can't understand why none of your love affairs seem to work out, unless you deliberately pick out men you know you'll have to drop. You just don't *want* them to come out right. Like Rick Prescott, always getting mixed up with girls he really doesn't care about, so he can have a free hand."

A form of fidelity for both of them, Ellenora had thought, perilously consoled, and the next instant scolded herself for lapsing into believing again. That was the way it went. As soon as she thought she was safe and strong, happily absorbed in her work either illustrating books or designing screens for a decorating firm, a crazy wire or card would come from across the world, and work, new friends, new self collapsed again. She should have had an affair with him that very first night, she argued sometimes, and then it would be all over and forgotten. It angered her that because she had denied herself to the one man she wanted she should be unable to go through an affair with any other man, as if he had demanded this vow of her. She strove so eagerly to find worthy superiority in her men friends that they could not get out of love with her and Ellenora fervently wished she could surrender to them instead of brewing her fantasy of true love out of nothing.

"Here we are!" Briggs's voice reminded her, and there they were at the Julien.

It was easier than she had imagined. She found she could walk right in the café door without a qualm. She didn't quite dare look around to see if anyone was there she knew, and she hastily ducked past Philippe's tables to the opposite corner in the back. Except for the new waiter at their table the place hadn't changed a bit, there were the same marble tables, the same pleasantly subdued excitement, but evidently she was cured, for her heart didn't turn over nor did she swoon with memories. She was glad this young man had obliged her to make the test.

"I understand pernod is the thing to drink here," he said, beaming. "I've never tried it."

It had turned out that they were almost old friends, having nearly met several times before. Ellenora's decorative screens had been given a nice plug by the household editor of *City Life* whom Briggs sometimes met in the office elevator; Ellenora had illustrated a children's book written in a hangover whimsy mood by one of Briggs's Caribbean author chums. At the *City Life* annual ball Ellenora and escort had left early because it was too rowdy at almost the exact moment when Briggs and Janie had left because it was too stuffy. These remarkable coincidences, patched up in the taxi coming down, served as a splendid background for a warm future friendship.

Briggs was feeling enormously pleased with himself. He looked around hoping someone he knew might be witnessing his arrival in this well-known spot with a beautiful new girl. He wouldn't have cared if even Janie could see him, because she was too smart a girl not to realize that any man would stand her up for a girl like Ellenora Carsdale. At least he thought so. Janie was a good scout, with brains, but the only reason he kept on with her was a lurking fear that he might not be able to do any better. Janie knew quite well where she stood, and as a matter of fact had gotten sore about it last night at the ball. She had made some crack about feeling pretty seedy in her Budget Shop navy blue taffeta in the midst of all the diamond-studded glamour girls with bare sun-tanned midriffs, but instead of telling her she looked fine Briggs had made the mistake of saying, "What do you care how you look, you've got more brains than any of them. Let's dance."

They had started quarreling about everything else, then, as they rumbaed, and Janie had said she was sick and tired of either getting all dressed up or else all undressed and then having him tell her what a fine brain she had. He tried to say that he wouldn't be offended if she complimented him on *his* brains and she had countered, grimly, "You would if I did it in bed."

After that they gave up trying to have a good time and went to Costello's bar on Third Avenue where he built up a big thing about brains being the only thing in the whole world he cared about next to money and porterhouse steak. Janie was calming down after a few bourbons on the rocks and after his admitting a dozen times that he had always been a dumbbell with a psychopathic worship for a real intellect, but then he overshot himself by leaning across the table to burble, "Why Janie, honest-to-God, if I had your brains you'd never see me again."

Janie's chief from United Nations came up just as she was about to blaze away and that was all that saved him then, but Briggs knew he had a great deal of fixing to do, and tonight he had planned orchids, poetry, diamond fizzes (she had some gin and he would bring some cheap champagne) and lots of talk about her good legs and her dandy complexion and her big old blue eyes.

Yet here he was with another girl a good fifty blocks from where he was supposed to be meeting Janie, and instead of talking about brains he was getting himself all worked up about art. In a minute or two he would telephone Janie, but first he would order drinks and sit for a while just in case this dear girl he had captured might elude him. She had started to tell him how Marius came to paint her, and of course he could not interrupt, so presently he forgot about Janie.

"It was one of those crazy mix-ups Marius was always getting into," Ellenora said, "the sort of thing that drove his friends to distraction. It was that hot, hazy summer my father died and Mrs. Addington, the one that's always the Empress Theodosia on a float for the benefit of blind miners, had given Mother a cottage on her estate near Pawling."

"Two pernods," Briggs murmured to the waiter.

"I'll have a martini," Ellenora said firmly, determined to have no holdovers from the Prescott days. "It was the summer of '36, the summer that Marius' friends had sold Mrs. Addington the idea of his doing a portrait of her. She always had the artist do two portraits of her, one in formal dress for her husband and one thrashing around on a chaise lounge with nothing on for the artist. Like the Duchess of Alba. She'd never seen any of Marius' painting but she'd heard he was a big he-man and that was enough."

"Was he married then?" Briggs asked, taking out his pencil.

"Oh please don't take this down," Ellenora implored hastily, and Briggs obediently put away his pencil. "Mrs. Addington wouldn't stand for any wives. She thought they were sort of obscene and an artist should be dedicated when she herself wasn't around. Anyway it was such a terrible summer that I've never forgotten it, because everything went wrong."

"How?" Briggs's pencil made another appearance and was frowned away.

"First Mother was annoyed because she said we were just to be a cover-up for Mrs. Addington's fun," Ellenora said. "Then Marius kept being delayed and wild wires kept coming from all the taverns along Route 9. After days and days he finally rolled up the driveway, drunk, in an ambulance he'd hired. Mrs. Addington had been told what an amusing character he was so for quite a while she thought it was all great fun. Then he started pouncing on the maids when he was supposed to be pouncing on Mrs. Addington. Then he chased Mother and then he insisted on painting me instead of Mrs. Addington. He was such a great big bear Mother was scared stiff of him, but I adored him. Mrs. Addington got jealous of Mother and told us we must leave, and Marius was so outraged he disappeared. Mrs. Addington sent detectives after him—"

"Poor guy," Briggs murmured. "He was always being hunted down."

"—and she tried to make him give back the two thousand advance. But his other creditors already had it so she took the portrait of me and gave it to the village thrift shop just for spite."

"Are there two *d*'s in Addington?" Briggs asked.

"Oh you couldn't print that," Ellenora cried out.

"No, I suppose not," Briggs sighed.

"You see now she claims to have discovered him," Ellenora said.

"It's tough on a guy being dead so anybody can say what they like about him and he can't deny it," Briggs said. "Everybody seems to have been his best friend but they were perfectly content not to know where he was for the last five or ten years. Nobody would give him a show but now all the dealers are claiming him. Take that picture of you, worth thousands now, and all Marius got out of it was a few weeks' board and a new passel of enemies. What I can't understand is how a man could go through life *always* breaking up his luck, making the same mistakes over and over."

"It's hard to understand," Ellenora agreed, adding half under her breath, "but awfully easy to do."

"Say, this stuff is good," Briggs exclaimed, holding up his glass. "Let's come here again sometime and spend more time on it."

He was nice, Ellenora admitted. Something about his glowing black eyes behind the horn-rimmed spectacles reminded her of Ricky—but as soon as this thought occurred she was disgusted with herself for always comparing, then always discarding some promising future for a past that was little more than a dream.

"I suppose you intend to write other things besides your magazine work," she said flatteringly. "Novels? Plays?"

Briggs's writing ambitions had gone no further than the desire to put off getting fired as long as possible, but Ellenora's words excited his fancy, and before he knew it he heard himself popping away with his thoughts on literature as if he was himself one of the anointed he had admired around the tropic beaches. He did not deny that his brain was teeming with ideas for novels though he managed to hint that his impossibly high literary standards prevented him from actually putting anything on paper. Or to be honest he wasn't really so full of basic plots for novels, it was just that he knew how he was going to go about writing them once the mood did strike him.

"The trouble with most novels is that they don't tell you the things you want to know about people," he said with an involuntary glance over his shoulder to make sure that Janie's sardonic little face was not behind him. "Now the minute I meet a man the first thing I want to know is how much money he makes, what rent he pays, whether his folks have money, whether his wife has a salary or income and if there's any inheritances expected. That's what makes him the way he is. I notice how he tips and what he considers the most important item on his budget. No matter what else we talk about it's a person's financial status that forms his point of view about everything else. I propose to X-ray each character's bankbook as soon as they enter so everything falls into place. Is that so crazy?"

Ellenora resisted a desire to burst out laughing. It wasn't so crazy. She had been vaguely wondering if he knew how expensive the Café Julien was and if he had enough money with him, or if he would appeal to her when the check came, and she would have to fork over her last five dollars.

"I think a character's situation should be clear," she said.

"For instance, here's what has me baffled about Marius," Briggs plunged ahead, earnestly. "They say he was always poor, but how poor is poor? He came to the café here and drank pernod which was eighty-five cents a glass. He went back and forth to Europe and even in those days a round trip would be three hundred dollars or more, wouldn't it? Some of his paintings brought him eight or nine hundred dollars, subtracting a third for his dealer, and he never sold more than one or two a year, but yet he always had women and wives and children and nobody starved to death. He often ate here in the Julien, they say, and even if he only had a beer and one egg it would be over a dollar. But he always had eggs Benedict. How?"

"People loaned him money and he never remembered it," Ellenora answered and went on patiently. "You see you can't figure out some people by arithmetic when they never lived by it themselves."

"Look how much other people are making out of him now, for instance," Briggs went on, tossing down his pernod as if it was a slug of rye and signaling the waiter for another. "Figure out that I've already made sixteen hundred dollars out of him without doing anything, more than he usually made in a year. Figure out the space rates of all the fellows writing articles on him, figure out the price dealers are getting for his stuff, the art teachers sucking out an extra course by lectures on him. Tot up the whole lot against his own figures—

Supposing I were to write a novel about him," said Briggs. "First, here's what I do."

He had produced a pencil and an envelope and was busily jotting down figures between gulps of his drink. Ellenora knew it was time for her to go, but her mind had become its usual blank as soon as statistics were mentioned and besides the waiter had brought two pernods again, regardless of her request for a martini. How clever of him, she reflected dreamily, and how pleasant it was to be here again, remembering only the gay moments and that ever present atmosphere of something delightful about to happen.

The café was crowded today, and people kept strolling around looking for tables or else pausing to speak warmly to acquaintances whose appeal was in having empty chairs at their tables. These fortunate table holders, possibly avoided as bores at any other time, could avenge themselves on old snubbers now by withholding invitations to sit; in answer to the eager "May I join you?" they could look coldly toward the door saying "I'm expecting friends" and perhaps win much better company. For his part the visitor never asked to sit unless he had first looked carefully around to see if finer friends were available. Everyone smiled a little, knowing the game so well and experiencing mischievous triumph in outmaneuvering the other.

Out of the corner of her eye Ellenora caught glimpses of Philippe toddling back and forth holding his tray aloft, steering himself by it as if it was an outboard motor that propelled his plump little body. She saw other familiar outposts pegged out across the room, the Van-Dyked old gourmet with the velvet-draped Brunhilde wife laying into an angry-looking lobster about to be drowned in Piper-Heidsieck. She saw the Wall Street Sunday painter who came to the Julien to watch the professional artists, and she saw the pompous painter and his sculptor wife who were Sunday brokers, keeping themselves artistically fit by playing the stock market. There was the savage drama critic, fearless in print but cravenly dragging his palsied old mother wherever he went as bomb shelter from exploding playwrights and actors. There was the voracious columnist who could wedge into any famous group by using his frightened little pregnant wife and golden-haired child to run resistance and was now, Ellenora saw, pushing them masterfully upon the unsuspecting university professor who leered wolfishly across the table at his latest pet pupil. Ellenora thought she detected reproachful glances at her own escort as if she had no right to be in this café without Ricky, and indeed she felt guilty herself. She noted with amusement that Briggs, who had vouchsafed such great curiosity about the Julien, was oblivious to everything but his literary mathematics. He passed his notes across for her inspection.

"Why don't you have your characters all checked by National Credit Association?" she inquired. "Make out a chart, like those maps in historical novels, with their credit ratings."

"Now you're kidding," Briggs accused, disappointed that she should be as skeptical as Janie. A furtive glance at the clock told him it was nearly seven and if he got hold of Janie by phone to head her off he might beguile his new friend into giving up her own date for him. He motioned for more drinks and excused himself to telephone. Ellenora picked up the paper, mystified by Briggs's figures, but then two and two making four had always baffled her. He was a nice young man, though, and she mustn't laugh at him.

"Eggs Benedict, $1.85," she saw had been crossed out, the idea of adding up Marius' own expenses abandoned in favor of assembling the sums other people were making out of him. As these figures were approximations and made no sense to her anyway she took his pencil and wrote down "Legitimate Expenses, Taxi $1.40, E. Carsdale Art School Tuition, $2000, Pen for keeping score $1.95—Pernods at $.85 each—" giggling.

"Here she is," she heard a voice beside her say and saw Philippe beaming at her. The next moment a mirage of Rick Prescott slipped into Briggs's seat opposite her and speechless, she picked up her glass as he picked up Briggs's. It couldn't be. But it was.

"I see you ordered for me," he said, offering her a cigarette. "Nice of you to hold a table, too."

At first her heart had done a complete flip at the incredible joy of seeing him and she looked around for Philippe to thank him for his demonstration of Julien magic but he had darted back to his own table, his stout little body quivering with suppressed chuckles. Then Rick's triumphant grin filled her with pent-up indignation that he should assume she would always

be there, ready to play whatever little games he chose until he
tired of it. This time she would show him that she was no
more a sitting duck for him. This time there would be no
pretty talk around the main issues. If she couldn't keep her
nature from always believing, then perhaps she could make it
find something worth believing. Don't you dare let him get
you again, she commanded herself fiercely, clenching her fist
tightly. Don't you dare.

"I'll never forgive you," she burst out.

The smile left Rick's face. She couldn't bear it.

"It's the third time you've forgotten my birthday," she
heard herself say. "I'd hoped for a bicycle."

The smile returned.

"Did you really think I'd forgotten that?" Rick asked reproachfully. He put down his glass and came around the table
to take her hand. "Just come out and see what's standing out
at the hitching post right now a-stomping away."

He reached for her other hand and she let him pull her to
her feet.

"With a handlebar basket for my skates?" she asked, letting
him lead her unresisting out the café door.

"My skates, too," he said and held open the outer door for
her. A cold blast of air came in. "Now shut your eyes and
count up to a little drink around the corner."

Here we go again, she sighed inwardly, not even aware that
she'd left her scarf in the café and was firmly clutching her
drink, as if it was a sure protection against folly. He kept a tight
grasp on her arm, hurrying her across the Square, neither of
them speaking, and turning the corner to his own apartment.

"But this isn't a bar," she said.

"Of course it isn't, my poor fallen creature," he said unlocking the door. "I have brought you here to reform you if
it is not too late. Now, sister, step inside the mission and tell
me what brought you to this pass."

It was the little games again, Ellenora thought desperately,
when there was so little time; she needed the truth not a paper hat and this time she wouldn't play.

"It was a soldier that set me off, sir," she said as he closed
the door behind her. "His regiment was to sail at dawn—ah
well, the old, old story."

PART FOUR

. . . we'll all go up to Cynthia's house . . .

THERE was no sign of Janie either at her home, Costello's bar, her girl friend's apartment, or in the U.N. lounge, Briggs's telephoning informed him. He was hardly more than an hour and a half late for their date and it made him sore that she should have gone out instead of waiting around like a lady for him to stand her up. He went back in the café and sat down, surmising from Ellenora's absence that she had gone to the powder room, since her gloves and scarf were still on the chair. He sipped his drink thoughtfully, trying to figure out what his approach should be to get her to go to the Earle party with him, and serve Miss Janie right, too.

"You're the new art man on *City Life*, aren't you?" Briggs looked up to find himself surrounded by half a dozen men, all seeming at first glance to be the same Hollywood country squire type in different sizes. The largest, a middle-aged, beery fellow in black beret, black flannel shirt and plaid jacket, was thrusting out his hand. "Saw you in the lobby as we came in. We've met before at the magazine. I'm Hoff Bemans."

"Oh yes," Briggs said, meaning oh no for he could not recall the man at all and he saw they were ready to pounce on his table.

"I spoke to you about appearing on my Fine Arts discussion panel on TV, you remember," Mr. Bemans said, firmly pulling out a chair. "Sit down, fellows. This is Briggs. These fellows were on my show just now. Ever been on TV?"

"No," said Briggs, extending a feeble paw to the bevy of panelists looming behind him, all looking alarmingly like spacemen with their black-rimmed goggles, berets, vast woolly mufflers and briefcases bulging with interplanetary secrets. Desperately he held up Ellenora's scarf to ward them away from his table. "I'm sorry, I'm with a friend—"

"The lady left with Mr. Prescott," the waiter interrupted.

Briggs looked at him blankly.

"I think she left note," the waiter said, pointing to the notepaper, which Briggs picked up, saw his own figures and then Ellenora's postscript about taxi and pernods which he couldn't understand unless somehow she had taken offense at his commercialism.

"They went across the Square," volunteered one of the panelists.

That would be his luck, Briggs thought irritably, and it was all Janie's fault, too. Assuming an air of knowing just what had happened, he paid the check offered by the waiter. He remembered Hoff Bemans very clearly all of a sudden as a fellow reputed to be always joining you with his friends and leaving you with his check.

"I understand you're doing the piece on Marius," Mr. Bemans said. "We talked about him today on the show, and of course you know I've done a biography of him, coming out next month. I knew him in the twenties, of course, and that's one reason I wanted to talk to you. These chaps are all avant-garde critics, teachers, editors. What say to a beer, fellows?"

"I can't," Briggs shouted, for the place was getting crowded and nothing less than a shout would deflect Bemans' chosen course. "If my friend should come back—"

"They won't be back," insisted the youngest space-man, leering.

It was the sort of thing that was always happening in Briggs's life and he wished he had hung on to Janie, now, just to have on hand in such emergencies.

"Anyway I'm due at a party at Mrs. Earle's," he said more feebly.

At this Bemans let out a cry of joy.

"Cynthia? Is Cynthia Earle having a party? Why, that's great. Come on, boys, we'll all go up to Cynthia's house, one of my oldest friends. What a gal!"

"Now wait a minute," Briggs protested, for he hated people who said gal even when it stood for gallon as was too often the case. "It isn't a party, really, it's a sort of symposium of what old friends of Marius remember about him, speeches, letters—"

"Fine! We're all vitally interested in Marius," Bemans said jovially, propelling Briggs outward through the café door while the others looked wistfully back at a passing tray of highballs. "Besides I get these guys to come on my program for no dough and the least I can do is try to give them a little treat afterwards. Always plenty of liquor at Cynthia's. Haven't seen her for years. Great old girl. Understand she's going to do her life story, is that right?"

Briggs muttered that rumors had reached him that the lady had a terrific book she wanted to write and was looking for a writer, a big name, who would write it for her and leave his big name off of it. Outside the Julien he tried to shake off Bemans' grasp with every intention of plunging back into the café or someplace far from these resolute companions closing around him.

"Scotty's station wagon will take us right there," Bemans said. "Pile in, boys, I'm going to show you one of the splendors of the Prohibition Era."

"I hope there's something to eat there, I'm starved," said the young man, evidently Scotty since he was unlocking the station wagon.

"Don't worry about that, and all free, too," Bemans cried.

"Look here," Briggs said firmly, backing away from the car. "I haven't any business taking all you people. I don't even know the woman. I'm only going because the magazine sent me. How can I show up with all of you bastards?"

"I guess you don't know Cynthia," Bemans said with a patronizing grin, cuddling his pipe in mittened hands. "I guarantee you Cynthia will be okay. Maybe a little beat up by this time, and that reminds me, fellows, a word of warning. Everybody stick together when it's time to go. Lady wolf got no chance if six little pigs stick together."

Everyone guffawed, piling into the car. Six little pigs and the lady wolf, by George, that was good, and they drove away quite overcome with laughter, as if their manly honor was constantly besieged by lecherous heiresses. Anecdotes to that effect were soon forthcoming, chief raconteur being Hoff Bemans who was oldest and loudest of the group and more richly stocked. Briggs could not listen, his mind on the ticklish question of whether bringing six extra guests to a dinner excused your being two hours late.

He recalled that Hoff Bemans was an old rear avant-gardist

with an inky finger in all the arts, who had set himself up as general handyman for the twenties, always ready to patch up a red carpet for Millay, Fitzgerald, Hemingway or Anderson, and a fast man with the blurb for anything from pottery exhibits to the new jazz. Years ago he had "returned to the soil" with the compliments of the Farm Home Finance Company, and was now quite the country squire, sprouting children regularly from his sturdy little peasant spouse from Minetta Lane, and singing the joys of the simple life in every bar on Third Avenue. He had a real old red barn on his place richly stocked with enough old *transitions* and his wife's old still lifes to keep their goat happy for years, a quaint old-time kitchen complete with Erector sets, broken toys, diapers, and old Chianti empties, and a fine old piny library stacked with Sears, Roebuck catalogues and bound volumes of *The Swan*, to which he contributed his quarterly tithe of three thousand words illuminating aesthetics. A good life and a good hearty man, Bemans, and it was too bad Briggs detested him so bitterly.

"Hey, where are you going?" he yelled suddenly as the car nipped past another red light up Fifth Avenue. "We've passed it."

"The Earle house is on Sixty-Fourth," Hoff said. "I know."

"But she said the old Beaux Arts studio building," Briggs said.

"What?" roared Hoff. "Turn back to Fortieth, Scotty, it's at her studio!"

The brakes were jammed so hard Hoff's pipe fell out.

"Damn, I wouldn't have come if I'd known that," he shouted angrily, replacing his pipe in his mouth. "Why couldn't she throw her party in the big house the way she used to? Confound these rich girls turning arty so nobody can have any fun any more. There ought to be a law. Studio, my foot! There won't be any place to sit down and we'll have her idea of a simple artist's supper and God knows what to drink."

Briggs felt that since none of them were invited they had small right to set up such a wail of righteous indignation, and as the car turned and sped downward again he had to listen to a chorus of complaints about the hardships wrought on friends by rich girls turning bohemian. They invited you to dinner and you went thinking for once you'd get a bang-up dinner in a fine house but what did you find? The hostess in an ominous-looking apron, the cook and butler dismissed, a great pot of the same old home spaghetti on a burner, a scraggly looking salad and a few knobs of cheese! Just what you would have had every day only you'd have had it better and more of it. It was the limit the way these rich girls tried to be simple and make everybody else suffer for it. But then most of the upper middle class was playing pioneer now, giving the money they saved by having no maid or nurse to their and their children's psychoanalysts, feeling some kind of grisly virtue in banging around Bendix and babies with their own sensitive untrained hands.

"The funny part is that it's now the artists and real poor have turned stuffy," said the driver, who Briggs fervently wished would pay more attention to the red lights than to his cosmic reflections. Back and front seats chimed in agreement to the observation and upbraided the new bohemia for wallowing in its middle-class euphoria of neo-modern furnishings, TV rooms, Sunday roasts, blended Scotch, and Howdy Doody. How different it was in the twenties, Hoff Bemans said, in the days of Marius and Dalzell Sloane and Ben Forrester! He assured his panel companions that in those days he would not have repaid their work with such miserable hospitality as he was now offering them, ah no. Rich people had fine homes in those days, places you were proud to take your friends, great parties it was a pleasure to crash.

Hoff was still puffing somberly at his pipe and shaking his head over the defections of the arty rich when they reached the Beaux Arts. They were soon rising upward in the trembling old elevator. Briggs was so unhappy wondering how to explain his associates that Bemans finally sensed it and patted him soothingly on the back.

"Nobody gets mad when unexpected men come to a party, son," he said kindly. "Especially Cynthia. It's just when you take women that it ain't etiquette."

This statement turned out to be absolutely true, for Cynthia's face on seeing her door full of strange men was a pleasure to see. She was glad to meet Mr. Briggs and as for his being late, why the spaghetti had hardly started to burn yet, though the anchovy sauce had been somewhat charred during the last round of martinis, but come in, come in, and how wonderful of him to bring so many marvelous people! It turned out that like many other well-known characters of the twenties whose friendship Hoff Bemans claimed, she did not recall ever having met him, but was happy to have him none the less. Briggs expected Hoff to be disconcerted by this, but he swaggered into the room, an arm about her shoulder confidently, reminding her of that night at Webster Hall, and those jolly treks up to the Cotton Club in Harlem, the time she came to a New Playwrights party on Cherry Lane with Otto Kahn and Horace Liveright, the time she came to a Salons of America auction ball at Schleffel Hall over on Third Avenue with Marius and got mixed up and bid against herself up to three hundred dollars for a Ben Forrester watercolor tagged at ten bucks. What good times those were and since they sounded perfectly plausible and Cynthia enjoyed hearing about them, Briggs began feeling proud of himself for having brought these fine fellows.

Cynthia was wearing her Tyrolean peasant outfit and everyone was telling her she didn't look a day over ten, a perfect child in fact. This flattery incited Cynthia to skip about and look up roguishly at the boys, all but fluttering her fan, and then look modestly downward with a clatter of eyelids, weighted as they were with layers of iridescent eye shadow and heavily beaded false eyelashes. Her golden hair was flowing freely tonight, bound Alice-in-Wonderland style with a gold ribbon. The large bare studio contained a great square couch on which several men and two women clustered; a dozen ladies in décolletage befitting a coronation party and men in dinner jackets stood in little groups holding warm martinis or New York State sherry. A large lumpy snowy-haired gentleman named Okie welcomed Briggs to the big work table on which the goblets and refreshments were laid out. Through the window could be seen the twinkling lights of Bryant Park and the red glow above Forty-Second Street.

"I understand you're doing the *City* piece on Marius," Okie said affably to Briggs, handing him a cocktail. "I'm doing a book and everybody here is interested in the man, critics, dealers, all friends of his. As a matter of fact this is sort of a belated wake for him, that's why you'll be interested, everybody telling what they remember of Marius and over there we have a tape recorder taking everything down. I think it's a great idea, a thing like this; as a matter of fact I suggested it to Cynthia. A get-together of all his oldest and dearest friends. Dalzell Sloane, the guy over there with the beard, and Ben Forrester, the big fellow with the funny-looking mustache, they just showed up."

"There are folks here that have been dead for twenty years," a wizened pixie-faced, brillo-haired little woman named Lorna Leahy said, giving Briggs a sunny smile. "I'll introduce you."

If he could hold out long enough and keep from getting tight, Briggs told himself, he should get enough material right here to finish up his piece without putting himself out in the least, so it was really a good thing that Janie and Ellenora had failed him after all.

"It's just like old times, by Jove!" Okie kept crying out, and the phrase summoned fatuous simpers to some faces; nostrils quivered sniffing out fragrant old memories, while to others the words brought an expression of helpless alarm as if some pesky visitor routed with desperate strategy had suddenly popped back in for his hat.

"Old times!" Ben Forrester muttered in Dalzell's ear. "Let's hope *they're* not here again."

Dalzell made no answer. He was the one who had dreaded most coming back into the world, yet here he was happier than he'd been in years. Maybe it was soft, as Ben would surely say, to have present pleasure obliterate years of defeat but the truth was he felt young again, he had money in his pocket, work ahead of him, and Cynthia was being nice to him. Odd, that seeing through her made him feel the more bound to her, as if her transparency was precious and must be protected. He wanted to have her go on thinking she was powerful, beautiful, and that all men were in love with her, because that was the Cynthia around which his youth had revolved; for the capricious vanity that was Cynthia's to be shattered meant the end of hope for him, too.

"What a kick Marius would get out of this!" exclaimed Okie. "I'd give a million dollars to see him walk in right now."

"The trick would be worth it," Ben said sardonically.

"Wouldn't you love to hear him when he saw the prices Severgny is charging for him?" Cynthia cried out.

"She'd ask us to throw him out for using such language," Ben whispered to Dalzell.

Dalzell felt his face reddening and he moved away from Ben imperceptibly. He didn't feel he understood the Ben he had come to know of late. The apparent ease with which dealers accepted their counterfeit Mariuses canceled Dalzell's sense of guilt but inflamed Ben's bitterness all the more. He was jealous of Marius now, as if the dead man had personally defeated him, and he would almost have been glad if some expert had spotted his own characteristic bold brush in a Marius half-finished water color. But none of these fine experts could even tell the break in the originals where Marius, drunk or bored with the picture, had had Trina finish the job, a vandalism obvious to any friend who knew how Marius worked or, for that matter, knew how Trina handled a broom. Dalzell feared that Ben's smoldering rage would boil over into a damaging public outburst and confession, and was glad to have Ben's attention caught by a pretty young art student sitting at his feet.

"Now that everybody's finished eating, let's get down to the business of the evening," Okie shouted, banging on the table with a tray for quiet. "What we're here for, as you know, is to put on record a permanent tribute to Marius. You all know of the books, exhibitions, articles about him and all that, but a few of us hit on the idea of making a Long Playing record of spontaneous reminiscences of Marius, tributes to him as man and as artist, the sort of thing that pops in your head just sitting around like this. We have Mrs. Earle's tape recorder and it will catch everything that's said. Later we cut it down to record size. I'm glad Hoff Bemans came in tonight, as he is familiar with radio discussions and has volunteered to act as sort of m.c. And what a thrill we'll have afterwards with the playback!"

What a perfectly marvelous way of paying tribute to Marius, people exclaimed, filling their glasses to pave the way for spontaneity. Older guests smiled as they recalled old Marius anecdotes they would narrate, and they could not help feeling relieved at the chance to shine in reflected spotlight, so to say, knowing that if the master himself had been present they would not have a chance to open their mouths.

Sitting on the floor beside Lorna Leahy in front of the table on which the recording machine rested young Briggs took out his ball-point pen and a notebook, and being moderately drunk adjusted his reading glasses for better hearing. He squinted intently at the notes he had already jotted down during the evening, and Lorna looked over his shoulder at them with considerable curiosity.

Cynthia's Studio Rent, $150 per mo.

Ford Foundation Grant to Busby—for study of Marius and his Group, $3000.

Guggenheim Fellowship to H. Bemans for Marius Biog., $2000.

Rockefeller Grant (Marsfield)—Color research from Delacroix to Marius, $4000, 2 yrs. travel.

Fulbright award (Canfield) Marius Contribution to American Thinking, $4000.

Last known Marius studio rent, $20. (Possessions seized for $80 unpaid.)

"All set, Charlie!" Okie motioned to the young man delegated to attend to the machine, and Hoff Bemans stepped over the groups clustered on the floor to take a position behind Lorna. But at this moment there was a commotion at the door. Cynthia and Severgny bustled out to the hall and came back leading the new arrival, a faded little woman in the most widowy of widow's weeds.

"Good heavens, it's Anna!" Lorna whispered. "Where did they dig her up? Look, she must have brought in some new pictures."

For Severgny was reverently placing on the table against the wall two small canvases, arranging the table lamps to illuminate the pictures while gasps of appropriate awe swept over the room. Dalzell Sloane felt Ben Forrester's hand suddenly grip his shoulder and their eyes met in something like fear.

"Just a minute while I introduce Anna Marius." Cynthia held the arrival by the arm. "Everybody knows how hard Mr. Severgny and Okie and I have been working all these months to locate traces of Marius' work and his family. We've been scouting all over the globe and now it turns out that Anna, here, Marius' first—ah—wife—was living right over on Staten Island, not even knowing Marius was dead till she read some-place about this meeting tonight. She says she never comes to Manhattan but made the trip just to bring us two of the can-vases she still had and here they are and here she is."

There was a round of polite applause and a ripple of excited murmurings as the lady sat down modestly in a corner.

"Was she legally married to him?" Briggs whispered to Lorna Leahy.

"Certainly not," Lorna muttered contemptuously. "Her real name is Anna Segal and she was always hanging around some artist or writer in Provincetown or Woodstock or Bleecker Street, wearing them down by sitting on their stairs till they'd come home and let her in, then running errands for them or begging for them. Marius was always throwing her out but she'd creep back and when he'd wake up with a hang-over there she'd be with a pick-me-up and ice bag ready, showing what a good wife she'd make. She was always losing her guys by marriage or death and now I suppose all she has left is Marius' bones. She's a ghoul, that's all."

The young man Okie had invited from CBS to operate the recording machine was testing sounds around the room and in a sudden blast of monkey chatter a cracked voice shouted, "*She's a ghoul, that's all,*" and then the apparatus was subdued.

"Okay, here we go," Hoff Bemans shouted. "Everybody just act natural and forget the record."

. . . the playback . . .

"WE should have had a professional regulate the whole thing," complained Cynthia much later, sitting on the floor wedged between Briggs's legs now that the young man had gotten a seat on the couch. He felt trapped and embarrassed by Cynthia's lively squirmings but she seemed quite uncon-scious of any undue intimacy, throwing a bare, braceleted arm over his knee or resting her sharp chin in deep thought on his thigh. "A professional could have picked up the right sounds instead of having all those whispers come bellowing out."

"It was a mistake letting Hoff Bemans try to m.c. it because he's a chronic air hog," said the young man from CBS. "He has to push in front of everybody the minute he sees a mike or a camera."

"He thinks he was chums with everybody just because he saw them eating in the same restaurant he did," Ben Forrester said. "Twenty years later he thinks he was at the same table, maybe in the same bed."

"I'll run it through again and cut out Hoff," said the young man.

Dalzell Sloane, Ben, Briggs, Okie and Severgny had stayed on for one more run-through although it was after two o'clock. Cynthia had graciously brought out her best brandy when the other guests left, for the evening had proved most unnerving for all. In the first playback private whispers and asides had come booming out drowning proper speeches and a dozen quarrels had started because someone waiting to hear his own pretty speech heard instead malicious remarks about himself made at the same time. Almost everyone had stalked out either wounded to the quick or eager to report the fiasco. Careful editing must be done by a chosen few, Cynthia had declared, and here they were, ears critically cocked, eyes on the Martell bottle. The machine whirred and voices came crackling out like popcorn.

"She's a ghoul—"

"Everybody knew Lorna meant Anna when that came out," Cynthia giggled, digging her elbow into a vulnerable angle of Briggs's lap. "But Anna just gave that patient martyr smile. Did you ever see so many yards of black on anyone in your life? That poor, rusty, humble Christian black! So like Anna! Go ahead, Charlie, skip the preliminaries."

The whirring began again.

"All the newspapers said was that it was an accident on a lonely mountain road in the Mexican interior. Nobody knows who was with him."

"You can bet it was some dame. We ought to demand an investigation and find who collected the accident insurance."

"For heaven's sake don't start anything like an investigation

*or we'll all be in trouble just for having known him. Don't you
know they've already got him pegged as a Commy just because he
was always painting ragged children and slums and beggars
and women slaving away?"*

*"Are they crazy? Marius never sympathized with Commies or
workers either. Those ragged kids were his own, the slums were
where he lived, the poor women were slaving to support him.
He'd a damn sight rather have painted Lord Fauntleroys and
well-fed beauties but he had to use what he had."*

*"Nonsense, Marius just liked to paint muscles and big bottoms
and hungry eyes and, boy, that's what he always had around!
Don't you remember how he used to say 'Kinetics!' There's your
secret for you, the hell with the rest."*

*"Wonder how he managed to lose Trina and that brood.
Didn't she write everybody a few years back trying to locate
him?"*

*"Trina was a she-devil. She must have eaten her young and
passed on or she'd be hounding Marius still, dead or alive. Still
she was always faithful, a monstrous faithful woman, he used to
say."*

*"That's just what drove him crazy, the sheer monotony of her
faithfulness. If she'd only be faithful once in a while, he always
complained, but oh no it was all the time, and it got him down."*

"At least he never needed to say that about Anna—"

"Good heavens," gasped Cynthia in alarm, "I had no idea
the damn machine was picking me up when I said that!"

*"—One martini and she'd start tearing her clothes off. Then
she joined Alcoholics Anonymous, remember, because she had
waked up one morning in bed with the janitor. From all I heard
she enjoyed him all the more sober."*

"Wait a minute, please," begged Cynthia. "Did Anna hear
that on the last playback? I think it's awful for people to listen to what other people say about them and make everybody
so uncomfortable."

"She was busy telling what an inspiration she was to Marius
about that time," Dalzell reassured her.

"Not that I wasn't telling the truth," Cynthia went on.
"Why, I heard she stayed with A.A. right through the Twelve
Steps, but one night she got tight and got into a surrealist art
class by mistake next door to the Twelve Steps Club and it

scared her into beginning all over in A.A. They call the art school the Thirteenth Step now, isn't that a scream?"

"I must say I thought Anna's statements were very interesting," Severgny said.

"Skip to that part, Charlie," said Cynthia, throwing her head back into Briggs's stomach so that he emitted a startled *woop*. "I missed part of that."

"'Anna,' he used to say to me, 'if it wasn't for you I'd be dead of starvation, Anna my sweets' and I'd always say, 'Now, ducky, you know your old friends don't mean to let you down this way, and if some of those that could help haven't come through, never writing and never putting anything your way, you mustn't be too hard on them, they're just thoughtless and maybe they'd rather have their bellies full of steak and Scotch whiskey at the St. Regis and ride around in their powder-blue Cadillacs than keep a genius from starving.' And Marius would be so darling he'd say, 'Anna, old girl, I can't say I blame them at that.' Why, if Marius would be here right now he wouldn't blame any of you for letting him down, he'd act as if all of you had always been his best friends.'"

"Listen here, Anna, don't look at me because I never let Marius down and if you're referring to the time you popped in on me and said Marius had to have eight dollars for his gas bill the reason I didn't give it to you was that I knew Marius was living with Trina up in Peekskill anyway—"

"Oh, Ben, I'm not accusing anyone, and as for Marius leaving me for Trina it wasn't because he was in love with her, it was only that she had that shack on the lake and the city was so hot. You know perfectly well he came back to me when the cold weather set in—"

"Good heavens, is she crying?" burst out Severgny, for unmistakable snuffles were being broadcast.

"Of course she's crying," said Cynthia. "Don't you remember how she always cried when she was trying to wheedle something out of you, saying it was for Marius? Imagine her showing up to play the grieving widow when she didn't even know he was dead till six weeks ago!"

"Has she tried to claim insurance and how much?" Briggs piped up, but the machine drowned out any answers.

"Now don't say Marius' friends let him down, just look at all *of us here honoring him tonight. The thing was Marius never appreciated what his friends did for him anymore than you did, Anna. He's the one who never wrote. Never a word except a card about five years ago from Vancouver asking me to send money to come back east."*

"Last I heard from him was from San Francisco saying the same thing. Didn't Cynthia say she got a card from Del Rio?"

"Wait a minute, what did he do with all that money if he never used it to come back?"

"Nobody ever sent him any money, Mr. Briggs, that's what I mean by letting him down—"

"People, people, we're here to tell stories about Marius not to abuse each other! This record is to be a tribute to Marius, a kind of bringing him to life, as it were—"

"If he was alive he wouldn't be invited here and Severgny and the other dealers wouldn't even handle his pictures because he owed them all, and what's more Marius wouldn't even know half of these people claiming to be his best friends."

"People, please, let's try to remember gay little things—"

"You mean like the time Cynthia Earle took Marius on a cruise, and her hair was black as a witch then and she was awfully yellow and skinny. Ha ha, I'll never forget Marius said it was the longest Hallowe'en he ever had—"

"Whose voice was that?" Cynthia cried out suddenly, leaping up so that Briggs fell backward on the bed, his notebook sliding down the crack next the wall where he rolled over to retrieve it. "Let's stop this right now, Charlie, till I find out who said that."

Nobody knew whose voice it had been, and since Charlie, the expert, had gone into the bathroom the machine was left on sputtering away, ignored by Cynthia who was shouting her indignation, all the angrier for Okie's roaring to her defense. He was accusing everyone of treason to that great benefactor, Mrs. Earle, who had done everything in the world for Marius, a big peasant oaf who didn't even appreciate a fine woman's love, let alone the trouble she had trying to help him make a name. No gratitude—

"Marius had just as much gratitude toward his benefactors as they had toward *their* benefactors," Ben Forrester interrupted. "When someone gave him money left them by their ancestor Marius always said he and the ancestor were the only ones who did anything to earn it."

"When I think of all I did for that swine," Cynthia cried indignantly. "And for all his wives, too. Why I even made him bring back a Spanish shawl for one of them when we came back from Trinidad. I was always decent to them. When I'd invite him to a party I'd always say now don't forget, do bring what's-her-name. No, you can't say I wasn't a real friend to Marius, Ben Forrester."

"Like your old man was a good friend to General Motors," Ben retorted. "You got your dividends. Then when you got through with him you never looked him up even though he was right down on Houston Street. Like everybody else here tonight. If they thought he was still struggling away down there they wouldn't even bother about him."

Ben was working up to something and Dalzell gave him a warning frown, fearing an explosion of Ben's pent-up bitterness. Ben got the signal and rose. Severgny caught the look and followed Ben to the door, picking up the pictures Anna had brought on his way.

"I never claimed to know the man, Ben," he said appeasingly. "I only have the *expertise*. For instance I have a suspicion these two pictures are phonies, and from the way you two looked at them I felt you had the same hunch. What about it?"

Ben busied himself sorting out their hats and coats from the hall.

"Why should you doubt them?" he asked guardedly.

"The background," Severgny said with a quiet smile. "Marius hasn't been east in the last seven years but one picture shows a Staten Island bus that only started running two years ago. I just happened to notice."

And the charred walls of an old brewery that had burned down only last year, Dalzell mentally added, and how could Marius have done that?

"I'd swear it was Marius' work," Dalzell said cautiously.

"Let's discuss them at the gallery when I've studied them longer." Severgny shrugged. "I think I should have a little chat with Anna. She may have talents none of us ever suspected."

Not Anna, Dalzell reflected, but who then? Who could have done that gnarled, tired truck horse like Marius? Not even Ben or himself. And if Severgny was beginning to suspect, where did that leave them?

"That's right, walk out on me!" Cynthia wailed woefully. "Walk out without so much as good-bye!"

Dalzell half-turned, but Ben significantly pushed him out the door.

"I'll call tomorrow, Cynthia dear," Severgny called out tenderly. "Get a good night's sleep. A pity the record was so unsatisfactory. Come on, gentlemen, poor Cynthia is utterly exhausted."

Dalzell hesitated, fancying he detected real woe in Cynthia's voice, but now was not the time to console her.

"Poor Cynthia, my foot! I'm not a bit exhausted," Cynthia wailed as the door closed on the three men. "I'm just the loneliest person in the whole world and everybody leaves me—"

"Cynthia dear, I'm here!" Okie cried out and in the hall the others heard her irritated retort, "Of course you're here, silly, there's never any getting rid of you."

"Cynthia, now, just a minute—"

"Oh go way, Okie, can't you ever learn when you're not wanted? For God's sake, Okie!"

With a heart-rending sob Cynthia flung herself about on her couch, face-down in the pillows, beating her fists into them with a great jangling of bracelets. Okie had planted himself doggedly in front of her, breathing heavily, his hands clenched at his sides.

"When you wish to apologize to me, Cynthia," he said in a choked proud voice, "I am willing to listen."

"Stop being such an ass!" wailed Cynthia. "You just want to stay and finish up my brandy the way you always do. Go way, I say."

She redoubled her sobs and pillow-beatings, kicking up her heels in anguish till a sandal flew off and hit Okie in the eye. It was more than even Okie could bear, especially since the young man named Charlie had come out of the bathroom and was staring at the scene with astonishment. Okie was so humiliated by this audience he could not restrain himself, and pointed a trembling finger at Cynthia's heaving back.

"Yes, you can say 'go way' but you should be glad there is

one man left for you to order around because all your other
men have run off years ago. I wasn't good enough for you,
then, oh no. I never got invited on the big house parties and
the cruises, oh no, you just had the big shots, I was always on
the outside. But I could take it, just like I took it from everybody else. I knew nobody liked me, but that didn't bother
me. I hung around and took all the snubs and insults, because
I knew if I hung around long enough the day would come
when none of you would find anybody else to take the dregs,
and that's why I've got the last laugh. You've got to have me
now because I'm the only one that will take the dregs, the
scraps of all of you."

"Go away!"

"All the time you used to kick me around and make fun of
me there were plenty others making fun of you, Cynthia, and
you can snoot and snub me to your heart's content, I knew
who they were really laughing at, and I could laugh too, my
girl, only I'm sorry for you, because you got nobody but me
and what would you do if you couldn't whistle me back?
Think about that, Cynthia, and see how you like being left
with nobody—nobody—"

Okie's voice broke with emotion and he gulped, looking
hungrily at Cynthia's shaking shoulders but she showed no
signs of listening to reason, just letting out little heartbroken
gasps as she clutched the velvet spread. Taking a long tremu-
lous breath, Okie cast a yearning look at the brandy bottle,
then tossed back his white head, clapped on his Homburg and
strode out of the door which the young man named Charlie
held open for him as if for a great star and followed him out.

Cynthia's sob stopped the instant the door closed and she
sat up, wiping her eyes. Looking around petulantly her gaze
fell on the space behind the couch where young Briggs had
fallen and was wedged between bed and wall, sleeping peacefully with his mouth wide open.

A triumphant smile lit up Cynthia's face.

"Left with nobody, er? Well, look who's here!" she said and
leaned over to yank him back up on the couch. The motion
woke Briggs who saw Cynthia's doting face above his and no
one else around. Hoff Bemans' warning not to be left alone
with the hostess rang an alarm in his brain, and he was out of

the door like a flash, almost pushing over Dalzell Sloane who was coming back down the hall.

"Thank Mrs. Earle for the nap, will you?" Briggs shouted, just making the elevator.

Dalzell opened the studio door gently and Cynthia gave a glad cry.

"Oh Dalzell, I knew you wouldn't leave me! I'm so lonely!" she cried, holding out her arms to him. "Promise me you'll never leave me again, never, no matter what! Am I so hideous, Dalzell, am I so old?"

The mascara and purple eyeshadow were streaking down her cheeks and her nose was red. Dalzell took out his handkerchief and carefully repaired her face which she held up to him trustingly.

"You're beautiful, Cynthia," he said. "You'll always be beautiful."

. . . the bore that walks like a man . . .

In the Pink Elephant bar around the corner from Cynthia's studio Okie stood at the bar, or rather rested himself upon it, continuing the long list of grievances that the evening had unleashed. To assure himself of a sympathetic ear he had gone so far as to invite the fellow Charlie What's-his-name for a nightcap. He had a suspicion that Cynthia's ignoring of his accusations had put him in a rather weak position with his audience, and he wanted to go over the whole thing and put it into what he referred to as "proper perspective."

"A gentleman can take only so much, Charlie," he declared, stirring his brandy and soda with a knobby forefinger. "Then the primitive man comes out as it did in me tonight. 'Try and whistle for me,' I said to her. They can all whistle for me—every damn one of the lot—see what good it does them. I took a lot from them."

"Sure you took a lot," agreed Charlie. "They were always trying to shake you."

"They couldn't do it, though," Okie said proudly. "I'll say that for myself, no matter how my feelings might have been hurt I stuck right along. Now I've got them all in my pocket, don't you see?"

"Sure," said Charlie. "You were right, too."

The intelligence of this comment brought an approving look from Okie, who studied his companion gravely.

"Where I made my mistake was not joining the Communist Party when I was your age," he mused.

The young man and bartender looked shocked.

"That would make me an ex-Commy, of course, right now and I could get even with the whole lot of them, Cynthia, Forrester and Sloane, all of them. I'd swear every one of them had a Party card at one time or other, and boy, it would take the rest of their lives to get out of that one. But I was too dumb to see ahead that far."

"You could be an ex-Commy without going to the trouble of being a Commy, couldn't you?" argued Charlie, rather pleased with this picture. "The real Commies wouldn't dare say you weren't one without giving themselves away. Go ahead, sic the F.B.I. on them, why don't you, and have yourself a ball watching them squirm."

"Other people do it, why shouldn't I?" said Okie reflectively.

"I think this guy really means it," Charlie observed to the bartender. "He's that mad at these characters, he'd turn 'em all in."

Okie shook his head with a sad, noble smile.

"No, my boy, anybody else would but I'm too much of a gentleman." He pounded the bar with his glass and the bartender, at a quick nod from Charlie, construed this as an order for two more drinks and poured them. "That's why I hate everybody, because they're not gentlemen. Do you realize that in all the years I've known Larry Whitfield he has never once invited me to lunch or to visit his big place there in the Berkshires? Do you believe me when I tell you that this dealer, Severgny, never once has taken me to his home or made any effort to know me? The bad manners! The rudeness! Like Ben Forrester, when he was riding high a couple of seasons there in Paris and could have taken me to some fine parties but oh no. I tell you people aren't gentlemen, that's all that hurts me!"

"Maybe they didn't want a Commy around," Charlie suggested, swigging his drink.

Okie whirled on him indignantly.

"How dare you call me a Commy?" he said.

"Wasn't you telling him you was a Commy?" asked the bartender coldly.

"No, he was telling me he was a gentleman," explained Charlie. He gave Okie a nudge. "Drink up, or the bar will close before we can order another. All that wine and sherry made me thirsty for a real drink. You should have saved your quarrel till after we'd finished the brandy."

Okie fixed bulging oyster eyes on his young friend belligerently.

"What quarrel are you referring to?" he demanded.

Charlie's jaw dropped.

"Well, when Mrs. Earle told you to go away and then you told her what you thought of her and—"

Okie put a hand on the lad's shoulder, groping past the shoulder padding to contact the shoulder proper.

"My dear fellow, can't you tell the difference between quarrels and the simple joking between friends? Cynthia and I enjoy putting on our little acts, but I'm surprised you were taken in by it. The reason I invited you here was that I thought you had a sense of humor. And now—ha ha, so you really didn't know Cynthia was kidding!"

"Were you joking about being a gentleman, too?" Charlie asked, which set the bartender off in silent chuckles of deep appreciation. Okie was looking at the bar check, holding it far away and then drawing it near his eyes.

"One-sixty!" he exclaimed incredulously. "What is this, El Morocco?"

He reached for his wallet cautiously as if it might bite off his hand and having located it in his inside coat pocket tugged away at it, evidently meeting with mighty resistance until his final capture of it almost lost him his balance. He fished some coins from his change pocket, extricated a reluctant one-dollar bill from the wallet, then restored it to its warm nest.

"I must say I don't see the point in paying out good money for drinks when we were having them free at Cynthia's," he grumbled.

Charlie looked at him in astonishment.

"But she ordered you out and you told her off, didn't you? You said what you thought of the whole lousy lot of them—"

"What?" Okie cried out, shocked. "You must have misunderstood the situation, my boy."

"What are you getting sore at me for?" Charlie said, nettled at Okie's reproving tone. "I thought you were a hundred per cent right. What kind of people are they, anyway?"

Okie straightened up, frowning at him beneath proud beetling gray brows.

"They are my friends, young man, friends of a lifetime, and I should think you would regard it an honor to meet them. Instead you stand here in this common saloon making derogatory remarks about your betters, insinuating that I myself behaved badly to our hostess—"

"I said I didn't blame you!" interrupted Charlie.

Okie lifted a forefinger admonishing silence.

"I shall apologize to poor Cynthia in the morning," he stated. "If she misunderstood our little joke as you seem to have done, then of course she will be upset until I make apologies."

"You're always going around apologizing," muttered Charlie, baffled and exasperated, seeing an end to nightcaps in Okie's final gesture of buttoning up his Chesterfield.

"Because I happen to be a gentleman, my dear fellow," Okie said haughtily. "Something you young upstarts know nothing about. Have you so much as uttered one word of thanks for my invitation to a nightcap, for instance? No. There you are."

"Thanks," said Charlie sulkily.

Reluctantly he followed Okie out and stood on the corner watching him swagger proudly eastward toward Fifth Avenue, noting that the Chesterfield was too snug but still seemed the proper armor.

. . . one has one's own life to live . . .

THE time had come, Elsie Hookley decided, to drop Jerry Dulaine. You took an interest in someone, knocked yourself out trying to help them get on their feet, defended them against a world of enemies, gave them the shirt off your back, and what thanks did you get? The person didn't want a shirt or to be on her feet. Your money, time and tender sympathy were all down the drain. Once you've made up your mind what a person ought to be you can't go back and be satisfied with them the way they are. Jerry had fascinated her as capable of magic transformation, but now that this had proved a false hope, Elsie felt righteously let down. She found daily justification for her decision to dismiss this friendship. There were the bills for objects Jerry had charged to her accounts all over town; there was the loan company to which Elsie had unwittingly given her name as sponsor now trying to collect from Elsie. There were the neighborhood tradesmen ringing Elsie's bell to ask for Miss Dulaine. And there was the cruel fact that the young lady herself kept away from Elsie's apartment and was never to be found by phone or knock in her own place. Once you have made up your mind to drop a person it is most inconsiderate of them not to come within dropping distance. Elsie had planned to keep a cool, polite distance, to keep her own counsel about what steps she was going to take in her own life—such as her intention of descending on her mother in Boston to wrest outright cash for splurging on the old family homestead just to show brother Wharton that from now on she was going to live on the same scale as he did.

"I'll simply make it clear to her I'm through trying to help people," Elsie told herself virtuously. "From now on I'm looking out for myself, and I shan't encourage her to tell me any of her troubles, either. When she tries to explain about all these financial mix-ups I will just shrug my shoulders."

There was no use denying that she had twinges of regret for the old happy days of friendship, and perhaps she was being unkind and unfair to her former protégée. But one had one's own life to live, after all. To avoid an open scene Elsie took pains to be out in the hours she thought Jerry would be in, and she had her lights out early at night in case Jerry might be tempted to drop in for a nightcap. But there were no encounters, and after congratulating herself on how well she was handling a rather awkward situation Elsie switched to the suspicion that it was Jerry who was avoiding her. This drove her crazy with curiosity. What was the girl up to?

Maybe she was keeping her distance out of shame at the failure of their recent enterprise. Still she'd never known Miss Dulaine to be ashamed of anything.

"The least I can do is to let her know I don't hold anything against her." Elsie relented a little as she helped Brucie locate a tick on his belly. "After all, there's no reason I should go to such extremes to punish her when she couldn't help the way things turned out. Even if she did hurt my feelings—"

Elsie did not try to define exactly how Jerry had hurt her feelings but hurt they were, and it was because Jerry had absolutely refused to cry on her shoulder or accept any consolation. She, Jerry, had shrugged off her benefactor as if their positions were reversed, and Elsie, with her heart full of belligerent defenses and excuses, found her charge rejecting them. Very well, Elsie had found new interests, but she would give her eyeteeth to know what Jerry was doing without her. It seemed hardly fair that Jerry betrayed no equivalent curiosity about her neighbor's new life.

"Haven't you gone yet, Iola?" Elsie called sharply to the kitchen. "I told you to leave as soon as you got things ready and I'll do the *scampi* when I feel like it. Now run along."

"I'm in no hurry, Miss Hookley," Iola whimpered. "I'd just as soon stay and fix 'em when you're ready."

She looked at her mistress dolefully, pale brown face smugly pious with love of duty, or was it, Elsie wondered suspiciously, malicious determination to bedevil her mistress by hanging around to see what was going on?

"Run along, I said," Elsie said firmly, and Iola with an audible sigh took off her apron and put on her coat and hat, looking reproachfully from Elsie to Brucie for being able to do without her.

"I been kinda scared lately, Miss Hookley," she said, standing in the doorway. "Couple times lately I seen somebody round this neighborhood look like that awful Portugee that used to devil me. If he starts bothering me again I just don't know what I'd do."

Elsie found another tick.

"I'd like to know how Brucie can get ticks in a city yard in winter," she said absently. "Good night, Iola. Nobody's going to bother you."

The door closed on another deep sigh. Elsie went to the kitchen and got out the ice bucket, fizz water and the bourbon. The shrimps were in the pan all ready for broiling in garlic butter, the avocados and salad greens waiting in the icebox, the chunk of provolone paired with the half-moon of Gruyère, the rice steaming gently on the stove. Elsie nodded approval and settled down in the living room with a highball.

She had just begun on her second when the door opened quietly and the young man whom Iola feared slipped into the room and grinning, without saying a word, poured himself a fine drink.

"You could at least knock, you little imp," Elsie said, not at all displeased. "I suppose you swiped my key and had a copy made."

He nodded happily.

"I like a lot of keys," he said. He looked around cautiously. "I saw Iola go. She won't come back, will she?"

Elsie laughed.

"You're still afraid of her. Iola can't hurt you."

"You never heard a dame scream like that one." Niggy shuddered. "Makes my blood run cold every time I think about it. I never knew a dame to start yelling when you made a little pass at her. She won't be back, will she?"

"Don't worry," Elsie reassured him. She looked over his suit, a gray with wider pin stripes than she had ever seen, and enough shoulder padding to float him in case of shipwreck. He flickered his sleeve self-consciously, catching her eye.

"Okay, I know. A little loud but that's my style. Nita likes it. Says it make me look like a South American millionaire," he said defensively. "Anyway I'm an intellectual now, I can dress any way I damn please. Look, can we talk or are you expecting somebody?"

Elsie motioned him to a chair.

"I expected you to phone," she said. "What are you up to in New York?"

"Old Brucie looks all right," answered Niggy as Brucie laid his head trustingly on his knees, waiting for the soothing scratch beneath the chin.

"He misses his fresh fish," Elsie said wickedly. Her guest's eyes flashed but he grinned and shrugged as she chuckled.

"Okay, you pulled me out of the fish pile but I wish I was there right now," he said. "At least I'd be making some dough."

He yanked a cigarette savagely out of a pack and lit it, his black eyes on Elsie waiting for her to say something, but Elsie kept her eyes on Brucie.

"Brains cost money," he said. "I was better off when I just had a boat."

He sounded injured and accusing, as if Elsie had made this unfair trade behind his back. Elsie laughed mockingly.

This angered the young man for he jumped up and poured himself another drink, planting himself in front of Elsie.

"All right, laugh, you know I was doing all right when you got hold of me. I made money on my boat, I played around with the waitresses at the Gull House, or the schoolteachers or the help around town, and it never cost a cent. They paid for everything. Then you fix me up with all the highbrows and rich dames and they want me on tap twenty-four hours a day and I'm lucky if I get a few meals out of it. Sure, I ride around in their cars, I drink their liquor, I sleep with their mothers or their daughters to break the monotony, but no cash, see, never a damn bit of cash."

"What's stopping you from going back to the Cape?" Elsie asked calmly, knowing he wanted something from her and enjoying the sense of power. She had every intention of giving in to his demands but she couldn't resist the desire to make him jump for his sugar.

Pouting sulkily, the lad's blue-shaven face with the snub nose and long upper lip and button eyes looked more than ever like a monkey's. Elsie found the resemblance charming and appealing. She pushed the dish of toasted almonds towards him and the nervous little monkey fingers snatched at them and stuffed them in his mouth as he talked.

"The guys there are all sore at me since I started running around with the summer people," he complained. "That's where you queered me year before last. And now that I've been around I don't want to go back to what I was. You said yourself I could paint as well as those mugs in the art classes. Sure, I can throw a couple of apples on a plate with a clam shell and a pop bottle and call it a still life but what kind of a living is that?"

"Who said it was a living?" Elsie said. "At least you met some new people through it. And now it seems you don't even paint, just go to cocktail parties and pontificate with the fine minds in my sister-in-law's intellectual group. Who pays for that, by the way?"

Niggy smirked annoyingly, and examined his fingernails.

"You've picked up a lot of camping tricks," Elsie said, deciding that she wouldn't give him a thing if he was going to act coy with her. Evidently sensing this Niggy changed his tactics.

"I worked nights in a garage up on the West Side," he said. "But damn it, Elsie, I can't go around with nice people, visit their homes and all that, maybe go on pleasure trips with them, if I have to drudge away in some dirty garage. A fellow's just got to get his hands on cash to keep up. Nita's been nice enough, letting me drive her car, letting me have some of Wharton's clothes—whatever isn't too big for me, passing out a ten-spot now and then, but I got my future to look out for."

"So?" Elsie said, determined to make it as difficult as possible.

Niggy was silent, scratching his crew cut moodily.

"Well, what's your problem?" Elsie persisted. "I take it you're sorry you gave up the fisherman's life but now you're too good for it. You like going around with rich people and highbrows only there's no money in it. You have to jump when they whistle but on the other hand you don't want them to stop whistling. Well?"

The young man took Brucie's head between his knees and gazed moodily into the dog's red-rimmed patient eyes.

"You can kid about the spot I'm in but you know you're the one that set me off," he muttered. "You're the one that told me it was easier to make upstairs than downstairs, the very words you used."

"It does sound like me," Elsie admitted, pleased. "I don't see why you hold it against me, Niggy. You got a summer in Gloucester out of it, you learned to talk Tanglewood, you helped make sets for summer arena theatres, you sat around the best beaches, then you jump into philosophy and literature and end up with my brother's wife. What more do you want?"

"Cash, like I told you," Niggy said. "So it looks like I've got to marry Isabella."

Elsie sat up straight, staring at him.

"Isabella?" she cried. "You're not referring to my niece, by any chance?"

Niggy nodded gloomily.

"What on earth is Nita thinking of to let you marry Isabella?" Elsie exclaimed indignantly. "My poor brother knocks himself out grooming the girl for a big marriage and then you step in and ruin everything, just because you've got Nita interested in you! What are you thinking of?"

The young man pushed Brucie aside and got to his feet. He downed another whiskey neat and this inspired Elsie to pour herself a revivifying swig. They banged their glasses down on the table at the same moment and looked at each other for a moment in silence.

"Look," Niggy said patiently. "When a fellow like myself gets mixed up with people like you he can't call the turns any more. He gets a lot of breaks, sure, but he has to take a lot of kicking around too, never knowing how soon the show is over. I got good and sick of that Gloucester setup, believe me, but I had to keep on till I was sure of what was next. I didn't even know what I was getting into with Nita, because we met first in the New School. It turns out she's your brother's wife, so most of the time she's busy doing the family social stuff and I'm hanging around somewhere waiting for a call. Then she thinks up a deal for me to teach Isabella art, and keeps me around, but it's a dog's life. Isabella has a dog's life, too, let me tell you."

"I shouldn't be surprised," Elsie murmured.

"Her father has her doing this, her mother has her doing that, and she can't do anything to suit them so she just sits in the Park all day or goes to double features with me, both of us in a jam, see, only she doesn't know about mine."

"She's no beauty, of course," Elsie observed.

Niggy shrugged.

"I don't care about women's looks," he said. "They all look the same to me in the long run. Anyway Isabella's got herself set on running away with me and getting married."

Elsie was aghast.

"I always knew you were a little devil, Niggy, but I must say I never dreamed you were capable of such a dirty trick as that! Marrying that poor girl just to get a living!"

"As if it was going to be any picnic for me!" Niggy retorted angrily. "She's the one that gets the bargain. She told me she never had any fun in her life till I came along. Does that mean I have any fun? I should say not! The whole damn family bores the living daylights out of me, especially that brother of yours, and Nita being so darn cutie all the time, pretending she doesn't know what the deal is because she's such a itty-bitty. The whole bunch makes me sick but I can't go back where I used to be, so I'm stuck."

Elsie pondered for a moment and an amusing idea struck her. Wharton had never tired of reminding her how much it cost the family to pay off her Baron and how he alone had saved the family honor. Someday she might be able to reply that the sacrifice was not all his.

"How much cash do you want and what would you do with it?" she asked.

The young man brightened.

"I could get by with a few hundred," he said eagerly. "I just want to clear out of town for a few months till I get some dames out of my hair. That jam between Nita and the kid is the toughest one but there's an old movie queen at the St. Moritz, too. I want some new territory. I'd like some fun, not this rat race."

"I went to the bank today so I've got some cash," Elsie said. "Maybe two hundred and some. And I'll give you a check."

Niggy was so excited he threw his arms around Brucie's neck and kissed him, an attention that made Brucie rise and draw back, growling ominously. Elsie went to the bedroom and got her wallet from the hatbox where she kept it. Two hundred and thirty, she counted out, and then carefully wrote out a check for three hundred. She always hated to give away cash outright, and on second thought took back three tens. Then she went back out and presented the money to her visitor. As soon as it touched his hands his cockiness returned.

"You're a good egg, Elsie," he stated. "I figured you wouldn't let me down, especially since you got me into this mess."

Little bastard, Elsie thought, highly delighted, reproaching her for giving him a leg up just as if she'd ruined his life! She decided she would invite him to share her *scampi* now that his business seemed settled, but she should have remembered that money in his hand always meant he would be out the door like a shot.

"You ought to be glad you have so many nice people as friends," she said primly.

"I only hope they lay off me for a while," Niggy said with his most impudent grin. "I'm fed up with nice people."

Elsie straightened up with a shocked expression.

"Ah, don't look so insulted, you know you're not nice people," Niggy exclaimed. For some reason, even though he had his money he was lingering by the door with a preoccupied air. What else did he want? Whatever it was she knew he wouldn't be long in telling her.

"I know a boat I could get for three thousand dollars," he announced. "Fellow in Boston. Wants me to come in with him taking fishing parties out, around Hyannis, summers, then take her down to the Keys winters. I'd be set for life, see."

Elsie saw. She sipped her drink reflectively, Niggy watching her out of the corner of his eye.

"Why not?" she said. "I'm going up to Boston tomorrow to settle some business with my mother. Meet me there and show me the boat. I'll be at her hotel."

Niggy jumped over a footstool to embrace her.

"Elsie, you're wonderful," he cried excitedly. "By George, if you were just a foot shorter I'd marry you tomorrow. Bye, now, till Boston."

He was gone, the door banged behind him. Elsie sat musing with a wry, doleful half smile that disturbed Brucie for he shook himself and ambled over to her, stood up and placed forepaws on her shoulders and licked her ear sympathetically.

"Dear Brucie, good old boy," Elsie said tenderly.

When she got up to put the shrimps in the broiler she saw that in his haste to leave the young man had left his cane. She looked at it incredulously and picked it up. It was Uncle's ram's-head cane, the very one she had feuded about with Wharton for so long, the one she had wanted for the express purpose of giving to Niggy.

"He got it anyway," Elsie marveled. Nita? Or Isabella? Whichever one had given it to him the idea struck Elsie as delicious and she felt more lonely than ever because there was no one with whom she dared share the joke. Presently she made up her mind and marched out to the hall and upstairs where she knocked on Jerry's door firmly. Getting no answer she knocked again and rang the buzzer. Then she tried the knob and to her surprise found the door was unlocked. She stepped inside and switched on the light.

The apartment was completely bare except for a barrel of junk in the middle of the bedroom. A pair of jet evening slippers were on top of the barrel and a crumpled magazine photograph of Collier McGrew.

. . . everybody needs a boat . . .

"I OUGHT to get in touch with Elsie," Jerry was admitting to her old friend Tessie over a jolly lunch at Louis and Armand's. "But I can't think of any way to make her understand."

"You can't even make me understand," Tessie said, shaking her head. "You say he never makes a pass?"

"Not what I'd call one," Jerry said. "A little kiss on the forehead, a little squeeze of the hand."

"He's not married, he's not queer, and he isn't a cripple, you say," pondered Tessie. "But he has you moved into his hotel, sets up your charge accounts again, gets you set with this TV job, and lets you have me stay with you. Crazy?"

Jerry laughed.

"No other signs of it," she said. "I thought when he had me meet his aunt that maybe he meant marriage but I count that out now. Sometimes I think he's rehabilitating me."

"I wouldn't stand for anybody doing social work on me," Tessie said. "Don't he ever say anything to give you a clue?"

"He likes me to tell him things about people," Jerry said. "I don't think he knows much about people, he's got such good manners he doesn't notice anything. But he gets a kick out of hearing inside stories about them. I guess I'm his court jester."

"What do you care so long as you've got no money worries?" Tessie said unconvincingly.

"Well he's managed to get me so hopped up about him that I don't know where I am," Jerry sighed. "I don't think he'd mind if I went out with other men but he has me so baffled I just stay home and wonder if he'll show up or telephone. How did I get into a fix like this?"

"You call this a fix," muttered Tessie. "There's just no limit to the kind of fixes a man can think up. Someday I'll tell you about my marriage."

Now that they were friends again they lunched together almost every day and reminded each other of old shared experiences, more fascinating now that they had nothing to lose by telling the truth. Tessie had quit the Lido and had dieted herself back into a modeling job with Jerry as her trainer. For the time being she was following Jerry's advice in everything just as Jerry had done with her when they first met. They needed each other again and after fifteen years of experience they could admit the need. Tessie had jumped from her playgirl career straight into a kind of super-respectable suburban life. It had to be super because $15,000-a-year husbands must live religiously on $25,000 in the excessively conventional manner demanded by wives who had been models, receptionists, or hat-check girls. After a few years of this struggle Tessie had run away with a jazz drummer, worked in the chorus line of whatever nightclub he played in, working her way down to the Lido in a determined effort to go to hell, after he left her. She was glad to start over again, however, after she and Jerry had compared notes, and she was shopping around now for a glossier respectability all over again.

"I never got over the kick of calling myself Mrs.," Tessie confessed. "Bill used to tell me I Missused myself so much everybody in Mount Kisco thought we couldn't possibly be married. I passed as Missus with Hotsy, too, of course, but it wasn't the same, not being on the level. Believe me, that's what I'm after now. Big church wedding, real wedding dress, big wedding ring, calling cards with a big Mrs. Somebody Junior the Fourth."

Jerry shook her head doubtfully.

"I can see the bridal suite on the *Ile de France* and the Do

Not Disturb sign on the hotel-room door," she said, "but the rest of it looks like a big bear trap to me. If you liked the life so much why did you knock yourself out to quit it?"

"I liked everything about it but Bill," Tessie said. "Him I just couldn't take. You don't know what it is to know everything a man's going to say. You get so you move heaven and earth to get the conversation around to where he won't have a chance to say it. That's marriage."

"Can we stand another brandy without falling on our facials?" Jerry asked, and answered the query by signaling the waiter for two more.

"You liked Bill well enough at first," Jerry said.

"Ever go out with a fellow who pretends he's conducting an orchestra every time any music plays?" Tessie demanded. "That was just one thing Bill did. When he was driving a car, making love, eating a steak—let him hear music and he's got to pretend he's Toscanini. It just embarrassed me to death. Maybe that's why I ran off with a drummer. At least Hotsy was a real drummer. But the real reason I left Bill was his damned boat."

It seemed that every time Bill met somebody he considered a valuable contact he got the conversation around to boats. Sailboats, motorboats, cabin cruisers, any kind of boat was his meat and he was always telling people if he had to choose between his old cruiser and Tessie he'd take the cruiser. The boredom, Tessie declared, of listening to him brag about his old *Bucephalus*, as he called her, and his troubles with the Miami Yacht Club and all the stuff about tides and bottom-scraping. If she was drinking it always ended with her making a scene and there was always somebody to take sides with Bill and say, "Aha, so the little lady is jealous of *Bucephalus*. No sporting blood, eh."

"I still don't see why you worked up such a grudge against his boat," Jerry said.

"His boat!" Tessie exclaimed scornfully. "He didn't have any boat, that was the whole trouble. Same as the orchestra. It was a pretend boat. Wait till you're married to a congenital liar and see what happens. Nobody else knows he's lying, so they end up hating you for trying to keep him off his favorite subject. I just hate boats, I'd have to say, and Bill would just give that jolly laugh of his and say, 'Believe it or not, Tess won't set foot on that boat to this day.' Funny thing, that was the only thing he ever bragged about, the dope."

It was fun having Tesise to go around with and it was fun being back uptown, safe in a beautifully impersonal hotel suite with a magic pencil that could buy anything from a hat to a Carey limousine. It was a more discreet, more cushioned life than that they had ever known together before but it was otherwise the same, and what Experience had taught them was that they liked it.

"You swear you won't ever tell anybody I was in the Lido line?" Tessie anxiously begged Jerry for the hundredth time. "I may tell a guy if I get matey with him but I don't want you to tell."

"I promise," Jerry said, "only you've got to promise not to tell that Collier McGrew isn't sleeping with me."

"I won't," Tessie said sympathetically. "I must say I simply don't dig it, though. He must like you, he does all this for you, he's not ashamed to take you places when he does come to town, he doesn't mind people talking—"

"Do they talk?" Jerry interrupted, startled.

"A big shot like that? Sure they do," Tessie said. "Everybody in the hotel and in the Fifth Avenue Credit Association knows who pays the bills even if he doesn't have a bed in your apartment. What's bad is that when a man doesn't put you to bed right at first he's likely to get over the urge."

"It kind of scares me," Jerry reflected. She wished she dared ask Elsie Hookley's advice but she couldn't get over the feeling that Elsie was bad luck for her. Just seeing Elsie would bring back the tense sick desperation of those days, the frantic hopes and fears, the daily failures, not to mention the danger of Elsie camping around her new home and scaring off McGrew. No, it had to be good-bye, Elsie, old dear.

"Why don't you go to an analyst about him?" Tessie suggested.

Jerry gave a short laugh.

"I'd feel like a fool showing up for psychoanalysis at this late date," she said. "I can save money by worrying. I figure it this way. He's a smart man, always too smart for the people he has to work with or for the people in his class, so he's always played a lone hand. He's like those birds, falcons, I guess, that peck out gazelles' eyes and throw the rest away. He pecks out just what he wants in people and throws the rest away. He likes my company when and where he likes it and he likes knowing he's trading that for something I want."

"Maybe he's got somebody else for the hay," Tessie said.

It was a disagreeable idea and Jerry winced.

"That would be my luck to get crazy over a man who's only crazy about my wizard brain," she said gloomily. "The gazelle's eyes falling in love with the hawk, that's about it."

They swirled their brandy glasses thoughtfully.

"How long do you give it, Jerry?" Tessie softly asked.

"I give myself forever, since I never felt like this before," Jerry said. "As for him—well, he might run for his life if I started something myself. Or maybe he expects me to. One of these days I'm afraid I'll take the chance."

"You've got that TV job, anyway," Tessie said. "What do you have to do, just line up celebrities for the show? Brother, who's that good-looking man looking at you?"

It was the producer of Jerry's show and he was only too eager to bring his good looks up for closer inspection. He had all sorts of program details to discuss with Jerry, including another drink around, and how about using this delightful young lady—

"Miss—I mean Mrs. Walton," Jerry said.

—in the fashion show. He had been admiring her carriage as she had darted in and out of the powder room and was sure she must have had show girl training. No? Well, it didn't matter. All he really wanted was her particular kind of statuesque beauty. He seemed so taken with Tessie and she with him that Jerry joined some friends at another table. In her absence the producer told Tessie he had heard Miss Dulaine was kept in great style by no less than Collier McGrew, and he wouldn't have dreamed she was the type, but maybe it was just Platonic. Tessie loyally assured him it was far from Platonic. They discovered they had both lived in Mount Kisco once, been married and divorced, and when Jerry rejoined them Tessie was telling all about the good times they used to have on her husband's cabin cruiser, the *Bucephalus*.

PART FIVE

. . . *view of the harbor* . . .

SOMEBODY had to take care of Marius' women before she
went stark mad, Cynthia Earle declared passionately. It was
true she had rashly opened the gates to trouble by sounding
off in print and on the air as a Marius collector, friend and
chief authority, but everybody else was doing the same. She
was better placed, however, so her telephone and doorbell
rang night and day with female supplicants. Gracie, Hedwig,
Jeannette, Natasha, Moira, Babsie—

Marius was the father of their children, their common-law
husband, their legal groom, their fiancé, anything that gave
them the right to protection or support from Marius admirers. Sometimes they even brought babies, and swore they had
made the trip on foot from suburban jungles or farther to
share in the great man's success, and nothing less than railroad fare home would budge them from Cynthia's handsome
home.

"Not a one of them attractive," Cynthia complained. "You
know how Marius used to sleep with people just out of morbid curiosity. And then Anna—my God—how was I to know
she was going to do a Rip Van Winkle? I admit I encouraged
her at first—I was so shocked she was still around—but I
never dreamed she'd come creeping up with her hat out every
time I turn around! Somebody's got to do something."

This was unfair, for Anna's technique had never been open
begging. She was a born poor relation and would not have
been a rich relation if she could because that would mean she
might have to do something for somebody else. No, in her
sweet, humble way she merely rang the doorbell of the big
house and collapsed on the doorstep, only sorry that it wasn't
snowing and that she didn't have her newborn babe in her
arms. As poor artist's neglected mate she followed these tactics shamelessly, according to Cynthia, and she had a way of
getting herself up in dusty, rusty clothes, with moldy fur col-
lars than which nothing looks poorer, and she would do this

no matter how many dresses you sent her, a deliberate trick so that the mere sight of her was a reproach to you. Here I am in rags, her pious smile said, and though I am not one to blame anyone I am sure you must be ashamed of that fine coat you're wearing.

Severgny, too, was regretting that the memorial exhibition was receiving so much publicity, for he too suffered from Anna and the increasing horde of Marius' avowed connections. Lawyers must be retained to investigate claims, bouncers must be placed strategically in the gallery to dispose of weird characters eager to make scenes. A long lost brother turned up on the West Coast smelling money from Marius' name in the papers, and was only brushed off by newspaper men discovering Marius' father living alone on a New Hampshire farm.

"Neither of those boys was any doggone good," said the old man. "Both of 'em run away from home soon as they was old enough to run, wild as they come, just like the Purvises, that's their mother's folks. Willard, he's the oldest, run off with a carnival one day at milking time, the way he would, that one, and Marius was always fooling around with his paints even after he was a big boy, anything to get out of work. I knowed they'd end up in trouble, but nobody's going to take my little farm away from me now to pay for their funerals or bail or whatever it is."

Nothing would convince the old man that Marius' new fame was on the up and up.

"Those New Yorkers wouldn't stop at anything," he said dourly. "It's some trick to make me look after his family. I told that woman of his to stop pestering me years ago and this is her way of getting back at me. I won't have any part of it and you can tell that good-for-nothing Willard for me to keep his nose out of it too, if he don't want to get in the same fix as his brother."

From a San Antonio art dealer who had made the trip to Marius' last known home in Mexico had come a small package of all his landlady there could find of his belongings, at least all that she had been unable to sell or find use for. These consisted of a notebook in which recipes, restaurant addresses hither and yon, telephone numbers, notes for future sketching grounds, bus schedules, and other odds and ends were jotted down; a dozen dunning letters forwarded from as many other addresses; some snapshots of children, probably his, in varying stages of growth; a roll of used film that the landlady had been too thrifty either to throw away or have developed. The letters were from Trina and her lawyer, all written after Marius' death and obviously unaware of it. They indicated that Trina had taken the children and walked out in a huff three years before in Vancouver, returned soon afterward repentant only to find Marius gone. The letters swung from her begging to be allowed to follow him and look after him wherever he was to wild denunciations and threats. The lawyer Trina had managed to hire as tracer and his stern promises of punishments to be visited as soon as the lost one returned to his family were certainly enough to keep a man on the run. At any rate it established that Trina was still on earth somewhere far away, or had been three months ago, and was likely to loom on the scene one of these days.

Something would certainly have to be done, Dalzell Sloane had agreed, but it took a lot of arguing to get Ben to see it that way.

"We've got to do it before Severgny or Cynthia start something," Dalzell kept insisting, and finally Ben assented.

He was still grousing about giving up a date with the young art student he had collected at Cynthia's party when they took off on the ferry from the Battery.

"Whatever we find out from Anna will make things worse," he prophesied.

"Not if we find it out before the others," Dalzell said. "Whatever it is we can put the lid on it—and her—before Trina shows up and blows up the whole apple cart."

"Women are bloodhounds," Ben said moodily. "Once they get their hooks in a man they can sniff him out the rest of his life across oceans and graves. Those old hooks have just got to get back in. You don't understand that because you always managed to clear out before they got their hooks into you."

Dalzell didn't say anything. There had been hooks all right, but emotional ones only that hurt the more for not hanging on. As for women sniffing out their prey it struck him that Ben himself had been offering his own persecutors the scent whenever they withdrew the hooks. Certainly the letters coming to Ben from his Southwestern ladies couldn't have found him so easily at Gerda Cahill's apartment, where he and Dalzell were staying, without being led. Ever since their fortunes had picked up, Ben had been restless, homesick Dalzell suspected, for his old familiar ties. We get sick of our clinging vines, he thought, but the day comes when we suspect that the vines are all that hold our rotting branches together. One without vines, like himself, knew all too well one's dry rot and longed for the old parasitical leaves to mask and bind it.

"What say we stay on the ferry and go right back to Manhattan?" Ben proposed as the boat bumped into the St. George slip. "What do you expect to find out anyway?"

"We'd just be thrashing the whole thing over every day till we found out the truth—or it found us out," Dalzell said doggedly, aware that he was irritating Ben with his obstinacy, but then Ben was constantly disappointing him, too, by his belligerent self-interest. They had expected each other to be not so much the friend they remembered as the creature made up of parts they needed most and it seemed unfair that the person had developed quite differently. Their first joy in discovering bonds of mutual necessity had changed subtly to an aggrieved surprise that their aims were so different. Their disappointment in each other was the familiar discovery of age: the old friend of his youth has failed him because he fails to give him back his youth.

At the St. George station Ben followed Dalzell to the Tottenville train which was waiting. It was midday, a time evidently not popular with Tottenville travelers for the only other passengers were a stout old German-looking couple laden with bundles, and a harassed young mother in a fishy-looking leopard coat with many glittering ornaments, twin girls in pink-flowered Easter outfits clinging to her knees and a fat little Hopalong Cassidy asleep in her arms, one boot hooked into the stirrup made by her purse handle.

"I hate this island," Ben said, looking out the window as the sleepy little villages slipped by like pictures through an ancient stereoscope, ivy-grown station shanties, old corner taverns with pointed roofs, winding roads with weather-beaten houses whose gardens were already turning green, the meadows and village four corners seeming unchanged through the centuries. "I know we used to claim this trip reminded us of the one from Paris out to St.-Germain-en-Laye—but I only came here when I was dead broke or in trouble, and you know how you blame a place for that."

Dalzell was beginning to feel excited and a little afraid. He would not admit that the expedition might be a mistake for no matter what trouble came of it the risk must be taken. Now that they were nearing Prince's Bay where the old German couple were getting off, he allowed himself to think of the possible consequences to himself and Ben.

"I agree that Anna has something up her sleeve all right," Ben said. "Anybody could tell that, but is it something we want to find out? We certainly don't want anybody shaking our sleeves, either."

"I don't think Cynthia suspects Anna. She hates her too much to give her any credit for mischief," Dalzell said. "But Severgny does. We've got to check before he does."

"I'd rather have Trina to deal with than Anna," Ben said. "At least there was never any doubt about where she stood, roaring all over the place like a storm trooper. But Anna was always changing her style, laying low and biding her time, sneaking up on you, sniveling and whining till she got what she was after. You can't lick the Anna type and we're fools to even tangle with her."

The young mother and her little family and the German couple had gotten off and they were the only passengers left by the time they got to Tottenville, the end of the line.

"The end of the world!" Ben muttered, looking around the station platform, but Dalzell felt a wave of old affection for this quaint remnant of a long-ago America. The Jersey shore was hardly a ferry's length away and the old roofless ferry was waiting to cross just as it always was while to his left the cobbled street led up the hill and around and the peaceful old houses followed the curve of the bay, their wide lawns sprawling down to water's edge. If the old Queens house had given them shelter and hiding in their bad times, the Island hereabouts had offered a healing vision of long ago to wipe out today. On summer days Dalzell had wandered through these roads, reminded of the old midwest lanes of his boyhood and the little foreign villages of now. For a moment of grateful memories he forgot Anna and their mission till Ben reminded him.

"I can't figure out how Anna happened to land in this territory," Ben pondered. "Sure, she used to hear Marius and the rest of us talk about it but what tidal wave threw her up here at this late date?"

A laundry truck from the Jersey ferry came up the hill and Dalzell flagged it as it turned, saving them the hour's walk to the old brewery where they were heading. It had gone out of business years ago but the building had stayed and only burned down last year, the driver informed them. Yet one of the pictures Anna had produced of Marius' had been of an old brewery horse grazing around the charred remains of the old brewery. "Home," the picture was titled in Marius' hand. The sight of this picture, offered by Anna as an old Marius that night at Cynthia's studio, was what had shocked Dalzell into action. He and Ben had the same sudden suspicion but Ben, aware of where it might lead, had wanted to forget it.

"All right, let's say Marius couldn't paint that picture unless he'd seen the place within the last year and that means he's still alive and maybe Anna's hiding him out here," Ben had said. "It also means he doesn't want to be found out. Why should we be the ones to track him down if he wants to be dead—that is, if he really isn't dead?"

Dalzell struggled to find a logical answer. All he knew was that for a cherished old friend to wish to be dead meant an unbearable wretchedness that must be alleviated. He had been lonely himself and he couldn't let old Marius suffer the same quiet terror if he could help it.

"It isn't just that he wants to be considered dead," Ben had argued. "It's that a whole industry has been piling up on his death. All these Marius worshippers only love a dead Marius and if it turns out he's alive they not only will lose money but will make his life worse than ever. And what about you and me? Do we confess to fixing up and painting a few bogus Mariuses, then bow out into Sing Sing? or maybe they have worse dungeons for artists than for axe killers."

"That's what we may be able to head off," Dalzell had said. "You know how Anna roused Severgny's suspicions right off claiming those new canvases were old ones from twenty years back. Then she gets Cynthia's back up. So both Severgny and Cynthia are going to check up on Anna and they're likely to find out more than they even dreamed of."

Ben reluctantly conceded the danger of this. But supposing Marius was still alive, what made Dalzell think he would not resent his old friends tracking him down?

Because, Dalzell said, of that one picture he had sent in by Anna, of the tired old brewery horse back on the ruins of his old stable.

"Marius called it 'Home,' " Dalzell said, "and I had the feeling that he meant it as a message to us."

The house was the only one for miles on the weed-grown road off the highway from the old brewery. It was that gaunt unpainted shingle house, barest symbol of home, often found on acres given over to truck farming, chickens, or temporary money-making where all funds go into the produce, not the worker. The project, long abandoned, left the husks of failure scattered over the field—unfinished sheds piled with rusted machine parts, post holes dug, broken-down chicken coops, empty paint buckets, scraps of tar paper. A few scraggly hens fluttered through the bushes and a collie was chasing a squawking rooster around the house. The mailbox at the head of the long lane was marked "Jensen," Anna's latest married name.

"Cut it out, Davey," a man's voice called out as the collie dropped his rooster chase to lunge vociferously toward the intruders.

"Marius," Dalzell breathed. "Ben, it *is* Marius."

"Either he doesn't know us or he isn't very glad to see us," Ben muttered.

"Come around the back way," Marius' voice came out.

The weary tone dampened their sudden excitement and they walked on hesitantly, wondering why they were here, frightened of what they might find. They saw him sitting in a low armchair by the kitchen stove, a blanket over his lap, a man indeed back from the grave. In the first shock of seeing him no one spoke. All that was left of the great ruddy-faced Marius was a gray skeleton with sunken blue eyes, deep lines rutting the hollow cheeks, the wide mouth drawn back in a bleak effort to smile, the hands, deeply veined, clutching the arms of his chair as if bracing against an expected attack. Dalzell's heart turned, thinking of what Marius must have been through to drain him of everything but fear.

"We got you!" Dalzell cried out, but he felt the trembling fear still in Marius' handclasp.

"You bastards!" Marius laughed weakly. "I should have known better than to trust Anna."

The kitchen was almost bare but they found a stool and chair and drew them up to the stove.

"It wasn't Anna. It was the brewery horse," Dalzell eagerly explained. "It worried us. If those last pictures were yours then we knew you had been in this section within the last year. And if somebody else had imitated you they were doing a better job than Ben and I have been doing and that worried us even more."

"What?" shouted Marius, and his laughter relieved the tension between them. "You rascals. Can't a man trust anybody even here in heaven?"

"At least you admit you're dead," Ben said. "Dalzell and I were afraid you'd try to palm yourself off as alive and bring your prices down. If you do I warn you it won't be worth our while doing any more of your work."

Marius was laughing weakly, brushing the tears from his gaunt cheeks.

"No sir, by God, I'm dead and I'm going to stay dead!" he declared and motioned Dalzell to bring out the bottle of bourbon handily sitting by the pump in the kitchen sink. "I never had it so good. But I can't trust anybody for long— Anna—even you fellows. Right now I'd like to just be an old brewery horse jogging home to graze till I hit the glue works, but it seems I'm a highwayman with a price on my head."

"How long had you been dead before you found out about it?" Ben asked.

"A good six months," Marius answered. He lit a cigarette Ben offered and looked for a moment from one to the other. "I guess I can tell you about it since you got me anyway."

"You've got us, too, don't forget," Dalzell reminded him. "We're all three in this together."

"I'd been living one jump ahead of the sheriff for years,"
Marius said. "Creditors, fights, dames, then borrowing this
guy's car—that is, without his knowing it— Well, I had about
every bone in my body broken when I wrecked it. The Indians
that found me dosed me with every herb and poison known
to man until all my livers and lights damn near blew up, but
I was afraid to go near any villages for fear I'd get arrested for
stealing the car or maybe some more of Trina's bloodhounds
might catch me. The Indians looked after me but I got stir-
crazy, sick of Mexico. I would have given my soul for one
hour at the Café Julien. An oil truck came along bound for
Acapulco and I hitched on and shipped out for New York on
a freighter as dishwasher. I'd heard from Anna a while back
that she'd got a farm here on insurance from some merchant
marine husband and I figured she'd take me in. I'd planned
before that to hide out in Rio but I thought Tottenville is further from civilization than Rio. I headed out here as soon as
the ship got in and sure enough there was old Anna, sweet
and silly as ever, broke and full of crazy ideas for making a
fortune—dog kennels, chickens, tearooms, you know."

"Did she know you were supposed to be dead?" Dalzell
asked.

"Sure, she was the one that told me. Seems she'd been trying to figure out some way of making something out of it, if
Trina wasn't going to beat her to it, and she was a little put
out when I showed up," he said. "I'd had pneumonia and
flu and malaria and everything else with the Indians and my
lungs and heart were pretty well shot, so I told her I wouldn't
last long and if she'd let me stay here I'd play dead for her.
No skin off her bottom. I did some pictures she could take in
and sell. Lousy. I've lost the touch somehow. It made me sore
she sold them so fast. But she saw being dead made me worth
a hell of a lot more to her so she managed to keep quiet. But
you know Anna. She'll botch it up. What I want to know is
what do I do next?"

"What do you do? Why, you come right back to New York
with Ben and me," Dalzell cried out impetuously. "Everybody will be so glad to have you back you'll get well in no
time. You stay with us in Gerda's apartment and we'll all work
together. We'll have a big celebration at the Julien."

"If I could sneak into the Julien for just one drink—" Marius said. And then he was shaking his head. He sighed, mopped his forehead with his handkerchief, then reached for his whiskey glass with trembling fingers.

"I can't risk it," he said. "I don't think I can take it any more." He grinned wryly. "Being dead has spoiled me. Gone soft."

"You're safe now, Marius, don't you see? You're a great man," Dalzell argued earnestly. "You've got the world on your side at last, and nothing to worry about. You should hear how they talk. Why, I promise you—"

He stopped at the skeptical expression on Ben's face and Marius' quizzical smile.

"You can't promise me anything and Ben knows it if you don't," Marius said quietly. "The minute I come to life I'm in trouble again."

"How about the rest of us?" Ben asked Dalzell. "People will think you and I cooked up the whole trick just to make money. They won't just accuse us of passing off bogus Marius for our own profits, they'll get us for hiding a fugitive—if Marius still is in trouble with police."

"I'm always in trouble with police." Marius shrugged. "But don't worry about signing my stuff because I'll stand up for it if the pinch comes. Just let's leave things the way they are."

"How?" Dalzell pondered.

"The most wonderful thing that ever happened to me was finding out I was dead that morning," Marius said. "No troubles, nothing to worry about but the cost of living. Damn it, why did you fellows have to spoil it? I always knew Trina and bill collectors would manage to drill a pipeline straight into my grave but I did think my old pals would respect the sleep of the dead."

"What did I tell you, Dalzell?" Ben nodded toward Dalzell, who felt helpless and defeated. Ben had been right, maybe, that they were safer to leave things as they were but when a lie was involved there was never any safety. Certainly with Anna as sole protector of the secret there was none. Through his mind there flitted all the possible reactions to the news that Marius was returned from the dead and right back in New York. There would be the initial amazement, the cries of joy, the eager questions, and then the slow mounting sense of outrage.

"If that isn't exactly like Marius!" he could hear Cynthia, Okie, Elsie Hookley, the dealers, all the old friends cry out indignantly. "That *would* be his idea of a fine practical joke, letting us go out on a limb for him, making fools of ourselves, while he has a good time laughing at us! How dare he! Here we are, knocking ourselves out to make him immortal and trying to forget what a big nuisance he always was, always broke, always in trouble, always having to be bailed out or nursed or helped! And now he pulls this! Believe me, I don't want to even see the man again."

In the silence he knew that this was in Ben's mind, too, and maybe in Marius'. Marius was looking out the window.

"I want you to go before Anna gets back from the city," he said. "She's gone down to New York for supplies for me, if I can ever get to working right again. I won't tell her you were here or that you know."

"You've seen the stuff they're writing about you, of course," Ben said. "Right up there with Titian and the old masters, my boy."

Marius threw up his hands.

"If I hadn't known it before I would have known I was dead when I read some of that bilge!" he said, and then shrugged. "What am I talking about? It was what I believed about myself. It was what made life worth living until—well, all of a sudden it—whatever it is—was gone. I was dead, all right. I couldn't figure it out. I couldn't paint. Me! Thought at first the damn harpies had killed it."

"Maybe too much liquor," Ben said.

Marius looked at him, astonished, and poured himself a new drink.

"There *can't* be too much liquor!" he said. "I decided maybe I was just under-drunk. And under-womanned. You know how a new dame can give you a fresh start. As soon as I'm well enough to light out I'll get a new one. Maybe that'll do it."

Ben and Dalzell exchanged an uneasy look.

"We've got some money for you," Dalzell said. "It's yours."

"Anna's brought me more than I ever had in my life," Marius said. "I've got it stashed away. In a couple of days I'll get the hell out of here, take the ferry to Perth Amboy and get a ship out of Hoboken for Greece, maybe Corsica. I got friends there. Always could work there, remember? If I don't get myself back there then count me out for good."

He threw off the blanket and got to his feet.

"See, I can get around," he said. "Damn it, now I've got to. I'll leave Anna some stuff to sell and she'll send me some dough. I'll be staying with Sophie, if she's still there and still loves me."

Dalzell pulled his wallet out with the last sixty dollars he had gotten for a Marius sketch.

"Here's a part payment," he said. "You let us know where to send any more we get."

"*If* we get—" Ben amended under his breath. "Look, Marius, do you mean you're going to let those dealers clean up over your dead body?"

"Looks like that's the only way they can do it," Marius said. He drummed on the table restlessly. "Now will you do something for me? Beat it and forget you saw me."

"Marius, couldn't you—couldn't we—" Dalzell began but with Marius and Ben looking at him whatever he wanted to offer fled from his brain. He felt angry that the love and warmth he felt for both his friends could not even reach them or do them any good, only the sixty dollars could help. He was bitterly disappointed that Marius alive, should destroy his dream of him, and he was angry with Ben for having been right.

"Come on, Sloane," Ben said. "Marius will let us know when he needs us. Let him stay dead now."

"Thanks, Ben," Marius said. "I'll do the same for you."

They heard him calling in the dog as they walked down the lane. At the road Dalzell stood still for a moment, looking back. A fog had rolled in from the bay and blurred out the meadow so the house seemed suspended in a ghostly haze, its two upstairs windows bleak eye sockets, its front porch railing the teeth in a death's head.

"What can we do?" Dalzell murmured.

"Nothing," Ben said gloomily. "Go back right where we

were when we first heard he was dead. Forget about today. Will you have to tell Cynthia the truth?"

No, Dalzell would not tell Cynthia, he said. He did not intend to tell Cynthia the truth about anything, he thought, for the truth was what she must be protected from.

"Funny, now that we've seen him alive, I'm convinced he really is dead," Ben said, puzzled.

They were silent walking across the meadow to the Hylan Boulevard bus, depressed with the certainty that they would never see Marius again.

. . . *olive branch in family tree* . . .

WHARTON sat stiffly upright in Elsie's cozy-looking club chair whose new slip cover cruelly disguised its broken coil springs all eager to snap at the sitter. He was going crazy. He *was* crazy! The curse of the Hookleys was upon him. He would be put away, probably in the very retreat his uncle and two cousins were patronizing—if that was the word and if they were Hookleys it was indeed the word—at this very minute. Poor Nita! How she would cry at being forced to certify him. Or *would* she cry? How did he know what might go on in that pretty but increasingly foreign little head?

He looked at Elsie, trying to keep his eyes from the corner behind her. Maybe it would be Elsie who would be the one to certify him. He was certain Elsie wouldn't like it one bit. She wouldn't like being deprived of her chief sport. It alarmed him that he could almost hear her forthright voice answering what he was thinking even while she was really saying something quite different.

"Wharton crazy? Nonsense!" It was exactly what she would say, of course. "He is obstinate, selfish, greedy, intolerably snobbish and in almost every way a monster but I will not have my brother called crazy."

"—must say I am immensely flattered at this sudden interest in my little home," Elsie was really saying.

Wharton drew a deep breath for strength and twisted around in his chair so his back would be to the corner, wincing at the punishment from the chair as he did so. No doubt Elsie had had the chair made especially for him. There! he thought in horror, I've got to stop *thinking*, that's all!

"My dear Elsie," he said tenderly, "you seem to regard a simple brotherly visit as an invasion of your privacy. I happened to be lunching at the Café Julien and thought it a good opportunity to see your flat and perhaps hear what news you brought from Boston. Do I really seem like such a *monster* to you?"

The very word popping out of his mouth upset him again and before he could stop himself he had looked at the corner by the fireplace and seen it again, or thought he was seeing it —the damnable ram's-head cane of Uncle Carpenter's. This time he stared at it steadily to make it go away, as you do when seeing double, but the cane would not go away. Impetuously he jumped up and walked over to it, touched it, more frightened than ever to find it real, the emerald eyes leering at him. If Elsie would only say something that would make it real, if it was real, or a hallucination if it was hallucination.

"I see Uncle's cane is in mint condition," he forced himself to say casually.

"Have you any objection?" Elsie snapped. "I suppose you think of me as a complete vandal, unworthy of the family precious treasures."

"No, no," Wharton protested. It was a real cane and he was not crazy but he'd opened himself up for a row and Elsie was raring to get at it so he'd have to find the explanation of how the cane got there in some more devious way.

"What about Mother?" Wharton asked firmly, sitting down in a kinder chair. "How did you find her and did she know you?"

"Of course she knew me," Elsie said coldly. "She simply refused to admit it. Mother is an imbecile, I grant you, but no more so now than she ever was, just more cunning, that's all."

"Perhaps she should be in an institution," Wharton said.

"What would you call that hotel?" Elsie answered sarcastically. "No, Wharton, Mother's act has never fooled me for one minute. She was always bored with her family and the pose of having no memory is very convenient for her, just as it was convenient for Father to pretend to be stone deaf."

This sort of talk from Elsie usually irritated Wharton to distraction but today he decided to be amused instead of getting Elsie's back up before he found out what he wished.

"Perhaps you're right," he conceded graciously. "Childhood is the happiest time, after all, so why shouldn't she want to spend her last years in a return to that happy state?"

"I never found anything happy in childhood and neither did you," Elsie stated pugnaciously. "I don't think I ever saw a smile on your face till the day you were allowed to clip your own coupons."

Wharton counted ten inwardly and went on again.

"I was surprised your visit was so short," he said. "You had told me, you recall, that you were considering opening the old house, and even making it your home again. I made no objections, you know. I didn't think it would be a wise move, for Boston is so changed—"

"Ridiculous!" Elsie said flatly.

"What I mean is that your old friends are scattered and even if you have some I don't know, still Boston does not have the—er—relaxed social life you enjoy here in New York. Besides you used to hate Boston."

That remarkably benign tone made Elsie look fixedly at her brother who was even bestowing a pat on Brucie's head, an unaccustomed compliment that made Brucie look questioningly at his mistress, then withdraw to a spot beside her where he too could watch the caller.

"I don't hate Boston," Elsie explained impatiently. "It's just little things I can't stand. The way the banks and restaurants and department stores are all like nursing homes, the very tone of voice the clerks have is that baby-talk you use on mental cases. 'Oh dear oh dear,' " she mimicked the soothing hushed voice, " 'we've spilled our nice gravy on our nice little jabot,' and 'aren't we the naughty girl overdrawing our nice little checking account.' "

"So you did go to the Trust and see Mr. Wheeling!" Wharton said. She must have got Mother to sign something or give her something, he thought, and in his exasperation he forgot his plan to use the honeyed approach but plunged to the heart of the matter. "I shall have the details of that later on, of course. What I should like explained, however, is just why you should purchase a boat and why you should be brazenly running all over Boston with a man who appears from all reports to be barely half your age. Why must you drag the Hookley name again through the mud—oh you don't care, I know that,—it's my wife and daughters who suffer. Actually bringing this bounder, whoever he may be, into my mother's hotel, foisting him on her as guest—"

"She cried whenever he started to go," Elsie said defensively. "Mother is lonely and she likes new people even if she just babbles."

"Elsie!" Wharton pointed his finger at her so menacingly that Brucie let out a yowl. "Carry on your routs or whatever they are in Greenwich Village where such things are common but I insist that you behave yourself in the places where my poor daughters have to bear the shame. As if poor Isabella's first year out hasn't been difficult enough as it is—"

His sister's voice tried to cut in twice before he would pause.

"Will you please listen to me now?" Elsie haughtily commanded. "It seems my good heart has run away with me again and what I did for you out of pure family pride only makes you abuse me the more."

"Now what?" Wharton exclaimed, knowing too well that no matter what deviltry he might suspect in his sister she was certain to have perpetrated something far worse.

"I merely was buying off a young man to save your daughter's good name, thank you very much," Elsie said, rising with a grand air and pulling her slightly soiled green quilted house robe about her. "You were so busy bullying Isabella about and scolding her for not doing the traditional things you never saw what was under your nose. The poor girl was being driven to running away with one of Nita's admirers."

Wharton's face paled and then the orchard shades came out on his sensitive nose, indicating the emotional confusion her words had aroused. He said nothing and Elsie's momentary glee in her advantage melted into sisterly concern.

"It's all right now, Wharton, dear," she said solicitously. "I saw what was going on and I felt it my duty to handle the situation as I saw best for the honor of the family. You say I have no proper family feeling but I'm very fond of Isabella in spite of your fears of my bad influence. I've had a little more worldly experience than you, Wharton, and I knew the man was not right for her. So—I sent him away. I shan't tell you the sum of money involved but then money doesn't mean as much to me as it does to you."

Wharton sat rigidly, staring at the cane unseeingly. Elsie, a little alarmed at this unprecedented collapse, started to speak again but he rose and lifted his hand wearily.

"Don't tell me any more now, Elsie," he begged. "I can't quite take it all in at once."

He shook out his kerchief and wiped his forehead in silence. Impressed into some sort of first aid Elsie clopped over to the bar in her wooden-soled sandals and poured out a brandy, turned to hand it to Wharton, but on second thought decided she needed one herself and poured another.

Wharton gulped the restorative. Pictures rose in his mind of the monkeylike little dark man at the restaurant wearing his old topcoat, the same little man in Nita's drawing room, the ram's-head cane, Isabella's constantly tear-stained, red-nosed lugubrious face, Nita coming in from one of her confounded culture classes with the "fellow student," the living room doors closing on the cozy laughter of the two scholars, Isabella peering in the library door and excitedly whispering, "Who's in there with Mother, Father? Can I go in?" These were the pictures but he couldn't make them fit together into any kind of meaning, and he knew he didn't want to. It was better to accept Elsie's meaning.

"I'm afraid I haven't been entirely fair to you, Elsie, my dear," he murmured. "I didn't realize that in exposing yourself to all this talk you were only saving Isabella."

"Of course you didn't realize," Elsie readily agreed. "You never do."

But Wharton did not react to the needle. It was no more sport than playing with a dead mouse, Elsie reflected, feeling unjustly deprived. There was something almost obscene, she felt, in Wharton sitting there all slumped over, letting her take cracks at him without striking back. It simply wasn't sporting. Quitting the game with the highest score just as his opponent has gotten warmed up for victory. Tears came to Elsie's eyes, and these Wharton saw. He got to his feet and patted her on the shoulder.

"I appreciate this, Elsie," he said, stiff-upper-lipping. "We'll talk it over another time."

We certainly will, Elsie thought, watching him make his way wearily out the door, we'll talk it over every time you bring up all you ever did for me, and you won't have a word to say.

But it wouldn't be the fun, she sighed, it would be just like losing a brother.

. . . *the café had three exits* . . .

DALZELL was having a *mazagran* in the Julien. There was small reason for him to be feeling content but he was, and he thought it was probably due to some basic masochism in his character that made surrender a relief if not a pleasure. He was down to his last twenty dollars, he had no idea where the next was coming from, but this was a state of affairs that seemed home to him. It was a pity that Ben was still angry with him, accusing him of messing up their prospects before they had gotten what they might out of them. He thought Ben was probably right: he *was* foolishly romantic and sentimental and it didn't do Marius or anybody else any good. But a person had to do the things he had to do.

"Mind if I join you, Mr. Sloane?"

It was the young fellow from *City Life* standing beside him. Dalzell motioned to the seat opposite and Briggs sat down heavily, placing a fat briefcase on the chair beside him.

"Don't let me forget that," he said. "Have you ever noticed that you can tell a person's looking for a job because they carry a fat briefcase? Like new wallets. You don't catch a fellow with lots of cash carrying a brand-new wallet."

He threw down a very new leather wallet on the table contemptuously.

"When you see a man trying to build up his morale with that sort of front you can tell his morale is pretty low," he said.

"Yours is low, I take it." Dalzell smiled.

"So-so," said Briggs gloomily. "I suppose you heard I lost my job, right after the Marius piece came out. It seems *City*

Life hired me because I didn't know anything about art.
Seems they like the simple average citizen approach to everything—science, medicine, books, everything. They only use
the intellectual angle on sports and business. Well I started
out fine from their point of view, then I had to interview so
many artists and museum people that I got too smart. I was
using fancy words and technical phrases. Would you believe it
that six months ago I thought *gouache* was some sort of
Spanish cowboy?"

"You should have kept it that way," Dalzell said sympathetically.

Briggs signaled Karl and ordered Scotch.

"It's not so bad because I had saved some money—four
hundred and ten bucks," he said. "I figured that what I
learned about painting would have cost me a couple of hundred in school, too, so that's something. And finding out I
was really a writer would have cost me maybe a thousand
bucks worth of psychoanalysis. Oh, I'm ahead."

"You don't have to take care of a family, then," Dalzell
said.

Briggs shook his head.

"I'm not married yet but if things get tough I may have
to," he said rather gloomily. "Oh I don't mean I'd marry a
rich wife—not that I see anything wrong in your marrying
Mrs. Earle as the papers say. I guess you've known her a long
time and you aren't doing it for money anyway."

"No," Dalzell answered, embarrassed. "It isn't that."

"That's good, because I've noticed men who marry for
money have trouble getting their hands on any cash," Briggs
said. "They're always borrowing from fellows like me who
have to work. They get a lot of credit on the strength of their
wife's credit but that's what hangs them because they can't
get their mitts on spending money."

"Thanks for the warning," Dalzell said.

"A girl with a small steady salary is the thing," Briggs said.
"This girl I know, Janie. I've moved into her apartment and
we can keep going on her paycheck while I work on this
novel I'm planning and wait for a job. It works out fine like
this. I tell her marriage would only tie her down."

Someone was waving from the doorway and Briggs nudged

Dalzell. Okie came toward their table, sweeping a hand over his long white pompadour.

"May I offer good wishes, Sloane?" he said pompously. "I just left Cynthia at the Gallery cocktail party and she was kicking up her heels and acting like a child bride. What in the world made you give in to her?"

"You seem to think I was drugged," Dalzell said, nettled, even though he had known he would have to grow more armor than ever now.

"You've hardly seen her for years and you hardly know the same people any more," Okie went on pleasantly. "You've never been married and you've no idea how difficult Cynthia makes things for her husbands. I do. I've seen them all. And they were all rich and influential in their own right, too."

"Maybe that was the trouble," Briggs put in.

"If I'd known Cynthia really wanted to get married after being through the mill five times already—" Okie began and paused meditatively.

"Only four," Dalzell corrected him.

Okie looked from Dalzell to Briggs, but Briggs did not take his briefcase off the chair since he wanted Okie to go away and let him continue discussing his own affairs.

"What happened to Ben Forrester?" Okie asked abruptly.

"He went back West," Dalzell said. "He found he hated New York now and he couldn't paint here."

"Was he really good?" Briggs asked.

"Ben Forrester and Dalzell Sloane here paved the way for half the successful young painters today," Okie declared generously. "Maybe they didn't have too much success but what they tried out was the fertilizer for the talent blooming today. How do you like that for appreciation, Sloane?"

"If it's a trade-last I can't think of anything to equal being called fertilizer," Dalzell said.

Okie burst into a loud haw-haw and decided to leave on the note of good humor since neither of them had invited him to sit down. There seemed to be no other table free and he put on his hat.

"This place is getting awfully common," he said fretfully. "No wonder they talk of converting it into apartments. I prefer the Florida Bar nowadays myself."

He clapped his Homburg over his locks and sauntered proudly out.

"I think you're wrong in your figuring, Sloane," he turned to call back from the door. "I think you're Number Six."

. . . the farewell banquet . . .

BY eight o'clock it began to be apparent to even the dullest tourist that this was no ordinary night at the Café Julien. Guests who had dropped in for a single apéritif, en route to an inexpensive dinner at San Remo or Grand Ticino's in the Italian quarter, stayed on through curiosity drinking up their dinner money very slowly, ordering a new round just as importunate newcomers were about to snatch their table from under them. They could see important-looking elderly gentlemen in dinner clothes peep in the café door, then proceed onward into the private dining room at the rear. It must be the Silurian annual banquet, someone hinted, the Silurians being newspapermen who had been in the trade twenty-five years.

"How could anybody afford to dine here if he's been in newspaper work that long?" argued others. It was a dinner honoring Romany Marie, or Barney Gallant, or survivors of the Lafayette Escadrille, others said, recalling similar occasions in the past. It was a banquet of real estate men commemorating their grief in selling the Julien to a mysterious concern rumored to be about to change it into apartments. This last theory was gaining credence when the unfamiliar sight of Monsieur Julien himself gave old-timers the clue to what was going on. Yes, it was a dinner of the Friends of Julien, an association of gourmets of great distinction, and what was more sensational was the whisper that this was their farewell dinner. Photographers from newspapers and magazines were setting up impressive-looking apparatus in every corner and mousy little people who inhabited the cheap little rooms upstairs and were never seen in the glamorous café suddenly showed their frightened little faces at the door. Hoff Bemans, leading his guest panelists into the café for a rewarding drink at anybody else's expense, spotted Dalzell Sloane and beckoned his men to crowd around that table, so that when Briggs returned from the men's room he could scarcely squeeze in.

"By George, I've done it again!" Hoff exclaimed proudly. "I didn't even know the Café was going to go out of business and here I stumbled right into the big night. So that's the old master, Julien himself!"

Monsieur Julien was a gay bachelor of sixty who made enough from the café bearing his name to live and usually dine at the Plaza. He was the last of a formidable dynasty of French chefs, inheriting the great reputation without the faintest culinary interest. But after a youthful struggle against the public insistence that all Juliens must be cooks he had surrendered. Very well, he would accept the unearned but profitable mantle. Cooking contests, cook books, food columns, canned dainties, all must have his name as sponsor. Wherever he went he was questioned about this dish or that sauce. At first he had sighed candidly, "I assure you if I had a pair of eggs and a greased griddle on the stove I would still starve to death." Later on in his career he answered more archly, "Ah, if I were to tell you how I make that dish then you would be Julien and what would I be?"

His grandfather had been proprietor of the famous Julien's in Paris and had founded the New York branch early in the century. All over the world there were people who quivered at the name. Even those who had never tasted *escargots Julien* quickly realized they must pretend they knew, and would sniff the air and paw the ground like truffle hounds, sighing, "Ah, Julien's!" Having put by a nice fortune paying French salaries and charging American prices the old gentleman was finally done in by the shrewdness of his equally thrifty employees who sold furniture and dishes under his very nose and found many convenient ways of rewarding themselves. The Paris place vanished in World War One and the New York café had been about to give up in 1929 when a group of wealthy gentlemen from all over the eastern seaboard (and one very proud member from Seattle) decreed that the name of Julien must not perish. All those who had swooned over a Julien lobster bisque or cassoulet of duck Julien-Marie (or said they had) vowed with their hands on their checkbooks that Julien's must go on. The finest lawyers, bankers, jurists, all manner of men of affairs co-operated to insure future security. Monsieur Julien was put on salary and to keep the venture from smacking of Depression opportunism the group called itself simply the Friends of Julien, standing by the thin of the thirties to reap profits in the forties. Self-made men, lacking in clubs and college backgrounds, listed membership in the Friends of Julien beside their names in *Who's Who* for it hinted of world travel and financial standing.

Most of the Friends were by no means habituées but appeared only at the annual dinner where they toasted bygone days, the chef, the wine steward, the bartender, and above all the great Julien. Julien, who appeared in the kitchen only for photographers, always wept over these unearned tributes to his magic touch with a field salad and permitted himself to quote elegies to his skill from old rivals—Moneta, the Ambassador's Sabatini, Henri Charpentier; and he summoned sentimental memories of days when the incomparable Escoffier of London's Carlton called personally on Papa Julien to pay his respects to the only man in the world he deigned to call "Maître," or so Julien *fils* declared. The anecdotes grew more impressive each year and convinced by his own publicity Julien made himself instead of his forebears the hero.

This evening's banquet had finally gotten under way in the private room but the café guests continued to dawdle, sending emissaries back to spy on the feast and report back who was there and what was being said. The waiters' unusual speed in presenting checks as a method of clearing the café only made the guests more obstinately determined to stay on enjoying the splendid affair by proxy. Caught in the spirit of the occasion Hoff Bemans was ordering round after round of highballs, figuring that he might stick Dalzell Sloane with the check by carefully timing his own departure or if Sloane got away first there was a very young first novelist along who had been on his panel and would be too shy to protest. On the program that evening Hoff had made insulting and derogatory remarks concerning the young man's work and youthful pomposity but he vaguely felt letting him buy the drinks would atone for this. For that matter no reason why old Sloane shouldn't have it since he would be getting into Cynthia Earle's pocket any minute.

"Thought your *City Life* piece on Marius didn't quite come off," Hoff said genially to Briggs. "Some good things in it but as a whole it just didn't come off."

"Thanks," Briggs said absently. He was staring at the young novelist wondering what it felt like to have your name on a fat book, and have people talking about it as if it meant something. The novel had worried him because the author's method wasn't like his own at all. Instead of building his characters on a sensible economic structure this fellow built them on what they had to eat and drink from the breast right through Schrafft's and the Grand Central Oyster Bar; whatever they elected to eat was evidently supposed to mean something about their hidden natures. Even their retching was recorded and it didn't indicate they had had a bad oyster but meant they were having an emotional *crise*. When they weren't eating, this author's characters were all put through boarding schools and colleges, all Ivy League, no matter how poor they talked, and Briggs, having worked his way through a minor university, was irritated at having to work his way again through these fictional characters' education. What did people like about that kind of book? Maybe it was the deep sex meaning the fellow gave to those menus, for the hero was always drawing some high-bosomed girl into his arms between courses, the hot oatmeal pounding through his veins.

"I read your book," Briggs roused himself to tell the young man.

"Thanks," said the author gratefully. Briggs noted that whatever fine liquors his characters enjoyed their creator was limiting himself to simple beer, though this economy might later be regretted when he found he had to pay for his comrades' expensive tastes.

Hoff was continuing the discussion on Marius' show, pointing out errors in the critics' reviews due perhaps to their not having consulted Mr. Bemans' recent book on the subject. The *Times* critic, for example, persisted in linking Marius' work with that of Forrester and Sloane which was utterly idiotic because neither Ben nor Dalzell could paint the simplest apple to resemble Marius' touch. Hoff wished Dalzell to tell Cynthia Earle, moreover, that he felt very hurt that his contribution to the Marius Long Playing Record had been cut out and he considered that was probably the real reason the project had been such a flop. Without his key words the thing hadn't jelled, had not, as he liked to put it, "quite come off."

The café had never been noisier or more crowded. Everyone was shouting to be heard and from the private dining room there were periodic roars of applause. As the banquet progressed curious changes were taking place all over the restaurant. Certain of the banqueters were slipping out to the café between their gourmet dishes to freshen up their palates with quick shots of rye or invigorating martinis and later on grew sociable enough to draw up chairs and make acquaintance with the café customers. Some of these truants urged their new friends to return to the banquet with them, gave them their own places and went back to the café for more informal fun. Before the dinner was even half over the personnel of the Friends' table had changed in such a surprising fashion that there was a lively sprinkling of sports jackets and dark shirts and these strangers were being served roast duckling with the finest of Chambertin while out in the café their legitimate highballs and rubbery canapés were being finished by distinguished drunken Friends. It was in this interchange that Hastings Hardy wound up at Dalzell's table while Briggs, done out of his rightful place, found himself in the private dining room drinking toasts to personalities he'd never heard of. He had arrived at the moment when Monsieur Julien was making the great salad with his own hands—that is to say he took into his own sacred hands various ingredients deftly offered by assistants and poured them personally into the bowl. In the solemn hush induced by this traditional rite cooks' caps could be seen bobbing around corners as they strained to see; other diners bent their heads reverently, and down in the lower kitchen the seafood chef was sustaining himself with mighty swigs of Martell in his pride that Monsieur Julien had thought his sole good enough to claim as his own handiwork.

Toasts had been made to famous dishes, countries, high-living monarchs and again and again to Monsieur Julien until the master was shaken to tears, and many others were moved to blow their noses heartily. To restore calm the oldest living member rose to propose a health, he said, to that great chef, Henri Charpentier, inventor of the *Crêpe Suzette* which had brought happiness to so many thousands. The applause inspired Monsieur Julien to interpolate that Charpentier, excellent genius though he was, had been surpassed by Sabatini, king of them all, next of course to Escoffier.

" 'Born with the gift of laughter and a sense that the world is mad,' " shouted one of the café intruders joyously, but a neighbor yanked him down by his brown-checked coattail hissing, "You ass, not THAT Sabatini."

"Five generations of kings Sabatini served," Monsieur Julien went on unperturbed, his black eyes flashing proudly around the table, "including Umberto and the Czar of all the Russias. As for Charpentier's *Crêpe Suzette*, can it really compare in delicacy and sheer originality with the *Coeur Flottant* Sabatini created especially for that queen among women, Mary Garden?"

A Friend who had spent the last three courses in the café returned in time to catch the last words and squeezing into the group snatched up Briggs's glass and shouted a ringing toast to Mary Garden, King Umberto and the Czar himself, then sat down on the nonexistent chair dragging napery, silver, dishes and six kinds of greens to the floor with him. It was too bad that the photographer chanced to get a fine shot of this disorderly scene for it spoiled the nostalgic sentimental tone of the accompanying article on "Farewell to the Café Julien" and made many ministers give thanks that this palace of sin was finally to be routed by clean-minded citizens.

It was this picture, showing Briggs wiping salad off the fallen comrade with Monsieur Julien handing him a napkin with Gallic courtesy, that turned out to be lucky for Briggs. The very day the picture appeared he was offered the job of restaurant reporter on a tabloid. It meant postponing his literary career which grieved him but was a great relief to Janie, who loved him devotedly and without illusions.

. . . *the nightcap* . . .

THE café crowd had thinned out a half hour before closing time when Ellenora and Rick Prescott came in for their nightcap. They had been coming in every night again, and tonight's news that the rumors of the Julien's approaching end were all too true filled them with dismay and foreboding. They had fallen in love with what they had seemed to be in these surroundings: these were the selves they knew: when they set foot inside these doors each became again what the other desired. Now that they were together so much elsewhere, their ordinary selves surrendered to each other, they were secretly conscious of a dimension missing. Fulfillment, so long desired, was somehow not enough. They had to have the Julien about them, Philippe beside them, the marble-topped table between them, their reflections in the wall mirrors a supporting chorus.

They had spent nights and days in Ricky's apartment telling each other everything about themselves, listening eagerly, but failing to fit the new portrait to the image of love they had been cherishing. Rick wanted to absolve himself of past follies and errors by confessing everything, recklessly handing over material for an ordinary lifetime of reproaches, for part of his love for Ellenora was his sense of guilt, a comfortable feeling of you-dear-darling-girl-to-forgive-me-for-all-the-ways-I-have-wronged-you. She was never to be spared, Ellenora thought, a little frightened at the role he had given her of forever forgiving him and then consoling him for having hurt her, inviting more hurt by understanding and forgiving it. She would have liked to shut her ears to his admission of other, lesser loves, but he had to know that she understood. She would have liked to know where they were heading for, now that they were lovers, but she understood her part well enough to realize she was to be near when he needed her, accept what he offered, ask no questions. It was enough that there *was* love, and the woman's duty was always to guard it, to have it ready when the man needed it.

"Calling Mr. Prescott!" The telephone operator stood in the café doorway and beckoned Rick. He blinked, puzzled.

He had spent hours in this spot waiting for a call from Ellenora that never had come. Now she was here beside him and the call was just catching up.

It was Jerry Dulaine, he found when he went out to the booth. She wanted to tell him about her new job, and maybe get some advice. She was working on a television show about problems of career girls. She had moved to the Hotel Delorme on Park Avenue if he'd like to call on her.

Rick hesitated. In his confessional orgy he hadn't said anything to Ellenora about Jerry, maybe because it didn't matter or maybe because you only tell about the closed episodes. He didn't like refusing Jerry when all she asked was some friendly encouragement. He was glad things were looking up for her, he said, and he'd drop around one of these days. Maybe he would at that, he reflected, going back to the café. His eyes lit up, seeing Ellenora at their table, just as he liked to think of her, sweetly waiting for him. Where would they go to hide from their real selves when the Julien vanished?

"Wrong Prescott," he said, pulling out his chair and sitting down happily as if their feet entwined under the same café table was home enough for him.

. . . the bird's gone . . .

October was as hot as August that year and the wreckers were shirtless under the midday sun, their bare backs glistening with perspiration. Rick Prescott had been leaning against the park fence watching them for a long time, thinking ruefully that of all the happy workers in the world wreckers were undoubtedly the most enthusiastic. The whole back wall of the building was down now, and the top floors, but the handsome Victorian Gothic façade with the imposing marble steps still stood, and it was disconcerting to look through the paneless café windows straight into open garden. Now the crimson entrance canopy was a tumbled pile of rags on the sidewalk, the white letters C A F E J U L I E N almost indiscernible under rubble, and next the thick laurel vines fell in a great heap of gleaming green leaves that seemed to be still breathing and quivering with life.

"That laurel must be near a hundred years old," a workman beside Rick said. "The walls come down easy enough but those vines are strong as iron. You wouldn't think it."

"My poor birds!" quavered a woman's voice behind them. She was a rouged and dyed old lady elaborately dressed in the fashion of pre-World War One, the low-crowned beaver hat atop her pompadour laden with birds and flowers, long peg-top brown velvet skirt almost concealing her high black kid shoes, a green changeable silk duster floating about her. She was dabbing at her mascaraed eyes with a lacy handkerchief and looked at Rick appealingly. "Their nest was right outside my window and now they're homeless. I used to feed them on the sill every morning for thirty years and more. Oh what will they do now the vine is gone?"

"Don't worry about your birds, lady," the workman said, nudging Rick. "They've gone South by now. Probably got a lot bigger nest down there in Miami."

"Do you really think so? Oh. I'm so glad." The old lady smiled tremulously. "I've cried every night worrying about them ever since they started tearing down the building. My room—right over the café window there—went yesterday. Thank you so much."

She hobbled slowly across the park and the workman winked at Rick.

"Betcha she never came out of her room till they tore the place down," he murmured. "She comes here and watches every day."

"I didn't realize people lived upstairs," Rick said.

"A lot of old-timers lived in those little rooms," the man said. "You see 'em wandering around the Park now, like her, all in kinda mummy clothes. A lot of queer old birds flushed out of their nests. They used that side entrance."

Rick took the cigarette he offered and lit it. He thought, as he walked on, that tonight at midnight he would bring Ellenora over here and they would sit on the park bench right opposite the old café with a split of champagne. The loving-cup would be the little Venetian glass slipper from Ellenora's dressing table and they would drink it the very minute of the old closing time. In the light of the street lamp at midnight they would see the old entrance steps up to the doorway and shadows would reconstruct the old café. The idea cheered him up and he quickened his steps, smiling a little to himself as he always did when he thought of something to tell Ellenora. He remembered that he hadn't told her yet he was being sent to Peru for six months but the funny thing was he didn't have to tell anything important to Ellenora because he felt she knew, without words. It was like his knowing she would always be waiting, sitting there at the café table, charming extravagant little hat—a "lady" hat as he always called Ellenora's hats—tilted at the chic angle, feathery wisp of veil or scarf making a smoke ring around her eager, radiant little face. Ellenora—keeping beautiful New York for him.

Sitting at the café table?—Rick stopped short, frightened. The nest was gone. He felt a sudden panic at the thought of his dream without the Julien frame. Where would he be sure of her waiting, loving, knowing? He couldn't, wouldn't dare leave her again with no Julien walls to hold her. He hurried frantically across the Park toward his apartment where she would be waiting—where she *had* to be waiting.

Dalzell Sloane looked again at the young man rushing past him, certain that he had seen him somewhere before. He frowned and then it came to him that the familiarity was only in the resemblance to Monty Douglass, the film actor. He walked on to the ruins of the Café Julien and sat down on a park bench opposite. It was odd that he didn't feel sad, he reflected, but then the Café had been gone from him long, long before the building came down. If it had been there in full glory at this very minute he would not have gone in, probably, for his new self might not belong there. He was not accustomed to his new self, yet, the Dalzell Sloane who was painting portraits of Hasting Hardy's entire family, at a fine fee, the Dalzell Sloane who would presently have to report at Elizabeth Arden's as he had promised to pick up Cynthia. He sighed a little, knowing just how it would be.

"Mrs. Sloane wants you to wait here until she's through," he was sure one of the beauteous young ladies would inform him. "She said for you to be sure and wait."

He would stand in a corner, fearful of smashing the jeweled perfume bottles or damaging the elegant, perfumed creatures gliding in and out, and sometimes a honey-voiced young lady would call him Mr. Earle and tell him his wife was almost through. He wondered, idly, if all of Cynthia's husbands had been called Mr. Earle after her first one since none of the other names had stuck, and whether he might not end up signing his paintings Dalzell Earle. It really didn't matter, he thought, any more than anything that happened to his new self mattered, for there was no more Dalzell Sloane than there was any more Marius or Julien. No good looking around the old neighborhood for souvenirs of the vanished past. He went to the curb and flagged a taxi.

The red-haired man sitting on the nearest bench watched him get into the cab, made a move to wave to him but thought better of it and resumed writing in the notebook spread open with his briefcase as desk.

What Dennis Orphen was writing was this:

It must be that the Julien was all that these people really liked about each other for now when they chance across each other in the street they look through each other, unrecognizing, or cross the street quickly with the vague feeling that here was someone identified with unhappy memories—as if the other was responsible for the fall of the Julien. Curious, too, that everyone connected with the café looks so small on the street. The arrogance and dignity of the old waiters is now wrapped up in a bundle under their arms when you catch a glimpse of one of them, shriveled and bent, scuttling down a subway kiosk; the men of affairs who had spent hours sipping their brandy and liquers, reading their papers with lordly ease, are suddenly old and harassed-looking, home and family harness collaring them for good, their café egos stowed away in vest pocket pill-boxes like morphine grains.

The Café Julien was gone and a reign was over. Those who had been bound by it fell apart like straws when the baling cord is cut and remembered each other's name and face as part of a dream that would never come back.

THE GOLDEN SPUR

For Margaret De Silver

1

THE HOTEL STATIONERY was Wedgwood blue like the wallpaper, delicately embossed with a gold crest and a motto, *In virtu vinci*, a nice thought, whatever it meant, for a hotel. Nice paper, too. Paper like that could make a writer of you, if anything could.

He took the whole pack from the desk and inserted it among his other papers in the briefcase with his pajamas, shirt, the monogrammed Hotel De Long ashtray, hand towels, and dainty lavender soap. Too bad there were only two hotel postcards left. Anyone seeing that view of the De Long lobby, magnified beyond recognition, jeweled with tropic blossoms, oriental rugs, divans, and liveried pages would assume that seductive sirens and fabulous adventurers lurked behind the potted palms. Actually, Jonathan had observed only a few old crones and decrepit gentlemen hobbling or wheeling through the modest halls last evening. He chose, however, to believe the postcards. That was the city as he had pictured it, and he wished he had a stock of them to keep sending out as camouflage for the cheaper quarters he had to find.

He addressed one card to Miss Tessie Birch, R.F.D., Silver City, Ohio.

"Dear Aunt Tessie. No time for good-by. Will write when I get more leads. J."

His window was on a court within hand-shaking distance of other windows, but a wedge of the street below was visible and there rose the contented purr of the city, a blend of bells, whirring motors, whistles, buildings rising, and buildings falling. The stage was set, the orchestra tuning up, and in a moment he would be on, Jonathan thought. Curious he felt no panic, as if his years of waiting in the wings had prepared him to take over the star role. But it was more as if he were released from a long exile in an alien land to come into his own at last. In a window across the court he could glimpse a fair young man seated at a desk, idly smoothing his hair and smiling as if at some happy secret. The figure moved, and it dawned on Jonathan that the window was a mirror, the young man with the secret was himself.

He looked around to see if there was more magic to be discovered in the room. He'd certainly gotten his seven dollars' worth. Last night he had sat up till three, marveling at the new life so suddenly opened to him, trying to organize the plan he had outlined before leaving Silver City. Again he flipped through the fat little red notebook, on the flyleaf of which was written: CONSTANCE BIRCH, NEW YORK CITY, 1927. Beneath his mother's name was written: PROPERTY OF JONATHAN JAIMISON, NEW YORK CITY, 1956. The old names his mother had listed and those he had added from the references in her letters Jonathan had already checked in this year's telephone directory with little success. Beside each name he had jotted the connection with his mother and the last known address. Two names offered possibilities. The first was:

"Claire Van Orphen, author. Typed mss. Last Xmas card 1933. Care Pen and Brush Club."

The Pen and Brush Club, he had found, was right in the vicinity, and a note might bring results. Second to Miss Van Orphen as a source was another but more famous writer, Alvine Harshawe, whose early work his mother had been privileged to type. She had continued to collect his press notices for years after she had returned to Ohio and married Jaimison, Senior.

"Copied Alvine's last act today and he was so pleased he took me to celebrate at The Golden Spur," she had written in her diary, which Jonathan knew almost by heart.

The Golden Spur still existed, he'd found, and Jonathan planned to ask there for Harshawe.

He knew the "Hazel" mentioned frequently in the diary had shared rooms on Horatio Street with his mother, and "George" had been her fiancé, a rich young lawyer. George's opinions on literature were faithfully quoted. He seemed to awe Jonathan's mother, but then she was awed by everybody she had ever encountered in New York, just as she found all places incredibly charming, such as the Horatio Street rooming house, the Hotel Brevoort (where George and Hazel took her to Sunday breakfast and where the public stenographer graciously gave her some work), the Black Knight,

Chumley's (where all the great writers and artists congregated in better style than at The Golden Spur), the Washington Square Bookstore ("Alvine's friend Lois works there"), Romany Marie's, the Café Royale, and other romantic names that Jonathan could not find in the directory.

Tucking the priceless little notebook in his inside coat pocket, Jonathan considered the wisdom of trying to find Miss Van Orphen this very day. The wall clock registered eleven-forty. A printed notice advised that guests would be charged for another day after one o'clock. Better wait until he was settled in permanent quarters, he decided. No use fooling himself that the mystery of these many years could be unraveled in a day. Let's get on with it, then, he told himself, and picked up his briefcase.

The corridor appeared deserted, and he seized the chance to nip in an open door where he could see a stack of postcards on the desk. He had barely time to slip them in his pocket when an ancient hump-backed porter materialized in the doorway. His withered old neck stretched out of the De Long uniform like a turtle's, and the watery eyes under wrinkled lizard lids blinked suspiciously at Jonathan, the old nose sniffing stolen postcards, towels, ashtrays, and precious soap.

"I must have missed him," Jonathan said nervously.

"He checked out an hour ago," said the porter, suspicions allayed. "Maybe you could catch him at the funeral parlor."

"That's so," said Jonathan.

"Or maybe his home," offered the porter. "He was just staying here to fix up the Major's affairs, all that legal stuff. Did you come for the funeral?"

"Yes," said Jonathan. "I—I got the word in Ohio."

"The Major would have appreciated your coming all that way just to bury him," said the porter. "He was a great one for appreciating little favors like that. They don't come any finer than the Major is what we say here."

"That's what I always said," Jonathan agreed, edging out the door past the porter. Lucky to touch hunchbacks, he remembered. "I hope I'm not late for the funeral."

"You'll make it," said his friend with a dry cackle. "The Major wouldn't let anybody hustle him. Things have got to be done just right, you know how he was."

"That's so," said Jonathan and returned the smart salute, grateful to the dead Major for his unexpected protection. He had one friend in New York, it seemed, even if the bond was a peculiar one. He was still glowing when he came out on the street. It was a wonderful July day created especially to surprise and delight the timid visitor. The street of old brick houses with their fanlights over white doorways, trellised balconies of greenery, magnolia trees, vined walls, cats sunning themselves in windows, was not so different from the residential streets in hundreds of home towns far away. Even little saplings on the sidewalk sprouted leaves, and pigeons strutted along the gutter until routed by a street sprinkler bearing a sign: KEEP NEW YORK CLEAN. A dirty but friendly baptism, Jonathan thought, brushing the mud from his trousers.

"Is this the way to Aunt Nellie's Carolina Tea Room?" a lady in a hatful of violets called out to him, leaning out of a taxicab door.

Jonathan was flattered to be taken for a seasoned New Yorker, and he pointed impulsively to a restaurant sign down the street. The lady beamed gratitude and with a flower-hatted companion clambered out of the cab, backsides first. The sign turned out to advertise MAC'S BAR AND GRILL, Jonathan saw on closer inspection, but maybe the ladies wouldn't know the difference.

Along the way doormen, decked out in more braid than banana generals, were being propelled by clusters of peanut-sized Poms and chows on mighty leashes, braking to allow each hydrant and every passing pooch to be checked. A dog was a necessity in this city, Jonathan deduced, and promised himself that one of these days he would have one, a Great Dane, say, something to give his doorman a real workout, a big-shot dog to show the world. He'd never had a dog, but now he would have everything the old Jonathan had never dared to want, for this was his city, and his mother's secret was the key to its treasure.

"I'm not a Jaimison," he murmured to himself over and over, and his stride grew longer, his head higher. "I could be anybody—*anybody!*"

Before him lay Washington Square.

Only eighteen hours in New York, and he loved everything, every inch of it. Ah, the square! He crossed Waverly and stood at the corner by the playground. He beamed at the ferociously determined child aiming a scooter straight at him, and jumped out of the way of a chain of girl roller-skaters advancing rhythmically toward him. An enormous-busted, green-sweatered girl with a wild bush of hair, black skin-tight pants outlining thick thighs and mighty buttocks, came whooping along, clutching the legs of a screaming bearded young man she bore on her shoulders.

"Let me down, now! Now you let me down!" he yelled, waving his arms. A short muscular girl with ape face and crew-cut, in stained corduroy shorts and red knee socks, ran behind, shouting with laughter.

"Didn't I tell you that Shirley is the strongest dyke in Greenwich Village?"

The big gorilla girl stopped abruptly, letting the young man fall headlong over her shoulders and sprawl crabwise over the green.

"Don't you dare call me a dyke!" she shouted, shaking the smaller girl by the shoulders.

The lad snatched the moment to pick himself up, with a sheepish grin at Jonathan, and tore down the street, combing his long, sleek locks as he ran.

"Go ahead, Shirley, pick up this one, go ahead!" the small girl yelled, pointing at Jonathan while she wriggled neatly out of her attacker's hands. Too startled to move for a few seconds, Jonathan saw the big girl's eye fall on him with a speculative smile. He clutched his briefcase and ran, the girls howling behind him. He made for the fenced-in space where the smallest kiddies, drunk with popsicles, were wobbling on teeter-totters or reeling behind their buggies. He knocked one of these live dolls over and quickly snatched it up in his arms as Big Shirley came toward him.

"Look out, he's going to throw the kid at you, Shirley!" the short girl yelled warning. "Come on, let's go."

They loped away, stopping for the younger ape to leap expertly onto Shirley's back. With a sigh of relief, Jonathan set down the howling child carefully.

"Thank you very much, sir," he said to the child, picking

up the raspberry Good Humor his savior had dropped and
restoring it to the open red mouth. He remembered that he
hadn't had anything to eat since last night's hamburger in the
station and he was ravenous. A benign white-haired old gentleman, wide-brimmed black hat on lap, black ribbons fluttering from his spectacles, sat on a bench reading a paperback
copy of *The Dance of Life*. Reassured by the title, Jonathan
coughed to get his attention.

"Could you tell me where I can get a cup of coffee here?"
he asked.

Without looking up from his reading, the gentleman
reached in his pocket and handed out a quarter before turning a page. Jonathan stared at the coin in his palm.

"Thank you, sir," he said. "Thank you very much."

How strange New Yorkers were, he marveled, but he
would get used to their ways. He crossed the park and wandered up a side street. Golden letters on a window, where a
menu was pasted, announced that this was Aunt Nellie's
Carolina Tea Room. His two old ladies were several blocks off
course, he thought, unless Mac of the Bar and Grill had set
them right. Perhaps they were inside right now, jubilantly
wolfing the farm-style apple-peanut surprise, home-boiled
country eggs, barn-fresh milk, cottage-made cocoa, garden-
good lettuce sandwiches. Rejecting these gourmet temptations, Jonathan turned in the other direction.

Lunch hour had filled the streets, and Jonathan studied the
people, fearing they were frowning at his best gray tropical
tweed because it was last year's style. His confidence melted
even more—as his confidence always had a way of doing—
after a couple addressed him in Spanish, and a girl asked him
directions in Swedish. On second thoughts, he might be too
dressed-up to pass as a native New Yorker. The standard costume seemed to be loose sport shirts and slacks, or even
shorts proudly exhibiting knobby shins, hairy calves, and
gnarled knees. Certainly these people were nothing like those
natty cosmopolitans pictured in *Esquire* and the movies. As
for the girls, he tried not to notice them. After his encounter
in the park he figured that they must be a stronger breed than
those back home.

Ah, New York! A flying pebble nicked him in the eye, and

as he was blindly trying to shake it out he found he was caught up in a crowd around a demolition operation that took up the whole block. Evidently something dramatic was about to happen, for all eyes stared skyward intently. Maybe the Mayor himself was about to appear on the roofless tower and beg for their ears. Jonathan nudged his way to the front and stared upward too.

A giant crane was the star performer, lifting its neck heavenward, then dropping a great iron ball gently down to a doomed monster clock in the front wall of the structure, tapping it tenderly, like a diagnostician looking for the sore spot. Does it hurt here? here? or here? Wherever it hurts must be target for the wham, and wham comes next, with the rubble hurtling down into the arena with a roar. A pause, and then the eager watchers followed the long neck's purposeful rise again, the rhythmical lowering of the magic ball, the blind grope for the clock face, and then the avalanche once more. The cloud of dust cleared, and a cry went up to see the clock still there, the balcony behind it falling. "They can't get the clock," someone exulted. "Not today! Hooray for the clock!" The spectators smiled and nodded to one another. Good show. Well done, team!

Jonathan returned the congratulatory smile of the fat little man on his right bearing a bag of laundry on his back, and composed a graver expression for the scowling neighbor on his other side. This was a ruddy-faced, agate-eyed man, bareheaded, with gray-streaked pompadour and mustache, carrying an attaché case and a rumpled blue raincoat over his arm.

"Do you realize the bastard who runs that blasted contraption gets sixty dollars an hour?" he asked Jonathan. "Sixty dollars an hour—twenty, thirty times what a college professor makes. And time and a half for overtime. Figure it out for yourself. Seven, eight hundred dollars a day just for sitting on his can in that little box and pressing buttons."

"Is that a fact?" Jonathan asked, feeling richer at the mention of such large sums. He moved closer with the vague hope that money was contagious.

"Destruction is what pays today," said his neighbor, twisting his mustache savagely. "Wreckers, bomb-builders, poison-makers. Who buys creative brains today?"

"Nobody," Jonathan said, glad to know some answers.

"Name me one constructive, intellectual activity that pays a living," pursued the quizmaster.

"You got me," Jonathan said.

He accepted a bent cigarette from the pack offered by the man, who was now brooding silently.

"Can you tell me if there's something special about this particular wrecking to bring out such a crowd?" Jonathan asked.

The gentleman snorted.

"Of course I can tell you. In the first place this was a splendid old landmark and people like to see the old order blown up. Then there is the glorious dirt and uproar which are the vitamins of New York, and of course the secret hope that the street will cave in and swallow us all up."

Jonathan looked down uneasily at the boards underfoot.

"Dear old Wanamaker's." His companion sighed. "If I had paid their nasty little bill, perhaps they would never have come to this. Well, mustn't get sentimental."

Another avalanche of rubble roared into the pit.

"Eight hundred dollars a day is a lot of money for pushing buttons," Jonathan thought aloud.

"Entertainers must be paid," the other man said and walked away.

What a brilliant fellow! Jonathan thought, looking after him regretfully. He remembered that he was hungry and started looking for a lunchroom, rejecting one because it looked too expensive, others because they looked too cheap, too crowded, or too empty. After wandering up and down, he stood still finally in front of an auction gallery he had passed three times, pretending to admire a gold sedan chair. On the other side of the street was a great glass and chromium supermarket advertising its opening with valuable favors to be given away to every customer. He might buy a bun, he thought, thus entitling him to the valuable favor, and come back and eat it in the sedan chair. Or— Then a sign swinging out over a dark doorway next to the auction window caught his eye.

THE GOLDEN SPUR, he read mechanically and stared at the red and gold swinging horseshoe.

The Golden Spur! His mother's Golden Spur, the place she used to go to meet the Man, the place she went with her famous friends, but above all, the place where the great romance had started, the place, indeed, where Jonathan came in.

So the place did exist—not the grand Piranesi palace he had vaguely imagined, with marble stairs leading forever upward to love and fame, but a dingy little dark hole he must have passed before without noticing. He lit a cigarette with trembling fingers. If The Golden Spur was real, then all of it was real. His mother had stood on this very spot, and suddenly her image leaped up, not the pale face on the pillow he remembered from long ago, but the stranger, Connie Birch, the girl who had written the letters, the girl who met her lover in The Golden Spur. He saw her as she looked in the old snapshots, the thin, chiseled face with shining, appealing eyes (*Oh, do like me, do try to like me, please*), the coronet of thick fair braids, the parted lips half-smiling, the eager when-where-who expectant aura that must have attracted its own happy answers. This was the girl whose trail he must find, the girl who had written her sister (he had that letter with him too):

"Oh Tessie, please don't expect me to marry John Jaimison when I come home to visit because I don't care how he hounds me, my life is here. I've told you how lovely all the marvelous people I meet at Miss Van Orphen's are to me when I go there to type her stories. Hazel, the girl I live with, prefers a wild time at cabarets but I'd much rather listen to the important people at Miss Van Orphen's. Then there is the restaurant where the writers and artists go, The Golden Spur, and I've met the most exciting man there and Tessie, he's going to be famous and how could I ever go back to John after being in love with a really great man?"

Jonathan took a step toward the magic door and then stood still, desperately trying to steel himself for the part he had chosen to play and that had seemed so simple, so right, when Aunt Tessie had told him the truth in Silver City just forty-eight hours before.

"Once you get on the track, things will come to you like in a dream," Aunt Tessie had said. "Keep thinking of all those stories your mother used to tell you every night, stories about people and places she knew in New York, like that Golden

Spur where she met all those famous ones. Think of the ones she used to find mentioned in the magazines, always cutting out their pictures and all that."

"I remember," Jonathan had said.

"I never got it straight in my own mind," Aunt Tessie had confessed. "Used to go in one ear and out the other like all those stories girls tell about their good times away from home, all those beaux, all fine men, all better than the home-town boys. 'After my time in New York,' your poor mother used to complain to me, 'how can you expect me to marry John Jaimison?' 'You were glad enough to get engaged to him before you went away,' I told her, 'and he did wait for you.' 'But Tessie, you just don't understand, I see everything different now,' she kept at me, crying her eyes out. 'I'm used to geniuses, men with great minds, now, and John Jaimison doesn't think about anything but selling Silver City flour products. All he reads is sales letters, all he writes is orders. All he does is brag about the Jaimison family, and how they're the biggest old family in middle Ohio and how proud I'll be to be allowed at their family reunions. Oh, Tessie,' your mother says to me, 'you can't see me marrying John Jaimison and going to those awful reunions!'"

"Of course not!" Jonathan had answered Aunt Tessie. "Why did you let it happen?"

"I said to her, 'Connie,' I said, 'what you say is true and I do understand how New York City changed your ideas about men, but honey,' I said, 'the point is he's still willing to marry you and in your condition you'd better snap him up, the sooner the quicker!' So!"

"Maybe he did suspect," Jonathan had said. "Maybe that was why he dumped Mother and me on you just three years after they married."

"John Jaimison turned her in just the way he turned in his car when it went bad," Aunt Tessie said. "He didn't suspect, he was just naturally a Jaimison, a small-minded man. He beefed about her turning tubercular on him as if he'd been sold a pig in a poke, and what a tussle it was getting money out of him for the doctors and you! Hard enough to catch him, and when I did he'd complain, 'You can't get blood out of a turnip, Tessie Birch,' and I'd say, 'Out of a Jaimison turnip you can't even get turnip juice.' But there, I never meant to tell you the truth about yourself!"

"I only wish you'd told me years ago," said Jonathan. "I needn't have gone to all those Jaimison reunions, with the old man bawling me out for not getting ahead, telling everybody that the Jaimison genius had skipped a generation. I only wish you could tell me who my true father was."

"I never thought it mattered, Jonny-boy," Aunt Tessie had said. "Connie told so many stories about New York. Don't you remember?"

"The bedtime stories she told got mixed up in my mind," he said. "The Golden Spur people weren't any more real than the King of the Golden River."

"It'll all fit together," Aunt Tessie consoled him. "You'll find your answer."

"I'll find the answer," Jonathan repeated aloud, as if Aunt Tessie were right there before The Golden Spur urging him on.

Through a gap in the plum velvet café curtains he could see the bar and was heartened to recognize his friend from the excavation standing inside. He breathed deep of the heady New York air, that delirious narcotic of ancient sewer dust, gasoline fumes, roasting coffee beans, and the harsh smell of sea that intoxicates inland nostrils.

Then he pushed open the door.

A long bar stretched before him back to dark stalls with dim stable lanterns perched on their newel posts. Framed photographs of the great horses of old covered the wainscoted walls, horseshoes and golden spurs hung above the bar itself, and photographed clippings of old racing forms. Jonathan examined these souvenirs, noting that all that was left of the sporting past were the bowling alley ads posted on the bulletin board. These were overshadowed by notices of summer art shows, off-Broadway entertainments, jazz concerts, night courses in Method Acting, sketching, folk-singing hootenannies, poetry readings, ballet and language groups. Penciled scraps of paper were Scotch-taped to the wall, advertising cars, scooters, beach shacks, lofts, or furniture for trade or sale. Homesick Californian with driver's license asked for free trip back to North Beach. A new espresso café on Bleecker Street wanted a man to get up a mimeographed Village news sheet in return for "nominal" pay and free cakes and coffee. A Sunday painter offered free dental service in exchange for model. An unemployed illustrator would teach the Chachacha or even the Charleston for her dinners.

"Brother, she's hungry!" Jonathan heard a feminine voice say over his shoulder and turned to see a big girl with shrimp-pink hair laughing at his absorption. He drew away, embarrassed at being caught in tourist innocence.

The girl got her cigarettes from the cigarette machine and sauntered back to the dining booths, throwing him a friendly, mocking smile. He took a stool at the bar and saw, farther down, his neighbor from the excavation applying himself to a highball with deep satisfaction. Near him a man with a skimpy gray goatee, in a plaid shirt and scalp-tight beret, was reading a copy of *Encounter* with a beer in hand. He had a mountain of pennies stacked in front of him, and now he raised his glass for a refill. The bartender silently counted off fifteen coppers. Conscious of Jonathan's interest in this little game, the man looked up from his magazine and stared at Jonathan, frowning.

"Excuse me," he said. "You remind me of somebody."

"I do?" Jonathan asked, well pleased to look like somebody.

The man studied him, frowning, then shook his head.

"I can't place it," he said.

"My name's Jaimison," Jonathan offered.

"Don't know any Jaimison," said the man.

He looked like a real Villager, Jonathan thought in deep admiration, ageless, jaunty, wearing his faded bohemian uniform with the calm assurance of the true belonger. (I must scrap this tourist outfit of mine and get one like his, Jonathan thought.) He was somewhere between thirty and sixty; the bags under the eyes and deep furrows between the tangled brows might testify to dissipation instead of years, for the sharp-cut sardonic face was otherwise unlined, the figure trim.

"Two double Bloody Marys on the rocks, Dan," a female voice pleaded from the dark recesses of the dining booths.

"So Lize is back in the Village," said the Villager.

"They always come back," said the bartender. "Will somebody tell me why?"

As no one answered, Jonathan seized the opportunity.

"Alvine Harshawe, for instance," he said boldly. "Has he come back?"

The bartender selected a tomato-juice can from under the counter thoughtfully.

"I'll have one of those too," added Jonathan. "Bloody Mary."

"Harshawe, Harshawe," mused the bartender. "Must be a night customer. Harshawe, eh? Maybe he comes in here and I just don't know him by name. Lots of good customers, my best friends, I don't know the names."

"Dan never heard of Alvine Harshawe!" The shrimp-haired girl was back again, standing by the goateed man, watching her drinks being made. "Don't you love Dan for that, Earl? Imagine not hearing of Alvine Harshawe."

The girl picked up the two drinks the bartender pushed toward her.

"Writers don't come in this bar," she said to Jonathan. "Try the White Horse."

"Just a minute, Lize," said the goateed man reproachfully.

"I forgot about Earl here," the girl amended. "I mean the hardcover big shots—like Harshawe."

She retreated to the dark dining section again with her two gory potions, and Jonathan took the third.

"A writer's got to go where columnists can see him," the goateed Villager stated. "Alvine Harshawe could be dying of thirst in the middle of the Sahara. Suddenly there's an oasis, a regular Howard Johnson job, with fifty-nine flavors bubbling up in all directions. Terrific. But if Lenny Lyons isn't at it, I won't go, Alvine says."

"So he dries up, who cares?" said the bartender.

"Don't be silly, Lyons would be there all right," said the fellow named Earl. "You don't catch Alvine taking a chance on no publicity."

"Outside of this guy Harshawe being a big shot, what else have you got against him, Earl?" inquired the bartender, polishing the rimless spectacles that made him look like a respectable white-collar worker.

"What have I got against him?" mused Earl. "Why, he's my oldest friend, that's all."

"Now we're getting somewhere," said the bartender approvingly.

Jonathan, ears alerted, moved closer.

"Then he did use to come here?" he asked.

"Everybody used to come to the Spur," the man said carelessly, "until they could afford not to."

"Supposing we don't get these writers like Lize says," argued the bartender. "Who needs writers when we're already stinking with painters?"

"Painters have got to drink, especially these days," Earl observed. "A painter can't turn out the stuff they have to do now without being loaded."

The bartender subtracted a fresh supply of pennies from the board and pushed another beer across the counter.

"That's where you're wrong, Earl," he said. "I know more about artists than you do. After all, I'm the bartender here. The way I size it up is that they got to paint sober, then they're so disgusted with what they done they got to get stoned."

"And wreck the joint," said Earl. "Look at the crack in that table where Hugow and Lew Schaffer bashed it."

Jonathan looked admiringly at the damaged table indicated.

"The place sure seems quiet with Hugow out of town." The bartender sighed. "Ah, what the hell, painting's no kind of work for those guys. They got to let off steam, beat up their girl, kick in a door. It's only human nature as I see it."

"Sure," said Jonathan. "Human nature, that's all."

"Artists get away with more human nature than anybody else," Earl muttered morosely to Jonathan.

"Hugow sure gets away with murder," the bartender agreed. "Dames? They're all over him. What's he got?"

"Same thing he always had," Earl said. "Only it works better now that his stuff sells big, now that he's the champ."

"Hugow's a great guy. Why shouldn't he be making up for all his bad times?" The bartender turned to Jonathan for agreement. "Can you blame him? You know Hugow."

"No, I'm afraid I don't know any artists," Jonathan said, flattered at the assumption. "Is he a great painter?"

The question seemed to require thought.

"He gets away with it," finally said the bartender. "I guess that's great enough."

The gentleman who had spoken to Jonathan at the excavation had kept to himself at the end of the bar but was listening.

"Art is all you hear in this bar nowadays," he explained to Jonathan. "We used to have brains. Real conversation."

"Speakeasy days," said Earl. "Brains, bathtub booze, and blind staggers. We had our champs then, too."

Jonathan longed to have the discussion continue, but Earl had scooped the last few pennies into his pocket and vanished before Jonathan could summon up the courage to ask about the champs of those other days, for one of them must have been his true father. His head throbbed with vague anticipation. He felt as if he had just pushed the magic button that was to open up the gates to his mother's past and his own future.

What and who was waiting to guide him? he wondered. He knew he would follow without any questions, no matter where he was led. His guides were closer than he knew.

2

L IZE BRITTEN and Darcy Trent having lunch at the Spur, stuck with each other at last, meant that the season was over, the summer drought was on. It meant that all the men—or the men Darcy and Lize shared—had taken to the hills, gone off on their Guggenheims, off to Rome or Mexico or Greece, off to Yaddo, MacDowell, Huntington Hartford, back to their wives or mothers for a free vacation.

There was nobody left in town except the outsiders, the summer faculties and students of the university, the deserted husbands, the tourists, and the creeps. From Hudson Street to First Avenue, in haunts old and new, Lize and Darcy cruised, pretending not to see each other but finally obliged to exchange a lipstick, borrow a dime to phone, until their year-long feud was crossed off in mutual loneliness. The chances were they would have another big showdown come September—oh, they'd manage to fix each other's wagon somehow during the summer, as they always did, but for the time being hostilities must go in the deep freeze, for they had plenty in common and good reason to unite.

Just two weeks ago that popular artist named Hugow, the Spur's leading attraction, had been whisked off to Cape Cod by that insatiable lady art dealer Cassie Bender. Brazen kid-naping, Darcy called it. Rescue was Lize's private word. Whichever way you looked at it, Darcy was left out in the cold. Deserted. Double-crossed.

"He never said a word!" Darcy kept saying, for good-by was a word Darcy never heard, as Lize and the Spur regulars knew full well. "It's the awful shock that gets me!"

"But he hadn't showed up at the studio for weeks!" Lize reminded her.

"I knew how to find him," Darcy muttered, for she had the same talent Lize herself had for tracking men; their itineraries lit up like the arteries on an anatomy chart the first time she met them. "But now he's really gone, don't you understand?"

Good thing you understand it at last yourself, old thing, Lize wanted to say, but she was not unkind. Darcy's eyes were puffed and her face swollen from weeping bitter brandied tears. She had chosen the darkest booth in the farthest corner of the Spur to wallow in her grief in private, but since she continued to heave and snuffle there could be no secret about her broken heart. This frank exhibition was what had won over Lize. A stiff upper lip would have challenged her, but for her old rival Darcy to make a public show of her defeat brought out the sportsman in Lize.

"Hell, Hugow was always sleeping with Cassie Bender!" she now offered as soothing consolation. "A guy's got to eat."

"I knew he did when he was living with you, Lize." Darcy sniffled into her handkerchief. "But what you don't seem to understand is that our relationship was different. Hugow was absolutely frank with me about everything, that's what I always liked about him. Most men are such liars. But when he went to Chicago that time with her and I hit the ceiling, he said I must be crazy to think of such a thing. 'Cassie Bender is my dealer, you little dope,' he said. 'You don't go around sleeping with your bread and butter. Sure, I go places with her, take her home and all that—I'd do the same for Kootz or Sidney Janis or Pierre Matisse. It's business. I like to make a buck and Cassie sells me, but as for an affair, you must be kidding.' Oh, he was perfectly honest about it."

Lize blinked.

"You knew Hugow before I did, Lize," Darcy said, "and you've got to admit he never lied. He was always honest."

"Maybe he just lied to himself," Lize suggested, a little dazed.

Darcy nodded emphatically.

"That's just it. He was so honest that if he had to lie he'd lie to himself too, don't you see?"

Lize was silent, a feat that took all her strength. It would have been so easy to say, "Yes, Hugow was always honest, as you say. Only last year when *I* was living with him and accused him of sleeping with *you* he burst out laughing. 'That dumb kid,' he says, 'are you out of your mind? Look here,' he says, 'I'll level with you. I've got my share of male egotism, call it plain vanity, so believe me I don't make passes at any dame that asks me why don't I paint like Grandma Moses. I could learn, she tells me. Listen, Lize,' he says, 'you must know how a crack like that would paralyze a man with my ego.' So we both had a good laugh, and a few months later you moved in and I was wondering what hit me. Old honest Hugow."

Anyhow Hugow didn't ever chase a woman, Lize was forced to admit. He was a softhearted fellow, and if a woman climbed into his bed he didn't kick her out. He made a brave stab at being independent, keeping his studio strictly for himself, but Lize had managed to move in, the same as the other girls, and Darcy after her. Poor guy. The technique was so simple you'd think the sap would have learned some defense tricks.

You got into the sacred old studio first with a crowd, after an opening or to see a new picture he might be feeling good about, and then you managed to hang around, helping clean up after the others left. So you stayed that one night and then if he didn't phone you afterward—which he never did, sober —you went back for something you'd left. This time you brought a toothbrush and an office dress, in case you stayed again. Next time you casually left a suitcase, because you'd just lost your apartment and couldn't find a place to move yet, you told him. So there you were, in. Poor old Hugow, it was so easy, but damn his hide, he did always manage to get away, even though he couldn't get you out.

It was a consolation to know he'd walked out on her successor just as he had on her the year before, Lize told herself.

"You might have guessed what you were in for, seeing how he treated everybody else before you," she said.

"But Lize, with me it was *serious!*" Darcy patiently protested. "I don't know how to explain it, but I *understood* Hugow, and none of you others ever had. I just happen to understand the artistic temperament, and that's where you failed him, you see."

Again Lize exercised stern self-control to keep from reminding Darcy that they'd covered the same artists in their time with about the same scores. And as for "failing" Hugow—she'd blow her top if she listened to Darcy go on about why she, Lize, and the others had never been right for Hugow anyway. With Darcy's little voice quavering on and on, Lize found herself brooding all over again about her own season with Hugow. Maybe she would have lasted longer if she'd realized that he took that crazy painting of his seriously. But how could you guess that a grown man thought it mattered whether he made a green or purple blob on the canvas? You could understand his being pleased when people liked it or when he got a big check for it, but to think the stuff mattered all by itself—as if it were a machine that would work, depending on a line being here instead of there. Crazy! Luckily she'd kept her mouth shut when he was in one of his sunk moods, though heaven knows she'd wanted to say, "Why in God's name do you go on with something that makes you so miserable?" She'd just let him fool around with the stuff while she quietly got the studio fixed up with a kitchen unit, a few rugs and chairs from the Salvation Army Furniture Store. She had just gotten to the point where she was inviting other couples in for hamburgers and beer, and the grocer was calling her Mrs. Hugow, when he simply disappeared.

Somebody mentioned something about a shack he used sometimes up in Rockland County and that maybe he'd gone up there to work. His friends didn't seem worried or even surprised. But days passed, and no word from him. Lize would come home from the office and then hang around The Golden Spur, hoping for some news of him. But nobody told her anything. That's the way Hugow always was— his pals shrugged—maybe he'd turn up tomorrow, maybe next week.

If she'd known more about his work she would have soon suspected that he wasn't coming back—at least not to her. She would have noticed that he or one of his cronies was slipping into the studio whenever she wasn't there and taking out stuff he needed. That his newest canvas was gone should have told her something, but she wasn't sure which was the new one because all his pictures looked alike to Lize. Great lozenges of red and white ("I love blood," he always said), black and gray squares ("I love chess," he'd say), long green spikes ("I love asparagus"). All Lize had learned about art from her life with painters was that the big pictures were for museums and the little ones for art.

Lize remembered that the first inkling of real trouble was when she heard that Darcy Trent, who had been at loose ends

ever since Lew Schaffer went back to his wife, was commuting to work from Rockland County.

Well!

Lize never allowed two and two to make four until she was
good and ready. So she went on hanging around the empty
studio for a couple of weeks more, knowing what was up all
right, and having it rubbed in whenever she went to The
Golden Spur or The Big Hat or The Barrel. Whoever was
Hugow's girl was queen of the crowd, in a way, with all the
hangers-on clambering to sit with her. But the minute the
grapevine had the word that she'd been bounced, the boys
who wanted to paint like Hugow and the ones who just
wanted to be around a big shot all faded away when she
hailed them. Sometimes the whole bar would clear out—a
party somewhere, they didn't dare ask her in case Hugow and
the new girl (Darcy) would be there. Lize found herself stuck
with a moist-eyed Hugow-worshiper, Percy Wright, whom
everybody had been ducking for years, but at least he had
money enough for them to close the bars together. The poor
mug actually got the idea he was *stealing* Hugow's girl, and
Lize let him think so.

Percy wasn't as spooky as the crowd thought, even if he did
have money (too much to be a respected artist and too little
to be a respected snob). He was in some Wall Street office,
but his analyst had set him painting, so he had started hanging around the Spur, trying to pin artists down to depth
conversations on Old Masters, when the proper thing was to
pop off on galleries, dealers, and critics. Lize was bored by
his constant boasting to strangers that she had once been
Hugow's girlfriend, as if this meant Hugow's talents would
automatically rub off on him now.

Still, his spaniel adoration was consoling. He had inherited
his mother's old brownstone house in Brooklyn Heights and
lived there alone with two floors rented out. He was flattered
when Lize started leaving her things there, a make-up kit,
douche-bag, then a suitcase "just while she was looking for an
apartment." To please her, he let her persuade him to give a
couple of big parties, thinking it would establish him with the
artist crowd. But, just as Lize had feared, the good guys

didn't show up, knowing Hugow wouldn't be there, and the guests were the dregs of all the Left Banks in the world, North Beach, Truro, Paris, or Rome, all knights of the open house, ready to spring at the pop of a cork, ready to stand by through thick of bourbon to thin of wine. Percy didn't mind the expense of these sodden revels that seemed to drag on for days, for he had learned Brooklyn hosts must always be taxed high for wrenching guests from their beloved dingy Manhattan bars, but he resented having their taxi fares back home extorted from him. Lize reproached him for being mean and stingy, but he retorted sulkily that he was *not* stingy, he just didn't like to spend money on other people, that was all. The parties didn't get him anywhere, Lize saw, and she was Indian-marked by her new escort. No use nagging him into buying drinks for the crowd in their own bailiwick, either, for Percy soon set up a squawk. Cash! Money in general was sacred enough, but *cash!*

In spite of these mistakes in adjusting, Percy bloomed under Lize's bullying, as everyone could see. This must have been the same nagging Hugow himself had gotten, he figured, and that set him up as Hugow's equal. He put on some weight, which made him look almost virile. He took to using a sun lamp, grew a little sprig of mustache, wore black-rimmed glasses, tuned his apologetic voice a few notes lower, walked on the balls of his feet, and all in all acted like a man important enough to be kicked around by an ex-girlfriend of Artist Hugow.

Lize had been regarding her time with Percy Wright as a sabbatical year, doing the things outsiders and tourists did—the theater, good restaurants, driving around week-ends in Percy's MG, and getting what she could without wounding him in the wallet directly. If a guy could produce enough background, music, and scenery changes, a girl could stand almost anybody. Her pride was saved, too. Some people even thought that orchestra seats at a good show and The Embers afterward was socially a big step up from Hugow's bed in an East Tenth Street dump. And she had a chance to case the field for somebody better. There were fellows in her office—she worked in a printing outfit near Grand Central—who made passes and asked for lunch dates, but they were mostly commuting husbands, scared to miss more than one train, and likely to shout "Yippee!" when they went to a Village spot. Lize had gone for them when she first started working in New York, but after doing the artist bit you couldn't go back to business types, except maybe once in a while. Percy never suspected, being so faithful to Hugow himself that he couldn't imagine a Hugow woman would go anywhere but back to Hugow, and Darcy Trent had that situation covered. Percy often said how glad he was that the master had consolation for losing Lize.

Lize had a rangy Southwest style and was at her best in trim slacks and sport coats or tailored suits that hung negligently on her lean frame with a fine Bond Street air. Dolled up for a big evening, freckles lightly dusted (those freckles were as good as any collateral for assuring the simple sophisticates of her sterling honesty!), a fillet of rosebuds or butterflies in her close-cropped sorrel hair, a great pouf of satin ribbon on the sleek hips, a dangle of beads at the ears and over the boyish bosom, Lize drew the interest of men of all sexes, but Darcy Trent managed all right too.

Darcy was a wood violet, not as diminutive as she appeared at first glance, but small-boned, small-nosed, small-faced, and given to tiny gestures and a tiny baby voice. She seemed womanly and practical too, and you thought Darcy must be like those small iron pioneer women in the Conestoga wagons, whipping men and children across the prairies, sewing, building, plowing, cooking, nursing, saving her menfolks from their natural folly and improvidence. The fact was that Darcy had never darned a sock, seldom made her own bed, thought coffee was born in delicatessen containers and all food grew in frozen packages. Her practicality exhibited itself in tender little cries of, "But you'll be sick, honey, if you don't eat something after all that bourbon! You must eat! Here, eat this pretzel." In other crises she could figure out efficiently in her head that four people sharing a taxi wouldn't be much more than four subway fares, and that way they could carry their drinks along. She was very firm too in insisting that a man coming out of a week-end binge still reeking of stale smoke and rye should keep away from his job Monday unless he shaved and changed his shirt.

Darcy was delicate in color, almost fading into background, but strong and gamy like those tiny weed-flowers whose roots push up boulders. A man felt that here was a real woman, an old-fashioned girl with her little footsies firmly on the ground, someone to count on, someone always behind you. Darcy's pretty feet were more likely to be on the wall or tangled up in sheets than on the ground, and as for being behind her man, he found out sooner or later she was really on his back. Alas, little women are as hard to throw out as Amazons, especially a confiding little creature like Darcy who had no place to go until there was another back to jump on. Between backs Darcy had no existence, like a hermit crab caught in a shuttle from one stolen shell to another.

Now that Hugow had vanished with Cassie Bender and her damnable station wagon—it was always transporting some artist and his canvases to some place his true mate couldn't get at him—Darcy, the little pioneer woman, had given up completely. She didn't show up at her job in the portrait photographer's studio on West Fifty-Seventh Street for three days on account of her tendency to cry all the time, and after that she was afraid to go in, having a hunch she was automatically fired. She sat around Hugow's studio, hoping there was some mistake, but knowing better. You would have thought she'd stay away from The Golden Spur, where the ritual of brushing off Hugow's cast-off ladies was as rigorously practiced as suttee, but there she was every day or night, getting what Lize had got the year before.

It was "Hello, Al, how's everything? Anybody sitting here —oh, you're just leaving? . . . Hello, Lester, have a beer with me—oh, you're joining friends? . . . What's that, waiter, you say this booth is reserved? Don't be silly! Reserved booths in the Spur, ha, ha! . . . Oh, you mean because I'm just one person—but supposing somebody else . . . oh, well . . ."

The crushing blow was when some fellow conspirator of Hugow's (probably Lew Schaffer, her old lover) had gotten into the studio when Darcy was out and cleaned out all Hugow's smaller possessions. The stuff, in a cardboard suitcase, was under the bar of The Golden Spur at this very minute, waiting for somebody on the way to Provincetown to pick it up. Hugow was really not to blame, Darcy had been insisting up to this point, everything was the fault of Cassie Bender and his other false friends. But to be deserted like this, left in that rat-ridden old slummy studio with the improvements she had generously installed for his comfort—the makeshift shower, dressing mirror, the wardrobe for her dresses, the cute make-up table—it was as if he was saying, here, take the works, my dear girl, you were so anxious to move in. Oh, that was cruel of Hugow, and so ungrateful.

"I think it was darned decent of him to leave you the place," Lize observed after some thought. "He could have locked you out and changed the key" (as he finally did to me, Lize added privately). "You'd been telling him all along you couldn't get an apartment, remember, so I think he meant to be nice, giving it up to you. After all, he loved that lousy dump."

Darcy was beginning to be sorry she'd bleated all her woes to Lize if they were going to be thrown right back at her. She recalled with relief that she hadn't confessed that Lew Schaffer had treated her the same way—walked out of his place after she'd fixed it up so pretty, walked right back to his wife. She'd been stuck with the rent until she'd unloaded it on some Vassar girls who wanted to Live. She'd found out that Lew had retrieved the place the minute she'd moved out to Nyack after Hugow. Men were sneaky that way. But twice stuck like that! Well, at least Lize didn't know that part.

"I never meant I wanted to live way over in that slum all alone," Darcy said. "Bowery bums sleeping on the doorstep and juvenile delinquents slinking up and down the fire escapes. And fifty dollars a month! Sure, it's cheap when you're dividing it, but all that by yourself for a dump where you're afraid to be alone."

Lize, smitten with a brilliant inspiration, looked meditatively at Darcy.

"Oh, I know I look a wreck," Darcy said defensively. "You don't need to tell me."

"I was just thinking your hair's cute with that lock falling down," Lize said.

For some time Lize had been trying to figure out a way of getting back with the old crowd on her own without losing Percy altogether. He had a big inferiority, with every right to it, and a mean way of getting even when he was wounded. She didn't want to break off till she was sure what came next. This week Percy's sister's family from Buffalo were visiting the Brooklyn house, which gave Lize a good excuse to stay out of the picture in a Village hotel. Whatever came of this Percy would have to admit was largely his fault.

"I was so hurt when you didn't want your family to meet me," she could say to him when the time came.

"I think this is a good chance to break with Percy," Lize said to Darcy.

"I can't understand how you endured him this long, Lize," Darcy said, absorbed in admiring her hair in her pocket mirror. "Hugow couldn't get over it. He just despised Percy, always sidling up to him—'May I join you people? I do hate to miss a word of Hugow's conversation.' Blah blah blah."

"No more blah blah to Percy than Hugow once he gets going," Lize retorted in a burst of obstinate loyalty.

Hugow, Hugow, Hugow—the way damn fool women carried on about him—sometimes not seeing him for years, too —you would think he was the Great Lover of the Ages, a perfect panther of a man, wonderfully equipped, wonderfully insatiable, every nuance at his command. Well, it just wasn't that way at all, and all his men friends, who were sure that was it, were plain stupid. Ask the women (not that they'd admit the truth). There was the big rush at the outset, while he was on a binge between pictures, a hungry-farm-boy technique, that was all; then you could wait for weeks for another pass, living right with him, too. That was what got you,—the cruel, indifferent, teasing withdrawal, all the worse because he had no idea he was being heartless. He could be lying on the bed right beside you, buck naked, absently flipping your eager hands off his body like so many horseflies, till you got so hurt you had to go off to some corner and bawl, with him lying there staring at the ceiling with nothing on his mind but how blue is sky and how black is night. He got under your skin that way, and damn his hide, he could always get any woman back—fifty years from now he could whistle through his old gums and they would all come flying up from hell to warm up his old bones. Other men—like Lew Schaffer and all the artists Lize and Darcy had run through—became just part of the everyday scenery after an affair was over. Like Lize or Darcy, who never left any trace of their past love.

Oh yes, there was usually a lipstick and a babushka left by Lize in a drawer. And Darcy's potato. ("There's nothing so beautiful in the whole world as a potato, I don't care what you artists say. A potato has everything," was Darcy's very own stand in all aesthetic arguments.) Darcy's potato crept into one painting or another like a Kilroy-was-here mark. Lew Schaffer had done a saint with potato eyes sprouting all over it, for instance, and Mrs. Schaffer had screamed, "So you've been sleeping with Darcy Trent!"

But Hugow got into your blood, kept you itching for him and hanging on shamelessly long after you knew he was through. Lize wondered how long before Darcy would admit it was hopeless.

"How do you mean this is a good chance to break with Percy?" Darcy suddenly asked. "How could you afford to go on staying at the Albert?"

"I could move into the studio with you," Lize said triumphantly.

Darcy's eyes widened.

"Oh no! What would people say, two girls living together! Oh, Lize, we couldn't, we just wouldn't dare!"

"Don't be so old-fashioned, for God's sake!" Lize said impatiently. There was something in what Darcy said, of course. Lize could already anticipate the snickering around The Golden Spur set when the news got out.

"It splits the rent, and you say you're scared alone. Okay, forget it," Lize said, but she had no intention of giving up the idea.

"I'm sorry, I always think of appearances." Darcy was sniveling again, and Lize could have given her a good slap. She looked toward the bar to see if any fresh company had arrived. The young man who had been reading the bulletin board was still there and, meeting his eye, Lize gave him a warm, friendly smile, which she saw had the proper energizing effect, for he started edging down the bar at once, pleased but hesitant.

"I think we can work something out," Lize murmured to Darcy absently, and waited for the right moment.

*

Jonathan had been stealing curious glances at the two young women in the back, even while his ears were tuned to the bar talk. He wondered if his mother had had just such a girlfriend who could, if he found her now, tell him all the intimate little confidences he longed to know. It was hard to picture his gentle mother in these surroundings, and surely she had never been as sophisticated as these two girls seemed.

The improbable red of the taller one's hair impressed him as stylish, while the smaller one's bright orange skirt lit up the dark corner like a forest blaze—an inviting touch, he thought. (Lize had been thinking that in that brassy hue little Darcy looked like a rather flashy mouse.) Jonathan was heartened to see that these two clean-cut New Yorkers were not above working over a good old American steak, and after Lize's friendly smile he was sure they were not formidable cosmopolitans after all, but simple, foursquare American girls. Never in the world would he have suspected the scrambled montage of bars, beds, and bushes behind their open, homespun faces. They were modern versions of his mother, Jonathan thought. He was considering a move to take the booth next to theirs when he felt a hand on his arm.

It was his companion of the wrecking scene.

"Come have a drink with me, young man," said the gentleman. "I have a class in precisely fifteen minutes and I defy anyone to face that sea of cretin faces without an anesthetic."

As Jonathan hesitated, his new friend went on confidentially, "I overheard you asking about Alvine Harshawe. It so happens that I recall seeing him here many years ago. He was just coming up then—some powerful stories in *The Sphere* and a play in the experimental theater. People used to point him out, that sort of thing."

"What was he like?" Jonathan asked eagerly.

The professor shrugged.

"Too sure of himself for my taste. Of course I was older and had done some writing of my own, but Harshawe was the comer, and the Spur was the writers' speakeasy."

"I'd like to know all I can about the Spur in those days," Jonathan said.

The professor studied him shrewdly.

"Another thesis on the twenties and thirties, eh?" he said. "Just what my colleague in the English Department has been working on for ten years. The Speakeasy as a Forcing Bed for Literature is her angle, I believe. I'm sure she'd be glad to share the background picture with you, because I'm the one who gave it to her, ha, ha."

He signaled for drinks, which Jonathan regarded uneasily.

"Place was horsy at first because the owner was a retired cowboy, got thrown by a wild horse in the rodeo at the old Madison Square Garden and won the place in a roll of dice. Fixed it all up with these racing prints and used to hobble around on crutches in his tight pants and satin shirts, Western style. Fought with a drunk and got thrown right through his own window, there. The place kept the horsy decor after he left, but then the jazz musicians took over till jazz went uptown; then it got the actors from the little theater upstairs, and finally the artists. Harshawe hasn't been even heard of in this place since the abstract wave took over."

"Did you know people who came here, say, around nineteen twenty-eight?" Jonathan asked.

"A few," said the gentleman. "I had just started teaching here in the East then, and I used to come in here with a student occasionally, and they would always point out the characters."

"Phone call, Doctor Kellsey," said the bartender. "What do I tell her this time?"

"Damn it, does a light go on all over the city every time I step into a bar?" cried Dr. Kellsey indignantly. "You told her once, didn't you, that Doctor Kellsey hadn't been in for weeks?"

"This is a different lady, Doctor," said the bartender.

"Ah. My wife. In that case tell her you don't know any Doctor Kellsey." He waited till the bartender hung up. "What did she say?"

"Said I was lucky," said the bartender.

"Damn these female bloodhounds," said the professor. He paid his bill and then fished out a card, which he handed to Jonathan.

"Here's where you can reach me if you'd like to get more

information. Always glad to talk over the old days with a fellow researcher. Helpful to both of us."

He gave Jonathan a genial handclasp that warmed his heart and hurried out.

DR. WALTER KELLSEY, KNOWLTON ARMS, GRAMERCY PARK, Jonathan read on the card. He copied it carefully in his little red notebook, glowing with the compliment of being taken for a fellow academician.

"Got a light, Buster?"

Startled, Jonathan looked up to see the tall girl with the pink hair beside him. He lit a match for her.

"Come on back and have a drink with us," she said, taking his arm. "No sense in being lonesome. Darcy and I are back here."

"I ought to be out looking for a room," he said, allowing himself to be led into the dark recesses, "and a job."

"It's too nice a day to be outdoors," protested the girl and nudged him gently into the booth. "Isn't that so, Darcy?"

Jonathan saw that the other girl was none too pleased at his intrusion.

"Really, Lize!" she exclaimed reprovingly.

"Okay, I picked him up, so what?" Lize looked him over with obvious satisfaction. "Doesn't he look like somebody, Darcy?"

"Doesn't everybody?" snapped Darcy.

She knew Lize had been getting bored with her damp sorrow, finagling for the last half-hour to get the eye of the stranger at the bar. Oh, he was good-looking in a clean, strapping Midwest way, and he did stand out in the Spur's galaxy of battered, beat-up gallants, but personally she preferred that battered, beat look on a man. At least you knew what they must have done to get that way, and what they were likely to go on doing. This eager, dewy-eyed Buster was too healthy to trust, apt to invite you for a chase over the moors, or to romp around a dance floor, clapping his hands over his head or swinging you around by the ponytail. Health was all right for women—God knows they needed it!—but a man ought to have something more special, an eyepatch, a broken nose, a battle scar, or a tired gimp like Hugow's. That was Darcy's theory. But Lize was on the prowl again, ready to snatch up the first thing that came along, now that she'd made up her mind to ditch Percy.

"You one of those college creeps?" Darcy asked Jonathan politely. "Is that why you got stuck with that stuffy professor?"

"Kellsey isn't stuffy except when he's on the wagon," Lize said severely. "Personally I like him. He's just a good-natured old slob that hates everybody, that's all. Be fair."

"He was very kind to me," Jonathan said. "He's going to help me on my research."

"I'm not going back to work this afternoon," Lize stated. "I think we should stick around here and get acquainted. Were you looking for a room on the bulletin board?"

Surprised that she had noticed, Jonathan nodded.

"I thought as much," Lize said. "You can relax, because we've got the place for you."

"Me?"

"Darcy needs a man to stay in Hugow's studio," Lize said, at which Darcy's crumpled little face tried to stiffen into an expression of moral outrage.

"Really, Lize!"

"It's all right, I'll be there too," Lize said. "Get it?"

Darcy looked at her with unwilling admiration.

"There's only the couch in the studio and the broken-down Hi-Riser in the back room," she said. "It has mice in it —just baby mice, though."

"He could have the couch," Lize said, who knew the place as well as Darcy did, after all.

"That's awfully good of you," Jonathan said, startled. "Are you sure you really would like to—I mean—"

"Listen to him," Lize said. "With his looks. Isn't he a beauty?"

She smiled at Jonathan meditatively.

"I love his hair," she mused. "I wonder what a real sharp crew-cut would do for him."

"You're always cutting people's hair," complained Darcy. "I had to cut Hugow's all over again to get it the way I liked it."

"Well, Cassie's probably sent him to a real barber by this time," Lize said maliciously; then, relenting, "Okay, Darcy, you can cut it this time. Can't she, Jack?"

"Jonathan," he said, embarrassed, not sure they were serious about anything.

Lize clapped her hand on his knee affectionately.

"Now I call that cute," she said. "Don't you, Darcy?"

Darcy was sulking, as if a new baby brother had put her nose out of joint.

"What's he doing looking for this Harshawe?" she grumbled. "Is he FBI or something?"

"We can help him get the lowdown on everybody once we get settled, eh, Darcy?" Lize chuckled. "Is that all right with you, Jonathan, moving in with us? We'll all save money by it."

It must be a perfectly ordinary New York custom, Jonathan thought.

"Everything's in a mess over there," Darcy said. "There's only some moldy marmalade and stuffed olives and shaving cream, but you're welcome."

She was cheering up under the prospect of company and taking an interest in the list of needed supplies Lize was jotting down. A little alarmed at the speed with which things were moving, Jonathan suggested he had better spend the rest of the afternoon looking around for a job.

"You sit right here, Bud," Lize commanded. "Everybody gets their jobs right here in the Spur, you might as well learn that right now. Why don't you take that café job up there on the bulletin board?"

"Do you think I could do it?" Jonathan asked.

This question struck both girls as irrelevant. If a job was what you wanted, you took whatever came along and found out later whether you could do it or not. If you got fired you still had your week's pay and came back to the Spur to hang around till another job turned up.

Jonathan was speechless with wonder at the amazing kindness of city women. Not only did the two new friends insist on dividing the check in three equal parts when it came, but they gave him explicit directions for getting to the Then-and-Now Café on Bleecker Street to apply for the job, and further information on getting to the new home he was to share with them. Then they left to do their marketing and to pick up Lize's suitcase at the Albert.

Jonathan took out his little red book after they left and wrote down his new address on the flyleaf. Before he gave up the booth, he wrote a note to the Miss Claire Van Orphen mentioned in his mother's letters, asking for an interview.

That's the way you did things in New York, he said to himself. Go right after 'em before you have time to think.

3

THE NOTE forwarded to her from the Pen and Brush Club had given Claire Van Orphen a full morning of reflections on the past. Some young man—the signature was unknown to her—would like to call on her on purely personal business connected with Constance Birch. He realized, the writer said, that a busy author like Miss Van Orphen must have had a dozen secretaries, and Constance Birch had worked for her less than a year—1928 it had been. But the experience had meant so much to his mother (for he was Constance Birch's son) that he dared to hope Miss Van Orphen might retain some recollections of her. Since his mother's death years ago he had regretted the lost opportunities for not having known her better, and now that he was in New York he was trying to enrich his picture of her by meeting those who had known her during her own New York period.

Constance Birch, Miss Van Orphen mused, putting down the note and frowning into space. What in heaven's name could she remember about her beyond the fact that she'd been the last secretary she had been able to afford? A pale, sweet, quiet little creature, Claire recalled, so shy you thought she'd be afraid to go home at night when she had to type late. Not at all, the girl had assured her. It was true that she had to cross that dark block under the El to get to her room, but she had the habit of stopping in a very nice bar for a sandwich and a beer, and there was always some nice fellow there going in her direction.

Well, I certainly can't tell her son about that, Claire reflected. Nor about the literary tea Claire had given—oh, those were the lavish days—in the Brevoort banquet suite, with Connie helping her in her nice unobtrusive way, and the surprising way the child had passed out in Claire's room later, passed out cold, as if there wasn't enough to do after a party.

"I'd never tasted champagne before, Miss Van Orphen," she had explained when she revived, greatly mortified. "And I'd never met so many famous men. Wasn't it awful?"

For the life of her Claire couldn't remember the girl's face or much of anything except that she was so obliging you couldn't fire her for her inexperience, and she didn't get on your nerves like the more hard-boiled efficient ones did, who charged more, besides. She did remember how anxious the girl was to learn city ways and yet how singularly blind she was to them. For instance, she always wore tennis shoes and simple little cotton dresses she made by hand, oblivious to the stylish touches from the *Vogues* she studied. Her pale cheeks would flush with excitement when she had to type a letter to some well-known editor, and she would stare with wide, eager eyes when Claire was on the telephone, then stammer, "M-Miss Van Orphen, excuse me, I couldn't help overhearing —do you really know Susan Glaspell personally? My!" Yes, her candid naïveté had made Claire feel sinfully worldly, she recalled, though there had been curious features about it. Like the time it had struck Claire that the child was available almost any hour of day or night and therefore must be having a friendless sort of life, so she decided to take her to The Black Knight for dinner, that being a popular speakeasy below the square where Claire had been taken once by an editor. On the way down Claire had felt a few qualms about introducing the little country girl to the kind of Village life she herself did not know or even wholly approve. It puzzled and amused her that, when they entered, several patrons, and the owner himself, cried out, "Hello, Connie."

"I thought you said you'd never been here," Claire said.

"Oh, I didn't know you meant Sam's," Connie said. "We just call it Sam's, you see."

Aside from those little kinks, Claire remembered nothing remarkable about her except that she had typed a serial Claire had sold to the *Delineator*, almost her last success. Well, all she could do for the young man, Claire thought, was to fill him in on the general background of Greenwich Village in the late twenties, the way biographers did when they ran short of personal facts.

Having so little to tell him, she would have the added embarrassment of disillusioning the lad about his mother's fine connections. Obviously the slight contact with Claire had been built up after the girl had gone back home and married the old steady beau. Claire recalled Christmas cards signed

"Connie, with appreciation for all your kindnesses my wonderful year in New York." She would certainly have to do something for the boy, have him come to the cocktail lounge for tea—the canapés were free. Sometimes a talented guest played the old grand piano, and there were young people around once in a while, so the place didn't seem such an elderly retreat.

It had been a long time since any stranger had looked her up, and Claire began to brighten. In the old days people they'd met on trips were always telephoning the Van Orphen girls—"You told us in Florence to be sure and look you up when we got to New York." It used to put the girls on their mettle, trying to put on a good show at home for those fascinating worldly strangers. Bea wasn't on hand for the sister act any more, of course; she had to manage alone now.

Claire pushed aside the avocado plant she was nursing in its glass of water on the window sill, and selected a pen from the glass slipper on her desk. She addressed an envelope to Mr. Jonathan Jaimison at the East Tenth Street address and began writing her note.

One thing Claire had no worry about was her clothes. She might be obliged to live in a cell, uncertain of selling a line she wrote, uncertain of the dear moments she could be granted with Bea, too modest to cling to successful old friends, but at least she need never worry about her appearance. She was happy in that knowledge.

Friends and relatives had scolded her years ago for throwing away all her money on clothes. "You'll have to go into your capital first thing you know," they warned. But in these difficult years Claire was glad of her wardrobe because good, really good clothes never go out of style, she said, and she'd rather feel a good three-hundred-dollar Molyneux dress on her back, even if it was thirty years old, than a brand-new budget-shop print, which she couldn't afford anyway. The ever-rising room rent in her modest hotel took a huge bite out of her vanishing income and dwindling royalties, but the backlog of fine clothes made her feel secure.

She had had to give up her original nice little suite for a bed-sitting-room barely large enough to hold her huge wardrobe trunk and hatboxes. The file cabinet had had to go to the cellar, but that was just as well. Instead of its testifying to her long, honorable professional career as a writer, those drawers full of manuscripts with attached lists of rejections and future publishing possibilities (now largely out of business) were rude reminders of a lifetime of misspent hopes. The simple little desk with its six pigeon-holes, tiny Swiss typewriter in the drawer, notebook and vase of pencils on top, were equipment enough for her present literary activities. The published pieces, the travel books and Christmas juveniles, were on the closet shelf, wrapped in cellophane. The stories she was always writing—for she could not stop the silly habit any more than she could stop saying Now-I-lay-me every night—she kept hidden in orderly stacks under the bed.

In the always-open trunk, stuffed closet, and bulging dresser drawers there were enough costumes for Claire to appear in different combinations for years to come. Some of the older creations, dating back to Paquin and Worth, remained in almost mint condition or only "slightly foxed," as the booksellers would say, and some of the post–World War I numbers seemed to be coming back in style. It was a pity that social life had deteriorated to the point where formal evening dress was seldom—indeed, where Claire was concerned, never —required any more. She had wistful moments of shaking out the bouffant rainbow tulle *robe de style*, the jewel-encrusted beige satin, the ruby velvet with richly embroidered panniers, the bronze lamé décolleté with flying wisps of gold-dotted net, and she would vow that if she ever got her hands on a good fat sum again it would pay her to go on an ocean cruise—they still dressed for dinner there, she was sure—just to get the good out of these treasures. She thought of the places where the gowns had appeared—the opera houses, the embassy balls, the garden parties, the state affairs honoring Colonel Van Orphen. All vanished and forgotten, wiped out, it seemed, almost in a day.

Every morning around half past ten, having had her instant coffee and an orange in her room at seven, Claire went to the Planet Drug Store around the corner and had an egg sandwich or Danish and a real coffee. This was the big adventure of the day, for all sorts of people dropped in at the fountain for a cup of coffee and chat with the counterman or with one another. They seldom started conversations with Claire, and although she realized her careful ensembles with matching hats and gloves intimidated them, she simply could not bring herself, a well-bred woman of over sixty, to step outdoors without hat and proper accessories. However, the counterman called her "baby," as he called all the ladies, and she could listen to the chatter, sometimes quite strange, and mull it over in her room later. There was a young man who talked about Shape Notes and the Fa Sol La Singers, from the West Virginia hills, and some television actors who talked about "bennies" and "dexies," and there was talk about show openings, reducing diets (these were always recited over chocolate sodas), new jokes, hospital experiences with explicit details that made Claire wince, and gloomy business talk by neighborhood merchants having a coffee or seltzer break.

"What do you do for a hangover, Jake?" the battered-looking haberdasher from next door begged to know.

"I just don't go there any more," said the counterman, and to his and Claire's amazement this made the gourmets split their sides laughing and became the great goody to be revived every day with wild shouts of joy. After this daily dip into the world, Claire retired to her room to write until her night meal of beans or spaghetti from the Horn & Hardart Retail Store, or, for a change, a tin of corned beef or a chicken leg and a pastry. She allowed herself the hotel dinner once a week. It was not fair that economizing on food should make you put on weight, but it was sadly true, and Claire had the devil's own time squeezing into her old gowns. The young woman at the hotel news stand was always gesturing to her that an under-arm seam had popped or that a top hook wasn't fastened. She further annoyed Claire with her helpful comments that her rouge or lipstick was crooked or too thick, and had she read that rouge wasn't fashionable any more? Claire always thanked her politely and continued making up the same way, placing a circle of fuchsia rouge in the exact center of each cheek and working it up toward the eyes as she had been doing since her first Harriet Hubbard Ayer beauty kit.

Once or twice a week, after she had revised an old love story or sold a little garden piece to a home magazine, she celebrated by walking over to a certain bar out of range of her hotel and treating herself to a Manhattan cocktail, sometimes two. When the frozen faced bartender or one of the oldtimers would spot the somewhat formidable lady in her hat, gloves, and carefully chosen afternoon costume rounding the corner, he would warn, "Here comes Miss Manhattan," and the customers would tip to the end of the bar like the balls on a bagatelle board, leaving one whole row of stools free for the lady.

"Good afternoon, Frank," Claire always said, assuming her place on the stool with dignity and speaking in her clear world-traveler voice, "A Manhattan, if you please. With cherry, thank you." After she had paid her bill, adjusted her veil, and marched out to the street, bartender and oldtimers would shake their heads and declare (as if they were Beau Brummells themselves) that nowhere in the world could there be found any outfits to equal those contrived by Miss Manhattan. In this they were quite wrong.

There was a twin of Claire's trunk in a hotel storage cellar on West Fifty-sixth Street, in which were many duplicates of Claire's collection. This trunk was the long-forgotten property of Mrs. Kingston Ball, née Beatrice Van Orphen, Claire's twin sister. Beatrice and Claire had dressed alike and done everything together until they were twenty-eight, when Bea, always the bolder of the two, declared the end of twinship. They had just lost another lover who, like all his predecessors, couldn't make up his mind which twin he preferred and was intimidated by there being two of everything. If there must be a pair, then he should have both or none; one would only make him feel cheated, as if he'd got only one book-end. Bea prophesied that this vertigo would attack every suitor they ever would get to the end of their days (somehow they got only one beau between them at a time) and they were blocking each other's futures. Claire was shattered and hurt by this proposal, as if she were to be stripped of her very skin, but Beatrice was determined. From now on she would tint her hair lighter and wear it short, and, since Claire loved their former style of dress, she could keep their dressmaker and Bea would buy ready-made. They would begin new, separate lives.

It was a bewildering blow to Claire to realize that this re-
volt had been simmering in her dear twin's head for years. It
embarrassed Claire to think of her fatuous complacency, never
dreaming of any divergence in their ideas on any subject. Her
sense of humiliation (for she felt she had somehow fallen below Bea's standards) made her accept Bea's program without
protest. When Bea burst into contrite tears at the final parting, saying, "It'll be much better for you too, going it alone,"
Claire gently comforted her with "Of course, dear, we're just
standing in each other's way."

So Bea moved to a hotel near Carnegie Hall, for she would
concentrate on their musical interests. Claire would pursue
her budding literary career and live downtown as before.
They would have different social engagements, take trips separately, affect different restaurants. This strategy, murder for
poor Claire, worked out well for Bea. When Claire chose a
Scandinavian cruise, Bea took Hawaii and there met and wed
Mr. Ball, a widower. At his death she returned to her old
hotel in New York but never to active twinship again. By that
time the wound had been assuaged for Claire by her trickle of
literary success—garden and travel articles and love stories for
family magazines; she too was content with occasional meetings which usually did nothing but reveal how far apart they
had drifted.

When Claire, carefully corseted and squeezed into the plum
velvet suit with moleskin toque and scarf, came up to Bea's
gloomy hotel for lunch, Bea hastily whisked her through the
long lobby, past the overstuffed Gothic sofas where the passé
(let's face it) international musical greats sat all day reviewing
the American scene. In the coffee shop Bea would pounce on
the darkest corner table, half ashamed and half protective,
suspecting the quizzical looks from the amusing young men
of her present circle, fervently hoping that her current pet
would not see her and guess her true age by Claire's costume.
She knew that Claire did not look any more of a period piece
than the majestic old Brunhildes and Isoldes wafting their
moth-eaten velvets through the hotel corridors, but it seemed
worse to flaunt your antiquity as Claire did than to be merely
eccentric.

On the other hand, when Bea arrived down at Claire's

hotel for the Washington Square summer concerts, wearing a jaunty strapless print sundress, gold barefoot sandals exposing red-painted toes, shoulder bones stabbing out behind like stunted wings, arms bare except for the costume jewelry and short white gloves, flowered ribbon bandeau on the close-cut blond hair, large Caribbean straw handbag swinging from her elbow, Claire led her to the very darkest corner of *her* gloomy dining room, feeling the sour glances of the lobby crones, reading bitchy meanings into the remarks of the nasty desk clerk that Bea was so sure she had beguiled.

"She's my sister, my own twin, and I love her, of course," each lady said after these reunions, "but we have nothing in common—nothing!"

All the same Claire longed for the day when Bea would need her and they could be together again.

4

A MAN is lucky if he discovers his true home before it is too late. True mate and true calling are part of this geographical felicity, but they seem to fall magically into place once the home is found. Virtues that have been drying up in the cocoon bloom and flourish, imp becomes saint, oaf becomes knight errant, Pekingese turns lion.

Jonathan recognized New York as home. His whole appearance changed overnight, shoulders broadened, apologetic skulk became swagger; he looked strangers in the eye and found friendship wherever he turned. With the blight of Jaimison heritage removed, his future became marvelously incalculable, the city seemed born fresh for his delight. He took for granted that his mother's little world, into which he had dropped, was the city's very heart.

Within a month he knew more of New York than he had ever known about the whole state of Ohio. True, each day he learned something that upset whatever he'd learned the day before, but after all the world went round, didn't it? He had an address, and he had a job which allowed him time to pursue his private program. The job was collecting historical tidbits about the neighborhood for a giveaway news-sheet in the new espresso café called Then-and-Now. The café was in the basement of a Bleecker Street real-estate firm that wanted to siphon off excess profits for tax purposes. Jonathan received thirty dollars a week, free sandwiches, cakes, and coffee, a desk, and a percentage of any ads he brought in. His new friend, Dr. Kellsey, adopted the café and furnished him with old Village lore. His other new friend, Earl Turner, was generous with editorial advice too, for he had once edited a glittering magazine called *The Sphere*. Mimeographed copies of *Café News* were stacked on the café's pastry counter, and to make sure the owners would consider it a success Jonathan saw to it that the sheets disappeared with speed.

A safe rule, Jonathan thought, was to assume that whatever would seem amazing in Silver City was the proper thing in New York. In Silver City people fussed over where they lived, the size and number of rooms, the suitable neighborhood, the right furniture. All New Yorkers, however, fell into whatever bed was nearest and called it home. In Silver City you lived with your family. In New York you lived with anybody but your family. The sofa might be full of mice just as the cot was full of rocks and the trundle full of nits, but for all Jonathan cared they could have been jumping with aardvarks. It was New York!

He was fortunate in having as roommates two ladies who were authorities on everything that mattered, and Jonathan listened gratefully to Darcy and Lize. The Golden Spur, they explained, was the cultural and social hub of New York City, which was bounded on the south by the San Remo, on the east by Vasyk's Avenue A bar, on the west by the White Horse, and on the north by Pete's Tavern. Friends who had deserted this area for uptown New York or the suburbs were crossed off as having gone to the bad. All connection with respectable family background had best be kept dark. Anybody with a tube of paint and a board was an artist. But writers were not writers unless decently unpublished or forever muffled by a Foundation placebo. The Word came only through grapevine gossip, never through print. The printed word on any subject was for squares. Although he had not met them, Jonathan felt on intimate terms with all the characters Darcy and Lize discussed, and soon was giving his own opinion on their affairs without hesitation. Hugow, Cassie Bender, Percy, Lew—they were his instant best friends, unseen.

It would take a little time, of course, to get used to living with two girls, having them stumble over his sleeping body in the studio on their way to bed at dawn. He had been gauche enough to propose that he move his bed to the windowless storeroom, a suggestion that brought a look of blank bewilderment to the girls' faces.

"What's the matter with your sleeping right here in the studio?" demanded Lize.

"What's so good about the junkroom?" Darcy pondered, equally baffled.

"I mean I'd be out of your way." Jonathan floundered. "I mean you'd be free to use this room for your dates and if you wanted to cook you could get to the kitchen without falling over me."

"Why would I be bringing a date to *my* place?" Lize asked Darcy in great mystification. "What makes him think we knock ourselves out cooking supper for a date?"

"I think it's kinda sweet of him, Lize," Darcy said tenderly, studying Jonathan with her little head sidewise, like a mother hen. He blushed and wondered whether she was measuring the depths of his naïveté or merely planning a new haircut for him.

"For your information, Buster, and strictly for the records," Lize told him firmly, "any date of mine takes me out, see. Home is for when you don't get a date or want to change your clothes. I've passed the stage where I date a guy just to save him money."

Darcy began to giggle.

"That would be the day," she said.

"Forget moving your bed," Lize said. "What I want to know is whether you can cook."

Jonthan had been used to cooking his own meals at Aunt Tessie's. No trick to it. Put some butter in a pan on the stove, throw in a piece of meat or can of something, and when it starts smoking, eat it.

"Steak? Hamburgers?" Lize asked with a light in her eye.

Especially steak and hamburgers. Ham and eggs.

"Didn't I tell you?" Lize cried triumphantly to Darcy. "I knew he was just the boy for us."

Jonathan was glad they allowed him to prove his helpfulness by fixing hamburgers for them that very night. The kitchen was his, they cried, from now on. Eager as he was to please, it took several days to learn just what was expected of him as cook, since the girls took off for their work before noon and never came home till there was no place else to go. Jonathan could use the kitchen table as a desk with no culinary distractions except at night, or rather at daybreak. The girls, though their programs after office hours seemed identical to him, did not hunt in pairs, but they did come home at approximately the same time, i.e., around four in the morning, after the bars had closed. Jonathan soon adjusted to this schedule, assuming it was typically New York. If he was awake he was glad to fix them bedtime scrambled eggs, but other times they did not disturb him.

Then one night he was roused by a little visitor groping her way into his bed. In the dim light from the street lamp he saw that it was Darcy, haloed in curlers, garbed in a pajama top, and greased as for the Channel swim, with some pleasant-smelling ointments. Flattered, he made room for her and she snuggled silently into place. The poor girl must be a sleep-walker, he deduced, and he should be ashamed for taking advantage of her infirmity, but, as often happens, his conscience arrived too late. All he could do was mumble, "Darcy, I'm terribly sorry this happened. I promise you I won't let it happen again, if you'll forgive me."

"Now you're waking me up!" wailed Darcy impatiently. "Can't you be quiet?"

"I just want to apologize—" But Darcy was fast asleep.

A few nights later he was wakened by Lize's sprawling into bed beside him.

"Just looking for a light," said Lize, extending a cigarette which he drowsily managed to light for her, but it seems she needed other comforts too. Taken off guard, conscience failed to strike, and since Lize had not a stitch on she must have had some dim inkling that the beast might be near. This time Jonathan reflected that an apology was not in order, nor even a thank you, but certain things mystified him. He knew it was his provincialism, and he would soon learn city ways, but—

"Do you always smoke—I mean—in bed?" he asked her cautiously, looking at the cigarette still dangling from her fingers.

"Hell, a girl has to do something." Lize yawned.

He had feared that these episodes, in which he blamed himself for taking advantage of their hospitality, would result in a change of atmosphere, but it finally dawned on him that they were no more important or meaningful than the midnight hamburger. City women were wonderful, he decided, but very strange. He heard them arguing over the comparative merits of their diaphragms and had the good sense to know they were not speaking of singing. In any case he was resolved to dodge further service as diaphragm-tester.

He also had the good sense to keep his private mission a secret from them, hoping they would not ask him about it, but
he need not have worried.

The girls never asked questions about a man's private interests or listened when he tried to tell them. For them it was
enough that he was a man and that he was there. Who needs
a *talking* man?

They were both dear girls, Jonathan thought, looking after
his interests and approving of everything he said and did in a
way no one in Silver City had ever done. They liked the plaid
shirt and moccasins he'd gotten on Eighth Street, just like
Earl Turner's, they understood his passion to grow a beard as
the flag of his emancipation from Home and Family, and then
applauded his change of mind due to the initial itching. It
was funny, Jonathan thought, when you considered how constantly these girls disagreed when they were together, how
similar their tastes really were when you got one of them
alone.

Both girls claimed to be afraid of their Tenth Street slum
neighborhood but would spring out at any hour of the night
to go any place else fearlessly. Coming *home* was what got
them, each said, and maybe this wasn't fear of marauders but
a sense of defeat in the evening's operations. In any case,
after a while Lize took to dropping into Jonathan's espresso
spot before closing time, for his protection going home. As
soon as Darcy found this out, she insisted they divide his time
equally, night for night. Protecting these young ladies from
hoodlums was not just a matter of walking them across town
and home, Jonathan discovered. It meant collecting nightcaps
along the way, invariably ending up at The Golden Spur to
check up on who was there, what they'd missed, and to make
sure that home was all there was left of the night.

In spite of their new truce, Darcy was distrustful of Lize.
She warned Jonathan of his danger on one of their walks
home.

"You've got to watch out for that Lize," Darcy said. "She
claims she walked out on Percy, but he told me himself that
he's the one that made the break. You can say what you want
to about Percy, maybe he is a creep and nobody wants him

around, but he's no liar, and he told me she's trying to get him to take her back. Talks about you all the time just to make him jealous. I hate seeing her try to use you the way she does. I try to sleep on the outside so she can't go barging in on you in the night—oh, Lize doesn't stop at anything, you know, where there's a man."

The next night Lize favored him with the same warning about danger from little Darcy, who was really stronger than he guessed. Jonathan thanked them both. He found he could keep them from harping on his danger by introducing Hugow's name, for this was a topic of which they never tired. It was a lesson in female psychology to hear that although Hugow had cruelly deserted each of them they bore him no grudge, for he had more than atoned by treating the other one badly too. The real villain in the case was that gallery woman, Cassie Bender, who was forever swooping down on some unsuspecting artist just as a girl was making out with him. A snob, they pronounced her, forcing Hugow to leave the old bars he loved for great champagne dos uptown with movie stars and Texas millionaires, the sort of thing Hugow detested, downright vulgar really, especially if you weren't invited.

Worse than snob, Lize cried, Cassie Bender was a common whore.

"Slept with every artist she ever handled," affirmed Darcy. "They all admit it when you pin them down."

Jonathan noticed that these caddish admissions were "pinned down" in the girls' own beds, but somehow this did not reflect on their own virtue.

"I swear I'm not going to break in any more artists for that old nympho," declared Lize, and both girls looked thoughtfully at Jonathan.

"I guess Hugow is a very fine painter," Jonathan said quickly. "Do you consider him better than Schaffer or the others?"

The girls pondered this for a moment, as if they had not thought of it before. They must have some opinion, he added, since they centered their private lives on painters.

"I don't see that there's much difference." Darcy shrugged. "They just think so because Cassie Bender gives them a line. One is the best one year and another the next. Cassie ruins them."

Jonathan gathered that Cassie Bender's real crime was her connection with that enemy, Art. She created a world of fame for a man and, common whore that she was, could lock other girls out of his life for weeks on end (as she was doing now with Hugow) just to get work out of him! Smart business-woman, nuts! She'd just been lucky enough to grab a big chunk from some rich old goat years ago. She had started her stable with that and now could buy her own pets.

"Wait till she gets a load of Jonathan here," Lize said.

"Me?" Jonathan was startled.

Darcy clapped her hands and studied him with fresh appreciation.

"Wow," she said. "I never thought of that."

"She'll buy him a box of paints just as an excuse to get her mitts on him too," Lize predicted. "I shouldn't be surprised if she doesn't line him up as a Hugow replacement."

"Wow," Darcy said.

"That's the Bender bitch for you," Lize said. "One of these days we'll come down here and find no pigskin briefcase, no electric razor, no tan raincoat on the hook, no Jonathan, just Cassie Bender's Lincoln streaking up the avenue."

"I'll bet he'd go, too," accused Darcy.

Jonathan wondered wistfully if his ignorance of painting would prevent him from meeting this predatory temptress, but he thanked his friends and said nothing could persuade him to leave his new home.

More important than the finding of a home with experienced guardians was the adoption of The Golden Spur as Jonathan's club. Earl Turner, the world traveler and personal friend of the great Harshawe, was responsible for this move. Before you looked for a job or a home or a girl, Earl instructed Jonathan, you must establish your bar base in a new city, just as you would choose a fraternity on entering a university. Look them all over carefully, he counseled, every bar people mentioned in the Village area—Minetta Tavern, White Horse Inn, San Remo, Leroy, Jumble Shop—all offering their special brands of social security. Compare their advantages and disadvantages. Is this a tourist trap, a "Left Coast" hang-out, or is it on the Bird Circuit, a meeting place for queers? Once you've made your choice, you conduct your social and business life there, since your home, mate, and job are bound to switch constantly. Make the owner or bartender your friend, use the place as a mailing and phone address, make your appointments there. Note the hours best suited for con-fidential talks there, the time for crashing a big party, the days when the roast beef is fresh and when it is hash; learn which barflies to duck.

Even if The Golden Spur had not recommended itself to Jonathan because of his mother's association with it, he would have chosen it. There was, as Earl pointed out, a nice diversity in the patrons. There were the college-faculty types, superior of their kind, for had they been average they would be sucking up to their departmental chiefs over in the Faculty Club or angling for academic advancement and traveling fel-lowships in stuffier environments. They wouldn't care to be caught bending elbows with the Spur's wild artists. The Spur artists were all "modern" in that they were against the previ-ous generation, though generations in art were not much longer than cat generations.

In season, these individuals flooded the bar Monday nights, flushed down in the preview champagne from the Upper East Side gallery openings, and on Friday nights from the show closings. The star of the occasion, at other times perhaps an inarticulate modest painter, then appeared with his brand-new claque, a tangle of patrons, dealers, and a change of blondes, himself now loud with triumph and ready to lick his weight in wildcats, which often turned out to be necessary. It's a mad-house, everyone cried joyously on these nights, a real mad-house, let's never go home.

Now that it was midsummer, the Spur's daytime character had a more tranquil aspect. Summer bachelors, whose absent wives disapproved of such places, strengthened themselves with a few scotches to face their shrouded rooms in the new luxury apartments nearby. Somber Adult Education students, in town to slurp up enough culture to nourish them through the long dry winter in some Midwest Endsville, sipped beer at the bar and dreamed of a wild Greenwich Village nymphomaniac who would oblige them to forget their careers. Young housewives in pants and sandals, hair in curlers under scarves, dropped in for a beer with their last-minute supermarket purchases and looked wistfully around for the no-good boy friends they'd given up to marry good providers. There were the old-timers, fixed in their own grooves of this drink on this stool at this bar at this time every day, year in, year out, so that they never heeded the changes in patrons from touts and bookies to little-theater people to neighborhood factory- and shop-workers, to whatever there was now.

Since Jonathan had accepted the Spur as the hub of New York life, it was only fitting he should invite Miss Claire Van Orphen to meet him there. It struck him as a favorable omen that chance had made him spend his first night in New York in the Hotel De Long, under the very roof of his mother's old patron. He read encouraging warmth in the note hinting that her memories of his mother were pleasant.

"Claire Van Orphen? Never heard of her," said his literary monitor, Earl Turner. Seeing Jonathan's face fall, Earl added kindly, "She must have been a best-seller in her day, that's why I never knew her."

Claire had dressed herself with care in the rose-spangled chiffon from a 1924 seasonal sale in a Paris boutique. In the hall mirror she saw that the dipping hemline might date it, and she evened it with gold safety pins. In a softly lit tearoom she would pass nicely, she thought, and the beige silk cape would cover any defects.

As with many writers, Claire's powers of observation worked only in unfamiliar territory, being comfortably off-duty on her daily beat. She had passed the Village Barn, Nick's, Ricky's, and a dozen other spots regularly for years without seeing them. The nasty little man at her hotel desk looked surprised when she asked how to get to the Golden Spur, and she thought it must be due to something racy about the place.

"It's right under your nose, Miss Van Orphen," he said with his customary sneer. "Right around the corner next to the auction gallery."

Even so, she would have walked past the place if a young

man had not stepped out and called her by name. She could not help smiling back at the engaging face.

"You must be Jonathan," she said. "How did you know me?"

Jonathan could not answer that the regal attire was exactly the costume he expected of a lady author, so he stammered that his mother had described her often. This gave Claire a twinge of uneasiness, for she had so little to tell him about his mother. She could not bear to disappoint him. What a dear young man he was too, with his twinkling brown eyes and quick smile that radiated a warmth uncommon in the world today! The gallant way he urged her to keep on her cape because of the air-conditioning inside moved her almost to tears, so long had it been since any man had been so solicitous.

Gratefully Claire vowed to herself she would do anything to help this dear lad get whatever it was he wanted. He was surprised that she had never been in the Golden Spur, since it was, he understood, the cultural center of Village life. Claire hastily assured him that she had, of course, often heard its praises sung and was happy to be there. She was flattered that he took for granted she would have a cocktail instead of sherry, and when he instructed the waiter to make her Manhattan dry, not sweet, she did not confess that the sweetness and the maraschino were what she liked best in a Manhattan. What a fascinating life she must have led among all the famous characters in this neighborhood, Jonathan said, and Claire nodded and smiled mysteriously into her glass, happier than she had been in years.

But nagging away behind her immense enjoyment of this adventure was the worrisome problem of digging up memories of his mother. For the life of her, Claire could not conjure up any but the palest picture of Connie Birch. A soft voice, yes, a very nice voice, unobtrusive, almost apologetic, she remembered, though the accent was corn-belt with that little bleat over the short "a"s and the resolute pounce on every "r." She must have had something special, though, Claire reflected, or else her mate had had, to produce such a remarkable offspring. It pained Claire to think of how obtuse she had been all her life, never seeing the true nature of those close to her—her own sister, for instance!—and now this boy's mother; granted she had been too much the lady to stare, polite blindness was surely no virtue in a writer. How nice it would be if she could produce a few intimate little vignettes to justify the young man's seeking her out!

Already Claire tingled with possessive pride in him, beaming when other patrons spoke to him, wishing fervently that sister Bea, who had many young men, could witness the way he introduced her, as if she were Edith Wharton. "This is Miss Van Orphen, Claire Van Orphen!"

She laughed at the story of his night in her hotel and of discussing with a porter the funeral of the newly deceased major he'd never known. Claire declared this to be a most amazing coincidence, for this would have been the funeral of her good friend Major Wedburn. Glad to gain time before she must answer questions about his mother, Claire chattered eagerly about the late Major Wedburn, such a distinguished military historian, pompous perhaps, but most impressive. He used to invite her every year to Ladies' Day at the Salmagundi Club and then was so amusingly discreet lest someone gossip about their residing in the same hotel! They exchanged manuscripts for criticism, which was nice, and had other professional contacts.

"Why, Major Wedburn was the one who sent Constance Birch to me for typing!" Claire suddenly interrupted herself, overjoyed to have found one small nugget, and in her relief invented words of admiration the Major had used at the time. Claire was ordinarily truthful, but she did want to prolong the interview. She made a bold decision to invent other little tidbits as coming from the late Major.

"That's the sort of thing I need," Jonathan said gratefully. "Sometimes I have only first names to go by; then my Aunt Tessie remembered others. When a name would be in the news, Mother would tell Aunt Tessie all about meeting the person with you or at your big parties."

Big parties indeed, Claire reflected wistfully, remembering the episode at the Brevoort, almost certain that it was the last time in nearly thirty years that she had entertained over six people at once.

"For instance, she wrote of meeting Alvine Harshawe with you," Jonathan went on, producing his little red notebook, "and there was a famous lawyer, George, who often called on you."

"George?" Claire repeated, her face reddening with embarrassment, for this nice boy's mother had certainly done some exaggerating, to say the least! Alvine Harshawe indeed! Claire found his work much too gamy for her own taste, but she would have been glad to claim his acquaintance. She could not deny knowing the man without calling the lad's mother a liar, so she improvised. "She must have met Harshawe when she was researching for the Major, who knew him well"—it *could* be!—"and the lawyer would have been George Terrence. George handled our family affairs for years."

She saw that the young man had his pencil poised alertly above the little red notebook.

"Of course I don't see much of him nowadays, because we haven't much for him to do any more," Claire said a little uneasily. "And he and Hazel have the place in Stamford, so—"

"Of course that is the George Mother meant!" Jonathan exclaimed. "Terrence, eh? All I knew was that the girl Mother lived with on Horatio Street was named Hazel and that later she married this lawyer named George. How do you spell Terrence?"

Claire spelled it out mechanically for him and gave the address outside Stamford where the Terrences lived. She was thoroughly baffled now. She could have sworn that Connie Birch had never been around during George's calls. But on the other hand she had not realized that the girl George married had been Connie's roommate. It was hard to believe that stuffy, ambitious Hazel had ever shared bohemian quarters with a colorless little nobody from the Midwest. But, if Connie had lived with Hazel, of course she had met George.

"I will write and ask them for an appointment," Jonathan said, pocketing his book again, beaming. "They're sure to have a lot to tell me."

Thinking of the Terrences' rigidly circumscribed social life of the past fifteen years, Claire wondered, and felt a little sad.

"I'll write them a note too," she said firmly. No matter how stuffy they had become, they surely could not fail to be charmed by Jonathan. Goodness knows, anyone as anxious to play the social game as Hazel Terrence could always use an extra young man, and George had always set himself up as such a liberal (carefully cushioned on a solid old capitalist tradition), which certainly meant being kind to strangers, didn't it? Claire thought, a little ruefully, that, although she was too proud to ask the Terrences any favor for herself, she had no compunction about asking for the young stranger. There was so little she could do for him; she had not really earned a second Manhattan. To deserve it she began improvising compliments that had been paid to Constance Birch. The Major, for instance, often mentioned the girl's outstanding ladylike qualities in a crass age. The Terrences—yes, it must have been the Terrences—often had remarked that little Miss Birch was too fine, her standards too high, for the vulgar struggle of the big city. Indeed—here the dryness of the second Manhattan must have affected Claire's ordinary prudence—she believed it was George Terrence himself who had advised the sweet child to go back to the simple decencies of her Ohio home. " 'Go and marry the boy back home,' " she improvised. "Those were his very words."

"Mr. Terrence advised that!" exclaimed Jonathan. "Then perhaps he was the one—"

"Unless it was Harshawe," Claire amended. "Or someone in the poetry group she attended, I remember—she was so different from the modern girl of the time, you see; we'd gone from the flapper to much worse, and such a plain old-fashioned girl stood out. I do hope you appreciate what a genuine lady your mother was, Jonathan, one of those shy, innocent little creatures everyone tries to protect. We all missed her when she went home, but we were glad for her sake. As George Terrence said—"

She paused, at a loss for more plausible remarks from George, but Jonathan took no notice, for he was consulting his precious notebook.

"Here's what my mother wrote about her friend Hazel's fiancé," he reported. " 'George is practically certain to be a great lawyer, another Clarence Darrow.' "

What a desperately romantic young woman the boy's mother must have been, Claire thought.

"Dear me, George Terrence was much too modest to make

a trial lawyer," she corrected him gently. "Very brilliant on briefs, of course, and highly regarded, but—"

"He might be the man!" Jonathan said, pursuing his own thoughts. "He didn't marry Hazel till Mother had gone back to Ohio and gotten married herself, don't you see?"

"No, I don't see," Claire confessed.

"All I have to go on is the fact that my real father was a very famous man," Jonathan explained.

"Mr. Jaimison?"

"No, I mean my *real* father, the man my mother was in love with before she married," Jonathan said. "He might have been a famous lawyer, mightn't he? And George Terrence, as you say, took a great interest in her?"

Claire's mouth fell open.

"You can't mean what you're saying." She choked. "Not that quiet, sweet little girl. My dear boy, you're not going to ask George a question like that!"

"I shan't ask him directly," Jonathan reassured her. "I just want to meet him and find out what he can tell me about my mother, and I can judge from that. If it turns out I'm the heir to a great legal mind, I will know what to expect of myself."

She mustn't spoil this beautiful friendship by behaving in a panicky, spinsterish way, Claire told herself. Be cool, be debonair.

"Of course," she said quite casually. "I felt better about my literary potentialities when I learned a great-grandfather had once published a novel. It's like money in the bank, knowing there are certain genes you can count on."

"I knew you'd understand," Jonathan said. "All my life before this I didn't think I could count on anything but the Jaimison pigheadedness. Now I can be anything. For instance, if my father was a great writer—"

"Like Alvine Harshawe." Claire smiled.

Jonathan blushed, but defensively admitted that it was a possibility. He had taken to keeping an extensive literary journal himself, he said, writing at his espresso shop, which, so far, was pleasantly ignored by the cake-and-ice-and-coffee set.

"I had no idea young people nowadays took anything but martinis," Claire said. "Do they really go for ice cream?"

"Sometimes they're on 'tea,' or else heroin," Jonathan said.

"They keep off alcohol because they don't want to mix their kicks, you see."

Claire nodded approvingly.

"Very sensible, I'm sure," she said, taking a dainty sip of her Manhattan. "I've always felt one gets more out of life by enjoying one pleasure at a time."

There, now! she thought, proud of herself for having smothered her virtuous instinct to warn Jonathan against dope fiends, drunkards, and harlots. But the pitfalls were everywhere, waiting to trip her into some horrid puritanism that would limit the youth's confidence. To be on safe ground she asked about his room and if he found New York lonely.

"I couldn't ever be lonely in this town," Jonathan said dreamily, "even if I lived all alone instead of with these two girls."

"It must be jolly," Claire said, catching her breath. "I mean it must be so much more interesting with two than just living with one."

She was steeled to babble on about the sheer common sense of triangular living or multiple-mistressing, but was saved by a man beckoning to Jonathan from the telephone corner. While Jonathan was gone to confer with his friend, Claire looked about her, filled with the joy of being brought —perhaps shocked—back to life. The hunting prints and racehorse pictures on the wall struck her as masterpieces of art, the flyblown lamps perfect period gems, the stables as booths a most original decorating caprice, and now Jonathan was bringing toward her the stranger with a little goatee and a plaid shirt exactly like Jonathan's.

"This is Earl Turner, Miss Van Orphen," Jonathan said triumphantly, as if he had finally brought the heads of two great nations together. "You're both writers so you must have lots to talk about. Earl tells me I have to go right over to see about a fire in my building—"

"It's all over now," Earl explained. "It's just that Hugow wants Jonathan to let him in and get out some canvases he left in there. Valuable paintings, that sort of thing."

"Earl will look after you," Jonathan assured her. "You've helped me so much, and I'll call you again next week."

He grasped her hand with a radiant, innocent smile, as if illegitimacy, opium-smoking, two mistresses, and a house on fire were all on the good ship *Lollipop*. He dropped a bill on the check. Claire sat back as he hurried out, and his friend in the beret slid into the seat. Claire saw that the friend was a man over fifty, and she knew from experience that there's nothing irks a man over fifty more than being stuck with a woman his own age. Earl's glum expression agreed with her guess.

"It's an interesting little place," she said politely. "Such interesting types, don't you think? Those artists at the bar, for instance."

"They're waiting for their girls to come in from work and buy them a drink," Earl said morosely.

"Interesting!" Claire said firmly, but she felt weak and deserted and knew she should leave.

She could feel the fine self-confidence built up by young Jonathan melting away under the bored expression of her companion. He scarcely glanced at her, classifying her no doubt as a dull family friend of Jonathan's, entitled to the respect due her age but nothing more. He looked beyond her to greet new and young arrivals, drumming on the table as he smoked. Stubbornly Claire took her time finishing her drink.

The Spur was filling up with the pre-dinner crowd now, all races and all costumes, bohemian, white-collar, beach, collegiate, Hollywood. There was an undercurrent of muffled anticipation in the air, and the special timbre in the murmuring voices, the secret knowledge in the gurgling laughter, the searching look in the eyes of everyone seemed faintly sinister to Claire. The revelation of what Jonathan Jaimison was seeking here, his sudden departure, and the letdown after her initial excitement left her frightened and unnerved, as if all this were building up to the real opera, in which there was no part for her. It annoyed her that her hands shook as she drew on her rose-colored gloves and that Jonathan's friend should be watching her now.

"Pretty rough crowd for you, I'm afraid," he said.

"Not for me, Mr. Turner," Claire said with dignity. "I find the people most attractive. The blond girl you bowed to looks fascinating."

"Fascinating indeed!" Earl said. "She just got back from

Greece, where she's been living on money she got from selling her baby. Couldn't afford an abortion, you see, so she
went ahead and made a nice deal out of the kid, if you call
that fascinating. Now she'll make a career out of breeding."

He wanted to shock her, Claire knew, and steeled herself.

"Enterprising, then," she said lightly. "Girls today are so
clever. I suppose that nice boy—or is it a girl?—with her is
on 'tea.'"

Earl snorted derisively.

"He never made that kind of money," he said. "He's lucky
to scrape enough together for Dexedrine and beer."

"A pity," Claire said wildly. "He looks so intelligent, you'd
think his habits would be more original."

Earl was looking at her now with puzzled amusement.

"You think he ought to live up to that long hair?" he said.

"Why not?" Claire asked and rose to go. She would be the
stately literary figure that Jonathan assumed her to be, she
told herself defiantly, not the timid spinster. "At least he looks
an artist."

"Trust the buckeye boys to play the tourist's dream," Earl
said. "Like the drugstore cowboys."

Maybe he wasn't being deliberately rude, Claire decided.

"I'm sorry I don't know your work, Mr. Turner," she said
graciously. "Jonathan said you were a writer. I'm sure I've
heard the name."

"Probably from the time when I edited *The Sphere*," Earl
said, mollified. "Of course that was some time ago."

Some time ago indeed, Claire thought, for the magazine
had come and gone a good twenty years ago.

"Such a brilliant magazine!" Claire said. "I was so sorry to
see it fail. Well, good night, Mr. Turner."

"Wait," said Earl. "I'll walk you to your hotel."

The polite gesture seemed to surprise Mr. Turner himself as
much as it did Claire, but it had been a long time since anyone had remembered *The Sphere*.

"No reason you should know my work," he said as they
walked up Fifth Avenue. "I haven't published anything recently."

"Nor have I, Mr. Turner," Claire admitted. "There doesn't
seem to be the demand, do you think?"

"Certainly not for me." Earl gave a mirthless laugh. "Frankly I never got back in my own stride after rewriting all the world's leading geniuses for *Sphere*."

"I'm sure you're much too modest," said Claire. "I'm afraid you're being too severe an editor of your own work."

"Well, in a way," Earl conceded, and was moved to tell Claire of his foolish perfectionism that made his stories too good to sell or for that matter even to write. They stood in the lobby of the Hotel De Long, eagerly chattering of literary matters, ignoring the avid eyes and ears of the elderly witches and aging beaux propped along the wall sofas.

"You should make them into a book," Claire advised. "I must remember the name of that editor at Dutton's for you."

The lobby heads swiveled unanimously as the two literary friends moved toward the elevator and were lost, alas. In Miss Van Orphen's tiny room (she was glad her little plants were blooming so nicely) they continued their discussion with great animation over glasses of instant coffee laced with a few drops of Christmas brandy. When Claire reported the delicious recipe the Planet's soda jerk had for hangover ("I just don't go there any more"), Earl declared she had the makings of a perfect little vignette for *The New Yorker*.

Claire promised that she would certainly try to write it, for it had been a long time since she had had any editorial inspiration. Earl acknowledged that it had been a rare pleasure for him, too, to exchange ideas with a fellow writer. They should meet often. As a first step he would call on her this very week and give her his constructive suggestions on whatever manuscripts she had on hand.

A wonderful day, Claire thought, and all due to the invasion of New York by young Jonathan Jaimison. In her gratitude she wrote a note before she went to bed to the George Terrences, urging them to see Connie Birch's son by all means. And then—because it was cruel to have a red-letter day and no one to share it—she had to write a note to sister Bea, imploring her to name a day for lunch, for it had been weeks, months. You just had to have someone, Claire told herself, tears in her eyes. Even when you knew they were bored with you, as Bea was with her, you had to have someone to *tell*.

5

H UGOW sat on the cracked stone stoop of the brown tenement on East Tenth Street and watched the fire ceremonials going on across the street. He had been so interested in the black and gold medieval-looking firemen's uniforms, the loudspeaker directions from the chief, the beautiful red engines, and the hose snaking in and out of windows that it took a minute to penetrate that the fire was in his own building. It was a small fire, put out almost at once, but he had panicked, thinking of the canvases he had stored in the fourth-floor studio. He was shaken, too, with the evidence that his hunch to rush home had been justified.

Last night, for instance, he had been swigging Tom Collinses on the terrace of Cassie Bender's shore house four hundred miles away when he was suddenly smitten with a passionate, overwhelming hunger. And for what?

For hunger.

He wanted to throw up the whole scene, the fine yellow gin, the perfect studio Cassie had fixed for him, the successful authors and actors and art-lovers and Bennington girls—"the cream of the Cape," as Cassie said—their Good Conversation; Christ, how sick you could get of Good Conversation. "Good Talk." There was no such thing as Good Talk. Talk was Talk and worse than marijuana for getting you high and nowhere. Sure, he talked too much when he was drunk, but he had the sense to be ashamed afterward, ashamed for diluting the pure classic joy of drinking with the cheap vice of yakking. He had wanted to throw up the fine Cape Cod air, the beach, the crystalline sunshine, Cassie's smothering love, and the rooms full of intelligent appreciators, and get back to a slum full of overturned ashcans, Bowery bums sprawling over the doorstep, lousy barflies who insulted him, jerks, Eagle jerks, Cub jerks, people who hated him for himself alone and not just because he was doing all right. He wanted to get back to a studio that had no comforts, just light and nobody in it; he wanted a new girl, someone who didn't understand him and that he couldn't understand, so that they could run through each other fast with no dead vines clinging, as in most of his other affairs. He wanted to *want*, that was it, he wanted to see something far off floating up like a forever-lost kite out of all possible range, something to blind and dazzle him so he could work for it. He wanted dirt, limitless oceans of dirt, so he could have the intense need for clean, he wanted loneliness so he could suffer the old ache of yearning for human contact.

The urge was so overpowering that he had walked past the pretty girl waiting for him to bring her a drink, pushed through the little groups on the terrace, down the sunflower path through the vegetable garden, through the tangle of bayberry bushes down the hill to the highway, the martini glass still in his hand. A butcher's truck stopped for him and turned him over at a gas station to an oil truck headed for Brooklyn. Hugow had to fight carsickness all the way down, but it wasn't the riding or the bumps, it was being fed up with being fed. Fat-cat-sick, that's what it was. Death. He had to get back to the screaming panic of the city. He had to get back to his own Village, to the half-finished canvas he had deserted. He had to find again that green, the wonderful green, the true paint-green, the unearthly sea-bottom moon-green, not the lousy nature-green of trees and grass. He'd almost gotten it once, then Darcy bugged him and he bolted and left everything in the old Tenth Street studio. When he got down there finally and saw the fire, he knew the picture had been calling for him, calling for help, and that had scared him, reminding him once again—as if he needed to be told—that what came from his brush was his own blood.

He could have gotten there earlier, but he had waited to be sure Darcy wouldn't be around, so he could sneak out his canvases without a scene. The crowd collected for the fire had drifted away, the Chinese laundry in the basement had been flooded, Chu Chu was out front, screaming curses at the cops and firemen.

Hugow had rushed up the steps, was putting his key in the lock when a cop's hand closed over it.

"What's your name, bud?"

"Hugow. I want to get into my studio."

"Hugo, eh. So you got a studio here. Funny there ain't no Hugo name here."

"It's the fourth floor rear."

"Fourth floor rear, eh. 'Jaimison, Trent, Britten. Fourth Floor Rear.' No Hugo. Let's have that key, bud, before you go making trouble for yourself."

You can't argue with cops—not when there was a chance of Darcy's popping along to make things worse. Even old Chu's recognizing him did no good, since he shook his fist at Hugow in his crazy-mad way, shouting that those evil artists upstairs must have set the fire in his honest laundry, throwing their turpentine rags around. Hugow had to withdraw, finally having extracted the information that the whole place was under guard until there was no chance that the original blaze would spread upstairs. No one would be admitted without credentials. After a moment's puzzled speculation on what had brought Lize and Darcy under the same roof, Hugow turned his attention to the third name. If he could get hold of this Jaimison he might be able to get in. Somebody at The Golden Spur would know who was staying here with the girls, Hugow was sure—the bartender, Earl Turner, or Lew Schaffer. He went to the candy store on the corner and phoned the Spur. Sure enough, Earl Turner was around and said the fellow Jaimison who was camping out with Lize and Darcy was right there. Earl promised to see that he came over to let Hugow get in and collect his stuff before the girls showed up.

"What goes on here anyway?" Hugow asked as an afterthought. "Is this a design for living?"

"Wasn't it always?" Earl answered.

It had been several weeks since Hugow had been in his old neighborhood, and he walked around Tompkins Square while he waited, dropping into the Czech bar for a beer, buying a bagel at a Polish delicatessen, and thinking that for all its many nationalities and mixed customs it was a mean, thin-spirited, hostile neighborhood. That was the East Side, rich and poor, all the way up till you got to Yorkville. He'd spent three years in the Tenth Street studio and was glad to be out of it, glad he'd lined up a new place way over on the West Side near Houston. The lights coming on around Tompkins Square and the fading daylight gave a romantic glow to the old houses, the "fudge light" that made madonnas out of the fat old shrews yelling out windows for their children or drag-

ging them along the streets with a whack and a cuff; it made
kindly peasants out of the suspicious, foxy merchants waiting
in the doors of their shops to short-change any crippled blind
man, especially if he was a brother. You could live on the East
Side all your life and still be a stranger. It must be the Italians
who warmed up the West Side, for they laughed and sang and
loved their babies: they wore pink shirts and red dresses so
their flying clotheslines were really glad rags. The East Side
was too near Vermont, maybe that did it, Hugow mused,
happy with this fancy, Vermont, where the country itself was
always trying to throw off the people, like a beautiful wild
horse that will never let itself be conquered by inferior riders.

The bums were the only good thing about the East Side,
Hugow thought, getting back to the stoop opposite his studio. At this time of day they had drifted down to the Bowery
missions for their handouts, but they'd be back later with
their half-pints of muscatel as nightcap before bedding down
in the entry halls or stoops along here. The Third Avenue El
used to hold them in as much by its safe shadows as by its
posts stretched out like a lifeline all the way down to Foley
Square. When the structure was torn down, leaving the avenue shorn of shade, bald as the Siberian steppes, the bewildered bums spilled all over to the side streets, rootless and
compassless, churning east and west, river to river, still calling
the Bowery home, but the Bowery was now an overblown
matron without her stays. There was no home except other
bums, bottles, empty doorways, a sunny stoop in winter, a
shady one in summer. The Bowery was only in the uncaged,
prowling, alley-happy heart. Like mine, Hugow thought, always on the prowl for something to louse up his life.

He lit a cigarette and watched for the Jaimison man, wondering if he belonged to Lize or to Darcy. Either one would
serve to get himself off the hook. It was a relief to be free of
Cassie too, good old Cassie who was always rescuing him and
had sustained him during his last work. Funny how a woman
and a picture got finished for him at the same time. Funny
that, whoever she was, she could never reach him again, her
warmth could do nothing for his chill, the empty chill of
finished work, the chill that he knew was a piece of dying.
For this he could only be revived by a fresh love, simple and

childish, or worldly and artificial, or perhaps a wild, nettle-some, raging affair of action, drama, brutal encounters without affection or any plane of communication. No one could say he was unfaithful. The word unfaithful was not for him, nor the word promiscuous, nor the words irresponsible or ungrateful, because a man who has never been chaste, faithful, responsi-ble, or grateful could not become *not* those things. Say he was a person of prodigious needs, using everything and everybody as his personal fuel. Only when he was drained, between pic-tures as he was now, did he become a human being, simple, lonesome, and sweet, making the friends and loves then that would feed him later.

The blond young man hurrying down the street must be Jaimison, Hugow surmised, and went to meet him. Having heard of the great Hugow, Jonathan was surprised to find him no Viking Apollo with a thundering baritone voice, but a man shorter than himself, with a hesitant apologetic drawl, an in-dolent way of walking that partly concealed a slight limp, long grayish-brown hair that he shook out of his eyes impatiently, a pointed sort of face, fawnlike when he focused his intense gray eyes on you, through you, perhaps beyond you. He was in slacks and sport shirt and needed a shave. After the brief mutual examination, Hugow took Jonathan's arm.

"So you're the replacement," he said. "You paint?"

"I'd like to," Jonathan said politely.

"Either you paint or you don't paint," Hugow said. "Did Earl tell you what I wanted? I've got to get the rest of my pic-tures out of the place before Darcy shows up and gives me a bad time. The cop thinks I'm a burglar, so you have to spon-sor me."

At the entrance there were now only two cops and Chu, who was angrily boarding up his broken window. Jonathan unlocked the door, and they climbed the three flights to the top floor. Jonathan had gotten used to coming home to a hurricane of feminine disorder, realizing after only a few weeks' training that the trim perfection of two young ladies' working appearance could not be achieved without a wild trail of bath towels, shoes, powder, bobby pins, scattered hose, coffee cups, tousled pajamas, empty milk bottles, and basins of soaking lingerie. Now he felt embarrassed and scooped up a tangle of wet nylons.

"I usually throw everything in a closet," he mumbled apologetically. "I'm the last one out in the morning."

Hugow took a look around the room and threw up his hands.

"They've taken over, I see that much. This is what women mean when they say they want to look after you. How do you manage to fit into this picture?"

"We're in and out at different times," Jonathan said. "We don't interfere with each other."

Hugow went to the kitchen. The dishes from a spaghetti supper of two nights before were in the rusty sink, and a half-gallon chianti bottle with an inch of red in the bottom stood on the floor. Hugow opened the closet door, where a shredded broom and a balding floor mop leaned. He reached up to yank a pulley which brought down from mysterious heights a clutch of canvases strapped together. He handed them to Jonathan. He reached up again and triumphantly fetched down a bottle labeled BURKE SPRINGS BOURBON. He noted that it was almost full and nodded with satisfaction.

"First thing you have to learn about a dame is whether to hide your bottles high or low. You have to hide them high for Darcy," he explained. "I'm surprised Lize didn't spot it, though."

He took a drink from the bottle and handed it to Jonathan.

"Lize and Darcy! How do you like that!" He laughed. "Thank God it's you in the middle and not me this time. I guess I owe you something for taking Darcy off my neck. I suppose they're both sore at me now."

"They blame it all on Cassie Bender," Jonathan said.

Hugow frowned.

"I forgot about Cassie," he said. "She's the one that's cursing me out right now, I suppose. I should have sent a wire or phoned collect or— Oh hell, I can't be apologizing to Cassie all my life, can I?"

"Not for the same thing, I guess," Jonathan said, and this seemed to please Hugow for he slapped him on the back approvingly.

"Too bad you aren't an artist or you could take on Cassie

too," he said. "Never mind, you've got your work cut out
with Lize and Darcy. How'd you happen to get trapped?"

"We thought it would save money," Jonathan said.

"More power to you, man," Hugow said skeptically.
"Maybe you can handle those things better than I can. Let's
get a move on before they can jump on us. You and I can cart
my stuff over to my new studio. They don't know where this
one is, that's a break."

Hugow opened a closet door, peered under the cot, took a
last look around the studio, found a tin can of evident value
to him, which he handed to Jonathan with the whisky bottle.

"You take these. Let's go."

There seemed no question that Jonathan would come with
him, and Jonathan thrust the bottle into his pocket and followed down the stairs. A bearded old bum, pockets overflowing with rags, grinned and pointed urgently at Jonathan's
bottle.

"I'm a Harvard man too," he said. "How about it?"

"Get your own brand," Hugow said, flipping a coin at him.

They walked down First Avenue, down toward Houston,
where they would get the Houston Street crosstown, Hugow
said, which would let them off near his new studio. He was always so glad to get back to Manhattan, he said, that he started
walking as soon as he hit the beloved pavements so as to get
the empty, clean smell of the country sunshine out of his system and let God's own dirt back in. He stopped at a pushcart
and bought a bag of plum tomatoes. In the shadow of a
boarded-up tenement building a group of derelicts were quarreling quietly over a bottle. The light from a basement bar next
door shone upon a huge figure of a man blocking the street.

"Doesn't anybody want to buy my blood?" he was saying
in a tired singsong. "I have very good blood. Doctors give a
hundred dollars a pint for my blood. Don't somebody want
to buy?"

Outlined by the traffic lights and lamps above and below,
he stood motionless, like a wax display figure on sale, one
great hand uplifted, commanding Hugow and Jonathan to
stop. He had no dangling rags and bags as the other bums
did, but his outfit had a mission-neat, mothball, decayed
shabbiness, vest, jacket, pants, shoes in the same varying

shades of ghoul green as his skin, and the wide-brimmed moldy old Quaker hat. The large bulbous nose, the greenish-gray hair and lashes, the gray-white eyes, all had the deathly color of leather buried for centuries in Davy Jones's locker, and the neatly rolled cloth bundle under his arm seemed a mariner's kit. His complexion was the curious paste of Dutch blondes mixed with blue-black native, with no gold or glow of tropic sun coming through. He must have been drowned a long time, Jonathan thought.

"Do you wish to buy my blood, sir?" the man murmured.

He was still standing there, motionless, as Hugow and Jonathan got on the bus. Hugow looked back out the window, and Jonathan saw that he was smiling radiantly.

"That's what I've been needing," he said. "God, how I love New York. Did you see that green?"

"Mushroom color, I thought," Jonathan said.

Hugow shook his head dreamily.

"The green I love, the green that is everything but green," he murmured. "I should have bought his blood just to see what makes it."

Jonathan said nothing, afraid he might strike the wrong note and cut off this beautiful new friendship at its very birth. This rare creature, this great god who seemed to be the heart of The Golden Spur circle, had taken him in as one of his own kind without hesitation. Jonathan felt as if a wild bird had flown to his shoulder and one false move would frighten it away. Now *he*, like the others, would be one of Hugow's willing slaves. He forgot about Claire Van Orphen left in the Spur, he forgot what chores were expected of him at the café, he was in the beatific glow of the master's favor.

At Varick Street, Hugow motioned to him to pick up the canvases and get off the bus. They turned a corner and stopped in an alleyway behind an old wooden warehouse. Hugow unlocked the door and they entered a pitch-black hall and fumbled their way up rickety wooden stairs. At the third flight a skylight let in enough light to show the way, and through a tiny half-moon window Jonathan glimpsed the twinkling lights of the North River craft and the Jersey shore beyond. The loose boards clattered underfoot, and a piece of stair rail broke off in his hand and rattled down the steps.

"I figured if I got a place crummy enough, I could keep out dames for a while," Hugow explained. "A guy's got to have a little time to himself, right?"

"They couldn't find their way here," Jonathan said.

"Women find their way any place," Hugow said. "They know where you're going before you've even made up your mind. But I'm safe for a while here, thank God."

Jonathan lit matches while Hugow fiddled with the latch. It turned out a key wasn't necessary, for the door fell open at the first push.

"Damn those kids," said Hugow.

But the burglar was a female and seemed to have made herself at home.

The girl was sprawled over a battered Victorian sofa, her long legs in black leotards flung up over the back. A pair of candle stumps dripped into saucers on an empty packing crate beside her and cast a glow over a dark face, sullen in sleep, with a tangle of thick black hair falling over it. She opened her eyes as they entered the loft.

"Iris!" Hugow exclaimed. "How'd you find it?"

"Asked around the bars," she said. "Mad?"

"Tickled to death. How'd you get in?"

"Beer opener." She sat up, yawning, and looked at them defiantly. "No use getting excited just because you forgot to invite me. I can't get into my room because the sublet is still there."

"What about your tryout?" he asked.

"Flopped. I flopped, especially. I was run out of Westport."

"So hello," Hugow said and tousled her hair.

She stood up and stretched herself lazily, like an enormous cat. She was taller than Hugow. Jonathan could not take his eyes away from her, fascinated by the tawny sheen of her skin and by her voice, which was rough and dark, with breaks in it like a boy's.

"There's nothing in the icebox but ice," she said.

"Ice is all we need," Hugow said, taking the bottle out of Jonathan's pocket. "This is my best friend. Better ask him his name."

"Jonathan Jaimison," said Jonathan.

"You're a writer?"

"Oh yes," Jonathan said, pleased. "Yes, I think so."

"Isn't this place great, Jonathan, boy?" Hugow demanded. "Look at that window. Look at those rafters."

Jonathan nodded but he could not take his eyes off the girl. Why, this was love at first sight, he thought. It had something to do with Hugow's adopting him and the man selling blood and the half-moon glimpse of river lights and the way the dark girl in the candlelight lit up the room with her voice and flash of laughter. Did she know it was love too? She was staring at him with her thick black brows drawn together.

"You look like someone," she said.

"Who?" Jonathan asked eagerly.

"Maybe somebody in the news," she said. "I'll remember later."

Hugow found jelly glasses and set them out with a tray of ice and his bag of plum tomatoes. He pulled out a lopsided brown leather chair, into which he sank happily.

"Beautiful!" he said, and Jonathan agreed enthusiastically. It was a barn of a place, really, floored only in the middle, with the rafters spreading out under low eaves at both sides. Etched on the big window, the West Side highway strung red and green lights into a dark yonder. A folded cot leaned against the long plank table.

"Wonderful to be back." Hugow sighed, fondling his drink. "Cozy nest, fine drink, fine old friends. Then Iris! My hunches are always good. I got the message about the fire in the studio and then the message that Iris was here. Amazing!"

"I knew if I had sent you a real message you would never show up," Iris said.

Hugow winked at Jonathan.

"Iris is a quick study," he said.

"You taught me," said Iris.

Jonathan looked from one to the other, feeling very much left out. They were a thing, no doubt about it. You could feel the current crackling between them, even though they were half the room's length apart and not looking at each other. He felt miserable and suffocated with love for both of them. If they were lovers, he should have the decency to clear out, but he couldn't bear to leave them, or the beautiful room fur-

nished so sumptuously in shadows, distant lights, and unknown desires.

"Iris is going to be a great actress, Jonathan," Hugow said.

"I know it," Jonathan said sincerely. "You can tell."

"Can you really?" Iris asked eagerly, fixing her eyes on
Jonathan. They were great dark eyes that seemed to drink in
more darkness, brimming over with night, he thought, orphan
eyes, deserted-wife eyes, slave eyes, beggar eyes. Even with her
white teeth gleaming in a fleeting smile she seemed utterly
dark, only reflecting outside color like the black river yonder.
It was a relief to have Hugow break the spell.

"Iris is almost twenty-one, so she thinks she knows what
the score is," Hugow said banteringly. "Three years in New
York, what the hell? Wait till you're forty-five and doubt sets
in."

"Hugow never has had any doubts," Iris said.

He should go now, Jonathan thought, forcing himself to
move toward the door. Hugow jumped up and clutched his
arm.

"Stick!" Hugow's lips formed the command.

Jonathan sat down again. Hugow was hungry and talked of
going to either Ticino's or the Bocce place. Jonathan, mindful that he could get free cakes, sandwiches, and coffee at his
place of employment, tentatively suggested the Then-and-
Now. Iris said nothing for the simple reason that she had fallen
asleep, her dark eyebrows tangled in a frown, but even with
the eyes closed a deep black unhappiness clouded her face.

"Iris is my one good deed," Hugow confided. "I broke it
up when I saw I was going to louse up her life for her."

"Where does she come from?" Jonathan asked.

Hugow shrugged.

"Middle West, or maybe upstate. Far enough away so she
can live her own life. I picked her up when I did a backdrop
for a little theater over The Golden Spur. She was in the cast
and got some notice. I don't know whether it was because
she can really act or because she looks so goddam tragic."

"I'm hungry," Iris said unexpectedly, then sighed. "But I
am so tired."

It was agreed that Hugow would run around the corner
and bring back pizzas and peperoni and more bourbon.

"You can look after Iris," he said. "Do you mind?"

Mind!

Now he was alone with Iris, here was his opportunity to register, but without Hugow he couldn't think of a word to say. Jonathan could scarcely breathe when she bent forward and put a hand impulsively on his.

"I'm so glad you stayed," she said in an intense whisper. "You see I just did something that scares me terribly and I've got to tell somebody—not Hugow—to make it go away. I mean I came so close to—well, please let me tell you and promise not to mention it again or tell Hugow."

Jonathan could nod at least.

"You see I had this wonderful part, and if the tryout was any good we were to come in to Broadway next month. But I was all wrong for it. Oh, I never dreamed I could be so bad! We flopped and it's my fault. So I got my sleeping pills and came here and—"

"You mean you were going to—" Jonathan choked.

"Please don't tell Hugow," she implored, clasping her hands together. "He's got guts and he thinks I have too. But I just couldn't stand living if I thought I was no good as an actress. There's just nothing else in life for me."

"Not even—Hugow?" Jonathan ventured.

She smiled at his innocence.

"You mean because he was my first lover. But you see that was all mixed up with my first job in the theater where Hugow was the scene designer, and it was my first year in the Village, and he was my first famous man. Hugow stood for the whole picture, don't you see? That's the way a girl's mind works."

That was the way it must have been with his mother, Jonathan thought.

"Hugow was good for me," Iris acknowledged. "I was flattered that the great man liked a kid like me. He thought I was older and when he found out I was just eighteen he panicked. We were shacked up in Rockland County, but he packed me up and sent me back to town. I was so embarrassed to be treated like a child after all. 'Marry some nice guy,' he said, can you imagine? 'Have some kids, live a nice normal life.'"

"Do they always say that?" Jonathan asked, surprised. "That's just what the man said to my mother."

"What man?"

What man, indeed?

"Something like that happened to my mother, that's all," he said. "At least you didn't listen to him. You stuck to your guns."

Forget about his mother, he advised himself sharply, think Iris, Iris, Iris.

"Oh, but do you know what I said to him? You won't believe me!" Iris covered her face with her hands at the memory. "I burst out crying, if you please, and said, 'But I don't want a normal life. I don't want a nice guy. I just want you!' Oh, I was such a little stupid, Jonathan!"

How in the world could Hugow have resisted such charming naïveté? Jonathan marveled, wishing he had been on hand to console her.

"I thought my heart was broken. Honestly!" Iris's great sooty eyes begged him to forgive her childishness. "I must have been a pest, hanging around the Bender Gallery, phoning Cassie Bender to try to find him, lurking outside the Spur. Wasn't it too silly of me? As if he was Gregory Peck! Not that Hugow isn't a dear, but really!"

"I'm glad you're over it," Jonathan said sincerely.

She flashed him a sad, grateful smile.

"I am too. As soon as I got a job touring in a Chekhov revival I forgot him like that! Awful of me, wasn't it?"

But she was here tonight, Jonathan reflected.

"It might start up again," he suggested.

"You don't know me, Jonathan." She shook her head firmly. "I've grown up. When I close a door I really close it."

He was very pleased to hear this. That was exactly the way he was himself, he said.

"I'm fond of Hugow still," Iris granted. "After all, I admire him as an artist. And we still can laugh over how crazy I was. And I wouldn't hurt him for anything in the world."

"Certainly not," Jonathan said, elated by the faint warning and promise in her voice. "But what about the sleeping pills? Would you have gone through with it?"

"If you hadn't come in?" Iris shook her cloudy hair and

considered for an intense moment. "I don't know, Jonathan, I really don't know myself. Maybe if I hadn't fallen asleep first. Then when you said you could tell I would be a great actress I wanted to live, because you made me believe in myself again."

Jonathan glowed with happiness. He had saved this lovely girl without even knowing he was doing so. She was leaning toward him, and he could not keep from kissing her tempestuously. He kissed the tiny mole that finished off the corner of her mouth like a beauty patch, and he looked with delight at the slow smile that transfigured her dark face with light.

"Do you know something, Jonathan?" No, he thought, utterly bemused by the way she murmured his name. "I knew something about you too, the instant we met. I knew you were going to be somebody different and really great. Like me. I could tell."

"You could?"

"I could tell, Jonathan."

It must be the real thing with her as it was with him. But he wouldn't want to hurt Hugow, his new friend. He heard his step on the stairs and went to the door with one of the candles to light the way.

Hugow beckoned him out to the hall and handed him some packages.

"Beer for breakfast too," he said. "Stick around till I get rid of the kid. She's a sweet kid and hasn't many pals, but I don't want to start this up again, you know how it is. Don't want to hurt her, but—"

"She oughtn't to be alone," Jonathan said cautiously. "I shouldn't tell you, but she's got some sleeping pills—"

He was surprised at Hugow's mocking retort.

"Pay no mind to that sleeping-pill bit. She's stagestruck, don't forget. There's always got to be an act."

Unsympathetic, Jonathan thought, but that would make his own sympathy more welcome to her. Iris made no move to play hostess but lay back regally on the couch, accepting cigarettes and drinks. Jonathan was happier than he'd ever been in his life, he thought, knowing she liked him and that Hugow wanted him there. He suggested warily taking Iris off Hugow's hands by inviting her to the Then-and-Now for a café Saigon.

"Iris thinks that espresso coffee tastes like wet blotters," Hugow said. "You fix us some highballs instead, Jonny-boy."

"Jonny-boy"—just what his mother and Aunt Tessie called him.

Jonathan went into the kitchen, glad to be useful in so many ways. He wondered how he could go about getting Iris to himself, since Hugow had been firm about not wanting her there. Each had made it clear that the last thing they wanted was to reopen their affair. Pondering how to handle the situation, he brought the ice back into the room in time to surprise the two friends locked in a passionate embrace. They sprang apart guiltily, snatching for cigarettes; Hugow lighted them both busily from a candle.

Jonathan stopped in his tracks, baffled. Even though they didn't want to hurt each other—

"I've got the ice," he mumbled idiotically. Then, as neither spoke, he hurried on. "It's a good icebox. Makes a lot, so you don't need to worry about running out of ice. Lots better than the old one over on Tenth Street."

"That so?" said Hugow. He was examining his cigarette intently. So was Iris. They didn't look at him, and he tried not to look at them. He dropped the ice tray on the sofa and backed toward the door.

"I've got to be running along," he said and went on explaining, as if any explaining was needed. "I've got to go to the espresso, see, then it's a long way over to East Tenth—"

"Sure you don't want to stay here?" Hugow murmured absently.

"Couldn't possibly," Jonathan babbled, burning with embarrassment. "Lize and Darcy expecting me, see, and I—see, I wouldn't want to hurt them."

He was out of the door, stumbling down the stairs, paying no mind to the glint of the river lights through the half-moon window, muttering, "Wouldn't want to hurt Lize and Darcy, see, can't go round hurting people. . . ."

Wait till he found out who he was, he thought, and could stand up to any situation. Iris would discover that he was indeed Somebody. A legal wizard, maybe, he thought wildly, if he was the child of George Terrence. A real writer, as big as Hugow in another way, if his father proved to be Alvine

Harshawe. He thought of the pile of Harshawe published works in the drawer of his desk at the café, works he was reading carefully in the hope of finding some veiled allusion to his mother or a plausible connection with her life. He thought of the journal he had always kept, as people do who have no one they trust to understand them. Tonight he would write a sardonic bit about Iris and the folly of sudden love.

Jonathan walked hurriedly toward the shop, across Carmine Street, still smarting at being an unwanted third. He was being properly punished for losing sight of his true quest, that was it. Tomorrow he would confer with Earl Turner as to an interview with Harshawe. Miss Van Orphen was arranging a visit with the George Terrences for him too. Before he dared to fall in love he must find his guiding star.

6

A T FIRST Earl Turner showed only a pessimistic interest in Jonathan's attempts to get a response from Alvine Harshawe.

"That guy wouldn't give five minutes to his own mother if she wasn't photogenic," he said. "Maybe he's in Hollywood, or China. You wrote him at his agent's and at the Cape Cod address and at the town house. Nothing much you can do now."

"The *Times* said Zanuck was coming to New York expressly to see him about their picture," Jonathan said.

This was news to Earl, and apparently very interesting, for he meditated in silence for some time.

"You leave this to me," he said finally. "If Harshawe's in town I'll go see him personally and fix it up."

Jonathan was enormously grateful for this kind offer, having no idea that his good friend was going to "fix it up" for him by first putting the bite on Harshawe for himself. Earl had been beating his brains trying to figure out a way of asking Alvine for money again without having to crawl. It irked him that his recurrent need to beg emphasized the hopelessness of his own career and the triumphant infallibility of Alvine's. No chance of their positions ever being reversed. Oh no. Fate, that cheap opportunist, never lets a winner down.

"There's a piece about him in *Esquire*," Jonathan said. "It says he misses the old days in the Village when he was in dire straits."

"I miss those old dire straits too," said Earl. "Dire straits, my foot! Better than being broke, I can tell you."

It was a good thing to have Jonathan's interests as an opening wedge to call Alvine, Earl thought; anything to vary the monotony of his usual routine. Every time he made his touch he found himself making grandiose allusions to big deals in the offing and the loan being only for a fortnight. Old Alvine never failed to shrug ironically, foreseeing in his damnably rude way that Earl wouldn't have the nerve to show up again for years, then not to beg but to borrow again, past loans never mentioned as if time had worn away interest and principal.

Galling to admit that Alvine, as always, was his last resort. Earl's system of Paul-Peter financing had caught up with him, as it did periodically, and suddenly there were all Pauls and no Peters. Creditors seemed to be converging on him from all over the world. It must be Earl Turner Festival Year, he thought, and all of these pests were as menacing as if the debts were for hundreds instead of piddling little fives and tens. Whenever a stranger glanced twice at him on the street, he knew he must be a collector. When an old friend crossed a street toward him he knew there was some buck or two he had forgotten to repay. Even the sun coming out was just a promise of tomorrow's rain, a reminder that the very heavens had their own collector. His wretched hotel, the One Three (not to be called Thirteen) had been goading him with ultimatums. So, on our knees again to old Alvine, Earl had thought gloomily.

At least the case of Jonathan Jaimison was a change of gambit, and there was a chance that Alvine would like the crazy angle.

If he could get through all the flunkies and chichi to Alvine, that is. The great man's stock must be slipping, however, for his agent's secretary readily admitted that he might be reached on the agent's cabin cruiser up at the City Island yacht basin, or else at his own town house. Earl tried the house number, and sure enough, Alvine himself got on the phone. How the hell did Earl know that he was here hiding out?

"Broke?" he asked. "What is it—bail, rent, blackmail?"

"All three, as usual," Earl said. "But that's only incidental. I can put it to you in about fifteen minutes when I see you. It's an episode from your past, fella, that might interest you if you've got the time. Nothing serious—maybe funny."

Alvine was in the mood to be curious. Earl should drop in around twelve and tell him his story. Earl could have been there in five minutes but he passed the time in Central Park feeding the ducks, then strolled slowly eastward, scattering peanut shells and thinking about old times.

His usual daydream was running through his head, the one about Alvine, with the background changed now to East

Sixty-fourth Street. The picture was always the same. It was the one where Earl saw himself at the wheel of his Cadillac-Rolls-Jaguar-or-whatever, slowing up to notice workmen busily piling up furniture on the sidewalk. Some officials are standing about, and then Alvine himself comes out of the house, pleading with the officials. Earl sees at once what is up—Alvine is being dispossessed. Hastily he leaps out of the car and rushes up to the scene, bulging wallet in his hand.

"Why didn't you tell me things were bad?" he demands of Alvine kindly, thrusting bills into everyone's hands. "Didn't I tell you I would pay you back someday when you needed it? Now the tables are turned and I'm tickled to death to help you out of the jam, old pal. Come, come, Alvine, no blubbering—good heavens, man, what else would you expect from your oldest friends? Let's be systematic about this, now. Men, put that furniture back where you found it; I'm taking care of everything, spot cash. And you, Alvine, buck up, old chap, men don't cry! No, don't explain! The main thing is I've got everything under control, so let's forget it and go have a drink. Twenty-One okay with you? What do you mean your clothes are too seedy? Hell, man, they know me—a tie is all that's necessary. Okay, hop in, and we'll stop off at Bronzini's and buy a dozen."

Earl knew that the grade of his daydreams had not improved since his Peabody High School days, but he was hooked by them, no matter how cheap, the way he was still hooked by Almond Joy candy bars, sneaking into telephone booths to wolf them down. He absently fumbled in his pocket now to see if he might buy one, knowing that he should be careful of his change. This brought on another dream, the one about finding money in the street, and his eyes darted expertly along the gutter. He had stopped hoping to find bills of any larger denomination than a twenty, reasoning they would be too hard to explain and too hard to change in his circle. You could change an imaginary ten-dollar bill easy enough, but a dream fifty could get you in trouble. Actually he had found coins on several occasions and was always scrounging around in mud puddles and in the teeth of oncoming trucks to pick up dream quarters that turned out to be real bottle caps. Once, spotting a possible dime in a gutter, he had bent over so suddenly his bursitis nipped him in the back and he couldn't straighten up while a Fifth Avenue bus braked to a screeching halt at his very coattails. Since then he had made it a sporting rule not to bend over for anything less than a dream quarter.

The Harshawe house suddenly leaped out of the block at him, and there was no use denying that the imminence of seeing old Alvine again—in a matter of seconds—excited Earl, and he knew a silly grin was on his face as if he were right in the presence of Scott Fitzgerald. He forced himself to stand quietly a moment before the little brownstone house that flaunted its iron balconies and old-fashioned lamp-posts in the teeth of the surrounding modern apartment houses. He reminded himself of Alvine's childish weaknesses—his pose of hating New York for its social demands, his pretense of hating publicity. He wasn't seeing a soul this time, he had assured Earl on the phone, just wallowing in solitude and work, and was only pausing in his intense concentration long enough to see Earl.

Satisfied that his grin had changed from hero-worship to sardonic detachment, Earl was ready to proceed. Following Alvine's instructions, he rang the caretaker's basement apartment and was told to go on up to the third floor, where Mr. Harshawe was still in bed. The living rooms were done up for the summer, the furniture in shrouds, the smell of camphor all over, floors bare, shades all drawn.

"That you, Turner?" Harshawe's voice boomed from behind an open door, and there was Alvine lying in bed, unshaven, bags under his eyes, hair a little grayer than five years ago falling over the crooked black eyebrows, the brown eyes still keenly probing, calculating every flaw in your own appearance. He was a big hunk of man, Earl noted, and all those years of gracious living had left their mark. Earl patted his own flat belly with quiet ostentation, as if it were the result of rigid abstinence.

One thing that never changed about Alvine was the wild disorder of his bedrooms, no matter which wife was in charge. He always had great giant beds, for he wrote, ate, snoozed, read, entertained, did everything in bed. "Alvine's playpen," his present wife, Peggy, called it, and was constantly complaining about the difficulty of making Alvine get out of pajamas. There were stacks of newspapers, every edition, magazines, notebooks, manuscripts, proofsheets, a bathrobe, and a typewriter skidding over the counterpane. A tray with a box of potato chips and a highball glass was on a chair, and a half-opened suitcase on the floor spilled out a tangle of shirts, socks, and ties. No sign of any feminine life, Earl noted, but then in all of Alvine's ménages the female was boxed up out of sight whenever Earl made his calls.

"You old bastard," Alvine greeted him, propping pillows behind his head and sizing up his guest. "I made out a check over there under the ashtray, if that's what you're looking for."

Earl flinched. Same old Alvine. Kick 'em right in the teeth before they can put on their poor little show.

"I was merely looking for wife tracks," Earl said coolly. "Don't tell me you've booted Number Four."

"I left Peg up at Chatham with a houseful of crumbs and waiting for more," Alvine said. "Anything to keep a man from working. 'You're so dull when you work, honey.'" Alvine mimicked his wife's boarding-school accent. "Or 'Really, dear, you're not having brandy before breakfast?'"

"She'll be sore you left," Earl ventured.

"Peg? She'll act sore but she'll really be glad she can sound off about my opinions without me shutting her up," Alvine said sourly. "She won't have to apologize to her pals for my insulting them. Oh, she'll give me hell but she'll be having a ball. Have a drink, or is it too early for a dedicated littérateur like yourself?"

Earl poured himself a short one from the Jack Daniel's bottle on the dresser and noted the empty glasses and overflowing ashtrays on floor and chairs.

"Big night?"

Alvine gave an impatient snort.

"You're as bad as a wife, Turner," he said. "You find somebody in bed an hour or so after you've managed to drag your own can out, and right off you start pointing and yelling big night, big night, aren't you ashamed, it's after ten, Bergdorf's is open, Saks is open, Irving Trust is open, get up, get busy, do something, do your crossword puzzle, tear up your mail, get on all the phones, start apologizing for last night and tomorrow too, while you're at it, get on the ball, don't just lie there minding your own business."

"Well, now, Alvine, really—" Earl protested.

"I should have married you, Turner," Alvine said. "I could have had four wives' worth of nagging without changing mistresses."

"Sorry, old man. I forget I'm day people and you were always night people," Earl said.

"Who says we're people?" Alvine yawned. "There's the check, don't you want it?"

Earl picked up the check and put it in his pocket. The minute he had it there he didn't give a damn what Alvine said. Needle away, boy, he thought, nothing bothers me now. Maybe he'd get around to his Jonathan errand and maybe he wouldn't.

"What happened to that system you used to have of getting advances from publishers?" Alvine asked. "They used to be tickled to death to hand you out advances on a mere idea. They were so sure they wouldn't have to bother reading anything. What spoiled it? Did you turn in a manuscript?"

Earl laughed too, as if it were a great joke instead of being in a small way—two chapters—all too true.

"I haven't had an idea myself in ten years," Alvine admitted graciously. "Sit down and talk, man, fill me in."

You got mad at Alvine, insulted and humiliated by him, but you couldn't resist when he raised his little finger toward you. So Earl sat down on a chair full of *Esquires* and *Trues* and told him what the old ironworker had told him in a Myrtle Avenue bar about his son being a junkie and pinning the stuff on the old man. . . .

"This fellow tells you this for true?" Alvine yawned again, and when Earl nodded, Alvine snorted. "Earl, how many times do I have to tell you that what a simple workman tells you in a low bar in a Brooklyn accent isn't necessarily true? You're safer swiping straight from De Maupassant or O. Henry, somebody out there in good old public domain. These bar confessions are always straight out of *Reader's Digest* or the *Post*, magazines a literary type like yourself wouldn't be reading. No, my friend, I'd be afraid to use that little idyll. And nobody likes a worker hero any more, anyway."

That was good old Alvine for you, first encouraging you to talk, then knocking your wind out.

"Who said anything about that?" Earl said. "The junkie is your hero these days. Where have you been?"

He knew he shouldn't have flared up, trying to take Alvine down, but the damned check in his pocket made him feel like an equal. He was ashamed as soon as he saw Alvine's eyebrow shoot up in its old Clark Gable way. You shouldn't take advantage of your betters, Earl reminded himself savagely, especially a great genius who hasn't had an idea in ten years. The genius had poured himself another drink and Earl held out his glass to the spout, reflecting that the old boy was hitting the bottle but then, with the favorites, the bottle never hit back as it certainly would with himself.

"Otherwise, how's life?" Alvine asked amiably, pushing himself up with another pillow to watch his caller—to count his crow's feet, Earl thought, see the grease spots on his shirt.

"Nothing new. A review now and then—eight bucks for fifteen hundred words of new criticism in a little magazine, or forty for six hundred words of old criticism in the Sunday book sections. A pulp rewrite of a De Maupassant."

"I mean what kind of place do you live, what about dames?" Alvine interrupted.

Material, Earl thought. The sonofabitch was always scratching for material like a dog scratching for fleas.

"I'm in this Hotel One Three, men only," Earl said. "Way over east in what they call the New Village. A real fleabag. Signs in the lobby, NO LOITERING IN THE LOBBY, kind of funny considering that the lobby is only five feet square. Signs in your room, ONLY ONE PERSON AT A TIME IN THIS ROOM. FOOD IN ROOM FORBIDDEN, and all that. I have a little electric plate hidden."

Earl saw that Alvine was amused. Probably already figuring how he could use the stuff. Okay, let him have it.

"A fellow there wrote a song from the signs," he said obligingly. " 'Won't you loiter in the lobby of my heart.' "

Good. The master was grinning.

"Dames?" Alvine persisted.

"A few favors from old friends, that's all," Earl said. "They throw me out regularly. Damn it, I'm a lonely man."

"Lonely!" shouted Alvine, suddenly coming to life. "What do you know about loneliness! Why, you're not even married!"

Earl had to laugh.

"Let alone four times like me. Oh, it's no laughing matter," Alvine went on bitterly. "You played it smart so you've still got your freedom. But me. There's nothing left of a man after he's parceled himself out to women four ways—five years lost here, five there, eight there, another six here . . . Believe me, that's loneliness! This door of your past to keep shut, that one mustn't touch, this one a booby trap—so what the hell have you got left of your own life? You can't even run around naked in your own mind!"

"You can think about all those front-page reviews of your books," Earl said with what he hoped was a good-natured chuckle. "Or having supper with the royal family after your play opens. Or editors wrastling on your doorstep. Don't get me crying over you, old man. It isn't that tough."

Alvine reached out for the highball glass on the floor and poured himself a drink.

"Write a story about a poor old writing stiff, a very complicated, well-educated, rich old author, perfectly adjusted to his lousy environment. Don't you see that great new Cinderella angle? The poor old slob, when he walks in a restaurant strangers flock to his table, put their drinks on his check; they visit his country home with their picnic hampers, they pick his roses, throw their banana peels around, urge their kids to swim in his pool, and when he shows up—it's his home, after all— they tell him they don't see what's so hot about his books or plays; in fact they don't even know them. They have no intention of leaving until they're chased off, so they can tell how mean he is. They ask if it's true he's 'interracial,' is it true that O'Hara writes all his stuff for him, that his present wife was a call girl in Las Vegas, that his mother spends most of her time in a straitjacket, that his kids are test-tube products, and that he's been living on dope ever since he left the breast—"

Earl had to shout to override Alvine's tirade.

"Stop breaking my heart!" he cried. "Who would read an old story like that? Talk about bar confessions! Where's your sympathetic character? Where's your struggle? Who cares about one man's most embarrassing moment?"

"Oh forget it!" Alvine said, lying back wearily. "Forget I said a word. It was just that I thought with your determination to write and my determination not to, between us we'd make one hell of an author."

Earl knew he shouldn't let Alvine get his goat but it always happened and he hated himself—and Alvine more—for it. He hated that wave of affection Alvine always felt for the person he had just kicked in the face. Good old Earl, he would say, how lovable of him to be a confirmed flop! He might be a nuisance but never a competitor. Other old pals might forge ahead and get stuffy—take old George Terrence, for example! —but you could count on old Earl to be down there at the bottom of the ladder, looking up at you like a dumb old mutt that can never learn the tricks.

What burned Earl was that Alvine no longer made any pretense of believing in his big projects, as if they were windy lies or so unfeasible that only poor gullible Earl would be taken in. He might have pulled off one of his deals, Earl thought, if he hadn't felt Alvine's skeptical eyes on him. Skeptical, hell—absolutely certain of Earl's failure. If others were always so damned sure you'd need the safety net, you usually ended up in it. You did what people expected of you. Look at Alvine. Everybody from high school on had always expected Alvine to make good, so he did. Everything worked out tick-tock. He turned out a play or novel, then sat back for years on his yacht or somebody else's and let the profits roll in—television, Hollywood, road companies, musical adaptations, foreign rights, revivals, with every gossip columnist beating the drum for him. Industrious, they called him, when every little word earned its own living again and again for years without Alvine's turning a hand. Yet people were always saying to Earl, "Why don't you get down to work, Turner, write something?" Sell something, was what they meant. He wished suddenly that Alvine would get sore at him, dignify him with a little decent jealousy, tell him to go to hell, get him off this hook somehow, let him fail in his own way without rubbing in how easy it was for others to succeed.

Well, they were each other's oldest friends. Not that it meant they liked each other. Some old friends went to their

graves without learning to like each other, without even getting to know each other.

Earl and Alvine had become friends through geographical
necessity at first—graduated from the same Schenectady high
school, into the West Side Y, then Greenwich Village, always
planning to write, talking endlessly about writing, getting
down all those upstate characters and legends, yak-yak-yak.
Earl realized he should have got the picture then and there,
because while he rolled into bed at daylight, perfectly content with their discussions, Alvine went right to his damned
typewriter to get it all down. Next time they'd meet, Alvine
would have a fat manuscript to read to him instead of resuming their talk as Earl wanted to do. "Where's your story,
Turner? The one you talked about all week?" Alvine would
ask. Earl would explain that the material needed more time;
he was too much the perfectionist to rush right in and mess
up a great idea before he was ripe for it. He never could get
over Alvine's reckless plunge from idea to typewriter. Cheating, he thought; not really playing the game. You could have
a depth talk about murder, couldn't you, without tearing
right out and killing somebody? Earl had a vague feeling of
having been robbed, too, he wasn't sure of what. But what
had he said that always set off Alvine without starting his
own motor?

When Earl got the *Sphere* editorial job they shared an apartment with George Terrence, a rich young lawyer, on Irving
Place. By that time Alvine had published some sketches about
Schenectady boyhood, things about places and people Earl
knew as well as Alvine did. Editing them for *The Sphere*, Earl
felt robbed again. They were bits he intended to put in his
novel when he got around to it, only now it was too late.
They didn't see much of each other after Alvine married his
literary agent, Roberta somebody, and don't think she wasn't
a big pusher for his success, typing, selling, making him into
a big enough shot for his next three wives. Not that Alvine
ever gave any of them credit. He could use up their money,
their life stories, their profitable connections and then complain they blocked his work.

"Do you mean to tell me you still hang around the Spur?"
Alvine asked. "Next you'll be telling me that you still get

grain alcohol from the mad druggist and make your own gin in the umbrella stand."

"At least the Spur is still alive," Earl said, remembering not to get sore. He wished he dared remind his chum of those old days when they were tickled to death to gouge the cash out of old George Terrence for a night at the Spur. "How about visiting it one of these nights?"

He was surprised that Alvine didn't laugh at the idea.

"Damned if I wouldn't like to, Turner," he said thoughtfully. "I need to freshen up on that background for the thing I'm working on, but how can I drop in a place like that and get the real picture?"

Conceited bastard.

"You mean you'd be recognized right away so your fans would tear your clothes off," Earl said, oh, very sympathetically.

Alvine nodded.

"Not that bad, but you know how it is. Old has-beens needling me for making it when they never could with their genius. Dames yakking about my mystique and their boyfriends sore and claiming I'm trying to rape them."

"I see your problem," Earl said. "Still, maybe I could handle the stampede. There's a young fellow around there now looking for you, and we could pick him up. He wants to know if you remember his mother. She had some pleasant memories of you."

"Pleasant memories," Alvine mused. "Sounds like a belated paternity suit."

You're not kidding, Earl thought. No reason for that big grin.

"Just the thing for writer's block," Alvine said. "A paternity suit ought to start you thinking. A real blockbuster."

So it was going to be a big joke.

"Her name was Connie Birch," Earl said. "She typed for you. Mean anything?"

"There was a Connie," Alvine recalled. "Sure. I promised to pay for the typing when I sold the piece. Lived way over on Horatio, Connie did. What became of her?"

"Died some twenty years ago. You can cross her off the bill."

"Dead or alive, Connie's got forty bucks coming to her," Alvine stated piously. "I'll settle with her heirs."

"You used to get 'em to type for free if you slept with them," Earl said. He could still get mad remembering how lucky Alvine used to be. "What was the deal with Connie?"

"Don't be a cad, Turner," mocked Alvine.

"You mean you don't remember," diagnosed Earl. "Anyway, this kid, Jonathan Jaimison, is crazy to see you and hear about his mother's New York past. Maybe he wants to write a book."

This was the wrong approach.

"Too many goddam writers already," Alvine said. "Why does anybody want to pick a lousy trade like that?"

"Look who's complaining," Earl said. "Nothing in it for Harshawe, of course. Just a million bucks and a passel of Pulitzers."

"I've never had a Pulitzer," Alvine corrected him with a rather brave, wistful smile. "A drama prize once, never any for my novels. Worst damn play I ever wrote, too."

So you did know that much, Earl thought.

"The picture deal was all loused up, you know."

Now wasn't that just too bad? Earl kept silent.

"Oh sure, I've had a couple of book-club breaks," Alvine granted, getting the message that he needn't expect sympathy. "But I've never gotten the critical reception for my novels that the plays get. That's why it's a challenge to me. I'm thinking of concentrating on novels, get out of this damn Broadway muck, give myself a chance to breathe. Keep to myself."

"Here?"

"Could be. Peg hates New York." He must have been mulling over what Earl had said earlier, for he said, "Say, what does this Jaimison kid you were telling me about, Connie's kid, look like?"

"You, come to think of it," Earl said. "By George, he does!"

Alvine sat up straight, both eyebrows up, incredulous but pleased.

"No kidding," Earl went on with delight. "I've been trying to think who he reminded me of all along. He's blond, and his eyes are different from yours—instead of his looking right through a person as you do, you can look right through him. But the build and profile are straight Harshawe, by George."

"Clean-cut American youth, standard model, that's all." Alvine shrugged, but he was amused. "Maybe I'll look him up at that. I ought to know more about that generation."

"For the new novel," guessed Earl, but Alvine only smiled enigmatically. Okay, make a big secret of it, Earl thought, but then Alvine always claimed it was no good talking about his writing, the way it was no good talking about cooking or dancing or singing—you just did it or you didn't, that was all there was to it. The born genius.

"What about you, Turner?" Alvine asked. "What do you want out of your writing, anyway? Dough? Kicks? Immortality?"

"I just want to be overestimated," Earl shouted, "like everybody else, goddammit."

Alvine burst out laughing. He liked that. He liked other people's hard-bought cynicism, but Earl was embarrassed at having betrayed himself. Now that he was standing up, ready to go, Alvine was suddenly crazy to have him stay. Have another drink—okay, one for the road then, and what have you read of the current trash? "You always read more than I do," Alvine said graciously. "When a book's bad I'm disgusted with the whole trade, and when it's good I wonder how such an oaf could turn out such good stuff. But you've got real critical sense." So Earl was beguiled again into trying to placate the master, telling him all the things wrong with Faulkner, Hemingway, Sartre, and the English crowd, till Alvine was crowing happily.

"We'll have a night going the rounds," he promised. "I'll have a look at this Jonathan kid."

Oh sure. Earl had sense enough to know that Alvine's geniality came over him only when the guest was headed for the door. Now was the time to leave.

He was able to congratulate himself, once outside, that this time he had not stayed too long. He had lived so long in cheap little hotel rooms that whenever he got into a regular home he couldn't bear to leave. He was as sensitive as the next one, but hints that hosts wanted to dine or sleep or go out bounced off Earl's consciousness once he was lost in home-hunger, standing in the door, half in, half out, not sitting down again, mind you, but not gone either. The few times before when he had succeeded in visiting the Harshawe ménage, he knew well enough he had overstayed, and it was funny too, because the minute he got in the door he kept watching Alvine anxiously to see if he looked bored or annoyed, which he did in a very short time. Then Earl got privately enraged and stayed on out of pure stubbornness. He could laugh at himself afterward.

"I know what old Alvine will have put on my gravestone when I go upstairs," he merrily told people. " 'We Thought He'd Never Go.' "

A good visit on the whole, Earl thought, walking down Lexington. Alvine had cheered him up in spite of everything. Suddenly he realized he had not even looked at the check. Maybe Alvine, who thought like a cagey rich man these days, was letting him have a measly fifty. Earl's lip curled. Already he regretted not having given a few straight criticisms of the last masterpiece, instead of buttering him up exactly like the disgusting toadies Alvine always managed to make of everybody around him. He regretted the faint twitch of affection he had felt when Alvine asked if he had time to wait for the restaurant next door to send up a bite of lunch. A real proof of Alvine's friendship, Earl had first thought, wanting to have an intimate little snack right there, just the two of them, instead of taking him out to phony chic spots like the Pavilion or Twenty-One, where his phony success friends would crowd around him. On second thoughts, the hell with this cozy little snack business, why didn't he invite him to those good places where he could meet those phony new pals? If phoniness was what he liked, his old pal Turner could be as phony as they come.

Earl reached in his vest pocket and took out the check. For two cents he'd tear it up and mail the pieces back to the old bastard. Then he peered at the figure written out. Three hundred dollars. Yes, three hundred dollars.

Three hundred cool dollars just like that. He stood still, breathing deep of the wonderful diamond-studded air, looking down beautiful Lexington Avenue, a street paved with gold, saw the little jewelry-store window right beside him and decided instantly he would go in and buy the silver wristwatch on the blue velvet.

It was true that Hotel One Three had promised to lock him out of his room if he did not pay today, but such catastrophes would not happen to a man armored with this beautiful check. A fine sense of accomplishment flooded his being, as if his own honest labor and not Alvine's generosity had brought about this reward.

Then a pang of irritation beset him, and he wondered how in heaven's name this piece of paper could be translated into cash. If he presented it to the hotel they would take out not only what he owed but a month in advance and probably raise the rate besides for such a rich guest. If he tried to get the bartender at The Golden Spur to okay it, then he would have to pay the old tabs he'd been hanging up at the Spur, and, besides paying all the customers from whom he'd borrowed a dollar or two over the years, he'd have to loan them money. He saw a branch of the bank on which Alvine's check had been written and thought of starting an account on the spot, but it would be days before he could draw on it. Passing a Riker's luncheonette, he saw that today there was steak-and-kidney pie, and it reminded him that he hadn't eaten today, and very little yesterday. Visions of great steaks of the past rose before his gaze; he thought of Cavanagh's, old Billy the Oysterman's, and the old Luchow's before it went Hollywood. He realized he was still walking and the great places he thought of were far, far away. Keene's Chop House then, he thought, and his mouth watered at the dream of those fat chops with Old Mustie Ale and a go at George Terrence's pipe always preserved there. But even Thirty-sixth Street was far away. And what good was a three-hundred-dollar check anywhere—no better than his cash treasure of a dollar and sixteen cents.

He was one of those doomed people who simply were not made to have money, he thought indignantly, child of eight generations of solid, substantial, bumbling Americans, born back in their rent—back eight generations with compound interest, the way old George Terrence, for instance, was born on top of eight generations of trust funds, so that he was honored as a success in his career before he'd made a dollar. He and Alvine used to sneer in the old times when their roommate, old George Terrence, would complain of being broke—less than fifty bucks in his wallet, maybe—might have to sell a bond, go into his savings, then after that go into one of his trust funds, and after that into his stocks, and then get an advance on the inheritance from his grandmother, then from his mother or uncle. Men like George honestly thought that to be broke meant just that. No, Earl conceded, George had never experienced the thrill of finding an extra one-dollar bill in his pocket after a week-end party—hell, George probably didn't even know they made one-dollar bills. George never had the exquisite ecstasy of spotting a dime in the gutter—dimes he knew, as any other born rich man does, merely as the coin used in tipping. Poor George had nothing but unlimited credit and could never be made to understand how a man with a big check in one pocket and a dollar sixteen in another could still be financially inconvenienced.

The gourmet lunch would have to be forgone, Earl saw. The sensible thing was to take the bus down, get some provender in that new supermarket near the Spur, stock up on coffee and eggs, and fix up a snack on his electric plate in his room. Once in the market he added a pint of milk and a bun to his eggs and coffee order, but when he offered his coins to the cashier she suddenly took a close squint at them—why hadn't she done this to the other people's money? he wondered—and cried out, "This quarter is no good!" The ladies behind him, who were battering at him with their pushcarts, stared indignantly at him. Crook. Pickpocket. Blackmailer. Forger. It seemed, the cashier stated with growing suspicion, that the coin was offensively Canadian and never mind about its being worth twenty-seven cents in United States money, it was worthless in the supermarket. Earl, goaded by the righteous scornful eyes of the ladies wheeling about him menacingly, took the milk and bun off his order and skulked out.

He started on the walk back to the Hotel One Three, automatically ducking back and forth across streets, swerving around corners from Sixth to Broadway and east across Fourteenth to avoid passing a certain dry-cleaner's, a certain drugstore, Teddy's Barbershop, Smart Shirts, Inc., a dentist's office, and a few bars, in all of which he owed varying sums. It occurred to him that he had almost worn out his present neighborhood, but where was there left for him to move? He had lived up and down town, East Side, West Side, in furnished rooms and fleabags from Chinatown to Harlem, pushed by creditors from Avenue A to Chelsea and even across the river to Hoboken, where he had holed up in a six-dollar room on River Street, living on beer and free broth from the Clam Broth House, then swung back across and up to Yorkville, Spanish Harlem, down again to the dingier fringes of the East Thirties, then westward ho again, widening his orbit as obliged by his little debts. He needed a helicopter, he thought savagely, to skip his pursuers and land *bingo* right in his own bed. Only a day ago he had been speculating on how long before he maneuvered himself right out of the city into the Atlantic Ocean. Never mind, all this would be changed when he cashed his check, and he should be glad he didn't have to make this simple trip by way of Woodlawn Cemetery.

The walk cleared his mind and he began appreciating the wonder of Alvine's forking over three hundred bucks. He began to figure out little tranquillity pills to various creditors, and he visualized the new suit—almost new, in the window of the Third Avenue Pawn Shop near Twelfth Street. He had promised himself that he would buy it with the first eighteen dollars he laid his hands on. Already he was enjoying the anticipated cries of joy from all those creditors as he passed out tens, and twenties.

"What's all the excitement?" he heard himself saying. "Didn't I tell you I would pay it later?"

Figuring all he had to pay out left him with the sudden desolate realization that a fortune had passed through his hands and nothing was left for Baby. Supposing he did manage by some miracle to cash the damn check, by night he would be as broke and desperate as he had been yesterday. Yes, and hungry too.

Earl did not realize that his feet had frozen into the sidewalk, as if his mind had commanded *Whoa* and they waited like patient old cart horses for a new command. His hand absently groped in his vest pocket, where, surprisingly enough, the check still reposed. As long as it was there, uncashed, he was a rich man. As long as he didn't cash it there was a choice left open. He could, for instance, simply take off for Mexico on a cheap flight and live pleasantly for six months. Write a novel. Like *Under the Volcano*, maybe. Mexico would do it for him. The instant this grandiose idea occurred to him, he knew it had been garaged in the back of his brain all along. His feet seemed to recognize the change of plan, for they automatically turned around and started in the other direction. Earl was not sure where they were taking him, but the knowledge of the uncashed check in his pocket gave him a dizzy glow of unlimited power.

At the corner of Twelfth Street he caught sight of a couple coming toward him, the lady in paisley-trimmed horsehair picture hat, flowered taffeta suit, and purple gloves definitely Claire Van Orphen, the young man Jonathan. In a flash he knew what he would do.

"Friends!" He made a deep bow to her and another to Jonathan. "I was just about to call both of you to say good-by."

"Good-by, Mr. Turner!" Claire exclaimed in dismay. "Where are you going?"

"Acapulco," he said. "Later the interior. I can really write in Mexico."

He would have gone on babbling, for he did feel guilty at having done so well for himself on a mission that was supposed to benefit Jonathan, but while he was casting about for some definite word to give the boy, Claire placed a detaining hand on his arm.

"But you can't go, Mr. Turner," she cried. "I've just been telling Jonathan the good news. You remember your theory about updating my old stories? The switch, you called it. Making the heroine the villain and vice versa? You said they would sell in a minute that way."

"I couldn't have been that definite, come now," Earl said warily. "I only revised them as a little game."

"You said in the old days the career girl who supported the family was the heroine, and the idle wife was the baddie," Claire said gleefully. "And now it's the other way round. In the soap operas, the career girl is the baddie, the wife is the goodie because she's better for *business*, didn't he say that, Jonathan? Well, you were right. CBS has bought the two you fixed, and Hollywood is interested. Jonathan and I have been looking for you all over. Isn't it wonderful?"

Earl drew a pack of cigarettes from his pocket, negligently selected one, and offered the pack to Jonathan. He felt quite faint.

"Not surprising when you know the score as I do," he said. "One does learn a little in twenty-five, thirty years of professional writing."

"You see you can't go away now, with all my other manuscripts for you to revise," Claire said anxiously. "And I have your check right here in my purse, fifty-fifty, just as we said."

"Check?" Earl repeated vaguely.

Mexico vanished. Escape vanished. There was nothing but checks.

"Supposing we stop in here at Longchamps and talk about it over a brandy?" he said, exuberant confidence suddenly overwhelming him. "I've just left Alvine Harshawe and he is delighted at the idea of meeting Jonathan, here. We talked for hours about you, boy. Wants to see you. Any day now you'll be hearing from him."

"Maybe I should telephone him," Jonathan suggested radiantly.

"Wait a bit. I'll be in touch with him again," Earl counseled. "Never fear, I'll fix it up. Come on, now we celebrate."

Claire was already being seated at a sidewalk table.

"You must let me be the hostess, then," she said.

"If we must we must," Earl said with a gallant shrug.

7

THE Then-and-Now Café did so little business that Jonathan worried over its survival. The real-estate man upstairs, who owned the building and half a block of houses beyond, was well pleased, however. A nice little capital loss, he gloated, rubbing his hands happily, just the break he needed. Moreover, he proposed to put more money into it for the same mysterious tax reasons, and since Dr. Kellsey's generous suggestions had not seduced trade so far, he was invited to submit more of his profit-proof ideas.

It was Dr. Kellsey's inspiration to have the walls covered with blown-up photographs of Pfaff's Beer Hall (of the 1850s), O. Henry's hotel on West Eighteenth Street, Henry James's early home on Mercer Street, Stephen Crane looking like a Bowery bum, John Masefield tending bar at Luke O'Connor's saloon, Richard Harding Davis dining on the Brevoort *terrasse*, and other nineteenth-century literary figures of the quarter. These reminders that other writers had been there before them merely annoyed the new crop of poets, subtly hinting that they themselves might end up tomorrow as blown-up "Thens" on these very walls. Dr. Kellsey himself realized this and thought all the better of the idea. Besides, he enjoyed his position as chief and sometimes only customer, with a big table to himself and no wide-eyed apprentice poets to watch him pour cognac into his espresso under the table, a routine that put him into a nostalgic mood for the old Prohibition days.

Jonathan was learning something new about the city every day, but there was no use trying to make today's lesson fit onto yesterday's. Each day the blackboard was erased and you began all over, yesterday's conclusions canceled by today's findings. Darcy, for instance, had confided often in Jonathan that there was something dangerously feeble-minded about a girl (Lize) who could hook up with a creep like Percy Wright. But now Darcy went the rounds at night with this very same creep, generously making him spend a couple of dollars at the Then-and-Now sometimes, admonishing Jonathan not to mention this to Lize.

"She'd really flip," Darcy prophesied. "It burns her up that so many men fall for me when she tries to hang on to them. God knows she's been doing her best to get Percy back but she hasn't figured out yet that I'm the reason he's holding out. He's just too nice a guy for Lize, that's all. He's kinda cute, too, the way he hangs onto his budget until you get him gassed enough to forget it. He says we aren't being fair to Lize, when she's so hot for him, but I say let's face it, Lize is just one of those women that can't hold a man, that's all, it's not his fault."

Jonathan obediently wiped Darcy's earlier statements about Percy from his memory and with the same open mind listened to Lize's stories of Percy pursuing her, begging her to come back. Sometimes Percy himself, deserted in some bar when both girls had found better fish to fry, attached himself to Jonathan and confided his own troubles, which were not frustrations in love but anguish that his idol, Hugow, was unmistakably shunning him. It was because Hugow's girls could not keep from falling for his unworthy self, Percy sighed. He told Jonathan it was not all roses having that terrible power over women, always breaking up homes, but what could a man do?

"If Hugow would only let me explain the situation," Percy said wistfully.

Jonathan told him he must not blame himself too much. It occurred to him that there was truth in every lie if you waited long enough, and you might as well believe everything while you waited.

Earl Turner said he was helping Claire Van Orphen "update" her fiction, and Miss Van Orphen's story was that she was helping Earl Turner get back on his feet professionally. Jonathan admired both of these people and felt fortunate in their friendship, just as he did about Dr. Kellsey's. The doctor brought his class papers to correct at a table in the Then-and-Now, enlivening this chore with helpful hints to Jonathan on his newssheet. He summoned his anecdotes of the past by running a beautifully manicured hand through his lordly gray mane, then pressing the hand to his closed eyes, a fascinating gesture that Jonathan could not resist imitating. Sometimes he caught himself performing in unison with the doctor and would peep out through the fingers over his eyes to see if his friend had noticed. Then the doctor would shake his mane (Jonathan would do the same), smile sadly (Jonathan would return the smile), and both would sigh, perhaps over the beauty of the past, perhaps over the folly of youth, perhaps over their shared sensitivity.

Jonathan took pride and comfort in the doctor's remark that he was the only young person who had the gift of curiosity. Students used to have it, oh yes indeed, the doctor said, but not any more. Everybody used that new word "empathy," said the doctor, but actually the word for the present age was "apathy." Apathy was what drove him to drink, said the doctor, apathy laced with either hostility or sheer ignorance in the young, apathy mixed with resentment and moral complacency in his wife, apathy with long-suffering and sulky envy in his lady-friend and departmental associate, Miss Anita Barlowe.

"But you, my dear Jonathan, you are eager to know things!" the doctor had said. "You want to know what I can tell you, what anybody can tell you, and you listen, too, by George. You make me feel alive."

So Jonathan was glad to have the doctor peer over his shoulder the night he was writing his historical items for the week.

"Have you mentioned that Poe wrote 'The Raven' over here on Carmine Street?" asked the doctor.

"Last week I said he wrote it on Third Street above Bertolotti's," said Jonathan. "They gave us an ad."

"Ah yes, I keep forgetting that the function of history is to bring in advertising," Dr. Kellsey said. "How about noting that Stokes killed Jim Fisk over Josie Mansfield right in the Broadway Central Hotel just below Third Street? Mention that the hotel was redecorated with the tiles and fixings from the old Waldorf Peacock Alley. And say that poor old Hurstwood, in *Sister Carrie*, spent his last days there—committed suicide there, didn't he?"

"Will they think of that as a plug?" Jonathan debated.

Dr. Kellsey sipped his coffee judiciously.

"Very well, then take the Brevoort. Jenny Lind stayed there, and in Edward Sheldon's play *Romance*—played by

Doris Keane, incidentally—her suitors unhitched the horses and drew her carriage right from the theater to the hotel. And it wasn't even air-conditioned then."

"That was the *old* Brevoort," demurred Jonathan.

"Try the Fifth Avenue Hotel, then, across the street from where Mabel Dodge had her peyote party forty years ago."

"No ad in that," Jonathan objected cautiously. "The Narcotics Squad might get after them."

The doctor chuckled.

"By George, you're getting to be a regular public-relations man. Must run in your family, that knack, or maybe it's plain Scotch caution."

Jonathan winced. Any reminder of the Jaimison family virtues sickened him, and it depressed him that his friend could find any trace of them in him. He made up his mind to tell the doctor the circumstances that made him definitely non-Jaimison, though Earl Turner had advised him against confiding in anyone else for fear it would block useful information. He opened his mouth to give a mere hint, but the doctor's delighted interest brought out everything Jonathan could remember from his mother's documents. When the doctor lifted a skeptical eyebrow over a point or two—"Are you sure she meant The Golden Spur and not The Gilded Lantern; that was a gypsy tearoom? And are you sure she took a poetry course at the night school, because I myself was teaching there then?"—Jonathan pounded the desk, ready to offer affidavits.

"Of course I'm sure. What surprises me is that you didn't know her yourself since you were teaching there. Look." Jonathan pulled the snapshot of his mother from his pocket and pressed it on the table before Kellsey. "Doesn't the name Connie Birch mean anything to you?"

The doctor obligingly took out two other pairs of glasses from his briefcase and studied the picture intently. Then he folded up both pairs of spectacles, readjusted his regular glasses, and handed back the picture to Jonathan. He stared at him in solemn silence for a moment.

"My boy," he said impressively, "we have here a most extraordinary coincidence. I did know your mother. She was in my poetry class. It was the braids that reminded me, and the unusual wide eyes. Connie. Yes sir, little Connie Birch. Amazing."

Jonathan felt faint and gripped the desk. Through a whirling mist he saw the doctor's fine hand rumpling through the handsome mane and heard his classroom Barrymore voice echo dimly in his ears.

"The very child who took me first to The Golden Spur, as a matter of fact," he was saying. "I forget names, but I was new here then, and this dear child with braids around her head had cried when I read Alan Seeger's poem, 'I have a rendezvous with death—' "

"Yes, yes," cried Jonathan. "She always cried over that."

"I invited her out after class for a beer and sandwich to comfort her," said the doctor, his rich voice choked with memories. "I found her naïveté refreshing, but it was she who suggested The Golden Spur. Usually I dropped in to Lee Chumley's, maybe the Brevoort or Jumble Shop. It surprised me that she should know such an out-of-bounds place as the Spur. Sporting types, jazz singers, writers looking for color, wandering trollops—yes, I was shocked to see that my naïve little student was devoted to this place."

"And after that—"

"After that I often took her there after class," recalled the doctor, stroking his head rhythmically as if this stimulated a special department of his memory. "She was always affected by love poems, and I'm afraid I got in the way of specializing in them—Sara Teasdale, Millay, Taggard—just because of the charming way this little student reacted to them. Gave me an excuse to console her, you see."

"You saw her home, then," Jonathan said, beginning to wonder uneasily if he had pressed the wrong button. He admired and respected Dr. Kellsey but he was not sure he wanted a closer connection.

The doctor reflected on this question and then nodded.

"I must have," he said. "It's true I was having some marriage problems at that time—in fact my wife was having me followed, as I recall, and my friend Miss Barlowe was having my wife followed—ha, ha—so little Connie Birch was my only refuge. Yes, she led me to the Spur. Curious, eh?"

"She wanted to meet someone there, perhaps," Jonathan

suggested. "She knew Alvine Harshawe, don't forget, and he went there."

Dr. Kellsey shook his head fondly.

"Your mother was far too sensitive a girl for a big extrovert like Harshawe," he said. "Oh yes, she pointed him out to me —strange I remembered the incident without realizing it was Connie Birch—but a delicate child who cries over poetry would never be taken in by your Harshawes."

"But there was someone," Jonathan persisted. "She did meet some man at the Golden Spur—don't you remember any of her friends?"

The doctor twisted his mustache meditatively and stared into the dark street outside.

"I don't remember how I got the impression she was alone in New York and without friends," he mused. "I re-member being surprised when Louis, the old waiter at the Brevoort Café, spoke to her by name when I took her there. And I was startled to run into her at a Pagan Ball at Web-ster Hall—she'd come all alone, she said, imagine! Strange, come to think of it."

"She must have known someone would be there," Jona-than suggested.

The doctor frowned thoughtfully into space.

"I didn't recognize her because her braids were down, the hair flowing. I knew she didn't realize the type of party it would be. Later I looked around for her to take her home, but she'd disappeared. Frightened, I think, for it was a real brawl."

He stopped short. A sharp suspicion had crossed his mind that he had indeed found Connie that night, must have taken her home, for how else could he account for having been found by police next noon asleep in Abingdon Square in his tattered Hamlet costume? God knows his wife had flung it in his face often enough later so that he couldn't deny it.

Jonathan wondered if his mother had ever been frightened at the idea of anything, especially a wild party. Even in her weakest stage of invalidism she welcomed any excitement. He was sure she was like himself, always ready to accept whatever occurred as the normal.

"Don't you think she went alone to the party and to the Spur because she knew a certain man would be there?" he asked. "She said in her letter that this well-known man would always be there and would walk her home later."

The doctor's eyebrows lifted. He looked pleased.

"I did get some recognition for my reviews in the *New Republic* then," he admitted thoughtfully.

Jonathan choked back an impatient exclamation. He hadn't foreseen this angle and he wished he could keep the doctor from pursuing it.

"It was a long time ago, my boy," said the doctor with a faintly mysterious smile. "And the whole episode had slipped my mind until now, but I assure you I would certainly have known if your mother was seriously interested in some other man."

Here was the closest he had come to an actual friend of his mother's, and it was leading nowhere, or if it was leading anywhere it was no place Jonathan wanted to look. He knew the doctor was studying him carefully and he became very busy at the typewriter, determined to drop the subject. But the doctor's speculative gaze made him uneasy, and he found himself tousling his hair in the doctor's familiar gesture. Presently the doctor rose and put his papers back in the briefcase.

"Remarkable," he murmured. "Incredible. I must put my mind to it and see what comes up. I'll do my best for you, my boy."

The tender way in which he said "my boy" made Jonathan berate himself for asking the doctor's aid. He rose politely to say good night, and the doctor stepped beside him.

"We seem to be almost exactly the same height," he said. "You have perhaps half an inch in your favor, due probably to all that spinach and orange juice of your generation. Well, good night."

"If she wasn't meeting Harshawe, what about George Terrence, the lawyer?" Jonathan cried after him. "Miss Van Orphen is sure Terrence went to the Spur in those days."

"Claire Van Orphen must be getting on in years now," said Dr. Kellsey. "I used to meet her at little affairs at the New School in the old days. She's probably a little confused about the past. It's hardly possible that a legal eagle of Terrence's standing would have haunted the Spur."

"But my mother knew him well," Jonathan insisted, unwilling to let the older man go without some leading answers.

The doctor raised skeptical shoulders.

"My little Connie? George Terrence? Possibly, possibly."

He gave Jonathan a soothing pat on the shoulder and tossed his hair back. Jonathan was annoyed to find himself tossing his own head again and meeting the doctor's quixotic smile.

"Amazing," murmured the doctor as he strode out.

He was humming, Jonathan noted with misgiving. Earl Turner had been right in advising him to confide in no one. Instead of getting helpful information he had let himself in for some unappealing doubts, for the doctor's suspicions had been quite obvious. Might as well be a Jaimison, Jonathan brooded, as to find his veins coursing with academic ink. He had a lightning vision of himself in future trudging over dreary campuses, briefcase bulging with student papers, growing a mustache like the doctor's, cultivating a rolling classroom voice, goading young Jonathans into becoming future Harshawes who would have all the fun and glory while he poured bourbon whisky over his poor frustrations.

"Can't you shut up the joint now?" a female voice urged, and there was Lize in the doorway. "Come on over to the Spur with me. This place is a morgue, how do you stand it?"

Lize didn't explain how she happened to be wandering in this dead end at one o'clock in the morning. She motioned Jonathan to a waiting cab when he locked the door, and he saw that the seat of the cab was taken up by the sleeping person of Percy Wright.

"Come on, we'll take the jump seats," Lize commanded. She cast a disapproving glance at the third passenger. "I asked him to meet me at Jack Delaney's after work for a talk—I wanted to borrow fifty bucks and I knew I'd have to get him stoned to get it—and the silly thing thought I wanted to come back to him and he got all emotional, blubbering away about not wanting to hurt me and all that, so I kept lining up double grasshoppers for him, and look at him! I had to tear out the lining of his coat to get the dough to pay the check. *I'm* perfectly sober. What's the matter with men?"

The sleeping figure mumbled.

"Don't try to wake up and be a nuisance now," Lize admonished him. "We'll drop off at the Spur and shoot him off to Brooklyn with the cabby."

She gave instructions to the driver and turned to give Jonathan a warm smile and a fond pat on the knee.

"I drove past half a dozen times to get you," Lize said, "but you always have that old goat from the college in there. What on earth do you pal around with him for? He's old enough to be your father."

"How could he be my father?" Jonathan exclaimed, stricken. "You have no right to say so—I mean, he's not as old as he looks."

"Okay, okay," Lize said, quite surprised by his fire. "You don't need to shout or we'll wake Junior here. I'm only asking what the old boy's got on you that you're so nice to him."

She patted him on the knee again.

"Dr. Kellsey hasn't got anything on me," Jonathan said tensely. "He's nothing to me—nothing at all."

Dr. Kellsey, after leaving Jonathan in the Then-and-Now, walked down the midnight streets in a kind of trance, crossing Seventh Avenue with speeding taxis shouting at him, finding an exotic charm in the smell of decaying bananas near a market, oblivious to the moist August heat. Bleecker Street along here had not changed much from the Bleecker Street he had known when he first came out of the West in the twenties. Granted that he had never been a man to observe his surroundings, his mind being taken up with a great file of indignant letters he had never gotten around to writing to deans, editors, women, creditors, anybody. In the early days he was always half-sprinting along Bleecker, he recalled, because he was due at class, or due to meet his wife for a showdown, and all along the way the little magic doors used to send out fragrant invitations to stop in the back room for a bracer.

Tonight, however, he was wafted along on a mysterious dream and he passed the strident bar cries of even the San Remo without turning his head. Jonathan's story, and the amazing discovery that he himself figured in it, had shaken his mind. The misty wraith of Connie Birch befogged everything. He was determined to fetch up a clearer picture and a proper sequence of memories, but so far he had experienced only the lightning flash of recognition at her photograph and name, a fleeting echo of a soft, apologetic twang, a hint of unexpectedly eager lips in a dark vestibule with sweet words lost in the roar of passing El trains. There was more, oh, there surely was more to it, but when he tried to force his memory through the door and up the stairs he lost the Connie image and the lips. He had been drunk at the time, that could always be guaranteed for episodes of this nature at that period, or else he had drowned guilt later in a healing binge. But this episode was special, Dr. Kellsey moaned, pleading with himself to produce clearer proof. The possibilities in Jonathan's story seemed to have transformed the world for him, and in his vague new rapture he walked across Washington Square and all the way up Broadway across Union Square and Gramercy Park to the Knowlton Arms.

There was an untapped quart of Old Taylor in his closet, and the idea had struck Kellsey that he might induce the proper memory chain by repeating the conditions of the original scene—plunge himself, say, into an alcoholic haze. He accepted the phone slips the desk clerk handed him, two calls from his wife and two, of course, from Anita, but he crumpled them into the wastebasket without noting the messages they'd left, only musing on how infallibly the two ladies kept neck and neck in their race to brand their ownership on him, almost as if—he did not know how right he was—they were partners against him instead of rivals *for*. Certainly their taunts at him were similar. "Too selfish to raise a family like any decent, normal man . . . too neurotic to live a proper married life. . . . No wonder he disliked children—probably couldn't have any himself." He grinned, thinking of their combined wrath when they found out about Connie Birch.

Tonight Dr. Kellsey entered his pleasant large bed-sitting-room with a purposeful air. Instead of getting into pajamas as he usually did, he pulled the serape over the open bed and rearranged the cushions. He turned on the pretty little lights over the unusable fireplace, hummed the march motif from

The Love for Three Oranges (his favorite opera) as he tested the effect of the three-way floor-lamp—should all three speeds glare down on the rather shabby Chinese rug, or should just one muted bulb gently spotlight the big easy chair with the table of Vichy, cigarettes, and glasses hospitably beside it? He adjusted his prized *shoji* screen around the refrigerator with the electric plate and toaster on top, carefully closed the bathroom door, and then removed his tan cord coat, damp with perspiration from his brisk walk, hung it over the "gentleman," and put on his best black Chinese silk robe, quite as if he were expecting a lady of distinction.

Gratified that the ice was plentiful, he planted a bowl of it with his bottle and giant glass on the table, poured himself a generous sampling, and sank down into the chair, ready to entertain as many dreams of the past as Old Taylor could induce. Old Taylor would, sooner or later, get rid of his damnable monitor, the fear of losing his job, fear of scandal, fear of commitments, fear of failure, the composite bogey that had made his sober existence so disgustingly continent and had blacked out the bold Rabelaisian adventures that he would have liked to brighten his memories if they had not threatened his position. Yes, he had to admit that half the time the monitor, with its blessed anesthesia, had been an ally against his accusing wife and angry mistress, enabling him to shout, "How can I be blamed for something I did not know I was doing?" When he was braced alcoholically for his classes, there was never a passable female student that he had not considered hungrily and, properly loaded, approached. Even complaisant girls, however, either froze or fled at their professor's greedy but classical advances. An unexpected goose or pinch on the bottom as they were mounting the stairs ahead of him, a sudden nip at the earlobe as they bent over the book he offered, a wild clutch at thigh, or a Marxian (Harpo) dive at bosom, a trousered male leg thrust between theirs as they passed his seat to make them fall in his lap, where he tickled their ribs—all these abrupt overtures sent them flying in terror. Brought to his senses by their screams, Kellsey retreated hastily. Some of the more experienced girls, after adjusting their skirts, blouses, coiffures, and maidenly nerves, realized that this was only a hungry man's form of courtship. They reminded themselves that old, famous, and rich men played very funny games, and they prepared themselves for the next move. But Kellsey, repulsed, became at once the haughty, sardonic, woman-hating pedant, leaving the poor dears with a confused impression that they were the ones who had behaved badly, and sometimes, baffled by his subsequent hostility and bad grades, they even apologized.

Deborah was his wife, Anita was his mistress, but Amnesia had been his true friend, the doctor reflected candidly, permitting him to stare straight through some little sophomore trollop who thought she had something on him after his passes of the previous evening. Amnesia gave him back his arrogance and dignity, the proper contempt for students and fellow men that was necessary to a teacher. But alas, Amnesia had also taken away the love of his life—little Connie Birch. If, as he was determined to believe, a child had come of that dim encounter, then he was romantic enough to be convinced it was true love. He assured himself there was proof in the mere fact that he had been drawn toward young Jonathan from the moment of their first meeting, and he detected family resemblances now. He took a long drag of his drink and forced his mind into the period when he had taught Connie. He knew well enough he would have turned the case over to Amnesia if it were not that his true love was conveniently dead.

"The biggest thing in my whole life, and I can't remember it." He sighed, and he thought that poor forgotten little Connie was the only woman who had ever given him anything.

There was Deborah, still his legal wife, though long since living apart from him. She had been a blind date when he had been teaching out in UCLA in 1926. He had drowned his distaste for her in corn whisky, and next thing he knew she'd accused him of getting her in a family way and he must marry her. A plain, smug little party, morally convinced that "sex" itself, let alone her groom's idea of honeymoon pranks, was woman's cross, Deborah had later confessed that the pregnancy was a lie to win his hand in wedlock. Walter was so burned over this trick that it was all he could do to put up a polite husbandly front for his job's sake. Deborah was perfectly satisfied to be let alone, now that she was a missus, and

they managed to work out a successful façade. Deborah did
his secretarial work, as well as working for other faculty members, so she was on the inside track of academic promotions
and finaglings. Presently she became secretary to a rich foundation whose board members were too busy to attend meetings, and powerful decisions were left to mousy little Mrs.
Kellsey.

Deborah's *sub rosa* importance enraged Walter except in his
periods of pious sobriety, when he was allowed to share it and
flaunt it in the faces of his colleagues. Her grapevine information got him a fellowship at the right time, and got him the
New York job when she was promoted to the foundation's
New York office. Drunk and in his right mind he hated and
feared her, but in his nightmares of remorse, financial catastrophes, or professional embarrassments, he turned to her.
These were their happiest times, he wallowing in shame and
she wallowing in virtue. If his reform lasted as long as his
binge, then the doctor became fully as smug as Deborah.
They dressed up to attend banquets and foundation affairs together, where Deborah's undercover power was lost in her official insignificance. She was glad, then, of her extra status as
faculty wife, and the doctor was equally glad of his temporary
edge over her. Penance done and complacency soon exploded, he went back to his other doghouse, the one kept in
constant readiness for him by Anita Barlowe, an assistant professor in his department with whom he had conducted an affair for several years.

This was a curiously spasmodic romance, grounded regularly whenever Anita insisted he divorce Deborah and marry
her, and sparked again by their common jealousy of some associate's triumph. Anita took a spiteful comfort in keeping
him away from his foundation-superior wife, and Kellsey took
a manly satisfaction in having one woman clever enough to
catch his subtle gibes at her. They usually went to bed together quite happily and got up infuriated, physically appeased but psychologically defeated.

The greatest thing they had together was a permanent fight
subject (i.e., divorce), money in the bank, you might say,
when they were bored and their love needed a neat whip. Of
course he was bound to Deborah too by a perpetual fight

subject, i.e., she had tricked him into marriage, yes. But hadn't he got along better career-wise through her wifely conniving? Yes. Hadn't she pulled the right wires many a time to save his ungrateful hide? Yes. What would he have done without her? Plenty, the doctor thought to himself, but he knew none of it would have been good, which was unforgivable of her.

What burned both women everlastingly was the memory of the time Anita had pounced on Deborah and demanded she give a divorce because Walter had never loved her anyway and why did she go on refusing him his freedom? Because he never asked for it, Deborah had replied with one of her smug smiles. Never even mentioned such a thing, she repeated, how very, very strange for Miss Barlowe to ask. Hysterical and humiliated, Anita had tried to pin down the doctor, who was properly enraged that she should have approached his wife. He had never loved Deborah, true. But did he want to marry Anita? No. After this climactic scene Deborah deliberately started calling herself Mrs. Walter Kellsey instead of plain Deborah Kellsey, Anita went into analysis with a Dr. Jasper who looked like a caricature of Kellsey (that helped a lot), and Kellsey resumed his secret binges and blackouts.

Trying to concentrate on his long-ago student romances, Dr. Kellsey was plagued by reminders of the two women who dogged his career. Everything he ever did seemed for the purpose of spiting or appeasing one or the other, and he wondered if there was anything left in him of untainted personal feeling. His surprising burst of joy at the mere hint he might be a father, for instance. Was this an example of a long-mocked philoprogenitive instinct, evidence that he had more of the simple average male in him than he'd ever suspected? Or was it malicious glee at turning the tables on Deborah for that unforgivable old lie about her pregnancy? Or was it a delicious slap at Anita for her bitchy taunts that he feared a "normal married relationship" with a "normal female" like herself because he knew he was sterile? Old Taylor blinked consolingly at him in the lamp glow, calling him back to that magic long ago when something or other had happened.

The Spur had been a speakeasy then, yes. He hadn't gotten mixed up with Anita yet—that didn't start till World War II—

but he was still tangled with Deborah, yes. And he used the excuse of his weekly night class to make a night of it, yes. And he had split-second images of that pale sweet girl and himself in a booth, in a dark vestibule, in a kitchen making drinks (the doctor took another gulp of his kindly potion, for now he was on the right track), trying to dance to a squeaky record from *The Vagabond King*, and falling down in a laughing huddle, with the girl and the record whirring round and round and round, and the ruff getting in his way when he tried to kiss—yes, he was in the Hamlet costume still. . . .

Each time he got to the record part the curtain descended. Doggedly the doctor went back from the Spur to the classroom, to Alan Seeger, to blond braids, carried the story along faster, upstairs, kitchen, gramophone, *Vagabond King*, giggling, sprawl—but the blackout always stopped him there. Just once he got past it to a third shadowy image, another man, an objectionably sneering presence, and a wave of poignant indignation swept over Kellsey that there was always some last-minute intruder, the triumph was always being snatched from under his nose, he was always too late. . . .

The telephone rang. Only Anita would telephone him this late, and it meant she had been phoning around for him all evening. He must have forgotten a date with her. He listened to the ring, clutching his glass, blaming Anita for spoiling his dream continuity, finally snatched the receiver and heard her whimpering reproaches you-said-you-said, you-always-you-always, you-never-you-never—

"Anita," he interrupted sternly, "you sound as if you'd been drinking."

He grinned with evil satisfaction at the outraged sputtering this accusation brought forth and when it died down he spoke with pious kindliness. "If you're in condition by Friday, then, my dear, I'll meet you to talk over all these problems you find in our relationship. I have certain things to tell you."

There! If she will break in upon a man's private dream life, let her stew over the consequences.

8

JONATHAN'S note to Mrs. George Terrence at Green Glades, Stamford, arrived in the same mail as a certain letter in green ink to Mr. Terrence. George recognized the ominous green ink, for it was the third such letter he had received, and he fervently hoped his wife and daughter would have mail of their own to distract their attention.

"Who in the world writes you in green ink, George?" his wife inquired, but he was glad she was preoccupied with her own letter.

"I'll read it later," he said, stuffing it into his pocket. "Nothing of any importance comes on Saturday, you know. Why are you scowling over your own letter, my dear?"

"Someone is bothering me again about an old roommate," Hazel said crossly. "I do think it's a nuisance to be expected to keep up with everyone you've ever known."

"That's not like you, dear," George remonstrated severely, glad to have the subject of green ink sidetracked. "As I recall your stories, you had some very happy times at college."

Both George and Hazel were excessively loyal, as a rule, to any demands from their alma maters, though George had been miserably lost at Yale and Hazel had barely finished one semester at Sweetbriar.

"This wasn't a college friend," Hazel said. "This is concerned with a girl I lived with when I was studying the theater. You wouldn't remember her."

Their daughter Amy, who had been patiently staring at the *Stamford Times* society page while her parents loitered over their coffee and mail, looked up.

"I never knew you were interested in the theater, Mother," she said. "I've never heard you mention it."

"I never mentioned it because I forgot all about it. I was young and foolish, like most girls," Hazel said impatiently. "There were all sorts of little drama groups starting up then. Naturally I would never have seriously considered going on the stage."

"I do recall your having a few lines in some little production on Cherry Lane," her husband said, knowing well enough the lasting wound a newspaper criticism of the performance had made on Hazel. "Some of my best clients make their fortune in the theater."

"I can't see why they should write you in green ink," Hazel said, goaded.

"I see no reason why they shouldn't," said George.

Daughter Amy observed the grimly set smiles on each parent's face and sighed, recognizing the signs. Father and Mother were about to engage in one of their obscure duels, flailing delicately at each other with lace-edged kerchiefs that concealed from the observer the weapon and the wound. She had never understood what hidden taunt started the hostilities, but she really couldn't care less. She wondered again how they had endured each other all these years, or did they have some normal human feelings invisible to outsiders? In the tense silence she applied herself dutifully to the newspaper items her mother had marked—MISS ALLIMAN'S PLANS, ETHEL FEIST A BRIDE, JOHANNA TRUE TO WED, and other careful hints that Daughter Amy was being left at the post.

"How nice about Ethel," Amy murmured sweetly.

"About this old friend you lived with, my dear," George said to his wife. "It wouldn't have been that nice child from the West, little Connie Whatsername?"

A petulant frown came to Hazel's fair brow.

"Now, why in the world did that come into your head?" she cried. "I thought it was strange that Claire Van Orphen should be writing me about her after all these years, but after all, Connie did do some work for Claire. Then this son writes me, as if I were a blood relation instead of a chance connection of his mother's. But you barely met her. I cannot understand how you should remember her at all."

His wife's irritation soothed George's own uneasiness, and he pushed his chair back from the table with an indulgent laugh.

"I see I need a lawyer for my answer to that," he said. His wife and daughter fetched a dutiful laugh. "What I need is a good lawyer" had been George's joke for years, but the laughers, aware only of George's highly successful legal career, never realized how true it was.

In his entire life George Terrence had never been able to present his own case in any matter, seeing the vulnerability of his own side more clearly than any other, his fine professional mind cruelly operating as prosecutor against G. Terrence, defendant. He took a dour, rueful satisfaction in arguing himself out of the good spots in any situation, sternly denying himself jubilation over triumphs, complacency over good fortune. Detaching himself from his person, he had watched people exploit his money, name, and abilities with ironical amusement. In time he acquired a monumental complacency over his brilliant victory over complacency, and his lengthy sardonic stories of defeats and minor mistakes were more boringly egotistical than other men's boasting.

As a precocious only child of a rich, cultured old family, he conceded (intellectually) that he had no more rights to the pet pony, the toy railroad, the privileges and spending money than the sturdy playmates who were constantly appropriating them. It seemed to him that the superior man degraded himself by fighting over material possessions and proved himself by gracefully conceding. He acquired a defensive ironic bluster and a haughty sulkiness that consoled his pride but did not protect him. At Yale other boys got girls and popularity using George's expensive clothes, cars, credit, and family contacts. They bragged of their rich society pal George Terrence, without letting George share the luster. He stood on street corners in New Haven, watching classmates he hardly knew race by in his Packard, wearing his sport jackets, their arms around lovely girls who would, he knew, rebuff him. (A rumor had gotten around that George Terrence kissed with his mouth closed!)

When he started his career in a distinguished firm on William Street in New York, he took a modest apartment on Irving Place and soon found that, through the pressuring of friends, he was sharing the place with two agreeable younger men interested in literature. At least he wouldn't be lonesome, George was told. It was true he did not suffer in that respect. The young men kept the apartment lively with their girlfriends and all-night gab-fests, and when one or the other was conducting a big love affair, George was likely to find himself locked out. They were as strange to New York City as he was, but they were not handicapped by conscience over privilege as was George. They crashed debutante parties, barged in on good people's dinners, borrowed money from him cheerfully, passed his bootleg gin around, and laughed heartily over his occasionally ironic outbursts.

It had comforted George to know, as he used to sit in his hall room preparing his brief while the living room rang with merry voices, that fun might be fun, but he was the one with the money, the background, and the industry to succeed. Harshawe, a tall, quiet, arrogant fellow, had had a novel accepted for publication, which gave him the edge over Turner, his friend. Harshawe was too tall to wear George's suits, but shirts, sporty vests, ties, socks, and jackets were acceptable. Turner confided in George rather bitterly that the reason Harshawe slaved so hard at his writing was his inferiority about not being a college man. Neither man could understand George's unwillingness to use his Yale Club privileges, where a man could have his liquor in the locker, swim, lounge about, and finally they bullied George into taking them there. It was embarrassing for George, since both interlopers knew all the routine of getting in better than he did, and nobody there knew him or, if anyone did, had a warm greeting that would set up his stock. He felt like an impostor and inwardly vowed never to put himself through such a miserable trial again.

Three months later, however, coming out of Grand Central Station on a Sunday and needing cash, he braved the club. He half expected to be refused entrance, actually. Once inside he saw a familiar pair of long legs stretched out in a big chair, showing Argyle socks made most positively by Mrs. Terrence, Sr., a newspaper obscuring the face, a highball glass nearby, with the arm reaching for it encased in a familiar Terrence tweed. It was Harshawe, who greeted him with lazy good humor.

"How did you manage to get in?" George asked, mystified.

Harshawe shrugged and nodded toward his glass.

"Sit down and have a drink, Terrence," he said hospitably. "Oh, I like the place. I drop in every day to read the papers and have a smoke or a drink."

George wouldn't have known how to manage this himself, so he said, "But how do they let you in?"

"I use your name," Harshawe said. And at that moment a boy came up to him and said, "Your call is ready, Mr. Terrence."

"Thanks, Joey," Harshawe said and rose to stroll over to the telephone, leaving George frozen with outrage, staring after him. In a burst of courage he snatched the *Wall Street Journal*, of all things, which Harshawe had been reading, and resolutely plumped himself down in Harshawe's chair. There was a touch on his arm.

"Pardon me, sir," the boy said firmly, "that's Mr. Terrence's chair, and I don't believe he's quite finished with his paper."

By this time George Terrence was madder than he'd ever been in his life, but, being unaccustomed to shabby shows of temper or pettishness, he could think of no way of handling the situation. All he could do was to gulp down Harshawe's drink and stalk out, forgetting to cash his check. He went straight to the apartment, packed up his things, and moved to the Hotel Lafayette. His anger appeased, his conscience bothered him about allowing a poor underprivileged, undereducated chap of inferior breeding to upset him. He sent a check for the quarter's rent on the apartment, said he had decided the Hotel Lafayette was more convenient for him, and graciously urged both Harshawe and Turner to be his guests at the Yale Club whenever they chose. The gesture restored George's *amour propre*, though it was periodically shaken whenever the three dined at the club and many members slapped Harshawe and Turner on the back, waiters beamed at them, but no one remembered George. The others did the ordering, made the suggestions, sent dishes back as they chose, and in all made George deeply relieved to get back to the Lafayette, where he could enjoy the pale eminence of being the youngest man in the café.

He was doing well in his profession, but when George did well nobody seemed to know it. Other, bolder members of the firm took entire credit in court for George's briefs. George tried to tell himself that the office and people who counted knew it was he who had done the real work, just as the important people at the Yale Club knew he was the real George Terrence, didn't they? But he ought to have learned that people believed whomever shouted the loudest and pushed the hardest. Crushed between his office pals and his old roommates, George appealed to psychoanalysis, a process that occupied two years and afforded that eager healer named Dr. Jasper a good living and some much-needed experience. In the nick of time Hazel Browne flung herself upon George and married him, remaining awed and grateful for this triumph, insisting on being bullied and masterminded, so that there was nothing for George to do but oblige her.

When people praised the powerful change in his character, George declared it was all due to his superb analysis. Hazel dutifully agreed, never realizing how colossal her own part had been in the transformation. She forgave George for his wild playboy youth, ruthless philandering, fascinating mistresses, and mythical past until George had the pleased conviction that he'd really had all that. Hazel must be right. It was the facts that erred. He allowed Hazel to worship him as a man of the world and dropped an occasional allusion that kept her ever fearful that she might lose him yet to the sexpots surely clamoring for him.

It was a good marriage for these twenty-odd years, with Hazel putting her whole soul into living up to the Terrence tradition of unimpeachable respectability and George always hoping to live it down. When their opposite views might have led to bickering they used their daughter as a buffer, and had grown so accustomed to speaking to each other through her that they hardly thought of her as a person but as an intercom.

"Your mother had a charming habit of being late for appointments when I was courting her." George now addressed his daughter. "While I waited in her living room her roommate very graciously entertained me. Naturally I remembered her kindness."

"I'm sure she was trying to get herself invited," Hazel said to her daughter. "Poor Connie didn't have many beaux as I recall her. At any rate I cannot understand why I should have to give out interviews to her relatives after all these years. Why should Claire Van Orphen suggest it? What could I possibly have to say about her?"

"What do you think Mother should do about it?" Amy obligingly passed the query to her father.

"If I were your mother I should write a nice little note inviting the party to come in for tea if he is in the neighborhood," George said judiciously, feeling for the offensive green-inked envelope in his pocket. "I gather that little Connie has passed on and they merely want to patch up some memories about her. No harm."

Hazel bit her lip.

"I still don't see why she should have mentioned me. You can tell your father, Amy, that I did write a polite note saying that we didn't get into the city often and that I didn't see how I could tell him anything about his mother. But he wants to see your father too. I think it's very strange. And he suggested coming out today."

A stranger asking to take up his own valuable time was a different matter entirely, and George was on the verge of protesting that the intruder must certainly be put off, but Hazel took the words out of his mouth.

"It's all very well to say I should have him here, but when we only see our daughter once a month and when your father prizes his reading time at home above every other consideration—"

"Not above an old friendship," George said, perverse as usual. "If it's Connie's son, of course I will see him, whether your mother cares to or not, Amy, my dear. It's certainly too late to put him off now, anyway."

Both Hazel and George were getting red in the face, the only outward indication that they were having what would be in other families a knockdown fight. Amy looked from one to the other parent with languid curiosity. This was a game her parents had been playing as long as she could remember, a game which excluded her, but it afforded her privacy and freedom.

Many was the time they conducted a polite discussion through Amy regarding the suitability of a school, a dress, a companion for her, both their faces getting redder and redder but their voices never rising in their careful "your father"ing and "your mother"ing. Amy could have gone off to the wrong college with the wrong people in the wrong clothes without her absence being noticed. She knew that her meticulously coiffured, massaged, and prim-mannered mother lived in awe of her trim, neatly turned-out father, quite as if his possible disapproval meant violence or excommunication instead of a delicately sardonic comment or a mere cough. Amy had given up puzzling over what their hold was on each other, devoting herself to the full-time job of concealing her life from them. If they were flaring up now, the cause was certainly more trivial than usual, a silly matter of receiving or not receiving somebody's son.

Mrs. Terrence, always the first to surrender, beckoned the Chinese houseman, Lee, who had been popping his head in the door every few minutes.

"Lee's in a hurry to clear up because he's going to the ballgame," she said. "Do you want to come with me to the Flower Show, Amy?"

"That sounds very nice, Mother," Amy said obediently.

"Mustn't let your mother tire you out," George Terrence admonished. "I'm sure you have lots of studying to do. Sometimes these special summer courses are tougher than the regular ones. Get back in time for a little rest before you leave, my child."

"Thank you, Father, I will," Amy said.

"She'll have all day Sunday," her mother said, "since she has to go back tonight."

George waited till the two ladies had left the table and Lee had started brushing up before he went into the library to his desk. He had to think, but he could never put his mind to anything properly if there was a chance that Hazel would interrupt. She had been remarkably suspicious today about his dreadful mail, he thought, and what with her twittering about little Connie Birch's son, she'd gone out of her way to be irritating. After a few moments he heard her calling, "George, we're off now. Tell your father we're leaving, Amy, dear." At the moment George felt like snarling, "So you're going, then for God's sake be off," but he controlled himself.

He wished fervently that something, anything, would keep his womenfolk away till he could collect his thoughts. He hoped he had remembered to ask where they were going, that was all, and if they were walking to be sure they wore the right shoes. He didn't care if they went barefooted, really, but he did care about showing interest. At any rate they were gone, and the next minute he heard Lee taking out the station-wagon, putting off toward the highway. Thank God.

George fumbled in his desk drawer for a minute before he remembered that he had destroyed the other two letters. He had kept them for a few weeks, intending to give them a completely detached legal study, but there had never come a moment when he could even think about them without panic. Their destruction had seemed to relieve his mind for a while, but the worry had only gone underground, and sprang up at sight of this last communication.

George spread the note on the desk before him, then covered his eyes with his hand. It was childish. He needed a brandy. Standing at the french windows, shot glass of brandy in hand, he looked out at the lush garden, the espaliered pear trees against the stone wall, the purple-blossomed Empress of China trees fringing the rock pool, the heliotrope-bordered paths, the twin fig trees by the gate. What would *you* do? he asked each one of them in turn and went back to his desk, forcing himself to read the letter.

"Dear Terrence: You know damn well I'll keep writing until I get some action or an answer. As a matter of fact, I like to write you. It gives me a chance to unload some old burns and a private laugh or two, like the laugh of you always calling yourself Roger Mills of Toronto. I knew who you were the first time you picked me up at the King Cole Bar but I went along with the Roger bit for laughs. I never could figure out why you picked me, when the other boys were so much prettier, but I suppose a closet queen has to pick the mutt type like yours truly to keep off suspicion.

"I wasn't planning to keep at the trade, really, not having your problem of being too afraid of dames to lay them. I could say you made me what I am today if I wanted to be real mean, doll, but you saved me financially that summer and I thank you. I know I saved you too, for you confessed you couldn't go for a dame that wanted you until you'd gotten excited over me. (I thought I'd mention that bit if I have to write to your wife, who, I guess, was the only one you ever made out with.) You taught me to like nice things, though, and Roger-George-baby I've got to have them now for an amusing little punk of my own that I've got on the hook just the way you got me.

"I'm a lousy actor, as any critic will tell you, so I can always get a job, but I can't make enough to keep this little punk in the luxuries I taught him to need. I'm laying it on the line, Rogie-Podgie, I'm nuts about this boy and it's driving me crazy when he has to screw some old woman for his bar tab. Love and honor are at stake when I repeat I've got to have $5000 to square things or I write Mrs. T. about that little summer's idyll. Daughter Amy—yes, I know you did make it once, anyway—will be grateful that she owes her existence to your great good friend and pupil.

"I'll be waiting, let's say till the first."

George looked at the writing again, commanding his mind to detach itself from his panic and take charge as it would do for a frightened client. The green letters curled around one another like snakes, y's and g's and f's had corkscrew tails, capitals writhed through loops before identifying themselves, even the letter T managed to spiral on its cross. You didn't need any legal training to deduce that the writer was abnormal, even criminal. How simple it would be if this were a client's problem instead of his own!

"Send the chap to me," George could hear himself loftily advising the worried client. "I'll get him to show exactly what he has on you and in that way get a line on his own record. You'll find we can scare him off, lucky to get away without a prison sentence. Leave it to me."

Hah. Leave it to me. Not when he was his own client, George thought morosely.

If only he dared consult Doctor Jasper . . . But it had been Dr. Jasper, after all, who'd gotten him into this mess. He'd been an eager young psychiatrist in those days, all hopped up over the new science, and George was his first paying customer. He'd believed in the doctor implicitly, George thought with a sigh, probably because it was all new and exciting and he was as eager to be a guinea pig as Jasper was to have one. If you're so afraid to sleep with a girl, said the doctor, then try it out with your own sex, maybe that's the answer, let's have everything out in the open. Once you know, then we can handle the problem. Jasper never expected he would be taken seriously, then, by anybody. Lucky Hazel appeared on the scene about then and simplified everything; no further dealings with old Jasper.

George picked up the note and tore it up carefully, made a little snake nest in the ashtray of the pieces, and set a match to them. A slight sound outside made him look up from this operation. Someone was coming up the garden path, the pebbles crackling underfoot. George stayed motionless, smitten by the dread that the green-ink writer himself might have cornered him. He realized he could be seen from the garden and, from the sound of the footsteps pausing, knew the intruder must be directly outside the window, no doubt staring at him. George forced himself to walk toward the window. He saw with almost a sob of relief that the young man was a stranger with only warm friendliness on the fair, smiling face. He pushed open the french windows, half locked by rose vines.

"The bus driver told me this was the Terrence place," the stranger said.

"I am George Terrence," George said.

"I wrote Mrs. Terrence I would pay a call today. I'm Jonathan Jaimison. My mother—"

George felt a wave of deep affection for this young man, unexpected savior of his peace.

"Connie's boy!" he exclaimed, holding out both hands with an enthusiasm that would have astounded his family. "What a splendid surprise. Do come in—no, no, right this way, never mind those tulips, just step over them."

As it had never occurred to Jonathan that he would not be welcome, he was pleased but not surprised at the warmth of his reception. He sat back in the elaborately comfortable red leather chair George had directed him to, accepted a cigarette and a stout highball, refused George's urgent offer of a sandwich, coffee, cake, icewater, protesting that he had breakfasted late. He would not stay long; all he wished was information about his mother's New York life from those who must have known her best. Miss Van Orphen had suggested—

"Splendid!" George Terrence exclaimed happily. "Yes, a splendid idea of Claire's. I must get in touch with her one of these days, it's been so long. A pity Hazel, Mrs. Terrence, isn't here, since she was such a dear friend of your mother's."

"Perhaps I'd better come back some day when Mrs. Terrence is in," Jonathan suggested tentatively.

Indeed he must not think of leaving, George insisted. After all he too had known the young man's mother, perhaps in some ways even better than his wife had. There had been times Connie Birch had confided in him, for instance, while he waited for Hazel to dress or come home for an appointment.

"You mean she confided in you about her—love life, say?" Jonathan leaned forward eagerly. "About the men she knew?"

George realized that, in his anxiety to detain his caller, he had gone too far. He had only the vaguest memory of Connie; all he remembered was his disappointment when the door used to open on Hazel's roommate instead of Hazel herself.

"No, no, nothing like that," he said hastily. "Surely you never thought your mother was not circumspect in every way. No, we discussed her work with my firm's clients, the Misses Van Orphen, and music, books—"

"But she did know several men," Jonathan persisted, and then asked doubtfully, "You don't mean to say she was not—attractive to men?"

George saw he was on the wrong tack.

"My dear boy, she was charming! Utterly charming," he declared. "You must see that in her pictures." He wished the boy would produce a photograph to nudge his memory. "As a matter of fact, if my wife had been late a few more times I cannot guarantee what might have happened."

"She wrote my aunt that you—or the man her roommate was engaged to—was tremendously clever," Jonathan told him. "She seemed to feel as you did, that if you had not been already committed—well, you know how those things are. You were a man of the world, she said, and had so much to teach a girl."

"She said that?" George was touched.

"You explained Marx to her," Jonathan said, "and Freud and that sort of thing."

Those had been courting subjects in that day, George recollected with some embarrassment. Now he did have a sudden picture of sitting on a sofa with the sweet girl, reading aloud from Freud while she consoled him with bootleg gin and orange juice till Hazel came home. He could almost swear there had been a slight hassle, a furtive embrace, a scurrying when Hazel's key sounded in the lock.

"I do want to find out the man in her life then," Jonathan said. "It wasn't you, sir, that winter of nineteen twenty-eight?"

"Nineteen twenty-eight," George repeated, and his eyes fell on the ashtray, where he fully expected to see green ashes. "Why do you ask?"

"I'm looking for my father," Jonathan confessed. "I was hoping it might be you, now that we've met."

The ashes were gray like any other ashes, George saw. A sweet sense of relief was surging through him, and an excitement was beginning in the back of his brain that meant a subtle, hidden point was about to be flushed out into service. He carried the ashtray to the window and poured the contents over the rosebush with great precision.

"Ashes are splendid for the soil, you know," George said.

Hazel Terrence would have been astonished at the behavior of her husband that Saturday afternoon. He had always professed a manly aversion to the details of the home, he disliked all social encounters that demanded small talk, and he particularly avoided contact with the younger generation.

Yet here he was showing Jonathan Jaimison over the grounds, pointing out the foundations of the old mill, leading him through the grape arbors and confessing his ambition to have a real vineyard (Hazel would have been surprised to hear this), explaining the herb garden with great pride: *this* was what you did with the *Waldmeister* in May-wine making, this was tarragon, this was rosemary, delicious with roast lamb, this was mint—by Jove, they'd have a julep!

"Next time you come up we must take you for a swim in the brook," George said, as if this was only the beginning of a deep intimacy. Hazel would never have dreamed he knew or cared so much about the flowers she and Lee nursed so tenderly. Her firm, dimpled jaw would have dropped to hear her husband's deferential interest in this young man's opinions on the state of the world and his benign advice on futures for talented lads. She would not have believed her ears had she heard the many times George exclaimed, "Splendid! How right you are!" to the stranger's shyly offered remarks.

Hazel had given up trying to break into her husband's moody silence at dinner with her harmless little anecdotes of town scandals, a tiff with the butcher, a pleasant encounter with an old neighbor, a report on a new supermarket's advantages. George had a way of smiling at her across the carefully chosen table flowers and shutting her up with "My dear, must we clutter up our minds with all this trivia? Isn't it hard enough to manage our own major patterns without dragging in the inconsequentials? We are not curious about others' private lives."

But here was her same George eagerly asking young Jaimison for more and more trivia, listening with deep absorption to a description of the Then-and-Now Café, nodding approvingly at Jonathan's praise of Claire Van Orphen.

"A splendid soul," said George. "I was fortunate enough to handle their father's estate and got to know the two sisters very well, particularly Claire, a most talented woman. And this writer friend you mention, Earl Turner, was an old friend of mine, too. We shared an apartment once with Harshawe, the now famous Harshawe, of course, and frankly I always felt Turner had the better brains. I've often thought of looking him up sometime, but since my semi-retirement we spend very little time in New York—my wife hates it."

Me hate New York! Hazel would have exclaimed, had she heard this statement—as if I had any choice about it! And "looking up" any old friend of his past was the last thing in the world George Terrence would ever want to do.

Whenever Jonathan suggested leaving, George Terrence thought of something else to detain him. So The Golden Spur was still going. Amazing. Jonathan must tell him more. Mrs. Terrence would be heartbroken to have missed him, and she should certainly be back before four. Living in the wilderness as he did, George warmly assured his guest, he found news of the great artistic world a godsend. It was seldom, moreover, that he found a young man who had so many of the same interests and reactions to life that he himself had had at that age. He was only surprised that Jonathan, with the acute perceptiveness he displayed on all subjects, had not taken up law.

"You really think so?" Jonathan asked, highly pleased. "As a matter of fact I did think of law at one time. My mother talked about it when I was still in primary school. Perhaps she was thinking of you."

Another wave of tenderness for his wife's long-lost room-mate came over George. In the course of their talk a far clearer memory of Connie had emerged, and he had fleeting pictures of himself and Hazel, all dressed up for some fancy social affair (it was Hazel who had started him on accepting these invitations), while little Connie lonesomely bade them have fun. Connie had been shy, just as he was, and he should have noticed more things—her interest in him, for instance. But Hazel had rushed him through to the altar so fast he hadn't had time to be even polite. Connie had written him a little verse on his birthday, though, by Jove, he suddenly remembered.

"Your mother was a very fine person, very sensitive," George said broodingly. "Too bad you're not a lawyer. I could be of some use to you now in getting started in New York."

Jonathan had the impulse to declare that he would plunge at once into the study of law if it would please this kind gentleman. He stole furtive glances at him, telling himself that in spite of his being a good four inches taller than Mr. Terrence, and blonder and blue of eye, there was a suspicious resemblance in the set of the ears, the shape of the brow, even in the timbre of their voices, though this might have been because his host's academic style of delivery was contagious. Jonathan was always susceptible to other people's mannerisms and he was already handling his cigarette in the same way George did, waving it like a baton to illustrate some remark, then plunging it up to his lips as if to stop an emergency hole in the dike. George, suddenly glancing over, caught Jonathan in the very act of synchronizing the gesture with his, and smiled.

"A daughter is all very well," George went on confidentially, "but a man who has worked his way to the top in his profession, learned a lot along the way, has a lot to give, needs a son to carry on, don't you see? For instance, if you were my boy—"

But I am, I am, Jonathan wanted to cry out, quite carried away as George paused to light another cigarette, I could be! He did not speak, but he had a feeling that George Terrence had the same thought. Under the circumstances they could not come out openly with the idea. But they would know, and that was the main thing.

"I think I am only being realistic when I admit to you that my daughter is not a clever girl," George said suddenly. "Her mother and I have had to make all her decisions, and we are grateful that she is a good, obedient child. She has had the best upbringing and every opportunity, but she has no ambition such as I always had, very little interest in society even, clings to her home so much she did not want to go further off to college than New York. I dare say in our old age this sort of clinging will be a comfort. And yet . . ."

He sighed and stroked his chin. Jonathan stroked his own chin in sympathy.

Suddenly his host banged his fist down.

"By Jove, it's not too late even now!" he exclaimed. "I'll put you in our office as a starter, send you to school nights, no reason you shouldn't make the most of a good legal mind such as yours. Not necessarily in the courts of law precisely, but there are other angles. How about that?"

"That's too good of you, sir," was all Jonathan could say.

George Terrence wrote something on a card, which he handed to Jonathan.

"This may be a day you'll remember all your life," he said. "I'll be making arrangements for you, and you come to the office a week from Wednesday. I'll come in myself!"

Behind him on the mantelpiece a cuckoo flew out of a clock, and Jonathan jumped up at the stroke of four, remembering he should take the four-thirty train back to the city. Mr. Terrence leaped up at the same time as a pair of black cocker spaniels tumbled through the french windows.

"Good heavens, the girls must be back!" he said. "Wait while I tell them you're here."

*

Jonathan stared blissfully at the card in his hand as George left. Incredible that his future should be solved so simply and suddenly. He wandered around the library, studying the family portraits with new interest, measuring his resemblance to them. It occurred to him that if George Terrence was really his father, then it would be awkward meeting his wife. She might even see the resemblance and feel bitterly toward the old girl friend who had betrayed her. Perhaps she already knew. Jonathan found himself weighing all angles of the situation with the shrewd legal slant of which he felt suddenly possessed. Naturally she would be considering the danger of financial claims. Jonathan was smitten with embarrassment. That his desire to claim a parent might be construed as a raid on the family fortune had not occurred to him before, and he fixed his gaze broodingly on the garden, stroking his chin just as George Terrence did when pondering a problem.

He heard a feminine voice enunciate softly but firmly, "I'm sorry, my dear, but you'll simply have to explain that my head is killing me and I must lie down. I'm going straight up to bed. Amy can speak to him."

There was a patient sigh from George, a soothing murmur from another feminine voice, and then the library door opened again to admit George, smiling rather grimly, followed by a young woman.

"This is my daughter Amy, Jonathan," George said. "You must meet this young man, my dear, child of one of your mother's and my very old friends. Will you excuse me, Jonathan, while I go upstairs and see what I can do to relieve my wife?"

"I'm afraid I'll have to say good-by now, Mr. Terrence," Jonathan said nervously, stretching out his hand. "The station bus will be along any minute."

He stopped short. Mechanically he went on shaking the hand of the young lady, dropped it, and grasped George's outstretched hand.

"Amy can drive you to the station, can't you, my dear? Take the Volkswagen, and Lee can pick it up at the station later," George urged. "Amy has to take the same train back, don't you, my dear?"

"I'll be glad to look after Mr. Jaimison, Father," Amy said, and then their eyes met.

Jonathan stared at her incredulously. He barely noticed George Terrence clasping his hand again in farewell.

"We'll be seeing each other, of course, Jonathan," George Terrence called out from the door. "This has been most interesting. Sorry Mrs. Terrence is under the weather. Ah well, the ladies—you understand!"

Jonathan did not hear. Amy stared back at him defiantly.

"There—there must be some mistake," he stammered. "I had no idea you were—I mean—"

"Hush!" She seized his arm petulantly and pulled him toward the garden door. "Come along, they know we have to make that train. They'll be arguing for hours. Why did you have to come here? What have you told him about me?"

"But I came to see him about my own problems! I never even dreamed—"

"I knew it would happen sometime," Amy said, leading him across the terrace to the lower gate where the Volkswagen stood. He got in while she waited to wave dutifully toward the house. Jonathan took the cue and waved too.

"Oh, they can't see us," she said, taking the wheel. "I was just waving good-by to Amy Terrence like I always do."

"I'm confused," Jonathan said, once they were on the highway. "You are Iris Angel, aren't you?"

"Now I am. I thought you'd come out to tell Father, for a bad minute."

"But I didn't know—I still don't understand."

"Anyway, you didn't goof when you saw me, so I forgive you," she said. "I absolutely shook when I saw you there!"

"But which are you, Amy or Iris?" Jonathan asked, mystified. "Aren't they your real parents?"

"Of course they are, when I'm with them," Amy said with an obvious effort to be patient with childish questions. "I'm Amy Terrence for them. You don't think they'd ever let me be anything else, do you? But the minute I'm out of their sight I'm Iris Angel."

Jonathan thought it strange that to his own daughter a great lawyer like George Terrence should be as unsympathetic as a Jaimison.

"But he understands ambition so well," he said. "You could have explained to him."

"Explain!" Iris mocked him. "There's no explaining to your family. You can waste your whole life fighting them, if you're a fighter. But I'm no fighter, and how can you fight when they make you doubt yourself? I'm an actress and the only way I can survive is to play the part called for. They want their Amy, so I play Amy Terrence for them, and everybody's happy with no argument. See?"

"We're in the same spot," he confessed. "I couldn't start being myself till I'd blanked out the Jaimisons."

He started to blurt out his own story but had the good sense to reserve the vital facts. Iris was fascinated with the hints he gave, and they agreed it was small wonder they had been drawn to each other at first meeting. They were still congratulating each other on the coincidence when they got off the train. At daybreak they were learning even more about each other, lying on Iris's floor on Waverly Place.

Amy Terrence had had secret names for herself all during her childhood, but "Iris Angel" was the one she stuck to after her fifteenth birthday. By that time she took for granted that the girl Amy was a dummy daughter invented by her parents, a proper doll wound up by them for family performances, while the real creature, Iris Angel, used the dummy as armor to hide her private self.

To all appearances Amy had been a quiet little girl, approved but scarcely noticed by teachers in the convent school, later practicing her piano, ballet, skating, and languages at home exactly as required, showing neither unseemly aptitude nor more apathy than was stylish. It had been a mighty feat of silent diplomacy for her to make her father feel it was his inspiration to allow her to live in New York for special courses instead of going to Vassar. A colleague in George Terrence's office had a daughter doing this very thing. The two men agreed that their daughters were too timid and overbred for modern times, and girls' schools would make them worse. The thing to do—if the girls were ever to hold their own in the race for husbands—was to push them out of the nest, put them on their own (suitably protected, of course) to prepare them for the day when no more spoon-feeding was possible.

The colleague's nice little daughter was persuaded to take Amy into her nice little flat in a nice little made-over house in nice little Turtle Bay. All four parents congratulated themselves on their liberal point of view, and they chuckled at the paradox of their own modernity and their daughters' shy Victorianism. They reminded one another of what mature men and women they had been at that age and what irony to have hatched these tender doves.

Amy dutifully followed her parents' suggestions in registering for secretarial courses, art and cooking classes. She had membership cards at the Museum of Modern Art and the Metropolitan, season tickets for the Philharmonic, charge accounts at suitable stores. She then proceeded to ignore the whole plan and quietly set about getting into the theater, visiting producers and agents with a doggedness that would have amazed her parents. She got a part as a bawd in a *Merry Wives of Windsor* production that played only two weeks but established her, in her own mind at least. She took a basement apartment on Waverly Place as Iris Angel, but arranged with her roommate to keep the Amy Terrence name on the Turtle Bay apartment. For three years she had managed to conceal her true activities, rushing up to her proper apartment when her roommate alerted her that a parent was imminent, appearing at the Connecticut parental home on alternate week ends in the guise of docile student-daughter.

A number of things had happened to Amy during that time. She had taken her turn at falling in love with the painter Hugow, dogged his footsteps through Village bars, phoned him at least twice a day, managed to be seduced by him, had the usual agonies of an abortion, and then was rescued by a summer stock job in Canada. For her parents' information she was on a painting trip with an art class. She then followed him to Haiti and spent three blissful months with him while her roommate dispatched prefabricated notes from Europe, where she and Amy were supposed to be on a tour of the château country.

After her first few panics Amy had become so expert in conducting her two lives that she switched from Iris to Amy as easily as she played her other stage roles. She was helped in the masquerade by two factors. One was the fact that her shy girl friend was in an equally dangerous spot, having a serious affair with a married university teacher and needing reciprocal protection, and the second was the convenient blindness induced by the imperturbable complacency and complete self-absorption of George and Hazel Terrence. Devoted parents as they were, they had never taken their responsibilities easily but had worried and consulted and nagged over every tooth, every mouthful, every sneeze, every freckle of their little girl, smothering her with their anxieties till they lost sight of the girl herself. Secretly she was their weapon against each other. Such a good child, such an obedient daughter, such a treasure! But what heaven to have her being good and obedient some place else, leaving them to their mature, well-organized selfishness!

Amy must have sensed her position the day she was born and seen the advantage it gave her for her own selfish ends. She could have been plotting like a trusty in prison, building complete confidence in good little Amy all those years, while grooming Iris Angel for the escape. She had seldom uttered a thought in the company of her parents, always listening obsequiously, receiving their admonitions with a prim "Yes, Father," "I shall certainly think about that, Father." "Thank you very much, Mother, I am sure you are right."

Fortunately neither George nor Hazel liked the theater, certainly not in its new off-Broadway aspects, so Amy did not feel her Iris Angel identity was imperiled. At first she had feared not disapproval of her stage ambitions but interference in them. There would have been formal discussions, Mother would have escorted her to auditions arranged through suitable social channels, Father would insist on a program of plays to be studied, private tutors would be chosen from distinguished old stars of their own day who would teach her how to beat her breast and nibble the scenery. She knew they would explain to their circle that they had chosen theatrical training for her as invaluable for a future hostess, not really as a career.

If her parents had been able to forget themselves long enough to really observe their little girl, they would have noted that her manners became glibber every year, her Yes,

Fathers, and Thank you, Mothers popped out mechanically, while Amy stared into space, increasingly bored by her daughterly role. Hugow and her stage and Village pals never once doubted her Iris Angel personality. Amy would have died of shame had they discovered her bourgeois background, but luckily they were too self-centered to be curious.

Now that Jonathan had found her out, she was surprised that it was a great relief to tell him everything. She had never thought of her double life as wrong; it was merely complicated at times, and inconvenient. Sometimes she was Amy, and sometimes she was Iris, she explained to Jonathan, never both at once, any more than a two-timing husband plays both his roles at once. Besides, it was absolutely necessary if she was to get what she wanted from life.

"I just do what other girls do, only they don't use two names," she said. "They just keep fighting it out with their families, but with parents like mine, I wouldn't have had a chance. I had to play it like a stage part."

Jonathan was such an admiring audience that she played up the part, describing narrow escapes from discovery both by her family and by her Iris Angel set. Now that she was Iris Angel again, her black hair fell loosely out of its prim arrangement, her arms and legs swung freely, she seemed bigger, as if even her flesh had been compressed in her Amy role. The voice changed from the colorless precision to the appealing huskiness that had first attracted him.

Funny, Jonathan kept remarking, that she should have to throw off her family mark to find her own identity, whereas his own problem was the opposite. It made the reasons for liking each other all the stronger, they told each other solemnly. Presently Iris bethought herself of danger and implored Jonathan not to betray her confidences. He was shocked at the idea.

"I am only wondering what would happen if your parents found out the extent of your Iris Angel life," he said. "As an actress, of course, you may have another name. But your union card, your contracts and lease here, and the false Iris Angel background you've given out . . . Can they stop you from appearing in a play, let's say?"

Iris had raised herself on one elbow on the rug where they lay and she was staring at him curiously.

"Or you find yourself unjustly accused in an accident," Jonathan went on, "and your double identity comes out. What is your legal position—"

He stopped when Iris put a hand over his mouth.

"You're just like Father!" she cried. "I can't stand it if you're turning out to get legal about everything. Jonathan, you scare me! Stop looking like Father."

"Do I really?"

"You do! You put your fingers together when you say the word 'legal' as if you were praying, just the way he does, and I can't stand it! It makes me afraid of you. You even say 'splendid' just the way he does."

Jonathan trembled.

"You know I wouldn't tell your father—" he started to assure her, but she interrupted him.

"What I don't understand is why you should have called on my parents," Iris said. "Mother never mentioned having lived in the Village or studying the theater. Until that note of yours came I never heard her mention your mother's name. And I simply can't believe she had all those beaux and dates as your mother said. Oh no. You've no idea how stuffy she is. Even worse than Father."

Curious that Iris had caught the resemblance in him to her father. If he couldn't make any headway with his wishful thinking about Alvine Harshawe, he would be content to be the byblow of a distinguished legal brain, Jonathan decided. Iris's long arms drew him closer, and joy filled him that he had found father and true love at the same time.

"Do you really want to go in Father's office as he said, and study law, Jonathan?" Iris said dreamily. "It will take years and years, darling, and there are so many other wonderful things we might be doing together. Why should he pick on you to be his successor?"

"Don't you see, it's because—" Jonathan started and then froze. Good God!

If he'd found a father in George Terrence, then he'd found not his true love but a sister!

"What is it, darling? If you're worrying about Hugow, you mustn't," Iris whispered. "The past is the past."

Jonathan forced himself to draw away from the warm golden cheek against his, and untangled his legs from the long brown ones. It was an effort to get to his feet.

The past was the past all right, and he should never have stirred it up.

"I've got to go," he said. "I mean we mustn't—I shouldn't —it's a mistake—oh, Iris, I do love you. Good-by."

He dashed out before she could speak, which was well, because any word from her would have brought him back. The faster he walked, the more frightened he was by the wheels he had set in motion which he must now brake as best he could.

Obviously he could not explain to Iris, and he dared not see her. His only hope was to get proof somehow that George Terrence was not his father. Until then he would hide.

For the first time he wished he had left an escape hole, even if it led back to Jaimison, Sr.

9

E VER since Jonathan Jaimison had brought magic into Claire Van Orphen's life she had been fervently longing for her twin sister, Bea. It was no use reminding herself that Bea felt no reciprocal yearning, and had never kept an engagement with her without postponing it at least twice. Bea was perfectly sweet about gossiping over the phone for an hour, but all Claire needed to do was say, "It's such fun talking, let's have lunch," and Bea was ready to hang up, almost as if she felt her good nature was being taken advantage of. Then Claire would pick up her poor pride and remember not to phone for weeks, because it was too obvious that Bea used the phone not to keep in touch with her but to keep her away.

Earl Turner doesn't find me such a bore, Claire told herself, and if I know Bea she would be mighty flattered to have an ex-*Sphere* editor like Earl call on her the way he does on me. And Jonathan is the sort of attractive young man she is always making a fool of herself over. And if she could just see me having my Manhattans at The Golden Spur with those two men, she would do her damnedest to make them like her best, the way she always used to do.

But Bea hardly listened to Claire's reports of her new life, or if she did hear she put her own interpretation on Claire's news. Maybe her little books on gardening, travel, careers, or kiddy life, and the occasional nice little love stories in nice women's magazines, weren't great literary triumphs, Claire conceded, but my word, it did mean something to do a job well enough to have it sold at a counter, and it wouldn't have hurt Bea to throw her a compliment. Oh, Bea tried to be kind, but her compliments were always laced with insults.

"I do think you're amazing to go on and on writing those little things you do, Claire," Bea would say. "I must send you that little avant-garde magazine my friend writes for. I'm sure you could catch on to the modern manner. It's such a shame to waste your talents on this other sort of thing. You really should catch up with the times, dear."

Well, what about those sales to TV of the old stories Earl had revamped? What about the old one he'd turned upside down and sold to the *Post*? Even Bea wouldn't dare call TV old hat. Claire didn't want to risk having the joy of her new triumphs crushed, and didn't confide them at first. Not over the phone, she said to herself. But how she ached for the old blind loyalty of their younger days! What good was happiness if you couldn't tell it to a loved one, share it and double the joy?

She herself, at least, tried to put on an act of being interested in Bea's obsession with the music world, all the green-room tattle about the Met and Balanchine and Bing and Lenny Bernstein, all the inside chatter that the ladies around Carnegie Hall feasted on. She may have worked too hard at feigning interest, Claire reflected, for Bea usually shut up abruptly after some comment from her sister. Once she had been downright angry, Claire recalled, after telling stories about Bing all during lunch so that Claire innocently asked how long she'd known Mr. Bing. It turned out Bea had never even met him and was annoyed when Claire expressed surprise at such passionate interest in a man she did not even know.

As Earl says, I probably bug her more than she bugs me, Claire sorrowfully admitted.

In the night the new loneliness for someone to share her success, the ache for Bea, the sister of long ago was unbearably painful. Maybe they could take a cruise together, the way they did when they were girls. They could talk over the family history, go over memories of Father and that dreadful second wife of his (still alive in a nursing home in Baltimore, determined to hang on till every penny was gone). They could fill in the gaps of old stories they had forgotten. They might even live together again.

The idea of suggesting this to Bea was too bold for Claire to entertain at first, but it grew on her more and more. She had a vague suspicion that Bea's money must be running out. Bea had never mentioned what sort of financial conditions her husband had left, but there had been astonishingly little insurance, and once she had told Claire she was lucky not to have had a smart businessman husband like hers to lose half her capital by "shrewd" investments. Claire had confessed that her own ignorance of money matters was all that saved her from the poorhouse. She had stubbornly rejected all expert advice on reinvestments, and therefore still had her small income, which sufficed, with her intermittent royalties. But Bea had always lived on a much higher scale, joking about her creditors and about Claire's naïve terror of bills. It struck Claire that perhaps Bea had been avoiding her lately because she didn't want Claire to guess that the game was up and that the bills were closing in.

Bea had not seemed impressed or even curious when Claire hinted at her new fortune, probably thinking it was only a matter of a few hundred dollars instead of dizzy thousands, with more to come. If Bea would only meet her halfway, a quarter of the way—no, if she would only open the door and let Claire come all the way alone, Claire would offer her a choice of Paris or Rome for a year or two. Claire could hear her heart thumping in terror at the thought of leaving her dear little closet of a room and the new friendships Jonathan had brought to her. But if that was the only way to win back her twinship . . .

She began to speculate on how she could get around Bea without that proud beauty flaring up at any implication she wasn't on top of the world as always. Maybe she would have to make all the arrangements before she even put it up to Bea. Maybe she would have to buy a cooperative apartment in Bea's own neighborhood, the West Fifties or Central Park South, and simply announce to her that a home was waiting just a few doors away, with no troublesome change of habits involved.

But *what about me?* Claire shuddered. At the thought of giving up her breakfasts at the Planet Drugstore, her two-Manhattan binge at Mac's Bar and Grill, her little book gossip with Jo and Lois at the Washington Square Book Store, the Sunday twilight walk through Washington Square, with the young people clustered around the fountain, plunking their banjos and chanting their hillbilly songs, the Good-morning-Miss-Van-Orphen all down the street, in Henry's delicatessen, where she bought her staples, in Schwarz's stationery shop, where she bought her *Times*, Claire felt a childish panic. Childish, oh, definitely. If she was going to win her way back to twinship she would have to grow up as Bea had and face change fearlessly—yes, even enthusiastically. Bea would see that they were indeed sisters.

Claire's twin, Mrs. Kingston Ball, was having her hair done in her hotel room by Madame Orloff-Gaby. Madame Orloff was another hotel widow, picking up a living by tinting other tenants' hair, doing their nails, walking their dogs, feeding their birds, or reading to them in her Russian accent, all her services costing only half the standard charge. Bea was given to claiming that it was not the cheapness that made her loyal to Madame but the marvelous musical background gladly shared with her clientele. In her Odessa youth Madame had been a singer, a true mezzo, as she would tell you, but a great career was nipped in the bud by a stupid coach who tried to make her into a lyric soprano. It was a miracle, she said, that the creature had left her with even a speaking voice. It was indeed a lovely voice, Beatrice felt, chocolate-rich, rumbling around in dark baritone cellars and exuding confidence and consolation. You could tell Madame Orloff absolutely anything, for she'd been everywhere and seen everything. Nothing surprised her, yet she was always interested, always deeply sympathetic, supporting you in any folly, or even crime, if that was your mood. Today had been an unusually quiet session, Bea silent and brooding, and Madame gracefully taking the cue. Finally, however, as she took the pins out of her customer's hair, she ventured gently, "Mrs. Ball is troubled about something today."

"Do I seem cross?" Bea asked apologetically. "I'm sorry. Yes, I am bothered. It's about my sister, you know, the one who lives down in Greenwich Village."

"I've seen her with you in the hotel," Madame said. "She is in trouble and has come to you?"

"No, Claire's all right. It's just that she's suddenly gotten the idea we should live together," Bea said. "We did when we were young, and had to do everything together till I flipped and got out. But now here we are, getting on in years, both of us alone, and Claire's idea is that the time has come for us to close ranks, so to speak. Go to the grave together, I guess."

Madame Orloff's smooth plump hands deftly arranged the other's locks, then patted the top of the head as a kind of sign-off. She took a cigarette pack from her apron pocket, offered one to Bea, and lit them both before she leaned back in the low slipper chair behind Bea, who continued to sit frowning at the mirror. Although bright sunshine leaked through the window, the heavy rose-embroidered curtains were drawn and the electric lights were on. ("There is nothing the matter with my complexion," Bea always said ruefully, "except daylight.")

"We got a very nice tint today, dear," Madame said, eying the image in the mirror. "I added just a dash more of the silver to soften the gold. Very softening. Points up the eyes. So you may live with your sister, then. It would save expenses, eh?"

Bea gave a preoccupied nod.

"It makes perfectly good sense, of course," she said. "I don't know why I'm so bitchy about it. Poor Claire. I almost snapped her head off when she first suggested it. Now why should I blaze up and be so damn nasty when Claire is so patient and amiable?"

"Being twins, you are opposites, that's all."

Bea shook her new crop of silvery blond softly curled locks.

"I don't think so at all. I think we're just two lefts or two rights and we don't complement each other at all. I'm not sure I don't understand Claire because I don't understand myself or whether I understand both of us too damn well."

"It looks so gay, being twins," said Madame.

"I suppose we got a kick when we were little with Mama always showing us off and everybody taking second looks." Bea tried an Oriental effect with her gray eye pencil. "Then I took to having tantrums when Mama would say, 'The twins want this' or 'The twins say that,' as if I personally had no identity at all. Claire loved it because she was shyer and felt that being two was a protection. But I hated seeing my own weaknesses doubled. I was stubborn—you know how stubborn I can be, Madame! No matter what I liked, I was bound to do the exact opposite of what my twin did: Half the time I never knew what I wanted because this mean streak made me automatically take the track contrary to Claire."

"Perhaps you are more alike than you wish." Madame smiled understandingly.

"Sure we are." Bea sighed and rubbed out the experiment in gray shadows around the eyes. "We're probably just one fat case of schizophrenia between us."

"She wants you to leave the hotel?" Madame tried to keep the fear of losing a steady sixty dollars a month out of her voice.

"She sold some film rights and thought of investing in a co-operative apartment right near the Hotel des Artistes—yes, I grant you, it sounds good. She has it worked out even to having a Japanese couple keep house for us, but then I hit the ceiling. It's her money and she means it so well and goodness knows I need money these days, but I said I wouldn't dream of leaving this hotel; then I was ashamed and said I'd think it over, but she was so hurt. She just can't see—"

"You don't get on at all," Madame deduced.

Bea took a comb and began carefully to rearrange her hair in less formal style. Madame subdued the disapproval in her eyes.

"It would mean being clamped back into the grave," Bea went on intensely. "Breakfast and dinner and over our nightcaps remembering anecdotes about Grandpa Sterling's Packard, and do I remember Father getting ossified at our coming-out dance at Sherry's, and can I still do my imitation of Laurette Taylor in *Peg o' My Heart*, and what fun those tango lessons were at the Castles'. My God, Sonia, I like to watch life while it's going on, be in it if I can, but Claire won't let you. She's got to drag you back fifty years to those good old days when I'm damned sure I didn't have any fun, watched and chaperoned and shadowed every minute. It's as if she has to have a transfusion from the past every day in order to get through the present, and it makes you feel so old and sunk and hopeless, as if everything's over, the game is up, good-by, world!"

Madame Orloff listened to Bea's outburst with a thoughtful smile.

"I live in the past too, Mrs. Ball," she admitted. "Perhaps I bore you too, talking about old days in Paris and Moscow."

"Never!" Bea assured her. "You see I don't know your past, so it seems alive, but my own past and Claire's is dead. I can't have her burying me in it—I really can't. You must see how interested I am in young ideas."

Madame chuckled.

"No one could say Mrs. Ball lives in the past, certainly," she said. "Indeed not. But you say she will pay all expenses?"

"She says she's making pots of money now," Bea said moodily. "I can't believe it's by her writing, but on the other hand Claire is not one to lie. Neither of us ever cared anything about money"—she gave a dry laugh—"that is, so long as we always had it. But now, with everything hocked and all my bills piling up . . . It would be heaven not to have those worries. And when I have my frightful headaches or rheumatic spells, believe me, I whimper around for some of my own kin just as much as Claire does. The thought of being left alone to die . . ."

"Don't tell me you have such morbid thoughts." Madame laughed incredulously. "You who are always so gay and full of life."

"I don't give in to them, that's all," Bea said. "But if I took on Claire it would be giving in. Not only that, but I'd have to give up my private life."

Madame stumped out her cigarette and studied her hands. Bea, holding the hand mirror, examined a wrinkle in her neck and impatiently turned out the dresser lamps.

"Luis," Madame said quietly.

Bea flung her cigarette into the bowl already filled with barely touched cigarette stubs and lit another one.

"It would be good-by, Luis," Madame murmured. "Good-by, those charming Sunday lunches."

Bea blew a smoke ring jauntily. It was amusing the way she maintained those little flapper mannerisms, Madame thought, blowing bangs out of her eyes, pouting, tossing her head, shrugging her shoulders, ishkabibble. Was it Clara Bow?

"That can't go on forever, anyway," Bea said. "You don't need to tell me."

"What *can* go on forever?" Madame said. "I always say, So far, so good. A family motto. You have gotten some entertainment and some consolation from Luis, as you have from other young men in the past. And the sister would not understand."

"It would be utterly out of the question," Bea said. "Claire's no fool. She's read everything, even if she hasn't lived it. I wouldn't even dare sneak any *chéris* into the set-up, so I'd be furious with Claire for making me give up Luis, and I'll never forgive Luis if I give up Claire's money for him. Maybe if Luis wasn't such a rude little beast—"

"He resents having to have his love bought," Madame said.

"The way I feel about Claire buying me, I guess," Bea said.

"You could give him the money to go back to the island," Madame suggested. "You say he's homesick."

"He says they'd make fun of him if he went back," Bea said morosely. "All he ever wanted in his life was to get to Miami. When he was a kid diving for pennies when the ships docked he'd follow the women tourists and say, 'Take me to Miami, mama, take me to Miami!' He was still saying it when I found him in that inn back in the hills, and I promised I'd take him."

"And you did." Madame chuckled. "Only it turned out to be New York."

"Everybody on the island was mocking him by that time, calling him Mr. Miami," Bea went on, brooding. "I bought him clothes, and he was just too grateful, that was all, so I brought him here, afraid I'd lose him in Miami. Now he says if he ever goes back, they will follow him down the streets yelling, 'Mr. Miami, Mr. Miami.' I suppose I made him the little monster he's turned out to be."

"You were a very unhappy, lonely woman when you met him," Madame reminded her. "Rushing off to Rome or Rio or London, packing and unpacking to keep from thinking."

"I missed my husband dreadfully," Bea said. "It got worse every year instead of better. Claire wanted me to live with her then, but how could a pious virgin comfort a haunted widow? Not that the trips did any good either. Wherever I'd go I'd say, 'How K. would have loved this,' and it didn't seem right to enjoy myself."

"K. loved travel?" encouraged Madame.

Bea laughed as a thought struck her.

"That was the funny part of it. If K. had been alive he wouldn't even have gone, because he hated going any place. If I'd bullied him into it he would only have loused it up for me. I'd have been in a rage all the time with him lying in bed in the hotel refusing to budge, or roaring around the ship's bar about women dragging their men away from home and making them change their bartenders. I don't know why on God's earth I missed him after he was dead, because I missed him more when he was alive."

Both ladies burst out laughing.

"We miss the man we wish he had been." Madame sighed pensively. "We never quite believe he is really what he is."

Bea, pleased at the way Madame articulated her thoughts with such understanding, reached for her purse, and Madame withheld a faint breath of relief. Instead of losing this steady income, perhaps she could double it, was the thought that hopped into her head.

"Perhaps your twin is not such a pious virgin after all," she said seductively. "Now that she is successful, as you say, perhaps she would like to be rejuvenated too—a nice rinse, the proper make-up, an introduction to an amusing man, eh?"

Bea considered this, then shook her head.

"I doubt it. The only man she went out with in the last twenty years, so far as I know, was our friend Major Wedburn, who lived in her hotel. That couldn't have been anything. No, I'm afraid it would be me joining Claire's life instead of her joining mine."

She leafed through her checkbook, frowning and clucking softly at the stubs. Then, with a deep sigh, she wrote out the check for Madame, fanning it idly for a moment while Madame's eyes followed its flutter. Bea was thinking that once she'd given Claire a definite no she could scarcely dare ask for the small loan she desperately needed. She gave her pretty reconstructed coiffure an impatient shake, as if she could shake off her utterly selfish, unfair attitude about poor Claire. She hadn't even asked for details of Claire's new success, she had been so stunned by the decision that was being forced upon her. Instead of being mad at Claire she should be mad at Luis for making her into such a silly old fool, really. But she didn't dare get mad at Luis. She was darned lucky to have him at any price, at his own good time, and they both knew it.

"Does Luis still live with that old actor?" Madame asked.

"Luis shares Gordon's apartment, yes," Bea said haughtily, knowing exactly what Madame was driving at.

"I was thinking your sister might like the old actor," said Madame soothingly. "Being on TV, you know."

"If you mean we could start double-dating again, no," said Bea. "Thank you, no."

Madame lifted her majestic figure out of the chair, collected the tools of her operations into a large green leather bag, folded her green working smock, and zipped it inside the bag. Bea was still fluttering the check with a vague feeling that while it was in motion it could not be subtracted from her slender balance. Madame regarded her indulgently.

"Maybe it would be a good thing to get used to your sister again little by little," she suggested.

"I hate getting used to anything," Bea said. "I hate the very words. I don't think you're alive if you let yourself get used to things."

"Think of it as a test curl before the permanent," Madame said. "Start doing little things together again—going to movies, the theater. Go see her in this new life she says she is having. What would it be to you—only a few hours a week while you postpone the decision."

"I suppose it would help me stall for time." Bea reflected. "I could stay with her for a week or two."

"Twice I went back to my husband and got used to him all over again," Madame said. "I still did not like what I had to get used to, but it was a sensible thing to do. When he died, my conscience was clear and I could dislike him with justice. He left me his collection of military buttons of great sentimental value. I was able to trade it for passage to America."

Bea wasn't listening. There were tears in her eyes as she thought of how horrid Claire's importunings were obliging her to be, and how unfair it was of her dear twin to make her face her foolish weaknesses. Good people forced you to use them, betray them, hate yourself. . . . Bea dabbed at her eyes angrily and handed Madame her well-earned check.

10

E ARL TURNER would have been mightily surprised to know the effect that his visit had upon Alvine Harshawe.

Alvine himself was surprised. At first there was his usual impatience at having his day shot full of holes by a morning caller. But then he was obliged to concede, in all fairness, that he couldn't hold this against old Earl. For the last five— no, ten—years he'd been holding out his day like a live target for anybody to shoot full of holes. He could not claim that his precious train of thought had been wrecked by that ghost from the past, for the simple reason that his thoughts didn't come in trains any more, or, if they did, they stood loaded on the siding, like a freightful of lumber waiting for a powerful engine to shove it to port. Mostly ideas came to him somewhat like office memos, stamped and questioned by the higher-ups before they reached him, the idea and its dismissal in the same message. "Why bother? Chekhov did this once and for all in *Three Sisters*." "You're sticking your neck out with this stale Steinbeck." "Why try to top Graham Greene?"

Why try? That was the hook to get each idea out of the way before he even tackled it. He was as bad as those conceited old stage stars rich enough to float through society for years, protesting that they just couldn't find a play that was good enough. In the same way he was always telling himself it was no use starting work before lunch or before Peg got out of the house, so then it was always too late. God knows it was no use trying to retrieve an inspiration after he'd mentioned it to Peg and she'd made her usual comment, "Do you really think people are interested in that sort of thing?" He didn't kid himself that anything or anybody was deliberately blocking his work; he didn't permit himself that alibi. On the other hand a man who'd worked as hard as he had at other times didn't just stop out of laziness. It wasn't all his own fault. What he really could say was his own fault was the easy way he deferred to Peg's plans, which never had anything to do with his work. That was why he'd been nursing the notion of skipping out, getting off Peg's social leash and holing up in the place where he'd done his best work.

That meant, of course, the New York house, which was closed most of the time and which Peg loathed. Maybe the old magic would start flowing again, he had figured, and even though he'd be lonesome and uncomfortable, used as he was to having Peg around, it was all the better for his work that she wouldn't be there.

One reason Peg wasn't keen on the place was that it was a holdover from Kay, his third wife, who had lived there with him for three tempestuous years. Kay he always regarded with a certain admiration as his emotional wife, always ready to throw a vase (cheap) or glass (empty), choking and panting in her rage, howling and abject in her penitence. The emotions all had to do with property, he had discovered. No bereft mother or betrayed virgin could storm as Kay did over his refusal to give her control of his finances. How childishly happy she was over the first book he dedicated to her, and what a tantrum when she discovered this did not entitle her to all the royalties! He'd managed to get out of that marriage with his shirt—in fact more shirts than she realized. He had been forced to give her this house as part of the divorce settlement —"My first real home since I left Sweden as a tiny little girl," she had pleaded sentimentally, then put it on sale that very same day. Alvine had foxed her by buying it back himself. The couple Kay had hired still lived in the basement, looking after things in return for their rent, and available for extra domestic service when he and Peg came to town.

Well, he supposed Peg couldn't be expected to like the house any more than she could be asked to like old Earl Turner, who wasn't in the *Social Register* or even in the telephone book. But Earl, like the house, belonged to the good old time when inspiration was flowing, and for that reason Alvine had rather welcomed his visit.

Looking back, he reflected that Earl was probably the closest friend that he'd ever had—that is, they'd been around the same places at the same time with the same ambition. Then Alvine had gotten married and later famous—two conditions that forbade a man to have a best friend. Best friends from that time on were his agent, his producer, his director, his leading man, his editor, his broker, plug them in and out of the switchboard as the deals changed. You lost one set of friends with each marriage, another when it dissolved, gaining smaller and smaller batches each time you traded in a wife. Mostly now his friends belonged to Peg, had to be okayed by Peg. Peg liked "amusing" people. By amusing she meant rich or titled or European social, certainly no literary clowns.

Alvine thought when it came right down to it he liked old Earl a damn sight better than he liked Peg. All day long he kept wishing he'd gone along with him, wherever the hell he was headed. Some crummy joint, probably the ideal setting for the new novel. Earl knew the spots all right. Lucky Earl! But let Alvine Harshawe try to get that kind of background! Let him try to pick up a conversation in a waterfront bar. Somebody was sure to spot him. Alvine Harshawe of all people! Was he there snooping for a story or was he really on the skids, as so many would love to hear?

He envied Earl, who could roam all over the city, from arty Park Avenue salon to Bowery mission, talk to strangers, do and go as he pleased, pack away enough juicy human material for a dozen Zolas. Not that he'd ever make use of it, bless his lazy old heart, except conversationally. The more he thought about Earl's opportunities and his own prison of fame, the more drab his present life with Peg seemed. (Wasn't this sterile period Peg's fault?) For years he'd been wanting to write about an ordinary young man involved in an ordinary situation with some ordinary everyday people. The Harshawe trademark, of course, was taut high drama in strange colorful backgrounds, and it was Alvine's plan to apply the same kind of swashbuckle to an everyday plot. But what did he know about everyday? Earl knew, because he wasn't hamstrung by a social dame like Peg.

The idea of envying poor old Earl set Alvine to sulking all day, and he was not cheered by his agent's good news of foreign royalties nor by viewing photographs of his agent's three sons, all great guys and a credit to the father. He began thinking of the son old Earl had found for him and by bedtime, after a few nightcaps, his head was bursting with the possibilities of the case. Could be, could be, he muttered dreamily over and over, and wished now he had gotten more particulars from Earl. He couldn't sleep as the situation began to branch out like a brand-new comedy plot.

What does a man do when he finds he has a ready-made son, twenty-six years old, mind you, by a female he scarcely remembers? Alvine found himself chortling out loud every few minutes. It was great, really great, he thought. In the first place he needed to find out for his comedy what a young man today was like, and here was one handed to him on a platter. By George, he'd announce him as his son, too. What would people say? he wondered.

It was characteristic of Alvine that he thought first of his public and only afterward of his wife. His earlier wives would have taken such news of a mystery son in their stride, he thought—Roberta would have been noble and modern, Ad would have cried a little, Kay would have seen it as a threat to her financial security—but what would Peg do? Alvine sat up and lit a cigarette, grinning. He had been with Peg longer than with the others, eight years—too goddam long, really— and the one thing he knew about her was that Peg didn't care what he did so long as he was in proper evening clothes. He could insult his host, rape the guest of honor, fall on his face with blind staggers, but by George, let him be dressed, black or white tie! All her complaints had to do with his being in a dirty old sweater or T shirt when he did whatever he did wrong—maybe was late or loud or lecherous. No matter how they'd quarreled over something, he could always win her over by dressing up for some fat nothing of a little party. She was prouder of him for having kept his waistline, he reflected, than for keeping his reputation.

What would really make her burn would be the embarrass-ment, Alvine realized. Peg embarrassed easy, God knew, and here was a real first-rate embarrasser in any family. She would think of all the little trivial social things before the big major thing hit her—like would this son move in with them and would they have to take him places with them and was he going to call her Mummy and all that. Or she might surprise him by throwing a real fit. Alvine figured, with an increasing glow of pleasure, that it might be the means of chickening out of this marriage. He hadn't written—or at least finished— any work since the wedding day. All his other women had kept at him in one way or other to get-to-work, write-write-write—you're-such-a-genius, or we-need-the-dough-for-that-cabin-cruiser or you-owe-it-to-your-public so get down on that typewriter and DO something. They stopped him in his tracks with their helpful yakking. He had thought, when he married Peg, it was going to be an inspiration just to be left alone. It had been amusing, at first, to see people's faces when Peg would say, "My goodness, how do I know what he's writing? I hope it's a space book because that's all I read." The other wives had always been ready to explain him and his work. It had amused him too that Peg, herself a much-admired beauty, was never jealous of the fuss women made over him. Indeed she never saw anything, wherever they went, but women's clothes, men's clothes, and interior decorations. She was always so absorbed in these subjects that when he described some brawl or contretemps that had occurred she would say, "Why, Ally Harshawe, you're making that up! I was right there."

It seemed to Alvine he could do nicely without ever having to hear "Why, Ally, you're making that up!" at the end of every one of his anecdotes. He could stand not hearing her brag of never reading her husband's works, too. His taunt of "illiteracy" only made her preen herself with a yawning, "Darling, you always said I was just a fine big animal." So he was stuck with a fine big animal who took all one winter to read just one of the space novels she often mentioned! He had gone back to separate bedrooms after being kept awake by paperback Ray Bradburys slithering off the bed all night.

He couldn't honestly say he'd lost anything by not writing these last few years. Peg often pointed out to him how much more famous he was now than when she'd married him. There hadn't been any new Harshawe, just revivals of the first two hit plays and all the usual anthologies and reprints of his stories. They'd traveled a lot, been interviewed all over the world, visited maharajahs and accepted decorations or honors. Damn it, you didn't have time to write if you wanted to keep your fame in good condition. Peg was disgustingly right in that, but that didn't stop him from wishing to God he could just sit down and knock something off like he used to. He could do it, too, if he could get Peg, that fine animal, off his neck. How these fine animals hung on, he marveled—he couldn't kid himself she loved him too much, but she loved the life he offered, and she wouldn't give that up.

Hell, he liked the life too, that was the trouble. He liked it best in those rare periods when he was left alone, though. He liked sleeping alone, and best of all staying awake alone, enjoying his insomnia, thinking his own crazy thoughts that Peg could never understand, listening to the all-night programs on the radio, reading a paragraph here and there about the secret of lobster gumbo or Gregory Peck's love life, figuring out what came next in his own life. The finding of a long-lost son would certainly shake things up.

"Peg, my dear, I'd like you to meet an old son of mine, Jonathan. . . ."

The thought tickled Alvine and he dozed off on it, the bedside radio gently clucking away, piping its program straight into his dream about Son Jonathan who was zooming around on a space-ship chased by his agent's three husky oafs in their space-helmets. This blurred into a Long John program about UFOs. The flying-saucer people, it said, particularly the Venusians (a pair of Venusian visitors having been interviewed by a reliable Hightstown, New Jersey, expert; absolutely a fact, affidavits right there in black and white) have a real brotherly interest in our civilization and will not do anything hostile to Earth until we're in a position to threaten them. A Mrs. Ethel Holm, ordinary housewife of Dingman's Ferry, Pennsylvania, also testified she found a very friendly attitude in the two Martians who landed their saucer in her back yard, and she testified in a signed statement right there in black and white so you knew it was God's truth that neither one had lifted a hand to her when she accepted their gentlemanly offer to take her for a ride around Clarion, a small sort of summer-resort planet behind the moon. Drowsily Alvine tried to fish the Jonathan image out of the planetarium ceiling.

Son Jonathan, a cross between a funny-paper space-man and a musical-comedy angel, materialized from a foam-rubber cloud, but just as he was changing into the Creature from the Black Lagoon Alvine woke himself up enough to reach out and switch the dial to Big Joe's all-night show, where more earthly experts discussed alcoholism. One man declared he was not alcoholic, just allergic to alcohol. A mere bite of rum-cake would set him off, stirring his allergy so hard he didn't show up for work for three weeks, you wouldn't believe what an allergy. Glad to have his new son driven out of outer space, Alvine sat up and poured himself a stout highball. He switched to a West Virginia station where a gentleman farmer was describing how he bored holes in his prize beefsteak tomatoes, filled them with vodka, let them age in the icebox, then ate them for breakfast. The Built-in-Snapper. Delicious. Alvine was about to yell out to Peg to fetch him some beef-steak tomatoes, when he remembered she wasn't there, that he was alone with his darling insomnia.

If he did get rid of Peg, chasing her out with a secret son, he'd probably get somebody else, he reflected, sitting up wide awake now. He didn't want a helpmeet or inspiration or even a bed-broken round-the-clock lay, but he did like to yell out to somebody, say around four a.m., and get a response. If Peg were here and had stumbled, yawning, into the room at his cry, dragging her blanket behind her like Linus, the kid in the *Peanuts* strip, she would have slipped sleepily in the bed be-side him, taking a sip of his nightcap, but then she would have complained, "I don't see why you kick about my space books when you listen to the stuff all night on the radio." And then they would have heckled each other back to sepa-rate beds again. So why pretend he was missing Peg? He switched back to Long John on WOR and poured himself some more allergy.

Now some very sincere fellows on the air were talking about the darrows, not outer-space people but the ones that live in the bowels of the earth. A scientific fact! It seems the way the experts discovered the existence of these darrows was that an ordinary everyday steel-worker took an elevator from the tower of an unfinished building—this was in Chicago a while back, affidavits in black and white on request—down to the basement. Down there the car slid sidewise—the fellow was sort of surprised—and started plunging down another shaft for almost two miles. Then the cage door opened and the darrows, these little fellows with big pointed heads, started talking to him, and they couldn't have been decenter if he'd worn his lodge pin. They had nothing against the

Earth—naturally, they lived in it—and they intended no mischief; they were just out to get Chicago. Similar elevator adventures had occurred in Providence, Rhode Island, and in West Yonkers, all absolutely bona fide, sworn to in black and white by ordinary people. The darrows were, if anything, even friendlier than the Venusians, though of course not so personable. All they asked was to destroy Chicago, the wickedest city in the world. An Elizabeth, New Jersey, cop, a guest of Long John, added that these darrows often surfaced to take night jobs, naturally in work involving extreme heat. Many people reported seeing them working away after midnight in that little bakery near the station in Perth Amboy.

Now there was a tranquilizing thought, Alvine mused. When Peg asked him if they would have to take the new son around to parties, he would tell her to go ahead by herself, he and the boy were going to look up some darrows over in Perth Amboy. Or they might hunt for some of their own, up around the Con-Ed diggings in Columbus Circle, say. Take an elevator down to the basement of the St. Moritz after dinner . . .

"Be sure and dress, then," Peg would say.

Alvine, awake, leafed indolently through the magazine sprawling open on the bed. Dr. Norman Vincent Peale's face smiled benignantly out at him, advising a young man unhappily engaged to a selfish beauty to give up looking for beauty and get himself a girl who had something on the ball spiritually. That's the ticket, Alvine thought. He closed his eyes, wondering if his life would have been richer had he settled down with Jonathan's mother, dear long-ago Connie, instead of skittering around from wife to wife, Venusians to darrows, jumping from flying saucers in Massachusetts Bay to instant sons in Greenwich Village. The more he thought about it the more repugnant the thought of going back to the Cape became, and the more intrigued he was by the idea of the kid, Jonathan. He would stick around town for a while longer, he resolved. He would go downtown and hunt out the boy.

My son Jonathan. It couldn't be. And yet— One thing was sure, he wouldn't pass up the opportunity of announcing to Peg that the boy was his. If the idea of a long-ago love coming to light made her holler, then he would simply say it all happened when he was in his white tie and Meyer Davis's orchestra was playing.

"That makes it legitimate." Alvine chuckled.

The people were the same, the places were the same, but suddenly there was a difference. It seemed to Jonathan that the city had been coquetting with him, persuading him it belonged to him until he was confident, then mocking him for his complacency.

It took all his will-power to keep from calling Iris, and he spent hours trying to write an explanation of his flight the other night that would not reveal the true dilemma. He was so sure she was hurt and unhappy that the note from her was a grievous shock to his pride.

"Jonathan, dear, I know you've wondered why I haven't been in to see you at the Espresso after our heavenly night— I longed to see you—but a part has come up for me in the new Jeff Abbott play and I am studying every minute for the audition next week. I'm not daring to see a soul—not even Hugow—because this means so much to me. So here I am, shut up like a nun as we have to be when the big chance comes along. Please don't be hurt because you do understand your Iris is first of all an actress. Love, love, love."

There, Jonathan told himself, that makes it easier, but it was disconcerting to have his own role switched. In the same way he felt betrayed by Miss Van Orphen when he called up to apologize for not keeping in touch with her lately and had to listen to her own apologies.

"I've been meaning to invite you for cocktails soon to meet my sister Beatrice," Claire said. "I've told her about you, and she wants to meet you. But Earl Turner is working with me over my old stories for this wonderful TV producer, and I haven't had a minute. I owe it all to you, Jonathan, because you brought Earl into my life and it's been so lucky! Please don't think I'm ungrateful, you dear boy. We'll get in touch with you the first possible minute."

He went to The Golden Spur, hoping to chance on Earl there and find out if he had heard from Alvine Harshawe, but he was pounced on by Percy Wright instead, which meant that he was quarantined for the evening. Even Hugow failed

him, but then, as the bartender and everybody else in the
Spur realized, Hugow was deep in preparations for a great
new show.

Dr. Kellsey alone was loyal, relaxing at the café table with
his espresso and flask of brandy. But this was no longer any
comfort to Jonathan. Instead he found the friendship increasingly oppressive. There seemed a new note of possessiveness
in the doctor. His invitations to a midnight steak at Delaney's
or a nightcap at Luchow's had a note of command. He spoke
of having Jonathan dine with a lady friend of his, an assistant
in the English department who worked with him occasionally.

"I'd just like to see her face when I introduce you," said
the doctor, and when Jonathan looked perplexed he explained
mysteriously, "You see she never knew me when I was your
age."

The doctor spoke of moving to a larger apartment in his
building, a place ideal for two bachelors. He wanted to know
if Jonathan didn't think it was a capital idea. When Jonathan,
taken off guard, agreed, the doctor nodded with satisfaction.

"I thought you'd get tired of shacking up with those two
little harpies." He gave him a knowing wink. "I dare say you
have to sleep with both of them."

The doctor gave a roar at Jonathan's embarrassment and
patted him fondly on the back.

"Confidentially, I wouldn't mind it myself," he admitted,
chuckling and wiping tears of laughter from his eyes. "I must
say I can't see myself turning down a nice piece of cake like
that, even though I was just as shy as you are, when I was
your age."

"It's nothing like that," Jonathan protested, but the doctor
brushed him aside.

"Nothing to be ashamed of, boy, we've got to have it. Only
thing is the living with women! Always tidying up your papers
so you can't work, or hiding the liquor, and their own junk all
over the place. How can you write your novel there?"

"But I'm not writing a nov—"

"Nonsense, you don't have to keep it a secret from me. I
know the signs. My guess has been right along that you're
writing a novel about The Golden Spur, and I'm all for it,
boy, because I always wanted to write it myself. So you've got

to have privacy, not women. Women are forever washing either their hair or their stockings. No wonder you're looking worried lately."

There was no use trying to persuade the doctor that he was perfectly satisfied with his living arrangements, and since the doctor had not openly stated that he expected Jonathan to move in with him, Jonathan could not risk offending him by a premature refusal. He decided to simplify his position by finding a room of his own some place else, maybe in Earl Turner's old hotel.

But before he could make any move, trouble started in the Tenth Street studio. Lize, after a fight with Darcy, took off for a printers' convention in Atlantic City. Darcy was going to stay home from work, she said, because she had a "virus," and wasn't it lucky she had Jonathan to look after her? This meant that she had time to wash her hair and launder her stockings and lingerie constantly, draping them over his books and shelves, using his shirts as housegowns, his socks as house-slippers, his writing table as ironing board. She implored him to come home early, bringing a sandwich, and exclaimed what a relief it was to have Lize out of the way so they could really get acquainted. When Jonathan found his books dumped on the floor to make room for gallon jugs of wine, Darcy explained that it was because she had decided to go on the wagon and that always required a stock of wine on hand.

"Everybody else goes on the wagon, why shouldn't I, just for spite?" she said in answer to Jonathan's baffled query. "It always makes people so mad. They think you're on the wagon so you can put something over on them. Lize will be furious. It does give you an edge in a fight, you know." Later she added dreamily, "Anyway I like the way everything looks so crazy when you aren't drinking."

Too kindhearted to desert under these circumstances Jonathan found Darcy waiting up for him at night, and often sitting on a stool watching him like a cat while he pretended to sleep. Too ashamed to confess his fear of living alone with a female, he developed a prodigious snore to protect himself.

"You have the nicest snore of any man I know," Darcy told him. "I really mean that sincerely. It makes me want to cuddle right up."

He tried to spend as little time as possible at the café to avoid Dr. Kellsey. He would move out of his apartment that very night, he vowed, but when he got home there was Darcy, waiting to confide in him, over a chianti nightcap, the fruits of her serious meditations.

"A couple has the most fun," Darcy said. "A person by themselves has to keep thinking up things to do."

She held out her glass, and Jonathan obediently poured more wine into it. It struck him that Darcy drank more when she was "on the wagon" than she did when she was drinking.

"I think we shouldn't pour it out from the jug like this," she said, looking at the gallon jug of chianti on the table with sudden displeasure. "I think we should pour some off into a vase or something. It looks nicer."

Jonathan found a milk bottle and carefully decanted a portion.

"Oh, fill it up," ordered Darcy.

Jonathan did. It left the jug almost empty.

"I mean when you're a couple you can do things together," she said and waved at the kitchen table where they sat. "Like this. When a girl gets home she wants somebody to have a nightcap with. And they can do other things together, like— oh, like going to auctions or double features and doing cross-word puzzles, I don't know.

"One of the reasons I broke off with Hugow," Darcy went on, ignoring Jonathan's blink of surprise, "was that he never liked doing things together. Half the time he never even told me where the party was till it was all over. I guess I'm just an old-fashioned girl but I don't think it looks nice for a girl to go to a party alone, especially if she hasn't been asked."

"Don't you have to be asked?" Jonathan inquired.

Darcy gave him a pitying look and patiently explained that in New York City people didn't get invitations to parties, you just found out where they were. Oh some uptown women like Cassie Bender passed out invitations, but it wasn't to have people come, it was just a mean way of trying to keep people out. Hugow, for instance, never liked invitation parties or jigger measures or blue-white hair or avocados.

"Too mushy, he said," Darcy explained, holding out her glass. "You see what I mean about a couple having fun, don't you?"

"Like you and Percy," Jonathan said.

"Oh, Percy drags me," Darcy said impatiently. "I can't go a step without him tagging along. It's all right for an hour or two, we talk about Hugow and all that, but I guess I just don't like rich men. A person like Lize would think a girl was crazy to say that, but that's the way I am. Is that the end of the chianti?"

It was, Jonathan said hopefully, but Darcy recalled there was a spot of rum in the kitchen, and one real drink would not seriously affect her wagon, and it was such fun talking things over.

"You take a rich man and what have you got?" she said, holding out her hands and ticking off her points on her fingers. "You've got dinner in some dingy little Armenian dive or Chinatown where there's no bar to run up the tab, you've got a neighborhood movie rerun, you've got waiters hiding from you once the place knows the kind of tipper he is, you've got pink plastic pop beads instead of pearls and cologne instead of perfume for your birthday, and the only reason you get taxis instead of subways is that he gets that thing claustrophobia in subways. That's your rich man for you."

"Was he that bad with Lize?" Jonathan murmured.

"Of course not." Darcy blazed. "Lize is big enough to clobber him into expensive places like the Stork Club and she can get him blotto and carry him home, but I don't think that looks nice and besides I'm not big enough."

Her eye traveled from her empty glass to the empty milk bottle to the empty jug and to the alarm clock on the icebox. It was after two. Jonathan, reading her mind, said that the liquor store had closed hours ago.

"I don't have to drink," Darcy said. "A little wine, that's all, especially lately, now that I've been thinking over things. Living with a girl like Lize makes you see how you could waste your life with the wrong men. Hugow, for instance, was all wrong for me, that's why I walked out. Not so much his being an artist as his being so much older. Of course my folks always hoped I would marry a real-estate man or car dealer, somebody solid."

Jonathan took the glasses to the sink and washed them. Darcy stabbed a cigarette into her lips and waited for him to light it, nodding approvingly as he emptied the ashtray.

"That's what I mean, a younger man takes more interest in the home, washing dishes and straightening things up, not just chasing after women all the time. All the time Hugow lived here he never made the bed once, honestly it was embarrassing. I could always tell he'd had some new woman in when I'd come home and find the bed all made up. I knew he hadn't done it himself. Older men just don't care about nice things, they can't seem to take their mind off sex. That's why you and I get on, Jonathan, don't you think? Take Lize, she doesn't care if the place is a dump, but I mind terribly. Look at that lumpy old couch! Cracked old plaster walls, beat-up old chairs, dirty old curtains! It's all right for a girl like Lize, but for nice people like you and me, Jonathan, I mean, I could just cry."

If Darcy was going to cry, and she was, it meant another all-night session of confessions, and Jonathan had no consolations to offer, even to himself.

"I thought you liked the place when Hugow had it," he said.

"I wouldn't take Hugow back if he was the last man on earth." Darcy sniffled, dabbing at her eyes with a handy dish-towel. "I saw him in the Spur with that Angel girl the other night and I walked right past without speaking, that's the way I feel."

"With—" Jonathan came to attention suddenly.

"That dopey kid that's been following him around for years, says she's on the stage, but she's really just on the prowl for Hugow, that's all, following him around till he's too tired to go anywhere but bed."

Moral indignation was drying Darcy's tears. Jonathan wanted to ask questions but then he would have to listen to cruel answers. So Iris wasn't seeing Hugow any more, so she was absorbed in preparing for an audition next week and was simply so concentrated on this big chance that she forgot everything else. Dedicated! "Like a nun"!

Bad enough to have to renounce the girl you loved because she might be your sister. Bad enough to renounce a possible father because you'd rather make him a father-in-law. But to have your misery compounded by having the girl indifferent to your show of will-power, busy as she was claiming credit for her own, then lying to him!

Was the whole city out to betray his blind confidence?

"I can understand his going back to Cassie Bender"— Darcy was stroking her infinitely well-known wounds— "because she's just like a mother, that's why I was never, no never, the least bit jealous of her like Lize used to be, but what does he see in that big goony-eyed kid? Why we all used to laugh the way she'd come into the Spur and just sit and moon at him, never talking, just watching like she was hyp- notized or something. That was three years ago, and now she's at it again, all goofy-eyed. Goodness knows you'd think she'd have learned she wasn't his type by this time."

Yes, you'd think so, Jonathan said to himself, but you couldn't learn when you didn't like the lesson. He ought to learn that Iris was carrying a torch for Hugow just like all the other girls, just as he had suspected at the very first. He ought to be angry now at hearing Darcy's news, but he wasn't mad at Iris, he was mad at Darcy for telling. It meant he had been foolishly trusting in Hugow too, so sure Hugow had no more interest in Iris and was a real friend, even though he no longer came to the espresso café to see him. Earl Turner too busy, Miss Van Orphen occupied, Iris gone, Dr. Kellsey a vague menace—there was no one left but Darcy, and Darcy without Lize to balance things was almost intolerable.

"Don't you think that's a good idea?" He heard Darcy's voice babbling urgently. She had found a miniature bottle of Southern Comfort and was sipping it. "After all, that awful little dive where you work can't make any money for you."

"It's not a dive," Jonathan said.

"Of course it's a dive, dopey," Darcy said. "Nobody goes there but your old goat professor and some funny-looking eggheads and social workers. It's a front for something, push- ers or spies or bookies—just like the Metropolitan Museum and that Eighth Avenue subway station—and you ought to get out before you get caught. I mean you should get a job

with the real-estate people right in their office, because you'd
be wonderful in real estate, Jonathan."

She had her head cocked, with that pouting smile that
meant she was feeling cuddly and would wiggle onto his lap
in a minute if he didn't stand up, which he did, pretending to
want a drink of water.

"You'd make a lot of money and wouldn't have to be
spending your savings and you'd have first crack at some nice
little apartment in the West Village, over on Horatio or Bank,
maybe. We could live there. Let Lize keep this place, if she
won't get out."

"We," Darcy had said.

"We could have a big housewarming and invite Hugow and
the whole Spur crowd and everybody would bring a bottle,"
Darcy went on dreamily, still holding out her hand as if it en-
circled a wineglass, though this had fallen on the floor and
was rolling about with a life of its own. "We'd make friends
with the cop so we could make noise all night if we wanted,
and we'd always have room for company to stay, that's the
thing I like about being a couple, don't you? If we had to we
could get married, too."

"Percy would want to live in Brooklyn, though," Jonathan
said cautiously.

"Now Jonathan, you know perfectly well I'm not talking
about Percy," Darcy said impatiently, then relented and flung
her arms around his waist exuberantly. "You know I mean us.
I'm surprised I didn't think of it before, but then Lize was all
over the place."

Jonathan winced, marveling that such a tiny girl could have
such a powerful hug.

"I don't think I'd be good at real estate," he quibbled, but
this only brought more reassuring hugs from Darcy. Her
curlered little head was strategically thrust against his breast-
bone and was butting him into retreat toward the living
room. He remembered his magic words just in time.

"Scrambled eggs!" he cried, pushing her aside. "I'll make
scrambled eggs, and maybe there's bacon left."

It worked, as it always did after his first error. Darcy was de-
toured by the flurry of cooking but not entirely appeased. She
watched his operations pensively, ate her share, and handed

him her plate to wash. He was able to get into bed and turn off the lights without further personal talk, and pretended to be fast asleep when he heard her call out plaintively from the bedroom, "All men ever think about is cooking."

There was no more time to be lost. As soon as the coast was clear, Jonathan escaped.

It should have but certainly would not have consoled Cassie Bender's shattered vanity to know that Hugow's flight from her magnificent summer party brought happiness to many vacationists now drifting back to the city. There were all the artists whose work she had rejected, all the ladies whose artist boy friends she had snatched, all the Cape summer people who were not important enough to be invited to her Big Do, and then the anonymous strangers who loved any story about an honest, poor artist putting a rich, snobbish, overaged lady dealer on the spot.

"What I like best is the idea of old Bender being stranded on the Cape with no man of her own"—Cape oldtimers chuckled—"like everybody else."

For there is no place on earth a man is so rare and so prized as Cape Cod. A clever woman plotted for months ahead to round one up for summer, so that instead of being one of the ravening packs of Extra Women she could qualify socially as a "couple," a couple on the Cape meaning one man and at least four women—wife, mother, sister, girl friend, and possible house guest.

"I'll bet she's still burning," gloated Darcy Trent. "She stole him from me and thought she could show him off as her private property and she got what was coming to her. I *knew* he had something like that in his mind when he left me!"

"But what about the big show she's supposed to give him in the fall?" Lize said. "Maybe she'll get even with him by calling it off."

This was exactly the reprisal urged on Mrs. Bender by her faithful maid and confidante, Beulah.

"You done too much for that Hugow," Beulah said. "You gotta lay it on the line now, kick him right out of our gallery."

God, how she'd like to be able to do it, Cassie thought, but there was no point in telling Beulah why she couldn't.

"He's been kicking you around long enough," Beulah said. "It ain't gonna get any better, and what's more you ain't gonna get any younger. That's not saying you look your age."

Beulah was understanding, too damned understanding, Cassie often felt. She knew too much. She could never be fired, certainly.

"You don't act your age either, that's the trouble," said the sage, dusting the knickknacks on her mistress's dressing table as Cassie lay in bed. "Time you settled down. Have the same man to breakfast two days running, take your make-up off when you go to bed, and all like that."

"My own fault for letting friendship louse up a good sex deal." Cassie whimpered. "I get to liking a guy and trying to help him out of jams, and first thing I've lost myself a good lover. If you want to know something, Beulah, the older I get the more I love that stuff."

"What else you going to do with men?" Beulah said. "That's all they're good for, so you got to make the most of it. You ain't going to get anything else out of 'em."

"After all I've done for him he makes me the laughingstock of the whole Cape." Cassie's tears began to gush again as they had been doing for weeks. "Then all of New York hears about it and men wonder what I did to make him skip. I'll be lucky to find any more lovers. In another ten years— damn it, Beulah, all a hotblooded woman can get in her fifties is a choice of drunks. A drunk who snivels about the good old days, or one that breaks up the joint getting into the mood, or else one that falls asleep before he even begins."

Beulah gave her mistress a comforting smack on the bottom as she passed the bed where Cassie sprawled. Cassie was large, fair, and showy, handsomer in her forties than she had been in her eager, shrill, and scrawny youth, before her hair had turned to gold. Nobody knew what had happened to her husbands or where she had found the mysterious millionaire who had set her up in her own gallery. Beulah had heard that Mrs. Bender had gone into the art racket as an excuse to raid the art quarters of cities all over the world for lovers, but Beulah declared that was just the mother in her. She was the same way herself, just couldn't stand seeing a good man lonesome and starved for love when there was a good bed in her room going to waste.

Cassie was forty-three—well, all right, forty-eight, if you're going to count every lost week end—and Hugow's betrayal had happened at birthday time, when she was frightened enough by the half-century mark reaching out for her before she'd even begun to have her proper quota of love. She was making more and more passes at the wrong men, then trying to recoup with stately cultural pronouncements in her refined Carolina accent, which she kept polished up like her grandfather's shotgun, ready to bring recalcitrant suitors into line. In this crucial period she wavered between her passionate need to be thought of as a splendid roll in the hay and her other urge—a good retreat position really—to be recognized as a Lady.

One trouble, which Cassie refused to admit, was that she forgot to adjust her courting technique to her encroaching avoirdupois. It was one thing for an impulsive, jolly girl to jump on an attractive stranger's lap, crying out that she just loved that Down East accent, but a hundred and sixty pounds of solid female doing the same thing was likely to cause buckling in the property before it was even sold. Gay solo dances, skirts flung overhead to stereophonic cha-cha in bohemian cellar parties might have incited men to lust at one time but now only brought on the janitor complaining of loosened plaster, or an astonished exclamation from younger fry: "Good God, Cassie doesn't wear pants!"

I mustn't ever go to those artists' dives downtown again, Cassie reminded herself over and over. It's all right whooping around in the country places with the old ones, the ones that have it made, like Sandy Calder and that set—even Eleanor Roosevelt or Emily Post couldn't lose anything by that—but it's these young, jealous little bastards that can ruin you, blabbing and getting things in the papers. The trouble is when the party gets wild I forget I have my professional name and dignity. Instead of going home, I go wild too.

Loving men and love as she did, Cassie had a constant struggle to maintain a proper aloofness. Those handsome, fleshy arms were ever ready to be flung around the nearest animate object while she nuzzled its head in her banquet-style decolletage. It was no feather-bed embrace, however, but more a bruising hug from a statue, for Cassie's flesh had no nonsense about it, a nose could be broken on those marble breasts, and young men, touched by the demonstration of warmth, were surprised to find no cuddle comfort here, but more the implacable rejection of a good unyielding mattress. No soft little-boy cosseting, no waste of affection, there was work to be done. With their heads butting into inhospitable crannies and curves of Cassie's neck and torso, they would hear her voice, a Charleston-lady coo to the last, rising above them, as far off and seductive as a steamship whistle inviting them to tropic islands. "This darling man must see me home." Cassie would be third-personing him fondly, and sometimes, it was said, he was never seen again, and only Cassie could tell whether he had escaped or been broken on the wheel.

Beulah's set in Harlem knew much more about Cassie's prodigious appetite for love than Cassie's artist set did. They followed her affairs as they did TV's *Brighter Day*, pleased with her triumphs, shedding tears over her failures. Beulah declared herself as one who believed in minding her own business: she was not like some, noseying in and blabbing one madam's business to the other. This was the pious prologue to each installment of Cassie Bender's Loves, absolving the narrator of all guilt, enabling her to enjoy it the more comfortably, just as confession perfumes the sin. In Beulah's accounts she herself had the leading part, giving full details on all the advice and general theosophizing which guided a grateful Mrs. Bender to success in love and business.

"No sir," Beulah reported herself as saying to Mrs. Bender only a few days before, "you do plenty enough for those paint men without giving them the run of your bed. You do for them and do and do, like this Mr. Hugow, and they takes what they wants when they wants it and then walks out, leaving you bawling. Then you kick some fine rich customer out of your bed the minute Mr. Hugow feels like coming back, and that ain't right. 'I knows all that, Beulah,' she says (here Beulah imitated the whining ofay lady voice), 'but these rich buyers of mine is too old and anyway by the time I've poured enough scotch into us to close the deal I'm so punched up I want to get in the hay with a real man, somebody where I don't have to do all the work. When that damn Hugow shows up I forget I'm mad at him, and there goes the ball-game.' 'Don't you be a fool,' I tells her, 'you hang on to those old men or they'll take away your gallery and you won't have those painters to lay around with.' "

That turned out to be one of Beulah's soundest warnings, though it came much too late, even if Cassie had ever been in the mood to heed it. Right now Cassie had no intention of letting Beulah crow over her good guessing but allowed the girl to believe her weeping was caused by a mere broken heart. She was out of pocket plenty too, since her tender solicitude for Hugow's comfort, the redecorating and repairing of the cottage for his studio, and his own casual treatment of cash, had nicked her bank account. Her grandiose plans for his fall exhibition, too, went far beyond the expenses allowed for business, but she had been excited and, let's face it, hopeful that she and Hugow could make a permanent team. Broken heart, wasted generosity, wounded pride—all these Beulah understood, but if she had any inkling that the Bender business was in imminent danger of collapsing, the tenderhearted girl would have demanded her two weeks' pay, cash, and flown out the door, for, as she herself would say, a person's got theyself to think of.

So Cassie, after her first stormy declaration that she wanted no part of Hugow's work, now saw that she could not afford the luxury of pride or revenge. The boom had been lowered from another direction. She should have seen it coming and insured against it. After all, the once doting gentleman who had put her in business was well on in years and had been due to pass on any minute in the last decade. But he had no family to interfere with his private expenditures; he had kept his interest in Mrs. Bender and their financial arrangements a secret through all the years, spreading his beneficences through several banks. Asking no questions had been one of Cassie's virtues, but it was only because she thought she knew the answers. Of course he would pop off one day, but of course arrangements, in his discreet, thorough way, would have been made for the continuance of the Bender Gallery.

But the gentleman had absconded, just as Hugow had, and it was no excuse that his flight had been through the pearly gates. Cassie had waited, after the newspaper reports of his passing, to hear from the estate manager, his lawyer, or his bank, but weeks passed and nothing happened. In the hysteria of the Hugow business she had found time to ask her own bank to look into the gentleman's last papers to see how her inheritance was to be handled. The bank reported there was no provision made. The gentleman, cautious to the very end, had left nothing to indicate any connection with the Bender Gallery or with Mrs. Cassie Bender. His bequests in other directions had been infuriatingly generous, according to the report, the largest going to a completely unknown woman.

"Why, the old goat!" Cassie raged when she heard of this from her lawyer. All those years—her best years, at that—she had been the old man's darling, graciously accepting his largesse in return for assembling a masterly collection of horns for him, and the monster had been unfaithful to her! When he had taken her to the Lafayette for lunch—yes, it was that long ago—and told her he could not see her again as he was on the threshold of sixty and could not do her justice, he must have been already starting something new! It was a sentimental lunch, Cassie recalled savagely, accompanied by her tears and the final affectionate clasp of some nice bonds and his word that the gallery would be supported indefinitely.

Instead of throwing out Hugow, she would have to beg him to stay, Cassie saw. She would make money on him, for he was on the way up, but she had to make it a big plunge, double his prices, build up the show as if he were another Pollock, which God knows he was not likely to be. And then what? Why, he would drop her for a bigger dealer, naturally.

So Cassie wept and raged and cursed, partly at the dead gentleman who had been no gentleman and at the lover who had decamped and now must be wheedled back and rewarded with the greatest show of his life. It was a gamble, but she had to do it, even if she had to close shop later on. So here she was, knocking herself out buttering up Texas tycoons and museum heads, hiring the most expensive public-relations firm, planning the most de luxe preview party, playing with her credit, and running after Hugow in all his wretched dives where she knew they jeered at her importunations.

If she hadn't been desperate, and if he hadn't become her most profitable talent, Cassie would have loved to play a vengeful game with him, letting him make all the moves, not committing herself to a show until she was good and ready, letting him realize how necessary she was. But she was in too precarious a spot.

Her lawyer was the one who gave her hope. "Perhaps the fortunate lady who got the quarter-million you expected to get is interested in art," he suggested. "It may be she knew the gentleman's taste and may even have discussed continuing with the investment on her own."

It was not much of a hope but it was worth a try, and after some preliminary investigation Cassie managed to write a discreet note to the heiress hinting that a partnership might be arranged that would be not only just but profitable. While she waited for this barely possible rescue she was obliged further to humble herself with pleasant, even merry, little notes to Hugow as if nothing in the world had happened between them but the exhibition plans.

"If this show is a sell-out," Cassie declared to Beulah, "I'm going to take my cut and buy myself the best-looking lover you ever saw."

"What if it's a flop?" Beulah chuckled.

If it's a flop, we're out of business, Cassie could have answered, but instead she said, "Then I'll start looking around for that first husband of mine, if I can remember his name."

Hugow was immensely relieved that Cassie showed no bitterness toward him. He was lazy about business and a coward about making enemies by switching dealers, framers, even waiters. Maybe he'd sneak out someday, the way he did with his women, but he was glad now that he didn't have to offend Cassie further.

Cassie plunged into preparations for the show and at the same time kept on the trail of her dead sponsor's heiress with propositions of partnership and appeals to sentiment. When her lawyer reported no reaction to her pleas, she meditated on the possibilities of polite blackmail. The late gentleman had been so experienced in clandestine affairs that he had left no trace of evidence of his past attentions, and her claim would have to be on a personal basis. The problems multiplied, Cassie made giddier and giddier plans, until both her gallery's future and Hugow's show were given hope by an unexpected visitor.

11

ALVINE HARSHAWE was in a foul mood the day he set out to find this Jonathan kid old Earl had told him about. For weeks he had been lingering around New York, enjoying himself in his own little sport of driving his agent and wife crazy. He quibbled and postponed closing the movie deal, allowed Peg to bombard him with telegrams and phone calls begging him to return to the Cape.

"My wife doesn't like the terms," he told his agent.

"My agent won't let me leave town till this is set," he told Peg.

Guests, important English directors, Italian film stars, "fun people," were due on Chipsie's yacht, Peg moaned, and he must realize his poor Peg couldn't entertain them alone. They didn't want to see her, they wanted their lion, as she knew perfectly well. Alvine knew it better than she did, and thought it did Peg good to be reminded of it once in a while. He'd pop up, he thought, just as they were all bored stiff and ready to go, then watch how they decided to stay, with the king back on the throne.

But suddenly Peg's telegrams stopped. After a few days came her cable triumphantly announcing that dear old Chipsie (Lord Eyvanchip, of course) had felt so sorry for her loneliness that he had simply kidnaped her to join the party sailing down to the Caribbean, dropping off at spots as whim suggested. She might leave the party in a month or even go on to the Mediterranean and then to Paris.

What am I supposed to do with four loose weeks on my hands? Alvine felt like bellowing indignantly across the ocean. He'd be damned if he'd fly over to join her in Paris, if that was what she was counting on. But she had not even suggested it, he thought with some surprise. What could be more baffling to a husband who yearns for his freedom than to have it handed to him gift-wrapped? Alvine pondered over Peg's unprecedented silence, studied her last cable for some clue, and became increasingly outraged.

And then the truth hit him.

It could not be—oh, *couldn't* it?—that for the first time a wife was shaking *him*! Alvine had never believed in fighting to get or hold any woman. Shake them loose little by little was his system, and let them drop off by themselves. Always the good people, the richest and most famous, stayed on his side through all of his divorces, dropped the old wife when he did, accepted whatever new wife he presented. Chipsie, being rich and titled, would never have stopped off had he known Alvine was not there. Chipsie couldn't stand boring wives, having just gotten rid of his own. Why, that made Chipsie a free man now, and this thought brought Alvine up short.

Peg wouldn't go in for any hanky-panky, he was sure of that, at least not for kicks or for spite and certainly not for mere love, but she was a snob. No use kidding himself that she wouldn't rather be Lady Chipsie than a mere author's wife if she had the chance, and the minute he had the thought Alvine knew what the game was. Peg was getting back at him with a ladyship. Alas! His agent had heard talk confirming the suspicion! What made Alvine burn was to think what a smug ass he'd been, so sure he was the one who pulled all the strings. He would never have dawdled around New York, half the time in his house and other times lounging around his agent's cabin cruiser up at City Island, drinking with a couple of actor guests at night, waking up at Port Jefferson or some Connecticut port, then starting all over next day—oh, never would he have enjoyed this except for the pleasure of infuriating old Peg.

But there was Peg hitting it off with old Chipsie and his world of envious enemies chuckling to think the arrogant Harshawe had been kicked out!

Raging about for some way of restoring his vanity, he remembered Earl Turner's talk of the kid who might be his son and he knew that was the answer. Let tricky old Peg have it right between the eyes. Winning a ladyship wouldn't be such a triumph if people knew it was a consolation prize after having her husband bring home a full-grown bastard son. Alvine set out at once to get Earl and find the boy Jonathan. He'd make the first move.

He took a cab from the City Island yacht basin, intending to stop off at the Sixty-fourth Street house and clean up, but it was a hot afternoon and he needed a drink after several days of salt air and bourbon. He dropped off at a dingy First Avenue bar where no necktie was demanded, then made another start downtown, with a few stopovers at some Third Avenue bars.

"Anybody ever tell you you're the spit and image of Alvine Harshawe?" the bartender in the first bar asked, after his second scotch.

"No," said Alvine.

"Of course he's a good bit taller and ten, twelve years younger, ha ha"—what was so funny about that? Alvine wondered testily—"but there's a resemblance, if you were dressed right. Many's the time I've fixed him up after a big night. The screwdriver's his drink."

"Must try it next time," Alvine said and paid his check.

At the next bar, where he ordered a screwdriver, a fish-faced blond man bared shark's teeth and extended a fin, saying, "You don't know me from Adam, but, by George, my mother's one of your greatest fans. I don't read Westerns myself, Mr. Steinbeck, but let me buy you a drink anyway."

"Buy your mother a drink," Alvine snarled and marched out.

He caught a glimpse in a shop-window mirror of an unshaven big bum in a stained white jacket and faded slacks. He smiled grimly, thinking of how Peg would carry on if she saw him going about New York like that. Never mind, he was a free man now, the hell with Peg. A wave of affection for his old pal Earl came over him, and he thought it would be only fair to appeal to Earl, show him that even foxy Harshawe could get in a jam. The trouble was he never took note of Earl's address, being sure he'd never want to look him up. He remembered something about the Hotel One Three and got a cab to cruise around the East Side looking for it, but it was no use. He and the cabby stopped off at Luchow's and had some drinks until a waiter came up with a necktie, suggesting that Alvine put it on. Alvine had a counter-suggestion and stalked out, too outraged to call the inside headwaiter, who knew him well.

Never mind, Earl was bound to be at one of the old haunts. Alvine had a dim recollection of a café Earl had mentioned on

Bleecker Street, where the boy Jonathan worked, the place that used to be their favorite bakery lunch, but where was that? The poor good old days in the Village with a mailbox full of rejection slips were blessedly dim in Alvine's memory, and all that he remembered, as they passed the lane of lights on Fourteenth Street, was the feeling of excitement, promise, and youth, a wonderful feeling that he had never expected to recapture. He paid off the cabby, forgetting about Peg and revenge in the sudden joy of the moment.

"Sure you'll be okay, bud?" the cabby called after him for some reason, but Alvine waved him on, amused at the unnecessary concern.

The clock in the Con Edison building beamed down familiarly, and Alvine, surprised that night had come so swiftly, thought then of the old days in George Terrence's apartment on Irving Place when the same clock had beamed in their window and bonged them awake each morning. Old George had been top man then, with his money and family, decent in his way, and it was probably a shame the way they used to exploit him, use his charge accounts, sign his name at restaurants, use his clothes and liquor and girls. Once in a while Alvine had encountered him in later years, and it gave him an inner laugh to see how their positions had changed, George now eager to be host instead of sulking at being "used," as in the old days. Old Earl Turner had had the edge then, for a brief period, having a salaried editorial job instead of being a chancy freelance writer. Where was old Earl right now anyway?

Alvine wandered down toward the square, stopped in a corner bar for a double Johnny Walker to sustain the pleasant glow of memories. When he came out, the neighborhood seemed to him to have changed beyond recognition, old landmarks swallowed up by great new apartment houses and supermarkets. The Planet Drug Store was still there, where they used to drop in for contraceptives, leaving the girl standing, all innocence, on the corner. On such a night as this, mused Alvine, in such a place he had made his preparations for a pass at Connie Birch, while she waited outside, clutching his manuscript. The boy Earl talked of was surely his, Alvine thought, crossing a side street now, pleased to recognize the old auction gallery, with the hamburger stand next door now a pizzeria, and the old candy store now a bar. He looked in, half expecting Earl to be there with a welcome, but nobody spoke to him, the drink was terrible, and the seedy-looking customers scowled at the stranger.

Alvine found himself passing the Planet Drug Store again and realized that he had forgotten his way around this neighborhood. He began to be annoyed with Earl, and the good feeling blurred into a suspicion that Earl had ganged up with Peg, but that was fantastic, of course, for Peg was a snob. "Fantastic, fantastic," he muttered, going down the street. Coming upon his reflection in a window unexpectedly explained why women on the street gave him a wide berth. He laughed aloud, thinking again how embarrassed Peg would be if she could see him looking like a panhandler. It made him feel good to be a natural part of this neighborhood instead of visiting it as a well-dressed slummer. Earl would like to see him like this, that much was certain.

"Do you know Earl Turner?" he asked in the next bar, a dark place, clammy and stenchy with stale air-conditioning.

"He hasn't been in lately," the bartender said.

What was the boy's name?

"How about Jonathan?" Alvine asked.

"He'll be around later, maybe, after midnight," said the man.

Alvine stood at the end of the bar and ordered. He laughed aloud again, thinking how fantastic it would seem to Earl to come in and find him there. Fantastic, he repeated, absolutely fantastic. There were several empty seats at the bar and at the tables but Alvine did not want to commit himself to such a permanent step, for the customers were not ordinary bar types or even bohemian types but seemed a collection of Rorschach blobs in the watery pink light. Another curious feature of this bar was that no one looked at Alvine or nudged someone to point at him. He was so accustomed to ignoring such attention, staring straight at his drink or at his *vis à vis*, that the absence of it made him look around more carefully, squinting at the blobs to make them form reasonable contours. Good God, I'm drunk, he suddenly decided as the blobs began twinning and tripling before his gaze. This particular kind of old-fashioned plain drunkenness had not happened to him since the old Village days, and now that he recognized it, he was amused and delighted with the game.

"It's the old rotgut," he reflected aloud.

With the fine labels to which he was accustomed at home, he could sip highballs for hours, knowing his Plimsoll line was reached when he retreated into icy silence, subtly insulting Peg's gayer guests by an occasional sardonic grunt that would make them turn anxiously, knowing the king was bored. He would saunter out of the room, bearing his glass, indicating that even drinking with such company was intolerable and that he preferred bed or a really intelligent talk with the cook or the dogs. No crazy, fascinating multiple visions such as his bar tour tonight was affording him. No three-headed long-eared blobs drinking triple drinks. Just boredom, blah blah boredom.

"Rotgut, yes," said the blob next to him. "But I find it has a tang to it that the good stuff doesn't have. They've got a brandy here that is terrific, sort of like sword-swallowing. We'll have some and you'll see what I mean."

The blob turned out to be absolutely right. The brandy was black and brackish, thick and smoky.

"The swords are rusty," said Alvine, gulping. "Instant tonsillectomy. Fantastic."

He found this curious sensation even more charming than the other effects. Instead of going down the little red lane, this raging drink shot up to the top of his head, where it separated the cerebrum from the cerebellum in one clean cut and then bubbled mischievously behind his eyeballs, so that the blobs all around changed their shapes with dizzying speed.

"Are you a darrow, by any chance?" he asked his friend, for the blob was now elongating into a pointed head which might conceivably have made him a Martian or Venusian except that he was too short.

"How did you know?" asked the sword-swallower. "My name is Wright, Percy Wright, but my grandmother was a darrow from Plainfield."

"Did she work nights in a bakery in Perth Amboy?" Alvine asked, intensely interested.

The fellow did not think she had, but he conceded that there were a lot of things about the darrows that he had never known. He did not know how often the darrows came up out of the earth, for instance, but he recalled an uncle who had to have a cement slab over his grave in Maryland because he kept floating out at high tide and indeed had once been waterborne in a tornado right into the village bar that had been his ruin. The wind had blown in the saloon door, and there was the uncle, perpendicular, pushed right up to the bar, ready for a nightcap.

"Fantastic, those darrows," said Alvine, delighted.

Out of the corner of his eye he could see the darrow's head lengthening and then squashing down like an accordion, an accordion with a tiny mustache. Under ordinary circumstances Alvine meticulously avoided that borderline in drinking when he was not master of the situation. He disliked slovenly drinking because he respected alcohol too much, he claimed, to see it degraded, used as a mask, weapon, or means to an end. Tonight was different.

He looked around to see if there were any other darrows present, but the bar was too dark to see well. His companion clung to him whenever Alvine started to leave, for he complained that nobody appreciated him in this bar, his girl friends were always insisting that he wait for them there and then they always came late and latched on to some other guy. It did strike Alvine that whenever his friend hailed a newcomer the person shied away to the farthest end of the bar or else left, probably afraid of darrows.

"Darcy, come have a drink with us!" the friend cried to a girl who walked by, a beautiful little blob of a girl with penetrating oyster eyes, or no, little clam eyes, tiny little Seine clam eyes that cut right through you.

"Not unless you get rid of that bum," said the girl. "You been down to the waterfront?"

"Now, wait a minute, Darcy. Now, Darcy."

The darrow began to cry, and the girl melted away into the Seine mud.

"Bitch," said Alvine, pulling up his friend, who kept sliding from his stool. "They're all bitches, popping off with the first title that comes along."

Rage at Peg came over him again but he couldn't remember what Peg looked like, except for the clam eyes. A fresh drink of the delicious house brandy made him happy again, and he thought of how Peg would screech if she saw him bring home all these blobs. His companion clutched his arm and maneuvered them to a vacant booth near the bar, where he laid his head down on the table and sobbed, little hiccupy sobs. Alvine watched his head stretch and contract like Silly Putty until the rhythm of it made him sleepy. He tried to keep his eyes open by staring at a menu card.

"Golden Spur." He made out the words finally. "I used to know the place once. Let's go there."

The darrow was sleeping now, snores punctuated with tiny hiccups. A disgusting lot, these darrows, Alvine thought. He tried to get up, but the other's legs sprawled out, locking him in.

"Okay," Alvine said, giving up and sliding back. "Might as well have another brandy."

"The boss says we can't serve you any more," said the waiter.

"Make it Johnny Walker, then," said Alvine agreeably, but the waiter had gone.

"Better get out of here before Percy comes to," far-off voices said, and then other far-off voices sounded familiar, addressing him by name.

"You get his other arm, Jonathan," the voice said. "Come on, Alvine, we'll get you to a cab. Here we go."

"Nasty lot, those darrows," Alvine said in the cab drowsily. "Where the hell were you, Earl, old boy? Looked for you all day. Let's go to Golden Spur. Old times' sake. Got to meet my son."

He was peacefully asleep.

"There's your end of the rainbow for you!" Earl exclaimed sarcastically. "You were so hot to find the guy, and see what you've got now. I don't know what on earth got into him, but here's your hero for the taking. This is the way it happens."

"He was looking for me!" Jonathan said unhappily. "Don't ever tell him we found him, Earl."

"You think it would bother him?" Earl laughed. "It's material, isn't it? Nothing bothers a genius but lack of material! Come on, we'll get him to bed."

*

"A good guy is always on the spot," Earl Turner said. "Everybody wants to take a crack at him. He doesn't have a chance. You've got to be a real bastard to get out of a jam, excuse the expression."

Jonathan looked at his notebooks stacked with his laundry package on the unpainted table of his room at the Hotel One Three.

"I should have left word where I was moving," he said.

Earl snorted.

"You can't tell a woman you're leaving until you're gone," he said. "Darcy wouldn't have let you get away, and Lize would have tied you up."

Jonathan knew it was true. What worried him was how he could resist capture once they started after him.

"I don't suppose I dare go in the Spur." He meditated. "All those messages on the bulletin board for me to get in touch. I can't go to the café on account of Dr. Kellsey. He's waiting for me to move into his apartment with him. He says he owes it to me."

There had been an unsigned note to "J.J." also, that would have been from Iris, saying, "The past is the past, but what about the future?" Earl had relayed other mysterious messages to him and had brought a letter from George Terrence.

"I can't tell you how disappointed I was when you did not appear for your appointment," it said. "Thinking it over, however, I could understand your hesitancy. We are both, I think, aware of our true relationship, though we have not discussed it candidly. I can see that the secrecy of the relationship would be a burden to you, since you want definite cause to cut yourself from the Jaimison name. I myself should like to sign papers admitting my paternity, which papers could be shown under special circumstances, but for appearances' sake I should like to 'adopt' you. This would avoid unpleasant effects on my wife and family, for I would propose this step to Hazel as a sentimental gesture toward her old friend.

"I think this will put you in a much happier position. I shall proceed with these arrangements, confident that you will get in immediate touch with the office. I cannot tell you how much it will mean to me to be united with my unknown son."

Jonathan gloomily handed the letter to Earl. Weighed down with his own problems as he was, he was still able to note with surprise the new sporty jacket Earl was wearing, the natty shoes and pink shirt. Success had gone straight to his back, evidently.

"What about Alvine?" Earl asked, after scanning the note. "He'll be out in another couple of weeks. Every day he asks about you. It's damned awkward, after I laid it on for you."

"He doesn't know how we found him?" Jonathan asked.

"He doesn't remember what happened after he took the elevator in the Big Hat bar and landed in the bowels of the earth with a tribe of darrows," Earl said dryly. "They told him we were expected, so he waited for us. And that's the story he told that made his agent and the doctor hustle him off to the hospital. Oh, he's still mixed up, all right, but it's just shock."

"I haven't got over the shock myself," said Jonathan.

"With Alvine it's the shock of having something go wrong for once in his damn life," Earl said. "A wife leaves him instead of him leaving her. Shock number one. Then the shock of hunting for me instead of me hunting for him. A guy like Alvine can't adjust to upsets like that. He's either kingpin or crybaby."

Earl looked at his watch. Now that he had a wristwatch, Jonathan noticed that he was forever looking at it, as if important people were waiting for him elsewhere. Apparently it was gratifying to use this gesture instead of having it used against him.

"Well, do you want to come along and see him or not? I can see why you don't feel like claiming him right now as your rightful parent, but so far as I'm concerned I like him better as a drunken slob than I ever did as the king of cats." Earl frowned at Jonathan. "Okay, you were looking for a big hero daddy and you back away when you come on him getting thrown out of a bar."

It was the truth, and Jonathan couldn't understand himself.

"I guess I was disappointed on account of my mother," he said. "I couldn't picture her with him. I didn't want to."

"If he hadn't been flipping he wouldn't have even bothered to look for you, just think of that," Earl said. "You would still be hoping to find him, hoping he was your man."

"I know."

"So you've got your wish, and whenever that happens it's always too late and all crossed up. He's got it in his old bull head that a lost bastard turning up in his life will put him one up on his wife. He wants to throw you in her face. I guess that isn't the way you pictured it."

"No."

"I told him I'd bring you up if I found you," Earl said. "Can't say I blame you for chickening out, but I'd like to help Alvine right now. I used to get sore at Alvine always being on top of the world, everything working out for him, but damn it, I don't like a big man down. Funny, eh? I'm used to Alvine always running the show. I'm used to being jealous. That's my security. Alvine's my old North Star, I mean he's got to be up there in the sky."

That was how he felt too, Jonathan thought. He was ashamed to admit that his dream of a father was of a man infinitely superior to John Jaimison, a man it would be a victory to claim, not a responsibility. It was no triumph to be captured himself, to round out some frustrated man's picture of himself as a father. He hadn't asked Fate to send him a great man who appeared to have gone off his rocker and stood in need of a son's tender devotion. Damn it, he'd done his time as dutiful son, yessirring and nosirring. He didn't want to begin that all over with a new candidate. He wondered why it had never occurred to him that his father would expect him to make up to him for the lost years—as if he owed it to him.

"I hoped I'd never see this damn dump again!" Earl exclaimed in sudden petulance. He yanked down the mottled yellow shade on the narrow court window, and the fabric tore off the roll. He swore. "Same view of garbage cans, dead cats, and broken baby carriages. I'm through with all that. Why do I have to rub my nose in it again just for some kid that thought he wanted to find a father and then wants to hide out?"

Jonathan was embarrassed.

"It was getting too much for me," he said patiently. "The girls and Mr. Terrence and Dr. Kellsey all expecting to take me over before I'd found out what I wanted. I was so sure Alvine Harshawe was the answer, then coming on him that night blubbering and wild, I couldn't believe it—"

"I couldn't believe it myself," Earl interrupted. "I couldn't believe I wasn't laughing, either, because he'd been so snotty about not wanting to go to the Spur for fear his public would mob him. I could have laughed, but the funny part was that I hated it. Hated seeing him stuck with a punk like Percy, a guy he'd never speak to in his right mind. I'd like to take you up to him, damn it. I'd like to see him get the edge on Peg the way he always had."

"I don't want it that way," Jonathan said.

Earl kicked the fallen shade angrily under the bed.

"If he really thought I was his own son he wouldn't use me to get even, that's all," Jonathan said. "Later on he'd probably admit it was all a joke on her, but the joke would be on me."

This made Earl meditate for a moment. Then he brought out more missives from his pocket and tossed them to Jonathan.

"Dan said these telegrams were forwarded around town to the Spur," he said. "You may have something there about Alvine. Maybe you'll think differently in a week or two when he comes around. Maybe he'll change his tune too. I'm staying at the De Long now if you need me. Don't expect me to come back to this fleabag again."

"It's only temporary," Jonathan said.

"I've stayed here temporarily all my life, boy," Earl said. "Don't get started."

"I hate the word 'permanent,'" said Jonathan. "I've got to pull out of the café job before it's too late. But what can I do? How will I get by?"

"You've got nothing to worry about," Earl said. "You're young, you've got looks, you've got a blue suit and a pair of black shoes, hell, the world is your oyster. All you need is a list of bar mitzvahs, walk right in, eat all you want, help yourself to a fat drink, shake hands, say Irving never looked better. You won't starve."

No use expecting sympathy from a battle-scarred trooper like Earl.

After the door closed, Jonathan looked at the telegrams. All were from John Jaimison, Senior, summoning Jonathan to visit him at the Hotel Sultana on Central Park West as soon as possible.

12

FOUR MONTHS ago Jonathan would have been outraged that his own special city should be defiled by the presence of a real Jaimison. He would have been indignant that the city had broken its promise of asylum and let in the enemy. He would have been shocked that his kind Aunt Tessie had given away his hiding place.

It surprised him that his chief feeling was mild astonishment that these people still existed when they had been erased from his own mind. The letter from Aunt Tessie explained a little.

"I wouldn't have given him the address but I got the idea it has something to do with money. I heard he was going to New York to see a specialist and it struck me he might be wanting to make up to you for everything before he dies. Now Jonny-boy, you take whatever you can get out of him, and don't open your mouth about his not being your own father. Goodness knows he gave you as bad a time as your own father could have, so let him pay for it. You go see him and be smart. Let's see if he'll let go a few dollars at last, ha ha."

Jonathan decided Aunt Tessie's theory must be right. He needn't worry that the old man would have made a trip to New York to retrieve a lost child, when he had not noticed his absence all this time. Nothing to be afraid of, really, in facing him again. If he wanted to atone, let him atone plenty.

Walking toward the park from the Seventy-second Street subway, however, Jonathan had time to worry about what kind of scene he would have to face, supposing the old man had reached a state of sniveling penitence. He might be propped up on his deathbed, surrounded by nurses and weeping Florence, and expecting Jonathan to join in tears of mutual forgiveness. But it was too late to back out now. In no time he heard himself being announced from the hotel desk, and there was his stepmother at the door of 9 B, one hand extended and the other at her lips.

"He's resting," she whispered. "He just got back from the specialist's examination."

At least she showed no signs of weeping.

"Pretty sick, eh?" Jonathan whispered back, tiptoeing into the vestibule.

Florence threw up her hands.

"You know your father," she said.

Jonathan looked startled.

"He will overdo," she said. "So when he had to make this trip I made him promise to see this expert. A hundred dollars a visit, so he must be good. And this hotel—twenty dollars a day, mind you, without counting the garage rent. Well, well, Jonathan!"

As she talked her little brown eyes shopped over his person busily, price-tagging his corduroy slacks and checked shirt, recognizing his old sport jacket and mentally throwing it out. Her frown centered on his hair as if the barbering bore Darcy's own signature. He followed her gingerly through the vestibule. Evidently there would be no deathbed scene, judging from her high spirits.

"My goodness, Jonathan, you certainly haven't got the New York look yet!" she exclaimed. "I should have thought you'd have a whole new suit by this time. Those trousers—"

"Cost eighteen dollars," Jonathan said obligingly.

If Florence was reducing him to his net merchandise value, Jonathan was just as curious about the obvious rise in the fortunes of the Jaimisons. Packages with the Saks Fifth Avenue label were piled on the hall chair, a new fur stole hung over its back, and the living room revealed not only an expensive view of Central Park but a corner bar cabinet with a full bottle of scotch visible. A closer look at his stepmother showed that she had gotten herself up to hold her own in the great city. The effect was not a New York look but the small-town look multifold. The rouge was redder, the jaw firmer, the coiffure browner and kinkier, the bracelets bigger and noisier, the Alice-blue silk dress bluer and tighter, the patent-leather sandals higher-heeled.

The smell of prosperity was here, Jonathan thought, mystified. A familiar cough announced the emergence of Mr. Jaimison himself from the bedroom. He stood for a moment framed in the doorway, squinting his eyes, mustache and famous Jaimison nose quivering as if testing the psychic temperature of the room. Jonathan squinted back, surprised that his onetime father was shorter and stockier than he remembered, but then he had usually seen him in lordly command of a desk or steering wheel. Without his props of authority the old man seemed at a loss for a moment; then he squared his shoulders and plunged masterfully across the room, arms swinging as if ready to put up a stiff defense. He cleared his throat.

"Well, son," he said, giving Jonathan's hand a firm disciplinary squeeze.

Jonathan cleared his own throat.

"Well, sir," he said and returned the other's bleak smile.

"I guess you never expected to see me in New York City," said Mr. Jaimison, plumping himself down in the regal wing chair his wife pushed toward him. "Never expected to find you here either, for that matter, but that's life, eh? I had this business matter to attend to—we'll talk about that later—and I promised Florence that while we were here I'd let a specialist go over me just to satisfy her, but let me tell you, I'm not as close to the cemetery as you think."

"I didn't—" But there was really no use, as Jonathan knew, in trying to make conversation, for Jaimison, Senior, always pitched right into a strident monologue, which was a deaf man's privilege.

"Yes sir, do you know what this doctor told me? Said I had a little liveliness in the kidneys, perfectly natural in a man of sixty, they say, a touch of firming up in the arteries, usual too, and they tell me I've got the liver of a man of forty. Doctor couldn't believe it. 'You've got the liver of a man of forty— maybe thirty-five,' he says. How about that? Ha ha ha!"

"Ha ha ha!" said Florence, nodding toward Jonathan in an invitation to join the fun.

"Ha," ventured Jonathan, and wondered if he was expected to ask for a peek at this splendid organ.

"Tell Jonathan what he said about your heart," she urged and leaned toward Jonathan confidentially. "I thought it was a heart attack but it was only gas. Ha ha ha."

"Ha," agreed Jonathan and nodded politely while Mr. Jaimison delivered a full medical report, straight A's from si-nuses to urine, minuses where it would have been promiscuous to be plus, prophecies of future gains and natural losses declaimed in the cheery manner of a smooth treasurer reassuring doubtful stockholders. When he paused to cough for emphasis, Jonathan coughed in sympathy; when he bared his dentures in a stiff smile, Jonathan arranged one on his own face. For there was no doubt about it, the old man was doing his best to be civil, flailing his olive branch around like a horsewhip, determined to bring up a bucket of bubbling geniality from the long-dry well. But why? Jonathan wondered.

Having finished off the medical report, Jaimison, Senior, launched into an equally gratifying and equally confidential description of his new Chevy, enumerating on his fingers (with Jonathan checking the tabulation involuntarily on his own fingers) the reasons he had chosen this car against other candidates, the real reason being that he never changed his mind about anything, so why would he change his car? During this talk Florence's eyes kept seeking out Jonathan's anxiously for approval, and if he smiled her hard enameled face cracked open wide enough to show a king's ransom in porcelain caps. When she saw his eyes straying in the direction of the bar, she whispered, "The lawyer sent the bottle to us as a gift. Would you like a highball? Okay?"

Extraordinary, Jonathan thought, nodding dumbly. The spectacle of a drink in Jonathan's hands stopped Mr. Jaimison's oration sharply. Forgetting his new warmth, he gave a disapproving snort. He himself never drank except for business, just as he never laughed except for business. It infuriated him that a man could drink half your bottle before your eyes and not even make a fool of himself. If he would only fall on his face, have a fit, or do something to give a non-drinker legitimate excuse to feel superior! However, an admonitory glance from his wife made him content to mutter only, "More accidents from drunken driving."

"I've never had a car," Jonathan said.

"Throw away your money on taxis, eh." Mr. Jaimison grunted.

"Now, Father," chided Florence, evidently bent on maintaining a truce. She startled Jonathan by giving him a conspiratorial wink, saying, "You know how your father always travels by car, business or pleasure, ever since we bought the

Chevy for our honeymoon. He isn't really himself till he's behind the wheel."

No need to remind him of that, Jonathan thought, remembering the blue Chevy tooling up Aunt Tessie's driveway
in response to a dozen or more pleas from her for Jonathan's
schooling, clothes, or even for simple advice. He recalled how
determinedly the gentleman had shunted off appeals by
launching into endless travelogues on trips he had just taken
with his new wife through the Great Smokies, the New England lakes, the Berkshires, the Adirondacks, Route this and
Thruway that, detour here and ferry there, just jump in the
car and away, away through those great open spaces between
Esso and Gulf. Dizzy from these vicarious tours, discouraged
by the inability to interrupt, Jonathan would give up and
dreamily observe the caller's evasion tactics. He had a vague
image of Jaimison *père*, in the plaid cap and goggles of the
early motorist, perpetually gypsying through cloverleafs and
underpasses, skyways and byways, oblivious to everything but
Stop and Go, knowing it was South by Dr. Pepper signs and
Hot Shoppes, North by tonic ads and Howard Johnsons (allowing for the recent exchange of these clues), but happy in
the one sure thing that he was safe at the wheel. What a
fortress! Nobody and nothing could ever get at a man behind
the wheel of his own God-given car. Nor was there any talent
in the world as valuable as Mr. Jaimison's superior gift for
parking.

"Your father thinks you should have a car," Florence said
radiantly, just as Jonathan was musing that he hated the automobile.

"Every good citizen ought to have a car," stated Mr.
Jaimison. "Something to show for himself, as I see it."

"Maybe Jonathan thinks owning his own home is most important for a young man." Florence again smiled at him with
the coy wink. "Okay?"

Jonathan mumbled something about cars and houses being
furthest from his mind, but Mr. Jaimison did not hear him,
nor did he hear Florence's murmured explanation that Father
should really get a hearing aid, and didn't Jonathan think the
high cost would be justified? Jonathan wanted to reply that
next to his gift for parking, Father enjoyed his deafness, for all

he ever wanted to hear from anybody was "Yes, sir." He didn't want to hear persiflage, or requests for loans, or tales of woe, and the resulting lack of wear and tear on his emotions kept his brow unfurrowed, his eye clear, and his pockets full. What were the pair of them getting at, anyway, with their talk of cars and houses? There must be money in it somewhere, just as Aunt Tessie had prophesied, and Jonathan began dreaming of hundred-dollar bills, or why not five-hundred-dollar bills? Whose face was on a five-hundred-dollar bill? he wondered. For all he knew it might be that of Jaimison, Senior. He'd take whatever the old buzzard offered, he decided, and run.

But Mr. Jaimison had gotten on an even more curious subject as he twirled his cigar. He hoped, he said, that Jonathan had not been permanently discouraged by failing to make good in Silver City. He would admit frankly that Florence had blamed him for not taking a firm hand with him when Jonathan was falling down on his jobs, but the way things were turning out now he would guarantee that Jonathan could go right back home and open his own offices as big as you please and have the town behind him in no time.

"I don't say you could do it alone, mind you," said Mr. Jaimison, "but I've built up a solid business reputation back there, and with me behind you you've got nothing to worry about. I'd retire in another few years from the mills, anyway, and with our own business started I could step in full time. I looked at offices for you in the Gas Building—"

"Offices? For me?" Jonathan thought the drink must be affecting his own hearing, gulped it down hastily, and then decided another one would clear his head. He jumped up and poured it, not even seeing Mr. Jaimison's instinctive gesture of disapproval. Florence gave a little gasp and leaped up to snatch Jonathan's glass and plant a coaster firmly beneath it before restoring it to him. Mr. Jaimison watched this operation and Jonathan's greedy gulping of the second drink with tight lips.

"I did not realize that alcohol was so necessary to you, Jonathan," he said.

"Everybody has his own fuel," Jonathan said. "You have to have gas, and I have to have alcohol."

Mr. Jaimison saw no reason to reply to this flippancy. He drummed his fingers on the arm of his chair.

"Now about your office," he began firmly. "I can see that you can be set up by the first of the year. Give you time to straighten out here in New York and get back home and look over the situation. Being on the spot myself will save you a lot, of course, while the lawyers are speeding up the settlement—"

"What's he talking about?" Jonathan asked Florence.

"The inheritance," Florence said. "Your father had to handle the whole thing when nobody knew where you were, and then the chance to buy this real-estate business came along at the same time, so he thought he'd settle that too, advancing you the money himself. Too good a chance for you to invest in a permanent job, so to say."

Jonathan looked from one to the other glassily. Either he was dreaming or they were both crazy.

"I guess you'll be glad to get back home, eh, son," said Jaimison, Senior, with a benign chuckle. "We Jaimisons never like city life. I suppose I've traveled through every sizable city in the country and you can have them all—Detroit, Columbus, New York. Another thing. That money will be a nice little fortune back home, but it wouldn't last you five years in New York. I guess you realize that."

"What money?" Jonathan asked patiently.

"This money we're telling you about," said Mr. Jaimison with a hint of his old irascibility. "The money this party left your mother when he died. Naturally they had to come to me trying to locate her, and I handled it as far as I could till Tessie told us how to locate you, get your signature on things and all that. The way I see it, you'll be set up in a foolproof business for life and can hold your head up with the rest of them. The lawyer—he sent me that scotch you're drinking, by the way—says I've done everything his client would have asked by way of protecting your interests. You'll be seeing him."

Jonathan made an involuntary move toward the bottle, but Florence forestalled him, hastily pouring out a few drops into his glass.

"Jonathan's more surprised than we were." Florence giggled. "Wasn't it foxy of your mother never to mention any of those investments she was making in New York when she worked here?"

"Had me paying through the nose for years, mind you, and all the time this fortune tucked away in New York!" Mr. Jaimison interrupted. "By George, I was mad when I found out, but, come to think it over, it works out all the better all around. Seems her employer invested her money so well that it's mounted to real sizable proportions. A couple hundred thousand dollars is a neat little nest egg, Jonathan, even in these times."

"Whose nest egg? What employer?" Jonathan shouted.

Florence put a finger to her lips, smiling.

"I don't blame you for being excited. Your father didn't write because he didn't know where to find you at first and he kept holding off the lawyer while he sort of got things ready and straightened out the details. The Major, it seems, never knew of your mother's death, so that had to be straightened out."

"Major?"

"Her employer, Major Wedburn," Mr. Jaimison said. "I don't suppose you ever heard of him, either. I never listened to your mother gabbing away about New York, so I daresay it's my own fault for not knowing she was making a whacking lot of money, but—"

Major Wedburn. The man whose funeral was being mourned by the De Long that first day in New York. Claire Van Orphen had said Connie Birch had typed for him. So the Major had left her a fortune in the guise of "investments." Jonathan sat clutching the arms of his chair, trying to keep his thoughts from plunging toward the inevitable conclusion, while Jaimison, Senior, talked on and on, waving envelopes and papers at him, thrusting memos into his hand, and sugaring his voice resolutely.

"Why don't you want your offices to be in the Gas Building, my boy?"

"Because I don't like gas," Jonathan said feebly. "Anyway, I don't need any offices."

Mr. Jaimison was controlling his impatience admirably.

"But I leased them for five years out of my own pocket!"

he said. "Naturally I knew you'd settle with me later. There's your real-estate business all set up for you, son."

"Not real estate!" Jonathan cried, seeing Darcy's greedy little face.

"Okay, your father could get you into the bank," Florence said with a firm nod to her husband. "You've got to have everything safely settled. These people trying to get your mother to back them because they had claims on the Major are likely to come after you, and you'd have no protection."

"Once you're dug in they can't get at you," said Mr. Jaimison. "Let 'em sue. Claiming the Major wanted his money used to support a dirty little art gallery. Claiming there's some mistake somewhere."

"Show him the letters," Florence urged. "You'll see that your father was very clever, planning your protection from those sharks."

Jonathan read the letters Jaimison, Senior, thrust into his hand as a final argument. Cassie Bender wished Mrs. Jaimison to be her partner in the Bender Art Gallery, inasmuch as they seemed to have been partners in the late Major's affections. In a later letter Mrs. Bender reminded Mrs. Jaimison of how much they both owed him, and how beholden they both should be to his well-known tastes, creating a monument of sorts to his beloved memory, carrying on his torch, so to speak. A third letter begged the fortunate heiress to regard herself as heir to the Major's responsibilities as well as to his rewards, and Mrs. Bender was confident the Bender Art Gallery was the Major's prime concern before his untimely end.

"She doesn't know my mother died." Jonathan cut into the buzz of Jaimison's voice going on about stocks, percentages, taxes.

"We ignored her letters, of course," Mr. Jaimison said, a note of weariness creeping into his tone, for it was only his wife's admonitory glances and headshakes that kept his temper down. "As I say, we've saved you all we could."

"But she's right," Jonathan said. "I must talk this over with her."

"Jonathan!"

This time Mr. Jaimison's honest rage over his son's blind stupidity was too much for him and he shook his fists in the air.

"Twenty-five years old, and the boy still can't think straight! Twenty-five years old!" he exploded.

"Twenty-six," interrupted Jonathan, his courage restored by the exhibition of the old Jaimison temper. "Born November twenty-eighth, nineteen twenty-nine, just six months and a half after your wedding day."

There now, see what that brings up, old boy, he exulted.

"Premature, yes, yes," Mr. Jaimison snapped back savagely. "The only time in your whole career that you weren't backward!"

"Father, now Father!" pleaded Florence with an imploring glance at Jonathan. "All of us having such a nice reunion here, and the future so rosy, and here we are quarreling. It does seem, Jonathan, that you ought to be grateful to your father for protecting your interests after the way you ran away without so much as good-by, and the lawyer hunting for you too."

"I'll see him myself," Jonathan said, stuffing papers into his pocket.

"But what are your plans? You've got to plan your future, son, all that money going to waste instead of into a nice business," Mr. Jaimison wailed. "What will you do?"

"I'm going into the art business," Jonathan said. "Just like Mrs. Bender said. Sort of a monument to my—I mean to Major Wedburn. Good-by, sir, and look out for that liver."

In the hall he heard his name called and saw Jaimison, Senior, standing in the doorway, mopping his forehead helplessly. He mopped his own brow as the elevator went down, then put his handkerchief away.

"Maybe it was one of the Major's habits too," he reassured himself.

He came out into the early autumn twilight of the park and sat down on the first bench he saw. He felt giddy. He saw the Sultana lights go on and wondered if it was all a dream. But there were the papers in his pocket. He glanced at the address on Cassie Bender's letter. Her gallery was just across the park.

Jonathan headed eastward.

13

C LAIRE VAN ORPHEN looked smaller and older when Jonathan finally paid her a visit. Just a few months made a difference after sixty, he thought, or was it the trimly modern black wool suit, paler make-up, and tidier coiffure that her sister's influence had brought about? To tell the truth he could not conjure up a picture of her old self, blurred as it was by his intense concern with his own problems, and having seen only himself in her eyes.

"Don't you think it's too grand for me?" she asked, with an apologetic wave toward the McKinley plush decor of the De Long Presidential suite. "I've been budgeting and scrimping for so many years I can't enjoy splurging unless I balance it by doing without something else. My sister Beatrice is just the opposite. That's one reason our plan to live together didn't work out."

Jonathan looked admiringly at the sooty but imposing chandeliers, the huge marble fireplace with its electric logs, the balding bear rug sprawled over the faded rose carpet. Arched doors at either end of the room were closed on one side and on the other to reveal bedroom walls gay with frolicking cupids, bluebirds, and butterflies from a giddier period. There was a combined air of Victorian closed parlors and musty potpourri that seemed deliciously romantic to Jonathan, more luxurious by far than Cassie Bender's bleak modernity.

"It's exactly the way my mother described it when she worked for you," he said. "So this was the place."

"Indeed no, my rooms were much simpler," Claire corrected him. "This was always Major Wedburn's suite, right up to the day he died. He kept it just this way no matter where he was traveling. I took over his lease, thinking of Beatrice, of course, but instead it turns out to be useful for Earl Turner, my collaborator. He has the Major's library there." She nodded toward the closed doors. "You know Earl Turner. Oh dear, I forget. You introduced us."

"I haven't seen him for some time," Jonathan said. "I'm

afraid he went to some trouble to contact Alvine Harshawe for me and it—well, it didn't work out as he thought."

"We've been so busy on our scripts, as I told you," Claire said tactfully, remembering that Earl was annoyed with the young man. "He feels we must ride our luck while we've got it. Goodness knows how long we can last. Do you mind ready-made Manhattans?"

"I missed our little parties," Jonathan said, sinking into a titanic overstuffed chair beside her coffee table. "So many things have been happening."

He did look different, Claire thought. Was it the handsome vest or was it something about the eyes? She wished she had not been affected by Earl's and George Terrence's disappointment in him, but it had been naughty of him to get poor George Terrence in such a state, especially since she had been the one responsible for their meeting. And Hazel phoning around like a mad creature, saying George kept confessing to a mysterious past and getting himself analyzed and that she was coming into the city to help with her daughter's career, and why had Claire set him off with that sinister young man anyway? Hazel was a fool, true enough, but still—

"I hope everything is going well," she said, feeling guilty for the many times she had had to refuse his visits in the last few months because of her own new preoccupations. How selfish of her, no matter how mischievous he had been with others, when he had brought so much light and luck into her lonely old age! It was the old ones who were the heartless ones, drawing all the blood they could out of the young and then shrugging them off. Even as she was repenting she found herself peeping at her watch to see how much time she had before the conference with the CBS director.

Jonathan had been eager to share his news with his mother's old friend, but he saw now that her life was filled without him, and there seemed no way to begin again.

"I've had a little luck," he said, but it was no good wasting his dramatic confidence on the polite, strained atmosphere. Besides, people accustomed to advising and helping you were often ruffled when you became independent, as if they liked your need of them more than they liked you.

"I came to ask you about Major Wedburn," Jonathan said. "I should like to have known that man."

Claire could not keep back a laugh.

"You and the Major! I can't think of a funnier combination!"

"I'm sure we would have gotten on," Jonathan protested. "That's why I want to know more about him."

"I'm afraid you would have found him pompous, but he was a great gentleman for all his quirks," Claire said. "Our families were very close. I was touched when he left me the Cecilia Beaux portrait of his grandfather, which hangs in the bedroom."

"My mother spoke of a Cecilia Beaux picture," Jonathan said. "Funny she never mentioned the Major."

"Very strange," Claire said. She and Earl had come to the private conclusion that Jonathan's mother had been a very strange young woman in many ways. She was glad to be asked about the Major instead of Connie Birch, for she knew her disapproval would show.

"He must have been a gay old dog," said Jonathan.

"I don't think anyone could ever have called the Major a gay dog," Claire said. "A man of the world, I grant you, but a most discreet one. I daresay there were women in his life, but he took care that no one knew it."

"Then he could have had a secret affair," Jonathan persisted.

Now what made him pry into that?

"He was a secretive man, very fussy about hiding his lady friends from the world, and from each other," she said, controlling her impatience with the young man's curiosity. "At one time he was courting my sister Bea and myself at the very same time, and we didn't check till years later. He'd been playing us against each other. I suppose he fancied himself a strategist."

Jonathan smiled.

"Sometimes a man has to be," he said, thinking of Lize and Darcy.

"Bea was put out when she found he had left me the portrait," Claire said and sighed. "But then Bea has been very touchy these last few weeks. Quite by chance I bought a new suit at Bonwit's, and it turned out Bea had bought the identical suit that very morning at Bergdorf's. Our minds used to work like that in the old days. But Bea was so horrified at being a twin again that she raged at me. Sent her suit right back. Do you know that I cried myself to sleep for the first time in twenty years? No one can hurt you like your own twin!"

Tears came to her eyes again and she only nodded sadly when Jonathan asked permission to look at the picture.

In the bedroom Jonathan studied the portrait of the Major's grandfather seated at a great desk, quill pen in hand, open record book before him, a pair of black Dachshunds at his feet. He was a stout dark man, and though Jonathan could trace no resemblance to himself, in an odd way he looked familiar. The strong Roman nose, the beetling eyebrows, the bullish shoulders—why, he might have been Jaimison, Senior! He was grasping the pen as if it were a steering wheel, the notebook was a ledger in which he was adding up his toll fees, the keen gaze was searching beyond for the next Howard Johnson. Quite shaken, Jonathan came back to Miss Van Orphen's side.

"The Major looked just like him." Claire answered Jonathan's unspoken question.

"There must have been something else about him," Jonathan mused, "something my mother found and loved."

Good heavens, not the Major too!

"Oh, no!" Claire said, wincing. "You can't do this to my old friend, Jonathan! I don't care how dead your mother is, she ought to be ashamed of herself, stirring up the poor Major's ashes, a fine man she barely knew—no, no!"

"But you yourself told me he admired her so much!" Jonathan protested, confused by her genuine indignation. "You told me he advised her to go back home and marry and have children. You told me—"

"I was making it up!" Claire cried. "I couldn't remember anything except that he had sent her to me for typing, but I didn't want to disappoint you, so I made up little lies!"

"They weren't lies," Jonathan said. "It was truer than you know. That's why he left his money to her, and now it's going to be mine. I tried to tell you before, but you were always busy on your work. Major Wedburn was my father."

Claire drew a long breath, poured another drink from her shaker, and filled Jonathan's glass as an afterthought. Everything was so upsetting—Bea's recent tantrums, the Terrences in her life again, and now the shock about the Major.

"Why do you young people have to stir up everything?" she burst out passionately and was immediately contrite. "Oh dear, it's not your fault. Forgive me. I should be thinking of how upsetting it must be for you, finding that your mother had so many lovers."

"But that explains so much to me," Jonathan said, surprised that she did not see this. "She wanted to be whatever anybody expected her to be, because she never knew what she was herself. That's the way I am, you see. And now that I know the Major had several different lives too, I understand myself better."

Claire was silent, trying to piece together these missing pieces from the Major's past. It was hard to work up sex jealousy thirty years later, but she could, at least, feel a sense of outraged decency that her first and only affair, a romantic secret between her and the Major, should have its memory fouled by that appalling young woman. How blind she had been not to see it all under her nose, but as usual she always missed the obvious, thinking of the little typist with her wide, eager eyes as charmingly naïve, and herself, ten years older, so worldly-wise! Thinking herself sophisticated with her one love affair in thirty-odd years, when the little country mouse, barely twenty, was having an affair with every man she met as if it were no more than a curtsy! And the Major leaving a fortune to the girl, tacitly admitting his paternity! But then old men always fancied themselves as dangerously fertile, and a girl could persuade the canniest Casanova that his merest handclasp had born fruit. George Terrence, of course—"of course" indeed, when she had never even guessed it at the time—was intent on producing living proof of a guilty past to cover up that brief experiment in homosexuality. Bea had told her about it. Bea always knew those things. Her little circle uptown doted on such tidbits about priggish old gentlemen like George.

"It did seem to me that Alvine Harshawe was the logical man in your mother's life," Claire said. "I understand he admitted it freely to his wife when her divorce suit claimed he was sterile. Of course he can't convince anyone he's sane when he insists on staying on in Harkness Pavilion, soaking up background for a psychiatric play, so Earl says. But what your mother wrote fitted him far more than it did George or the Major."

"I found that what she said fitted everyone," Jonathan explained. "She thought every man she met in New York was Prince Charming and whatever they asked must be the proper thing. She was afraid to seem ignorant or small-town. It's the way I am. That's why we were misfits in our small town. People there—especially the Jaimisons—are *proud* of their ignorance because it's been in the family such a long time."

Claire felt herself melting again under his radiant smile. He shouldn't be blamed for shaking up all these little tempests, and she would say as much to Earl. Considering their own change of luck, they had no right to mistrust the boy's windfall, no matter how preposterous the circumstances.

"I'm investing the Major's money in the way I believe he would approve," Jonathan confided. He handed one of his new cards to her.

"Jonathan Jaimison, Associate Director, Bender Gallery," she read aloud in bewilderment.

"Mrs. Bender thinks I have inherited the Major's natural flair," Jonathan said. "The lawyers consider it a good deal."

Now why should he have to apologize for coming up in the world? Jonathan asked himself.

"But what about your own talent?" Claire said.

"I never could find out what it was," he said. "All I know is that I do appreciate other men's talents, and this way I have a career of other people's talents. I hoped you'd understand."

Claire knew she was squinting suspiciously at the card, trying not to speak out her doubts and warnings, when she should be rejoicing at his news. But that Mrs. Bender! The Major would surely be shocked at such a collaboration. She read in the boy's face that she was failing him, not responding at all as he expected. But he was old enough to know she could not help being loyal to her own generation.

"I'm afraid the Major's tastes in art were totally opposed to the Bender Gallery's," she said bravely. "Winslow Homer was his idol, you know, and he loved Albert Ryder. When the gallery next door had a few Hugow paintings on show I remember the Major getting absolutely indignant."

Jonathan's face clouded.

"I thought of him as more cosmopolitan," he said. "I thought he was someone I'd want to be like."

"The Major was terribly proud of his family," Claire said. "He always tried to go to the family reunions at Christmas in Hartford. And he loved touring around the country in his Lincoln, until the last few years. He was a very conservative man."

Maybe family reunions were different in Hartford, Jonathan thought gloomily, and maybe touring the country in a Lincoln was not as dreary as in a Jaimison vehicle.

"You don't think we'd have gotten on, then," he said.

"I can't picture your having a thing in common," Claire said, shaking her head. "Indeed this all seems incredible, Jonathan."

She was relieved to see Earl Turner come in at that moment.

"Just left the Spur," he told Jonathan. "They tell me you don't come in any more since you made it uptown. Can't say I blame you now the West Coast bums have moved in. The old crowd seems drifting down to The Big Hat."

For a man who had come to success after decades of failure, Earl looked very morose, Jonathan thought. The frozen boyishness now seemed old and dried, petulant more than cynical. The familiar beret was gone, that was it, and the revealed bony bald head added years.

"So Cassie Bender's got you under her wing," he said, tossing back the card Claire passed to him. "It's part of the course. And the grapevine has it that your family came to the city and handed you a fat check."

"Something on that order," Jonathan said.

"Maybe you could advance me twenty until the first," Earl said.

Claire looked at him in amazement.

"Why, Earl, you just got a check for five thousand dollars!"

Earl threw up his hands.

"I can't help it!" he said. "You spend your life thinking in two-bit terms, and that's the only money that's real. Now, when I realize it's my own dough I'm spending it doesn't seem right. With nobody trailing me with duns, nobody hounding me to pay up, honest to God, I get withdrawal symptoms! My whole system is geared for the old way."

"Never mind," Claire comforted him. "It probably won't last."

"It's not just money," Earl said. "At the Spur I started to tell Dan about the new series we're doing for CBS and I saw he didn't believe me, but I didn't believe myself either. Damn it, it was true! I was bragging. It's all right to lie, but a man can't brag when it's true."

He rose impatiently and started toward the library doors.

"I'll straighten out that ending before our man gets here. We have twenty minutes," he said.

"Shall I reserve a table downstairs for dinner?" Claire asked him. "It's roast beef night."

"I can't eat the slops here," Earl said. "We can order tuna-fish sandwiches sent over from the Planet."

"I wish you'd visit the gallery sometime," Jonathan said, unwilling to accept their indifference.

"I can't see how that old warhorse Cassie Bender hooked a smart kid like you for a patsy," Earl observed. "It just doesn't figure."

"She hasn't hooked me. I think of it as the opportunity of a lifetime!" Jonathan exclaimed. "I'll be traveling all over, meeting wonderful people—look at my credit cards! Cassie arranged everything for me. I know what people say—"

It was no use, he saw by their shocked faces. He picked up his own card and the credit cards he had childishly flaunted and stuck them back in his wallet. It was tiresome having to defend bighearted, overbearing Cassie wherever he went. It was no use expecting these old friends to receive him back into their arms, eager for his confidences. Old people thought only of themselves. Each one alone might be his champion, but together—and he had combined them himself!—they closed ranks, leaving the young intruder outside once again.

"I just wanted to say hello," he said. "I'll run along now."

The boy's feelings must have been hurt, Claire thought remorsefully, but after all one had one's own work and one's own life to live. The young never seemed to understand that.

But you had so little time left, and it seemed as if you dared not stop running for a minute. You didn't run to win the prize as you did in youth. Indeed your dimming eyes could not tell if you'd passed the goal or not. You went on running because in the end that was the only prize there was—to be alive, to be in the race.

14

D R. KELLSEY was amazed to find himself installed in the larger apartment next to his old one within a month after he'd suggested it to the landlord of Knowlton Arms. He had been talking of this change for twenty years and it might have taken that long again to put his decision into effect. But here he was, books, screen, and pictures moved over in a trice, the studio couch for Jonathan in the living-room alcove, snug as you please, his own couch in the bedroom, empty closet and dressing room for Jonathan, separate door to bedroom so they could have their privacy. Everything settled but Jonathan, and he had left that to the last.

Now the die was cast, the professor reflected, a little frightened at the *definiteness* of things. Jonathan had been evasive when the hint to share his quarters had first been made, but he was a shy lad and would need to see that the place was all ready for him, no trouble was involved, and any responsibility was on the doctor's side. As they were both sensitive fellows they probably would be embarrassed to admit their secret relationship in so many words, but Jonathan must have recognized the facts just as the doctor had.

What worried the doctor was the problem of his lady friend, Anita. She had been urging this move on him for years, as part of her program for his divorcing Deborah and marrying her. A larger apartment would only mean to her that he had surrendered at last, and he would be in for a bad time explaining first the move and then Jonathan. The excuse of "private reasons" was a red flag to women anyway, sure to make them flip.

Pondering these matters sent Dr. Kellsey into a flip of his own for the period between the close of his summer term and the opening of the fall term. He spent this vacation, as he often had done in the past, in civilized drinking, a relaxation conducted in his two-and-a-half room apartment exactly as it had been in his one-and-a-half. It meant days on days unshaven, pajamaed, phone unhooked, incinerator clanking with empty bottles and broken glasses, a copper bowl of quarters by the hall door to hand out to liquor deliverers, delicatessen messengers, then a rehabilitation period presaged by a doctor's visit, drugstore deliveries, valet and laundrymen bringing and taking, a visiting barber, the public stenographer, newspapers, signs indicating reform was under way. Finally, the phone back on the hook, the hand and voice a little shaky but curable by the usual restoratives, the professor was ready to resume a gentleman's life, academic duties organized, the new autumn taken in stride.

He had not heard from his messages to Jonathan but was not concerned—young men were always dilatory—and it gave him time to butter up Anita meanwhile. He had agreed to meet her uptown at five and then escort her to Cassie Bender's preview party.

Pausing for a pair of quick ones at the club made him late at the start, and he had built up an even greater sense of guilt by the time he glimpsed Anita standing in the green glass shadows of the Lever Building. It struck him that she looked uncommonly calm for a girl who'd been kept waiting on a street corner for a good half hour. He had feared to find her pacing up and down, angry little eyes rolling from north to south to wristwatch, lighting a cigarette to place in holder, puff-puff and throw away, then lighting another in that fierce way she had, as if she was cooking his goose, but good, and snorting out smoke like Fafner himself.

"Hi!" she cried, waving her purse at him as merrily as any film star welcoming photographers. "Here I am."

No reproaches for breaking dates. No words about being late. Suspiciously Dr. Kellsey gave her his arm and they turned up Park.

"Good to see you," he said experimentally. Instead of saying, "Well, it's about time," Anita turned on him a radiant smile. Now that he was about to break up with her, he realized that years of familiarity had blinded him to Anita's good points. The sharp gypsy-dark face had good features, nostrils flaring a bit like a nervy racehorse's, upper lip too long and sulky, true, and the thin mouth shirred into a sort of bee-bite in the middle, fixed for a perpetual umlaut. Or an *œuf* or *œil*. More likely *eek*, he reflected. But good chin lines, he admitted generously, good planes, photogenically speaking, decent figure; she always boasted of walking right out of the store in standard size 12, triple-A shoe size 8, 32 bra—oh, there was nothing the matter with Anita's looks except that a mean fairy had taken them over at birth, squinching up everything somehow.

"I didn't mind waiting," she said. "I love watching the characters in this neighborhood. They fit the new architecture, all spare and bleak and hollow-looking. I'm sure their X-rays look like the blueprints for a modern skyscraper."

"The women with all their organs out and the men with all their ulcers in," Walter retorted, feeling thrown off by her beamish mood, unable to utilize his prepared defense.

"No, really, there is a kind of stark purity—a sort of Mondrian quality that gets me," Anita said dreamily.

"What about a Hugow quality, since this is his day?" Walter said, falling at once into the clumsy-witted state that Anita's arch fantasy moods always threw him.

"Now, Walter, please!" Anita twittered. "Hugow has depth, mystery, all the things you lack, darling, so of course you wouldn't understand. Oh, poor Cassie Bender will make a fortune out of this show."

Walter glanced uneasily at the sunny uptilted countenance usually clouded with discontent, and sure to be when he got around to giving her his news. Yes, she had the smug well-fed look of someone who had just done in her best friend for his own good. And here she was with a good word for Hugow ("terribly overrated" was her usual opinion of him) and a tender word for Cassie Bender ("a vulgar nymphomaniac" was her habitual epithet). The simple exhibition of good humor alarmed Walter much more than her needling could. In fact Anita's caustic view of their acquaintances was a major charm for him, blotting out his own aching jealousy of all forms of success and permitting him the nice role of bighearted forgiver. ("Now, now, Anita, let's be fair. No one can be that bad, dear girl, they must have *something*.") And if she wasn't going to attack him for his neglect, he would have to make the first move himself.

"I'm sorry to have missed your calls and our usual Friday dinners," he began, "but I was busy moving, you see—"

"So they told me at the club," Anita interrupted. "Don't give it a thought, Walter. I understood perfectly."

"But you see a strange thing happened," he went on doggedly. "It turns out there is a young chap in town who is the son of an old friend of mine, that is to say, she was a pupil of mine years ago."

"You do too much for your students, Walter," Anita said. "I've often told Dr. Jasper that that is our only trouble."

Suddenly the reason for her serenity dawned on the professor. Why, of course! She had just left her analyst's couch and had had her ego stroked for an hour by Dr. Jasper! He'd forgotten she had started that again. For a few hours after each consultation she enjoyed a state of glorious euphoria that merely having the money to buy analysis gives some people. Walter began steaming all over at the thought of the intimate revelations in Anita's folder on her "relationship" with himself. No use getting into that old psychoanalysis hassle, though, when there were bigger arguments ahead.

"He's given me so much help in adjusting to our relationship," Anita said somberly.

Help. Adjust. Relationship. How he hated the words, Walter thought irritably. Anita's problem was not a sense of inadequacy in herself but in her feeling overadequate to handle other people's inadequacies. She certainly didn't need a doctor to reassure her of her superiority. What she really wanted was for everybody else to be analyzed into admitting their wretched inferiority.

"He says the reason you don't have the normal philoprogenitive instincts is because you are compensated by being the father image to your students," Anita confided.

Father image!

"Does he think I was born a father image?" Dr. Kellsey exclaimed. "What about the students I had of my own age years ago? Doesn't this shrinker know there are a lot of other images in his old sample case? Doesn't he—"

He stopped, for Anita was giggling girlishly.

"I do think you're jealous of Dr. Jasper," she said. "That always happens and you're afraid I'm transferring."

Transfer! But he mustn't let her throw him. Instead he pointed toward the latest glass building under construction.

"Goldfish, that's what these damn architects would have us turn into!" he declaimed. "But the trouble is that some of us are toads and ought to be decently hidden."

Anita gave a silvery laugh.

"Oh, Walter, don't waste your marvelous epigrams on poor little me," she cried. "There'll be all sorts of clever people at Cassie's who can appreciate your wit properly."

"Look, we don't have to go to this show," Dr. Kellsey burst out. "I'm sick of this Hugow worship wherever I go. I can't stand that faded blond art madam, either. Let's skip it and have a quiet steak down at Costello's where we can talk."

Anita drew a white-gloved hand from his arm and batted her beadies at him reproachfully.

"I didn't realize you felt so hostile toward Cassie Bender," she said.

"Hostile!" echoed Dr. Kellsey savagely.

"And you can't downgrade Hugow's painting. Everyone says he's the best this year," she said.

Now the professor was really angry.

"I'm sick of this new cultural Gay Payoo," he shouted. "I can't stand Picasso or baseball or Louis Armstrong or boxers or folksongs or people's children or new faces, but if I open my mouth to say so a crowd closes in on me ready to get me deported. What about a little freedom of thought? You're as bad as the others, Anita, afraid to have an opinion of your own."

"Just because I don't agree with you, Wally, isn't that it?" Anita laughed, infuriatingly, above his heckling. "Come along, you silly boy, there'll be champagne and you'll love it. La la la."

She was humming "Three Coins in the Fountain" again and fondly resumed his arm. The shrinker had certainly filled her up with self-confidence this time, Walter thought, and he wondered how long before it would start chipping off like the lipstick and eyeshadow. Whatever was making her so satisfied made him jealous, but then he was jealous of everybody nowadays, jealous of the President of the United States for all that free rent and gravy, jealous of cops for their freedom to sock anybody who annoyed them, jealous of students who could skip his classes, jealous of Hugow or anybody stupid enough to believe in his own genius, jealous of happy believers and bold infidels, and jealous of young men with a whole lifetime ahead to louse themselves up as they wished. Ridiculous to be jealous of poor old Anita, especially when she had his bad news coming to her.

"All right, then, let's go," he snapped, taking long strides to throw off Anita's prim little high-heeled steps, her thighs never parting as if afraid of wandering rapists. "I haven't much time because I must see this young chap I mentioned, the son of my old student—"

"What's his name?" Anita asked. "Who was his mother?"

He had almost forgotten.

"He is Jonathan Jaimison," he said. "Mother was Connie Birch."

"I can't understand this sentimentality over an old student," Anita said. "You always claim your classes are just one big moronic sea, so what did this one do to stamp her?"

The familiar indications of a fight soothed and warmed Dr. Kellsey. There was chance of a little sport after all.

"It was long before your time, my dear," he said. "I had just come East and barely begun my classes. This girl had a slender talent—"

"You've always hated slender talents." Anita was now smoldering nicely. "Why do you have to waste time on her son?"

They had reached the entrance to the brownstone where Cassie Bender's modern window stood out, bravely anachronistic.

"For very special reasons that I can't go into right here," he said, amused to watch the chipping-off process begin in earnest as Anita, scowling thunderously, drew back and stoned him with a look. "The father image, as you call it, owes something to the father seeker, wouldn't your good Dr. Jasper say? Here is a too permissive young man with no sense of security in a sea of hostilities and unrewarding relationships. It is my plan to help him to adjust or project, rather, by taking him into my home as if he were, let us say, a son image."

"You wouldn't!" Anita choked. "You mean you took that apartment for him instead of for us! You really meant it to be good-by."

Now he did feel guilty and remorseful, for the poor girl looked white and wild under her careful make-up. As soon as she had put his plan into words he realized that he couldn't say good-by to Anita, any more than he could say good-by to his conscience or, for that matter, to his wife.

"It's to help the boy out till he can look out for himself," he said cautiously. "Think of him as a lost boy, Anita, without friends or money in this big city, no place to turn but to that father image you mention. You shouldn't criticize me, Anita, for feelings you used to scold me for lacking!"

Ha. He was turning the tables on her, and Anita was too smart not to know it. She was sniffling a little but softening. They went into the gallery, through the hall to the glass-roofed patio, where the party was assembling under a chandelier mobile.

"At least you can be decent to Cassie," Anita muttered in his ear as the gallery queen swooped toward them, white bosom bursting from purple velvet beamed toward them like truck headlights. "I'm so glad you came early," cried Cassie, clasping a hand of each guest. "The most marvelous news for you! I want you to meet my new partner, this heavenly, heavenly creature, Jonathan Jaimison. Darling, come meet Dr. Kellsey and Anita Barlowe, such distinguished scholars."

"Jonathan Jaimison?" Anita said, looking at Dr. Kellsey.

The young man was far too handsome, Anita thought, but then that sort of looks always went fast, thank God. Cassie was crowing over him in that revolting possessive hungry, sexy way she had, pawing him as she introduced him. But Dr. Kellsey's face was more interesting at the moment than Cassie's new partner, who was vigorously shaking the doctor's hand.

"I don't think I heard right," said Dr. Kellsey. "Did Mrs. Bender say she had a new partner? But that can't be you, Jonathan."

"Yes, it is a surprise, isn't it?" Jonathan said happily. "I couldn't think of a better use for my money than to buy into a business like this."

"I'm teaching him everything I know!" said Cassie with a splendid gesture.

"That's so generous of you," said Anita sweetly. "And so like you."

She could tell that her lover was thoroughly unprepared for this encounter, and, whatever the situation was, it comforted her to have him be the one to squirm for a change.

"So you've left the café," Dr. Kellsey said, "and the East Tenth Street apartment."

"I've caged him in the downstairs studio next door," Cassie said merrily. "Wasn't that clever of me?"

"It's best to be near Teacher, isn't it, Mr. Jaimison?" Anita asked Jonathan. "One never knows when one will need a lesson."

She was annoying Dr. Kellsey, she knew, but she felt she had the right. Poor lost boy with no money and no home indeed! A millionaire, from the way he was dressed, and the talk about buying the business!

"I knew his mother, you see," Dr. Kellsey mumbled, trying to collect his wits in the face of Anita's curled lip. "It was a long time ago. I found some old snapshots, Jonathan, that perhaps might help you in your research."

"Good," said Jonathan. "But I've dropped that research. I've been meaning to tell you."

"I see," said Dr. Kellsey, smiling but stricken. "That happens, of course, to all researchers, as Miss Barlowe here can tell you. The researcher comes upon findings that don't fit in with his preconception, so he loses interest in the game."

Anita was pleased and touched to be mentioned and moved closer. She could tell by the professor's trembling voice and nervous mustache twigging that he was immensely disturbed. Jonathan too was aware of a new sarcastic note in his old friend's voice.

"It was a game, as you say," he conceded warily. "As soon as I talked to Mrs. Bender I saw that here was my future."

"It's absolutely miraculous!" Cassie Bender linked arms with Jonathan, enveloping new visitors in her perfumed aura, clutching one, smiling at another, and speaking into a third one's ear. "You've no idea what a flair this boy has! Don't you agree, Dr. Kellsey, that *appreciation* is a talent in itself? Absolutely apart from criticism or promotion or diagnostic approach? Jonathan *appreciates*."

"It must be heaven," Anita murmured.

"Why, I'd never even heard of Percy Wright until Jonathan

brought him to my attention. Wright has taken a good deal from Hugow, true, but Hugow's at his peak and Wright is new, one of the new romantics."

"Hard Edge," explained Jonathan.

"But Soft Middle," said Cassie.

"Ah," said the doctor.

"Champagne?" Jonathan motioned toward the bar. "There's scotch if you'd rather."

"I prefer Hugow," the doctor said absently. "Where is he?"

"He still stands up, doesn't he?" Cassie agreed. "But he makes me so mad when he won't come in! He says he can't stand openings and being talked about as if he was dead. He says the kind of people who like him make him want to give up art and drive a hack. Just between us, I'm glad to find a *gentleman* painter like Percy, after my struggles with Hugow."

"We've tripled his prices," Jonathan reminded her. "Sold out, too."

Cassie was loaded, he thought, and more Southern belle by the minute.

"Then you're no longer the little lost boy without friends or home," Anita said to him with a charming smile, edging away from her escort's savage nudge. "You've found yourself."

"Of course Dr. Kellsey was a great help to me," Jonathan said, knowing he had failed the doctor miserably and wondering how he could atone for getting lucky. "You understood me, sir, and it meant a lot to me."

It meant too much for the professor.

"Ah, but I was mistaken all the while," he said. "It wasn't the father image you sought, after all, but the mother image. And now you've found your true mother."

Too bad Cassie missed that one, Anita thought. Men were so bitchy.

"How much he looks like Dr. Jasper!" she whispered to Walter. "It's amazing!"

"Really, Anita!" reproved the doctor. In his annoyance, the professor rejected the highball offered by Jonathan, suggesting pointedly to Anita that they must leave. It was Jonathan who was the offender now, greeting new visitors as Cassie drew him away.

"You were so right about Mother Cassie," Anita murmured, following Dr. Kellsey to the exit. "She's absolutely clucking today. I suppose she's sleeping with your little hero. Let's go before she makes us look at the pictures. I can't understand what anybody finds in Hugow."

There was his old Anita, the professor rejoiced, the shrinker's salve all worn away and the dear acidulous, embittered girl back again.

"Now, now," he rebuked her gently. "Cassie isn't all that bad, and you can't miss the basic strength in Hugow, crude though it is. Sure you don't want to stay for the crowd? It would be interesting to see how Jonathan handles them in his new role."

"I hate that Spur crowd and Cassie's rich oafs and the disgusting noises the critics make," Anita said. "Let's go to Costello's for a little honest air—unless, of course, you're afraid your wife will be there."

"Nonsense, Deborah would never be in a place like that," he said, which started Anita all over on a very old tack.

"Like that? Like what? You mean it's too good for me and not good enough for your wife? Or maybe she'll be at that new apartment of yours, meant for everybody but me."

It was like old times, before Jonathan had stirred up his life. The professor tucked Anita's hand under his arm when they got into the taxi and gently reminded her that a man's wife did have first rights to his apartment, new or old. By the time they got out at Costello's for steak and quiet talk they weren't speaking to each other.

It was good to be back in the ring.

The Hugow opening was a sensational success by Golden Spur standards. One minute before eight, the hour the party was slated to close, an entire new saloonful of art-lovers roared in from the Muse's farthest reaches. A sea of arms reached in the air for drinks as if for basketballs and passed them over heads of immobilized figures. Museum directors, critics, dilettantes were pushed into the paintings they admired; oldtimers accustomed to snubbing each other found themselves glued together, buttocks to buttocks, lipstick to hairy ear, beard to bra. The barstool artflies took over, and Jonathan's nightmare began.

"Jonathan, you stinker, get out the hooch, you know where the bitch keeps it! . . . Can you imagine that jerk locking up the bar when his old pals walk in? . . . Hugow would kill the guy if he knew they were holding out on his old friends. . . . Get it out, you dirty scab."

The more distinguished guests were being knocked down as they fought for their minks under the mountains of duffel coats, and leather jackets, and there were cries of "Thief! . . . Get the police. . . . Get Hugow! Get a doctor."

Jonathan's efforts to sneak more bottles into the party only reminded his old buddies that he was in a position now to do even more for them, and they despised him for it.

"I got to have forty-five bucks for my loft, Jonny-boy. If I get Hugow to put down a few lines on a card, how much will you pay for it?"

Whatever he said or did was wrong and brought forth jeers, none louder than when Cassie obliged him to announce the doors were being locked. He knew they regarded him as an informer now, but he hated himself too, wishing he could be put out with them instead of putting them out. He had looked forward to this great day as a kind of debut for himself, the more so because Cassie had kept postponing it for greater thunder. He would show his old friends that he was going to be a friend indeed. He had hoped to show Hugow too, but the artist had disappeared on some private binge, and Jonathan found himself agreeing with Cassie that an artist should be more *responsible*, more *mature*, more *considerate*.

"Is that what I'm going to be?" he asked himself, shocked. "Am I going to think Percy Wright is a finer painter because he takes off his hat in elevators?"

Long before the mob had poured in, Cassie, following her usual practice, had siphoned off the plummier guests to her own private quarters for caviar and champagne and inside chatter.

"Do get rid of everybody and come back here," she begged Jonathan. "Tell them I have a headache or passed out or anything."

"Jonny is Cassie Bender's bouncer!" jeered someone as Jonathan tried to guide a sneaker-footed stumbler to the door, and Jonathan was annoyed at Cassie for humiliating him, at the victim, at himself, and at the taunter for speaking the truth. His anger gave him strength to push the intruders outward, though they rushed out as suddenly as they had advanced when word spread that the Jackson Gallery party further down the avenue was still on. There was a hint that Hugow himself had gone to that party instead of his own, which made everyone gleeful.

In the gallery Jonathan stood panting from his exertions, brushing his sleeves, straightening his tie and hair; a regular bouncer, he thought, and his name in gold letters on a door meant just that. He picked his way over the floor littered with broken glasses, sandwiches, and forgotten rubbers to the patio which led to Cassie's exclusive quarters, where the cream of the party was assembled, the big shots he would now be able to swing behind deserving talent, providing the talent didn't double-cross him first. He wished he were going with the mob to the other party, cardless, thirsty, mannerless, tie-less, absolutely free.

Immature, irresponsible, he told himself.

Cassie was arranged on her favorite sofa, one plump but shapely leg thrown across the other high enough to reveal chiffon ruffles and a charming suspicion—no, it couldn't be!—of pubic curls, coquettishly hidden as soon as the peek was offered. One gray millionaire sat at her feet for the view of lower joys, while another leaned over the back of the sofa, gazing down hungrily into the generous picnic of her decol-letage. Cassie waved her cigarette holder around both admir-ers and spoke in her Lady Agatha accent of the mystique of art collecting. Jonathan pretended not to see her gracious gesture making room at her feet for him to crouch, look, lis-ten, and learn. He sipped his whisky doggedly, feeling like a child left with the dreary grown-ups while the other boys were having fun in forbidden playgrounds. These important personages of the art world had no value in themselves, only when presented to men like Hugow for their needs. None of them would ever be friends or people in their own right, he thought. Just as he was speculating on how soon he could break loose from his new duties, he saw George Terrence coming toward him, smiling.

"My dear boy, you look as if you'd seen a ghost! Don't apologize, I understand now why you didn't answer my letters, and believe me, I think it's splendid. I've taken up painting for my nerves, on the advice of my doctor, and I will say that there's nothing like it. I don't blame you a bit for preferring it to the law. Even my wife is taking it up. In fact, she just purchased a Hugow from Mrs. Bender, that's why we came."

A lean, lantern-jawed, crew-cut man of distinction, barber-tanned and vested in lamé brocade suddenly detached himself from a manly cluster around the fireplace and reached a beautiful hand toward George.

"Roger Mills, as I live and breathe," he said. "How long has it been—let's see, ten, twenty—no, don't tell me—why, I believe it's nearly twenty-five years, isn't it?" He smiled brilliantly at Jonathan and favored him with the next handclasp. "So you're one of Roger's protégés, too. I've heard about you from Mrs. Kingston Ball, Miss Van Orphen's sister."

"I think you're mistaken about my name," George Terrence said, taking a firm grip on Jonathan's arm as Jonathan was trying to get away. "Terrence is the name. Would you like to meet Mrs. Terrence, Jonathan? She's been anxious to meet you, now that we're so interested in artists."

The trimly dieted little matron summoned from her corner was the same one who had avoided him as Connie Birch's son but was eager to make amends to the promising dealer and was equally pleased to meet the glitter-vested Mr. Gordon.

"Did I hear you mention Claire Van Orphen?" she asked him. "Claire and Beatrice used to call on us years ago. And Mr. Jaimison here is the son of a dear old friend as well as a friend of Claire's. What a lot we have to talk over!"

"Indeed, indeed," said the stranger. "I knew your husband before he was your husband, Mrs. Terrence, when he was quite the gay bachelor, in fact, eh, Roger?"

Mrs. Terrence burst into arch giggles.

"You don't need to remind me, sir," she cried. "George was a very naughty boy when I first knew him and I did my best to reform him. But do you know I do love hearing him tell about his escapades, because sex standards are so much freer now, don't you think, Mr. Gordon, and what shocked us then just seems amusing these days? I really blush at my own ignorance more than at George's naughty affairs. Imagine George using an alias, like royalty!"

Mr. Gordon toyed with the jeweled buttons of his vest and looked from Mrs. Terrence's bisque-matted façade to George Terrence's steely smile.

"Indeed," he said. "So you knew about Roger Mills."

Mrs. Terrence giggled again.

"That was so clever of George. His family owned the Roger Cotton Mills, so sometimes he called himself Roger Cotton and sometimes Roger Mather when he was out on a lark. I nearly died laughing, but it would have shocked me if I'd known it once."

"It still shocks me, Mrs. Terrence," said the stranger.

Jonathan wanted to leave the happily reunited old friends to their reminiscences, but this time it was Mrs. Terrence who detained him.

"My daughter has told me about you," she said. "Really my taking up art, modern art, that is, has made Amy and me much closer, just as it has made George and me understand each other. You must let us come and browse around the newer galleries, Jonathan, because you're the expert and we're amateurs."

"What made you take it up?" asked the stranger, brooding. "Nerves—like Roger's here?"

"Oh no," said the lady. "I knew it was all right because Mrs. Crysler was collecting modern art."

"Don't go, Jonathan," exclaimed George. "Please stay," cried Hazel and Mr. Gordon. "Come sit with me, Jonathan," commanded Cassie.

It was a trap, he thought gloomily. He thought wistfully of the pack of gallery-flies prowling through the night, battering on doors to be let in, brawling and bruising down to The Golden Spur, and he thought those were the real backers of art, those were the providers, the blood-donors, and Cassie's salon of critics, guides, and millionaires, were the free-loaders, free-loading on other people's genius, other people's broken hearts, and, when it came to that, other people's money.

Well, he'd learned something more about himself, and if all he'd lost was some of Major Wedburn's money, that was okay.

He didn't have to save his life by collaboration with the enemy, did he? He found Percy Wright trying to be sick in Cassie's bathroom.

"It's not the liquor, it's my awful problems!" Percy gasped. "I mean, naturally I'm terribly flattered that you and Cassie have taken me up and let me meet these great people, but I still admire Hugow—my master, really—and I want to tell him he mustn't blame me for my prices boosting and those reviewers saying he's through, because he isn't. Would I still be trying to paint like him if he was through, I mean? And if he gets through, where does that leave my work when it's like his?"

Yes, it was a problem, Jonathan agreed.

"I'll make a fortune when my show comes on," Percy said, "but nobody likes my money anyway. You'd think it was leprosy, the way Darcy nags me about it. But how can I stop my stuff from selling?"

"You can buy me out," said Jonathan, inspired. "Be a dealer. That's where you belong. Everybody you like will like you."

"You wouldn't sell," Percy said, cheered at once.

Jonathan handed him a towel filled with ice and a fresh glass of scotch, and the deal was started.

Jonathan hurried down Madison and looked for lights from the side-street galleries along the way where other opening parties had been held. By this time the old crowd must be heading toward The Golden Spur for post mortems and wakes, and he stood waving for a cab. A green taxi was parked in front of a Hamburger Heaven and as he waited the driver came out of the restaurant with a paper bag. He opened the cab door.

"Just the man we're hunting. Get in," he said. "How do you like this job? The best thing I ever painted."

Hugow took off his cap and grinned.

"I knew it," said Jonathan. "You're still in your green period."

"My fare's buying Pernod, a love potion rich debutantes give to taxi-drivers—green, of course."

Iris was hurrying out of the liquor store with her package.

"Darling, we've been looking all over for you," she cried, climbing in. "We've got everything ready for the trip."

"You never guessed I'd be at the gallery," Jonathan said.

"I figured you'd be too smart to stick that one out," Hugow said.

"I was only watching your doodlings pull in a fortune," Jonathan said. "It gets boring."

"Hugow's got it all spent already," Iris said.

It was lovely to be in each other's arms in the back seat of a taxi once again. It didn't matter that she'd been with Hugow, and the truth had no part in love anyway, except for the truth of finding each other at the right moment.

"Not spent, invested," said Hugow, heading the car north. "There won't be any money in art in the year two thousand, so I'm in a new business, the coming one."

Jonathan didn't care what business it was so long as they were all together once more.

"Demolition, that's my business now," said Hugow. "Cab for a hobby, demolition for real. My firm's hoping for this contract."

"The Metropolitan?"

They were passing the Museum, heading for the park entrance.

"We call that a ball job in my business," said Hugow. "The iron ball, that's our god. I'm picking up the lingo too. No art corn, just the simple, brutal words."

"Already it's arty," said Jonathan. " 'Demolition' for 'wrecking.' I've got some money to invest in it myself."

"I'll take it," Hugow said.

Jonathan wondered where Hugow was taking them, but if nobody else wanted The Golden Spur, he'd be the last to suggest it. He wanted to ask Iris where she had been all these weeks, but she was here now. Wasn't that all that mattered?

"Your parents were at the show," he told Iris.

"Parents are getting into everything now, spoiling all the fun," Iris complained. "Now mother wants to go back into the theater, she says, now that she knows about me. I told them all about me so I could leave for good, but instead they wanted to come too. Father painting, mind you! That's what that analyst Dr. Jasper did!"

They were tooling over to the West Side Highway. Maybe Hugow was taking them up to his shack up in Rockland County, where they would freeze to death. Maybe he'd turn around before they hit the bridge and go down to the Spur after all. Iris had her head cozily on his shoulder and was babbling away between sandwiches and drinks about the frightful hazards of getting on good terms with your family after all these years.

"That's why I love you so much," she said. "You simply have no family pride, Jonathan."

"On the contrary, I am very proud of my family," Jonathan said. "The Jaimisons happen to be one of the oldest families in Ohio."

He was very glad that Hugow had turned back downtown, perhaps to the Spur, where they could begin all over.

CHRONOLOGY

NOTE ON THE TEXTS

NOTES

Chronology

<table>
<tr><td>1896</td><td>Born in family home at 53 West North Street in Mt. Gilead, Ohio, on November 28, the second of three daughters of Roy King Powell and Hattie Sherman Powell. (In later years Powell habitually gives her birth year as 1897. Father, b. August 24, 1869, and mother, b. March 24, 1872, are both from the Mt. Gilead area. Father is of Welsh-Irish descent, while family tradition claims the mother's family, while mostly English, is also part Cherokee. Father works at series of jobs, including night manager of a local hotel and traveling salesman selling perfume, bedding, cherries, cookies, and coffins. Sister Mabel born July 11, 1895.)</td></tr>
<tr><td>1899</td><td>Sister Phyllis born December 29 at 115 Cherry Street.</td></tr>
<tr><td>1903</td><td>Mother dies, probably the result of a botched abortion, on December 6, in Shelby, Ohio.</td></tr>
<tr><td>1904–6</td><td>Lives with series of relatives in central Ohio, while father is on the road as traveling salesman. (Later remembers: "a year of farm life with this or that aunt, life in small-town boarding houses, life with very prim strict relatives, to rougher life in the middle of little factory towns.")</td></tr>
<tr><td>1907–9</td><td>Father marries Sabra Stearns, a former schoolteacher and cashier, in 1907. Family is reunited in a large farmhouse outside Cleveland. Stepmother proves to be abusive and is despised by Powell and her sisters, all of whom eventually run away from home. Becomes an early and precocious reader; favorite writers include Alexandre Dumas, Victor Hugo, and Charles Dickens. Begins to write stories, plays, and sketches.</td></tr>
<tr><td>1910–14</td><td>When stepmother burns some of her notebooks in the summer of 1910, runs off to live with her maternal aunt, Orpha May Sherman Steinbrueck, in Shelby. Aunt encourages Powell's literary ambitions. ("She gave me music lessons and thought I had genius and when I wrote</td></tr>
</table>

crude little poems and stories, she cherished them, positive that I was another Jean Webster or Ella Wheeler Wilcox.") Attends Shelby High School, where she is made yearbook editor in her senior year.

1914–17   With the financial assistance of her aunt, neighbors, and the school itself, matriculates in the fall of 1914 at Lake Erie College in Painesville, Ohio. Publishes stories in the *Lake Erie Record*, beginning in early 1915. Works during summer of 1915 as maid and waitress at a resort near the college; writes diary addressed to a fictional friend named "Mr. Woggs." Proves a barely adequate student at Lake Erie, but distinguishes herself in extracurricular activities, serving as editor of the *Lake Erie Record* in her senior year, writing and performing her own plays, and playing the part of Puck in an outdoor production of *A Midsummer Night's Dream*. Spends the summer of 1916 as a counselor at Camp Caho in Michigan. Works for a Shelby newspaper, the *Globe*, for most of the summer of 1917.

1918   Graduates from Lake Erie College and moves to Pomfret, Connecticut, where she writes, works on a farm, and does some suffragist campaigning throughout the northeastern corner of the state. Studies seriously but informally with author and photographer Ella Boult, who also lives in Pomfret. Moves on September 2 to 353 West 85th Street in New York City. Attempts to enlist in the U.S. Navy in October, but is hospitalized for a month when physical examination indicates that she is suffering from Spanish influenza.

1919   Does extensive free-lance writing for a wide variety of magazines and newspapers, while working at a succession of jobs. Appears as an extra in *Footlights and Shadows*, a silent film starring Olive Thomas.

1920   Lives at 569 West End Avenue and is employed by the Interchurch World Movement, where her duties include working in support of Armenian famine relief. Early in the year, meets a co-worker, Joseph Roebuck Gousha (b. August 20, 1890), a poet and critic from Pittsburgh who has also recently arrived in New York City; they attend Broadway plays together and take long walks in Tarrytown and on Staten Island. Marries Gousha on November 20 at the Church of the Transfiguration on 29th Street in Manhattan. After a honeymoon at the Hotel Pennsylvania on Seventh Avenue near Pennsylvania Station, Powell and her husband decide to maintain separate households, but then move in together at 31 Riverside Drive.

1921 Son Joseph R. Gousha Jr., known as "Jojo," is born on August 22 at St. Luke's Hospital in Manhattan after difficult delivery. Powell remains in hospital with son for three weeks.

1922 Begins her first novel, *Whither*, an autobiographical work about her early days in New York; writes mostly in Central Park and in the Children's Room of the New York Public Library. Joseph abandons writing and begins successful career in advertising.

1923 It becomes obvious that Jojo is mentally impaired (possibly autistic, a condition then not identified; he will be classified and ministered to as "retarded" or "schizophrenic" throughout most of his life, although his capacity for memorization and certain intellectual tasks is on the genius level). Joseph's financial success permits the family to hire Louise Lee as nurse and caretaker for Jojo (Lee remains with the household until 1954). Family begins practice of renting a summer beach cottage in Mt. Sinai, Long Island.

1924 Moves with family to 46 West Ninth Street in Greenwich Village. *Whither* is accepted by the Boston publisher Small, Maynard.

1925 *Whither* is published and almost immediately disavowed by Powell. Writes a second novel, *She Walks In Beauty*, which she will always describe as her first. Begins novel *The Bride's House*. After disagreements with Joseph, spends several weeks in Ohio with her sisters and Orpha May Steinbrueck. Jojo's disturbances are increasingly blatant and alarming. Powell establishes a deeply devoted, and possibly romantic, friendship with the leftist playwright John Howard Lawson late in the year.

1926   *The Bride's House* is completed but remains unpublished
        along with *She Walks In Beauty*. Father dies in July after a
        paralytic stroke. Powell's social circle includes Charles
        Norman, Eugene Jolas, Jacques LeClercq, Esther An-
        drews, and Canby Chambers, and she becomes acquainted
        with Ernest Hemingway, John Dos Passos, and Theodore
        Dreiser. Begins writing book reviews for the New York
        Evening Post, to which she will contribute for more than
        three decades.

1927   Spends most of the year working on plays, short stories,
        and free-lance work for magazines, while trying to find a
        publisher for her two unpublished novels (later claims
        that *She Walks In Beauty* was turned down by 36 pub-
        lishers).

1928   Lives at 106 Perry Street in Greenwich Village. *She Walks
        In Beauty* is published by Brentano's, to generally favor-
        able reviews and unremarkable sales. Joseph is briefly un-
        employed in the fall and Powell responds by writing a first
        draft of "The Party," a play (later retitled *Big Night*) sat-
        irizing the advertising world, in a period of three weeks.
        Starts work on novel *Dance Night*.

1929   *The Bride's House* is published; it meets with less success
        than her previous book. Jojo, sporadically violent and out
        of control, is now confined to hospitals or special schools
        much of the time. Powell becomes a close friend of Mar-
        garet Burnham De Silver, a wealthy woman whose schiz-
        ophrenic daughter is resident in the same New Jersey
        institution as Jojo. Another close friend is the editor
        Coburn Gilman, who becomes Powell's favorite drinking
        companion. Late in the year, Powell has what is diag-
        nosed as a heart attack at the family vacation home on
        Long Island and is brought back by taxi to New York,
        where she is hospitalized for several weeks. (Attack is
        probably symptom of a chest teratoma that she will suffer
        from until 1949.)

1930   *Dance Night* is published by Farrar & Rinehart; its poor
        sales and negative reviews depress Powell, who will always
        consider this her finest novel. Visits Bermuda in the sum-
        mer with Margaret De Silver. Earns some of her living

collaborating with nightclub comedian Dwight Fiske on bawdy song-stories. (Many of these are later published in Fiske's collections *Without Music* in 1933 and *Why Should Penguins Fly?* in 1934.)

1931   Begins work on two novels, *Come Back to Sorrento* and a book she originally calls the "Lila" novel, which becomes *Turn, Magic Wheel*. Begins keeping a detailed diary with some regularity, a practice she continues for the rest of her life. An early play, *Walking Down Broadway*, is purchased for $7,500 and loosely adapted into a film directed by Erich von Stroheim (the film, which is taken away from von Stroheim and partially reshot, is retitled *Hello, Sister!* and released in 1933). The family moves in October to 9 East Tenth Street.

1932   *Come Back to Sorrento* is published by Farrar & Rinehart, who against Powell's wishes retitle it *The Tenth Moon*. Spends beginning of the year in California, working as a screenwriter, but receives no film credits. *Big Night* is selected for production by the Group Theater, and Powell is anxious about what she calls the "heavy footed literalism" of their staging. The play is directed by Cheryl Crawford, then, late in the rehearsal period, by Harold Clurman; the cast includes Stella Adler, J. Edward Bromberg, and Clifford Odets. Begins work on novel *The Story of a Country Boy*, based in part on memories of her maternal cousin Charles Miller.

1933   *Big Night* opens in January; receives harsh reviews and closes after four days, although it is praised by Robert Benchley in *The New Yorker*. Powell begins work on another play, *Jig-Saw*. Completes *The Story of a Country Boy*. Forms friendship with Edmund Wilson; friendship with John Dos Passos deepens. At the end of the year, there is a rupture, apparently final, with John Howard Lawson.

1934   Begins work on satirical novel *Turn, Magic Wheel*. *Jig-Saw* is produced by the Theater Guild, with Spring Byington, Ernest Truex, and Cora Witherspoon in leading roles; production is a modest success, and play is published by Farrar & Rinehart. *The Story of a Country Boy* is published to poor sales and undistinguished reviews; film rights are sold to Warner Brothers and First National Pictures for $12,500.

1935   Continues work on *Turn, Magic Wheel*; Farrar & Rinehart are mystified by her self-proclaimed "new style" of urban comedy, and John Farrar suggests that she put the novel aside, "not necessarily destroy." Visits Havana and Key West with Joseph and old friend Harry Lissfelt. *Man of Iron*, a film loosely derived from *The Story of a Country Boy*, is released to poor reviews.

1936   *Turn, Magic Wheel* is published by Farrar & Rinehart, to excellent reviews and moderate sales. British edition is published by John Constable; the reviews are even more enthusiastic. (Powell will continue to have a small but avid following in England.) Moves again to Hollywood in the fall; earns a large salary as a screenwriter and is promised an extended contract, guaranteeing her up to $1500 a week; dislikes writing for the movies and returns to New York.

1937   Works on novel *The Happy Island* while taking amphetamine diet pills. Attempts to produce a play, *Red Dress*, based on *She Walks In Beauty*, with Norman Bel Geddes.

1938   *The Happy Island* is published; it is a critical and financial failure. Jojo is moved to Gladwyne Colony in Valley Forge, Pennsylvania, where he lives for most of the next 14 years.

1939   Signs with Scribner's, where her new editor is Max Perkins, famous for his work with F. Scott Fitzgerald, Ernest Hemingway, and Thomas Wolfe. Appears as a regular guest analyzing popular songs on radio program *Music and Manners*, featuring Ann Honeycutt. Briefly employed as book critic for *Mademoiselle*; describes the work as a "kindergarten" job. Through Dos Passos, becomes increasingly friendly with Gerald and Sara Murphy, and spends weekends with them at their homes in East Hampton and Snedens Landing, New York. Works much of the year on novel *Angels on Toast*, writing part of it in a Coney Island hotel.

1940   *Angels on Toast* published by Scribner's, to good reviews and marginal sales. Begins work on *A Time To Be Born*, based in part on the career of Clare Boothe Luce.

1941   After a dream about her childhood in late January starts to sketch out what becomes *My Home Is Far Away*, a novel closely based on childhood experiences. At year's end, she helps rewrite a musical comedy, *The Lady Comes Across*; other participants in the project include composer Vernon Duke, lyricist John Latouche, choreographer George Balanchine, and actors Jessie Matthews, Mischa Auer, Joe E. Lewis, and Gower Champion.

1942   *The Lady Comes Across* closes in January after two performances. John Latouche remains one of Powell's closest friends. *A Time To Be Born*, published by Scribner's, becomes Powell's best-selling book to date by far, and is reprinted four times in the first year. The family moves in September to duplex at 35 East Ninth Street.

1943   Works steadily on *My Home Is Far Away*, which she envisions as the beginning of a trilogy. Writes in her diary: "In the new book, I want to trace corruption, private and public, through innocence and love—possibly learning that only by being prepared for all evil can evil be met." Begins work on novel "The Destroyers," later retitled *The Locusts Have No King*.

1944   *My Home Is Far Away* is published; it is dedicated to her cousin John Franklin Sherman, who was also raised by Orpha May Steinbrueck and is serving overseas. Begins "Marcia," the second volume of her projected trilogy (the novel is never finished, and less than 100 pages of draft survive). Edmund Wilson publishes a mixed review of *My Home Is Far Away* in *The New Yorker* in November; it hurts Powell deeply and nearly ruptures their friendship.

1945   In the summer, visits Ohio for what will be the last reunion with her two sisters.

1946   Incorporates the fascination and horror she feels listening to radio broadcasts of the United States atomic bomb tests on Bikini Atoll into the final scene of *The Locusts*

Have No King, which she now plans as a deliberately "post-war" novel. Takes an automobile trip to Florida with Margaret De Silver, where they visit with Esther Andrews, Canby Chambers, and Pauline Pfeiffer Hemingway. Undergoes a hysterectomy in the fall; tells friends she has been "spayed." Works on *The Locusts Have No King* throughout the year.

1947   Meets Malcolm Lowry during his visit to Manhattan to promote his recently published novel *Under the Volcano*; the two become friends and correspondents. Max Perkins dies in June. Powell attends to John Dos Passos after an automobile accident in September on Cape Cod, which costs him an eye and kills his wife, Katy. Hospitalized for more than two weeks after being attacked and badly beaten by Jojo in November.

1948   *The Locusts Have No King* is published by Scribner's. Powell deems it an "admirable, superior work—no holes of plot as in other works—and a sustained intelligence dominating the farcical and exaggerated so that it had more unity and structural solidity than anything I ever did." The novel receives favorable reviews but sales are mediocre. To Powell's surprise, her English publisher, John Constable, rejects the book. Visits Haiti and Key West in March.

1949   Pressure within Powell's chest is finally diagnosed as a teratoma, a rare tumor that often includes fragments of hair and teeth, which has become so acute that her ribs are cracking from its pressure. Tumor is successfully removed in April. Powell believes the growth a "failed twin" and nicknames it "Terry Toma." Accepts a month-long residency during the summer at the MacDowell Colony, but is irritated by the colony's regulations and traditions and remains stymied in her work on "Marcia." Sister Mabel Powell Pocock dies in October.

1950   Unable to make headway with her new project, a "novel of Washington Square" entitled *The Wicked Pavilion*. Feeling the need for a drastic change, moves in October with financial aid from Margaret De Silver to Paris, where she lives at the Hotel Lutetia on the Left Bank. Renews old friendships with Eugene Jolas and Libby Holman, and meets Samuel Beckett, Jean-Paul Sartre, and Simone de Beauvoir; dislikes France and finds Parisians "the most moralizing people in the world." Cuts her stay short when Chinese intervention in the Korean War suggests to her that a global conflict may be imminent.

1951   Stays briefly in London in January before returning to New York. Jojo has an unusually good year and spends a considerable amount of time at home, encouraging parents' hopes for further improvement. Writes in her diary on July 29: "Incredible that after working steadily on this novel, with very few sidetracks except wretched and futile attempts at money . . . I have gotten no further than 12 pages or so." Cuts her ties with Scribner's when they refuse, after her repeated urgings, to bring out a collection of her short stories. Rosalind Baker Wilson (daughter of Edmund Wilson) brings Powell to Houghton Mifflin.

1952   *Sunday, Monday and Always*, a collection of short stories, is published in June by Houghton Mifflin and receives excellent notices, with many reviewers using the occasion to celebrate Powell's work in general. In the fall, London-based publisher W. H. Allen agrees to bring out *The Locusts Have No King*, *Sunday, Monday and Always*, and the forthcoming novel, *The Wicked Pavilion*, in England, restoring Powell to print there for the first time in several years. Becomes active supporter of Adlai Stevenson in his presidential campaign against Dwight D. Eisenhower. Works sporadically on "Yow," a children's book about cats, which she does not finish.

1953   The demolition of Powell's beloved Hotel Lafayette and the adjoining Hotel Brevoort helps provide impetus to complete *The Wicked Pavilion*. Powell takes photographs of the rubble and models the novel's "Café Julien" on the Lafayette. In her diary, lists the novels that have most influenced her: *Sister Carrie* (Dreiser), *Dodsworth* (Lewis), *Sentimental Education* (Flaubert), *Satyricon* (Petronius), *Daniel Deronda* (Eliot), *Dead Souls* (Gogol), *Lost Illusions* and *The Distinguished Provincial* (Balzac), *Our Mutual Friend* and *David Copperfield* (Dickens), and *Jenny* (Undset).

1954 Meets Gore Vidal in March and forms friendship. Frequents the Cedar, a bar on University Place, where she meets many artists, including Franz Kline. *The Wicked Pavilion* is published in October; it is reviewed on the front page of the New York *Herald Tribune* book review and appears for a week on the *New York Times* bestseller list. Afraid of Jojo's violence, she and Joseph look into the possibility of a prefrontal lobotomy; Dos Passos convinces them not to go ahead with the operation. Louise Lee suffers a debilitating stroke in March and does not return to the Gousha household; this upsets Jojo greatly and his parents reluctantly confine him more or less permanently to the New York state hospital system.

1955 Begins a residency in April at Yaddo, arts colony outside Saratoga Springs, New York, and is happier there than at the MacDowell Colony; begins a new novel, later published as *A Cage for Lovers*. Through the writer and bookstore owner Peter Martin, meets the young Jacqueline Miller (later Rice), who becomes one of her closest friends and later serves as her executor. In November, endures first in series of severe nosebleeds; she is told in December that she is suffering from anemia. Contributes book reviews regularly to the New York *Post*.

1956 Rewrites *Angels on Toast* as a paperback for Fawcett Books under the title *A Man's Affair*. Writes television script based on story "You Should Have Brought Your Mink."

1957 Completes novel *A Cage for Lovers*, after a long series of rewrites demanded by the publisher; the book is published in October with little fanfare or appreciation. Joseph is informed in December by his advertising agency that he will be retired on January 1, 1958.

1958 Family finances collapse after Joseph's retirement. By October, the family is forced to move from 35 East Ninth Street, and begins a series of residencies in hotels and sublets. Powell writes a great deal of free-lance work and searches for a job. At the suggestion of Malcolm Cowley, Viking Press contracts Powell for a novel that will become *The Golden Spur*.

1959   Margaret De Silver rescues Powell and Joseph from their poverty with a generous trust fund.

1960   Powell and Joseph move to 43 Fifth Avenue. Powell spends much of the spring at Yaddo, where she becomes close friends with novelist Hannah Green, but leaves after another violent nosebleed. Joseph is diagnosed with rectal cancer in May; an operation relieves pain but his health continues to deteriorate. Powell returns to Lake Erie College to receive an honorary doctorate.

1961   Powell is hospitalized for anemia; doctors suggest removal of a growth, which she refuses. Spends much of the year taking care of her husband.

1962   Joseph dies on February 14. Margaret De Silver dies on June 1. *The Golden Spur* is published by Viking in October. Edmund Wilson's "Dawn Powell: Greenwich Village in the Fifties," the most significant critical piece on Powell's work during her lifetime, is published in *The New Yorker*.

1963   *The Golden Spur* is nominated for the National Book Award but does not win. Powell works with Lee Adams and Charles Strouse on a musical comedy version of *The Golden Spur*. Moves to a penthouse at 95 Christopher Street, prompting a lawsuit from her former landlords at 43 Fifth Avenue. Autobiographical sketch "What Are You Doing In My Dreams?" is published in *Vogue*. Begins work on "Summer Rose," a novel.

1964   Returns to Lake Erie College in May to lecture, meet with students, and deliver graduation address. The American Academy of Arts and Letters presents her with the Marjorie Peabody Waite Award for lifetime achievement in literature. Powell finds herself in more professional demand than in the past, with regular offers for well-paid free-lance work and a significantly higher advance for her next novel. Her health is poor; she has begun to lose weight and suffers from anemia. Diagnosed with colon cancer in August, she realizes that she is probably mortally ill. *The Golden Spur* musical project is indefinitely postponed.

1965   Completes "Staten Island, I Love You" for *Esquire*, a rem-
             iniscence of her walks with Joseph Gousha 45 years earlier.
             Continues to work on "Summer Rose." Her weight drops
             to 105 pounds. Enters St. Luke's Hospital in September,
             where she refuses a colostomy. Returns to her home,
             where she is tended by Hannah Green and Jacqueline
             Miller Rice, and visited often by Coburn Gilman. Signs a
             hastily drawn will in which she donates her body to med-
             ical research; returns to St. Luke's by ambulance. Dies on
             the afternoon of November 14. (In 1970 the Cornell Med-
             ical Center contacts Jacqueline Miller Rice about the re-
             turn of Powell's remains; Rice gives Cornell authority to
             bury them in New York City Cemetery on Hart Island, the
             city's potter's field.)

Note on the Texts

This volume contains four novels by Dawn Powell that were first published between 1944 and 1962: *My Home Is Far Away* (1944), *The Locusts Have No King* (1948), *The Wicked Pavilion* (1954), and *The Golden Spur* (1962). This volume prints the texts of the first American editions for each of these novels. Although these novels were published in England, Powell's involvement in the preparation of the English editions was minimal, and her editors made changes based on British conventions of spelling and usage.

According to an entry in her diary dated January 27, 1941, Powell began writing *My Home Is Far Away* after having a dream about her childhood. "Unfortunately my fever brought back so many childhood memories with such brilliant clarity that it seems almost imperative to write a novel about that—the three sisters, the stepmother, Papa. This is bad because the new idea is so much work and the old one now seems wooden. Wrote a start from 3 to 5 A.M. in bed with temperature." The novel took shape during the next three years. On April 25, 1942, Powell wrote in her diary that she was "dissatisfied with novel—which is not like me. But it is the longest, most expansive book I've ever attempted and I'm afraid I have not the actual capacity for handling this big a theme. I still like it and feel cheated that I can't linger more over it and make it richer, which is what it needs." By February 1944, Powell was more confident about her handling of autobiographical material in the novel, writing that "I haven't the faintest notion of whether it's good or bad but at least now it is going very fast. It pours out spontaneously now that it is more fictionalized." Powell's diary records conflicting attitudes toward the progress of *My Home Is Far Away* as the novel neared completion. In February 1944, she remarked that she was "actually bored" by the book and "eager to get to the other one which permits the special kind of writing I like," but the following month she wrote, "I'm just beginning to think this novel may be of value. . . . I write and rewrite each chapter half a dozen times with pleasure—perhaps because the material is so limitless." On May 15, 1944, Powell claimed that she was "exhausted" by the novel and "not sure of it, even"; three days later, she wrote, "Book back on right foot—up to page 260 now, after throwing out a great deal—forty pages or so." She submitted the finished version of *My Home Is Far Away* to Maxwell Perkins, her editor at Scribner's, on July 25, 1944, noting in her diary that she was "pleased with ending and other features of end more than beginning or earlier part." The book was published by Scribner's in October 1944. Powell had envisioned it as the first part of a trilogy and worked on a sequel to *My Home Is Far Away*, tentatively called "Marcia," throughout the 1940s and 1950s. Only a fragmentary draft survives of "Marcia," which was never completed. This volume prints the text of the 1944 Scribner's edition of *My Home Is Far Away*.

The Locusts Have No King was called "The Destroyers" when Powell began writing the novel in 1943. The book developed slowly and evolved as a response, at least in part, to the end of World War II. In a letter to Perkins written in the summer of 1946, she described the book as "a follow-up of *A Time To Be Born*, which dealt with New York in the beginning follies of war. This book deals with the more desperate follies of post-war Manhattan—the exaggerated drive to perdition of a nation now conditioned to destruction." Diary entries from the summer of 1946 contain references to the atomic bomb tests in the Pacific which figure as the background to the novel's final scene; there is also a description of the novel as "a love story, the New York love story of a triangle marking time. The love story is serious and important and tragic to the people in it, but a matter of cosmic burlesque to all casual outsiders. Therefore the book has a serious main story in the setting of ageless laughter." She sent an incomplete draft of the novel to Perkins in April 1947 and received his comments shortly before his death in June 1947. (John Hall Wheelock replaced Perkins as Powell's editor.) By November 1947, Powell wrote that she was able to "see end of novel clearly now—day of atom bomb (Bikini). Lesson—cling to whatever is fine." The book was finished in late 1947 or early 1948, and it was published by Scribner's on April 26, 1948. This volume prints the 1948 Scribner's text of *The Locusts Have No King*.

In January 1950, while visiting Gerald and Sara Murphy in Snedens Landing, New York, Powell read parts of *The Creevey Papers*, a collection of letters to and from Thomas Creevey (1768–1838), a member of Parliament. Powell wrote in her diary that she "became fascinated, especially at Mrs. Creevey's letters to her husband from Bath in which she refers to 'that Wicked Pavilion'—the place everyone enjoys till after midnight, drinking so they cannot get up till noon, and then with heads." Two days later, in an entry dated January 31, 1950, Powell wrote, "Started novel about Cafe Lafayette. Wrote seven pages. Called *The Wicked Pavilion*. If this goes it will be due to Murphy weekend—early bed in strange, river atmosphere and without the dull callers." The following week she wrote that the novel "seems to have already been written in my head waiting for the title (and focal point of the Lafayette) to release it." In a letter to John Hall Wheelock dated September 18, 1950, Powell wrote that "reading the gossipy letters of French ladies and all the letters in the *Creevey Papers*, it struck me how sad it was that the vivid realness of the life as described by these ordinary letter-writers—the customs, the town talk, the scandal, the financial and personal problems of a Londoner or Parisian—was never really done in a novel. . . . I felt compelled to do my own favorite city the service the old letter-writers did for their times." After this promising start, however, the novel progressed slowly. Despite "working steadily" on *The Wicked Pavilion*, Powell noted on July 29, 1951, "I have gotten no further than 12 pages or so and this is due to talking to blank wall." She began to make headway with the novel in the summer of 1952 and continued to work on it throughout the remainder of 1952 and 1953; it was completed in February 1954. Having left Scribner's in September 1951, Powell submitted the novel to Houghton Mifflin, which had published a collection of her short stories, *Sunday, Monday and Always*, in 1952. *The Wicked Pavilion* was published by Houghton Mifflin in the autumn of 1954. This volume prints the 1954 Houghton Mifflin text of *The Wicked Pavilion*.

Powell began writing *The Golden Spur* in March 1958, shortly after making some preliminary notes for a "Cedar novel" (referring to the Cedar Tavern, the Greenwich Village bar on which The Golden Spur of the book is based). She worked on the novel for the next four years. Because of Powell's dissatisfaction with the editing of her novel *A Cage for Lovers* (1957), she left Houghton Mifflin, which had published her previous three books, in 1958. Malcolm Cowley, a senior editor at Viking, recommended that his firm publish *The Golden Spur* and commented on drafts of the novel. When Powell submitted a finished version of *The Golden Spur* to Viking in 1962, Helen Taylor, one of the editors there, suggested revisions. Powell rejected Taylor's recommendations, writing in her diary on September 27, 1962, "I was so dimmed by doubting publisher, editors that I could not sustain my original explosion of life technique until literal-minded editing made me so mad I tore back into it, throwing out every suggestion that had been made and being more myself than ever." *The Golden Spur* was published on October 5, 1962. The text of the 1962 Viking Press edition of *The Golden Spur* is printed here.

This volume presents the texts of the original printings chosen for inclusion here, but it does not attempt to reproduce nontextual features of their typographic design. The texts are presented without change, except for the correction of typographical errors. Spelling, punctuation, and capitalization are often expressive features and are not altered, even when inconsistent or irregular. The following is a list of typographical errors corrected, cited by page and line number: 5.28, that.'; 14.22, Wallis'; 25.15, asafedita; 35.11, Kraus'; 41.7, Lois asked; 49.21, Lois and; 51.14, Lois hung; 51.19, Lois protested; 58.25, Willardsville; 66.32, come; 96.14, away; 100.19, poth; 118.33, Grant) a; 174.25, her; 194.35, funiture; 208.31, Carson's; 254.27, don't; 268.39, *Day*"; 279.3, simple tastes; 287.33, saying-; 290.4, Strafford's; 307.36, Murray.; 315.4, Lily; 316.8, Staffords'; 337.16, Barlowe's; 345.3, *paellae*; 377.26, its; 378.26, *Swann*; 388.24, owners; 402.17, *chihuaha*; 413.23, reverance; 414.10, you're; 419.27, Pepper?) Frederick; 421.28, wrinkles,"; 431.37, benefit.; 442.26, brassiére; 458.1, Surat; 468.1, act to; 478.7, more."; 506.1, televisions; 509.15, everyday; 515.1, irreplacable; 530.18, one 'clock; 549.32, "ignorance"; 559.11, not; 560.31, ones'; 577.2, ¶"Good; 610.33, Hookley's; 613.7, ARE RICH; 613.36, Mulligans'; 615.37, holds barred; 623.32, load; 634.17, hotly; 648.10, kindly.; 654.16, said; 664.4, a a; 670.24, Martel; 671.12 *there's*; 675.28, me Cynthia; 679.10, belligerantly; 683.5, provalone; 693.2, gazelle's; 694.21, curiousity; 698.3, St. Germain; 718.8, noiser; 718.37, Martel; 737.13, River.'; 747.30, week ends; 754.21, gentleman." I; 755.25, satisfation; 791.8, break.'; 796.33, acknowledged." I; 801.23, positions'; 814.23, Pavillon; 816.16, forgone; 822.25, "The Raven"; 822.35, Hearstwood; 830.6, *shogi*; 834.27, always-; 841.39, absence's; 845.26, enthusaism; 846.31, to was; 864.21, Panhard; 868.7, substracted; 880.14, displeasure." I; 901.33, "adopt".

Notes

In the notes below, the reference numbers denote page and line of this volume. No note is made for material included in standard desk-reference books such as Webster's *Collegiate*, *Biographical*, and *Geographical* dictionaries. For further biographical information than is contained in the chronology, see Tim Page, *Dawn Powell: A Biography* (New York: Henry Holt, 1998); Tim Page, ed., *The Diaries of Dawn Powell: 1931–1965* (South Royalton, Vermont: Steerforth Press, 1995); Tim Page, ed., *Selected Letters of Dawn Powell: 1913–1965* (New York: Henry Holt, 1999).

MY HOME IS FAR AWAY

14.34–36   "I slept . . . Duty"]   Opening lines of "Beauty and Duty" by Ellen Sturgis Hooper (1818–41).

22.3   "Little Orphan Annie"]   "Little Orphant Annie" (1888), poem by James Whitcomb Riley.

28.12–14   Buster Brown . . . Little Nemo]   Buster Brown and his friend Mary-Jane were featured in R. F. Outcault's comic strip *Buster Brown* (1902–20); Little Nemo, in Winsor McCay's comic strip *Little Nemo in Slumberland*, undergoes a series of extravagant dreams.

30.17–34   Our little farm . . . chance.]   J. F. Kerrigan's song "Give an Honest Irish Lad a Chance" was published in 1881.

35.31   "Oh the moon . . . Red Wing]   "Red Wing," song (1907) by Thurland Chattaway and Kerry Mills.

36.16–17   "Oh, Bedelia . . . Bedelia."]   "Bedelia," song (1903) by William Jerome and Jean Schwartz.

38.1–3   Lady Maccabees . . . Corps]   Lady Maccabees, women's branch of the Maccabees, a fraternal mutual aid and social organization; D.A.R., Daughters of the American Revolution, patriotic community service organization founded in 1890; Eastern Star, Masonic organization for women; Women's Relief Corps, women's auxiliary of the Grand Army of the Republic, an organization for Civil War veterans.

48.17–18   "Just because . . . goo-goo eyes,"]   "Just Because She Made Dem Goo-goo Eyes" (1900), words by John Queen, music by Hughie Cannon.

48.18–19   "Won't . . . Bailey,"]   Song (1902), words and music by Hughie Cannon.

48.19   "Two Little Girls in Blue."]   Song (1893), words and music by Charles Graham.

57.13   "Moxie"]   Popular soft drink invented by Augustin Thompson of Lowell, Massachusetts, in 1886.

85.20   Big Four]   Local nickname for the midwestern railroad line that serviced Cleveland, Cincinnati, Chicago, and St. Louis.

89.9   Lillian Russell]   American stage star and famous beauty (1861–1922) whose vehicles included *The Grand Duchess* (1890) and, with the burlesque team Weber and Fields, *Fiddle-dee-dee* and *Whoop-dee-doo*.

89.17   Eddie Foy]   Vaudeville entertainer (1856–1928) whose starring vehicles included *Piff! Paff! Pouf!* (1904) and *The Earl and the Girl* (1905).

104.18–19   "Sandolphin . . . Angel of Prayer,"]   Cf. Henry Wadsworth Longfellow, "Sandalphon" (1858), lines 5–6: "Of Sandalphon, the Angel of Glory, / Sandalphon, the Angel of Prayer?"

104.20   the Flower Song]   Tenor aria from Act II of Georges Bizet's *Carmen* (1875).

108.24   'Hello, Central,']   "Hello, Central, Give Me Heaven," song (1901) by Charles K. Harris about a little girl who wants to telephone her dead mother.

110.8–11   "Last Days of Pompeii," . . . Horatio Alger]   *The Last Days of Pompeii*, novel (1834) by Edward Bulwer-Lytton (1803–73); E.D.E.N. Southworth, popular American author (1819–99) whose novels included *The Missing Bride* (1855) and *The Hidden Hand* (1859); *Lucile*, verse romance (1860) by Edward Robert Bulwer Lytton (1831–91), writing under the pseudonym Owen Meredith; Dinah Maria Mulock Craik (1826–87), author best known for the novel *John Halifax, Gentleman* (1857) and the children's tale *The Little Lame Prince* (1875); *If I Were King* (1902), historical drama by Justin Huntly McCarthy (1860–1936); *Wormwood: A Drama of Paris* (1890), novel by Marie Corelli (1855–1924); G. A. Henty (1832–1902), English juvenile adventure novelist whose books included *With Clive in India* (1884) and *By Pike and Dyke* (1890); Horatio Alger Jr. (1832–99), American writer whose books for boys included the series *Ragged Dick*, *Luck and Pluck*, and *Tattered Tom*.

111.6–7   *St. Nicholas Magazine*]   Illustrated magazine for children published from 1873 to 1925.

129.7   'If I Had a Thousand Lives.']   "If I Had a Thousand Lives to Live" (1908), song by Sylvester Maguire and Alfred Solman.

130.8   "Hee Haw! And Her Name was Maud,"]   *And Her Name Was Maud*, Fred Opper's comic strip about a mule named Maud, appeared under that title roughly from 1926 to 1932, although Maud had already featured in Opper's Sunday comics for many years, going back to the early 1900s.

132.36   Mabel Taliaferro] Stage and movie actress (1887–1979) whose films included *Cinderella* (1911) and *The Three of Us* (1915).

143.33   *The Green Fairy Book . . . The Blue Fairy Book*] Children's books by Andrew Lang (1844–1912).

147.26   "The Whistler and His Dog"] Song (1905) by Arthur Pryor.

157.24   "Work for the Night is Coming,"] Song (1864) by Annie L. Walker and Lowell Mason.

157.30   *Snowbound*] John Greenleaf Whittier's *Snow-Bound: A Winter Idyl* (1866).

160.26   "Angel's Serenade,"] Italian song "La Serenata" (1867) by Marco Marcellinao Marcello and Gaetano Braga.

164.3–4   *Tales of a Wayside Inn*] Book-length cycle of tales in verse (1863) by Henry Wadsworth Longfellow.

169.15   "My Mother Calls Me William,"] Cf. "Jest 'Fore Christmas" by Eugene Field: "Father calls me William, sister calls me Will, / Mother calls me Willie, but the fellers call me Bill!"

171.13   "Too Much Mustard"] Song (1911) by Cecil Macklin.

183.10   E. P. Roe . . . Holmes] Edward Payson Roe (1838–88), American clergyman and author of novels including *Barriers Burned Away* (1872) and *Near to Nature's Heart* (1876); Charlotte Braeme (1836–84), English author of romance novels such as *Dora Thorne* (1880); Edward Bulwer-Lytton (1803–73), English novelist; Mary Jane Holmes (1825–1904), American novelist best known for *Lena Rivers* (1856).

186.14–15   *The Calling . . . the Limberlost*] *The Calling of Dan Matthews* (1909) by Harold Bell Wright; *The Beloved Vagabond* (1906) by W. J. Locke; *A Girl of the Limberlost* (1909) by Gene Stratton Porter.

190.14   "Till the Sands of the Desert Grow Cold,"] Song (1911), words by George Graff Jr., music by Ernest Ball.

190.14–15   "Put On Your Old Gray Bonnet,"] Song (1909), words by Stanley Murphy, music by Percy Wenrich.

190.15–16   "Come, Josephine, in My Flying Machine."] Song (1910), words by Alfred Bryan, music by Fred Fisher.

192.37   "Glow Worm,"] "The Glow Worm" (1902), German song by Paul Lincke, popularized with English lyrics by Lilla Cayley Robinson in 1907.

197.15   'On Mobile Bay,'] Song (1910), words by Earle C. Jones, music by Charles N. Daniels.

201.29   Chautauqua] The Chautauqua community, founded in 1874 in Jamestown, New York, was designed to promote intellectual and spiritual development. Subsequently "Chautauqua" came to be used as a generic term for various troupes that traveled throughout the country presenting cultural and exotic entertainments.

201.39   Rabindranath Tagore] Indian poet (1861–1941) who won the Nobel Prize for Literature in 1913.

202.23   "Cavalleria Rusticana"] One-act opera (1890) by Pietro Mascagni (1863–1945).

203.32   G.A.R.] The Grand Army of the Republic, an organization for Union veterans.

THE LOCUSTS HAVE NO KING

241.1   THE LOCUSTS HAVE NO KING] On December 30, 1947, Powell sent the following letter describing her intentions in this novel to Michael Sadleir, an English publisher who turned the book down.

Dear Mr. Sadleir:

Very likely my new novel will be out here by the time page proofs have reached you. Scribners's—(I'm getting proofreading jitters as you see so I put apostrophes everywhere just to be sure and are there two b's in my publisher?)—is slating it for February. The name is The Locusts Have No King and it deals with postwar New York in the satirical vein of A Time To Be Born and The Happy Island. New York is not the same city it was, being overrun now with Americans. From all I hear the West and Midwest holes they left vacant are being filled with New York aesthetes lapping up water and oxygen and Nature's well-turned ankles with explorer's glee, pumping away at briar pipes and bedirndled third wives and persisting in trying to crack the native soul by being folksy instead of decently snobbish.

This, of course, has nothing to do with my novel, which I think you will like. I have a perfectly wonderful young lady in it who supplies the love interest and supplies and supplies. She is not the heroine. She is that young, resolutely gay girl who appears to most sedately scholarly men in their early middle age and batters away at them with public jeers at their work and jubilantly pursues a course of humiliating and teasing them that invigorates, debilitates and somehow appeals to their sense of the preposterous so that they feel oddly protective and sorry for her. Eventually my Frederick—(you see I have named him after the hero of Sentimental Education, but don't tell Flaubert)—finds she is the one who needs pity.

How did I come to mention a minor figure first? Or the love interest? Probably due to the six or seven generations of patent medicine flowing through my veins that makes me point out the chocolate flavor instead of the tonic itself.

The theme, as you so perspicaciously gathered from the Biblical title, deals with the disease of destruction sweeping through our times—no leader is needed, each person is out to destroy whatever valuable or beautiful thing life has. The moral is that in an age of destruction one must cling to whatever remnants of love, friendship, or hope above and beyond reason that one has, for the enemy is all around, ready to snatch it. You will see that I refer to the enemy not as Fascism, Communism, Mammon or anything but the plague of destructivism—inherent in human nature but released in magnified potency since the war.

This solemn message is "packaged," as we say in our advertising, in a possibly exaggerated comedy form—no more exaggerated than Hogarth's pictures of similar days. There are a splendid pair of high-salaried hard-drinking lady Babbitts with artistic yens, a quartette of midnight friends (male) who would not know each other by day but who view everybody's business (particularly their catastrophes) with a philosophic pleasure. The weighing of disaster and heartbreak is their nightly chore, harmless and gratifying. The reader can view my noble hero and heroine (Frederick and Lyle) not only through their ideas of themselves and each other but through the mocking laughter of people who do not even know them, other people who knew them "when"—in fact, these two poor nice creatures are given to the reader in the same impartial way all of us are given to our friends: through their own eyes, through their enemies' eyes, through talk behind their backs since they are more or less public figures . . .

You may be surprised—and I expect severe censure from my own countrymen—that in this period of 1945–1946 these articulates (new word) do not refer to the war. Too realistic, perhaps, but their eyes are on the future and the main chance. Gourmets about to sit down to a superb dinner already steaming up their nostrils do not waste time talking of lunch.

Edmund Wilson, the critic, insists I have been writing "existential" novels for years, before Sartre. I object, for my novels are based on the fantastic designs made by real human beings earnestly laboring to maladjust themselves to fate. There is no principle for them to prove—they may disobey the law of gravity as they please. My characters are not slaves to an author's propaganda. I give them their heads. They furnish their own nooses.

(Collection Temple University Libraries)

245.24   *"Salut e figli masci!"*]   Traditional Italian toast: "Health and masculine children!"

252.30   Ward McAllister]   American lawyer (1827–95) and arbiter of taste and conduct for New York society; author of *Society As I Have Found It* (1890).

261.37–38   Zorach marble mother-and-child]   Lithuanian-born American sculptor William Zorach (1887–1966) was known for his simplified human and animal forms based on ancient statuary; his 1930 marble sculpture *Mother and Child* is now at the Metropolitan Museum of Art.

273.26   *Everybody's Doing It*]   Song (1911) by Irving Berlin.

275.40   Schillinger method]   Joseph Schillinger, Russian-American music
theorist, propounded his compositional method, involving the application of
complex mathematical techniques, in *The Schillinger System of Musical
Composition* (1941).

276.2   *Two Little Girls in Blue*]   Popular song (1893), words and music by
Charles Graham.

278.13   Marsh]   Painter Reginald Marsh (1898–1954), a friend of Powell.

285.22   *Student Prince*]   *The Student Prince* (1924), operetta by Sigmund
Romberg.

288.5–6   Roland Young . . . Ernest Truex]   Roland Young, comic character actor who appeared in such films as *Ruggles of Red Gap* (1935), *The Man
Who Could Work Miracles* (1936), and *Topper* (1937); Ernest Truex, comic
actor featured in films including *It's a Wonderful World* (1939) and *Slightly
Honorable* (1940).

288.32   *The Knights*]   Comedy (424 B.C.) by Aristophanes.

296.19   O.W.I.]   Office of War Information.

315.1   Hudson Dusters]   New York street gang of the late 19th and early
20th centuries, originating in Hell's Kitchen; their name was said to derive
from their use of cocaine.

315.4   Lillie Langtry's]   Popular English stage actress (1853–1929), known
as the Jersey Lily.

316.18   *Lil Abner . . . Bruce Gentry*]   *Li'l Abner*, comic strip (1934–77) by
Al Capp, chronicled the outlandish inhabitants of Dogpatch; *Bruce Gentry*,
comic strip (1945–52) by Ray Bailey, involved the adventures of aviators in
South America.

317.2   Kenneth Roberts]   Historical novelist (1885–1957) whose best-
selling books included *Rabble in Arms* (1933) and *Northwest Passage* (1937).

325.16   *A Bicycle Built for Two*]   "Daisy Bell," song (1892) by Harry
Dacre.

347.6   Dale Carnegie]   Carnegie (1888–1955) was a lecturer, founder of a
chain of self-improvement schools, and author of the best seller *How to Win
Friends and Influence People* (1936).

353.39   Babbitt]   Protagonist of Sinclair Lewis's satirical novel (1922).

379.3   Candide]   Naïve hero of Voltaire's comic novel (1759).

410.39   *Penny*]   Comic strip (1943–70) by Harry Haenigsen, about the
daily life of a teenage girl.

415.25   Johnson office]   Name for the Motion Picture Producers and
Distributors of America, more commonly called the Hays office or the Breen

office. In 1930 the MPPDA adopted a production code regulating the moral content of movies, which remained in effect until 1966.

431.31   Peter Blume] Russian-born American painter (1906–92), a friend of Powell.

432.24   *"Cha Ta"*] "Ja-Da" (1918), song by Bob Carleton, popularized by Beatrice Lillie.

445.6–7   *You Won't Be Satisfied Until You Break My Heart*] Song (1945) by Freddy James and Larry Stock.

445.8   Veronica Lake] Hollywood actress (1919–73) whose films included *This Gun for Hire* (1942) and *The Blue Dahlia* (1946).

450.8–9   *Anniversary Waltz*] Song (1941) by Dave Franklin and Al Dubin.

455.30   Word Revolution . . . Jolas] Eugene Jolas (1894–1952), American journalist and poet, was founder and co-editor with Maria Jolas of *transition* (1926–38), where he published his 1929 manifesto "Revolution of the Word." Jolas was a close friend of Powell.

455.35   Southern Agrarian] One of the group of Southern writers associated with the Nashville-based magazine *The Fugitive* (1922–25) who published the manifesto *I'll Take My Stand* (1930) advocating a return to regional and agrarian values; prominent members of the movement included Robert Penn Warren, Allen Tate, and John Crowe Ransom.

458.1   Valeska Surratt] Vaudeville and silent film actress (1882–1962) whose films included *The Soul of Broadway* (1915) and *The Victim* (1916).

475.10   the Boyg] Powerful monster who appears only as a voice in darkness in Henrik Ibsen's *Peer Gynt* (1867).

480.19–20   *The Pumpkinification of Claudius*] *Apocolocyntosis divi Claudii* (The Pumpkinification of the Divine Claudius), satire by Seneca the Younger (4 B.C.–A.D. 65).

480.23   Al Capp or Caniff] Al Capp (1909–79), creator of the comic strip *Li'l Abner*; Milton Caniff (1907–88), creator of the comic strips *Terry and the Pirates*, *Male Call*, and *Steve Canyon*.

481.26   *The girl that I marry*] "The Girl That I Marry," song by Irving Berlin from the score of *Annie Get Your Gun* (1946).

497.1–2   that guy in *Pygmalion*] Professor Henry Higgins, who remolds the flower seller Eliza Doolittle in Bernard Shaw's 1912 comedy.

498.31   Bikini] The United States detonated two atomic bombs at Bikini atoll, in the Marshall Islands of the central Pacific, on July 1 and 25, 1946. Both tests were broadcast live on the radio in the United States. Designed to measure the effect of atomic weapons on naval vessels, the tests were the first nuclear explosions to take place since the bombing of Hiroshima and Nagasaki in August 1945.

THE WICKED PAVILION

501.2–7   ". . . oh this wicked . . . Papers]   The Creevey Papers, a collection of letters, journals, and notebooks of the member of Parliament Thomas Creevey (1768–1838), was published in 1903.

505.16   Mr. Orphen]   Dennis Orphen is the hero of Powell's Turn, Magic Wheel (1936) and a minor character in A Time To Be Born (1942).

508.28   Pennell]   The American artist and author Joseph Pennell (1857–1926), who spent much of his career in Europe.

518.8   The Life of the Bee]   Best-selling entomological study (1901) by Maurice Maeterlinck (1862–1947).

523.15   Laurencin]   Marie Laurencin (1885–1956), French painter and decorative artist.

524.25   Vincent Sheean . . . Walter Duranty]   Vincent Sheean (1899–1974) was an author and widely syndicated columnist, best known for his memoir Personal History (1935); Walter Duranty (1884–1957), New York Times correspondent known for sympathetic coverage of Stalin's Russia, whose books included I Write as I Please (1935).

534.38   Frank Benson]   Popular New York–based painter and etcher (1862–1951) known for his depictions of wildlife, sporting, and hunting scenes.

579.12   Leonard Lyons']   Gossip columnist (1904–76); his column The Lyons Den was nationally syndicated.

585.7   "Rose of Washington Square,"]   Song (1920) by Ballard Macdonald and James F. Hanley, popularized by Fanny Brice.

654.2   Duchess of Alba]   Goya's 1795 painting "La Maja Desnuda" ("The Nude Maja") is thought by many to be a portrait of the Duchess of Alba, who may have been Goya's mistress.

663.11   transitions]   Little magazine (1926–38) edited by Elliot Paul and Eugene Jolas (see note 455.30); one of the most influential organs of experimental literature and art, its contributors included Gertrude Stein, James Joyce, André Breton, William Carlos Williams, and Hart Crane.

665.13   Otto Kahn . . . Horace Liveright]   Kahn (1867–1934), American banker and arts patron; Liveright (1886–1933), writer, producer, and the publisher of works by Hemingway, Dreiser, and O'Neill.

697.34   Hopalong Cassidy]   Fictional hero of Western novels by Clarence Mulford (1883–1956), later the basis for movies and a television series.

714.22   Lafayette Escadrille] A French fighter squadron made up of American volunteers that began flying missions in April 1916, a year before the U.S. entered World War I. In January 1918 it became the 103rd Pursuit Squadron of the U.S. army air corps.

719.11–12   'Born . . . mad,'] Cf. the first line of *Scaramouche: A Romance of the French Revolution* (1921) by the Italian-born English novelist Rafael Sabatini (1875–1950).

719.21   Mary Garden] Scottish-born opera singer (1874–1967).

THE GOLDEN SPUR

727.4   *In virtu vinci*] I triumph in virtue.

732.7   *The Dance of Life*] Study (1923) by sexologist and philosopher Havelock Ellis.

734.17   Wanamaker's] The block-long department store on Fourth Avenue between East 9th and 10th streets was built in 1862 and demolished in 1956; Powell witnessed its destruction.

737.13   King of the Golden River] Fairy tale (1851) by John Ruskin.

738.17   *Encounter*] Liberal anti-communist literary and cultural magazine based in London, published from 1953 to 1990.

739.31   Lenny Lyons] See note 579.12.

742.7   Yaddo, MacDowell, Huntington Hartford] Yaddo and the Mac-Dowell Colony, long-established artists' colonies; wealthy financier Hunting-ton Hartford (b. 1911), a noted collector and patron of the arts.

743.20–21   Kootz . . . Matisse] The art dealers Samuel Kootz, Sidney Janis, and Pierre Matisse owned galleries in New York City.

743.39   Grandma Moses] Anna Mary Robertson Moses (1860–1961), known popularly as "Grandma Moses," American folk artist who began painting in her seventies and created more than 1500 works before her death. Her work received wide acclaim after her one-woman show at the Gallery St. Etienne in New York in 1940.

760.13   Susan Glaspell] American novelist, playwright, and political ac-tivist (1882–1948); a co-founder of the Provincetown Players.

760.31   *Delineator*] Magazine for women (1873–1937) edited by Theodore Dreiser from 1907 to 1910. During the last years of its run (before it merged with the *Pictorial Review*) it emphasized women's fashions.

762.18   Paquin and Worth] Paris fashion houses founded by designers Jeanne Paquin (1869–1936) and Charles Frederick Worth (1825–95).

763.10   Shape Notes and the Fa Sol La Singers] Shaped-note singing is a traditional style of religious singing in the American South, using hymnals in which the shapes of notes indicate pitch; the Fa Sol La Singers were a group who made recordings in this style in the early 1930s.

782.3   on the good ship *Lollipop*] Signature song of the child star Shirley Temple, first performed in the film *Bright Eyes* (1934).

818.2   *Under the Volcano*] Novel (1947) by Malcolm Lowry.

822.31   Stokes . . . Josie Mansfield] Edward Stokes fatally shot financial speculator James Fisk in 1872 after quarreling over a business transaction and over Fisk's mistress, the actress Josie Mansfield.

822.35   *Sister Carrie*] Novel (1900) by Theodore Dreiser.

822.40   Edward Sheldon's play *Romance*] Successful play (1913) by the popular playwright (1886–1946) whose other stage works included *The Boss* (1911) and *The Garden of Paradise* (1914).

823.1   Doris Keane] American stage actress (1881–1945).

823.6   where Mabel Dodge had her peyote party forty years ago] Mabel Dodge, later Mabel Dodge Luhan (1879–1962), often hosted salons in her apartment at 23 Fifth Avenue from 1912 to 1918, when she moved to New Mexico.

824.10–11   Alan Seeger's poem, 'I have a rendezvous with death—'] Poem (1916) that enjoyed widespread popularity following its publication a few months after Seeger's death while fighting with the French Foreign Legion during World War I.

824.27   Taggard] Genevieve Taggard (1894–1948), poet and anthologist who was Powell's friend during the 1920s.

830.1   *The Love for Three Oranges*] Opera (1921) by Sergei Prokofiev.

834.7   *The Vagabond King*] Light opera (1925) by Rudolf Friml.

864.23   Laurette Taylor] Stage actress (1884–1946) who achieved great success in J. Hartley Manners' comedy *Peg o' My Heart* (1912).

864.24   the Castles'] Vernon (1887–1918) and Irene (1893–1969) Castle achieved national fame by popularizing ballroom dancing.

865.31   Clara Bow] Movie actress (1905–65) known for her portrayal of jazz-era flappers, and sometimes called the "It Girl"; her films included *Parisian Love* (1925), *The Plastic Age* (1925), and *Dancing Mothers* (1926).

874.19   Long John] Long John Nebel had a long-running late-night talk show on New York radio station WOR; his guests frequently discussed extraterrestrial and paranormal phenomena.

876.23   Dr. Norman Vincent Peale's]   Minister (1898–1993) and author of
the best seller *The Power of Positive Thinking*.

887.31   Sandy Calder]   Alexander Calder (1898–1976), painter, sculptor,
and printmaker.

925.25   Fafner]   The dragon who guards the Nibelung gold in Richard
Wagner's *Der Ring des Nibelungen*; he is killed in Act II of *Siegfried* (1876).

928.32   "Three Coins in the Fountain"]   Song (1954) by Sammy Cahn
and Jule Styne.

Library of Congress Cataloging-in-Publication Data

Powell, Dawn, 1896–1965.
  [Novels. Selections]
  Novels, 1944–1962 / Dawn Powell.
      p. cm. — (The Library of America ; 127)
    Contents: My home is far way — The locusts have no king —
The wicked pavilion — The golden spur.
  ISBN 1–931082–02–2 (alk. paper)
    1. New York (N.Y.)—Fiction. 2. Ohio—Fiction. I. Title: My
home is far away. II. Title: Locusts have no king. III. Title:
Wicked pavilion. IV. Title: Golden spur. V. Title. VI. Series.
PS3531.O936   A6   2001B
813'.52—dc21   00–054596

THE LIBRARY OF AMERICA SERIES

The Library of America fosters appreciation and pride in America's literary heritage by publishing, and keeping permanently in print, authoritative editions of its best and most significant writing. An independent nonprofit organization, it was founded in 1979 with seed money from the National Endowment for the Humanities and the Ford Foundation.

This book is set in 10 point Linotron Galliard,
a face designed for photocomposition by Matthew Carter
and based on the sixteenth-century face Granjon. The paper is
acid-free Ecusta Nyalite and meets the requirements for permanence
of the American National Standards Institute. The binding
material is Brillianta, a woven rayon cloth made by
Van Heek-Scholco Textielfabrieken, Holland.
The composition is by The Clarinda
Company. Printing and binding by
R.R.Donnelley & Sons Company.
Designed by Bruce Campbell.